Bagombo Snuff Box

Bagombo Snuff Box

Uncollected Short Fiction

Kurt Vonnegut

G. P. PUTNAM'S SONS

New York

G. P. Putnam's Sons
Publishers Since 1838
a member of
Penguin Putnam Inc.
375 Hudson Street
New York, NY 10014

A list of permissions can be found on page 297.

Library of Congress Cataloging-in-Publication Data

Vonnegut, Kurt.
Bagombo snuff box : uncollected short fiction /
Kurt Vonnegut.
p.   cm.
ISBN 0-399-14505-2
ISBN 0-399-14526-5 (Limited Edition)
1. United States—Social life and customs—
20th century—Fiction.
I. Title.
PS3572.05B34   1999   99-13665 CIP
819'.54—dc21

The text of this book is set in Transitional 521.
Book design by Amanda Dewey

Printed in the United States of America
1   3   5   7   9   10   8   6   4   2

This book is printed on acid-free paper. ∞

F

As in my other works of fiction:

All persons living and dead are purely coincidental, and should not be construed. No names have been changed in order to protect the innocent. Angels protect the innocent as a matter of Heavenly routine.

In memory of my first agents,
Kenneth Littauer
and Max Wilkinson,
who taught me how to write

Contents

Preface

Kurt Vonnegut has achieved wide recognition as one of the best American novelists of the second half of the twentieth century, on the strength of such works as *Slaughterhouse-Five, Cat's Cradle, Breakfast of Champions,* and *Bluebeard.* His skills as a short story writer have attracted less attention. In the first decade and more of his career, Vonnegut's short fiction enjoyed a wide readership in the leading magazines of the day. Throughout the fifties and early sixties, he wrote many stories, which were published in *Collier's, The Saturday Evening Post, Cosmopolitan, Argosy, Redbook,* and other magazines. Twenty-three stories were collected in *Welcome to the Monkey House;* now, with this volume, the others can be found in a single collection, too.

Vonnegut's short fiction commanded a ready market, appearing in the best of the glossy wide-circulation magazines, and remained in demand while those publications thrived. It was ingenious, varied, and well written. Collected in *Welcome to the Monkey House,* or as anthologized, it has continued to find a readership. As popular fiction, these stories are accomplished in their energy, humor, and insight. It is important that the twenty-odd known stories not collected in *Monkey House* be preserved in book form, for they have their place in the Vonnegut canon as surely as his acclaimed novels. It is in these stories where he honed his skills that we see evolve the range of Vonnegut's talents, and the topics and techniques further developed in his later work.

Vonnegut began writing short stories in the late 1940s, while employed in public relations at General Electric in Schenectady, New York. Earlier, he had cut his teeth on journalism: while attending Shortridge High School in Indianapolis (1936–1940), he had been a regular contributor to and managing editor of its daily newspaper, *The Shortridge Echo,* and in college he worked on *The Cornell Daily Sun.* In his columns he creates characters, and one begins to see the humor and witty social iconoclasm evident in the mature work. The war intervened, with the dramatic circumstances that would be the stuff of his masterpiece, *Slaughterhouse-Five,* yet Vonnegut's course to becoming a writer had already been set.

After the war, popular magazines featuring short stories flourished in the United States. The late forties and early fifties were still a largely television-free era, with a steady demand for entertaining reading material. In 1949, Vonnegut sent "Report on the Barnhouse Effect" to *Collier's.* Knox Burger, who was fiction editor there, recognized the author's name from Cornell, where Burger had been editor of the campus humor magazine, *The Widow,* and gave the story his attention. After some revisions, "Barnhouse" became Vonnegut's first story to be accepted for publication. Burger was helpful also in introducing Vonnegut to Kenneth Littauer and Max Wilkinson, two agents with long experience in guiding aspiring writers. Their advice on the writing of a well-made story was invaluable (and even finds its way into the eight rules Vonnegut sets forth in his introduction to this collection). Having soon placed more stories, and with the apparent assurance of a market for his fiction, Vonnegut quit General Electric, moved to Cape Cod, and devoted himself full-time to writing.

. · . · .

This collection includes stories that draw on Vonnegut's World War Two experiences. The events on which *Slaughterhouse-Five* was based are by now widely known: how Vonnegut was captured by the Germans at the Battle of the Bulge, was held as a prisoner of war in Dresden, was sheltered in an underground meat storage room when that city was incinerated in massive air raids, and after the Nazi defeat wandered briefly in a Germany awash in refugees before he was reunited with American forces. "*Der Arme Dolmetscher*," "Souvenir," and "The Cruise of *The Jolly Roger*" treat the aftermath of war with a varying mix of humor and poignancy.

Many of the stories offer fascinating insights into attitudes and pre-occupations of Americans in the fifties. At General Electric the motto was "Progress is our most important product," a slogan that sums up the decade's optimism and the extension of the wartime can-do spirit. There was widespread belief in the ability of science and technology to go on improving everyday life. The assumption of a stable society that could offer the average family a happy home, financial advancement, and living conditions made easier and more glamorous by ever better gadgetry provides the context for these stories. Vonnegut questions this rosy vision, however, by showing that such ostensible progress may come at human cost. Thus do the home owners in "The Package" discover the inadequacy of the glitz embodied in their new gadget-laden house in a high-income suburb and decide they prefer the solidity of their old lives, and thus does the community of "Poor Little Rich Town" come to choose old ways over new and modest means over the affluence promised by developers. The theme is repeated in Vonnegut's first novel, the contemporary *Player Piano* (1952), and in much of his later fiction.

Pretense does not fare well in these stories. People who put on airs are usually exposed, often by children. Youngsters expose the egotistical gangster in "A Present for Big Saint Nick," and a nine-year-old trips up the show-off salesman in "Bagombo Snuff Box." At times pretense becomes a way of getting through life, as it does for the star performer's husband in "Unpaid Consultant," who invents an imaginary role for himself in order to retain a sense of importance. Kitty Cahoun, of "Custom-Made Bride," rebels against the pretense of the "Falloleen" role into which her designer husband would mold her. And young Kiah of "The Powder-Blue Dragon" finds only disillusionment in his attempt to pretend his way into a more sophisticated world by way of an exotic sports car. Such stories prefigure the warning sounded in *Mother Night*: "We are what we pretend to be, so we must be careful about what we pretend to be."

As in the novels, occupation often determines identity—at least in the case of men. Father-son relationships, which recur also in the novels, may help define the identities of both parent and child—see "This Son of Mine." The relationship is seldom comfortable, partly because of its propensity to impose an identity on the son, and partly because the father fears how he may be viewed by the son.

If there is one aspect of the stories that, more than any other, may make them seem dated, it is the roles of the women. After all, large numbers of married women in this era did not work outside the home, and they often took their standard for how they should dress, cook, decorate, entertain, or parent from some of the very magazines in which these stories appeared. While one would hardly expect stories written in the fifties to exhibit the kind of sensitivity to women's concerns so powerfully expressed in the novels *Galápagos* and *Bluebeard*, they already point that way. Even the romantic tales "A Night for Love" and "Find Me a Dream" demonstrate the burdensome expectations that can be placed on women in a man's world. "Lovers Anonymous," published in 1963, treats humorously the social awkwardness occasioned by the newly emergent "women's liberation."

The short story requires quick character definition, and these stories reveal how adept Vonnegut was at establishing a recognizable personality in a few paragraphs. That facility carries over into the novels, where character often seems subservient to message. Indeed, the more psychologically complex personalities, *Mother Night*'s Howard Campbell or *Bluebeard*'s Rabo Karabekian, for instance, are developed with a minimum of physical description. Some of the characterizations in these stories—the high school band director George M. Helmholtz, who is featured in three, comes to mind—might be prototypes for those in the novels.

Several stories rely on a convenient narrator, someone like a storm window salesman or a financial advisor, with access to many different social settings. Such a person can enter the homes of rich celebrities, as happens in "Custom-Made Bride" and "Unpaid Consultant," and deliver matter-of-fact observations. These narrators lend the immediacy of an intimate voice, a presence who, by virtue of being there, authenticates the account. Often theirs is the perspective of sound common sense that keeps the bizarre grounded in the everyday, and their wry commentary or ironic tone is a source of humor.

Vonnegut's humorous stories fit that American tradition of the tall tale epitomized by Mark Twain. "Tom Edison's Shaggy Dog," which appears in *Welcome to the Monkey House*, is the classic example of the form. Both "Mnemonics" and "Any Reasonable Offer" in this collection rise to an abrupt joke ending. Untraditional is Vonnegut's use of humor in science fiction stories. He characteristically seizes on the comic possibilities of the otherworldly settings and bizarre events typical of science fiction. "Thanasphere" belongs in the category of comic science fiction, the story combining space travel (then only an exciting prospect) and conventional notions of the spirits of the dead being "up there." If the story's humor is tinged with poignancy, that, too, is characteristic of Vonnegut. *Player Piano* and *The Sirens of Titan*, novels cast in the science fiction mode, abound in plot developments that are at once comic and painful, as does the classic short story "Epicac," which appears in *Welcome to the Monkey House*.

Television contributed to the end of Vonnegut's career as a short story writer. The magazines that had been eager buyers of stories suffered from losses of readership and advertising revenues. And the audience for magazine stories turned increasingly to television for entertainment, while the advertisers who were the magazines' lifeblood found the new medium irresistible. Some magazines folded, some changed format, some shrank. Vonnegut switched to writing novels—first paperback originals, *The Sirens of Titan* (1959) and *Mother Night* (1961), and then, beginning with *Cat's Cradle* (1963), hardcover. All of his novels, now fourteen in number, remain in print.

As mentioned earlier, *Welcome to the Monkey House* (1968) included twenty-three stories. Of these, eleven had appeared in an earlier collection, now out of print and a rare find, *Canary in a Cat House* (1961). "Hal

Irwin's Magic Lamp," included in that collection but not in *Monkey House*, is included also here, though in a different version from the original. The rest remained uncollected. Preparing a study (*The Short Fiction of Kurt Vonnegut*, Greenwood Press, 1997) took me into musty archives, retrieving Vonnegut contributions from bound volumes of *The Saturday Evening Post, Collier's,* and other magazines. It seemed obvious that these scattered tales deserved a proper home of their own, just as those in print in *Welcome to the Monkey House* have. Naturally I was delighted that Kurt Vonnegut shared my enthusiasm for the idea.

One curiosity for those interested in literary details. "*Der Arme Dolmetscher*" (The Poor Interpreter) is referred to on the copyright page of *Welcome to the Monkey House* and was included in the manuscript of that collection, but does not appear in the published work. The citation says that it appeared in *The Atlantic Monthly* with the title "Das Ganz Arm Dolmetscher," although in fact *Atlantic* used the shorter, grammatically correct title. Another curiosity: Although it did not appear until July 1955, it may have been accepted much earlier; the headnote describes Vonnegut as working at General Electric, when he had left the company by 1950.

Peter Reed

Bagombo Snuff Box

Introduction

My longtime friend and critic Professor Peter Reed, of the English Department at the University of Minnesota, made it his business to find these stories from my distant past. Otherwise, they might never have seen the light of day again. I myself hadn't saved one scrap of paper from that part of my life. I didn't think I would amount to a hill of beans. All I wanted to do was support a family.

Peter's quest was that of a scholar. I nevertheless asked him to go an extra mile for me, by providing an informal preface to what is in fact his rather than my collection.

God bless you, Dr. Reed, I think.

. . . . .

These stories, and twenty-three of similar quality in my previous hardcover collection, *Welcome to the Monkey House*, were written at the very end of a golden age of magazine fiction in this country. For about fifty years, until 1953, say, stories like these were a mild but popular form of entertainment in millions of homes, my own included.

This old man's hope has to be that some of his earliest tales, for all their mildness and innocence and clumsiness, may, in these coarse times, still entertain.

They would not be reprinted now, if novels I had written around the same time had not, better late than never, received critical attention. My children were adults by then, and I was middle-aged. These stories, printed in magazines fat with fiction and advertising, magazines now in most cases defunct, were expected to be among the living about as long as individual lightning bugs.

That anything I have written is in print today is due to the efforts of one publisher, Seymour "Sam" Lawrence (1927–1994). When I was broke in 1965, and teaching at the Writers' Workshop at the University of Iowa all alone, completely out of print, having separated myself from my family on Cape Cod in order to support them, Sam bought rights to my books, for peanuts, from publishers, both hardcover and softcover, who had given up on me. Sam thrust my books back into the myopic public eye again.

CPR! Cardiopulmonary resuscitation of this author who was all but dead!

Thus encouraged, this Lazarus wrote *Slaughterhouse-Five* for Sam. That made my reputation. I am a Humanist, and so am not entitled to expect an afterlife for myself or anyone. But at Seymour Lawrence's memorial service at New York City's Harvard Club five years ago, I said this with all my heart: "Sam is up in Heaven now."

I returned to Dresden, incidentally, the setting for *Slaughterhouse-Five*, on October 7th, 1998. I was taken down into the cellar where I and about a hundred other American POWs survived a firestorm that suffocated or incinerated 135,000 or so other human beings. It reduced the "Florence of the Elbe" to a jagged moonscape.

While I was down in that cellar again, this thought came to me: "Because I have lived so long, I am one of the few persons on Earth who saw an Atlantis before it disappeared forever beneath the waves."

Short stories can have greatness, short as they have to be. Several knocked my socks off when I was still in high school. Ernest Hemingway's "The Short Happy Life of Francis Macomber" and Saki's "The Open Window" and O. Henry's "The Gift of the Magi" and Ambrose Bierce's "An Occurrence at Owl Creek Bridge" spring to mind. But there is no greatness in this or my other collection, nor was there meant to be.

My own stories may be interesting, nonetheless, as relics from a time, before there was television, when an author might support a family by writing stories that satisfied uncritical readers of magazines, and earning thereby enough free time in which to write serious novels. When I became a full-time free-lance in 1950, I expected to be doing that for the rest of my life.

I was in such good company with a prospectus like that. Hemingway had written for *Esquire*, F. Scott Fitzgerald for *The Saturday Evening Post*, William Faulkner for *Collier's*, John Steinbeck for *The Woman's Home Companion*!

Say what you want about me, I never wrote for a magazine called *The Woman's Home Companion*, but there was a time when I would have been most happy to. And I add this thought: Just because a woman is stuck alone at home, with her husband at work and her kids at school, that doesn't mean she is an imbecile.

Publication of this book makes me want to talk about the peculiar and beneficial effect a short story can have on us, which makes it different from a novel or movie or play or TV show.

If I am to make my point, though, you must first imagine with me a scene in the home of my childhood and youth in Indianapolis, in the middle of the previous Great Depression. The previous Great Depression lasted from the stock market crash on October 24th, 1929, until the Japanese did us the favor, for the sheer hell of it, of bombing our comatose fleet of warships in Pearl Harbor, on December 7th, 1941. The little yellow bastards, as we used to call them, were bored to tears with the Great Depression. So were we.

Imagine that it is 1938 again. I am sixteen again. I come home again from yet another lousy day at Shortridge High School. Mother, who does not work outside the home, says there is a new *Saturday Evening Post* on the coffee table. It is raining outside, and I am unpopular. But I can't turn on a magazine like a TV set. I have to pick it up, or it will go on lying there, dead as a doornail. An unassisted magazine has no get-up-and-go.

After I pick it up, I have to make all one hundred sixty pounds of male adolescent meat and bones comfortable in an easy chair. Then I have to leaf through the magazine with my fingertips, so my eyes can shop for a story with a stimulating title and illustration.

Illustrators during the golden age of American magazine fiction used to get as much money as the authors whose stories they illustrated. They were often as famous as, or even more famous than, the authors. Norman Rockwell was their Michelangelo.

While I shop for a story, my eyes also see ads for automobiles and cigarettes and hand lotions and so on. It is advertisers, not readers, who pay the true costs of such a voluptuous publication. And God bless them for doing that. But consider the incredible thing I myself have to do in turn. I turn my brains on!

That isn't the half of it. With my brains all fired up, I do the nearly impossible thing that you are doing now, dear reader. I make sense of idiosyncratic arrangements, in horizontal lines, of nothing but twenty-six phonetic symbols, ten Arabic numerals, and perhaps eight punctuation marks, on a sheet of bleached and flattened wood pulp!

But get this: While I am reading, my pulse and breathing slow down. My high school troubles drop away. I am in a pleasant state somewhere between sleep and restfulness.

OK?

And then, after however long it takes to read a short story, ten minutes, say, I spring out of the chair. I put *The Saturday Evening Post* back on the coffee table for somebody else.

OK?

So then my architect dad comes home from work, or more likely from no work, since the little yellow bastards haven't bombed Pearl Harbor yet. I tell him I have read a story he might enjoy. I tell him to sit in the easy chair whose cushion is still dented and warmed by my teenage butt.

Dad sits. I pick up the magazine and open it to the story. Dad is tired and blue. Dad starts to read. His pulse and breathing slow down. His troubles drop away, and so on.

Yes! And our little domestic playlet, true to life in the 1930s, dear reader, proves exactly what? It proves that a short story, because of its physiological and psychological effects on a human being, is more closely related to Buddhist styles of meditation than it is to any other form of narrative entertainment.

What you have in this volume, then, and in every other collection of short stories, is a bunch of Buddhist catnaps.

Reading a novel, *War and Peace*, for example, is no catnap. Because a novel is so long, reading one is like being married forever to somebody nobody else knows or cares about. Definitely not refreshing!

Oh sure, we had radios before we had TV. But radios can't hold our attention, can't take control of our emotions, except in times of war. Radios can't make us sit still. Unlike print and plays and movies and boob tubes, radios don't give us anything for our restless eyes to do.

Listen: After I came home from World War Two, a brevet corporal twenty-two years old, I didn't want to be a fiction writer. I married my childhood sweetheart Jane Marie Cox, also from Indianapolis, up in Heaven now, and enrolled as a graduate student in the Anthropology Department of the University of Chicago. But I didn't want to be an anthropologist, either. I only hoped to find out more about human beings. I was going to be a journalist!

To that end, I also took a job as a police reporter for the Chicago City News Bureau. The News Bureau was supported by all four Chicago dailies back then, as a sensor for breaking news, prowling the city night and day, and as a training ground. The only way to get a job on one of those papers, short of nepotism, was to go through the News Bureau's hazing first.

But it became obvious that no newspaper positions were going to open up in Chicago or anywhere else for several years. Reporters had come home from the war to reclaim their jobs, and the women who had replaced them would not quit. The women were terrific. They should not have quit.

And then the Department of Anthropology rejected my M.A. thesis, which proved that similarities between the Cubist painters in Paris in 1907 and the leaders of Native American, or Injun, uprisings late in the nineteenth century could not be ignored. The Department said it was unprofessional.

Slowly but surely, Fate, which had spared my life in Dresden, now began to shape me into a fiction writer and a failure until I was a bleeding forty-seven years of age! But first I had to be a publicity hack for General Electric in Schenectady, New York.

While writing publicity releases at GE, I had a boss named George. George taped to the outside of his office door cartoons he felt had some bearing on the company or the kind of work we did. One cartoon was of two guys in the office of a buggy whip factory. A chart on the wall showed their business had dropped to zero. One guy was saying to the other, "It can't be our product's quality. We make the finest buggy whips in the world." George posted that cartoon to celebrate how GE, with its wonderful new products, was making a lot of other companies feel as though they were trying to sell buggy whips.

A broken-down movie actor named Ronald Reagan was working for the company. He was on the road all the time, lecturing to chambers of commerce and power companies and so on about the evils of socialism. We never met, so I remain a socialist.

While my future two-term president was burbling out on the rubber-chicken circuit in 1950, I started writing short stories at nights and on weekends. Jane and I had two kids by then. I needed more money than GE would pay me. I also wanted, if possible, more self-respect.

There was a crazy seller's market for short stories in 1950. There were four weekly magazines that published three or more of the things in every issue. Six monthlies did the same.

I got me an agent. If I sent him a story that didn't quite work, wouldn't quite satisfy a reader, he would tell me how to fix it. Agents and editors back then could tell a writer how to fine-tune a story as though they were pit mechanics and the story were a race car. With help like that, I sold one, and then two, and then three stories, and banked more money than a year's salary at GE.

I quit GE and started my first novel, *Player Piano*. It is a lampoon on GE. I bit the hand that used to feed me. The book predicted what has indeed come to pass, a day when machines, because they are so dependable and efficient and tireless, and getting cheaper all the time, are taking the halfway decent jobs from human beings.

I moved our family of four to Cape Cod, first to Provincetown. I met Norman Mailer there. He was my age. He had been a college-educated infantry private like me, and he was already a world figure, because of his great war novel *The Naked and the Dead*. I admired him then, and do today. He is majestic. He is royalty. So was Jacqueline Onassis. So was Joe DiMaggio. So is Muhammad Ali. So is Arthur Miller.

We moved from Provincetown to Osterville, still on the Cape. But only three years after I left Schenectady, advertisers started withdrawing their money from magazines. The Buddhist catnaps coming out of my typewriter were becoming as obsolete as buggy whips.

One monthly that had bought several of my stories, *Cosmopolitan*, now survives as a harrowingly explicit sex manual.

That same year, 1953, Ray Bradbury published *Fahrenheit 451*. The title refers to the kindling point of paper. That is how hot you have to get a book or a magazine before it bursts into flame. The leading male character makes his living burning printed matter. Nobody reads anymore. Many ordinary, rinky-dink homes like Ray's and mine have a room with floor-to-ceiling TV screens on all four walls, with one chair in the middle.

The actors and actresses on all four walls of TV are scripted to acknowledge whoever is sitting in the chair in the middle, even if nobody is sitting in the chair in the middle, as a friend or relative in the midst of things. The wife of the guy who burns up paper is unhappy. He can afford only three screens. His wife can't stand not knowing what's happening on the missing fourth screen, because the TV actors and actresses are the only people she loves, the only ones anywhere she gives a damn about.

Fahrenheit 451 was published before we and most of our neighbors in Osterville even owned TVs. Ray Bradbury himself may not have owned one. He still may not own one. To this day, Ray can't drive a car and hates to ride in airplanes.

In any case, Ray was sure as heck prescient. Just as people with dysfunctional kidneys are getting perfect ones from hospitals nowadays, Americans with dysfunctional social lives, like the woman in Ray's book, are getting perfect friends and relatives from their TV sets. And around the clock!

Ray missed the boat about how many screens would be required for a successful people-transplant. One lousy little Sony can do the job, night and day. All it takes besides that is actors and actresses, telling the news, selling stuff, in soap operas or whatever, who treat whoever is watching, even if nobody is watching, like family.

"Hell is other people," said Jean-Paul Sartre. "Hell is other real people," is what he should have said.

You can't fight progress. The best you can do is ignore it, until it finally takes your livelihood and self-respect away. General Electric itself was made to feel like a buggy whip factory for a time, as Bell Labs and others cornered patents on transistors and their uses, while GE was still shunting electrons this way and that with vacuum tubes.

Too big to fail, though, as I was not, GE recovered sufficiently to lay off thousands and poison the Hudson River with PCBs.

By 1953, Jane and I had three kids. So I taught English in a boarding school there on the Cape. Then I wrote ads for an industrial agency in

Boston. I wrote a couple of paperback originals, *The Sirens of Titan* and *Mother Night*. They were never reviewed. I got for each of them what I used to get for a short story.

I tried to sell some of the first Saab automobiles to come into this country. The doors opened into the wind. There was a roller-blind behind the front grille, which you could operate with a chain under the dashboard. That was to keep your engine warm in the wintertime. You had to mix oil with your gasoline every time you filled the tank of those early Saabs. If you ever forgot to do that, the engine would revert to the ore state. One engine I chipped away from a Saab chassis with a cold chisel and a sledge looked like a meteor!

If you left a Saab parked for more than a day, the oil settled like maple syrup to the bottom of the gas tank. When you started it up, the exhaust would black out a whole neighborhood. One time I blacked out Woods Hole that way. I was coughing like everybody else, I couldn't imagine where all that smoke had come from.

Then I took to teaching creative writing, first at Iowa, then at Harvard, and then at City College in New York. Joseph Heller, author of *Catch-22*, was teaching at City College also. He said to me that if it hadn't been for the war, he would have been in the dry-cleaning business. I said to him that if it hadn't been for the war, I would have been garden editor of *The Indianapolis Star.*

Now lend me your ears. Here is Creative Writing 101:

1. Use the time of a total stranger in such a way that he or she will not feel the time was wasted.
2. Give the reader at least one character he or she can root for.
3. Every character should want something, even if it is only a glass of water.
4. Every sentence must do one of two things—reveal character or advance the action.

5. Start as close to the end as possible.

6. Be a sadist. No matter how sweet and innocent your leading characters, make awful things happen to them—in order that the reader may see what they are made of.

7. Write to please just one person. If you open a window and make love to the world, so to speak, your story will get pneumonia.

8. Give your readers as much information as possible as soon as possible. To heck with suspense. Readers should have such complete understanding of what is going on, where and why, that they could finish the story themselves, should cockroaches eat the last few pages.

The greatest American short story writer of my generation was Flannery O'Connor (1925–1964). She broke practically every one of my rules but the first. Great writers tend to do that.

Ms. O'Connor may or may not have broken my seventh rule, "Write to please just one person." There is no way for us to find out for sure, unless, of course, there is a Heaven after all, and she's there, and the rest of us are going there, and we can ask her.

I'm almost sure she didn't break rule seven. The late American psychiatrist Dr. Edmund Bergler, who claimed to have treated more professional writers than any other shrink, said in his book *The Writer and Psychoanalysis* that most writers in his experience wrote to please one person they knew well, even if they didn't realize they were doing that. It wasn't a trick of the fiction trade. It was simply a natural human thing to do, whether or not it could make a story better.

Dr. Bergler said it commonly required psychoanalysis before his patients could know for whom they had been writing. But as soon as I finished his book, and then thought for only a couple of minutes, I knew it was my sister Allie I had been writing for. She is the person the stories in this book were written for. Anything I knew Allie wouldn't like I crossed out. Everything I knew she would get a kick out of I left in.

Allie is up in Heaven now, with my first wife Jane and Sam Lawrence and Flannery O'Connor and Dr. Bergler, but I still write to please her. Allie was funny in real life. That gives me permission to be funny, too. Allie and I were very close.

In my opinion, a story written for one person pleases a reader, dear reader, because it makes him or her a part of the action. It makes the reader feel, even though he or she doesn't know it, as though he or she is eavesdropping on a fascinating conversation between two people at the next table, say, in a restaurant.

That's my educated guess.

Here is another: A reader likes a story written for just one person because the reader can sense, again without knowing it, that the story has boundaries like a playing field. The story can't go simply anywhere. This, I feel, invites readers to come off the sidelines, to get into the game with the author. Where is the story going next? Where should it go? No fair! Hopeless situation! Touchdown!

Remember my rule number eight? "Give your readers as much information as possible as soon as possible"? That's so they can play along. Where, outside the Groves of Academe, does anybody like a story where so much information is withheld or arcane that there is no way for readers to play along?

The boundaries to the playing fields of my short stories, and my novels, too, were once the boundaries of the soul of my only sister. She lives on that way.

Amen.

Kurt Vonnegut

Thanasphere

At noon, Wednesday, July 26th, windowpanes in the small mountain towns of Sevier County, Tennessee, were rattled by the shock and faint thunder of a distant explosion rolling down the northwest slopes of the Great Smokies. The explosion came from the general direction of the closely guarded Air Force experimental station in the forest ten miles northwest of Elkmont.

Said the Air Force Office of Public Information, "No comment."

That evening, amateur astronomers in Omaha, Nebraska, and Glenwood, Iowa, reported independently that a speck had crossed the face of the full moon at 9:57 p.m. There was a flurry of excitement on the news wires. Astronomers at the major North American observatories denied that they had seen it.

They lied.

In Boston, on the morning of Thursday, July 27th, an enterprising newsman sought out Dr. Bernard Groszinger, youthful rocket consultant for the Air Force. "Is it possible that what crossed the moon was a space-ship?" the newsman asked.

Dr. Groszinger laughed at the question. "My own opinion is that we're beginning another cycle of flying-saucer scares," he said. "This time everyone's seeing spaceships between us and the moon. You can tell your readers this, my friend: No rocket ship will leave the earth for at least another twenty years."

He lied.

He knew a great deal more than he was saying, but somewhat less than he himself thought. He did not believe in ghosts, for instance—and had yet to learn of the Thanasphere.

Dr. Groszinger rested his long legs on his cluttered desktop, and watched his secretary conduct the disappointed newsman through the locked door, past the armed guards. He lit a cigarette and tried to relax before going back into the stale air and tension of the radio room. IS YOUR SAFE LOCKED? asked a sign on the wall, tacked there by a diligent security officer. The sign annoyed him. Security officers, security regulations only served to slow his work, to make him think about things he had no time to think about.

The secret papers in the safe weren't secrets. They said what had been known for centuries: Given fundamental physics, it follows that a projectile fired into space in direction x, at y miles per hour, will travel in the arc z. Dr. Groszinger modified the equation: Given fundamental physics and one billion dollars.

Impending war had offered him the opportunity to try the experiment. The threat of war was an incident, the military men about him an irritating condition of work—*the experiment* was the heart of the matter.

There were no unknowns, he reflected, finding contentment in the dependability of the physical world. Young Dr. Groszinger smiled, thinking of Christopher Columbus and his crew, who hadn't known what lay ahead of them, who had been scared stiff by sea monsters that didn't exist. Maybe the average person of today felt the same way about space. The Age of Superstition still had a few years to run.

But the man in the spaceship two thousand miles from earth had no unknowns to fear. The sullen Major Allen Rice would have nothing surprising to report in his radio messages. He could only confirm what reason had already revealed about outer space.

The major American observatories, working closely with the project, reported that the ship was now moving around the earth in the predicted orbit at the predicted velocity. Soon, anytime now, the first message in history from outer space would be received in the radio room. The broadcast could be on an ultra-high-frequency band where no one had ever sent or received messages before.

The first message was overdue, but nothing had gone wrong—nothing *could* go wrong, Dr. Groszinger assured himself again. Machines, not men, were guiding the flight. The man was a mere observer, piloted to his lonely vantage point by infallible electronic brains, swifter than his own. He had controls in his ship, but only for gliding down through the atmosphere, when and if they brought him back from space. He was equipped to stay for several years.

Even the man was as much like a machine as possible, Dr. Groszinger thought with satisfaction. He was quick, strong, unemotional. Psychiatrists had picked Major Rice from a hundred volunteers, and predicted that he would function as perfectly as the rocket motors, the metal hull, and the electronic controls. His specifications: Husky, twenty-nine years of age, fifty-five missions over Europe during the Second World War without a sign of fatigue, a childless widower, melancholy and solitary, a career soldier, a demon for work.

The Major's mission? Simple: To report weather conditions over enemy territory, and to observe the accuracy of guided atomic missiles in the event of war.

Major Rice was fixed in the solar system, two thousand miles above the earth now—close by, really—the distance from New York to Salt Lake City, not far enough away to see much of the polar icecaps, even. With a telescope, Rice could pick out small towns and the wakes of ships without much trouble. It would be breathtaking to watch the enormous blue-and-green ball, to see night creeping around it, and clouds and storms growing and swirling over its face.

Dr. Groszinger tamped out his cigarette, absently lit another almost at once, and strode down the corridor to the small laboratory where the radio equipment had been set up.

Lieutenant General Franklin Dane, head of Project Cyclops, sat next to the radio operator, his uniform rumpled, his collar open. The General stared expectantly at the loudspeaker before him. The floor was littered with sandwich wrappings and cigarette butts. Coffee-filled paper cups stood before the General and the radio operator, and beside the canvas chair where Groszinger had spent the night waiting.

General Dane nodded to Groszinger and motioned with his hand for silence.

"Able Baker Fox, this is Dog Easy Charley. Able Baker Fox, this is Dog Easy Charley . . ." droned the radio operator wearily, using the code names. "Can you hear me, Able Baker Fox? Can you—"

The loudspeaker crackled, then, tuned to its peak volume, boomed: "This is Able Baker Fox. Come in, Dog Easy Charley. Over."

General Dane jumped to his feet and embraced Groszinger. They laughed idiotically and pounded each other on the back. The General snatched the microphone from the radio operator. "You made it. Able Baker Fox! Right on course! What's it like, boy? What's it feel like? Over." Groszinger, his arm draped around the General's shoulders, leaned forward eagerly, his ear a few inches from the speaker. The radio operator turned the volume down, so that they could hear something of the quality of Major Rice's voice.

The voice came through again, soft, hesitant. The tone disturbed Groszinger—he had wanted it to be crisp, sharp, efficient.

"This side of the earth's dark, very dark just now. And I feel like I'm falling—the way you said I would. Over."

"Is anything the matter?" asked the General anxiously. "You sound as though something—"

The Major cut in before he could finish: "There! Did you hear that?"

"Able Baker Fox, we can't hear anything," said the General, looking perplexed at Groszinger. "What is it—some kind of noise in your receiver? Over."

"A child," said the Major. "I hear a child crying. Don't you hear it? And now—listen!—now an old man is trying to comfort it." His voice seemed farther away, as though he were no longer speaking directly into his microphone.

"That's impossible, ridiculous!" said Groszinger. "Check your set, Able Baker Fox, check your set. Over."

"They're getting louder now. The voices are louder. I can't hear you very well above them. It's like standing in the middle of a crowd, with everybody trying to get my attention at once. It's like . . ." The message trailed off. They could hear a shushing sound in the speaker. The Major's transmitter was still on.

"Can you hear me, Able Baker Fox? Answer! Can you hear me?" called General Dane.

The shushing noise stopped. The General and Groszinger stared blankly at the speaker.

"Able Baker Fox, this is Dog Easy Charley," chanted the radio operator. "Able Baker Fox, this is Dog Easy Charley. . . ."

Groszinger, his eyes shielded from the glaring ceiling light of the radio room by a newspaper, lay fully dressed on the cot that had been brought in for him. Every few minutes he ran his long, slender fingers through his tangled hair and swore. His machine had worked perfectly, *was* working perfectly. The one thing he had not designed, the damn man in it, had failed, had destroyed the whole experiment.

They had been trying for six hours to reestablish contact with the lunatic who peered down at earth from his tiny steel moon and heard voices.

"He's coming in again, sir," said the radio operator. "This is Dog Easy Charley. Come in, Able Baker Fox. Over."

"This is Able Baker Fox. Clear weather over Zones Seven, Eleven, Nineteen, and Twenty-three. Zones One, Two, Three, Four, Five, and Six overcast. Storm seems to be shaping up over Zones Eight and Nine, moving south by southwest at about eighteen miles an hour. Over."

"He's OK now," said the General, relieved.

Groszinger remained supine, his head still covered with the newspaper. "Ask him about the voices," he said.

"You don't hear the voices anymore, *do* you, Able Baker Fox?"

"What do you mean, I don't hear them? I can hear them better than I can hear you. Over."

"He's out of his head," said Groszinger, sitting up.

"I heard that," said Major Rice. "Maybe I am. It shouldn't be too hard to check. All you have to do is find out if an Andrew Tobin died in Evansville, Indiana, on February 17, 1927. Over."

"I don't follow you, Able Baker Fox," said the General. "Who was Andrew Tobin? Over."

"He's one of the voices." There was an uncomfortable pause. Major Rice cleared his throat. "Claims his brother murdered him. Over."

The radio operator had risen slowly from his stool, his face chalk-white. Groszinger pushed him back down and took the microphone from the General's now limp hand.

"Either you've lost your mind, or this is the most sophomoric practical joke in history, Able Baker Fox," said Groszinger. "This is *Groszinger* you're talking to, and you're dumber than I think you are if you think you can kid me." He nodded. "Over."

"I can't hear you very well anymore, Dog Easy Charley. Sorry, but the voices are getting louder."

"Rice! Straighten out!" said Groszinger.

"There—I caught that: Mrs. Pamela Ritter wants her husband to marry again, for the sake of the children. He lives at—"

"Stop it!"

"He lives at 1577 Damon Place, in Scotia, New York. Over and out."

General Dane shook Groszinger's shoulder gently. "You've been asleep five hours," he said. "It's midnight." He handed him a cup of coffee. "We've got some more messages. Interested?"

Groszinger sipped the coffee. "Is he still raving?"

"He still hears the voices, if that's what you mean." The General dropped two unopened telegrams in Groszinger's lap. "Thought you might like to be the one to open these."

Groszinger laughed. "Went ahead and checked Scotia and Evansville, did you? God help this army, if all the generals are as superstitious as you, my friend."

"OK, OK, you're the scientist, you're the brain-box. That's why I want *you* to open the telegrams. I want you to tell me what in hell's going on."

Groszinger opened one of the telegrams.

HARVEY RITTER LISTED FOR 1577 DAMON PLACE, SCOTIA. GE ENGINEER. WIDOWER, TWO CHILDREN. DECEASED WIFE NAMED PAMELA. DO YOU NEED MORE INFORMATION? R. B. FAILEY, CHIEF, SCOTIA POLICE

He shrugged and handed the message to General Dane, then opened the other telegram:

RECORDS SHOW ANDREW TOBIN DIED IN HUNTING ACCIDENT FEBRUARY 17, 1927. BROTHER PAUL LEADING BUSINESSMAN. OWNS COAL BUSINESS STARTED BY ANDREW. CAN FURNISH FURTHER DETAILS IF NEEDED. F. B. JOHNSON, CHIEF, EVANSVILLE P.D.

"I'm not surprised," said Groszinger. "I expected something like this. I suppose you're firmly convinced now that our friend Major Rice has found outer space populated by ghosts?"

"Well, I'd say he's sure as hell found it populated by something," said the General.

Groszinger wadded the second telegram in his fist and threw it across the room, missing the wastebasket by a foot. He folded his hands and affected the patient, priestlike pose he used in lecturing freshman physics classes. "At first, my friend, we had two possible conclusions: Either Major Rice was insane, or he was pulling off a spectacular hoax." He twiddled his thumbs, waiting for the General to digest this intelligence. "Now that we know his spirit messages deal with real people, we've got to conclude that he has planned and is now carrying out some sort of hoax. He got his names and addresses before he took off. God knows what he hopes to accomplish by it. God knows what we can do to make him stop it. That's your problem, I'd say."

The General's eyes narrowed. "So he's trying to jimmy the project, is he? We'll see, by God, we'll see." The radio operator was dozing. The General slapped him on the back. "On the ball, Sergeant, on the ball. Keep calling Rice till you get him, understand?"

The radio operator had to call only once.

"This is Able Baker Fox. Come in, Dog Easy Charley." Major Rice's voice was tired.

"This is Dog Easy Charley," said General Dane. "We've had enough of your voices, Able Baker Fox—do you understand? We don't want to hear any more about them. We're onto your little game. I don't know what your angle is, but I do know I'll bring you back down and slap you on a rock pile in Leavenworth so fast you'll leave your teeth up there. Do we understand each other?" The General bit the tip from a fresh cigar fiercely. "Over."

"Did you check those names and addresses? Over."

The General looked at Groszinger, who frowned and shook his head. "Sure we did. That doesn't prove anything. So you've got a list of names and addresses up there. So what does that prove? Over."

"You say those names checked? Over."

"I'm telling you to quit it, Rice. Right now. Forget the voices, do you hear? Give me a weather report. Over."

"Clear patches over Zones Eleven, Fifteen, and Sixteen. Looks like a solid overcast in One, Two, and Three. All clear in the rest. Over."

"That's more like it, Able Baker Fox," said the General. "We'll forget about the voices, eh? Over."

"There's an old woman calling out something in a German accent. Is Dr. Groszinger there? I think she's calling his name. She's asking him not to get too wound up in his work—not to—"

Groszinger leaned over the radio operator's shoulder and snapped off the switch on the receiver. "Of all the cheap, sickening stunts," he said.

"Let's hear what he has to say," said the General. "Thought you were a scientist."

Groszinger glared at him defiantly, snapped on the receiver, and stood back, his hands on his hips.

"—saying something in German," continued the voice of Major Rice.

"Can't understand it. Maybe you can. I'll give it to you the way it sounds: *'Alles geben die Götter, die unendlichen, ihren Lieblingen, ganz. Alle—'"*

Groszinger turned down the volume. *"'Alle Freuden, die unendlichen, alle Schmerzen, die unendlichen, ganz,'"* he said faintly. "That's how it ends." He sat down on the cot. "It's my mother's favorite quotation—something from Goethe."

"I can threaten him again," said the General.

"What for?" Groszinger shrugged and smiled. "Outer space *is* full of voices." He laughed nervously. *"There's* something to pep up a physics textbook."

"An omen, sir—it's an omen," blurted the radio operator.

"What the hell do you mean, an omen?" said the General. "So outer space is filled with ghosts. That doesn't surprise me."

"Nothing would, then," said Groszinger.

"That's exactly right. I'd be a hell of a general if anything would. For all I know, the moon is made of green cheese. So what. All I want is a man out there to tell me that I'm hitting what I'm shooting at. I don't give a damn what's going on in outer space."

"Don't you see, sir?" said the radio operator. "Don't you see? It's an omen. When people find out about all the spirits out there they'll forget about war. They won't want to think about anything but the spirits."

"Relax, Sergeant," said the General. "Nobody's going to find out about them, understand?"

"You can't suppress a discovery like this," said Groszinger.

"You're nuts if you think I can't," said General Dane. "How're you going to tell anybody about this business without telling them we've got a rocket ship out there?"

"They've got a right to know," said the radio operator.

"If the world finds out we have that ship out there, that's the start of World War Three," said the General. "Now tell me you want that. The enemy won't have any choice but to try and blow the hell out of us before we can put Major Rice to any use. And there'd be nothing for us to do but try and blow the hell out of them first. Is that what you want?"

"No, sir," said the radio operator. "I guess not, sir."

"Well, we can experiment, anyway," said Groszinger. "We can find out as much as possible about what the spirits are like. We can send Rice into a wider orbit to find out how far out he can hear the voices, and whether—"

"Not on Air Force funds, you can't," said General Dane. "That isn't what Rice is out there for. We can't afford to piddle around. We need him right there."

"All right, all right," said Groszinger. "Then let's hear what he has to say."

"Tune him in, Sergeant," said the General.

"Yes, sir." The radio operator fiddled with the dials. "He doesn't seem to be transmitting now, sir." The shushing noise of a transmitter cut into the hum of the loudspeaker. "I guess he's coming in again. Able Baker Fox, this is Dog Easy Charley—"

"King Two X-ray William Love, this is William Five Zebra Zebra King in Dallas," said the loudspeaker. The voice had a soft drawl and was pitched higher than Major Rice's.

A bass voice answered: "This is King Two X-ray William Love in Albany. Come in W5ZZK, I hear you well. How do you hear me? Over."

"You're clear as a bell, K2XWL—twenty-five thousand megacycles on the button. I'm trying to cut down on my drift with a—"

The voice of Major Rice interrupted. "I can't hear you clearly, Dog Easy Charley. The voices are a steady roar now. I can catch bits of what they're saying. Grantland Whitman, the Hollywood actor, is yelling that his will was tampered with by his nephew Carl. He says—"

"Say again, K2XWL," said the drawling voice. "I must have misunderstood you. Over."

"I didn't say anything, W5ZZK. What was that about Grantland Whitman? Over."

"The crowd's quieting down," said Major Rice. "Now there's just one voice—a young woman, I think. It's so soft I can't make out what she's saying."

"What's going on, K2XWL? Can you hear me, K2XWL?"

"She's calling my name. Do you hear it? She's calling my name," said Major Rice.

"Jam the frequency, dammit!" cried the General. "Yell, whistle—do something!"

Early-morning traffic past the university came to a honking, bad-tempered stop, as Groszinger absently crossed the street against the light, on his way back to his office and the radio room. He looked up in surprise, mumbled an apology, and hurried to the curb. He had had a solitary break-fast in an all-night diner a block and a half from the laboratory building, and then he'd taken a long walk. He had hoped that getting away for a couple of hours would clear his head—but the feeling of confusion and helplessness was still with him. Did the world have a right to know, or didn't it?

There had been no more messages from Major Rice. At the General's orders, the frequency had been jammed. Now the unexpected eavesdrop-pers could hear nothing but a steady whine at 25,000 megacycles. General Dane had reported the dilemma to Washington shortly after midnight. Perhaps orders as to what to do with Major Rice had come through by now.

Groszinger paused in a patch of sunlight on the laboratory building's steps, and read again the front-page news story, which ran fancifully for a column, beneath the headline "Mystery Radio Message Reveals Possible Will Fraud." The story told of two radio amateurs, experimenting illegally on the supposedly unused ultra-high-frequency band, who had been amazed to hear a man chattering about voices and a will. The amateurs had broken the law, operating on an unassigned frequency, but they hadn't kept their mouths shut about their discovery. Now hams all over the world would be building sets so they could listen in, too.

"Morning, sir. Nice morning, isn't it?" said a guard coming off duty. He was a cheerful Irishman.

"Fine morning, all right," agreed Groszinger. "Clouding up a little in the west, maybe." He wondered what the guard would say if he told him what he knew. He would laugh, probably.

Groszinger's secretary was dusting off his desk when he walked in. "You could use some sleep, couldn't you?" she said. "Honestly, why you men don't take better care of yourselves I just don't know. If you had a wife, she'd make you—"

"Never felt better in my life," said Groszinger. "Any word from General Dane?"

"He was looking for you about ten minutes ago. He's back in the radio room now. He's been on the phone with Washington for half an hour."

She had only the vaguest notion of what the project was about. Again, Groszinger felt the urge to tell about Major Rice and the voices, to see what effect the news would have on someone else. Perhaps his secretary would react as he himself had reacted, with a shrug. Maybe that was the spirit of this era of the atom bomb, H-bomb, God-knows-what-next bomb—to be amazed at nothing. Science had given humanity forces enough to destroy the earth, and politics had given humanity a fair assurance that the forces would be used. There could be no cause for awe to top *that* one. But proof of a spirit world might at least equal it. Maybe that was the shock the world needed, maybe word from the spirits could change the suicidal course of history.

General Dane looked up wearily as Groszinger walked into the radio room. "They're bringing him down," he said. "There's nothing else we can do. He's no damn good to us now." The loudspeaker, turned low, sang the monotonous hum of the jamming signal. The radio operator slept before the set, his head resting on his folded arms.

"Did you try to get through to him again?"

"Twice. He's clear off his head now. Tried to tell him to change his frequency, to code his messages, but he just went on jabbering like he couldn't hear me—talking about that woman's voice."

"Who's the woman? Did he say?"

The General looked at him oddly. "Says it's his wife, Margaret. Guess that's enough to throw anybody, wouldn't you say? Pretty bright, weren't we, sending up a guy with no family ties." He arose and stretched. "I'm going out for a minute. Just make sure you keep your hands off that set." He slammed the door behind him.

The radio operator stirred. "They're bringing him down," he said.

"I know," said Groszinger.

"That'll kill him, won't it?"

"He has controls for gliding her in, once he hits the atmosphere."

"If he wants to."

"That's right—if he wants to. They'll get him out of his orbit and back to the atmosphere under rocket power. After that, it'll be up to him to take over and make the landing."

They fell silent. The only sound in the room was the muted jamming signal in the loudspeaker.

"He don't want to live, you know that?" said the radio operator suddenly. "Would you want to?"

"Guess that's something you don't know until you come up against it," said Groszinger. He was trying to imagine the world of the future—a world in constant touch with the spirits, the living inseparable from the dead. It was bound to come. Other men, probing into space, were certain to find out. Would it make life heaven or hell? Every bum and genius, criminal and hero, average man and madman, now and forever part of humanity— advising, squabbling, conniving, placating . . .

The radio operator looked furtively toward the door. "Want to hear him again?"

Groszinger shook his head. "Everybody's listening to that frequency now. We'd all be in a nice mess if you stopped jamming." He didn't want to hear more. He was baffled, miserable. Would Death unmasked drive men to suicide, or bring new hope? he was asking himself. Would the living desert their leaders and turn to the dead for guidance? To Caesar . . . Charlemagne . . . Peter the Great . . . Napoleon . . . Bismarck . . . Lincoln . . . Roosevelt? To Jesus Christ? Were the dead wiser than—

Before Groszinger could stop him, the sergeant switched off the oscillator that was jamming the frequency.

Major Rice's voice came through instantly, high and giddy. ". . . thousands of them, thousands of them, all around me, standing on nothing, shimmering like northern lights—beautiful, curving off in space, all around the earth like a glowing fog. I can see them, do you hear? I can see them now. I can see Margaret. She's waving and smiling, misty, heavenly, beautiful. If only you could see it, if—"

The radio operator flicked on the jamming signal. There was a footfall in the hallway.

General Dane stalked into the radio room, studying his watch. "In five minutes they'll start him down," he said. He plunged his hands deep into his pockets and slouched dejectedly. "We failed this time. Next time, by God, we'll make it. The next man who goes up will know what he's up against—he'll be ready to take it."

He put his hand on Groszinger's shoulder. "The most important job you'll ever have to do, my friend, is to keep your mouth shut about those spirits out there, do you understand? We don't want the enemy to know we've had a ship out there, and we don't want them to know what they'll come across if they try it. The security of this country depends on that being our secret. Do I make myself clear?"

"Yes, sir," said Groszinger, grateful to have no choice but to be quiet. He didn't want to be the one to tell the world. He wished he had had nothing to do with sending Rice out into space. What discovery of the dead would do to humanity he didn't know, but the impact would be terrific. Now, like the rest, he would have to wait for the next wild twist of history.

The General looked at his watch again. "They're bringing him down," he said.

At 1:39 p.m., on Friday, July 28th, the British liner *Capricorn*, two hundred eighty miles out of New York City, bound for Liverpool, radioed that an unidentified object had crashed into the sea, sending up a towering geyser on the horizon to starboard of the ship. Several passengers were said to have seen something glinting as the thing fell from the sky. Upon reaching the scene of the crash, the *Capricorn* reported finding dead and stunned fish on the surface, and turbulent water, but no wreckage.

Newspapers suggested that the *Capricorn* had seen the crash of an experimental rocket fired out to sea in a test of range. The Secretary of Defense promptly denied that any such tests were being conducted over the Atlantic.

In Boston, Dr. Bernard Groszinger, young rocket consultant for the Air Force, told newsmen that what the *Capricorn* had observed might well have been a meteor.

"That seems quite likely," he said. "If it was a meteor, the fact that it reached the earth's surface should, I think, be one of the year's most important science news stories. Usually meteors burn to nothing before they're even through the stratosphere."

"Excuse me, sir," interrupted a reporter. "Is there anything out beyond the stratosphere—I mean, is there any name for it?"

"Well, actually the term 'stratosphere' is kind of arbitrary. It's the outer shell of the atmosphere. You can't say definitely where it stops. Beyond it is just, well—dead space."

"Dead space—that's the right name for it, eh?" said the reporter.

"If you want something fancier, maybe we could put it into Greek," said Groszinger playfully. "*Thanatos*, that's Greek for 'death,' I think. Maybe instead of 'dead space' you'd prefer 'Thanasphere.' Has a nice scientific ring to it, don't you think?"

The newsmen laughed politely.

"Dr. Groszinger, when's the first rocket ship going to make it into space?" asked another reporter.

"You people read too many comic books," said Groszinger. "Come back in twenty years, and maybe I'll have a story for you."

Mnemonics

Alfred Moorhead dropped the report into his *Out* basket, and smiled to think that he had been able to check something for facts without referring to records and notes. Six weeks before, he couldn't have done it. Now, since he had attended the company's two-day Memory Clinic, names, facts, and numbers clung to his memory like burdocks to an Airedale. The clinic had, in fact, indirectly cleared up just about every major problem in his uncomplicated life, save one—his inability to break the ice with his secretary, Ellen, whom he had silently adored for two years. . . .

"Mnemonics is the art of improving the memory," the clinic's instructor had begun. "It makes use of two elementary psychological facts: You remember things that interest you longer than things that don't, and pictures stick in your mind better than isolated facts do. I'll show you what I mean. We'll use Mr. Moorhead for our guinea pig."

Alfred had shifted uncomfortably as the man read off a nonsensical list and told him to memorize it: "Smoke, oak tree, sedan, bottle, oriole." The instructor had talked about something else, then pointed to Alfred. "Mr. Moorhead, the list."

"Smoke, oriole, uh—" Alfred had shrugged.

"Don't be discouraged. You're perfectly normal," the instructor had said. "But let's see if we can't help you do a little better. Let's build an image, something pleasant, something we'd like to remember. Smoke, oak tree, sedan—I see a man relaxing under a leafy oak tree. He is smoking a pipe, and in the background is his car, a yellow sedan. See it, Mr. Moorhead?"

"Uh-huh." Alfred *had* seen it.

"Good. Now for 'bottle' and 'oriole.' By the man's side is a vacuum bottle of iced coffee, and an oriole is singing on a branch overhead. There, we can remember that happy picture without any trouble, eh?" Alfred had nodded uncertainly. The instructor had gone on to other matters, then challenged him again.

"Smoke, sedan, bottle, uh—" Alfred had avoided the instructor's eyes.

When the snickering of the class had subsided, the instructor had said, "I suppose you think Mr. Moorhead has proved that mnemonics is bunk. Not at all. He has helped me to make another important point. The images used to help memory vary widely from person to person. Mr. Moorhead's personality is clearly different from mine. I shouldn't have forced my images on him. I'll repeat the list, Mr. Moorhead, and this time I want you to build a picture of your own."

At the end of the class, the instructor had called on Alfred again. Alfred had rattled the list off as though it were the alphabet.

The technique was so good, Alfred had reflected, that he would be able to recall the meaningless list for the rest of his life. He could still see himself and Rita Hayworth sharing a cigarette beneath a giant oak. He filled her glass from a bottle of excellent wine, and as she drank, an oriole brushed her cheek with its wing. Then Alfred kissed her. As for "sedan," he had lent it to Aly Khan.

Rewards for his new faculty had been splendid and immediate. The promotion had unquestionably come from his filing-cabinet command of business details. His boss, Ralph L. Thriller, had said, "Moorhead, I didn't know it was possible for a man to change as much as you have in a few weeks. Wonderful!"

His happiness was unbroken—except by his melancholy relationship with his secretary. While his memory worked like a mousetrap, paralysis still gripped him whenever he thought of mentioning love to the serene brunette.

Alfred sighed and picked up a sheaf of invoices. The first was addressed to the Davenport Spot-welding Company. He closed his eyes and a shimmering tableau appeared. He had composed it two days previous, when Mr. Thriller had given him special instructions. Two davenports faced each other. Lana Turner, sheathed in a tight-fitting leopard skin, lay on one. On the other was Jane Russell, in a sarong made of telegrams. Both of them blew kisses to Alfred, who contemplated them for a moment, then reluctantly let them fade.

He scribbled a note to Ellen: *Please make sure Davenport Spot-welding Company and Davenport Wire and Cable Company have not been confused in our billing.* Six weeks before, the matter would certainly have slipped his mind. *I love you,* he added, and then carefully crossed it out with a long black rectangle of ink.

In one way, his good memory was a curse. By freeing him from hours of searching through filing cabinets, it gave him that much more time to worry about Ellen. The richest moments in his life were and had been— even before the Memory Clinic—his daydreams. The most delicious of these featured Ellen. Were he to give her the opportunity to turn him down, and she almost certainly would, she could never appear in his fantasies again. Alfred couldn't bring himself to risk that.

The telephone rang. "It's Mr. Thriller," said Ellen.

"Moorhead," said Mr. Thriller, "I've got a lot of little stuff piled up on me. Could you take some of it over?"

"Glad to, chief. Shoot."

"Got a pencil?"

"Nonsense, chief," said Alfred.

"No, I mean it," said Mr. Thriller grimly. "I'd feel better if you wrote this down. There's an awful lot of stuff."

Alfred's pen had gone dry, and he couldn't lay his hands on a pencil without getting up, so he lied. "Okay, got one. Shoot."

"First of all, we're getting a lot of subcontracts on big defense jobs, and a new series of code numbers is going to be used for these jobs. Any number beginning with Sixteen A will designate that it's one of them. Better wire all our plants about it."

In Alfred's mind, Ava Gardner executed a smart manual of arms with a rifle. Emblazoned on her sweater was a large 16A. "Right, chief."

"And I've got a memo here from . . ."

Fifteen minutes later, Alfred, perspiring freely, said, "Right, chief," for the forty-third time and hung up. Before his mind's eye was a pageant to belittle the most flamboyant dreams of Cecil B. DeMille. Ranged about Alfred was every woman motion picture star he had ever seen, and each brandished or wore or carried or sat astride something Alfred could be fired for forgetting. The image was colossal, and the slightest disturbance might knock it to smithereens. He had to get to pencil and paper before tragedy struck. He crossed the room like a game-stalker, hunched, noiselessly.

"Mr. Moorhead, are you all right?" said Ellen, alarmed.

"Mmm. Mmm!" said Alfred, frowning.

He reached the pencil and pad, and exhaled. The picture was fogging, but it was still there. Alfred considered the ladies one by one, wrote down their messages, and allowed them to dissolve.

As their numbers decreased, he began to slow their exits in order to savor them. Now Ann Sheridan, the next-to-the-last in line, astride a western pony, tapped him on the forehead with a lightbulb to remind him of the name of an important contact at General Electric—Mr. Bronk. She blushed under his gaze, dismounted, and dissolved.

The last stood before him, clutching a sheaf of papers. Alfred was stumped. The papers seemed to be the only clue, and they recalled nothing. He reached out and clasped her to him. "Now, baby," he murmured, "what's on *your* mind?"

"Oh, Mr. Moorhead," sighed Ellen.

"Oh, gosh!" said Alfred, freeing her. "Ellen—I'm sorry, I forgot myself."

"Well, praise be, you finally remembered *me*."

Any Reasonable Offer

A few days ago, just before I came up here to Newport on a vacation, in spite of being broke, it occurred to me there isn't any profession—or racket, or whatever—that takes more of a beating from its clients than real estate. If you stand still, they club you. If you run, they shoot.

Maybe dentists have rougher client relationships, but I doubt it. Give a man a choice between having his teeth or a real estate salesman's commission extracted, and he'll choose the pliers and novocaine every time.

Consider Delahanty. Two weeks ago, Dennis Delahanty asked me to sell his house for him, said he wanted twenty thousand for it.

That afternoon I took a prospect out to see the house. The prospect walked through it once, said that he liked it and he'd take it. That evening he closed the deal. With Delahanty. Behind my back.

Then I sent Delahanty a bill for my commission—five percent of the sale price, one thousand dollars.

"What the hell are you?" he wanted to know. "A busy movie star?"

"You knew what my commission was going to be."

"Sure, I knew. But you only worked an hour. A thousand bucks an hour! Forty thousand a week, two million a year! I just figured it out."

"Some years I make ten million," I said.

"I work six days a week, fifty weeks a year, and then turn around and pay some young squirt like you a thousand for one hour of smiles and small talk and a pint of gas. I'm going to write my congressman. If it's legal, it sure as hell shouldn't be."

"He's my congressman, too, and you signed a contract. You read it, didn't you?"

He hung up on me. He still hasn't paid me.

Old Mrs. Hellbrunner called right after Delahanty. *Her* house has been on the market for three years, and it represents about all that's left of the Hellbrunner family's fortune. Twenty-seven rooms, nine baths, ballroom, den, study, music room, solarium, turrets with slits for crossbowmen, simulated drawbridge and portcullis, and a dry moat. Somewhere in the basement, I suppose, are racks and gibbets for insubordinate domestics.

"Something is very wrong," said Mrs. Hellbrunner. "Mr. Delahanty sold that awful little cracker-box of his in one day, and for four thousand more than he paid for it. Good heavens, I'm asking only a quarter of the replacement price for my house."

"Well—it's a very *special* sort of person who would want your place, Mrs. Hellbrunner," I said, thinking of an escaped maniac. "But someday he'll come along. They say there's a house for every person, and a person for every house. It isn't every day I get someone in here who's looking for something in the hundred-thousand-dollar range. But sooner or later—"

"When you accepted Mr. Delahanty as a client, you went right to work and earned your commission," she said. "Why can't you do the same for me?"

"We'll just have to be patient. It's—"

She, too, hung up, and then I saw the tall, gray-haired gentleman standing in the office doorway. Something about him—or maybe about me—made me want to jump to attention and suck in my sagging gut.

"Yessir!" I said.

"Is this yours?" he said, handing me an ad clipped from the morning paper. He held it as though he were returning a soiled handkerchief that had fallen from my pocket.

"Yessir—the Hurty place. That's mine, all right."

"This is the place, Pam," he said, and a tall, somberly dressed woman joined him. She didn't look directly at me, but at an imaginary horizon over my left shoulder, as though I were a headwaiter or some other minor functionary.

"Perhaps you'd like to know what they're asking for the place before we go out there," I said.

"The swimming pool is in order?" said the woman.

"Yes, ma'am. Just two years old."

"And the stables are usable?" said the man.

"Yessir. Mr. Hurty has his horses in them now. They're all newly white-washed, fireproof, everything. He's asking eighty-five thousand for the place, and it's a firm price. Is that within your price range, sir?"

He curled his lip.

"I said that about price range, because some people—"

"Do we look like any of them?" said the woman.

"No, you certainly don't." And they didn't, either, and every second they were looking more like a four-thousand-two-hundred-fifty-dollar com-mission. "I'll call Mr. Hurty right away."

"Tell him that Colonel and Mrs. Bradley Peckham are interested in his property."

The Peckhams had come by cab, so I drove them to the Hurty estate in my old two-door sedan, for which I apologized, and, to judge from their expression, rightly so.

Their town car, they related, had developed an infuriating little squeak, and was in the hands of a local dealer, who had staked his reputation on getting the squeak out.

"What is it you do, Colonel?" I asked, making small talk.

His eyebrows went up. "Do? Why, whatever amuses me. Or in time of crisis, whatever my country needs most."

"Right now he's straightening things out at National Steel Foundry," said Mrs. Peckham.

"Rum show, that," said the Colonel, "but coming along, coming along."

At the Hurty threshold, Mr. Hurty himself came to the door, tweedy, booted, and spurred. His family was in Europe. The Colonel and his wife, once I had made the formal introductions, ignored me. The Peckhams had some distance to go, however, before offending four thousand dollars' worth of my pride.

I sat quietly, like a Seeing Eye dog or overnight bag, and listened to the banter of those who bought and sold eighty-five-thousand-dollar estates with urbane negligence.

There were none of your shabby questions about how much the place cost to heat or keep up, or what the taxes were, or whether the cellar was dry. Not on your life.

"I'm so glad there's a greenhouse," said Mrs. Peckham. "I had such high hopes for the place, but the ad didn't mention a greenhouse, and I just prayed there was one."

"Never underestimate the power of prayer," I said to myself.

"Yes, I think you've done well with it," the Colonel said to Hurty. "I'm glad to see you've got an honest-to-God swimming pool, and not one of these cement-lined puddles."

"One thing you may be interested in," said Hurty, "is that the water isn't chlorinated. It's passed under ultraviolet light."

"I should hope so," said the Colonel.

"Um," said Hurty.

"Have you a labyrinth?" said Mrs. Peckham.

"How's that?" said Hurty.

"A labyrinth made of box hedge. They're awfully picturesque."

"No, sorry," said Hurty, pulling on his mustache.

"Well, no matter," said the Colonel, making the best of it. "We can put one in."

"Yes," said his wife. "Oh, dear," she murmured, and placed her hand over her heart. Her eyes rolled, and she started to sink to the floor.

"Darling!" The Colonel caught her about the waist.

"Please—" she gasped.

"A stimulant!" commanded the Colonel. "Brandy! Anything!"

Hurty, unnerved, fetched a decanter and poured a shot.

The Colonel's wife forced some between her lips, and the roses returned to her cheeks.

"More, darling?" the Colonel asked.

"A sip," she whispered.

When she'd finished it off, the Colonel sniffed the glass. "By George, but that's got a lovely bouquet!" He held out the glass to Hurty, and Hurty filled it.

"Jove!" said the Colonel, savoring, sniffing. "First-rate. Mmm. You know, it's a vanishing race that has the patience really to know the exquisite things in life. With most, it's gulp, gulp, and they're off on some mad chase again."

"Sure," said Hurty.

"Better, dear?" the Colonel asked his wife.

"Much. You know how it is. It comes and goes."

I watched the Colonel take a book from the shelves. He looked in the front, possibly to make sure it was a first edition. "Well, Mr. Hurty," he said, "I think it must show in our eyes how much we like the place. There are some things we'd change, of course, but by and large—"

Hurty looked to me.

I cleared my throat. "Well," I lied, "there are a number of people very interested in this property, as you might expect. I think you'd better make your offer official as soon as possible, if it's really to your liking."

"You aren't going to sell it to just *anybody*, are you?" said the Colonel.

"Certainly not!" lied Hurty, trying to recapture some of the élan he had lost during the labyrinth and brandy episodes.

"Well," said the Colonel, "the legal end can be handled quickly enough when the time comes. But first, if you don't mind, we'd like to get the feel of the place—get the newness out of it."

"Yes, of course, certainly," said Hurty, slightly puzzled.

"Then you don't mind if we sort of wander about a bit, as though it were already ours?"

"No, I guess not. I mean, certainly not. Go right ahead."

And the Peckhams did, while I waited, fidgeting in the living room, and Hurty locked himself in his study. They made themselves at home all afternoon, feeding the horses carrots, loosening the earth about the roots of plants in the greenhouse, drowsing in the sun by the swimming pool.

Once or twice I tried to join them, to point out this feature or that, but they received me as though I were an impertinent butler, so I gave it up.

At four, they asked a maid for tea, and got it—with little cakes. At five, Hurty came out of his study, found them still there, covered his surprise admirably, and mixed us all cocktails.

The Colonel said he always had *his* man rub the inside of martini glasses with garlic. He asked if there was a level spot for polo.

Mrs. Peckham discussed the parking problems of large parties, and asked if there was anything in the local air that was damaging to oil paintings.

At seven, Hurty, fighting yawns, excused himself, and telling the Peckhams to go on making themselves at home, he went to his supper. At eight, the Peckhams, having eddied about Hurty and his meal on their way to one place or another, announced that they were leaving.

They asked me to drop them off at the town's best restaurant.

"I take it you're interested?" I said.

"We'll want to talk a little," said the Colonel. "The price is certainly no obstacle. We'll let you know."

"How can I reach you, Colonel, sir?"

"I'm here for a rest. I prefer not to have anyone know my whereabouts, if you don't mind. I'll call you."

"Fine."

"Tell me," said Mrs. Peckham. "How did Mr. Hurty make his money?"

"He's the biggest used-car salesman in this part of the state."

"Aha!" said the Colonel. "I knew it! The whole place had the air of new money about it."

"Does that mean you don't want it after all?" I asked.

"No, not exactly. We'll simply have to live with it a little while to see what can be done about it, if anything."

"Could you tell me specifically what it was you didn't like?" I asked.

"If you can't see it," said Mrs. Peckham, "no one could possibly point it out to you."

"Oh."

"We'll let you know," said the Colonel.

Three days passed, with their normal complement of calls from Delahanty and Mrs. Hellbrunner, but without a sign from Colonel Peckham and his lady.

As I was closing my office on the afternoon of the fourth day, Hurty called me.

"When the hell," he said, "are those Peckham people going to come to a boil?"

"Lord knows," I said. "There's no way I can get in touch with them. He said he'd call me."

"You can get in touch with them anytime of night or day."

"How?"

"Just call my place. They've been out here for the past three days, taking the newness out of it. They've damn well taken something out of me, too. Do the liquor and cigars and food come out of your commission?"

"If there is a commission."

"You mean there's some question about it? He goes around here as though he has the money in his pocket and is just waiting for the right time to give it to me."

"Well, since he won't talk with me, you might as well do the pressuring. Tell him I've just told you a retired brewer from Toledo has offered seventy-five thousand. That ought to get action."

"All right. I'll have to wait until they come in from swimming, for cock-tails."

"Call me back when you've got a reaction, and I'll toot out with an offer form all ready to go."

Ten minutes later he did. "Guess what, brain-box?"

"He bit?"

"I'm getting a brand-new real estate agent."

"Oh?"

"Yes indeedy. I took the advice of the last one I had, and a red-hot prospect and his wife walked out with their noses in the air."

"No! Why?"

"Colonel and Mrs. Peckham wish you to know that they couldn't possibly be interested in anything that would appeal to a retired brewer from Toledo."

It was a lousy estate anyhow, so I gaily laughed and gave my attention to more substantial matters, such as the Hellbrunner mansion. I ran a boldface advertisement describing the joys of life in a fortified castle.

The next morning, I looked up from my work to see the ad, torn from the paper, in the long, clean fingers of Colonel Peckham.

"Is this yours?"

"Good morning, Colonel. Yessir, it is."

"It sounds like *our* kind of place," said the voice of Mrs. Peckham.

We crossed the simulated drawbridge and passed under the rusty portcullis of their kind of place.

Mrs. Hellbrunner liked the Peckhams immediately. For one thing, they were, I'm pretty sure, the first people in several generations to admire the place. More to the point, they gave every indication of being about to buy it.

"It would cost about a half-million to replace," said Mrs. Hellbrunner.

"Yes," said the Colonel. "They don't build houses like this anymore."

"Oh!" gasped Mrs. Peckham, and the Colonel caught her as she headed for the floor.

"Quick! Brandy! Anything!" cried Colonel Peckham.

When I drove the Peckhams back to the center of town, they were in splendid spirits.

"Why on earth didn't you show us this place first?" said the Colonel.

"Just came on the market yesterday," I said, "and priced the way it is, I don't expect it'll be on the market very long."

The Colonel squeezed his wife's hand. "I don't expect so, do you, dear?"

. · . · .

Mrs. Hellbrunner still called me every day, but now her tone was cheery and flattering. She reported that the Peckhams arrived shortly after noon each day, and that they seemed more in love with the house on each visit.

"I'm treating them just like Hellbrunners," she said craftily.

"That's the ticket."

"I even got cigars for him."

"Pour it on. It's all tax-deductible," I cheered.

Four nights later, she called me again to say that the Peckhams were coming to dinner. "Why don't you sort of casually drop in afterward, and just happen to have an offer form with you?"

"Have they mentioned any figures?"

"Only that it's perfectly astonishing what you can get for a hundred thousand."

I set my briefcase down in the Hellbrunner music room after dinner that evening. I said, "Greetings."

The Colonel, on the piano bench, rattled the ice in his drink.

"And how are *you*, Mrs. Hellbrunner?" I said. One glance told me she had never in all her life been worse.

"I'm fine," she said hoarsely. "The Colonel has just been speaking very interestingly. The State Department wants him to do some troubleshooting in Bangkok."

The Colonel shrugged sadly. "Once more to the colors, as a civilian this time."

"We leave tomorrow," said Mrs. Peckham, "to close our place in Philadelphia—"

"And finish up at National Steel Foundry," said the Colonel.

"Then off to Bangkok they go," quavered Mrs. Hellbrunner.

"Men must work, and women must weep," said Mrs. Peckham.

"Yup," I said.

The next morning, the telephone was ringing when I unlocked my office door.

It was Mrs. Hellbrunner. Shrill. Not like old family at all. "I don't *believe* he's going to Bangkok," she raged. "It was the price. He was too polite to bargain."

"You'll take less?" Up to now, she'd been very firm about the hundred-thousand figure.

"Less?" Her voice became prayerful. "Lord—I'd take fifty to get rid of the monster!" She was silent for a moment. "Forty. Thirty. Sell it!"

So I sent a telegram to the Colonel, care of National Steel Foundry, Philadelphia.

There was no reply, and then I tried the telephone.

"National Steel Foundry," said a woman in Philadelphia.

"Colonel Peckham, please."

"Who?"

"Peckham. Colonel Bradley Peckham. *The* Peckham."

"We have a Peckham, B. C., in Drafting."

"Is he an executive?"

"I don't know, sir. You can ask him."

There was a click in my ear as she switched my call to Drafting.

"Drafting," said a woman.

The first operator broke in: "This gentleman wishes to speak to Mr. Peckham."

"*Colonel* Peckham," I specified.

"Mr. Melrose," called the second woman, "is Peckham back yet?"

"Peckham!" Mr. Melrose shouted. "Shag your tail. Telephone!"

Above the sound of room noises, I heard someone ask, "Have a good time?"

"So-so," said a vaguely familiar, faraway voice. "Think we'll try Newport next time. Looked pretty good from the bus."

"How the hell do you manage tony places like that on your salary?"

"Takes a bit of doing." And then the voice became loud, and terribly familiar. "Peckham speaking. Drafting."

I let the receiver fall into its cradle.

I was awfully tired. I realized that I hadn't had a vacation since the end of the war. I had to get away from it all for a little while, or I would go mad. But Delahanty hadn't come through yet, so I was stone broke.

And then I thought about what Colonel Bradley Peckham had said about Newport. There *were* a lot of nice houses there—all beautifully staffed, furnished, stocked, overlooking the sea, and for sale.

For instance, take this place—the Van Tuyl estate. It has almost everything: private beach *and* swimming pool, polo field, two grass tennis courts, nine-hole golf course, stables, paddocks, French chef, at least three exceptionally attractive Irish parlor maids, English butler, cellar full of vintage stuff—

The labyrinth is an interesting feature, too. I get lost in it almost every day. Then the real estate agent comes looking for me, and he gets lost just as I find my way out. Believe me, the property is worth every penny of the asking price. I'm not going to haggle about it, not for a minute. When the time comes, I'll either take it or leave it.

But I've got to live with the place a little longer—to get the newness out—before I tell the agent what I'm going to do. Meanwhile, I'm having a wonderful time. Wish you were here.

The Package

hat do you know about that?" said Earl Fenton. He unslung his stereoscopic camera, took off his coat, and laid the coat and the camera on top of the television-radio-phonograph console. "Here we go on a trip clean around the world, Maude, and two minutes after we come back to our new house, the telephone rings. That's civilization."

"For you, Mr. Fenton," said the maid.

"Earl Fenton speaking . . . Who? . . . You got the right Fenton? There's a *Brudd* Fenton on San Bonito Boulevard. . . . Yes, that's right, I did. Class of 1910 . . . Wait! No! Sure I do! Listen, you tell the hotel to go to hell, Charley, you're my guest. . . . Have we got room?"

Earl covered the mouthpiece and grinned at his wife. "He wants to know if we've got room!" He spoke into the telephone again. "Listen,

Charley, we've got rooms I've never been in. No kidding. We just moved in today—five minutes ago. . . . No, it's all fixed up. Decorator furnished the place nice as you please weeks ago, and the servants got everything going like a dollar watch, so we're ready. Catch you a cab, you hear? . . .

"No, I sold the plant last year. Kids are grown up and on their own and all—young Earl's a doctor now, got a big house in Santa Monica, and Ted's just passed his bar exams and gone in with his Uncle George— Yeah, and Maude and I, we've just decided to sit back and take a well-earned— But the hell with talking on the phone. You come right on out. Boy! Have we got a lot of catching up to do!" Earl hung up and made clucking sounds with his tongue.

Maude was examining a switch panel in the hallway. "I don't know if this thingamajig works the air-conditioning or the garage doors or the windows or what," she said.

"We'll get Lou Converse out here to show us how everything works," said Earl. Converse was the contractor who had put up the rambling, many-leveled "machine for living" during their trip abroad.

Earl's expression became thoughtful as he gazed through a picture window at the flagstone terrace and grill, flooded with California sunshine, and at the cartwheel gate that opened onto the macadam driveway, and at the garage, with its martin house, weathercock, and two Cadillacs. "By golly, Maude," he said, "I just finished talking to a ghost."

"Um?" said Maude. "Aha! See, the picture window goes up, and down comes the screen. Ghost? Who on earth?"

"Freeman, Charley Freeman. A name from the past, Maude. I couldn't believe it at first. Charley was a fraternity brother and just about the biggest man in the whole class of 1910. Track star, president of the fraternity, editor of the paper, Phi Beta Kappa."

"Goodness! What's he doing coming here to see poor little us?" said Maude.

Earl was witnessing a troubling tableau that had been in the back of his mind for years: Charley Freeman, urbane, tastefully clothed, was having a plate set before him by Earl, who wore a waiter's jacket. When he'd invited Charley to come on out, Earl's enthusiasm had been automatic, the reflex of a man who prided himself on being a plain, ordinary, friendly fellow, for all of his success. Now, remembering their college relationship, Earl found that the prospect of Charley's arrival was making him uncomfortable. "He was a rich kid," Earl said. "One of those guys"—and his voice was tinged with bitterness—"who had everything. You know?"

"Well, hon," said Maude, "you weren't exactly behind the door when they passed out the looks and brains."

"No—but when they passed out the money, they handed me a waiter's jacket and a mop." She looked at him sympathetically, and he was encouraged to pour out his heart on the subject. "By golly, Maude, it does something to a man to go around having to wait on guys his same age, cleaning up after 'em, and seeing them with nice clothes and all the money in the world, going off to some resort in the summer when I had to go to work to pay next year's tuition." Earl was surprised at the emotion in his voice. "And all the time they're looking down on you, like there was something wrong with people who weren't handed their money on a silver platter."

"Well, that makes me good and mad!" Maude said, squaring her shoulders indignantly, as though to protect Earl from those who'd humiliated him in college. "If this great Charley Freeman snooted you in the old days, I don't see why we should have him in the house now."

"Oh, heck—forgive and forget," Earl said gloomily. "Doesn't throw me anymore. He seemed to want to come out, and I try to be a good fellow, no matter what."

"So what's the high-and-mighty Freeman doing now?"

"Don't know. Something big, I guess. He went to med school, and I came back here, and we kind of lost touch." Experimentally, Earl pressed a button on the wall. From the basement came muffled whirs and clicks, as machines took control of the temperature and humidity and purity of the atmosphere about him. "But I don't expect Charley's doing a bit better than this."

"What were some of the things he did to you?" Maude pursued, still indignant.

Earl waved the subject away with his hand. There weren't any specific incidents that he could tell Maude about. People like Charley Freeman hadn't come right out and said anything to humiliate Earl when he'd waited on them. But just the same, Earl was sure that he'd been looked down on, and he was willing to bet that when he'd been out of earshot, they'd talked about him, and . . .

He shook his head in an effort to get rid of his dour mood, and he smiled. "Well, Mama, what say we have a little drinkie, and then take a tour of the place? If I'm going to show it to Charley, I'd better find out how a few of these gimcracks work, or he'll think old Earl is about as at home in a setup like this as a retired janitor or waiter or something. By golly, there goes the phone again! That's civilization for you."

"Mr. Fenton," the maid said, "it's Mr. Converse."

"Hello, Lou, you old horse thief. Just looking over your handiwork. Maude and I are going to have to go back to college for a course in electrical engineering, ha ha. . . . Eh? Who? . . . No kidding. They really want to? . . . Well, I guess that's the kind of thing you have to expect to go through. If they've got their heart set on it, okay. Maude and I go clean around the world, and two minutes after we're home, it's like the middle of Grand Central Station."

Earl hung up and scratched his head in mock wonderment and weariness. In reality, he was pleased with the activity, with the bell-ringing proof that his life, unlike his ownership of the plant and the raising of his kids and the world cruise, was barely begun.

"What now?" said Maude.

"Aw, Converse says some fool home magazine wants to do a story on the place, and they want to get the pictures this afternoon."

"What fun!"

"Yeah—I guess. I dunno. I don't want to be standing around in all the pictures like some stuffed shirt." To show how little he cared, he interested himself in another matter. "I don't know why she wouldn't, considering what we paid her, but that decorator really thought of everything, you know?" He'd opened a closet next to the terrace doors and found an apron, a chef's hat, and asbestos gloves inside. "By golly, you know, that's pretty rich. See what it says on the apron, Maude?"

"Cute," said Maude, and she read the legend aloud: "'Don't shoot the cook, he's doing the best he can.' Why, you look like a regular Oscar of the Waldorf, Earl. Now let me see you in the hat."

He grinned bashfully and fussed with the hat. "Don't know exactly how one of the fool things is supposed to go. Feel kind of like a man from Mars."

"Well, you look wonderful to me, and I wouldn't trade you for a hundred stuck-up Charley Freemans."

They wandered arm in arm over the flagstone terrace to the grill, a stone edifice that might have been mistaken from a distance for a branch post office. They kissed, as they had kissed beside the Great Pyramid, the Colosseum, and the Taj Mahal.

"You know something, Maude?" said Earl, a great emotion ballooning in his breast. "You know, I used to wish my old man was rich, so you and I could have had a place like this right off—bing!—the minute I got out of college and we got married. But you know, we couldn't have had this moment looking back and knowing, by God, we made every inch of the way on our own. And we understand the little guy, Maude, because we were little guys once. By gosh, nobody born with a silver spoon in their mouth can buy that understanding. A lot of people on the cruise didn't want to look at all that terrible poverty in Asia, like their consciences bothered them. But us—well, seeing as how we'd come up the hard way, I don't guess we had much on our consciences, and we could look out at those poor people and kind of understand."

"Uh-huh," said Maude.

Earl worked his fingers in the thick gloves. "And tonight I'm going to broil you and me and Charley a sirloin steak as thick as a Manhattan phone book, and deserve every ounce of it, if I do say so myself."

"We aren't even unpacked."

"So what? I'm not tired. Got a lot of living to do, and the quicker I get at it, the more I'll get done."

Earl and Maude were in the living room, Earl still in his chef's outfit, when Charley Freeman was ushered in by the maid.

"By golly!" said Earl. "If it isn't Charley!"

Charley was still thin and erect, and the chief mark of age upon him was the graying of his thick hair. While his face was lined, it was still confident and wise-looking, was still, in Earl's opinion, subtly mocking. There was so much left of the old Charley, in fact, that the college relationship, dead for forty years, came alive again in Earl's mind. In spite of himself, Earl felt resentfully servile, felt crude and dull. His only defense was the old one—hidden resentment, with a promise that things would be very different before long.

"Been a long time, hasn't it, Earl?" Charley said, his voice still deep and virile. "You're looking fine."

"Lot of water can go under the bridge in forty years," said Earl. He was running his finger nervously over the rich fabric of the sofa. And then he remembered Maude, who was standing rigid, thin-lipped behind him. "Oh, excuse me, Charley, this is my wife, Maude."

"This is a pleasure I've had to put off for a long time," said Charley. "I feel I know you, Earl spoke of you so much in college."

"How do you do?" said Maude.

"Far better than I had any reason to expect six months ago," said Charley. "What a handsome house!" He laid his hand on the television-radio-phonograph console. "Now, what the devil do you call this?"

"Huh?" said Earl. "TV set. What's it look like?"

"TV?" said Charley, frowning. "TV? Oh—abbreviation for 'television.' That it?"

"You kidding me, Charley?"

"No, really. There must be more than a billion and a half poor souls who've never seen one of the things, and I'm one of them. Does it hurt to touch the glass part?"

"The tube?" Earl laughed uneasily. "Hell, no—go ahead."

"Mr. Freeman's probably got a tube five times as big as this one at home," said Maude, smiling coldly, "and he's kidding us along like he doesn't even know this is a TV set, the tube's so small."

"Well, Charley," said Earl, cutting briskly into the silence that followed Maude's comment, "and to what do we owe the honor of this visit?"

"For old times' sake," said Charley. "I happened to be in town, and I remem—"

Before Charley could elaborate, he was interrupted by a party composed of Lou Converse, a photographer from *Home Beautiful*, and a young, pretty woman writer.

The photographer, who introduced himself simply as Slotkin, took command of the household, and as he was to do for the whole of his stay, he quashed all talk and activities not related to getting the magazine pictures taken. "Zo," said Slotkin, "und de gimmick is de pagatch, eh?"

"Baggage?" said Earl.

"*Package*," said the writer. "See, the angle on the story is that you come home from a world cruise to a complete package for living—everything anybody could possibly want for a full life."

"Oh."

"It's complete," said Lou Converse, "complete right down to a fully stocked wine cellar and a pantry filled with gourmet specialties. Brand-new cars, brand-new everything but wine."

"Aha! Dey vin a condezt."

"He sold his factory and retired," said Converse.

"Maude and I figured we owed ourselves a little something," said Earl. "We held back all these years, putting money back into the business and all, and then, when the kids were grown up and the big offer came for the plant, we all of a sudden felt kind of crazy, and said, 'Why not?' And we just went ahead and ordered everything we'd ever wanted."

Earl glanced at Charley Freeman, who stood apart and in the background, half smiling, seeming to be fascinated by the scene. "We started out, Maude and I," said Earl, "in a two-room apartment down by the docks. Put that in the story."

"We had love," said Maude.

"Yes," said Earl, "and I don't want people to think I'm just another stuffed shirt who was born with a wad of money and blew himself to this setup. No, sir! This is the end of a long, hard road. Write that down. Charley remembers me back in the old days, when I had to work my way through school."

"Rugged days for Earl," said Charley.

Now the center of attention, Earl felt his self-confidence returning, and he began to see Charley's coming back into his life at this point as a generous act of fate, a fine opportunity to settle the old scores once and for all. "It wasn't the work that made it rugged," Earl said pointedly.

Charley seemed surprised by Earl's vehemence. "All right," he said, "then the work wasn't rugged. It was so long ago I can remember it either way."

"I mean it was tough being looked down on because I wasn't born with a silver spoon in my mouth," said Earl.

"Earl!" said Charley, smiling in his incredulity. "As many fatheads as we had for fraternity brothers, not one of them for a minute looked down—"

"Make ready for de pigdures," Slotkin said. "Stardt mit de grill—breadt, saladt, und a big, bloody piece of meadt."

The maid brought a five-pound slab of steak from the freezer, and Earl held it over the grill. "Hurry up," he said. "Can't hold a cow at arm's length all day." Behind his smile, however, he was nettled by Charley's bland dismissal of his college grievances.

"Hold it!" said Slotkin. The flashbulbs went off. "Good!"

And the party moved indoors. There, Earl and Maude posed in room after room, watering a plant in the solarium, reading the latest book before the living room fireplace, working push-button windows, chatting with the maid over the laundry console, planning menus, having a drink at the rumpus room bar, sawing a plank in the workshop, dusting off Earl's gun collection in the den.

And always, there was Charley Freeman at the rear of the entourage, missing nothing, obviously amused as Maude and Earl demonstrated their packaged good life. Under Charley's gaze, Earl became more and more restless and self-conscious as he performed, and Slotkin berated him for wearing such a counterfeit smile.

"By God, Maude," said Earl, perspiring in the master bedroom, "if I ever have to come out of retirement—knock on wood—I can go on television as a quick-change artist. This better be the last picture, by golly. Feel like a darn clotheshorse."

But the feeling didn't prevent his changing once more at Slotkin's command, this time into a tuxedo. Slotkin wanted a picture of dinner by candlelight. The dining room curtains would be drawn, electrically, to hide the fact of midafternoon outdoors.

"Well, I guess Charley's getting an eyeful," said Earl, distorting his face as he punched a collar button into place. "I think he's pretty darn impressed." His voice lacked conviction, and he turned hopefully to Maude for confirmation.

She was sitting at her dressing table, staring mercilessly at her image in the mirror, trying on different bits of jewelry. "Hmm?"

"I said I guess Charley's pretty impressed."

"*Him,*" she said flatly. "He's just a little *too* smooth, if you ask me. After the way he used to snoot you, and then he comes here all smiles and good manners."

"Yeah," said Earl, with a sigh. "Doggone it, he used to make me feel like two bits, and he still does, looking at us like we were showing off instead of just trying to help a magazine out. And did you hear what he said when I came right out and told him what I didn't like about college?"

"He acted like you just made it up, like it was just in your mind. Oh, he's a slick article, all right. But I'm not going to let him get my goat," said Maude. "This started out as the happiest day of our lives, and it's going to go on being that. And you want to know something else?"

"What's that?" Backed by Maude, Earl felt his morale rising. He hadn't been absolutely sure that Charley was inwardly making fun of them, but Maude was, and she was burned up about it, too.

Her voice dropped to a whisper. "For all his superior ways, and kidding us about our TV set and everything, I don't think the great Charley Freeman amounts to a hill of beans. Did you see his suit—up close?"

"Well, Slotkin kept things moving so fast, I don't guess I got a close look."

"You can bet *I* did, Earl," said Maude. "It's all worn and shiny, and the cuffs are a sight! I'd die of shame if you went around in a suit like that."

Earl was startled. He had been so on the defensive that it hadn't occurred to him that Charley's fortunes could be anything but what they'd been in college. "Maybe a favorite old suit he hates to chuck out," he said at last. "Rich people are funny about things like that sometimes."

"He's got on a favorite old shirt and a favorite old pair of shoes, too."

"I can't believe it," murmured Earl. He pulled aside a curtain for a glimpse of the fairyland of the terrace and grill, where Charley Freeman stood chatting with Slotkin and Converse and the writer. The cuffs of Charley's trousers, Earl saw with amazement, were indeed frayed, and the heels of his shoes were worn thin. Earl touched a button, and a bedroom window slithered open.

"It's a pleasant town," Charley was telling them. "I might as well settle here as anywhere, since I haven't very strong reasons for living in any particular part of the country."

"Zo eggspensif!" said Slotkin.

"Yes," said Charley, "I'd probably be smart to move inland, where my money'd go a little farther. Lord, it's incredible what things cost these days!"

Maude laid her hand on Earl's shoulder. "Seems kind of fishy, doesn't it?" she whispered. "You don't hear from him for forty years, and all of a sudden he shows up, down-and-out, to pay us a big, friendly call. What's he after?"

"Said he just wanted to see me for old times' sake," said Earl.

Maude sniffed. "You believe that?"

The dining room table looked like an open treasure chest, with the flames of the candelabra caught in a thousand perfect surfaces—the silver, the china, the facets of the crystal, Maude's rubies, and Maude's and Earl's proud eyes. The maid set steaming soup, prepared for the sake of the picture, before them.

"Perfect!" said Slotkin. "So! Now talk."

"What about?" said Earl.

"Anything," said the woman writer. "Just so the picture won't look posed. Talk about your trip. How does the situation in Asia look?"

It was a question Earl wasn't inclined to chat about lightly.

"You've been to Asia?" said Charley.

Earl smiled. "India, Burma, the Philippines, Japan. All in all, Maude and I must have spent two months looking the situation over."

"Earl and I took every side trip there was," said Maude. "He just had to see for himself what was what."

"Trouble with the State Department is they're all up in an ivory tower," said Earl.

Beyond the glittering camera lens and the bank of flashbulb reflectors, Earl saw the eyes of Charley Freeman. Expert talk on large affairs had been among Charley's many strong points in college, and Earl had been able only to listen and nod and wonder.

"Yes, sir," said Earl, summing up, "the situation looked just about hopeless to everybody on the cruise but Maude and me, and it took us a while to figure out why that was. Then we realized that we were about the only ones who'd pulled themselves up by their bootstraps—that we were the only ones who really understood that no matter how low a man is, if he's got what it takes, he can get clean to the top." He paused. "There's nothing wrong with Asia that a little spunk and common sense and know-how won't cure."

"I'm glad it's that easy," said Charley. "I was afraid things were more complicated than that."

Earl, who rightly considered himself one of the easiest men on earth to get along with, found himself in the unfamiliar position of being furious with a fellow human being. Charley Freeman, who evidently had failed as Earl had risen in the world, was openly belittling one of Earl's proudest accomplishments, his knowledge of Asia. "I've seen it, Charley!" said Earl. "I'm not talking as just one more darn fool armchair strategist who's never been outside his own city limits!"

Slotkin fired his flashbulbs. "One more," he said.

"Of course you're not, Earl," said Charley. "That was rude of me. What you say is very true, in a way, but it's such an oversimplification. Taken by itself, it's a dangerous way of thinking. I shouldn't have interrupted. It's simply that the subject is one I have a deep interest in."

Earl felt his cheeks reddening, as Charley, with his seeming apology, set himself up as a greater authority on Asia than Earl. "Think maybe I'm entitled to some opinions on Asia, Charley. I actually got out and rubbed elbows with the people over there, finding out how their minds work and all."

"You should have seen him jawing away with the Chinese bellboys in Manila," said Maude, challenging Charley with her eyes to top *that*.

"Now then," said the writer, checking a list, "the last shot we want is of you two coming in the front door with your suitcases, looking surprised, as though you've just arrived. . . ."

In the master bedroom again, Earl and Maude obediently changed back into the clothes they'd been wearing when they first arrived. Earl was studying his face in a mirror, practicing looks of pleased surprise and trying not to let the presence of Charley Freeman spoil this day of days.

"He's staying for supper and the night?" asked Maude.

"Oh heck, I was just trying to be a good fellow on the phone. Wasn't even thinking when I asked him to stay here instead of at the hotel. I could kick myself around the block."

"Lordy. Maybe he'll stay a week."

"Who knows? Slotkin hasn't given me a chance to ask Charley much of anything."

Maude nodded soberly. "Earl, what does it all add up to?"

"All what?"

"I mean, have you tried to put any of it together—the old clothes, and his paleness, and that crack about doing better now than he'd had any right to expect six months ago, and the books, and the TV set? Did you hear him ask Converse about the books?"

"Yeah, that threw me, too, because Charley was the book kind."

"All best-sellers, and he hadn't heard of a one! And he wasn't kidding about television, either. He really hasn't seen it before. He's been out of circulation for a while, and that's for sure."

"Sick, maybe," said Earl.

"Or in jail," whispered Maude.

"Good gosh! You don't suppose—"

"I suppose something's rotten in the state of Denmark," said Maude, "and I don't want him around much longer, if we can help it. I keep trying to figure out what he's doing here, and the only thing that makes sense is that he's here with his fancy ways to bamboozle you out of money, one way or another."

"All right, all right," said Earl, signaling with his hands for her to lower her voice. "Let's keep things as friendly as we can, and ease him out gently."

"How?" said Maude, and between them they devised what they considered a subtle method for bringing Charley's visit to an end before supper.

"Zo . . . zo much for dis," the photographer said. He winked at Earl and Maude warmly, as though noticing them as human beings for the first time. "Denk you. Nice pagatch you live." He had taken the last picture. He packed his equipment, bowed, and left with Lou Converse and the writer.

Putting off the moment when he would have to sit down with Charley, Earl joined the maid and Maude in the hunt for flashbulbs, which Slotkin had thrown everywhere. When the last bulb was found, Earl mixed martinis and sat down on a couch that faced another, on which Charley sat.

"Well, Charley, here we are."

"And you've come a distance, too, haven't you, Earl?" said Charley, turning his palms upward to indicate the wonder of the dream house. "I see you've got a lot of science fiction on your shelves. Earl, this house *is* science fiction."

"I suppose," said Earl. The flattery was beginning, building up to something—a big touch, probably. Earl was determined not to be spellbound by Charley's smooth ways. "About par for the course in America, maybe, for somebody who isn't afraid of hard work."

"What a course—with this for par, eh?"

Earl looked closely at his guest, trying to discover if Charley was belittling him again. "If I seemed to brag a little when those fool magazine people were here," he said, "I think maybe I've got a little something to brag about. This house is a lot more'n a house. It's the story of my life, Charley—my own personal pyramid, sort of."

Charley lifted his glass in a toast. "May it last as long as the Great Pyramid at Gizeh."

"Thanks," said Earl. It was high time, he decided, that Charley be put on the defensive. "You a doctor, Charley?"

"Yes. Got my degree in 1916."

"Uh-huh. Where you practicing?"

"Little old to start practicing medicine again, Earl. Medicine's changed so much in this country in recent years, that I'm afraid I'm pretty much out of it."

"I see." Earl went over in his mind a list of things that might get a doctor in trouble with the law. He kept his voice casual. "How come you suddenly got the idea of coming to see me?"

"My ship docked here, and I remembered that this was your hometown," said Charley. "Haven't any family left, and trying to start life all over on this side again, I thought I'd look up some of my old college friends. Since the boat landed here, you were the first."

That was going to be Charley's tale, then, Earl thought—that he had been out of the country for a long time. Next would come the touch. "Don't pay much attention to the college gang, myself," he said, unable to resist a small dig. "Such a bunch of snobs there that I was glad to get away and forget 'em."

"God help them if they didn't outgrow the ridiculous social values of college days," said Charley.

Earl was taken aback by the sharpness in Charley's voice, and not understanding it, he hastily changed the subject. "Been overseas, eh? Where, exactly, Charley?"

"Earl!" Maude called from the dining room, according to the plan. "The most awful thing has happened."

"Oh?"

Maude appeared in the doorway. "Angela"—she turned to Charley to explain—"my sister. Earl, Angela just called to say she was coming here with Arthur and the children before dinner, and could we put them up for the night."

"Gosh," said Earl, "don't see how we can. There're five of them, and we've only got two guest rooms, and Charley here—"

"No, no," said Charley. "See here, tell them to come ahead. I planned to stay at the hotel, anyway, and I have some errands to run, so I couldn't possibly stay."

"Okay, if you say so," said Earl.

"If he's got to go, he's got to go," said Maude.

"Yes, well, got a lot to do. Sorry." Charley was on his way to the door, having left his drink half finished. "Thanks. It's been pleasant seeing you. I envy you your package."

"Be good," said Earl, and he closed the door with a shudder and a sigh.

While Earl was still in the hallway, wondering at what could become of a man in forty years, the door chimes sounded, deep and sweet. Earl opened the door cautiously to find Lou Converse, the contractor, standing on the doorstep. Across the street, Charley Freeman was getting into a taxi.

Lou waved to Charley, then turned to face Earl. "Hello! Not inviting myself to dinner. Came back after my hat. Think I left it in the solarium."

"Come on in," said Earl, watching Charley's taxi disappear toward the heart of town. "Maude and I are just getting set to celebrate. Why not stay for dinner and, while you're at it, show us how some of the gadgets work?"

"Thanks, but I'm expected home. I can stick around a little while and explain whatever you don't understand. Too bad you couldn't get Freeman to stay, though."

Maude winked at Earl. "We asked him, but he said he had a lot of errands to run."

"Yeah, he seemed like he was in kind of a hurry just now. You know," Converse said thoughtfully, "guys like Freeman are funny. They make you feel good and bad at the same time."

"What do you know about that, Maude?" said Earl. "Lou instinctively felt the same way we did about Charley! How do you mean that, exactly, Lou, about feeling good and bad at the same time?"

"Well, good because you're glad to know there are still some people like that in the world," said Converse. "And bad—well, when you come across a guy like that, you can't help wondering where the hell your own life's gone to."

"I don't get you," said Earl.

Converse shrugged. "Oh, Lord knows we couldn't all dedicate our lives the way he did. Can't all be heroes. But thinking about Freeman makes me feel like maybe I could have done a little more'n I have."

Earl exchanged glances with Maude. "What did Charley tell you he'd been doing, Lou?"

"Slotkin and I didn't get much out of him. We just had a few minutes there while you and Maude were changing, and I figured I'd get the whole story from you sometime. All he told us was, he'd been in China for the last thirty years. Then I remembered there was a big piece about him in the paper this morning, only I'd forgotten his name. That's where I found out about how he sunk all his money in a hospital over there and ran it until the Commies locked him up and finally threw him out. Quite a story."

"Yup," Earl said bleakly, ending a deathly silence, "quite a story, all right." He put his arm around Maude, who was staring through the picture window at the grill. He squeezed her gently. "I said it's quite a story, isn't it, Mama?"

"We really did ask him to stay," she said.

"That's not like us, Maude, or if it is, I don't want it to be anymore. Come on, hon, let's face it."

"Call him up at the hotel!" said Maude. "That's what we'll do. We'll tell him it was all a mistake about my sister, that—" The impossibility of any sort of recovery made her voice break. "Oh, Earl, honey, why'd he have to pick today? All our life we worked for today, and then he had to come and spoil it."

"He couldn't have tried any harder not to," Earl sighed. "But the odds were too stiff."

Converse looked at them with incomprehension and sympathy. "Well, heck, if he had errands he had errands," he said. "That's no reflection on your hospitality. Good gosh, there isn't another host in the country who's got a better setup for entertaining than you two. All you have to do is flick a switch or push a button for anything a person could want."

Earl walked across the thick carpet to a cluster of buttons by the bookshelves. Listlessly, he pressed one, and floodlights concealed in shrubbery all around the house went on. "That isn't it." He pressed another, and a garage door rumbled shut. "Nope." He pressed another, and the maid appeared in the doorway.

"You ring, Mr. Fenton?"

"Sorry, a mistake," said Earl. "That wasn't the one I wanted."

Converse frowned. "What is it you're looking for, Earl?"

"Maude and I'd like to start today all over again," said Earl. "Show us which button to push, Lou."

The No-Talent Kid

It was autumn, and the leaves outside Lincoln High School were turning the same rusty color as the bare brick walls in the band rehearsal room. George M. Helmholtz, head of the music department and director of the band, was ringed by folding chairs and instrument cases, and on each chair sat a very young man, nervously prepared to blow through something or, in the case of the percussion section, to hit something, the instant Mr. Helmholtz lowered his white baton.

Mr. Helmholtz, a man of forty, who believed that his great belly was a sign of health, strength, and dignity, smiled angelically, as though he were about to release the most exquisite sounds ever heard by human beings. Down came his baton.

Blooooomp! went the big sousaphones.

Blat! Blat! echoed the French horns, and the plodding, shrieking, querulous waltz was begun.

Mr. Helmholtz's expression did not change as the brasses lost their places, as the woodwinds' nerve failed and they became inaudible rather than have their mistakes heard, while the percussion section sounded like the Battle of Gettysburg.

"A-a-a-a-ta-ta, a-a-a-a-a-a, ta-ta-ta-ta!" In a loud tenor, Mr. Helmholtz sang the first-cornet part when the first cornetist, florid and perspiring, gave up and slouched in his chair, his instrument in his lap.

"Saxophones, let me hear you," called Mr. Helmholtz. "Good!"

This was the C Band, and for the C Band, the performance was good. It couldn't have been more polished for the fifth session of the school year. Most of the youngsters were just starting out as bandsmen, and in the years ahead of them they would acquire artistry enough to move into the B Band, which met the next hour. And finally the best of them would gain positions in the pride of the city, the Lincoln High School Ten Square Band.

The football team lost half its games and the basketball team lost two-thirds of theirs, but the band, in the ten years Mr. Helmholtz had been running it, had been second to none until the past June. It had been the first in the state to use flag twirlers, the first to use choral as well as instrumental numbers, the first to use triple-tonguing extensively, the first to march in breathtaking double time, the first to put a light in its bass drum. Lincoln High School awarded letter sweaters to the members of the A Band, and the sweaters were deeply respected, and properly so. The band had won every statewide high school band competition for ten years—save the showdown in June.

While members of the C Band dropped out of the waltz, one by one, as though mustard gas were coming out of the ventilation, Mr. Helmholtz continued to smile and wave his baton for the survivors, and to brood inwardly over the defeat his band had sustained in June, when Johnstown High School had won with a secret weapon, a bass drum seven feet in diameter. The judges, who were not musicians but politicians, had had eyes and ears for nothing but this Eighth Wonder of the World, and since then Mr. Helmholtz had thought of little else. But the school budget was already lopsided with band expenses. When the school board had given him the last special appropriation he'd begged so desperately—money to wire the plumes of the bandsmen's hats with flashlight bulbs and batteries for night games—the board had made him swear like a habitual drunkard that, so help him God, this was the last time.

Only two members of the C Band were playing now, a clarinetist and a snare drummer, both playing loudly, proudly, confidently, and all wrong. Mr. Helmholtz, coming out of his wistful dream of a bass drum bigger than the one that had beaten him, administered the coup de grâce to the waltz by clattering his stick against his music stand. "All righty, all righty," he said cheerily, and he nodded his congratulations to the two who had persevered to the bitter end.

Walter Plummer, the clarinetist, responded gravely, like a concert soloist receiving an ovation led by the director of a symphony orchestra. He was small, but with a thick chest developed in summers spent at the bottom of swimming pools, and he could hold a note longer than anyone in the A Band, much longer, but that was all he could do. He drew back his tired, reddened lips, showing the two large front teeth that gave him the look of a squirrel, adjusted his reed, limbered his fingers, and awaited the next challenge to his virtuosity.

This would be Plummer's third year in the C Band, Mr. Helmholtz thought, with a mixture of pity and fear. Nothing could shake Plummer's determination to earn the right to wear one of the sacred letters of the A Band, so far, terribly far away.

Mr. Helmholtz had tried to tell Plummer how misplaced his ambitions were, to recommend other fields for his great lungs and enthusiasm, where pitch would be unimportant. But Plummer was in love, not with music, but with the letter sweaters. Being as tone-deaf as boiled cabbage, he could detect nothing in his own playing about which to be discouraged.

"Remember," said Mr. Helmholtz to the C Band, "Friday is challenge day, so be on your toes. The chairs you have now were assigned arbitrarily. On challenge day it'll be up to you to prove which chair you really deserve." He avoided the narrowed, confident eyes of Plummer, who had taken the first clarinetist's chair without consulting the seating plan posted on the bulletin board. Challenge day occurred every two weeks, and on that day any bandsman could challenge anyone ahead of him to a contest for his position, with Mr. Helmholtz as judge.

Plummer's hand was raised, its fingers snapping.

"Yes, Plummer?" said Mr. Helmholtz. He had come to dread challenge day because of Plummer. He had come to think of it as Plummer's day. Plummer never challenged anybody in the C Band or even the B Band, but stormed the organization at the very top, challenging, as was unfortunately the privilege of all, only members of the A Band. The waste of the A Band's time was troubling enough, but infinitely more painful for Mr. Helmholtz were Plummer's looks of stunned disbelief when he heard Mr. Helmholtz's decision that he hadn't outplayed the men he'd challenged.

"Mr. Helmholtz," said Plummer, "I'd like to come to A Band session that day."

"All right—if you feel up to it." Plummer always felt up to it, and it would have been more of a surprise if Plummer had announced that he wouldn't be at the A Band session.

"I'd like to challenge Flammer."

The rustling of sheet music and clicking of instrument case latches stopped. Flammer was the first clarinetist in the A Band, a genius whom not even members of the A Band would have had the gall to challenge.

Mr. Helmholtz cleared his throat. "I admire your spirit, Plummer, but isn't that rather ambitious for the first of the year? Perhaps you should start out with, say, challenging Ed Delaney." Delaney held down the last chair in the B Band.

"You don't understand," said Plummer. "You haven't noticed I have a new clarinet."

"Hmm? Oh—well, so you do."

Plummer stroked the satin-black barrel of the instrument as though it were King Arthur's sword, giving magical powers to whoever possessed it. "It's as good as Flammer's," said Plummer. "Better, even."

There was a warning in his voice, telling Mr. Helmholtz that the days of discrimination were over, that nobody in his right mind would dare to hold back a man with an instrument like this.

"Um," said Mr. Helmholtz. "Well, we'll see, we'll see."

After practice, he was forced into close quarters with Plummer again in the crowded hallway. Plummer was talking darkly to a wide-eyed freshman bandsman.

"Know why the band lost to Johnstown High last June?" asked Plummer, seemingly ignorant of the fact that he was back-to-back with Mr. Helmholtz. "Because they stopped running the band on the merit system. Keep your eyes open on Friday."

Mr. George M. Helmholtz lived in a world of music, and even the throbbing of his headache came to him musically, if painfully, as the deep-throated boom of a bass drum seven feet in diameter. It was late afternoon on the first challenge day of the new school year. He was sitting in his living room, his eyes covered, awaiting another sort of thump—the impact of the evening paper, hurled against the clapboards of the front of the house by Walter Plummer, the delivery boy.

As Mr. Helmholtz was telling himself that he would rather not have his newspaper on challenge day, since Plummer came with it, the paper was delivered with a crash.

"Plummer!" he cried.

"Yes, sir?" said Plummer from the sidewalk.

Mr. Helmholtz shuffled to the door in his carpet slippers. "Please, my boy," he said, "can't we be friends?"

"Sure—why not?" said Plummer. "Let bygones be bygones, is what I say." He gave a bitter imitation of an amiable chuckle. "Water over the dam. It's been two hours now since you stuck the knife in me."

Mr. Helmholtz sighed. "Have you got a moment? It's time we had a talk, my boy."

Plummer hid his papers under the shrubbery, and walked in. Mr. Helmholtz gestured at the most comfortable chair in the room, the one in which he'd been sitting. Plummer chose to sit on the edge of a hard one with a straight back instead.

"My boy," said the bandmaster, "God made all kinds of people: some who can run fast, some who can write wonderful stories, some who can paint pictures, some who can sell anything, some who can make beautiful music. But He didn't make anybody who could do everything well. Part of the growing-up process is finding out what we can do well and what we can't do well." He patted Plummer's shoulder. "The last part, finding out what we can't do, is what hurts most about growing up. But everybody has to face it, and then go in search of his true self."

Plummer's head was sinking lower and lower on his chest, and Mr. Helmholtz hastily pointed out a silver lining. "For instance, Flammer could never run a business like a paper route, keeping records, getting new customers. He hasn't that kind of a mind, and couldn't do that sort of thing if his life depended on it."

"You've got a point," said Plummer with unexpected brightness. "A guy's got to be awful one-sided to be as good at one thing as Flammer is. I think it's more worthwhile to try to be better rounded. No, Flammer beat me fair and square today, and I don't want you to think I'm a bad sport about that. It isn't that that gets me."

"That's mature of you," said Mr. Helmholtz. "But what I was trying to point out to you was that we've all got weak points, and—"

Plummer waved him to silence. "You don't have to explain to me, Mr. Helmholtz. With a job as big as you've got, it'd be a miracle if you did the whole thing right."

"Now, hold on, Plummer!" said Mr. Helmholtz.

"All I'm asking is that you look at it from my point of view," said Plummer. "No sooner'd I come back from challenging A Band material, no sooner'd I come back from playing my heart out, than you turned those C Band kids loose on me. You and I know we were just giving 'em the feel of challenge days, and that I was all played out. But did you tell them that? Heck, no, you didn't, Mr. Helmholtz, and those kids all think they can play better than me. That's all I'm sore about, Mr. Helmholtz. They think it means something, me in the last chair of the C Band."

"Plummer," said Mr. Helmholtz, "I have been trying to tell you something as kindly as possible, but the only way to get it across to you is to tell it to you straight."

"Go ahead and quash criticism," said Plummer, standing.

"Quash?"

"Quash," said Plummer with finality. He headed for the door. "I'm probably ruining my chances for getting into the A Band by speaking out like this, Mr. Helmholtz, but frankly, it's incidents like what happened to me today that lost you the band competition last June."

"It was a seven-foot bass drum!"

"Well, get one for Lincoln High and see how you make out then."

"I'd give my right arm for one!" said Mr. Helmholtz, forgetting the point at issue and remembering his all-consuming dream.

Plummer paused on the threshold. "One like the Knights of Kandahar use in their parades?"

"That's the ticket!" Mr. Helmholtz imagined the Knights of Kandahar's huge drum, the showpiece of every local parade. He tried to think of it with the Lincoln High School black panther painted on it. "Yes, sir!" When the bandmaster returned to earth, Plummer was astride his bicycle.

Mr. Helmholtz started to shout after Plummer, to bring him back and tell him bluntly that he didn't have the remotest chance of getting out of C Band ever, that he would never be able to understand that the mission of a band wasn't simply to make noises but to make special kinds of noises. But Plummer was off and away.

Temporarily relieved until next challenge day, Mr. Helmholtz sat down to enjoy his paper, to read that the treasurer of the Knights of Kandahar, a respected citizen, had disappeared with the organization's funds, leaving behind and unpaid the Knights' bills for the past year and a half. "We'll pay a hundred cents on the dollar, if we have to sell everything but the Sacred Mace," the Sublime Chamberlain of the Inner Shrine had said.

Mr. Helmholtz didn't know any of the people involved, and he yawned and turned to the funnies. He gasped, turned to the front page again. He looked up a number in the phone book and dialed.

"Zum-zum-zum-zum," went the busy signal in his ear. He dropped the telephone into its cradle. Hundreds of people, he thought, must be trying to get in touch with the Sublime Chamberlain of the Inner Shrine of the Knights of Kandahar at this moment. He looked up at his flaking ceiling in prayer. But none of them, he prayed, was after a bargain in a cart-borne bass drum.

He dialed again and again, and always got the busy signal. He walked out on his porch to relieve some of the tension building up in him. He would be the only one bidding on the drum, he told himself, and he could name his price. Good Lord! If he offered fifty dollars for it, he could probably have it! He'd put up his own money, and get the school to pay him back in three years, when the plumes with the electric lights in them were paid for in full.

He was laughing like a department store Santa Claus, when his gaze dropped from heaven to his lawn and he espied Plummer's undelivered newspapers lying beneath the shrubbery.

He went inside and called the Sublime Chamberlain again, with the same results. He then called Plummer's home to let him know where the papers were mislaid. But that line was busy, too.

He dialed alternately the Plummers' number and the Sublime Chamberlain's number for fifteen minutes before getting a ringing signal.

"Yes?" said Mrs. Plummer.

"This is Mr. Helmholtz, Mrs. Plummer. Is Walter there?"

"He was here a minute ago, telephoning, but he just went out of here like a shot."

"Looking for his papers? He left them under my spirea."

"He did? Heavens, I have no idea where he was going. He didn't say anything about his papers, but I thought I overheard something about selling his clarinet." She sighed, and then laughed. "Having money of their own makes them awfully independent. He never tells me anything."

"Well, you tell him I think maybe it's for the best, his selling his clarinet. And tell him where his papers are."

It was unexpected good news that Plummer had at last seen the light about his musical career. The bandmaster now called the Sublime Chamberlain's home again for more good news. He got through this time, but was disappointed to learn that the man had just left on some sort of lodge business.

For years, Mr. Helmholtz had managed to smile and keep his wits about him in C Band practice sessions. But on the day after his fruitless efforts to find out anything about the Knights of Kandahar's bass drum, his defenses were down, and the poisonous music penetrated to the roots of his soul.

"No, no, no!" he cried in pain. He threw his white baton against the brick wall. The springy stick bounded off the bricks and fell into an empty folding chair at the rear of the clarinet section—Plummer's empty chair.

As Mr. Helmholtz retrieved the baton, he found himself unexpectedly moved by the symbol of the empty chair. No one else, he realized, no matter how untalented, could fill the last chair in the organization as well as Plummer had. Mr. Helmholtz looked up to find many of the bandsmen contemplating the chair with him, as though they, too, sensed that something great, in a fantastic way, had disappeared, and that life would be a good bit duller on account of that.

During the ten minutes between the C Band and B Band sessions, Mr. Helmholtz hurried to his office and again tried to get in touch with the Sublime Chamberlain of the Knights of Kandahar. No luck! "Lord knows where he's off to now," Mr. Helmholtz was told. "He was in for just a second, but went right out again. I gave him your name, so I expect he'll call you when he gets a minute. You're the drum gentleman, aren't you?"

"That's right—the drum gentleman."

The buzzers in the hall were sounding, marking the beginning of another class period. Mr. Helmholtz wanted to stay by the phone until he'd caught the Sublime Chamberlain and closed the deal, but the B Band was waiting—and after that it would be the A Band.

An inspiration came to him. He called Western Union and sent a telegram to the man, offering fifty dollars for the drum and requesting a reply collect.

But no reply came during B Band practice. Nor had one come by the halfway point of the A Band session. The bandsmen, a sensitive, high-strung lot, knew immediately that their director was on edge about something, and the rehearsal went badly. Mr. Helmholtz stopped a march in the middle because somebody outside was shaking the large double doors at one end of the rehearsal room.

"All right, all right, let's wait until the racket dies down so we can hear ourselves," Mr. Helmholtz said.

At that moment, a student messenger handed him a telegram. Mr. Helmholtz tore open the envelope, and this is what he read:

DRUM SOLD STOP COULD YOU USE A STUFFED CAMEL ON WHEELS STOP

The wooden doors opened with a shriek of rusty hinges. A snappy autumn gust showered the band with leaves. Plummer stood in the great opening, winded and perspiring, harnessed to a drum as big as a harvest moon!

"I know this isn't challenge day," said Plummer, "but I thought you might make an exception in my case."

He walked in with splendid dignity, the huge apparatus grumbling along behind him.

Mr. Helmholtz rushed to meet him. He crushed Plummer's right hand between both of his. "Plummer, boy! You got it for us. Good boy! I'll pay you whatever you paid for it," he cried, and in his joy he added rashly, "And a nice little profit besides. Good boy!"

"Sell it?" said Plummer. "I'll give it to you when I graduate. All I want to do is play it in the A Band as long as I'm here."

"But Plummer," said Mr. Helmholtz, "you don't know anything about drums."

"I'll practice hard," said Plummer. He backed his instrument into an aisle between the tubas and the trombones, toward the percussion section, where the amazed musicians were hastily making room.

"Now, just a minute," said Mr. Helmholtz, chuckling as though Plummer were joking, and knowing full well he wasn't. "There's more to drum playing than just lambasting the thing whenever you take a notion to, you know. It takes years to be a drummer."

"Well," said Plummer, "the quicker I get at it, the quicker I'll get good."

"What I meant was that I'm afraid you won't be quite ready for the A Band for a little while."

Plummer stopped his backing. "How long?" he asked.

"Oh, sometime in your senior year, perhaps. Meanwhile, you could let the band have your drum to use until you're ready."

Mr. Helmholtz's skin began to itch all over as Plummer stared at him coldly. "Until hell freezes over?" Plummer said at last.

Mr. Helmholtz sighed. "I'm afraid that's about right." He shook his head. "It's what I tried to tell you yesterday afternoon: Nobody can do everything well, and we've all got to face up to our limitations. You're a fine boy, Plummer, but you'll never be a musician—not in a million years. The only thing to do is what we all have to do now and then: smile, shrug, and say, 'Well, that's just one of those things that's not for me.'"

Tears formed on the rims of Plummer's eyes. He walked slowly toward the doorway, with the drum tagging after him. He paused on the doorsill for one more wistful look at the A Band that would never have a chair for him. He smiled feebly and shrugged. "Some people have eight-foot drums," he said, "and others don't, and that's just the way life is. You're a fine man, Mr. Helmholtz, but you'll never get this drum in a million years, because I'm going to give it to my mother for a coffee table."

"Plummer!" cried Mr. Helmholtz. His plaintive voice was drowned out by the rumble and rattle of the big drum as it followed its small master down the school's concrete driveway.

Mr. Helmholtz ran after him. Plummer and his drum had stopped at an intersection to wait for a light to change. Mr. Helmholtz caught him there and seized his arm. "We've got to have that drum," he panted. "How much do you want?"

"Smile," said Plummer. "Shrug! That's what I did." Plummer did it again. "See? So I can't get into the A Band, so you can't have the drum. Who cares? All part of the growing-up process."

"The situations aren't the same!" said Mr. Helmholtz. "Not at all the same!"

"You're right," said Plummer. "I'm growing up, and you're not."

The light changed, and Plummer left Mr. Helmholtz on the corner, stunned.

Mr. Helmholtz had to run after him again. "Plummer," he wheedled, "you'll never be able to play it well."

"Rub it in," said Plummer.

"But look at what a swell job you're doing of pulling it," said Mr. Helmholtz.

"Rub it in," Plummer repeated.

"No, no, no," said Mr. Helmholtz. "Not at all. If the school gets that drum, whoever's pulling it will be as crucial and valued a member of the A Band as the first-chair clarinet. What if it capsized?"

"He'd win a band letter if it didn't capsize?" said Plummer.

And Mr. Helmholtz said this: "I don't see why not."

Poor Little Rich Town

Newell Cady had the polish, the wealth, the influence, and the middle-aged good looks of an idealized Julius Caesar. Most of all, though, Cady had know-how, know-how of a priceless variety that caused large manufacturing concerns to bid for his services like dying sultans offering half their kingdoms for a cure.

Cady could stroll through a plant that had been losing money for a generation, glance at the books, yawn and tell the manager how he could save half a million a year in materials, reduce his staff by a third, triple his output, and sell the stuff he'd been throwing out as waste for more than the cost of installing air-conditioning and continuous music throughout the plant. And the air-conditioning and music would increase individual productivity by as much as ten percent and cut union grievances by a fifth.

The latest firm to hire him was the Federal Apparatus Corporation, which had given him the rank of vice-president and sent him to Ilium, New York, where he was to see that the new company headquarters were built properly from the ground up. When the buildings were finished, hundreds of the company's top executives would move their offices from New York City to Ilium, a city that had virtually died when its textile mills moved south after the Second World War.

There was jubilation in Ilium when the deep, thick foundations for the new headquarters were poured, but the exultation was possibly highest in the village of Spruce Falls, nine miles from Ilium, for it was there that Newell Cady had rented, with an option to buy, one of the mansions that lined the shaded main street.

Spruce Falls was a cluster of small businesses and a public school and a post office and a police station and a firehouse serving surrounding dairy farms. During the second decade of the century it experienced a real estate boom. Fifteen mansions were built back then, in the belief that the area, because of its warm mineral springs, was becoming a spa for rich invalids and hypochondriacs and horse people, as had Saratoga, not far away.

In 1922, though, it was determined that bathing in the waters of the spring, while fairly harmless, was nonetheless responsible for several cases of a rash that a Manhattan dermatologist, with no respect for upstate real estate values, named "Spruce Falls disease."

In no time at all the mansions and their stables were as vacant as the abandoned palaces and temples of Angkor Thom in Cambodia. Banks foreclosed on those mansions that were mortgaged. The rest became property of the town in lieu of unpaid taxes. Nobody arrived from out of town to bid for them at any price, as though Spruce Falls disease were leprosy or cholera or bubonic plague.

Nine mansions were eventually bought from the banks or the town by locals, who could not resist getting so much for so little. They set up housekeeping in maybe six rooms at most, while dry rot and termites and mice and rats and squirrels and kids wrought havoc with the rest of the property.

"If we can make Newell Cady taste the joys of village life," said Fire Chief Stanley Atkins, speaking before an extraordinary meeting of the volunteer firemen on a Saturday afternoon, "he'll *use* that option to buy, and

Spruce Falls will become *the* fashionable place for Federal Apparatus executives to live. Without further ado," said Chief Atkins expansively, "I move that Mr. Newell Cady be elected to full membership in the fire department and be named head judge of the annual Hobby Show."

"*Audaces fortuna juvat!*" said Upton Beaton, who was a tall, fierce-seeming sixty-five. He was the last of what had been the first family of Spruce Falls. "Fortune," he translated after a pause, "favors the bold, that's true. But gentlemen—" and he paused again, portentously, while Chief Atkins looked worried and the other members of the fire department shifted about on their folding chairs. Like his forebears, Beaton had an ornamental education from Harvard, and like them, he lived in Spruce Falls because it took little effort for a Beaton to feel superior to his neighbors there. He survived on money his family had made during the short-lived boom.

"But," Beaton said again, as he stood up, "is this the kind of fortune we want? We are being asked to waive the three-year residence requirement for membership in the fire department in Mr. Cady's case, and thereby all our memberships are cheapened. If I may say so, the post of judge of the Hobby Show is of far greater significance than it would seem to an outsider. In our small village, we have only small ways of honoring our great, but we, for generations now, have taken pains to reserve those small honors for those of us who have shown such greatness as it is possible to achieve in the eyes of a village. I hasten to add that those honors that have come to me are marks of respect for my family and my age, not for myself, and are exceptions that should probably be curtailed."

He sighed. "If we waive this proud tradition, then that one, and then another, all for money, we will soon find ourselves with nothing left to wave but the white flag of an abject surrender of all we hold dear!" He sat, folded his arms, and stared at the floor.

Chief Atkins had reddened during the speech, and he avoided looking at Beaton. "The real estate people," he mumbled, "swear property values in Spruce Falls will quadruple if Cady stays."

"What is a village profited if it shall gain a real estate boom and lose its own soul?" Beaton asked.

Chief Atkins cleared his throat. "There's a motion on the floor," he said. "Is there a second?"

"Second," said someone who kept his head down.

"All in favor?" said Atkins.

There was a scuffling of chair legs, and faint voices, like the sounds of a playground a mile away.

"Opposed?"

Beaton was silent. The Beaton dynasty of Spruce Falls had come to an end. Its paternal guidance, unopposed for four generations, had just been voted down.

"Carried," said Atkins. He started to say something, then motioned for silence. "Shhh!" The post office was next door to the meeting hall, in the same building, and on the other side of the thin partition, Mr. Newell Cady was asking for his mail.

"That's all, is it, Mrs. Dickie?" Cady was saying to the postmistress.

"That's more'n some people get around here in a year," said Mrs. Dickie. "There's still a little second-class to put around. Maybe some for you."

"Mmm," said Cady. "That the way the government teaches its people to sort?"

"Them teach me?" said Mrs. Dickie. "I'd like to see anybody teach me anything about this business. I been postmistress for twenty-five years now, ever since my husband passed on."

"Um," said Cady. "Here—do you mind if I come back there and take a look at the second-class for just a minute?"

"Sorry—regulations, you know," said Mrs. Dickie.

But the door of Mrs. Dickie's cage creaked open anyway. "Thank you," said Cady. "Now, suppose, instead of holding these envelopes the way you were, suppose you took them like this, and uh—ah—putting that rubber cap on your thumb instead of your index finger—"

"My land!" cried Mrs. Dickie. "Look at you go!"

"It would be even faster," said Cady, "if it weren't for that tier of boxes by the floor. Why not move them over here, at eye level, see? And what on earth is this table doing back here?"

"For my children," said Mrs. Dickie.

"Your children play back here?"

"Not real children," said Mrs. Dickie. "That's what I call the plants on the table—the wise little cyclamen, the playful little screw pine, the temperamental little sansevieria, the—"

"Do you realize," said Cady, "that you must spend twenty man-minutes and heaven knows how many foot-pounds a day just detouring around it?"

"Well," said Mrs. Dickie, "I'm sure it's awfully nice of you to take such an interest, but you know, I'd just feel kind of lost without—"

"I can't help taking an interest," said Cady. "It causes me actual physical pain to see things done the wrong way, when it's so easy to do them the right way. Oops! Moved your thumb right back to where I told you not to put it!"

"Chief Atkins," whispered Upton Beaton in the meeting hall.

"Eh?"

"Don't you scratch your head like that," said Beaton. "Spread your fingers like this, see? *Then* dig in. Cover twice as much scalp in half the time."

"All due respect to you, sir," said Atkins, "this village could do with a little progress and perking up."

"I'd be the last to stand in its way," said Beaton. After a moment he added, "'Ill fares the land, to hastening ills a prey, where wealth accumulates, and men decay.'"

"Cady's across the street, looking at the fire truck," said Ed Newcomb, who had served twenty years as secretary of the fire department. The Ilium real estate man, who had put stars in every eye except Beaton's, had assured Newcomb that his twenty-six-room Georgian colonial, with a little paper and paint, would look like a steal to a corporation executive at fifty thousand dollars. "Let's tell him the good news!" Newcomb's father had bought the ark at a bank foreclosure sale. He was the only bidder.

The fire department joined its newest member by the fire truck and congratulated him on his election.

"Thanks," said Cady, tinkering with the apparatus strapped to the side of the big red truck. "By George, but there's a lot of chrome on one of these things," he said.

"Wait till you see the new one!" said Ed Newcomb.

"They make the damn things as ornamental as a merry-go-round," said Cady. "You'd think they were playthings. Lord! What all this plating and gimcrackery must add to the cost! New one, you say?"

"Sure," said Newcomb. "It hasn't been voted on yet, but it's sure to pass." The joy of the prospect showed on every face.

"Fifteen hundred gallons a minute!" said a fireman.

"Two floodlights!" said another.

"Closed cab!"

"Eighteen-foot ladders!"

"Carbon dioxide tank!"

"And a swivel-mounted nozzle in the turret smack-spang in the middle!" cried Atkins above them all.

After the silence that followed the passionate hymn to the new truck, Cady spoke. "Preposterous," he said. "This is a perfectly sound, adequate truck here."

"Mr. Cady is absolutely right," said Upton Beaton. "It's a sensible, sturdy truck, with many years of dependable service ahead of it. We were foolish to think of putting the fire district into debt for the next twenty years, just for an expensive plaything for the fire department. Mr. Cady has cut right to the heart of the matter."

"It's the same sort of thing I've been fighting in industry for half my life," said Cady. "Men falling in love with show instead of the job to be done. The sole purpose of a fire department should be to put out fires and to do it as economically as possible."

Beaton clapped Chief Atkins on the arm. "Learn something every day, don't we, Chief?"

Atkins smiled sweetly, as though he'd just been shot in the stomach.

The Spruce Falls annual Hobby Show took place in the church basement three weeks after Newell Cady's election to the fire department. During the intervening twenty-one days, Hal Brayton, the grocer, had stopped adding bills on paper sacks and bought an adding machine, and had moved his counters around so as to transform his customer space from a jammed box canyon into a racetrack. Mrs. Dickie, the postmistress, had moved her leafy children and their table out of her cage and had had the lowest tier of mailboxes raised to eye level. The fire department had voted down scarlet and blue capes for the band as unnecessary for firefighting. And startling figures had been produced in a school meeting proving beyond any doubt that it would cost seven dollars, twenty-nine cents, and six mills more per student per year to maintain the Spruce Falls Grade School than it would to ship the children to the big, efficient, centralized school in Ilium.

The whole populace looked as though it had received a powerful stimulant. People walked and drove faster, concluded business more quickly, and every eye seemed wider and brighter—even frenzied. And moving proudly through this brave new world were the two men who were shaping it, constant companions after working hours now. Newell Cady and Upton Beaton. Beaton's function was to provide Cady with the facts and figures behind village activities and then to endorse outrageously Cady's realistic suggestions for reforms, which followed facts and figures as the night the day.

The judges of the Hobby Show were Newell Cady, Upton Beaton, and Chief Stanley Atkins, and they moved slowly along the great assemblage of tables on which the entries were displayed. Atkins, who had lost weight and grown listless since informed public opinion had turned against the new fire truck, carried a shoe box in which lay neat stacks of blue prize ribbons.

"Surely we won't need all these ribbons," said Cady.

"Wouldn't do to run out," said Atkins. "We did one year, and there was hell to pay."

"There are a lot of classes of entries," explained Beaton, "with first prizes in each." He held out his hand to Atkins. "One with a pin, please, Chief." He pinned a ribbon to a dirty gray ball four feet in diameter.

"See here," said Cady. "I mean, aren't we going to talk this over? I mean, we shouldn't all merrily go our own ways, should we, sticking ribbons wherever we happen to take a notion to? Heavens, here you're giving first prize to this frightful blob, and I don't even know what it is."

"String," said Atkins. "It's Ted Batsford's string. Can you believe it—

the very first bit he ever started saving, right in the center of this ball, he picked up during the second Cleveland administration."

"Um," said Cady. "And he decided to enter it in the show this year."

"Every show since I can remember," said Beaton. "I knew this thing when it was no bigger than a bowling ball."

"So for brute persistence, I suppose we should at last award him a first prize, eh?" Cady said wearily.

"At last?" said Beaton. "He's always gotten first prize in the string-saving class."

Cady was about to say something caustic about this, when his attention was diverted. "Good Lord in heaven!" he said. "What is that mess of garbage you're giving first prize to now?"

Atkins looked bewildered. "Why, it's Mrs. Dickie's flower arrangement, of course."

"*That* jumble is a flower arrangement?" said Cady. "I could do better with a rusty bucket and a handful of toadstools. And you're giving it first prize. Where's the competition?"

"Nobody enters anybody else's class," said Beaton, laying a ribbon across the poop deck of a half-finished ship model.

Cady snatched the ribbon away from the model. "Hold on! Everybody gets a prize—am I right?"

"Why, yes, in his or her own class," said Beaton.

"So what's the point of the show?" demanded Cady.

"Point?" said Beaton. "It's a show, is all. Does it have to have a point?"

"Damn it all," said Cady. "I mean that it should have some sort of mission—to foster an interest in the arts and crafts, or something like that. Or to improve skills and refine tastes." He gestured at the displays. "Junk, every bit of it junk—and for years these misguided people have been getting top honors, as though they didn't have a single thing more to learn, or as though all it takes to gain acclaim in this world is the patience to have saved string since the second Cleveland administration."

Atkins looked shocked and hurt.

"Well," said Beaton, "you're head judge. Let's do it your way."

"Listen, Mr. Cady, sir," Atkins said hollowly, "we just can't not give—"

"You're standing in the way of progress," said Beaton.

"Now then, as I see it," said Cady, "there's only one thing in this whole room that shows the slightest glimmer of real creativity and ambition."

There were few lights in Spruce Falls that went off before midnight on the night of the Hobby Show opening, though the town was usually dark by ten. Those few nonparticipants who dropped in at the church to see the exhibits, and who hadn't heard about the judging, were amazed to find one lonely object, a petit-point copy of the cover of a woman's magazine, on view. Pinned to it was the single blue ribbon awarded that day. The other exhibitors had angrily hauled home their rejected offerings, and the sole prizewinner appeared late in the evening, embarrassed and furtive, to take her entry home, leaving the blue ribbon behind.

Only Newell Cady and Upton Beaton slept peacefully that night, with feelings of solid, worthwhile work behind them. But when Monday came again, there was a dogged cheerfulness in the town, for on Sunday, as though to offset the holocaust of the Hobby Show, the real estate man had been around. He had been writing to Federal Apparatus Corporation executives in New York, telling them of the mansions in Spruce Falls that could virtually be stolen from the simple-hearted natives and that were but a stone's throw from the prospective home of their esteemed colleague Mr. Newell Cady. What the real estate man had to show on Sunday were letters from executives who believed him.

By late afternoon on Monday, the last bitter word about the Hobby Show had been spoken, and talk centered now on the computation of capital gains taxes, the ruthless destruction of profit motives by the state and federal governments, the outrageous cost of building small houses—

"But I tell you," said Chief Atkins, "under this new law, you don't have to pay *any* tax on the profit you make off of selling your house. All that profit is just a paper profit, just plain, ordinary inflation, and they don't tax you on that, because it wouldn't be fair." He and Upton Beaton and Ed Newcomb were talking in the post office, while Mrs. Dickie sorted the late-afternoon mail.

"Sorry," said Beaton, "but you have to buy another house for at least as much as you got for your old one, in order to come under that law."

"What would I want with a fifty-thousand-dollar house?" said New-comb, awed.

"You can have mine for that, Ed," said Atkins. "That way, you wouldn't have to pay any tax at all." He lived in three rooms of an eighteen-room white elephant his own father had bought for peanuts.

"And have twice as many termites and four times as much rot as I've got to fight now," said Newcomb.

Atkins didn't smile. Instead, he kicked shut the post office door, which was ajar. "You big fool! You can't tell who might of been walking past and heard that, what you said about my house."

Beaton stepped between them. "Calm down! Nobody out there but old Dave Mansfield, and he hasn't heard anything since his boiler blew up. Lord, if the little progress we've had so far is making everybody that jumpy, what's it going to be like when we've got a Cady in every big house?"

"He's a fine gentleman," said Atkins.

Mrs. Dickie was puffing and swearing quietly in her cage. "I've bobbed up and down for that bottom tier of boxes for twenty-five years, and I can't make myself stop it, now that they're not there anymore. Whoops!" The mail in her hands fell to the floor. "See what happens when I put my thumb the way he told me to?"

"Makes no difference," said Beaton. "Put it where he told you to, be-cause here he comes."

Cady's black Mercedes came to a stop before the post office.

"Nice day, Mr. Cady, sir," said Atkins.

"Hmmm? Oh yes, I suppose it is. I was thinking about something else." Cady went to Mrs. Dickie's cage for his mail, but continued to talk to the group over his shoulder, not looking at Mrs. Dickie at all. "I just figured out that I go eight-tenths of a mile out of my way every day to pick up my mail."

"Good excuse to get out and pass the time of day with people," said Newcomb.

"And that's two hundred forty-nine point six miles per year, roughly," Cady went on earnestly, "which at eight cents a mile comes out to nine-teen dollars and ninety-seven cents a year."

"I'm glad to hear you can still buy something worthwhile for nineteen dollars and ninety-seven cents," said Beaton.

Cady was in a transport of creativeness, oblivious of the tension mounting in the small room. "And there must be at least a hundred others who drive to get their mail, which means an annual expenditure for the hundred of one thousand, nine hundred and ninety-seven dollars, not to mention man-hours. Think of it!"

"Huh," said Beaton, while Atkins and Newcomb shuffled their feet, eager to leave. "I'd hate to think what we spend on shaving cream." He took Cady's arm. "Come on over to my house a minute, would you? I've something I think you'd—"

Cady stayed put before Mrs. Dickie's cage. "It's not the same thing as shaving cream at all," he said. "Men have to shave, and shaving cream's the best thing there is to take whiskers off. And we have to get our mail, certainly, but I've found out something apparently nobody around here knows."

"Come on over to my house," said Beaton, "and we'll talk about it."

"It's so perfectly simple, there's no need to talk about it," said Cady. "I found out that Spruce Falls can get rural free delivery, just by telling the Ilium post office and sticking out mailboxes in front of our houses the way every other village around here does. And that's been true for years!" He smiled, and glanced absently at Mrs. Dickie's hands. "Ah, ah, ah!" he chided. "Slipping back to your old ways, aren't you, Mrs. Dickie?"

Atkins and Newcomb were holding open the door, like a pair of guards at the entrance to an execution chamber, while Upton Beaton hustled Cady out.

"It's a great advantage, coming into situations from the outside, the way I do," said Cady. "People inside of situations are so blinded by custom. Here you people were, supporting a post office, when you could get much better service for just a fraction of the cost and trouble." He chuckled modestly, as Atkins shut the post office door behind him. "One-eyed man in the land of the blind, you might say."

"A one-eyed man might as well be blind," declared Upton Beaton, "if he doesn't watch people's faces and doesn't give the blind credit for the senses they do have."

"What on earth are you talking about?" said Cady.

"If you'd looked at Mrs. Dickie's face instead of how she was doing her work, you would have seen she was crying," said Beaton. "Her husband died in a fire, saving some of these people around the village you call blind. You talk a lot about wasting time, Mr. Cady—for a really big waste of time, walk around the village someday and try to find somebody who doesn't know he can have his mail brought to his door anytime he wants to."

The second extraordinary meeting of the volunteer firemen within a month finished its business, and the full membership, save one fireman who had not been invited, seemed relaxed and contented for the first time in weeks. The business of the meeting had gone swiftly, with Upton Beaton, the patriarch of Spruce Falls, making motions, and the membership seconding in chorus. Now they waited for the one absent member, Newell Cady, to arrive at the post office on the other side of the thin wall to pick up his Saturday-afternoon mail.

"Here he is," whispered Ed Newcomb, who had been standing watch by the window.

A moment later, the rich voice came through the wall. "Good heavens, you've got all those plants in there with you again!"

"Just got lonesome," said Mrs. Dickie.

"But my dear Mrs. Dickie," said Cady, "think of—"

"The motion's been carried, then," said Chief Atkins in a loud voice. "Mr. Beaton is to be a committee of one to inform Mr. Cady that his fire department membership, unfortunately, is in violation of the by-laws, which call for three years' residence in the village prior to election."

"I will make it clear to him," said Beaton, also speaking loudly, "that this is in no way a personal affront, that it's simply a matter of conforming to our by-laws, which have been in effect for years."

"Make sure he understands that we all like him," said Ed Newcomb, "and tell him we're proud an important man like him would want to live here."

"I will," said Beaton. "He's a brilliant man, and I'm sure he'll see the wisdom in the residence requirement. A village isn't like a factory, where you can walk in and see what's being made at a glance, and then look at the books and see if it's a good or bad operation. We're not manufacturing or selling anything. We're trying to live together. Every man's got to be his own expert at that, and it takes years."

The meeting was adjourned.

The Ilium real estate man was upset, because everyone he wanted to see in Spruce Falls was out. He stood in Hal Brayton's grocery store, looking at the deserted street and fiddling with his fountain pen.

"They're *all* with the fire engine salesman?" he said.

"They're all going to be paying for the truck for the next twenty years," said Upton Beaton. He was tending Brayton's store while Brayton went for a ride on the fire engine.

"Red-hot prospects are going to start coming through here in a week, and everybody goes out joy-riding," said the real estate man bitterly. He opened the soft drink cooler and let the lid fall shut again. "What's the matter—this thing broken? Everything's warm."

"No, Brayton just hasn't gotten around to plugging it in since he moved things back the way they used to be."

"You said he's the one who doesn't want to sell his place?"

"One of the ones," said Beaton.

"Who else?"

"Everybody else."

"Go on!"

"Really," said Beaton. "We've decided to wait and see how Mr. Cady adapts himself, before we put anything else on the market. He's having a tough time, but he's got a good heart, I think, and we're all rooting for him."

Souvenir

Joe Bane was a pawnbroker, a fat, lazy, bald man, whose features seemed pulled to the left by his lifetime of looking at the world through a jeweler's glass. He was a lonely, untalented man and would not have wanted to go on living had he been prevented from playing every day save Sunday the one game he played brilliantly—the acquiring of objects for very little, and the selling of them for a great deal more. He was obsessed by the game, the one opportunity life offered him to best his fellow men. The game was the thing, the money he made a secondary matter, a way of keeping score.

When Joe Bane opened his shop Monday morning, a black ceiling of rainclouds had settled below the valley's rim, holding the city in a dark pocket of dead, dank air. Autumn thunder grumbled along the misty hillsides. No sooner had Bane hung up his coat and hat and umbrella, taken off his rubbers, turned on the lights, and settled his great bulk on a stool

behind a counter than a lean young man in overalls, shy and dark as an Indian, plainly poor and awed by the city, walked in to offer him a fantastic
pocketwatch for five hundred dollars.

"No, sir," said the young farmer politely. "I don't want to borrow money
on it. I want to sell it, if I can get enough for it." He seemed reluctant to
hand it to Bane, and cupped it tenderly in his rough hands for a moment
before setting it down on a square of black velvet. "I kind of hoped to hang
on to it, and pass it on to my oldest boy, but we need the money a whole
lot worse right now."

"Five hundred dollars is a lot of money," said Bane, like a man who had
been victimized too often by his own kindness. He examined the jewels
studding the watch without betraying anything of his inner amazement.
He turned the watch this way and that, catching the glare of the ceiling
light in four diamonds marking the hours three, six, nine, and twelve, and
the ruby crowning the winder. The jewels alone, Bane reflected, were worth
at least four times what the farmer was asking.

"I don't get much call for a watch like this," said Bane. "If I tied up five
hundred dollars in it, I might be stuck with it for years before the right
man came along." He watched the farmer's sunburned face and thought
he read there that the watch could be had for a good bit less.

"There ain't another one like it in the whole county," said the farmer, in
a clumsy attempt at salesmanship.

"That's my point," said Bane. "Who wants a watch like this?" Bane, for
one, wanted it, and was already regarding it as his own. He pressed a button on the side of the case and listened to the whirring of tiny machinery
striking the nearest hour on sweet, clear chimes.

"You want it or not?" said the farmer.

"Now, now," said Bane, "this isn't the kind of deal you just dive head-
first into. I'd have to know more about this watch before I bought it." He
pried open the back and found inside an engraved inscription in a foreign
language. "What does this say? Any idea?"

"Showed it to a schoolteacher back home," said the young man, "and
all she could say was it looked a whole lot like German."

Bane laid a sheet of tissue paper over the inscription, and rubbed a pencil back and forth across it until he'd picked up a legible copy. He gave the

copy and a dime to a shoeshine boy loitering by the door and sent him down the block to ask a German restaurant proprietor for a translation.

The first drops of rain were spattering clean streaks on the sooty glass when Bane said casually to the farmer, "The cops keep pretty close check on what comes in here."

The farmer reddened. "That watch is mine, all right. I got it in the war," he said.

"Uh-huh. And you paid duty on it?"

"Duty?"

"Certainly. You can't bring jewelry into this country without paying taxes on it. That's smuggling."

"Just tucked it in my barracks bag and brought her on home, the way everybody done," said the farmer. He was as worried as Bane had hoped.

"Contraband," said Bane. "Just about the same as stolen goods." He held up his hands placatingly. "I don't mean I can't buy it, I just want to point out to you that it'd be a tricky thing to handle. If you were willing to let it go for, oh, say a hundred dollars, maybe I'd take a chance on it to help you out. I try to give veterans a break here whenever I can."

"A hundred dollars! That's all?"

"That's all it's worth, and I'm probably a sucker to offer that," said Bane. "What the hell—that's an easy hundred bucks for you, isn't it? What'd you do—cop it off some German prisoner or find it lying around in the ruins?"

"No, sir," said the farmer, "it was a little tougher'n that."

Bane, who was keenly sensitive to such things, saw that the farmer, as he began to tell how he'd gotten the watch, was regaining the stubborn confidence that had deserted him when he'd left his farm for the city to make the sale.

"My best buddy Buzzer and me," said the farmer, "were prisoners of war together in some hills in Germany—in Sudetenland, somebody said it was. One morning, Buzzer woke me up and said the war was over, the guards were gone, the gates were open."

Joe Bane was impatient at first with having to listen to the tale. But it was a tale told well and proudly, and long a fan of others' adventures for want of any of his own, Bane began to see, enviously, the two soldiers walking through the open gates of their prison, and down a country road in the hills early on a bright spring morning in 1945, on the day the Second World War ended in Europe.

The young farmer, whose name was Eddie, and his best buddy Buzzer walked out into peace and freedom skinny, ragged, dirty, and hungry, but with no ill will toward anyone. They'd gone to war out of pride, not bitterness. Now the war was over, the job done, and they wanted only to go home. They were a year apart, but as alike as two poplars in a windbreak.

Their notion was to take a brief sightseeing tour of the neighborhood near the camp, then to come back and wait with the rest of the prisoners for the arrival of some official liberators. But the plan evaporated when a pair of Canadian prisoners invited the buddies to toast victory with a bottle of brandy they'd found in a wrecked German truck.

Their shrunken bellies gloriously hot and tingling, their heads light and full of trust and love for all mankind, Eddie and Buzzer found themselves swept along by a jostling, plaintive parade of German refugees that jammed the main road through the hills, refugees fleeing from the Russian tanks that growled monotonously and unopposed in the valley behind and below them. The tanks were coming to occupy this last undefended bit of German soil.

"What're we runnin' from?" said Buzzer. "The war's over, ain't it?"

"Everybody else is runnin'," said Eddie, "so I guess maybe we better be runnin', too."

"I don't even know where we are," said Buzzer.

"Them Canadians said it's Sudetenland."

"Where's that?"

"Where we're at," said Eddie. "Swell guys, them Canadians."

"I'll tell the world! Man," said Buzzer, "I love everybody today. Whoooooey! I'd like to get me a bottle of that brandy, put a nipple on it, and go to bed with it for a week."

Eddie touched the elbow of a tall, worried-looking man with close-cropped black hair, who wore a civilian suit too small for him. "Where we runnin' to, sir? Ain't the war over?"

The man glared, grunted something, and pushed by roughly.

"He don't understand English," said Eddie.

"Why, hell, man," said Buzzer, "why'n't you talk to these folks in their native tongue? Don't hide your candle under a bushel. Let's hear you sprecken some Dutch to this man here."

They'd come alongside a small, low black roadster, which was stalled on the shoulder of the road. A heavily muscled square-faced young man was tinkering with the dead motor. On the leather front seat of the car sat an older man whose face was covered with dust and several days' growth of black beard, and shaded by a hat with the brim pulled down.

Eddie and Buzzer stopped. "All right," said Eddie. "Just listen to this: *Wie geht's?*" he said to the blond man, using the only German he knew.

"*Gut, gut,*" muttered the young German. Then, realizing the absurdity of his automatic reply to the greeting, he said with terrible bitterness, "*Ja! Geht's gut!*"

"He says everything's just fine," said Eddie.

"Oh, you're fluent, mighty fluent," said Buzzer.

"Yes, I've traveled extensively, you might say," said Eddie.

The older man came to life and yelled at the man who was working on the motor, yelled shrilly and threateningly.

The blond seemed frightened. He went to work on the motor with redoubled desperation.

The older man's eyes, bleary a moment before, were wide and bright now. Several refugees turned to stare as they passed.

The older man glanced challengingly from one face to the next, and filled his lungs to shout something at them. But he changed his mind, sighed instead, and his spirits collapsed. He thrust his face in his hands.

"Wha'd he say?" said Buzzer.

"He don't speak my particular dialect," said Eddie.

"Speaks low-class German, huh?" said Buzzer. "Well, I'm not goin' another step till we find somebody who can tell us what's goin' on. We're Americans, boy. Our side won, didn't it? What we doin' all tangled up with these Jerries?"

"You—you Americans," said the blond, surprisingly enough in English. "Now you will have to fight them."

"Here's one that talks English!" said Buzzer.

"Talks it pretty good, too," said Eddie.

"Ain't bad, ain't bad at all," said Buzzer. "Who we got to fight?"

"The Russians," said the young German, seeming to relish the idea. "They'll kill you, too, if they catch you. They're killing everybody in their path."

"Hell, man," said Buzzer, "we're on their side."

"For how long? Run, boys, run." The blond swore and hurled his wrench at the motor. He turned to the old man and spoke, scared to death of him.

The older man released a stream of German abuse, tired of it quickly, got out of the car, and slammed the door behind him. The two looked anxiously in the direction from which the tanks would come, and started down the road on foot.

"Where you guys headed?" said Eddie.

"Prague—the Americans are in Prague."

Eddie and Buzzer fell in behind them. "Sure gettin' a mess of geography today, ain't we, Eddie?" said Buzzer. He stumbled, and Eddie caught him. "Oh, oh, Eddie, that old booze is sneakin' up on me."

"Yeah," said Eddie, whose own senses were growing fuzzier. "I say to hell with Prague. If we don't ride, we don't go, and that's that."

"Sure. We'll just find us some shady spot, and sit and wait for the Russians. We'll just show 'em our dog tags," said Buzzer. "And when they see 'em, bet they give us a big banquet." He dipped a finger inside his collar and brought out the tags on their string.

"Oh my, yes," said the blond German, who had been listening carefully, "a wonderful big banquet they'll give you."

The column had been moving more and more slowly, growing more packed. Now it came to a muttering halt.

"Must be a woman up front, tryin' to read a road map," said Buzzer.

From far down the road came an exchange of shouts like a distant surf. Restless, anxious moments later, the cause of the trouble was clear: The column had met another, fleeing in terror from the opposite direction. The Russians had the area surrounded. Now the two columns merged to form an aimless whirlpool in the heart of a small village, flooding out into side lanes and up the slopes on either side.

"Don't know nobody in Prague, anyhow," said Buzzer, and he wandered off the road and sat by the gate of a walled farmyard.

Eddie followed his example. "By God," he said, "maybe we oughta stay right here and open us up a gun shop, Buzzer." He included in a sweep of his hand the discarded rifles and pistols that were strewn over the grass. "Bullets and all."

"Swell place to open a gun shop, Europe is," said Buzzer. "They're just crazy about guns around here."

Despite the growing panic of the persons milling about them, Buzzer dropped off into a brandy-induced nap. Eddie had trouble keeping his eyes open.

"Aha!" said a voice from the road. "Here our American friends are."

Eddie looked up to see the two Germans, the husky young man and the irascible older one, grinning down at them.

"Hello," said Eddie. The cheering edge of the brandy was wearing off, and queasiness was taking its place.

The young German pushed open the gate to the farmyard. "Come in here, would you?" he told Eddie. "We have something important to say to you."

"Say it here," said Eddie.

The blond leaned down. "We've come to surrender to you."

"You've come to what?"

"We surrender," said the blond. "We are your prisoners—prisoners of the United States Army."

Eddie laughed.

"Seriously!"

"Buzzer!" Eddie nudged his buddy with the toe of his boot. "Hey, Buzzer—you gotta hear this."

"Hmmmm?"

"We just captured some people."

Buzzer opened his eyes and squinted at the pair. "You're drunker'n I am, by God, Eddie, goin' out capturin' people," he said at last. "You damn fool—the war's over." He waved his hand magnanimously. "Turn 'em loose."

"Take us through the Russian lines to Prague as American prisoners, and you'll be heroes," said the blond. He lowered his voice. "This is a famous German general. Think of it—you two can bring him in as your prisoner!"

"He really a general?" said Buzzer. "Heil Hitler, Pop."

The older man raised his arm in an abbreviated salute.

"Got a little pepper left in him, at that," said Buzzer.

"From what I heard," said Eddie, "me and Buzzer'll be heroes if we get just us through the Russian lines, let alone a German general."

The noise of a tank column of the Red Army grew louder.

"All right, all right," said the blond, "sell us your uniforms, then. You'll still have your dog tags, and you can take our clothes."

"I'd rather be poor than dead," said Eddie. "Wouldn't you, Buzzer?"

"Just a minute, Eddie," said Buzzer, "just hold on. What'll you give us?"

"Come in the farmyard. We can't show you here," said the blond.

"I even heard there was some Nazis in the neighborhood," said Buzzer. "Come on, give us a little peek here."

"Now who's a damn fool?" said Eddie.

"Just want to be able to tell my grandchildren what I passed up," said Buzzer.

The blond was going through his pockets. He pulled out a fat roll of German currency.

"Confederate money!" said Buzzer. "What else you got?"

It was then that the old man showed them his pocketwatch, four diamonds, a ruby, and gold. And there, in the midst of a mob of every imaginable sort of refugee, the blond told Buzzer and Eddie that they could have the watch if they would go behind a wall and exchange their ragged American uniforms for the Germans' civilian clothes. They thought Americans were so dumb!

This was all so funny and crazy! Eddie and Buzzer were so drunk! What a story they would have to tell when they got home! They didn't want the watch. They wanted to get home alive. There, in the midst of a mob of every imaginable sort of refugee, the blond was showing them a small pistol, as though they could have that, too, along with the watch.

But it was now impossible for anybody to say any more funny stuff and still be heard. The earth shook, and the air was ripped to shreds as armored vehicles from the victorious Soviet Union, thundering and backfiring, came up the road. Everybody who could got out of the way of the juggernaut. Some were not so lucky. They were mangled. They were squashed.

Eddie and Buzzer and the old man and the blond found themselves behind the wall where the blond had said the Americans could swap their uniforms for the watch and civilian clothes. In the uproar, during which anybody could do anything, and nobody cared what anybody else did, the blond shot Buzzer in the head. He aimed his pistol at Eddie. He fired. He missed.

That had evidently been the plan all along, to kill Eddie and Buzzer. But what chance did the old man, who spoke no English, have to pass himself off to his captors as an American? None. It was the blond who was going to do that. And they were both about to be captured. All the old man could do was commit suicide.

Eddie went back over the wall, putting it between himself and the blond. But the blond didn't care what had become of him. Everything the blond needed was on Buzzer's body. When Eddie peered over the wall to see if Buzzer was still alive, the blond was stripping the body. The old man now had the pistol. He put its muzzle in his mouth and blew his brains out.

The blond walked off with Buzzer's clothes and dog tags. Buzzer was in his GI underwear and dead, without ID. On the ground between the old man and Buzzer, Eddie found the watch. It was running. It told the right time. Eddie picked it up and put it in his pocket.

The rainstorm outside Joe Bane's pawnshop had stopped. "When I got home," said Eddie, "I wrote Buzzer's folks. I told 'em he'd been killed in a fight with a German, even though the war was over. I told the Army the same thing. I didn't know the name of the place where he'd died, so there was no way they could look for his body and give him a decent funeral. I had to leave him there. Whoever buried him, unless they could recognize

GI underwear, wouldn't have known he was American. He could have been a German. He could have been anything."

Eddie snatched the watch from under the pawnbroker's nose. "Thanks for letting me know what it's worth," he said. "Makes more sense to keep it for a souvenir."

"Five hundred," said Bane, but Eddie was already on his way out the door.

Ten minutes later, the shoeshine boy returned with a translation of the inscription inside the watch. This was it:

"To General Heinz Guderian, Chief of the Army General Staff, who cannot rest until the last enemy soldier is driven from the sacred soil of the Third German Reich. ADOLF HITLER."

The Cruise of
The Jolly Roger

During the Great Depression, Nathan Durant was homeless until he found a home in the United States Army. He spent seventeen years in the Army, thinking of the earth as terrain, of the hills and valleys as enfilade and defilade, of the horizon as something a man should never silhouette himself against, of the houses and woods and thickets as cover. It was a good life, and when he got tired of thinking about war, he got himself a girl and a bottle, and the next morning he was ready to think about war some more.

When he was thirty-six, an enemy projectile dropped into a command post under thick green cover in defilade in the terrain of Korea, and blew Major Durant, his maps, and his career through the wall of his tent.

He had always assumed that he was going to die young and gallantly.

But he didn't die. Death was far, far away, and Durant faced unfamiliar and frightening battalions of peaceful years.

In the hospital, the man in the next bed talked constantly of the boat he was going to own when he was whole again. For want of exciting peacetime dreams of his own, for want of a home or family or civilian friends, Durant borrowed his neighbor's dream.

With a deep scar across his cheek, with the lobe of his right ear gone, with a stiff leg, he limped into a boatyard in New London, the port nearest the hospital, and bought a secondhand cabin cruiser. He learned to run it in the harbor there, christened the boat *The Jolly Roger* at the suggestion of some children who haunted the boatyard, and set out arbitrarily for Martha's Vineyard.

He stayed on the island but a day, depressed by the tranquility and permanence, by the feeling of deep, still lakes of time, by men and women so at one with the peace of the place as to have nothing to exchange with an old soldier but a few words about the weather.

Durant fled to Chatham, at the elbow of Cape Cod, and found himself beside a beautiful woman at the foot of a lighthouse there. Had he been in his old uniform, seeming as he'd liked to seem in the old days, about to leave on a dangerous mission, he and the woman might have strolled off together. Women had once treated him like a small boy with special permission to eat icing off cakes. But the woman looked away without interest. He was nobody and nothing. The spark was gone.

His former swashbuckling spirits returned for an hour or two during a brief blow off the dunes of Cape Cod's east coast, but there was no one aboard to notice. When he reached the sheltered harbor at Provincetown and went ashore, he was a hollow man again, who didn't have to be anywhere at any time, whose life was all behind him.

"Look up, please," commanded a gaudily dressed young man with a camera in his hands and a girl on his arm.

Surprised, Durant did look up, and the camera shutter clicked. "Thank you," said the young man brightly.

"Are you a painter?" asked his girl.

"Painter?" said Durant. "No—retired Army officer."

The couple did a poor job of covering their disappointment.

"Sorry," said Durant, and he felt dull and annoyed.

"Oh!" said the girl. "There's some real painters over there."

Durant glanced at the artists, three men and one woman, probably in their late twenties, who sat on the wharf, their backs to a silvered splintering pile, sketching. The woman, a tanned brunette, was looking right at Durant.

"Do you mind being sketched?" she said.

"No—no, I guess not," said Durant bearishly. Freezing in his pose, he wondered what it was he'd been thinking about that had made him interesting enough to draw. He realized that he'd been thinking about lunch, about the tiny galley aboard *The Jolly Roger*, about the four wrinkled wieners, the half-pound of cheese, and the flat remains of a quart of beer that awaited him there.

"There," said the woman, "you see?" She held out the sketch.

What Durant saw was a big, scarred, hungry man, hunched over and desolate as a lost child. "Do I really look that bad?" he said, managing to laugh.

"Do you really feel that awful?"

"I was thinking of lunch. Lunch can be pretty terrible."

"Not where we eat it," she said. "Why not come with us?"

Major Durant went with them, with the three men, Ed, Teddy, and Lou, who danced through a life that seemed full of funny secrets, and with the girl, Marion. He found he was relieved to be with others again, even with these others, and his step down the walk was jaunty.

At lunch, the four spoke of painting, ballet, and drama. Durant grew tired of counterfeiting interest, but he kept at it.

"Isn't the food good here?" said Marion, in a casual and polite aside.

"Um," said Durant. "But the shrimp sauce is flat. Needs—" He gave up. The four were off again in their merry whirlwind of talk.

"Did you just drive here?" said Teddy, when he saw Durant staring at him disapprovingly.

"No," said Durant. "I came in my boat."

"A boat!" they echoed, excited, and Durant found himself center stage.

"What kind?" said Marion.

"Cabin cruiser," said Durant.

Their faces fell. "Oh," said Marion, "one of those floating tourist cabins with a motor."

"Well," said Durant, tempted to tell them about the blow he'd weathered, "it's certainly no picnic when—"

"What's its name?" said Lou.

"*The Jolly Roger*," said Durant.

The four exchanged glances, and then burst into laughter, repeating the boat's name, to Durant's consternation and bafflement.

"If you had a dog," said Marion, "I'll bet you'd call it Spot."

"Seems like a perfectly good name for a dog," said Durant, reddening.

Marion reached across the table and patted his hand. "Aaaaaah, you lamb, you musn't mind us." She was an irresponsibly affectionate woman, and appeared to have no idea how profoundly her touch was moving the lonely Durant, in spite of his resentment. "Here we've been talking away and not letting you say a word," she said. "What is it you do in the Army?"

Durant was startled. He hadn't mentioned the Army, and there were no insignia on his faded khakis. "Well, I was in Korea for a little while," he said, "and I'm out of the Army now because of wounds."

The four were impressed and respectful. "Do you mind talking about it?" said Ed.

Durant sighed. He did mind talking about it to Ed, Teddy, and Lou, but he wanted very much for Marion to hear about it—wanted to show her that while he couldn't speak her language, he could speak one of his own that had life to it. "No," he said, "there are some things that would just as well stay unsaid, but for the most part, why not talk about it?" He sat back and lit a cigarette, and squinted into the past as though through a thin screen of shrubs in a forward observation post.

"Well," he said, "we were over on the east coast, and . . ." He had never tried to tell the tale before, and now, in his eagerness to be glib and urbane, he found himself including details, large and small, as they occurred to him, until his tale was no tale at all, but a formless, unwieldy description of war as it had really seemed: a senseless, complicated mess that in the telling was first-rate realism but miserable entertainment.

He had been talking for twenty minutes now, and his audience had finished coffee and dessert, and two cigarettes apiece, and the waitress was getting restive about the check. Durant, florid and irritated with himself, was trying to manage a cast of thousands spread over the forty thousand square miles of South Korea. His audience was listening with glazed eyes, brightening at any sign that the parts were about to be brought together into a whole and thence to an end. But the signs were always false, and at last, when Marion swallowed her third yawn, Durant blew himself in his story through the wall of his tent and fell silent.

"Well," said Teddy, "it's hard for us who haven't seen it to imagine."

"Words can hardly convey it," said Marion. She patted Durant's hand again. "You've been through so much, and you're so modest about it."

"Nothing, really," said Durant.

After a moment of silence, Marion stood. "It's certainly been pleasant and interesting, Major," she said, "and we all wish you bon voyage on *The Jolly Roger*."

And there it ended.

Back aboard *The Jolly Roger*, Durant finished the stale quart of beer and told himself he was ready to give up—to sell the boat, return to the hospital, put on a bathrobe, and play cards and thumb through magazines until doomsday.

Moodily he studied his charts for a course back to New London. It was then he realized that he was only a few miles from the home village of a friend who had been killed in the Second World War. It struck him as wryly fitting that he should call on this ghost on his way back.

He arrived at the village through an early-morning mist, the day before Memorial Day, feeling ghostlike himself. He made a bad landing that shook the village dock, and tied up *The Jolly Roger* with a clumsy knot.

When he reached the main street, he found it quiet but lined with flags. Only two other people were abroad to glance at the dour stranger.

He stepped into the post office and spoke to the brisk old woman who was sorting mail in a rickety cage.

"Pardon me," said Durant, "I'm looking for the Pefko family."

"Pefko? Pefko?" said the postmistress. "That doesn't sound like any name around here. Pefko? They summer people?"

"No—I don't think so. I'm sure they're not. They may have moved away a while ago."

"Well, if they lived here, you'd think I'd know. They'd come here for their mail. There's only four hundred of us year around, and I never heard of any Pefko."

The secretary from the law office across the street came in and knelt by Durant, and worked the combination lock of her mailbox.

"Annie," said the postmistress, "you know about anybody named Pefko around here?"

"No," said Annie, "unless they had one of the summer cottages out on the dunes. It's hard to keep track of who is in those. They're changing hands all the time."

She stood, and Durant saw that she was attractive in a determinedly practical way, without wiles or ornamentation. But Durant was now so convinced of his own dullness that his manner toward her was perfunctory.

"Look," he said, "my name is Durant, Major Nathan Durant, and one of my best friends in the Army was from here. George Pefko—I know he was from here. He said so, and so did all his records. I'm sure of it."

"Ohhhhhh," said Annie. "Now wait, wait, wait. That's right—certainly. Now I remember."

"You knew him?" said Durant.

"I knew *of* him," said Annie. "I know now who you're talking about: the one that got killed in the war."

"I was with him," said Durant.

"Still can't say as I remember him," said the postmistress.

"You don't remember him, probably, but you remember the family," said Annie. "And they *did* live out on the dunes, too. Goodness, that was a long time ago—ten or fifteen years. Remember that big family that talked Paul Eldredge into letting them live in one of his summer cottages all winter? About six kids or more. That was the Pefkos. A wonder they didn't freeze to death, with nothing but a fireplace for heat. The old man came out here to pick cranberries, and stayed on through the winter."

"Wouldn't exactly call this their hometown," said the postmistress.

"George did," said Durant.

"Well," said Annie, "I suppose one hometown was as good as another for young George. Those Pefkos were wanderers."

"George enlisted from here," said Durant. "I suppose that's how he settled on it." By the same line of reasoning, Durant had chosen Pittsburgh as his hometown, though a dozen other places had as strong a claim.

"One of those people who found a home in the Army," said the postmistress. "Scrawny, tough boy. I remember now. His family never got any mail. That was it, and they weren't church people. That's why I forgot. Drifters. He must have been about your brother's age, Annie."

"I know. But I tagged after my brother all the time in those days, and George Pefko never had anything to do with his gang. They kept to themselves, the Pefkos did."

"There must be somebody who remembers him well," said Durant. "Somebody who—" He let the sentence die on a note of urgency. It was unbearable that every vestige of George had disappeared, unmissed.

"Now that I think about it," said Annie, "I'm almost sure there's a square named after him."

"A square?" said Durant.

"Not really a square," said Annie. "They just call it a square. When a man from around here gets killed in a war, the town names some little plot of town property after him—a traffic circle or something like that. They put up a plaque with his name on it. That triangle down by the village dock—I'm almost sure that was named for your friend."

"It's hard to keep track of them all, *these* days," said the postmistress.

"Would you like to go down and see it?" said Annie. "I'll be glad to show you."

"A plaque?" said Durant. "Never mind." He dusted his hands. "Well, which way is the restaurant—the one with a bar?"

"After June fifteenth, any way you want to go," said the postmistress. "But right now everything is closed and shuttered. You can get a sandwich at the drugstore."

"I might as well move on," said Durant.

"As long as you've come, you ought to stay for the parade," said Annie.

"After seventeen years in the Army, that would be a real treat," said Durant. "What parade?"

"Memorial Day," said Annie.

"That's tomorrow, I thought," said Durant.

"The children march today. School is closed tomorrow," said Annie. She smiled. "I'm afraid you're going to have to endure one more parade, Major, because here it comes."

Durant followed her apathetically out onto the sidewalk. He could hear the sound of a band, but the marchers weren't yet in sight. There were no more than a dozen people waiting for the parade to pass.

"They go from square to square," said Annie. "We really ought to wait for them down by George's."

"Whatever you say," said Durant. "I'll be closer to the boat."

They walked down the slope toward the village dock and *The Jolly Roger*.

"They keep up the squares very nicely," said Annie.

"They always do, they always do," said Durant.

"Are you in a hurry to get somewhere else today?"

"Me?" said Durant bitterly. "Me? Nothing's waiting for me anywhere."

"I see," said Annie, startled. "Sorry."

"It isn't your fault."

"I don't understand."

"I'm an Army bum like George. They should have handed me a plaque and shot me. I'm not worth a dime to anybody."

"Here's the square," said Annie gently.

"Where? Oh—that." The square was a triangle of grass, ten feet on a side, an accident of intersecting lanes and a footpath. In its center was a low boulder on which was fixed a small metal plaque, easily overlooked.

"George Pefko Memorial Square," said Durant. "By golly, I wonder what George would make of that?"

"He'd like it, wouldn't he?" said Annie.

"He'd probably laugh."

"I don't see that there's anything to laugh about."

"Nothing, nothing at all—except that it doesn't have much to do with anything, does it? Who cares about George? Why should anyone care about George? It's just what people are expected to do, put up plaques."

The bandsmen were in sight now, all eight of them, teenagers, out of step, rounding a corner with confident, proud, sour, and incoherent noise intended to be music.

Before them rode the town policeman, fat with leisure, authority, leather, bullets, pistol, handcuffs, club, and a badge. He was splendidly oblivious to the smoking, backfiring motorcycle beneath him as he swept slowly back and forth before the parade.

Behind the band came a cloud of purple, seeming to float a few feet above the street. It was lilacs caried by children. Along the curb, teachers looking as austere as New England churches called orders to the children.

"The lilacs came in time this year," said Annie. "Sometimes they don't. It's touch-and-go."

"That so?" said Durant.

A teacher blew a whistle. The parade halted, and Durant found a dozen children bearing down on him, their eyes large, their arms filled with flowers, their knees lifted high.

Durant stepped aside.

A bugler played taps badly.

The children laid their flowers before the plaque on George Pefko Memorial Square.

"Lovely?" whispered Annie.

"Yes," said Durant. "It would make a statue want to cry. But what does it mean?"

"Tom," called Annie to a small boy who had just laid down his flowers, "why did you do that?"

The boy looked around guiltily. "Do what?"

"Put the flowers down there," said Annie.

"Tell them you're paying homage to one of the fallen valiant who selflessly gave his life," prompted a teacher.

Tom looked at her blankly, and then back at the flowers.

"Don't you know?" said Annie.

"Sure," said Tom at last. "He died fighting so we could be safe and free. And we're thanking him with flowers, because it was a nice thing to do."

He looked up at Annie, amazed that she should ask. "Everybody knows that."

The policeman raced his motorcycle engine. The teacher shepherded the children back into line. The parade moved on.

"Well," said Annie, "are you sorry you had to endure one more parade, Major?"

"It's true, isn't it," murmured Durant. "It's so damn simple, and so easy to forget." Watching the innocent marchers under the flowers, he was aware of life, the beauty and importance of a village at peace. "Maybe I never knew—never had any way of knowing. This *is* what war is about, isn't it. This."

Durant laughed. "George, you homeless, horny, wild old rummy," he said to George Pefko Memorial Square, "damned if you didn't turn out to be a saint."

The old spark was back. Major Durant, home from the wars, was somebody.

"I wonder," he said to Annie, "if you'd have lunch with me, and then, maybe, we could go for a ride in my boat."

Custom-Made Bride

I am a customer's man for an investment counseling firm. I'm starting to build a clientele and to see my way clear to take, in a modest way, the good advice I sell. My uniform—gray suit, Homburg hat, and navy blue overcoat—is paid for, and after I get a half-dozen more white shirts, I'm going to buy some stock.

We in the investment counseling business have a standard question, which goes, "Mr. X, sir, before we can make our analyses and recommendations, we'd like to know just what it is you want from your portfolio: income or growth?" A portfolio is a nest egg in the form of stocks and bonds. What the question tries to get at is, does the client want to put his nest egg where it will grow, not paying much in dividends at first, or does he want the nest egg to stay about the same size but pay nice dividends?

The usual answer is that the client wants his nest egg to grow *and* pay a lot of dividends. He wants to get richer fast. But I've had plenty of unusual answers, particularly from clients who, because of some kind of mental block, can't take money in the abstract seriously. When asked what they want from their portfolio, they're likely to name something they're itching to blow money on—a car, a trip, a boat, a house.

When I put the question to a client named Otto Krummbein, he said he wanted to make two women happy: Kitty and Falloleen.

Otto Krummbein is a genius, designer of the Krummbein Chair, the Krummbein Di-Modular Bed, the body of the Marittima-Frascati Sports Racer, and the entire line of Mercury Kitchen Appliances.

He is so engrossed in beauty that his mental development in money matters is that of a chickadee. When I showed him the first stock certificate I bought for his portfolio, he wanted to sell it again because he didn't like the artwork.

"What difference do the looks of the certificate make, Otto?" I said, bewildered. "The point is that the company behind it is well managed, growing, and has a big cash reserve."

"Any company," said Otto, "that would choose as its symbol this monstrosity at the top of the certificate, this fat Medusa astride a length of sewer pipe and wrapped in cable, is certainly insensitive, vulgar, and stupid."

When I got Otto as a client, he was in no condition to start building a portfolio. I got him through his lawyer, Hal Murphy, a friend of mine.

"I laid eyes on him for the first time two days ago," said Hal. "He came wandering in here, and said in a casual, fogbound way that he thought he might need a little help." Hal chuckled. "They tell me this Krummbein is a genius, but I say he belongs on Skid Row or in a laughing academy. He's made over two hundred and thirty-five thousand dollars in the past seven years, and—"

"Then he is a genius," I said.

"He's blown every dime of it on parties, nightclubbing, his house, and clothes for his wife," said Hal.

"Hooray," I said. "That's the investment advice I always wanted to give, but nobody would pay for it."

"Well, Krummbein is perfectly happy with his investments," said Hal.

"What made him think he might just possibly need a little help was a call from the Internal Revenue Service."

"Oh, oh," I said. "I'll bet he forgot to file a declaration of estimated income for the coming year."

"You lose," said Hal. "This genius has never paid a cent of income taxes—ever! He said he kept expecting them to send him a bill, and they never did." Hal groaned. "Well, brother, they finally got around to it. Some bill!"

"What can I do?" I asked.

"He's got bundles of money coming in all the time—and insists on being paid in cashier's checks," said Hal. "You take care of them while I try to keep him out of prison. I've told him all about you, and he says for you to come out to his house right away."

"What bank does he use?" I said.

"He doesn't use a bank, except to cash the checks, which he keeps in a wicker basket under his drafting table," said Hal. "Get that basket!"

Otto's home and place of business is thirty miles from town, in a wilderness by a waterfall. It looks, roughly, like a matchbox resting on a spool. The upper story, the matchbox, has glass walls all the way around, and the lower story, the spool, is a windowless brick cylinder.

There were four other cars in the guest parking area when I arrived. A small cocktail party was in progress. As I was skirting the house, wondering how to get into it, I heard somebody tapping on the inside of a glass wall above. I looked up to see the most startling and, in a bizarre way, one of the most beautiful women of my experience.

She was tall and slender, with a subtly muscled figure sheathed in a zebra-striped leotard. Her hair was bleached silver and touched with blue, and in the white and perfect oval of her face were eyes of glittering green, set off by painted eyebrows, jet black and arched. She wore one earring, a barbaric gold hoop. She was making spiral motions with her hand, and I understood at last that I was to climb the spiral ramp that wound around the brick cylinder.

The ramp brought me up to a catwalk outside the glass walls. A towering, vigorous man in his early thirties slid back a glass panel and invited me in. He wore lavender nylon coveralls and sandals. He was nervous, and there was tiredness in his deep-set eyes.

"Mr. Krummbein?" I said.

"Who else would I be?" said Otto. "And you must be the wizard of high finance. We can go into my studio, where we'll have more privacy, and then"—pointing to the woman—"you can join us in a drink."

His studio was inside the brick cylinder, and he led me through a door and down another spiral ramp into it. There were no windows. All light was artificial.

"Guess this is the most modern house I've ever been in," I said.

"Modern?" said Otto. "It's twenty years behind the times, but it's the best my imagination can do. Everything else is at least a hundred years behind the times, and that is why we have all the unrest, this running to psychiatrists, broken homes, wars. We haven't learned to design our living for our own times. Our lives clash with our times. Look at your clothes! Shades of 1910. You're not dressed for 1954."

"Maybe not," I said, "but I'm dressed for helping people handle money."

"You are being suffocated by tradition," said Otto. "Why don't you say, 'I am going to build a life for myself, for my time, and make it a work of art'? Your life isn't a work of art—it's a thirdhand Victorian whatnot shelf, complete with someone else's collection of seashells and hand-carved elephants."

"Yup," I said, sitting down on a twenty-foot couch. "That's my life, all right."

"Design your life like that Finnish carafe over there," said Otto, "clean, harmonious, alive with the cool, tart soul of truth in our time. Like Falloleen."

"I'll try," I said. "Mostly it's a question of getting my head above water first. What is Falloleen, a new miracle fiber?"

"My wife," said Otto. "She's hard to miss."

"In the leotard," I said.

"Did you ever see a woman who fitted so well into surroundings like this—who seems herself to be designed for contemporary living?" said

Otto. "A rare thing, believe me. I've had many famous beauties out here, but Falloleen is the only one who doesn't look like a piece of 1920-vintage overstuffed furniture."

"How long have you been married?" I said.

"The party upstairs is in celebration of one month of blissful marriage," said Otto, "of a honeymoon that will never end."

"How nice," I said. "And now, about your financial picture—"

"Just promise me one thing," he said, "don't be depressing. I can't work if I'm depressed. The slightest thing can throw me off—that tie of yours, for instance. It jars me. I can't think straight when I look at it. Would you mind taking it off? Lemon yellow is your color, not that gruesome maroon."

Half an hour later, tieless, I felt like a man prowling through a city dump surrounded by smoldering tire casings, rusting bedsprings, and heaps of tin cans, for that was the financial picture of Otto Krummbein. He kept no books, bought whatever caught his fancy, without considering the cost, owed ruinous bills all over town for clothes for Falloleen, and didn't have a cent in a savings account, insurance, or a portfolio.

"Look," said Otto, "I'm scared. I don't want to go to prison, I didn't mean to do anything wrong. I've learned my lesson. I promise to do anything you say. Anything! Just don't depress me."

"If you can be cheerful about this mess," I said, "the Lord knows I can. The thing to do, I think, is to save you from yourself by letting me manage your income, putting you on an allowance."

"Excellent," said Otto. "I admire a bold approach to problems. And that will leave me free to work out an idea I got on my honeymoon, an idea that is going to make millions. I'll wipe out all this indebtedness in one fell swoop!"

"Just remember," I said, "you're going to have to pay taxes on that, too. You're the first man I ever heard of who got a profitable idea on his honeymoon. Is it a secret?"

"Moonlight-engineered cosmetics," said Otto, "designed expressly, according to the laws of light and color, to make a woman look her best in the moonlight. Millions, zillions!"

"That's swell," I said, "but in the meantime, I'd like to go over your bills to see exactly how deep in you are, and also to figure out what allowance you could get by on at a bare minimum."

"You could go out to supper with us tonight," said Otto, "and then come back and work undisturbed here in the studio. I'm sorry we have to go out, but it's the cook's day off."

"That would suit me fine," I said. "That way I'll have you around to answer questions. There ought to be plenty of those. For instance, how much is in the basket?"

Otto paled. "Oh, you know about the basket?" he said. "I'm afraid we can't use that. That's special."

"In what way?" I said.

"I need it—not for me, for Falloleen," said Otto. "Can't I keep that much, and send you all the royalty checks that come in from now on? It isn't right to make Falloleen suffer because of my mistakes. Don't force me to do that, don't strip me of my self-respect as a husband."

I was fed up, and I stood irritably. "I won't strip you of anything, Mr. Krummbein," I said. "I've decided I don't want the job. I'm not a business manager, anyway. I offered to help as a favor to Hal Murphy, but I didn't know how bad working conditions were. You say I'm trying to strip you, when the truth is that your bones were bleached white on the desert of your own prodigality before I arrived. Is there a secret exit out of this silo," I said, "or do I go out the way I came in?"

"No, no, no," said Otto apologetically. "Please, sit down. You've got to help me. It's just that it's a shock for me to get used to how bad things really are. I thought you'd tell me to give up cigarettes or something like that." He shrugged. "Take the basket and give me my allowance." He covered his eyes. "Entertaining Falloleen on an allowance is like running a Mercedes on Pepsi-Cola."

In the basket was five thousand–odd dollars in royalty checks from manufacturers and about two hundred dollars in cash. As I was making out a receipt for Otto, the studio door opened above us, and Falloleen, forever identified in my mind with a Finnish carafe, came down the ramp grace-fully, carrying a tray on which were three martinis.

"I thought your throats might be getting parched," said Falloleen.

"A voice like crystal chimes," said Otto.

"Must I go, or can I stay?" said Falloleen. "It's such a dull party without you, Otto, and I get self-conscious and run out of things to say."

"Beauty needs no tongue," said Otto.

I dusted my hands. "I think we've got things settled for the time being. I'll get down to work in earnest this evening."

"I'm awfully dumb about finances," said Falloleen. "I just leave all that to Otto—he's so brilliant. Isn't he!"

"Yup," I said.

"I was thinking what fun it would be to take our whole party to Chez Armando for dinner," said Falloleen.

Otto looked askance at me.

"We were just talking about love and money," I said to Falloleen, "and I was saying that if a woman loves a man, how much or how little money the man spends on her makes no difference to her. Do you agree?"

Otto leaned forward to hear her answer.

"Where were you brought up?" said Falloleen to me. "On a chicken farm in Saskatchewan?"

Otto groaned.

Falloleen looked at him in alarm. "There's more going on here than I know about," she said. "I was joking. Was that so awful, what I said? It seemed like such a silly question about love and money." Comprehension bloomed on her face. "Otto," she said, "are you broke?"

"Yes," said Otto.

Falloleen squared her lovely shoulders. "Then tell the others to go to Chez Armando without us, that you and I want to spend a quiet evening at home for a change."

"You belong where there are people and excitement," said Otto.

"I get tired of it," said Falloleen. "You've taken me out every night since God knows when. People must wonder if maybe we're afraid to be alone with each other."

. . . .

Otto went up the ramp to send the guests on their way, leaving Falloleen and me alone on the long couch. Fuddled by her perfume and beauty, I said, "Were you in show business, Mrs. Krummbein?"

"Sometimes I feel like I am," said Falloleen. She looked down at her blue fingernails. "I certainly put on a show wherever I go, don't I?"

"A marvelous show," I said.

She sighed. "I guess it should be a good show," she said. "I've been designed by the greatest designer in the world, the father of the Krummbein Di-Modular Bed."

"Your husband designed you?"

"Didn't you know?" said Falloleen. "I'm a silk purse made out of a sow's ear. He'll design you, too, if he gets the chance. I see he's already made you take off your tie. I'll bet he's told you what your color is, too."

"Lemon yellow," I said.

"Each time he sees you," said Falloleen, "he'll make some suggestion about how to improve your appearance." She ran her hands dispassionately over her spectacular self. "Step by step, one goes a long way."

"You were never any sow's ear," I said.

"One year ago," she said, "I was a plain, brown-haired, dowdy thing, fresh out of secretarial school, starting to work as secretary to the Great Krummbein."

"Love at first sight?" I said.

"For me," murmured Falloleen. "For Otto it was a design problem at first sight. There were things about me that jarred him, that made it impossible for him to think straight when I was around. We changed those things one by one, and what became of Kitty Cahoun, nobody knows."

"Kitty Cahoun?" I said.

"The plain, brown-haired, dowdy thing, fresh out of secretarial school," said Falloleen.

"Then Falloleen isn't your real name?" I said.

"It's a Krummbein original," said Falloleen. "Kitty Cahoun didn't go with the decor." She hung her head. "Love—" she said, "don't ask me any more silly questions about love."

· · . · ·

"They're off to Chez Armando," said Otto, returning to the studio. He handed me a yellow silk handkerchief. "That's for you," he said. "Put it in your breast pocket. That dark suit needs it like a forest needs daffodils."

I obeyed, and saw in a mirror that the handkerchief really did give me a little dash, without being offensive. "Thanks very much," I said. "Your wife and I've been having a pleasant time talking about the mysterious disappearance of Kitty Cahoun."

"What ever did become of her?" said Otto earnestly. A look of abject stupidity crossed his face as he realized what he'd said. He tried to laugh it off. "An amazing and amusing demonstration of how the human mind works, wasn't it?" he said. "I'm so used to thinking of you as Falloleen, darling." He changed the subject. "Well, now the maestro is going to cook supper." He laid his hand on my shoulder. "I absolutely insist that you stay. Chicken à la Krummbein, asparagus tips à la Krummbein, potatoes à la—"

"I think I ought to cook supper," said Falloleen. "It's high time the bride got her first meal."

"Won't hear of it," said Otto. "I won't have you suffering for my lack of financial acumen. It would make me feel terrible. Falloleen doesn't belong in a kitchen."

"I know what," said Falloleen, "we'll both get supper. Wouldn't that be cozy, just the two of us?"

"No, no, no, no," said Otto. "I want everything to be a surprise. You stay down here with J. P. Morgan, until I call you. No fair peeking."

"I refuse to worry about it," said Otto, as he, Falloleen, and I cleared away the supper dishes. "If I worry, I can't work, and if I can't work, I can't get any money to bail me out of this mess."

"The important thing is for somebody to worry," I said, "and I guess I'm it. I'll leave you two lovebirds alone up here in the greenhouse while I go to work."

"Man must spend half his time at one with Nature," said Otto, "and half at one with himself. Most houses provide only a muddy, murky in-between." He caught my sleeve. "Listen, don't rush off. All work and no play make Jack a dull boy. Why don't the three of us just have a pleasant social evening, so you can get to know us, and then tomorrow you can start getting down to brass tacks?"

"That's nice of you," I said. "But the quicker I get to work, the quicker you'll be out of the woods. Besides, newlyweds don't want to entertain on their first evening at home."

"Heavens!" said Otto. "We're not newlyweds anymore."

"Yes we are," said Falloleen meekly.

"Of course you are," I said, opening my briefcase. "And you must have an awful lot to say to each other."

"Um," said Otto.

There followed an awkward silence in which Otto and Falloleen stared out into the night through the glass walls, avoiding each other's eyes.

"Didn't Falloleen put on one too many earrings for supper?" said Otto.

"I felt lopsided with just one," said Falloleen.

"Let me be the judge of that," said Otto. "What you don't get is a sense of the whole composition—something a little off-balance here, but lo and behold, a perfect counterbalance down there."

"So you won't capsize," I said, opening the studio door. "Have fun."

"It didn't really jar you, did it, Otto?" said Falloleen guiltily.

I closed the door.

The studio was soundproofed, and I could hear nothing of the Krummbeins' first evening at home as I picked over the wreckage of their finances.

I intruded once, with a long list of questions, and found the upstairs perfectly quiet, save for soft music from the phonograph and the rustle of rich, heavy material. Falloleen was turning around in a lazy sort of ballet, wearing a magnificent evening gown. Otto, lying on the couch, watched her through narrowed lids and blew smoke rings.

"Fashion show?" I said.

"We thought it would be fun for me to try on all the things Otto's bought me that I haven't had a chance to wear," said Falloleen. Despite her heavy makeup, her face had taken on a haggard look. "Like it?" she said.

"Very much," I said, and I roused Otto from his torpor to answer my questions.

"Shouldn't I come down and work with you?" he asked.

"Thanks," I said, "but I'd rather you wouldn't. The perfect quiet is just what I need."

Otto was disappointed. "Well, please don't hesitate to call me for anything."

An hour later, Falloleen and Otto came down into the studio with cups and a pot of coffee. They smiled, but their eyes were glazed with boredom.

Falloleen had on a strapless gown of blue velveteen, with ermine around the hem and below her white shoulders. She slouched and shuffled. Otto hardly glanced at her.

"Ah-h-h!" I said. "Coffee! Just the thing! Style show all over?"

"Ran out of clothes," said Falloleen. She poured the coffee, kicked off her shoes, and lay down at one end of the couch. Otto lay down at the other end, grunting. The peace of the scene was deceptive. Neither Otto nor Falloleen was relaxed. Falloleen was clenching and unclenching her hands. Every few seconds Otto would click his teeth like castanets.

"You certainly look very lovely, Falloleen," I said. "Are those by any chance moonlight-engineered cosmetics you're wearing?"

"Yes," said Falloleen. "Otto had some samples made up, and I'm a walking laboratory. Fascinating work."

"You're not in moonlight," I said, "but I'd say the experiment was a smashing success."

Otto sat up, refreshed by praise of his work. "You really think so? We had moonlight for most of our honeymoon, and the idea practically forced itself on me."

Falloleen sat up as well, sentimentally interested in the subject of the honeymoon. "I loved going out to glamorous places every evening," she said, "but the evening I liked best was the one when we went canoeing, just the two of us, and the lake and the moon."

"I kept looking at her lips there in the moonlight," said Otto, "and—"

"I was looking at your eyes," said Falloleen.

Otto snapped his fingers. "And then it came to me! By heaven, something was all wrong with ordinary cosmetics in the moonlight. The wrong colors came out, blues and greens. Falloleen looked like she'd just swum the English Channel."

Falloleen slapped him with all her might.

"Whatja do that for?" bellowed Otto, his face crimson from the blow. "You think I've got no sense of pain?"

"You think I haven't?" seethed Falloleen. "You think I'm striated plywood and plastic?"

Otto gasped.

"I'm sick of being Falloleen and the style show that never ends!" Her voice dropped to a whisper. "She's dull and shallow, scared and lost, unhappy and unloved."

She twitched the yellow handkerchief from my breast pocket and wiped it across her face dramatically, leaving a smear of red, pink, white, blue, and black. "You designed her, you deserve her, and here she is!" She pressed the stained handkerchief into Otto's limp hand. Up the ramp she went. "Good-bye!"

"Falloleen!" cried Otto.

She paused in the doorway. "My name is Kitty Cahoun Krummbein," she said. "Falloleen is in your hand."

Otto waved the handkerchief at her. "She's as much yours as she is mine," he said. "You wanted to be Falloleen. You did everything you could to be Falloleen."

"Because I loved you," said Kitty. She was weeping. "She was all your design, all for you."

Otto turned his palms upward. "Krummbein is not infallible," he said. "There was widespread bloodshed when the American housewife took the Krummbein Vortex Can Opener to her bosom. I thought being Falloleen would make you happy, and it's made you unhappy instead. I'm sorry. No matter how it turned out, it was a work of love."

"You love Falloleen," said Kitty.

"I love the way she looked," said Otto. He hesitated. "Are you really Kitty again?"

"Would Falloleen show her face looking like this?"

"Never," said Otto. "Then I can tell you, Kitty, that Falloleen was a crashing bore when she wasn't striking a pose or making a dramatic entrance or exit. I lived in terror of being left alone with her."

"Falloleen didn't know who she was or what she was," Kitty sobbed. "You didn't give her any insides."

Otto went up to her and put his arms around her. "Sweetheart," he said, "Kitty Cahoun was supposed to be inside, but she disappeared completely."

"You didn't like anything about Kitty Cahoun," said Kitty.

"My dear, sweet wife," said Otto, "there are only four things on earth that don't scream for redesigning, and one of them is the soul of Kitty Cahoun. I thought it was lost forever."

She put her arms around him tentatively. "And the other three?" she said.

"The egg," said Otto, "the Model-T Ford, and the exterior of Falloleen."

"Why don't you freshen up," said Otto, "slip into your lavender negligee, and put a white rose behind your ear, while I straighten things out here with the Scourge of Wall Street?"

"Oh, dear," she said. "I'm starting to feel like Falloleen again."

"Don't be afraid of it," said Otto. "Just make sure this time that Kitty shines through in all her glory."

She left, supremely happy.

"I'll get right out," I said. "Now I know you want to be alone with her."

"Frankly, I do," said Otto.

"I'll open a checking account and hire a safe-deposit box in your name tomorrow," I said.

And Otto said, "Sounds like your kind of thing. Enjoy, enjoy."

Ambitious Sophomore

George M. Helmholtz, head of the music department and director of the band of Lincoln High School, was a good, fat man who saw no evil, heard no evil, and spoke no evil, for wherever he went, the roar and boom and blast of a marching band, real or imagined, filled his soul. There was room for little else, and the Lincoln High School Ten Square Band he led was, as a consequence, as fine as any band on earth.

Sometimes, when he heard muted, wistful passages, real or imagined, Helmholtz would wonder if it wasn't indecent of him to be so happy in such terrible times. But then the brasses and percussion section would put sadness to flight, and Mr. Helmholtz would see that his happiness and its source could only be good and rich and full of hope for everyone.

Helmholtz often gave the impression of a man lost in dreams, but there was a side to him that was as tough as a rhinoceros. It was that side that raised money for the band, that hammered home to the school board, the Parent Teacher Association, Chamber of Commerce, Kiwanis, Rotary, and Lions that the goodness and richness and hope that his band inspired cost money. In his fund-raising harangues, he would recall for his audiences black days for the Lincoln High football team, days when the Lincoln stands had been silent, hurt, and ashamed.

"Half-time," he would murmur, and hang his head.

He would twitch a whistle from his pocket and blow a shrill blast. "Lincoln High School Ten Square Band!" he'd shout. "Forward—harch! Boom! Ta-ta-ta-taaaaaa!" Helmholtz, singing, marching in place, would become flag twirlers, drummers, brasses, woodwinds, glockenspiel and all. By the time he'd marched his one-man band up and down the imaginary football field once, his audience was elated and wringing wet, ready to buy the band anything it wanted.

But no matter how much money came in, the band was always without funds. Helmholtz was a spender when it came to band equipment, and was known among rival bandmasters as "The Plunger" and "Diamond Jim."

Among the many duties of Stewart Haley, Assistant Principal of Lincoln High, was keeping an eye on band finances. Whenever it was necessary for Haley to discuss band finances with Helmholtz, Haley tried to corner the bandmaster where he couldn't march and swing his arms.

Helmholtz knew this, and felt trapped when Haley appeared in the door of the bandmaster's small office, brandishing a bill for ninety-five dollars. Following Haley was a delivery boy from a tailor shop, who carried a suit box under his arm. As Haley closed the office door from inside, Helmholtz hunched over a drawing board, pretending deep concentration.

"Helmholtz," said Haley, "I have here an utterly unexpected, utterly unauthorized bill for—"

"Sh!" said Helmholtz. "I'll be with you in a moment." He drew a dotted line across a diagram that was already a black thicket of lines. "I'm just putting the finishing touches on the Mother's Day formation," he said. "I'm trying to make an arrow pierce a heart and then spell 'Mom.' It isn't easy."

"That's very sweet," said Haley, rattling the bill, "and I'm as fond of mothers as you are, but you've just put a ninety-five-dollar arrow through the public treasury."

Helmholtz did not look up. "I was going to tell you about it," he said, drawing another line, "but what with getting ready for the state band festival and Mother's Day, it seemed unimportant. First things first."

"Unimportant!" said Haley. "You hypnotize the community into buying you one hundred new uniforms for the Ten Square Band, and now—"

"Now?" said Helmholtz mildly.

"This boy brings me a bill for the hundred-and-first uniform!" said Haley. "Give you an inch and—"

Haley was interrupted by a knock. "Come in," said Helmholtz. The door opened, and there stood Leroy Duggan, a shy, droll, slope-shouldered sophomore. Leroy was so self-conscious that when anyone turned to look at him he did a sort of fan dance with his piccolo case and portfolio, hiding himself as well as he could behind them.

"Come right in, Leroy," said Helmholtz.

"Wait outside a moment, Leroy," said Haley. "This is rather urgent business."

Leroy backed out, mumbling an apology, and Haley closed the door again.

"My door is always open to my musicians," said Helmholtz.

"It will be," said Haley, "just as soon as we clear up the mystery of the hundred-and-first uniform."

"I'm frankly surprised and hurt at the administration's lack of faith in my judgment," said Helmholtz. "Running a precision organization of a hundred highly talented young men isn't the simple operation everyone seems to think."

"Simple!" said Haley. "Who thinks it's simple! It's plainly the most tangled, mysterious, expensive mess in the entire school system. You say a hundred young men, but this boy here just delivered the hundred-and-first uniform. Has the Ten Square Band added a tail gunner?"

"No," said Helmholtz. "It's still a hundred, much as I'd like to have more, much as I need them. For instance, I was just trying to figure out how to make *Whistler's Mother* with a hundred men, and it simply can't be done." He frowned. "If we could throw in the girls' glee club we might make it. You're intelligent and have good taste. Would you give me your ideas on the band festival and this Mother's Day thing?"

Haley lost his temper. "Don't try to fuddle me, Helmholtz! What's the extra uniform for?"

"For the greater glory of Lincoln High School!" barked Helmholtz. "For the third leg and permanent possession of the state band festival trophy!" His voice dropped to a whisper, and he glanced furtively at the door. "Specifically, it's for Leroy Duggan, probably the finest piccoloist in this hemisphere. Let's keep our voices down, because we can't discuss the uniform without discussing Leroy."

The conversation became tense whispers.

"And what's the matter with Leroy's wearing one of the uniforms you've already got?" said Haley.

"Leroy is bell-shaped," said Helmholtz. "We don't have a uniform that doesn't bag or bind on him."

"This is a public school, not a Broadway musical!" said Haley. "Not only have we got students shaped liked bells, we've got them shaped like telephone poles, pop bottles, chimpanzees, and Greek gods. There's going to have to be a certain amount of bagging and binding."

"My duty," said Helmholtz, standing, "is to bring the best music out of whoever chooses to come to me. If a boy's shape prevents him from making the music he's capable of making, then it's my duty to get him a shape that will make him play like an angel. This I did, and here we are." He sat down. "If I could be made to feel sorry for this, then I wouldn't be the man for my job."

"A special uniform is going to make Leroy play better?" said Haley.

"In rehearsals, with nobody but fellow musicians around," said Helmholtz, "Leroy has brilliance and feeling that would make you weep and faint. But when Leroy marches, with strangers watching, particularly girls, he gets out of step, stumbles, and can't even play 'Row, Row, Row Your Boat.'" Helmholtz brought his fist down on the desk. "And that's not going to happen at the state band festival!"

The bill in Haley's hand was rumpled and moist now. "The message I came to deliver today," he said, "remains unchanged: You can't get blood out of a turnip. The total cash assets of the band are seventy-five dollars, and there is absolutely no way for the school to provide the remaining twenty—absolutely none."

He turned to the delivery boy. "That is my somber message to you, as well," he said.

"Mr. Kornblum said he was losing money on it as it was," said the delivery boy. "He said Mr. Helmholtz came in and started talking, and before he knew it—"

"Don't worry about a thing," said Helmholtz. He brought out his checkbook and, with a smile and a flourish, wrote a check for twenty dollars.

Haley was ashen. "I'm sorry it has to turn out this way," he said.

Helmholtz ignored him. He took the parcel from the delivery boy and called to Leroy, "Would you come in, please?"

Leroy came in slowly, shuffling, doing his fan dance with the piccolo case and portfolio, apologizing as he came.

"Thought you might like to try on your new uniform for the band festival, Leroy," said Helmholtz.

"I don't think I'd better march," said Leroy. "I'd get all mixed up and ruin everything."

Helmholtz opened the box dramatically. "This uniform's special, Leroy."

"Every time I see one of those uniforms," said Haley, "all I can think of is a road company of *The Chocolate Soldier*. That's the uniform the stars wear, but you've got a hundred of the things—a hundred and one."

Helmholtz removed Leroy's jacket. Leroy stood humbly in his shirtsleeves, relieved of his piccolo case and portfolio, comical, seeing nothing at all comical in being bell-shaped.

Helmholtz slipped the new jacket over Leroy's narrow shoulders. He buttoned the great brass buttons and fluffed up the gold braid cascading from the epaulets. "There, Leroy."

"Zoot!" exclaimed the delivery boy. "Man, I mean zoot!"

Leroy looked dazedly from one massive, jutting shoulder to the other, and then down at the astonishing taper to his hips.

"Rocky Marciano!" said Haley.

"Walk up and down the halls, Leroy," said Helmholtz. "Get the feel of it."

Leroy blundered through the door, catching his epaulets on the frame.

"Sideways," said Helmholtz, "you'll have to learn to go through doors sideways."

"Only about ten percent of what's under the uniform is Leroy," said Haley, when Leroy was out of hearing.

"It's all Leroy," said Helmholtz. "Wait and see—wait until we swing past the reviewing stand at the band festival and Leroy does his stuff."

When Leroy returned to the office, he was marching, knees high. He halted and clicked his heels. His chin was up, his breathing shallow.

"You can take it off, Leroy," said Helmholtz. "If you don't feel up to marching in the band festival, just forget it." He reached across his desk and undid a brass button.

Leroy's hand came up quickly to protect the rest of the buttons. "Please," he said, "I think maybe I could march after all."

"That can be arranged," said Helmholtz. "I have a certain amount of influence in band matters."

Leroy buttoned the button. "Gee," he said, "I walked past the athletic office, and Coach Jorgenson came out like he was shot out of a cannon."

"What did the silent Swede have to say?" said Helmholtz.

"He said that only in this band-happy school would they make a piccolo player out of a man built like a locomotive," said Leroy. "His secretary came out, too."

"Did Miss Bearden like the uniform?" said Helmholtz.

"I don't know," said Leroy. "She didn't say anything. She just looked and looked."

Late that afternoon, George M. Helmholtz appeared in the office of Harold Crane, head of the English Department. Helmholtz was carrying a heavy, ornate gold picture frame and looking embarrassed.

"I hardly know how to begin," said Helmholtz. "I—I thought maybe I could sell you a picture frame." He turned the frame this way and that. "It's a nice frame, isn't it?"

"Yes, it is," said Crane. "I've admired it often in your office. That is the frame you had around John Philip Sousa, isn't it?"

Helmholtz nodded. "I thought maybe you'd like to frame some John Philip Sousa in your line—Shakespeare, Edgar Rice Burroughs."

"That might be nice," said Crane. "But frankly, the need hasn't made itself strongly felt."

"It's a thirty-nine-dollar frame," said Helmholtz. "I'll let it go for twenty."

"Look here," said Crane, "if you're in some sort of jam, I can let you have—"

"No, no, no," said Helmholtz, holding up his hand. Fear crossed his face. "If I started on credit, heaven only knows where it would end."

Crane shook his head. "That's a nice frame, all right, and a real bargain. Sad to say, though, I'm in no shape to lay out twenty dollars for something like that. I've got to buy a new tire for twenty-three dollars this afternoon and—"

"What size?" said Helmholtz.

"Size?" said Crane. "Six-seventy, fifteen. Why?"

"I'll sell you one for twenty dollars," said Helmholtz. "Never been touched."

"Where would you get a tire?" said Crane.

"By a stroke of luck," said Helmholtz, "I have an extra one."

"You don't mean your spare, do you?" said Crane.

"Yes," said Helmholtz, "but I'll never need it. I'll be careful where I drive. Please, you've got to buy it. The money isn't for me, it's for the band."

"What else would it be for?" said Crane helplessly. He took out his bill-fold.

When Helmholtz got back to his office, and was restoring John Philip Sousa to the frame, Leroy walked in, whistling. He wore the jacket with the boulder shoulders.

"You still here, Leroy?" said Helmholtz. "Thought you went home hours ago."

"Can't seem to take the thing off," said Leroy. "I was trying a kind of experiment with it."

"Oh?"

"I'd walk down the hall past a bunch of girls," said Leroy, "whistling the piccolo part of 'The Stars and Stripes Forever.'"

"And?" said Helmholtz.

"Kept step and didn't miss a note," said Leroy.

The city's main street was cleared of traffic for eight blocks, swept, and lined with bunting for the cream of the state's youth, its high school bands. At one end of the line of march was a great square with a reviewing stand. At the other end were the bands, hidden in alleys, waiting for orders to march.

The band that looked and sounded best to the judges in the reviewing stand would receive a great trophy, donated by the Chamber of Commerce. The trophy was two years old, and bore the name of Lincoln High School as winner twice.

In the alleys, twenty-five bandmasters were preparing secret weapons with which they hoped to prevent Lincoln's winning a third time—special effects with flash powder, flaming batons, pretty cowgirls, and at least one three-inch cannon. But everywhere hung the smog of defeat, save over the bright plumage of the ranks of Lincoln High.

Beside those complacent ranks stood Stewart Haley, Assistant Principal, and, wearing what Haley referred to privately as the uniform of a Bulgarian rear admiral, George M. Helmholtz, Director of the Band.

Lincoln High shared the alley with bands from three other schools, and the blank walls on either side echoed harshly with the shrieks and growls of bands tuning up.

Helmholtz was lighting pieces of punk with Haley's lighter, blowing on them, and passing them in to every fourth man, who had a straight, cylindrical firework under his sash.

"First will come the order 'Prepare to light!'" said Helmholtz. "Ten seconds later, 'Light!' When your left foot strikes the ground, touch your punk to the end of the fuse. The rest of you, when we hit the reviewing stand, I want you to stop playing as though you'd been shot in the heart. And Leroy—"

Helmholtz craned his neck to find Leroy. As he did so, he became aware of a rival drum major, seedy and drab by comparison with Lincoln's peacocks, who had been listening to everything he said.

"What can I do for you?" said Helmholtz.

"Is this the Doormen's Convention?" said the drum major.

Helmholtz did not smile. "You'd do well to stay with your own organization," he said crisply. "You're plainly in need of practice and sprucing up, and time is short."

The drum major walked away, sneering, insolently spinning his baton.

"Now, where's Leroy got to, this time?" said Helmholtz. "He's a disciplinary problem whenever he puts on that uniform. A new man."

"You mean Blabbermouth Duggan?" said Haley. He pointed to Leroy's broad back in the midst of another band. Leroy was talking animatedly to a fellow piccoloist, who happened to be a very pretty girl with golden curls tucked under her cap. "You mean Casanova Duggan?" said Haley.

"Everything's built around Leroy," said Helmholtz. "If anything went wrong with Leroy, we'd be lucky to place second. . . . Leroy!"

Leroy paid no attention.

Leroy was too engrossed to hear Helmholtz. He was too engrossed to notice that the insolent drum major, who had lately called Helmholtz's band a Doormen's Convention, was now examining his broad back with profound curiosity.

The drum major prodded one of Leroy's shoulder pads with the rubber tip of his baton. Leroy gave no sign that he felt it. The drum major laid his hand on Leroy's shoulder and dug his fingers several inches into it. Leroy went on talking.

With an audience gathering, the drum major began a series of probings with his baton, starting from the outside of Leroy's shoulder and moving in toward the middle, trying to locate the point where padding stopped and Leroy began.

The baton at last found flesh, and Leroy turned in surprise. "What's the idea?" he said.

"Making sure your stuffing's all in place, General," said the drum major. "Spring a leak, and we'll be up to our knees in sawdust."

Leroy reddened. "I don't know what you're talking about," he said.

"Ask your boyfriend to take off his jacket so we can all see his rippling muscles," the drum major said to Leroy's new girl. He challenged Leroy, "Go on, take it off."

"Make me," said Leroy.

"All righty, all righty," said Helmholtz, stepping between the two.

"You think I can't?" said the drum major.

Leroy swallowed and thought for a long time. "I know you can't," he said at last.

The drum major pushed Helmholtz aside and seized Leroy's jacket by its shoulders. Off came the epaulets, then the citation cord, then the sash. Buttons popped off, and Leroy's undershirt showed.

"Now," said the drum major, "we'll simply undo this, and—"

Leroy exploded. He hit the drum major's nose, stripped off his buttons, medals, and braid, hit him in the stomach, and went over to get his baton, with the apparent intention of beating him to death with it.

"Leroy! Stop!" cried Helmholtz in anguish. He wrenched the baton from Leroy. "Just look at you! Look at your new uniform—wrecked!" Trembling, he touched the rents, the threads of missing buttons, the misshapen padding. He raised his hands in a gesture of surrender. "It's all over. We concede—Lincoln High concedes."

Leroy was wild-eyed, unrepentant. "I don't care!" he yelled. "I'm glad!"

Helmholtz called over another bandsman and gave him the keys to his car. "There's a spare uniform in the back," he said numbly. "Go get it for Leroy."

The Lincoln High School Ten Square Band swung smartly along the street, moving toward the bright banners of the reviewing stand. George M. Helmholtz smiled as he marched along the curb beside it. Inside he was ill, angry, and full of dread. With one cruel stroke, Fate had transformed his plan for winning the trophy into the most preposterous anticlimax in band history.

He couldn't bear to look at the young man on whom he had staked everything. He could imagine Leroy with appalling clarity, slouching along, slovenly, lost in a misfit uniform, a jumble of neuroses and costly fabrics. Leroy was to play alone when the band passed in review. Leroy, Helmholtz reflected, would be incapable even of recalling his own name at that point.

Ahead was the first of a series of chalk marks Helmholtz had made on the curb earlier in the day, carefully measured distances from the reviewing stand.

Helmholtz blew his whistle as he passed the mark, and the band struck up "The Stars and Stripes Forever," full-blooded, throbbing, thrilling. It raised the crowd on its toes and put roses in its cheeks. The judges leaned out of the reviewing stand in happy anticipation of the coming splendor.

Helmholtz passed another mark. "Prepare to light!" he shouted. And a moment later, "Light!"

Helmholtz smiled glassily. In five seconds the band would be before the reviewing stand, the music would stop, the fireworks would send American flags into the sky. And then, playing alone, Leroy would tootle pathetically, ridiculously, if he played at all.

The music stopped. Fireworks banged, and up went the parachutes. The Lincoln High School Ten Square Band passed in review, lines straight, plumes high, brass flashing.

Helmholtz almost cried as American flags hung in air from parachutes. Among them, like a cloudburst of diamonds, was the Sousa piccolo masterpiece. Leroy! Leroy!

The bands were massed before the reviewing stand. George M. Helmholtz stood at parade rest before his band, between the great banner bearing the Lincoln High Black Panther on a scarlet field and Old Glory.

When he was called forward to receive the trophy, the bandmaster crossed the broad square to the accompaniment of a snare drum and a piccolo. As he returned with thirty pounds of bronze and walnut, the band played "Lincoln's Foes Shall Wail Tonight," words and music by George M. Helmholtz.

When the parade was dismissed, Assistant Principal Haley hurried from the crowd to shake Helmholtz's hand.

"Shake Leroy's hand," said Helmholtz. "He's the hero." He looked around for Leroy, beaming, and saw the boy was with the pretty blond piccolo player again, more animated than ever. She was responding warmly.

"She doesn't seem to miss the shoulders, does she?" said Helmholtz.

"That's because *he* doesn't miss them anymore," said Haley. "He's a man now, bell-shaped or not."

"He certainly gave his all for Lincoln High," said Helmholtz. "I admire school spirit in a boy."

Haley laughed. "That wasn't school spirit—that was the love song of a full-bodied American male. Don't you know anything about love?"

Helmholtz thought about love as he walked back to his car alone, his arms aching with the weight of the great trophy. If love was blinding, obsessing, demanding, beyond reason, and all the other wild things people said it was, then he had never known it, Helmholtz told himself. He sighed, and supposed he was missing something, not knowing romance.

When he got to his car, he found that the left front tire was flat. He remembered that he had no spare. But he felt nothing more than mild inconvenience. He boarded a streetcar, sat down with the trophy on his lap, and smiled. He was hearing music again.

Bagombo
Snuff Box

T his place is new, isn't it?" said Eddie Laird.
        He was sitting in a bar in the heart of the city. He was the only cus-
tomer, and he was talking to the bartender.

"I don't remember this place," he said, "and I used to know every bar in
town."

Laird was a big man, thirty-three, with a pleasantly impudent moon
face. He was dressed in a blue flannel suit that was plainly a very recent
purchase. He watched his image in the bar mirror as he talked. Now and
then, one of his hands would stray from the glass to stroke a soft lapel.

"Not so new," said the bartender, a sleepy, fat man in his fifties. "When
was the last time you were in town?"

"The war," Laird said.

"Which war was that?"

"Which war?" Laird repeated. "I guess you have to ask people that nowadays, when they talk about war. The second one—the Second *World* War. I was stationed out at Cunningham Field. Used to come to town every weekend I could."

A sweet sadness welled up in him as he remembered his reflection in other bar mirrors in other days, remembered the reflected flash of captain's bars and silver wings.

"This place was built in 'forty-six, and been renovated twice since then," the bartender said.

"Built—and renovated twice," Laird said wonderingly. "Things wear out pretty fast these days, don't they? Can you still get a plank steak at Charley's Steak House for two dollars?"

"Burned down," the bartender said. "There's a J. C. Penney there now."

"So what's the big Air Force hangout these days?" Laird said.

"Isn't one," the bartender said. "They closed down Cunningham Field."

Laird picked up his drink, and walked over to the window to watch the people go by. "I halfway expected the women here to be wearing short skirts still," he said. "Where are all the pretty pink knees?" He rattled his fingernails against the window. A woman glanced at him and hurried on.

"I've got a wife out there somewhere," Laird said. "What do you suppose has happened to *her* in eleven years?"

"A wife?"

"An ex-wife. One of those war things. I was twenty-two, and she was eighteen. Lasted six months."

"What went wrong?"

"Wrong?" Laird said. "I just didn't want to be owned, that's all. I wanted to be able to stick my toothbrush in my hip pocket and take off whenever I felt like it. And she didn't go for that. So . . ." He grinned. "*Adiós*. No tears, no hard feelings."

He walked over to the jukebox. "What's the most frantically popular song of the minute?"

"Try number seventeen," the bartender said. "I guess I could stand it one more time."

Laird played number seventeen, a loud, tearful ballad of lost love. He listened intently. And at the end, he stamped his foot and winked, just as he had done years before.

"One more drink," Laird said, "and then, by heaven, I'm going to call up my ex-wife." He appealed to the bartender. "That's all right, isn't it? Can't I call her up if I want to?" He laughed. "'Dear Emily Post: I have a slight problem in etiquette. I haven't seen or exchanged a word with my ex-wife for eleven years. Now I find myself in the same city with her—'"

"How do you know she's still around?" the bartender said.

"I called up an old buddy when I blew in this morning. He said she's all set—got just what she wants: a wage slave of a husband, a vine-covered cottage with expansion attic, two kids, and a quarter of an acre of lawn as green as Arlington National Cemetery."

Laird strode to the telephone. For the fourth time that day, he looked up his ex-wife's number, under the name of her second husband, and held a dime an inch above the slot. This time, he let the coin fall. "Here goes nothing," Laird said. He dialed.

A woman answered. In the background, a child shrieked and a radio blabbed.

"Amy?" Laird said.

"Yes?" She was out of breath.

A silly grin spread over Laird's face. "Hey—guess what? This is Eddie Laird."

"Who?"

"Eddie Laird—Eddie!"

"Wait a minute, would you, please?" Amy said. "The baby is making such a terrible racket, and the radio's on, and I've got brownies in the oven, just ready to come out. I can't hear a thing. Would you hold on?"

"Sure."

"Now then," she said, winded, "who did you say this was?"

"Eddie Laird."

She gasped. "Really?"

"Really," Laird said merrily. "I just blew in from Ceylon, by way of Baghdad, Rome, and New York."

"Good heavens," said Amy. "What a shock. I didn't even know if you were alive or dead."

Laird laughed. "They can't kill me, and by heaven, they've sure tried."

"What have you been up to?"

"Ohhhhh—a little bit of everything. I just quit a job flying for a pearling outfit in Ceylon. I'm starting a company of my own, prospecting for uranium up around the Klondike region. Before the Ceylon deal, I was hunting diamonds in the Amazon rain forest, and before that, flying for a sheik in Iraq."

"Like something out of *The Arabian Nights*," said Amy. "My head just swims."

"Well, don't get any glamorous illusions," Laird said. "Most of it was hard, dirty, dangerous work." He sighed. "And how are you, Amy?"

"Me?" said Amy. "How is any housewife? Harassed."

The child began to cry again.

"Amy," said Laird huskily, "is everything all right—between us?"

Her voice was very small. "Time heals all wounds," she said. "It hurt at first, Eddie—it hurt very much. But I've come to understand it was all for the best. You can't help being restless. You were born that way. You were like a caged eagle, mooning, molting."

"And you, Amy, are *you* happy?"

"Very," said Amy, with all her heart. "It's wild and it's messy with the children. But when I get a chance to catch my breath, I can see it's sweet and good. It's what *I* always wanted. So in the end, we both got our way, didn't we? The eagle and the homing pigeon."

"Amy," Laird said, "could I come out to see you?"

"Oh, Eddie, the house is a horror and I'm a witch. I couldn't stand to have you see me like this—after you've come from Ceylon by way of Baghdad, Rome, and New York. What a hideous letdown for someone like you. Stevie had the measles last week, and the baby has had Harry and me up three times a night, and—"

"Now, now," Laird said, "I'll see the real you shining through it all. I'll come out at five, and say hello, and leave again right away. Please?"

On the cab ride out to Amy's home, Laird encouraged himself to feel sentimental about the coming reunion. He tried to daydream about the best of his days with her, but got only fantasies of movie starlet–like nymphs dancing about him with red lips and vacant eyes. This shortcoming of his imagination, like everything else about the day, was a throwback to his salad days in the Air Force. All pretty women had seemed to come from the same mold.

Laird told the cab to wait for him. "This will be short and sweet," he said.

As he walked up to Amy's small, ordinary house, he managed a smile of sad maturity, the smile of a man who has hurt and been hurt, who has seen everything, who has learned a great deal from it all, and who, incidentally, has made a lot of money along the way.

He knocked and, while he waited, picked at the flaking paint on the door frame.

Harry, Amy's husband, a blocky man with a kind face, invited Larry in.

"I'm changing the baby," Amy called from inside. "Be there in two shakes."

Harry was clearly startled by Laird's size and splendor, and Laird looked down on him and clapped his arm in comradely fashion.

"I guess a lot of people would say this is pretty irregular," Laird said. "But what happened between Amy and me was a long time ago. We were just a couple of crazy kids, and we're all older and wiser now. I hope we can all be friends."

Harry nodded. "Why, yes, of course. Why not?" he said. "Would you like something to drink? I'm afraid I don't have much of a selection. Rye or beer?"

"Anything at all, Harry," Laird said. "I've had kava with the Maoris, scotch with the British, champagne with the French, and cacao with the Tupi. I'll have a rye or a beer with you. When in Rome . . ." He dipped into his pocket and brought out a snuff box encrusted with semiprecious gems. "Say, I brought you and Amy a little something." He pressed the box into Harry's hand. "I picked it up for a song in Bagombo."

"Bagombo?" said Harry, dazzled.

"Ceylon," Laird said easily. "Flew for a pearling outfit out there. Pay was fantastic, the mean temperature was seventy-three, but I didn't like the monsoons. Couldn't stand being bottled up in the same rooms for weeks at a time, waiting for the rain to quit. A man's got to get out, or he just goes to pot—gets flabby and womanly."

"Um," said Harry.

Already the small house and the smells of cooking and the clutter of family life were crowding in on Laird, making him want to be off and away. "Nice place you have here," he said.

"It's a little small," Harry said. "But—"

"Cozy," said Laird. "Too much room can drive you nuts. I know. Back in Bagombo, I had twenty-six rooms, and twelve servants to look after them, but they didn't make me happy. They mocked me, actually. But the place rented for seven dollars a month, and I couldn't pass it up, could I?"

Harry started to leave for the kitchen, but stopped in the doorway, thunderstruck. "Seven dollars a month for twenty-six rooms?" he said.

"Turned out I was being taken. The tenant before me got it for three."

"Three," Harry murmured. "Tell me," he said hesitantly, "are there a lot of jobs waiting for Americans in places like that? Are they recruiting?"

"You wouldn't want to leave your family, would you?"

Harry was conscience-stricken. "Oh, no! I thought maybe I could take them."

"No soap," said Laird. "What they want is bachelors. And anyway, you've got a nice setup here. And you've got to have a specialty, too, to qualify for the big money. Fly, handle a boat, speak a language. Besides, most of the recruiting is done in bars in Singapore, Algiers, and places like that. Now, I'm taking a flier at uranium prospecting on my own, up in the Klondike, and I need a couple of good Geiger counter technicians. Can you repair a Geiger counter, Harry?"

"Nope," said Harry.

"Well, the men I want are going to have to be single, anyway," said Laird. "It's a beautiful part of the world, teeming with moose and salmon, but rugged. No place for women or children. What *is* your line?"

"Oh," said Harry, "credit manager for a department store."

"Harry," Amy called, "would you please warm up the baby's formula, and see if the lima beans are done?"

"Yes, dear," said Harry.

"What did you say, honey?"

"I said yes!" Harry bellowed.

A shocked silence settled over the house.

And then Amy came in, and Laird had his memory refreshed. Laird stood. Amy was a lovely woman, with black hair, and wise brown affectionate eyes. She was still young, but obviously very tired. She was prettily dressed, carefully made-up, and quite self-conscious.

"Eddie, how nice," she said with brittle cheerfulness. "Don't you look well!"

"You, too," Laird said.

"Do I really?" Amy said. "I feel so ancient."

"You shouldn't," Laird said. "This life obviously agrees with you."

"We *have* been very happy," Amy said.

"You're as pretty as a model in Paris, a movie star in Rome."

"You don't mean it." Amy was pleased.

"I do," Laird said. "I can see you now in a Mainbocher suit, your high heels clicking smartly along the Champs-Élysées, with the soft winds of the Parisian spring ruffling your black hair, and with every eye drinking you in—and a gendarme salutes!"

"Oh, Eddie!" Amy cried.

"Have you been to Paris?" said Laird.

"Nope," said Amy.

"No matter. In many ways, there are more exotic thrills in New York. I can see you there, in a theater crowd, with each man falling silent and turning to stare as you pass by. When was the last time you were in New York?"

"Hmmmmm?" Amy said, staring into the distance.

"When were you last in New York?"

"Oh, I've never been there. Harry has—on business."

"Why didn't he take you?" Laird said gallantly. "You can't let your youth slip away without going to New York. It's a young person's town."

"Angel," Harry called from the kitchen, "how can you tell if lima beans are done?"

"Stick a lousy fork into 'em!" Amy yelled.

Harry appeared in the doorway with drinks, and blinked in hurt bewilderment. "Do you have to yell at me?" he said.

Amy rubbed her eyes. "I'm sorry," she said. "I'm tired. We're both tired."

"We haven't had much sleep," Harry said. He patted his wife's back. "We're both a little tense."

Amy took her husband's hand and squeezed it. Peace settled over the house once more.

Harry passed out the drinks, and Laird proposed a toast.

"Eat, drink, and be merry," Laird said, "for tomorrow we could die."

Harry and Amy winced, and drank thirstily.

"He brought us a snuff box from Bagombo, honey," said Harry. "Did I pronounce that right?"

"You've Americanized it a little," said Laird. "But that's about it." He pursed his lips. "*Bagombo.*"

"It's very pretty," said Amy. "I'll put it on my dressing table, and not let the children near it. Bagombo."

"There!" Laird said. "*She* said it just right. It's a funny thing. Some people have an ear for languages. They hear them once, and they catch all the subtle sounds immediately. And some people have a tin ear, and never catch on. Amy, listen, and then repeat what I say: *'Toli! Pakka sahn nebul rokka ta. Si notte loni gin ta tonic.'*"

Cautiously Amy repeated the sentence.

"Perfect! You know what you just said in Buhna-Simca? 'Young woman, go cover the baby, and bring me a gin and tonic on the south terrace.' Now then, Harry, you say, *'Pilla! Sibba tu bang-bang. Libbin hru donna steek!'*"

Harry, frowning, repeated the sentence.

Laird sat back with a sympathetic smile for Amy. "Well, I don't know, Harry. That might get across, except you'd earn a laugh from the natives when you turned your back."

Harry was stung. "What did I say?"

"'Boy!'" Laird translated. "'Hand me the gun. The tiger is in the clump of trees just ahead.'"

"*Pilla!*" Harry said imperiously. "*Sibba tu bang-bang. Libbin hru donna steek!*" He held out his hand for the gun, and the hand twitched like a fish dying on a riverbank.

"Better—much better!" Laird said.

"That *was* good," Amy said.

Harry brushed off their adulation. He was grim, purposeful. "Tell me," he said, "are tigers a problem around Bagombo?"

"Sometimes, when game gets scarce in the jungles, tigers come into the outskirts of villages," Laird said. "And then you have to go out and get them."

"You had servants in Bagombo, did you?" Amy said.

"At six cents a day for a man, and four cents a day for a woman? I guess!" Laird said.

There was the sound of a bicycle bumping against the outside of the house.

"Stevie's home," Harry said.

"I want to go to Bagombo," Amy said.

"It's no place to raise kids," Laird said. "That's the big drawback."

The front door opened, and a good-looking, muscular nine-year-old boy came in, hot and sweaty. He threw his cap at a hook in the front closet and started upstairs.

"Hang up your hat, Stevie!" Amy said. "I'm not a servant who follows you around, gathering things wherever you care to throw them."

"And pick up your feet!" said Harry.

Stevie came creeping down the stairway, shocked and perplexed. "What got into you two all of a sudden?" he said.

"Don't be fresh," Harry said. "Come in here and meet Mr. Laird."

"*Major* Laird," said Laird.

"Hi," said Stevie. "How come you haven't got a uniform on, if you're a Major?"

"Reserve commission," Laird said. The boy's eyes, frank, irreverent, and unromantic, scared him. "Nice boy you have here."

"Oh," Stevie said, "*that* kind of a Major." He saw the snuff box, and picked it up.

"Stevie," Amy said, "put that down. It's one of Mother's treasures, and it's not going to get broken like everything else. Put it down."

"Okay, okay, okay," said Stevie. He set the box down with elaborate gentleness. "I didn't know it was such a treasure."

"Major Laird brought it all the way from Bagombo," Amy said.

"Bagombo, Japan?" Stevie said.

"Ceylon, Stevie," Harry said. "Bagombo is in Ceylon."

"Then how come it's got 'Made in Japan' on the bottom?"

Laird paled. "They export their stuff to Japan, and the Japanese market it for them," he said.

"There, Stevie," Amy said. "You learned something today."

"Then why don't they say it was made in Ceylon?" Stevie wanted to know.

"The Oriental mind works in devious ways," said Harry.

"Exactly," said Laird. "You've caught the whole spirit of the Orient in that one sentence, Harry."

"They ship these things all the way from Africa to Japan?" Stevie asked.

A hideous doubt stabbed Laird. A map of the world swirled in his mind, with continents flapping and changing shape and with an island named Ceylon scuttling through the seven seas. Only two points held firm, and these were Stevie's irreverent blue eyes.

"I always thought it was off India," Amy said.

"It's funny how things leave you when you start thinking about them too hard," Harry said. "Now I've got Ceylon all balled up with Madagascar."

"And Sumatra and Borneo," Amy said. "That's what we get for never leaving home."

Now four islands were sailing the troubled seas in Laird's mind.

"What's the answer, Eddie?" Amy said. "Where *is* Ceylon?"

"It's an island off Africa," Stevie said firmly. "We studied it."

Laird looked around the room and saw doubt on every face but Stevie's. He cleared his throat. "The boy is right," he croaked.

"I'll get my atlas and show you," Stevie said with pride, and ran upstairs.

Laird stood up, weak. "Must dash."

"So soon?" Harry said. "Well, I hope you find lots of uranium." He avoided his wife's eyes. "I'd give my right arm to go with you."

"Someday, when the children are grown," Amy said, "maybe we'll still be young enough to enjoy New York and Paris, and all those other places— and maybe retire in Bagombo."

"I hope so," said Laird. He blundered out the door, and down the walk, which now seemed endless, and into the waiting taxicab. "Let's go," he told the driver.

"They're all yelling at you," said the driver. He rolled down his window so Laird could hear.

"Hey, Major!" Stevie was shouting. "Mom's right, and we're wrong. Ceylon *is* off India."

The family that Laird had so recently scattered to the winds was together again, united in mirth on the doorstep.

"*Pilla!*" called Harry gaily. "*Sibba tu bang-bang. Libbin hru donna steek!*"

"*Toli!*" Amy called back. "*Pakka sahn nebul rokka ta. Si notte loni gin ta tonic.*"

The cab pulled away.

That night, in his hotel room, Laird put in a long-distance call to his second wife, Selma, in a small house in Levittown, Long Island, New York, far, far away.

"Is Arthur doing any better with his reading, Selma?" he asked.

"The teacher says he isn't dull, he's lazy," Selma said. "She says he can catch up with the class anytime he makes up his mind to."

"I'll talk to him when I get home," Laird said. "And the twins? Are they letting you sleep at all?"

"Well, I'm getting two of them out of the way at one crack. Let's look at it that way." Selma yawned agonizingly. "How's the trip going?"

"You remember how they said you couldn't sell potato chips in Dubuque?"

"Yes."

"Well, *I* did," said Laird. "I'm going to make history in this territory. I'll stand *this* town on its ear."

"Are you—" Selma hesitated. "Are you going to call *her* up, Eddie?"

"Naaaaah," Laird said. "Why open old graves?"

"You're not even curious about what's happened to her?"

"Naaaaah. We'd hardly know each other. People change, people change." He snapped his fingers. "Oh, I almost forgot. What did the dentist say about Dawn's teeth?"

Selma sighed. "She needs braces."

"Get them. I'm clicking, Selma. We're going to start living. I bought a new suit."

"It's about time," Selma said. "You've needed one for *so* long. Does it look nice on you?"

"I think so," Laird said. "I love you, Selma."

"I love you, Eddie. Good night."

"Miss you," Laird said. "Good night."

The Powder-Blue
Dragon

A thin young man with big grimy hands crossed the sun-softened asphalt of the seaside village's main street, went from the automobile dealership where he worked to the post office. The village had once been a whaling port. Now its natives served the owners and renters of mansions on the beachfront.

The young man mailed some letters and bought stamps for his boss. Then he went to the drugstore next door on business of his own. Two summer people, a man and a woman his age, were coming out as he was going in. He gave them a sullen glance, as though their health and wealth and lazy aplomb were meant to mock him.

He asked the druggist, who knew him well, to cash his own personal check for five dollars. It was drawn on his account at a bank in the next town. There was no bank in the village. His name was Kiah.

Kiah had moved his money, which was quite a lot, from a savings account into checking. The check Kiah handed the druggist was the first he had ever written. It was in fact numbered 1. Kiah didn't need the five dollars. He worked off the books for the automobile dealer, and was paid in cash. He wanted to make sure a check written by him was really money, would really work.

"My name is written on top there," he said.

"I see that," said the druggist. "You're certainly coming up in the world."

"Don't worry," said Kiah, "it's good." Was it ever good! Kiah thought maybe the druggist would faint if he knew how good that check was.

"Why would I worry about a check from the most honest, hardworking boy in town?" The druggist corrected himself. "A checking account makes you a big man now, just like J. P. Morgan."

"What kind of a car does he drive?" asked Kiah.

"Who?"

"J. P. Morgan."

"He's dead. Is that how you judge people, by the cars they drive?" The druggist was seventy years old, very tired, and looking for somebody to buy his store. "You must have a very low opinion of me, driving a secondhand Chevy." He handed Kiah five one-dollar bills.

Kiah named the Chevy's model instantly: "Malibu."

"I think maybe working for Daggett has made you car-crazy." Daggett was the dealer across the street. He sold foreign sports cars there, and had another showroom in New York City. "How many jobs you got now, besides Daggett?"

"Wait tables at the Quarterdeck weekends, pump gas at Ed's nights." Kiah was an orphan who lived in a boardinghouse. His father had worked for a landscape contractor, his mother as a chambermaid at the Howard Johnson's out on the turnpike. They were killed in a head-on collision in front of the Howard Johnson's when Kiah was sixteen. The police had said the crash was their fault. His parents had no money, and their secondhand Plymouth Fury was totaled, so they didn't even have a car to leave him.

"I worry about you, Kiah," said the druggist. "All work and no play. Still haven't saved enough to buy a car?" It was generally known in the village that Kiah worked such long hours so he could buy a car. He had no girl.

"Ever hear of a Marittima-Frascati?"

"No. And I don't believe anybody else ever heard of one, either."

Kiah looked at the druggist pityingly. "Won the Avignon road race two years in a row—over Jaguars, Mercedes, and everything. Guaranteed to do a hundred and thirty on an open stretch. Most beautiful car in the world. Daggett's got one in his New York place." Kiah went up on his tiptoes. "Nobody's ever seen anything like it around here. Nobody."

"Why don't you ever talk about Fords or Chevrolets or something I've heard of? Marittima-Frascati!"

"No class. That's why I don't talk about them."

"Class! Listen who's talking about class all the time. He sweeps floors, polishes cars, waits tables, pumps gas, and he's got to have class or nothing."

"You dream your dreams, I'll dream mine," Kiah said.

"I dream of being young like you in a village that's as pretty and pleasant as this one is," said the druggist. "You can take class and—"

Daggett, a portly New Yorker who operated his branch showroom only in the summer, was selling a car to an urbane and tweedy gentleman as Kiah walked in.

"I'm back, Mr. Daggett," Kiah said.

Daggett paid no attention to him. Kiah sat down on a chair to wait and daydream. His heart was beating hard.

"It's not for me, understand," the customer was saying. He looked down in amazement at the low, boxy MG. "It's for my boy. He's been talking about one of these things."

"A fine young-man's car," Daggett said. "And reasonably priced for a sports car."

"Now he's raving about some other car, a Mara-something."

"Marittima-Frascati," said Kiah.

Daggett and the customer seemed surprised to find him in the same room.

"Mmmm, yes, that's the name," the customer said.

"Have one in the city. I could get it out here early next week," said Daggett.

"How much?"

"Fifty-six hundred and fifty-one dollars," said Kiah.

Daggett gave a flat, unfriendly laugh. "You've got a good memory, Kiah."

"Fifty-six hundred!" the customer said. "I love my boy, but love's got to draw the line somewhere. I'll take this one." He took a checkbook from his pocket.

Kiah's long shadow fell across the receipt Daggett was making out.

"Kiah, please. You're in the light." Kiah didn't move. "Kiah, what is it you want? Why don't you sweep out the back room or something?"

"I just wanted to say," Kiah said, his breathing shallow, "that when this gentleman is through, I'd like to order the Marittima-Frascati."

"You what?" Daggett stood angrily.

Kiah took out his own checkbook.

"Beat it!" Daggett said.

The customer laughed.

"Do you want my business?" Kiah asked.

"I'll take care of your business, kid, but good. Now sit down and wait." Kiah sat down until the customer left.

Daggett then walked toward Kiah slowly, his fists clenched. "Now, young man, your funny business almost lost me a sale."

"I'll give you two minutes, Mr. Daggett, to call up the bank and find out if I've got the money, or I'll get my car someplace else."

Daggett called the bank. "George, this is Bill Daggett." He interjected a supercilious laugh. "Look, George, Kiah Higgins wants to write me a check for fifty-six hundred dollars. . . . That's what I said. I swear he does. . . . Okay, I'll wait." He drummed on the desktop and avoided looking at Kiah.

"Fine, George. Thanks." He hung up.

"Well?" Kiah said.

"I made that call to satisfy my curiosity," said Daggett. "Congratulations. I'm very impressed. Back to work."

"It's my money. I earned it," Kiah said. "I worked and saved for four years—four lousy, long years. Now I want that car."

"You've got to be kidding."

"That car is all I can think about, and now it's going to be mine, the damnedest car anybody around here ever saw."

Daggett was exasperated. "The Marittima-Frascati is a plaything for maharajas and Texas oil barons. Fifty-six hundred dollars, boy! What would that leave of your savings?"

"Enough for insurance and a few tanks of gas." Kiah stood. "If you don't want my business . . ."

"You must be sick," said Daggett.

"You'd understand if you'd been brought up here, Mr. Daggett, and your parents had been dead broke."

"Baloney! Don't tell me what it is to be broke till you've been broke in the city. Anyway, what's the car going to do for you?"

"It's going to give me one hell of a good time—and about time. I'm going to do some living, Mr. Daggett. The first of next week, Mr. Daggett?"

The midafternoon stillness of the village was broken by the whir of a starter and the well-bred grumble of a splendid engine.

Kiah sat deep in the lemon-yellow leather cushions of the powder-blue Marittima-Frascati, listening to the sweet thunder that followed each gentle pressure of his toe. He was scrubbed pink, and his hair was freshly cut.

"No fast stuff, now, for a thousand miles, you hear?" Daggett said. He was in a holiday mood, resigned to the bizarre wonder Kiah had wrought. "That's a piece of fine jewelry under the hood, and you'd better treat it right. Keep it under sixty for the first thousand miles, under eighty until three thousand." He laughed. "And don't try to find out what she can really do until you've put five thousand on her." He clapped Kiah on the shoulder. "Don't get impatient, boy. Don't worry—she'll do it!"

Kiah switched on the engine again, seeming indifferent to the crowd gathered around him.

"How many of these you suppose are in the country?" Kiah asked Daggett.

"Ten, twelve." Daggett winked. "Don't worry. All the others are in Dallas and Hollywood."

Kiah nodded judiciously. He hoped to look like a man who had made a sensible purchase and, satisfied with his money's worth, was going to take it home now. The moment for him was beautiful and funny, but he did not smile.

He put the car in gear for the first time. It was so easy. "Pardon me," he said to those in his way. He raced his engine rather than blow his brass choir of horns. "Thank you."

When Kiah got the car onto the six-lane turnpike, he ceased feeling like an intruder in the universe. He was as much a part of it as the clouds and the sea. With the mock modesty of a god traveling incognito, he permitted a Cadillac convertible to pass him. A pretty girl at its wheel smiled down on him.

Kiah touched the throttle lightly and streaked around her. He laughed at the speck she became in his rearview mirror. The temperature gauge climbed, and Kiah slowed the Marittima-Frascati, forgiving himself this one indulgence. Just this once—it had been worth it. This was the life!

The girl and the Cadillac passed him again. She smiled, and gestured disparagingly at the expanse of hood before her. She loved his car. She hated hers.

At the mouth of a hotel's circular driveway, she signaled with a flourish and turned in. As though coming home, the Marittima-Frascati followed, purred beneath the porte cochere and into the parking lot. A uniformed man waved, smiled, admired, and directed Kiah into the space next to the Cadillac. Kiah watched the girl disappear into the cocktail lounge, each step an invitation to follow.

As he crossed the deep white gravel, a cloud crossed the sun, and in the momentary chill, Kiah's stride shortened. The universe was treating him like an intruder again. He paused on the cocktail lounge steps and looked over his shoulder at the car. There it waited for its master, low, lean, greedy for miles—Kiah Higgins's car.

Refreshed, Kiah walked into the cool lounge. The girl sat alone in a corner booth, her eyes down. She amused herself by picking a wooden swizzle stick to bits. The only other person in the room was the bartender, who read a newspaper.

"Looking for somebody, sonny?"

Sonny? Kiah felt like driving the Marittima-Frascati into the bar. He hoped the girl hadn't heard. "Give me a gin and tonic," he said coldly, "and don't forget the lime."

She looked up. Kiah smiled with the camaraderie of privilege, horsepower, and the open road.

She nodded back, puzzled, and returned her attention to the swizzle stick.

"Here you are, sonny," said the bartender, setting the drink before him. He rattled his newspaper and resumed his reading.

Kiah drank, cleared his throat, and spoke to the girl. "Nice weather," he said.

She gave no sign that he'd said anything. Kiah turned to the bartender, as though it were to him he'd been speaking. "You like to drive?"

"Sometimes," the bartender said.

"Weather like this makes a man feel like really letting his car go full-bore." The bartender turned a page without comment. "But I'm just breaking her in, and I've got to keep her under fifty."

"I guess."

"Big temptation, knowing she's guaranteed to do a hundred and thirty."

The bartender put down his paper irritably. "What's guaranteed?"

"My new car, my Marittima-Frascati."

The girl looked up, interested.

"Your what?" the bartender said.

"My Marittima-Frascati. It's an Italian car."

"It sure don't sound like an American one. Who you driving it for?"

"Who'm I driving it for?"

"Yeah. Who owns it?"

"Who you think owns it? *I* own it."

The bartender picked up his paper again. "*He* owns it. He owns it, and it goes a hundred and thirty. Lucky boy."

Kiah replied by turning his back. "Hello," he said to the girl, with more assurance than he thought possible. "How's the Cad treating you?"

She laughed. "My car, my fiancé, or my father?"

"Your car," Kiah said, feeling stupid for not having a snappier retort.

"Cads always treat me nicely. I remember you now. You were in that darling little blue thing with yellow seats. I somehow didn't connect you with the car. You look different. What did you call it?"

"A Marittima-Frascati."

"Mmmmmm. I could never learn to say that."

"It's a very famous car in Europe," Kiah said. Everything was going swimmingly. "Won the Avignon road race two years running, you know."

She smiled a bewitching smile. "No! I *didn't* know that."

"Guaranteed to go a hundred and thirty."

"Goodness. I didn't think a car could go that fast."

"Only about twelve in the country, if *that*."

"Certainly isn't many, is it? Do you mind my asking how much one of those wonderful cars costs?"

Kiah leaned back against the bar. "No, I don't mind. Seems to me it was somewhere between five and six."

"Oh, between *those*, is it? Quite something to be between."

"Oh, I think it's well worth it. I certainly don't feel I've thrown any money down a sewer."

"That's the important thing."

Kiah nodded happily, and stared into the wonderful eyes, whose admiration seemed bottomless. He opened his mouth to say more, to keep the delightful game going forever and ever, when he realized he had nothing more to say. "Nice weather."

A glaze of boredom formed on her eyes. "Have you got the time?" she asked the bartender.

"Yes, ma'am. Seven after four."

"What did you say?" asked Kiah.

"Four, sonny."

A ride, Kiah thought, maybe she'd like to go for a ride.

The door swung open. A handsome young man in tennis shorts blinked and grinned around the room, poised, vain, and buoyant. "Marion!"

he cried. "Thank heaven you're still here. What an angel you are for waiting for me!"

Her face was stunning with adoration. "You're not very late, Paul, and I forgive you."

"Like a fool, I let myself get into a game of doubles, and it just went on and on. I finally threw the game. I was afraid I'd lose you forever. What've you been up to while you've been waiting?"

"Let me see. Well, I tore up a swizzle stick, and I, uh— Ohhhhhh! I met an extremely interesting gentleman who has a car that will go a hundred and thirty miles an hour."

"Well, you've been slickered, dear, because the man was lying about his car."

"Those are pretty strong words," Marion said.

Paul looked pleased. "They are?"

"Considering that the man you called a liar is right here in this room."

"Oh, my." Paul looked around the room with a playful expression of fear. His eyes passed over Kiah and the bartender. "There are only four of us here."

She pointed to Kiah. "That boy there. Would you mind telling Paul about your Vanilla Frappé?"

"Marittima-Frascati," Kiah said, his voice barely audible. He repeated it, louder. "Marittima-Frascati."

"Well," Paul said, "I must say it sounds like it'd go two hundred a second. Have you got it here?"

"Outside," Kiah said.

"That's what I meant," Paul said. "I must learn to express myself with more precision." He looked out over the parking lot. "Oho, I see. The little blue jobbie. Ver-ry nice, scary but gorgeous. And that's yours?"

"I said it was."

"Might be the second-fastest car in these parts. Probably is."

"Is that a fact?" Kiah said sarcastically. "I'd like to see the first."

"Would you? It's right outside, too. There, the green one."

The car was a British Hampton. Kiah knew the car well. It was the one he'd begun saving for before Daggett showed him pictures of the Marittima-Frascati.

"It'll do," Kiah said.

"Do, will it?" Paul laughed. "It'll do yours in, and I'll bet anything you like."

"Listen," said Kiah, "I'd bet the world on my car against yours, if mine was broken in."

"Pity," said Paul. "Another time, then." He explained to Marion, "Not broken in, Marion. Shall we go?"

"I'm ready, Paul," she said. "I'd better tell the attendant I'll be back for the Cadillac, or he'll think I've been kidnapped."

"Which is exactly what is about to happen," said Paul. "Be seeing you, Ralph," he said to the bartender. They knew each other.

"Always glad to see you, Paul," said Ralph.

So Kiah now knew the names of all three, but they didn't know what his name was. Nobody had asked. Nobody cared. What could matter less than what his name was?

Kiah watched through a window as Marion spoke to the parking attendant, and then eased herself down into the passenger seat of the low-slung Hampton.

Ralph asked the nameless one this: "You a mechanic? Somebody left that car with you, and you took it out for a road test? Better put the top up, because it's gonna rain."

The rear wheels of the powder-blue dragon with the lemon-yellow leather bucket seats sprayed gravel at the parking attendant's legs. A doorman beneath the porte cochere signaled for it to slow down, then jumped for his life.

Kiah was encouraging it softly, saying, "That's good, let's go, let's go. I love yah," and so on. He steered, and shifted the synchromesh gears so the car could go ever faster smoothly, but he felt doing all that was really unnecessary, that the car itself knew better than he did where to go and how to do what it had been born to do.

The only Marittima-Frascati for thousands of miles swept past cars and trucks as though they were standing still. The needle of the temperature gauge on the padded dashboard was soon trembling against the pin at the extreme end of the red zone.

"Good girl," said Kiah. He talked to the car sometimes as though it were a girl, sometimes as though it were a boy.

It overtook the Hampton, which was going only a hair over the speed limit. The Marittima-Frascati had to slow a lot, so it could run alongside the Hampton and Kiah could give Marion and Paul the finger.

Paul shook his head and waved Kiah on, then applied his brakes to drop far behind. There would be no race.

"He's got no guts, baby," said Kiah. "Let's show the world what guts are." He pressed the accelerator to the floor. As blurs loomed before him and vanished, he kept it there.

The engine was shrieking in agony now, and Kiah said in a matter-of-fact tone, "Explode, explode."

But the engine didn't explode or catch fire. Its precious jewels simply merged with one another, and the engine ceased to be an engine. Nor was the clutch a clutch anymore. That allowed the car to roll into the break-down lane of the highway, powered by nothing but the last bit of momentum it would ever have on its own.

The Hampton, with Paul and Marion aboard, never passed. They must have gotten off at some exit far behind, Kiah thought.

Kiah left the car where it died. He thumbed a ride back to the village, without having to give his lift a story of any kind. He returned to Daggett's showroom and acted as though he was there to work. The MG was still on the floor. The man who said he would buy it for his son had changed his mind.

"I gave you the whole day off," said Daggett.

"I know," said Kiah.

"So where's the car?"

"I killed it."

"You what?"

"I got it up to one forty-four, when they said it could only do one thirty-five."

"You're joking."

"Wait'll you see," said Kiah. "That's one dead sports vehicle. You'll have to send the tow truck."

"My God, boy, why would you do such a thing?"

"Call me Kiah."

"Kiah," echoed Daggett, convinced he was dealing with a lunatic.

"Who knows why anybody does anything?" said Kiah. "I don't know why I killed it. All I know is I'm glad it's dead."

A Present for
Big Saint Nick

Big Nick was said to be the most recent heir to the power of Al Capone. He refused to affirm or deny it, on the grounds that he might tend to incriminate himself.

He bought whatever caught his fancy, a twenty-three-room house outside Chicago, a seventeen-room house in Miami, racehorses, a ninety-foot yacht, one hundred fifteen suits, and among other things, controlling interest in a middleweight boxer named Bernie O'Hare, the Shenandoah Blaster.

When O'Hare lost sight in one eye on his way to the top of his profession, Big Nick added him to his squad of bodyguards.

Big Nick gave a party every year, a little before Christmas, for the children of his staff, and on the morning of the day of the party, Bernie

O'Hare, the Shenandoah Blaster, went shopping in downtown Chicago with his wife, Wanda, and their four-year-old son, Willy.

The three were in a jewelry store when young Willy began to complain and cling to his father's trousers like a drunken bell-ringer.

Bernie, a tough, scarred, obedient young thug, set down a velvet-lined tray of watches and grabbed the waist of his trousers. "Let go my pants, Willy! Let go!" He turned to Wanda. "How'm I supposed to pick a Christmas present for Big Nick with Willy pulling my pants down? Take him off me, Wan. What ails the kid?"

"There must be a Santa Claus around," said Wanda.

"There ain't no Santy Clauses in jewelry stores," said Bernie. "You ain't got no Santy Claus in here, have you?" he asked the clerk.

"No, sir," said the clerk. His face bloomed, and he leaned over the counter to speak to Willy. "But if the little boy would like to talk to old Saint Nick, I think he'll find the jolly old elf right next—"

"Can it," said Bernie.

The clerk paled. "I was just going to say, sir, that the department store next door has a Santa Claus, and the little—"

"Can'tcha see you're making the kid worse?" said Bernie. He knelt by Willy. "Willy boy, there ain't no Santy Clauses around for miles. The guy is full of baloney. There ain't no Santy next door."

"There, Daddy, there," said Willy. He pointed a finger at a tiny red figure standing by a clock behind the counter.

"Cripes!" said Bernie haggardly, slapping his knee. "The kid's got a eye like a eagle for Santy Clauses." He gave a fraudulent laugh. "Why, say, Willy boy, I'm surprised at you. That's just a little *plastic* Santy. He can't hurt you."

"I hate him," said Willy.

"How much you want for the thing?" said Ernie.

"The plastic Santa Claus, sir?" said the bewildered clerk. "Why, it's just a little decoration. I think you can get one at any five-and-ten-cent store."

"I want that one," said Bernie. "Right now."

The clerk gave it to him. "No charge," he said. "Be our guest."

Bernie dropped the Santa Claus on the terrazzo floor. "Watch what

Daddy's going to do to Old Whiskers, Willy," he said. He brought his heel down. "Keeeeee-runch!"

Willy smiled faintly, then began to laugh as his father's heel came down again and again.

"Now you do it, Willy," said Bernie. "Who's afraid of *him*, eh?"

"I'll bust his ol' head off," said Willy gleefully. "Crunch him up!" He himself trampled Father Christmas.

"That was *real* smart," said Wanda. "You make me spend all year trying to get him to like Santa Claus, and then you pull a stunt like that."

"I hadda do something to make him pipe down, didn't I?" said Bernie. "Okay, okay. Now maybe we can have a little peace and quiet so I can look at the watches. How much is this one with the diamonds for numbers?"

"Three hundred dollars, sir, including tax," said the clerk.

"Does it glow in the dark? It's gotta glow in the dark."

"Yes, sir, the face is luminous."

"I'll take it," said Bernie.

"Three hundred bucks!" said Wanda, pained. "Holy smokes, Bernie."

"Whaddya mean, holy smokes?" said Bernie. "I'm ashamed to give him a little piece of junk like this. What's a lousy three-hundred-dollar watch to Big Nick? You kick about this, but I don't hear you kicking about the way the savings account keeps going up. Big Nick *is* Santy Claus, whether you like it or not."

"I don't like it," said Wanda. "And neither does Willy. Look at the poor kid—Christmas is ruined for him."

"Aaaaah, now," said Bernie, "it ain't that bad. It's real warmhearted of Big Nick to wanna give a party for the kids. I mean, no matter how it comes out, he's got the right idea."

"Some heart!" said Wanda. "Some idea! He gets dressed up in a Santa Claus suit so all the kids'll worship him. And he tops that off by makin' the kids squeal on their parents."

Bernie nodded in resignation. "What can I do?"

"Quit," said Wanda. "Work for somebody else."

"What else I know how to do, Wan? All I ever done was fight, and where else am I gonna make money like what Big Nick pays me? Where?"

A tall, urbane gentleman with a small mustache came up to the adjoining counter, trailed by a wife in mink and a son. The son was Willy's age, and was snuffling and peering apprehensively over his shoulder at the front door.

The clerk excused himself and went to serve the genteel new arrivals.

"Hey," said Bernie, "there's Mr. and Mrs. Pullman. You remember them from last Christmas, Wan."

"Big Nick's accountant?" said Wanda.

"Naw, his lawyer." Bernie saluted Pullman with a wave of his hand. "Hi, Mr. Pullman."

"Oh, hello," said Pullman without warmth. "Big Nick's bodyguard," he explained to his wife. "You remember him from the last Christmas party."

"Doing your Christmas shopping late like everybody else, I see," said Bernie.

"Yes," said Pullman. He looked down at his child, Richard. "Can't you stop snuffling?"

"It's psychosomatic," said Mrs. Pullman. "He snuffles every time he sees a Santa Claus. You can't bring a child downtown at Christmastime and not have him see a Santa Claus *some*where. One came out of the cafeteria next door just a minute ago. Scared poor Richard half to death."

"I won't have a snuffling son," said Pullman. "Richard! Stiff upper lip! Santa Claus is your friend, my friend, everybody's friend."

"I wish he'd stay at the North Pole," said Richard.

"And freeze his nose off," said Willy.

"And get ate up by a polar bear," said Richard.

"*Eaten* up by a polar bear," Mrs. Pullman corrected.

"Are you encouraging the boy to hate Santa Claus?" said Mr. Pullman.

"Why pretend?" said Mrs. Pullman. "*Our* Santa Claus *is* a dirty, vulgar, prying, foulmouthed, ill-smelling fake."

The clerk's eyes rolled.

"Sometimes, dear," said Pullman, "I wonder if you remember what we were like before we met that jolly elf. Quite broke."

"Give me integrity or give me death," said Mrs. Pullman.

"Shame comes along with the money," said Pullman. "It's a package deal. And we're in this thing together." He addressed the clerk. "I want something terribly overpriced and in the worst possible taste, something, possibly, that glows in the dark and has a barometer in it." He pressed his thumb and forefinger together in a symbol of delicacy. "Do you sense the sort of thing I'm looking for?"

"I'm sorry to say you've come to the right place," said the clerk. "We have a model of the *Mayflower* in chromium, with a red light that shines through the portholes," he said. "However, *that* has a clock instead of a barometer. We have a silver statuette of Man o' War with rubies for eyes, and *that's* got a barometer. Ugh."

"I wonder," said Mrs. Pullman, "if we couldn't have Man o' War welded to the poop deck of the *Mayflower?*"

"You're on the right track," said Pullman. "You surprise me. I didn't think you'd ever get the hang of Big Nick's personality." He rubbed his eyes. "Oh Lord, what does he need, what does he need? Any ideas, Bernie?"

"Nothing," said Bernie. "He's got seven of everything. But he says he still likes to get presents, just to remind him of all the friends he's got."

"He *would* think that was the way to count them," said Pullman.

"Friends are important to Big Nick," said Bernie. "He's gotta be told a hunnerd times a day everybody loves him, or he starts bustin' up the furniture an' the help."

Pullman nodded. "Richard," he said to his son, "do you remember what you are to tell Santa Claus when he asks what Mommy and Daddy think of Big Nick?"

"Mommy and Daddy love Big Nick," said Richard. "Mommy and Daddy think he's a real gentleman."

"What're you gonna say, Willy?" Bernie asked his own son.

"Mommy and Daddy say they owe an awful lot to Big Nick," said Willy. "Big Nick is a kind, generous man."

"Ev-ry-bo-dy loves Big Nick," said Wanda.

"Or they wind up in Lake Michigan with cement overshoes," said Pullman. He smiled at the clerk, who had just brought him the *Mayflower* and Man o' War. "They're fine as far as they go," he said. "But do they glow in the dark?"

· · · ·

Bernie O'Hare was the front-door guard at Big Nick's house on the day of the party. Now he admitted Mr. and Mrs. Pullman and their son.

"Ho ho ho," said Bernie softly.

"Ho ho ho," said Pullman.

"Well, Richard," said Bernie to young Pullman, "I see you're all calmed down."

"Daddy gave me half a sleeping tablet," said Richard.

"Has the master of the house been holding high wassail?" said Mrs. Pullman.

"I beg your pardon?" said Bernie.

"Is he drunk?" said Mrs. Pullman.

"Do fish swim?" said Bernie.

"Did the sun rise?" said Mr. Pullman.

A small intercom phone on the wall buzzed. "Yeah. Nick?" said Bernie.

"They all here yet?" said a truculent voice.

"Yeah, Nick. The Pullmans just got here. They're the last. The rest are sitting in the living room."

"Do your stuff." Nick hung up.

Bernie sighed, took a string of sleighbells from the closet, turned off the alarm system, and stepped outside into the shrubbery.

He shook the sleighbells and shouted. "Hey! It's Santy Claus! And Dunder and Blitzen and Dancer and Prancer! Oh, boy! They're landing on the roof! Now Santy's coming in through an upstairs bedroom window!"

He went back inside, hid the bells, bolted and chained the door, reset the alarm system, and went into the living room, where twelve children and eight sets of parents sat silently.

All the men in the group worked for Nick. Bernie was the only one who looked like a hoodlum. The rest looked like ordinary, respectable business-men. They labored largely in Big Nick's headquarters, where brutality was remote. They kept his books and gave him business and legal advice, and applied the most up-to-date management methods to his varied enter-prises. They were a fraction of his staff, the ones who had children young enough to believe in Santa Claus.

"Merry Christmas!" said Santa Claus harshly, his big black boots clumping down the stairs.

Willy squirmed away from his mother and ran to Bernie for better protection.

Santa Claus leaned on the newel post, a cigar jutting from his cotton beard, his beady eyes traveling malevolently from one face to the next. Santa Claus was fat and squat and pasty-faced. He reeked of booze.

"I just got down from me workshop at the Nort' Pole," he said challengingly. "Ain't nobody gonna say hi to ol' Saint Nick?"

All around the room parents nudged children who would not speak.

"Talk it up!" said Santa. "This ain't no morgue." He pointed a blunt finger at Richard Pullman. "You been a good boy, heh?"

Mr. Pullman squeezed his son like a bagpipe.

"Yup," piped Richard.

"Ya sure?" said Santa suspiciously. "Ain't been fresh wit' grown-ups?"

"Nope," said Richard.

"Okay," said Santa. "Maybe I got a electric train for ya, an' maybe I don't." He rummaged through a pile of parcels under the tree. "Now, where'd I put that stinkin' train?" He found the parcel with Richard's name on it. "Want it?"

"Yup," said Richard.

"Well, *act* like you want it," said Santa Claus.

Young Richard could only swallow.

"Ya know what it cost?" said Santa Claus. "Hunnerd and twenny-four fifty." He paused dramatically. "*Wholesale.*" He leaned over Richard. "Lemme hear you say t'anks."

Mr. Pullman squeezed Richard.

"T'anks," said Richard.

"T'anks. I guess," said Santa Claus with heavy irony. "You never got no hunnerd-and-twenny-four-fifty train from your old man, I'll tell you that. Lemme tell you, kid, he'd still be chasin' ambulances an' missin' payments on his briefcase if it wasn't for me. An' don't nobody forget it."

Mr. Pullman whispered something to his son.

"What was that?" said Santa. "Come on, kid, wha'd your old man say?"

"He said sticks and stones could break his bones, but words would never hurt him." Richard seemed embarrassed for his father. So did Mrs. Pullman, who was hyperventilating.

"Ha!" said Santa Claus. "That's a hot one. I bet he says that one a hunnerd times a day. What's he say about Big Nick at home, eh? Come on, Richard, this is Santa Claus you're talkin' to, and I keep a book about kids that don't tell the trut' up at the Nort' Pole. What's he really t'ink of Big Nick?"

Pullman looked away as though Richard's reply couldn't concern him less.

"Mommy and Daddy say Big Nick is a real gentleman," recited Richard. "Mommy and Daddy love Big Nick."

"Okay, kid," said Santa, "here's your train. You're a good boy."

"T'anks," said Richard.

"Now I got a big doll for little Gwen Zerbe," said Santa, taking another parcel from under the tree. "But first come over here, Gwen, so you and me can talk where nobody can hear us, eh?"

Gwen, propelled by her father, Big Nick's chief accountant, minced over to Santa Claus. Her father, a short, pudgy man, smiled thinly, strained his ears to hear, and turned green. At the end of the questioning, Zerbe exhaled with relief and got some of his color back. Santa Claus was smiling. Gwen had her doll.

"Willy O'Hare!" thundered Santa Claus. "Tell Santy the trut', and ya get a swell boat. What's your old man and old lady say about Big Nick?"

"They say they owe him a lot," said Willy dutifully.

Santa Claus guffawed. "I guess they do, boy! Willy, you know where your old man'd be if it wasn't for Big Nick? He'd be dancin' aroun' in little circles, talking to hisself, wit'out nuttin' to his name but a flock of canaries in his head. Here, kid, here's your boat, an' Merry Christmas."

"Merry Christmas to you," said Willy politely. "Please, could I have a rag?"

"A rag?" said Santa.

"Please," said Willy. "I wanna wipe off the boat."

"Willy!" said Bernie and Wanda together.

"Wait a minute, wait a minute," said Santa. "Let the kid talk. *Why* you wanna wipe it off, Willy?"

"I want to wipe off the blood and dirt," said Willy.

"Blood!" said Santa. "Dirt!"

"Willy!" cried Bernie.

"Mama says everything we get from Santa's got blood on it," said Willy. He pointed at Mrs. Pullman. "And that lady says he's dirty."

"No I didn't, no I didn't," said Mrs. Pullman.

"Yes you did," said Richard. "I heard you."

"My father," said Gwen Zerbe, breaking the dreadful silence, "says kissing Santa Claus isn't any worse than kissing a dog."

"Gwen!" cried her father.

"I kiss the dog all the time," said Gwen, determined to complete her thought, "and I never get sick."

"I guess we can wash off the blood and dirt when we get home," said Willy.

"Why, you fresh little punk!" roared Santa Claus, bringing his hand back to hit Willy.

Bernie stood quickly and clasped Santa's wrists. "Please," he said, "the kid don't mean nothing."

"Take your filt'y hands off me!" roared Santa. "You wanna commit suicide?"

Bernie let go of Santa.

"Ain't you gonna say nuttin'?" said Santa. "I t'ink I got a little apology comin'."

"I'm very sorry, Santa Claus," said Bernie. His big fist smashed Santa's cigar all over his face. Santa went reeling into the Christmas tree, clawing down ornaments as he fell.

Childish cheers filled the room. Bernie grinned broadly and clasped his hands over his head, a champ!

"Shut them kids up!" Santa Claus sputtered. "Shut them up, or you're all dead!"

Parents scuffled with their children, trying to muzzle them, and the children twisted free, hooting and jeering and booing Santa Claus.

"Make him eat his whiskers, Bernie!"

"Feed him to the reindeers!"

"You're all t'rough! You're all dead!" shouted Santa Claus, still on his back. "I get bums like you knocked off for twenty-five bucks, five for a hunnerd. Get out!"

The children were so happy! They danced out of the house without their coats, saying things like, "Jingle bells, you old poop," and "Eat tinsel, Santy," and so on. They were too innocent to realize that nothing had changed in the economic structure in which their parents were still embedded. In so many movies they'd seen, one punch to the face of a bad guy by a good guy turned hell into an earthly paradise.

Santa Claus, flailing his arms, drove their parents after them. "I got ways of findin' you no matter where you go! I been good to you, and this is the thanks I get. Well, you're gonna get thanks from me, in spades. You bums are all gonna get rubbed out."

"My dad knocked Santa on his butt!" crowed Willy.

"I'm a dead man," said O'Hare to his wife.

"I'm a dead woman," she said, "but it was almost worth it. Look how happy the children are."

They could expect to be killed by a hit man, unless they fled to some godforsaken country where the Mafia didn't have a chapter. So could the Pullmans.

Saint Nicholas disappeared inside the house, then reappeared with another armload of packages in Christmas wrappings. His white cotton beard was stained red from a nosebleed. He stripped the wrappings from one package, held up a cigarette lighter in the form of a knight in armor. He read the enclosed card aloud: "'To Big Nick, the one and only. Love you madly.'" The signature was that of a famous movie star out in Hollywood.

Now Saint Nicholas showed off another pretty package. "Here's one comes all the way from a friend in Italy." He gave its red ribbon a mighty yank. The explosion not only blew off his bloody beard and fur-trimmed red hat, but removed his chin and nose as well. What a mess! What a terrible thing for the young to see, one would think, but they wouldn't have missed it for the world.

After the police left, and the corpse was carted off to the morgue, dressed like Kris Kringle from the neck down, O'Hare's wife said this: "I don't think this is a Christmas the children are going to forget very soon. I know I won't."

Their son Willy had a souvenir that would help him remember. He had found the greeting card that came with the bomb. It was in the shrubbery. It said, "Merry Christmas to the greatest guy in the world." It was signed "The Family."

There would be a rude awakening, of course. The fathers were going to have to find new jobs, ho ho.

Unpaid Consultant

Most married women won't meet an old beau for cocktails, send him a Christmas card, or even look him straight in the eye. But if they happen to need something an old beau sells—anything from an appendectomy to venetian blinds—they'll come bouncing back into his life, all pink and smiling, to get it for wholesale or less.

If a Don Juan were to go into the household appliance business, his former conquests would ruin him inside of a year.

What I sell is good advice on stocks and bonds. I'm a contact man for an investment counseling firm, and the girls I've lost, even by default, never hesitate to bring their investment problems to me.

I am a bachelor, and in return for my services, which after all cost me nothing, they sometimes offer me that jewel beyond price—the home-cooked meal.

The largest portfolio I ever examined, in return for nostalgia and chicken, country style, was the portfolio of Celeste Divine. I lost Celeste in high school, and we didn't exchange a word for seventeen years, until she called me at my office one day to say, "Long time no see."

Celeste Divine is a singer. Her hair is black and curly, her eyes large and brown, her lips full and glistening. Painted and spangled and sheathed in gold lamé, Celeste is before the television cameras for one hour each week, making love to all the world. For this public service she gets five thousand dollars a week.

"I've been meaning to have you out for a long time," said Celeste to me. "What would you say to home-cooked chicken, Idaho potatoes, and strawberry shortcake?"

"Mmmmmmmmmm," I said.

"And after supper," said Celeste, "you and Harry and I can sit before a roaring fire and talk about old times and old friends back home."

"Swell," I said. I could see the firelight playing over the columns of figures, *The Wall Street Journal*, the prospectuses and graphs. I could hear Celeste and her husband Harry murmuring about the smell of new-mown hay, American Brake Shoe preferred, moonlight on the Wabash, Consolidated Edison three-percent bonds, cornbread, and Chicago, Milwaukee, St. Paul, and Pacific common.

"We've only been away from here for two years," said Celeste, "but it seems like a lifetime, so much has happened. It'll be good to see somebody from back home."

"You really came up fast, didn't you, Celeste," I said.

"I feel like Cinderella," said Celeste. "One day, Harry and I were struggling along on his pay from Joe's Greasing Palace, and the next day, everything I touched seemed to turn to gold."

It wasn't until I'd hung up that I began wondering how Harry felt.

Harry was the man I'd lost Celeste to. I remembered him as a small, good-looking, sleepy boy, who asked nothing more of life than the prettiest wife in town and a decent job as an automobile mechanic. He got both one week after graduation.

· · · ·

When I went to the Divine home for supper, Celeste herself, with the body of a love goddess and the face of a Betsy Wetsy, let me in.

The nest she'd bought for herself and her mate was an old mansion on the river, as big and ugly as the Schenectady railroad station.

She gave me her hand to kiss, and befuddled by her beauty and perfume, I kissed it.

"Harry? Harry!" she called. "Guess who's here."

I expected to see either a cadaver or a slob, the remains of Harry, come shuffling in.

But there was no response from Harry.

"He's in his study," said Celeste. "How that man can concentrate! When he gets something on his mind, it's just like he was in another world." She opened the study door cautiously. "You see?"

Lying on his back on a tiger-skin rug was Harry. He was staring at the ceiling. Beside him was a frosty pitcher of martinis, and in his fingers he held a drained glass. He rolled the olive in it around and around and around.

"Darling," said Celeste to Harry, "I hate to interrupt, dear."

"What? What's that?" said Harry, startled. He sat up. "Oh! I beg your pardon. I didn't hear you come in." He stood and shook my hand forthrightly, and I saw that the years had left him untouched.

Harry seemed very excited about something, but underneath his excitement was the sleepy contentment I remembered from high school. "I haven't any right to relax," he said. "Everybody in the whole damn industry is relaxing. If I relax, down comes the roof. Ten thousand men out of jobs." He seized my arm. "Count their families, and you've got a city the size of Terre Haute hanging by a thread."

"I don't understand," I said. "Why are they hanging by a thread?"

"The industry!" said Harry.

"What industry?" I said.

"The catchup industry," said Celeste.

Harry looked at me. "What do *you* call it? Catchup? Ketchup? Catsup?"

"I guess I call it different things at different times," I said.

Harry slammed his hand down on the coffee table. "There's the story of the catchup-ketchup-catsup industry in a nutshell! They can't even get together on how to spell the name of the product. If we can't even hang together that much," he said, "we'll all hang separately. Does one automobile manufacturer call automobiles 'applemobiles,' and another one 'axlemobiles,' and another one 'urblemowheels'?"

"Nope," I said.

"You bet they don't," said Harry. He filled his glass, motioned us to chairs, and lay down again on the tiger skin.

"Harry's found himself," said Celeste. "Isn't it marvelous? He was at loose ends so long. We had some terrible scenes after we moved here, didn't we, Harry?"

"I was immature," said Harry. "I admit it."

"And then," said Celeste, "just when things looked blackest, Harry blossomed! I got a brand-new husband!"

Harry plucked tufts of hair from the rug, rolled them into little balls, and flipped them into the fireplace. "I had an inferiority complex," he said. "I thought all I could ever be was a mechanic." He waved away Celeste's and my objections. "Then I found out plain horse sense is the rarest commodity in the business world. Next to most of the guys in the catchup industry, I look like an Einstein."

"Speaking of people blossoming," I said, "your wife gets more gorgeous by the minute."

"Hmmmmm?" said Harry.

"I said, Celeste is really something—one of the most beautiful and famous women in the country. You're a lucky man," I said.

"Yeah, yeah—sure," said Harry, his mind elsewhere.

"You knew what you wanted, and you got it, didn't you?" I said to Celeste.

"I—" Celeste began.

"Tell me, Celeste," I said, "what's your life like now? Pretty wild, I'll bet, with the program and the nightclub appearances, publicity, and all that."

"It is," said Celeste. "It's the most—"

"It's a lot like the industry," said Harry. "Keep the show moving, keep the show moving—keep the catchup moving, keep the catchup moving.

There are millions of people who take television for granted, and there are millions of people taking catchup for granted. They want it when they want it. It's got to be there—and it's got to be right. They don't stop to think about how it got there. They aren't interested." He dug his fingers into his thighs. "But they wouldn't get television, and they wouldn't get catchup if there weren't people tearing their hearts out to get it to 'em."

"I liked your record of 'Solitude' very much, Celeste," I said. "The last chorus, where you—"

Harry clapped his hands together. "Sure she's good. Hell, I said we'd sponsor her, if the industry'd ever get together on anything." He rolled over and looked up at Celeste. "What's the story on chow, Mother?" he said.

At supper, conversation strayed from one topic to another, but always settled, like a ball in a crooked roulette wheel, on the catchup industry.

Celeste tried to bring up the problem of her investments, but the subject, ordinarily a thriller, fizzled and sank in a sea of catchup again and again.

"I'm making five thousand a week now," said Celeste, "and there are a million people ready to tell me what to do with it. But I want to ask a friend—an old friend."

"It all depends on what you want from your investments," I said. "Do you want growth? Do you want stability? Do you want a quick return in dividends?"

"Don't put it in the catchup industry," said Harry. "If they wake up, if I can wake 'em up, OK. I'd say get in catchup and stay in catchup. But the way things are now, you might as well sink your money in Grant's Tomb, for all the action you'll get."

"Um," I said. "Well, Celeste, with your tax situation, I don't think you'd want dividends as much as you'd want growth."

"It's just crazy about taxes," said Celeste. "Harry figured out it was actually cheaper for him to work for nothing."

"For love," said Harry.

"What company are you with, Harry?" I said.

"I'm in a consulting capacity for the industry as a whole," said Harry.

The telephone rang, and a maid came in to tell Celeste that her agent was on the line.

I was left alone with Harry, and I found it hard to think of anything to say—anything that wouldn't be trivial in the face of the catchup industry's impending collapse.

I glanced around the room, humming nervously, and saw that the wall behind me was covered with impressive documents, blobbed with sealing wax, decked with ribbons, and signed with big black swirling signatures. The documents were from every conceivable combination of human beings, all gathered in solemn assembly to declare something nice about Celeste. She was a beacon to youth, a promoter of Fire Prevention Week, the sweetheart of a regiment, the television discovery of the year.

"Quite a girl," I said.

"See how they get those things up?" said Harry. "They really look like something, don't they?"

"Like nonaggression pacts," I said.

"When someone gets one of these, they think they've got something—even if what it says is just plain hogwash and not even good English. Makes 'em feel good," said Harry. "Makes 'em feel important."

"I suppose," I said. "But all these citations are certainly evidence of affection and respect."

"That's what a suggestion award should look like," said Harry. "It's one of the things I'm trying to put through. When a guy in the industry figures out a better way to do something, he ought to get some kind of certificate, a booby-dazzler he can frame and show off."

Celeste came back in, thrilled about something. "Honey," she said to Harry.

"I'm telling him about suggestion awards," said Harry. "Will it keep a minute?" He turned back to me. "Before you can understand a suggestion a guy made the other day," he said, "you've got to understand how catchup is made. You start with the tomatoes out on the farms, see?"

"Honey," said Celeste plaintively, "I hate to interrupt, but they want me to play Dolley Madison in a movie."

"Go ahead, if you want to," said Harry. "If you don't, don't. Now where was I?"

"Catchup," I said.

As I left the Divine home, I found myself attacked by a feeling of doom. Harry's anxieties about the catchup industry had become a part of me. An evening with Harry was like a year of solitary confinement in a catchup vat. No man could come away without a strong opinion about catchup.

"Let's have lunch sometime, Harry," I said as I left. "What's your number at the office?"

"It's unlisted," said Harry. He gave me the number very reluctantly. "I'd appreciate it if you'd keep it to yourself."

"People would always be calling him up to pick his brains, if the number got around," said Celeste.

"Good night, Celeste," I said. "I'm glad you're such a success. How could you miss with that face, that voice, and the name Celeste Divine? You didn't have to change a thing, did you?"

"It's just the opposite with catchup," said Harry. "The original catchup wasn't anything like what we call catchup or ketchup or catsup. The original stuff was made out of mushrooms, walnuts, and a lot of other things. It all started in Malaya. *Catchup* means 'taste' in Malaya. Not many people know that."

"I certainly didn't," I said. "Well, good night."

I didn't get around to calling Harry until several weeks later, when a prospective client, a Mr. Arthur J. Bunting, dropped into my office shortly before noon. Mr. Bunting was a splendid old gentleman, stout, over six feet tall, with the white mustache and fierce eyes of an old Indian fighter.

Mr. Bunting had sold his factory, which had been in his family for three generations, and he wanted my suggestions as to how to invest the proceeds. His factory had been a catchup factory.

"I've often wondered," I said, "how the original catchup would go over in this country—made the way they make it in Malaya."

A moment before, Mr. Bunting had been a sour old man, morbidly tidying his life. Now he was radiant. "You know catchup?" he said.

"As an amateur," I said.

"Was your family in catchup?" he said.

"A friend," I said.

Mr. Bunting's face clouded over with sadness. "I and my father," he said hoarsely, "and my father's father made the finest catchup this world has ever known. Never once did we cut corners on quality." He gave an anguished sigh. "I'm sorry I sold out!" he said. "There's a tragedy for someone to write: A man sells something priceless for a price he can't resist."

"There's a lot of that going on, I guess," I said.

"Being in the catchup business was ridiculous to a lot of people," said Mr. Bunting. "But by glory, if everybody did his job as well as my grandfather did, my father did, and I did, it would be a perfect world! Let me tell you that!"

I nodded, and dialed Harry's unlisted telephone number. "I've got a friend I'd like very much to have you meet, Mr. Bunting," I said. "I hope he can have lunch with us."

"Good, fine," said Mr. Bunting. "And now the work of three generations is in the hands of strangers," he said.

A man with a tough voice answered the telephone. "Yeah?"

"Mr. Harry Divine, please," I said.

"Out to lunch. Back at one," said the man.

"Gee, that's too bad. Mr. Bunting," I said, hanging up, "it would have been wonderful to get you two together."

"Who is this person?"

"Who is he?" I said. I laughed. "Why, my friend Harry is Mr. Catchup himself!"

Mr. Bunting looked as though he'd been shot in the belly. "Mr. Catchup?" he said hollowly. "That's what they used to call me. Who's he with?"

"He's a consultant for the whole industry," I said.

The corners of Mr. Bunting's mouth pulled down. "I never even heard of him," he said. "My word, things happen fast these days!"

As we sat down to lunch, Mr. Bunting was still very upset.

"Mr. Bunting, sir," I said, "I was using the term 'Mr. Catchup' loosely. I'm sure Harry doesn't claim the title. I just mean that catchup was a big thing in *his* life, too."

Mr. Bunting finished his drink grimly. "New names, new faces," he said. "These sharp youngsters, coming up fast, still wet behind the ears, knowing all the answers, taking over—do they know they've got a heritage to respect and protect?" His voice quivered. "Or are they going to tear everything down, without even bothering to ask why it was built that way?"

There was a stir in the restaurant. In the doorway stood Celeste, a bird of paradise, creating a sensation.

Beside her, talking animatedly, demanding her full attention, was Harry.

I waved to them, and they crossed the room to join us at our table. The headwaiter escorted them, flattering the life out of Celeste. And every face turned toward her, full of adoration.

Harry, seemingly blind to it all, was shouting at Celeste about the catchup industry.

"You know what I said to them?" said Harry, as they reached our table.

"No, dear," said Celeste.

"I told them there was only one thing to do," said Harry, "and that was burn the whole damn catchup industry down to the ground. And next time, when we build it, by heaven, let's *think*!"

Mr. Bunting stood, snow white, every nerve twanging.

Uneasily I made the introductions.

"How do you do?" said Mr. Bunting.

Celeste smiled warmly. Her smile faded as Mr. Bunting looked at Harry with naked hate.

Harry was too wound up to notice. "I am now making a historical study of the catchup industry," he announced, "to determine whether it never left the Dark Ages, or whether it left and then scampered back."

I chuckled idiotically. "Mr. Bunting, sir," I said, "you've no doubt seen Celeste on television. She's—"

"The communications industry," said Harry, "has reached the point where it can send the picture of my wife through the air to forty million homes. And the catchup industry is still bogged down, trying to lick thixotropy."

Mr. Bunting blew up. "Maybe the public doesn't *want* thixotropy licked!" he bellowed. "Maybe they'd rather have good catchup, and thixotropy be damned! It's flavor they want! It's quality they want! Lick thixotropy, and you'll have some new red bilge sold under a proud old name!" He was trembling all over.

Harry was staggered. "You know what thixotropy is?" he said.

"Of course I know!" said Bunting, furious. "And I know what good catchup is. And I know what you are—an arrogant, enterprising, self-serving little pipsqueak!" He turned to me. "And a man is judged by the company he keeps. Good day!" He strode out of the restaurant, grandly.

"There were tears in his eyes," said Celeste, bewildered.

"His life, his father's life, and his grandfather's life have been devoted to catchup," I said. "I thought Harry knew that. I thought everybody in the industry knew who Arthur J. Bunting was."

Harry was miserable. "I really hurt him, didn't I?" he said. "God knows, I didn't want to do that."

Celeste laid her hand on Harry's. "You're like Louis Pasteur, darling," she said. "Pasteur must have hurt the feelings of a lot of old men, too."

"Yeah," said Harry. "Like Louis Pasteur—that's me."

"The old collision between youth and age," I said.

"Big client, was he?" said Harry.

"Yes, I'm afraid so," I said.

"I'm sorry," said Harry. "I can't tell you how sorry. I'll call him up and make things right."

"I don't want you to say anything that will go against your integrity, Harry," I said. "Not on my account."

Mr. Bunting called the next day to say that he had accepted Harry's apology.

"He made a clean breast of how he got into catchup," said Mr. Bunting, "and he promised to get out. As far as I'm concerned, the matter is closed."

I called up Harry immediately. "Harry, boy, listen!" I said. "Mr. Bunting's business isn't *that* important to me. If you're right about catchup and the Buntings are wrong, stick with it and fight it out!"

"It's all right," said Harry, "I was getting sick of catchup. I was about to move on, anyway." He hung up. I called him back, and was told that he had gone to lunch.

"Do you know where he's eating?"

"Yeah, right across the street. I can see him going in."

I got the address of the restaurant and hailed a cab.

The restaurant was a cheap, greasy diner, across the street from a garage. I looked around for Harry for some time before realizing that he was on a stool at the counter, watching me in the cigarette machine mirror.

He was wearing coveralls. He turned on his stool, and held out a hand whose nails were edged in black. "Shake hands with the new birdseed king," he said. His grip was firm.

"Harry, you're working as a mechanic," I said.

"Not half an hour ago," said Harry, "a man with a broken fuel pump thanked God for me. Have a seat."

"What about the catchup business?" I said.

"It saved my marriage and it saved my life," said Harry. "I'm grateful to the pioneers, like the Buntings, who built it."

"And now you've quit, just like that?" I snapped my fingers.

"I was never in it," said Harry. "Bunting has promised to keep that to himself, and I'd appreciate it if you'd do the same."

"But you know so much about catchup!" I said.

"For eighteen months after Celeste struck it rich and we moved here," said Harry, "I walked the streets, looking for a job suitable for the husband of the famous and beautiful Celeste."

Remembering those dark days, he rubbed his eyes, reached for the catchup. "When I got tired, cold, or wet," he said, "I'd sit in the public library, and study all the different things men could do for a living. Making catchup was one of them."

He shook the bottle of catchup over his hamburger, violently. The bottle was almost full, but nothing came out. "There—you see?" he said. "When you shake catchup one way, it behaves like a solid. You shake it another way, and it behaves like a liquid." He shook the bottle gently, and catchup poured over his hamburger. "Know what that's called?"

"No," I said.

"Thixotropy," said Harry. He hit me playfully on the upper arm. "There—you learned something new today."

Der Arme
Dolmetscher

I was astonished one day in 1944, in the midst of front-line hell-raising, to learn that I had been made interpreter, *Dolmetscher* if you please, for a whole battalion, and was to be billeted in a Belgian burgomaster's house within artillery range of the Siegfried Line.

It had never entered my head that I had what it took to dolmetsch. I qualified for the position while waiting to move from France into the front lines. While a student, I had learned the first stanza of Heinrich Heine's "Die Lorelei" by rote from a college roommate, and I happened to give those lines a dogged rendition while working within earshot of the battalion commander. The Colonel (a hotel detective from Mobile) asked his Executive Officer (a dry-goods salesman from Knoxville) in what language the lyrics were. The Executive withheld judgment until I had bungled through "*Der Gipfel des Berges foo-unk-kelt im Abendsonnenschein.*"

"Ah believes tha's Kraut, Cuhnel," he said.

My understanding in English of the only German I knew was this: "I don't know why I am so sad. I can't get an old legend out of my head. The air is cool and it's getting dark, and quiet flows the Rhine. The peak of the mountain twinkles in evening sunshine."

The Colonel felt his role carried with it the obligation to make quick, headstrong decisions. He made some dandies before the Wehrmacht was whipped, but the one he made that day was my favorite. "If tha's Kraut, whassat man doin' on the honey-dippin' detail?" he wanted to know. Two hours later, the company clerk told me to lay down the buckets, for I was now battalion interpreter.

Orders to move up came soon after. Those in authority were too harried to hear my declarations of incompetence. "You talk Kraut good enough foah us," said the Executive Officer. "Theah ain't goin' to be much talkin' to Krauts where weah goin'." He patted my rifle affectionately. "Heah's what's goin' to do most of youah interpretin' fo' ya," he said. The Executive, who had learned everything he knew from the Colonel, had the idea that the American Army had just licked the Belgians, and that I was to be stationed with the burgomaster to make sure he didn't try to pull a fast one. "Besides," the Executive concluded, "theah ain't nobody else can talk Kraut at all."

I rode to the burgomaster's farm on a truck with three disgruntled Pennsylvania Dutchmen who had applied for interpreters' jobs months earlier. When I made it clear that I was no competition for them, and that I hoped to be liquidated within twenty-four hours, they warmed up enough for me to furnish the interesting information that I was a *Dolmetscher.* They also decoded "Die Lorelei" at my request. This gave me command of about forty words (par for a two-year-old), but no combination of them would get me so much as a glass of cold water.

Every turn of the truck's wheels brought a new question: "What's the word for 'army'? . . . How do I ask for the bathroom? . . . What's the word for 'sick'? . . . 'well'? . . . 'dish'? . . . 'brother'? . . . 'shoe'?" My phlegmatic instructors tired, and one handed me a pamphlet purporting to make German easy for the man in the foxhole.

"Some of the first pages are missing," the donor explained as I jumped from the truck before the burgomaster's stone farmhouse. "Used 'em for cigarette papers," he said.

It was early morning when I knocked at the burgomaster's door. I stood on the step like a bit player in the wings, with the one line I was to deliver banging around an otherwise empty head. The door swung open. *"Dolmetscher,"* I said.

The burgomaster himself, old, thin, and nightshirted, ushered me into the first-floor bedroom that was to be mine. He pantomimed as well as spoke his welcome, and a sprinkling of *"Danke schön"* was adequate dolmetsching for the time being. I was prepared to throttle further discussion with *"Ich weiss nicht, was soll es bedeuten, dass ich so traurig bin."* This would have sent him padding off to bed, convinced that he had a fluent, albeit shot-full-of-*Weltschmerz*, *Dolmetscher*. The stratagem wasn't necessary. He left me alone to consolidate my resources.

Chief among these was the mutilated pamphlet. I examined each of its precious pages in turn, delighted by the simplicity of transposing English into German. With this booklet, all I had to do was run my finger down the left-hand column until I found the English phrase I wanted, and then rattle off the nonsense syllables printed opposite in the right-hand column. "How many grenade launchers have you?" for instance, was *Vee feel grenada vairfair habben zee?* Impeccable German for "Where are your tank columns?" proved to be nothing more troublesome than *Vo zint eara pantzer shpitzen?* I mouthed the phrases: "Where are your howitzers? How many machine guns have you? Surrender! Don't shoot! Where have you hidden your motorcycle? Hands up! What unit are you from?"

The pamphlet came to an abrupt end, toppling my spirits from manic to depressive. The Pennsylvania Dutchman had smoked up all the rear-area pleasantries, the pamphlet's first half, leaving me with nothing to work with but the repartee of hand-to-hand fighting.

As I lay sleepless in bed, the one drama in which I could play took shape in my mind. . . .

DOLMETSCHER (*to* BURGOMASTER'S DAUGHTER): I don't know what will become of me, I am so sad. (*Embraces her.*)

BURGOMASTER'S DAUGHTER (*with yielding shyness*): The air is cool, and it's getting dark, and the Rhine is flowing quietly.

(DOLMETSCHER *seizes* BURGOMASTER'S DAUGHTER, *carries her bodily into his room.*)

DOLMETSCHER (*softly*): Surrender.

BURGOMASTER (*brandishing Luger*): Ach! Hands up!

DOLMETSCHER and BURGOMASTER'S DAUGHTER: Don't shoot!

(*A* map, *showing disposition of American First Army, falls from* BURGO-MASTER'S *breast pocket.*)

DOLMETSCHER (*aside, in English*): What is this supposedly pro-Ally burgomaster doing with a map showing the disposition of the American First Army? And why am I supposed to be dolmetsching with a Belgian in German? (*He snatches .45 automatic pistol from beneath pillow and aims at* BURGOMASTER.)

BURGOMASTER and BURGOMASTER'S DAUGHTER: Don't shoot! (BURGOMASTER *drops Luger, cowers, sneers.*)

DOLMETSCHER: What unit are you from? (BURGOMASTER *remains sullen, silent.* BURGOMASTER'S DAUGHTER *goes to his side, weeps softly.* DOLMETSCHER *confronts* BURGOMASTER'S DAUGHTER.) Where have *you* hidden your motorcycle? (*Turns again to* BURGOMASTER.) Where are your howitzers, eh? Where are your tank columns? How many grenade launchers have you?

BURGOMASTER (*cracking under terrific grilling*): I—I surrender.

BURGOMASTER'S DAUGHTER: I am so sad.

(*Enter* GUARD DETAIL *composed of Pennsylvania Dutchmen, making a routine check just in time to hear* BURGOMASTER *and* BURGOMASTER'S DAUGHTER *confess to being Nazi agents parachuted behind American lines.*)

Johann Christoph Friedrich von Schiller couldn't have done any better with the same words, and they were the only words I had. There was no chance of my muddling through, and no pleasure in being interpreter for a full battalion in December and not being able to say so much as "Merry Christmas."

I made my bed, tightened the drawstrings on my duffel bag, and stole through the blackout curtains and into the night.

Wary sentinels directed me to Battalion Headquarters, where I found most of our officers either poring over maps or loading their weapons. There was a holiday spirit in the air, and the Executive Officer was honing an eighteen-inch bowie knife and humming "Are You from Dixie?"

"Well, bless mah soul," he said, noticing me in the doorway, "here's old 'Sprecken Zee Dutch.' Speak up, boy. Ain't you supposed to be ovah at the mayah's house?"

"It's no good," I said. "They all speak Low German, and I speak High."

The executive was impressed. "Too good foah 'em, eh?" He ran his index finger down the edge of his murderous knife. "Ah think we'll be runnin' into some who can talk the high-class Kraut putty soon," he said, and then added, "Weah surrounded."

"We'll whomp 'em the way we whomped 'em in Nawth Ca'lina and Tennessee," said the Colonel, who had never lost on maneuvers back home. "You stay heah, son. Ah'm gonna want you foah mah pussnel intupretah."

Twenty minutes later I was in the thick of dolmetsching again. Four Tiger tanks drove up to the front door of Headquarters, and two dozen German infantrymen dismounted to round us up with submachine guns.

"Say sumpin'," ordered the Colonel, spunky to the last.

I ran my eye down the left-hand columns of my pamphlet until I found the phrase that most fairly represented our sentiments. "Don't shoot," I said.

A German tank officer swaggered in to have a look at his catch. In his hand was a pamphlet, somewhat smaller than mine. "Where are your howitzers?" he said.

The Boy Who
Hated Girls

George M. Helmholtz, head of the music department and director of the band of Lincoln High School, could sound like any musical instrument. He could shriek like a clarinet, mumble like a trombone, bawl like a trumpet. He could swell his big belly and roar like a sousaphone, could purse his lips sweetly, close his eyes, and whistle like a piccolo.

At eight o'clock one Wednesday night, he was marching around the band rehearsal room at the school, shrieking, mumbling, bawling, roaring, and whistling "Semper Fidelis."

It was easy for Helmholtz to do. For almost half of his forty years, he'd been forming bands from the river of boys that flowed through the school. He'd sung along with them all. He'd sung so long and wished so hard for his bands that he dealt with life in terms of them alone.

Marching beside the lusty pink bandmaster, his face now white with awe and concentration, was a gangly sixteen-year-old named Bert Higgens. He had a big nose, and circles under his eyes. Bert marched flappingly, like a mother flamingo pretending to be injured, luring alligators from her nest.

"*Rump-yump, tiddle-tiddle, rump-yump, burdle-burdle,*" sang Helmholtz. "Left, right, *left*, Bert! El-bows *in*, Bert! Eyes off *feet*, Bert! Keep on *line*, Bert! Don't turn *head*, Bert! Left, right, *left*, Bert! Halt—one, *two!*"

Helmholtz smiled. "I think maybe there was some improvement there."

Bert nodded. "It's sure been a help to practice with you, Mr. Helmholtz."

"As long as you're willing to work at it, so am I," said Helmholtz. He was bewildered by the change that had come over Bert in the past week. The boy seemed to have lost two years, to become what he'd been in his freshman year: awkward, cowering, lonely, dull.

"Bert," said Helmholtz, "are you sure you haven't had any injury, any sickness recently?" He knew Bert well, had given him trumpet lessons for two years. He had watched Bert grow into a proud, straight figure. The collapse of the boy's spirits and coordination was beyond belief.

Bert puffed out his cheeks childishly as he thought hard. It was a mannerism Helmholtz had talked him out of long before. Now he was doing it again. Bert let out the air. "Nope," he said.

"I've taught a thousand boys to march," said Helmholtz, "and you're the first one who ever forgot how to do it." The thousand passed in review in Helmholtz's mind—ranks stretching to infinity, straight as sunbeams. "Maybe we ought to talk this over with the school nurse," said Helmholtz. A cheerful thought struck him. "Unless this is girl trouble."

Bert raised one foot, then the other. "Nope," he said. "No trouble like that."

"Pretty little thing," said Helmholtz.

"Who?" said Bert.

"That dewy pink tulip I see you walking home with," said Helmholtz.

Bert grimaced. "Ah-h-h-h—her," he said. "Charlotte."

"Charlotte isn't much good?" said Helmholtz.

"I dunno. I guess she's all right. I suppose she's OK. I haven't got anything against her. I dunno."

Helmholtz shook Bert gently, as though hoping to jiggle a loose part into place. "Do you remember it at all—the feeling you used to have when you marched so well, before this relapse?"

"I think it's kind of coming back," said Bert.

"Coming up through the C and B bands, you learned to march fine," said Helmholtz. These were the training bands through which the hundred men of the Lincoln High School Ten Square Band came.

"I dunno what the trouble is," said Bert, "unless it's the excitement of getting in the Ten Square Band." He puffed his cheeks. "Maybe it's stopping my lessons with you."

When Bert had qualified for the Ten Square Band three months before, Helmholtz had turned him over to the best trumpet teacher in town, Larry Fink, for the final touches of grace and color.

"Say, Fink isn't giving you a hard time, is he?" said Helmholtz.

"Nope," said Bert. "He's a nice gentleman." He rolled his eyes. "Mr. Helmholtz—if we could practice marching just a couple more times, I think I'll be fine."

"Gee, Bert," said Helmholtz, "I don't know when I can fit you in. When you went to Fink, I took on another boy. It just so happened he was sick tonight. But next week—"

"Who is he?" said Bert.

"Norton Shakely," said Helmholtz. "Little fellow—kind of green around the gills. He's just like you were when you started out. No faith in himself. Doesn't think he'll ever make the Ten Square Band, but he will, he will."

"He will," agreed Bert. "No doubt about it."

Helmholtz clapped Bert on the arm, to put some heart into him. "Chin up!" he sang. "Shoulders back! Go get your coat, and I'll take you home."

As Bert put on his coat, Helmholtz thought of the windows of Bert's home—windows as vacant as dead men's eyes. Bert's father had wandered away years before—and his mother was seldom there. Helmholtz wondered if that was where the trouble was.

Helmholtz was depressed. "Maybe we can stop somewhere and get a soda, and maybe play a little table tennis afterward in my basement," he said. When he'd given Bert trumpet lessons, they'd always stopped somewhere for a soda, and then played table tennis afterward.

"Unless you'd rather go see Charlotte or something," said Helmholtz.

"Are you kidding?" said Bert. "I hate the way she talks sometimes."

The next morning, Helmholtz talked with Miss Peach, the school nurse. It was a symposium between two hearty, plump people, blooming with hygiene and common sense. In the background, rickety and confused, stripped to the waist, was Bert.

"By 'blacked out,' you mean Bert fainted?" said Miss Peach.

"You didn't see him do it at the Whitestown game last Friday?" said Helmholtz.

"I missed that game," said Miss Peach.

"It was right after we'd formed the block L, when we were marching down the field to form the pinwheel that turned into the Lincoln High panther and the Whitestown eagle," said Helmholtz. The eagle had screamed, and the panther had eaten it.

"So what did Bert do?" said Miss Peach.

"He was marching along with the band, fine as you please," said Helmholtz. "And then he just drifted out of it. He wound up marching by himself."

"What did it feel like, Bert?" said Miss Peach.

"Like a dream at first," said Bert. "Real good, kind of. And then I woke up, and I was alone." He gave a sickly smile. "And everybody was laughing at me."

"How's your appetite, Bert?" said Miss Peach.

"He polished off a soda and a hamburger last night," said Helmholtz.

"What about your coordination when you play games, Bert?" said Miss Peach.

"I'm not in sports," said Bert. "The trumpet takes all the time I've got."

"Don't you and your father throw a ball sometimes?" said Miss Peach.

"I don't have a father," said Bert.

"He beat me at table tennis last night," said Helmholtz.

"All in all, it was quite a binge last night, wasn't it?" Miss Peach said.

"It's what we used to do every Wednesday night," said Bert.

"It's what I do with all the boys I give lessons to," said Helmholtz.

Miss Peach cocked her head. "You used to do it with Bert?"

"I take lessons from Mr. Fink now," said Bert.

"When a boy reaches the Ten Square Band," said Helmholtz, "he's beyond me, as far as individual lessons are concerned. I don't treat him like a boy anymore. I treat him like a man. And he's an artist. Only an artist like Fink can teach him anything from that point on."

"Ten Square Band," mused Miss Peach. "That's ten on a side—a hundred in all? All dressed alike, all marching like parts of a fine machine?"

"Like a block of postage stamps," said Helmholtz proudly.

"Uh-huh," said Miss Peach. "And all of them have had lessons from you?"

"Heavens, no," said Helmholtz. "I've only got time to give five boys individual lessons."

"A lucky, lucky five," said Miss Peach. "For a little while."

The door of the office opened, and Stewart Haley, the Assistant Principal, came in. He had begun his career as a bright young man. But now, after ten years of dealing with oversize spirits on undersize salaries, his brightness had mellowed to the dull gloss of pewter. A lot of his luster had been lost in verbal scuffles with Helmholtz over expenses of the band.

In Haley's hand was a bill. "Well, Helmholtz," he said, "if I'd known you were going to be here, I'd have brought another interesting bill with me. Five war-surplus Signal Corps wire-laying reels, complete with pack frames? Does that ring a bell?"

"It does," said Helmholtz, unabashed. "And may I say—"

"Later," said Haley. "Right now I have a matter to take up with Miss Peach—one that makes your peculation look like peanuts." He rattled the bill at Miss Peach. "Miss Peach—have you ordered a large quantity of bandages recently?"

Miss Peach paled. "I—I ordered thirty yards of sterile gauze," she said. "It came this morning. And it's thirty yards, and it's gauze."

Haley sat down on a white stool. "According to this bill," he said, "somebody in this grand institution has ordered and received two hundred yards of silver nylon ribbon, three inches wide—treated to glow in the dark."

He was looking blankly at Helmholtz when he said it. He went on looking at Helmholtz, and color crept into his cheeks. "Hello again, Helmholtz."

"Hi," said Helmholtz.

"Down for your daily shot of cocaine?" said Haley.

"Cocaine?" said Helmholtz.

"How else," said Haley, "could a man get dreams of cornering the world output of nylon ribbon treated to glow in the dark?"

"It costs much less to make things glow in the dark than most people realize," said Helmholtz.

Haley stood. "So it was you!"

Helmholtz laid his hand on Haley's shoulder and looked him in the eye. "Stewart," he said, "the question on everybody's lips is, How can the Ten Square Band possibly top its performance at the Westfield game last year?"

"The big question is," said Haley, "How can a high school with a modest budget like ours afford such a vainglorious, Cecil B. DeMille machine for making music? And the answer is," said Haley, "We can't!" He jerked his head from side to side. "Ninety-five-dollar uniforms! Biggest drum in the state! Batons and hats that light up! Everything treated to glow in the dark! Holy smokes!" he said wildly. "The biggest jukebox in the world!"

The inventory brought nothing but joy to Helmholtz. "You love it," he said. "Everybody loves it. And wait till you hear what we're going to do with those reels and that ribbon!"

"Waiting," said Haley. "Waiting."

"Now then," said Helmholtz, "any band can form block letters. That's about the oldest stuff there is. As of this moment our band is the only band, as far as I know, equipped to write longhand."

In the muddled silence that followed, Bert, all but forgotten, spoke up. He had put his shirt back on. "Are you all through with me?" he said.

"You can go, Bert," said Miss Peach. "I didn't find anything wrong with you."

"Bye," said Bert, his hand on the doorknob. "Bye, Mr. Helmholtz."

"So long," said Helmholtz. "Now what do you think of that?" he said to Haley. "Longhand!"

Just outside the door, Bert bumped into Charlotte, the dewy pink tulip of a girl who often walked home with him.

"Bert," said Charlotte, "they told me you were down here. I thought you were hurt. Are you all right?"

Bert brushed past her without a word, leaning, as though into a cold, wet gale.

"What do I think of the ribbon?" said Haley to Helmholtz. "I think this is where the spending of the Ten Square Band is finally stopped."

"That isn't the only kind of spree that's got to be stopped," said Miss Peach darkly.

"What do you mean by that?" said Helmholtz.

"I mean," said Miss Peach, "all this playing fast and loose with kids' emotions." She frowned. "George, I've been watching you for years—watching you use every emotional trick in the books to make your kids march and play."

"I try to be friends," said Helmholtz, untroubled.

"You try to be a lot more than that," said Miss Peach. "Whatever a kid needs, you're it. Father, mother, sister, brother, God, slave, or dog—you're it. No wonder we've got the best band in the world. The only wonder is that what's happened with Bert hasn't happened a thousand times."

"What's eating Bert?" said Helmholtz.

"You won him," said Miss Peach. "That's what. Lock, stock, and barrel—he's yours, all yours."

"Sure he likes me," said Helmholtz. "Hope he does, anyway."

"He likes you like a son likes a father," said Miss Peach. "There's a casual thing for you."

Helmholtz couldn't imagine what the argument was about. Everything Miss Peach had said was obvious. "That's only natural, isn't it?" he said. "Bert doesn't have a father, so he's going to look around for one, naturally, until he finds some girl who'll take him over and—"

"Will you please open your eyes, and see what you've done to Bert's life?" said Miss Peach. "Look what he did to get your attention, after you stuck him in the Ten Square Band, then sent him off to Mr. Fink and forgot all about him. He was willing to have the whole world laugh at him, just to get you to look at him again."

"Growing up isn't supposed to be painless," said Helmholtz. "A baby's one thing, a child's another, and a man's another. Changing from one thing to the next is a famous mess." He opened his eyes wide. "If we don't know that, who does?"

"Growing up isn't supposed to be hell!" said Miss Peach.

Helmholtz was stunned by the word. "What do you want me to do?"

"It's none of my business," said Miss Peach. "It's a highly personal affair. That's the way you made it. That's the way you work. I'd think the least you could do would be to learn the difference between getting yourself tangled up in a boy and getting yourself tangled up in ribbon. You can cut the ribbon. You can't do that to a boy."

"About that ribbon—" said Haley.

"We'll pack it up and send it back," said Helmholtz. He didn't care about the ribbon anymore. He walked out of the office, his ears burning.

Helmholtz carried himself as though he'd done nothing wrong. But guilt rode on his back like a chimpanzee. In his tiny office off the band rehearsal room, Helmholtz removed stacks of sheet music from the washbasin in the corner and dashed cold water in his face, hoping to make the chimpanzee go away at least for the next hour. The next hour was the rehearsal period for the Ten Square Band.

Helmholtz telephoned his good friend Larry Fink, the trumpet teacher.

"What's the trouble this time, George?" said Fink.

"The school nurse just jumped all over me for being too nice to my boys. She says I get too involved, and that's a very dangerous thing."

"Oh?"

"Psychology's a wonderful science," said Helmholtz. "Without it, everybody'd still be making the same terrible mistake—being nice to each other."

"What brought this on?" said Fink.

"Bert," said Helmholtz.

"I finally let him go last week," said Fink. "He never practiced, came to the lessons unprepared. Frankly, George, I know you thought a lot of him, but he wasn't very talented. He wasn't even very fond of music, as near as I can tell."

Helmholtz protested with all his heart. "That boy went from the C Band to the Ten Square in two years! He took to music like a duck to water."

"Like a camel in quicksand, if you ask me," said Fink. "That boy busted his butt for you, George. And then you busted his heart when you handed him on to me. The school nurse is right: You've got to be more careful about who you're nice to."

"He's even forgotten how to march. He fell out of step and spoiled a formation, forgot where he was supposed to go, at half-time at the Findlay Tech game."

"He told me about it," said Fink.

"Did he have any explanation?"

"He was surprised you and the nurse didn't come up with it. Or maybe the nurse figured it out, but didn't want anybody else to know."

"I still can't imagine," said Helmholtz.

"He was drunk, George. He said it was his first time, and promised it would be his last. Unfortunately, I don't believe we can count on that."

"But he still can't march," said Helmholtz, shocked. "When just the two of us practice alone, with nobody watching, he finds it impossible to keep in step with me. Is he drunk all the time?"

"George," said Fink, "you and your innocence have turned a person who never should have been a musician into an actor instead."

From the rehearsal room outside Helmholtz's office came the cracks and slams of chairs being set up for the Ten Square Band. Bandsmen with a free period were doing that. The coming hour was ordinarily a perfect one for the bandmaster, in which he became weightless, as he sang the part of this instrument or that one, while his bandsmen played. But now he feared it.

He was going to have to face Bert again, having been made aware in the interim of how much he might have hurt the boy. And maybe others.

Would he be to blame, if Bert went on to become an alcoholic? He thought about the thousand or more boys with whom he had behaved like a father, whether they had a real father or not. To his knowledge, several had later become drunks. Two had been arrested for drugs, and one for burglary. He lost track of most. Few came back to see him after graduation. That was something else it was time to think about.

The rest of the band entered now, Bert among them. Helmholtz heard himself say to him, as privately as he could, "Could you see me in my office after school?" He hadn't a clue of what he would say then.

He went to his music stand in front, rapped his baton against it. The band fell silent. "Let's start off with 'Lincoln's Foes Shall Wail Tonight.'" The author of the words and music was Helmholtz himself. He had written them during his first year as bandmaster, when the school's bandsmen at athletic events and parades had numbered only fifty. Their uniforms fit them purely by chance, and in any case made them look, as Helmholtz himself had said at the time, like "deserters from Valley Forge." That was twenty years before.

"Everybody ready?" he said. "Good! Fortissimo! Con brio! A-one, a-two, a-three, a-four!" Helmholtz stayed earth-bound this time. He weighed a ton.

When Bert came to his office after school, Helmholtz had an agenda. He wanted the lonely boy to stop disliking Charlotte. She appeared to be a warm person, who could lead Bert into a social life apart from the band and Helmholtz. He thought it important, too, that the dangers of alcohol be discussed.

But the talk wouldn't go at all as planned, and Helmholtz sensed that it wouldn't as soon as Bert sat down. He had self-respect on a scale Helmholtz had never seen him exhibit before. Something big must have happened, thought Helmholtz. Bert was staring straight at him, challenging, as though they were equals, no longer man and boy.

"Bert," Helmholtz began, "I won't beat around the bush. I know you were drunk at the football game."

"Mr. Fink told you?"

"Yes, and it troubled me."

"Why didn't you realize it at the time?" said Bert. "Everybody else did. People were laughing at you because you thought I was sick."

"I had a lot on my mind," said Helmholtz.

"Music," said Bert, as though it were a dirty word.

"Certainly music," said Helmholtz, taken aback. "My goodness."

"*Nothin'* but music," said Bert, his gaze like laser beams.

"That's often the case, and why not?" Again Helmholtz added incredulously, "My goodness."

"Charlotte was right."

"I thought you hated her."

"I like her a lot, except for the things she said about you. Now I know how right she was, and I not only like her, I love her."

Helmholtz was scared now, and unused to that. This was a most unpleasant scene. "Whatever she said about me, I don't think I'd care to hear it."

"I won't tell you, because all you'd hear is music." Bert put his trumpet in its case on the bandmaster's desk. The trumpet was rented from the school. "Give this to somebody else, who'll love it more than I did," he said. "I only loved it because you were so good to me, and you told me to." He stood. "Good-bye."

Bert was at the door before Helmholtz asked him to stop, to turn around and look him in the eye again, and say what Charlotte had said about him.

Bert was glad to tell him. He was angry, as though Helmholtz had somehow swindled him. "She said you were completely disconnected from real life, and only pretended to be interested in people. She said all you paid attention to was music, and if people weren't playing it, you could still hear it in your head. She said you were nuts."

"Nuts?" echoed Helmholtz wonderingly.

"I told her to stop saying that," said Bert, "but then you showed me how really nutty you are."

"Please tell me how. I need to know," said Helmholtz. But a concert band in his head was striking up Tchaikovsky's *1812 Overture*, complete with the roar of cannons. It was all he could do not to sing along.

"When you gave me marching lessons," Bert was saying, "and I was act-ing drunk, you didn't even notice how crazy it was. You weren't even there!"

A brief silence followed a crescendo in the music in the bandmaster's head. Helmholtz asked this question: "How could that girl know anything about me?"

"She dates a lot of other bandsmen," said Bert. "She gets 'em to tell her the really funny stuff."

Before leaving for home at sunset that day, Helmholtz paid a visit to the school nurse. He said he needed to talk to her about something.

"Is it that Bert Higgens again?" she said.

"I'm afraid it's even closer to home than that," he said. "It's me this time. It's I. It's me."

This Son
of Mine

The factory made the best centrifugal pumps in the world, and Merle Waggoner owned it. He'd started it. He'd just been offered two million dollars for it by the General Forge and Foundry Company. He didn't have any stockholders and he didn't owe a dime. He was fifty-one, a widower, and he had one heir—a son. The boy's name was Franklin. The boy was named for Benjamin Franklin.

One Friday afternoon father and son went out of Merle's office and into the factory. They walked down a factory aisle to Rudy Linberg's lathe.

"Rudy," said Merle, "the boy here's home from college for three days, and I thought maybe you and him and your boy and me might go out to the farm and shoot some clay pigeons tomorrow."

Rudy turned his sky-blue eyes to Merle and young Franklin. He was Merle's age, and he had the deep and narrow dignity of a man who had learned his limitations early—who had never tried to go beyond them. His limitations were those of his tools, his flute, and his shotgun.

"Might try crows," he said.

Rudy stood at attention like the good soldier he was. And like an old soldier, he did it without humility, managed to convey that he was the big winner in life, after all. He had been Merle's first employee. He might have been a partner way back then, for two thousand dollars. And Rudy'd had the cash. But the enterprise had looked chancy to him. He didn't seem sorry now.

"We could set up my owl," said Rudy. He had a stuffed owl to lure crows. He and his son, Karl, had made it.

"Need a rifle to get at the crows out there," said Merle. "They know all about that owl of yours and Karl's. Don't think we could get any closer to 'em than half a mile."

"Might be sport, trying to get at 'em with a scope," said Franklin softly. He was tall and thin, in cashmere and gray flannel. He was almost goofy with shyness and guilt. He had just told his father that he wanted to be an actor, that he didn't want the factory. And shock at his own words had come so fast that he'd heard himself adding, out of control, the hideously empty phrase, "Thanks just the same."

His father hadn't reacted—yet. The conversation had gone blandly on to the farm, to shooting, to Rudy and Karl, to Rudy and Karl's new station wagon, and now to crows.

"Let's go ask my boy what he's got on tomorrow," said Rudy. It was a formality. Karl always did what his father wanted him to do, did it with profound love.

Rudy, Merle, and Franklin went down the aisle to a lathe thirty feet from Rudy's. Merle's chin was up. Rudy looked straight ahead. Franklin looked down at the floor.

Karl was a carbon copy of his father. He was such a good mimic of Rudy that his joints seemed to ache a little with age. He seemed sobered by fifty-one years of life, though he'd lived only twenty. He seemed instinctively wary of safety hazards that had been eliminated from the factory by the time he'd learned to walk. Karl stood at attention without humility, just as his father had done.

"Want to go shooting tomorrow?" said Rudy.

"Shoot what?" said Karl.

"Crows. Clay pigeons," said Rudy. "Maybe a woodchuck."

"Don't mind," said Karl. He nodded briefly to Merle and Franklin. "Glad to."

"We could take some steaks and have supper out there," said Merle. "You make the steak sauce, Rudy?"

"Don't mind," said Rudy. He was famous for his steak sauce, and had taught the secret to his son. "Be glad to."

"Got a bottle of twenty-year-old bourbon I've been saving for something special," said Merle. "I guess tomorrow'll be special enough." He lit a cigar, and Franklin saw that his father's hand was shaking. "We'll have a ball," he said.

Clumsily Merle punched Franklin in the kidneys, man to man, trying to make him bubble. He regretted it at once. He laughed out loud to show it didn't matter, laughed through cigar smoke that stung his eyes. The laugh drove smoke into the walls of his lungs. Pleasure fled. On and on the laugh went.

"Look at him, Rudy!" said Merle, lashing the merriment onward. "Foot taller'n his old man, and president of what at Cornell?"

"Interfraternity Council," murmured Franklin, embarrassed. He and Karl avoided looking at each other. Their fathers had taken them hunting together maybe a hundred times. But the boys had hardly spoken to each other, had exchanged little more than humorless nods and head shakes for hits and misses.

"And how many fraternities at Cornell?" said Merle.

"Sixty-two," said Franklin, more softly than before.

"And how many men in a fraternity?" said Merle.

"Forty, maybe," said Franklin. He picked up a sharp, bright spiral shaving of steel from the floor. "There's a pretty thing," he said. He knew his father's reaction was coming now. He could hear the first warning tremors in his voice.

"Say sixty fraternities," said Merle. "Say forty men in each . . . Makes twenty-four hundred boys my boy's over, Rudy! When I was his age, I didn't have but six men under me."

"They aren't under me, Father," said Franklin. "I just run the meetings of the Council and—"

The explosion came. "You run the show!" roared Merle. "You can be as damn polite about it as you want to, but you still run the show!"

Nobody said anything.

Merle tried to smile, but the smile curdled, as though he were going to burst into tears. He took the strap of Rudy's overalls between his thumb and forefinger and rubbed the faded denim. He looked up into Rudy's sky-blue eyes.

"Boy wants to be an actor, Rudy," he said. And then he roared again. "That's what he said!" He turned away and ran back to his office.

In the moment before Franklin could make himself move, Rudy spoke to him as if nothing were wrong.

"You got enough shells?" said Rudy.

"What?" said Franklin.

"You got enough shells? You want us to pick up some?" said Rudy.

"No," said Franklin. "We've got plenty of shells. Half a case, last time I checked."

Rudy nodded. He examined the work in Karl's lathe and tapped his own temple. The tapping was a signal Franklin had seen many times on hunts. It meant that Karl was doing fine.

Rudy touched Karl's elbow lightly. It was the signal for Karl to get back to work. Rudy and Karl each held up a crooked finger and saluted with it. Franklin knew what that meant, too. It meant, "Good-bye, I love you."

Franklin put one foot in front of the other and went looking for his own father.

Merle was sitting at his desk, his head down, when Franklin came in. He held a steel plate about six inches square in his left hand. In the middle of the plate was a hole two inches square. In his right hand he held a steel cube that fitted the hole exactly.

On the desktop were two black bags of jeweler's velvet, one for the plate and one for the cube. About every ten seconds Merle put the cube through the hole.

Franklin sat down gingerly on a hard chair by the wall. The office hadn't changed much in the years he'd known it. It was one more factory room, with naked pipes overhead—the cold ones sweaty, the hot ones dry. Wires snaked from steel box to steel box. The green walls and cream trim were as rough as elephant hide in some places, with alternating coats of paint and grime, paint and grime.

There had never been time to scrape away the layers, and barely enough time, overnight, to slap on new paint. And there had never been time to finish the rough shelves that lined the room.

Franklin still saw the place through child's eyes. To him it had been a playroom. He remembered his father's rummaging through the shelves for toys to amuse his boy. The toys were still there: cutaway pumps, salesmen's samples, magnets, a pair of cracked safety glasses that had once saved Rudy Linberg's blue eyes.

And the playthings Franklin remembered best—remembered best because his father would show them to him, but never let him touch—were what Merle was playing with now.

Merle slipped the cube through the square hole once more. "Know what these are?" he said.

"Yes, sir," said Franklin. "They're what Rudy Linberg had to make when he was an apprentice in Sweden."

The cube could be slipped through the hole in twenty-four different ways, without letting the tiniest ray of light pass through with it.

"Unbelievable skill," said Franklin respectfully. "There aren't craftsmen like that coming along anymore." He didn't really feel much respect. He was simply saying what he knew his father wanted to hear. The cube and the hole struck him as criminal wastes of time and great bores. "Unbelievable," he said again.

"It's unbelievable, when you realize that Rudy didn't make them," said Merle, "when you realize what generation the man who made them belongs to."

"Oh?" said Franklin. "Who did make them?"

"Rudy's boy," said Merle. "A member of your generation." He ground out his cigar. "He gave them to me on my last birthday. They were on my desk, boy, waiting for me when I came in—right beside the ones Rudy gave me so many years ago."

Franklin had sent a telegram on that birthday. Presumably, the telegram had been waiting on the desk, too. The telegram had said, "Happy Birthday, Father."

"I could have cried, boy, when I saw those two plates and those two cubes side by side," said Merle. "Can you understand that?" he asked. "Can you understand why I'd feel like crying?"

"Yes, sir," said Franklin.

Merle's eyes widened. "And then I guess I did cry—one tear, maybe two," he said. "Because—you know what I found out, boy?"

"No, sir," said Franklin.

"The cube of Karl's fitted through the hole of Rudy's!" said Merle. "They were interchangeable!"

"Gosh!" said Franklin. "I'll be darned. Really?"

And now he felt like crying, because he didn't care, couldn't care—and would have given his right arm to care. The factory whanged and banged and screeched in monstrous irrelevance—Franklin's, all Franklin's, if he just said the word.

"What'll you do with it—buy a theater in New York?" Merle said abruptly.

"Do with what, sir?" said Franklin.

"The money I'll get for the factory when I sell it—the money I'll leave to you when I'm dead," said Merle. He hit the word "dead" hard. "What's Waggoner Pump going to be converted into? Waggoner Theaters? Waggoner School of Acting? The Waggoner Home for Broken-Down Actors?"

"I—I hadn't thought about it," said Franklin. The idea of converting Waggoner Pump into something equally complicated hadn't occurred to him, and appalled him now. He was being asked to match his father's passion for the factory with an equal passion for something else. And Franklin had no such passion—for the theater or anything else.

He had nothing but the bittersweet, almost formless longings of youth.

Saying he wanted to be an actor gave the longings a semblance of more fun than they really had. Saying it was poetry more than anything else.

"I can't help being a little interested," said Merle. "Do you mind?"

"No, sir," said Franklin.

"When Waggoner Pump becomes just one more division of General Forge and Foundry, and they send out a batch of bright young men to take over and straighten the place out, I'll want something else to think about—whatever it is you're going to do."

Franklin itched all over. "Yes, sir," he said. He looked at his watch and stood. "If we're going shooting tomorrow, I guess I'd better go see Aunt Margaret this afternoon." Margaret was Merle's sister.

"You do that," said Merle. "And I'll call up General Forge and Foundry, and tell them we accept their offer." He ran his finger down his calendar pad until he found a name and telephone number. "If we want to sell, I'm to call somebody named Guy Ferguson at something called extension five-oh-nine at something called the General Forge and Foundry Company at someplace called Ilium, New York." He licked his lips. "I'll tell him he and his friends can have Waggoner Pump."

"Don't sell on my account," said Franklin.

"On whose account would I keep it?" said Merle.

"Do you have to sell it today?" Franklin sounded horrified.

"Strike while the iron's hot, I always say," said Merle. "Today's the day you decided to be an actor, and as luck would have it, we have an excellent offer for what I did with my life."

"Couldn't we wait?"

"For what?" said Merle. He was having a good time now.

"Father!" cried Franklin. "For the love of heaven, Father, please!" He hung his head and shook it. "I don't know what I'm doing," he said. "I don't know for sure what I want to do yet. I'm just playing with ideas, trying to find myself. Please, Father, don't sell what you've done with your life, don't just throw it away because I'm not sure I want to do that with my life, too! Please!" Franklin looked up. "I'm not Karl Linberg," he said. "I can't help it. I'm sorry, but I'm not Karl Linberg."

Shame clouded his father's face, then passed. "I—I wasn't making any odious comparisons there," said Merle. He'd said exactly the same thing many times before. Franklin had forced him to it, just as he had forced him now, by apologizing for not being Karl Linberg.

"I wouldn't want you to be like Karl," said Merle. "I'm glad you're the way you are. I'm glad you've got big dreams of your own." He smiled. "Give 'em hell, boy—and be yourself! That's all I've ever told you to do with your life, isn't it?"

"Yes, sir," said Franklin. His last shred of faith in any dreams of his own had been twitched away. He could never dream two million dollars' worth, could never dream anything worth the death of his father's dreams. Actor, newspaperman, social worker, sea captain—Franklin was in no condition to give anyone hell.

"I'd better get out to Aunt Margaret's," he said.

"You do that. And I'll hold off telling Ferguson or whatever-his-name-is anything until Monday." Merle seemed at peace.

On his way through the factory parking lot to his car, Franklin passed Rudy and Karl's new station wagon. His father had raved about it, and now Franklin took a good look at it—just as he took good looks at all the things his father loved.

The station wagon was German, bright blue, with white-sidewall tires, its engine in the rear. It looked like a little bus—no hood in front, a high, flat roof, sliding doors, and rows of square windows on the sides.

The interior was a masterpiece of Rudy and Karl's orderliness and cabinet work, of lockers and niches and racks. There was a place for everything, and everything was in its place—guns, fishing tackle, cooking utensils, stove, ice chest, blankets, sleeping bags, lanterns, first-aid kit. There were even two niches, side by side, in which were strapped the cases of Karl's clarinet and Rudy's flute.

Looking inside admiringly, Franklin had a curious association of thoughts. His thoughts of the station wagon were mixed with thoughts of a great ship that had been dug up in Egypt after thousands of years. The ship had been fitted out with every necessity for a trip to Paradise—every necessity save the means of getting there.

"Mistuh Waggonuh, suh!" said a voice, and an engine raced.

Franklin turned to see that the parking lot guard had seen him coming, had now brought him his car. Franklin had been spared the necessity of walking the last fifty feet to it.

The guard got out and saluted smartly. "This thing really go a hundred and twenty-five, like it says on the speedometer?" he said.

"Never tried," said Franklin, getting in. The car was a sports car, windy and skittish, with room for two. He had bought it secondhand, against his father's wish. His father had never ridden in it. It was fitted out for its trip to Paradise with three lipstick-stained tissues, a beer can opener, a full ashtray, and a road map of Illinois.

Franklin was embarrassed to see that the guard was cleaning the windshield with his handkerchief. "That's all right, that's all right," he said. "Forget it." He thought he remembered the guard's name, but he wasn't sure. He took a chance on it. "Thanks for everything, Harry," he said.

"George, suh!" said the guard. "George Miramar Jackson, suh!"

"Of course," said Franklin. "Sorry, George. Forgot."

George Miramar Jackson smiled brilliantly. "No offense, Mistuh Waggonuh, suh! Just remember next time—George Miramar Jackson, suh!" In George's eyes there blazed the dream of a future time, when Franklin would be boss, when a big new job would open up indoors. In that dream, Franklin would say to his secretary, "Miss So-and-So? Send for—" And out would roll the magical, magnificent, unforgettable name.

Franklin drove out of the parking lot without dreams to match even George Miramar Jackson's.

At supper, feeling no pain after two stiff cocktails and a whirlwind of mothering at Aunt Margaret's, Franklin told his father that he wanted to take over the factory in due time. He would become the Waggoner in Waggoner Pump when his father was ready to bow out.

Painlessly, Franklin moved his father as profoundly as Karl Linberg had with a steel plate, a steel cube, and heaven knows how many years of patient scree-scraw with a file.

"You're the only one—do you know that?" choked Merle. "The only one—I swear!"

"The only one what, sir?" said Franklin.

"The only son who's sticking with what his father or his grandfather or sometimes even his great-grandfather built." Merle shook his head mournfully. "No Hudson in Hudson Saw," he said. "I don't think you can even cut cheese with a Hudson saw these days. No Flemming in Flemming Tool and Die. No Warner in Warner Street. No Hawks, no Hinkley, no Bowman in Hawks, Hinkley, and Bowman."

Merle waved his hand westward. "You wonder who all the people are with the big new houses on the west side? Who can have a house like that, and we never meet them, never even meet anybody who knows them? They're the ones who are taking over instead of the sons. The town's for sale, and they buy. It's their town now—people named Ferguson from places called Ilium.

"What is it about the sons?" said Merle. "They're your friends, boy. You grew up with them. You know them better than their fathers do. What is it? All the wars? Drinking?"

"I don't know, Father," said Franklin, taking the easiest way out. He folded his napkin with a neat finality. He stood. "There's a dance out at the club tonight," he said. "I thought I'd go."

"You do that," said Merle.

But Franklin didn't. He got as far as the country club's parking lot, then didn't go in.

Suddenly he didn't want to see his friends—the killers of their fathers' dreams. Their young faces were the faces of old men hanging upside down, their expressions grotesque and unintelligible. Hanging upside down, they swung from bar to ballroom to crap game, and back to bar. No one pitied them in that great human belfry, because they were going to be rich, if they weren't already. They didn't have to dream, or even lift a finger.

Franklin went to a movie alone. The movie failed to suggest a way in which he might improve his life. It suggested that he be kind and loving and humble, and Franklin was nothing if he wasn't kind and loving and humble.

. · . · .

The colors of the farm the next day were the colors of straw and frost. The land was Merle's, and it was flat as a billiard table. The jackets and caps of Merle and Franklin, of Rudy and Karl, made a tiny cluster of bright colors in a field.

Franklin knelt in the stubble, cocking the trap that would send a clay pigeon skimming over the field. "Ready," he said.

Merle threw his gun to his shoulder, squinted down the barrel, grimaced, and lowered the gun once more. "Pull!" he said.

Franklin jerked the lanyard of the trap. Out flew the clay pigeon.

Merle fired one barrel and then, with the pigeon out of range, clowningly fired the other. He'd missed. He'd been missing all afternoon. He didn't seem to mind much. He was, after all, still the boss.

"Behind it," said Merle. "I'm trying too hard. I'm not leading." He broke down his gun and the empty shells popped out. "Next?" he said. "Karl?"

Franklin loaded another clay pigeon into the trap. It was a very dead pigeon. So would the next one be. Karl hadn't missed all afternoon, and after Karl came Rudy, who hadn't missed, either.

Surprisingly, neither had Franklin. Not giving a damn, he had come to be at one with the universe. With brainless harmony like that, he'd found that he couldn't miss.

If Merle's shots hadn't been going wild, the only words spoken might have been a steady rhythm of "Ready . . . Pull . . . Ready . . . Pull." Nothing had been said about the murder of Franklin's small dream—the dream of being an actor. Merle had made no triumphant announcement about the boy's definitely taking over the factory someday.

In the small world of a man hunched over, Franklin cocked the trap and had a nightmarish feeling that they had been shooting clay pigeons for years, that that was all there was to life, that only death could end it.

His feet were frozen.

"Ready," said Franklin.

"Pull!" said Karl.

Out went the clay pigeon. *Bang* went the gun, and the bird was dust.

Rudy tapped his temple, then saluted Karl with a crooked finger. Karl returned the salute. That had been going on all afternoon—without a trace of a smile. Karl stepped back and Rudy stepped up, the next cog in the humorless clay-pigeon-destroying machine.

It was now Karl's turn to work the trap. As he and Franklin changed places, Franklin hit him on the arm and gave him a cynical smile. Franklin put everything into that blow and the smile—fathers and sons, young dreams and old dreams, bosses and employees, cold feet, boredom, and gunpowder.

It was a crazy thing for Franklin to do. It was the most intimate thing that had ever passed between him and Karl. It was a desperate thing to do. Franklin had to know if there was a human being inside Karl and, if so, what the being was like.

Karl showed a little of himself—not much. He showed he could blush. And for a split second, he showed that there was something he'd like to explain to Franklin.

But all that vanished fast. He didn't smile back. "Ready," he said.

"Pull!" said Rudy.

Out went the clay pigeon. *Bang* went the gun, and the bird was dust.

"We're going to have to find something harder for you guys and easier for me," said Merle. "I can't complain about the gun, because the damn thing cost me six hundred dollars. What I need is a six-dollar gun I can hold responsible for everything."

"Sun's going down. Light's getting bad," said Rudy.

"Guess we better knock off," said Merle. "No question about who the old folks' champion is, Rudy. But the boys are neck-and-neck. Ought to have some kind of shoot-off."

"They could try the rifle," said Rudy. The rifle leaned against the fence, ready for crows. It had a telescope. It was Merle's.

Merle brought an empty cigarette pack from his pocket and stripped off the foil. He handed the foil to Karl. "You two boys hang this up about two hundred yards from here."

Franklin and Karl trudged along the fence line, trudged off two hundred yards. They were used to being sent together on errands one of them could have handled alone—were used to representing, ceremoniously, their generation as opposed to their fathers'.

Neither said anything until the foil was tacked to a fence post. And then, as they stepped back from the target, Karl said something so shyly that Franklin missed it.

"Beg your pardon?" said Franklin.

"I'm—I'm glad you're not gonna take over the factory," said Karl. "That's good—that's great. Maybe, when you come through town with a show, I'll come backstage and see you. That all right? You'll remember me?"

"Remember you?" said Franklin. "Good gosh, Karl!" For a moment he felt like the actor he'd dreamed briefly of being.

"Get out from under your old man," said Karl, "that's the thing to do. I just wanted to tell you—in case you thought I was thinking something else."

"Thanks, Karl," said Franklin. He shook his head weakly. "But I'm not going to be an actor. I'm going to take over when Father retires. I told him last night."

"Why?" said Karl. "Why?" He was angry.

"It makes the old man happy, and I don't have any better ideas."

"You can do it," Karl said. "You can go away. You can be anything you want!"

Franklin put his hands together, then opened them to form a flower of fatalism. "So can anybody."

Karl's eyes grew huge. "I can't," he said. "I can't! Your father doesn't just have you. He's got his big success." He turned away, so Franklin couldn't see his face. "All my old man's got is me."

"Oh, now, listen," said Franklin. "Hey, now!"

Karl faced him. "I'm what he'd rather have than the half of Waggoner Pump he could have had for two thousand dollars!" he said. "Every day of my life he's told me so. Every day!"

"Well, my gosh, Karl," said Franklin, "it is a beautiful relationship you've got with your father."

"With my father?" said Karl incredulously. "With yours—with yours.

It's him I'm supposed to get to love me. He's supposed to be eating his heart out for a son like me. That's the big idea." He waved his arms. "The station wagon, the duets, the guns that never miss, the damn-fool son that works on hand signals—that's all for your father to want."

Franklin was amazed. "Karl, that's all in your head. You are what your own father would rather have than half of Waggoner Pump or anything!"

"I used to think so," said Karl.

"The plate and cube you made," said Franklin, "you gave them to my father, but they were really a present for yours. And what perfect presents from a son to a father! I never gave my father anything like that—anything I'd put my heart and soul into. I couldn't!"

Karl reddened and turned away again. "I didn't make 'em," he said. He shivered. "I tried. How I tried!"

"I don't understand."

"My father had to make 'em!" said Karl bitterly. "And I found out it didn't make any difference to him who made 'em, just as long as your father thought I'd made 'em."

Franklin gave a sad, low whistle.

"When my old man did that, he rubbed my nose in what the big thing was to him." Karl actually wiped his nose on his jacket sleeve.

"But Karl—" said Franklin.

"Oh, hell," Karl said, tired. "I don't blame him. Sorry I said anything. I'm OK—I'm OK. I'll live." He flicked the foil target with a fingertip. "I'm gonna miss, and the hell with 'em."

Nothing more was said. The two trudged back to their fathers. It seemed to Franklin that they were leaving behind all they'd said, that the rising wind was whirling their dark thoughts away. By the time they had reached the firing line, Franklin was thinking only of whiskey, steak, and a red-hot stove.

When he and Karl fired at the foil, Franklin ticked a corner. Karl hit it in the middle. Rudy tapped his temple, then saluted Karl with a crooked finger. Karl returned the salute.

After supper, Rudy and Karl played duets for flute and clarinet. They played without sheet music, intricately and beautifully. Franklin and Merle could only keep time with their fingers, hoping that their tapping on the tabletop sounded like drums.

Franklin glanced at his father. When their eyes met, they decided that their drumming wasn't helping. Their drumming stopped.

With the moment to think about, to puzzle him pleasantly, Franklin found that the music wasn't speaking anymore of just Rudy and Karl. It was speaking of all fathers and sons. It was saying what they had all been saying haltingly, sometimes with pain and sometimes with anger and sometimes with cruelty and sometimes with love: that fathers and sons were one.

It was saying, too, that a time for a parting in spirit was near—no matter how close anyone held anyone, no matter what anyone tried.

A Night
for Love

Moonlight is all right for young lovers, and women never seem to get tired of it. But when a man gets older he usually thinks moonlight is too thin and cool for comfort. Turley Whitman thought so. Turley was in his pajamas at his bedroom window, waiting for his daughter Nancy to come home.

He was a huge, kind, handsome man. He looked like a good king, but he was only a company cop in charge of the parking lot at the Reinbeck Abrasives Company. His club, his pistol, his cartridges, and his handcuffs were on a chair by the bed. Turley was confused and upset.

His wife, Milly, was in bed. For about the first time since their three-day honeymoon, in 1936, Milly hadn't put up her hair in curlers. Her hair was all spread out on her pillow. It made her look young and soft and mysterious. Nobody had looked mysterious in that bedroom for years. Milly opened her eyes wide and stared at the moon.

Her attitude was what threw Turley as much as anything. Milly refused to worry about what was maybe happening to Nancy out in the moonlight somewhere so late at night. Milly would drop off to sleep without even knowing it, then wake up and stare at the moon for a while, and she would think big thoughts without telling Turley what they were, and then drop off to sleep again.

"You awake?" said Turley.

"Hm?" said Milly.

"You decided to be awake?"

"I'm staying awake," said Milly dreamily. She sounded like a girl.

"You think you've been staying awake?" said Turley.

"I must have dropped off without knowing it," she said.

"You've been sawing wood for an hour," said Turley.

He made her sound unattractive to herself because he wanted her to wake up more. He wanted her to wake up enough to talk to him instead of just staring at the moon. She hadn't really sawed wood while she slept. She'd been very beautiful and still.

Milly had been the town beauty once. Now her daughter was.

"I don't mind telling you, I'm worried sick," said Turley.

"Oh, honey," said Milly, "they're fine. They've got sense. They aren't crazy kids."

"You want to guarantee they're not cracked up in a ditch somewhere?" said Turley.

This roused Milly. She sat up, frowned, and blinked away her sleepiness. "You really think—"

"I really think!" said Turley. "He gave me his solemn promise he'd have her home two hours ago."

Milly pulled off her covers, put her bare feet close together on the floor. "All right," she said. "I'm sorry. I'm awake now. I'm worried now."

"About time," said Turley. He turned his back to her, and dramatized his responsible watch at the window by putting his big foot on the radiator.

"Do—do we just worry and wait?" said Milly.

"What do you suggest?" said Turley. "If you mean call the police to see if there's been an accident, I took care of that detail while you were sawing wood."

"No accidents?" said Milly in a small, small voice.

"No accidents they know of," said Turley.

"Well—that's—that's a little encouraging."

"Maybe it is to you," said Turley. "It isn't to me." He faced her, and he saw that she was now wide awake enough to hear what he had been wanting to say for some time. "If you'll pardon me saying so, you're treating this thing like it was some kind of holiday. You're acting like her being out with that rich young smart-aleck in his three-hundred-horsepower car was one of the greatest things that ever happened."

Milly stood, shocked and hurt. "Holiday?" she whispered. "Me?"

"Well—you left your hair down, didn't you, just so you'd look nice in case he got a look at you when he finally brought her home?"

Milly bit her lip. "I just thought if there was going to be a row, I didn't want to make it worse by having my hair up in curlers."

"You don't think there should be a row, do you?" said Turley.

"You're the head of the family. You—you do whatever you think is right." Milly went to him, touched him lightly. "Honey," she said, "I don't think it's good. Honest I don't. I'm trying just as hard as I can to think of things to do."

"Like what?" said Turley.

"Why don't you call up his father?" said Milly. "Maybe he knows where they are or what their plans were."

The suggestion had a curious effect on Turley. He continued to tower over Milly, but he no longer dominated the house, or the room, or even his little barefoot wife. "Oh, great!" he said. The words were loud, but they were as hollow as a bass drum.

"Why not?" said Milly.

Turley couldn't face her anymore. He took up his watch at the window again. "That would just be great," he said to the moonlit town. "Roust L. C. Reinbeck himself out of bed. 'Hello—L.C.? This is T.W. What the hell is your son doing with my daughter?'" Turley laughed bitterly.

Milly didn't seem to understand. "You've got a perfect right to call him or anybody else, if you really think there's an emergency," she said. "I mean, everybody's free and equal this time of night."

"Speak for yourself," Turley said, overacting. "Maybe you've been free and equal with the great L. C. Reinbeck, but I never have. And what's more, I never expect to be."

"All I'm saying is, he's human," said Milly.

"You're the expert on that," said Turley. "I'm sure I'm not. He never took me out dancing at the country club."

"He never took me out dancing at the country club, either. He doesn't like dancing." Milly corrected herself. "Or he didn't."

"Please, don't get technical on me this time of night," said Turley. "So he took you out and did whatever he likes to do. So whatever that was, you're the expert on him."

"Honey," said Milly, full of pain, "he took me out to supper once at the Blue Mill, and he took me to a movie once. He took me to *The Thin Man*. And all he did was talk, and all I did was listen. And it wasn't romantic talk. It was about how he was going to turn the abrasives company back into a porcelain company. And he was going to do the designing. And he never did anything of the kind, so that's how expert I am on the great Louis C. Reinbeck." She laid her hand on her bosom. "I'm the expert on you," she said, "if you want to know who I'm the expert on."

Turley made an animal sound.

"What, sweetheart?" said Milly.

"Me," said Turley, impatient. "What you're an expert on—me?"

Milly made helpless giving motions Turley didn't see.

He was standing stock-still, winding up tighter and tighter inside. Suddenly he moved, like a cumbersome windup man. He went to the telephone on the bedside table. "Why *shouldn't* I call him up?" he blustered. "Why shouldn't I?"

He looked up Louis C. Reinbeck's number in the telephone book clumsily, talked to himself about the times the Reinbeck company had gotten him up out of bed in the middle of the night.

He misdialed, hung up, got set to dial again. His courage was fading fast.

Milly hated to see the courage go. "He won't be asleep," she said. "They've been having a party."

"They've been having a what?" said Turley.

"The Reinbecks are having a party tonight—or it's just over."

"How you know that?" said Turley.

"It was in this morning's paper, on the society page. Besides," Milly continued, "you can go in the kitchen and look and see if their lights are on."

"You can see the Reinbeck house from our kitchen?" said Turley.

"Sure," said Milly. "You have to get your head down kind of low and over to one side, but then you can see their house in a corner of the window."

Turley nodded quizzically, watched Milly, thought about her, hard. He dialed again, let the Reinbecks' telephone ring twice. And then he hung up. He dominated his wife, his rooms, and his house again.

Milly knew that she had made a very bad mistake in the past thirty seconds. She was ready to bite off her tongue.

"Every time the Reinbecks do anything," said Turley, "you read every word about it in the paper?"

"Honey," said Milly, "all women read the society page. It doesn't mean anything. It's just a silly something to do when the paper comes. All women do it."

"Sure," said Turley. "Sure. But how many of 'em can say to theirselves, 'I could have been Mrs. Louis C. Reinbeck'?"

Turley made a great point of staying calm, of being like a father to Milly, of forgiving her in advance. "You want to face this thing about those two kids out there in the moonlight somewhere?" he said. "Or you want to go on pretending an accident's the only thing either one of us is thinking about?"

Milly stiffened. "I don't know what you mean," she said.

"You duck your head a hundred times a day to look at that big white house in the corner of the kitchen window, and you don't know what I mean?" said Turley. "Our girl is out in the moonlight somewhere with the kid who's going to get that house someday, and you don't know what I mean? You left your hair down and you stared at the moon and you hardly heard a word I said to you, and you don't know what I mean?" Turley shook his big, imperial head. "You just can't imagine?"

The telephone rang twice in the big white house on the hill. Then it stopped. Louis C. Reinbeck sat on a white iron chair on the lawn in the moonlight. He was looking out at the rolling lovely nonsense of the golf course and, beyond that and below, the town. All the lights in his house were out. He thought his wife, Natalie, was asleep.

Louis was drinking. He was thinking that the moonlight didn't make the world look any better. He thought the moonlight made the world look worse, made it look dead like the moon.

The telephone's ringing twice, then stopping, fitted in well with Louis's mood. The telephone was a good touch—urgency that could wait until hell froze over. "Shatter the night and then hang up," said Louis.

Along with the house and the Reinbeck Abrasives Company, Louis had inherited from his father and grandfather a deep and satisfying sense of having been corrupted by commerce. And like them, Louis thought of himself as a sensitive maker of porcelain, not grinding wheels, born in the wrong place at the wrong time.

Just as the telephone had rung twice at the right time, so did Louis's wife appear as though on cue. Natalie was a cool, spare Boston girl. Her role was to misunderstand Louis. She did it beautifully, taking apart his reflective moods like a master mechanic.

"Did you hear the telephone ring, Louis?" she said.

"Hm? Oh—yes. Uh-huh," said Louis.

"It rang and then it stopped," said Natalie.

"I know," said Louis. He warned her with a sigh that he didn't want to discuss the telephone call or anything else in a flat, practical Yankee way.

Natalie ignored the warning. "Don't you wonder who it was?"

"No," said Louis.

"Maybe it was a guest who left something. You didn't see anything around, did you, that somebody left?"

"No," said Louis.

"An earring or something, I suppose," said Natalie. She wore a pale-blue cloudlike negligee that Louis had given her. But she made the negligee meaningless by dragging a heavy iron chair across the lawn, to set it next to Louis's. The arms of the chairs clicked together, and Louis jerked his fingers from between them just in time.

Natalie sat down. "Hi," she said.

"Hi," said Louis.

"See the moon?" said Natalie.

"Yup," said Louis.

"Think people had a nice time tonight?" said Natalie.

"I don't know," said Louis, "and I'm sure they don't, either." He meant by this that he was always the only artist and philosopher at his parties. Everybody else was a businessman.

Natalie was used to this. She let it pass. "What time did Charlie get in?" she said. Charlie was their only son—actually Louis Charles Reinbeck, Junior.

"I'm sure I don't know," said Louis. "He didn't report in to me. Never does."

Natalie, who had been enjoying the moon, now sat forward uneasily. "He is home, isn't he?" she said.

"I haven't the remotest idea," said Louis.

Natalie bounded out of her chair.

She strained her eyes in the night, trying to see if Charlie's car was in the shadows of the garage. "Who did he go out with?" she asked.

"He doesn't talk with me," said Louis.

"Who is he with?" said Natalie.

"If he isn't by himself, then he's with somebody you don't approve of," said Louis.

But Natalie didn't hear him. She was running into the house. Then the telephone rang again, and went on ringing until Natalie answered.

She held the telephone out to Louis. "It's a man named Turley Whitman," she said. "He says he's one of your policemen."

"Something wrong at the plant?" said Louis, taking the phone. "Fire, I hope?"

"No," said Natalie, "nothing as serious as that." From her expression, Louis gathered that something a lot worse had happened. "It seems that our son is out with Mr. Turley's daughter somewhere, that they should have been back hours ago. Mr. Turley is naturally very deeply concerned about his daughter."

"Mr. Turley?" said Louis into the telephone.

"Turley's my first name, sir," said Turley. "Turley Whitman's my whole name."

"I'm going to listen on the upstairs phone," whispered Natalie. She gathered the folds of her negligee, ran manlike up the stairs.

"You probably don't know me except by sight," said Turley. "I'm the guard at the main-plant parking lot."

"Of course I know you—by sight and by name," said Louis. It was a lie. "Now what's this about my son and your daughter?"

Turley wasn't ready to get to the nut of the problem yet. He was still introducing himself and his family. "You probably know my wife a good deal better'n you know me, sir," he said.

There was a woman's small cry of surprise.

For an instant, Louis didn't know if it was the cry of his own wife or of Turley's. But when he heard sounds of somebody trying to hang up, he knew it had to be on Turley's end. Turley's wife obviously didn't want her name dragged in.

Turley was determined to drag it in, though, and he won out. "You knew her by her maiden name, of course," he said, "Milly—Mildred O'Shea."

All sounds of protest at Turley's end died. The death of protests came to Louis as a shocking thing. His shock was compounded as he remembered young, affectionate and pretty, mystifying Milly O'Shea. He hadn't thought of her for years, hadn't known what had become of her.

And yet at the mention of her name, it was as though Louis had thought of her constantly since she'd kissed him good-bye in the moonlight so long before.

"Yes—yes," said Louis. "Yes, I—I remember her well." He wanted to cry about growing old, about the shabby ends brave young lovers came to.

From the mention of Milly's name, Turley had his conversation with the great Louis C. Reinbeck all his own way. The miracle of equality had been achieved. Turley and Louis spoke man to man, father to father, with Louis apologizing, murmuring against his own son.

Louis thanked Turley for having called the police. Louis would call them, too. If he found out anything, he would call Turley at once. Louis addressed Turley as "sir."

Turley was exhilarated when he hung up. "He sends his regards," he said to Milly. He turned to find himself talking to air. Milly had left the room silently, on bare feet.

Turley found her heating coffee in the kitchen on the new electric stove. The stove was named the Globemaster. It had a ridiculously compli-cated control panel. The Globemaster was a wistful dream of Milly's come true. Not many of her dreams of nice things had come true.

The coffee was boiling, making the pot crackle and spit. Milly didn't notice that it was boiling, even though she was staring at the pot with ter-rible concentration. The pot spit, stung her hand. She burst into tears, put the stung hand to her mouth. And then she saw Turley.

She tried to duck past him and out of the kitchen, but he caught her arm.

"Honey," he said in a daze. He turned off the Globemaster's burner with his free hand. "Milly," he said.

Milly wanted desperately to get away. Big Turley had such an easy time holding her that he hardly realized he was doing it. Milly subsided at last, her sweet face red and twisted. "Won't—won't you tell me what's wrong, honey?" said Turley.

"Don't worry about me," said Milly. "Go worry about people dying in ditches."

Turley let her go. "I said something wrong?" He was sincerely bewil-dered.

"Oh, Turley, Turley," said Milly, "I never thought you'd hurt me this way—this much." She cupped her hands as though she were holding something precious. Then she let it fall from her hands, whatever her imagination thought it was.

Turley watched it fall. "Just because I told him your name?" he said.

"When—when you told him my name, there was so much else you told him." She was trying to forgive Turley, but it was hard for her. "I don't suppose you knew what else you were telling him. You couldn't have."

"All I told him was your name," said Turley.

"And all it meant to Louis C. Reinbeck," said Milly, "was that a woman down in the town had two silly little dates with him twenty years ago, and she's talked about nothing else since. And her husband knows about those two silly little dates, too—and he's just as proud of them as she is. Prouder!"

Milly put her head down and to one side, and she pointed out the kitchen window, pointed to a splash of white light in an upper corner of the window. "There," she said, "the great Louis C. Reinbeck is up in all that light somewhere, thinking I've loved him all these years." The floodlights on the Reinbeck house went out. "Now he's up there in the moonlight somewhere—thinking about the poor little woman and the poor little man and their poor little daughter down here." Milly shuddered. "Well, we're not poor! Or we weren't until tonight."

The great Louis C. Reinbeck returned to his drink and his white iron lawn chair. He had called the police, who had told him what they told Turley—that there were no wrecks they knew of.

Natalie sat down beside Louis again. She tried to catch his eye, tried to get him to see her maternal, teasing smile. But Louis wouldn't look.

"You—you know this girl's mother, do you?" she said.

"Knew," said Louis.

"You took her out on nights like this? Full moon and all that?"

"We could dig out a twenty-year-old calendar and see what the phases of the moon were," said Louis tartly. "You can't exactly avoid full moons, you know. You're bound to have one once a month."

"What was the moon on our wedding night?" said Natalie.

"Full?" said Louis.

"New," said Natalie. "Brand-new."

"Women are more sensitive to things like that," said Louis. "They notice things."

He surprised himself by sounding peevish. His conscience was doing funny things to his voice because he couldn't remember much of anything about his honeymoon with Natalie.

He could remember almost everything about the night he and Milly O'Shea had wandered out on the golf course. That night with Milly, the moon had been full.

Now Natalie was saying something. And when she was done, Louis had to ask her to say it all over again. He hadn't heard a word.

"I said, 'What's it like?'" said Natalie.

"What's what like?" said Louis.

"Being a young male Reinbeck—all hot-blooded and full of dreams, swooping down off the hill, grabbing a pretty little town girl and spiriting her into the moonlight." She laughed, teasing. "It must be kind of god-like."

"It isn't," said Louis.

"It isn't godlike?"

"Godlike? I never felt more human in all my life!" Louis threw his empty glass in the direction of the golf course. He wished he'd been strong enough to throw the glass straight to the spot where Milly had kissed him good-bye.

"Then let's hope Charlie marries this hot little girl from town," said Natalie. "Let's have no more cold, inhuman Reinbeck wives like me." She stood. "Face it, you would have been a thousand times happier if you'd married your Milly O'Shea."

She went to bed.

"Who's kidding anybody?" Turley Whitman asked his wife. "You would have been a million times happier if you'd married Louis Reinbeck." He was back at his post by the bedroom window, back with his big foot on the radiator.

Milly was sitting on the edge of the bed. "Not a million times, not two times, not the-smallest-number-there-is times happier," said Milly. She was wretched. "Turley—please don't say anything more like that. I can't stand it, it's so crazy."

"Well, you were kind of calling a spade a spade down there in the kitchen," said Turley, "giving me hell for telling the great Louis Reinbeck your name. Let me just call a spade a spade here, and say neither one of us wants our daughter to make the same mistake you did."

Milly went to him, put her arms around him. "Turley, please, that's the worst thing you could say to me."

He turned a stubborn red, was as unyielding as a statue. "I remember all the big promises I made you, all the big talk," he said. "Neither of us thinks company cop is one of the biggest jobs a man can hold."

Milly tried to shake him, with no luck. "I don't care what your job is," she said.

"I was gonna have more money than the great L. C. Reinbeck," said Turley, "and I was gonna make it all myself. Remember, Milly? That's what really sold you, wasn't it?"

Her arms dropped away from him. "No," she said.

"My famous good looks?" said Turley.

"They had a lot to do with it," said Milly. His looks had gone very well with the looks of the prettiest girl in town. "Most of all," she said, "it was the great Louis C. Reinbeck and the moon."

The great Louis C. Reinbeck was in his bedroom. His wife was in bed with the covers pulled up over her head. The room was cunningly contrived to give the illusion of romance and undying true love, no matter what really went on there.

Up to now, almost everything that had gone on in the room had been reasonably pleasant. Now it appeared that the marriage of Louis and Natalie was at an end. When Louis made her pull the covers away from her face, when Natalie showed him how swollen her face was with tears, this was plainly the case. This was the end.

Louis was miserable—he couldn't understand how things had fallen to pieces so fast. "I—I haven't thought of Milly O'Shea for twenty years," he said.

"Please—no. Don't lie. Don't explain," said Natalie. "I understand."

"I swear," said Louis. "I haven't seen her for twenty years."

"I believe you," said Natalie. "That's what makes it so much worse. I wish you had seen her—just as often as you liked. That would have been better, somehow, than all this—this—" She sat up, ransacked her mind for the right word. "All this horrible, empty, aching, nagging regret." She lay back down.

"About Milly?" said Louis.

"About Milly, about me, about the abrasives company, about all the things you wanted and didn't get, about all the things you got that you didn't want. Milly and me—that's as good a way of saying it as anything. That pretty well says it all."

"I—I don't love her. I never did," said Louis.

"You must have liked the one and only time in your life you felt human," said Natalie. "Whatever happened in the moonlight must have been nice—much nicer than anything you and I ever had."

Louis's nightmare got worse, because he knew Natalie had spoken the truth. There never had been anything as nice as that time in the moonlight with Milly.

"There was absolutely nothing there, no basis for love," said Louis. "We were perfect strangers then. I knew her as little as I know her now."

Louis's muscles knotted and the words came hard, because he thought he was extracting something from himself of terrible importance. "I—I suppose she is a symbol of my own disappointment in myself, of all I might have been," he said.

He went to the bedroom window, looked morbidly at the setting moon. The moon's rays were flat now, casting long shadows on the golf course, exaggerating the toy geography. Flags flew here and there, signifying less than nothing. This was where the great love scene had been played.

Suddenly he understood. "Moonlight," he murmured.

"What?" said Natalie.

"It had to be." Louis laughed, because the explanation was so explosively simple. "We had to be in love, with a moon like that, in a world like that. We owed it to the moon."

Natalie sat up, her disposition much improved.

"The richest boy in town and the prettiest girl in town," said Louis, "we couldn't let the moon down, could we?"

He laughed again, made his wife get out of bed, made her look at the moon with him. "And here I'd been thinking it really had been something big between Milly and me way back then." He shook his head. "When all it was was pure, beautiful, moonlit hokum."

He led his wife to bed. "You're the only one I ever loved. An hour ago, I didn't know that. I know that now."

So everything was fine.

"I won't lie to you," Milly Whitman said to her husband. "I loved the great Louis C. Reinbeck for a while. Out there on the golf course in the moonlight, I just had to fall in love. Can you understand that—how I would have to fall in love with him, even if we didn't like each other very well?"

Turley allowed as how he could see how that would be. But he wasn't happy about it.

"We kissed only once," said Milly. "And if he'd kissed me right, I think I might really be Mrs. Louis C. Reinbeck tonight." She nodded. "Since we're calling spades spades tonight, we might as well call that one a spade, too. And just before we kissed up there on the golf course, I was thinking what a poor little rich boy he was, and how much happier I could make him than any old cold, stuck-up country club girl. And then he kissed me, and I knew he wasn't in love, couldn't ever be in love. So I made that kiss good-bye."

"There's where you made your mistake," said Turley.

"No," said Milly, "because the next boy who kissed me kissed me right, showed me he knew what love was, even if there wasn't a moon. And I lived happily ever after, until tonight." She put her arms around Turley. "Now kiss me again the way you kissed me the first time, and I'll be all right tonight, too."

Turley did, so everything was all right there, too.

. · . · .

About twenty minutes after that, the telephones in both houses rang. The burden of the messages was that Charlie Reinbeck and Nancy Whitman were fine. They had, however, put their own interpretation on the moonlight. They'd decided that Cinderella and Prince Charming had as good a chance as anybody for really living happily ever after. So they'd married.

So now there was a new household. Whether everything was all right there remained to be seen. The moon went down.

Find Me
a Dream

If the Communists ever expect to overtake the democracies in sewer pipe production, they are certainly going to have to hump some—because just one factory in Creon, Pennsylvania, produces more pipe in six months than both Russia and China put together could produce in a year. That wonderful factory is the Creon Works of the General Forge and Foundry Company.

As Works manager, Arvin Borders told every rookie engineer, "If you don't like sewer pipe, you won't like Creon." Borders himself, a forty-six-year-old bachelor, was known throughout the industry as "Mr. Pipe."

Creon is the Pipe City. The high school football team is the Creon Pipers. The only country club is the Pipe City Golf and Country Club. There is a permanent exhibit of pipe in the club lobby, and the band that plays for the Friday-night dances at the club is Andy Middleton and His Creon Pipe-Dreamers.

One Friday night in the summertime, Andy Middleton turned the band over to his piano player. He went out to the first tee for some peace and fresh air. He surprised a pretty young woman out there. She was crying. Andy had never seen her before. He was twenty-five at the time.

Andy asked if he could help her.

"I'm being very silly," she said. "Everything is fine. I'm just being silly."

"I see," said Andy.

"I cry very easily—and even when there's nothing at all to cry about, I cry," she said.

"That must be kind of confusing for people who are with you," he said.

"It's a mess," she said.

"It might come in handy in case you ever have to attend the funeral of someone you hate," he said.

"It isn't going to be very handy in the pipe industry," she said.

"Are you in the pipe industry?" he said.

"Isn't everybody in Creon in the pipe industry?" she said.

"I'm not," he said.

"How do you keep from starving to death?" she said.

"I wave a stick in front of a band . . . give music lessons . . . things like that," he said.

"Oh, God—a musician," she said, and she turned her back.

"That's against me?" he said.

"I never want to see another musician as long as I live," she said.

"In that case," he said, "close your eyes and I'll tiptoe away." But he didn't leave.

"That's your band—playing tonight?" she said. They could hear the music quite clearly.

"That's right," he said.

"You can stay," she said.

"Pardon me?" he said.

"You're no musician," she said, "or that band would have made you curl up and die."

"You're the first person who ever listened to it," he said.

"I bet that's really the truth," she said. "Those people don't hear anything that isn't about pipe. When they dance, do they keep any kind of time to the music?"

"When they what?" he said.

"I said," she repeated, "when they dance."

"How can they dance," he said, "if the men spend the whole evening in the locker room, drinking, shooting crap, and talking sewer pipe, and all the women sit out on the terrace, talking about things they've overheard about pipe, about things they've bought with money from pipe, about things they'd like to buy with money from pipe?"

She started weeping again.

"Just being silly again?" he said. "Everything still fine?"

"Everything's fine," she said. The demoralized, ramshackle little band in the empty ballroom ended a number with razzberries and squeals. "Oh God, but that band hates music!" she said.

"They didn't always," he said.

"What happened?" she said.

"They found out they weren't ever going anywhere but Creon—and they found out nobody in Creon would listen. If I went and told them a beautiful woman was listening and weeping out here, they might get back a little of what they had once—and make a present of it to you."

"What's your instrument?" she said.

"Clarinet," he said. "Any special requests—any melodies you'd like to have us waft from the clubhouse while you weep alone?"

"No," she said. "That's sweet, but no music for me."

"Tranquilizers? Aspirin?" he said. "Cigarettes, chewing gum, candy?"

"A drink," she said.

Shouldering his way to the crowded bar, a bar called The Jolly Piper, Andy learned a lot of things about the sewer pipe business. Cleveland, he learned, had bought a lot of cheap pipe from another company, and Cleveland was going to be sorry about it in about twenty years. The Navy had specified Creon pipe for all buildings under construction, he learned, and nobody was going to be sorry. It was a little-known fact, he learned, that the whole world stood in awe of American pipe-making capabilities.

He also found out who the woman on the first tee was. She had been brought to the dance by Arvin Borders, bachelor manager of the Creon Works. Borders had met her in New York. She was a small-time actress, the widow of a jazz musician, the mother of two very young daughters.

Andy found out all this from the bartender. Arvin Borders, "Mr. Pipe" himself, came into the bar and craned his neck, looking for somebody. He was carrying two highballs. The ice in both glasses had melted.

"Still haven't seen her, Mr. Borders," the bartender called to him, and Borders nodded unhappily and left.

"Who haven't you seen?" Andy asked the bartender.

And the bartender told him all he knew about the widow. He also gave Andy the opinion, out of the corner of his mouth, that General Forge and Foundry Company headquarters in Ilium, New York, knew about the romance and took a very dim view of it. "You tell me where, in all of Creon," the bartender said to Andy, "a pretty, young New York actress could fit in."

The woman went by her stage name, which was Hildy Matthews, Andy learned. The bartender didn't have any idea who her husband had been.

Andy went into the ballroom to tell his Pipe-Dreamers to play a little better for a weeping lady on the golf course, and he found Arvin Borders talking to them. Borders, an earnest, thickset man, was asking the band to play "Indian Love Call" very loud.

"Loud?" said Andy.

"So she'll hear it, wherever she is, and come," said Borders. "I can't imagine where she got to," he said. "I left her on the terrace, with the ladies, for a while—and she just plain evaporated."

"Maybe she got fed up with all the talk about pipe," said Andy.

"She's very interested in pipe," said Borders. "You wouldn't think a woman who looked like that would be, but she can listen to me talk shop for hours and never get tired of it."

"'Indian Love Call' will bring her back?" said Andy.

Borders mumbled something unintelligible.

"Pardon me, sir?" said Andy.

Borders turned red and pulled in his chin. "I said," he said gruffly, "'It's our tune.'"

"I see," said Andy.

"You boys might as well know now—I'm going to marry that girl," said Borders. "We're going to announce our engagement tonight."

Andy bowed slightly. "Congratulations," he said. He put his two high-balls down on a chair, picked up his clarinet. "'Indian Love Call,' boys—real loud?" he said.

The band was slow to respond. Nobody seemed to want to play much, and everybody was trying to tell Andy something.

"What's the trouble?" said Andy.

"Before we play, Andy," said the pianist, "you ought to know just who we're playing for, whose *widow* we're playing for."

"Whose widow?" said Andy.

"I had no idea he was so famous," said Borders. "I mentioned him to your band here, and they almost fell off their chairs."

"Who?" said Andy.

"A dope fiend, an alcoholic, a wife-beater, and a woman-chaser who was shot dead last year by a jealous husband," said Borders indignantly. "Why anybody would think there was anything wonderful about a man like that I'll never know," he said. And then he gave the name of the man, a man who was probably the greatest jazz musician who had ever lived.

"I thought you weren't ever coming back," she said, out of the shadows on the first tee.

"I had to play a special request," said Andy. "Somebody wanted me to play 'Indian Love Call' as loud as I could."

"Oh," she said.

"You heard it and you didn't come running?" he said.

"Is that what he expected me to do?" she said.

"He said it was your tune," he said.

"That was his idea," she said. "He thinks it's the most beautiful song ever written."

"How did you two happen to meet?" he said.

"I was dead broke, looking for any kind of work at all," she said. "There was a General Forge and Foundry Company sales meeting in New York. They were going to put on a skit. They needed an actress. I got the part."

"What part did they give you?" he said.

"They dressed me in gold lamé, gave me a crown of pipe fittings, and introduced me as 'Miss Pipe Opportunities in the Golden Sixties,'" she said. "Arvin Borders was there," she said. She emptied her glass. "Kismet," she said.

"Kismet," he said.

She took his highball from him. "I'm sorry," she said, "I'm going to need this one, too."

"And ten more besides?" he said.

"If it takes ten more to get me back to all those people, all those lights, all that pipe," she said, "I'll drink ten more."

"The trip's that tough?" he said.

"If only I hadn't wandered out here," she said. "If only I'd stayed up there!"

"One of the worst mistakes a person can make, sometimes, I guess," he said, "is to try to get away from people and think. It's a great way to lose your forward motion."

"The band is playing so softly I can hardly hear the music," she said.

"They know whose widow's listening," he said, "and they'd just as soon you didn't hear them."

"Oh," she said. "They know. You know."

"He—he didn't leave you anything?" he said.

"Debts," she said. "Two daughters . . . for which I'm really very grateful."

"The horn?" he said.

"It's with him," she said. "Please—could I have one more drink?"

"One more drink," he said, "and you'll have to go back to your fiancé on your hands and knees."

"I'm perfectly capable of taking care of myself, thank you," she said. "It isn't up to you to watch out for me."

"Beg your pardon," he said.

She gave a small, melodious hiccup. "What a terrible time for that to happen," she said. "It doesn't have anything to do with drinking."

"I believe you," he said.

"You don't believe me," she said. "Give me some kind of a test. Make me walk a straight line or say something complicated."

"Forget it," he said.

"You don't believe I love Arvin Borders, either, do you?" she said. "Well, let me tell you that one of the things I do best is love. I don't mean pretending to love. I mean really loving. When I love somebody, I don't hold anything back. I go all the way, and right now I happen to love Arvin Borders."

"Lucky man," he said.

"Would you like to hear exactly how much I have already learned about pipe?" she said.

"Go ahead," he said.

"I read a whole book about pipe," she said. "I went to the public library and got down a book about pipe and nothing else but pipe."

"What did the book say?" he said.

From the tennis courts to the west came faint, crooning calls. Borders was now prowling the club grounds, looking for his Hildy. "Hildeee," he was calling. "Hildy?"

"You want me to yell yoo-hoo?" said Andy.

"Shhh!" she said. And she gave the small, melodious hiccup.

Arvin Borders wandered off into the parking lot, his cries fading away in the darkness that enveloped him.

"You were going to tell me about pipe," said Andy.

"Let's talk about you," she said.

"What would you like to know about me?" he said.

"People have to ask you questions or you can't talk?" she said.

He shrugged. "Small-time musician. Never married. Big dreams once. Big dreams all gone."

"Big dreams of what?" she said.

"Being half the musician your husband was," he said. "You want to hear more?"

"I love to hear other people's dreams," she said.

"All right—love," he said.

"You've never had that?" she said.

"Not that I've noticed," he said.

"May I ask you a very personal question?" she said.

"About my ability as a great lover?" he said.

"No," she said. "I think that would be a very silly kind of question. I think everybody young is basically a great lover. All anybody needs is the chance."

"Ask the *personal* question," he said.

"Do you make any money?" she said.

Andy didn't answer right away.

"Is that too personal?" she said.

"I don't guess it would kill me to answer," he said. He did some figuring in his head, gave her an honest report of his earnings.

"Why, that's very good," she said.

"More than a schoolteacher, less than a school janitor," he said.

"Do you live in an apartment or what?" she said.

"A big old house I inherited from my family," he said.

"You're really quite well off when you stop to think about it," she said. "Do you like little children—little girls?"

"Don't you think you'd better be getting back to your fiancé?" he said.

"My questions keep getting more and more personal," she said. "I can't help it, my own life has been so personal. Crazy, personal things happen to me all the time."

"I think we'd better break this up," he said.

She ignored him. "For instance," she said, "I pray for certain kinds of people to come to me, and they come to me. One time when I was very young, I prayed for a great musician to come and fall in love with me—and he did. And I loved him, too, even though he was the worst husband a woman could have. That's how good I am at loving."

"Hooray," he said quietly.

"And then," she said, "when my husband died and there was nothing to eat and I was sick of wild and crazy nights and days, I prayed for a solid, sensible, rich businessman to come along."

"And he did," said Andy.

"And then," she said, "when I came out here and ran away from all the people who liked pipe so much—do you know what I prayed for?"

"Nope," he said.

"A man to bring me a drink," she said. "That was all. I give you my word of honor, that was all."

"And I brought you two drinks," he said.

"And that isn't all, either," she said.

"Oh?" he said.

"I think that I could love you very much," she said.

"A pretty tough thing to do," he said.

"Not for me," she said. "I think you could be a very good musician if somebody encouraged you. And I could give you the big and beautiful love you want. You'd definitely have that."

"This is a proposal of marriage?" he said.

"Yes," she said. "And if you say no, I don't know what I'll do. I'll crawl under the shrubbery here and just die. I can't go back to all those pipe people, and there's no place else *to* go."

"I'm supposed to say yes?" he said.

"If you feel like saying yes, then say yes," she said.

"All right—" he said at last, "yes."

"We're both going to be so glad this happened," she said.

"What about Arvin Borders?" he said.

"We're doing him a favor," she said.

"We are?" he said.

"Oh, yes," she said. "On the terrace there, a woman came right out and said it would ruin Arvin's career if he married a woman like me—and you know, it probably would, too."

"That was the crack that sent you out here into the shadows?" he said.

"Yes," she said. "It was very upsetting. I didn't want to hurt anybody's career."

"That's considerate of you," he said.

"But you," she said, taking his arm, "I don't see how I could do anything for you but a world of good. You wait," she said. "You wait and see."

Runaways

They left a note saying teenagers were as capable of true love as anybody else—maybe more capable. And then they took off for parts unknown.

They took off in the boy's old blue Ford, with baby shoes dangling from the rearview mirror, with a pile of comic books on the burst backseat.

A police alarm went out for them right away, and their pictures were in the papers and on television. But they weren't caught for twenty-four hours. They got all the way to Chicago. A patrolman spotted them shopping together in a supermarket there, caught them buying what looked like a lifetime supply of candy, cosmetics, soft drinks, and frozen pizzas.

The girl's father gave the patrolman a two-hundred-dollar reward. The girl's father was Jesse K. Southard, governor of the state of Indiana.

That was why they got so much publicity. It was exciting when an ex–

reform school kid, a kid who ran a lawn mower at the governor's country club, ran off with the governor's daughter.

When the Indiana State Police brought the girl back to the Governor's Mansion in Indianapolis, Governor Southard announced that he would take immediate steps to get an annulment. An irreverent reporter pointed out to him that there could hardly be an annulment, since there hadn't been a marriage.

The governor blew up. "That boy never laid a finger on her," he roared, "because she wouldn't let him! And I'll knock the block off any man who says otherwise."

The reporters wanted to talk to the girl, naturally, and the governor said she would have a statement for them in about an hour. It wouldn't be her first statement about the escapade. In Chicago she and the boy had lectured reporters and police on love, hypocrisy, persecution of teenagers, the insensitivity of parents, and even rockets, Russia, and the hydrogen bomb.

When the girl came downstairs with her new statement, however, she contradicted everything she'd said in Chicago. Reading from a three-page typewritten script, she said the adventure had been a nightmare, said she didn't love the boy and never had, said she must have been crazy, and said she never wanted to see the boy again.

She said the only people she loved were her parents, said she didn't see how she could make it up to them for all the heartaches she had caused, said she was going to concentrate on schoolwork and getting into college, and said she didn't want to pose for pictures because she looked so awful after the ordeal.

She didn't look especially awful, except that she'd dyed her hair red, and the boy had given her a terrible haircut in an effort to disguise her. And she'd been crying some. She didn't look tired. She looked young and wild and captured—that was all.

Her name was Annie—Annie Southard.

When the reporters left, when they went to show the boy the girl's latest statement, the governor turned to his daughter and said to her, "Well, I certainly want to thank you. I don't see how I can ever thank you enough."

"You thank me for telling all those lies?" she said.

"I thank you for making a very small beginning in repairing the damage you've done," he said.

"My own father, the governor of the state of Indiana," said Annie, "ordered me to lie. I'll never forget that."

"That isn't the last of the orders you'll get from me," he said.

Annie said nothing out loud, but in her mind she placed a curse on her parents. She no longer owed them anything. She was going to be cold and indifferent to them for the rest of her days. The curse went into effect immediately.

Annie's mother, Mary, came down the spiral staircase. She had been listening to the lies from the landing above. "I think you handled that very well," she said to her husband.

"As well as I could, under the circumstances," he said.

"I only wish we could come out and say what there really is to say," said Annie's mother. "If we could only just come out and say we're not against love, and we're not against people who don't have money." She started to touch her daughter comfortingly, but was warned against it by Annie's eyes. "We're not snobs, darling—and we're not insensitive to love. Love is the most wonderful thing there is."

The governor turned away and glared out a window.

"We *believe* in love," said Annie's mother. "You've seen how much I love your father and how much your father loves me—and how much your father and I love you."

"If you're going to come out and say something, say it," said the governor.

"I thought I was," said his wife.

"Talk money, talk breeding, talk education, talk friends, talk interests," said the governor, "and then you can get back to love if you want." He faced his women. "Talk happiness, for heaven's sake," he said. "See that boy again, keep this thing going, marry him when you can do it legally, when we can't stop you," he said to Annie, "and not only will you be the unhappiest woman alive, but he'll be the unhappiest man alive. It will be a mess you can truly be proud of, because you will have married without having met a single condition for a happy marriage—and by single condition I mean one single, solitary thing in common.

"What did you plan to do for friends?" he said. "His gang at the pool-room or your gang at the country club? Would you start out by buying him a nice house and nice furniture and a nice automobile—or would you wait for him to buy those things, which he'll be just about ready to pay for when hell freezes over? Do you like comic books as well as he does? Do you like the same kind of comic books?" cried the governor.

"Who do you think you are?" he asked Annie. "You think you're Eve, and God only made one Adam for you?"

"Yes," said Annie, and she went upstairs to her room and slammed the door. Moments later music came from her room. She was playing a record.

The governor and his wife stood outside the door and listened to the words of the song. These were the words:

They say we don't know what love is,
Boo-wah-wah, uh-huh, yeah.
But we know what the message in the stars above is,
Boo-wah-wah, uh-huh, yeah.
So hold me, hold me, baby,
And you'll make my poor heart sing,
Because everything they tell us, baby,
Why, it just don't mean a thing.

Eight miles away, eight miles due south, through the heart of town and out the other side, reporters were clumping onto the front porch of the boy's father's house.

It was old, cheap, a carpenter's special, a 1926 bungalow. Its front windows looked out into the perpetual damp twilight of a huge front porch. Its side windows looked into the neighbors' windows ten feet away. Light could reach the interior only through a window in the back. As luck would have it, the window let light into a tiny pantry.

The boy and his father and his mother did not hear the reporters knocking. The television set in the living room and the radio in the kitchen were both on, blatting away, and the family was having a row in the dining room, halfway between them.

The row was actually about everything in creation, but it had for its subject of the moment the boy's mustache. He had been growing it for a month and had just been caught by his father in the act of blacking it with shoe polish.

The boy's name was Rice Brentner. It was true, as the papers said, that Rice had spent time in reform school. That was three years behind him now. His crime had been, at the age of thirteen, the theft of sixteen automobiles within a period of a week. Except for the escapade with Annie, he hadn't been in any real trouble since.

"You march into the bathroom," said his mother, "and you shave that awful thing off."

Rice did not march. He stayed right where he was.

"You heard your mother," his father said. When Rice still didn't budge, his father tried to hurt him with scorn. "Makes him feel like a man, I guess—like a great big man," he said.

"Doesn't make him look like a man," said his mother. "It makes him look like an I-don't-know-what-it-is."

"You just named him," said his father. "That's exactly what he is: an I-don't-know-what-it-is." Finding a label like that seemed to ease the boy's father some. He was, as one newspaper and then all the newspapers had pointed out, an eighty-nine-dollar-and sixty-two-cent-a-week supply clerk in the main office of the public school system. He had reason to resent the thoroughness of the reporter who had dug that figure from the public records. The sixty-two cents galled him in particular. "An eighty-nine-dollar-and-sixty-two-cent-a-week supply clerk has an I-don't-know-what-it-is for a son," he said. "The Brentner family is certainly covered with glory today."

"Do you realize how lucky you are not to be in jail—rotting?" said Rice's mother. "If they had you in jail, they'd not only shave off your mustache, without even asking you about it—they'd shave off every hair on your head."

Rice wasn't listening much, only enough to keep himself smoldering comfortably. What he was thinking about was his car. He had paid for it with money he himself had earned. It hadn't cost his family a dime. Rice now swore to himself that if his parents tried to take his car away from him, he would leave home for good.

"He knows about jail. He's been there before," said his father.

"Let him keep his mustache if he wants to," said his mother. "I just wish he'd look in a mirror once to see how silly it makes him look."

"All right—let him keep it," said his father, "but I'll tell you one thing he isn't going to keep, and I give you my word of honor on that, and that's the automobile."

"Amen!" said his mother. "He's going to march down to a used-car lot, and he's going to sell the car, and then he's going to march over to the bank and put the money in his savings account, and then he's going to march home and give us the bankbook." As she uttered this complicated promise she became more and more martial until, at the end, she was marching in place like John Philip Sousa.

"You said a mouthful!" said her husband.

And now that the subject of the automobile had been introduced, it became the dominant theme and the loudest one of all. The old blue Ford was such a frightening symbol of disastrous freedom to Rice's parents that they could yammer about it endlessly.

And they just about did yammer about it endlessly this time.

"Well—the car is going," said Rice's mother, winded at last.

"That's the end of the car," said his father.

"And that's the end of me," said Rice. He walked out the back door, got into his car, turned on the radio, and drove away.

Music came from the radio. The song told of two teenagers who were going to get married, even though they were dead broke. The chorus of it went like this:

We'll have no fancy drapes—
No stove, no carpet, no refrigerator.
But our nest will look like a hunk of heaven,
Because love, baby, is our interior decorator.

Rice went to a phone booth a mile from the Governor's Mansion. He called the number that was the governor's family's private line.

He pitched his voice a half-octave higher, and he asked to speak to Annie.

It was the butler who answered. "I'm sorry, sir," he said, "but I don't think she's taking any calls just now. You want to leave your name?"

"Tell her it's Bob Counsel," said Rice. Counsel was the son of a man who had gotten very rich on coin-operated laundries. He spent most of his time at the country club. He was in love with Annie.

"I didn't recognize your voice for a minute there, Mr. Counsel," said the butler. "Please hold on, sir, if you'd be so kind."

Seconds later Annie's mother was on the phone. She wanted to believe so desperately that the caller was the polite and attractive and respectable Bob Counsel that she didn't even begin to suspect a fraud. And she did almost all the talking, so Rice had only to grunt from time to time.

"Oh Bob, oh Bob, oh Bob—you dear boy," she said. "How nice, how awfully nice of you to call. It was what I was *praying* for! She *has* to talk to somebody her own age. Oh, her father and I have talked to her, and I guess she heard us, but there's such a gap between the generations these days.

"This thing—this thing Annie's been through," said Annie's mother, "it's more like a nervous breakdown than anything else. It isn't really a nervous breakdown, but she isn't herself—isn't the Annie we know. Do you understand what I'm trying to say?"

"Yup," said Rice.

"Oh, she'll be so glad to hear from you, Bob—to know she's still got her old friends, her real friends to fall back on. Hearing your voice," said the governor's wife, "our Annie will know everything's going to get back to normal again."

She went to get Annie—and had a ding-dong wrangle with her that Rice could hear over the telephone. Annie said she hated Bob Counsel, thought he was a jerk, a stuffed shirt, and a mamma's boy. Somebody thought to cover the mouthpiece at that point, so Rice didn't hear anything more until Annie came on the line.

"Hullo," she said emptily.

"I thought you might enjoy a ride—to kind of take your mind off your troubles," said Rice.

"What?" said Annie.

"This is Rice," he said. "Tell your mother you're going to the club to play tennis with good old Bob Counsel. Meet me at the gas station at Forty-sixth and Illinois."

So half an hour later, they took off again in the boy's old blue Ford, with baby shoes dangling from the rearview mirror, with a pile of comic books on the burst backseat.

The car radio sang as Annie and Rice left the city limits behind:

Oh, baby, baby, baby,
What a happy, rockin' day,
'Cause your sweet love and kisses
Chase those big, black blues away.

And the exhilarating chase began again.

Annie and Rice crossed the Ohio border on a back road and listened to the radio talk about them above the sound of gravel rattling in the fenders.

They had listened impatiently to news of a riot in Bangalore, of an airplane collision in Ireland, of a man who blew up his wife with nitroglycerine in West Virginia. The newscaster had saved the biggest news for last—that Annie and Rice, Juliet and Romeo, were playing hare and hounds again.

The newscaster called Rice "Rick," something nobody had ever called him, and Rice and Annie liked that.

"I'm going to call you Rick from now on," said Annie.

"That's all right with me," said Rice.

"You look more like a Rick than a Rice," said Annie. "How come they named you Rice?"

"Didn't I ever tell you?" said Rice.

"If you did," she said, "I've forgot."

The fact was that Rice had told her about a dozen times why he was named Rice, but she never really listened to him. For that matter, Rice never really listened to her, either. Both would have been bored stiff if they had listened, but they spared themselves that.

So their conversations were marvels of irrelevance. There were only two subjects in common—self-pity and something called love.

"My mother had some ancestor back somewhere named Rice," said Rice. "He was a doctor, and I guess he was pretty famous."

"Dr. Siebolt is the only person who ever tried to understand me as a human being," said Annie. Dr. Siebolt was the governor's family physician.

"There's some other famous people back there somewhere, too—on my mother's side," said Rice. "I don't know what all they did, but there's good blood back there."

"Dr. Siebolt would hear what I was trying to say," said Annie. "My parents never had time to listen."

"That's why my old man always got burned up at me—because I've got so much of my mother's blood," said Rice. "You know—I want to do things and have things and live and take chances, and his side of the family isn't that way at all."

"I could talk to Dr. Siebolt about love—I could talk to him about anything," said Annie. "With my parents there were just all kinds of things I had to keep bottled up."

"Safety first—that's their motto," said Rice. "Well, that isn't my motto. They want me to end up the way they have, and I'm just not that kind of a person."

"It's a terrible thing to make somebody bottle things up," said Annie. "I used to cry all the time, and my parents never could figure out why."

"That's why I stole those cars," said Rice. "I just all of a sudden went crazy one day. They were trying to make me act like my father, and I'm just not that kind of man. They never understood me. They don't understand me yet."

"But the worst thing," said Annie, "was then my own father ordered me to lie. That was when I realized that my parents didn't care about truth. All they care about is what people think."

"This summer," said Rice, "I was actually making more money than my old man or any of his brothers. That really ate into him. He couldn't stand that."

"My mother started talking to me about love," said Annie, "and it was all I could do to keep from screaming, 'You don't know what love is! You never have known what it is!'"

"My parents kept telling me to act like a man," said Rice. "Then, when I really started acting like one, they went right through the roof. What's a guy supposed to do?" he said.

"Even if I screamed at her," said Annie, "she wouldn't hear it. She never listens. I think she's afraid to listen. Do you know what I mean?"

"My older brother was the favorite in our family," said Rice. "He could do no wrong, and I never could do anything right, as far as they were concerned. You never met my brother, did you?"

"My father killed something in me when he told me to lie," said Annie.

"We sure are lucky we found each other," said Rice.

"What?" said Annie.

"I said, 'We sure are lucky we found each other,'" said Rice.

Annie took his hand. "Oh yes, oh yes, oh yes," she said fervently. "When we first met out there on the golf course, I almost died because I knew how right we were for each other. Next to Dr. Siebolt, you're the first person I ever really felt close to."

"Dr. who?" said Rice.

In the study of the Governor's Mansion, Governor Southard had his radio on. Annie and Rice had just been picked up, twenty miles west of Cleveland, and Southard wanted to hear what the news services had to say about it.

So far he had heard only music, and was hearing it now:

Let's not go to school today,
Turtle dove, turtle dove.
Let's go out in the woods and play,
Play with love, play with love.

The governor turned the radio off. "How do they *dare* put things like that on the air?" he said. "The whole American entertainment industry does nothing but tell children how to kill their parents—and themselves in the bargain."

He put the question to his wife and to the Brentners, the parents of the boy, who were sitting in the study with him.

The Brentners shook their heads, meaning that they did not know the answer to the governor's question. They were appalled at having been called into the presence of the governor. They had said almost nothing— nothing beyond abject, rambling, ga-ga apologies at the very beginning. Since then they had been in numb agreement with anything the governor cared to say.

He had said plenty, wrestling with what he called the toughest decision of his life. He was trying to decide, with the concurrence of his wife and the Brentners, how to make the runaways grow up enough to realize what they were doing, how to fix them so they would never run away again.

"Any suggestions, Mr. Brentner?" he said to Rice's father.

Rice's father shrugged. "I haven't got any control over him, sir," he said. "If somebody'd tell me a way to get control of him, I'd be glad to try it, but . . ." He let the sentence trail off to nothing.

"But what?" said the governor.

"He's pretty close to being a man now, Governor," said Rice's father, "and he's just about as easy to control as any other man—and that isn't very easy." He murmured something else, which the governor didn't catch, and shrugged again.

"Beg your pardon?" said the governor.

Rice's father said it again, scarcely louder than the first time. "I said he doesn't respect me."

"By heaven, he would if you'd have the guts to lay down the law to him and make it stick!" said the governor with hot righteousness.

Rice's mother now did the most courageous thing in her life. She was boiling mad about having all the blame put on her son, and she now squared the governor of Indiana away. "Maybe if we'd raised our son the way you raised your daughter," she said, "maybe then we wouldn't have the trouble we have today."

The governor looked startled. He sat down at his desk. "Well said, madam," he said. He turned to his wife. "We should certainly give our child-rearing secret to the world."

"Annie isn't a bad girl," said his wife.

"Neither's our boy a bad boy," said Rice's mother, very pepped up, now that she'd given the governor the works.

"I—I'm sure he isn't," said the governor's wife.

"He isn't a bad boy anymore. That's the big thing," blurted Rice's father. And he took courage from his wife's example, and added something else. "And that little girl isn't what you'd call real little, either," he said.

"You recommend they get married?" said the governor, incredulous.

"I don't know what I recommend," said Rice's father. "I'm not a recommending man. But maybe they really do love each other. Maybe they really were made for each other. Maybe they really would be happy for the rest of their lives together, starting right now, if we'd let 'em." He threw his hands up. "I don't know!" he said. "Do you?"

Annie and Rice were talking to reporters in a state police barracks outside of Cleveland. They were waiting to be hauled back home. They claimed to be unhappy, but they appeared to be having a pretty fine time. They were telling the reporters about money now.

"People care too much about money," said Annie. "What is money, when you really stop to think about it?"

"We don't want money from her parents," said Rice. "I guess maybe her parents think I'm after their money. All I want is their daughter."

"It's all right with me, if they want to disinherit me," said Annie. "From what I've seen of the rich people I grew up with, money just makes people worried and unhappy. People with a lot of money get so worried about how maybe they'll lose it, they forget to live."

"I can always earn enough to keep a roof over our heads and keep from starving," said Rice. "I can earn more than my old man does. My car is completely paid for. It's all mine, free and clear."

"I can earn money, too," said Annie. "I would be a lot prouder of working than I would be of what my parents want me to do, which is hang around with a lot of other spoiled people and play games."

A state trooper now came in, told Annie her father was on the telephone. The governor of Indiana wanted to talk to her.

"What good will talk do?" said Annie. "Their generation doesn't understand our generation, and they never will. I don't want to talk to him."

The trooper left. He came back a few minutes later.

"He's still on the line?" said Annie.

"No, ma'am," said the trooper. "He gave me a message for you."

"Oh, boy," said Annie. "This should really be good."

"It's a message from your parents, too," the trooper said to Rice.

"I can hardly wait to hear it," said Rice.

"The message is this," said the trooper, keeping his face blankly official, "you are to come home in your own car whenever you feel like it. When you get home, they want you to get married and start being happy as soon as possible."

Annie and Rice crept home in the old blue Ford, with baby shoes dangling from the rearview mirror, with a pile of comic books on the burst backseat. They came home on the main highways. Nobody was looking for them anymore.

Their radio was on, and every news broadcast told the world the splendid news: Annie and Rice were to be married at once. True love had won another stunning victory.

By the time the lovers reached the Indiana border, they had heard the news of their indescribable happiness a dozen times. They were beginning to look like department store clerks on Christmas Eve, jangled and exhausted by relentless tidings of great joy.

Rice turned off the radio. Annie gave an involuntary sigh of relief. They hadn't talked much on the trip home. There didn't seem to be anything to talk about: everything was so settled—everything was so, as they say in business, finalized.

Annie and Rice got into a traffic jam in Indianapolis and were locked for stoplight after stoplight next to a car in which a baby was howling. The parents of the child were very young. The wife was scolding her husband, and the husband looked ready to uproot the steering wheel and brain her with it.

Rice turned on the radio again, and this is what the song on the radio said:

We certainly fooled them,
The ones who said our love wasn't true.
Now, forever and ever,
You've got me, and I've got you.

In almost a frenzy, with Annie's nerves winding ever tighter, Rice changed stations again and again. Every station bawled of either victories or the persecution of teenage love. And that's what the radio was bawling about when the old blue Ford stopped beneath the porte cochere of the Governor's Mansion.

Only one person came out to greet them, and that was the policeman who guarded the door. "Congratulations, sir . . . madam," he said blandly.

"Thank you," said Rice. He turned everything off with the ignition key. The last illusion of adventure died as the radio tubes lost their glow and the engine cooled.

The policeman opened the door on Annie's side. The door gave a rusty screech. Two loose jelly beans wobbled out the door and fell to the immaculate blacktop below.

Annie, still in the car, looked down at the jelly beans. One was green. The other was white. There were bits of lint stuck to them. "Rice?" she said.

"Hm?" he said.

"I'm sorry," she said, "I can't go through with it."

Rice made a sound like a faraway freight whistle. He was grateful for release.

"Could we talk alone, please?" Annie said to the policeman.

"Beg your pardon," said the policeman as he withdrew.

"Would it have worked?" said Annie.

Rice shrugged. "For a little while."

"You know what?" said Annie.

"What?" said Rice.

"We're too young," said Annie.

"Not too young to be in love," said Rice.

"No," said Annie, "not too young to be in love. Just too young for about everything else there is that goes with love." She kissed him. "Good-bye, Rice. I love you."

"I love you," he said.

She got out, and Rice drove away.

As he drove away, the radio came on. It was playing an old song now, and the words were these:

> Now's the time for sweet good-bye
> To what could never be,
> To promises we ne'er could keep,
> To a magic you and me.
> If we should try to prove our love,
> Our love would be in danger.
> Let's put our love beyond all harm.
> Good-bye—sweet, gentle stranger.

2BR02B

Everything was perfectly swell.

There were no prisons, no slums, no insane asylums, no cripples, no poverty, no wars.

All diseases were conquered. So was old age.

Death, barring accidents, was an adventure for volunteers.

The population of the United States was stabilized at forty million souls.

One bright morning in the Chicago Lying-In Hospital, a man named Edward K. Wehling, Jr., waited for his wife to give birth. He was the only man waiting. Not many people were born each day anymore.

Wehling was fifty-six, a mere stripling in a population whose average age was one hundred twenty-nine.

X rays had revealed that his wife was going to have triplets. The children would be his first.

Young Wehling was hunched in his chair, his head in his hands. He was so rumpled, so still and colorless as to be virtually invisible. His camouflage was perfect, since the waiting room had a disorderly and demoralized air, too. Chairs and ashtrays had been moved away from the walls. The floor was paved with spattered dropcloths.

The room was being redecorated. It was being redecorated as a memorial to a man who had volunteered to die.

A sardonic old man, about two hundred years old, sat on a stepladder, painting a mural he did not like. Back in the days when people aged visibly, his age would have been guessed at thirty-five or so. Aging had touched him that much before the cure for aging was found.

The mural he was working on depicted a very neat garden. Men and women in white, doctors and nurses, turned the soil, planted seedlings, sprayed bugs, spread fertilizer. Men and women in purple uniforms pulled up weeds, cut down plants that were old and sickly, raked leaves, carried refuse to trash burners.

Never, never, never—not even in medieval Holland or old Japan—had a garden been more formal, been better tended. Every plant had all the loam, light, water, air, and nourishment it could use.

A hospital orderly came down the corridor, singing under his breath a popular song:

> If you don't like my kisses, honey,
> Here's what I will do:
> I'll go see a girl in purple,
> Kiss this sad world toodle-oo.
> If you don't want my lovin',
> Why should I take up all this space?
> I'll get off this old planet,
> Let some sweet baby have my place.

The orderly looked in at the mural and the muralist. "Looks so real," he said, "I can practically imagine I'm standing in the middle of it."

"What makes you think you're not in it?" said the painter. He gave a satiric smile. "It's called *The Happy Garden of Life,* you know."

"That's good of Dr. Hitz," said the orderly.

He was referring to one of the male figures in white, whose head was a portrait of Dr. Benjamin Hitz, the hospital's chief obstetrician. Hitz was a blindingly handsome man.

"Lot of faces still to fill in," said the orderly. He meant that the faces of many of the figures in the mural were blank. All blanks were to be filled with portraits of important people either on the hospital staff or from the Chicago office of the Federal Bureau of Termination.

"Must be nice to be able to make pictures that look like something," said the orderly.

The painter's face curdled with scorn. "You think I'm proud of this drab? You think this is my idea of what life really looks like?"

"What's your idea of what life looks like?"

The painter gestured at a foul dropcloth. "There's a good picture of it," he said. "Frame that, and you'll have a picture a damn sight more honest than this one."

"You're a gloomy old duck, aren't you?" said the orderly.

"Is that a crime?" said the painter.

"If you don't like it here, Grandpa—" The orderly finished the thought with the trick telephone number that people who didn't want to live any-more were supposed to call. The zero in the telephone number he pro-nounced "naught."

The number was 2BR02B.

It was the telephone number of an institution whose fanciful sobri-quets included "Automat," "Birdland," "Cannery," "Catbox," "Delouser," "Easy Go," "Good-bye, Mother," "Happy Hooligan," "Kiss Me Quick," "Lucky Pierre," "Sheepdip," "Waring Blender," "Weep No More," and "Why Worry?"

"To Be or Not to Be" was the telephone number of the municipal gas chambers of the Federal Bureau of Termination.

The painter thumbed his nose at the orderly. "When I decide it's time to go," he said, "it won't be at the Sheepdip."

"A do-it-yourselfer, eh?" said the orderly. "Messy business, Grandpa.

Why don't you have a little consideration for the people who have to clean up after you?"

The painter expressed with an obscenity his lack of concern for the tribulations of his survivors. "The world could do with a good deal more mess, if you ask me," he said.

The orderly laughed and moved on.

Wehling, the waiting father, mumbled something without raising his head. And then he fell silent again.

A coarse, formidable woman strode into the waiting room on spike heels. Her shoes, stockings, trench coat, bag, and overseas cap were all purple, a purple the painter called "the color of grapes on Judgment Day."

The medallion on her purple musette bag was the seal of the Service Division of the Federal Bureau of Termination, an eagle perched on a turnstile.

The woman had a lot of facial hair—an unmistakable mustache, in fact. A curious thing about gas chamber hostesses was that no matter how lovely and feminine they were when recruited, they all sprouted mustaches within five years or so.

"Is this where I'm supposed to come?" she asked the painter.

"A lot would depend on what your business was," he said. "You aren't about to have a baby, are you?"

"They told me I was supposed to pose for some picture," she said. "My name's Leora Duncan." She waited.

"And you dunk people," he said.

"What?" she said.

"Skip it," he said.

"That sure is a beautiful picture," she said. "Looks just like heaven or something."

"Or something," said the painter. He took a list of names from his smock pocket. "Duncan, Duncan, Duncan," he said, scanning the list. "Yes—here you are. You're entitled to be immortalized. See any faceless body here you'd like me to stick your head on? We've got a few choice ones left."

She studied the mural. "Gee," she said, "they're all the same to me. I don't know anything about art."

"A body's a body, eh?" he said. "All righty. As a master of the fine art, I recommend this body here." He indicated the faceless figure of a woman who was carrying dried stalks to a trash burner.

"Well," said Leora Duncan, "that's more the disposal people, isn't it? I mean, I'm in service. I don't do any disposing."

The painter clapped his hands in mock delight. "You say you don't know anything about art, and then you prove in the next breath that you do know more about it than I do! Of course the sheaf carrier is wrong for a hostess! A snipper, a pruner—that's more your line." He pointed to a figure in purple who was sawing a dead branch from an apple tree. "How about her?" he said. "You like her at all?"

"Gosh—" she said, and she blushed and became humble. "That—that puts me right next to Dr. Hitz."

"That upsets you?" he said.

"Good gravy, no!" she said. "It's—it's just such an honor."

"Ah, you admire him, eh?" he said.

"Who doesn't admire him?" she said, worshipping the portrait of Hitz. It was the portrait of a tanned, white-haired, omnipotent Zeus, two hundred forty years old. "Who doesn't admire him?" she said again. "He was responsible for setting up the very first gas chamber in Chicago."

"Nothing would please me more," said the painter, "than to put you next to him for all time. Sawing off a limb—that strikes you as appropriate?"

"That is kind of like what I do," she said. She was demure about what she did. What she did was make people comfortable while she killed them.

And while Leora Duncan was posing for her portrait, into the waiting room bounded Dr. Hitz himself. He was seven feet tall, and he boomed with importance, accomplishments, and the joy of living.

"Well, Miss Duncan! Miss Duncan!" he said, and he made a joke. "What are you doing here? This isn't where the people leave. This is where they come in!"

"We're going to be in the same picture together," she said shyly.

"Good!" said Dr. Hitz. "And say, isn't that some picture?"

"I sure am honored to be in it with you," she said.

"Let me tell you, I'm honored to be in it with you. Without women like you, this wonderful world we've got wouldn't be possible."

He saluted her and moved toward the door that led to the delivery rooms. "Guess what was just born," he said.

"I can't," she said.

"Triplets!" he said.

"Triplets!" she said. She was exclaiming over the legal implications of triplets.

The law said that no newborn child could survive unless the parents of the child could find someone who would volunteer to die. Triplets, if they were all to live, called for three volunteers.

"Do the parents have three volunteers?" said Leora Duncan.

"Last I heard," said Dr. Hitz, "they had one, and were trying to scrape another two up."

"I don't think they made it," she said. "Nobody made three appointments with us. Nothing but singles going through today, unless somebody called in after I left. What's the name?"

"Wehling," said the waiting father, sitting up, red-eyed and frowzy. "Edward K. Wehling, Jr., is the name of the happy father-to-be."

He raised his right hand, looked at a spot on the wall, gave a hoarsely wretched chuckle. "Present," he said.

"Oh, Mr. Wehling," said Dr. Hitz, "I didn't see you."

"The invisible man," said Wehling.

"They just phoned me that your triplets have been born," said Dr. Hitz. "They're all fine, and so is the mother. I'm on my way in to see them now."

"Hooray," said Wehling emptily.

"You don't sound very happy," said Dr. Hitz.

"What man in my shoes wouldn't be happy?" said Wehling. He gestured with his hands to symbolize the carefree simplicity. "All I have to do is pick out which one of the triplets is going to live, then deliver my maternal grandfather to the Happy Hooligan, and come back here with a receipt."

Dr. Hitz became rather severe with Wehling, towered over him. "You don't believe in population control, Mr. Wehling?" he said.

"I think it's perfectly keen," said Wehling.

"Would you like to go back to the good old days, when the population of the earth was twenty billion—about to become forty billion, then eighty billion, then one hundred and sixty billion? Do you know what a drupelet is, Mr. Wehling?" said Hitz.

"Nope," said Wehling, sulking.

"A drupelet, Mr. Wehling, is one of the little knobs, one of the little pulpy grains, of a blackberry," said Dr. Hitz. "Without population control, human beings would now be packed on the surface of this old planet like drupelets on a blackberry! Think of it!"

Wehling continued to stare at the spot on the wall.

"In the year 2000," said Dr. Hitz, "before scientists stepped in and laid down the law, there wasn't even enough drinking water to go around, and nothing to eat but seaweed—and still people insisted on their right to reproduce like jackrabbits. And their right, if possible, to live forever."

"I want those kids," said Wehling. "I want all three of them."

"Of course you do," said Dr. Hitz. "That's only human."

"I don't want my grandfather to die, either," said Wehling.

"Nobody's really happy about taking a close relative to the Catbox," said Dr. Hitz sympathetically.

"I wish people wouldn't call it that," said Leora Duncan.

"What?" said Dr. Hitz.

"I wish people wouldn't call it the Catbox, and things like that," she said. "It gives people the wrong impression."

"You're absolutely right," said Dr. Hitz. "Forgive me." He corrected himself, gave the municipal gas chambers their official title, a title no one ever used in conversation. "I should have said 'Ethical Suicide Studios,'" he said.

"That sounds so much better," said Leora Duncan.

"This child of yours—whichever one you decide to keep, Mr. Wehling," said Dr. Hitz. "He or she is going to live on a happy, roomy, clean, rich planet, thanks to population control. In a garden like in that mural there." He shook his head. "Two centuries ago, when I was a young man, it was a hell that nobody thought could last another twenty years. Now centuries of peace and plenty stretch before us as far as the imagination cares to travel."

He smiled luminously.

The smile faded when he saw that Wehling had just drawn a revolver.

Wehling shot Dr. Hitz dead. "There's room for one—a great big one," he said.

And then he shot Leora Duncan. "It's only death," he said to her as she fell. "There! Room for two."

And then he shot himself, making room for all three of his children.

Nobody came running. Nobody, it seemed, had heard the shots.

The painter sat on the top of his stepladder, looking down reflectively on the sorry scene. He pondered the mournful puzzle of life demanding to be born and, once born, demanding to be fruitful . . . to multiply and to live as long as possible—to do all that on a very small planet that would have to last forever.

All the answers that the painter could think of were grim. Even grimmer, surely, than a Catbox, a Happy Hooligan, an Easy Go. He thought of war. He thought of plague. He thought of starvation.

He knew that he would never paint again. He let his paintbrush fall to the dropcloths below. And then he decided he had had about enough of the Happy Garden of Life, too, and he came slowly down from the ladder.

He took Wehling's pistol, really intending to shoot himself. But he didn't have the nerve.

And then he saw the telephone booth in a corner of the room. He went to it, dialed the well-remembered number: 2BR02B.

"Federal Bureau of Termination," said the warm voice of a hostess.

"How soon could I get an appointment?" he asked, speaking carefully.

"We could probably fit you in late this afternoon, sir," she said. "It might even be earlier, if we get a cancellation."

"All right," said the painter, "fit me in, if you please." And he gave her his name, spelling it out.

"Thank you, sir," said the hostess. "Your city thanks you, your country thanks you, your planet thanks you. But the deepest thanks of all is from future generations."

Lovers
Anonymous

Herb White keeps books for the various businesses around our town, and he makes out practically everybody's income tax. Our town is North Crawford, New Hampshire. Herb never got to college, where he would have done well. He learned about bookkeeping and taxes by mail. Herb fought in Korea, came home a hero. And he married Sheila Hinckley, a very pretty, intelligent woman practically all the men in my particular age group had hoped to marry. My particular age group is thirty-three, thirty-four, and thirty-five years old, these days.

On Sheila's wedding day we were twenty-one, twenty-two, and twenty-three. On Sheila's wedding night we all went down to North Crawford Manor and drank. One poor guy got up on the bar and spoke approximately as follows:

"Gentlemen, friends, brothers, I'm sure we wish the newlyweds nothing but happiness. But at the same time I have to say that the pain in our hearts will never die. And I propose that we form a permanent brotherhood of eternal sufferers, to aid each other in any way we can, though Lord knows there's very little anybody can do for pain like ours."

The crowd thought that was a fine idea.

Hay Boyden, who later became a house mover and wrecker, said we ought to call ourselves the Brotherhood of People Who Were Too Dumb to Realize That Sheila Hinckley Might Actually Want to Be a Housewife. Hay had boozy, complicated reasons for suggesting that. Sheila had been the smartest girl in high school, and had been going like a house afire at the University of Vermont, too. We'd all assumed there wasn't any point in serious courting until she'd finished college.

And then, right in the middle of her junior year, she'd quit and married Herb.

"Brother Boyden," said the drunk up on the bar, "I think that is a sterling suggestion. But in all humility I offer another title for our organization, a title in all ways inferior to yours except that it's about ten thousand times easier to say. Gentlemen, friends, brothers, I propose we call ourselves 'Lovers Anonymous.'"

The motion carried. The drunk up on the bar was me.

And like a lot of crazy things in small, old-fashioned towns, Lovers Anonymous lived on and on. Whenever several of us from that old gang happen to get together, somebody is sure to say, "Lovers Anonymous will please come to order." And it is still a standard joke in town to tell anybody who's had his heart broken lately that he should join LA. Don't get me wrong. Nobody in LA still pines for Sheila. We've all more or less got Sheilas of our own. We think about Sheila more than we think about some of our other old girls, I suppose, mainly because of that crazy LA. But as Will Battola, the plumber, said one time, "Sheila Hinckley is now a spare whitewall tire on the Thunderbird of my dreams."

Then about a month ago my good wife served a sordid little piece of news along with the after-dinner coffee and macaroons. She said that Herb and Sheila weren't speaking to each other anymore.

"Now, what are you doing spreading idle gossip like that for?" I said.

"I thought it was my duty to tell you," she said, "since you're the lover-in-chief of Lovers Anonymous."

"I was merely present at the founding," I said, "and as you well know, that was many, many years ago."

"Well, I think you can start *un*-founding," she said.

"Look," I said, "there aren't many laws of life that stand up through the ages, but this is one of the few: People who are contemplating divorce do not buy combination aluminum storm windows and screens for a fifteen-room house." That is my business—combination aluminum storm windows and screens, and here and there a bathtub enclosure. And it was a fact that very recently Herb had bought thirty-seven Fleetwood windows, which is our first-line window, for the fifteen-room ark he called home.

"Families that don't even eat together don't keep together very long," she said.

"What do you know about their eating habits?" I wanted to know.

"Nothing I didn't find out by accident," she said. "I was collecting money for the Heart Fund yesterday." Yesterday was Sunday. "I happened to get there just when they were having Sunday dinner, and there were the girls and Sheila at the dinner table, eating—and no Herb."

"He was probably out on business somewhere," I said.

"That's what I told myself," she said. "But then on my way to the next house I had to go by their old ell—where they keep the firewood and the garden tools."

"Go on."

"And Herb was in there, sitting on a box and eating lunch off a bigger box. I never saw anybody look so sad."

The next day Kennard Pelk, a member of LA in good standing and our chief of police, came into my showroom to complain about a bargain storm window that he had bought from a company that had since gone out of business. "The glass part is stuck halfway up and the screen is rusted out," he said, "and the aluminum is covered with something that looks like blue sugar."

"That's a shame," I said.

"The reason I turn to you is, I don't know where else I can get service."

"With your connections," I said, "couldn't you find out which penitentiary they put the manufacturers in?"

I finally agreed to go over and do what I could, but only if he understood that I wasn't representing the entire industry. "The only windows I stand behind," I said, "are the ones I sell."

And then he told me a screwy thing he'd seen in Herb White's rotten old ell the night before. Kennard had been on his way home in the police cruiser at about two a.m. The thing he'd seen in Herb White's ell was a candle.

"I mean, that old house has fifteen rooms, not counting the ell," said Kennard, "and a family of four—five, if you count the dog. And I couldn't understand how anybody, especially at that time of night, would want to go out to the ell. I thought maybe it was a burglar."

"The only thing worth stealing in that house is the Fleetwood windows."

"Anyway, it was my duty to investigate," said Kennard. "So I snook up to a window and looked in. And there was Herb on a mattress on the floor. He had a bottle of liquor and a glass next to him, and he had a candle stuck in another bottle, and he was reading a magazine by candlelight."

"That was a fine piece of police work," I said.

"He saw me outside the window, and I came closer so he could see who I was. The window was open, so I said to him, 'Hi—I was just wondering who was out here,' and he said, 'Robinson Crusoe.'"

"Robinson Crusoe?" I said.

"Yeah. He was very sarcastic with me," said Kennard. "He asked me if I had the rest of Lovers Anonymous with me. I told him no. And then he asked me if a man's home was still his castle, as far as the police were concerned, or whether that had been changed lately."

"So what did you say, Kennard?"

"What was there *to* say? I buttoned up my holster and went home."

Herb White himself came into my showroom right after Kennard left. Herb had the healthy, happy, excited look people sometimes get when they come down with double pneumonia. "I want to buy three more Fleetwood windows," he said.

"The Fleetwood is certainly a product that everybody can be enthusiastic about," I said, "but I think you're overstepping the bounds of reason. You've got Fleetwoods all around right now."

"I want them for the ell," he said.

"Do you feel all right, Herb?" I asked. "You haven't even got furniture in half the rooms we've already made wind-tight. Besides, you look feverish."

"I've just been taking a long, hard look at my life, is all," he said. "Now, do you want the business or not?"

"The storm window business is based on common sense, and I'd just as soon keep it that way," I replied. "That old ell of yours hasn't had any work done on it for I'll bet fifty years. The clapboards are loose, the sills are shot, and the wind whistles through the gaps in the foundation. You might as well put storm windows on a shredded wheat biscuit."

"I'm having it restored," he said.

"Is Sheila expecting a baby?"

He narrowed his eyes. "I sincerely hope not," he said, "for her sake, for my sake, and for the sake of the child."

I had lunch that day at the drugstore. About half of Lovers Anonymous had lunch at the drugstore. When I sat down, Selma Deal, the woman back of the counter, said, "Well, you great lover, got a quorum now. What you gonna vote about?"

Hay Boyden, the house mover and wrecker, turned to me. "Any new business, Mr. President?"

"I wish you people would quit calling me Mr. President," I said. "My marriage has never been one hundred percent ideal, and I wouldn't be surprised that was the fly in the ointment."

"Speaking of ideal marriages," said Will Battola, the plumber, "you didn't by chance sell some more windows to Herb White, did you?"

"How did you know?"

"It was a guess," he said. "We've been comparing notes here, and as near as we can figure, Herb has managed to give a little piece of remodeling business to every member of LA."

"Coincidence," I said.

"I'd say so, too," said Will, "if I could find anybody who wasn't a member and who still got a piece of the job."

Between us, we estimated Herb was going to put about six thousand dollars into the ell. That was a lot of money for a man in his circumstances to scratch up.

"The job wouldn't have to run more than three thousand if Herb didn't want a kitchen and a bathroom in the thing," said Will. "He's already got a kitchen and a bathroom ten feet from the door between the ell and the house."

Al Tedler, the carpenter, said, "According to the plans Herb gave me this morning, there ain't gonna *be* no door between the ell and the house. There's gonna be a double-studded wall with half-inch Sheetrock, packed with rockwood batts."

"How come double studding?" I asked.

"Herb wants it soundproof."

"How's a body supposed to get from the house to the ell?" I said.

"The body has to go outside, cross about sixty feet of lawn, and go in through the ell's own front door," said Al.

"Kind of a shivery trip on a cold winter's night," I said. "Not many bodies would care to make it barefoot."

And that was when Sheila Hinckley White walked in.

You often hear somebody say that So-and-So is a very well preserved woman. Nine times out of ten So-and-So turns out to be a scrawny woman with pink lipstick who looks as if she had been boiled in lanolin. But Sheila really is well preserved. That day in the drugstore she could have passed for twenty-two.

"By golly," Al Tedler said, "if I had that to cook for me, I wouldn't be any two-kitchen man."

Usually when Sheila came into a place where several members of LA were sitting, we would make some kind of noise to attract her attention and she would do something silly like wiggle her eyebrows or give us a wink. It didn't mean a thing.

But that day in the drugstore we didn't try to catch her eye and she didn't try to catch ours. She was all business. She was carrying a big red book about the size of a cinder block. She returned it to the lending library in the store, paid up, and left.

"Wonder what the book's about," said Hay.

"It's red," I said. "Probably about the fire engine industry."

That was a joke that went a long way back—clear back to what she'd put under her picture in the high school yearbook the year she graduated. Everybody was supposed to predict what kind of work he or she would go into in later life. Sheila put down that she would discover a new planet or be the first woman justice of the Supreme Court or president of a company that manufactured fire engines.

She was kidding, of course, but everybody—including Sheila, I guess— had the idea that she could be anything she set her heart on being.

At her wedding to Herb, I remember, I asked her, "Well now, what's the fire engine industry going to do?"

And she laughed and said, "It's going to have to limp along without me. I'm taking on a job a thousand times as important—keeping a good man healthy and happy, and raising his young."

"What about the seat they've been saving for you on the Supreme Court?"

"The happiest seat for me, and for any woman worthy of the name of woman," she said, "is a seat in a cozy kitchen, with children at my feet."

"You going to let somebody else discover that planet, Sheila?"

"Planets are stones, stone-dead stones," she said. "What I want to discover are my husband, my children, and through them, myself. Let somebody else learn what she can from stones."

After Sheila left the drugstore I went to the lending library to see what the red book was. It was written by the president of some women's college. The title of it was *Woman, the Wasted Sex, or, The Swindle of Housewifery*.

I looked inside the book and found it was divided in these five parts:

I. 5,000,000 B.C.–A.D. 1865, The Involuntary Slave Sex

II. 1866–1919, The Slave Sex Given Pedestals

III. 1920–1945, Sham Equality—Flapper to Rosie the Riveter

IV. 1946–1963, Volunteer Slave Sex—Diaper Bucket to Sputnik

V. Explosion and Utopia

Reva Owley, the woman who sells cosmetics and runs the library, came up and asked if she could help me.

"You certainly can," I said. "You can throw this piece of filth down the nearest sewer."

"It's a very popular book," she said.

"That may be," I said. "Whiskey and repeating firearms were very popular with the redskins. And if this drugstore really wants to make money, you might put in a hashish-and-heroin counter for the teenage crowd."

"Have you read it?" she asked.

"I've read the table of contents," I said.

"At least you've *opened* a book," she said. "That's more than any other member of Lovers Anonymous has done in the past ten years."

"I'll have you know I read a great deal," I said.

"I didn't know that much had been written about storm windows." Reva is a very smart widow.

"You can sure be a snippy woman, on occasion," I said.

"That comes from reading books about what a mess men have made of the world," she said.

The upshot was, I read that book.

What a book it was! It took me a week and a half to get through it, and the more I read, the more I felt as if I were wearing long burlap underwear.

Herb White came into my showroom and caught me reading it. "Improving your mind, I see," he said.

"If something's improved," I said, "I don't know what it is. You've read this, have you?"

"That pleasure and satisfaction was mine," he said. "Where are you now?"

"I've just been through the worst five million years I ever expect to spend," I said. "And some man has finally noticed that maybe things aren't quite as good as they could be for women."

"Theodore Parker?" said Herb.

"Right," I said. Parker was a preacher in Boston about the time of the Civil War.

"Read what he says," said Herb.

So I read out loud: "'The domestic function of woman does not exhaust her powers. To make one half the human race consume its energies in the functions of housekeeper, wife and mother is a monstrous waste of the most precious material God ever made.'"

Herb had closed his eyes while I read. He kept them closed. "Do you realize how hard those words hit me, with the—with the wife I've got?"

"Well," I said, "we all knew you'd been hit by something. Nobody could figure out what it was."

"That book was around the house for weeks," he said. "Sheila was reading it. I didn't pay any attention to it at first. And then one night we were watching Channel Two." Channel Two is the educational television station in Boston. "There was this discussion going on between some college professors about the different theories of how the solar system had been born. Sheila all of a sudden burst into tears, said her brains had turned to mush, said she didn't know anything about anything anymore."

Herb opened his eyes. "There wasn't anything I could say to comfort her. She went off to bed. That book was on the table next to where she'd been sitting. I picked it up and it fell open to the page you just read from."

"Herb," I said, "this isn't any of my business, but—"

"It's your business," he said. "Aren't you president of LA?"

"You don't think there really *is* such a thing!" I said.

"As far as I'm concerned," he said, "Lovers Anonymous is as real as the Veterans of Foreign Wars. How would *you* like it if there was a club whose sole purpose was to make sure you treated your wife right?"

"Herb," I said, "I give you my word of honor—"

He didn't let me finish. "I realize now, ten years too late," he said, "that I've ruined that wonderful woman's life, had her waste all her intelligence and talent—on what?" He shrugged and spread his hands. "On keeping house for a small-town bookkeeper who hardly even finished high school, who's never going to be anything he wasn't on his wedding day."

He hit the side of his head with the heel of his hand. I guess he was punishing himself, or maybe trying to make his brains work better. "Well," he said, "I'm calling in all you anonymous lovers I can to help me put things right—not that I can ever give her back her ten wasted years. When we get the ell fixed up, at least I won't be underfoot all the time, expecting her to cook for me and sew for me and do all the other stupid things a husband expects a housewife to do.

"I'll have a little house all my own," he said, "and I'll be my own little housewife. And anytime Sheila wants to, she can come knock on my door and find out I still love her. She can start studying books again, and become an oceanographer or whatever she wants. And any handyman jobs she needs done on that big old house of hers, her handy neighbor—which is me—will be more than glad to do."

With a very heavy heart I went out to Herb's house early that afternoon to measure the windows of the ell. Herb was at his office. The twin girls were off at school. Sheila didn't seem to be at home, either. I knocked on the kitchen door, and the only answer I got was from the automatic washing machine.

"Whirr, gloop, rattle, slup," it said.

As long as I was there, I decided to make sure the Fleetwoods I'd already installed were working freely. That was how I happened to look in through the living room window and see Sheila lying on the couch. There were books on the floor around her. She was crying.

When I got around to the ell I could see that Herb had certainly been playing house in there. He had a little kerosene range on top of the woodpile, along with pots and pans and canned goods.

There was a Morris chair with a gasoline lantern hanging over it, and a big chopping block next to the chair, and Herb had his pipes and his magazines and his tobacco laid out there. His bed was on the floor, but it was nicely made, with sheets and all. On the walls were photographs of Herb in the Army, Herb on the high school baseball team, and a tremendous print in color of Custer's Last Stand.

The door between the ell and the main house was closed, so I felt free to climb in through a window without feeling I was intruding on Sheila. What I wanted to see was the condition of the sash on the inside. I sat down in the Morris chair and made some notes.

And then I leaned back and lit a cigarette. A Morris chair is a comfortable thing. Sheila came in without my even hearing her.

"Cozy, isn't it?" she said. "I think every man your age should have a hideaway. Herb's ordered storm windows for his Shangri-la, has he?"

"Fleetwoods," I said.

"Good," she said. "Heaven knows Fleetwoods are the best." She looked at the underside of the rotten roof. Pinpricks of sky showed through. "I don't suppose what's happening to Herb and me is any secret," she said.

I didn't know how to answer that.

"You might tell Lovers Anonymous and their Ladies' Auxiliary that Herb and I have never been this happy before," she said.

I couldn't think of any answer for that, either. It was my understanding that Herb's moving into the ell was a great tragedy of recent times.

"And you might tell them," she said, "that it was Herb who got happy first. We had a ridiculous argument about how my brains had turned to mush. And then I went upstairs and waited for him to come to bed—and he didn't. The next morning I found he'd dragged a mattress out here and was sleeping like an angel. ·

"I looked down on him, so happy out here, and I wept. I realized that he'd been a slave all his life, doing things he hated in order to support his mother, and then me, and then me and the girls. His first night out here was probably the first night in his life that he went to sleep wondering who he might be, what he might have become, what he still might be."

"I guess the reason the world seems so upside down so often," I said, "is that everybody figures he's doing things on account of somebody else. Herb figures this whole ell business is a favor to you."

"Anything that makes him happier is a favor to me," she said.

"I read that crazy red book—or I'm reading it," I said.

"Housewifery *is* a swindle, if a woman can do more," she said.

"You going to do more, Sheila?"

"Yes," she said. She had laid out a plan whereby she would get her degree in two years, with a combination of correspondence courses, extension courses, and a couple of summer sessions at Durham, where the state university is. After that she was going to teach.

"I never would have made a plan like that," she told me, "if Herb hadn't called my bluff to the extent he did. Women are awful bluffers sometimes.

"I've started studying," she went on. "I know you looked through the window and saw me with all my books, crying on the couch."

"I didn't think you'd seen me," I said. "I wasn't trying to mind some-body else's business. Kennard Pelk and I both have to look through win-dows from time to time in the line of duty."

"I was crying because I was understanding what a bluffer I'd been in school," she said. "I was only pretending to care about the things I was learning, back in those silly old days. Now I *do* care. That's why I was cry-ing. I've been crying a lot lately, but it's good crying. It's about discovery, it's about grown-up joy."

I had to admit it was an interesting adjustment Sheila and Herb were making. One thing bothered me, though, and there wasn't any polite way I could ask about it. I wondered if they were going to quit sleeping with each other forever.

Sheila answered the question without my having to ask it.

"Love laughs at locksmiths," she said.

About a week later I took the copy of *Woman, the Wasted Sex, or, The Swindle of Housewifery* to a luncheon meeting of LA at the drugstore. I was through with the thing, and I passed it around.

"You didn't let your wife read this, did you?" Hay Boyden asked.

"Certainly," I said.

"She'll walk out on you and the kids," said Hay, "and become a rear ad-miral."

"Nope," I said.

"You give a woman a book like this," said Al Tedler, "and you're gonna have a restless woman on your hands."

"Not necessarily," I said. "When I gave my wife this book I gave her a magic bookmark to go with it." I nodded. "That magic bookmark kept her under control all the way through."

Everybody wanted to know what the bookmark was.

"One of her old report cards," I said.

Hal Irwin's Magic Lamp

Hal Irwin built his magic lamp in his basement in Indianapolis, in the summer of 1929. It was supposed to look like Aladdin's lamp. It was an old tin teapot with a piece of cotton stuck in the spout for a wick. Hal bored a hole in it for a doorbell button, which he hooked up to two flashlight batteries and a buzzer inside. Like many husbands back then, he had a workshop in the basement.

The idea was, it was a cute way to call servants. You'd rub the teapot as if it were a magic lamp, and you'd push the button on the side. The buzzer'd go off, and a servant, if you had one, would come and ask you what you wished.

Hal didn't have a servant, but he was going to borrow one from a friend. Hal was a customers' man in a brokerage house, and he knew his business inside out. He'd made half a million dollars on the stock market, and nobody knew it. Not even his wife.

He made the magic lamp as a surprise for his wife. He was going to tell her it was a magic lamp. And then he was going to rub it and wish for a big new house. And then he was going to prove to her that it really was a magic lamp, because every wish was going to come true.

When he made the lamp, the interior decorator was finishing up the insides of a big new French château Hal had ordered built out on North Meridian Street.

When Hal made that lamp, he and Mary were living in a shotgun house down in all the soot at Seventeenth and Illinois Street. They'd been married two years, and Hal hadn't had her out more than five or six times. He wasn't being stingy. He was saving up to buy her all the happiness a girl could ever ask for, and he was going to hand it to her in one fell swoop.

Hal was ten years older than Mary, so it was easy for him to buffalo her about a lot of things, and one of the things was money. He wouldn't talk money with her, never let her see a bill or a bank statement, never told her how much he made or what he was doing with it. All Mary had to go by was the piddling allowance he gave her to run the house, so she guessed they were poor as Job's turkey.

Mary didn't mind that. That girl was as wholesome as a peach and a glass of milk. Being poor gave her room to swing her religion around. When the end of the month came, and they'd eaten pretty well, and she hadn't asked Hal for an extra dime, she felt like a little white lamb. And she thought Hal was happy, even though he was broke, because she was giving him a hundred million dollars' worth of love.

There was only one thing about being poor that really bothered Mary, and that was the way Hal always seemed to think she wanted to be rich. She did her best to convince him that wasn't true.

When Hal would carry on about how well other folks were doing—about the high life at the country clubs and the lakes—Mary'd talk about the millions of folks in China who didn't have a roof over their heads or anything to eat.

"Me doing velly well for Chinaman," Hal said one night.

"You're doing very well for an American or for an anything!" Mary said. She hugged him, so he'd be proud and strong and happy.

"Well, your successful Chinaman's got a piece of news for you," Hal said. "Tomorrow you're gonna get a cook. I told an employment agency to send one out."

Actually, the person arriving the next day, whose name was Ella Rice, wouldn't be coming to cook, and wasn't from an employment agency. She already had a job with a friend of Hal's whom Mary didn't know. The friend would give her the day off so she could play the part of a jinni.

Hal had rehearsed her at the friend's house, and he would pay her well. She needed the extra money. She was going to have a baby in about six weeks, she thought. All she had to do was put on a turban when the time came, when Hal showed Mary his magic lamp, and rubbed it and rang its buzzer. Then she would say, "I am the jinni. What do you want?"

After that, Hal would start wishing for expensive things he already owned, which Mary hadn't seen yet. His first wish would be for a Marmon town car. It would already be parked out front. Every time he made a wish, starting with that one, Ella Rice would say, "You got it."

But that was tomorrow, and today was today, and Mary thought Hal didn't like her cooking. She was a wonderful cook. "Honey," she said, "are my meals that bad?"

"They're great. I have no complaints whatsoever."

"Then why should we get a cook?"

He looked at her as though she were deaf, dumb, and blind. "Don't you ever think of my pride?" he asked her. He put his hand over her mouth. "Honeybunch, don't tell me again about people dying like flies in China. I am who I am where I am, and I've got pride."

Mary wanted to cry. Here she thought she'd been making Hal feel better, and she'd been making him feel worse instead.

"What do you think I think when I see Bea Muller or Nancy Gossett downtown in their fur coats, buying out the department stores?" Hal said. "I think about you, stuck in this house. I think, Well, for crying out loud, I used to be president of their husbands' fraternity house! For crying out loud, me and Harve Muller and George Gossett used to be the Grand

Triumvirate. That's what they used to call the three of us in college—the Grand Triumvirate! We used to run the college, and I'm not kidding. We founded the Owl's Club, and I was president.

"Look where they live, and look where we live," Hal went on. "We oughta be right out there with 'em at Fifty-seventh and North Meridian! We oughta have a cottage right next to 'em at Lake Maxinkuckee! Least I can do is get my wife a cook."

Ella Rice arrived at the house the next day at three o'clock as planned. In a paper bag she had the turban Hal had given her. Hal wasn't home yet. Ella was supposed to pretend to be the new cook instead of a jinni until Hal arrived at three-thirty. Which she did.

What Hal hadn't counted on, though, was that Mary would find Ella so likable, but so pitiful, not a cook, but a fellow human being in awful trouble. He had expected them to go to the kitchen to talk about this and that, what Hal liked to eat, and so on. But Mary asked Ella about her pregnancy, which was obvious. Ella, who was no actress, and at the end of her rope in any case, burst into tears. The two women, one white, one black, stayed in the living room and talked about their lives instead.

Ella wasn't married. The father of her child had beaten her up when he found out she was pregnant, and then taken off for parts unknown. She had aches and pains in many places, and no relatives, and didn't know how much longer she could do housework. She repeated what she had told Hal, that her pregnancy still had six weeks to go, she thought. Mary said she wished she could have a baby, but couldn't. That didn't help.

When Hal parked the new Marmon out front and entered the house, neither woman was in any condition to enjoy the show he had planned. They were a mess! But he imagined his magic lamp would cheer them up. He went to get it from the closet where he had hidden it upstairs, then brought it into the living room and said, "My goodness! Look what I just found. I do believe it's a magic lamp. Maybe if I rub it a jinni will appear, and she will make a wish come true." He hadn't considered hiring a black man to play the jinni. He was scared of black men.

Ella Rice recognized her cue, and got off the couch to do the crazy thing the white man was going to pay for. Anything for money. It hurt her a lot to stand, after sitting still for a half-hour. Even Hal could see that.

Hal wished for a Marmon, and the jinni said, "You got it." The three went out to the car, and Hal told them to get in, that it was his, paid for in full. The women sat in the backseat, and Mary said to Ella, not to Hal, "Thanks a lot. This is wonderful. I think I'm going nuts."

Hal drove up North Meridian Street, pointing out grand houses left and right. Every time he did that, Mary said that she wouldn't want it, that Hal could throw his magic lamp out the window, as far as she was concerned. What she was really upset about was the humiliating use he was making of her new friend Ella.

Hal stopped in front of a French château on which workmen were putting finishing touches. He turned off the motor, rubbed the lamp, buzzed the buzzer, and said, "Jinni, give me a new house at 5644 North Meridian Street."

Mary said to Ella, "You don't have to do this. Don't answer him."

Ella got mad at Mary now. "I'm getting *paid!*" Everything Ella said was in a dialect typical of a person of her race and class and degree of education back then. Now she groaned. She was going into labor.

They took Ella Rice to the city hospital, the only one that admitted black people. She had a healthy boy baby, and Hal paid for it.

Hal and Mary brought her and the baby back to their new house. The old house was on the market. And Mary, who couldn't have a baby herself, fixed up one of the seven bedrooms for mother and child, with cute furniture and wallpaper and toys the baby wasn't old enough to play with. Mother and child had their own bathroom.

The baby was christened in a black church, and Mary was there. Hal wasn't. He and Mary were hardly speaking. Ella named the baby Irwin, in honor of the people who were so good to her. His last name was the same as hers. He was Irwin Rice.

Mary had never loved Hal, but had managed to like him. It was a job. There weren't many ways for women to earn their own money back then, and she hadn't inherited anything, and wouldn't unless Hal died. Hal was no dumber than most men she'd known. She certainly didn't want to be alone. They had a black yard man and a black laundress, and a white housemaid from Ireland, who lived in the mansion. Mary insisted on doing the cooking. Ella Rice offered to do it, at least for herself. But nobody except Mary was allowed to cook.

She hated the new house so much, and the gigantic car, which embarrassed her, that she couldn't even like Hal anymore. This was very tough on Hal, extremely tough, as you can well imagine. Not only was he not getting love, or what looked like love, from the woman he'd married, but she was giving ten times more love than he'd ever gotten, and nonstop, to a baby as black as the ace of spades!

Hal didn't tell anybody at the office about the situation at home, because it would have made him look like a weakling. The housemaid from Ireland treated him like a weakling, as though Mary were the real power, and crazy as a bedbug.

Ella Rice of course made her own bed, and kept her bedroom and bathroom very neat. Things didn't seem right to her, either, but what could she do? Ella nursed the baby, so its food was all taken care of. Ella didn't eat downstairs with the Irwins. Not even Mary considered that a possibility. Ella didn't eat with the servants in the kitchen, either. She brought upstairs whatever Mary had prepared especially for her, and ate it in her bedroom.

At the office, anyway, Hal was making more money than ever, trading stocks and bonds for others, but also investing heavily for himself in stocks, never mind bonds, on margin. "On margin" meant he paid only a part of the full price of a stock, and owed the rest to the brokerage where he worked. And then the stock's value would go up, because other people wanted it, and Hal would sell it. He could then pay off his debt to the brokerage, and the rest of the profit was his to keep.

So he could buy more stock on margin.

Three months after the magic-lamp episode, the stock market crashed. The stocks Hal had bought on margin became worthless. All of a sudden, everybody thought they were too expensive at any price. So what Hal Irwin owed to his brokerage, and what his brokerage owed to a bank in turn, was more than everything he owned—the new house, the unsold old house, the furniture, the car, and on and on. You name it!

He wasn't loved at home even in good times, so Hal went out a seventh-story window without a parachute. All over the country, unloved men in his line of work were going out windows without parachutes. The bank foreclosed on both houses, and took the Marmon, too. Then the bank went bust, and anybody with savings in it lost those savings.

Mary had another house to go to, which was her widowed father's farm outside the town of Crawfordsville. The only place Ella Rice could think of to go with her baby was the black church where the baby had been baptized. Mary went there with them. A lot of mothers with babies or children, and old people, and cripples, and even perfectly healthy young people were sleeping there. There was food. Mary didn't ask where it came from. That was the last Mary would see of Ella and Irwin Rice. Ella was eating, and then she would nurse the baby.

When Mary got to her father's farmhouse, the roof was leaking and the electricity had been shut off. But her father took her in. How could he not? She told him about the homeless people in the black church. She asked him what he thought would become of them in such awful times.

"The poor take care of the poor," he said.

Coda to My Career
as a Writer
for Periodicals

Some of these stories have been edited for this book, with minor and major glitches repaired, which editors and I should have repaired before they were printed the first time. Rereading three of them so upset me, because the premise and the characters of each were so promising, and the denouement so asinine, that I virtually rewrote the denouement before I could stop myself. Some "editing"! They are "The Powder-Blue Dragon," "The Boy Who Hated Girls," and "Hal Irwin's Magic Lamp." As fossils, they are fakes on the order of Piltdown Man, half human being, half the orangutan I used to be.

No matter how clumsily I wrote when I was starting out, there were magazines that would publish such orangutans. And there were others that, to their credit, would not touch my stuff with rubber gloves. I wasn't offended or ashamed. I understood. I was nothing if not modest. I remember a cartoon I saw long ago, in which a psychiatrist was saying to a patient, "You don't have an inferiority complex. You *are* inferior." If the patient could afford a psychiatrist, he was earning a living somehow, despite his genuine inferiority. That was my case, too, and the evidence seems to be that I got better.

Thanks to popular magazines, I learned on the job to be a fiction writer. Such paid literary apprenticeships, with standards of performance so low, don't exist anymore. Mine was an opportunity to get to know myself. Those who wrote for self-consciously literary publications had this advantage, their talent and sophistication aside: They already knew what they could do and who they were.

There may be more Americans than ever now embarking on voyages of self-discovery like mine, by writing stories, come hell or high water, as well as they can. I lecture at eight colleges and universities each year, and have been doing so for two decades. Half of those one hundred sixty institutions have a writer-in-residence and a course in creative writing. When I quit General Electric to become a writer, there were only two such courses, one at the University of Iowa, the other at Stanford, which my President's daughter now attends.

Given that it is no longer possible to make a living writing short stories, and that the odds against a novel's being successful are a thousand to one, creative-writing courses could be perceived as frauds, as would pharmacy courses if there were no drugstores. Be that as it may, students themselves demanded creative writing courses while they were demanding so many other things, passionately and chaotically, during the Vietnam War.

What students wanted and got, and what so many of their children are getting, was a *cheap* way to externalize what was inside them, to see in black-and-white who they were and what they might become. I italicize *cheap* because it takes a ton of money to make a movie or a TV show. Never mind that you have to deal with the scum of the earth if you try to make one.

There are on many campuses, moreover, local papers, weeklies or monthlies, that publish short stories but cannot pay for them. What the heck, practicing an art isn't a way to earn money. It's a way to make one's soul grow.

Bon voyage.

. · . · ·

I still write for periodicals from time to time, but never fiction, and only when somebody asks me to. I am not the dynamic self-starter I used to be. An excellent alternative weekly in Indianapolis, *NUVO*, asked me only a month ago to write an essay for no pay on the subject of what it is like to be a native Middle Westerner. I have replied as follows:

"Breathes there the man, with soul so dead, who never to himself has said, this is my own, my native land!"

This famous celebration of no-brainer patriotism by the Scotsman Sir Walter Scott (1771–1832), when stripped of jingoistic romance, amounts only to this: Human beings come into this world, for their own good, as instinctively territorial as timber wolves or honeybees. Not long ago, human beings who strayed too far from their birthplace and relatives, like all other animals, would be committing suicide.

This dread of not crossing well-understood geographical boundaries still makes sense in many parts of the world, in what used to be Yugoslavia in Europe, for example, or Rwanda in Africa. It is, however, now excess instinctual baggage in most of North America, thank God, thank God. It lives on in this country, as obsolescent survival instincts often do, as feelings and manners that are by and large harmless, that can even be comical.

Thus do I and millions like me tell strangers that we are Middle Westerners, as though we deserved some kind of a medal for being that. All I can say in our defense is that natives of Texas and Brooklyn are even more preposterous in their territorial vanity.

Nearly countless movies about Texans and Brooklynites are lessons for such people in how to behave ever more stereotypically. Why have there been no movies about supposedly typical Middle Western heroes, models to which we, too, might then conform?

All I've got now is an aggressively nasal accent.

. · . · ·

About that accent: When I was in the Army during the Second World War, a white Southerner said to me, "Do you *have to talk* that way?"

I might have replied, "Oh, yeah? At least my ancestors never owned slaves," but the training session at the rifle range at Fort Bragg in North Carolina seemed neither the time nor the place to settle his hash.

I might have added that some of the greatest words ever spoken in American history were uttered with just such a Jew's-harp twang, including the Gettysburg Address of Abraham Lincoln of Illinois and these by Eugene V. Debs of Terre Haute, Indiana: "While there is a lower class I am in it, while there is a criminal element I am of it; while there is a soul in prison, I am not free."

I would have kept to myself that the borders of Indiana, when I was a boy, cradled not only the birthplace of Eugene V. Debs, but the national headquarters of the Ku Klux Klan.

Illinois had Carl Sandburg and Al Capone.

Yes, and the thing on top of the house to keep the weather out is the *ruff*, and the stream in back of the house is the *crick*.

Every race and subrace and blend thereof is native to the Middle West. I myself am a purebred Kraut. Our accents are by no means uniform. My twang is only fairly typical of European-Americans raised some distance north of the former Confederate States of America. It appeared to me when I began this essay that I was on a fool's errand, that we could be described en masse only as what we weren't. We weren't Texans or Brooklynites or Californians or Southerners, and so on.

To demonstrate to myself the folly of distinguishing us, one by one, from Americans born anywhere else, I imagined a crowd on Fifth Avenue in New York City, where I am living now, and another crowd on State Street in Chicago, where I went to a university and worked as a reporter half a century ago. I was not mistaken about the sameness of the faces and clothing and apparent moods.

But the more I pondered the people of Chicago, the more aware I became of an enormous presence there. It was almost like music, music unheard in New York or Boston or San Francisco or New Orleans.

It was Lake Michigan, an ocean of pure water, the most precious substance in all this world.

Nowhere else in the Northern Hemisphere are there tremendous bodies of pure water like our Great Lakes, save for Asia, where there is only Lake Baikal. So there is something distinctive about native Middle Westerners, after all. Get this: When we were born, there had to have been incredible quantities of fresh water all around us, in lakes and streams and rivers and raindrops and snowdrifts, and no undrinkable salt water anywhere!

Even my taste buds are Middle Western on that account. When I swim in the Atlantic or the Pacific, the water tastes all wrong to me, even though it is in fact no more nauseating, as long as you don't swallow it, than chicken soup.

There were also millions and millions of acres of topsoil around us and our mothers when we were born, as flat as pool tables and as rich as chocolate cake. The Middle West is not a desert.

When I was born, in 1922, barely a hundred years after Indiana became the nineteenth state in the Union, the Middle West already boasted a constellation of cities with symphony orchestras and museums and libraries, and institutions of higher learning, and schools of music and art, reminiscent of the Austro-Hungarian Empire before the First World War. One could almost say that Chicago was our Vienna, Indianapolis our Prague, Cincinnati our Budapest, and Cleveland our Bucharest.

To grow up in such a city, as I did, was to find such cultural institutions as ordinary as police stations or firehouses. So it was reasonable for a young person to daydream of becoming some sort of artist or intellectual, if not a policeman or fireman. So I did. So did many like me.

Such provincial capitals, which is what they would have been called in Europe, were charmingly self-sufficient with respect to the fine arts. We

294 | Kurt Vonnegut

sometimes had the director of the Indianapolis Symphony Orchestra to supper, or writers and painters, or architects like my father, of local renown.

I studied clarinet under the first-chair clarinetist of our symphony orchestra. I remember the orchestra's performance of Tchaikovsky's *1812 Overture*, in which the cannons' roars were supplied by a policeman firing blank cartridges into an empty garbage can. I knew the policeman. He sometimes guarded street crossings used by students on their way to or from School 43, my school, the *James Whitcomb Riley School*.

It is unsurprising, then, that the Middle West has produced so many artists of such different sorts, from world-class to merely competent, as provincial cities and towns in Europe used to do.

I see no reason this satisfactory state of affairs should not go on and on, unless funding for instruction in and celebration of the arts, and especially in public school systems, is withdrawn.

Participation in an art is not simply one of many possible ways to make a living, an obsolescent trade as we approach the year 2000. Participation in an art, at bottom, has nothing to do with earning money. Participation in an art, although unrewarded by wealth or fame, and as the Middle West has encouraged so many of its young to discover for themselves so far, is a way to make one's soul grow.

No artist from anywhere, however, not even Shakespeare, not even Beethoven, not even James Whitcomb Riley, has changed the course of so many lives all over the planet as have four hayseeds in Ohio, two in Dayton and two in Akron. How I wish Dayton and Akron were in Indiana! Ohio could have Kokomo and Gary.

Orville and Wilbur Wright were in Dayton in 1903 when they invented the airplane.

Dr. Robert Holbrook Smith and William Griffith Wilson were in Akron in 1935 when they devised the Twelve Steps to sobriety of Alcoholics Anonymous. By comparison with Smith and Wilson, Sigmund Freud was a piker when it came to healing dysfunctional minds and lives.

Beat that! Let the rest of the world put that in their pipes and smoke it, not to mention Cole Porter, Hoagy Carmichael, Frank Lloyd Wright, and Louis Sullivan, Twyla Tharp and Bob Fosse, Ernest Hemingway and Saul Bellow, Mike Nichols and Elaine May. Toni Morrison!

Larry Bird!

New York and Boston and other ports on the Atlantic have Europe for an influential, often importunate neighbor. Middle Westerners do not. Many of us of European ancestry are on that account ignorant of our families' past in the Old World and the culture there. Our only heritage is American. When Germans captured me during the Second World War, one asked me, "Why are you making war against your brothers?" I didn't have a clue what he was talking about. . . .

Anglo-Americans and African-Americans whose ancestors came to the Middle West from the South commonly have a much more compelling awareness of a homeland elsewhere in the past than do I—in Dixie, of course, not the British Isles or Africa.

What geography can give all Middle Westerners, along with the fresh water and topsoil, if they let it, is awe for a fertile continent stretching forever in all directions.

Makes you religious. Takes your breath away.

Grateful acknowledgment is made to the following publications, where the stories collected here first appeared:

Argosy, for "A Present for Big Saint Nick" (published as "A Present for Big Nick") and "Souvenir."

The Atlantic Monthly, for *"Der Arme Dolmetscher."*

Cape Cod Compass, for "The Cruise of *The Jolly Roger."*

Collier's, for "Any Reasonable Offer," "Mnemonics," "The Package," "Poor Little Rich Town," and "Thanasphere."

Cosmopolitan, for "Bagombo Snuff Box," © 1954 Hearst Communications, Inc.; "Find Me a Dream," © 1961 Hearst Communications, Inc.; "The Powder-Blue Dragon," © 1954 Hearst Communications, Inc.; and

International Policy Exchange Series

Published in collaboration with the
Center for International Policy Exchanges
University of Maryland

Series Editors
Douglas J. Besharov
Neil Gilbert

SCHOOL of
PUBLIC POLICY

YOUTH LABOR IN TRANSITION

Inequalities, Mobility, and Policies in Europe

Edited by

JACQUELINE O'REILLY

JANINE LESCHKE

RENATE ORTLIEB

MARTIN SEELEIB-KAISER

PAOLA VILLA

OXFORD
UNIVERSITY PRESS

OXFORD
UNIVERSITY PRESS

Oxford University Press is a department of the University of Oxford. It furthers
the University's objective of excellence in research, scholarship, and education
by publishing worldwide. Oxford is a registered trade mark of Oxford University
Press in the UK and certain other countries.

Published in the United States of America by Oxford University Press
198 Madison Avenue, New York, NY 10016, United States of America.

© Oxford University Press 2019

Library of Congress Cataloging-in-Publication
Data Names: O'Reilly, Jacqueline, 1964– editor. | Leschke, Janine, editor. |
Ortlieb, Renate, editor. | Seeleib-Kaiser, Martin, editor. | Villa, Paola, 1949– editor.
Title: Youth labor in transition : inequalities, mobility, and policies in Europe /
edited by Jacqueline O'Reilly, Janine Leschke, Renate Ortlieb,
Martin Seeleib-Kaiser, and Paola Villa.
Description: New York, NY : Oxford University Press, [2019] |
Series: International policy exchange series | Includes bibliographical references and index.
Identifiers: LCCN 2018028252| ISBN 9780190864798 (jacketed : alk. paper) |
ISBN 9780190864811 (epub) | ISBN 9780190864828 (online component)
Subjects: LCSH: Youth—Employment—Europe. | Young adults—Employment—Europe. |
Labor policy—Europe. | School-to-work transition—Europe.
Classification: LCC HD6276.E82 U6645 2019 | DDC 331.3/47094—dc23
LC record available at https://lccn.loc.gov/2018028252

9 8 7 6 5 4 3 2 1

Printed by Sheridan Books, Inc., United States of America

CONTENTS

ACKNOWLEDGMENTS

Writing at a time of ongoing Brexit negotiations, we cannot understate what an enormous privilege it has been to work with so many intelligent, diligent, and good-humored people on this project from across Europe. From Ireland to Turkey and from Greece to Estonia, we have had the pleasure and intellectual stimulation of discussing this work with research organizations from 19 countries and 25 research partners, alongside external academic reviewers and policy stakeholders. The chapters in this book are only a small part of the vast quantity of work produced during the course of the project. An extensive round of working papers, policy briefs, and videos are available on the project website, Strategic Transitions for Youth Labour in Europe (STYLE; http://www.style-research.eu), via EurActiv, and in contributions to the STYLE e-handbook (http://www.style-handbook.eu). Thank you to all of you who have made this such a vibrant and productive project.

This book would not have been possible without the generous investment provided by the European Union's Seventh Framework Programme for research, technological development, and demonstration under grant agreement No. 613256. We are very grateful for the careful guidance and support provided by our project officers at the European Commission, Dr. Georgios Papanagnou and Marc Goffart. Their support was excellent on many dimensions, ensuring not only that we achieved our contractual and administrative obligations but also that our endeavors contributed to a high-quality international academic debate. The views expressed here are those of the authors and do not necessarily reflect the official opinions of the European Union. Neither the European Union institutions and bodies nor any person acting on their behalf may be held responsible for the use that may be made of the information contained therein.

We extend a massively warm thank-you to the people who kept the big administrative and financial wheels on this project turning, allowing us to roll on with the heart of the academic endeavor. You really have been a great team to work with. Providing good-humored and outstanding professional support, that so often went well beyond the call of duty, and your job descriptions, thank you: John Clinton, Francesca Anderson, Chris Matthews, Alison Gray, Rosie Mulgrue, Andrea Mckoy, and Prof. Aidan Berry from the University of Brighton Business School.

The editors are grateful to the contributors for their patience in responding to our numerous requests for revisions to their original manuscripts. All the contributors have expressed their gratitude to us for the excellent English language editing provided by Niamh Warde. She was always meticulously constructive and good humored in helping transform our (at times impenetrable) academic prose into readable English, together with the careful support of Daniela Benati in preparing the manuscript.

The editors and authors also thank the following individuals for participating in STYLE project meetings and providing critically constructive feedback on draft chapters: Brendan Burchell (University of Cambridge, UK), Günther Schmid (Berlin Social Science Center (WZB), Germany), Colette Fagan (University of Manchester, UK), Maria Jepsen (ETUI, Belgium), Glenda Quintini (Organization for Economic Co-operation and Development, France), Jochen Clasen (University of Edinburgh, UK), Mark Stuart (University of Leeds, UK), Bent Greve (University of Roskilde, Denmark), Marge Unt (Coordinator of EXCEPT, Tallinn University, Estonia), Chiara Saraceno (Collegio Carlo Alberto, Italy), Paweł Kaczmarczyk (University of Warsaw, Poland), Jan Brzozowski (Krakow University of Economics, Poland), Claire Wallace (University of Aberdeen, UK), Traute Meyer (University of Southampton, UK), Nigel Meager (IES, UK), Marc Cowling (University of Brighton, UK), Fatoş Gökşen (Koç University, Turkey), Niall O'Higgins (ILO, Switzerland), Ruud Muffels (University of Tilburg, the Netherlands), Marc van der Meer (University of Tilburg, the Netherlands), Eskil Wadensjö (SOFI, Stockholm University, Sweden), Ute Klammer (University of Duisburg-Essen, Germany), Jale Tosun (Coordinator of CUPESSE, University of Heidelberg, Germany), Katarina Lindahl (European Commission, DG EMPLOY), Thomas Biegert (Berlin Social Science Center (WZB), Germany), Zeynep Cemalcilar (Koç University, Turkey), Torild Hammer (Norwegian Social Research, Norway), Agata Patecka (SOLIDAR), Ramon Pena-Casas (OSE, Belgium), Karen Roiy (Business Europe), and Giorgio Zecca and Clementine Moyart (European Youth Forum). We thank our commissioning editor at Oxford University Press, Dana Bliss; the series editor, Neil Gilbert; and particularly Doug Besharov, who provided very valuable advice when he attended our meeting in Krakow in January 2017.

We are also grateful for the further comments on earlier drafts provided remotely by Jose Luis Arco-Tirado (University of Granada, Spain), Jason Heyes (University of Sheffield, UK), Anne Horvath (European Commission), Maria Iacovou (University of Cambridge, UK), Russell King (University of Sussex, UK), Bernhard Kittel (University of Vienna, Austria), Martin Lukes (University of Economics, Prague, Czech Republic), William Maloney (Newcastle University, UK), Emily Rainsford (Newcastle University, UK), Bettina Schuck (University of Heidelberg, Germany), Peter Sloane (Swansea University, UK), Nadia Steiber (University of Vienna, Austria), Robert Strohmeyer (University of Mannheim, Germany), Mihaela Vancea (Pompeu Fabra University, Spain), Jonas Felbo-Kolding (University of Copenhagen, Denmark), Mihails Hazans (University of Latvia, Latvia), Felix Hörisch (University of Heidelberg, Germany), Øystein Takle Lindholm (Oslo and Akershus University College of Applied Sciences, Norway), Tiiu Paas and Andres Võrk (University of Tartu, Estonia), Magnus Paulsen Hansen (Copenhagen Business School, Denmark), and the Q-Step Team (University of Kent, UK).

Earlier versions of the chapters were presented and discussed at project meetings kindly hosted by the following partner organizations: CROME, University of Brighton (UK), Koç University (Turkey), Grenoble École de Management (France), Institute for Employment Studies (UK), Copenhagen Business School (Denmark), University of Turin (Italy), and the Krakow University of Economics (Poland). Thank you for making our serious discussions so convivial.

Some of the chapters have been presented at numerous international conferences, including the International Sociological Association in Yokohama, 2014; a mini-conference of the Society for the Advancement of Socio-Economics held at the London School of Economics, July 2015, held in conjunction with the EU-funded cupesse.eu project; a special session at the Council for European Studies meeting in Philadelphia with former EU Commissioner László Andor, 2016, and held in conjunction with the EU-funded negotiate-research.eu and Livewhat projects; a special session at the Work, Employment and Society conference at the University of Leeds, 2016, held in conjunction with the EU-funded except-project.eu and cupesse.eu; and a special stream at the European Social Policy Association conference (ESPAnet) at Erasmus University, Rotterdam, 2016, held in conjunction with the EU-funded negotiate-research.eu.

In addition to the expert academic advice, authors also benefited from discussing their early findings with local advisory boards across Europe; these boards were composed of a number of non-governmental organizations, charities, public policymakers, and trade union and employers' organizations. In particular, we are grateful for the regular participation and discussions with Christine Lewis (UNISON), Katerina Rudiger (CIPD), Edward Badu (North London Citizens, UK), Menno Bart and Even Hagelien (EUROCIETT), Alvin Carpio (Young Fabians, UK), Abi Levitt and Ronan McDonald (Tomorrow's

People, UK), Liina Eamets (Estonian Agricultural Registers and Information Board), Tomáš Janotík and Mária Mišečková (Profesia, Slovakia), Aime Lauk (Statistics Estonia), Anne Lauringson and Mari Väli (Estonian Unemployment Insurance Fund), Martin Mýtny (Oracle, Slovakia), and Tony Mernagh (Brighton and Hove Economic Partnership). Supporting this communications platform, Natalie Sarkic-Todd and Irene Marchi have been wonderful partners in helping promote the results of this research through EurActiv. We thank you all very much for your participation in this project; it has really enriched our discussions.

Last but not least, the fecundity of our research team was evidenced not only in their numerous publications but also in the arrival of 11 babies born to researchers on this project (2013–2017)—a vibrant testament to the youthfulness of our researchers and their ability to combine academic careers alongside making transitions to having families of one, two, and, in some cases, three children. I hope the parents look back on the time spent on this project as a good investment, and that when their own children grow up, they can see what their mums and dads were up to late at night.

We hope that some of the findings from this research will be of benefit to young people making their way through the challenging transitions from youth to adulthood in Europe and further afield. All royalties from the printed version of this book will be donated to the Child Development Fund (www.childfund-stiftung.de) to support the educational needs of disadvantaged children in East Africa through school and vocational school fellowships that are particularly focused on supporting young girls.

This has been an enormously rewarding project, and we feel very privileged to have had the opportunity to contribute some of our energy to understanding and explaining the problems that need to be addressed concerning youth labor in transition.

Jacqueline O'Reilly, Janine Leschke, Renate Ortlieb,
Martin Seeleib-Kaiser, and Paola Villa
Brighton, Copenhagen, Graz, Tübingen, and Trento, July 2017

ABBREVIATIONS AND ACRONYMS

COUNTRIES

AT	Austria
BE	Belgium
BG	Bulgaria
CH	Switzerland
CY	Cyprus
CZ	Czech Republic
DE	Germany
DK	Denmark
EE	Estonia
EL	Greece
ES	Spain
FI	Finland
FR	France
HR	Croatia
HU	Hungary
IE	Ireland
IS	Iceland
IT	Italy
LT	Lithuania
LU	Luxembourg
LV	Latvia

MK	Macedonia
MT	Malta
NL	Netherlands
NO	Norway
PL	Poland
PT	Portugal
RO	Romania
SE	Sweden
SI	Slovenia
SK	Slovakia
TR	Turkey
UK	United Kingdom
US	United States

ALMP	active labor market policy
BHPS	British Household Panel Survey
CCI	cultural and creative industry
CEE	Central and Eastern Europe
CSRs	country-specific recommendations
DG	Directorate General
EC	European Commission
ECB	European Central Bank
EES	European Employment Strategy
EMCO	European Commission Employment Committee
EPL	employment protection legislation
ESS	European Social Survey
EST	employment status trajectories
ETUC	European Trade Union Confederation
EU	European Union
EU-LFS	European Union Labour Force Survey
EURES	European Employment Services
Eurofound	European Foundation for the Improvement of Living and Working Conditions
Eurostat	Statistical Office of the European Union
EU-SILC	European Union Survey on Income and Living Conditions
EU2 2007	accession countries to the EU: Bulgaria and Romania
EU8 2004	accession countries to the EU: Czech Republic, Estonia, Hungary, Latvia, Lithuania, Poland, Slovakia, and Slovenia
EU28	European Union 28 countries
EVS	European Values Study
EWCS	European Working Conditions Survey
FTE	full-time equivalent

GDP	gross domestic product
HPAC	hierarchical age–period–cohort (regression model)
ICT	Information/Communication Technologies Sector
ILO	International Labour Organization
ISCED	International Standard Classification of Education
ISCO	International Standard Classification of Occupations
ISEI	International Socio-Economic Index of Occupational Status
KM	Kaplan–Meier (estimator)
LABREF	Labour Market Reforms Database
LFS	Labor Force Survey
LIFO	last-in, first-out
LMI	labor market intermediary
MISSOC	Mutual Information System on Social Protection
NACE	Statistical Classification of Economic Activities
NCDS	National Child Development Study
NEET	not in employment, education, or training
NGO	non-governmental organization
OECD	Organization for Economic Co-operation and Development
OLM	occupational labor markets
OM	optimal matching
OMC	open method of coordination
ONS-LS	Office for National Statistics Longitudinal Study
PES	public employment services
PIAAC	Programme for the International Assessment of Adult Competencies
PPS	purchasing power standards
R&D	research and development
SES	Structure of Earnings Survey
STW	school-to-work
STYLE	Strategic Transitions for Youth Labour in Europe (FP7 project)
TCN	third-country national
TLM	transitional labor market
UK-LFS	UK Quarterly Labour Force Survey
VET	vocational education and training
WVS	World Values Survey
YEI	Youth Employment Initiative
YG	Youth Guarantee

A glossary of labor market terms is available from the European Union at http://ec.europa.eu/eurostat/statistics-explained/index.php/Category:Labour_market_glossary.

CONTRIBUTORS

MEHTAP AKGÜÇ
Centre for European Policy Studies
Brussels, Belgium

MIROSLAV BEBLAVÝ
Centre for European Policy Studies
Brussels, Belgium

ADELE BERGIN
Economic and Social Research Institute
Dublin, Ireland

GABRIELLA BERLOFFA
Department of Economics and
Management
University of Trento
Trento, Italy

WERNER EICHHORST
Institute of Labor Economics
Bonn, Germany

MARIANNA FILANDRI
Department of Culture, Politics and
Society
University of Turin
Turin, Italy

MAIRÉAD FINN
School of Social Work and Social Policy
Trinity College Dublin
Dublin, Ireland

VLADISLAV FLEK
Department of International Relations
and European Studies
Metropolitan University Prague
Prague, Czech Republic

RAFFAELE GROTTI
Economic and Social Research Institute
Dublin, Ireland

KARI P. HADJIVASSILIOU
Institute for Employment Studies
Brighton, United Kingdom

GÁBOR HAJDU
Institute for Sociology
Centre for Social Sciences of the
Hungarian Academy of Sciences
Budapest, Hungary

MARTIN HÁLA
Department of International Business
Metropolitan University Prague
Prague, Czech Republic

LUCIA MÝTNA KUREKOVÁ
Slovak Governance Institute
Bratislava, Slovakia

JANINE LESCHKE
Department of Business and Politics
Copenhagen Business School
Frederiksberg, Denmark

MASSIMILIANO MASCHERINI
European Foundation for the
Improvement of Living and Working
Conditions
Dublin, Ireland

JAAN MASSO
Faculty of Economics and Business
Administration
University of Tartu
Tartu, Estonia

ELEONORA MATTEAZZI
Department of Sociology and Social
Research
University of Trento
Trento, Italy

GABRIELE MAZZOLINI
Department of Economics, Quantitative
Methods and Business Strategy
University of Milan-Bicocca
Milan, Italy

FERNANDA MAZZOTTA
Department of Economics and Statistics
University of Salerno
Salerno, Italy

SEAMUS MCGUINNESS
Economic and Social Research Institute
Dublin, Ireland

MÁRTON MEDGYESI
Institute for Sociology
Hungarian Academy of Sciences
Budapest, Hungary

MARÍA GONZÁLEZ MENÉNDEZ
Department of Sociology
University of Oviedo
Oviedo, Spain

MARTINA MYSÍKOVÁ
Institute of Sociology of the Czech
Academy of Sciences
Prague, Czech Republic

ILDIKÓ NAGY
Institute for Sociology
Hungarian Academy of Sciences
Budapest, Hungary

TIZIANA NAZIO
Department of Culture, Politics and
Society & Collegio Carlo Alberto
University of Turin
Turin, Italy

JACQUELINE O'REILLY
University of Sussex Business School for
Legal Reasons
University of Sussex
Brighton, United Kingdom

RENATE ORTLIEB
Department of Human Resource
Management
University of Graz
Graz, Austria

LAVINIA PARISI
Department of Economics and Statistics
University of Salerno
Salerno, Italy

MARIA PETMESIDOU
Department of Social Administration and
Political Science
Democritus University of Thrace
Thrace, Greece

HELEN RUSSELL
Economic and Social Research Institute
Dublin, Ireland

ALINA ȘANDOR
Department of Economics and
Management
University of Trento
Trento, Italy

MARTIN SEELEIB-KAISER
Institute of Political Science
University of Tübingen
Tübingen, Germany

MAURA SHEEHAN
International Centre for Management and
Governance Research
Edinburgh Napier University
Edinburgh, Scotland

ENDRE SIK
TÁRKI Social Research Institute
Budapest, Hungary

MARK SMITH
Department of People, Organizations and
Society
Grenoble School of Management
Grenoble, France

THEES F. SPRECKELSEN
Department of Social Policy and
Intervention
University of Oxford
Oxford, United Kingdom

ARIANNA TASSINARI
Institute for Employment Studies
Brighton, United Kingdom

MARYNA TVERDOSTUP
Faculty of Economics and Business
Administration
University of Tartu
Tartu, Estonia

KURT VANDAELE
European Trade Union Institute
Brussels, Belgium

PAOLA VILLA
Department of Economics and
Management
University of Trento
Trento, Italy

SILVANA WEISS
Department of Human Resource
Management
University of Graz
Graz, Austria

ADELE WHELAN
Economic and Social Research Institute
Dublin, Ireland

FLORIAN WOZNY
Institute of Labor Economics
Bonn, Germany

ZUZANA ŽILINČÍKOVÁ
Slovak Governance Institute
Bratislava, Slovakia

CAROLINA V. ZUCCOTTI
Mighraion Policy Centre
European University Institute
Florence, Italy

1

COMPARING YOUTH TRANSITIONS IN EUROPE

JOBLESSNESS, INSECURITY, INSTITUTIONS,
AND INEQUALITY

**Jacqueline O'Reilly, Janine Leschke, Renate Ortlieb,
Martin Seeleib-Kaiser, and Paola Villa**

1.1. INTRODUCTION

In the immediate aftermath of the Great Recession (2008–2009), European youth joblessness soared, especially in those countries facing the largest financial difficulties. Youth were particularly hard hit in Southern Europe, Ireland, and the Baltic countries. For some countries, this was not a new problem. For decades preceding the crisis, they had struggled with the problem of successfully integrating young people into paid work (Furlong and Carmel 2006).

The Great Recession exacerbated early career insecurity, which had already been evident before the crisis. Unstable, short-term, and poorly paid jobs have resulted from regulatory trends that began in the early 1990s. Employment protection legislation (EPL) was weakened in order to enhance labor market flexibility, enabling firms to respond quickly to changes. This was achieved through the liberalization of temporary contracts and in some cases a reduction of benefit entitlement for young people (Smith et al., this volume; Leschke and Finn, this volume). Measures to render labor markets more flexible have been actively supported by policy recommendations at the European Union (EU) level, with limited concern about the consequences for youth, both before and during the economic crisis (Smith and Villa 2016). The analyses presented in this volume show that focusing solely on youth unemployment is not enough to understand

1

the consequences of the Great Recession for young people; we also need to understand how employment insecurity affects youth labor transitions, their long-term impact, and how these are mediated by labor market institutions and policies.

Institutional settings for the integration of youth differ remarkably across Europe, despite attempts made in recent years to overcome national and regional weaknesses following recommendations made at the EU level (Wallace and Bendit 2009; O'Reilly et al. 2015). Countries with more robust and embedded vocational education and training (VET) systems and with integrated employer involvement have traditionally been able to create more stable transition pathways from education to employment (Hadjivassiliou et al., this volume; Grotti, Russell, and O'Reilly, this volume). Those with more fragmented coordination have faced greater challenges and in some cases inertia (Petmesidou and González Menéndez, this volume).

The current evolution of youth labor markets reveals traditional and emerging forms of segmentation along education/class, nationality/ethnicity, and, to some degree, gender dimensions. Some countries are better able to contain labor market segmentation between well-protected prime-age workers and poorly protected younger workers. In others, segmentation has resulted in the involuntary concentration of young workers in temporary and precarious jobs, or it has left them without hope of finding a decent job.

In this chapter, we outline the key problems and challenges associated with analyzing youth joblessness and employment insecurity from a cross-European perspective.[1] First, we briefly contextualize European youth employment trends. Second, we identify how the problem of youth unemployment has been defined in both research and policy frameworks. Third, we outline comparative approaches to evaluating countries' performance. Fourth, we discuss how we conceptualize and compare sustainable youth transitions. Fifth, we consider how inequalities among youth vary by the intersection of gender, parental background, and ethnicity. Finally, we conclude by summarizing the contributions to this volume and suggesting that a more comprehensive approach to policymaking requires understanding both the dynamics of economic production regimes and the effects of inequalities emanating from the family sphere of social reproduction.

1.2. CONTEXTUALIZING EUROPEAN YOUTH EMPLOYMENT TRENDS

Some of the trends in youth employment during the Great Recession could be contextualized in relation to broader global and historical changes to the organization of work resulting from technological change, globalization, and demographic transformation, but these only tell part of the story. These three trends are major drivers affecting aggregate labor demand and supply, in addition to policy decisions in advanced industrialized countries, but their effects on youth labor markets are not unilinear. The impact of global trends is mediated through labor market institutions, and distinctive patterns of local demand for young workers have their roots in employers' behavior before the Great Recession (Grotti et al., this volume). Although youth unemployment soared after the economic crisis, the causes of this are complex and vary between different categories of youth, as well as between different countries.

From a long-term perspective, the decline of manufacturing jobs in the northern hemisphere has decimated sectors that traditionally supported the integration of large cohorts of young men through apprenticeships. The speed of recent technological change is reshaping work on new digital platforms, but the impact of these changes on employment is neither theoretically nor empirically fully understood (Vivarelli 2014), and the consequences for young people are ambivalent. On the one hand, youth have an advantage over older generations if systems of VET adequately respond to the technological trends and changing job opportunities, where labor market entrants benefit from their up-to-date competencies. On the other hand, as low-skill jobs diminish, young people with few or limited qualifications encounter higher barriers to entering the labor market. Although the digital economy opens up new opportunities for consumers, it raises various challenges for workers, related to the types of jobs it generates and how these are regulated. This includes questions about remuneration, social protection, and, more generally, externalization of risks to workers—for example, in the emerging gig economy, in which young people are increasingly finding employment (Jepsen and Drahokoupil 2017; Lobel 2017; Neufeind et al., 2018). In addition, occupational choice becomes more difficult for young people because job profiles continuously change and investment in a specific vocational training or university study program may quickly become outdated. As a result, certain groups of young people may be "left behind" in the process of accelerated technological change.

Processes of globalization allow companies to relocate more easily and to reap the benefits of low-cost production regions. Although many jobs have been moved to the Far East, in the European context firms do not have to move to very distant shores. Instead, they can often relocate to destinations in Central and Eastern Europe and thereby create employment for young people in Europe's periphery. Nevertheless, unemployment continues to be high in these eastern regions, and it is unclear to what extent offshoring and globalization affect the overall volume of youth labor in Europe. Firms relocate not only due to wage–cost differences but also as a consequence of lower labor standards and more employer-friendly labor law. Relocations or the threat of relocations to regions with low labor standards pose a challenge for national and European policymakers by restricting the policy options available. Nevertheless, despite these global trends, Grotti et al. (this volume) show how young Europeans are more likely to find work in service sector jobs of retail, accommodation and food, and health and social work—sectors involving face-to-face delivery that are not as vulnerable to offshoring strategies.

We might expect demographic changes would have a favorable effect on youth employment opportunities because the number of workers per retiree is projected to decline substantially in the EU28 (Eurostat 2015). Projected population trends indicate an uneven distribution of where these are rising or declining across individual EU member states: Half of the EU member states are projected to show rising population trends and the other half declining trends between 2014 and 2080. Population numbers are predicted to rise by more than 30% in 8 of the 28 EU member states, whereas they are predicted to decline by approximately 30% or more in 6 member states (for details, see Eurostat 2015). To meet potential future labor shortages, immigration trends can only partly compensate for declining fertility rates and increasing life expectancy, so it should, in theory, be easier for young people to find work. But as Blanchflower and Freeman (2000) and Gruber and Wise (2010) show, these demographic trends have not resulted in more jobs for youth across the Organization for Economic Co-operation and Development (OECD) countries. What is more likely is that young people will have to work longer and are likely to receive lower pensions in the future.

Although these global trends of accelerated technological change, globalization, and demographic transformation mark a significant change to the world of work, it is not easy to untangle their specific impact on youth employment. The relationship between cause and effect is complex and varied, not only in explaining the differential outcomes between groups of countries but also in explaining the outcomes among different groups of young people in these countries. Rather than viewing "youth unemployment" as a unitary problem, a more refined understanding of what kind of problem this is needs to be specified.

1.3. IDENTIFYING THE PROBLEM OF YOUTH UNEMPLOYMENT

Endeavors to define the "problem" of youth unemployment have generated a number of contested interpretations as to its causes and possible solutions; these interpretations also affect the way policy is developed to address the problem. Some countries have attributed the rapid increase in youth unemployment to a "deficit model" in their school-to-work (STW) institutions or to the nature of segmented labor markets, in which young people are institutionally marginalized, or they have allotted blame to a "welfare dependency" culture, which may be producing young people without sufficient "grit" or the right set of mental skills to find employment (Pohl and Walther 2007; Wallace and Bendit 2009). The consequences of the economic crisis have prioritized the problem of youth employment and underemployment for policymakers. The solutions developed have included reforms of (pre)vocational training and a modernization of educational institutions. Countries have pursued various paths of "activation," either through enabling active labor market policies (ALMPs), such as training measures, or through more coercive steps that include obligatory activation and job take-up with benefit sanctions in the event of noncompliance (Hadjivassiliou et al., this volume). Despite diverse experiences across Europe, the distinction proposed by Scarpetta, Sonnet, and Manfredi (2010) between "poorly integrated new entrants" and young people who are "left behind" offers a very succinct means to identify the key universal trends and policy issues examined in this book.

Poorly integrated new entrants are young people who, although qualified, experience persistent difficulties in accessing stable employment. They are caught in a series of short-term, insecure, and poorly paid jobs that frequently do not correspond well to their qualifications (McGuinness, Bergin, and Whelan, this volume); such insecure employment is often interspersed by intermittent periods of unemployment and/or inactivity. This group of poorly integrated new entrants accounted for approximately 20%–30% of all youth aged 15–29 years in OECD countries in 2005–2007; these youth are particularly prevalent in France, Greece, Spain, and Italy (Scarpetta et al. 2010).

The second group of *youth left behind* is made up of young people who are characterized by inability, discouragement, or unwillingness to enter the labor market; who face multiple disadvantages; and who are more likely to have no qualifications, to come from an immigrant/minority background, and/or to live in disadvantaged/rural/remote areas (Eurofound 2012; TUC 2012; Roberts and MacDonald 2013). The size of this group can be estimated by the number of young people not in employment, education, or training, known as "NEETs." Although the concept of NEETs has been highly contested for covering a very diverse group of young people—including unqualified early school-leavers, qualified graduates taking time off to find work, and youth with family caring responsibilities—it has become a widely recognized international benchmark for measuring country performance (Mascherini, this volume).

According to Eurostat data, the share of NEETs among the 15- to 29-year-old age group in the EU28 was 13.2% in 2007; it reached its peak at 15.9% in 2013 and then fell slightly to 14.8% by 2015 (for 2015, see Figure 1.1).[2] Country variations in the share of NEETs in the EU28 range from less than 8% (DK, LU, SE, and NL) to more than 25%. The highest NEET rate is found in Italy—25.7% in 2015; Greece, Bulgaria, and Romania all have NEET rates greater than 20%. The NEET rate for Turkey is as high as 27.9%.

In addition to national NEET rates, Figure 1.1 also presents youth unemployment rates and youth unemployment ratios. These three indicators are to be viewed as complementary in that they measure different phenomena.

The *unemployment rate* is the proportion of youth actively searching for a job as a percentage of all those in the same age group who are either employed or unemployed; students are excluded from this measure. The *unemployment ratio*

Percent

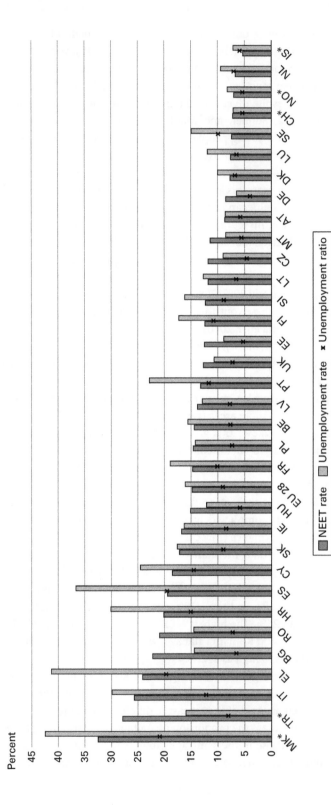

Figure 1.1 Youth unemployment rates, unemployment ratios, and NEET rates in 2015 (young people aged 15–29 years).
Source: Eurostat EU-LFS.

includes students as part of the total population against which youth unemployment is calculated. Because they are measured against a wider population, unemployment ratios are lower than unemployment rates. Ratios provide an indicator of the proportion of youth searching for a job vis-à-vis the relative share of youth in education. The *NEET rate* is the percentage of the youth population not in education or training among all young people in the same age group, including those who are working or studying or both; it can be interpreted as a measure that reflects the fragility of STW transitions in a particular country.

These three indicators vary significantly between countries (see Figure 1.1). Countries with similar NEET rates can have very different levels of youth unemployment rates or ratios. For example, if we compare Sweden, Portugal, and the United Kingdom—three seemingly different countries—we find some interesting points of comparison. The youth unemployment rate in Portugal is very high at greater than 20%. However, Portugal's youth unemployment ratio is fairly similar to that of Sweden at approximately 10%–12%, and these are both higher than the ratio of approximately 7% in the United Kingdom. This tells us that there are relatively more students in the United Kingdom than in Sweden or Portugal compared to those who are unemployed. But the NEET rates in the United Kingdom and Portugal are fairly similar at approximately 13%, which tells us that transitions to work or education and training are more effective in Sweden than in the former two countries. It is the careful interpretation of these data and the interrelationships between them that shape priorities on policy agendas.

Debates about which indicators should be used are both political and academic in nature. They are academic in terms of how we should appropriately measure and interpret the phenomena of youth unemployment and underemployment, and they are political in terms of emphasizing their significance and the importance of different policies developed to address the particular problem that is measured. These indicators also reflect the varying performance of countries, the overall macroeconomic and labor market conditions, and the effectiveness of institutional settings—particularly labor regulation—in facilitating young people's transitions to sustainable employment.

1.4. COMPARING COUNTRY PERFORMANCE

A comprehensive comparison of developments in youth labor market transitions across Europe presents a number of challenges. Early comparative work either tended to focus on a small selection of countries (Marsden and Ryan 1986) or emphasized the distinctive profile of particular types of countries associated with coordinated market economies (e.g., Germany) in contrast with liberal market economies (e.g., the United Kingdom). The *varieties of capitalism* approach emphasized the more successful integration and higher skill trajectories of youth in more coordinated economies (Hall and Soskice 2001). The key dimension of comparison was the relationship between business organizations, VET systems, and policymakers—the institutions that comprise the economic sphere of production (O'Reilly, Smith, and Villa 2017).

Variation across countries as regards occupational, company-specific skills, or generalist skill regimes also has very different effects on the speed, type, and quality of transitions that young people make (Russell, Helen, and Philip J. O'Connell 2001; Brzinsky-Fay 2007). In their comprehensive volume on transitions from education to work in Europe, Gangl, Müller, and Raffe (2003) find that countries in which youth have higher levels of education, and those with large-scale systems of vocational training, provide young people with a better start in their working lives. Van der Velden and Wolbers (2003) take a broader view of the impact of institutional conditions on transition outcomes. These authors test for the effects of various institutional indicators, including measures for the structure of training systems, the structure of collective bargaining and wage-setting mechanisms, and the stringency of employment protection. In this direct comparison between competing institutional hypotheses, the structure of training systems again turns out to be the most important predictor of cross-national differences in transition patterns. Boeri and Jimeno (2015), in a study on the divergence of unemployment in Europe, stress that youth unemployment is a main driver of these cross-country differences. According to their findings, the divergence is largely caused by differences in labor market institutions (including collective bargaining, wage-setting mechanisms, EPL, and labor market regulation) and their interactions with demand shocks, including fiscal consolidation.

One way to approach large, cross-national comparisons has been the use of welfare regime typologies with a number of aggregate indicators and dimensions to distinguish between different families of countries with related practices (for a critical summary of these approaches, see O'Reilly 2006; Ferragina and Seeleib-Kaiser 2011; Arts and Gelissen 2012). Ferragina and Seeleib-Kaiser argue that the main point of contention in these debates is that typologies are usually based on ideal types, not on real types. Two further critiques of regime approaches are that (1) they assume an overarching rationale rather than focusing on specific and sometimes contradictory policy logics and structures (Keck and Saraceno 2013) and (2) typologies tend toward a more static picture of regime types that overestimates path dependency (Hadjivassiliou et al., this volume). Despite these limitations, typologies are often used as pragmatic heuristic devices that allow us to make summary comparisons of a large number of countries. More recently established approaches have been adapted to specifically address the issue of youth transitions (Wallace and Bendit 2009).

Walther and Pohl (2005) put forward a typology of youth transition regimes building on established welfare regime typologies. They include dimensions that go beyond social protection measures and consider, in particular, education and training, the regulation of labor markets, the role of occupational profiles, and job mobility in structuring labor market entry, as well as mechanisms of "doing gender" (Pohl and Walther 2007, 545–46). They distinguish between five youth transition regimes: universalistic (DK, FI, and SE); employment-centered, which is primarily based on dual training (AT and DE), both school-based (FR) and mixed (NL); liberal (IE and UK); subprotective (EL, ES, IT, and PT); and post-socialist (BG, PL, RO, SK, and SI) (Pohl and Walther 2007).

This regime typology provides a useful analytical framework that is specifically focused on youth transitions. However, as a number of contributors in this volume show, youth transition regimes are in flux because of the impact of the Great Recession; policy reforms have created new forms of regime hybridization as countries attempt to adjust to these shocks (Hadjivassiliou et al., this volume; Petmesidou and González Menéndez, this volume).

The impact of the Great Recession on country performance is well illustrated using the most common measure—youth unemployment rates (Figure 1.2). Although most countries have started to show decreases in youth unemployment since it peaked in approximately 2013, youth unemployment rates were on average still 4 percentage points (pp) higher in 2015 for 15- to 29-year-olds than before the crisis. Whereas the difference between countries recording the lowest and those recording the highest youth unemployment rates (for 15- to 29-year-olds) was 14.1 pp in 2008, the difference was 34.8 pp in 2015 (see Figure 1.2). Some countries are beginning to improve their performance since the economic crisis, including some countries in Eastern Europe, the Baltic States, and the United Kingdom and Ireland; however, for Southern European countries, the situation has deteriorated even further.

Despite the diversity of labor market conditions and the youth unemployment rate across Europe, there is a universally shared experience of growing early career insecurity associated with youth labor transitions. Drawing on a range of different methodological approaches and data sources, the chapters in this volume present evidence on youth transitions and policy interventions for a range of countries within these various regime "types." The chapters are not exclusively inspired by STW transition regimes; rather, they also frequently cite more general welfare regime typologies in order to capture a broader perspective that goes beyond immediate STW transitions and also covers the effects of early career insecurity.

1.5. CONCEPTUALIZING AND COMPARING SUSTAINABLE YOUTH TRANSITIONS

The concept of sustainable youth transitions can be traced back to the notion of transitional labor markets developed by Schmid (2008). His work has a broader

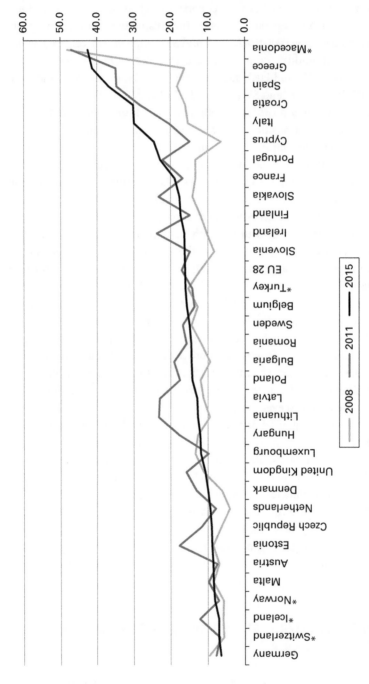

Figure 1.2 Evolution of youth unemployment rates (% total labor force, aged 15–29 years): 2008, 2011, and 2015.
Source: Eurostat EU-LFS.

focus than this volume in examining transitions ranging from early entry to parenthood and later-life transitions out of the labor market. A key preoccupation of this approach with a view to social risk management is to identify policies and institutions that enable integrative and maintenance transitions (which enable people to stay in employment by moving between different forms of flexible employment) in contrast to exclusionary transitions (which result in unemployment or inactivity) (O'Reilly 2003). In particular, it considers the interfaces of education and the labor market, the labor market and private life, and transitions between different employment statuses within the labor market. In identifying innovative policies that focus on supporting employment continuity rather than job security—by securing transitions over the life course and thereby managing social risks—Schmid's perspective is a precursor to more recent debates on sustainable employment and the flexicurity approach (see Smith et al., this volume; Leschke and Finn, this volume; Petmesidou and González Menéndez, this volume; Berloffa et al., this volume).

As the conceptual focus on measuring transitions has become more pertinent, it has been facilitated by the availability of large-scale, cross-national, and, in some cases, longitudinal data sets. Labor market research has increasingly moved from comparing stocks of employed and unemployed people toward an analysis of flows between a large set of different labor market statuses and life states. There has been a rising level of sophistication in terms of data and methods in how transitions have been examined (Brzinsky-Fay 2007; Flek, Hála, and Mysíková, this volume; Berloffa et al., this volume). These have ranged from simple year-on-year comparisons of transitions from one state to another using cross-sectional data to more complex longitudinal analysis that follows individuals over a longer time period (Zuccotti and O'Reilly, this volume).

As well as tracing these patterns, attention has also been given to qualitative distinctions between integrative, maintenance, and exclusionary transitions around employment (O'Reilly, Cebrián, and Lallement 2000; Schmid 2008; Leschke 2009). The use of sequence analysis to measure youth transitions has enabled distinctions between countries in which speedy or delayed transitions are more common (Brzinsky-Fay 2007; Quintini and Manfredi 2009; Berloffa et al., this volume; Filandri, Nazio, and O'Reilly, this volume). This type of analysis can identify universal trends as well as dominant patterns within particular countries.

Alongside the growing sophistication of the measures used to capture youth transitions, there is also some debate concerning the age limits to youth. The chapters in this volume use a variety of age ranges, depending on the focus of their research question. The decision to go beyond an upper age limit of 24 years that is often used arbitrarily or by statistical convention provides a more comprehensive picture of the longer term consequences of early career insecurity for youth trajectories. Using a broader age band is particularly relevant given the increasingly extended duration of participation in education and the raising of the school-leaving age. Furthermore, it allows us to take into consideration not only STW but also labor market transitions and the quality of employment in the early phase of youth working life. Early career insecurity can also have effects on young people in their early thirties—and not only in Southern Europe (Flek et al., this volume; Berloffa et al., this volume). Depending on the analytical aim of the respective chapters and the underlying data used, contributors here take into account youth up to the age of 34 years. Some of the chapters also stress the relevance of disaggregating youth either by age group (Hadjivassiliou et al., this volume; Leschke and Finn, this volume) or by the phase in their working life (Berloffa et al., this volume).

The volume's emphasis on transitions also highlights the importance of developing a dynamic analysis of labor market trajectories that goes beyond conventional analysis of stocks of labor. Several authors propose innovative solutions to overcome static approaches and commonly used indicators such as temporary jobs. These approaches include an analysis of longitudinal data and labor market flows (Flek et al., this volume) and a composite analysis of multidimensional features of job insecurity (Berloffa et al., this volume) or job quality (Russell, Leschke, and Smith 2015; Filandri et al., this volume).

Comparisons of youth trajectories presented in the volume include dimensions of occupational class, education, gender, age, and parental background. A novel additional dimension is the comparisons of youth trajectories that take account of ethnicity, nationality, and migration status, as well as more established cleavages and patterns of segmentation.

1.6. ESTABLISHED AND EMERGING FORMS OF SEGMENTATION AND INTERSECTING INEQUALITIES

Youth labor markets are a particularly apposite space for identifying both established and emerging forms of labor market segmentation. We are able not only to compare contemporary divisions between young people's labor market trajectories but also to trace the longer term legacies related to their parents' labor market experiences by drawing on extensive comparable cross-national data sources to identify patterns of commonality and difference in intersecting inequalities (Berloffa, Matteazzi, and Villa, this volume; Zuccotti and O'Reilly, this volume). In terms of gender differences, young women had higher levels of educational attainment than men before the Great Recession, but they also had slightly higher rates of unemployment. By 2015, young men (aged 15–29 years) had marginally overtaken young women's unemployment rates on the EU28 average (16.5 vs. 15.7, respectively), with 17 countries having more favorable outcomes for women than for men. During the Great Recession, unemployment rates increased for both young men and young women; however, the trend was steeper for men in male-dominated sectors, particularly in construction and manufacturing (Eurostat 2017; Grotti et al., this volume). In 2015, young women (aged 15–29 years) were still more likely than young men to be NEET (16.7% compared to 13.0%, respectively) for EU28 (Eurostat 2017; Mascherini, this volume). Gender differences have decreased during the economic crisis not because of increasing gender equality but, rather, because of the rising shares of male NEETs.

Youth unemployment is also disproportionately higher, employment rates are lower, and working conditions are poorer for those from certain Black and minority ethnic backgrounds, as well as for some migrant workers (Akgüç and Beblavý, this volume; Spreckelsen, Leschke, and Seeleib-Kaiser, this volume). Some authors conflate ethnic differences as being largely attributable to migration, whereas others recognize that there is a long-standing community of non-White nationals within their societies that experiences very different employment trajectories depending on their ethnicity (Crul, Schneider, and Lelie 2012; Zuccotti and O'Reilly, this volume). Individuals with low levels of educational attainment or with disabilities also have more difficulty entering and remaining in employment in all countries (on educational attainment, see Gangl 2003; on disabilities and vulnerability, see Halvorsen et al. 2017; see also Hart et al. 2015).

One of the underlying reasons for poorer labor market integration of some ethnic and migrant youth and—more generally—of youth from low-income families is that they are less likely to participate in further formal education than their peers, although some ethnic groups have a higher propensity to pursue higher education (Zuccotti and O'Reilly, this volume). Gendered and ethnic segmentation in the take-up of particular vocational pathways can perpetuate these inequalities, with transitions taking place into less valued and less rewarded occupations, while those not participating in VET systems become labor market outsiders (Charles et al. 2001; Becker 2003; Alba 2011; Gundert and Mayer 2012; Gökşen et al. 2016). The specific institutional and societal context—in interplay with effectively implemented policies to address intersecting inequalities—affects the quality of youth transitions (Krizsan, Skjeie, and Squires 2012; Gökşen et al. 2016).

The research presented in this volume shows that we cannot assume that disadvantage in the labor market can be simply read off from a series of particular socioeconomic characteristics of an individual. The experiences of unemployment and labor market transitions vary by the intersection of gender and parental background (Filandri et al. this volume; Berloffa, Matteazzi, and Villa, this volume; Mazzotta and Parisi, this volume; Medgyesi and Nagy, this volume). This analysis constitutes the components of the sphere of social reproduction of labor (O'Reilly et al. 2017). It is in this realm that family differences, as well as those of ethnicity, migration status, and educational attainment, influence and interact with the inequality in youth transitions observed in the sphere of economic production (Spreckelsen et al., this volume; Mascherini, this volume; Zuccotti and O'Reilly, this volume; Ortlieb, Sheehan, and Masso, this volume). The effect of these disadvantages depends on institutional arrangements supporting equality of integration (Gökşen et al. 2016; Hadjivassiliou et al. 2016). Policies can be targeted at institutions of economic production such as VET systems, EPL, and employers; they can focus on the sphere of social reproduction by seeking to improve individual young people's "employability" skills and attitudes and by addressing disadvantaged families (or not); or they can have a more integrated focus on the two domains (O'Reilly et al. 2017).

The youth transitions examined in this book look at different groups of young people, the way they feel about their options (including their attitudes toward and values about work), and how policy communities can enable them to overcome the negative consequences of disengagement. Collectively, the research presented here illustrates the importance of policy initiatives directed at labor market institutions, such as VET systems, EPL, and unemployment benefits, as well as focusing on employers' patterns of recruitment and the role of trade unions.

This research also goes beyond conventional perspectives focused solely on the sphere of economic production by drawing attention to the very significant role of the family in shaping young people's futures and the social reproduction of labor (O'Reilly et al. 2017) and also to the more recent evidence on youth migration trajectories as a distinctive characteristic of the recent phase of youth unemployment in Europe (O'Reilly et al. 2015). Moving beyond STW transitions, this broader approach includes an analysis of the longer term consequences of insecure employment and how these consequences are shaped by institutions. We also distinguish between different categories of youth, which allows us to identify both universal trends and country-specific differences that affect transition trajectories. As a result, these findings provide a more nuanced and informed approach with regard to effective policymaking in different countries.

1.7. ORGANIZATION OF THE BOOK

The book is organized into four parts. Part I examines problematic youth transitions into employment and recent trends as to where young people find work, how well countries perform, and how this affects policy responses. In Part II, we examine how the family shapes youth labor market transitions. The chapters in Part II use different methodological approaches to address two key transitions for youth: finding work and leaving home. Part III examines youth migration transitions across Europe. Using quantitative and qualitative approaches, the chapters in Part III focus on the situation of young EU migrant workers abroad, when they return home, and the role of labor market intermediaries in shaping these transitions. Part IV identifies some of the key policy challenges emerging from our analysis. Chapters in Part IV critically assess the concept of NEETs and vulnerable transitions for disadvantaged men and women from ethnic backgrounds, the challenges posed by overeducation, new forms of self-employment, the values and attitudes of young people, and their propensity to engage with trade unions. Drawing on this extensive evidence, we argue that the increasing levels of precariousness, mobility, and inequality in youth labor markets require a comprehensive raft of policies targeted at the spheres of economic production and social reproduction to engage employers more effectively and address inequalities stemming from the family.

1.7.1. Part I: Comparing Problematic Youth Transitions to Work

In Part I, we examine problematic youth transitions into employment. This opens with Chapter 2 by Grotti, Russell, and O'Reilly, which examines the sectors in which young people (aged 16–24 years) are most frequently employed before and after the Great Recession. Drawing on data from the European Union Labor Force Survey (EU-LFS) for 23 countries between 2007 and 2014, the authors find that youth employment continues to be unevenly distributed across sectors and that regardless of the different proportions emerging, many countries share striking similarities in this distribution. The authors ask whether the decline in jobs for youth is attributable to shrinkage in these sectors related to long-term trends in the overall structure of the economy or to the effects of the Great Recession (i.e., a hiring freeze, as in previous recessions, and the dissolution of temporary contracts, which are mainly held by young workers). Using a shift-share analysis, they identify the sectors in which young people have been most vulnerable to job losses so as to assess whether or not jobs for youth have deteriorated by examining *where* the changing employment status of these jobs has seen a decline in full-time permanent opportunities and a growth in part-time and/or temporary work. The evidence is sobering: Job opportunities in "youth-friendly" sectors have declined during the recession, and the quality of this employment has deteriorated.

Adopting a comparative perspective to assess STW transition regimes, Chapter 3 by Hadjivassiliou et al. asks how well countries have performed during the Great Recession and whether lessons can be learned from these experiences. Drawing on Pohl and Walther's (2007) comparative framework of STW transition regimes, the authors assess the youth labor market performance of eight countries (SE, DE, FR, NL, ES, TR, EE, and PL) belonging to five different institutional clusters and the effect of recent policy innovations. They analyze the cross-cluster variation by key institutional dimensions: youth employment policy governance structure (e.g., level/mode of policy coordination and social partners' role); the structure of education and training systems (e.g., VET and apprenticeships) and the nature of linkages with the labor market; and dominant labor market and welfare policy models (e.g., EPL, wage-formation systems, ALMPs, and the structure of social assistance and benefits systems). Their findings indicate that the institutional configurations of STW regimes in Europe are currently experiencing a degree of flux and hybridization. Evidence of convergence in policy instruments emerges, although differential performance persists. A combination of institutional and macroeconomic factors, together with a common trend of progressive deterioration in the quality of youth transitions across the board, are likely to present significant obstacles for the future.

Providing a critique of recent labor market policies and institutional outcomes in Europe, Chapter 4 by Smith et al. identifies challenges to attempts to engage in a coherent reconceptualization of European employment policy from a youth perspective. First, they argue that there has been an over-reliance on supply side policies to address labor market challenges. Second, the external pressures of macroeconomic stability (including fiscal consolidation), rather than a coherent strategy toward sustainable labor market outcomes, have driven labor market reforms. Third, reform has been based on a downward pressure on job security (i.e., EPL) and a strengthening of employability security through ALMPs, despite slack labor demand. Fourth, because of over-reliance on quantitative targets, there is a lack of consideration of the impact of precariousness and early career insecurity on young people. Finally, reforms have failed to integrate a gender and life course perspective to reflect the realities of labor market participation. In terms of policy implications, the authors call for a renewed perspective on what constitutes an "efficient" labor market, alongside the integration of quality outcomes. They seek to identify policies that could develop durable and resilient labor markets for postcrisis Europe, particularly for the generation entering work.

Using a dynamic version of the flexicurity matrix, Chapter 5 by Leschke and Finn analyzes trade-offs and vicious and virtuous relationships between external and internal numerical flexibility and income security for youth (aged 15–24 and 25–29 years). In all European countries, youth are more likely to be unemployed than adults; they also have a higher likelihood of being in temporary employment. Moreover, young people have more difficulty fulfilling eligibility criteria for unemployment benefits, including minimum contributory periods and means testing in secondary benefit schemes. Drawing on EU-LFS data for 2007, 2009, and 2013, Leschke and Finn estimate the access of young people to unemployment benefits and also their participation in short-time working schemes. This analysis is complemented by an institutional analysis to chart recent changes in unemployment benefit criteria that are directly or indirectly targeted at youth. The results show that after initial improvements geared toward making unemployment benefit systems more encompassing, benefit coverage among youth has once again decreased in a number of countries in the wake of the crisis, highlighting the deficits in protection of young people against economic shocks.

To address these concerns, Petmesidou and González Menéndez in Chapter 6 disentangle and critically examine the complex routes of policy learning and policy transfer within and between different regimes of youth employment transitions. Their stringent analysis provides practical insights differentiating between successful innovations at different regional, national, and European levels. They comparatively examine the possibilities of, and barriers to, policy transfer and innovation between different STW transition regimes in Europe. Examining the policymaking machinery, they ask whether or not this facilitates experimentation with new, proactive youth employment measures. Their analysis shows that factors related to policy development and operational delivery (e.g., the role of evidence, the ability of decision-makers to tolerate risks, and the role of specific actors in forging learning and transfer) are crucial in enabling or hindering effective policy innovation. They conclude by calling attention to the usefulness of cross-national analysis for understanding the interplay between institutional and process factors that drive or hinder knowledge transfer and policy innovation for building resilient bridges to the labor market for young people.

1.7.2. Part II: Transitions Around Work and the Family

A particularly innovative contribution of this volume is its inclusion of an analysis of the sphere of social reproduction related to the role of the family in shaping youth labor market transitions. In Part II, we bring together a number of contributors who use diverse methodological approaches to focus on patterns of flows as well as on the quality of employment into which young people can move. A key element shared by these contributions is to provide innovative approaches to examining transitions and to situate these in relation to family circumstances. For some young people, unemployment is a frictional experience; for others, long-term vulnerability is part of a generational family legacy. The chapters deploy different methodological approaches to address key transitions for youth in finding work and leaving home.

Examining flows between labor market statuses, Chapter 7 by Flek, Hála, and Mysíková compares youth (aged 15–34 years) and prime-age individuals (aged 35–56 years) over various stages of the Great Recession (2008–2012). They examine youth labor market dynamics in four countries (Austria, France, Poland, and Spain) that are illustrative of very different institutional settings and macroeconomic shocks. A particularly novel aspect of this study is the decomposition into "inflows" into and "outflows" out of unemployment for youth and prime-age individuals. The main result is that young workers are more likely to move between employment and unemployment—in both directions—compared to prime-age workers. This is instructive for assessing the gap in the labor market prospects of the two age groups. In summary, the authors find that young people "churn" through the (secondary) labor market relatively more frequently than their prime-age counterparts. These patterns are consistent across countries with substantially different labor market performances, institutions, and EU membership history, although the length of time it takes unemployed youth to find work varies from country to country. Higher levels of schooling and work experience are key factors influencing the probability of exiting unemployment and moving into employment.

Using a dynamic approach to evaluate youth labor market performance, Chapter 8 by Berloffa et al. illustrates an innovative methodology for grouping employment status sequences and also proposes a new definition of employment quality based on four dimensions: employment security, income security, economic success, and a positive match between education and occupation. The authors use longitudinal data (2006–2012) for 17 countries from the European Union Survey of Income and Living Conditions (EU-SILC) to examine youth (aged 16–34 years) employment outcomes in two different phases of their working life: labor market entry and approximately 5 years after exiting education. They analyze how the quality of employment obtained and the trajectory followed vary according to gender, education, country groups, and time periods (i.e., before and during the Great Recession). Their findings suggest that there is still a pressing need to enhance women's chances to remain continuously in employment and to enable them to move up in the labor income distribution. Loosening the rules on the use of temporary contracts actually generates more difficulties for women and low-educated individuals; it also appears to worsen youth employment prospects in general.

Asking how long young people (aged 19–34 years) should wait to find the right job, Chapter 9 by Filandri, Nazio, and O'Reilly examines the difference the family makes in this "waiting" decision. They use cross-sectional and longitudinal EU-SILC data (2005–2012) for five countries (Finland, France, Italy, Poland, and the United Kingdom), which are illustrative of different transition regimes. They also compare whether taking the first available opportunity or holding out for something better affects the quality of jobs that young people are able to secure. In addition, they explore whether early experiences of unemployment affect later occupational conditions in terms of pay and skill levels. Comparing the impact of family status on the transitions and timing affecting young people, their findings show reinforced patterns of stratification: Young people from work-rich, higher occupational status families were able to make better transitions in terms of job quality than was the case for lower status families. These results raise significant questions about the locus for policy interventions in addressing the legacies of family inequalities for young people today.

Berloffa, Matteazzi, and Villa undertake an analysis of intergenerational inequality and social mobility in Chapter 10. They investigate how this transmission varies for young men and women (aged 25–34 years) across a range of different groups of countries. Using the 2011 EU-SILC ad hoc module on the intergenerational transmission of disadvantages, they estimate the extent to which parents' employment during young people's adolescence affects their employment status at approximately 30 years of age. They find that having had a working mother during adolescence reduces the likelihood of being workless for both sons and daughters at approximately age 30 years in all country groups, except in the Nordic countries; the effects of fathers' working condition are less widespread across countries. This suggests that the consequences of different labor market institutions, family models, and welfare regimes on the intergenerational transmission of worklessness are not very clear-cut. In all country groups (except the Nordic countries), policies should pay attention to mothers' employment—not only when their children are in their early years of life but also during their adolescence. Helping mothers to remain in or re-enter the labor market might have important consequences for the future employment prospects of both their daughters and their sons.

Considering the decision by young people (aged 18–34 years) to leave or to return to the parental home, Chapter 11 by Mazzotta and Parisi examines the effects of partnership and employment before and after the onset of the economic crisis (2005–2013) for different groups of countries. They find that the Great Recession has reduced the probability of leaving home and increased the probability of returning, with differences across country groups. The probability of leaving home decreased in Continental countries at the beginning of the Great Recession, but it remained stable in Southern and Eastern Europe. Southern European countries show an increase in returns home throughout the entire period. Finally, leaving and returning home seem more closely linked to partnership than to employment; at the same time, starting a new family is indirectly affected by employment.

How young adults (aged 18–34 years) who are co-residing with their parents contribute to household expenses has not received significant attention to date in the literature on youth transitions. In Chapter 12, Medgyesi and Nagy draw on EU-SILC 2010 data for 17 EU countries to examine how resources are pooled in these households. They find that income sharing in the household attenuates income differences between household members because it helps those with low resources. At the same time, income sharing in the household tends to increase inequalities for young adults living with their parents. Some young adults stay at home longer in order to enjoy better economic well-being, some stay longer as a strategy to overcome the difficulties faced in the labor market or the housing market or both, whereas others remain at home longer in order to support their family of origin.

The evidence presented by the chapters in Part II indicates the persistent importance of family resources (or the lack of them) in affecting the capability to move out of joblessness (Berloffa, Matteazzi, and Villa, this volume; Mazzotta and Parisi, this volume). In some cases, family resources allow some young people to "wait" for the right opportunity (Filandri et al., this volume). For other young people, it is not a question of "waiting" as they have nowhere else to go; while some stay at home to support other family members (Medgyesi and Nagy, this volume). Flek et al. (this volume) show that waiting longer than six months can have deleterious long-term effects that may culminate in becoming youth who are "left behind." The extent to which young people are able to act is clearly shaped by the resources on which they can rely. Whether these are private family resources or collective public goods or agencies will vary by country, region, and class.

1.7.3. Part III: Transitions Across Europe

One of the distinctive characteristics of the recent period of youth unemployment has been the increased level of labor mobility across Europe (O'Reilly et al. 2015). A range of European initiatives that includes directives, social security coordination, and information services has sought to encourage EU cross-border labor mobility so as to contribute to better labor market matching by remedying intra-EU skill gaps and skill shortages. EU cross-border labor mobility of often young and high-qualified workers has become particularly important since the 2004 and 2007 accessions of Central and Eastern European countries (Galgóczi, Leschke, and Watt 2009, 2012). The trend has been further enhanced and diversified with the Great Recession, which led to increased flows of Southern Europeans to the North as a result of the economic downturn in their own countries (Kahanec and Zimmermann 2016).

Recent intra-EU labor migration might represent a key tool for remedying youth unemployment by providing work opportunities for young unemployed in the countries with more abundant work opportunities (Berg and Besharov 2016). Migration experience might provide important individual-level benefits and give signals to employers who value a set of skills and characteristics that living and working abroad help to develop. These can range from cognitive language skills to noncognitive skills such as independence, self-initiative, intercultural competence, and increased flexibility. However, migration can also lead to suboptimal labor allocation, with substantial numbers of migrant workers being employed below their skill levels and often facing poorer working conditions than their peers when they return home (Clark and Drinkwater 2008; Johnston, Khattab, and Manley 2015).

To examine young migrants' (aged 15–35 years) labor market integration, in Chapter 13 Akgüç and Beblavý use pooled data from the European Social Survey (2002–2015). They analyze labor market outcomes (unemployment, hours worked, contract type, and overqualification) across an aggregate of European destination countries by migrant origin (Southern European, Eastern European, intra-EU, and non-EU) vis-à-vis natives. They show that young migrants of all origin clusters have poorer labor market outcomes than nationals. In particular, after controlling for education, gender, age, country, and year effects, migrants from Eastern and Southern Europe display important differences vis-à-vis nationals in terms of having a higher propensity to be unemployed, to be employed on a temporary employment contract, and to be overqualified. Moreover, the analysis reveals a gender gap in women's disfavor.

Building on this analysis and deepening it, Chapter 14 by Spreckelsen, Leschke, and Seeleib-Kaiser examines the quantitative and qualitative labor market integration of young recent migrants (aged 20–34 years) in Germany and the United Kingdom. The assumption is that because of different reservation wages and variations in the applicable migration policy regimes, migrants from Central Eastern Europe (EU8), Bulgaria and Romania (EU2), Southern Europe, and the remaining EU will have qualitatively different outcomes in destination labor markets. Using German microcensus data and the UK-LFS, the chapter focuses descriptively on levels of employment and income; on marginal, fixed-term, and (solo) self-employment; and on overqualification of migrants compared to nationals before and after the economic crisis. The authors find that despite institutional differences and policy regimes regarding EU migrant workers, young EU migrant citizens are well integrated into the labor markets of both the two destination countries (particularly the United Kingdom) in terms of employment rates. However, their qualitative labor market integration seems to mirror the existing stratification across regions of Europe: EU8 and EU2 citizens often work in precarious and atypical employment, youth from Southern Europe take a middle position, and youth from the remaining EU countries do as well, or better, on several indicators than their national peers.

The entry route of young migrants from Eastern European countries (EU8) into a foreign labor market is a central focus of Chapter 15 by Ortlieb and Weiss. Focusing on the Austrian labor market, an important destination for EU8 migrants, these authors examine the role of labor market intermediaries (LMIs), such as public employment services, online job portals, and temporary work agencies, in facilitating this transition. Based on semistructured interviews with representatives of employers, LMIs, and young migrants (aged 18–34 years), they find that online job portals are the most common LMIs used and that the information services offered by LMIs are more relevant than matchmaking and administrative services. The relevance of LMI types and services varies across sectors. To varying degrees, LMIs fulfill specific functions in these sectors, such as reducing transaction costs, managing risks associated with the employment relationship, and building networks. The results can inform the design of policy measures aimed at improving the labor market opportunities of young migrants from Eastern Europe, such as the provision of cost-free information and matchmaking services and monitoring of LMIs in order to prevent exploitation of young migrants, and they can also inform future theoretical models accounting for youth migration.

Finally, going beyond understanding what happens to young people when they move abroad to find work, we also examine what happens when, and if, they return home. In Chapter 16, Masso et al. examine the labor market trajectories of return migrants to Estonia and Slovakia. They analyze how the characteristics of young return migrants (aged 18–34 years) differ from those of their peers who either stayed in Estonia and Slovakia or are still working in another European country. They also investigate the short-term labor market outcomes of returnees relative to the two other groups. The analysis is based on national LFS data sets from 2009–2013. The authors find that return migrants, in both countries, are more likely to be young, male, and overqualified before their return compared to stayers. Return migrants in Slovakia initially face a higher risk of short-term unemployment, but they exit unemployment registries faster than stayers. In contrast, Estonian returnees who register with the labor office exit the registry at a slower pace than the unemployed in general. Masso et al.'s findings can inform policymaking aimed at reintegrating young return migrants into home-country labor markets under changing economic conditions and varied welfare support structures.

Altogether, the four chapters in Part III provide fresh insights into the experiences of young migrants during the Great Recession. Although European youth (particularly from a number of Central and Eastern countries of origin and—more recently—Southern Europe) show relatively high mobility and have comparatively high employment rates, some of them are also more prone to skills–occupation mismatch, atypical working conditions, and vulnerability compared to nationals in the destination countries to which they migrate.

1.7.4. Part IV: Challenging Futures for Youth

Drawing this volume to a close, the chapters in Part IV identify a number of key issues that will remain significant in future years. These chapters focus on the concept of NEETs; the consequences of overeducation, gender, and ethnic differences; the promises and drawbacks of youth self-employment; young people's attitudes; and what possibilities there are for trade unions to organize the next generation of young workers.

Starting with the concept of NEETs, Mascherini provides an overview in Chapter 17 of the origin of the concept and how it entered the European policy agenda. He reviews the characteristics, evolution, and composition of the NEET population in Europe using EU-LFS data. He then proposes disaggregating the NEET indicator so as to better address the heterogeneity of different subgroups of young people categorized as NEETs. These subgroups include re-entrants into the labor market or education, the short- and long-term unemployed, young people unavailable because of illness or disability, young people unavailable because of family responsibilities, discouraged workers, and other inactives. The chapter discusses the diversity of member states in terms of size and composition of the NEET population, as well as their STW transition patterns. This is linked with an analysis of the first year of the implementation of the European Youth Guarantee and the concrete measures adopted by member states in order to address the needs of the different subgroups of NEETs.

In contrast to the NEET population, the problem of overeducation is perceived as a consequence of the expansion of higher education and the lack of appropriately skilled jobs for graduates. Well-qualified young people may have to enter employment that is below their qualification level, which in turn can have long-term consequences for their future labor market success. Drawing on EU-LFS data to construct quarterly time series of both youth (aged 15–24 years) and adult (aged 25–64 years) overeducation between 1997 and 2011 for 29 European countries, Chapter 18 by McGuinness, Bergin, and Whelan assesses the rate of overeducation among various age cohorts across countries and over time. Using time-series techniques, the authors find that youth overeducation is substantially driven by the composition of education provision, aggregate labor demand, and labor market flexibility.

Gender and ethnicity differences after a period of nonemployment are the focus of Chapter 19 by Zuccotti and O'Reilly. Their analysis is based on the Office for National Statistics Longitudinal Study, a large-scale data set from England and Wales that follows employment and occupational outcomes for individuals from 2001 (aged 16–29 years) to 2011 (aged 26–39 years). Being NEET in 2001 leads to approximately 17 pp less chance of being employed 10 years later (while controlling for comparable levels of education, social background, and neighborhood deprivation). However, this penalty varies across ethnic groups. The NEET scar is less severe among Indian and Bangladeshi men than among White British men by more than half. In contrast, the scars appear to be deeper for Pakistani and Caribbean women than for White British women.

Self-employment for youth has been widely promoted at the national and European level as a response to changing labor market conditions (European Commission 2010). But how beneficial is self-employment for young people? Is it a new form of precarious and poor-quality employment? Despite considerable interest among policymakers in measures to stimulate self-employment and entrepreneurship, there is limited comparative evidence about the nature and quality of self-employment, as well as the job-creation propensities of these enterprises. Ortlieb, Sheehan, and Masso address this gap in Chapter 20 using a comparative mixed methods approach. In addition to a range of secondary data sources, they draw on in-depth interviews with founders of business start-ups (aged 18–34 years) in six countries—Estonia, Germany, Ireland, Poland, Spain, and the United Kingdom—focusing on two industries (cultural and creative, and communication technologies). The analysis takes account of the differences between self-employed people who work as sole traders—sometimes under conditions that have been termed "bogus self-employment"—and those business founders who run an enterprise with employees. The findings suggest that for some young people, self-employment presents an option that offers high-quality jobs. A group of young self-employed people report that they can use and further develop their skills, and they appreciate the high degrees of autonomy and flexibility. However, the actual volume of jobs created through self-employment is rather low. Moreover, job quality is impaired by poor social protection, with negative consequences especially in the long term. Policies need to address the high risks associated with self-employment in relation to unemployment, health care, and pension benefits.

Another dimension of future challenges discussed in this volume relates to changing attitudes toward and values regarding work among young people compared to previous generations. In Chapter 21, Hajdu and Sik conceptualize and operationalize different aspects of work values. They draw on international data sets (World Values Survey/European Values Study, European Social Survey, and International Social Survey Programme) to test for more than 30 countries whether work values differ across birth cohorts, age groups, and periods. The most important result is that significant gaps do not exist among the birth cohorts regarding the centrality of work, employment commitment, or extrinsic and intrinsic work values. Consequently, the authors argue that generations are not significantly divided in their work values in contemporary Europe.

The final challenge examined here looks at the problem of low youth unionization in Europe. Chapter 22 by Vandaele argues that the low and decreasing rate of youth unionization in the majority of European countries is not the outcome of a generational shift in attitudes and beliefs regarding the value of trade unions. Rather, this is a result of the decline of union membership as a social practice and the diminishing exposure of young people to unionism at the workplace. The chapter illustrates with a number of examples that unions have a large amount of agency in developing effective, tailor-made strategies for organizing young workers and thereby strengthening their collective voice.

1.8. CONCLUSIONS

The book draws to a close by providing an integrated analysis of the findings of all the research presented in the volume. We discuss the challenges of comparing youth transitions across countries and the importance of using a wider range of indicators and a more comprehensive policy focus. First, we argue that the concept of economic production encapsulates some of the key dimensions and foci for policy initiatives related to VET, labor market flexibility, insecurity, and mobility. Second, we contend that an exclusive focus on this domain risks undervaluing the continued importance of the sphere of social reproduction, the role of family legacies, and how these affect established and emerging forms of inequality. Third, we propose that given the complexity and variety of youth transitions, policy initiatives need to attend simultaneously to both dimensions so as to develop multifocused strategies for ensuring successful youth transitions. The final chapter concludes with an outlook on what directions are required for future policymaking and research targeted at identifying sustainable bridges that facilitate youth labor market transitions.

NOTES

1 The research presented here draws evidence from an EU-funded interdisciplinary research project involving 25 partners from 19 European countries, including Turkey (http://www.style-research.eu). This was funded from the European Union's Seventh Framework Programme for research, technological development, and demonstration under grant agreement No. 613256.
2 The NEET share is higher if we consider the age group 20–34 years, which stood at 18.9% in 2015—this is approximately 17.6 million young people in the EU28 (Eurostat 2017, EU-LFS, not shown).

REFERENCES

Alba, Richard. 2011. "Schools and the Diversity Transition in the Wealthy Societies of the West." *American Behavioral Scientist* 55 (12): 1616–34.

Arts, Wil, and John Gelissen. 2012. "Models of the Welfare State." In *The Oxford Handbook of the Welfare State,* edited by Francis Castles, Stephan Leibfried, Jane Lewis, Herbert Obinger, and Christopher Pierson, 569–83. Oxford: Oxford University Press.

Becker, Rolf. 2003. "Educational Expansion and Persistent Inequalities of Education: Utilizing Subjective Expected Utility Theory to Explain Increasing Participation Rates in Upper Secondary School in the Federal Republic of Germany." *European Sociological Review* 19 (1): 1–24.

Berg, Ellen L., and Douglas J. Besharov. 2016. "Patterns of Global Migration." In *Adjusting to a World in Motion: Trends in Global Migration and Migration,* edited by Douglas J. Besharov and Mark H. Lopez, 58–79. Oxford: Oxford University Press.

Blanchflower, David G., and Richard B. Freeman. 2000. "The Declining Economic Status of Young Workers in OECD Countries." In *Youth Employment and Joblessness in Advanced Countries*, edited by David G. Blanchflower and Richard B. Freeman, 19–56. Chicago: University of Chicago Press.

Boeri, Tito, and Juan F. Jimeno. 2015. *The Unbearable Divergence of Unemployment in Europe.* CEP Discussion Paper 1384. London: London School of Economics.

Brzinsky-Fay, Christian. 2007. "Lost in Transition? Labour Market Entry Sequences of School Leavers in Europe." *European Sociological Review* 23 (4): 409–22.

Charles, Maria, Marlis Buchmann, Susan Halebsky, Jeanne M. Powers, and Marisa M. Smith. 2001. "The Context of Women's Market Careers: A Cross-National Study." *Work and Occupations* 28 (3): 371–96.

Clark, Ken, and Stephen Drinkwater. 2008. "The Labour-Market Performance of Recent Migrants." *Oxford Review of Economic Policy* 24 (3): 495–516.

Crul, Maurice, Jens Schneider, and Frans Lelie. 2012. *The European Second Generation Compared: Does the Integration Context Matter?* Amsterdam: Amsterdam University Press.

Eurofound. 2012. *NEETs—Young People Not in Employment, Education or Training: Characteristic, Costs and Policy Responses in Europe.* Luxembourg: Publications Office of the European Union.

Eurostat. 2015. "People in the EU—Population Projections." http://ec.europa.eu/eurostat/statistics-explained/index.php/People_in_the_EU_-_population_projections

Eurostat. 2017. "Statistics on Young People Neither in Employment nor in Education or Training." http://ec.europa.eu/eurostat/statistics-explained/index.php/Statistics_on_young_people_neither_in_employment_nor_in_education_or_training

Ferragina, Emanuele, and Martin Seeleib-Kaiser. 2011. "Thematic Review: Welfare Regime Debate: Past, Present, Future?" *Policy & Politics* 39 (4): 583–611.

Furlong, Andy, and Fred Cartmel. 2006. "Social Change and Labour Market Transitions." In *Young People and Social Change*, edited by Andy Furlong and Fred Cartmel, 34–51. Berkshire, UK: McGraw-Hill.

Galgóczi, Béla, Janine Leschke, and Andrew Watt, eds. 2009. *EU Labour Migration Since Enlargement: Trends, Impacts and Policies.* Aldershot, UK: Ashgate.

Galgóczi, Béla, Janine Leschke, and Andrew Watt, eds. 2012. *EU Migration and Labour Markets in Troubled Times: Skills Mismatch, Return and Policy Responses.* Aldershot, UK: Ashgate.

Gangl, Markus. 2003. "Returns to Education in Context: Individual Education and Transition Outcomes in European Labour Markets." In *Transitions from Education to Work in Europe: The Integration of Youth into EU Labour Markets*, edited by Markus Gangl and Walter Müller, 156–85. Oxford: Oxford University Press.

Gangl, Markus, Walter Müller, and David Raffe. 2003. "Conclusions: Explaining Cross-National Differences in School-to-Work Transitions." In *Transitions from Education to Work in Europe: The Integration of Youth into EU Labour Markets*, edited by Markus Gangl and Walter Müller, 277–305. Oxford: Oxford University Press.

Gökşen, Fatoş, Alpay Filiztekin, Mark Smith, Çetin Çelik, İbrahim Öker, and Sinem Kuz. 2016. "Vulnerable Youth and Gender in Europe." STYLE Working Paper 4.3. Brighton, UK: CROME, University of Brighton. http://www.style-research.eu/publications/working-papers

Gruber, Jonathan, and David A. Wise. 2010. *Social Security Programs and Retirement Around the World: The Relationship to Youth Employment.* Chicago: University of Chicago Press.

Gundert, Stefanie, and Karl U. Mayer. 2012. "Gender Segregation in Training and Social Mobility of Women in West Germany." *European Sociological Review* 28 (1): 59–81.

Hadjivassiliou, Kari P., Catherine Rickard, Chiara Manzoni, and Sam Swift. 2016. "Database of Effective Youth Employment Measures in Selected Member States." STYLE Working Paper 4.4b. Brighton, UK: CROME, University of Brighton. http://www.style-research.eu/publications/working-papers

Hall, Peter A., and David Soskice. 2001. *Varieties of Capitalism: The Institutional Foundations of Comparative Advantage.* Oxford: Oxford University Press.

Halvorsen, Rune, Bjørn Hvinden, Jerome Bickenbach, Delia Ferri, and Ana Marta Guillén Rodriguez, eds. 2017. *The Changing Disability Policy System: Active Citizenship and Disability in Europe.* London: Routledge.

Hart, Angie, Claire Stubbs, Stefanos Plexousakis, Maria Georgiadi, and Elias Kourkoutas. 2015. "Aspirations of Vulnerable Young People in Foster Care." STYLE Working Paper 9.3. Brighton, UK: CROME, University of Brighton. http://www.style-research.eu/publications/working-papers

Jepsen, Maria, and Jan Drahokoupil, 2017. "The Digital Economy and Its Implications for Labour." *Transfer* 23 (3): 103–7.

Johnston, Ron, Nabil Khattab, and David J. Manley. 2015. "East Versus West? Over-Qualification and Earnings Among the UK's European Migrants." *Journal of Ethnic and Migration Studies* 41 (2): 196–218.

Kahanec, Martin, and Klaus Zimmermann. 2016. *Labor Migration, EU Enlargement, and the Great Recession.* Berlin: Springer.

Keck, Wolfgang, and Chiara Saraceno. 2013. "The Impact of Different Social-Policy Frameworks on Social Inequalities Among Women in the European Union: The Labour-Market Participation of Mothers." *Social Politics* 20 (3): 297–328.

Krizsan, Andrea, Hege Skjeie, and Judith Squires. 2012. *Institutionalizing Intersectionality: The Changing Nature of European Equality Regimes.* Basingstoke, UK: Palgrave Macmillan.

Leschke, Janine. 2009. "The Segmentation Potential of Non-Standard Employment: A Four-Country Comparison of Mobility Patterns." *International Journal of Manpower* 30 (7): 692–715.

Lobel, Orly. 2017. "The Gig Economy and the Future of Employment and Labor Law." *University of San Francisco Law Review* 51 (1): 51–74.

Marsden, David, and Paul Ryan. 1986. "Where Do Young Workers Work? Youth Employment by Industry in Various European Economies." *British Journal of Industrial Relations* 24 (1): 83–102.

Neufeind, Max, Jacqueline O'Reilly, and Florian Ranft. ed. 2018. *Work in the Digital Age: Challenges of the Fourth Industrial Revolution.* London: Rowman and Littlefield.

O'Reilly, Jacqueline, ed. 2003. *Regulating Working Time Transitions in Europe.* Cheltenham, UK: Elgar.

O'Reilly, Jacqueline. 2006. "Framing Comparisons: Gendering Perspectives on Cross-National Comparisons of Welfare and Work." *Work, Employment & Society* 20 (4): 731–50.

O'Reilly, Jacqueline, Inmaculada Cebrián, and Michel Lallement. 2000. *Working Time Changes: Social Integration Through Transitional Labour Markets.* Cheltenham, UK: Elgar.

O'Reilly, Jacqueline, Werner Eichhorst, András Gábos, Kari Hadjivassiliou, David Lain, Janine Leschke, Seamus McGuinness, et al. 2015. "Five Characteristics of Youth Unemployment in Europe: Flexibility, Education, Migration, Family Legacies, and EU Policy." *Sage Open* 5 (1): 1–19. doi:10.1177/2158244015574962.

O'Reilly, Jacqueline, Mark Smith, and Paola Villa. 2017. "The Social Reproduction of Youth Labour Market Inequalities: The Effects of Gender, Households and Ethnicity." In *Making Work More Equal: A New Labour Market Segmentation Approach*, edited by Damian Grimshaw, Colette Fagan, Gail Hebson, and Isabel Tavora, 249–67. Manchester, UK: Manchester University Press.

Pohl, Axel, and Andreas Walther. 2007. "Activating the Disadvantaged: Variations in Addressing Youth Transitions Across Europe." *International Journal of Lifelong Education* 26 (5): 533–53. doi:10.1080/02601370701559631.

Quintini, Glenda, and Thomas Manfredi. 2009. *Going Separate Ways? School-to-Work Transitions in the United States and Europe.* OECD Social, Employment and Migration Working Paper 90. Paris: OECD.

Roberts, Steven, and Robert MacDonald. 2013. "Introduction for Special Section of Sociological Research Online: The Marginalised Mainstream: Making Sense of the 'Missing Middle' of Youth Studies." *Sociological Research Online* 18 (1). http://www.socresonline.org.uk/18/1/21.html

Russell, Helen, and Philip J. O'Connell. 2001. "Getting a Job in Europe: The Transition from Unemployment to Work Among Young People in Nine European Countries." *Work, Employment and Society* 15 (1): 1–24.

Russell, Helen, Janine Leschke, and Mark Smith. 2015. "Balancing Flexibility and Security in Europe: The Impact on Young People's Insecurity and Subjective Well-Being." STYLE Working Paper 10.3. Brighton, UK: CROME, University of Brighton. http://www.style-research.eu/publications/working-papers

Scarpetta, Stefano, Anne Sonnet, and Thomas Manfredi. 2010. "Rising Youth Unemployment During the Crisis: How to Prevent Negative Long-Term Consequences on a Generation?" OECD Social, Employment and Migration Paper 106. Paris: OECD.

Schmid, Günther. 2008. *Full Employment in Europe: Managing Labour Market Transitions and Risks.* Cheltenham, UK: Elgar.

Smith, Mark, and Paola Villa. 2016. "Flexicurity Policies to Integrate Youth Before and After the Crisis." STYLE Working Paper 10.4. Brighton, UK: CROME, University of Brighton. http://www.style-research.eu/publications/working-papers

TUC. 2012. "Youth Unemployment and Ethnicity." London: Trade Union Congress. https://www.tuc.org.uk/sites/default/files/BMEyouthunemployment.pdf

Van der Velden, Rolf K. W., and Maarten H. J. Wolbers. 2003. "The Integration of Young People into the Labour Market: The Role of Training Systems and Labour Market Regulation." In *Transitions from Education to Work in Europe: The Integration of Youth into EU Labour Markets*, edited by Markus Gangl and Walter Müller, 186–211. Oxford: Oxford University Press.

Vivarelli, Marco. 2014. "Innovation, Employment and Skills in Advanced and Developing Countries: A Survey of Economic Literature." *Journal of Economic Issues* 48 (1): 123–54.

Wallace, Claire, and René Bendit. 2009. "Youth Policies in Europe: Towards a Classification of Different Tendencies in Youth Policies in the European Union." *Perspectives on European Politics and Society* 10 (3): 441–58. doi:10.1080/15705850903105868.

Walther, Andreas, and Axel Pohl. 2005. "Thematic Study on Policies for Disadvantaged Youth in Europe: Final Report to the European Commission." Tübingen: Institute for Regional Innovation and Social Research. http://ec.europa.eu/employment_social/social_inclusion/docs/youth_study_en.pdf.

PART I

COMPARING PROBLEMATIC YOUTH TRANSITIONS TO WORK

2

WHERE DO YOUNG PEOPLE WORK?

Raffaele Grotti, Helen Russell, and Jacqueline O'Reilly

2.1. INTRODUCTION

A considerable body of comparative research on youth labor markets has focused on differences in school-to-work (STW) transitions and their impact on
youth employment. Much of this research has examined institutional factors,
comparing the performance of different vocational education and training
(VET) systems, the effectiveness of active labor market policies, wage-setting
arrangements, or the need for young people to have greater employability skills.
However, surprisingly little attention has been given to employers' behavior or
to identifying which sectors of the economy are more open to employing young
people and how these have changed over time. This chapter seeks to address this
gap by examining where young people (aged 16–24 years) have been employed—
prior to and since the Great Recession of 2008–2009.

2.2. COMPARING YOUTH TRANSITIONS
ACROSS COUNTRIES AND SECTORS

2.2.1. Country Comparisons

Comparative employment research has drawn on a range of different analytical
frameworks that can be used to understand youth employment. These range
from polarized "ideal types," such as the *Varieties of Capitalism* (Hall and Soskice
2001), to more complex typologies encompassing a broader range of variables
(O'Reilly 2006). These typologies focus not only on VET systems, wage setting,

trade unions, and employers' organizations but also on labor market policies and labor market characteristics, as well as cognitive conceptions of what kind of problem youth unemployment represents for policymakers (Russell and O'Connell 2001; Wallace and Bendit 2009; Buchmann and Kriesi 2011).

Using a multidimensional approach, Pohl and Walther (2007) classify countries into five types of "youth transition regimes": *universalistic* (Denmark, Finland, and Sweden); *employment-centered*, primarily based on dual training (Austria and Germany), but also including school-based (France) or mixed (Netherlands) training; *liberal* (Ireland and the United Kingdom); *subprotective* (Cyprus, Italy, Greece, Portugal, and Spain); and *post-socialist*, which includes a mixed liberal and employment-centered approach (e.g., Baltic states, Bulgaria, Romania, Slovenia, and Slovakia). This comparative framework provides a parsimonious heuristic device for making systematic comparisons of trends in youth employment between countries (for a fuller discussion of this typology, see Hadjivassiliou et al., this volume).

2.2.2. Sectorial Comparisons

Here, we are interested in differences in youth employment not only between countries and regime types but also between sectors within countries—a topic that has received surprisingly little attention (Marsden and Ryan 1986). Cross-national research has tended to focus either on macroeconomic factors and the effects of labor market policies or on supply-side comparisons of youth "employability." More qualitative sectorial studies of employer engagement have either examined differences within one country (Simms, Gamwell, and Hopkins 2017) or evaluated the impact of labor market policies in particular sectors, again often within one country (Lewis and Ryan 2008). Overall, there has been a remarkably limited examination of the role of employers and of sectorial trends in understanding changes in youth employment from a cross-national perspective.

An early comparative study from Marsden and Ryan (1986) asked, "Where do young workers work?" These authors established that youth employment was not evenly distributed across sectors; in fact, services and some areas of manufacturing were more open to youth than other sectors (Marsden and Ryan 1986, 85). Within countries, considerable variation between "youth-friendly" sectors emerged, but this distribution was very similar across all six countries the authors examined. At the time this research was carried out (1972), and focusing only on male youth, the most popular sectors were footwear, clothing, wood products, and textiles—all largely manufacturing jobs.

More recent studies by Blanchflower and Freeman (2000), using Organization for Economic Co-operation and Development (OECD) data from 1994, have revealed the persistent uneven distribution of youth employment across sectors. Blanchflower and Freeman distinguished between "youth-intensive" industries, in which there is a higher ratio of younger to older workers,[1] and they found that young people (aged 16–24 years) were more likely to be employed in hotels and restaurants, retail, and repair than in utilities, education, or public administration. Two sectors (hotel and restaurants, and retail) accounted for 39% of all young workers in Germany and France in 1994. Gender differences were also identifiable, with young men being disproportionately employed in construction and young women disproportionately in the health sector. Like Marsden and Ryan before them, these authors found that "the uniformity of these patterns across countries is striking and suggests that, differences in school to work transition patterns notwithstanding, what happens to the youth labor market depends critically on developments in a limited set of sectors in all countries" (p. 47).

2.2.3. Gender Segregation

Greater attention has been given to sectorial comparison of the changing composition of employment in studies on gender segregation and the Great Recession. Bettio and Verashchagina (2014) found that the concentration of women in the public sector and in services shielded them from the worst job losses. Rubery and Rafferty (2013) also emphasize the role of gender segregation in their analysis of the crisis in the United Kingdom; they argue that recession and restructuring may induce changes in segregation through substitution that will result in higher unemployment rates for women. Kelly et al. (2014) show that gender segregation in Ireland fully accounts for the observed gender differential in unemployment rates during the recent recession: The hyper-concentration of young men in construction was a significant factor in the disproportionate rise in male youth unemployment.

This body of research indicates that not only is youth employment concentrated in particular sectors but also this varies significantly by gender. As a result, we might expect the consequences for youth employment opportunities to be sensitive to how these sectors were affected by the Great Recession.

2.2.4. Comparing the Quality of Employment

In addition to the quantity of jobs created or destroyed, there has also been a long-running interest in the quality of youth employment. Marsden and Ryan (1986) were also interested in understanding the quality of employment that young people can access and how pay rates affect their employment opportunities. They argued that young people have greater difficulty entering jobs where adult wages are high and jobs are well protected. Employers are more likely to view young people as less productive and relatively expensive compared to older workers, if they are expected to treat them on similar terms of employment. Young workers are likely to find it easier to enter low-wage, low-skilled jobs, for which there is less competition from older workers. In sectors where employers can pay apprentices lower rates of pay, this has encouraged higher rates of youth employment. The quality of these jobs could be enhanced where there was a good apprenticeship system in place, as evidenced by Germany, which overall has a much higher proportion of skilled young workers compared to other countries.

More recent analysis from Blanchflower and Freeman (2000, 49) expected the youth share of employment for 20- to 24-year-olds to increase between 1985 and 1994. Demographic trends with falling numbers of youth, increased educational participation, and the growth of a youth-friendly service sector should have led to an increase in the youth share of employment. Instead, this share fell, and the quality of youth employment and earnings deteriorated in nearly all OECD countries. Blanchflower and Freeman attribute this to the worsening conditions of low-paid and less skilled jobs.

2.2.5. Declining Demand for Youth Labor

In addition to the previously mentioned deterioration, Blanchflower and Freeman (2000) argue that there has been a "massively declining labor demand for young workers" (p. 54). A similar finding has been provided in a more recent analysis from Boeri and Jimeno (2015, 4). The latter authors attribute the explosion of European youth joblessness since the Great Recession to a massive elimination of jobs held by young people and to a hiring freeze by employers. Indeed, employers' first response to decreases in demand is to stop recruiting and to not renew temporary contracts when they expire. Boeri and Jimeno argue that the destruction of jobs for young people came about with the "dissolution of temporary contracts, while at the same time employment rates among older workers were increasing" (p. 4). As Boeri and Jimeno acknowledge, this is a distinct feature of the Great Recession. In previous economic downturns, older workers were incentivized to leave the labor market via early retirement plans. In the recent period, fiscal consolidation has led to increasing retirement ages to the detriment of employment among young people. Boeri and Jimeno cite this as one example of a more general thesis: Reforms that are effective in normal times may not be desirable during major recessions. However, older workers are not a direct substitute for younger workers because they have different skills and experience that employers value (Eichhorst et al. 2014).

Countries also show different capacities for integrating young people. Despite country similarities in the distribution of youth-friendly jobs across sectors, there was significant variation between countries in the proportions of employed youth. The Marsden and Ryan (1986) study found that some countries, such as Italy, had very low shares of youth employment, whereas these rates were much higher in the United Kingdom. Country differences clearly have had a long-term impact on how many young people are integrated into paid work, where that work is located, and the status it is accorded. This variation is likely to derive from both long-term processes (related to change in the economic structure and labor market institutional characteristics) and short-term cyclical effects, which elicit different national policy responses (Blanchflower and Freeman 2000; O'Higgins 2012; Boeri and Jimeno 2015).

Some accounts of the declines in youth employment attribute them to the impact of the economic crisis on particular sectors. Okun's law predicts that the depth of the recession, measured as a decline in gross domestic product (GDP), has a direct correlation with the rise in unemployment. However, O'Higgins (2012) suggests that Okun's law is not well supported in the European case. For example, Ireland experienced a 12% drop in GDP and a disproportionally large fall of 53% in youth employment; the explanation, he argues, while including an account of other countries, is largely related to a fall in aggregate labor demand (O'Higgins 2012, 21). Boeri and Jimeno (2015) draw a similar conclusion to that of O'Higgins (2012). Although they argue that Okun's law can account for approximately 50% of the change in youth jobs in Europe, it does not explain the "unbearable divergence of unemployment in Europe." This divergence, they believe, is the product of both shocks of varying intensity and different labor market responses. Policy options include increasing wage flexibility or employment flexibility, where this can mean either cuts in the number of hours worked or cuts in the number of people employed. Whether youth unemployment is a long-term structural characteristic related to labor market institutions or the result of short-term cyclical effects is contested; Boeri and Jimeno (2015, 4) suggest that even long-term structural characteristics fluctuate too much over time.

2.2.6. Research Questions

Evidence from this literature suggests three possible lines of investigation to understand how sectorial differences affected youth employment rates during the Great Recession. First, changes to the overall size of youth-friendly sectors can explain why the youth job market worsened, or in a few cases improved. We can hypothesize that part of the explanation for the growth in youth unemployment is related to how the size of these sectors changed since 2007. Did young people lose their jobs because the sector shrunk as a result of economic shock and the recession? This would be a reasonable expectation in countries in which youth were disproportionately employed in the construction sector and in which there had been a housing bubble leading up to 2007 (Boeri and Jimeno 2015). Or, second, did the fall in youth employment come about because employers' propensity to employ young workers declined? This would be evidenced by a decline in the youth:older worker ratio. Third, was the growth of youth unemployment only a consequence of the destruction of temporary jobs; that is, was it easier to get rid of young people, especially in dualist labor markets? Or, have youth job opportunities continued to deteriorate with the growth of lower quality employment, in the way identified by Blanchflower and Freeman (2000)?

2.3. RESEARCH DESIGN, DATA, MEASURES, AND METHODS

To answer the previous questions, we draw on European Union Labour Force Survey (EU-LFS) data, examining where young people (aged 16–24 years) have been employed and how this changed between 2007 and 2014. First, we examine the descriptive statistics on youth unemployment and labor force participation trends for the five country groups over three decades (from 1983, where possible, to 2014). The 23 countries considered have been chosen in order to maximize the time span over which we can assess the trends. At the same time, so as to have consistent aggregate measures, the countries chosen have data for the entire period.[2] We present aggregate trends for two measures: the youth unemployment rate and the youth labor force participation rate.

The youth unemployment rate represents the share of unemployed youth among the active—that is, employed or unemployed—youth labor force population. Students and other inactive youth are not included in this estimate. In contrast, the labor force participation rate records the share of economically active youth over the total youth population, including those who are inactive. We decided to complement the measure of unemployment rate with the measure of participation rate in order to provide a more comprehensive picture of the nonemployment phenomenon among youth and of the heterogeneity among country groups in the forces that have driven unemployment trends. Indeed, focusing only on the unemployment rate risks missing important aspects of the phenomenon (O'Reilly et al. 2015). This is because variations in the unemployment rate may be the result both of flows between unemployment and employment and of flows from unemployment or employment to inactivity, and vice versa (O'Higgins 2012; Berloffa et al., this volume; Flek, Hála, and Mysíková, this volume); for a discussion of measures of youth not in employment, education, or training (NEETs), see Mascherini (this volume).

Second, we select 11 countries that represent the five country groups to provide a more in-depth analysis identifying where young people have been employed and how this has changed over three time points: before (2007), during (2010), and after (2014) the Great Recession. The countries selected are Denmark and Sweden for the universalistic group; France, Germany, and the Netherlands representing the employment-centered countries; Ireland and the United Kingdom for the liberal countries; Italy and Spain for the subprotective countries; and Hungary and Poland representing the post-socialist countries. By including pairs of countries for each regime type, we can also identify differences within these categories.

Third, we use a shift-share analysis to address our research question as to whether young people lost their jobs because a sector reduced in size or because it became less youth friendly, suggesting a reduction in employers' propensity to employ young people. This allows us to disaggregate changes in employment by economic activity. It also enables us to answer our third research question regarding the deteriorating quality of jobs for youth by drawing on other relevant characteristics relating to employment status (full-time/part-time and permanent/temporary employment) and demography (age and gender). This method is particularly suitable for our purposes. It allows us to decompose aggregate changes in total employment resulting from different driving forces: the structural change in the overall size of sectors (growth effect), the change in the proportion of youth workers in each sector (share effect), and the interaction between these two forces (interaction effect).

More formally, where Y_t is the share of youth over total employment in year t, we can write

$$Y_t = \sum_i T_{i,t} p_{i,t}$$

where $T_{i,t}$ represents total employment in sector i in year t, and $p_{i,t}$ is the share of youth employment over total employment in sector i in year t. Then, based on these two quantities, we can decompose the changes in the share of youth employment as follows:

$$\Delta Y_t = Y_t - Y_{t-1} =$$

$$= \sum_i \left(T_{i,t} - T_{i,t-1} \right) p_{i,t-1} \qquad \text{Growth effect}$$

$$+ \sum_i \left(p_{i,t} - p_{i,t-1} \right) T_{i,t-1} \qquad \text{Share effect}$$

$$+ \sum_i \left(p_{i,t} - p_{i,t-1} \right) \left(T_{i,t} - T_{i,t-1} \right) \quad \text{Interaction effect}$$

This equation can be further decomposed to disaggregate changes in youth employment by subgroups—for example, distinguishing between males and females or distinguishing youth according to their employment status (i.e., full-time, part-time, or temporary employment). In these cases, the aggregate changes, as well as the contribution of the different effects, do not change but are simply further disaggregated by additional characteristics.

Throughout the chapter, we define employment in accordance with the International Labour Organization definition. Under this definition, anyone working at least 1 hour during the reference week is considered employed, which includes, for example, students working part-time. This has possible implications for the comparative dimension of the study because in some countries, such as the Nordic states, students are more likely to work than in others, leading to a higher estimation of youth employment.

The self-employed are included with the employed, except when we examine temporary/permanent contracts, because this characteristic applies only to employees. Less than 5% of employed youth are self-employed, with the exception of Poland, Spain, and especially Italy (see Ortlieb, Sheehan, and Masso, this volume). As we will show, the results that exclude the self-employed are in line with the results for total employment.

Finally, in the decomposition analyses, the categorization of the sectors is based on the NACE statistical classification of economic activities in the EU (Eurostat 2008).[3] Shift-share analysis furnishes descriptive understandings of the shifting trends over time and allows us to investigate whether changes in youth employment are driven by structural shifts in the growth or shrinkage of particular economic sectors or whether they are attributable to changes in employers' propensity to employ young people.[4]

2.4. TRENDS IN YOUTH UNEMPLOYMENT AND ACTIVITY RATES

The recession of 2008–2009 marked the end of a period of fairly continuous growth in youth employment during the early years of the millennium. Since 2008, youth unemployment has soared dramatically in subprotective, liberal, and post-socialist countries (Figure 2.1). The subprotective countries have had some of the highest levels of youth unemployment, even since the mid-1980s, while

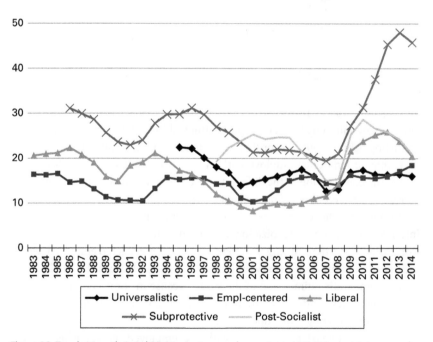

Figure 2.1 Trends in youth (aged 16–24 years) unemployment rate in 11 EU countries, grouped by youth transition regime: 1983–2014 (%).
Source: EU-LFS; authors' analysis.

youth unemployment rates were also high in liberal countries during the 1980s. Toward the end of that decade, youth unemployment began to fall in both regions, but then it increased again coming into the mid-1990s. Until the Great Recession in 2008–2009, youth unemployment had been falling across most regions. The exception to this trend was the post-socialist countries, which experienced very high levels of youth unemployment in the 1990s. However, by the mid-2000s, this was also beginning to change, mainly driven by Poland and Slovakia, so that by 2007 the overall levels for this group of countries were converging with the levels in other European countries. The fluctuating trend in unemployment characterizing the employment-centered regime did not result in substantial variation between the beginning of our observational window and the pre-recession period, although notable variations were present during that time. The universalistic countries, which we observe from the mid-1990s, experienced a decline in youth unemployment up until the end of the century, which was mainly driven by reductions in youth unemployment in Sweden and, above all, in Finland. Overall, prior to the Great Recession, trends in the rate of youth unemployment appeared to be converging over time between country groups. Indeed, at the outset of the recession, youth unemployment ranged from 12% to 15% for all groups of countries apart from the subprotective, which registered a value of 19%.

With the onset of the recession, more variation between country groups can be observed. At one extreme, there are the universalistic and employment-centered countries, where youth unemployment grew slightly at the very beginning of the recession and then stabilized. Germany had experienced rising levels of youth unemployment up until 2005 (Kohlrausch 2012), but, unlike any other country, youth unemployment fell there during the recession. At the other extreme, in the subprotective countries, where youth unemployment was already very high—driven especially by Spain and Greece—the rate more than doubled to staggeringly high levels with the onset of the recession in 2008. In the middle are the liberal and post-socialist countries, which witnessed a notable increase in youth unemployment in the first years of the recession and a subsequent decrease. However, these declines have not counterbalanced the steep growth in the immediate postcrisis period. In these two country groups, the countries driving the upward trends were Ireland, Latvia, and Lithuania. By 2014, we observed a convergence between country groups, with the youth unemployment rate ranging from 16% to 21% everywhere, apart from the subprotective cluster, which has a youth unemployment rate of 46%.

Looking at unemployment rates only, however, may hide important dynamics of the phenomenon. For example, the unemployment rate does not capture the outflow of individuals from the pool of the active population, which is more widespread among youth than among prime-age workers (see Flek et al., this volume). Greater difficulties in making the transition from school to work can lead young people to stay longer in education. Several countries in fact witnessed increases in enrollments in higher education during the Great Recession (OECD 2013). The recession may also have led to "discouragement" among young people, who gave up on the labor market when job search failed. The problem of NEETs highlights this latter issue (see Mascherini, this volume). For these reasons, the picture presented previously should be interpreted in light of the evolution of youth labor market participation (Figure 2.2). Unemployment dynamics can thus be seen as the result of both demand- and supply-side factors.

Here, we see that the universalistic countries have the highest levels of youth labor market participation and that this has been fairly constant over the observed period. Overall, for the other countries, there is a fall in youth labor market participation rates from the 1980s until the late 1990s, arguably because of the increasing number of young people staying on in education. From the late 1990s onward, youth participation stabilized up until the recession in the liberal and employment-centered countries. In the post-socialist countries, after a steep decline, youth participation stabilized around the mid-2000s, while the subprotective countries experienced an uninterrupted decline.

With the onset of the Great Recession, young people started to exit again from the labor market in four country groups out of five. The post-socialist group is

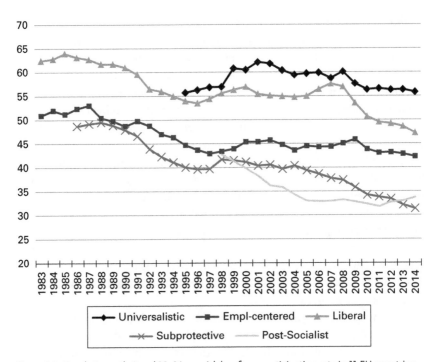

Figure 2.2 Trends in youth (aged 16–24 years) labor force participation rate in 11 EU countries, grouped by youth transition regime: 1983–2014 (%).
Source: EU-LFS; authors' analysis.

the exception. A particularly marked decline is observed for the liberal and the subprotective groups.

The combined trends in youth unemployment and labor market participation provide a more complete picture of the consequences of recession for youth in terms of jobs lost. This is particularly true for the young people in the liberal group and especially in the subprotective group, who experienced the highest decline in labor market participation and the largest increase in unemployment. The phenomenon of youth exclusion from the labor market is far more substantial if we consider both indicators jointly, as discussed by Blanchflower and Freeman (2000).

The heaviest consequences of the Great Recession have been paid by Mediterranean youth, where almost one in two young people were unemployed in the last phase of the recession. If we do not limit our focus to the active youth population but expand our attention toward the labor market participation of youth, the scenario is even more stark. Indeed, the trends for labor force participation show that a growing share of youth is giving up or postponing employment and moving into inactivity. The consequences of this latter trend depend on the extent to which young people are remaining longer in education or are stuck in other forms of "inactivity" (see Mascherini, this volume).

2.5. CROSS-NATIONAL VARIATION IN THE YOUTH SHARE OF EMPLOYMENT

As Marsden and Ryan (1986) noted, countries vary significantly in terms of the proportion of all employment occupied by young people; this characteristic persists, as evidenced in Table 2.1, which reports the share of youth (aged 16–24 years) employment among total (aged 16–64 years) employment. Overall, the universalistic and liberal countries together with the Netherlands and Germany had the highest youth shares of employment. In 2014, this ranged from nearly 15% in Denmark and the Netherlands to approximately 10% in Finland and Germany. Seven years previously, Ireland would have topped the list, along with a number of post-socialist countries, where young people accounted for a sizable percentage of all those at work. However, by 2014, many of these countries had seen a decimation of young people in employment: Ireland experienced a fall in the youth share from 16% to just under 8% during this period; the youth share of employment was also halved in Spain and Portugal, with a drop from just under 10% of all employment in 2007 to less than 5% in 2014.

The youth share of employment fell by between 1 and 2 percentage points (pp) in most of the other countries considered between 2007 and 2014. The only exceptions are the universalistic countries, where youth employment decreased only slightly or even increased, as was the case in Sweden. The countries with the

Table 2.1 Youth employment (ages 16–24 years) as a share of total employment (ages 16–64 years) in 23 EU countries: 2007, 2010, and 2014 (%)

Transition regime	Country	2007	2010	2014
Universalistic	Denmark	14.4	14.7	14.5
	Norway	13.2	13.1	12.8
	Sweden	9.9	11.0	11.2
	Finland	11.5	10.2	10.8
Liberal	United Kingdom	13.9	13.0	12.8
	Ireland	16.1	10.4	7.9
Employment-centered	Netherlands	15.5	15.1	14.8
	Germany	11.7	11.2	10.2
	France	9.3	8.9	8.0
	Belgium	8.2	7.5	6.9
	Luxembourg	6.4	6.3	5.4
Post-socialist	Lithuania	8.3	6.9	8.3
	Latvia	12.7	9.1	8.0
	Estonia	10.6	8.2	8.0
	Poland	9.7	8.7	7.1
	Hungary	6.7	5.9	6.4
	Slovakia	9.9	7.1	6.3
	Czech Republic	7.9	6.8	6.2
	Romania	8.8	7.3	6.1
Subprotective	Portugal	9.1	7.2	5.9
	Spain	9.9	6.5	4.5
	Italy	6.5	5.5	4.3
	Greece	6.9	5.6	4.2

Source: EU-LFS; authors' analysis.

lowest proportion of working youth in 2007 were Luxembourg, Italy, Hungary, and Greece, where youth younger than 25 years accounted for approximately 6% of all workers. By 2014, these shares had fallen to approximately 4% of all employment in Italy and Greece.

However, an employer "hiring freeze" (interpreted as employers' lower propensity to employ young people aged 16–24 years as a share of the 16- to 64-year-old population) is not the only factor that might influence the declining youth share of employment. Increased enrollment in school and a greater number of NEETs may also have contributed to this trend. Demographic trends might likewise have played a role. Declining fertility or rising emigration could lead to a shrinking youth population and a consequent reduction in the youth labor supply.[5]

2.6. IN WHICH SECTORS ARE YOUNG PEOPLE EMPLOYED?

Looking in more detail at sectorial patterns, we focus separately by gender on developments in 11 countries (with 2 or 3 countries representing each country group).[6] Table 2.2 reports the three main sectors in which female and male youth were employed in the periods pre (2007) and post (2014) the Great Recession (Tables A2.2a and A2.2b in the Appendix report the complete figures for females and males, respectively).

A common feature of employment for young women across all 11 countries examined is the importance of the wholesale and retail sector (labeled D in Table 2.2). This sector accounts for more than one in three jobs for young women in Denmark and the Netherlands and for one in four jobs in Ireland, the United Kingdom, Spain, Italy, and Poland (2014 figures). The lowest this figure falls is 19% in Germany. There are, however, differences in the importance of other sectors as employers of young women across countries and country groups. The health sector (K) accounts for a significantly higher proportion of female youth employment in the universalistic countries (Denmark and Sweden) and the employment-centered countries (Germany, France, and the Netherlands), whereas in the liberal and subprotective countries, the accommodation and food sector (F) is the second highest employer of young women, accounting for between 14% and 22% of their total employment. The two post-socialist countries, and to a lesser extent Germany and Italy, have a distinctly high level of manufacturing sector (B) employment. However, in all four of these countries, manufacturing employment declined between 2007 and 2014.

The wholesale and retail sector also accounts for a significant proportion of employment for young men in all 11 countries, suggesting that there are lower barriers to entry in this sector. In 2014, the proportion of young men employed in wholesale/retail varied from 33% in the Netherlands to 14% in Hungary. Country variation appears to be somewhat greater for young men than for young women; in particular, there is wide divergence in the importance of manufacturing. Pre-recession, in 2007, manufacturing accounted for approximately one-third of male youth employment in Germany, Hungary, and Poland but only for 13%–15% in Denmark, the Netherlands, Ireland, and the United Kingdom. Over time, the proportion of young men employed in the manufacturing sector decreased in all countries except Ireland, Hungary, and Poland, but the fall was particularly sharp in Denmark, Sweden, and Spain.

Because of the housing bubble, a distinctively high percentage of young men were employed in construction (C) in Spain and Ireland in 2007—34% and 27%,

Table 2.2 The three main sectors in which youth (aged 16–24 years) are employed in 11 EU countries by gender: 2007 and 2014 (employment shares)

Country	Period	Female			Male		
		1st	2nd	3rd	1st	2nd	3rd
Denmark	2007	D (34.0)	K (17.7)	F (11.4)	D (29.5)	B (15.2)	C (14.4)
	2014	D (34.4)	K (18.1)	F (14.4)	D (30.3)	F (10.5)	C (10.3)
Sweden	2007	D (22.8)	K (20.8)	F (14.0)	D (18.8)	H (14.2)	C (13.9)
	2014	D (21.1)	K (20.2)	F (14.1)	D (17.8)	H (13.9)	B (11.7)
Ireland	2007	D (30.6)	F (16.2)	K (10.7)	C (33.5)	D (19.9)	B (13.5)
	2014	D (29.1)	F (22.2)	K (14.2)	D (25.1)	F (19.2)	B (13.8)
United Kingdom	2007	D (28.0)	F (13.8)	K (13.1)	D (25.5)	C (16.3)	B (14.3)
	2014	D (24.6)	F (16.9)	K (16.4)	D (22.2)	F (13.3)	B (13.3)
Germany	2007	D (19.4)	K (19.3)	B (15.0)	B (34.2)	D (14.2)	C (13.1)
	2014	K (22.5)	D (18.6)	B (12.7)	B (28.9)	D (17.6)	C (12.8)
France	2007	D (22.1)	K (17.4)	H (11.0)	C (20.8)	B (19.9)	D (18.3)
	2014	D (23.7)	K (19.9)	H (10.2)	D (18.8)	B (16.5)	C (16.3)
Netherlands	2007	D (31.3)	K (18.6)	F (13.8)	D (27.8)	B (12.9)	H (11.8)
	2014	D (37.1)	K (19.4)	F (12.6)	D (33.4)	F (15.2)	H (11.8)
Spain	2007	D (30.9)	F (13.8)	B (10.6)	C (27.0)	B (20.9)	D (15.9)
	2014	D (27.4)	F (20.8)	K (11.8)	D (20.9)	F (15.8)	B (14.6)
Italy	2007	D (23.5)	B (17.1)	F (14.5)	B (29.0)	C (19.3)	D (17.5)
	2014	D (24.7)	F (21.6)	L (14.6)	B (27.3)	D (18.6)	F (15.6)
Hungary	2007	D (25.2)	B (23.0)	F (10.7)	B (34.2)	C (14.9)	D (14.2)
	2014	B (20.1)	D (19.5)	F (14.2)	B (34.1)	D (13.5)	C (11.2)
Poland	2007	D (31.1)	B (16.2)	A (9.0)	B(32.1)	D (18.5)	A (14.7)
	2014	D (31.1)	B (14.8)	F (10.4)	B (35.0)	D (16.6)	C (13.8)

Symbols

A Agriculture	E Transport and communication	I Public administration
B Manufacturing	F Accommodation and food	J Education
C Construction	G Financial activities	K Health and social work
D Wholesale and retail	H Real estate, business	

Note: For each country, the table shows the shares of youth employment in the first three main sectors.
Source: EU-LFS; authors' analysis.

respectively. This left young men particularly exposed to the subsequent crash, and by 2014 the percentages employed in construction had fallen to under 7% in both cases. In the other countries, excluding the Netherlands, construction remains an important source of employment for young men, accounting for at least 1 in 10 jobs.

The changes in the distribution of youth across sectors could simply reflect overall shifts in the employment structure. In the following section, we consider whether sectors have also changed in their propensity to employ young people.

2.7. DID EMPLOYERS HAVE A WEAKER PROPENSITY TO EMPLOY YOUNG PEOPLE DURING THE GREAT RECESSION?

In Section 2.5, we showed that the youth share of total employment declined during the period 2007–2014 in all observed countries except Denmark and Sweden. Here, we deepen this analysis and investigate whether and to what extent employers' preferences for youth labor vary across sectors. Table 2.3 shows the share of youth within each sector. This allows us to see the concentration of youth within particular sectors—and their under-representation in others—and how these vary over time.

The highest youth share is found in the accommodation and food sector, which is particularly high at 46% in Denmark and the Netherlands. The youth share in this sector is much lower in the subprotective countries, although young people are still over-represented. Over time, however, the reliance on youth in this sector decreased in the majority of countries.

Wholesale and retail is also a youth-intensive sector: In 2007, young people accounted for more than one-fourth of those employed in this sector in Denmark, the Netherlands, Ireland, and the United Kingdom, but they accounted for less than 10% in Italy and Hungary. Over time, the youth share of employment in wholesale and retail decreased in almost all countries, and particularly in Ireland and Spain, again suggesting that youth are particularly exposed to a hiring freeze or labor shedding in this sector in some countries. Ireland and Spain also experienced the largest decline in the youth share in construction (17 pp and 10 pp, respectively). Notable decreases of between 3.5 pp and 5 pp are also present in France, Italy, the United Kingdom, and the Netherlands.

Beyond these marked changes, and with the exception of Denmark and Sweden, the decline in the youth share was observed in all sectors, reflecting young people's declining employment share across the economy as a whole. This evidence substantiates the argument made by Blanchflower and Freeman (2000) that there is a long-term tendency of employers to lower their propensity to employ young people. The negative impact on young people has been exacerbated during the crisis by a lower propensity of employers to hire young people and the dissolution of temporary contracts, by and large held by young people (Boeri and Jimeno 2015). We examine these trends more formally using a shift-share analysis.

Table 2.3 Youth employment (ages 16–24 years) as a share of total employment (ages 16–64 years) by sector in 11 EU countries: 2007, 2010, and 2014 (%)

Sector	Denmark			Sweden			Germany			France			Netherlands		
	2007	2010	2014	2007	2010	2014	2007	2010	2014	2007	2010	2014	2007	2010	2014
Agriculture	20.0	17.2	14.8	13.4	13.2	12.7	12.1	10.6	10.2	9.0	6.3	6.2	20.2	17.2	16.5
Manufacturing	11.1	8.4	8.0	9.0	7.3	7.3	12.4	11.7	10.1	8.7	8.3	7.3	10.8	8.5	7.5
Construction	16.2	15.5	13.5	12.7	13.6	12.7	13.2	12.3	11.3	15.6	13.5	10.9	12.0	11.4	8.6
Wholesale and retail	30.5	32.3	33.7	16.4	18.5	18.3	14.5	14.5	13.0	13.4	13.2	12.8	30.8	31.6	30.0
Transport and communication	11.3	10.6	10.0	10.0	8.8	8.7	7.6	8.1	7.7	6.8	7.0	7.0	14.6	12.5	9.5
Accommodation and food	43.9	46.5	45.8	31.3	34.6	35.4	21.1	20.7	18.2	19.9	20.4	17.0	45.6	46.7	44.6
Financial services	6.7	6.3	6.4	5.8	6.9	7.8	8.6	9.8	8.6	6.0	6.7	6.5	7.8	5.7	4.0
Real estate, professional	9.9	10.6	10.5	8.8	10.8	9.7	9.3	9.8	8.1	8.5	7.6	6.4	12.9	12.6	11.7
Public administration	5.1	6.5	4.2	2.8	3.7	4.4	9.2	7.0	7.3	4.9	5.1	4.7	6.0	5.6	3.4
Education	4.9	5.7	6.8	4.0	5.2	7.0	9.3	8.4	8.0	5.1	5.1	5.3	5.7	7.2	7.1
Health and social work	8.9	9.8	9.3	7.1	8.4	9.4	11.7	11.0	10.8	6.9	6.4	5.8	10.0	11.0	8.8
Arts and other services	16.0	22.0	22.0	13.5	16.1	18.6	10.4	11.3	9.8	11.4	12.2	10.4	17.3	19.7	12.8

Sector	Ireland 2007	Ireland 2010	Ireland 2014	United Kingdom 2007	United Kingdom 2010	United Kingdom 2014	Spain 2007	Spain 2010	Spain 2014	Italy 2007	Italy 2010	Italy 2014	Hungary 2007	Hungary 2010	Hungary 2014	Poland 2007	Poland 2010	Poland 2014
Agriculture	6.9	6.7	5.9	13.6	10.8	12.5	7.7	7.6	6.0	5.1	4.4	4.2	5.4	5.3	6.2	8.5	6.8	5.5
Manufacturing	11.9	7.2	6.0	10.2	9.9	9.5	9.7	4.7	3.3	7.1	5.2	4.3	8.2	6.4	7.4	10.2	8.6	8.2
Construction	21.8	10.2	4.8	14.9	11.5	11.1	12.5	6.5	2.8	9.5	7.9	4.8	7.4	6.6	7.1	9.1	10.5	8.4
Wholesale and retail	27.4	21.0	14.9	26.0	25.3	22.1	13.7	9.7	6.2	8.4	7.7	6.1	8.3	7.4	7.6	15.4	13.5	10.9
Transport and communication	8.2	4.9	4.7	9.7	7.8	7.7	7.5	5.2	2.9	4.3	3.9	2.9	5.8	4.8	4.3	7.6	7.4	6.6
Accommodation and food	30.9	25.1	22.4	37.0	33.1	35.9	13.6	10.8	9.9	14.7	14.1	13.2	13.5	14.2	14.6	26.1	21.9	19.2
Financial services	16.7	7.1	4.4	14.3	9.3	10.8	5.1	2.3	1.6	3.7	3.1	1.3	7.2	4.1	3.6	9.1	9.4	5.0
Real estate, professional	13.1	6.6	5.9	9.7	9.9	9.3	7.7	4.5	3.1	5.7	4.7	3.1	5.4	3.5	5.1	9.5	7.4	6.4
Public administration	5.8	3.7	1.1	7.5	6.2	5.5	4.5	4.1	1.2	2.6	1.8	1.2	5.5	6.6	6.4	6.5	6.7	3.2
Education	6.9	6.5	3.6	5.5	6.3	7.9	6.1	4.5	3.8	1.1	1.1	0.5	2.0	2.1	2.8	3.4	3.6	2.5
Health and social work	8.5	5.6	5.0	8.5	8.8	9.6	6.3	5.4	3.6	2.7	2.3	2.3	2.7	2.8	4.1	3.8	3.7	2.6
Arts and other services	21.6	17.7	12.7	20.1	21.5	19.6	14.5	12.4	8.3	9.5	9.6	8.4	7.0	7.4	7.4	12.7	13.2	9.1

Source: EU-LFS; authors' analysis.

The heterogeneity in the experience of youth employment among countries could be a result of several different factors. It could be the result of an
overall shrinkage in the sector in question (shift) or of a declining share of youth
employed in the same sector. Using a shift-share analysis, we can decompose
changes in the total share of youth employment in 2007–2010 and 2010–2014
by sector. This method enables us to measure how much of the changes in youth
employment are due to changes in the size of sectors (growth or sector effect), to
changes in the utilization of youth labor within sectors (share effect), and to the
interaction between these two forces (interaction term) (Figure 2.3).[7]

The first thing to note is that in all countries and in both periods, changes in
youth employment are driven by the share effect, namely by the fact that during
the recession young people are more likely to be dismissed (or less likely to be
hired) compared to older people. For example, the great decrease in youth employment that we observe for Spain in the first phase of the recession (–3.35) is
almost entirely due to the share effect (–3.31). This supports the argument that
employers have lowered their propensity to employ young people, both by im-
posing a hiring freeze and through the dissolution of temporary contracts.

In some cases, we observe growth and share effects operating in opposite
directions at the same time. For example, in the Netherlands in the second period, the growth effect increases youth employment (+0.35), but the share effect

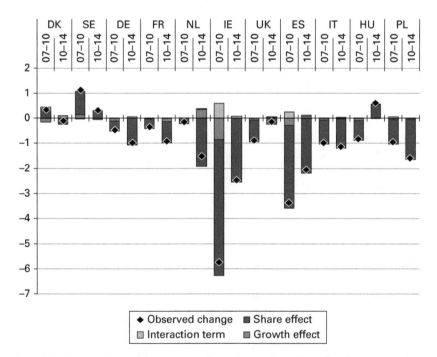

Figure 2.3 Decomposition of changes in youth employment as a share of total employment in
11 EU countries, 2007–2010 and 2010–2014 (percentage points).
Source: EU-LFS; authors' analysis.

decreases it (–1.91). We could interpret this as being the result, on the one hand, of the expansion of some sectors that traditionally give employment to youth and, on the other hand, to a decline over time in the use of youth within these sectors. This is what has happened for the wholesale and retail sector in the Netherlands.

Although differences between countries exist in the contribution of each sector to the total share effect, the overall changes have been mainly driven by construction, manufacturing, and wholesale and retail (results not shown but available upon request). Shifts in manufacturing played a particularly important role in reducing youth employment in the first phase of the recession; this was attributable to sector shrinkage, but also to a reduction in the use of youth labor. Countries especially affected by shifts in manufacturing were Ireland and the subprotective and post-socialist countries. Construction has also been a major driver of youth unemployment especially in Spain and Ireland (where both growth and share effects contributed to falling employment rates). The wholesale and retail sector played a major role in growing youth unemployment in the liberal countries, Spain, and Poland, where the reduced use of youth within this sector contributed to the overall decline in youth employment.

Beyond this general picture, it is worth investigating which young workers have been most affected by the recession. As a first step in this direction, we look at whether changes in youth employment have been driven mainly by shifts in male or in female employment. We do so by carrying out a shift-share analysis and decomposing the changes in youth employment by gender (Figure 2.4).[8] Here, we only report the share component because it has emerged as the factor that drives overall youth employment and because it addresses the issue of whether employers have lowered their propensity to employ youth. Because these results are derived from a further decomposition of the effects presented in Figure 2.3 (and in Table A2.4), the overall changes as well as the total share effect are identical.

When youth employment changes are disaggregated by gender, a clear and unique pattern does not emerge. On the one hand, changes in overall employment were driven in the universalistic and employment-centered countries by changes in female employment. This holds in the case of both employment increases (Denmark and Sweden) and decreases. On the other hand, in the subprotective and post-socialist countries, the overall changes were driven by changes in male employment. These different patterns are not surprising. Indeed, compared with employment-centered and especially with universalistic countries, countries belonging to the subprotective and post-socialist groups are characterized by considerably lower female labor market participation, implying a lower capacity of women's employment to drive changes in overall employment. It is also worth noting that whenever we observe increases in the share of youth employment, these are driven by an increased share of female employment.

A further step in studying how the recession has hit youth employment is to focus on which types of job creation and destruction have benefited or disadvantaged the youth population. We do this in Section 2.8, employing a shift-share

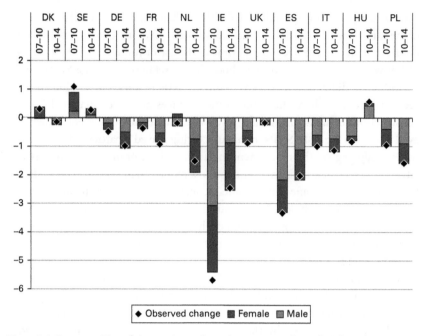

Figure 2.4 Decomposition of changes in youth employment as a share of total employment in 11 EU countries, 2007–2010 and 2010–2014; share effect by gender (percentage points). *Source*: EU-LFS; authors' analysis.

analysis to decompose changes in youth employment by whether employment is full- or part-time and on a permanent or temporary contract.

2.8. HAS THE QUALITY OF YOUTH EMPLOYMENT DETERIORATED?

In addition to the fall in employment, the situation of young people may also have worsened because of a reduction in the quality of their jobs. Were youth displaced because they were employed in jobs characterized by less secure employment contracts? Or did the youth share of temporary and part-time jobs increase because young people were increasingly hired via less desirable forms of employment contract (Blanchflower and Freeman 2000)?

First, we decompose share effects by working arrangement, distinguishing between full-time and part-time employment (Figure 2.5). Focusing on the share effects, which we have shown to drive a reduction of youth employment, we see that it is the component related to full-time employment that drives the youth employment decline; that is, the driving force is the fall in the proportion of full-time jobs that are available to young people. In some cases, the use of part-time employment among youth increased across sectors. This is the case of the

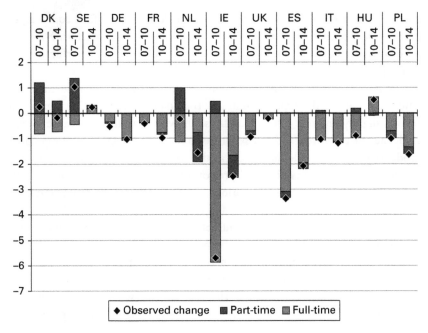

Figure 2.5 Decomposition of changes in youth employment as a share of total employment in 11 EU countries, 2007–2010 and 2010–2014; share effect by working arrangement (percentage points).
Source: EU-LFS; authors' analysis.

universalistic countries in both phases of the recession. Overall, the larger losses in full-time employment have resulted in the decline in youth employment. An emblematic example is the Netherlands during the first phase of the recession, where the decrease in youth employment resulted from two opposite forces: the increase in part-timers (+0.98) and the decrease in full-timers (–1.13)—that is, the growth in part-time jobs did not compensate for the fall in full-time work.

Whenever we observe an overall increase in youth employment, this is often attributable to an increase in young people working part-time rather than any increase in full-time jobs, which overall have decreased. The universalistic countries in the first period are an example of this dynamic, which has been driven by the wholesale and retail sector.

Overall, we have shown that job destruction for young people mainly occurred in full-time employment; there was some decrease in part-time jobs, and in some cases, it led to an increase in youth unemployment. Young people were more at risk of remaining jobless because of an employer hiring freeze; where they were able to find work, this was more likely to be in economically less desirable jobs. The use of full-time employment declined in all sectors virtually everywhere in both phases of the recession. In the few cases in which full-time work has increased, the growth has been negligible. The generalized decline in youth employment is mainly attributable to the declining full-time component; changes in the wholesale and retail, construction, and manufacturing sectors have been driving the trend, with the collapse of full-time job opportunities for young people.

The next step is to investigate another characteristic of the employment relationship, namely the type of contract. The analysis presented in Figure 2.6 reports slightly different results than those shown so far; this is because we exclude the self-employed, as discussed in Section 2.3. Focusing on employees only produces some negligible differences in the size of the changes, but the results follow the same patterns observed previously: decreases in the share of youth employment in all countries and periods, with the exception of Sweden in both periods, Denmark in the first period, and Hungary in the second period.

The share effects of the type of contract used to employ young people largely mirror those presented for full-time and part-time employment. Again, the outflow of youth from the labor market mainly derives from the loss of better jobs. Changes in the share of youth in employment are driven by declines in the share of youth in permanent employment. However, in the few cases in which we observe the youth share increasing, this comes from increases in both permanent

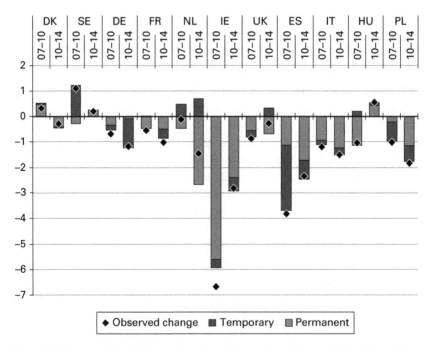

Figure 2.6 Decomposition of changes in youth employment as a share of total employment in 11 EU countries, 2007–2010 and 2010–2014; share effect by employment relationship (percentage points).
Source: EU-LFS; authors' analysis.

and temporary youth employment, with the creation of permanent jobs driving the changes.

Great heterogeneity is also visible between countries. Of course, this is due both to the impact of the recession on total employment and to the overall use of temporary employment. For example, we observe the highest decrease (−2.56) in temporary employment in Spain in the first phase of the recession, as predicted by Boeri and Jimeno (2015). This is not very surprising because Spain, among the 11 countries selected, is probably the country where the impact of the recession was greatest, and it is also the country where temporary forms of employment are more widespread.

As regards variations in growth and share effects for permanent and temporary employment across sectors, the results reflect the patterns presented in Section 2.7. Manufacturing, construction, and wholesale and retail are the sectors that have driven the decline in permanent employment for youth during the recession. This has occurred both via the shrinkage of sectors and via the declining utilization of youth within sectors.

There are a couple of caveats that should be underlined. First, in interpreting the sizes of the decomposed changes, we have to keep in mind that these changes also reflect the sizes of the groups. For example, if we observe the largest contribution of part-time employment in the Netherlands, it is probably because the Netherlands is the country where part-time employment is more widespread. The same holds for temporary employment in Spain.

Second, we have to consider that changes in the share of youth are also a product of the inflow/outflow of those aged 25 years or older into and out of employment. For example, Boeri and Jimeno (2015, 3) observed that a characteristic of this specific recession is that the employment rates of older people increased in most countries as pension reforms progressively increased retirement age. This, also, is a factor that contributes to accounting for the heterogeneous experience of youth unemployment across countries. Therefore, at least in principle, we might observe changes in the share of youth employment even in cases in which youth employment does not change but older people's employment does. In this sense, these analyses furnish a picture of youth employment from a different perspective—looking at the composition of employment—and complement the pictures provided by the study of the unemployment and labor force participation rates.

2.9. CONCLUSIONS

We set out to understand which sectors of the economy are more likely to employ young people and how this changed between 2007 and 2014. Drawing on research from the 1980s, the study illustrated the persistently uneven distribution of youth employment across sectors, regardless of cross-national differences in youth transition regimes. Even as the relative importance of different sectors has changed within these economies with the growth of service employment, job opportunities for youth are dominated by particular sectors. These differences have persisted and become more entrenched since the Great Recession. Young people (aged 16–24 years) have historically been more likely to find work in low-wage, low-skilled jobs where there is less competition from older workers. Despite growth in youth-friendly sectors, demographic trends showing a contraction in younger cohorts of workers, and increasing levels of youth participation in education, youth employment continues to fall, and it was falling even prior to the Great Recession. Boeri and Jimeno (2015) argue that the collapse of the youth labor market is attributable not only to a hiring freeze by employers but also to the heavy destruction of jobs held by young people through the dissolution of temporary contracts in response to the sharp deterioration in the economy and despite incentive structures shaped by policy. Blanchflower and Freeman (2000) suggested that the quality of employment and earnings for young people in these sectors has deteriorated in nearly all OECD countries because of the worsening conditions of low-paid and less skilled jobs. To test these arguments, we conducted a shift-share analysis for the period from 2007 to 2014 to examine whether these predicted trends explained overall European patterns in youth employment, and how they were affected by gender and employment status.

The share of youth employment (ages 16–24 years) relative to the total population (ages 16–64 years) has fallen over the period considered (2007–2014). This is demonstrated in our findings from a shift-share analysis. Part of this fall is attributable to the impact of the recession on reducing the overall levels of employment in some sectors—for example, construction and manufacturing. But this is only part of the explanation. It was not only that the size of the sector shrank but also that the share of employed youth fell even in sectors that were more resilient. Second, the quality of jobs for youth has deteriorated, as predicted by Blanchflower and Freeman (2000). We have seen that better quality employment declined in favor of part-time and temporary jobs during this relatively short period from 2007 to 2014.

These findings clearly contribute to improving a relatively neglected understanding of cross-national sectorial differences as to where young people find work. By drawing on earlier studies, we illustrated the persistence of this sectorial variability, despite cross-country differences. One of the clearest findings from this research is the need first to understand that youth job opportunities are very specific to sectors and that this applies regardless of country. Second, the engagement of employers is key to improving youth opportunities for work (Lewis and Ryan 2008; Simms et al., 2017). Our research evidence indicates that employers have lowered their propensity to employ youth (combining a hiring freeze with the dissolution of temporary contracts), possibly for some of the reasons outlined by Marsden and Ryan (1986) with regard to wages, productivity, and training costs. But closer attention needs to be given to understanding how wage rates, labor market policies, and the costs of training make employers less disposed to recruiting young people. Hadjivassiliou et al. (this volume) illustrate how countries perform better where employers are closely engaged in STW transition regimes and VET systems. Here, employers see an incentive to participate. In more fragmented regimes where there is greater inertia in the ability to involve employers through different policy channels, the outcomes for youth have been devastating, especially in subprotective countries (see Petmesidou and González Menéndez, this volume). One of the key challenges in terms of policy learning and transfer requires mobilizing employers and professional bodies within multi-agency forms of governance to deliver effective programs to overcome some of the deleterious consequences for youth that have become evident in the past decade.

NOTES

1 This is similar to the youth-share statistic we report later.
2 The aggregate measures do not take into account the size of the countries (or sample size); rather, each country has a weight of one.
3 Since 2008, the applied version of NACE is "Rev. 2" (Revision 2). In the change from Rev. 1.1 to Rev. 2, some activities were disaggregated, whereas others were collapsed. In order to maximize the comparability of our data over time, we built a new classification based on the two versions (see Table A2.1 in the Appendix). The main changes involved in the shift to NACE Rev. 2 are related to the creation of a new Section J, "Information and communication," which includes activities that in Rev. 1.1 were spread across different categories. Although it was not possible to entirely eliminate potential bias, we reduced its effects by collapsing the new category with the old category I, "Transport, storage and communications." Finally, because of their small sizes, we excluded the categories "Activities of households as employers" and "Activities of extraterritorial organisations and bodies."
4 See Smith, Fagan, and Rubery (1998) for a comparable approach used to examine the use of part-time employment in Europe.
5 Significant variations between countries are also present in this respect. On the one hand, we observe in our sample for the post-socialist countries and Ireland a marked decline in the share of youth among the total population aged 16–64 years—of between 4 pp and 6 pp between 2007 and 2014. On the other hand, the share of youth increased in the universalistic countries. At the same time, Ireland is also the country in which the share of youth in employment declined the most, whereas Denmark and Sweden are the only countries in which youth in work increased.
6 The complementary figures for the whole working population are shown in Table A2.3 in the Appendix.

7 Results of the shift-share analysis presented in Figure 2.3 are also reported in Table A2.4 in the Appendix.
8 Results are also reported in Table A2.5 in the Appendix. The same table also reports the shift-share results decomposed by working arrangement and employment relationship that will be discussed later.

REFERENCES

Bettio, Francesca, and Alina Verashchagina. 2014. "Women and Men in the 'Great European Recession.'" In *Women and Austerity: The Economic Crisis and the Future for Gender Equality*, edited by Maria Karamessini and Jill Rubery, 57–81. Abingdon, UK: Routledge.

Blanchflower, David G., and Richard B. Freeman. 2000. "The Declining Economic Status of Young Workers in OECD Countries." In *Youth Employment and Joblessness in Advanced Countries*, edited by David G. Blanchflower and Richard B. Freeman, 19–56. Chicago: University of Chicago Press.

Boeri, Tito, and Juan Francisco Jimeno. 2015. "The Unbearable Divergence of Unemployment in Europe." CEP Discussion Paper 1384. London: Centre for Economic Performance, London School of Economics.

Buchmann, Marlis C., and Irene Kriesi. 2011. "Transition to Adulthood in Europe." *Annual Review of Sociology* 37: 481–503.

Eichhorst, Werner, Tito Boeri, An De Coen, Vincenzo Galasso, Michael Kendzia, and Nadia Steiber. 2014. "How to Combine the Entry of Young People in the Labour Market with the Retention of Older Workers?" *IZA Journal of European Labor Studies* 3 (19): 1–23.

Eurostat. 2008. *Statistical Classification of Economic Activities in the European Community*. NACE Rev. 2. Luxembourg: Office for Official Publications of the European Communities.

Hall, Peter A., and David Soskice. 2001. *Varieties of Capitalism: The Institutional Foundations of Comparative Advantage*. Oxford: Oxford University Press.

Kelly, Elish, Gillian Kingston, Helen Russell, and Frances McGinnity. 2014. "The Equality Impact of the Unemployment Crisis." *Journal of the Statistical and Social Inquiry Society of Ireland* 44: 71–85.

Kohlrausch, Bettina. 2012. *Youth Unemployment in Germany: Skill Biased Patterns of Labour Market Integration*. Berlin: Friedrich-Ebert-Stiftung.

Lewis, Paul, and Paul Ryan. 2008. "A Hard Sell? The Prospects for Apprenticeship in British Retailing." *Human Resource Management Journal* 18 (1): 3–19.

Marsden, David, and Paul Ryan. 1986. "Where Do Young Workers Work? Youth Employment by Industry in Various European Economies." *British Journal of Industrial Relations* 24 (1): 83–102.

O'Higgins, Niall. 2012. "This Time It's Different? Youth Labour Markets During 'the Great Recession.'" IZA Discussion Paper 6434. Bonn: Institute for the Study of Labor.

O'Reilly, Jacqueline. 2006. "Framing Comparisons: Gendering Perspectives on Cross-National Comparisons of Welfare and Work." *Work, Employment and Society* 20 (4): 731–50.

O'Reilly, Jacqueline, Werner Eichhorst, András Gábos, Kari Hadjivassiliou, David Lain, Janine Leschke, Seamus McGuinness, et al. 2015. "Five Characteristics of Youth Unemployment in Europe: Flexibility, Education, Migration, Family Legacies, and EU Policy." *SAGE Open* 5 (1): 1–19. doi:10.1177/2158244015574962.

Organization for Economic Co-operation and Development. 2013. *Education at a Glance 2013: OECD Indicators*. Paris: Organization for Economic Co-operation and Development. http://www.oecd.org/education/eag2013.htm

Pohl, Axel, and Andreas Walther. 2007. "Activating the Disadvantaged— Variations in Addressing Youth Transitions Across Europe." *International Journal of Lifelong Education* 26 (5): 533–53.

Rubery, Jill, and Anthony Rafferty. 2013. "Women and Recession Revisited." *Work, Employment and Society* 27 (3): 414–32.

Russell, Helen, and Philip J. O'Connell. 2001. "Getting a Job in Europe: The Transition from Unemployment to Work Among Young People in Nine European Countries." *Work, Employment and Society* 15 (1): 1–24.

Simms, Melanie, Sophie Gamwell, and Benjamin Hopkins. 2017. "Understanding Employer Engagement in Youth Labour Market Policy in the UK." *Human Resource Management Journal*. Special Issue (November): 548–64.

Smith, Mark, Colette Fagan, and Jill Rubery. 1998. "Where and Why Is Part-Time Work Growing in Europe?" In *Part-Time Prospects: International Comparisons of Part-Time Work in Europe, North America and the Pacific Rim*, edited by Jacqueline O'Reilly and Colette Fagan, 35–56. London: Routledge.

Wallace, Claire, and René Bendit. 2009. "Youth Policies in Europe: Towards a Classification of Different Tendencies in Youth Policies in the European Union." *Perspectives on European Politics and Society* 10 (3): 441–58. doi:10.1080/15705850903105868.

APPENDIX

Table A2.1 Classification of sectors based on NACE Rev. 1.1 and NACE Rev. 2

	NACE Rev. 1.1 (up to 2007)		NACE Rev. 2 (from 2008 onward)	Sector
A	Agriculture, hunting and forestry	A	Agriculture, forestry and fishing	Agriculture
B	Fishing			
C	Mining and quarrying	B	Mining and quarrying	Manufacturing
D	Manufacturing	C	Manufacturing	
E	Electricity, gas and water supply	D	Electricity, gas, steam and air conditioning supply	
		E	Water supply, sewerage, waste management and remediation activities	
F	Construction	F	Construction	Construction
G	Wholesale and retail trade: repair of motor vehicles, motorcycles and personal and household goods	G	Wholesale and retail trade: repair of motor vehicles and motorcycles	Wholesale and retail
H	Hotels and restaurants	I	Accommodation and food service activities	Accommodation and food
I	Transport, storage and communications	H	Transportation and storage	Transport and communication
		J	Information and communication	
J	Financial intermediation	K	Financial and insurance activities	Financial activities
K	Real estate, renting and business activities	L	Real estate activities	Real estate, business; Professional and technical activities
		M	Professional, scientific and technical activities	
		N	Administrative and support service activities	
L	Public administration and defence; compulsory social security	O	Public administration and defence; compulsory social security	Public administration

Table A2.1 Continued

	NACE Rev. 1.1 (up to 2007)		NACE Rev. 2 (from 2008 onward)	Sector
M	Education	P	Education	Education
N	Health and social work	Q	Human health and social work activities	Health and social work
O	Other community, social and personal services activities	R	Arts, entertainment and recreation	Arts and other services
		S	Other service activities	
P	Activities of private households as employers and undifferentiated production activities of private households	T	Activities of households as employers; undifferentiated goods- and services-producing activities of households for own use	Excluded (small size sectors)
Q	Extraterritorial organizations and bodies	U	Activities of extraterritorial organizations and bodies	

Table A2.2a Distribution of employed youth (aged 16–24 years) across sectors in 11 EU countries, 2007 and 2014 (%), females

Sector	Denmark		Sweden		Germany		France		Netherlands	
	2007	2014	2007	2014	2007	2014	2007	2014	2007	2014
Agriculture	2.1	0.8	1.4	1.0	1.4	0.7	1.3	0.8	1.9	1.4
Manufacturing	10.1	5.2	6.1	4.1	15.0	12.7	10.8	8.7	5.7	3.2
Construction	1.0	0.9	1.0	1.2	1.0	1.6	1.0	1.4	0.4	0.3
Wholesale and retail	34.0	34.4	22.8	21.1	19.4	18.6	22.1	23.7	31.3	37.1
Transport and communication	3.8	3.7	3.9	4.2	2.3	4.4	3.2	4.6	3.1	2.6
Accommodation and food	11.4	14.4	14.0	14.1	9.8	8.8	8.5	8.3	13.8	12.6
Financial activities	1.2	1.4	1.3	1.4	3.2	3.1	3.4	3.3	1.9	0.9
Real estate, business	6.9	6.4	11.5	11.1	9.7	10.0	11.0	10.2	11.0	11.3
Public administration	1.4	1.3	1.9	2.1	6.0	5.0	5.8	5.5	1.9	1.4
Education	3.0	4.6	6.9	9.3	5.9	7.6	6.6	6.0	3.6	4.7
Health and social work	17.7	18.1	20.8	20.2	19.3	22.5	17.4	19.9	18.6	19.4
Arts and other services	7.4	8.9	8.6	10.1	7.0	5.2	8.9	7.6	6.8	5.2

Sector	Ireland		United Kingdom		Spain		Italy		Hungary		Poland	
	2007	2014	2007	2014	2007	2014	2007	2014	2007	2014	2007	2014
Agriculture	0.4	1.0	0.6	0.3	2.0	2.6	1.6	1.5	1.4	2.2	9.0	4.9
Manufacturing	7.1	5.1	6.3	3.8	10.6	5.7	17.1	10.5	23.0	20.1	16.2	14.8
Construction	1.3	0.3	1.3	1.3	1.9	0.2	1.5	0.9	1.2	1.3	0.7	1.6
Wholesale and retail	30.6	29.1	28.0	24.6	30.9	27.4	23.5	24.7	25.2	19.5	31.1	31.1
Transport and communication	2.8	4.2	3.8	3.4	3.9	3.0	2.9	3.7	5.6	4.2	2.8	4.9
Accommodation and food	16.2	22.2	13.8	16.9	13.8	20.8	14.5	21.6	10.7	14.2	7.9	10.4
Financial activities	6.4	2.4	5.4	3.0	1.8	1.5	2.6	1.6	4.4	1.8	4.2	3.1
Real estate, business	8.4	7.3	9.3	8.3	9.7	8.4	13.5	10.0	6.9	6.9	5.9	8.7
Public administration	1.9	0.7	4.0	2.5	1.8	0.7	1.4	0.7	5.3	8.8	6.4	4.3
Education	4.9	5.4	5.0	9.5	5.9	8.5	2.3	1.3	4.6	5.9	4.8	6.1
Health and social work	10.7	14.2	13.1	16.4	8.7	11.8	5.8	9.1	4.6	8.3	4.2	4.3
Arts and other services	9.5	7.9	9.6	10.0	9.1	9.4	13.3	14.6	7.1	6.9	7.0	5.8

Source: EU-LFS; authors' analysis.

Table A2.2b Distribution of employed youth (aged 16–24 years) across sectors in 11 EU countries, 2007 and 2014 (%), males

Sector	Denmark		Sweden		Germany		France		Netherlands	
	2007	2014	2007	2014	2007	2014	2007	2014	2007	2014
Agriculture	5.5	3.9	3.7	2.9	3.1	1.9	5.1	3.3	5.6	3.8
Manufacturing	15.2	9.4	20.0	11.7	34.2	28.9	19.9	16.5	12.9	8.7
Construction	14.4	10.3	13.9	14.0	13.1	12.8	20.8	16.3	9.2	6.3
Wholesale and retail	29.5	30.3	18.8	17.8	14.2	17.6	18.3	18.8	27.8	33.4
Transport and communication	6.0	8.6	8.4	10.4	5.0	7.3	5.9	9.9	8.6	8.3
Accommodation and food	7.0	10.5	6.2	7.8	4.0	5.1	7.2	7.2	11.0	15.2
Financial activities	1.6	1.2	1.0	1.6	2.3	2.4	1.1	2.4	1.4	1.2
Real estate, business	6.3	7.6	14.2	13.9	7.0	7.2	9.1	8.2	11.8	11.8
Public administration	2.6	1.9	1.3	2.9	5.9	5.2	5.0	5.8	3.4	2.0
Education	2.3	4.4	2.6	4.8	3.9	3.2	1.5	4.3	1.6	2.8
Health and social work	5.1	6.0	5.1	5.9	4.7	5.5	3.0	3.7	2.7	3.2
Arts and other services	4.5	5.9	4.9	6.5	2.8	2.9	3.1	3.6	4.2	3.2

Sector	Ireland		United Kingdom		Spain		Italy		Hungary		Poland	
	2007	2014	2007	2014	2007	2014	2007	2014	2007	2014	2007	2014
Agriculture	3.7	6.0	1.9	2.0	4.5	8.7	4.0	4.8	5.3	6.2	14.7	11.4
Manufacturing	13.5	13.8	14.3	13.3	20.9	14.6	29.0	27.3	34.2	34.1	32.1	35.0
Construction	33.5	6.6	16.3	11.5	27.0	6.8	19.3	12.0	14.9	11.2	11.0	13.8
Wholesale and retail	19.9	25.1	25.5	22.2	15.9	20.9	17.5	18.6	14.2	13.5	18.5	16.6
Transport and communication	3.2	6.6	5.7	7.3	5.3	7.5	4.2	5.9	7.5	7.2	6.7	9.3
Accommodation and food	8.9	19.2	10.1	13.3	7.3	15.8	9.5	15.6	6.8	6.1	3.3	2.7
Financial activities	3.1	2.9	3.8	3.7	0.9	0.7	1.0	0.4	0.9	0.9	0.8	0.7
Real estate, business	7.0	7.6	7.4	10.0	7.0	7.3	7.1	6.9	5.0	5.7	6.4	5.0
Public administration	1.7	0.7	3.8	2.7	3.7	3.3	3.3	2.2	6.0	9.8	2.5	2.3
Education	1.0	2.3	2.4	3.7	2.2	4.0	0.5	0.4	0.9	1.6	0.9	0.6
Health and social work	1.0	2.8	1.9	3.9	1.3	2.7	1.1	1.4	1.3	1.2	0.8	0.6
Arts and other services	3.8	6.5	7.1	6.6	3.8	7.7	3.7	4.6	3.1	2.5	2.4	2.1

Source: EU-LFS; authors' analysis.

Table A2.3 Distribution of total employment (ages 16–64 years) across sectors in 11 EU countries, 2007 and 2014 (%)

Sector	Denmark			Sweden			Germany			France			Netherlands		
	2007	2010	2014	2007	2010	2014	2007	2010	2014	2007	2010	2014	2007	2010	2014
Agriculture	2.79	2.32	2.32	2.00	1.85	1.69	2.19	1.48	1.34	3.53	2.94	2.79	2.84	2.59	2.08
Manufacturing	16.57	13.86	13.38	15.45	13.34	12.17	23.79	22.20	21.58	16.97	15.40	14.00	13.45	11.63	10.91
Construction	7.09	5.88	6.05	6.39	6.73	6.69	6.61	6.78	6.85	7.10	7.52	6.88	6.33	6.11	5.32
Wholesale and retail	14.93	14.70	13.94	12.28	12.33	11.89	13.50	12.90	14.08	13.80	13.45	13.09	14.88	14.49	16.24
Transport and communication	6.29	8.82	8.96	6.25	9.30	9.39	5.65	8.15	7.83	6.40	8.42	8.48	6.31	9.18	7.84
Accommodation and food	2.97	3.30	3.95	3.20	3.47	3.44	3.70	3.90	3.84	3.63	3.89	3.61	4.20	4.45	4.32
Financial services	2.99	3.23	2.93	1.99	2.16	2.12	3.68	3.38	3.25	3.25	3.49	3.41	3.29	3.05	3.66
Real estate, professional	9.61	9.34	9.64	14.57	13.36	14.36	10.40	10.75	10.65	10.92	9.97	11.31	13.61	10.96	13.52
Public administration	5.73	5.89	5.57	5.74	5.95	6.43	7.54	7.49	7.17	10.03	10.23	9.54	6.88	7.34	6.70
Education	7.81	8.55	9.54	10.87	10.93	11.28	6.03	6.63	6.64	6.97	6.99	7.66	6.94	7.57	7.25
Health and social work	17.90	19.37	18.84	16.10	15.61	15.56	11.62	12.26	12.67	12.77	13.41	15.12	16.39	18.21	17.62
Arts and other services	5.31	4.74	4.87	5.17	4.98	5.00	5.31	4.08	4.10	4.63	4.29	4.12	4.88	4.41	4.53

Sector	Ireland			United Kingdom			Spain			Italy			Hungary			Poland		
	2007	2010	2014	2007	2010	2014	2007	2010	2014	2007	2010	2014	2007	2010	2014	2007	2010	2014
Agriculture	4.82	3.93	4.74	1.26	1.08	1.17	4.46	4.21	4.39	3.86	3.69	3.58	4.59	4.52	4.62	14.06	12.62	11.26
Manufacturing	14.16	13.31	12.83	14.18	11.85	11.65	16.99	15.13	14.12	22.26	20.85	21.14	24.22	23.49	24.34	24.13	22.45	23.30
Construction	13.61	6.54	5.85	8.26	7.85	7.39	13.28	9.01	5.94	8.54	8.62	6.94	8.47	7.35	6.33	7.00	8.21	7.55
Wholesale and retail	14.58	14.88	14.37	14.37	14.05	13.55	15.77	16.07	17.17	15.37	14.91	14.91	15.15	14.44	13.52	15.02	14.93	14.60
Transport and communication	5.85	9.08	9.09	6.84	8.60	8.90	6.22	8.05	8.51	5.54	7.25	7.48	7.73	9.35	8.93	6.48	7.63	8.18
Accommodation and food	6.44	6.86	7.32	4.50	5.13	5.40	7.19	7.44	8.17	5.05	5.30	5.92	4.19	4.11	4.21	1.94	2.22	2.13
Financial services	4.42	5.05	4.85	4.45	4.10	3.97	2.53	2.67	2.91	2.93	3.00	2.87	2.19	2.44	2.32	2.42	2.32	2.40
Real estate, professional	9.42	9.18	10.00	12.01	11.89	12.53	10.33	10.38	11.14	10.97	10.76	11.21	7.21	7.13	7.79	6.26	6.64	7.25
Public administration	5.02	5.71	5.20	7.17	6.46	6.06	6.43	8.07	7.48	6.30	6.47	6.05	7.01	8.28	9.47	6.22	6.61	6.77
Education	6.52	8.05	8.02	9.21	10.52	10.56	5.99	6.79	7.13	7.12	7.03	7.09	7.97	8.41	7.96	7.40	7.81	7.90
Health and social work	10.36	12.80	13.20	12.04	13.51	13.43	6.73	7.83	8.49	6.96	7.51	8.42	6.67	6.74	6.71	5.74	5.82	5.85
Arts and other services	4.81	4.59	4.54	5.70	4.95	5.39	4.08	4.34	4.55	5.10	4.60	4.39	4.60	3.74	3.81	3.34	2.76	2.80

Source: EU-LFS; authors' analysis.

Table A2.4 Decomposition of changes in youth employment (ages 16–24 years) as a share of total employment (ages 16–64 years) in 11 EU countries: 2007–2010 and 2010–2014 (percentage points)

Country	Period	Observed change	Growth effect	Share effect	Interaction term
Denmark	2007–10	0.28	–0.16	0.37	0.06
	2010–14	–0.15	0.09	–0.23	0.00
Sweden	2007–10	1.06	0.15	0.91	–0.01
	2010–14	0.26	–0.06	0.32	0.00
Ireland	2007–10	–5.68	–0.85	–5.41	0.58
	2010–14	–2.47	–0.01	–2.53	0.07
United Kingdom	2007–10	–0.92	–0.07	–0.86	0.00
	2010–14	–0.19	0.03	–0.24	0.02
Germany	2007–10	–0.51	–0.11	–0.41	0.01
	2010–14	–1.01	0.06	–1.06	0.00
France	2007–10	–0.39	–0.03	–0.38	0.02
	2010–14	–0.95	–0.13	–0.85	0.02
Netherlands	2007–10	–0.20	–0.07	–0.15	0.02
	2010–14	–1.53	0.35	–1.91	0.03
Spain	2007–10	–3.35	–0.28	–3.31	0.24
	2010–14	–2.06	0.07	–2.18	0.05
Italy	2007–10	–1.01	–0.07	–0.96	0.02
	2010–14	–1.16	–0.02	–1.18	0.04
Hungary	2007–10	–0.86	–0.09	–0.79	0.01
	2010–14	0.55	0.01	0.53	0.01
Poland	2007–10	–0.98	–0.04	–0.98	0.05
	2010–14	–1.61	–0.04	–1.59	0.02

Source: EU-LFS; authors' analysis.

Table A2.5 Decomposition of changes in youth employment (ages 16–24 years) as a share of total employment (ages 16–64 years): 2007–2010 and 2010–2014; share effect by gender, working arrangement, and employment relationship

Country	Period	Observed change in overall employment	Gender		Working arrangement		Observed change in employees only	Employment relationship	
			Male	Female	Full-time	Part-time		Permanent	Temporary
Denmark	2007–2010	0.28	-0.01	0.38	-0.81	1.19	0.35	0.48	0.05
	2010–2014	-0.15	-0.10	-0.14	-0.72	0.48	-0.26	-0.40	-0.05
Sweden	2007–2010	1.06	0.24	0.66	-0.45	1.36	1.13	-0.28	1.21
	2010–2014	0.26	0.10	0.22	0.18	0.13	0.23	0.19	0.05
Germany	2007–2010	-0.51	-0.18	-0.23	-0.35	-0.06	-0.66	-0.34	-0.19
	2010–2014	-1.01	-0.49	-0.57	-0.95	-0.11	-1.15	-0.09	-1.14
France	2007–2010	-0.39	-0.16	-0.22	-0.36	-0.03	-0.52	-0.47	0.01
	2010–2014	-0.95	-0.53	-0.31	-0.77	-0.07	-0.99	-0.49	-0.37
Netherlands	2007–2010	-0.20	-0.28	0.14	-1.13	0.98	-0.09	-0.48	0.48
	2010–2014	-1.53	-0.73	-1.18	-0.77	-1.14	-1.43	-2.67	0.70
Ireland	2007–2010	-5.68	-3.07	-2.35	-5.86	0.45	-6.66	-5.61	-0.31
	2010–2014	-2.47	-0.86	-1.67	-1.66	-0.87	-2.80	-2.39	-0.54
United Kingdom	2007–2010	-0.92	-0.43	-0.42	-0.70	-0.15	-0.85	-0.55	-0.27
	2010–2014	-0.19	-0.09	-0.15	-0.19	-0.05	-0.25	-0.69	0.33
Spain	2007–2010	-3.35	-2.17	-1.14	-3.10	-0.22	-3.80	-1.13	-2.56
	2010–2014	-2.06	-1.11	-1.06	-1.95	-0.23	-2.32	-1.72	-0.74

(continued)

Table A2.5 Continued

Country	Period	Observed change in overall employment	Gender		Working arrangement		Observed change in employees only	Employment relationship	
			Male	Female	Full-time	Part-time		Permanent	Temporary
Italy	2007–2010	–1.01	–0.60	–0.36	–1.06	0.10	–1.17	–0.94	–0.17
	2010–2014	–1.16	–0.72	–0.46	–1.13	–0.05	–1.48	–1.23	–0.28
Hungary	2007–2010	–0.86	–0.63	–0.15	–0.97	0.18	–1.01	–1.12	0.20
	2010–2014	0.55	0.43	0.09	0.62	–0.10	0.59	0.44	0.11
Poland	2007–2010	–0.98	–0.40	–0.58	–0.70	–0.28	–0.99	–0.22	–0.73
	2010–2014	–1.61	–0.89	–0.70	–1.35	–0.25	–1.81	–1.16	–0.61

Source: EU-LFS; authors' analysis.

3

HOW DOES THE PERFORMANCE OF SCHOOL-TO-WORK TRANSITION REGIMES VARY IN THE EUROPEAN UNION?

Kari P. Hadjivassiliou, Arianna Tassinari, Werner Eichhorst, and Florian Wozny

3.1. INTRODUCTION

The Great Recession has had a profound impact on the process of young people's school-to-work (STW) transitions, exacerbating the challenges already arising from the long-term structural transformations affecting youth labor markets across the European Union (EU). These challenges have been a catalyst for policy change. Following European Commission recommendations, many countries have embarked upon ambitious reform programs, including the introduction of the Youth Guarantee (YG), structural reforms of vocational education and training (VET), and activation policies.

This chapter tackles two central questions pertaining to the performance and evolution of STW transition regimes in Europe during the Great Recession. First, what role have institutional characteristics played in mediating and structuring the impact of the crisis on young people's labor market situation? Second, in what ways have policy changes introduced during the recession changed the structure and logic of European STW transition regimes?

Following an institutionalist approach, this chapter tackles these two analytical puzzles by means of a comparative case study design. We draw on the typology of "youth transition regimes" advanced by Pohl and Walther (2007) as a heuristic framework for comparison. First, we investigate how country-specific institutional configurations mediated the impact of the crisis on young people's labor market situation between 2007 and 2015 in a sample of eight member states belonging to different clusters. Our findings show that institutional legacies mattered considerably in determining the type and severity of the challenges that the different countries faced. However, institutional factors also interacted in complex ways with the broader macroeconomic conditions and the availability of fiscal resources.

Second, we analyze the main changes in STW transition regimes across five country clusters between 2007 and 2015. We review three policy domains: active labor market policies (ALMPs) and not in employment, education, or training (NEET) policies;[1] VET; and employment protection legislation (EPL). We assess the extent to which reforms have brought about substantial change in the underlying logic and design of STW transition regimes and whether these will lead to future improvements in performance. We focus on youth-specific employment policy areas in order to identify conflicting trends of convergence and persisting divergence in institutional design. We find that institutional configurations appear to be in a state of flux, blurring the distinctive characteristics and internal coherence of the STW transition regimes captured by Pohl and Walther's (2007) original typology and calling into question its continued heuristic validity. Considerable challenges persist despite intense reform activity, and the postcrisis quality of STW transitions appears to have deteriorated across all country clusters.

The chapter proceeds as follows. Section 3.2 outlines the theoretical and case study selection framework. Section 3.3 presents the institutional features and performance of each of the five STW transition regimes represented by the eight case study countries. Section 3.4 discusses the main trends and implications of institutional and policy change across clusters during the crisis, and section 3.5 concludes.

3.2. THEORETICAL AND CASE STUDY SELECTION FRAMEWORK

The notion of "transition regimes" developed by Pohl and Walther (2007) encompasses institutional and policy domains, including the structure of education and training systems, employment regulation and social security systems, and the focus of youth transition policies (whether their model of activation is "supportive" or "workfare"). The original conceptualization also includes cultural norms relating to interpretative frames of youth and the causes of labor market "disadvantage" dominating different clusters; we do not include these in our analysis here. Pohl and Walther distinguish between five main types of youth transition regimes: universalistic, liberal, employment-centered, subprotective, and post-socialist. The distinctive features of each ideal-typical regime are summarized in Table 3.1.

Although these clusters display considerable internal variation with regard to the institutional configurations of different countries, the typology can be a useful heuristic device for analyzing and conceptualizing broad patterns of convergence and variation in terms of policy design and institutional change across countries. Each regime type is characterized by specific challenges regarding the STW transition process, as well as by a distinctive logic in the design of STW transition policies.

On the basis of this typology, we conducted eight case studies in countries belonging to distinct regime types so as to compare the performance of differing institutional arrangements and the trajectory of institutional change between and within clusters between 2007 and 2015. The country case studies were chosen not only to exemplify the characteristics and challenges of each cluster but also to illustrate internal variation within clusters. The *universalistic model* is represented here by Sweden. Within the *employment-centered regime*, we analyzed the cases of Germany, the Netherlands, and France, which—despite broad similarities—differ in the focus of their STW transition models, especially in their VET systems. The United Kingdom typifies the *liberal regime*. The *subprotective regime*, typical of the Mediterranean countries, is exemplified by Spain. Finally, the Estonian and Polish case studies illustrate the *post-socialist regime,* which has adopted a mix of liberal and employment-centered approaches.

The case study methodology involved primary data collection through interviews with policymakers, employer organizations, trade unions, and academic experts in each country.[2] This work was complemented by an extensive review of policy documents and academic literature at the EU and national levels, as well as secondary data analysis of key statistical and evaluation data relating to youth labor market performance in the selected countries.

Section 3.3 considers how regimes' institutional features affect their performance regarding the effectiveness of young people's STW transitions, conceptualized in terms of the speed, ease, and quality of youth transitions (see Flek, Hála, and Mysíková, this volume; Berloffa et al., this volume; Filandri, Nazio, and O'Reilly, this volume). Although the quality of youth transitions encompasses a range of dimensions (incidence of informal, temporary, and/or precarious employment, and transition rates to permanent employment), here we focus on the type of employment contract (permanent vs. temporary) as an indicator of quality.

We measure country performance using a range of empirical indicators: total and long-term youth unemployment rate, youth unemployment ratio, employment rate within 3 years of completing education, NEET rate, educational attainment, and incidence of fixed-term employment.[3] A comparison of indicators between 2007 and 2015 captures how different regimes have mediated the impact of the Great Recession on young people's labor market situation. Our discussion

Table 3.1 Comparative framework

STW transition regime typology	Education system and VET	Focus of STW transition policies and ALMP	EPL and labor market regulation	Speed and quality of STW transitions
Universalistic (SE)	Inclusive education system High investment and high transitions in tertiary education Secondary role of VET	Supportive activation (Youth Guarantee) Human capital investment	"Flexicurity model": moderate/low EPL, inclusive social protection system; Corporatist tradition with collectively agreed minimum wages (including youth-related) that vary by sector	Fast and stable
Employment-centered (DE, FR, NL)	Selective and standardized education and training Prominence of VET (company- or school-based), including prevocational training and apprenticeships High levels of employer involvement	"Train-first" approach: focus on VET and apprenticeships as main labor market integration route Targeted ALMPs for vulnerable youth Occasional use of wage incentives and demand-side measures	EPL dualism between permanent and temporary employment Segmented social protection Corporatist tradition, but minimum wages set by legislation	Variable, but fast and stable for countries with large apprenticeship systems or VET take-up High levels of temporary employment Cyclical problems of low labor demand
Liberal (UK)	Comprehensive education system, predominance of general education Fragmented post-compulsory training Low status and standardization of VET Limited employer involvement	Supply-side, workfare activation model Focus on acquisition of employability skills and rapid labor market entry ("work-first" approach) Targeted remedial interventions for NEETs and vulnerable young people	Low levels of EPL Universalistic but minimal social protection Minimum wages set by legislation (differentiated for young people)	Fast but unstable; high incidence of low-quality employment Skills mismatch

Cluster	Education system	Labor market policy	Employment protection / wages	Transition outcomes
Subprotective (ES)	Comprehensive education system Low status and take-up of VET High levels of early school leaving Weak linkages between education system and labor market	Underdeveloped ALMP and low PES capacity Focus on acquisition of first work experience Wage subsidies	High EPL dualism between temporary and permanent employment Segmented social protection with high protection gaps; high familialism No age-related minimum wage	Lengthy and uncertain High levels of temporary employment Skills mismatch Low labor demand
Post-socialist/transitional (EE, PL)	Comprehensive education systems, predominance of general education Low prominence of VET (school- or company-based) Weak linkages between education system and labor market High levels of educational attainment	Combination of liberal and employment-centered policies ALMP relatively underdeveloped Focus on acquisition of employability skills (supply side) and stimulus of labor demand through wage subsidies	High EPL dualism, but considerable differences within cluster Minimum wages set with social partners' involvement, not differentiated by age	Variable length and stability High incidence of temporary/low-quality employment Skills mismatch

Source: Adapted from Pohl and Walther (2007).

of performance determinants mainly focuses on the interaction between three institutional dimensions: the structure of the education and training system (particularly VET); employment regulation; and labor market policy models, with a focus on the characteristics of ALMP. Although our emphasis here is more on supply-side policies, the issue of sufficient labor demand (and demand-side policies) is also of crucial importance for STW transitions. The Great Recession has affected member states differently in terms of both job destruction during the recession and job creation in the recovery years (Grotti, Russell, and O'Reilly, this volume). For instance, among the countries studied here, job separation rates increased sharply in Estonia and Spain, but to a lesser extent in the Netherlands, whereas Germany proved much more resilient throughout the crisis (European Central Bank 2014). This variation must be kept in mind when assessing differences in performance.

Section 3.4 analyzes how the regimes' institutional features have changed due to intense policy innovation activity during the crisis, focusing on policy changes introduced since 2015. In particular, we assess the effects that recent policy changes may have on both the quality of future STW transitions and the heuristic and conceptual validity of Pohl and Walther's (2007) typology in the current historical phase. Our analysis also draws upon Rubery's (2011) concept of "hybridization" of social models to capture the nature of ongoing institutional changes affecting youth transition policy regimes in Europe. This refers to the process whereby developments in new policy areas cross traditional boundaries and paths of development usually associated with distinct welfare regime typologies. This is useful for conceptualizing ongoing changes in youth employment policy, where processes of gradual institutional change (Streeck and Thelen 2005) and multifaceted policy innovations appear to be slowly transforming the logic and objectives of existing policy regimes toward increased liberalization (Streeck 2009), while attempting to address existing protection gaps. The hybridization concept captures the contradictory nature of existing policy innovations, emphasizing the need to reconsider the validity of existing typologies of youth transition regimes in light of recent developments.

3.3. INSTITUTIONAL FEATURES AND PERFORMANCE IN DIFFERENT YOUTH TRANSITION REGIMES

The ideal-typical institutional characteristics of each regime prior to the crisis, as captured in Pohl and Walther's (2007) heuristic typology, are summarized in Table 3.1, whereas our discussion focuses on our country case studies, whose features may deviate from those generalized in Pohl and Walther's typology.

3.3.1. Universalistic Cluster

The universalistic youth transition model—represented here by Sweden—is characterized by an inclusive education system, with diversified post-compulsory routes into general and vocational education and high levels of investment in tertiary education. The linkage between education and the labor market is col-linear, with employers increasingly playing a role in specifying and delivering training. Nonetheless, VET plays a secondary role in post-compulsory educa-tion compared to higher education (Wadensjö 2015). The education and training system's comprehensive and inclusive nature is considered an important factor in facilitating human capital acquisition and smooth STW transitions. The fact that a high share of students—well above the EU average—combines work and study also helps such transitions (Eurofound 2014).

Sweden's strong corporatist tradition of close cooperation between the so-cial partners and the state contributes to the effectiveness of STW transition mechanisms such as traineeships/internships (Eurofound 2014). The institution-alized nature of corporatist arrangements in universalistic countries means that collective agreements constitute important driving forces for labor market regu-lation and wage setting (see Table 3.1).

The unemployment rate for 15- to 24-year-olds in Sweden was equal to the EU average in 2015 but was far below the EU average for 25- to 29-year-olds (Table 3.2). In general, STW transitions are comparatively fast and stable. In 2015, approximately 83% of 15- to 34-year-olds were employed 3 years after completing education (Table 3.3). This explains why the long-term unemploy-ment rate (see Table 3.2) and the NEET rate are among the lowest across the eight countries considered here and also far below the EU average (see Table 3.3). Indeed, unemployment spells for young people tend to be rather short and refer to transitions between education paths. However, subgroups such as the less ed-ucated, the disabled, or migrants face considerable barriers to entering the labor market (Wadensjö 2015).

ALMPs are particularly well developed and funded, and the overall STW transition model is based on young people's early activation, implemented through a highly personalized approach. In Sweden, this is realized through a strong job guarantee and social assistance program (Wadensjö 2015). One ele-ment of such programs is intensive (and early) job search assistance, combined with personalized action plans that have proved to be effective short-term tran-sition mechanisms. Supported forms of employment also play an important role.

Since the early 2000s, and more markedly since the onset of the Great Recession, the quality and effectiveness of Sweden's education and training system have deteriorated, despite strong public investment (European Commission 2015a). Sweden is one of the few European countries where VET participa-tion has decreased since 2005 (Gonzalez Carreras, Kirchner, and Speckesser

Table 3.2 Unemployment rate, long-term unemployment rate, and unemployment ratio: 2007 and 2015 (%)

Country	Unemployment rate							Long-term unemployment rate				Unemployment ratio			
	15–24 years				25–29 years			15–24 years		25–29 years		15–24 years		25–29 years	
	2015		2007		2015		2007	2015	2007	2015	2007	2015	2007	2015	2007
	Total	Women	Total	Women	Total	Women	Total	Total	Total	Total	Total	Total	Total	Total	Total
Spain	48.3	48.0	18.1	21.7	28.5	28.1	9.0	35.0	10.1	44.1	14.7	16.8	8.7	24.3	7.7
France	24.7	23.4	18.8	19.5	14.0	13.7	10.1	28.8	24.3	35.3	32.3	9.1	7.2	11.9	8.8
Poland	20.8	20.9	21.7	23.8	10.1	9.8	10.6	29.2	34.6	35.9	45.5	6.8	7.1	8.5	8.7
Sweden	20.4	19.6	19.3	19.8	8.7	8.4	7.0	6.3	4.0	15.5	11.0	11.2	10.1	7.5	6.1
United Kingdom	14.6	12.9	14.3	12.5	6.0	5.6	4.9	21.9	15.7	28.7	23.7	8.6	8.8	5.1	4.2
Estonia	13.1	12.2	10.1	7.2	6.0	7.1	4.4	15.5	30.5	34.7	46.8	5.5	3.8	5.1	3.7
Netherlands	11.3	11.2	5.9	6.2	6.5	6.3	2.4	18.7	12.6	31.5	26.2	7.7	4.3	5.7	2.2
Germany	7.2	6.5	11.9	11.1	5.8	4.9	9.9	22.5	32.2	32.2	42.7	3.5	6.1	4.8	8.1
EU	20.4	19.5	15.5	15.9	12.4	12.3	8.7	32.4	26.4	43.0	36.8	8.4	6.8	10.2	7.1

Source: Eurostat (2015).

Table 3.3 Employment rate within 3 years of highest educational attainment (ISCED), NEET rate, and fixed-term employment rate for 15- to 29-year-olds: 2007 and 2015 (%)

Country	Employment rate within 3 years					NEET rate				Fixed-term (15–29 years)	
	Total		0–2 (ISCED)	3–4 (ISCED)	5–8 (ISCED)	15–24 years		25–29 years		Total	
	2015	2007	2015	2015	2015	2015	2007	2015	2007	2015	2007
Germany	86.9	77.8	44.1	87.3	92.4	6.2	12.0	12.3	16.9	38.1	41.5
Netherlands	84.8	84.3	67.6	83.9	89.1	4.7	3.5	10.6	7.6	44.2	37.0
Sweden	83.2	82.4	61.6	79.2	90.8	6.7	7.5	8.6	8.8	41.0	43.6
United Kingdom	76.9	79.3	41.2	72.8	85.5	11.1	11.9	15.4	14.9	11.3	10.3
Estonia	74.8	76.0	32.7	71.8	84.8	10.8	8.9	14.8	17.2	8.0	4.2
Poland	73.3	70.5	23.7	64.7	83.7	11.0	10.6	20.5	21.6	54.3	49.5
France	62.8	70.6	21.4	57.0	77.9	11.9	10.7	20.0	17.2	41.0	35.5
Spain	54.2	74.4	29.2	47.5	66.7	15.6	12.0	26.0	13.8	54.3	51.5
EU	**69.8**	**73.5**	**33.1**	**66.5**	**79.7**	**12.0**	**11.0**	**19.7**	**17.2**	**32.5**	**30.9**

Source: Eurostat (2015).

2015). Despite repeated attempts to increase the take-up of apprenticeships (Wadensjö 2015), their incidence remains low and primarily concentrated in craft occupations, suggesting a persistent prevalence of the "academic" higher education route as the privileged form of post-compulsory training.

This cluster's institutional setup is usually characterized as an example of "flexicurity" with extended welfare provision (Eurofound 2014; Leschke and Finn, this volume). However, over time, activation has become tougher and benefits less generous and more conditional. Unemployment benefits are income based and subject to membership in an unemployment insurance fund. Young school-leavers generally do not qualify for these benefits because they do not meet the income requirements, which discourages them from registering as unemployed (Albæk et al. 2015). However, they can access means-tested social assistance or less generous unemployment benefit through ALMPs.

The universalistic cluster is not internally homogeneous, and different regulatory regimes may apply to distinct groups in the labor market. For example, in contrast to Denmark, Sweden's EPL is relatively high for permanent employment, but relatively low for temporary employment, leading to labor market segmentation reflected in levels of temporary employment that surpass the EU average (see Table 3.3). However, unlike in France or Spain, fixed-term contracts act as a stepping stone to more stable and regular work.

The limited changes in unemployment rates and ratios, as well as contract types and transition speed, between 2007 and 2015 suggest that youth labor demand was not strongly affected by the recent crisis (Grotti et al., this volume).

3.3.2. Employment-Centered Cluster

Countries in the employment-centered transition cluster (DE, FR, and NL in this study) are characterized by selective and highly standardized education and training systems, with well-developed apprenticeship and national certification systems. The German education system's selectivity is clearly shown in the educational attainment data. Among the eight countries reviewed, Germany has the highest proportion of young people aged 20–24 years (70.7%) with medium ISCED (International Standard Classification of Education) levels and the lowest proportion (6.4%) with high ISCED levels, whereas France has high shares of youth with high ISCED levels, especially those aged 20–24 years (28.8%; Table 3.4).

Dual VET constitutes a core feature of the German education system, with apprenticeships providing the main form of VET at the upper secondary level. In the Netherlands, apprenticeships are slightly less prominent, whereas in France, school-based VET still dominates (Eurofound 2014). Employers are actively involved in defining the design and content of VET in Germany and the Netherlands, closely cooperating with VET providers, but this is not the case in France. STW transitions in Germany and the Netherlands are generally efficient,

Table 3.4 Educational attainment by age and ISCED level (2015)

Country	20–24 years			25–34 years		
	0–2	**3–4**	**5–8**	**0–2**	**3–4**	**5–8**
Spain	31.5	46.9	21.5	34.4	24.6	41.0
Germany	22.9	70.7	6.4	12.7	57.7	29.6
Netherlands	20	61.7	18.3	14.4	40.5	45.1
Estonia	16.7	69.5	13.8	10.8	48.6	40.6
United Kingdom	14.3	56.2	29.5	14.7	38.4	47.0
France	12.8	58.3	28.8	13.5	41.9	44.7
Sweden	12.7	69.8	17.5	12.1	41.4	46.5
Poland	9.2	76.3	14.5	6.1	50.7	43.2
EU	**17.3**	**65.5**	**17.2**	**16.6**	**45.6**	**37.9**

Source: Eurostat (2015).

especially for those with medium ISCED levels, indicating well-established VET systems, which also contribute to both countries having the lowest NEET rates (see Table 3.3). High degrees of occupational specificity (Gangl 2001; Brzinsky-Fay 2007) and strong involvement of relevant stakeholders (Gonzalez Carreras et al. 2015) in the German and Dutch training systems are important driving forces for smooth STW transitions.

Youth unemployment rates in Germany and the Netherlands are the lowest among all the countries reviewed. However, Dutch youth unemployment ratios for 15- to 24-year-olds are relatively high. This discrepancy between the two countries in the share of active young people in the labor market is especially strong for those aged 15–24 years and much less important for those aged 25–29 years, who are less affected by differences in the education systems (see Table 3.2). Long-term unemployment rates are rather average in both countries (see Table 3.3). The difference between short- and long-term unemployment rates is due to the fact that short-term unemployed people tend to participate overproportionally during periods of recovery. The situation in France is more difficult because both short- and long-term unemployment rates are high.

Germany and the Netherlands have strict EPL for permanent employment, whereas their EPL for temporary employment is much lower than the Organization for Economic Co-operation and Development (OECD) average. In France, EPL is high for both permanent and temporary employment. Despite these differences, temporary employment for 15- to 29-year-olds was above the EU average in all three countries in 2015. It must be noted that half of all fixed-term contracts relate to apprenticeships in Germany, which has a much better transition probability compared with France (see Table 3.3). Segmentation is also predominant in France, not only for disadvantaged but also for qualified youth (Eurofound 2014).

Differences in ALMPs in the three countries are related to their different education systems and general economic performance. The Netherlands has traditionally high ALMP spending (EU's highest spending in 2014), with a focus on mediation and re-employment or reintegration, especially for the most vulnerable groups (Bekker et al. 2015). Wage subsidies also play a role in France and the Netherlands for helping young people acquire work experience. In Germany, basic training and assistance for less educated youth are also gaining importance given the favorable labor market situation. Thus, the specific focus of ALMPs depends not only on the general orientation of a particular cluster but also on a country's current economic situation.

In this cluster, the welfare system is based on a social insurance model with benefits financed by taxes (as in Sweden) and individual contributions. Similar to Sweden, benefits are income based, but young people do not have universal access to benefits. Indeed, depending on their status, young people can be excluded from or receive reduced benefits. In Germany, for example, young people receive a reduced amount of social assistance if they still live in their parents' home, and they need the approval of their local authority if they wish to move out while still receiving benefits (Eichhorst, Wozny, and Cox 2015).

Likewise in the Netherlands, there is no automatic right of young people to either income or reintegration support (Bekker et al. 2015). According to the 2012 Work and Social Assistance Act (Wet Werk en Bijstand, WWB), young people (aged younger than 27 years) have to wait 1 month before claiming social assistance for the first time, and they must search for a job (or education/ training placement). The aim is to encourage them to either (re)engage with education or attach themselves to the labor market, thus avoiding becoming NEETs. A comparison of unemployment rates and ratios as well as contract types and transition speed between 2007 and 2015 suggests that youth labor demand has been negatively affected by the recent crisis in the Netherlands and even more so in France, leading to lower and more unstable employment. Conversely, Germany has experienced higher youth labor demand as a result of its exceptionally favorable economic situation, with improved labor market conditions in 2015 compared to 2007.

3.3.3. Liberal Cluster

Liberal youth transition regimes—the United Kingdom in this study—are characterized by a comprehensive education system, high flexibility, and fragmentation in post-compulsory education. VET delivery models are not standardized and are accessible through school-based programs combining academic study with vocational elements, broad vocational programs, or specialist occupational programs delivered at both school and the workplace.

VET focuses rather narrowly on delivering particular occupational skills, albeit with less specialization and lower quality standards than in the employment-centered model. Indeed, the United Kingdom's VET provision has been criticized as being too focused on basic skills and relatively low-level qualifications.

The liberal regime is also characterized by limited employer engagement in VET provision, with employers viewing themselves as "customers" of the education system as opposed to partners (Tassinari, Hadjivassiliou, and Swift 2016). In fact, the decoupling of the education system and labor market—as well as the lack of joint delivery or codesign of VET—has made skill mismatch a recurring concern. A significant minority still leaves secondary education without the necessary skills and qualifications to compete in the labor market.

Recent reforms in the United Kingdom—especially the Apprenticeship Trailblazer reforms—have attempted to increase employer involvement in designing and delivering apprenticeship standards (Hadjivassiliou et al. 2015). Although the policy intention is to foster a major change in the STW transition pattern (expanding apprenticeships and revamping technical education and VET), it is too early to assess whether this initiative will lead to a permanent path shift. Indeed, due its deeply entrenched structural characteristics—that is, a fragmented market-based skills system with high flexibility but variable quality, employer resistance to assuming a more active role as providers instead of consumers of VET, and lack of parity of esteem between vocational and academic qualifications—the United Kingdom's VET-related policy has been suffering from a perennial implementation gap between policy objectives and reality, which is likely to continue (Tassinari et al. 2016).

Despite efforts to expand apprenticeships among young people in recent years, there has been a step-change in growth for those aged 25 years or older, with only a moderate increase in apprenticeship take-up among those aged 19–24 years and a fall in the number of apprenticeships available to 16- to 18-year-olds (Hadjivassiliou et al. 2015). As already argued, this expansion of apprenticeships has so far been more about formalizing adult workers' skills than meeting the youth-related policy objective.

To date, the evidence is unclear as to whether increased employer ownership in the United Kingdom is enough to guarantee quality in the new apprenticeship standards (House of Commons Education Committee 2015). Even so, it is also acknowledged that the ongoing apprenticeship/VET reforms with the new emphasis on, inter alia, increased employer involvement in VET provision, greater standardization and coordination, and improved quality of apprenticeships/VET linked to a more general upskilling push—which is likely to become more pertinent post-Brexit—show signs of potential paradigmatic change in the United Kingdom's STW system (Tassinari et al. 2016).

The United Kingdom's educational attainment data reflect this cluster's distinctive feature, namely the relatively minor role of VET. Indeed, "academization" is highest for both 20- to 24-year-olds and 25- to 34-year-olds across all countries reviewed (see Table 3.4). For this reason, employability is an important concern for the United Kingdom's youth-related policy, as reflected in the work-first focus of youth-related ALMPs.

The liberal cluster is characterized by low EPL: The United Kingdom's EPL is one of the lowest in the OECD, resulting in a less segmented labor market—reflected, for example, in the (lower) proportion of young people in temporary employment, which, in 2014, stood at 14.7% for those aged 15–24 years (as opposed to an EU average of 43.4%; Eurostat 2015). However, weak EPL also helps give rise to hyper-precarious forms of employment such as zero-hours contracts, in which working hours are set by employer demand, leading to unpredictable/unstable income. This transfer of business risk from employer to employee is especially prevalent among young people; indeed, 36% of people employed on zero-hours contracts are aged 16–24 years (Office for National Statistics 2016).

ALMPs are not specifically targeted at young people, apart from some flagship initiatives (e.g., the Youth Contract program) targeting unemployed youth. Unlike the other clusters, subsidies play a minor role, with interventions mainly focused on supply-side measures (Hadjivassiliou et al. 2015). Although the United Kingdom's benefits system is universal, benefit levels are low and subject to increasingly stringent conditionality. Welfare reforms implemented after 2010 are generally aimed at encouraging young people to exit the benefits system quickly and achieve early labor market (re)integration by making rules governing access to benefits stricter and more punitive.

Youth unemployment and long-term unemployment rates (see Table 3.2) are comparatively low, achieved—as explained previously—by low EPL and strong conditionality for benefits. Whereas this reduces rigidities that are harmful for STW transitions, it also creates unstable working conditions: The employment rate 3 years after completing education tends toward the average for all education levels through high job turnover (see Table 3.3). In general, the United Kingdom is characterized by rapid but unstable STW transitions. Due to low EPL for permanent contracts, temporary contracts are rarely used (see Table 3.3). The United Kingdom's labor market seems to have performed relatively well in the recent crisis, although long-term unemployment remains considerably above the precrisis level and is recovering more slowly than short-term unemployment.

3.3.4. Subprotective Cluster

The subprotective model—Spain in this study—is characterized by nonselective and comprehensively structured compulsory education systems, albeit with relatively low-quality, underdeveloped VET and comparatively high early school-leaving (ESL) rates (Eurofound 2014). The structure of educational attainment reflects this cluster's nonselective education system and weak VET role. Indeed, the Spanish education system is rather polarized in that it has the lowest level of ISCED 3–4 attainment for those aged 20–24 years, and especially for those aged 25–34 years (see Table 3.4).

Education and training are centrally standardized, and the incidence of apprenticeships is comparatively low, although there have been efforts to make VET more flexible and more closely aligned to employers' skill needs (González Menéndez et al. 2015b).

The distinctive characteristics of the subprotective model include the relatively high EPL levels for permanent employees, as well as the relatively ungenerous benefits system, which in turn reflects this cluster's traditionally weak welfare state and limited benefit provision, especially to young people (Eurofound 2014). The Spanish labor market is highly segmented, with a high incidence of temporary employment, especially among youth, as a result of the gap in EPL between highly regulated permanent contracts and deregulated fixed-term contracts. However, whereas past reforms only reduced protection at the margins and thus increased segmentation, recent reforms also deregulated EPL for permanent contracts (González Menéndez et al. 2015b).

The employment rate 3 years after completing education in Spain is the lowest among all countries reviewed. In particular, individuals with medium or high educational attainment have to contend with comparatively low employment rates (see Table 3.3). This cluster's institutional features tend to generate the greatest difficulties for labor market entry, given large shares of low-skilled entrants, comparatively high EPL for permanent jobs, and the absence of a comprehensive social safety net (Gangl 2001; Brzinsky-Fay 2007). This makes STW transitions complex, lengthier, and unstable.

ALMPs are relatively underdeveloped, with challenges arising from the weak institutional capacities of the Public Employment Services (PES), although improving ALMP delivery and strengthening activation constitute some of the main areas of recent policy intervention. Spanish ALMPs seek to improve young people's skills or provide them with work experience (González Menéndez et al. 2015b). An increase in the supply of work experience and/or job placements for young people is pursued through hiring subsidies that reduce nonwage labor costs.

Institutional factors are overshadowed by a lack of labor demand in Spain as the main factor explaining poor performance in youth transitions. Indeed, the Spanish labor market was one of the most adversely affected by the recession and the ensuing severe fiscal consolidation efforts, which is why every indicator must be seen in the light of extremely low levels of youth labor demand.

Spain had the highest youth unemployment rate and ratio in 2015. The discrepancy between these indicators is high for those aged 20–24 years, and it is much higher than in 2007. Young people seem to be staying longer in education in view of the economic downturn (see Table 3.2). In addition, long-term youth unemployment, the NEET rate, and temporary employment are the highest in 2015 among the eight countries (see Tables 3.2 and 3.3). Aside from temporary employment, these indicators were close to or below the EU average in 2007, indicating how labor demand fluctuations can change our assessment of STW transition regimes.

3.3.5. Post-Socialist/Transitional Cluster

In both Estonia and Poland, compulsory education systems are comprehensive, with post-compulsory general education remaining a more popular choice than vocational education, partly because of VET's poor reputation and excessive rigidity (Ślęzak and Szopa 2015). In 2015, Poland had the lowest levels of low-qualified youth and the highest rate of medium ISCED attainment among those aged 20–24 years, partly because compulsory education lasts until age 18 years. Educational attainment in Estonia is closest to the EU average (see Table 3.4). In both countries, NEET rates are also slightly below the EU average for those aged 15–24 years. However, NEET rates for 25- to 29-year-olds are close to the EU average in Poland and five percentage points below average in Estonia.

VET in Poland is mostly school based, whereas in Estonia it involves a greater share of company-based training, albeit still within a school-based delivery model. In Estonia, apprenticeships account for only approximately 2% of students, whereas they are marginally more common in Poland (European Commission 2015a). Employer involvement in VET is relatively low, although there have recently been efforts to increase employer engagement in VET. The linkages between the education system and the labor market are also weak, resulting in considerable skills mismatch (McGuinness, Bergin, and Whelan, this volume).

Similar to the United Kingdom, low incidence of work-based training increases the need for ALMPs to enhance youth employability, especially by providing financial incentives for employers to hire young people. Both countries also focus on specializing and standardizing education paths in line with labor market needs (Eamets and Humal 2015; Ślęzak and Szopa 2015). In both countries, the policy instruments used to support STW transitions include training and/or employment subsidies to increase the supply of work-experience placements. Whereas ALMPs in Estonia mainly concentrate on less educated youth, in Poland they also target highly qualified young people, given that graduate unemployment is quite high.

In both countries, welfare benefits are a mix of universal and contribution-based systems without any specific focus on young people. But they differ in relation to EPL: Estonia has relatively low EPL for permanent employment and relatively high EPL for temporary employment; in Poland, EPL is much stricter for permanent as opposed to temporary employment, making the latter more attractive for employers. The incidence of temporary employment in 2015 among 15- to 29-year-olds was extremely high in Poland (54%), whereas it was the lowest (8%) in Estonia among the countries reviewed (see Table 3.3). Institutional rigidity—which hampers adjustments to labor market changes—is one major impediment to smooth STW transition in Poland. The youth employment rate within 3 years after completing education corresponds to the EU average in both countries, when all education levels are considered together.

However, educational attainment in Poland is very important: Those with the lowest levels of educational attainment face similar labor market entry barriers as in France (see Table 3.3). This is related to the Polish education system, which produces the lowest proportion of young people with low educational attainment, who may face a crowding-out effect by more highly educated youth, leading to overqualification (see Table 3.4). In 2015, the Polish unemployment and long-term unemployment rates were close to the EU average. Estonian unemployment rates were among the lowest in the EU in 2015, although they had dramatically increased during the first period of the crisis. Both countries have recovered rather well from the crisis: Unemployment rates in 2015 are similar to those in 2007, and long-term unemployment rates have considerably declined (Table 3.2).

3.4. INSTITUTIONS IN FLUX: HOW ARE YOUTH TRANSITION REGIMES CHANGING?

Although the recession has been a global phenomenon, there are significant differences between countries regarding its depth, duration, and impact on young people (European Central Bank 2014). Whereas Germany, the Netherlands, and Austria consistently recorded youth unemployment rates of less than or approximately 10%, other countries fared much worse (with France and Poland recording rates of greater than 20% and Spain and Greece rates of greater than 50%; Hadjivassiliou et al. 2015).

After the recessionary years (2008–2009), the most important policy prescription recommended (or imposed—in Greece, Ireland, and Portugal) by the EU and the European Central Bank was "fiscal consolidation." All the countries most severely hit by the economic downturn, notably Southern countries but also some in Central and Eastern Europe, were recommended to combine austerity policies to cut public deficit and debt with structural reforms (including labor market reforms—to introduce more "flexibility" combined with an expansion of ALMPs). This produced contradictory outcomes for young people. The resulting macroeconomic environment generated weak or insufficient labor demand in many member states—or, in the case of the subprotective cluster, dramatically reduced demand for labor—and further exacerbated young people's labor market situation, given that they face more elastic labor demand relative to adult workers (Eurofound 2014; Eichhorst, Marx, and Wehner 2016; Grotti et al., this volume).

These developments have resulted in (1) a dramatic rise in youth unemployment in most countries; (2) lengthier, unstable, and nonlinear STW transitions; (3) a deterioration of youth employment quality combined with greater precariousness; (4) increased discouragement and labor market detachment; and

(5) greater labor market vulnerability of disadvantaged youth, such as the low skilled, migrants, and the disabled. Although recession-related economic deterioration and subsequent job-poor recovery account for such developments, these are also rooted in persistent structural deficiencies such as poorly performing education and training systems, segmented labor markets, and low PES capacity. The degree to which these deficiencies adversely affect young people varies considerably between and even within clusters, although a general deterioration in the length and quality of STW transitions is observed in all five clusters.

Against this backdrop, it is unsurprising that considerable policy action at the EU and national levels has focused on reforming the institutional arrangements that structure the STW transition process (Smith et al., this volume). In Section 3.4.1, we discuss some of the most notable institutional changes observed in 2007–2015 across the eight countries in the five clusters reviewed, including the implementation of the YG (2013 onward).[4]

In view of this changing policy landscape, some of the characteristics of each regime are in a state of flux, although more in some clusters (subprotective) than in others (universalistic). Moreover, competing trends of convergence and persisting divergence in different policy areas across clusters appear to be emerging. The implications of these ongoing processes of institutional change for the coherence and applicability of the existing typologies of youth transition regimes, as well as the quality of STW transitions, are assessed in Section 3.4.2.

3.4.1. Trends in Institutional Change and Convergence

Between 2007 and 2015, there was a change in governance structures, institutional frameworks, and actual policies and mechanisms associated with each STW transition regime across all countries in the five clusters. In many countries, the introduction of the YG in 2013 acted as a catalyst for structural reforms.[5] We identify five areas in which institutional change was especially prominent in 2007–2015: the strengthening of ALMP and PES capacity, the decentralization and localization of governance and delivery of youth employment policy, targeting of NEET policies, reforms of VET and apprenticeships, and EPL reforms. Next, we discuss the parallel trends of convergence and persisting divergence in these policy areas across clusters.

3.4.1.1. Strengthening of ALMP and PES Capacity

The institutional field of ALMP was a focus of substantial policy innovation between 2007 and 2015, and it was subject to some contradictory trends regarding the trajectory of change. Countries in all five clusters have intervened to strengthen their ALMPs and related infrastructure, most notably PES, although this has not been matched overall by an increase in available resources.

The YG—the EU's flagship youth employment program—has arguably been a potentially important driver of change in this area. Its implementation combines measures to help young people into employment in the short term with comprehensive structural reforms aimed at introducing systemic change in the structuring of STW transitions. These include introducing properly designed activation policies, well-functioning PES, cross-sectoral partnerships, multiagency working and outreach measures aimed at NEETs and disengaged youth, and effective VET and apprenticeship policies (European Commission 2015b).

In Estonia, France, Poland, and Spain, the implementation of the YG has involved PES restructuring to provide young people with individualized support, foster better links with both employers and education and training providers, and adopt a more targeted and proactive approach toward supporting NEETs (European Commission 2015b). It seems that the YG has improved the capacity of the Spanish PES to play a more active role in addressing youth unemployment (González Menéndez et al. 2015b).

The countries reviewed have also introduced new or have strengthened existing ALMPs and brought about changes in their activation models. In some cases, this emanated from the YG's focus on properly designed activation policies, whereas in others such reforms were enacted independently. For example, the YG's specific focus on young people's integrated STW transitions represents a departure from Estonia's traditional lack of labor market policies targeted at youth. As such, it arguably represents a "new way of doing things," especially by focusing on increasing the combined effect of different measures for vulnerable youth (Eamets and Humal 2015). Focusing even more on early intervention and activation, Sweden's government has reinforced its YG with a gradual introduction of a 90-day guarantee (Wadensjö 2015; Forslund 2016). Moreover, there is a much stronger focus on closer cooperation between Swedish central and local government (and PES) to ensure that youth-related ALMPs have greater impact at the local level.

Independent of the YG, the United Kingdom also implemented a raft of youth-related ALMPs such as the Youth Contract, introduced in 2012 with a strong focus on early activation and/or education and training. Similarly, in the Netherlands, there has been a distinct reinforcement of activation combined with severe restrictions to benefit access for youth aged 18–27 years following the 2009 Investment in Youth Act (Eichhorst and Rinne 2014).

Although the YG concept—including its focus on early, personalized, and integrated interventions—has been welcomed, its implementation across the EU has unsurprisingly been patchy and uneven (Bussi 2014; Eurofound 2015; Eichhorst and Rinne 2017). Reflecting the different institutional setups, labor markets, and economic structures and performance, the scope for YG-related change at the national and/or regional level has varied considerably. In Germany and the Netherlands (employment-centered cluster) and Sweden (universalistic cluster), the focus of the YG has been on the continuation, upscaling, and improvement of existing measures, as well as on improved cooperation and cross-agency working, rather than on any major change (Weishaupt 2014; Düll 2016).

In Spain (subprotective cluster), the YG led to some policy innovation and provided the framework whereby local initiatives already in place were formalized as part of its implementation (Petmesidou and González Menéndez 2016; see also Petmesidou and González Menéndez, this volume).

However, the EU funds earmarked for the YG are viewed as being inadequate for its effective implementation (Dhéret and Morosi 2015; Eurofound 2015; International Labour Organization 2015; Eichhorst and Rinne 2017). The uneven absorption capacity of these funds across the EU—especially at the regional level—combined with a lack of mobilization of some countries has cast further doubt on their ability to successfully implement the YG (Bussi 2014; ETUC 2016).

These examples point to the emergence of a partly contradictory trend, in which changes in policy design to strengthen ALMPs' effectiveness have not been matched by adequate increases in capacity. With the exception of Germany and—to some extent—Sweden, in most other countries reviewed (EE, ES, NL, PL, and UK), such efforts have not been accompanied by an increase in funding commensurate to the magnitude of youth unemployment. In Spain—where youth unemployment rose dramatically during the Great Recession—substantial fiscal consolidation linked to its austerity program has led to PES recruitment freezes and thus affected PES capacity to help increasing numbers of young jobseekers (European Commission 2016). Likewise, the Polish PES did not receive additional funds (Ślęzak and Szopa 2015). Estonia, one of the countries with the most severe austerity, experienced adverse implications for PES capacity (Eamets and Humal 2015).

This focus on PES capacity indicates potential convergence regarding policy objectives across clusters. However, the ability of a PES to actually strengthen links and cooperation with both employers and education and training institutions is highly variable, often limited, or even missing (Dhéret and Morosi 2015). In both Spain and France, there has been concern about PES's capacity to adequately service the large number of unemployed young people (European Commission 2016). However, concerns about capacity in the delivery of ALMPs extend beyond PES. In Sweden, there are concerns that reinforced municipal responsibility for youth-related activation measures has not been accompanied by a commensurate realignment between municipalities and centrally financed PES for financial incentives for ALMPs, thus limiting the municipalities' outreach capacity (European Commission 2016).

3.4.1.2. Decentralization and Devolution of Responsibility
The extent to which major changes regarding governance structures and/or institutional frameworks underpinning STW transitions were implemented as a result of the YG varied across contexts, largely depending on the pre-existing institutional setup. However, across the clusters we can observe convergence in terms of greater decentralization and devolution of responsibility for supporting

effective STW transitions at the local level, combined with greater autonomy and flexibility in addressing the specific needs of young people, especially NEETs.

In Germany and the Netherlands, where the YG can be considered an upscaling of existing measures, change has mainly occurred in the form of ongoing decentralization and localization of the responsibility for supporting STW transitions from the national to the local level. The objective is to enhance the cooperation and cross-agency working of local partnerships and to provide more integrated services to disadvantaged youth (Düll 2016). In the Netherlands, the responsibility for delivering employment and youth care services has shifted since 2015 to local authorities (Bekker, van de Meer, and Muffels 2015; Bekker et al. 2015). In Germany, municipal-level initiatives such as the *Jugendberufsagenturen* in Hamburg have developed effective local models of one-stop shops offering integrated, multiagency services to young people (Gehrke 2015).

Although municipalities (and the state) have always been the main actors for youth-related policies in Sweden (Wadensjö 2015), their activation responsibility has been strengthened since January 2015, as they are now directly responsible for activating early school-leavers and following up NEETs for targeted support (Forslund 2016). Devolution is also occurring in the United Kingdom, where local authorities now have formal responsibility for tracking young people's participation in education or training and for supporting NEETs in finding suitable training (Hadjivassiliou et al. 2015).

There seems to be convergence—sometimes instigated by YG implementation rules—in setting up broader stakeholder partnerships to offer integrated services, especially to youth at risk. Most countries are improving or setting up new governance structures, such as stronger partnership working arrangements and broader stakeholder engagement to address fragmentation in youth-related policies (Eurofound 2015; International Labour Organization 2015). For example, the introduction of the YG in Spain has led to better PES coordination between different levels of government and improved interregional cooperation (European Commission 2016) while providing a new framework for policy transfer across several government levels (González Menéndez et al. 2015a; Petmesidou and González Menéndez, this volume). Nonetheless, such broader stakeholder involvement and partnership working is not always easy to achieve in contexts with no tradition, structures, or mechanisms for cross-agency collaboration (e.g., France and Poland).

Both Estonia and France have strengthened partnership working across government agencies (European Commission 2016). For example, *Pôle emploi* (French PES) and *missions locales* (local PES for youth) are negotiating an agreement to improve their partnership working and provide adequate services to young people (European Commission 2016). How successful this attempt will be is debatable. The coordination of actors has historically been problematic within the fragmented French STW transition system, which lacks an overarching coordinating structure and integrative logic (Smith, Toraldo, and Pasquier 2015;

European Commission 2016). Similarly, in Poland, the YG has stimulated enhanced cooperation between local-level employment offices (*Poviat*) and a wide range of organizations, such as academic career centers, local Voluntary Labor Corps (*Ochotnicze Hufce Pracy* (OHP)) units, social welfare centers, and schools (Weishaupt 2014). However, effective cooperation between PES and OHP regarding youth-related ALMPs remains a challenge (European Commission 2016). Early indications regarding YG implementation show that social partner and youth organizations' involvement has been very limited in most countries (Dhéret and Morosi 2015; Eurofound 2015).

3.4.1.3. Targeting of NEET Policies: Addressing Low Skilling and Early School Leaving

Another common pattern across clusters has been a stronger focus on NEETs, early school-leavers, and other at-risk youth groups (low qualified, from an ethnic minority/migrant background, or from a lower socioeconomic/disadvantaged background).

Education-related reforms have addressed low educational attainment. Policy interventions across all clusters have focused on reducing ESL age so that young people obtain the minimum labor market entry requirement of at least an upper secondary education qualification (European Commission 2015a; Hadjivassiliou 2016). In Spain, the 2013 education reform (*Ley Orgánica para la Mejora de la Calidad Educativa*) sought to reduce ESL by allowing those aged 15–17 years to enroll in basic professional training to obtain the upper secondary school qualification and eventually access higher level training (González Menéndez et al. 2015a, 2015b). In Sweden, given the large share (approximately 25%) of youth who have not successfully completed upper secondary education, so-called "education contracts" were introduced in 2015 to encourage unemployed young people aged 20–24 years to complete their upper secondary education (Wadensjö 2015; Forslund 2016).

There has also been an increased focus on targeting NEETs across all clusters (Mascherini, this volume). Training and education or activation measures, rehabilitation programs, more integrated services, and outreach activities to identify, register, and (re-)engage NEETs have all been used. This is crucial given the large numbers of NEETs who are not registered with PES and cannot access YG-related and other supportive interventions. Although many countries—including Spain and Germany—have set up online outreach tools, the engagement of unregistered, "hardest-to-reach" youth through grassroots actions (e.g., street outreach work) and multiagency working remains less common (Eurofound 2015; Hadjivassiliou 2016). This constitutes a serious limitation because online outreach tools (e.g., using Facebook and other social media and/or designated online platforms/portals to reach out to NEETs) cannot replace face-to-face interaction, especially when it comes to youth with more complex problems (International Classification of Functioning 2015).

Overall, it is fair to say that in many cases, the YG has provided an additional impetus in focusing on NEETs, although the actual implementation in countries with high youth unemployment falls short of initial expectations.

3.4.1.4. VET and Apprenticeships

VET and apprenticeships suggest elements of convergence across clusters, although changes may be confined to policy objectives rather than actual outcomes. There has been a universal effort to reform or strengthen the role of VET/apprenticeships in STW transitions, although the extent of change seems to be more far-reaching—at least in terms of policy intention—in the subprotective cluster (European Commission 2015a; González Menéndez et al. 2015b). Spain has recently embarked upon a major education reform to improve the links between its education system and the labor market. Royal Decree 1529/2012 laid the foundations for the gradual introduction of the dual-training principle in Spain's VET and sought to foster greater participation by companies (González Gago 2015; González Menéndez et al. 2015b). Recent education reform introduced more vocational pathways in lower secondary education and a new 2-year VET module to address ESL (González Gago 2015).

Since 2013, the United Kingdom (liberal cluster) has been implementing a major VET and apprenticeship reform. Apprenticeship Trailblazers seek to put employers at the heart of the apprenticeship system, representing a potential paradigm shift within the UK context (Tassinari et al. 2016). The reforms aim to promote VET and associated career pathways as a high-quality option and to expand apprenticeship take-up (Hadjivassiliou et al. 2015). Similar VET/apprenticeship reforms have been introduced in Estonia (2013), Sweden (2014), and France (2013 and 2014).

VET and apprenticeships may potentially become more important STW transition mechanisms, even in the liberal (UK) and the subprotective (ES) clusters, where they have traditionally been underdeveloped. However, introducing apprenticeship/VET reforms at the policy design level is not sufficient to bring about deep-seated institutional change. This requires a change in the attitude of training providers and employers, as well as increased partnership working between the two, which is not easily achieved in countries lacking such a tradition of cooperation, such as France, Poland, Spain, and the United Kingdom (Eurofound 2015; Hadjivassiliou, Tassinari, and Swift 2015; Ślęzak and Szopa 2015; Smith et al. 2015).

VET reforms also require strong and unequivocal employer support in terms of offering an adequate supply of quality placements and associated training (Eichhorst 2015). Change is also required in the attitude of young people and their families, whereby apprenticeship/VET is not viewed as a second-best option. Nonetheless, VET still suffers from a rather poor image in the subprotective (ES), post-socialist (EE and PL), and liberal (UK) clusters (Eamets and Humal 2015; González Menéndez et al. 2015b).

There is also concern about the education and training systems' ability to quickly adapt in line with the new VET/apprenticeship reforms to deal effectively with the current cohort of unemployed youth, as well as the gap between employer demand and the VET system's ability to respond satisfactorily (Eurofound 2015). These factors may act as barriers to deep institutional change in this policy area.

3.4.1.5. Flexibilization of Youth Labor Markets and EPL Reforms

Persistent labor market segmentation is evident across all five clusters, although the trajectory of change seems to be one of convergence toward greater "flexibilization," along with the loosening of EPL for prime-age workers rather than greater security. Reforms of EPL have focused on achieving a better balance in protection between those on permanent and those on temporary contracts, thus reducing existing dualisms. In the Netherlands, EPL changes since July 2015 seek to strengthen the position of workers on temporary contracts (Bekker et al. 2015). Similarly, in Spain, following the 2010 and 2012 labor market reforms, the deregulation of EPL for permanent contracts has reduced the dualism between temporary and permanent employment protection (González Menéndez et al. 2015a). The Estonian Employment Contracts Act (2009) introduced major reforms aimed at increasing labor market flexibility. In France, highly controversial and politically difficult EPL changes have proved to be more limited but in any case have sought to reduce labor market dualism.

However, it is too soon to gauge the impact of these changes on youth labor markets, especially against a backdrop of limited labor demand in some of the countries examined. More worryingly, existing evidence suggests that the share of temporary contracts among youth has even increased in countries (FR and ES) that deregulated EPL during the crisis (Eichhorst et al. 2016; Grotti, Russell, and O'Reilly, this volume). The available evidence suggests that attempts to loosen EPL for permanent contracts in highly dualized labor markets (FR and ES) are likely to result in worsening working conditions and more unstable employment for all workers rather than in easier STW transitions (Eichhorst and Rinne 2014; González Menéndez et al. 2015a, 2015b). Even the traditionally better performance of some STW regimes seems to come under question, with temporary, precarious employment rates increasing among young people in countries such as the Netherlands, thus pointing to a potential convergence toward lower quality of transitions across the board.

3.4.2. Assessing the Impact of Institutional Change on Youth Transition Regimes

The ongoing processes of institutional change in the targeting, design, and governance of ALMPs, the status of VET systems, and the design of EPL institutions are leading to a reconfiguration of European youth transition regimes. The five convergence trends in the trajectory of policy change during the crisis are accompanied by persisting divergence in institutional and fiscal capacity across countries that—together with dynamics of institutional path dependency—affect the depth and effectiveness of reform implementation and thus raise doubts about the possibility of substantial institutional change occurring in the short term.

Nonetheless, our analysis suggests that the STW transition regimes defined by Pohl and Walther's (2007) typology may be in a state of flux as a result of policy developments during the recent crisis. Rubery's (2011) "regime hybridization" concept is relevant here for capturing the nature of the ongoing institutional changes affecting the structure of youth transition policy regimes in Europe. Indeed, recent policy developments are blurring the distinctions between regimes and potentially altering the underlying logic structuring youth transitions in each cluster. Countries across all regimes have recently adopted reforms in regulation and policy instruments that do not belong to their "traditional" institutional legacy as captured by Pohl and Walther's typology. Furthermore, a tendency toward greater liberalization of employment regulation has been accompanied by increased policy activity in "new" areas, such as ALMPs, to address existing gaps in support and protection, in line with the trajectory identified by Rubery for European welfare regimes as a whole.

For example, reforms of VET and apprenticeship systems have achieved prominence in countries in the liberal and subprotective clusters, where these instruments have traditionally been secondary in importance, while at the same time the sustainability and effectiveness of VET have faced challenges in the employment-centered and universalistic cluster countries, where VET has traditionally been more established. The increased focus on "supportive" and targeted ALMPs—traditionally characteristics of the universalistic cluster—is now spreading to countries where such instruments were considerably less developed, such as those belonging to the subprotective and post-socialist clusters, largely as a result of the policy convergence process driven by the YG. At the same time, processes of labor market flexibilization are changing the institutional architecture of employment regulation toward greater liberalization across the board, including in countries traditionally characterized by entrenched dualisms in protection (i.e., subprotective or employment-centered clusters).

Although developing revised typologies was not an objective of our analysis, our findings show that it is necessary to consider institutional configurations and "clusters" as being dynamic, while continuing to devote attention to processes of institutional and structural change that may be altering the underlying logic of distinct youth transition regimes over time.

Although the limited number of countries in our sample did not allow us to systematically explore the internal "coherence" of the different youth transition regimes outlined by Pohl and Walther (2007), our analysis has shown that considerable variation exists across countries, even within clusters that share common underlying logics of institutional configuration. This suggests that although the "youth transition regime" concept can act as a useful heuristic, analytical device, generalizations at the cluster level in terms of performance need to be examined judiciously.

In terms of impact on performance, most reforms introduced in the aftermath of the Great Recession are very recent, making it difficult to estimate their potential to contribute to positive changes in the future quality and speed of STW transition to tackle performance challenges. However, some preliminary remarks can be made. In the universalistic cluster, where the main challenge arises from the difficult labor market integration of specific groups of disadvantaged youth, current efforts to improve the speed and targeting of activation measures may prove helpful. In the employment-centered and subprotective clusters, where a key youth-related challenge arises from high levels of labor market segmentation, the current policy trend of greater labor market flexibilization may actually be counterproductive in ensuring fast and secure transitions. Indeed, it has already resulted in higher levels of temporary and precarious employment—at least in the short term (Eichhorst et al. 2016).

Increasing PES capacity and strengthening ALMP comprise another fundamental area of intervention to help disadvantaged youth across clusters, especially in the subprotective and post-socialist regimes. Likewise, reforming VET to increase linkages between education and the labor market could help address the skills mismatch pervasive in the subprotective and liberal clusters. However, the depth of policy change in these areas remains limited by dynamics of institutional path dependency and the low availability of resources for effective implementation. The overall emerging picture is thus one in which policy changes aimed at strengthening *supportive* policy instruments—such as expanding ALMP and PES capacity and strengthening VET systems—are currently limited in their reach and potential effectiveness. At the same time, the trends of *liberalization and deregulation* of protective institutions, such as EPL, contribute to making young people's STW transitions potentially more unstable, at least in the short term.

3.5. CONCLUSIONS

Our comparative analysis has shown that countries' institutional configurations matter considerably in shaping the structure of young people's STW transitions and in mediating the impact of the Great Recession on youth unemployment. Drawing upon Pohl and Walther's (2007) concept of "youth transition regime" as a heuristic framework for comparison, we have assessed the performance of countries belonging to different clusters regarding the speed, ease, and quality of STW transitions. The divergence in performance between countries belonging to different regimes—which had already started in 2007 and has accelerated since 2009—shows the important role of institutional arrangements in shaping STW transitions in the fields of employment regulation, education and training, and ALMP.

In line with existing evidence, well-integrated VET systems with strong employer involvement and clear labor market connections alongside supportive ALMPs have emerged as important institutional characteristics that have historically facilitated the comparatively better performance in STW transitions of the universalistic (SE) and employment-centered (DE and NL) clusters. Therefore, it is unsurprising that recent policy interventions introduced by European countries during austerity, including the YG initiative, have focused on strengthening these two institutional areas. In VET, the focus has primarily been on expanding apprenticeships as a transition route and increasing linkages between training systems and the labor market by enhancing employer involvement. In ALMP, policy intervention has focused on improving PES capacity and diversifying existing activation measures to provide more personalized support to unemployed youth, including NEETs. Given the well-documented "scarring" effects of NEET status, this renewed NEET focus is welcome, as is the tailoring of responses across clusters in recognition of the NEET population's heterogeneity (Mascherini, this volume; Zuccotti and O'Reilly, this volume).

These areas of policy change could be viewed as a potential sign of convergence across regimes in terms of their underlying logic of STW transitions. However, the extent to which such policy changes can become embedded in other contexts crucially depends on existing institutional and coordination capacity, as well as the availability of resources. Indeed, VET systems are complexly interwoven within the broader institutional fabric, with the evidence suggesting that the potential for far-reaching change may be limited by dynamics of institutional path dependency (e.g., the lack of established mechanisms for social partner engagement and coordination). Likewise, the absence of pre-existing institutional infrastructures of coordination in numerous countries jeopardizes the success of attempts to improve PES capacity and establish effective partnership working between different agencies to engage difficult-to-reach youth.

Resource limitations—both fiscal and in terms of actors' capacity—also act as a barrier to more deep-seated institutional change, potentially making the transfer of "good practice" across regimes inherently difficult. Despite EU funding, in most cases reforms are being introduced against a backdrop of tight public finances and spending cuts, which undermines the effective implementation of policies such as the expansion of ALMP and PES capacity. Moreover, in the context of a fragile economic recovery in many countries—or second-dip recession in a few—employer capacity to provide training places (e.g., apprenticeships) and jobs to young people may be limited (Eurofound 2015).

Employment regulation has also emerged from our analysis as a key factor affecting the quality and nature of STW transitions. Differential levels of EPL between temporary and permanent employment have led many countries—especially in the subprotective and employment-centered clusters—to entrenched labor market segmentation, with young people being increasingly confined to the labor market's temporary segment. Since 2010, many countries have tried to tackle segmentation by deregulating permanent contracts (Eichhorst et al. 2016). Despite being more pronounced in the most segmented countries, such as France and Spain, this has also occurred in better-performing countries such as the Netherlands. While reducing segmentation, excessive flexibility can lead to low employment quality and high precariousness, as the experience of the liberal and post-socialist clusters shows. The trend emerging from reforms implemented during the Great Recession thus seems to point toward greater labor market flexibilization, which is not promising in terms of ensuring that transitions are stable and secure in the long term. Balancing flexibility and security in youth labor markets represents a key outstanding challenge that is yet to be fully confronted in all clusters.

Although institutional configurations are very important in shaping the structure, nature, and effectiveness of STW transitions, the performance of countries is also significantly shaped by macroeconomic trends, especially by levels of demand for youth labor. Divergence between countries in economic performance accounts for many of the observed differences with regard to the performance of youth labor markets. The comparatively positive performance of the Polish youth labor market is largely explained by the fact that Poland did not fall into a recession. Likewise, Germany, the Netherlands, and Sweden started recovering from the recession relatively sooner compared to the other countries, accounting for their comparatively better performance in youth employment.

In a context in which youth labor demand remains low, policy interventions focused solely on the supply side or that encourage flexibility will remain limited in their effectiveness. Our analysis illustrates how the institutional configurations of STW regimes in Europe are "in flux." The validity and applicability of established typologies, such as that of Pohl and Walther (2007), are limited in the present historical phase because of ongoing dynamics of regime hybridization (Rubery 2011). Current trends of emerging "convergence" across clusters in the design of youth-transition policy instruments may alter the logic of transition systems across regimes in the long term, making a new conceptualization of youth transition regimes necessary. However, currently, this institutional change remains limited in terms of impact and superficial in terms of actual implementation. Differences in performance across regimes persist, with some faring better than others, although at the same time a common, worrying trend can be identified across clusters: a progressive deterioration of the quality of youth transitions across the board, despite the positive policy intentions to strengthen and improve the efficacy of transition regimes.

NOTES

1   Although we are aware of the importance of other policy instruments such as in-work benefits, which may act as pull factors for what concerns the labor market transitions of young people, we are unable to address them in this chapter due to space constraints (see Smith et al., this volume).

2   This chapter is based on seven in-depth case studies completed in 2015. See STYLE Working Papers, WP3, Country reports, CROME. http://www.style-research.eu/publications/working-papers.

3   The different indicators capture different aspects of youth labor market performance. High youth unemployment rates reflect young people's difficulties in securing employment. However, this does not mean that the number of unemployed young people (aged 15–24 years) is large, because many in this age group are in full-time education (i.e., inactive). This may make meaningful comparisons between different countries difficult (Wadensjö 2015). A more reliable indicator is the youth unemployment ratio (O'Reilly et al. 2015).

4   Although the introduction of the YG by the European Commission in 2013 has been welcome, it has been subject to a number of criticisms, not least that it was introduced quite late and was accompanied by inadequate financial resources (Dhéret and Morosi 2015). According to International Labour Organization (2015) estimates, the proper implementation of the YG in EU28 requires spending of approximately €45 billion, whereas the available EU financial support—under the Youth Employment Initiative, which is funding the implementation of the YG across the EU—amounts to €6.4 billion.

5   All the country reports on the YG mentioned here were published by the European Commission in 2016 on the website http://ec.europa.eu/social/main.jsp?catId=1161.

REFERENCES

Albæk, Karsten, Rita Asplund, Erling Barth, Lena Lindahl, Kristine von Simson, and Pekka Vanhala. 2015. "Youth Unemployment and Inactivity. A Comparison of School-to-Work Transitions and Labour Market Outcomes in Four Nordic Countries." TemaNord 2015: 548. Copenhagen: Norden.

Bekker, Sonja, Marc van de Meer, and Ruud Muffels. 2015. "Barriers to and Triggers of Innovation and Knowledge Transfer in the Netherlands." STYLE Working Paper 4.1. Brighton, UK: CROME, University of Brighton. http://www.style-research.eu/publications/working-papers

Bekker, Sonja, Marc van de Meer, Ruud Muffels, and Ton Wilthagen. 2015. "Policy Performance and Evaluation: Netherlands." STYLE Working Paper 3.3. Brighton, UK: CROME, University of Brighton. http://www.style-research.eu/publications/working-papers

Brzinsky-Fay, Christian. 2007. "Lost in Transition? Labor Market Entry Sequences of School-Leavers in Europe." *European Sociological Review* 23 (4): 409–22.

Bussi, Margherita. 2014. *The Youth Guarantee in Europe*. Brussels: European Trade Union Institute.

Dhéret, Claire, and Martina Morosi. 2015. "One Year After the Youth Guarantee: Policy Fatigue or Signs of Action?" EPC Policy Brief. Brussels: European Policy Centre.

Düll, Nicola. 2016. "How to Best Combine Personalised Guidance, Work Experience and Training Elements Targeted at Vulnerable Youth? Practices and Lessons from Germany." Peer Review on "The Guarantee for Youth," Paris, April 7–8.

Eamets, Raul, and Katrin Humal. 2015. "Policy Performance and Evaluation: Estonia." STYLE Working Paper 3.3. Brighton, UK: CROME, University of Brighton. http://www.style-research.eu/publications/working-papers

Eichhorst, Werner. 2015. "Does Vocational Training Help Young People Find a (Good) Job?" IZA World of Labor. https://wol.iza.org/articles/does-vocational-training-help-young-people-find-good-job/long

Eichhorst, Werner, Paul Marx, and Caroline Wehner. 2016. "Labor Market Reforms in Europe: Towards More Flexicure Labor Markets?" IZA Discussion Paper 9863. Bonn: Institute for the Study of Labor.

Eichhorst, Werner, and Ulf Rinne. 2014. "Promoting Youth Employment Through Activation Strategies." Employment Working Paper 163. Geneva: International Labour Office.

Eichhorst, Werner, and Ulf Rinne. 2017. "The European Youth Guarantee: A Preliminary Assessment and Broader Conceptual Implications." IZA Policy Paper 128. Bonn: Institute for the Study of Labor.

Eichhorst, Werner, Florian Wozny, and Michael Cox. 2015. "Policy Performance and Evaluation: Germany." STYLE Working Paper 3.3. Brighton, UK: CROME, University of Brighton. http://www.style-research.eu/publications/working-papers

ETUC. 2016. *Towards a Real and Effective Youth Guarantee in Europe*. Brussels: European Trade Union Confederation.

Eurofound. 2014. *Mapping Youth Transitions in Europe*. Luxembourg: Publications Office of the European Union.

Eurofound. 2015. "Beyond the Youth Guarantee—Lessons Learned in the First Year of Implementation." Background document prepared for the informal EPSCO meeting of July 16–17, Luxembourg.

European Central Bank. 2014. "The Impact of the Economic Crisis on Euro Area Labour Markets." *ECB Monthly Bulletin* 2014 (October).

European Commission. 2015a. *Education and Training Monitor 2015*. Luxembourg: European Union.

European Commission. 2015b. *Youth Unemployment—European Semester Thematic Fiche*. Brussels: European Commission.

European Commission. 2016. The *Youth Guarantee Country by Country*. Brussels: European Commission. http://ec.europa.eu/social/main.jsp?catId=1161

Eurostat. 2015. *Being Young in Europe Today—2015 Edition*. Luxembourg: Publications Office of the European Union.

Forslund, Anders. 2016. "Strategies to Improve Labor Market Outcomes of Youth at Risk—The Swedish Experience." Country Paper presented at the High Level Learning Exchange on "Designing and Implementing Effective Strategies to Support the Integration and Retention in the Labor Market of Youth at Risk," Stockholm, February 18–19.

Gangl, Markus. 2001. "European Patterns of Labor Market Entry: A Dichotomy of Occupationalized Versus Non-Occupationalized Systems?" *European Societies* 3 (4): 471–94.

Gehrke, Anne-Marie. 2015. *WP7 Case Study: Jugendberufsagentur (JBA) "Nobody Should Be Lost."* Hamburg: CITISPYCE.

Gonzalez Carreras, Francisco J., Laura Kirchner Sala, and Stefan Speckesser. 2015. "The Effectiveness of Policies to Combat Youth Unemployment." STYLE Working Paper 3.2. Brighton, UK: CROME, University of Brighton. http://www.style-research.eu/publications/working-papers

González Gago, Elvira. 2015. "Co-ordination and Interdisciplinary Work as Key Answers to the NEETs—Spain." Peer review on "Targeting NEETs—Key Ingredients for Successful Partnerships in Improving Labor Market Participation," Oslo, September 24–25.

González Menéndez, María C., Ana M. Guillén, Begoña Cueto, Rodolfo Gutiérrez, F. Javier Mato, and Aroa Tejero. 2015a. "Barriers to and Triggers of Policy Innovation and Knowledge Transfer in Spain." STYLE Working Paper 4.1. Brighton, UK: CROME, University of Brighton. http://www.style-research.eu/publications/working-papers

González Menéndez, María C., F. Javier Mato, Rodolfo Gutiérrez, Ana M. Guillén, Begoña Cueto, and Aroa Tejero. 2015b. "Policy Performance and Evaluation: Spain." STYLE Working Paper 3.3. Brighton, UK: CROME, University of Brighton. http://www.style-research.eu/publications/working-papers

Hadjivassiliou, Kari P. 2016. "What Works for the Labor Market Integration of Youth at Risk." Thematic paper presented at the High Level Learning Exchange on "Designing and Implementing Effective Strategies to Support the Integration and Retention in the Labor Market of Youth at Risk," Stockholm, February 18–19.

Hadjivassiliou, Kari, Arianna Tassinari, Stefan Speckesser, Sam Swift, and Christine Bertram. 2015. "Policy Performance and Evaluation: United Kingdom." STYLE Working Paper 3.3. Brighton, UK: CROME, University of Brighton. http://www.style-research.eu/publications/working-papers

Hadjivassiliou, Kari, Arianna Tassinari, and Sam Swift. 2015. "Barriers to and Triggers of Policy Innovation and Knowledge Transfer in the UK." STYLE

Working Paper 4.1. Brighton, UK: CROME, University of Brighton. http://www.style-research.eu/publications/working-papers

House of Commons Education Committee. 2015. "Apprenticeships and Traineeships for 16 to 19 Year-Olds." Sixth Report of Session 2014–15. London: The Stationery Office Limited.

International Classification of Functioning. 2015. *Relevance and Feasibility of MLP Activity on Outreach Work with NEETs.* Brussels: European Commission.

International Labour Organization. 2015. "The Youth Guarantee Program in Europe: Features, Implementation and Challenges." Working Paper 4. Geneva: International Labour Organization Research Department.

Office for National Statistics. 2016. *Contracts That Do Not Guarantee a Minimum Number of Hours: September 2016.* Newport: Office for National Statistics.

O'Reilly, Jacqueline, Werner Eichhorst, András Gábos, Kari Hadjivassiliou, David Lain, Janine Leschke, et al. 2015. "Five Characteristics of Youth Unemployment in Europe: Flexibility, Education, Migration, Family Legacies, and EU Policy." *SAGE Open* 5 (1): 1–19. Advance online publication. doi:10.1177/2158244015574962.

Petmesidou, Maria, and María C. González Menéndez, eds. 2016. "Policy Learning and Innovation Processes Drawing on EU and National Policy Frameworks on Youth—Synthesis Report." STYLE Working Paper 4.2. Brighton, UK: CROME, University of Brighton. http://www.style-research.eu/publications/working-papers

Pohl, Axel, and Andreas Walther. 2007. "Activating the Disadvantaged— Variations in Addressing Youth Transitions Across Europe." *International Journal of Lifelong Education* 26 (5): 533–53.

Rubery, Jill. 2011. "Reconstruction Amid Deconstruction: Or Why We Need More of the Social in European Social Models." *Work, Employment and Society* 25 (4): 658–74.

Ślęzak, Ewa, and Bogumiła Szopa. 2015. "Policy Performance and Evaluation: Poland." STYLE Working Paper 3.3. Brighton, UK: CROME, University of Brighton. http://www.style-research.eu/publications/working-papers

Smith, Mark, Maria Laura Toraldo, and Vincent Pasquier. 2015. "Barriers to and Triggers of Innovation and Knowledge Transfer in France." STYLE Working Paper 4.1. Brighton, UK: CROME, University of Brighton. http://www.style-research.eu/publications/working-papers

Streeck, Wolfgang. 2009. *Re-Forming Capitalism. Institutional Change in the German Political Economy.* Oxford: Oxford University Press.

Streeck, Wolfgang, and Kathleen Ann Thelen, eds. 2005. *Beyond Continuity: Institutional Change in Advanced Political Economies.* Oxford: Oxford University Press.

Tassinari, Arianna, Kari Hadjivassiliou, and Sam Swift. 2016. "Plus ça change . . .? Innovation and Continuity in UK Youth Employment Policy in the Great Recession." *Politiche sociali / Social Policies* (2): 225–48.

Wadensjö, Eskil. 2015. "Policy Performance and Evaluation: Sweden." STYLE Working Paper 3.3. Brighton, UK: CROME, University of Brighton. http:// www.style-research.eu/publications/working-papers

Weishaupt, J. Timo. 2014. "Central Steering and Local Autonomy in Public Employment Services." Analytical Paper, PES-to-PES Dialogue. Brussels: European Commission.

4

STRESSED ECONOMIES, DISTRESSED POLICIES, AND DISTRAUGHT YOUNG PEOPLE

EUROPEAN POLICIES AND OUTCOMES FROM A YOUTH PERSPECTIVE

Mark Smith, Janine Leschke, Helen Russell, and Paola Villa

4.1. INTRODUCTION

This chapter assesses recent labor market policies and outcomes in Europe, with a focus on the impact upon young people.[1] Our point of departure is the inadequacy of moribund "flexicurity" policies that lost both their political sponsors and their credibility during the Great Recession.[2] These weaknesses were compounded by an overemphasis on flexibility measures, a gender-blind approach to policy, and limited consideration for the impact on young people.

The crisis facing young people on the labor market has become a growing concern for both policymakers and academic researchers. Whereas some of these concerns reflect long-standing challenges faced by young people entering the labor market, other issues are linked more specifically to outcomes and policy changes resulting from the severe economic downturn. These challenges have short-term (rising unemployment), medium-term (long-term unemployment and precariousness), and long-term consequences (scarring and delayed family formation) for the generation of youth that entered working life in the years of the Great Recession (see Part II of this volume).

Our critique of policies and outcomes is based on extensive analysis—as part of the STYLE project—of recent European and national policies for youth at the flexibility–security interface. This includes studies tracing and scrutinizing policy reforms—in particular, developments in active labor market policies (ALMPs) and unemployment insurance—using, among other sources, European comparative policy databases such as the Labour Market Reforms Database (LABREF) and the Mutual Information System on Social Protection (MISSOC) (Eamets et al. 2015; Smith and Villa 2016; also see Leschke and Finn, this volume). Another study under the project used quantitative analysis on European Social Survey (ESS) data to analyze the impact of flexicurity on young people's insecurity and subjective well-being (Russell, Leschke, and Smith 2015). Based on these studies and previous research by the authors (e.g., Smith and Villa 2013; Leschke, Theodoropoulou, and Watt 2014), we demonstrate in this chapter four key weaknesses in employment policy related to young people in Europe. First, there has been an over-reliance on supply-side policies and on quantitative targets. Second, labor market reforms have been driven by external pressures of macroeconomic stability rather than by a coherent strategy toward sustainable labor market outcomes. Third, reforms have been based on a downward pressure on job security and a strengthening of employability security through ALMPs, despite slack labor demand. Fourth, due to the over-reliance on quantitative targets, there is a lack of consideration by policymakers of the wider (subjective) impact of precariousness and early career insecurity on young people and their life courses. In identifying these four elements, we argue that employment policy, both European and national, has not been well adapted to the needs of young people. The consequences of all these four weaknesses in policymaking are particularly acute for young people and are frequently not taken into consideration.

The remainder of this chapter is divided into three sections. Section 4.2 explores the context of European employment policymaking, with a particular focus on the evolution of the European Employment Strategy (EES) and the position of young people within this pan-national framework for policy learning and development. Section 4.3 explores, in turn, the four key critiques of European employment policy and their impact on young people. Section 4.4 concludes with a consideration of the policy implications and a call for a renewed perspective on durable and resilient labor markets for young women and men transitioning from school to work.

4.2. YOUTH AND EUROPEAN UNION EMPLOYMENT POLICY

Within the European Union (EU), the most direct way to influence member states' employment policy is via labor law directives, which are often negotiated autonomously by the social partners in the area of working conditions. These initiatives, however, have been rather ineffective in setting EU-wide minimum standards during the past 15 years—at least at a cross-sectoral level (Falkner 2016). The EES has provided a framework whereby the EU exerts a soft influence on member states' employment policy.[3] The aim has been to achieve broadly

defined European-level goals in terms of labor market performance—in particular, a high level of employment—by way of benchmarking and best-practice
learning. These ideals were proposed in order to help member states improve
their labor market policies (including structural reforms) and achieve shared
goals—articulated through the "employment guidelines" and the "country-
specific recommendations" (CSRs). The extent to which the EES—based on the
voluntary open method of coordination (OMC)—influences national employment policies has been a question for researchers over the life of the strategy
as this innovative form of policymaking has evolved (Heidenreich and Zeitlin
2009; de la Porte and Pochet 2012; Copeland and ter Haar 2013; Smith and Villa
2013). Although direct links between European-level analysis and prescription
on employment policy, on the one hand, and national-level implementation, on
the other hand, have been difficult to draw, there is evidence of a number of
mechanisms whereby EU policy formulations have some influence on national
policymaking (Heidenreich 2009; de la Porte and Heins 2015).

The EES operates on the basis of employment guidelines and quantitative
headline targets to be achieved by the EU as a whole. These guidelines provide
concise and general guidance in terms of what is "expected" of member states
regarding the achievement of the different targets set within the general goal of
"high employment," as established in the Amsterdam Treaty. Over this period, EU
influence has been exercised via the OMC framed by the employment guidelines,
which form the basis for the country-specific reporting in the so-called National
Reform Programmes; specific guidance on national employment policy is provided via CSRs (issued by the European Commission (EC) and endorsed by the
Council of Ministers). These processes have been complemented by best-practice
events between national policymakers and the EC. Moreover, this has also been
a period in which European countries have been encouraged (by the EC and
the Organization for Economic Co-operation and Development (OECD)) to
make their labor markets more flexible (i.e., more responsive to changes), with
an emphasis on moving from job security (i.e., employment protection legislation (EPL)) to employment or employability security (i.e., smooth transitions
from unemployment to employment or directly between different jobs through
ALMPs), under the assumption that an increase in flexibility should lead to more
employment opportunities for all.[4] At the heart of the EES, there has been an
idealized view of the employment relationship and of good labor market performance, based on freeing up supply-side constraints. Indeed, flexibility has been
a theme of the EES since its early formulation, albeit with limited recognition
of the impact on youth in its diverse effects for insiders and outsiders. However,
as the economic context and the political leadership of member states have
changed, the policy buzzwords and foci on particular labor market problems, key
labor supply groups, and core solutions have also shifted. Over time, the policy
tools proposed for reaching the goals of the EES have evolved, shifting from flexibility toward flexicurity (for a critique, see Hansen and Triantafillou 2011).

The promotion of flexicurity was the policy approach that marked the period directly prior to the crisis (Wilthagen and Tros 2004), although without an explicit target group and with blindness toward differences in age and gender (Jepsen 2005; Plantenga, Remery, and Rubery 2008). The shift from "security of the job" to "security on the labor market" suggested by Wim Kok's (2003) report was often interpreted by policymakers at the national level as a prescription for reducing EPL and flexibilizing labor markets. This resulted in an underdevelopment of the security dimension[5]—at least before the crisis kicked in—which was also implied by an overemphasis on flexibility vis-à-vis security in the EU version of flexicurity (Heyes 2011).

Young people have not always been visible in the various formulations of the EES framework and have mainly been included where there have been chronic problems in certain member states. One of the most significant lines of action of the EES highlights the need to improve the quality of human capital through education and continuous training, in particular that of the most "disadvantaged" groups (women, older workers, low-skilled, migrants, and the disabled). Thus, education, particularly important for young people, has been a central plank of the EES since its inception and was further strengthened in 2010 when the new strategy, Europe 2020, was launched, providing guidelines for the new decade. In particular, Europe 2020 included some revisions of the EES by way of introducing two explicit headline targets on education. Indeed, an underlying principle of the "ideal labor market" proposed by the EES (throughout its many reformulations) has been the provision of high-quality education and skills. This should equip young people with the appropriate characteristics to enter employment; hence, failures in this area may result in high drop-out rates; youth unemployment; and not in employment, education, or training (NEET) status (see Mascherini, this volume).

Despite the position of education in the EES, analysis of the 477 CSRs issued by the EC over time (2000–2013) shows that young people were not identified as a group in need of specific employment policies.[6] Indeed, mention of younger workers was rather rare, likewise in the documentation and other mechanisms of the EES (Smith and Villa 2016). For example, in the early years of the EES (2000–2002) there were, on average, just 5 CSRs per year linked to youth out of the 50–60 issued each year. By contrast, older workers and women received more CSRs: 8–9 and 12–13, respectively. Only when the situation on the youth labor market deteriorated did we witness a greater focus on young people in the CSRs. In 2011 and 2012, there were 15 and 17 CSRs, respectively, that explicitly considered young people (Smith and Villa 2016, 19–20).

The impact of labor market reforms on young people received little attention before the economic recession of 2008–2009. So-called "reforms at the margin" in the name of flexicurity had been recommended and implemented in a number of member states—with dramatic consequences for young people, not taken into account by policymakers. Prior to the economic recession, several member states started deregulating their labor markets: Although this move enabled the entry of many young people into employment when the economy was growing, it turned into something of a boomerang effect when these young workers became among the first to lose their jobs during the severe recession (European Commission 2010; Leschke 2012; O'Reilly et al. 2015). As a result, the subsequent call to member states was to strengthen ALMP and to intervene with individualized and well-targeted policies of activation to prevent long-term youth unemployment (e.g., the Youth Guarantee (YG) in 2013). The evolving economic crisis meant that the emergence of high youth unemployment became a key theme. Against the backdrop of the EES, member states also responded to their own priorities (and political constraints) as well as to the various recommendations for reform from the EC.

The 2010 Youth on the Move flagship policy of Europe 2020 did place young people in a more prominent position within the employment strategy as one of the seven flagship policy areas. This followed the publication of the Youth Strategy Communication a year earlier, which again placed a heavy emphasis on education and training opportunities but also highlighted the principles of flexicurity as a means to ease youth transitions (European Commission 2009). The Youth on the Move policy documentation did recognize the risks associated with segmentation of young people on temporary contracts (European Commission 2010), but there were few targeted initiatives in this regard. Furthermore, the gender dimension to these policy proposals was almost completely absent, reflecting a long-term decline in the position of gender equality and gender-mainstreaming mechanisms within the EES (Villa 2013). The Youth Opportunities Initiative (2012–2013) led to more action as the effects of the crisis on young people became clear (European Commission 2011). The main area of action for this initiative was supporting the transition from school to work, particularly for those young people falling out of the system having failed to achieve an upper secondary education. But it also included intra-EU mobility and the use of the European Social Fund to support youth labor markets. Although these initiatives represented an increased focus on young people, an integrated approach to youth transitions and the challenges young people face on the labor market was still absent (Knijn and Plantenga 2012). These initiatives coalesced around the YG—an EU-wide scheme aimed at providing employment or training opportunities for all young people before they experience 4 months without work or training, in order to avoid the risk of long-term unemployment. The scheme was bold in its ambitions, reflecting acknowledgment of the scale of the problem facing European youth, but it was weak in its implementation (Bussi and Geyer 2013).

The somewhat ambivalent position of the EES toward youth has been mirrored in national policy priorities, leading to a situation in which concerns about the position of young people on the labor market have not been widely considered. Responses were reactive rather than proactive, and they often materialized only in the face of the deterioration of youth labor market prospects created by the

Great Recession. In Section 4.3, we explore in more detail the consequences of the relatively scant attention given to young people in European employment policymaking.

4.3. FAILED POLICIES AND OUTCOMES FOR YOUNG PEOPLE

4.3.1. Over-Reliance on Supply-Side Solutions and Quantitative Targets

Employment policy guidance from the EC and national-level policy implementation have been characterized by an over-reliance on supply-side solutions to high unemployment and low employment rates, with emphasis being placed on the activation of unemployed and inactive people and on the need for new forms of "flexible" contracts to encourage employers to recruit. The 2015 revised guidelines do call for "boosting demand for labor," but they focus on reducing "barriers" to job creation rather than on aggregate demand (see Section 4.3.3). Yet the subsequent guidelines call for "enhancing labor supply, skills and competences," underlying the ongoing reliance on supply-side approaches. In a sovereign debt crisis (that followed the 2008–2009 recession), there may well be constraints on policymakers' options (which are focused on labor market policies rather than on expansionary macroeconomic policies), but it is then also necessary to acknowledge the limitations of those options that, by definition, rely only on supply-side policy measures. For young people, the activation approach has been evident in the emphasis on educational investment, highlighting the idea that failings have been linked to inadequate qualifications rather than to the functioning of the labor market or to a lack of demand. Indeed, the reformulation of the EES under the Europe 2020 strategy reinforced this position, with the inclusion of education headline targets (reducing early school leaving and, in particular, raising the share of young people with tertiary education to 40%),[7] as well as the new skills and jobs agenda.

The emphasis on labor market flexibility could be considered to have been optimistic before the crisis and to have been unrealistic during the crisis and austerity period (Lehndorff 2014). The weaknesses of the supply-side philosophy were exposed during the crisis, with the consequences falling on young people. The EES has also been heavily focused on increasing the quantity of people in employment, with a limited (and then invisible) focus on job quality. This is most evident in the strong priority given to quantitative targets over quality outcomes and the creation of new atypical contracts. Also, the focus has been on soft law under the OMC in employment; indeed, the past decade and a half has seen very few labor law directives with binding and sanctionable content.[8] An exception is the 2008 Temporary Agency Work Directive—an issue that had long been in stalemate due to disagreement between the European-level social partners.

The employment rate headline target (75% of 20- to 64-year-olds to be employed in 2020, with specific national targets reflecting their current situation)[9] illustrates the dominance of quantitative over qualitative ambitions. In order to assess the development of employment in the EU and the member states, the employment rate indicator from the EU Labour Force Survey (EU-LFS) is used, which records any employment in the interview reference week of 1 hour or more. This implies that the employment rate headline indicator does not differentiate between regular full-time employment and employment with few hours, including marginal employment or involuntary part-time work. The heterogeneity of employment forms means that a single measure is inadequate for capturing and measuring experiences on the labor market. For example, Eurostat does not publish the full-time equivalent (FTE) employment rates on its web page, although using FTEs provides a very different picture—in particular, the (qualitative) employment integration of women and young people. The contrast is clearest in the Dutch case, in which female employment rates in the Eurostat definition are close to 70% and thus among the highest in Europe, whereas FTEs are only approximately 48% for 2015 and thus at the bottom of the European ranking.[10]

European initiatives establishing a complementary set of quality-of-work indicators include the 2001 Laeken indicators (with 10 quality-of-work dimensions) and the more recent deliberations of the Employment Committee of the Council, aimed at rendering these indicators more concise. Yet these initiatives have not been very fruitful in terms of visibility (for an extensive discussion, see Peña-Casas 2009; Bothfeld and Leschke 2012). A stronger focus on work-quality issues was first "overshadowed" by the flexicurity drive in European policies and then by the urgency of the economic crisis and rising unemployment (Bothfeld and Leschke 2012). On a more general level, even though there exist several European-level social indicator systems and scoreboards that include more qualitative indicators, when it comes to using them in a more concrete manner, they usually disappear into annexes or complementary assessment documents; also, the fact that there are several parallel social indicator systems and scoreboards does not make coherent reporting easy (Leschke 2016).

4.3.2. External Pressures on Employment Policy

The external pressures on national employment policymakers have been rising for all member states and have been very intense for those under financial assistance and experiencing the worst of the sovereign debt crisis (Scharpf 2011; de la Porte and Heins 2015). There has been a resulting high intensity of policymaking across the EU, as well as widespread reforms that have not necessarily been coherent with the founding vision of the EES or the aims of improving labor market performance—not least among those countries suffering most as a result of the Great Recession. Indeed, there are some member states that demonstrate a particularly high intensity of policymaking and appear to be struggling in the more turbulent waters created by the changing economic conditions. Both policy and youth labor market outcomes suggest that these countries are finding it difficult to "swim" in these shifting waters of the European economic and policy environment (Smith and Villa 2016). Equally, Hasting and Heyes (2016) suggest that these conditions have made it more difficult to develop security policies associated with the flexicurity approach. Contrariwise, there are some countries that seem to have developed policy more incrementally and to have refined their "swimming technique" in these choppy waters; these countries have more stable institutional environments and have had some success on youth labor markets (Smith and Villa 2016). The uneven distribution of these external pressures may lead to a further variety of outcomes across youth labor markets and poorer chances of convergence toward stronger labor market performance.

The contradictory outcomes of pressure for change due to high youth unemployment during the crisis, on the one hand, and austerity pressure for fiscal consolidation, on the other hand, can be illustrated by the developments in unemployment benefits over the course of the Great Recession (for other examples of incoherent developments in welfare policies, see Heise and Lierse 2011; Lehndorff 2014). Young workers are subject both to explicit disadvantage in terms of differential rules of access to unemployment benefit and to implicit disadvantage in access through their over-representation in temporary contracts and shorter tenure. Reliable unemployment benefits of sufficient generosity and duration render it possible to search for an adequate job, facilitating a better match between education and jobs (Gangl 2004), instead of forcing unemployed youth to take the first-best option. Indeed, the limited access of youth to unemployment benefit schemes in many countries has appeared on the national, international, and supranational agendas in light of high and rising (youth) unemployment in the early years of the economic recession (OECD 2011; European Commission 2011; Dullien 2013; Del Monte and Zandstra 2014). The previous focus on supply-side measures was no longer deemed effective because of the lack of realistic possibilities to bring large numbers of youth back into employment quickly. A number of European countries accordingly improved the situation of youth and other weakly covered groups—such as temporary workers—by permanently or temporarily increasing access, benefit levels, or benefit duration; lump-sum and one-off payments were also common instruments (Leschke and Finn, this volume). However, the initial positive developments in terms of benefit coverage were no longer visible in 2014 when the effects of austerity had kicked in. During the stimulus period (2008–2009), the focus in several countries was on relaxing eligibility and increasing benefit levels. Reforms relating to eligibility, in particular, even when not explicitly geared toward youth, usually have a disproportionate effect on the young unemployed given their shorter average tenure. The austerity period (2010–2014), in contrast, was characterized by tightening of eligibility and decreasing of benefit levels. However, there was still a limited number of countries that relaxed the qualifying criteria for youth during the austerity period; these reforms usually stipulated a strong link between passive benefit entitlements and participation in education and training programs (for details on institutional changes and outcomes, see European Commission 2014; MISSOC 2014; Leschke and Finn, this volume). Obviously, cutting income security in times of crisis is problematic because alternative income sources both in terms of job opportunities and wider household income are scarce (Mazzotta and Parisi, this volume).

Another example of external pressure on more inclusive employment policies is inherent in the way the EES has operated since the mid-2000s. The coordination of employment policy under the EES takes place together with the macroeconomic coordination. Since 2010, this is done in the framework of the so-called "European Semester," in which the countries submit both the National Reform Programme—as part of the EES—and a Stability and Convergence Programme. This implies that there is a general danger that qualitative employment and social targets may be subordinated to budgetary discipline, particularly in times of austerity. The fact that at the height of the crisis the Council of Ministers put fiscal discipline first on the list of country-specific recommendations confirms this view. We can observe a similar "hierarchy" in the 2010 guidelines, in which guidelines 1–3 deal with macroeconomic stability and guidelines 7–10 with employment and social policy (European Commission 2010). Leschke et al. (2014) demonstrate the contradictions between the recent EU economic governance reforms and the austerity measures, on the one hand, and the Europe 2020 inclusive growth target, on the other hand. Their analysis shows that the fiscal austerity bias, as evident in the national social spending projections, makes it very difficult to reduce poverty and social exclusion. Indeed, further doubts are raised by the fact that the national-specific targets on poverty reduction do not add up to achieve the EU-wide 2020 headline target and that countries use different poverty indicators in their reporting, ranging from at-risk-of-poverty after social transfers to low work-intensity households and long-term unemployment.

4.3.3. Mixed Implementation of Flexicurity Measures

The direction and tone of both EU and national policymaking have often been characterized by a downward pressure on EPL. In recent years, the focus has been, in particular, on decreasing EPL for permanent contracts, thereby narrowing the gap between EPL for permanent and temporary workers. Between 2008 and 2013 (most recent data), 12 out of 22 EU countries included in the OECD EPL database lowered EPL on permanent contracts (OECD 2016). Three countries (Greece, Portugal, and Spain) lowered EPL also for temporary contracts between 2008 and 2013; in all three of these countries, there were also reductions in EPL for permanent contracts (i.e., further increasing labor market flexibility). Although at times there have been measures to promote security, such measures were often triggered by situations of urgency (i.e., the youth unemployment crisis) and usually did not follow a steady upward logic. This reflects the mixed implementation of flexicurity measures and an ethos of deregulation. During the period of EU-led structural reform, much policy (and much research) has been driven by a focus on downward pressure on EPL. The declining position of job quality as a goal and the increasing emphasis on quantitative employment targets testifies to the increasingly explicit focus on liberalization of the labor market in order to raise the number of people in employment. Some authors claim that this has long been the goal of European employment policy (Hermann 2007; Amable, Demmou, and Ledezma 2009; Van Apeldoorn 2009), whereas others suggest that the changing political, economic, and social climate have reduced the scope for policies associated with a more secure and inclusive labor market (Villa and Smith 2014; Hastings and Heyes 2016).

The debate between the merits of more flexible hire-and-fire labor markets and more regulated protection of labor markets is not new and has driven policy and research debates for many years (OECD 1994). Comparisons of EPL over time and across countries are central to this debate. The evidence for the effects of EPL reduction is at best contradictory (Solow 1998, 2000; Simonazzi and Villa 1999; Freeman 2005; Aleksynska 2014). However, although the research suggests that there are limited effects of EPL reduction on "performance" and that the impact varies by specific target group (even proponents of the deregulation agenda admit that it is not easy to predict the impact of EPL reforms on young people (OECD 2004)), the propagation of the reform agenda in EC and European Central Bank (ECB) documents has continued. For example, recent ECB analysis of the limited impact of labor market reforms calls for more time, more reforms, and greater inter- and intracountry mobility (European Central Bank 2014, 67). This commitment on the part of European institutions reflects the hegemony of macroeconomic policy linked to monetary union, defining labor market policy in relation to its response to macro/finance shocks (European Commission 2012) rather than gearing labor market policy toward quality outcomes for participants. Indeed, closer reading of these documents shows that rather than being based on empirical evidence, the case continues to be made on the basis of economic theory and on prior expectations regarding the outcomes of EPL reduction.[11] Furthermore, some evidence shows the increasing inefficiency of labor markets, as measured by an outward-shifting Beveridge curve—a sign of declining "efficiency" in matching jobs to workers (Simonazzi and Villa 2016), with increasing risks for young people scarred by the crisis and the reform agenda. In addition, there is evidence of a strong divergence in the performance of EU labor markets despite a common reform agenda (Hastings and Heyes 2016).

Much of the reform agenda around reducing EPL has been conducted in the name of flexicurity as policymakers focus on the flexibility rather than the security dimension to the portmanteau (Eamets et al. 2015). Others have noted that flexicurity policies can have a disproportionate impact on young people, especially measures to reduce job security (Madsen et al. 2013). The youth labor market may have much to gain from effective balancing of flexibility and security (O'Reilly et al. 2015), but "reforms at the margin" (i.e., increasing flexibility for outsiders) risk increasing segmentation of youth labor markets and rising precariousness.

In order to illustrate the uneven implementation of flexicurity measures, we present here results from an analysis of the LABREF database to chart policy activity categorized as affecting different elements of the flexicurity model (see Smith and Villa 2016). In particular, we identify a subset of LABREF policy domains that fall under the three conventional flexicurity categories (see, e.g., Wilthagen and Tros 2004):[12] job security (i.e., EPL),[13] employment security (i.e., ALMP),[14] and income security (i.e., unemployment benefits and other welfare support measures).[15] In short, these policies were categorized according to whether they are ex ante likely to promote or diminish job security, employment security, and income security.[16] The focus is on the explicit intention of policymakers (as recorded in LABREF), not the actual impact of the measures enacted.

Figure 4.1 illustrates the intensity in policymaking categorized under the three elements of the flexicurity model by direction of policy (increasing or decreasing protection or coverage). The data demonstrate significant policy activity in the areas of both job security and employment security and less activity regarding income security. It is worth noting that whereas employment security measures are almost exclusively categorized as "increasing" (i.e., promoting employment security through changes in ALMP), job security measures and income security measures go in both directions (increasing and decreasing security)—not only over time but often also within the same year. This result holds across country groups and years.

When we focus on measures linked to job security (EPL), we observe that the Mediterranean group stands out with significant policy activity reducing job security; this is particularly stark during the austerity years. After the Mediterranean group, this pattern is most notable in the Central and Eastern European (CEE) countries. Elsewhere, there is evidence of policy activity reducing the level of job security across most country groups during the austerity years (least among the Nordic countries). However, the English-speaking countries have marked policy activity reducing income security in the austerity period. This is in contrast with the income security measures showing an increase in intensity in the crisis and austerity subperiods in all the other country groups—that is, Continental, Nordic, CEE, and Mediterranean.

The policies in Figure 4.1 relate to the whole labor market because young people are affected by wider changes in employment policy. However, it is also possible to analyze these flexicurity measures concentrating only on policies identified in LABREF as relating to young people. This focused policy activity

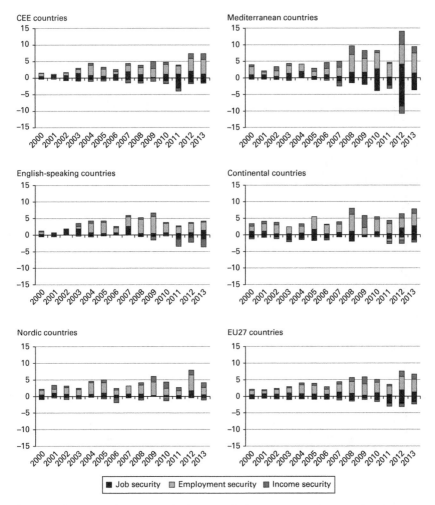

Figure 4.1 Flexicurity policy intensity by direction of policy (increasing/decreasing) and country group, 2000–2013 (average number of policies enacted per country).
Note: Figures below the Y axis (<0) indicate the average number of policies decreasing security, while those above the Y axis (>0) show the number of policies increasing security.
Source: LABREF database; authors' analyses.

shows an increasing share of flexicurity policies targeted at young people as the economic conditions deteriorated, rising from just 6% in the precrisis subperiod to 12% in the crisis subperiod and to 15% in the austerity subperiod.

This subset of policymaking for young people is almost exclusively focused on increasing employment security, but in the austerity subperiod we not only see a greater intensity of measures but also a greater diversity. In the final period, the promotion of employment security for young people accounts for approximately four-fifths of new policies (Table 4.1). The Nordic and Mediterranean countries stand out, with certain measures aimed at reducing job security for young people.

Table 4.1 Distribution of youth-focused flexicurity policies by country group and subperiod, 2000–2013 (% and number of policies)

	Job security (%)		Employment security (%)		Income security (%)		Total (%)	No.
	Increasing	Decreasing	Increasing	Decreasing	Increasing	Decreasing		
2000–2007								
Continental	–	–	100.0	–	–	–	100	26
Central and Eastern	–	–	100.0	–	–	–	100	20
Nordic	–	–	100.0	–	–	–	100	13
Mediterranean	–	–	100.0	–	–	–	100	10
English-speaking	–	–	100.0	–	–	–	100	7
EU27	–	–	100.0	–	–	–	100	76
2008–2009								
Continental	–	–	76.9	–	23.1	–	100	13
Central and Eastern	–	–	100.0	–	–	–	100	5
Nordic	–	–	100.0	–	–	–	100	7
Mediterranean	–	–	100.0	–	–	–	100	13
English-speaking	–	–	100.0	–	–	–	100	15
EU27	–	–	94.3	–	5.7	–	100	53
2010–2013								
Continental	–	–	84.0	4.0	8.0	4.0	100	25
Central and Eastern	4.0	2.0	84.0	2.0	6.0	2.0	100	50
Nordic	–	11.1	77.8	5.6	–	5.6	100	18
Mediterranean	1.8	12.7	80.0	1.8	3.6	–	100	55
English-speaking	–	–	80.0	10.0	–	10.0	100	20
EU27	1.8	6.0	81.5	3.6	4.2	3.0	100	168

Note: See Chapter 3, Section 3.3 for details.
Source: LABREF database; authors' analysis.

Overall, we see the main element of youth-focused policymaking in the area of ALMP, which we have broadly categorized as promoting employment security (i.e., security in the labor market through ALMP) in line with the conventional flexicurity model. However, during the austerity subperiod, we observe other measures too, and at the margins these policies appeared to be weakening rather than strengthening the "principles" of flexicurity. The concentration of reforms in countries subject to "Euro Pact" pressure increases the risks for already vulnerable workers in weak labor markets, particularly the young. In this context, it is important to expand the metrics for judging labor market performance and to go beyond shifts in much-criticized EPL measures.

4.3.4. Consequences of Early Career Insecurity and Precariousness

Although quality of employment and the wider consequences of insecurity have been neglected in policy developments, these are nevertheless crucial issues for understanding the impact of the crisis on young people in Europe.

Poor labor market integration and precariousness have negative consequences for all labor market participants, but for young people, early career insecurity can create longer-term consequences with regard to both labor market outcomes and family formation. The scarring effects of early unemployment for later career prospects and earnings have been found in many countries (Ackum 1991; Arulampalam, Gregg, and Gregory 2001; Burda and Mertens 2001). Precarious employment may have similar consequences. Chung, Bekker, and Houwing (2012) argue that the low and decreasing rate of transition from temporary jobs means that the current youth cohort may be facing long-term labor market risks and scarring processes. As our results show, there is also growing evidence that early career employment precariousness may have persistent effects on psychological well-being and health (Clark, Georgellis, and Sanfey 2001; Bell and Blanchflower 2011). In addition, McGuinness and Wooden (2009) show that skill mismatches in the early career can lead to a pathway of mismatched jobs, lower returns to qualifications, and unfulfilled potential (McGuinness, Bergin, and Whelan, this volume). Moreover, poor labor market integration of youth can also lead to delayed family formation or unfulfilled plans for having children (Scherer 2009).

There is evidence of a deterioration in the quality of work across a range of dimensions for young people who entered the workforce during the Great Recession. The proportion of young people working part-time involuntarily increased very substantially. Between 2007 and 2014, involuntary part-time work increased across the EU from 27% to 35% among those aged younger than 30 years, and this figure rose to 69% in Spain, 82% in Italy, 75% in Greece, and 72% in Romania.[17] Temporary contracts also became increasingly widespread and in some countries became the norm for young people (OECD 2014). Across the EU27, temporary employment among young people grew from 29% in the first quarter of 2005 to a peak of 34% in the third quarter of 2015.[18]

These objective trends in precarious work have other consequences, too. Feelings of subjective insecurity also increased among employed young people as a result not only of rising temporary work but also of perceived vulnerability to job loss and underemployment, as well as concerns about future prospects (Peiró, Sora, and Caballer 2012; Green et al. 2014). Data from the ESS show that across Europe between 2006 and 2008–2009, the proportion of the employed who believed it was "likely" or "very likely" that they would become unemployed in the next 12 months rose from 17% to 27% among those aged younger than 30 years, whereas the figure for those aged 30 years or older rose by 7 percentage points (Figure 4.2).[19] The rise in insecurity was particularly sharp in Estonia, Ireland, Portugal, and Spain, and young women experienced a greater increase in perceived insecurity than young men. As a consequence of these trends, the age gap in subjective insecurity widened, reflecting the disproportionate effect of the crisis on young people. Perceptions of wider employment security, or the extent to which employees perceive there to be opportunities outside their current job, were also adversely affected by the economic crisis (Russell et al. 2015).

In addition to increased insecurity and underemployment, labor market entrants are also particularly vulnerable to pay adjustments. In Ireland, for example, the austerity measures included significant cuts in entry-level salaries for public-sector workers such as nurses and teachers. Results from the Structure of

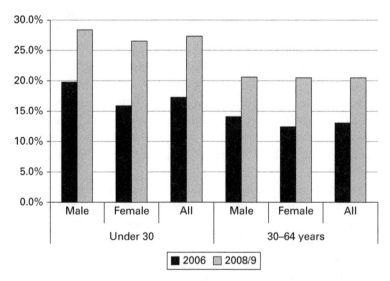

Figure 4.2 Subjective job insecurity, 2006 and 2008–2009: percentage of the employed who think it is "likely" or "very likely" that they will become unemployed in the next 12 months. *Source*: ESS Round 3 and ESS Round 4. Average across 20 countries; weighted by post-stratification weights.

Earnings Survey (SES) show that the ratio of youth earnings (aged younger than 30 years) to average earnings declined across 20 of 23 European countries between 2006 and 2014, illustrating that pay for young people fell further below the average.[20] These figures provide some examples of the range of quality-of-work impacts that are hidden in figures or targets that only measure employment rates and the quantity of jobs.

The effects of unemployment and insecurity on well-being are also invisible in the policy discussions described previously. The impact of both unemployment and job insecurity on psychological well-being is very well established, with longitudinal studies demonstrating a causal link (for reviews, see De Witte 2005; McKee-Ryan et al. 2005; Paul and Moser 2009). However, it is sometimes argued that labor market instability will have a weaker effect on well-being among young people because employment is less central to their self-identity or because they have fewer financial responsibilities and may have access to parental support (Jackson et al. 1983). Furthermore, the argument may be particularly relevant for young people that when unemployment becomes a social norm, the psychological impact is reduced (Clark 2003). The normalization of unemployment, inactivity, and temporary employment for younger workers could mean that the stigma attached to these statuses is reduced. A number of studies have found that the effect of unemployment on psychological well-being is greatest for prime-age workers and is weaker for young people and workers closer to retirement (Theodossiou 1998; Nordenmark and Strandh 1999), although this finding is not universal (McKee-Ryan et al. 2005). Our analyses of the ESS data showed that although overall the satisfaction gap between the employed and the unemployed was narrower for younger people, the effect was nonetheless significant and substantial (Russell et al. 2015). Unemployed young people had significantly lower life satisfaction compared to their employed peers in all but 1 of the 20 countries analyzed, and they had significantly lower well-being—measured by items in the WHO-5 Well-Being Index—in all but 4 countries.

Reduced life satisfaction is also observed among those who believe their job is insecure compared to those who feel secure. Figure 4.3 illustrates the gradient in life satisfaction scores by employment status. A significant difference in the life satisfaction of securely employed and insecurely employed young people is observed across all but six of the countries in the study,[21] and statistical models reveal that the relationship is just as strong for those aged younger than 30 years as for those aged 30 years or older (data not shown; available from authors upon request). In a number of countries—namely Belgium, Finland, Greece, and Norway—insecurely employed young people are just as dissatisfied as the unemployed (Figure 4.3).

The impact of unemployment and insecurity on the psychological well-being of individuals is often neglected by policymakers. Yet the costs for individuals and their families (Scherer 2009) are high. At the extreme, a number of studies have established a relationship between unemployment and increased suicide

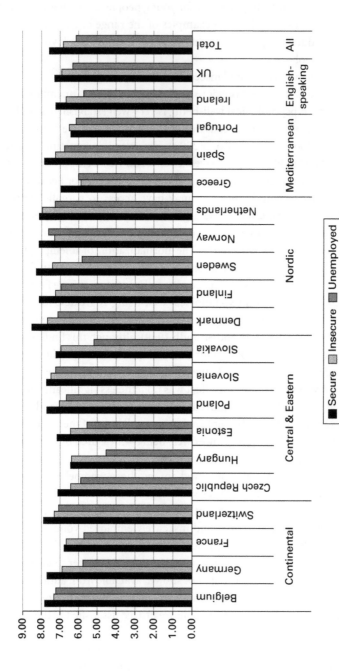

Figure 4.3 Life satisfaction among securely employed, insecurely employed, and unemployed young people younger than age 30 years, 2010.
Source: ESS 2010; authors' analysis.

rates among young men (Walsh 2011). The existing evidence suggests that young people struggling to gain a foothold in the increasingly precarious labor market may also pay a longer-term price for entering the labor market at the "wrong time." The longer-term consequences of precariousness for young people will partly depend on policy responses to assist transitions out of unemployment and out of temporary/insecure work into sustainable work.

4.4. CONCLUSIONS

This chapter develops a critique of EU and national employment policies in relation to young people, highlighting the results and outcomes for their labor market experiences and drawing on research conducted for the STYLE project. We identify four main areas of critique:

1. Employment policy has been strongly focused on supply-side measures that highlight the responsibility of individuals to equip themselves for jobs, with little consideration for the quality of employment.
2. Labor market policymaking has been driven largely by the external pressures of austerity, fiscal consolidation, and monetary stability rather than by coherence and a strategy aimed at a sustainable healthy labor market for participants.
3. There has been a partial implementation of flexicurity principles with a heavy focus on reductions in EPL for outsiders—a precrisis trend—without wider consideration of the consequences for young people, who were disproportionately affected by labor market flexibility during the crisis (via the heavy destruction of jobs held by young people and with the dissolution of temporary contracts). In the face of the youth unemployment crisis, the focus then turned to strengthening employment security by way of increasing ALMPs and also (temporarily) income security.
4. The focus on quantitative measures of labor market performance has meant that the subjective outcomes and quality measures have become something of a blind spot for policymakers, yet these outcomes are crucial for young people.

The EC's response to the declining position of flexicurity has been to call for a "healthy and dynamic" labor market model as the new framework for labor market policy in the Europe 2020 period (European Commission 2014, 75). However, the commitment of the EC and the ECB to the structural reform agenda suggests that the prospects for a healthy labor market—from the perspective of good matches with quality jobs and, more broadly, the well-being of young people—are likely to be limited, not least because an apparent underlying neoliberal agenda has increasingly dominated the EC employment project, pushing social goals down the agenda (Villa and Smith 2014): Young people have been a casualty of this policy direction.

Before the crisis, flexicurity was seen as the ideal institutional setting that could be viewed as a beacon for policymakers and the problems faced by European labor markets (O'Reilly et al. 2015). The so-called flexicurity model was a key element of the EES, though with an overemphasis on flexibility components compared to security dimensions. Also, there was something of a blind spot with regard to the consideration of young people within flexicurity models (Eamets et al. 2015), just as was the case for gender (Jepsen 2005). Moreover, flexicurity-driven policies faced a major challenge with the onset of the crisis (Hastings and Heyes 2016). Overall, young people tend to have worse flexibility–security outcomes in that their labor market situation is more precarious and they benefit less from income security, especially in the fiscal consolidation period. This is in line with previous literature indicating that vulnerable groups on the labor market, such as youth, the elderly, women, the long-term unemployed, and temporary employees, do not experience the same wins that regular employees might gain from flexibility–security policies (Leschke 2012).

The YG was a major policy initiative at the EU level, but it was based on a delayed recognition of the scale and consequences of the problems facing the youth labor markets (Bussi and Geyer 2013). The YG made a number of bold commitments designed to address the challenges facing a subsection—the so-called NEETs—of young people entering the labor market. Yet the implementation of the YG did not meet expectations (Dhéret and Morosi 2015). The question remains whether this was the embryo of a future policy for young people that lacked support or an inappropriate idea for the time, especially given financial constraints, poorly equipped public employment services to take on the task, and, importantly, poor labor demand in several member states. Part of the explanation rests with an employment policy that remains reactive and subservient to macroeconomic stability measures, but it is also important to consider the limits of European coordination. Policymaking in relation to employment at the European and national levels struggles to find a voice in turbulent economic times, and some countries are finding it difficult to implement coherent and durable reforms and instead are "splashing around," to use the words of Smith and Villa (2016). At the same time, young people are learning to swim at the start of their active economic life, and in some contexts the waters are very turbulent. The long-term consequences for national labor markets and individual young women and men are potentially severe.

Thus, the challenges in relation to employment policy for young people, in particular, remain. Flexicurity was a much-criticized concept, but for a while it provided a common theme around which guidance and justification for labor market reform could be grouped (Bekker 2012). The weaknesses were an overemphasis on the implementation of flexibility measures, coupled with economic circumstances creating slack demand when security, through employability on labor markets, was being promoted. These factors were compounded by an absence of a gender and life course perspective, including the perspective on youth in the original formulation. The economic circumstances will remain challenges for employment policy, but intelligent policy development that reflects the realities of generational and gender differences on modern European labor markets and addresses security measures more comprehensively and permanently can help address the policy weaknesses outlined here. Postcrisis, post-austerity, and post-flexicurity Europe requires the development of the "next big idea" around how to develop employment policy that is coherent, impactful, and relevant for young women and men as new entrants to the labor market, while capturing the imagination and commitment of policymakers at the European and national levels. This may require a return to hard-law measures, as evident in the labor law directives of the late 1990s and early 2000s, but it would be a considerable challenge to obtain sufficient support given the underlying policy approach of recent years. However, perhaps more important, the limitations of a primarily supply-side approach need to be addressed so that policymakers can place the promotion of quality employment opportunities at the heart of macro policymaking.

Based on this picture of incoherent policymaking and uncertain youth labor market outcomes, there is a need to (re)integrate the concept of quality into policies addressing the trajectories of young people (Berloffa et al., this volume), including school-to-work transitions. In this sense, with a view to longer-term outcomes, the notion of efficiency on the labor market needs be expanded to consider not only quantity or speed in finding jobs but also quality outcomes (e.g., good matching, job stability and/or continuity in employment, and decent earnings). As with gender inequalities, an impact assessment for generational differences is required to insure against unintended consequences of labor market policies that are not focused on youth but still have an effect on weaker participants because of subsequent changes in the overall institutional settings. At stake are lifelong consequences for today's young people.

NOTES

1 We thank Brendan Burchell, Jochen Clasen, Ruud Muffels, Magnus Paulsen Hansen, the participants at the STYLE meetings in Turin and Krakow, as well as Martin Seeleib-Kaiser and Jackie O'Reilly from the editorial team for critical comments on earlier versions of this chapter.

2 See Section 4.2 for an overview of flexicurity. For a critical discussion of the European Union approach to flexicurity, see Smith and Villa (2016) and Leschke and Finn (this volume).

3   The Open Method of Coordination (OMC) in employment policy, for simplicity termed European Employment Strategy (EES) in this chapter, was launched in 1997 and was formally included in the Amsterdam Treaty. From 2000, it was conducted as part of the Lisbon strategy, which was replaced in 2010 by the Europe 2020 strategy.

4   See the communication on the common principles of flexicurity (European Commission 2007). Also see the approach proposed in the European Commission's report, *Employment and Social Developments in Europe 2014*, for "a healthy labor market: Balancing employment protection legislation, activation and support" in the analysis of the impact of the recession on labor market institutions (European Commission 2015, 75).

5   The four EC flexicurity principles are flexible and reliable contractual arrangements, effective active labor market policies, comprehensive lifelong learning strategies, and modern social security systems.

6   Smith and Villa (2016) chart the evolution in the EES through a detailed analysis of the content of the 477 CSRs on employment policy issued over the period 2000–2013, identifying the CSRs directly and indirectly focused on young people. In the early years, only a limited number of countries received a recommendation that explicitly considered young people. It was subsequently acknowledged that young people were at a disadvantage in some countries, but the recommendations issued were rather generic. In 2007–2009, only three countries received a simple generic mention of the young without any precise suggestion as to what policy action to follow. It was only in 2011–2013 that the deterioration of youth employment opportunities was reflected in an increasing number of CSRs directly focused on policy recommendations for youth.

7   This despite the problem of "brain overflow" (Kaczmarczyk and Okólski 2008), particularly in the new member states, implying that high-skilled young workers from new member states are migrating to EU15 countries, where they often work under precarious conditions and below their skill levels (see Spreckelsen, Leschke, and Seeleib-Kaiser, this volume).

8   Although, even with regard to binding labor law directives, derogations are possible with regard to specific roles or activities or by means of collective agreements (e.g., on the working-time directive, see Eurofound 2015).

9   In contrast to the Lisbon strategy, there are no longer subtargets for women and older workers.

10   FTEs are only presented in the statistical annex of the specialized annual publication *Employment and Social Developments in Europe 2015* (European Commission 2016) and are thus not made widely available.

11   So-called "priors" are used as part of the justification for a further deregulatory agenda (see European Commission 2012).

12   Also see the chart reproduced in the *Employment and Social Developments in Europe 2014* report, illustrating the balance between EPL, ALMP, and unemployment benefits (European Commission 2015, 75).

13 This captures changes in EPL impacting on permanent and temporary, as well as individual and collective, contracts (Smith and Villa 2016).

14 ALMP measures were the only policies in LABREF that mapped clearly onto the employment security dimension of flexicurity.

15 This subset accounts for 2,216 policies (approximately two-thirds of all policies recorded in the database between 2000 and 2013). Using the additional information in the LABREF database on the direction of policy (i.e., increasing or decreasing), we can further categorize policies according to whether they strengthen or weaken different elements of the flexicurity model.

16 Information on the direction of reforms (whether they are ex ante likely to have an impact by increasing or decreasing security) is codified in LABREF by means of binary indicators. The taxonomy developed to construct the indicator of the direction of reforms (built on existing economic literature) needs to be interpreted with caution because some simplifications are inevitable. However, an indicator of direction is necessary when analyzing reforms in order to avoid mixing reforms bringing opposing changes in the policy settings (European Commission 2012, 66).

17 Eurostat database: "Involuntary part-time employment as percentage of the total part-time employment for young people by sex and age" (yth_empl_080) (Eurostat 2016).

18 Eurostat database: "Temporary employees as a percentage of the total number of employees, by sex and age (%)" (lfsq_etpga) (Eurostat 2016).

19 The analysis is based on 20 countries: BE, BG, CH, CY, DE, DK, EE, ES, FI, FR, HU, IE, NL, NO, PL, PT, SE, SI, SK, and UK. Each country was weighted to receive equal representation in the results (i.e., N is constrained to be equal for each country so that more highly populated countries do not dominate). Just under half of the ESS Round 4 interviews were carried out in 2009. The question in ESS Round 4 adds the qualification "unemployed and looking for work."

20 Authors' analysis of SES published results for 2006 and 2014. Table available from the authors on request. The SES excludes those employed in small establishments and those in the public administration/defense.

21 The difference between subjectively securely and insecurely employed young people is not statistically significant in BG, FR, HU, NL, PL, and CH. In the UK and CZ, the difference is only significant at the 10% level.

REFERENCES

Ackum, Susanne. 1991. "Youth Unemployment, Labor Market Programs and Subsequent Earnings." *Scandinavian Journal of Economics* 93 (4): 531–43.

Aleksynska, Mariya. 2014. *Deregulating Labor Markets: How Robust Is the Analysis of Recent IMF Working Papers?* Conditions of Work and Employment Series 47. Geneva: ILO.

Amable, Bruno, Lilas Demmou, and Ivan Ledezma. 2009. "The Lisbon Strategy and Structural Reforms in Europe." *Transfer: European Review of Labor and Research* 15 (1): 33–52.

Arulampalam, Wiji, Paul Gregg, and Mary Gregory. 2001. "Unemployment Scarring." *Economic Journal* 111 (November): 577–84.

Bekker, Sonja. 2012. *Flexicurity: The Emergence of a European Concept.* Social Europe Series 30. Cambridge: Intersentia.

Bell, David N. F., and David G. Blanchflower. 2011. "Young People and the Great Recession." *Oxford Review of Economic Policy* 27 (2): 241–67.

Bothfeld, Silke, and Janine Leschke. 2012. "'More and Better Jobs': Is Quality of Work Still an Issue—and Was It Ever?" *Transfer: European Review of Labor and Research* 18 (3): 337–53. [Special issue]

Burda, Michael C., and Antje Mertens. 2001. "Estimating Wage Losses of Displaced Workers in Germany." *Labor Economics* 8 (1): 15–41.

Bussi, Margherita, and Leonard Geyer. 2013. *Youth Guarantees and Recent Developments on Measures Against Youth Unemployment: A Mapping Exercise.* Background Analysis 04. Brussels: ETUI.

Chung, Heejung, Sonja Bekker, and Hester Houwing. 2012. "Young People and the Post-Recession Labor Market in the Context of Europe 2020." *European Review of Labor and Research* 18 (3): 301–17.

Clark, Andrew. 2003. "Unemployment as a Social Norm: Psychological Evidence from Panel Data." *Journal of Labor Economics* 21 (2): 323–51.

Clark, Andrew, Yannis Georgellis, and Peter Sanfey. 2001. "Scarring: The Psychological Impact of Past Unemployment." *Economica* 68: 221–41.

Copeland, Paul, and Beryl ter Haar. 2013. "A Toothless Bite? The Effectiveness of the European Employment Strategy as a Governance Tool." *Journal of European Social Policy* 23 (1): 21–36.

De la Porte, Caroline, and Elke Heins. 2015. "The New Era of European Integration? Governance of Labour Market and Social Policy Since the Sovereign Debt Crisis." *Comparative European Politics* 13 (1): 8–28.

De la Porte, Caroline, and Philippe Pochet. 2012. "Why and How (Still) Study the Open Method of Co-ordination (OMC)?" *Journal of European Social Policy* 22 (3): 336–49.

De Witte, Hans. 2005. "Job Insecurity: Review of the International Literature on Definitions, Prevalence, Antecedents and Consequences." *SA Journal of Industrial Psychology* 31 (4): 1–6.

Del Monte, Micaela, and Thomas Zandstra. 2014. "Common Unemployment Insurance Scheme for the Euro Area." Cost of Non-Europe Report PE 510.984. Brussels: European Parliamentary Research Service, European Added Value Unit.

Dhéret, Claire, and Martina Morosi. 2015. "One Year After the Youth Guarantee: Policy Fatigue or Signs of Action?" EPC Policy Brief, May 27. Brussels: European Policy Centre.

Dullien, Sebastian. 2013. "A Euro-Area Wide Unemployment Insurance as an Automatic Stabilizer: Who Benefits and Who Pays?" Paper prepared for the European Commission (DG EMPL). Brussels: European Commission.

Eamets, Raul, Miroslav Beblavý, Kariappa Bheemaiah, Mairéad Finn, Katrin Humal, Janine Leschke, Ilaria Maselli, and Mark Smith. 2015. "Mapping Flexibility and Security Performance in the Face of the Crisis." STYLE Working Paper 10.1. Brighton, UK: CROME, University of Brighton. http://www.style-research.eu/publications/working-papers

Eurofound. 2015. *Opting Out of the European Working Time Directive.* Luxembourg: Publications Office of the European Union.

European Central Bank. 2014. "The Impact of the Economic Crisis on the Euro Area Labor Markets." *ECB Monthly Bulletin* (October): 49–68.

European Commission. 2007. "Towards Common Principles of Flexicurity: More and Better Jobs Through Flexibility and Security." Communication from the Commission COM (2007) 359 final. http://eur-lex.europa.eu/legal-content/EN/TXT/?uri=COM:2007:0498:FIN

European Commission. 2009. "An EU Strategy for Youth—Investing and Empowering: A Renewed Open Method of Coordination to Address Youth Challenges and Opportunities." Communication from the Commission COM (2009) 200 final. https://ec.europa.eu/youth/sites/youth/files/youth-strategy-assessment-2009_en.pdf

European Commission. 2010. "Youth and Segmentation in EU Labor Markets." In *Employment in Europe 2010*, 117–54. Directorate-General for Employment, Social Affairs and Inclusion Directorate A. Luxembourg: Publications Office of the European Union.

European Commission. 2011. "Adapting Unemployment Benefit Systems to the Economic Cycle 2011." European Employment Observatory Review. Luxembourg: Publications Office of the European Union.

European Commission. 2012. "The Skill Mismatch Challenge in Europe." In *Employment and Social Development in Europe 2012*, 351–94. Luxembourg: Publications Office of the European Union.

European Commission. 2014. "Stimulating Job Demand: The Design of Effective Hiring Subsidies in Europe." European Employment Policy Observatory Review. Luxembourg: Publications Office of the European Union.

European Commission. 2015. "The Legacy of the Crisis: Resilience and Challenges." In *Employment and Social Developments in Europe 2014*, 43–103. Directorate-General for Employment, Social Affairs and Inclusion Directorate A. Luxembourg: Publications Office of the European Union.

European Commission. 2016. *Employment and Social Developments in Europe 2015.* Luxembourg: Publications Office of the European Union.

Eurostat. 2016. "Eurostat Database." http://ec.europa.eu/eurostat/data/database

Falkner, Gerda. 2016. "The European Union's Social Dimension." In *European Union Politics*, 5th ed., edited by Michelle Cini and Nieves Pérez-Solórzano Borragán, 269–80. Oxford: Oxford University Press.

Freeman, Richard B. 2005. "Labor Market Institutions Without Blinders: The Debate Over Flexibility and Labor Market Performance." *International Economic Journal* 19 (2): 129–45.

Gangl, Markus. 2004. "Welfare States and the Scar Effects of Unemployment: A Comparative Analysis of the United States and West Germany." *American Journal of Sociology* 109 (6): 1319–64.

Green, Francis, Alan Felstead, Duncan Gallie, and Hande Inanc. 2014. "Job-Related Well-Being Through the Great Recession." *Journal of Happiness Studies* 17 (1): 389–411.

Hansen, Magnus Paulsen, and Peter Triantafillou. 2011. "The Lisbon Strategy and the Alignment of Economic and Social Concerns." *Journal of European Social Policy* 21 (3): 197–209.

Hastings, Thomas, and Jason Heyes. 2016. "Farewell to Flexicurity? Austerity and Labour Policies in the EU." *Economic and Industrial Democracy*. Advance on-line publication. doi:10.1177/0143831X16633756.

Heidenreich, Martin. 2009. "The Open Method of Coordination: A Pathway to the Gradual Transformation of National Employment and Welfare Regimes?" In *Changing European Employment and Welfare Regimes*, edited by Martin Heidenreich and Jonathan Zeitlin, 10–36. London: Routledge.

Heidenreich, Martin, and Jonathan Zeitlin, eds. 2009. *Changing European Employment and Welfare Regimes*. London: Routledge.

Heise, Arne, and Hanna Lierse. 2011. *Budget Consolidation and the European Social Model: The Effects of European Austerity Programmes on Social Security Systems*. Berlin: Friedrich-Ebert-Stiftung.

Hermann, Christoph. 2007. "Neoliberalism in the European Union." *Studies in Political Economy* 79 (1): 61–89.

Heyes, Jason. 2011. "Flexicurity, Employment Protection and the Jobs Crisis." *Work, Employment and Society* 25 (4): 642–57.

Jackson, Paul R., Elizabeth M. Stafford, Michael H. Banks, and Peter B. Warr. 1983. "Unemployment and Psychological Distress in Young People: The Moderating Effect of Employment Commitment." *Journal of Applied Psychology* 68 (3): 525–35.

Jepsen, Maria. 2005. "Towards a Gender Impact Analysis of Flexicurity?" In *Employment Policy from Different Angles*, edited by Thomas Bredgaard and Flemming Larsen, 68–87. Copenhagen: Djøf Forlag.

Kaczmarczyk, Pawel, and Marek Okólski. 2008. "Demographic and Labor Market Impacts of Migration on Poland." *Oxford Review Economic Policy* 24 (3): 599–624.

Knijn, Trudie, and Janneke Plantenga. 2012. "Conclusions: Transitions to Adulthood, Social Policies and New Social Risks for Young Adults." In *Work, Family Policies and Transitions to Adulthood in Europe*, edited by Trudie Knijn, 202–15. Hampshire: Palgrave Macmillan.

Kok, Wim. 2003. "Jobs, Jobs, Jobs: Creating More Employment in Europe." Report of the Employment Taskforce. Brussels: European Commission.

Lehndorff, Steffen, ed. 2014. *Divisive Integration: The Triumph of Failed Ideas in Europe—Revisited*. Brussels: ETUI.

Leschke, Janine. 2012. "Has the Economic Crisis Contributed to More Segmentation in Labor Market and Welfare Outcomes?" Working Paper 02. Brussels: ETUI.

Leschke, Janine. 2016. "Zwischenbilanz und Verbesserungspotenziale der Europa-2020-Strategie." *WSI-Mitteilungen* 69 (1): 66–69.

Leschke, Janine, Sotiria Theodoropoulou, and Andrew Watt. 2014. "Towards Europe 2020? Austerity and the New Economic Governance in the EU." In *Divisive Integration: The Triumph of Failed Ideas in Europe—Revisited*, edited by Steffen Lehndorff, 295–329. Brussels: ETUI.

Madsen, Per Kongshøj, Oscar Molina, Jesper Møller, and Mariona Lozano. 2013. "Labor Market Transitions of Young Workers in Nordic and Southern European Countries: The Role of Flexicurity." *Transfer: European Review of Labor and Research* 19 (30): 325–43.

McGuinness, Seamus, and Mark Wooden. 2009. "Overskilling, Job Insecurity and Career Mobility." *Industrial Relations* 48 (2): 265–86.

McKee-Ryan, Frances, Zhaoli Song, Connie R. Wanberg, and Angelo J. Kinicki. 2005. "Psychological and Physical Well-Being During Unemployment: A Meta-Analytic Review." *Journal of Applied Psychology* 90 (1): 53–76.

MISSOC. 2014. "Comparative Tables on Social Protection, Situation on 1 July 2014." Mutual Information System on Social Protection. https://www.missoc.org

Nordenmark, Mikael, and Mattias Strandh. 1999. "Towards a Sociological Understanding of Mental Well Being Among the Unemployed: The Role of Economic and Psychosocial Factors." *Sociology* 33 (3): 577–97.

O'Reilly, Jacqueline, Werner Eichhorst, András Gábos, Kari Hadjivassiliou, David Lain, Janine Leschke, Seamus McGuinness, et al. 2015. "Five Characteristics of Youth Unemployment in Europe: Flexibility, Education, Migration, Family Legacies, and EU Policy." *SAGE Open* 5 (1): 1–19. doi:10.1177/2158244015574962.

Organization for Economic Co-operation and Development (OECD). 1994. *The OECD Jobs Study: Facts, Analysis, Strategies*. Paris: OECD.

Organization for Economic Co-operation and Development (OECD). 2004. "Employment Protection Legislation and Labor Market Performance." In *OECD Employment Outlook 2004*, 61–125. Paris: OECD.

Organization for Economic Co-operation and Development (OECD). 2011. "Income Support for the Unemployed: How Well Has the Safety-Net Held up During the 'Great Recession'?" In *Employment Outlook*, 15–83. Paris: OECD.

Organization for Economic Co-operation and Development (OECD). 2014. "Non-Regular Employment, Job Security and the Labor Market Divide." In *Employment Outlook*, 141–209. Paris: OECD.

Organization for Economic Co-operation and Development (OECD). 2016. "OECD Indicators of Employment Protection: Annual Time Series Data 1985–2013." Paris: OECD. http://www.oecd.org/els/emp/oecdindicatorsofem ploymentprotection.htm.

Paul, Karsten I., and Klaus Moser. 2009. "Unemployment Impairs Mental Health: Meta-Analyses." *Journal of Vocational Behavior* 74 (3): 264–82.

Peiró, José M., Beatriz Sora, and Amparo Caballer. 2012. "Job Insecurity in the Younger Spanish Workforce: Causes and Consequences." *Journal of Vocational Behavior* 80 (2): 444–53.

Peña-Casas, Ramón. 2009. "More and Better Jobs: Conceptual Frameworks and Monitoring Indicators of Quality of Work and Employment in the EU Policy Arena." Working Paper on the Reconciliation of Work and Welfare in Europe, REC-WP 06/2009. Edinburgh: University of Edinburgh.

Plantenga, Janneke, Chantal Remery, and Jill Rubery. 2008. *Gender Mainstreaming of Employment Policies: A Comparative Review of Thirty European Countries*. Luxembourg: Office for Official Publications of the European Communities.

Russell, Helen, Janine Leschke, and Mark Smith. 2015. "Flexicurity and Subjective Insecurity." STYLE Working Paper 10.3. Brighton, UK: CROME, University of Brighton. http://www.style-research.eu/publications/working-papers

Scharpf, Fritz W. 2011. "Monetary Union, Fiscal Crisis and the Preemption of Democracy." LEQS Paper 36. Cologne: Max Planck Institute for the Study of Societies.

Scherer, Stefani. 2009. "The Social Consequences of Insecure Jobs." *Social Indicators Research* 93 (3): 527–47.

Simonazzi, Annamaria, and Paola Villa. 1999. "Flexibility and Growth." *International Review of Applied Economics* 13 (3): 281–311.

Simonazzi, Annamaria, and Paola Villa. 2016. "Europe at a Crossroads: What Kind of Structural Reforms?" In *Den Arbeitsmarkt verstehen, um ihn zu gestalten*, edited by Gerhard Bäcker, Steffen Lehndorff, and Claudia Weinkopf, 273–82. Wiesbaden: Springer.

Smith, Mark, and Paola Villa. 2013. "Recession and Recovery: Making Gender Equality Part of the Solution." In *Gender and the European Labor Market*, edited by Francesca Bettio, Janneke Plantenga, and Mark Smith, 224–41. London: Routledge.

Smith, Mark, and Paola Villa. 2016. "Flexicurity Policies to Integrate Youth Before and After the Crisis." STYLE Working Paper 10.4. Brighton, UK: CROME,

University of Brighton. http://www.style-research.eu/publications/working-papers

Solow, Robert M. 1998. "What Is Labour-Market Flexibility? What Is It Good For?" Keynes Lecture in Economics. *Proceedings of the British Academy* 97: 189–211.

Solow, Robert M. 2000. "Unemployment in the United States and in Europe: A Contrast and the Reasons." Working Paper 331. Munich: CESifo.

Theodossiou, Ioannis. 1998. "The Effects of Low-Pay and Unemployment on Psychological Well-Being: A Logistic Regression Approach." *Journal of Health Economics* 17 (1): 85–104.

Van Apeldoorn, Bastiaan. 2009. "The Contradictions of 'Embedded Neoliberalism' and Europe's Multilevel Legitimacy Crisis: The European Project and Its Limits." In *Contradictions and Limits of Neoliberal European Governance—From Lisbon to Lisbon*, edited by Bastiaan van Apeldoorn, Jan Drahokoupil, and Laura Horn, 21–43. London: Palgrave.

Villa, Paola. 2013. "The Role of the EES in the Promotion of Gender Equality in the Labour Market: A Critical Appraisal." In *Gender and the European Labour Market,* edited by Francesca Bettio, Janneke Plantenga, and Mark Smith, 135–67. London: Routledge.

Villa, Paola, and Mark Smith. 2014. "Policy in Time of Crisis: Employment Policy and Gender Equality in Europe." In *Women and Austerity: The Economic Crisis and the Future for Gender Equality*, edited by Maria Karamessini and Jill Rubery, 273–94. London: Routledge.

Walsh, Brendan. 2011. "Well-Being and Economic Conditions in Ireland." Working Paper 11/27. Dublin: UCD School of Economics.

Wilthagen, Ton, and Frank Tros. 2004. "The Concept of 'Flexicurity': A New Approach to Regulating Employment and Labor Markets." *Transfer: European Review of Labour and Research* 10 (2): 166–86.

5

LABOR MARKET FLEXIBILITY
AND INCOME SECURITY

CHANGES FOR EUROPEAN YOUTH DURING THE GREAT RECESSION

Janine Leschke and Mairéad Finn

5.1. INTRODUCTION

This chapter examines how young people have been affected by the Great Recession. In particular, it analyzes the relationship between labor market flexibility and the income security of youth in Europe. Given the exponential increase in youth unemployment during the Great Recession, a specific focus is placed on institutional developments regarding unemployment benefits—a topic that has remained under-researched to date.[1]

To provide some context, young people in most European countries are more likely than adults to be working on temporary contracts with limited job security, and they are also likely to move in and out of unemployment more frequently (*external numerical flexibility*) (Organization for Economic Co-operation and Development (OECD) 2014; Flek, Hála, and Mysíková, this volume). At the same time, young people tend to have less access to unemployment benefits compared to adults, given that eligibility for such benefits (*income security*) usually depends on a certain minimum amount of time spent in employment within a specific reference period, often with additional requirements regarding thresholds for earnings or working hours. Unemployment benefits and social assistance are frequently means tested at the household level. Adequate unemployment benefit coverage not only renders young people more financially independent of their parents but also been shown to lead to better post-unemployment outcomes, including earnings and job stability (Gangl 2004). Moreover, there is evidence that due to (on average) lower tenure and work experience (important assets when employers are deciding who to retain and who to fire), young people do not benefit as much as adults from subsidized short-time working (Arpaia et al. 2010)—a measure that grants *internal numerical flexibility* to employers and at the same time (at least to a certain degree) sustains the income security of employees. Youth are thus faced with a situation in which they bear the brunt of a disproportionate share of external numerical labor market flexibility and at the same time lack income security.

Income security during unemployment has received considerable policy attention at the international, European, and national levels throughout the Great Recession, but particularly during the first years, as certain groups—such as youth and nonstandard workers—have suffered a disproportionate share of job losses. Prior to the Great Recession, little attention was paid to this issue (Eurofound 2003; Leschke 2008; Schulze Buschoff and Protsch 2008), particularly at the practical policy level.[2] More comprehensive unemployment benefit coverage for youth and nonstandard workers can be achieved by ensuring the availability and adequacy of lower tier schemes, such as social assistance, and via permanent or temporary changes to the eligibility criteria under unemployment insurance schemes.[3]

Particularly during the early years of the crisis, serious efforts were made in several countries to improve the income security of those groups that had been disproportionally hit by unemployment, including youth and temporary workers. These efforts focused both on sustaining employment (introduction of state-subsidized short-term working schemes or expansion of existing schemes to new groups) and on cushioning unemployment (more inclusive unemployment benefits). There was also increased concern about the income security of nonstandard workers and youth at the European and international levels, as evidenced by a number of publications (OECD 2010a; European Commission 2011a) and the explicit mentioning of the need for adequate social protection for fixed-term and self-employed workers under guideline 7 of the 2010 European Employment Strategy (Council of the European Union 2010). Moreover, a basic unemployment insurance for the Euro area, which could serve as an automatic stabilizer in downturns, has been discussed (Dullien 2013; Del Monte and Zandstra 2014). By contrast, austerity measures often targeted employment and social policies (Heise and Lierse 2011; Lehndorff 2014), which impacted on the initial expansionary adjustments to unemployment benefits in some countries.

Against this background, this chapter adopts a comparative European approach. It traces developments at the interface between numerical flexibility (both internal and external) and income security for youth during different phases of the Great Recession. We examine young (aged 15–24 years) and older (aged 25–29 years) youth separately so as to explore differences between these age groups. Older youth were also affected by the crisis, but given that they typically have more work experience, and thus longer tenure, we can expect them to do better than younger youth at the flexibility–security interface. Section 5.2 frames the chapter by discussing the European Union's approach to flexicurity and by describing possible interactions between labor market flexibility and income security. Section 5.3 briefly discusses developments in external and internal numerical flexibility for youth during different phases of the Great Recession. Section 5.4, the core of the chapter, examines income security during unemployment—a dimension that has thus far remained underexplored. First, we map the institutional changes occurring in the design of unemployment benefits in a number of European countries during the Great Recession, with the intention of making benefits more inclusive for youth and other particularly affected labor market groups. Second, we analyze benefit coverage for young and older youth compared to adults—based on special extracts of aggregate European Union Labour Force Survey (EU-LFS) data. The chapter concludes that youth are doing worse than adults on all examined dimensions of the flexibility–security interface. Despite initial expansionary measures regarding income security in a number of countries, it emerges that income security has been undermined for youth overall when the austerity period is taken into consideration.

5.2. RELATIONSHIPS BETWEEN LABOR MARKET FLEXIBILITY AND INCOME SECURITY

In examining the type of relationship that exists between labor market flexibility and income security, previous research has shown that nonstandard employment does not always act as a stepping stone to regular employment. On the contrary, nonstandard employment is often permanent or recurring, and—due to more limited job security—is frequently associated with transitions out of employment into either unemployment or inactivity (Anxo and O'Reilly 2000; Gash 2008; Muffels 2008; European Commission 2009; Leschke 2009; Berloffa et al., this volume). What little research is available on the income security of flexible workers shows that nonstandard workers are more likely to be excluded from access to unemployment benefits (to varying degrees, depending on the country and the group of workers in question). Once they qualify for access, they may actually be in a position to receive proportionately higher benefit levels because of the progressive nature of some of the systems (low benefit ceilings, flat-rate schemes, etc.; see Grimshaw and Rubery 1997; Talós 1999; Klammer and Tillmann 2001; Eurofound 2003; Leschke 2008; Schulze Buschoff and Protsch 2008), although in absolute terms the levels might not suffice to make ends meet.

Turning to the literature on flexicurity, there has been enduring criticism of the flexicurity concept as proposed by the European Commission during the second half of the Lisbon Strategy (European Commission 2007).[4] The European Trade Union Confederation (ETUC) has repeatedly questioned the shift in focus from job security granted by strict employment protection legislation (EPL) to more labor market flexibility combined with employment or employability security—to be achieved, for example, through active labor market policies (ALMPs) and lifelong learning measures. ETUC has also questioned the framing of flexibility and security as trade-offs, as well as the one-sided attribution of flexibility needs to employers and of security needs to employees (ETUC 2007). The Great Recession has put the flexicurity concept under further pressure (Heyes 2011; Ibsen 2011) and—in view of the youth unemployment crisis and the fact that workers with temporary contracts have been disproportionally affected—has also called into question the strong focus on labor market flexibility as opposed to cushioning security measures (Tangian 2007; Burroni and Keune 2011). In view of this criticism and in particular of the experience of the crisis, the Europe 2020 strategy has somewhat modified the EU's take on flexicurity. Under Europe 2020, the EU places more emphasis on the role of job security for those countries that have very segmented labor markets and thereby removes the focus from labor market adaptation via increasing external numerical flexibility.[5] Europe 2020 also calls attention to the importance of income security during transitions. More adequate social security benefits for some groups of nonstandard workers, namely fixed-term workers and the self-employed, were specifically mentioned in the 2010 integrated guidelines on economic and employment policies (Council of the European Union 2010, guideline 7). The most recent guidelines have returned to a rather vague formulation stipulating a design of social protection systems that "facilitates take-up for all those entitled to do so . . . and helps to prevent, reduce and protect against poverty and social exclusion through the life cycle" (Council of the European Union 2015, guideline 8). In addition, the positive role of internal flexibility devices—such as short-time working measures and working-time accounts—in buffering employment shocks is emphasized by the Commission in its agenda for new skills and jobs (European Commission 2010a).

A critical use of the flexicurity concept is particularly important with regard to youth, who—even more so since the onset of the crisis—tend to accumulate negative flexicurity outcomes (Madsen et al. 2013). Young people are more prone than adults to moving between fixed-term jobs (with limited job security) and unemployment (see Section 5.3); at the same time, because of contracts of shorter duration and thus greater difficulties in fulfilling the eligibility requirements for unemployment benefits, their access to benefits is considerable weaker than that of adults (see Section 5.4). Thus, the flexibility–security interface could be described as vicious (young people lose out on both dimensions because higher contractual flexibility means more frequent unemployment, which is less often covered by benefits).

As we show in this chapter, the crisis has not only triggered a change in discourse at the EU and international levels but also facilitated institutional change (although often only of a temporary nature), making unemployment benefits for youth and temporary workers more inclusive in a number of countries. In the second part of the crisis, some of these developments have been reversed again, or benefit eligibility for young unemployed has been made more conditional on participation in education or training measures. Wilthagen and Tros (2004), building on the concept of transitional labor markets developed by Schmid and Gazier (2002), have proposed a matrix combining different forms of flexibility, on the one hand, with different dimensions of security, on the other hand. Leschke, Schmid, and Griga (2007) and Schmid (2008)—working within the framework of transitional labor market theory—propose exploring the links between these dimensions more comprehensively by going beyond trade-offs and also examining cases in which both flexibility and security can be improved (termed *virtuous relationships*) and in which both can be undermined (termed *vicious relationships*). In this chapter, we focus in particular on the interface between numerical flexibility (both internal and external) and income security for youth, given that these dimensions have seen dynamic changes during the Great Recession.

5.3. TRACING CHANGES IN LABOR MARKET FLEXIBILITY FOR YOUTH DURING THE CRISIS

In this section, we examine developments regarding different components of labor market flexibility for youth during the crisis. Labor market transitions are a common phenomenon among young people. School-to-work transitions are often characterized by moves in and out of the labor market before a stable job is found (OECD 2010a). These transitions are a result of rather unstable first-time jobs (e.g., temporary contracts for probationary periods) or jobs that by definition are of shorter duration (e.g., training contracts). Some youth withdraw from the labor market for prolonged periods of time—for example, to return to education. Spells of unemployment (and inactivity) are therefore a frequent phenomenon among young people.

Figure 5.1 illustrates for the EU as a whole the disproportionate levels of unemployment and the different forms of nonstandard employment (temporary employment and part-time work) experienced by youth (aged 15–24 and 25–29 years). It shows data for the precrisis period (2007), stimulus period (2009), and austerity period (2013). Young people both started from higher levels (with the exception of part-time employment for the older youth group) than adults and were more affected by increases in unemployment and nonstandard employment over the course of the crisis. During the austerity period, unemployment lies at 23.3% for the younger and at 14.6% for the older youth group, compared with 8.8% for adults. The spread across Europe is large, with an unemployment

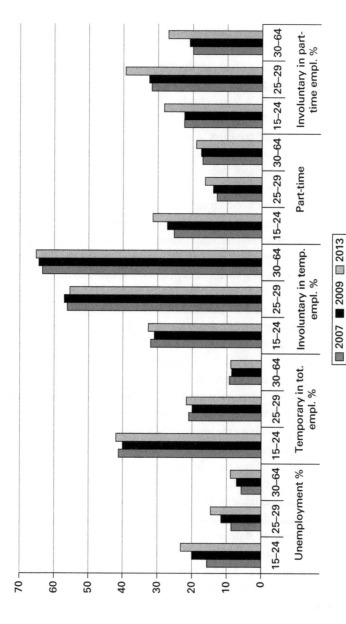

Figure 5.1 Development of unemployment and nonstandard employment in EU27 by age group and year (2007, 2009, and 2013).
Source: Eurostat EU-LFS, special extracts.

rate of 58.3% for youth (aged 15–24 years) in Greece and of 7.8% for youth in Germany. Temporary employment is the prime example for external numerical flexibility—here the share in 2013 lies at 42% for young youth and at 21.7% for older youth, while the adult share stands at 9%. Both youth groups have slightly higher temporary employment shares during the austerity period than before the crisis (2007), whereas the adult temporary employment rate in 2013 is still slightly below its 2007 level.

Temporary employment is often involuntary (inability to find a permanent job), and this is on average more pronounced among older youth and adults (approximately 55% and 65%, respectively) than among younger youth (approximately 33%) across the EU27. In most EU countries, more than half of the respondents in the age group of 15- to 24-year-olds are involuntarily in temporary employment. Only in Austria, Germany, and Denmark are the majority of temporary contracts of young youth composed of training contracts (Eurofound 2013).

There is a direct trade-off between external flexibility (in the form of temporary contracts) and job security because temporary employment by its nature enjoys less protection than regular employment. As a result of notice periods and severance pay, among other components, permanent employment is more protected than temporary employment. Temporary employment usually runs out after a predefined period based on a legal maximum number of successive fixed-term contracts and a maximum cumulated duration, as regulated by the European fixed-term work directive and other regulations. Countries vary substantially in the strictness of EPL for both permanent and temporary contracts (for details, see OECD 2013). Countries with lax rules regarding the dismissal of workers on permanent contracts usually have comparatively lower shares of people in temporary employment because labor market flexibility can already be achieved through hire-and-fire policies around permanent jobs—the United Kingdom is a case in point. Schömann and Clauwaert (2012), drawing on country studies, identify a clear trend during the Great Recession of many member states making their labor markets more flexible by changing the rules governing atypical contracts. They highlight, in particular, the trend toward increasing the maximum length of fixed-term contracts or the maximum possible number of renewals of such contracts. They also point to the creation in several member states of new types of contracts that are often less protected and are frequently targeted explicitly at young people (Schömann and Clauwaert 2012, Section 2.2 and Table 1). Reforms of rules on redundancy that undermine the protective role of individual and collective dismissal are also highlighted by Schömann and Clauwaert for a substantive number of European countries (Section 2.3 and Table 1). The latter trend is confirmed by a comparison of the 2008 and 2013 OECD indicators on strictness of EPL for individual and collective dismissals pertaining to regular contracts (OECD 2016; see also Berloffa et al., this volume).

Working-time accounts or short-time working measures also create flexibility for employers in times of slack demand. Both have been used during the Great Recession and particularly the economic recession of 2008–2009, with a slightly stronger focus on short-time working: Almost all countries that already had these publicly funded schemes in place before the crisis expanded the schemes to increase their reach,[6] while some other countries (BG, CZ, HU, NL, PL, SK, SI, LV, and LT) newly introduced such schemes temporarily during the crisis. Newly introduced schemes are usually less generous in terms of duration and benefits than those that are already established; however, they also usually cover a broader range of employees (Arpaia et al. 2010). Since the crisis, some countries have introduced temporary schemes covering specific types of firm or sector.[7] No such schemes exist in Cyprus, Estonia, or Malta, which suggests that in these countries, working-time reductions usually go hand in hand with wage cuts of the same proportion. In contrast to temporary employment, which is often involuntary (as noted at the beginning of this section), short-time working measures carry advantages for employees in that they have enabled job preservation and the avoidance of unemployment during the crisis (Hijzen and Martin 2012). Short-time working schemes partially compensate for lost wages through the unemployment benefit fund—topped up in some countries (e.g., Belgium) by sector-level funds either directly or via the employer.

In the past, short-time working measures were restricted in many countries to core workers—either explicitly by requiring that temporary workers be released first or implicitly by offering participation in these schemes only to workers who were eligible for unemployment benefits. During the crisis, however, several of these countries (e.g., AT, BE, FR, DE, and LU) deliberately opened up their schemes—either temporarily or permanently—to new groups of workers (for country details, see Arpaia et al. 2010; European Commission 2010b). The available empirical evidence indicates, however, that the positive impacts were limited to permanent workers (Hijzen and Venn 2011; Hijzen and Martin 2012).

Figure 5.2 illustrates the evolution of short-time working for both youth and adults before and during the Great Recession. It shows, on EU27 average, the share of people working fewer hours than usual during the interview reference week because of slack demand for technical or (usually) economic reasons as a share of total employment. In all years, adults emerge as being more likely than young people to participate in short-time working measures. In line with the expansion of these schemes to new groups of workers, among them the temporarily employed, participation peaked in 2009 for all groups (somewhat more pronouncedly for adults and older youth). The share subsequently declined, although it still stands at a higher level in 2013 than before the crisis for all three groups.

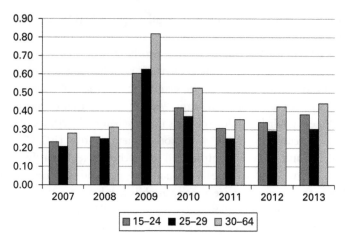

Figure 5.2 Evolution of short-time working (with or without partial benefits) in EU27 by age group, 2007–2013 (% of total employment).
Source: Eurostat EU-LFS, special extracts.

Figure 5.3 provides information on short-time working by country and age group for the year 2009 when stimulus measures peaked. The EU-LFS data have the advantage that they are comparable across countries; they do not, however, tell us anything about whether short-time working is compensated by partial unemployment benefits.[8] Using the information provided in Arpaia et al. (2010), we therefore group countries into those without compensation (/), those with long-standing and usually more generous schemes ($), and those with new, temporary, and usually less generous schemes (¤). Figure 5.3 illustrates that young youth (aged 15–24 years) were considerably more likely to participate in short-time working measures in 2009 in Denmark, the Netherlands, Latvia, Malta, and Lithuania—albeit with considerable variation in overall participation across these countries. In Belgium, Bulgaria, Greece, and Hungary, the participation of young youth was slightly higher than that of adults.

In conclusion, overall, in contrast to external numerical flexibility, in which youth (and particularly younger youth) are considerably over-represented, internal numerical flexibility, as captured here by short-time working, is less segmented than initially expected—at least when the EU-LFS indicator is used. It is younger rather than older youth who seem to have been over-represented in short-time working. Note that a positive assessment of short-time working only holds as long as it has prevented even sharper increases in unemployment. Also, in countries or sectors where no partial compensation of working-hour reduction is available, short-time working will have more adverse effects on the economic situation of affected workers.

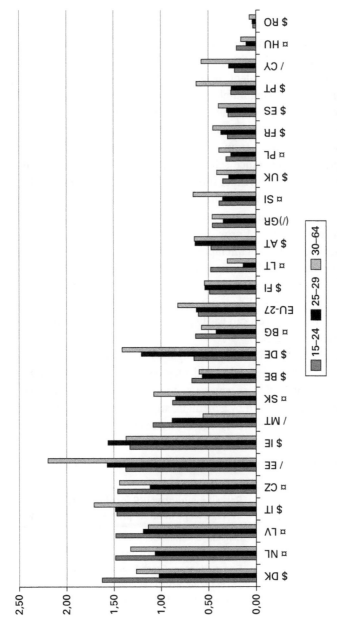

Figure 5.3 Short-time working (with or without partial wage replacement) by age group and country in EU27, 2009 (% of total employment).
Source: Eurostat EU-LFS, special extracts.

5.4. EVOLUTION OF INCOME SECURITY FOR UNEMPLOYED YOUTH DURING THE GREAT RECESSION

Turning to income security, substantial shares of unemployed people do not have access to unemployment (insurance) benefits. In part, this is deliberate policy (i.e., a link between contributions and benefits is intended), whereas in other cases there is "implicit disentitlement" (Standing 2002) whereby, as a result of the trend away from dependent, permanent, and full-time "standard employment relationships," growing numbers of unemployed workers cannot fulfill the qualifying criteria for unemployment insurance benefits.

Unemployment insurance benefits are the first tier of provision and are usually based on contributions from employers and employees. All EU countries have unemployment insurance schemes, although their eligibility conditions and benefit rates (generosity) differ substantially (Kvist, Straubinger, and Freundt 2013; OECD *Benefits and Wages*). In order to contextualize the following analysis of reforms of unemployment benefits during the stimulus and austerity periods of the crisis, Table 5.1 provides an overview of benefit generosity during an individual's initial phase of unemployment (1 or 2 months of unemployment). We depict benefit generosity using net replacement rates for single persons at 67% of average wages because this likely comes closest to the situation for an average young person. Table 5.1 does not take access to benefits into account in any way: Generous benefit levels can easily go hand in hand with exclusive benefits and vice versa (see Table 5.3).

An unemployed person who is not eligible for unemployment insurance or whose entitlement has been exhausted may be entitled to unemployment assistance, which is typically less generous, noncontributory, means tested at the household level, and financed by general taxation.[9] The fact that unemployment assistance is assessed at the household rather than the individual level implies

Table 5.1 Unemployment insurance benefit generosity of EU27 countries (in order of generosity) in 2013

Generosity (NRR)	Benefit insurance NRR for single person at 67% of average wage in initial phase of unemployment
Most generous (NRR > 71%)	Belgium, Slovenia, Denmark, Latvia, Luxembourg, Spain, Bulgaria, Portugal, Netherlands, Italy, Finland
Mid-level generous (NRR = 55%–70%)	France, Hungary, Czech Republic, Slovakia, Sweden, Germany, Austria, Estonia
Low-level generous (NRR = 41%–54%)	Lithuania, Ireland, Poland, Romania, Malta
Least generous (NRR < 40%)	Greece, United Kingdom

NRR, net replacement rates.
Source: OECD *Benefits and Wages*, 2013; authors' compilation.

that young people living at home have broader household means taken into consideration as part of their assessment (Eurofound 2013). Typically, unemployment assistance does not require qualifying periods; in cases in which it operates with qualifying periods, these are laxer than those for unemployment insurance benefits.[10] In some cases, unemployment assistance is restricted to certain categories, such as unemployed people with dependent family members; in some cases, youth or specific types of youth are explicitly excluded (see OECD *Benefits and Wages*).[11] In almost all EU countries, as a last tier, tax-funded social assistance subject to means testing exists.

This section seeks to highlight the exclusion of youth from access to unemployment benefits, which is an underexamined topic in comparative welfare-state research (Van Oorschot 2013). Our analysis makes special reference to changes during the first period of the crisis (2008–2009) and to developments throughout the austerity period (2010–2014). Given that unemployment benefit systems are designed to meet complex (and fast-changing) conditions, there is no room here to specify the different qualifying conditions and other design features, although some details are provided as they relate to youth (also as temporary workers).[12] Regularly updated comparative information on the design of unemployment benefit systems can be found in the European Commission's Labour Market Reforms (LABREF) database (2015), the European Commission's Mutual Information System on Social Protection (MISSOC) Comparative Tables database (2014), and the OECD *Benefits and Wages* series. Detailed comparative information on unemployment benefit schemes, particularly with regard to part-time workers, is also available from a special OECD (2010b) survey.

5.4.1. Review of Youth Integration in Unemployment Benefit Schemes

Young workers are subject to both explicit exclusion in terms of differential rules of access to unemployment benefits and implicit exclusion (Standing's (2002) "implicit disentitlement") from such benefits through their over-representation in temporary contracts and an average shorter tenure. Earnings or hours thresholds directly exclude those who work on low-hours, part-time contracts, while the qualifying period (usually a minimum contribution period within a given reference period) can further restrict the access of young people whose contracts are of short duration (for details and specific country examples, see Eurofound 2013; Leschke 2013). There are also rules affecting youth directly with both positive and negative consequences for benefit coverage. We provide some concrete examples in the following discussion.

Three countries explicitly exclude certain types of temporary workers from eligibility for unemployment benefits: the Czech Republic, Poland, and Slovakia (for details, see Eurofound 2013). In Slovakia, for example, all temporary workers were excluded from unemployment benefits until January 2013;

now temporary workers above a certain earnings threshold qualify more easily than permanent workers (2 years of employment within a reference period of 4 years, compared to a reference period of 3 years for permanent workers; Eurofound 2013).

In general, it is easier for young people (and temporary workers) to access unemployment benefits in countries that have short contribution periods within a long reference period (however, this says nothing about the generosity of the benefits received). According to Eurofound (2013), in practice it seems to be easiest for workers with short contract duration, in particular temporary workers, to qualify for unemployment benefits in France, Spain, Greece, Malta, and Finland. Qualifying conditions are likely to be most difficult to meet in the Netherlands, Ireland, Latvia, Poland, and Bulgaria (for details, see Eurofound 2013, 20–21).

Age also plays a role in access to benefits and is an explicit factor that can negatively impact on the access of young people. In the United Kingdom, for example, those younger than age 18 years are not entitled to any form of benefit, irrespective of what type of contract they have had (European Commission 2011a). On the other hand, the qualifying criteria for unemployment benefits in some countries can be more relaxed for youth or can include criteria other than a certain contributory period. In Finland, for instance, youth (aged 17–25 years) wishing to access unemployment insurance benefits can have a vocational qualification, 5 months' work history, or 5 months' participation in ALMPs. Romania grants graduates who are looking for work an exemption from qualifying periods for unemployment benefits (MISSOC 2014).

Young people can also be entitled to lower amounts and shorter benefit duration. In Italy and Ireland, for example, younger workers' benefit rates are lower than those of older workers (European Commission 2011a). Several countries make benefit duration dependent on the length of the contribution period (e.g., AT, BG, DE, and NL), which disproportionally affects younger workers with shorter employment tenure (MISSOC 2014).

5.4.2. Recent Reforms of Unemployment Benefit Schemes Affecting European Youth

This section examines reforms in unemployment benefit schemes throughout the crisis, dealing separately with the first ("stimulus") period (2008–2009) and the second ("austerity") period (2010–2014). The focus during the stimulus period was predominantly—although not exclusively—on opening up access to unemployment benefits, whereas during the austerity period, unemployment benefits were among the targets of austerity measures in several countries. A number of benefit reforms were explicitly geared toward youth, usually comprising direct links to education and training programs (see examples discussed later). The majority of reforms, however, were of a more general nature and were related to relaxing or tightening up qualifying conditions or to increasing or decreasing benefit levels that indirectly impact on youth. Here, we review the changes to unemployment benefit systems in the EU27 with regard to qualifying criteria, benefit levels (including one-off payments), and duration.[13] For country examples of these reforms, see the remainder of Section 5.4 and Table 5.2.

Table 5.2 Initial typology of EU27 countries with modifications in unemployment benefit systems directly or indirectly targeted at youth during the first period of crisis (2008–2009) and during the austerity period (2010–2014)

(Temporary) Modifications of	Direction of change	2008–2009	2010–2014
Eligibility (qualifying conditions)	Relaxed	Finland, Italy*, Latvia, Portugal, Sweden(*)	Portugal, Slovenia(*), Spain*
	Tightened	Ireland	Belgium*, Czech Republic, Denmark*·¹, Greece, Hungary, Romania
	Explicitly opened up to new groups of workers	France*, Italy(*), Spain	Czech Republic*, Italy*, Slovenia
Benefit levels	Increasing	Belgium, Bulgaria, Czech Republic, Netherlands, Poland, Slovenia	Belgium, Bulgaria, Slovenia
	Lump sum/one-off payment	France*, Greece, Italy, Spain	Spain
	Decreasing	Ireland(*)	Greece, Ireland*, Latvia, Poland, Portugal, Romania, Spain
Benefit duration	Increasing	Finland, Latvia, Lithuania, Portugal, Romania, Spain	Denmark
	Decreasing	Czech Republic, Denmark, France, Ireland, Poland	Greece

Notes: Because of the complexity and the variation of benefit systems, some of the changes are difficult to classify. In 2013, for example, the number of days for which unemployment benefit could be paid was capped in Greece. The maximum of 450 days within a 4-year period now cannot be extended if one becomes unemployed again, and this affects both benefit duration and general eligibility. We have therefore listed Greece in both rows. In addition, in some cases there are uncertainties as to the exact year in which the reforms became active.

* = Reform explicitly relating to youth.

(*) = Parts of the reform explicitly relating to youth.

1 = Refers to social assistance.

Source: Authors' depiction based on European Commission (2011a, 2011c), Eurofound (2013), Leschke (2013), MISSOC (2014), and LABREF (2015).

5.4.2.1. Stimulus Period (Economic Recession of 2008–2009)

In the first part of the recession (2008–2009), which was characterized in most countries by a number of measures to stimulate the economy, *qualifying criteria* were relaxed in Finland, France, Italy, Latvia, Portugal, Spain, and Sweden (Latvia and Portugal previously had rather strict qualifying criteria), with positive impacts on employees with short tenure (for details, see European Commission 2010c, 137; European Commission 2011a, 18–24). The relaxation was achieved by reducing contribution periods, increasing reference periods (or both), or opening up schemes explicitly to new groups of workers. Sweden, for example, temporarily lowered the condition of membership (in an unemployment insurance fund) for income-related unemployment benefits from 1 year to 6 months and—by abolishing the work requirement—made it possible for students to join an unemployment insurance fund (European Commission 2011a). In Italy, from 2009 to 2011, ordinary unemployment allowance was extended to apprentices with at least 3 months' tenure, while a broad group of employees—including fixed-term, temporary agency workers, and apprentices—was allowed to apply for exceptional unemployment benefits (European Commission 2011a). France made means-tested welfare benefits available to jobseekers aged between 18 and 25 years, who had previously been excluded. To prevent students from gaining access to this benefit, a relatively strict qualifying condition of 2 years' employment within 3 years was added, taking into account all types of employment contract (LABREF 2015). Several of the measures introduced in this time period were temporary.

A number of countries, including France, Greece, Italy, and Spain, granted temporary *lump-sum* or *one-off payments* to unemployed workers not eligible for regular unemployment benefits. In France, these were directly targeted at youth who did not fulfill the eligibility criteria for unemployment benefits (LABREF 2015).

Unemployment benefit levels were increased in Belgium, the Netherlands, Bulgaria, the Czech Republic, and Poland, as well as in Latvia and Finland (European Commission 2011b, 76–78). As an exception to this trend of improving the situation of groups with less coverage, Ireland substantially reduced the benefit level for young claimants (aged 18–24 years) in 2009. However, these reduced benefit rates did not apply to those participating in training or education programs (European Commission 2011c).

Benefit duration of unemployment insurance or assistance was increased in Finland, Romania, Latvia, and Lithuania, although in the latter case only in municipalities that had been hit particularly hard by the crisis (European Commission 2011b, 76–78). Targeting the benefit duration of persons already eligible for unemployment benefits, the Spanish government approved a temporary flat-rate unemployment assistance benefit payable for 6 months to all persons whose unemployment insurance benefits had expired.[14] A similar reform was carried out in Portugal. Conversely, Ireland, the Czech Republic, Poland, France, and Denmark decreased the maximum duration of unemployment benefits.[15] The Irish reform explicitly targeted young youth (aged <18 years) by reducing the duration of Job Benefit from 12 to 6 months for this age group (European Commission 2011a).

Second-tier systems such as social assistance were improved in a number of countries, as evidenced by increases to housing support, for example. Some countries (e.g., Estonia) had planned improvements to their unemployment benefit systems, which then were not implemented or were postponed because of the crisis. Only a few countries had reduced benefits during this initial crisis period as a part of fiscal consolidation measures (e.g., Ireland); in most cases, these reductions concerned benefit duration.

5.4.2.2. Austerity Period

During the economic recession (2008–2009), the focus was often on relaxing eligibility criteria and increasing benefit levels. The austerity period (2010–2014), by contrast, was characterized by tightening eligibility and decreasing benefit levels (see Table 5.2). Reforms relating to eligibility, even when not explicitly geared toward youth, have a particularly disproportionate effect on young unemployed given their shorter average tenure. However, there were also a few countries that relaxed qualifying criteria during this period, often with a view to supporting young people. These reforms usually stipulated a link between passive benefit entitlements and participation in education and training programs (European Commission 2014; MISSOC 2014).[16] Here, we provide details regarding a number of reforms explicitly targeting youth (marked with an asterisk in Table 5.2).

In Ireland, *benefit levels* for those aged 22–26 years were reduced further (a first reduction had already taken place in 2009). Higher rates apply if the jobseeker participates in education or training or has dependent children. Belgium and Denmark tightened *qualifying criteria* for youth: In 2012, Belgium increased the waiting period before benefit allowance is granted to 12 months for all recipients (previously it had stood at 6, 9, and 12 months). The Belgian benefit is now called "vocational development benefit" and requires proactive steps with regard to finding employment. In Denmark, since 2013, people younger than age 30 years and without education no longer receive social assistance.[17] There is an equivalent student benefit if youth embark on education, whereas those not ready for education will still receive social assistance if they participate in activation measures geared at inclusion in education. In Spain, Slovenia, and Italy, on the other hand, qualifying criteria for youth were relaxed during this period—the benefits to be accrued are usually short term and/or means tested. In Spain, for example, a temporary program was introduced in 2011 geared toward youth, long-term unemployed, and other vulnerable groups, making a means-tested flat-rate unemployment subsidy of 6 months dependent on participation in individualized training actions (European Commission 2011a). In Slovenia, qualifying conditions were relaxed for all unemployed in 2011 and were further relaxed for those younger than age 30 years in 2013. In Italy, since 2013, young people on apprenticeships are eligible for regular unemployment benefits. The Czech reform shortened the reference period for eligibility (making benefits more difficult to access) but at the same time opened up unemployment benefits to students fulfilling the eligibility criteria (Eurofound 2013). Table 5.2 provides a summary overview of countries that modified their unemployment benefit schemes during the stimulus and austerity periods.[18]

Clearly, Southern European and Central-Eastern European welfare systems show more activity in relation to changing policies for youth, particularly—but not exclusively—in the austerity period. Thus, it seems that the trend is for greater change in countries that were affected more severely by the Great Recession. At the same time, these countries had a tradition of benefit provision that was not as long-standing or as robust as in corporatist or Nordic countries—traditions that were more neoliberal or relied on familial ties. Moreover, Greece, Ireland, and Portugal—which received bailouts in exchange for implementing programs of economic adjustment described in the so-called Memoranda of Understanding—all feature in Table 5.2, with Ireland and Greece showing a profile of tightening conditions, whereas Portugal has a more mixed profile. Spain and Italy experienced more informal pressure to implement structural reforms. According to our analysis, Spain shows a mixed profile, whereas Italy has an expanding profile, albeit from a very low starting point in terms of benefit coverage, in particular.

5.4.3. Income Security: Access to Unemployment Benefits for Youth During the Crisis

The remainder of Section 5.4 examines the access of youth versus adults to unemployment benefits during different stages of the Great Recession. The aim is to explore the question as to whether youth were disproportionately affected during the crisis. Special extracts from aggregate EU-LFS data are used, and we present figures regarding persons who are registered with the Public Employment Service (PES) and are in receipt of unemployment benefit or assistance. We examine here exclusively the short-term unemployed (1 or 2 months).[19] Given that the EU-LFS information on people in receipt of unemployment benefits has been identified as unreliable as a result, among other things, of under- and misreporting (Immervoll, Marianna, and Mira D'Ercole 2004, 58–67),[20] when we report country results, we show relative distributions and changes over time in benefit coverage rather than absolute levels (for a similar strategy, see OECD 2011). It is unlikely that reporting errors will vary substantially between different age groups in the same country or over time. Table 5.3 uses ranges on benefit coverage in 2013 with regard to the adult population (aged 30–64 years) in order to put the following analysis into perspective.

As a first indication, Figure 5.4 highlights differences in unemployment benefit coverage for the EU27 by previous contract type, age, and for three time

Table 5.3 Coverage with unemployment insurance or assistance benefits as share of all unemployed adults (aged 30–64 years) in EU countries, 2013 (EU27 = 44.7%)

Coverage (%)	Countries
<20	Italy, Malta, Romania
≤ 20 < 35	Bulgaria, Lithuania, Poland, Slovakia
≥35 to <50	Cyprus, Estonia, Greece, Hungary, Latvia, Luxembourg, Portugal, Slovenia, Sweden, United Kingdom
≥50 to ≤65	Austria, Czech Republic, France, Spain
≥65	Belgium, Denmark, Finland, Germany

Notes: Duration of unemployment 1 or 2 months. Registered with PES and receiving benefits or assistance as percentage of all unemployed.
Source: Eurostat EU-LFS, special extracts.

points, using the main reason for having left the previous job as a proxy for permanent or temporary job prior to being unemployed. We calculate the coverage rate as those registered with the PES and receiving benefits or assistance as a percentage of all unemployed. Older youth (although only limited data are available) are doing better than younger youth in this respect, and if they have been on a permanent contract prior to unemployment, their coverage rate is

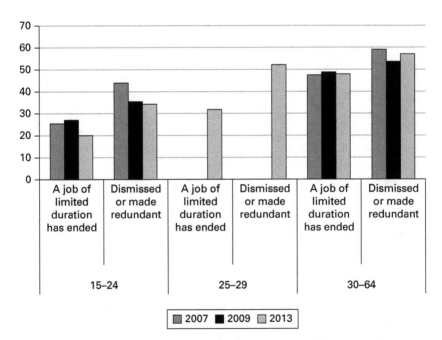

Figure 5.4 Short-term unemployed in receipt of unemployment benefit by previous contract type (temporary vs. permanent), age group, and year (2007, 2009, and 2013) in EU27 (% of all unemployed).
Source: Eurostat EU-LFS, special extracts.

in fact close to that for adults. Distinguishing now by previous contract type, temporary workers in all age groups are less likely than permanent employed to have access to unemployment benefits if they become unemployed. Previous temporary workers in the young youth group are least likely to have access. The differences across age may be due either to the explicit difference in youth access to benefits or to variations across age groups in the distribution of different types of temporary contracts or both. In line with the improvements in benefit design during the stimulus period, the situation of temporary workers seems to have improved somewhat in the first years of the crisis. However, the positive development stalled and indeed turned negative during austerity. This confirms our previously mentioned findings that national and supranational responses to the exclusion of certain labor market groups from benefit access were not sustained.

Figure 5.5 shows the benefit coverage of youth as a share of adults for all EU27 countries with complete data for 2013. With a few exceptions (RO, LT, and EE), in the majority of countries youth are considerably less likely to receive unemployment benefits than adults. On average, younger youth have a coverage rate corresponding to 30% of that of adults. Coverage for older youth corresponds to 70% of the adult rate. Regarding young youth in Germany, the United Kingdom, Belgium, and Austria, the coverage is approximately one-half that of adults. The examples of the United Kingdom and Germany show that for youth coverage, universal basic benefit schemes (as second-tier benefits) work relatively well. However, the benefits payable under these schemes are means tested and relatively low. In all other countries with available information, the younger youth share compared to adults lies under 40%, while it is below 20% in eight countries. Among the countries with very low youth coverage, the majority also have high temporary employment shares among youth, which points to a vicious relationship between flexibility and security. It is important to square these findings with youth unemployment rates, generosity of benefits, and other transition options such as apprenticeships or training or education with compensation.

Figure 5.6 shows relative changes in benefit coverage during the crisis period for young youth using 2007 as the basis. For ease of readability, we only display data for 2009 (the year of the recession when most money was spent on stimulus measures) and the most recent available year, 2013. The majority of countries with available information saw an increase in unemployment benefit coverage of youth during the first part of the crisis, with the most pronounced increases occurring in Slovenia, Portugal, Denmark, and Spain. Both improvements in access to unemployment benefit systems and also, importantly, changing characteristics of newly unemployed during the crisis will have played a role here.[21] When we compare 2007 precrisis data with 2013 austerity-period data, we see

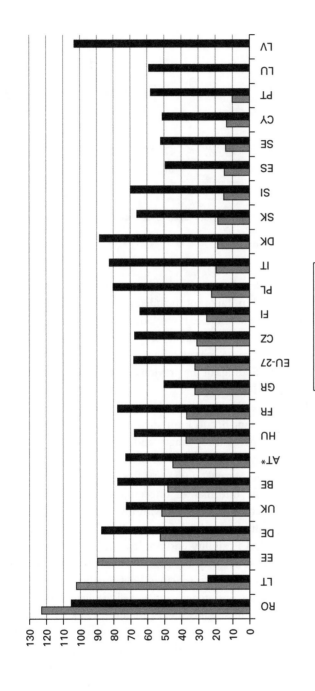

Figure 5.5 Benefit coverage of youth (aged 15–24 and 25–29 years) as share of adults (aged 30–64 years) by country, 2013.
Source: Eurostat EU-LFS, special extracts.

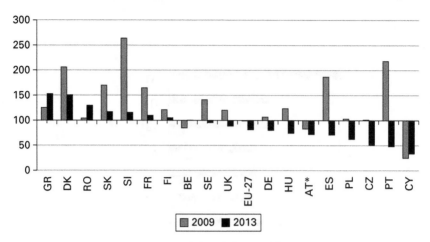

Figure 5.6 Evolution of benefit coverage for youth (aged 15–24 years) by country during crisis (stimulus and austerity periods); 2007 = 100.
Source: Eurostat EU-LFS, special extracts.

that only for a limited number of countries is this positive coverage trend still visible. It is most pronounced in Italy (not included in the figure), Greece, and Denmark—countries that have medium to low relative coverage rates of youth as compared to adults (see Figure 5.5). Benefit coverage was lower in 2013 than in 2007 in Spain, Portugal, and Cyprus, among others.

Table 5.4 summarizes the findings of the previous analysis, also including information for older youth and adults.

The analysis in this chapter has highlighted two important issues. First, it has emerged that it is important not to limit such a study to youth between ages 15 and 24 years or to merge the younger and older (aged 25–29 years) youth groups. Older youth have been shown to be better off than younger youth in terms of external (but not internal) numerical flexibility, although we still lack detailed and age-specific information on compensation during short-time working. Older youth are also better off with regard to income security. At the same time, both youth groups differ from adults in that they are more affected by external numerical flexibility and are less likely to enjoy internal numerical flexibility or income security. Second, this analysis has highlighted the complexity of unemployment benefit schemes; how greatly they vary across Europe in terms of both access and generosity, as well as availability of secondary schemes; and their frequent adjustment (not always in a strategic way, as seems to have been the case during the economic recession of 2008–2009). In this regard, comparative analysis on the dimension of benefit access is difficult. Attempts to create "simple" indices for benefit coverage—as they exist for benefit generosity—have so far not been successful (Alphametrics Ltd. 2009). The data testify to this complexity. Indeed, because the EU-LFS (in addition to

Table 5.4 Relative change in access to unemployment insurance and assistance benefits for EU27 countries before crisis (2007) and in stimulus (2009) and austerity (2013) periods

Age group (years)		Substantial decrease in access	Substantial increase in access	Missing data	EU27 (relative)	EU27 (absolute)
15–24	2009	CY	EL, SE, FR, SK, ES, DK, PT, SI, IT	IE, NL, BG, EE, LT, LU, LV, MT	99	−0.1
	2013	CY, PT, CZ, PL, ES, AT (2012), HU	RO, DK, EL, IT		81	−3.3
25–29	2009	EL	PL, UK, PT, CY, ES, SI, IT, RO	IE, NL, BG, EE, LT, LU, MT	100	0.1
	2013	EL, SE, AT (2012)	UK, PL, RO, SI, IT		85	−5.4
30–64	2009	LU	IT, PT, BG, LV, ES, EE, LT, MT	IE, NL	102	0.9
	2013	MT, RO	UK, ES, IT		104	1.7

Notes: Cut-off point for substantial decrease is <75% on 2007 value and for substantial increase is >125% on 2007 value. Duration of unemployment 1 or 2 months. Registered with PES and receiving benefits or assistance as percentage of all unemployed.
Source: Eurostat EU-LFS, special extracts.

other potential comparability weaknesses) does not allow a distinction between insurance and assistance benefits, we questioned the reliability of the information on benefit coverage rates in a cross-national perspective and therefore only used relative change within countries in our analysis.

5.5. CONCLUSIONS

The previous analysis has illustrated that youth are not only more likely to hold temporary contracts with limited job security and to experience unemployment with potential long-term scarring effects but also less likely to have access to unemployment benefits than adults. Limited unemployment benefit coverage comes about due to their lacking, or shorter-term, labor market experience, which translates into difficulties in fulfilling the eligibility conditions for access to unemployment benefits, given that these schemes are still predominantly modeled on so-called standard employment. This combination of external numerical flexibility and lower income security during unemployment can be termed a vicious relationship between flexibility and security and seems to be the predominant long-term trend despite temporary improvements during the economic recession (2008–2009).

In light of surging youth unemployment—and indeed a youth unemployment crisis—in a number of European countries, concern about the previously overlooked explicit or implicit limited access of youth to unemployment benefit schemes emerged on the international and supranational agenda (e.g., of the OECD and the European Commission). The previous focus on supply-side measures was no longer deemed very fruitful, given the lack of realistic possibilities to include large numbers of youth in employment again within a reasonable period of time. Several European countries—particularly, but not exclusively, during the economic recession (2008–2009)—accordingly improved income security for youth. More generally, temporary workers also experienced improvements with regard to access to and the generosity of unemployment benefit schemes. This was achieved by relaxing qualifying criteria, offering lump-sum or one-off payments, and increasing benefit levels or benefit duration. However, already during the economic recession (2008–2009), the reforms in terms of unemployment benefits not only took the direction of greater generosity. Although no countries restricted access to benefits during the stimulus period, and only Ireland cut benefit levels, a sizable number of countries shortened the duration of benefits. In the second crisis period (2010–2014), characterized by austerity policies, eligibility was tightened and benefit levels were reduced in many countries. There was still a focus in a few countries on improving the income security of youth, though usually conditional on participation in education or training. Increased coupling of benefit receipt with enforcement of education or training components for youth seems to be a more general recent trend according to our analysis. These developments have been summarized in Table 5.2.

More activity in relation to changing unemployment benefit policies is recorded for Southern European and Central-Eastern European welfare systems, the bulk of which were affected more severely by (youth) unemployment and at the same time had more limited unemployment benefit provisions than corporatist and Northern European countries. Several of the countries that were recommended to implement fiscal consolidation and structural reforms feature in Table 5.2 and for the most part show a profile of expanding eligibility during the severe recession of 2008–2009 and tightening conditions again at least on some dimensions thereafter, illustrating the short-term nature of upward adjustments.

Using the EU-LFS data on access to unemployment benefits and notwithstanding the limitations of these data (especially compositional effects, besides changes in access due to changing eligibility), our analysis reveals—in line with the institutional changes outlined previously—an improved situation in coverage for both the youth and adult groups during the economic recession of 2008–2009 (for details, see Table 5.4). When we take into account the austerity period, we see that on European average, both younger and older youth are worse off than before the Great Recession. This is not the case for adults. Accordingly, we can see that the benefit coverage of youth, which is considerably lower than that of adults to start with, has decreased further in a number of countries. This outcome highlights the weaknesses in the system for protecting against shocks and illustrates that the current design of unemployment benefit systems—despite short-term adjustments—tends to protect older workers with more secure employment contracts as opposed to younger workers, who carry the bulk of labor market flexibilization and at the same time lack an income-security cushion. This finding corroborates longer term dualization trends in labor market and social security systems between those who are well protected (more often people in standard employment) and those who are poorly protected (more often people in nonstandard employment), including along the lines of age, as highlighted, for example, by Seeleib-Kaiser, Saunders, and Naczyk (2012) for Germany and the United Kingdom.

Reliable unemployment benefits of a certain generosity and duration make it possible to search for an adequate job. Income security during transitions thus can facilitate a better match between skills and occupation instead of forcing unemployed youth to take the first best option—including informal or casual labor that will not contribute to increasing the tax and contribution base for funding social security schemes in the future. More comprehensive and reliable unemployment benefit coverage can also have other positive effects—both from the viewpoint of the individual and from that of wider society—in that it might place youth in a situation of independence from their families, in which they can consider forming families of their own. The trends we are witnessing and that were already evident before the Great Recession imply, however, that these functions of social protection are being weakened.

When examining the interface of flexibility and security in a comparative perspective, it is important to consider the context and potential functional equivalents. A case in point here are countries such as Spain, Portugal, Cyprus, and Slovakia, which combine very high youth unemployment and high temporary employment shares (external numerical flexibility) with very low relative benefit coverage rates (income security). On the other hand, the low benefit coverage rate for young youth in Denmark might be less problematic in light of Denmark's relatively small youth unemployment population and its generous education allowance and comparatively generous social assistance—both of which can act as functional equivalents. Similarly, short-time working measures also acted as functional equivalents to unemployment benefits during the period under observation, and young people were relatively well represented. Short-time working measures were newly introduced in a number of countries (often temporarily) and were also expanded to include new groups of workers. Such measures are an instrument of internal numerical flexibility that enables job preservation while at the same time often cushioning working-time reductions to a certain degree and thereby granting some income security.

In summary, although virtuous relationships between flexibility and security were strengthened for youth and other disadvantaged labor market groups in the first part of the crisis—when these groups had been severely affected by unemployment—this remained a short-term trend in most cases. In overemphasizing labor market flexibility to the detriment of income security, the more recent developments point again to trade-offs and vicious relationships and thereby continue the precrisis trend toward dualization and segmentation in accordance with age, gender, and other sociodemographic characteristics.

NOTES

1 We thank Ute Klammer, Igor Guardiancich, Martin Seeleib-Kaiser, Paola Villa, and Traute Meyer, as well as the participants at the Turin and Krakow STYLE meetings, for very comprehensive and useful comments on earlier versions of this chapter.

2 Notable exceptions are two studies commissioned by the European Parliament on indicators for monitoring the coverage of social security systems for people in flexible employment (Alphametrics Ltd. 2005, 2009).

3 Clasen and Clegg (2011) and Lefresne (2008), for example, provide country case studies addressing the extent to which benefit schemes have adapted—or have failed to adapt—in recent decades to the major changes affecting labor markets.

4 The Lisbon Strategy was launched by the European Commission in 2000, listing among its aims the generation of growth and of more and better jobs; in 2010, it was replaced by the Europe 2020 strategy for "smart, sustainable and inclusive growth."

5 See, for example, the discussion on the single open-ended contract, which, however, has been ardently criticized by ETUC.

6 For instance, opening them up to more firms than previously; less bureaucratic access conditions; and temporary increases in the level, duration, and/or coverage of public financial support.

7 Greece has introduced such schemes for small and medium-sized enterprises, while Sweden has for manufacturing, for example (LABREF 2015).

8 Note, however, that because of differences in the definition and delimitation of short-time working, the EU-LFS figures diverge somewhat from other available figures, including OECD and national-level data.

9 Based on country-specific information from OECD *Benefits and Wages*, 12 EU countries have unemployment assistance schemes (AT, DE, EE, EL, ES, FI, FR, IE, MT, PT, SE, and UK). However, in countries that do not have an unemployment assistance scheme, social assistance can act as a functional equivalent, although it is potentially more stigmatizing.

10 Examples are Estonia, Greece, and Portugal (OECD Benefits and Wages).

11 For example, in Ireland, Job Allowance is not available to those who are younger than age 18 years or who have been out of school for less than 3 months. It can, however, be paid to those in ALMPs or with dependents

(European Commission 2011a). In both Austria and Ireland, unemployment assistance cannot be accessed directly but, rather. only after unemployment insurance benefits have been exhausted.

12 EPL is another area of reform that is important for understanding this topic. However, we confine ourselves here to an analysis of policies and practices related to income security because this in itself is quite voluminous and complex. Furthermore, focusing on income security measures prioritizes the security offered to people outside of the working relationship and not just to those in work (as in the case of EPL).

13 Changes with regard to contributions that took place in a number of countries are not reviewed here because they do not usually have a direct impact on the coverage of nonstandard workers. They can, however, have an indirect impact if they create incentives to hire individuals on standard rather than nonstandard contracts (see, e.g., Spain, where in the past the government has tried to encourage employers to hire individuals on regular contracts by reducing related contributions).

14 Unemployment assistance in Spain is usually restricted to specific labor market groups, such as unemployed persons with family responsibilities or older workers. The special benefit introduced in January 2009 was abolished in February 2011; it had covered approximately 700,000 unemployed people (Sanz de Miguel 2011).

15 Denmark formerly had a comparatively long universal duration of unemployment insurance benefits of 4 years; in 2010, this was reduced to 2 years.

16 Labor market integration, for example, is promoted through one-off benefits, special benefits for the young, and benefits for partial and temporary employment (for details, see MISSOC 2014).

17 Given its level, Danish social assistance can be viewed as a functional equivalent to unemployment benefits.

18 It is important to note here that it is challenging to compile extremely comprehensive data on these developments. The difficulty lies in the frequent changes to policy, in the time limits imposed on some policies, and in the time that is needed to establish the impact of general policies on youth. Here, we draw on MISSOC and LABREF as sources, in addition to all publications that to our knowledge are available on the topic at the time of writing. However, our study represents a first effort at mapping this policy landscape, and we believe that more work is needed to fully complete the analysis. We do not distinguish between different causes for unemployment benefit reforms; although most will have been directly linked to the (unemployment) crisis, in some countries changes might also be part of a longer term reform agenda.

19 This allows us to get around issues such as varying average duration of unemployment (different long-term unemployment rates), differences in duration of unemployment insurance benefits, and timing of granting of unemployment assistance benefits across countries.

20 Differences in the wording of survey questions across countries play a crucial role here. Immervoll, Marianna, and Mira D'Ercole (2004) show for selected countries that the figures on unemployment benefit receipt rates from administrative data sources differ substantially from those from labor force surveys, with no clear direction in difference.

21 For instance, men were more affected by unemployment than women in the first part of the crisis, whereas—due to being more often in standard employment—they are usually more likely to fulfill eligibility criteria for unemployment benefits.

REFERENCES

Alphametrics Ltd. 2005. "Feasibility Study: Indicators on Coverage of Social Security Systems for People in Flexible Employment." Study commissioned by the European Commission, VC/2003/0228. Royston: Alphametrics Ltd.

Alphametrics Ltd. 2009. "Flexicurity: Indicators on the Coverage of Certain Social Protection Benefits for Persons in Flexible Employment in the European Union." Study commissioned by the European Commission, VC/2007/0780. Royston: Alphametrics Ltd.

Anxo, Dominique, and Jacqueline O'Reilly. 2000. "Working-Time Regimes and Transitions in Comparative Perspective." In *Working-Time Changes. Social Integration Through Transitional Labour Markets,* edited by Jacqueline O' Reilly, Inmaculada Cebrián, and Michel Lallement, 61–92. Cheltenham, UK: Elgar.

Arpaia, Alfonso, Nicola Curci, Eric Meyermans, Jörg Peschner, and Fabiana Pierini. 2010. "Short Time Working Arrangements as Response to Cyclical Fluctuations." Occasional Papers 64. Brussels: European Union.

Burroni, Luigi, and Maarten Keune. 2011. "Flexicurity: A Conceptual Critique." *European Journal of Industrial Relations* 17 (1): 75–91.

Clasen, Jochen, and Daniel Clegg, eds. 2011. *Regulating the Risk of Unemployment: National Adaptations to Post-Industrial Labour Markets in Europe.* Oxford: Oxford University Press.

Council of the European Union. 2010. "Council Decision of 21 October 2010 on Guidelines for the Employment Policies of the Member States (2010/707/ EU)." *Official Journal of the European Union L* 308: 46–51.

Council of the European Union. 2015. "Council Decision (EU) 2015/1848 on Guidelines for the Employment Policies of the Member States for 2015." *Official Journal of the European Union L* 268: 28–32.

Del Monte, Micaela, and Thomas Zandstra. 2014. "Common Unemployment Insurance Scheme for the Euro Area." Cost of Non-Europe Report PE 510.984. Brussels: European Parliamentary Research Service, European Added Value Unit.

Dullien, Sebastian. 2013. "A Euro-Area Wide Unemployment Insurance as an Automatic Stabilizer: Who Benefits and Who Pays?" Paper prepared for the European Commission (DG-EMPL). Brussels: European Commission.

Eurofound. 2003. *Flexibility and Social Protection: Reconciling Flexible Employment Patterns Over the Active Life Cycle with Security for Individuals.* Luxembourg: Publications Office of the European Union.

Eurofound. 2013. *Young People and Temporary Employment in Europe.* Luxembourg: Publications Office of the European Union.

European Commission. 2007. "Towards Common Principles of Flexicurity: More and Better Jobs Through Flexibility and Security." Communication from the Commission COM (2007) 359 final. http://eur-lex.europa.eu/legal-content/EN/TXT/?uri=COM:2007:0498:FIN

European Commission. 2009. "Labour Flows, Transitions and Unemployment Duration." In *Employment in Europe 2009*, 47–103. Luxembourg: Office for Official Publications of the European Communities.

European Commission. 2010a. "An Agenda for New Skills and Jobs: A European Contribution Towards Full Employment." Communication from the Commission COM (2010) 682 final. http://eur-lex.europa.eu/legal-content/EN/TXT/?uri=COM:2010:0682:FIN

European Commission. 2010b. "Labour Flows, Transitions and Unemployment Duration." In *Employment in Europe 2010*, 75–107. Luxembourg: Publications Office of the European Union.

European Commission. 2010c. *Labour Market and Wage Developments in 2009.* European Economy 5 (provisional version). Luxembourg: Publications Office of the European Union.

European Commission. 2011a. *Adapting Unemployment Benefits to the Economic Cycle 2011.* European Employment Observatory Review. Luxembourg: Publications Office of the European Union.

European Commission. 2011b. *Labour Market Developments in Europe, 2011.* European Economy 2. Brussels: Directorate-General of Economic and Financial Affairs.

European Commission. 2011c. *Youth Employment Measures 2010.* European Employment Observatory Review. Luxembourg: Publications Office of the European Union.

European Commission. 2014. *Stimulating Job Demand: The Design of Effective Hiring Subsidies in Europe 2014.* European Employment Policy Observatory Review. Luxembourg: Publications Office of the European Union.

European Trade Union Confederation. 2007. "Flexicurity will get nowhere without reinforcing rights for workers, says the ETUC" Press Release 13.09.2007. Brussels: European Trade Union Confederation. https://www.etuc.org/en/pressrelease/flexicurity-will-get-nowhere-without-reinforcing-rights-workers-says-etuc

Eurostat EU-LFS. n.d. European Union Labour Force Survey data, special extracts. http://ec.europa.eu/eurostat/web/microdata/european-union-labour-force-survey

Gangl, Markus. 2004. "Welfare States and the Scar Effects of Unemployment: A Comparative Analysis of the United States and West Germany." *American Journal of Sociology* 109 (6): 1319–64.

Gash, Vanessa. 2008. "Preference or Constraint? Part-Time Workers' Transitions in Denmark, France and the United Kingdom." *Work, Employment and Society* 22 (4): 655–74.

Grimshaw, Damian, and Jill Rubery. 1997. "Workforce Heterogeneity and Unemployment Benefits: The Need for Policy Reassessment in the European Union." *Journal of European Social Policy* 7 (4): 291–318.

Heise, Arne, and Hanna Lierse. 2011. *Budget Consolidation and the European Social Model: The Effects of European Austerity Programmes on Social Security Systems*. Berlin: Friedrich-Ebert-Stiftung.

Heyes, Jason. 2011. "Flexicurity, Employment Protection and the Jobs Crisis." *Work, Employment and Society* 25 (4): 642–57.

Hijzen, Alexander, and Sébastien Martin. 2012. "The Role of Short Term Working Schemes During the Global Financial Crisis and Early Recovery: A Cross Country Analysis." OECD Social, Employment and Migration Working Paper 144. Paris: OECD.

Hijzen, Alexander, and Danielle Venn. 2011. *The Role of Short-Time Work Schemes During the 2008–09 Recession*. OECD Social, Employment and Migration Working Paper 115. Paris: Organization for Economic Co-operation and Development.

Ibsen, Christian L., 2011. "Strained Compromises? Danish Flexicurity During Crisis." *Nordic Journal of Working Life Studies* 1 (1): 45–65.

Immervoll, Herwig, Pascal Marianna, and Marco Mira D'Ercole. 2004. "Benefit Coverage Rates and Household Typologies: Scope and Limitations of Tax-Benefit Indicators." OECD Social, Employment and Migration Working Paper 20. Paris: OECD.

Klammer, Ute, and Katja Tillmann. 2001. *Flexicurity: Soziale Sicherung und Flexibilisierung der Arbeits- und Lebensverhältnisse*. Düsseldorf: Ministerium für Arbeit und Soziales, Qualifikation und Technologie des Landes Nordrhein-Westfalen.

Kvist, Jon, Simon Grundt Straubinger, and Anders Freundt. 2013. "Measurement Validity in Comparative Welfare State Research: The Case of Measuring Welfare State Generosity." *European Journal of Social Security* 15 (4): 321–40.

LABREF. 2015. LABREF Labour Market Reforms database (European Commission and Employment Committee). https://webgate.ec.europa.eu/labref/public

Lefresne, Florence. 2008. "Regard comparatif sur l'indemnisation du chômage: la difficile sécurisation des parcours professionnels." Chronique Internationale de l'IRES 115. Paris: Istitut de Recherches Economiques et Sociales.

Lehndorff, Steffen, ed. 2014. *Divisive Integration: The Triumph of Failed Ideas—Revisited*. Brussels: ETUI.

Leschke, Janine. 2008. *Unemployment Insurance and Non-Standard Employment: Four European Countries in Comparison*. Wiesbaden: VS Verlag für Sozialwissenschaften.

Leschke, Janine. 2009. "The Segmentation Potential of Non-Standard Employment: A Four-Country Comparison of Mobility Patterns." *International Journal of Manpower* 30 (7): 692–715. [Special issue]

Leschke, Janine. 2013. "La crise economique a-t-elle accentué la segmentation du marché du travail et de la protection sociale? Une analyse des pays de l'UE (2008–2010)." *Revue Française des Affaires Sociales* 4: 10–33. [Special issue]

Leschke, Janine, Günther Schmid, and Dorit Griga. 2007. "On the Marriage of Flexibility and Security: Lessons from the Hartz-Reforms in Germany." In *Flexicurity and Beyond: Finding a New Agenda for the European Social Model*, edited by Henning Jørgensen and Per Kongshøj Madsen, 335–64. Copenhagen: Djøf Forlag.

Madsen, Per Kongshøj, Oscar Molina, Jesper Møller, and Mariona Lozano. 2013. "Labour Market Transitions of Young Workers in Nordic and Southern European Countries: The Role of Flexicurity." *Transfer: European Review of Labour and Research* 19 (3): 325–43.

MISSOC. 2014. "Comparative Tables." https://www.missoc.org/missoc-database/comparative-tables

Muffels, Ruud, ed. 2008. *Flexibility and Employment Security in Europe: Labour Markets in Transition*. Cheltenham, UK: Elgar.

Organization for Economic Co-operation and Development (OECD) "OECD Benefits and Wages. Country Policy Descriptions." http://www.oecd.org/els/soc/benefits-and-wages-country-specific-information.htm

Organization for Economic Co-operation and Development (OECD). 2010a. "How Good Is Part-Time Work?" In *Employment Outlook 2010*, 211–66. Paris: OECD.

Organization for Economic Co-operation and Development (OECD). 2010b. "Detailed Description of Part-Time Work Regulations and Unemployment Benefit Schemes Affecting Part-Time Workers." Supporting material for Chapter 4. "How Good Is Part-Time Work?" In *Employment Outlook 2010*. Paris: OECD.

Organization for Economic Co-operation and Development (OECD). 2011. "Income Support for the Unemployed: How Well Has the Safety-Net Held Up During the 'Great Recession'?" In *OECD Employment Outlook 2011*, 15–83. Paris: OECD.

Organization for Economic Co-operation and Development (OECD). 2013. "Protecting Jobs, Enhancing Flexibility: A New Look at Employment Protection Legislation." In *OECD Employment Outlook 2013*, 65–126. Paris: OECD.

Organization for Economic Co-operation and Development (OECD). 2014. "Non-Regular Employment, Job Security and the Labour Market Divide." In *OECD Employment Outlook 2014*, 141–209. Paris: OECD.

Organization for Economic Co-operation and Development (OECD). 2016. "OECD Indicators of Employment Protection. Annual Time Series Data 1985–2013." Paris: OECD. http://www.oecd.org/els/emp/oecdindicatorsofem ploymentprotection.htm

Sanz de Miguel, Pablo. 2011. "Government Endorses New Measures to Encourage Growth and Reduce Deficit." *EurWORK, European Observatory of Working Life*, March 1. Dublin: Eurofound. https://www.eurofound.europa.eu/is/ observatories/eurwork/articles/other/government-endorses-new-measures-to-encourage-growth-and-reduce-deficit

Schmid, Günther. 2008. *Full Employment in Europe: Managing Labour Market Transitions and Risks*. Cheltenham, UK: Elgar.

Schmid, Günther, and Bernard Gazier, eds. 2002. *The Dynamics of Full Employment: Social Integration Through Transitional Labour Markets*. Cheltenham, UK: Elgar.

Schömann, Isabelle, and Stefan Clauwaert. 2012. "The Crisis and National Labour Law Reforms: A Mapping Exercise." ETUI Working Paper 04. Brussels: European Trade Union Institute.

Schulze Buschoff, Karin, and Paula Protsch. 2008. "(A-)typical and (In-)Secure? Social Protection and 'Non-Standard' Forms of Employment in Europe." *International Social Security Review* 61 (4): 51–73.

Seeleib-Kaiser, Martin, Adam Saunders, and Marek Naczyk. 2012. "Shifting the Public–Private Mix: A New Dualization of Welfare." In *The Age of Dualization: The Changing Face of Inequality in Deindustrializing Societies*, edited by Patrick Emmenegger, Silja Häusermann, Bruno Palier, and Martin Seeleib-Kaiser, 151–75. New York: Oxford University Press.

Standing, Guy. 2002. *Beyond the New Paternalism: Basic Security as Equality*. London: Verso.

Talós, Emmerich, ed. 1999. *Atypische Beschäftigung: Internationale Trends und sozialstaatliche Regelungen*. Vienna: Manz.

Tangian, Andranik. 2007. "European Flexicurity: Concepts, Methodology and Policies." *Transfer: European Review of Labour and Research* 13 (4): 551–73.

Van Oorschot, Wim. 2013. "Comparative Welfare State Analysis with Survey-Based Benefit Recipiency Data: The 'Dependent Variable Problem' Revisited." *European Journal of Social Security* 15 (3): 224–48.

Wilthagen, Ton, and Frank Tros. 2004. "The Concept of 'Flexicurity': A New Approach to Regulating Employment and Labour Markets." *Transfer: European Review of Labour and Research* 10 (2): 166–86.

6

POLICY TRANSFER AND INNOVATION FOR BUILDING RESILIENT BRIDGES TO THE YOUTH LABOR MARKET

Maria Petmesidou and María González Menéndez

6.1. INTRODUCTION

The Great Recession has significantly aggravated problems with the labor market integration of youth that have been evident for several decades in some areas of Europe. The need to develop effective measures for sustained school-to-work (STW) transitions has become a paramount political concern on the European Union (EU) policy agenda. It has generated EU initiatives for a common focus among member states on comprehensive and integrated policies for youth at risk. This has accelerated mutual learning, policy transfer, and experimentation with new practices in order to build resilient bridges to the youth labor market. Drawing on the policy learning and transfer literature, we test the hypothesis that a distinction can be made between countries with policy machineries that facilitate both learning and experimentation with new, proactive youth employment measures and those exhibiting considerable inertia.

Our analysis covers eight EU member states (Belgium, Denmark, France, Greece, the Netherlands, Slovakia, Spain, and the United Kingdom) and one accession state (Turkey).[1] They represent a range of STW transition regimes (Walther and Pohl 2005; Hadjivassiliou et al., this volume) and welfare regimes exhibiting different levels of national performance relating to youth unemployment and its gender dimension (Gökşen et al. 2016a). The primary research consists of interviews conducted in each of the nine countries with policy experts, officials, academics, and researchers. It is complemented by an analysis of available secondary data.

We find that local/regional administrations and agencies are more likely to exchange knowledge on policy processes and tools among themselves and also to get involved in cross-country mutual policy learning. Most important, a mode of policy governance based on regional/local partnerships and networks of public services, professional bodies and education/training providers, employers, youth associations, and other stakeholders tends to stimulate policy experimentation. The role of policy entrepreneurs in promoting policy learning and transfer has also been ascertained in a few cases. However, for these manifestations of learning and innovation to yield results of sustained labor market integration of youth, a national policy environment is required that is conducive to coordinated sharing and diffusion of information and experience between different levels of administration and joint stakeholders' bodies.

Our hypothesis is proven true in this respect in that it brings to the fore a distinction between countries with more or less systematic interaction and feedback between all levels of administration—from the bottom up and vice versa—and those with poor channels of sharing and diffusion of policy knowledge. The factors accounting for the latter are, among others, overcentralized administrative structures, fragmentation/overlapping of competences, and bureaucratic inertia.

The remainder of this chapter consists of four sections. The first frames the research question and presents our conceptual and analytical framework, and the second lays out the research methodology. The third section assesses, at a macro level, the relevance of policy learning in the political/policy agenda of the countries studied and also examines the most significant channels of policy influence, transfer, and diffusion within and across various levels of governance (including the supranational level). It additionally provides a microanalysis of specific cases of more or less successful policy innovation with regard to the Youth Guarantee (YG; or a similar program) and apprenticeship schemes. We also reflect on the extent to which the gender dimension in STW transitions is taken into account in policy learning and innovation. The final section discusses the conclusions deriving from our findings.

6.2. RESEARCH QUESTION AND ANALYTICAL FRAMEWORK

Labor market and welfare policy arrangements in European countries are increasingly open to "recalibration" and transformation through complex policy learning and policy transfer routes that, as Dwyer and Ellison (2009, 390) state, "undermine traditional welfare regime characteristics, and both pluralise and deinstitutionalise sources of policy making." Available literature on policy transfer regarding work transitions has so far focused on globalization influences and transatlantic policy transfer with respect to welfare-to-work schemes and on the "iterative process" across Europe involving the adoption of "workfare" elements in social welfare policies and their subsequent adaptation within national traditions (Peck and Theodore 2001; Fergusson 2002; Dwyer and Ellison 2009). A systematic examination of policy learning and transfer across STW transition regimes at different levels of governance and with respect to the role and influence of key actors (state and nonstate, as well as supranational actors) is lacking. There has also been little research on the degree to which EU-level youth strategies since the late 2000s (particularly the Youth Opportunities Initiative) have been a "leverage" for policy learning and change—assessed in terms of the extent, direction, and effectiveness of policy innovation.

The presence of policy learning and transfer cannot be assumed to lead automatically to successful outcomes (Dwyer and Ellison 2009). Similarly, not all policy innovations are necessarily effective, and there is no clear evidence of an association between policy innovations' effectiveness and the type of policy transfer and learning, be it voluntary or coercive (Dolowitz and Marsh 2000) or soft or hard (Stone 2004). Nonetheless, some literature supports the hypothesis of a positive association between the degree of innovation/experimentation in employment policy and the strength of established processes of policy learning and transfer (Evans 2009; Legrand 2012). Accordingly, countries frequently experimenting with new, proactive youth employment measures and those exhibiting path dependence and inertia (European Commission 2011; Organization for Economic Co-operation and Development (OECD) 2015) appear to respectively exhibit stronger and weaker established processes of policy learning and transfer. In this chapter, we test this hypothesis with the aim of highlighting, for a number of European countries, institutional and governance aspects of STW transition policies that facilitate or hinder learning and innovation. We also examine EU influence in this respect.

We are interested in effective innovations, which we define as policy changes in objectives, programs, and delivery processes that are conducive to positive results with regard to the labor market and the social inclusion of youth (particularly of the most disadvantaged/disaffected young people). Our definition of (effective) innovation is in agreement with the European Commission's social innovation concept, defined as the development of "new ideas, services and models to better address social issues."[2]

Crucial, as a point of departure, is Hall's (1993, 278) definition of policy learning "as a deliberate attempt to adjust the goals or techniques of policy in response to past experience and new information." Hall further distinguishes between radical changes in the basic instruments of policy and in policy goals (second- and third-order changes, respectively), on the one hand, and piecemeal changes in the levels or settings of these instruments (first-order changes), on the other hand.[3] Also key are Streeck and Thelen's (2005) concepts for understanding institutional change, namely "layering" and "conversion." Here, we pay greater attention to the former, defined as "grafting of new elements onto an otherwise stable institutional framework," which—if it takes place for prolonged periods—can "significantly alter the overall trajectory of an institution's development" (Thelen 2004, 35; see also Hacker 2004). Streeck and Thelen's approach seeks to show that significant innovative, path-departing reforms can occur beyond "critical junctures" and/or strong "outside pressures." In this sense, it provides an insight into how Hall's first- and second-order changes may, in the long term, extensively alter the core objectives and role of an institution—resulting in radical change. These approaches identify major mechanisms of change and develop partly overlapping, partly complementary typologies.

In addition, we refer to a range of pathways along which policy change takes place: (1) through a more or less intentional policy learning and transfer process that—according to Dolowitz and Marsh (2000)—could consist in "copying," "emulation," and/or "inspiration" drawn from abroad; (2) in a context in which outside triggers may open up "windows of opportunity" for domestic policy entrepreneurs to push forward reform agendas (see Kingdon 1984; Roberts and King 1996); and (3) as a more or less coerced policy change and transfer (e.g., where EU funding or bailout deals are provided subject to certain conditions). The combination of mechanisms and pathways of policy change and innovation provide our analytical framework.

6.3. SELECTION/GROUPING OF COUNTRIES AND METHODOLOGY

We used a combination of three criteria for selecting the nine countries under study. First, we included countries that joined the EU at different stages of enlargement, and we also added an accession country. Second, drawing on Walther and Pohl's (2005) study of STW transition regimes and Gangl's (2001) analysis of labor market entry patterns, we selected countries spanning the entire range of categories differentiated by these authors. Walther and Pohl identified five STW transition regimes: the universalistic regime of Nordic countries, the employment-centered regime of Continental countries, the liberal regime of Anglo-Saxon countries, the subprotective regime of Mediterranean countries, and the post-socialist or transitional regime (with subprotective traits) in Central and Eastern European countries. In our study, these categories are represented, respectively, by Denmark; the United Kingdom; Belgium, France, and the Netherlands; Greece, Spain, and Turkey; and Slovakia. Labor market entry patterns provide a cross-cutting dimension: In Belgium, France, Spain, and the United Kingdom, labor market entry is driven by internal labor markets (ILM); in Denmark and the Netherlands, it is driven by occupational labor markets (OLM); and in Greece, it is driven by a mix of very high employment risks at the outset of careers with little volatility once in employment. The stronger role of job experience and worker mobility in ILM- compared to OLM-driven labor markets makes youth labor market outcomes much less favorable in the former case (Gangl 2001).

The third criterion concerns the scale of the youth problem in Europe, assessed in terms of the total and long-term youth unemployment rates and the poverty and social exclusion risks faced by youth not in employment, education, or training (NEETs). According to the STW transition regime literature, the severity of the youth problem varies significantly across regimes, as does the propensity to engage in policy experimentation at the national and local levels of government. This is the case even though innovative practices do not always imply successful youth employment outcomes—either in terms of efficiency (achieving the highest possible youth employment rate) or in terms of equity (significantly lowering the incidence of NEETs and the risk of poverty). Our aim is to highlight the factors driving or hindering effective innovation in terms of youth labor market outcomes.

As shown in Figure 6.1, Greece and Spain exhibit youth unemployment rates of greater than 50% and also experience comparatively high long-term youth

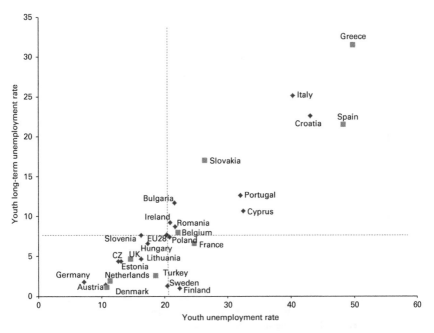

Figure 6.1 Comparison of countries on the severity of the "youth problem," as indicated by youth total and long-term unemployment rates (aged 15–24 years), 2014/2015. The youth unemployment rate refers to the 2015 annual rate, whereas the youth long-term unemployment rate refers to the 2014 rate. Unemployment is considered long term if its duration exceeds 12 months.
Note: We focus on the youth age range 15–24 years because this is the most commonly used age bracket in the youth unemployment official statistics of most EU countries.
Source: Figure drawn by the authors on the basis of Eurostat's EU-LFS and YOUTH data.

unemployment. Slovakia shares some similarities with Greece and Spain in that it scores highly on both these indicators. Denmark, the Netherlands, Germany, and Austria exhibit the lowest youth unemployment and long-term unemployment rates. Belgium and France have higher rates than the latter countries because they have been affected by rising total and long-term youth unemployment, although not as acutely as is the case in Southern Europe. The United Kingdom performs better than the previously mentioned two Continental countries but less well than the best performers (Germany, Austria, Denmark, and Netherlands).[4] In Turkey, the youth problem appears to be less severe than in most Continental, Eastern, and Southern European countries.[5]

Regarding NEETs and the at-risk-of-poverty and/or social exclusion rates (particularly among young females), the United Kingdom performs worse than the Continental and Scandinavian countries (Figures 6.2 and 6.3), with young women facing a higher risk of poverty and social exclusion and of being NEET. Belgium, Denmark, and France exhibit no substantial gender differences. In fact, in Denmark, young women fare slightly better than men in terms of these dimensions. In Greece and Spain, the "youth problem" in terms of disengagement from education, training, and employment is most acute. Greece is an outlier because it exhibits one of the highest NEET rates and risk of poverty and/

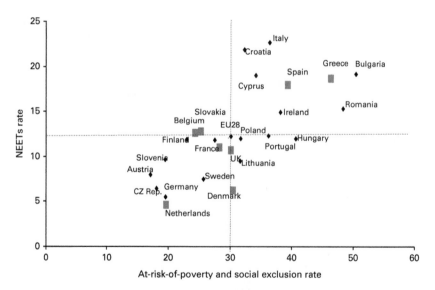

Figure 6.2 Comparison of countries on the severity of the "youth problem," as indicated by the NEET rate and the at-risk-of-poverty and/or social exclusion rate (males aged 15–24 years). The NEETs rates refers to 2014 and the at-risk-of-poverty and/or social exclusion rates to 2013; there are no data for Turkey on youth at-risk-of-poverty or social exclusion.

Note: The poverty and/or social exclusion indicator refers to the share of youth in at least one of the following conditions: (1) living below the poverty line (defined as 60% of median equivalized income); (2) experiencing severe material deprivation; and (3) living in a household with very low work intensity. This is a household indicator that is sensitive to cases where young people leave the parental home early (e.g., in Denmark).

Source: Figure drawn by the authors on the basis of the Eurostat YOUTH data.

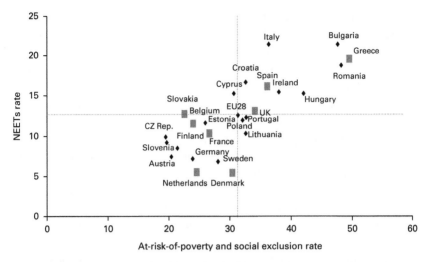

Figure 6.3 Comparison of countries on the severity of the "youth problem," as indicated by the NEET rate and the at-risk-of-poverty and/or social exclusion rate (females aged 15–24 years), The NEETs rates refers to 2014 and the at-risk-of-poverty and/or social exclusion rates refer to 2013; there are no data for Turkey on youth at-risk-of-poverty or social exclusion.
Note: The poverty and/or social exclusion indicator refers to the share of youth in at least one of the following conditions: (1) living below the poverty line (defined as 60% of median equivalized income); (2) experiencing severe material deprivation; and (3) living in a household with very low work intensity. This is a household indicator that is sensitive to cases where young people leave the parental home early (e.g., in Denmark).
Source: Figure drawn by the authors on the basis of the Eurostat YOUTH data.

or social exclusion among the young (particularly among young women) (see Mascherini, this volume).

Denmark, the United Kingdom, and the Netherlands exhibit the shortest (first) job search periods for the young, with no significant gender differences (approximately 5–11 months for 75% of the examined youth cohorts who had entered the labor market). Belgium and France follow with 16–27 months, with no significant gender differences either. The longest search periods are found in Greece and Spain (36–38 months, with a significant gender gap—in favor of men—in Spain). The transition to a first job is shorter in Slovakia, albeit with very pronounced gender differences (17 months for men and 29 months for women) (see Flek, Hála, and Mysíková, this volume).[6]

The nine countries we selected on the basis of the three criteria mentioned previously were divided into two groups. Group A is composed of Denmark, the Netherlands, and the United Kingdom, whereas Group B is made up of Belgium, France, Greece, Slovakia, Spain, and Turkey. Group A countries have lower youth unemployment rates and shorter job search periods for first entry into the labor market compared to Group B.

In the light of the analytical framework discussed previously, we examine differences and similarities between (and within) the two groups of countries. The analysis draws on data and information obtained through semistructured, in-depth interviews carried out in each of the nine countries with key stakeholders involved in the design and implementation of youth-related policies (high-ranking officials in ministries and relevant public services; in trade unions and employers' associations; in vocational education and apprenticeship services; and in youth organizations, firms, and other major relevant bodies), as well as with academics and researchers with a good grasp of policy issues and challenges regarding youth labor markets; policy learning and transfer within and across countries; and policy negotiation, planning, and implementation.

In countries with highly centralized policymaking processes, the majority of interviewees were selected from among officials and other stakeholders at the national level, whereas in countries with devolved power in policymaking, the interviews were conducted with informants at the regional/local level. A common template laid out the issues to be covered, but the interviews were adapted to each specific national case.

Table 6.1 depicts the number of interviews conducted in each country.[7] These took place in two rounds (June–September 2015 and December 2015 to January 2016). In the second round, case studies of schemes with an innovative potential were carried out. Because a comprehensive and integrated approach to STW transition (including apprenticeships) is at the forefront of EU initiatives providing a (more or less) convergent trend among member countries (Hadjivassiliou et al., this volume), the case studies selected in each country consisted of interventions under the YG (or similar scheme easing transition to the labor market) and apprenticeship schemes introducing innovation in the structure, management, and knowledge base of vocational education and training (VET). In some cases, persons interviewed during the first phase of the study were also included among the interviewees of the second phase. In the light of our thematic focus, the national teams also scrutinized the available literature for each country with the aim of understanding the major planks of academic and public debate on facilitators of or constraints on policy innovation.

6.4. THE DYNAMICS OF POLICY CHANGE AND INNOVATION

In this section, we lay out and compare the major channels of policy influence, transfer, and diffusion within and across various levels of governance (including the supranational level) in the countries studied. Specific instances of innovative schemes in each country are also analyzed. The aim is to highlight major aspects of institutional structures, governance patterns, and interactions among main players in policy design and delivery that facilitate or hinder policy learning and innovation.

6.4.1. "Enablers" of and "Barriers" to Policy Learning and Innovation

Institutional (and process) "enablers" and "barriers" in the sphere of policy learning and innovation are examined in the nine countries with regard to whether the political/policy environment is conducive or not to learning and

Table 6.1 Countries examined by STW regime, interviews conducted, and in-depth studies of specific schemes with innovative potential

| Countries and STW transition regimes | No. of (semistructured) interviews[a] | | Schemes studied in Phase 2 | |
	Phase 1	Phase 2	Schemes with holistic approach	Innovative apprenticeship schemes
Group A				
DK *Universalistic*	6	4	YG (in place before launching of EU initiative)	Operation Apprenticeship
UK *Liberal*	11	7	Youth Contract (similar to YG)	Apprenticeship Trailblazers
NL *Employment-centered (OLM)*	25		Pact for Youth-Unemployment-Free Zone in Mid-Brabant (South Netherlands)	Collaborative initiative in Amsterdam region
Group B				
FR *Employment-centered (ILM)*	8	8	Schemes integrated into YG	Second Chance Schools
BE *Employment-centered (ILM)*	3	4	Regional schemes for YG	JEEP (Jeunes, École, Emploi) program
Subprotective				
ES[b]	11	14	YG in three localities (Avilés, Gijón, Lugones)	Pilots of dual training in Asturias region
EL	14	7	Voucher for Labor Market Entry (main strand of YG so far)	Experimental Vocational Training Schools (tourism sector)
SK[c]	7	6	National Project Community Centers (Roma communities)	Dual VET initiated by Automotive Industry Association
TR	11	3	On-the-Job Training Program	Apprenticeship Program (dual system)

[a]The number of interviews varies depending on the scope of the literature available on the issues studied (for each country) and from which valuable information could be obtained.
[b]According to Gangl (2001), Spain clusters with the Northern European ILM countries (with high labor mobility), but it also shares the characteristic of family support to the young with the other Southern European countries under the subprotective regime.
[c]Post-socialist, but similarities with Southern European countries.
ILM, internal labor markets; OLM, occupational labor markets; STW, school-to-work.

innovation; the main mechanisms of policy change and innovation; and the pathways of learning and transfer. The information is presented schematically in Tables 6.2 and 6.3.

Denmark and the United Kingdom stand out as the countries whose policy environments are most oriented toward evidence-based policymaking. In Denmark, corporatist learning supports a highly coordinated sharing and diffusion of knowledge between different levels of administration and joint stakeholders' bodies. Recent reform in the apprenticeship-based VET system responds to the pressure for employment-relevant education and training in line with the requirements of the flexicurity model,[8] which—in a context of high reservation wages and collectively agreed minimum wages—creates strong pressures for young workers to perform productive work immediately after being hired. The strengthening of the link between benefit provisions to the young and the obligation to participate in education—in parallel with the introduction of a grade requirement for entering vocational education—placed VET at the center of the growth agenda of Danish politics.

Denmark is more of an exporter of policy ideas to other EU countries, particularly with regard to active labor market policies (ALMPs) and the concept of flexicurity. However, soft forms of learning across countries and through supranational channels are also important; for example, inspiration from the Swiss VET model has influenced reform in Denmark. As to the mechanism of change, the 2014 reform of the Danish VET system constitutes a case of institutional "layering," in which an element of "merit" (namely the "grade requirement") is attached to the existing institutional setup. The aim is to improve the quality and the perceived value of VET at the expense of its social integration role regarding youngsters who fail to achieve mainstream education standards. The latter function is undertaken by other programs targeted at disadvantaged youth (immigrants and youth with working-class backgrounds). In this way, however, disadvantaged young people run the risk of leaving education with inadequate qualifications. Gender considerations with regard to policy innovation play a minor role in Denmark, given the limited differences in unemployment rates for young men and young women. Recently, information campaigns and the use of student counselors have sought to address gender differences in educational choice. Additional mentoring services for young mothers have also been introduced (Gökşen et al. 2016a, 48–50).

In the United Kingdom, a strong liberal tradition impedes coordinated policy diffusion and feedback. Instead, we find high reliance on voluntarist learning (peer-to-peer learning, codes of conduct, etc.). EU initiatives and program-funding eligibility criteria are not a major stimulus of policy innovation. Cross-country learning and emulation concern mostly Anglo-Saxon and OECD countries. However, devolution of powers to the home nations has arguably created favorable conditions for the diffusion of good practices and has promoted a closer dialogue with EU policy initiatives by the devolved entities

Table 6.2 Aspects of policy learning and innovation (Group A countries)

Country	Political/policy environment conducive to policy learning, transfer, innovation (A) "Enablers"	Political/policy environment conducive to policy learning, transfer, innovation (A) "Barriers"	Pathways of learning and transfer (B) Within-country policy learning — Coordinated learning	Pathways of learning and transfer (B) Within-country policy learning — Voluntarist learning (peer-to-peer, codes of conduct, etc.)	Pathways of learning and transfer (B) Cross-country mutual learning (inspiration, copying, experimental emulation, etc.)	Pathways of learning and transfer (B) EU influence (OMC, European Semester, funding conditionality, "bailout" deals)	Mechanisms of policy learning and transfer (C) Incremental adjustment, fine-tuning, "layering," and/or redeployment of old institutions/measures for new purposes	Mechanisms of policy learning and transfer (C) Changes in policy instruments; new innovative schemes	Mechanisms of policy learning and transfer (C) Changes in specific or broad policy goals
Denmark	Robust evidence-based policymaking under corporatist governance	Weakening corporatist governance	Systematic bottom-up/top-down policy learning	Some evidence	Some inspiration (e.g., Swiss model for VET reform in Denmark) "Exporters" of policy ideas in the EU (ALMPs, flexicurity model)	EU program funding conditionality not a major stimulus "Exporters" of ALMPs	Strong evidence (e.g., of "layering")	—	Strengthening effectiveness of VET in meeting skills needs (at the expense of social integration role)
Netherlands	No strong tradition of ex-ante or ex-post evaluation research	Centralized youth policy governance cannot address regional/local challenges	Influence goes both ways, but more bottom-up initiatives through networking	As above	As above	As above	Evidence of incremental adjustment	Experimentation with network governance	"Triple helix" form of governance

(continued)

Table 6.2 Continued

Country	Political/policy environment conducive to policy learning, transfer, innovation (A)		Pathways of learning and transfer (B)				Mechanisms of policy learning and transfer (C)		
	"Enablers"	"Barriers"	Within-country policy learning		Cross-country mutual learning (inspiration, copying, experimental emulation, etc.)	EU influence (OMC, European Semester, funding conditionality, "bailout" deals)	Incremental adjustment, fine-tuning, "layering," and/or redeployment of old institutions/measures for new purposes	Changes in policy instruments; new innovative schemes	Changes in specific or broad policy goals
			Coordinated learning	Voluntarist learning (peer-to-peer, codes of conduct, etc.)					
United Kingdom	Robust evidence-based policymaking—Use of piloting, controlled experiments, etc.	Liberal tradition and market competition do not favor diffusion or feedback for strategic decision-making	Evidence used for fine-tuning—Devolution facilitates policy learning cross-regionally	High reliance on voluntarist learning—Dense network of think tanks and policy communities	Influence of OECD and other Anglo-Saxon countries—Apprenticeship Trailblazer initiative may imply emulation of other EU countries	As above	Strong evidence of incremental adjustment and fine-tuning	—	Apprenticeship Trailblazers: Shift of focus from education providers to employers

OMC, open method of coordination (a soft form of EU intergovernmental policy learning and regulation; see Smith et al., this volume).
Source: Compiled on the basis of the information provided by the country reports.

Table 6.3 Aspects of policy learning and innovation (Group B countries)

Country	Political/policy environment conducive to policy learning, transfer, innovation (A)		Pathways of learning and transfer (B)				Mechanisms of policy learning and transfer (C)		
			Within-country policy learning						
	"Enablers"	"Barriers"	Coordinated learning	Voluntarist learning (peer-to-peer, codes of conduct, etc.)	Cross-country mutual learning (inspiration, copying, experimental emulation, etc.)	EU influence (OMC, European Semester, funding conditionality, "bailout" deals)	Incremental adjustment, fine-tuning, and/or redeployment of old institutions/measures for new purposes	Changes in policy instruments; new innovative schemes	Changes in specific or broad policy goals
France	Strong monitoring and evaluation tradition	Institutional stasis due to "dirigiste" governance—"Policy fatigue"	Limited: Relatively poor coordination between different institutional actors	Limited: Low involvement of employers, union activism important in policy learning	Inspiration from EU (e.g., Second Chance Schools) and other EU countries (e.g., Germany)	OMC on ALMPs—EC recommendations and EU programs have accelerated measures for youth	Incremental changes	Second Chance Schools (innovation in pedagogical principles that set in train institutional diffusion process)	
Belgium	Piloting and evaluation widespread but no systematic feedback into policy design	Fragmentation of competencies causes inconsistent cooperation across regions and with other actors	Limited cross-regional learning (Synerjob program facilitates peer-to-peer learning)		Strong influence through soft forms of learning from other EU countries	As above	Increasing cross-regional cooperation in new programs	—	
Spain	Limited evaluation, mostly linked to EU-funded programs	Fragmentation of competencies and political competition—Some policy inertia	Formal channels limited to state and autonomous communities	Limited but evidence of informal networks	EU influence strong in terms of policy goals and resources; weaker in terms of outcomes—EU channels (mutual learning, expert networks) are important	OMC on ALMPs—EC/Troika recommendations and EU program requirements	—	YG national registry (links and recentralizes data)—Increased weight of evaluation	Path shift toward dual VET

(continued)

Table 6.3 Continued

Country	Political/policy environment conducive to policy learning, transfer, innovation (A)		Pathways of learning and transfer (B)				Mechanisms of policy learning and transfer (C)		
			Within-country policy learning						
	"Enablers"	"Barriers"	Coordinated learning	Voluntarist learning (peer-to-peer, codes of conduct, etc.)	Cross-country mutual learning (inspiration, copying, experimental emulation, etc.)	EU influence (OMC, European Semester, funding conditionality, "bailout" deals)	Incremental adjustment, fine-tuning, "layering," and/or redeployment of old institutions/measures for new purposes	Changes in policy instruments; new innovative schemes	Changes in specific or broad policy goals
Greece		Excessive bureaucratization and high degree of policy inertia—Path dependence	Limited diffusion, mostly through EU influence and bailout requirements	Limited dialogue— Some diffusion by domestic policy entrepreneurs	As above	Coerced transfer under bailout deal and EU program requirements	—	—	As above
Slovakia		Party political expediency limits innovation	No systematic feedback between different institutional actors	As above	As above	EC recommendations and EU program requirements	—	Experimentation with work-based interventions at local level	As above
Turkey	Absence of evaluation and rare piloting	Overcentralized and monolithic administrative structure	Fragmented project-based solutions, no systematic feedback	Very limited	Some copying and/ or emulation in context of World Bank-funded projects and accession process, but decreasing impact of latter	Eligibility criteria of EU and World Bank-funded programs and requirements of "acquis"	Redeployment of old instruments for introducing ALMPs by PES	Establishment of Vocational Qualifications Authority	—

OMC, open method of coordination (a soft form of EU intergovernmental policy learning and regulation; see Smith et al., this volume).

Source: Compiled on the basis of the information provided by the country reports.

(e.g., Wales). Although there is a well-established tradition of robust evidence-based policymaking, backed by a dense network of epistemic/policy communities and think tanks facilitating extensive piloting, trailblazers, and so forth, there is no systematic and coordinated flow of information into high levels of (strategic) policy decision-making. Accumulated evidence is used for fine-tuning policies and for changes in policy instruments—that is, mostly for first- and second-order changes, according to Hall's (1993) approach to policy change. A shift in policy goals is emerging in the VET field with the Apprenticeship Trailblazers initiative (discussed later). Regarding gender considerations, a number of programs (among others, Women's Start-Up and Inspiring the Future) are aimed at tackling gender segregation; increasing women's presence in science, technology, engineering, and mathematics; and keeping young parents in education (Gökşen et al. 2016a, 52–53).

Compared to Denmark, corporatist learning in the Netherlands is less robust. Nevertheless, bottom-up innovations are usually introduced through concerted action between various local stakeholders, as is the case, for instance, with the Youth Starter's Grant—the largest scheme for facilitating SWT transition, run by approximately 150 municipalities; the Pact for a Youth-Unemployment-Free Zone in the Mid-Brabant region; and innovative education reform practices in Amsterdam. Such initiatives embrace the "triple-" or "multi-helix" model, which consists of collaboration, at the local level, between public administration and services, educational institutions, and the market (Bekker, van de Meer, and Muffels 2015). There is no strong tradition of controlled experiments or systematic ex-post evaluation research. However, like Denmark, the Netherlands is an exporter of good practices, such as the integrated personalized approach to youth unemployment adopted under the European Commission YG initiative. Soft forms of cross-country learning exert an influence on policy innovation in this country as well. Interregional policy transfer and emulation is highly important: For instance, the "Brainport" model of network-based regional development (South Netherlands) that emerged in the late 1990s has provided inspiration and a blueprint for local actors' innovative initiatives in the Mid-Brabant region and the Amsterdam area. The major barriers to policy change are the centralized governance of youth policies and the lack of interaction/integration between policy domains, of concrete target setting, and of impact assessment of single policies and their combined effect. Current innovative initiatives seek to tackle these barriers from the bottom up.

European-level influence is more decisive in initiating policy change in Group B countries. Piloting, program evaluation, and impact assessment are performed less systematically, and even if program evaluation is widespread, it is difficult to ascertain whether the acquired evidence effectively feeds into policy design. In Belgium, significant institutional barriers emerge from fragmentation/overlapping of competences in the fields of education, training, and employment policy for youth between the two levels of government (federal and regional) and the different language communities. This condition significantly slows the sharing of information on good practices. At the same time, EU influence is extensive, while some new schemes (e.g., the Synerjob scheme, in which public employment services (PES) from the different regions work together to fill vacancies through mixed job-counseling teams) open up opportunities for an incremental adjustment in the direction of peer-to-peer learning across regions and language communities with the aim of strengthening interregional labor mobility.

France stands out with respect to monitoring and evaluation. It fits the evidence-based tradition (of Group A countries), particularly as regards its VET system, paired with a long-standing concern about youth unemployment. At the same time, a high degree of institutional stasis due to the *"dirigiste* tradition" (a strong directive action by the state) is identified as a barrier to innovation. Notwithstanding policy compartmentalization and "policy fatigue," the main enablers of and barriers to policy innovation in youth employment and education policies are public opinion and social tensions, which have sometimes triggered (or halted) reform, particularly in connection with labor contracts. The EU and other supranational bodies are identified as important sources of innovation. Regarding the intersection of vulnerable youth, gender, and employment, a significant innovative scheme launched in 2012—*Emplois d'avenir* (Jobs of the Future)—which comes under the French YG, consists of a holistic intervention (of subsidized work contracts, training/coaching, and counseling) and is addressed to youth from disadvantaged areas and disabled young people. Also since 2012, tackling the gender segregation of young people into male and female sectors has become a policy target (Gökşen et al. 2016a, 50–51).

In the other four countries, the range of policy innovation and knowledge diffusion is limited by highly centralized administration structures (in Greece and Turkey), excessive bureaucratization (in Greece), policy inertia and path dependence (in Spain), and the fact that political interests overrule policy decisions (mostly in Turkey). However, Slovakia, as well as a number of regional governments in Spain (particularly those where policy coordination between regions/localities is stronger), stand out as examples of innovative initiatives (e.g., the initiative by the automotive sector for VET reform in Slovakia and specific examples of policy learning and sharing of "good examples" in the regions of Aragon, Asturias, and others in Spain). In Greece, Slovakia, and Spain, EU-program and European Social Fund funding conditionality are significant drivers of policy change. This is partly the case in Turkey, too, with regard to the accession process. However, sometimes project-based initiatives for policy experimentation wither away as funding expires.

Greece has experienced coerced transfer under the EU bailout, particularly in the field of labor protection legislation, with reforms that were embraced in the successive rescue deals dismantling collective bargaining, introducing subminimum wages for youth, and increasing flexibility in hiring and dismissals. In Greece, Slovakia, and Spain, a path shift is underway in VET structures in an attempt to strengthen the dual system under the initiative provided in the context of the European Alliance for Apprenticeships and bilateral agreements between Germany (an exporter of the dual system) and six EU countries. Domestic policy entrepreneurs (the Automotive Industry Association in Slovakia and the Hellenic Chamber of Hotels in collaboration with the Greek–German Chamber of Industry and Commerce in Greece) played a significant role in seizing the opportunity for experimenting with the dual VET system under the influence of external stimuli. This experimental emulation paved the way for a wholesale reform of VET in Slovakia.

Gender mainstreaming in youth employment policies is not prevalent in the two Southern European countries. In Spain, a gender concern can be found only in two youth employment policies: (1) the 2012 entrepreneurship contract for young women (aged 16–30 years) in male-dominated industries and (2) the consideration of age 35 years (vs. 30 years for men) as the maximum age for capitalizing 100% of unemployment benefits in a lump sum for self-employment. In Greece, there are specific support schemes for women's entrepreneurship, but these do not particularly target *young* women. Likewise, some programs addressed to youth (Gates for Youth Entrepreneurship, Youth in Action, and European Youth Card) only marginally embrace a gender perspective.

In summary, in the Group A countries, a strong debate on the mismatch between the skills provided by the educational and VET systems and those required in the workplace constitutes a significant driver of policy change and innovation (see McGuinness, Bergin, and Whelan, this volume). In Denmark, under the universalistic STW transition regime and within a systematic framework of knowledge diffusion between all levels of governance and stakeholders' bodies, VET reform for tackling this mismatch reflects a "layering" change process. Under the liberal STW regime of the United Kingdom, despite robust ex-ante and ex-post policy evaluation, competition and choice leave little room for co-ordinated diffusion of evidence/knowledge that could feed into policy decisions (except for policy fine-tuning). And yet there is evidence of an incipient radical change that brings employers to the center of VET policy design and delivery. The Netherlands represents an interesting example of copying/emulation of innovative policies across regions.

In the Group B countries, EU stimuli and inspiration from other EU countries for policy change are found to be quite significant. Policy entrepreneurs can also play an important role in these initiatives. France, Greece, and Slovakia provide some examples of EU influence opening a "window of opportunity" for local policy entrepreneurs to act as pull factors for major reform in VET/education. In Greece, however, which exemplifies a case of coerced reform under the rescue deals, this has been of marginal impact so far. European stimuli fostering cooperation at the local/regional level constitute an important channel of innovative initiatives in Belgium and Spain. Turkey exhibits strong barriers to policy innovation mostly because of its overcentralized administrative structures, monolithic policy implementation institutions, and overruling of policy choices by political expediency.

Finally, even though there is much concern among EU countries about gender equality in the professional sphere, there is limited focus on the intersection of youth, gender, and employment in all the countries examined (see Gökşen et al. 2016a).

6.4.2. Case Studies of Policy Innovation

Following the brief, comparative macro perspective presented previously, this section further elucidates the foci of innovation on the basis of case studies of YG and apprenticeship policies. The schemes studied range from ambitious, novel initiatives at an early stage (in the case of the Netherlands) to well-established programs with a positive impact on youth labor markets (e.g., the YG in Denmark). Steps taken toward a holistic/integrated approach to youth unemployment triggered by the European Commission YG program, with little progress so far in terms of nationwide implementation (in Greece, Slovakia, and Spain), have also been included.

We use three interrelated (and partly overlapping) dimensions for analyzing and comparing policy innovations. The first dimension concerns the extent to which the selected policy schemes produce significant changes in the institutional setting and/or in the group of actors involved in their design and implementation. Of crucial importance is how the schemes impact on changes in policy governance by promoting more or less structured forms of cooperation between actors at different levels of administration and between major stakeholders (employers, trade unions, youth organizations, and others) with the aim of improving service provision to disadvantaged youth. The second dimension refers to changes in the way policy is formulated and in the policy toolkit with a view to reaching out to disadvantaged youth, improving the skill profile of young jobseekers, and providing integrated services. Third, we trace the main pathway(s) in which innovation takes place: (1) through more or less intentional policy learning (among domestic actors at different territorial levels and/or across countries); (2) via a push provided by policy entrepreneurs; and (3) through EU influence, mainly with regard to the flagship initiatives for youth (the YG and the European Alliance for Apprenticeships). Tables 6.4 and 6.5 briefly summarize the trends along these three dimensions in the two groups of countries.

Our case studies indicated three foci of innovation for addressing STW transition barriers and difficulties. First is a novel way of governance in policy design and delivery often referred to as a "triple" or "multiple" helix. This involves collaboration between the public administration, professional bodies and education/ training providers, employers, youth associations, and other stakeholders interested in employment growth and youth labor market integration. Second is a commitment to the YG through an integrated preventive and proactive approach.

Table 6.4 Summary of findings—YG or similar scheme

		Changes in governance	Changes in policy tool kit	Pathways of policy innovation		
		"Triple-" or "multi-helix" governance	Holistic intervention	Intentional learning, experimentation	Policy entrepreneurs	EU influence
Group A countries	DK	Active path in context of holistic interventions.	New measures focus on speeding up intervention and improving individual screening	Lessons drawn from previous schemes	—	"Exporter" of YG
	NL	Partnership- and network-based initiatives at regional level supporting comprehensive, integrated policies		Cross-regional learning very important	—	Important—Also "exporter" of policies
	UK	More interagency and joined-up partnership working under YG, with mixed results—"Payment by results" drives performance	Local tailoring important, limited collaboration in delivery	Lessons drawn from previous schemes	—	Important for regions with devolved government
Group B countries	FR	Limited evidence (partnerships often ad hoc)—Innovation linked to coordination of existing measures		As above	In some local *missions* and *Pôles emploi*	Important
	BE	Regional and local examples of establishing partnerships with nonstate actors and experimenting with holistic interventions		No systematic exchange of information between regions		Important
	ES	Multi-agent partnerships in local pilot interventions; Major challenge: coordination at national level	Established practice before YG in some localities but still a major challenge	Informal channels of information from bottom up	State in centralizing youth unemployment data—Local PES targeting specific groups	Important
	EL	Very limited partnerships; As above	Major challenge: experimenting with individually tailored services		—	Important
	SK	Local, collaborative, trust-based relationships; As above		Communities of practice exposed to international experience	In some localities, incubators of learning and innovation	Important

Source: Compiled on the basis of the information provided by the country reports (Turkey is omitted because there is no scheme similar to the YG or dual VET).

Table 6.5 Summary of findings—Apprenticeship Scheme

		Changes in governance	Changes in structure and knowledge/ pedagogic base of VET	Pathways of policy innovation		
		"Triple-" or "multi-helix" governance	Flexible learning process—Integrated approach	Intentional learning, experimentation	Policy entrepreneurs	EU influence
Group A countries	DK	Operation Apprenticeship launched by Confederation of Danish Industry	Emphasis on matching skills to needs of industry	Peer-to-peer learning and exchange of knowledge with training institutions and other key stakeholders	—	Important but also exporters of policies
	NL	Coalition of key stakeholders in Amsterdam region—Set vocational training in context of an integrated system of service provision		Cross-regional learning very important	—	As above
	UK	Apprenticeship Trailblazers imply significant shift in design and delivery of VET—New apprenticeship standards		Ongoing policy and peer learning	—	Little exchange of knowledge with the EU
Group B countries	FR	"Plural governance" of Second Chance Schools	Flexible learning process	Marseille model diffused to other regions/ localities	Local policy entrepreneurs mobilized key stakeholders	Important
	BE	JEEP program (Jeunes, École, Emploi), a network-based bottom-up initiative in the Forest municipality of Brussels		Diffusion to other municipalities	—	Important

ES	Different approaches by region	Employers can decide curricula	Individualized learning pathway (Basque region)—Learning across regions	Regional governments—Employers' associations	Important: Through European Alliance for Apprenticeship and bilateral agreements for cooperation with Germany
EL	Experimentation in tourism sector	Flexibility in course-based training and apprenticeship schedules following seasonality of tourism sector	Hellenic Chamber of Hotels and Greek–German Chamber of Industry and Commerce		As above
SK	Experimentation in automotive industry	New apprenticeship standards	Automotive Industry—Key actors drew on experience from other countries		As above

Source: Compiled on the basis of the information provided by the country reports (Turkey is omitted because there is no scheme similar to the YG or dual VET).

This combines services and provides comprehensive support, tailored to individual needs. Third is the strengthening of traineeships and apprenticeships, combining school- and work-based learning (dual VET), which are advocated by the European Commission as significant tools for enhancing youth employability, in parallel with the mobilization of employers to play a more active role in this respect.

Experimentation around a raft of policies for a YG is currently particularly visible in the Netherlands. This is illustrated by the case of two regions (Mid-Brabant and Amsterdam), which are implementing a preventive approach to youth unemployment that links the YG and dual training. The initiatives rest on cooperation between multiple agents. In the Amsterdam region, the aim is to embed vocational training in an integrated system of service provision embracing health, housing, family conditions, and labor market integration. The Mid-Brabant Pact is a partnership-based endeavor—signed by major stakeholders—for comprehensive and integrated interventions that are expected to lead to a Youth-Unemployment-Free Zone within 3 years (2015–2018). New policy tools include a youth monitor database linking schools, public employment offices, and local agencies, in addition to an umbrella network of partnerships that is hoped will foster rich, cross-industry learning—if network ties prove to be sustainable. Both cases involve extensive cross-regional learning, as mentioned previously, and introduce a partnership-based mode of policy governance. In this respect, the innovation consists in the "push for cooperation" that yields policy experimentation (Verschraegen, Vanhercke, and Verpoorten 2011).

Danish YG policies linked to dual training and apprenticeships stand out as the blueprint for the EC initiative for a YG. The key feature of this model is an active path that mixes education/training and work-first approaches in the context of holistic interventions that combine profiling the young by education and age—in order to activate them in a given period of time—with coaching, mentoring, and the development of basic skills. Recently, incremental changes have reinforced a path shift from rights to obligations for youth regarding education and employment (Carstensen and Ibsen 2016).

The United Kingdom is another front runner for ALMPs. A marketized logic dominates governance and delivery of policies in this country (e.g., the "payment-by-results" system). The negative aspects of this model, which slows down the coordinated use of knowledge for effective strategies targeting the most disadvantaged youth, were briefly highlighted in Section 6.4.1. These drawbacks are reflected in the persistently high NEET rate and the comparatively high risk of poverty and social exclusion among the young. The significant shift in the governance, design, and delivery of VET sought through the Apprenticeship Trailblazers initiative attempts to mobilize employers to play a central role in this respect (Hadjivassiliou, Swift, and Fohrbeck 2016).

Among Group B countries, initiatives for innovation in Belgium rest mostly with the relatively autonomous authorities (regions and language communities).

Flanders and the Brussels region take the lead for innovative partnership-based interventions and programs (e.g., the Jeunes, École, Emploi (JEEP) program, which provides guidance on training and job search to students before they leave compulsory education). The YG initiative has triggered some degree of central coordination through a national framework that fosters the use of local administrations' access to school data to prevent early school leaving, and the development of common conditionality criteria for unemployment benefit provision and of incentives for acquiring information/communication technologies and language skills (the latter are particularly important for labor mobility across language communities) (Martellucci and Lenaerts 2016).

In France, a most significant innovation in policy governance and in the structure and knowledge base of VET is linked with the introduction of Second Chance Schools (E2C) (European Commission 2013; Smith 2016). Their experimental introduction (in Marseille in 1997), institutional recognition, and further diffusion are closely linked with the role of local policy entrepreneurs in mobilizing regional/local stakeholders from the political, economic/corporate, and educational world to get involved in the design and operation of these new vocational education units in the context of a "plural governance." E2Cs signpost a significant shift in learning methodology from the mainstream qualification-based approach to the acquisition of competences in a flexible learning process that follows the student's progress. However, as for YG policies, a comprehensive outreach strategy for all young NEETs is lacking, the ability of the local PES (local "missions") to form partnerships with various local stakeholders is highly variable, and stakeholders' commitment is often low or ad hoc.

In Greece, Slovakia, and Spain, EU influence on introducing a comprehensive and integrated approach to youth unemployment and the NEETs problem, as well as upgrading and expanding VET, has been important. Nonetheless, interventions along these lines remain fragmented, with little positive effect on outcomes so far. In Spain, overly restrictive rules for participation in the YG program and a technically difficult registration process have excluded many low-skilled unemployed youth. Local partnerships forged with non-governmental organizations (NGOs) and with employers' associations to motivate the young to go to the PES to receive tailored services have been present in successful YG regional/local projects. Experimentation at the regional level aimed at mobilizing business-sector participation in the dual-training environment has been marked (e.g., in the Basque region; González Menéndez et al. 2016).

In Slovakia, experimental local community centers (some of them in the form of social enterprises) were formed by municipalities or by NGOs to support the social inclusion of marginalized social groups under the YG (with an emphasis on Roma youth). These have been inspired by similar organizations in Belgium and Germany through the diffusion of knowledge and expertise by research networks and international NGOs. Equally important are the knowledge and experience accumulated by principal officers in these centers, through their previous careers in similar policy settings and the relationships of trust they have helped develop with local agencies. Moreover, the Automotive Industry Association played the role of "policy entrepreneur" in creating the first pilot centers in dual vocational schools in 2002, which instigated a wholesale reform to strengthen dual training (Veselková 2016).

In Greece, a top-down experimental transfer is underway in the context of the German–Greek cooperation for developing dual VET and improving its image. Domestic actors, such as the Hellenic Chamber of Hotels and the Greek–German Chamber of Industry and Commerce, played the role of "pull factors" for external stimuli and created industry-based experimental vocational education schools in order to provide the skills needed in the tourism industry. The initiative is still at an incipient stage. Moreover, there has been very little development of comprehensive and integrated intervention under the YG (Petmesidou and Polyzoidis 2016).

In Turkey, the on-the-job training program operated by the PES shares some similarities with the active path under the YG, given that it seeks to help young people with low skills into available training places. However, there is no in-built integrated and individualized orientation. The system operates in a highly centralized way with little bottom-up or horizontal communication. Despite some recent EU-inspired institutional building (e.g., the Vocational Qualification Authority and the Directorate-General of Lifelong Learning), the absence of cooperation between existing institutions and firms maintains substantive inefficiencies in VET, which is further weakened by an extensive practice of apprenticeships in the informal economy (Gökşen et al. 2016b).

6.5. CONCLUSIONS

The hypothesis of a distinction between those countries frequently experimenting with new, proactive youth employment measures (Denmark, the Netherlands, the United Kingdom, and, to some extent, France) and those exhibiting considerable inertia (mainly Greece and Turkey, but also Belgium, Slovakia, and Spain) is clearly supported by our analysis. This distinction cuts across the typology of STW transition regimes and indicates a more complex picture of differences and similarities within and between regimes, as well as across regions/localities, with regard to policy learning and effective innovation in youth labor markets.

Our analysis shows that the urgency of the youth employment problem in many areas of Europe in the aftermath of the Great Recession led to a swathe of policy responses involving learning, transfer, and experimentation in order to address the complex needs of youth at risk. By drawing upon the main explanatory frameworks of policy learning and transfer, we recorded the following mechanisms of policy learning and innovation: *evidence-based incremental changes* in policy delivery and policy instruments (e.g., in Denmark and the

United Kingdom); *a "layering" process* with new elements being drafted on existing policies and altering their focus (e.g., in the VET field in Denmark); a *novel way of governance* (multi-actor/multi-agency partnerships) with the potential to trigger a paradigm shift in policy design and implementation in specific regions (e.g., in the Netherlands and less wide-ranging in Belgium and Spain) or in specific policy fields (VET in France, Slovakia, and the United Kingdom); and, finally, the *mobilization of policy entrepreneurs* (Greece and Slovakia)—mainly under the influence of EU-level initiatives (YG and European Alliance for Apprenticeships)—who introduce and develop new ideas and instruments.

Regarding the pathways of learning, these range from more or less systematic diffusion of policy knowledge among the different levels of administration to peer-to-peer learning (in Group A countries) and weak or absent diffusion channels (in Group B countries). In the latter group of countries, EU influence through conditions linked to program funding, mutual learning activities, country recommendations, or coerced transfer (under the bailout deal for Greece) has had varying degrees of importance.

Notably, devolution of policy functions tends to facilitate learning and experimentation with innovative interventions because local/regional administrations and agencies are more likely to exchange knowledge on policy processes and tools among themselves, as well as get involved in EU-wide mutual policy learning. However, for innovative initiatives to yield results with regard to sustained labor market integration of youth at the national level, a policy environment that is conducive to coordinated sharing and diffusion of knowledge between different levels of administration and joint stakeholders' bodies is required. In some countries (e.g., Denmark), corporatist governance highly supports systematic bottom-up and top-down learning and policy innovation, leading to significant policy outcomes (namely comparatively low youth unemployment rates and gender disparities). In other countries, fragmented governance and administrative inertia hinder coordinated learning exchange for effective innovation. Poor labor market outcomes in Group B countries partly reflect these conditions.

The following major barriers were identified: *Fragmentation* and often overlapping competencies among different levels of administration lead to inconsistent cooperation across regions and with other actors, thus slowing innovation diffusion (in Belgium and Spain); *overcentralized administrative structures*, dominance of fragmented, project-based solutions, and inability to convert such projects into long-term sustainable policies (in Greece and Turkey); and *political culture and values* (e.g., a strong liberal tradition in the United Kingdom) and party-political expediency (e.g., in Slovakia), which do not favor systematic and coordinated flow of information into high levels of (strategic) policy decision-making. Hence, the improvement of coordination capacities vertically and horizontally among key policy actors is crucial for facilitating the spread of good practices nationwide.

Regarding the major foci of policy learning, innovation, and change, these include integrated, personalized interventions of a YG type; the structure, management, and knowledge base of VET as a significant tool for enhancing youth employability; and new forms of policy governance creating scope for regional/ local experimentation. In Group A countries with developed vocational education "tracks" (e.g., Denmark and the Netherlands), the main policy challenges that involve learning and innovation concern VET upgrading, feedback mechanisms between VET and the labor market, and multi-actor/multi-agency forms of governance. How to mobilize employers—in collaboration with professional bodies and training providers—in order to reconsider the knowledge base, learning methodology, and delivery of VET and to develop new apprenticeship standards—is a key challenge also in France and the United Kingdom. In Group B countries, learning lessons from other countries' experience so as to improve the quality and capacity of PES operation is a crucial step toward developing integrated individualized services under the YG. Equally important is drawing experience from across Europe in order to develop robust VET systems and raise their public visibility and attractiveness for young people.

NOTES

1   The research inputs of the partner institutions that participated in Work Package 4 of the STYLE project are greatly acknowledged. We truly appreciate the contributions by the following colleagues: Martin B. Carstensen and Christian Lyhne Ibsen (Copenhagen Business School); Kari Hadjivassiliou, Arianna Tassinari, Sam Swift, and Anna Fohrbeck (Institute of Employment Studies, United Kingdom); Sonja Bekker, Marc van der Meer, and Ruud Muffels (Tilburg University); Mark Smith, Maria Laura Toraldo, and Vincent Pasquier (Grenoble École de Management); Marcela Veselková (Slovak Governance Institute); Elisa Martellucci, Gabriele Marconi, and Karolien Lenaerts (Centre for European Policy Studies); and Fatoş Gökşen, Deniz Yükseker, Sinem Kuz, and Ibrahim Öker (Koç University). Their analyses of policy learning and innovation in their countries have provided key insights for our comparative approach. Many thanks go also to our colleagues at Democritus University (Periklis Polyzoidis) and the University of Oviedo (Ana M. Guillén, Begoña Cueto, Rodolfo Gutiérrez, Javier Mato, and Aroa Tejero) for their valuable help. For critical comments and substantive suggestions on earlier drafts of the chapter, we thank Nigel Meager and the editors of the book. The usual disclaimer applies.

2   Accessible at http://ec.europa.eu/social/main.jsp?catId=1022. There is also a vast literature on innovation patterns regarding the interface between labor market institutions, technological/organizational regimes, and industrial competition. Such research examines innovation in the light of economic theory (e.g., the Schumpeterian view on innovation and entrepreneurship)

and focuses on the extent to which labor market deregulation and increasing flexibility promote or hamper innovation, productivity, and gross domestic product growth (Kleinknecht, van Schaik, and Zhou 2014). However, this literature is beyond our scope here.

3 Similarly, the Europeanization literature focusing on change induced by EU policy options (Radaelli 2003) distinguishes between inertia, absorption/ accommodation of new elements into domestic policies without significant change in the overall institutional settings, and wholesale changes in policy structures and processes.

4 Also see European Commission (2014), where Austria, Denmark, Germany, and the United Kingdom are among the countries with comparatively high rates of transitions from short-term unemployment to employment and from temporary to permanent employment (among all working-age groups). The Netherlands is a borderline case with its low transition rates from temporary to permanent employment but comparatively easy returns from short-term unemployment to permanent employment. Greece and Spain are among the worst performers in these two respects. Slovakia also exhibits low rates of return from short-term unemployment to employment.

5 Turkey shares some similarities with Southern European countries in terms of welfare patterns (Grütjen 2008), but there are significant differences in employment structure. In 2014, approximately one-fifth of the labor force was employed in agriculture (the rates for Italy, Portugal, and Spain ranged between 4% and 5%; in Greece. the share stood at 13%).

6 Turkey exhibits a much lower level of educational attainment for women, with 45% not having completed primary schooling (Gökşen et al. 2016a). Across EU countries, gender differences in terms of the educational field of study, vocational educational orientation, and the impact of parenthood are crucial for examining labor market entry (Mills and Präg 2014). However, these issues lie outside our scope here.

7 For a detailed presentation of the country studies, see the Working Papers and Synthesis Reports available at http://www.style-research.eu/publications/working-papers (under Work Package 4).

8 For a critical discussion of "flexicurity," see Smith et al. in this volume.

REFERENCES

Bekker, Sonja, Marc van de Meer, and Ruud Muffels. 2015. "Barriers to and Triggers of Policy Innovation and Knowledge Transfer in the Netherlands." STYLE Working Paper 4.1. Brighton, UK: CROME, University of Brighton. http://www.style-research.eu/publications/working-papers

Carstensen, Martin, and Christian Lyhne Ibsen. 2016. "Denmark—Brief Country Report." In *Policy Learning and Innovation Processes Drawing on EU and National Policy Frameworks on Youth—Synthesis Report*, edited by Maria Petmesidou and María C. González Menéndez, 103–9. STYLE Working Paper 4.2. Brighton, UK: CROME, University of Brighton. http://www.style-research.eu/publications/working-papers

Dolowitz, David, and David Marsh. 2000. "Learning from Abroad: The Role of Policy Transfer in Contemporary Policy Making." *Governance* 13 (1): 5–24.

Dwyer, Peter J., and Nick Ellison. 2009. "We Nicked Stuff from All Over the Place: Policy Transfer or Muddling Through?" *Policy & Politics* 37 (3): 389–407.

European Commission. 2011. *Peer Country Papers on Youth Guarantees*. Brussels: European Commission. http://ec.europa.eu/social/main.jsp?catId=964

European Commission. 2013. *Apprenticeship and Traineeship Schemes in EU27: Key Success Factors. A Guidebook for Policy Planners and Practitioners*. Brussels: European Commission. http://ec.europa.eu/education/policy/vocational-policy/doc/alliance/apprentice-trainee-success-factors_en.pdf

European Commission. 2014. *Employment and Social Developments in Europe 2014*. Luxembourg: Publications Office of the European Union. http://ec.europa.eu/social/main.jsp?catId=738&langId=en&pubId=7736

Evans, Mark. 2009. "New Directions in the Study of Policy Transfer." *Policy Studies* 30 (3): 237–41.

Fergusson, Ross. 2002. "Rethinking Youth Transitions." *Policy Studies* 23 (3/4): 173–90.

Gangl, Markus. 2001. "European Patterns of Labor Market Entry: A Dichotomy of Occupationalized Systems vs. Non-Occupational Systems?" *European Societies* 3 (4): 471–94.

Gökşen, Fatoş, Alpay Filiztekin, Mark Smith, Çetin Çelik, İbrahim Öker, and Sinem Kuz. 2016a. "Vulnerable Youth and Gender in Europe." STYLE Working Paper 4.3. Brighton, UK: CROME, University of Brighton. http://www.style-research.eu/publications/working-papers

Gökşen, Fatoş, Deniz Yükseker, Sinem Kuz, and Ibrahim Öker. 2016b. "Turkey—Brief Country Report." In *Policy Learning and Innovation Processes Drawing on EU and National Policy Frameworks on Youth—Synthesis Report*, edited by Maria Petmesidou and María C. González Menéndez, 63–67. STYLE Working Paper 4.2. Brighton, UK: CROME, University of Brighton. http://www.style-research.eu/publications/working-papers

González Menéndez, María C., Ana Marta Guillén, Begoña Cueto, Rodolfo Gutiérrez, Javier Mato, and Aroa Tejero. 2016. "Spain—Brief Country Report." In *Policy Learning and Innovation Processes Drawing on EU and National Policy Frameworks on Youth—Synthesis Report*, edited by Maria Petmesidou and María C. González Menéndez, 47–54. STYLE Working Paper 4.2. Brighton, UK: CROME, University of Brighton. http://www.style-research.eu/publications/working-papers

Grütjen, Daniel. 2008. "The Turkish Welfare Regime: An Example of the Southern European Model? The Role of the State, Market and Family in Welfare Provision." *Turkish Policy Quarterly* 8 (1): 111–29.

Hacker, Jacob S. 2004. "Privatizing risk without privatizing the welfare state: the hidden politics of social policy retrenchment in the United States". *American Political Science Review* 98(2): 243–260.

Hadjivassiliou, Kari P., Sam Swift, and Anna Fohrbeck. 2016. "UK—Brief Country Report." In *Policy Learning and Innovation Processes Drawing on EU and National Policy Frameworks on Youth—Synthesis Report*, edited by Maria Petmesidou and María C. González Menéndez, 68–88. STYLE Working Paper 4.2. Brighton, UK: CROME, University of Brighton. http://www.style-research.eu/publications/working-papers

Hall, Peter. 1993. "Policy Paradigms, Social Learning, and the State: The Case of Economic Policymaking in Britain." *Comparative Politics* 25 (3): 275–96.

Kingdon, John W. 1984. *Agendas, Alternatives and Public Policies.* Boston: Little Brown.

Kleinknecht, Alfred, Flore N. van Schaik, and Haibo Zhou. 2014. "Is Flexible Labor Good for Innovation? Evidence from Firm-Level Data." *Cambridge Journal of Economics* 38 (5): 1207–19.

Legrand, Timothy. 2012. "Overseas and Over Here: Policy Transfer and Evidence-Based Policymaking." *Policy Studies* 33 (4): 329–49.

Martellucci, Elisa, and Karolien Lenaerts. 2016. "Belgium—Brief Country Report." In *Policy Learning and Innovation Processes Drawing on EU and National Policy Frameworks on Youth—Synthesis Report*, edited by Maria Petmesidou and María C. González Menéndez, 18–28. STYLE Working Paper 4.2. Brighton, UK: CROME, University of Brighton. http://www.style-research.eu/publications/working-papers

Mills, Melinda, and Patrick Präg. 2014. "Gender Inequalities in the School-to-Work Transition in Europe." Short Statistical Report 4. Brussels: Rand Europe.

Organization for Economic Co-operation and Development (OECD). 2015. *Local Implementation of Youth Guarantees: Emerging Lessons from European Experiences.* Paris: OECD. http://www.oecd.org/cfe/leed/reports-local-youth.htm

Peck, Jamie, and Nik Theodore. 2001. "Exporting Workfare/Importing Welfare-to-Work: Exploring the Politics of Third Way Policy Transfer." *Political Geography* 20 (4): 427–60.

Petmesidou, Maria, and Periklis Polyzoidis. 2016. "Greece—Brief Country Report." In *Policy Learning and Innovation Processes Drawing on EU and National Policy Frameworks on Youth—Synthesis Report*, edited by Maria Petmesidou and María C. González Menéndez, 35–46. STYLE Working Paper 4.2. Brighton, UK: CROME, University of Brighton. http://www.style-research.eu/publications/working-papers

Radaelli, Claudio M. 2003. "The Europeanization of Public Policy." In *The Politics of Europeanization*, edited by Kevin Featherstone and Claudio M. Radaelli. Oxford: Oxford University Press.

Roberts, Nancy C., and Paula J. King. 1996. *Transforming Public Policy: Dynamics of Policy Entrepreneurship and Innovation*. San Francisco: Jossey-Bass.

Smith, Mark. 2016. "France—Brief Country Report." In *Policy Learning and Innovation Processes Drawing on EU and National Policy Frameworks on Youth—Synthesis Report*, edited by Maria Petmesidou and María C. González Menéndez, 27–34. STYLE Working Paper 4.2. Brighton, UK: CROME, University of Brighton. http://www.style-research.eu/publications/working-papers

Stone, Diane. 2004. "Transfer Agents and Global Networks in the 'Transnationalization' of Policy." *Journal of European Public Policy* 11 (3): 545–66.

Streeck, Wolfgang, and Kathleen Ann Thelen, eds. 2005. *Beyond Continuity: Institutional Change in Advanced Political Economies*. Oxford: Oxford University Press.

Thelen, Kathleen Ann. 2004. *How Institutions Evolve*. Cambridge: Cambridge University Press.

Verschraegen, Gert, Bart Vanhercke, and Rika Verpoorten. 2011. "The European Social Fund and Domestic Activation Policies: Europeanization Mechanisms." *Journal of European Social Policy* 21 (1): 55–72.

Veselková, Marcela. 2016. "Slovakia—Brief Country Report." In *Policy Learning and Innovation Processes Drawing on EU and National Policy Frameworks on Youth—Synthesis Report*, edited by Maria Petmesidou and María C. González Menéndez, 55–62. STYLE Working Paper 4.2. Brighton, UK: CROME, University of Brighton. http://www.style-research.eu/publications/working-papers

Walther, Andreas, and Axel Pohl. 2005. *Thematic Study on Policies for Disadvantaged Youth in Europe. Final Report to the European Commission*. Tübingen: Institute for Regional Innovation and Social Research. http://ec.europa.eu/employment_social/social_inclusion/docs/youth_study_en.pdf

PART II

TRANSITIONS AROUND WORK AND THE FAMILY

7

HOW DO YOUTH LABOR FLOWS DIFFER FROM THOSE OF OLDER WORKERS?

Vladislav Flek, Martin Hála, and Martina Mysíková

7.1. INTRODUCTION

This chapter analyzes youth labor market dynamics, their structure, and their policy implications. We focus on selected European Union (EU) countries (Austria, France, Poland, and Spain) during the various stages of the Great Recession (2008–2009, 2010–2011, and 2012), comparing the results for young people (aged 16–34 years) with those for prime-age individuals (aged 35–54 years). The choice of countries is based on two criteria: (1) sufficient differences in youth labor market performance and/or in labor market regulations[1] and (2) the availability/quality of data.[2] We concentrate on the possible presence of *common* trends across all the countries analyzed.

Our aim is to provide new evidence regarding differences between youth and prime-age labor market dynamics, thus calling attention to the overall presence of age-based labor market segmentation and even marginalization. To this end, we apply (1) the flow approach toward labor market dynamics (Blanchard and Diamond 1990; Elsby, Smith, and Wadsworth 2011) and (2) an analysis of the socioeconomic determinants of transitions in both directions between employment and unemployment (D'Addio 1998; Kelly et al. 2013; Flek, Hála, and Mysíková 2015).

Our analysis is based on an exploration of longitudinal data from the European Union Statistics on Income and Living Conditions (EU-SILC) in an innovative way. In Sections 7.2 and 7.3, we argue in detail that existing flow analyses based on longitudinal data lack comparisons across EU countries because of data limitations. For the same reason, they typically concern working-age populations as a whole rather than just youth. The cross-national analysis based on longitudinal data developed in this chapter represents a research novelty, but we must admit that it still far from constitutes full representativeness.

In general, youth labor market dynamics should be more pronounced compared to those of prime-age groups for many reasons. First, young people move relatively more frequently between the labor market and inactivity. In addition, two other key factors are worth noting: (1) Matching difficulties in the early years of working life lead to frequent job changes, with repeated unemployment spells in between; and (2) investment in firm-specific human capital is lower for young people; hence, when layoffs occur, the last-in, first-out (LIFO) rule is frequently applied (Bell and Blanchflower 2011). For the period of the Great Recession, there is still a lack of studies comparing the quantitative dimension of youth and prime-age labor market dynamics.

The *flow* approach views labor market transitions as a state-dependent process that simultaneously involves all the movements (flows) of individuals between employment, unemployment, and inactivity. It enables us to quantify the overall degree and structure of labor market dynamics over time, across countries, and for various age groups. We address the degree of difference between the gross flows and flow transition rates (transitional probabilities of moving from one labor market status to another) of young and prime-age individuals. The results should be instructive for assessing the gap between the labor market prospects of the two age groups.

The flows between labor market statuses, particularly between employment and unemployment, determine variations in unemployment rates (Petrongolo and Pissarides 2008). We focus on the link between the different unemployment performances in various countries, age groups, and periods and the concrete flow, which contributes decisively to the observed differences in the evolution of unemployment rates. Thus, our research results based on the "flow" decomposition of unemployment rate dynamics should be helpful for understanding differences in the evolution of youth and prime-age unemployment rates.

Research on youth labor market dynamics concentrates on school-to-work transitions (for an overview and/or most recent findings, see Albert, Toharia, and Davia 2008; Berloffa et al., this volume; Hadjivassiliou et al., this volume). We prefer instead to combine the flow approach outlined previously with a detailed analysis of the socioeconomic determinants of transitions between employment and unemployment. Our previous research (Flek and Mysíková 2016) shows that the flows in both directions between employment and unemployment are actually decisive for the overall youth labor market dynamics during the Great Recession.

When estimating the determinants of a likelihood of exiting employment and becoming unemployed, we intend to verify the significance of age, in particular. Furthermore, we estimate the determinants of moving from unemployment to employment, with an emphasis on the length of previous unemployment. With increasing unemployment duration, the unemployed are likely to be stigmatized and/or discouraged from further job search. Job-finding prospects may therefore be viewed as a diminishing function of unemployment duration, net of other socioeconomic characteristics of the unemployed (Machin and Manning 1999; Shimer 2012). Based on our results, we suggest country-specific adjustments in youth unemployment policy agendas.

To summarize, the chapter addresses the following key research questions:

1. How do youth labor market dynamics (expressed by the movements of young people between employment, unemployment, and inactivity) differ from the dynamics of the prime-age individuals?
2. Do the most marked differences between the evolutions of the youth and the prime-age unemployment rates lie in a relatively different exposure to job loss, in the prospects for exiting unemployment, or in transitions between inactivity and the labor market?
3. Does the age of a worker significantly affect the probability of job loss followed by unemployment? Or is the impact of the age variable actually offset by variables such as work experience or education?
4. How do job search durations vary between young and prime-age unemployed persons? At which unemployment duration does the job-finding probability of an unemployed person drop significantly and become already comparable to the gloomy employment prospects of a long-term unemployed individual?

Section 7.2 provides a literature overview with a deeper foundation of our research questions. We outline our methodological approach in Section 7.3 and also describe how we conduct cross-national comparative flow analyses using longitudinal EU-SILC data. In Section 7.4, we focus on the youth and prime-age flows and flow transition rates. This section continues with decompositions of unemployment dynamics and the identification of the driving forces (flows) that account for the different evolution of youth and prime-age unemployment rates. In Section 7.5, we analyze the determinants of youth and prime-age flows in both directions between employment and unemployment. Section 7.6 concludes the chapter.

7.2. LITERATURE OVERVIEW

The literature provides us with various partial arguments pointing to the specificity of youth labor market dynamics. Only a small fraction of young labor market entrants immediately manage to find stable and satisfactory employment. The rest are first faced with unemployment or with frequent job changes combined with repeated unemployment spells (for recent evidence, see Berloffa et al., this volume). This situation is often attributed to educational mismatch, to a lack of work experience, or to the absence of firm-specific skills on the part of young workers (International Labour Organization (ILO) 2013; McGuinness, Bergin, and Whelan, this volume).

The position of young adults in the labor market is more dynamic than that of prime-age participants even when education, skills, and other characteristics match the employer's requirements. Young employees are still more likely to be subject to layoffs—through the practice of fixed-term labor contracts or because of the LIFO rules and seniority-weighted redundancy payments (Bell and Blanchflower 2011). Higher outflows from employment to unemployment compared to those for the prime-age segment of the workforce thus indicate that young workers actually constitute a marginalized group in the sense established by Reich, Gordon, and Edwards (1973).

As shown most recently by Elsby et al. (2011), young people are also characterized by a relatively higher frequency of outflows from unemployment into employment and by shorter unemployment spells compared to the prime-age segment. Such a seemingly positive tendency is likely to be associated with the lower reservation wages of young unemployed, with their acceptance of less stable or less significant jobs, and with lower redundancy costs linked with their future layoffs (Blanchard 1999; Berloffa et al., this volume). Thus, the relatively high outflows of young people from unemployment into employment are again closely linked with a notion of youth as a marginalized group: Young people appear to be forced to accept jobs prevailingly on secondary labor markets, with frequent and relatively brief unemployment episodes in between.

Despite the reasonably good and varied amount of findings collected so far, we believe that an accurate, cross-national view on youth labor market dynamics during the Great Recession is still largely missing. This concerns the absence of a synthetic measure of such dynamics and their structure, as well as comparisons with the labor market dynamics of prime-age individuals. The flow approach seems a promising way to fill that gap. However, the existing longitudinal flow literature lacks comparisons across countries because of data limitations. Instead, it explores national data sources such as Labor Force Surveys (Gomes 2009; Elsby et al. 2011). Also, except for the latter authors, such flow analyses concern working-age populations as a whole rather than various age groups.

Elsby et al. (2011) deal explicitly with youth flows in the United Kingdom and report a higher youth labor market dynamics compared to the prime-age group. Higher youth outflow rates from employment to unemployment and vice versa appear to be in line with the theoretical assumptions of Reich et al. (1973) and Blanchard (1999). These rates confirm the presence of an age-based labor market segmentation and the marginalized status of young workers in the United Kingdom. Flek and Mysíková (2015) and Flek et al. (2015) address youth flows in the Czech Republic and provide some comparisons with neighboring countries and/or Spain, with similar conclusions to those reported by Elsby et al. (2011). Given the relatively small number of such studies, European youth flows still need to be analyzed in a broader cross-country perspective.

The Great Recession exacerbated the difficulties for young people on the labor market, creating a situation in which youth unemployment rates increased faster than prime-age unemployment rates (ILO 2013). Because the flows of workers between labor market statuses determine variations in unemployment rates (Petrongolo and Pissarides 2008; Dixon, Freebairn, and Lim 2011; Elsby et al. 2011; Shimer 2012), a link can be derived between the different unemployment performances in various countries, age categories, or periods, on the one hand, and the concrete flow (which contributes decisively to the observed differences), on the other hand. Labor market and activation policies should then focus on that particular flow. As noted by Elsby et al. (2011), "Policy that focused on encouraging outflows from unemployment may not be as relevant in an economy in which rises in unemployment were driven by changes in the rate of outflows from employment" (p. 4).[3]

When estimating the socioeconomic determinants of moving from employment to unemployment, we use a standard binary probit model. Kelly et al. (2013) use an analogous approach for analyzing the outflows from youth unemployment to employment in Ireland during the Great Recession. Our main aim is to verify the presence of age-based labor market segmentation, based on the higher exposure of young people to job loss followed by unemployment.

A negative relationship between job-finding probability and unemployment duration is referred to in the literature as the "duration dependence" (Machin and Manning 1999; Shimer 2012). We plan to verify its presence in both age categories of unemployed by performing estimates based on the discrete-time proportional hazard models developed by Cox (1972) and Jenkins (1997). Among others, Albert et al. (2008) use such models when analyzing school-to-work transitions in Spain. Other examples include retirement decisions in the United Kingdom (Disney, Emmerson, and Wakefield 2006) and employment decisions after the birth of the first child in Spain (Davia and Legazpe 2014). To our knowledge, there have been only two attempts to explore this model for analyzing exits from youth unemployment into employment (D'Addio 1998; Flek et al. 2015), and both of these point to the significance of duration dependence. As with the flow analysis, however, cross-country comparisons and comparisons between age groups are still scarce.

7.3. DATA AND METHODOLOGY

To our knowledge, this chapter represents one of the first attempts to use the matched longitudinal monthly data of the EU-SILC database for a comparative analysis of youth and prime-age labor market flows in Europe. Being relatively new, this approach requires some initial description of the data, followed by methodological notes on estimation strategies.

7.3.1. Labor Market Dynamics and Flow Decomposition of Unemployment Rates

Some European labor markets that are potentially suitable for reference purposes, such as that of Germany, were not yet included in the versions of longitudinal EU-SILC data sets used in our analysis. Some countries, typically Scandinavian, collected some of the relevant variables only for one selected person per household. In other potentially interesting cases, such as the United Kingdom, there were other technical obstacles to the results being comparable (e.g., a high share of missing information on monthly economic activity).

We deal with young people aged 16–34 years at the beginning of all analyzed periods (2008–2009, 2010–2011, and 2012). The prime-age population, aged 35–54 years, represents a reference group. The choice of the age interval 16–34 years to represent young people is relatively straightforward in that any study aimed at youth labor market dynamics has to involve at least the early stages of work careers of young people, including university graduates. Where appropriate, we decompose the youth age band into various subgroups (16–19, 20–24, 25–29, and 30–34 years) so as to examine the possible heterogeneity of this age group.

The EU-SILC data explored in Section 7.4 consider an individual as the unit of analysis. Only the respondents with full survey participation over the chosen subperiods have been selected for analysis. Our national subsamples are therefore pure panels, where all the reported month-to-month individual labor market statuses are matched. We use the longitudinal weights provided by Eurostat specifically for these subsamples—the standard means of minimizing the attrition bias. Regarding the calendar bias, we hope to avoid it by averaging the observed status changes over the subperiods analyzed.[4] Nonetheless, the retrospective nature of reports on economic activity and their self-declared character may lead to deviations from the ILO definition of unemployment.

We extract a 2-year period from longitudinal EU-SILC 2010 (version 5 of August 2014), which covers monthly economic activity for January 2008 through to December 2009, and another 2-year period from longitudinal EU-SILC 2012 (version 1 of August 2014), which includes data for January 2010 through to December 2011. Both of these subsamples provide chains of 23 monthly individual labor market statuses (i.e., employment, unemployment, and inactivity) and contain far more respondents than a single, 4-year panel of EU-SILC. We also add data for January through December 2012, from EU-SILC 2013 (version 2 of August 2015). The chains of monthly labor market statuses for a single year are obviously shorter (and thus less suitable for longitudinal analysis than the 2-year subsamples), but they enable us to incorporate the year 2012 into the analysis.

In the past month, an individual could be employed (E_{t-1}), unemployed (U_{t-1}), or inactive (I_{t-1}). In the current month, he or she can remain in an unchanged labor market status[5] or change it as follows: $(E_{t-1} \rightarrow U_t);(E_{t-1} \rightarrow I_t);(U_{t-1} \rightarrow E_t);(U_{t-1} \rightarrow I_t);(I_{t-1} \rightarrow E_t);(I_{t-1} \rightarrow U_t)$. Thus, the individual may move from previous to current status in six ways, and the corresponding numbers of individuals represent six gross labor market flows. Figure 7.1 in Section 7.4 compares the relative involvement of young and prime-age individuals in gross flows, where $UE = (U_{t-1} \rightarrow E_t)/(E_{t-1} + U_{t-1} + I_{t-1})$ and so forth for $EU, EI, \ldots$. This approach represents a standard proxy for aggregate and/or group-specific labor market fluidity (Blanchard and Diamond 1990).

In contrast, transitional probabilities λ presented later in Section 7.4 (see Figures 7.2 and 7.3) represent a first-order Markov process, where the probability of moving from the previous to the current status depends exclusively on the individual's previous status (Blanchard and Diamond 1990). For instance, an unemployed individual's average monthly job-finding probability is $\lambda^{UE} = (U_{t-1} \rightarrow E_t)/U_{t-1}$.

Next to this, we express a net change in unemployment in terms of the corresponding average monthly gross flows "in" $(E_{t-1} \rightarrow U_t; I_{t-1} \rightarrow U_t)$ and "out" of unemployment $(U_{t-1} \rightarrow E_t; U_{t-1} \rightarrow I_t)$, which are additionally rearranged as a product of the respective transition probability rate λ and the labor market stock (E, U, I) at time $(t - 1)$. A monthly average change in unemployment rate in percentage points is then decomposed into the contributions of the "ins" and the "outs" of unemployment. The third term shows the contribution of changes in the labor force to unemployment rate dynamics. Such a decomposition of unemployment rate dynamics was developed by Dixon et al. (2011) and applied in a slightly modified form also by Flek and Mysíková (2015). Table 7.1 in Section 7.4 reports results separately for the evolutions of the youth and prime-age unemployment rates.

7.3.2. Assessing the Determinants of Transitions Between Employment and Unemployment

In Section 7.5, the estimates consider an (un)employment spell as the unit of analysis, including multiple episodes. This leads to a different data organization, which is based on nonweighted subsamples. It must be admitted that a data organization of this kind makes the results potentially more prone to the calendar and/or attrition bias than in the case of the flow approach (presented in Section 7.4), which considers the individual as the unit of analysis. We concentrate initially on the determinants of transitions from employment to unemployment by using a probit model. In the 2-year subperiods, we extract from nonweighted samples all employment spells occurring at any time between the first month of the first year (January 2008 or January 2010) and the beginning of the second year (January 2009 or January 2011). For 2012, we concentrate on employment recorded in the first month (January 2012). For all of the three subperiods, we ascertain whether or not the transitions into unemployment occur during the following 11 months.

The dependent binominal variable in a probit model equals 1 if an employment status transitioned to unemployment during the observed period, and 0 otherwise. The individual and other characteristics (e.g., age, gender, education, work experience, household size, and population density) stand for independent explanatory variables. We report results in the form of average marginal effects for pooled samples (with a dummy for prime age) and then separately for the two age groups. Among a range of potentially relevant determinants, we do not analyze the impact of previous employment duration. We are aware that the length of an employment spell can affect the probability of losing a job (e.g., because of LIFO) but, unfortunately, job tenure is not available in the data. Instead, we capture the intensity of employment by years of work experience as a regressor.

For the duration model estimates, we collect all unemployment spells in our three nonweighted subsamples. As with the probit estimates, we refer later for simplicity to individuals, although some of them experienced multiple unemployment spells. The data used for estimations are naturally censored. We introduce a censoring indicator "1" if an unemployment spell terminates in employment and "0" in all other cases.[6]

The econometric analysis is developed in two steps. As the first step, we explore the Kaplan–Meier (KM) estimator (Kaplan and Meier 1958), which represents a nonparametric estimate of the survival function. For our purposes, "survival" means the duration of unemployment; time is measured in months. At this stage, we do not account for individual or other characteristics. Instead, we simply assume that the KM survival curves will decline over time in line with the emergence of closed spells that end in a move into employment. Log-rank tests would document how (in)significantly the KM curves for young and prime-age unemployed differ—in other words, whether the duration of job search differs significantly between the two age categories.

Second, we apply a discrete-time proportional hazard model (Cox 1972).[7] Our idea is to detect the "true" duration dependence of unemployment. Note that unemployed workers with "bad" characteristics (low education, etc.) tend to be less employable than those with "good" characteristics. This is likely to apply to unemployment spells of any length and leads to a selection of individuals with "bad" characteristics into long-term unemployment. But such "duration dependence" is actually spurious because it is explained by other variables and not by unemployment duration per se. In contrast, unemployment duration in and of itself may negatively affect the job-finding probability of unemployed individuals—even after controlling for their available characteristics and unobserved heterogeneity—because of the stigmatization and discouragement effects of long-term unemployment.

We assume that the baseline hazard function is piecewise constant in the chosen unemployment duration intervals (1–2 months, 3–4 months, 5–6 months, 7–10 months, 11–15 months, and 16–24 months), whereas the vector of covariates in the model equation indicates the impact of explanatory variables on the probability of moving in a randomly chosen time from unemployment into employment. For the sake of better interpretation, the estimated coefficients are transformed into hazard ratios. For the periods 2008–2009 and 2010–2011, unemployment spells lasting between 16 and 24 months represent a reference duration interval. For 2012, a reference interval stands for unemployment spells lasting between 11 and 12 months. The set of chosen covariates is analogous to the previous probit analysis.[8]

7.4. LABOR MARKET DYNAMICS AND THEIR AGE-BASED SPECIFICITY

7.4.1. Comparing the Youth and Prime-Age Gross Flows

Figure 7.1 reports gross flows for young (aged 16–34 years) and prime-age (aged 35–54 years) individuals in the four countries considered and suggests the presence of country-specific and age-based patterns in labor market dynamics during the Great Recession. The results are presented as percentages, where, for instance, *UE* relates the average monthly number of individuals involved in a gross flow from unemployment to employment to total labor market stocks (and so forth for *EU, EI, . . .*).

In both age groups, Austria and Spain record persistently higher aggregate fluidity of their labor markets compared to France and Poland. Viewed from another perspective, all the countries involved in our analysis display an approximately two or three times lower degree of aggregate fluidity of their labor markets compared to the United States and the United Kingdom, where between 5% and 7% of the working-age population change their labor market status every month or quarter (Gomes 2009). In this respect, our results are in line with the general view, which considers the Anglo-American labor markets to be considerably more fluid than the labor markets in Continental, Southern, or Eastern Europe.[9]

Figure 7.1 shows that young people are relatively more involved in gross flows compared to prime-age individuals. This holds true uniformly across all the analyzed countries and periods (1: 2008–2009; 2: 2010–2011; and 3: 2012). Thus, on aggregate, the position of young people on the labor market is much less stable. This result confirms the observations of Elsby et al. (2011) for the United Kingdom, who also established that young people "churn" through the labor market relatively more frequently.

The structure of the gross flows of young people is different from that of prime-age individuals. Whereas in the latter case, gross flows between employment and unemployment (*UE; EU*) are almost the only source of dynamics, the youth flows involve a relatively higher frequency of transitions between inactivity and the labor market (*IE; EI; UI; IU*). This is fully in line with intuition,

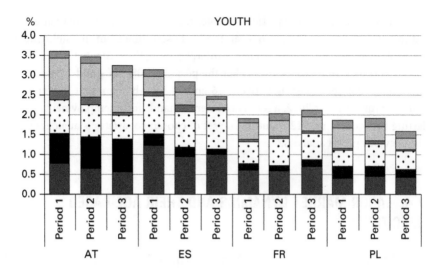

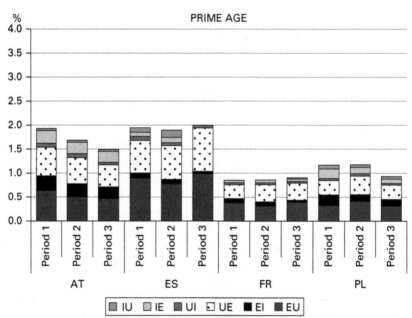

Figure 7.1 Gross flows as percentages of total matched labor market stocks in four European countries (monthly averages; period 1: 2008–2009; period 2: 2010–2011; period 3: 2012; youth: 16–34; prime age 35–54).

Sources: EU-SILC longitudinal UDB 2010, version 5 of August 2014; EU-SILC longitudinal UDB 2012, version 1 of August 2014; EU-SILC UDB 2013, version 2 of August 2015; authors' computations.

given that young people naturally tend to enter or exit the labor market relatively more frequently, particularly because of beginning/finishing education or because of taking/finishing parental leave.

The relatively higher frequency of transitions between inactivity and the labor market is not the sole specificity of youth labor market dynamics. The relative share of youth flows between employment and unemployment in both directions (*EU; UE*) is actually also higher compared to that of prime-age individuals. Figure 7.1 reveals that these two flows typically account for more than 50% of the entire youth labor market dynamics. Only Austria deviates persistently from this tendency because of its exceptionally high shares of youth transitions from employment to inactivity and vice versa (*EI; IE*).

7.4.2. The Youth and Prime-Age Transition Rates

Figures 7.2 and 7.3 present transition rates from employment to unemployment (λ^{UE}) and from unemployment to employment (λ^{UE}) for young and prime-age individuals for the three periods and the four countries considered.

The values of λ^{EU} in Figure 7.2 confirm that a young worker (aged 16–34 years) is more likely to become unemployed than a prime-age worker (aged 35–54 years). This finding stems from comparisons of the last two columns (i.e., of the two age groups) for each country and applies uniformly to the four countries and the three periods analyzed, irrespective of the existing institutional differences, different unemployment performances, or other national specificities. A disproportionally high exposure of young workers to unemployment appears to be a general phenomenon, suggesting the overall presence of an age-based segmentation and marginalization on European labor markets.

Figure 7.2 also documents heterogeneity in the risk of becoming unemployed within the youth age band (16–34 years). The lowest age categories (16–19 and/or 20–24 years) face the highest risk of becoming unemployed. But this is not to say that as the age of young workers increases, their risk of becoming unemployed becomes fully comparable with that of prime-age workers. Even the upper youth age category (30–34 years) typically faces a relatively higher risk of becoming unemployed compared to prime-age workers.

The job-finding rates $\left(\lambda^{UE}\right)$ in Figure 7.3 suggest that, with the sole exception of Austria in 2008–2009, a young unemployed person is relatively more "attractive" than a prime-age individual when firms hire new workers. This applies also to the job-finding rates $\left(\lambda^{IE}\right)$ of previously inactive young people (see Figures A7.1–A7.4 in the Appendix). As argued in more detail in the literature overview in Section 7.2, such tendencies will probably again label youth as a marginalized group, forced to accept less stable employment conditions compared to the prime-age segment of the workforce, with frequent subsequent transitions back into unemployment.

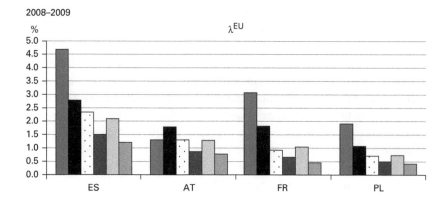

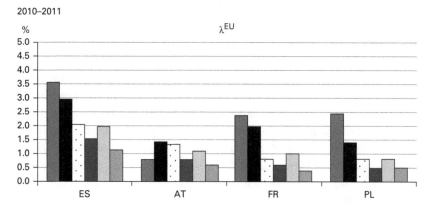

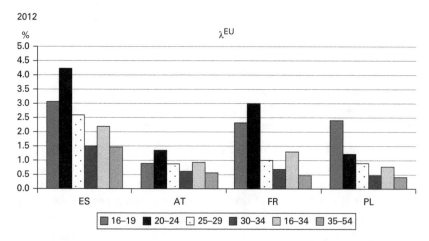

Figure 7.2 Transition rates from employment to unemployment for various age groups in four European countries (monthly averages, in %)
Sources: EU-SILC UDB 2010, version 5 of August 2014; EU-SILC UDB 2012, version 1 of August 2014; EU-SILC UDB 2013, version 2 of August 2015; authors' computations.

2008–2009

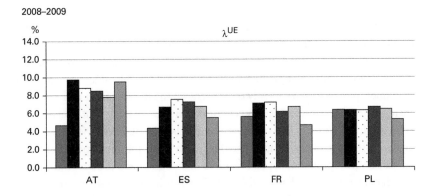

2010–2011

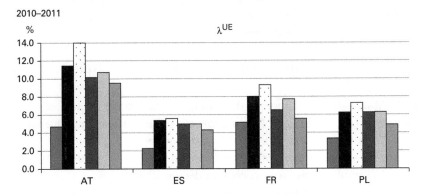

2012

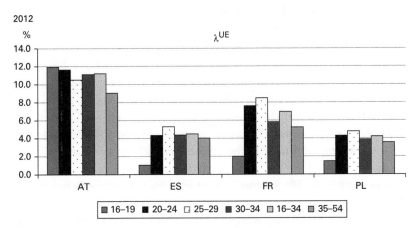

■ 16–19 ■ 20–24 □ 25–29 ■ 30–34 ▨ 16–34 ■ 35–54

Figure 7.3 Transition rates from unemployment to employment for various age groups in four European countries (monthly averages, in %).
Sources: EU-SILC UDB 2010, version 5 of August 2014; EU-SILC UDB 2012, version 1 of August 2014; EU-SILC UDB 2013, version 2 of August 2015; authors' computations.

One would presume that the lowest age categories of young unemployed transition back into education (inactivity) more frequently than the upper categories. This alternative transition channel should help them avoid remaining in unemployment and increase their job-finding chances in the future. However, our results presented in the Appendix suggest that even the lowest age categories of young unemployed remain mostly dependent on the labor market and that their transitions to education (inactivity) cannot be viewed as a relevant alternative.[10]

Our findings confirm the observations of Elsby et al. (2011) for the United Kingdom. The established (age-based) gaps in both job-loss and job-finding rates can be interpreted as typical features of marginalized groups in the sense of Reich et al. (1973) or Blanchard (1999). The results point to the need for additional policy measures aimed at higher employment stability and a better quality of jobs held by young people rather than at merely increasing their outflow rates from unemployment (inactivity) to employment.

7.4.3. Flow Decomposition of Unemployment Rate Dynamics

Table 7.1 decomposes changes in the unemployment rate for the four countries considered (AT, ES, FR, and PL) in terms of both movements into unemployment (from employment or inactivity) and movements out of unemployment (into employment or inactivity) over the periods 2008–2009, 2010–2011, and 2012. The results in the second column demonstrate the trend of disproportionate increases in youth unemployment rates compared to prime-age unemployment rates in the initial period of the Great Recession (2008–2009). As seen in the fourth column, these disproportionate increases in youth unemployment in 2008–2009 (in ES, FR, and PL) were generated decisively by inflows into unemployment from employment, which accounted for far higher increases in youth unemployment rates than in prime-age unemployment rates.

This is in line with our finding that the job-loss rates of young workers are persistently higher than those of prime-age workers. But in the fourth column of Table 7.1, we can see exactly how the inflows of workers into unemployment from employment contribute to the different evolutions of the unemployment rates of the two age groups. The contribution of inflows into unemployment from inactivity in the fifth column is also higher for young people, but this contribution to the different unemployment rate dynamics of the two age groups is much less relevant than the contribution of inflows of workers into unemployment from employment (likewise, the contribution of changes in the labor force in the last column is less relevant).

In contrast, had the outflows from unemployment to employment (in the seventh column in Table 7.1) been the only driver of unemployment rate dynamics, youth unemployment rates would actually have developed more favorably than prime-age unemployment rates. This confirms that the job-finding difficulties of the young unemployed cannot be viewed as the cause of disproportionate increases in youth unemployment rates in the initial stage of the Great Recession (2008–2009).

Table 7.1 Unemployment rate dynamics of young people (aged 16–34 years) and prime-age individuals (aged 35–54 years) in four European countries in 2008–2009, 2010–2011, and 2012 (monthly averages, in percentage points)

Country/period	$\Delta\left(\dfrac{U}{LF}\right)$	"Ins" (+)	$\lambda^{EU}\dfrac{I_{t-1}}{LF_t}$	$\lambda^{IU}\dfrac{E_{t-1}}{LF_t}$	"Outs" (−)	$-\lambda^{UE}\dfrac{U_{t-1}}{LF_t}$	$-\lambda^{UI}\dfrac{U_{t-1}}{LF_t}$	Contribution of changes in LF[a]
AT 2008–2009								
Prime age	0.0311	0.7845	0.7297	0.0548	−0.7599	−0.6685	−0.0914	0.0065
Youth	−0.1660	1.3498	1.1001	0.2498	−1.5124	−1.1797	−0.3327	−0.0034
AT 2010–2011								
Prime age	−0.0788	0.6160	0.5533	0.0628	−0.6992	−0.6127	−0.0866	0.0044
Youth	−0.2594	1.2005	0.9697	0.2308	−1.4543	−1.1670	−0.2873	−0.0056
AT 2012								
Prime age	−0.0012	0.5719	0.5354	0.0364	−0.5743	−0.5180	−0.0563	0.0012
Youth	0.0408	1.0867	0.8436	0.2431	−1.0120	−0.9025	−0.1095	−0.0339
ES 2008–2009								
Prime age	0.3080	1.1727	1.0535	0.1193	−0.8641	−0.7768	−0.0873	−0.0006
Youth	0.4432	1.9669	1.6931	0.2737	−1.4785	−1.3286	−0.1499	−0.0452
ES 2010–2011								
Prime age	0.1791	1.1002	0.9189	0.1813	−0.9041	−0.8088	−0.0953	−0.0170
Youth	0.1446	1.8244	1.4199	0.4045	−1.5977	−1.3550	−0.2426	−0.0821
ES 2012								
Prime age	0.0926	1.1173	1.1089	0.0084	−1.0321	−1.0091	−0.0230	0.0074
Youth	0.0036	1.5550	1.4727	0.0823	−1.5106	−1.4612	−0.0494	−0.0408

(continued)

Table 7.1 Continued

Country/period	$\Delta\left(\dfrac{U}{LF}\right)$	"Ins" (+)	$\lambda^{EU}\dfrac{I_{t-1}}{LF_t}$	$\lambda^{IU}\dfrac{E_{t-1}}{LF_t}$	"Outs" (−)	$-\lambda^{UE}\dfrac{U_{t-1}}{LF_t}$	$-\lambda^{IU}\dfrac{U_{t-1}}{LF_t}$	Contribution of changes in LF[a]
FR 2008–2009								
Prime age	0.0916	0.4532	0.4292	0.0240	−0.3623	−0.3276	−0.0347	0.0007
Youth	0.1252	1.1087	0.9230	0.1858	−0.9255	−0.8313	−0.0942	−0.0581
FR 2010–2011								
Prime age	−0.0407	0.3760	0.3504	0.0255	−0.4153	−0.3890	−0.0263	−0.0014
Youth	−0.0311	1.1350	0.8799	0.2551	−1.0941	−1.0059	−0.0881	−0.0721
FR 2012								
Prime age	0.0242	0.4447	0.4247	0.0200	−0.4196	−0.3879	−0.0317	−0.0009
Youth	0.1678	1.3437	1.0912	0.2525	−1.1115	−1.0138	−0.0977	−0.0645
PL 2008–2009								
Prime age	0.0648	0.4748	0.3910	0.0838	−0.4088	−0.3597	−0.0491	−0.0012
Youth	0.1974	0.9511	0.6529	0.2982	−0.6974	−0.6299	−0.0675	−0.0563
PL 2010–2011								
Prime age	0.0238	0.5294	0.4684	0.0611	−0.5063	−0.4518	−0.0545	0.0007
Youth	−0.0214	0.9993	0.6961	0.3032	−0.9643	−0.8663	−0.0980	−0.0564
PL 2012								
Prime age	0.0151	0.3902	0.3626	0.0276	−0.3796	−0.3475	−0.0321	0.0046
Youth	0.0855	0.8987	0.6498	0.2488	−0.7501	−0.7075	−0.0426	−0.0632

[a]Computed as $U_{t-1}\left(\dfrac{1}{LF_t}-\dfrac{1}{LF_{t-1}}\right)$. The results are affected by rounding.

Sources: EU-SILC UDB 2010, version 5 of August 2014; EU-SILC UDB 2012, version 1 of August 2014; EU-SILC UDB 2013, version 2 of August 2015; authors' computations.

After a short break in 2010–2011, when the development of youth unemployment rates started to resemble and sometimes even outperform prime-age unemployment rates, the most recent period covered by our data (2012) shows again the prevailing tendency of youth unemployment rates to increase more rapidly than prime-age rates. This could potentially be attributed to an only temporary effect of stimulus measures that were targeting the young unemployed disproportionally. Indeed, except for Spain, the 2012 balance of "ins" and "outs" reflects a new round of disproportionate increases in youth unemployment rates compared to prime-age unemployment rates. Similarly to 2008–2009, the main driver of these disproportions is seen in the fourth column in Table 7.1 and is embodied in a disproportionally high contribution of inflows of young workers from employment into unemployment.

Table 7.1 reveals the sources of different dynamics in youth unemployment rates. Surprisingly, the contributions of *outflows* from unemployment into employment in Spain and Austria were comparable in 2008–2009 and 2010–2011 (see the seventh column). The decisive source of strikingly different youth unemployment rate dynamics in these two countries was represented by a relatively much higher contribution of *inflows* of Spanish young workers into unemployment from employment (see the fourth column).

In 2012, France and Poland recorded the highest increases in youth unemployment rates. Both the stories behind these developments and the policy implications are somewhat different. In Poland, the only problem was embodied, at least in a given comparative perspective, in insufficient *outflows* from unemployment into employment (in the seventh column in Table 7.1). In contrast, France suffered simultaneously from relatively low "outs" and high "ins" of youth unemployment.

7.5. DETERMINING FACTORS OF TRANSITIONS BETWEEN EMPLOYMENT AND UNEMPLOYMENT

In this section, we provide an econometric analysis of the socioeconomic determinants of movements between employment and unemployment in both directions. In particular, we intend to verify within a multivariate framework the statistical significance of age for the risk of losing one's job and becoming unemployed. Then we concentrate on unemployment durations within both age groups of interest with the aim of detecting the presence of duration dependence of unemployment, net of other individual and additional characteristics influencing the job-finding probability of an unemployed person.

7.5.1. Transitions from Employment to Unemployment

Tables 7.2a–7.2c evaluate the factors influencing the probability of losing one's job and becoming unemployed. We present results for pooled samples of young and prime-age individuals in two specifications in the second and third columns. The first specification does not involve work experience and confirms

Table 7.2a Determinants of transitions of young people (aged 16–34 years) and prime-age individuals (aged 35–54 years) from employment to unemployment in four European countries: 2008–2009 (average marginal effects from probit model)

	AT				ES			
	Pooled	Pooled	Youth	Prime age	Pooled	Pooled	Youth	Prime age
Prime age	-0.048***	0.044**	—	—	-0.131***	-0.022**	—	—
Male	0.033***	0.045***	0.027	0.054***	-0.032***	-0.008	0.004	-0.012
Tertiary education	-0.150***	-0.156***	-0.228***	-0.138***	-0.199***	-0.109***	-0.099***	-0.112***
Secondary education	-0.100***	-0.090***	-0.087***	-0.096***	-0.138***	-0.078***	-0.064***	-0.082***
Experience (in years)	—	-0.006***	-0.005**	-0.006***	—	-0.004***	-0.009***	-0.003***
HH size 1	0.082***	0.101***	0.137***	0.089***	a	a	a	a
HH size 2	0.072***	0.090***	0.121***	0.081***	0.010	0.010	0.002	0.014
HH size 3	0.027*	0.038***	0.073***	0.025	0.009	0.003	-0.002	0.006
Densely populated area	0.004	-0.008	0.025	-0.025*	-0.038***	-0.02**	-0.053***	-0.004
Medium-populated area	-0.017	-0.018	-0.003	-0.024	-0.011	0.003	-0.015	0.013
Pseudo R^2	0.046	0.061	0.058	0.060	0.065	0.054	0.027	0.050
AUC	0.651	0.676	0.662	0.677	0.675	0.673	0.617	0.672
n	3,982	3,982	1,215	2,677	9,799	7,828	2,577	5,251

	FR				PL			
	Pooled	Pooled	Youth	Prime age	Pooled	Pooled	Youth	Prime age
Prime age	-0.102***	-0.000	—	—	-0.065***	0.024**	—	—
Male	0.004	0.015**	0.013	0.015**	0.007	0.017***	0.017	0.018**
Tertiary education	-0.101***	-0.105***	-0.178***	-0.069***	-0.121***	-0.123***	-0.144***	-0.126***
Secondary education	-0.045***	-0.037***	-0.065***	-0.026***	-0.046***	-0.041***	-0.071***	-0.025**
Experience (in years)	—	-0.007***	-0.019***	-0.004***	—	-0.006***	-0.011***	-0.004***
HH size 1	0.067***	0.069***	0.038	0.077***	a	a	a	a
HH size 2	0.028***	0.042***	0.050**	0.033***	0.025***	0.040***	0.035*	-0.041***
HH size 3	0.017*	0.026***	0.030	0.020**	-0.011	0.000	-0.019	0.011
Densely populated area	-0.003	-0.01	-0.026	-0.004	-0.006	-0.000	-0.022	0.012
Medium-populated area	-0.013	-0.013	-0.058***	0.004	-0.006	-0.003	-0.029	0.007
Pseudo R^2	0.061	0.095	0.083	0.065	0.036	0.063	0.053	0.059
AUC	0.682	0.725	0.700	0.694	0.631	0.688	0.666	0.683
n	7,449	7,449	2,387	5,018	8,782	8,694	3,097	5,597

[a]One- and two-person households are merged because of a low share of observations in the first category.

AUC, area under the curve; HH, household.

*$p < .10$.

**$p < .05$.

***$p < .01$.

Sources: EU-SILC UDB 2010, version 5 of August 2014; authors' computations.

Table 7.2b Determinants of transitions of young people (aged 16–34 years) and prime-age individuals (aged 35–54 years) from employment to unemployment in four European countries: 2010–2011 (average marginal effects from probit model)

	AT				ES			
	Pooled	Pooled	Youth	Prime age	Pooled	Pooled	Youth	Prime age
Prime age	-0.040***	0.034**	—	—	-0.115***	-0.011	—	—
Male	0.005	0.019*	0.024	0.024**	-0.021**	-0.001	-0.018	0.007
Tertiary education	-0.167***	-0.181***	-0.220***	-0.163***	-0.154***	-0.110***	-0.097***	-0.119***
Secondary education	-0.086***	-0.084***	-0.101***	-0.076***	-0.093***	-0.066***	-0.123***	-0.047***
Experience	—	-0.005***	-0.001	-0.006***	a	-0.005***	-0.006***	-0.005***
HH size 1	0.024	0.044***	0.029	0.049***	a	a	a	a
HH size 2	0.026**	0.045***	-0.001	0.064***	-0.013	0.000	-0.014	0.004
HH size 3	-0.012	0.000	-0.012	0.006	0.018*	-0.005	-0.010	-0.004
Densely populated area	0.014	0.005	0.033	-0.006	-0.050***	-0.022**	-0.036*	-0.017*
Medium-populated area	-0.004	-0.008	0.031	-0.023*	-0.030**	-0.002	-0.005	-0.001
Pseudo R^2	0.044	0.063	0.045	0.072	0.052	0.060	0.028	0.062
AUC	0.652	0.686	0.641	0.695	0.661	0.682	0.622	0.690
n	4,057	3,972	1,274	2,698	7,735	6,344	1,763	4,581

	FR				PL			
	Pooled	Pooled	Youth	Prime age	Pooled	Pooled	Youth	Prime age
Prime age	-0.104***	-0.006	—	—	-0.069***	0.034***	—	—
Male	-0.011*	0.002	-0.013	0.006	-0.030***	-0.016**	-0.033**	-0.007
Tertiary education	-0.108***	-0.113***	-0.196***	-0.076***	-0.173***	-0.170***	-0.160***	-0.185***
Secondary education	-0.043***	-0.038***	-0.078***	-0.023***	-0.074***	-0.062***	-0.056**	-0.061***
Experience	—	-0.006***	-0.019***	-0.004***	—	-0.006***	-0.014***	-0.005***
HH size 1	0.046***	0.053***	0.041	0.049***	a	a	a	a
HH size 2	0.025***	0.039***	0.034*	0.030***	0.027***	0.042***	0.052***	0.033***
HH size 3	0.015*	0.024***	0.020	0.017*	0.013	0.022***	0.025*	0.020**
Densely populated area	-0.021***	-0.014*	-0.029*	-0.007	0.003	0.004	-0.033**	0.026***
Medium-populated area	-0.003	0.002	-0.014	0.008	0.018**	0.021**	0.023	0.020**
Pseudo R^2	0.068	0.105	0.099	0.061	0.040	0.069	0.066	0.065
AUC	0.692	0.737	0.726	0.685	0.644	0.688	0.682	0.689
n	7,774	7,736	2,387	5,349	8,464	8,407	3,071	5,336

[a]One- and two-person households are merged because of a low share of observations in the first category.

AUC, area under the curve; HH, household.

*$p < .10$.

**$p < .05$.

***$p < .01$.

Source: EU-SILC UDB 2012, version 1 of August 2014; authors' computations.

Table 7.2c Determinants of transitions of young people (aged 16–34 years) and prime-age individuals (aged 35–54 years) from employment to unemployment in four European countries: 2012 (average marginal effects from probit model)

	AT				ES			
	Pooled	Pooled	Youth	Prime age	Pooled	Pooled	Youth	Prime age
Prime age			—		-0.051***	0.014	—	—
Male			-0.024**		-0.020***	-0.004	-0.030**	0.004
Tertiary education			-0.067***		-0.067***	-0.083***	-0.107***	-0.075***
Secondary education			-0.019		-0.062***	-0.07***	-0.100***	-0.059***
Experience			-0.003**		—	-0.005***	-0.010***	-0.004***
HH size 1			0.010		a	a	a	a
HH size 2			-0.028*		0.019**	0.022***	-0.007	0.034***
HH size 3			-0.029*		0.007	0.010	-0.016	0.020**
Densely populated area			0.026*		-0.021***	-0.019***	-0.013	-0.021***
Medium-populated area			0.003		-0.022**	-0.018**	-0.004	-0.022**
Pseudo R^2			0.044		0.031	0.051	0.045	0.047
AUC			0.668		0.634	0.667	0.648	0.666
n	b	b	1,596	b	9,003	8,927	2,424	6,503

	FR				PL			
	Pooled	Pooled	Youth	Prime age	Pooled	Pooled	Youth	Prime age
Prime age	−0.053***						—	
Male	−0.007						−0.025***	
Tertiary education	−0.062***						−0.071***	
Secondary education	−0.016**						−0.035**	
Experience	—						−0.007***	
HH size 1	0.019**						[a]	
HH size 2	0.010						0.004	
HH size 3	0.006						−0.013	
Densely populated area	0.011**						0.005	
Medium-populated area	0.009						0.003	
Pseudo R^2	0.054						0.049	
AUC	0.678						0.676	
n	8,629	[b]	[b]	[b]	[b]	[b]	3,702	[b]

[a]One- and two-person households are merged because of a low share of observations in the first category.

[b]For 2012, the share of employment spells transitioning into unemployment frequently amounts to less than 5%. Such results are omitted because of their presumably low representativeness.

AUC, area under the curve; HH, household.

*p < .10.

**p < .05.

***p < .01.

Source: EU-SILC UDB 2013, version 2 of August 2015; authors' computations.

the significantly lower probability of prime-age workers losing their jobs and becoming unemployed. The second specification includes work experience—a variable that proves significant in all cases. With added controls for work experience, the previously established age-group effect weakens substantially; in some cases, it loses its significance or even reverses. Austria and Poland represent the most illustrative cases in that in these two countries, the controls for work experience change the sign of the age-group effect.

The pooled models show uniformly that higher education levels significantly diminish the likelihood of losing one's job and becoming unemployed. In contrast, the effects of the remaining variables—such as gender, household size, or population density—are rather country specific or vary over time. Considering national specificities, it is worth noting that Spain is the only country in which gender has a significant effect on the probability of losing one's job and becoming unemployed in all subperiods analyzed. Female workers in Spain thus have a higher probability of becoming unemployed compared to men.

With added controls for work experience, this gender-based difference becomes insignificant. Women's lower work experience in Spain is thus responsible for their disadvantage in terms of sustaining employment and avoiding unemployment. This effect is not clearly apparent in any other country. In Austria, we can observe the opposite: Here, controls for work experience strengthen the men's disadvantage.

Among young people, the gender effect (both with and without controls for work experience) usually has no significant impact on the probability of losing one's job and becoming unemployed. This is not surprising because the gender difference in work experience cannot fully evolve at the beginning of working careers. But the gender gap in work experience may intensify during the life cycle, and women, especially in Spain, might suffer from a lack of such experience in the longer term.

The results of separate estimations for the two age groups also show that work experience significantly lowers the likelihood of losing one's job and becoming unemployed and that this effect is in most cases more evident among young workers. Higher education likewise significantly reduces the probability of losing one's job and becoming unemployed, and this effect is again typically stronger for young workers. Only in Spain is this specificity missing, thus indicating another difficulty faced by young workers in this country.

What really matters is not the age of a worker but, rather, his or her work experience and education. Our results confirm that young workers need to very quickly accrue relevant work experience because it diminishes their risk of becoming unemployed. The acquisition of higher education also appears to be an important factor in reducing the unemployment risk for young people.

7.5.2. Duration Dependence of Unemployment

Finally, we consider the differences in the duration of unemployment between young people and prime-age workers. Figure A7.5 in the Appendix provides evidence from KM functions. The graphs confirm our empirical findings presented in Section 7.4—as well as the conceptual considerations mentioned in the literature overview in Section 7.2—that young unemployed are unlikely to suffer from longer job search *compared* to prime-age unemployed.[11] But this is not to say that the problem of a prolonged duration of job search *within* the group of young unemployed should be ignored. As the Great Recession progressed, the survival functions in Figure A7.5 show dramatic declines in the job-finding prospects of young unemployed even in the shortest unemployment spells. This tendency is most apparent when comparing the periods 2008–2009 and 2012.

Austria shows its best performance within this general tendency. Figure A7.5 illustrates the gap between Austria and the remaining countries in terms of time needed by young unemployed to find a job: For instance, in 2010–2011, 44% of young Austrian unemployed managed to find a job after 4 months of unemployment duration; in France, Poland, and Spain, the shares were only 29%, 25%, and 21%, respectively. When comparing the situation after unemployment lasting for a minimum of 1 year in the same period, Austria again boasts the best job-finding prospects for young unemployed—this share amounted to 68%, as opposed to a mere 47% for Spain (58% for France and 53% for Poland).

Table 7.3 assesses the role of unemployment duration within a multivariate framework that also controls for a range of factors such as age, education, household size, and population density. The results in the first five rows of Table 7.3 show the impact of unemployment duration on individual job-finding probability in the form of hazard ratios. For each unemployment spell analyzed, the hazard ratio γ in Table 7.3 indicates the probability of leaving unemployment and becoming employed relative to a reference spell. For the periods 2008–2009 and 2010–2011, unemployment spells lasting between 16 and 24 months represent a reference duration interval. For 2012, a reference interval stands for unemployment spells lasting between 11 and 12 months.

Statistically insignificant hazard ratios γ would mean that there is actually no difference in job-finding prospects between the particular unemployment spell and the reference spell. The remaining rows in Table 7.3 show the hazard ratios that report the impact of explanatory variables. Suppose, for instance, that the hazard ratio reported for males takes the value "2"; then the probability that a man moves in a randomly chosen time from unemployment into employment would be, ceteris paribus, twice as high as for a woman.

In the initial stage of the Great Recession (2008–2009), the negative duration dependence of youth unemployment appeared to be absent in France and Austria.[12] This means that the individual and other characteristics of the young

Table 7.3 Youth hazard ratios of transition from unemployment to employment in four European countries (age category 16–34 years)

	2008–2009						2010–2011					2012			
	AT	AT[a]	ES	FR	FR[a]	PL	AT	ES	ES[a]	FR	PL	AT	ES	FR	PL
γ_1 (1–2 months)	4.029***	0.477	3.444***	1.514**	0.582	2.589***	3.637***	2.318***	1.137	1.977***	2.280***	6.127**	4.715***	4.965***	7.061***
γ_2 (3–4 months)	3.123***	0.629	3.517***	1.623**	0.743	3.357***	3.207***	2.578***	1.408	1.640***	3.128***	6.542***	5.186***	5.218***	9.670***
γ_3 (5–6 months)	2.451**	0.671	3.031***	1.607**	0.862	3.006***	2.600**	2.632***	1.608	1.699***	3.236***	2.118	6.736***	4.845***	9.282***
γ_4 (7–10 months)	1.458	0.524	2.067***	1.376*	0.894	2.924***	1.365	1.619***	1.110	1.457**	1.925***	2.934	3.208***	3.010***	5.447***
γ_5 (11–15 months)	2.336**	1.225	2.212***	0.958	0.759	1.323	1.595	2.132***	1.719***	1.361	1.551**	—	—	—	—
Male	1.446***	1.659**	1.092	0.911	0.884	1.421***	1.051	1.122*	1.159	1.032	1.416***	1.204	0.987	0.800**	1.355***
Tertiary education	1.248	1.409	1.380***	2.158***	3.061***	1.155	1.450*	1.381***	1.542***	1.774***	1.161	1.886*	1.646***	1.735***	1.921***
Secondary education	1.319**	1.907***	1.100	1.522***	1.759***	1.156	1.410**	1.112	1.165	1.446***	0.936	1.662**	1.434***	1.549***	1.257
Age 20–24 years	1.624***	2.206***	1.283**	1.024	1.034	1.341*	2.044***	1.722***	1.968***	1.283	1.817***	0.822	2.312***	2.499***	1.846**
Age 25–29 years	1.790***	2.390***	1.327***	0.876	0.804	1.37*	2.644***	2.036***	2.417***	1.378*	2.037***	0.662	2.244***	2.235***	1.888**
Age 30–34 years	1.616**	2.072**	1.289**	0.771	0.707	1.639***	2.045***	1.753***	2.042***	0.948	1.848***	0.774	2.133***	1.907***	1.625
HH size 1	1.618**	3.452***	b	1.732***	2.315***	b	1.279	b	b	1.690***	b	1.693**	b	1.357	b
HH size 2	1.905***	2.843***	1.440***	1.438***	1.521***	1.581***	1.012	1.332***	1.475***	1.524***	1.684***	1.034	1.327***	1.395***	1.354*
HH size 3	1.143	1.314	1.118	1.141	1.202	0.883	0.840	1.087	1.121	1.208*	1.233**	0.765	0.999	0.979	1.221*
Densely populated	0.738**	0.594**	0.766***	0.643***	0.534***	0.932	0.676***	0.636***	0.574***	1.429***	0.987	0.450***	0.693***	0.817*	1.116

Medium populated	1.027	0.939	0.847**	0.684***	0.588***	0.878	0.740*	0.775***	0.731***	0.944	0.946	0.553***	0.872	0.771*	0.797*
Constant	0.012***	0.058***	0.018***	0.046***	0.118***	0.013***	0.020***	0.013***	0.023***	0.020***	0.011***	0.027***	0.004***	0.005***	0.002***
Log-likelihood	−977.8	−970.4	−4,201.8	−1,731.4	−1,728.4	−1,863.4	−872.2	−3,476.0	−3,474.1	−2,007.6	−2,614.0	−463.3	−2,674.1	−1,329.3	−1,601.2
p value	—	0.000	—	—	0.007	—	—	—	0.024	—	—	—	—	—	—
n (unemployment spells)	541	541	2,237	896	896	1,077	466	1,952	1,952	1,014	1,376	315	2,133	981	1,378

Results with gamma frailty reported only when the likelihood ratio test of gamma variance (p value) significantly proved the impact of unobserved heterogeneity on model results.

bOne- and two-person households are merged because of a low share of observations in the first category.

HH, household.

*$p < .10$.

**$p < .05$.

***$p < .01$.

Sources: EU-SILC UDB 2010, version 5 of August 2014; EU-SILC UDB 2012, version 1 of August 2014; EU-SILC UDB 2013, version 2 of August 2015; authors' computations.

unemployed (and not the duration of unemployment per se) significantly affected their prospects of finding a job.

In contrast, those young unemployed in Poland whose unemployment spells lasted more than 10 months represented the risk group of young unemployed requiring targeting by additional policy measures, given that their chances of finding a job were not significantly better in comparison with the reference duration interval representing long-term unemployment (16–24 months). In Spain, the analogous risk group consisted of those young unemployed with unemployment spells exceeding 15 months (all shorter unemployment spells were associated with significantly higher job-finding probabilities).

As the Great Recession progressed, the duration dependence of youth unemployment started affecting developments in all the countries analyzed. Young Austrians who remained unemployed for more than 6 months in 2010–2011 (and for more than 4 months in 2012) represented the risk group of young unemployed. It follows that those young Austrian unemployed who did not find (or did not accept) a job relatively quickly faced sharply diminishing employment prospects. This suggests that stigmatization and/or discouragement effects of prolonged youth unemployment emerged in Austria with much briefer unemployment spells than in countries with considerably higher youth unemployment. The probable reason is that in countries with high levels of youth unemployment, longer unemployment durations are considered more "natural." The results for France and Poland confirm this assumption. In France, all young individuals who were unemployed for more than 10 months formed the risk group. This applied to both 2010–2011 and 2012. The results for Poland are very similar to those for France.

In Spain, the situation changed most dramatically between the two periods. In 2010–2011, all young unemployed with unemployment spells of between 1 and 10 months actually constituted the risk group in that their job-finding probabilities did not differ significantly from the employment prospects of long-term young unemployed (16–24 months). This further illustrates the depth of the youth unemployment problem in Spain. In contrast, the results for Spain in 2012 became comparable with those for France and Poland—the risk group of Spanish young unemployed was associated with unemployment durations exceeding 10 months.

The analysis of explanatory variables does not confirm the uniform presence of statistically significant gender- or education-based differences. But in Austria and France, the chance of finding a job gradually evolved in favor of young women. This is in line with Kelly et al. (2013), who report a lower probability of moving from unemployment to employment for young Irish men. In contrast, young Polish men have a consistently relatively higher chance of finding a job compared to young women in Poland. Spain shows no gender effects. Poland is also specific in that it lacks an education effect (except for tertiary education in 2012), whereas for the remaining countries we find convincing evidence that the chance of a young unemployed person finding a job increases with secondary and/or tertiary education. A young person aged 25–29 years has the highest probability of moving from unemployment to employment in the majority of countries and periods analyzed. This indicates that employers tend to avoid hiring the relatively immature young unemployed. Regarding household size, it negatively affects the probability of young unemployed finding a job, although with varying significance. A significantly higher job-finding probability (relative to a household consisting of four members or more) is associated almost exclusively with small households consisting, as a maximum, of two members. This might suggest that in the absence of other members in respondents' households (presumably their parents), who could contribute decisively to the common budget, the pressure to find a job imposed on young unemployed is significantly higher. However, this effect is not fully uniform—it is absent for Austria in 2010–2011.

The hazard ratios for densely populated areas are significant and lower than 1 (except for Poland in all three periods). This seems to contradict the assumption that larger cities provide more employment opportunities and thus better chances to exit from unemployment.[13] Our result can be associated with longer job search in the hope of gaining a better match or more opportunities to participate in the informal economy.

Table A7.1 in the Appendix suggests that prime-age hazard functions generally display a higher sensitivity of job-finding chances to the duration of unemployment episodes. Among other findings, the impact of age on the prospect of finding a job among prime-age unemployed is worth noting, especially the significant *negative* impact of age categories 45+ years. This suggests that the presumed skill obsolescence and deterioration in human capital associated with these age categories function as negative signals to potential employers and diminish the chances of older unemployed finding work.

7.6. CONCLUSIONS

Youth are relatively more involved in gross flows than are prime-age groups. This holds true uniformly across the four countries analyzed during the period 2008–2012 and supports the existing evidence of a higher aggregate fluidity of youth labor markets compared to prime-age markets. The main result stemming from the analysis of flow transition rates is that a young worker is more likely to move between employment and unemployment in both directions compared to a prime-age worker. This finding is in line with contemporary evidence for the United Kingdom. It can be interpreted as a typical feature of marginalized groups, which have to "churn" relatively more frequently through the (secondary) labor market.

The analysis of transition rates provides the following main conclusion: The policy priority should be to reduce the gap between the unemployment risks faced by a young and a prime-age worker. This gap is characteristic for all the labor markets analyzed and concerns countries with substantially different labor market performance, institutions, EU membership history, and other national specificities. Reducing the gap is important not only for generally improving the relative position of marginalized youth on the labor market but also for achieving more proportional evolutions in the youth and prime-age unemployment rates.

This chapter demonstrates that inflows of young workers into unemployment accounted for far higher increases in youth unemployment rates compared to prime-age unemployment rates. In contrast, had the outflows from unemployment to employment been the only driver of unemployment rate dynamics, youth unemployment rates would have developed more favorably than prime-age unemployment rates.

We analyzed in detail the determining factors of transitions from employment to unemployment. The results again stress the importance of a policy targeted at employment protection for young people, who need to gain work experience promptly after entering the labor market so as to minimize the probability of job loss. In addition, the effect of education on lowering the risk of job loss and becoming unemployed is apparent for individuals of any age; nonetheless, it seems that higher education decreases the probability of becoming unemployed more substantially for young workers.

Finally, we examined the extent to which the job-finding chances of young unemployed decline due to the duration of their unemployment, net of the impact of standard socioeconomic characteristics and unobserved heterogeneity of unemployed persons. Although the results for young unemployed appear to be generally favorable compared to those for prime-age unemployed, they simultaneously show growing negative duration dependence of youth unemployment as the Great Recession progressed. From 2010 onward, the job-finding prospects of young unemployed could be viewed as a diminishing function of unemployment duration in all countries analyzed. In 2012, the results nearly equalized across countries (except for Austria): With unemployment durations exceeding 10 months, the job-finding probability of a young unemployed person declines significantly, and those who remain unemployed for a longer time deserve additional policy attention.

Such a result may represent useful feedback for the European Youth Guarantee scheme, which promotes uniformly an offer to young people in the EU of a quality job, an apprenticeship, or training within 4 months after graduation or job loss. In contrast, our results demonstrate that the job-finding probability of a young unemployed person is already highest within the shortest unemployment spells. Although the information on unemployment durations and job-finding probabilities is never available ex ante to policymakers, it would appear that young people who are unemployed for a considerably longer time than 4 months are those who should be targeted by concentrated policy efforts and resources. This proposition is probably even more relevant for the ongoing post-recessionary period.

NOTES

1   Hadjivassiliou et al. (this volume) provide an overview of national specificities in youth labor market performance and in institutional arrangements of labor markets across the EU (including employment protection legislation, vocational education and training, active labor market policy, and collective bargaining). Our categorization of countries is analogous to that of Berloffa et al. (this volume), who analyze, among others, the clusters of Continental, Mediterranean, and Eastern European countries. Given the depth of our analysis, we concentrate on only a limited number of countries that reflect our categorization.

2   Section 7.3 discusses the data issues in more detail.

3   A common practice in this respect is to follow Petrongolo and Pissarides (2008) or Shimer (2012) in showing how much of the variance of the *steady-state* unemployment rate accounts for changes in the flow transition rates. Also see Elsby et al. (2011) for an application to youth unemployment rate dynamics in the United Kingdom. A credible compliance with this direction would require data gathered over a longer period of time than in the EU-SILC. This is why we limit ourselves to a "flow" decomposition of the *observed* changes in unemployment rates. Dixon et al. (2011) apply a similar framework to US data. Except for Flek and Mysíková (2015), such an approach has probably never been applied before to a cross-country analysis in Europe.

4   EU-SILC is an annual survey in which the monthly economic status is reported retrospectively. Respondents might not always recall correctly when they changed their labor market status. Although the precise month of such changes is potentially uncertain, it should not affect our results, which are based on monthly averages for the entire subperiods analyzed.

5   EU-SILC data do not account for direct job-to-job flows. This is why in our analysis an unchanged employment status can represent either maintaining the previous job or moving to another job.

6   A particular unemployment spell is left censored when it is already in progress at the beginning of the observed period, and it is right censored when it does not terminate by the end of the observed period. An additional, specific type of right censoring occurs when an unemployment spell ends in inactivity rather than in employment. The KM estimators applied take into account the right-censored data, whereas the left censoring remains unaddressed by techniques available to us. The seemingly easiest solution to this problem would be to remove the censored observations from the data set.

Unfortunately, this would probably make all the estimations of unemployment durations downward biased because longer unemployment spells are more likely to be censored compared to shorter ones. Note that in the case of probit model estimations, censoring is not an issue because we do not analyze the duration of *employment* there.

7　This model was implemented into a STATA routine (pmghaz) by Jenkins (1997). We utilize a refined version (pmghaz8) that has been applied, for example, by Disney et al. (2006), Albert et al. (2008), Davia and Legazpe (2014), and Flek et al. (2015).

8　Note that these variables may not capture all the existing differences among unemployed individuals, and their unobserved heterogeneity may lead to spurious duration dependence (Jenkins 1997; Machin and Manning 1999). To account for unobserved heterogeneity, we use the mixed proportional hazard model, in which the continuous hazard rate contains a gamma-distributed random variable with unit mean and unknown variance, which is to be estimated.

9　The results in Figure 7.1 do not involve the 55+ years age group. However, the share of elderly individuals in the working-age population and/or the specificity of their transitions are not large enough to qualitatively change the overall nature of the results (Flek and Mysíková (2015) report more details on flows among the elderly).

10　We do not report results for unemployment-to-education transitions of young people. However, Figure A7.4 in the Appendix presents the outflow rates from unemployment to inactivity for four age bands of young unemployed. In most countries and periods, these rates do not necessarily increase with lower age. Moreover, for the low age categories of young unemployed, the outflow rates from unemployment to inactivity are too low (usually lower than 1%) to represent any real alternative to unemployment. Austria can be viewed as the only exception.

11　Log-rank tests reveal that only in Austria (in the first subperiod analyzed) is the youth survival curve placed significantly above the prime-age survival curve; see Figure A7.5 in the Appendix.

12　For Poland and Spain, the controls for unobserved heterogeneity did not affect the significance of the results reported in Table 7.3 for the given period. For Austria and France, the results with gamma frailty are reported in additional columns because the likelihood ratio test of gamma variance (*p* value) proved the impact of unobserved heterogeneity on the significance of results—with added controls for unobserved heterogeneity, all the coefficients turned out to be insignificant. To eliminate spurious duration dependence, we decided not to discuss the results where the controls for unobserved heterogeneity proved the insignificance of duration intervals for job-finding probability.

13 D'Addio (1998) reports such an effect for young French women in the early 1990s.

REFERENCES

Albert, Cecilia, Luis Toharia, and María A. Davia. 2008. "To Find or Not to Find a First 'Significant' Job." *Revista de Economía Aplicada* 16 (46): 37–59.

Bell, David N. F., and David G. Blanchflower. 2011. "Young People and the Great Recession." *Oxford Review of Economic Policy* 27 (2): 241–67.

Blanchard, Olivier J. 1999. *European Unemployment: The Role of Shocks and Institutions*. Rome: Banca d'Italia.

Blanchard, Olivier J., and Peter A. Diamond. 1990. "The Cyclical Behavior of Gross Flows of US Workers." *Brookings Papers on Economic Activity* 21 (2): 85–156.

Cox, David R. 1972. "Regression Models and Life Tables." *Journal of the Royal Statistical Society, Series B (Methodological)* 34 (2): 187–220.

D'Addio, Anna C. 1998. "Unemployment Durations of French Young People: The Impact of Individual, Family and Other Factors on the Hazard Rate." CORE Discussion Paper 9851. Louvain-in-Neuve: Université Catholique de Louvain.

Davia, María A., and Nuria Legazpe. 2014. "Determinants of Employment Decisions After the First Childbirth in Spain." *Journal of Family and Economic Issues* 35 (2): 214–27.

Disney, Richard, Carl Emmerson, and Matthew Wakefield. 2006. "Ill Health and Retirement in Britain: A Panel Data-based Analysis." *Journal of Health Economics* 25 (4): 621–49.

Dixon, Robert, John Freebairn, and Guay C. Lim. 2011."Net Flows in the U.S. Labor Market, 1990–2010." *Monthly Labor Review* (February): 25–32.

Elsby, Michael W. L., Jennifer C. Smith, and Jonathan Wadsworth. 2011. "The Role of Worker Flows in the Dynamics and Distribution of UK Unemployment." Discussion Paper 5784. Bonn: Institute for the Study of Labor.

Flek, Vladislav, Martin Hála, and Martina Mysíková. 2015. "Duration Dependence and Exits from Youth Unemployment in Spain and the Czech Republic." *Economic Research* 28 (1): 1063–78.

Flek, Vladislav, and Martina Mysíková. 2015. "Unemployment Dynamics in Central Europe: A Labour Flow Approach." *Prague Economic Papers* 24 (1): 73–87.

Flek, Vladislav, and Martina Mysíková. 2016. "Youth Transitions and Labour Market Flows." STYLE Working Paper 5.2. Brighton, UK: CROME, University of Brighton. http://www.style-research.eu/publications/working-papers

Gomes, Pedro. 2009. "Labour Market Flows: Facts from the United Kingdom." Working Paper 367. London: Bank of England.

International Labour Organization. 2013. *Global Employment Trends for Youth 2013: A Generation at Risk.* Geneva: International Labour Organization.

Jenkins, Stephen P. 1997. "Sbe17: Discrete Time Proportional Hazards Regression." *STATA Technical Bulletin* 7 (39): 22–32.

Kaplan, Edward L., and Paul Meier. 1958. "Nonparametric Estimation from Incomplete Observations." *Journal of the American Statistical Association* 53 (282): 457–81.

Kelly, Elish, Seamus McGuinness, Philip J. O'Connell, David Haugh, and Alberto Gonzáles Pandiella. 2013. "Transitions in and out of Unemployment Among Young People in the Irish Recession." Economics Department Working Paper 1084. Paris: Organization for Economic Co-operation and Development.

Machin, Stephen, and Alan Manning. 1999. "The Causes and Consequences of Long-Term Unemployment in Europe." In *Handbook of Labor Economics*, edited by Orley C. Ashenfelter and David Card, 3085–139. Amsterdam: Elsevier.

Petrongolo, Barbara, and Christopher A. Pissarides. 2008. "The Ins and Outs of European Unemployment." *American Economic Review* 98 (2): 256–62.

Reich, Michael, David M. Gordon, and Richard C. Edwards. 1973. "Dual Labor Markets: A Theory of Labor Market Segmentation." *American Economic Review* 63 (2): 359–65.

Shimer, Robert. 2012. "Reassessing the Ins and Outs of Unemployment." *Review of Economic Dynamics* 15 (2): 127–48.

APPENDIX

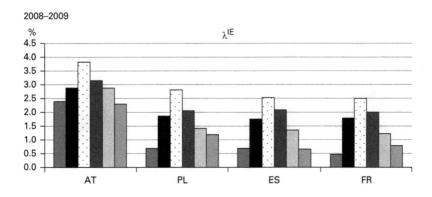

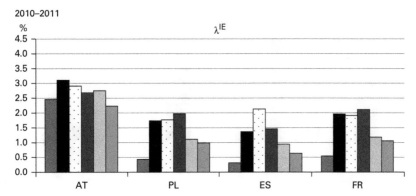

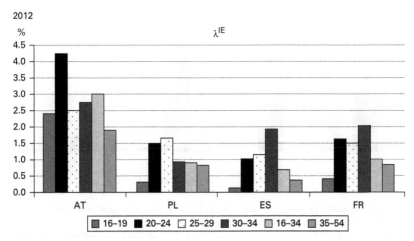

Figure A7.1 Transition rates from inactivity to employment for various age groups in four European countries (monthly averages, in %)

Sources: EU-SILC UDB 2010, version 5 of August 2014; EU-SILC UDB 2012, version 1 of August 2014; EU-SILC UDB 2013, version 2 of August 2015; authors' computations.

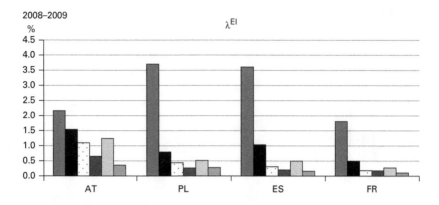

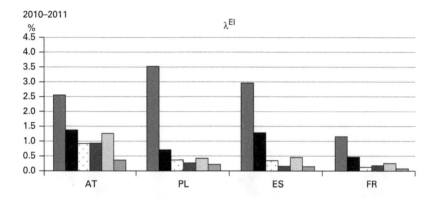

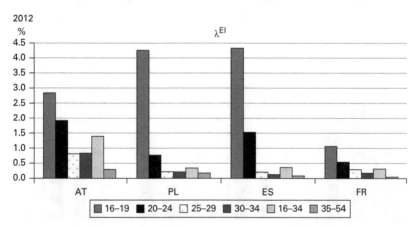

Figure A7.2 Transition rates from employment to inactivity for various age groups in four European countries (monthly averages, in %)

Sources: EU-SILC UDB 2010, version 5 of August 2014; EU-SILC UDB 2012, version 1 of August 2014; EU-SILC UDB 2013, version 2 of August 2015; authors' computations.

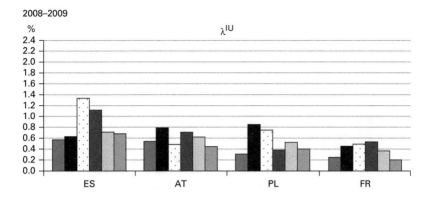

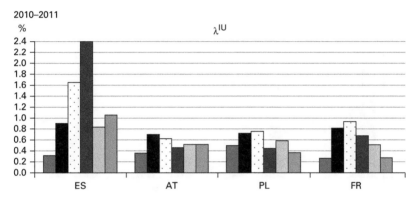

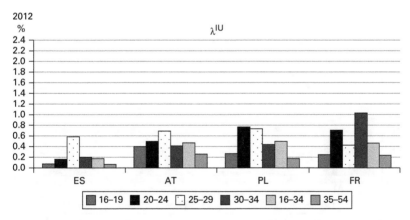

Figure A7.3 Transition rates from inactivity to unemployment for various age groups in four European countries (monthly averages, in %)
Sources: EU-SILC UDB 2010, version 5 of August 2014; EU-SILC UDB 2012, version 1 of August 2014; EU-SILC UDB 2013, version 2 of August 2015; authors' computations.

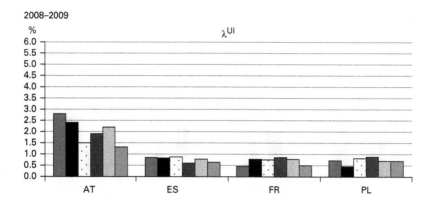

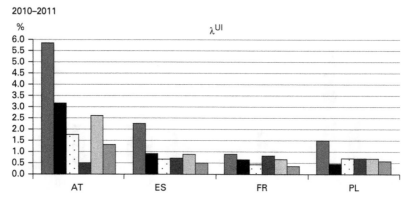

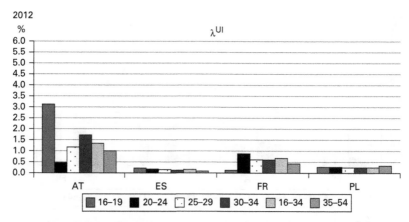

Figure A7.4 Transition rates from unemployment to inactivity for various age groups in four European countries (monthly averages, in %)

Sources: EU-SILC UDB 2010, version 5 of August 2014; EU-SILC UDB 2012, version 1 of August 2014; EU-SILC UDB 2013, version 2 of August 2015; authors' computations.

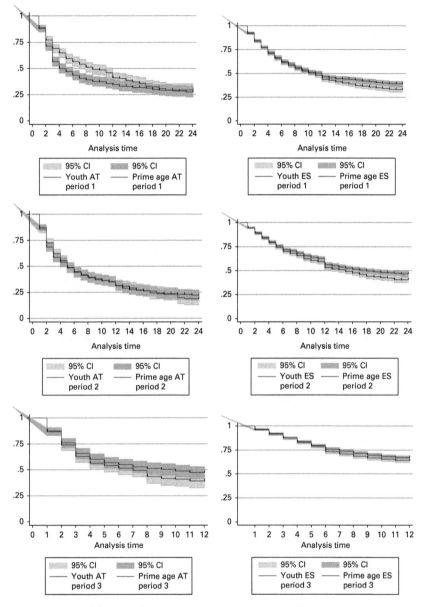

Figure A7.5 Survival functions for two age groups (16–34, 35–54) in four European countries (probabilities of remaining unemployed in %; 1: 2008–2009, 2: 2010–2011; 3: 2012)
Note: Analysis time: unemployment in months.
Sources: EU-SILC UDB 2010, version 5 of August 2014; EU-SILC UDB 2012, version 1 of August 2014; EU-SILC UDB 2013, version 2 of August 2015; authors' computations.

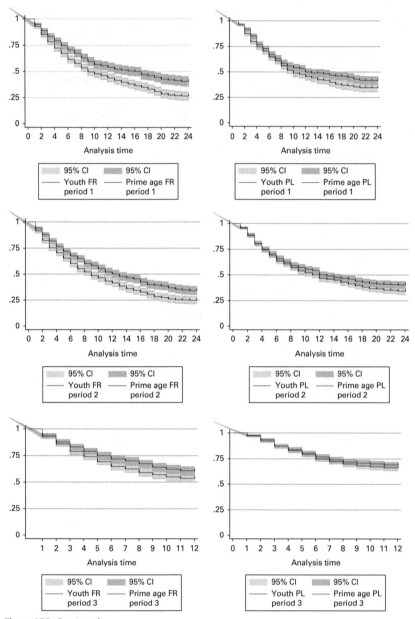

Figure A7.5 Continued

Table A7.1 Prime-age hazard ratios of transition from unemployment to employment in four European countries (age category 35–54 years)

	2008–2009				2010–2011				2012				
	AT	ES	FR	PL	AT	ES	FR	PL	AT	AT^a	ES	FR	PL
$\gamma_1^{(1\text{-}2 \text{ months})}$	9.106***	5.432***	2.062***	2.346***	4.956***	3.986***	1.691***	3.181***	6.297***	2.479	5.467***	4.480***	4.358***
$\gamma_2^{(3\text{-}4 \text{ months})}$	10.808***	5.193***	2.030***	4.833***	3.845***	3.710***	1.903***	5.116***	6.291***	3.870**	6.379***	3.811***	7.374***
$\gamma_3^{(5\text{-}6 \text{ months})}$	4.296***	4.583***	2.150***	3.972***	3.201***	3.562***	1.691***	3.668***	2.710	2.094	6.271***	3.597***	5.987***
$\gamma_4^{(7\text{-}10 \text{ months})}$	2.575**	3.203***	2.042***	3.195***	1.732	2.096***	1.358*	2.648***	1.822	1.632	3.574***	2.752**	3.303***
$\gamma_5^{(11\text{-}15 \text{ months})}$	2.139	2.262***	0.874	1.511	2.340**	3.197***	1.155	2.186***	–	–	–	–	–
Male	1.612***	1.026	0.982	1.421***	1.450***	1.271***	1.109	1.770***	1.179	1.372	1.146**	1.267*	1.951***
Tertiary education	1.530**	1.124	1.831***	1.316	1.336	1.273***	1.188	1.404	1.230	1.267	1.161	1.484*	1.516
Secondary education	1.602***	1.100	1.242	1.112	1.263*	1.011	1.257*	1.056	1.098	1.073	1.129	1.619***	1.271
Age 40–44 years	0.817	1.145*	0.766*	1.176	0.957	1.019	1.192	0.891	0.866	0.696	0.979	0.644**	1.018
Age 45–49 years	0.731**	1.038	0.824	0.737**	0.720**	0.997	0.967	0.918	0.739	0.582*	0.849*	0.777	0.818
Age 50–54 years	0.824	0.928	0.705**	0.687***	0.510***	0.771***	0.715**	0.748***	0.410***	0.260***	0.728***	0.490***	0.785
HH size 1	1.176	b	1.411**	b	0.646**	b	1.032	b	1.106	1.034	b	0.870	b
HH size 2	1.177	0.954	0.961	1.046	1.104	1.051	0.712**	0.823*	0.988	0.914	1.154	0.888	0.972
HH size 3	1.009	0.955	1.017	0.918	0.827	1.178**	0.825	0.784**	1.177	1.150	1.222**	0.863	0.926
Densely populated	0.641***	0.675***	0.796	0.951	0.428***	0.559***	1.326**	0.896	0.266***	0.166***	0.554***	0.897	0.899
Medium populated	0.685***	0.684***	1.104	1.044	0.721**	0.711***	1.146	0.802**	0.668**	0.559**	0.707***	0.827	0.845

(continued)

Table A7.1 Continued

| | 2008–2009 | | | | 2010–2011 | | | | 2012 | | | |
	AT	ES	FR	PL	AT	ES	FR	PL	AT	AT[a]	ES	FR	PL
Constant	0.014***	0.019***	0.027***	0.016***	0.046***	0.017***	0.030***	0.017***	0.037***	0.154*	0.009***	0.014***	0.005***
Log-likelihood	−996.8	−4,030.9	−1,326.9	−1,800.1	−997.3	−4,067.8	−1,677.3	−2,307.9	−532.0	−530.0	−3,629.6	−958.0	−1,305.7
p value	–	–	–	–	–	–	–	–	–	0.022	–	–	–
n (unemployment spells)	548	2,260	722	1,028	519	2,353	822	1,237	394	394	3,048	734	1,176

[a]Results with gamma frailty reported only when the likelihood ratio test of gamma variance (p value) significantly proved the impact of unobserved heterogeneity on model results.

[b]One- and two-person households are merged because of a low share of observations in the first category.

*p < .10.

**p < .05.

***p < .01.

HH, household.

Sources: EU-SILC UDB 2010, version 5 of August 2014; EU-SILC UDB 2012, version 1 of August 2014; EU-SILC UDB 2013, version 2 of August 2015; authors' computations.

8

HOW CAN YOUNG PEOPLE'S EMPLOYMENT QUALITY BE ASSESSED DYNAMICALLY?

Gabriella Berloffa, Eleonora Matteazzi, Gabriele Mazzolini, Alina Şandor, and Paola Villa

8.1. INTRODUCTION

The objective of this chapter is to present a dynamic approach that enables assessment of various aspects of youth labor market performance over a relatively long period of time. Standard analyses of labor market performance are usually based on indicators aimed at capturing young people's condition in the labor market at a single point in time (employment, unemployment, or inactivity rates; see Hadjivassiliou et al., this volume) or on estimations of the conditional probabilities of entering or leaving a certain status (see Flek, Hála, and Mysíková, this volume). More recently, some authors have turned their attention to the analysis of entire employment status trajectories. In this chapter, we argue that it is important—in order to be able to set priorities and design appropriate policies—to consider sequences of individual employment statuses over time that encompass information on the timing, length, and order in which changes of status occur.

Another aspect of labor market outcomes for which it is important to adopt a dynamic perspective is evaluation of the "quality" of employment. Researchers and policymakers are increasingly concerned with various employment dimensions, such as the security of jobs, a decent labor income, and a good match between educational qualifications and skills. Because it is increasingly common for individuals to move between different jobs, with possible unemployment spells in between, we need to go beyond the concepts of job security

237

and job quality and evaluate the quality and security of the individual employment condition over an appropriate period of time. In this chapter, we present the definition of employment quality illustrated in Berloffa et al. (2015). This definition is based on four dimensions (employment security, income security, income success, and successful match between education and occupation), which are identified using information covering a 2-year period.

An empirical application of this approach to analyzing young people's employment quality within a dynamic perspective is presented here. We distinguish between two different phases of young people's working lives: entry into the labor market (i.e., the transition from school to the first relevant employment experience) and the subsequent phase approximately 5 years after leaving full-time education. The analysis of these two phases is carried out using EU-SILC (European Union Statistics on Income and Living Conditions) longitudinal data over the period 2006–2012 for 17 countries. Our results suggest that adopting a dynamic approach to youth labor market performance allows a more accurate analysis of young people's employment paths and their quality. Empirical findings show that although males and females have similar chances of rapidly accessing paid employment after leaving education, women's labor market conditions deteriorate over the following few years. Consequently, there is still a pressing need to enhance women's chances of remaining continuously in employment and of moving up the labor income distribution. Relaxing the rules on the use of temporary contracts actually generates more difficulties for women and low-educated individuals, and it also appears to worsen youth employment prospects in general.

The remainder of the chapter is organized as follows. Section 8.2 reviews the relevant literature. Section 8.3 discusses the methodology and data used. Section 8.4 presents some descriptive statistics to show the extent to which individual trajectories and employment quality vary across European countries, gender, and educational attainment. Section 8.5 presents the empirical methodology and illustrates our main empirical findings. Section 8.6 concludes the chapter.

8.2. LITERATURE REVIEW

In the analysis of individual labor market performance, two aspects are of particular interest to researchers and policymakers: employment status and some job-related characteristics (job security, earnings, and match with level of education). Analysis of individual employment status is usually based on aggregate indicators referring to a single point in time (employment, unemployment, and inactivity) and on related trends (International Labour Organization 2015; European Commission 2016). More sophisticated studies also include the temporal dimension (European Commission Employment Committee 2009). Such studies generally consider the probabilities of entering or exiting a certain status (employment or unemployment), conditional on current or previous statuses, but they differ according to the type of conditionality considered. Some authors estimate simple status-dependent probabilities (Russell and O'Connell 2001; Uhlendorff 2006; Stewart 2007; Cappellari and Jenkins 2008; Berloffa, Modena, and Villa 2014); others use a duration analysis to capture different effects of previous statuses according to their length (Muller and Gangl 2003; Kalwij 2004; Dorsett and Lucchino 2013b). Some scholars consider only transitions between statuses of a specific length (Korpi et al. 2003), whereas others are interested in the long-term effect of youth unemployment on later labor market outcomes (employment status, earnings, etc.; Mroz and Savage 2006).

One drawback of these approaches is their focus on a single status change (education–employment, employment–unemployment). They often account for the length of previous spells yet discard other crucial information on labor market dynamics, such as the timing and the order in which events occur. The sequence analysis approach attempts to overcome these shortcomings by considering the complexity of a transition process involving several status changes over time (Shanahan 2000). Various authors have recently used this type of analysis to model longitudinal processes, such as school-to-work transitions and career trajectories (Scherer 2005; Brzinsky-Fay 2007; Quintini and Manfredi 2009; Dorsett and Lucchino 2013a).[1] All of these studies adopt the optimal matching (OM) technique to group individual sequences.[2] However, the use of OM to study life course events is a controversial choice. The most recurrent criticisms concern the lack of a theoretical basis for converting sequences into a model (Levine 2000) and the failure to account for the direction of time and the order of statuses across sequences (Wu 2000). Given these criticisms, research on OM has moved toward a fine-tuning of the methodology.[3] Notwithstanding the various extensions and improvements developed during the past decade, the classification of trajectories or sequences based on OM is still *data driven*. In the following section, we present an alternative, *outcome-driven* methodology for grouping individual trajectories. This approach does not rely on sequence alignment (OM) or data-reduction techniques (i.e., cluster analysis or discrepancy analysis) to group trajectories. Instead, we identify—on the basis of our research questions— the main outcomes we are interested in, and we group the individuals in our sample accordingly.[4] Further details regarding this methodology are discussed in Section 8.3.

Because labor markets are increasingly characterized by workers moving quite frequently between jobs, with possible unemployment spells in between, we need to adopt a dynamic perspective not only for individuals' employment statuses but also for the evaluation of other dimensions of their employment condition. For example, the need to combine flexibility and security in European labor markets (Smith et al., this volume) requires going beyond the concept of job security associated with type of contract and instead using a definition of individual employment security based on employment status trajectories (Berloffa et al. 2016). In this chapter, we present a new ambitious attempt to define a concept of "employment quality" within a dynamic perspective.

Numerous studies have explored the definition and implications of the complex and multidimensional concept of job quality (Green 2006; European Commission 2014, 172–79). Even when attention is restricted to objective (rather than subjective) job quality, the definition and the aspects considered vary noticeably across academic fields and studies. Nevertheless, there is some convergence on the features considered to be crucial for workers' well-being. These always include some indicators on the level of earnings (and earnings distribution) and on insecurity (i.e., unemployment risk).[5] Thus, our definition of employment quality encompasses four dimensions that we consider essential for the successful inclusion of young people in the labor market: employment security, income security, income success, and a good match between educational qualification and occupation. The last dimension is not usually considered in the literature on job quality. However, skill mismatch is a widespread and increasing phenomenon in Europe, especially for young people (European Commission 2012; European Central Bank 2014; International Labour Organization 2014a, 2014b; McGuinness, Bergin, and Whelan, this volume)[6] and for migrant workers (Spreckelsen, Leschke, and Seeleib-Kaiser, this volume). Generally, overqualified workers are less satisfied with their jobs and are more likely to leave them compared to their equally qualified and well-matched counterparts (Quintini 2011). Therefore, we include a good match between educational qualification and occupation as one of the key dimensions of employment quality (also see Berloffa et al. 2015).

8.3. DATA AND METHODOLOGICAL ISSUES

The approach presented in this chapter is based on two main tools of analysis: (1) a new "outcome-driven" methodology for grouping individual employment status trajectories (ESTs) and (2) a dynamic concept of employment quality. In the evaluation of youth labor market performance, these two tools can be used jointly or separately according to the specific aim of the analysis. As an example, we show how they can be employed to examine two different phases of youth working life: the first entry into the labor market and the subsequent phase approximately 5 years after exit from education.[7]

For young individuals exiting full-time education (first phase), a particularly important policy concern is whether they are able to enter and remain in employment for a sufficiently long period of time. In this phase, other aspects of employment quality are less relevant. Hence, we use only the first tool of analysis—that is, the features of individual ESTs in the first 3 years after leaving education. As in Berloffa, Mazzolini, and Villa (2015), we classify ESTs according to the outcome of interest—that is, the achievement of a "relevant" employment spell, defined as lasting for at least 6 consecutive months (see Section 8.3.1 for more details).

For the subsequent phase (approximately 5 years after education exit), it is important to examine whether individuals achieved a secure and successful employment condition and whether the shortcomings of lack of work experience are overcome. For the analysis of this phase, we combine the two tools of analysis, as in Berloffa et al. (2015). We identify those individuals who achieved a good-quality employment condition and disaggregate the group of those who did not achieve this outcome by the type of EST that characterizes their labor market experience during that same period. In this case, trajectory types are grouped according to the outcome of interest—that is, prevailing status and the frequency of status changes (for further details, see Section 8.3.2).

The empirical analysis makes use of EU-SILC longitudinal data covering the years from 2006 to 2012. The focus is on young people aged 16–34 years. The data make it possible to track individuals for a maximum of four interviews (i.e., 4 years), but our analysis is restricted to individuals with at least three consecutive interviews (i.e., 3 years) in order to increase the sample size. For the first phase, we consider only young individuals who left education during the 3 years covered by the three interviews. Because of data limitations, we are able to consider 17 countries (AT, BE, CZ, DK, EE, EL, ES, FI, FR, HU, IT, PL, PT, SE, SI, SK, and UK).[8] For the second phase, we consider young people who left education 3–5 years before the first interview.[9] We consider the same group of countries as for the first phase, except for Denmark (because of the low number of cases in some EST types) and the United Kingdom (because its definition of the income reference period is not consistent with that of the other countries and with the data used to identify employment status sequences). However, we are able to also include the Netherlands in the second phase of the analysis. In both phases, monthly information about self-declared employment statuses (e.g., employed, unemployed, inactive, and in education) is used to identify individual employment status sequences.[10]

8.3.1. First Phase: ESTs in the First 3 Years After Leaving Education

In the analysis of the early labor market experiences of young people, we consider their ESTs during the first 3 years after education exit. As discussed in Berloffa, Mazzolini, and Villa (2015), we classify them according to the time needed to reach, and the pathway that led to, the first relevant employment spell—that is, an employment spell lasting at least 6 consecutive months.[11] We distinguish between successful and unsuccessful trajectories according to the achievement or not of this outcome, and we identify various subtypes according to whether individuals experience a small number of long jobless spells (i.e., spells of unemployment or inactivity) or a large number of short employment and jobless spells. We also consider the decision to return to education after a sufficiently long period in employment or unemployment/inactivity. These criteria produce six different EST types:

> *Successful trajectories*
>> • *Speedy pathway*: The sequence presents a relevant employment spell within 6 months after leaving full-time education.
>> • *Long-search pathway*: The sequence presents a relevant employment spell after more than 6 months in unemployment or inactivity.
>> • *In & out successful pathway*: The sequence presents a relevant employment spell after various nonrelevant employment spells, interspersed by short periods in unemployment or inactivity.
> *Unsuccessful trajectories*
>> • *In & out unsuccessful pathway*: The sequence (similar to the *in & out successful pathway*) does not end in a relevant employment spell.
>> • *Continuous unemployment/inactivity pathway*: The sequence is characterized only by spells of unemployment or inactivity.
> *Return to education pathway*: The sequence is characterized by a long spell in education (at least 6 consecutive months) experienced 6 months after having left full-time education.

Figure 8.1 provides a graphical representation of individual employment trajectories pertaining to these six EST types. They are obtained by applying the previously specified criteria to the EU-SILC sample of young people for the first phase (i.e., during the first 3 years after education exit).

8.3.2. Second Phase: Employment Quality Approximately 5 Years After Leaving Education

As discussed in Berloffa et al. (2015), for the subsequent temporal phase of youth labor market experience, four dimensions are essential for assessing individuals' "employment quality": employment security, income security, income success, and education–occupation success. The definition of each dimension is presented in Table 8.1. Each dimension is evaluated during the two calendar years corresponding to the first two interviews.[12]

Identifying those young people who experience security and/or success is not enough from a policy standpoint because the group of those who have not achieved this outcome is quite heterogeneous. Indeed, individuals with frequent status changes require different policy interventions compared to individuals who remain for long periods in unemployment or inactivity. Therefore, we consider individual ESTs and group them according to their prevailing status and

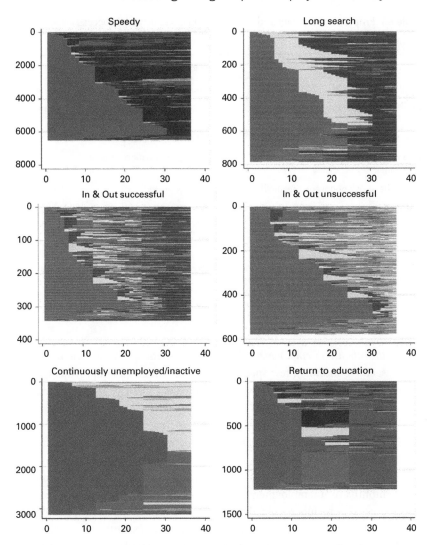

Figure 8.1 ESTs for young people in the first 3 years after leaving education (first phase) in 17 European countries.
Source: Berloffa, Mazzolini, and Villa (2015) based on EU-SILC longitudinal data (2006–2012).

the frequency of status changes.[13] In this group, returning to education for a relevant number of months may have important consequences for future prospects.
Hence, it cannot be mixed with other types of trajectories. Given these criteria,
we identify six EST types for the second phase:

1. *Almost always in employment*: All months in employment, with or
   without short spells in education (less than 6 consecutive months).

Table 8.1 Employment quality and its dimensions: Security and success

Employment quality

Security	Success
Employment security	Income success: Individuals' monthly earnings[a]
Spells of employment ≥ 6 months	Above the country–year–education median earnings
Spells of nonemployment ≤ 3 months	Not diminishing over time
Income security: Individuals' annual earnings[b]	Education–occupation success[c]
Above the at-risk-of-poverty threshold	Not overeducated
Not diminishing over time	Not moving down the occupational ladder over time

[a]Monthly earnings are computed by dividing the declared annual labor income by the number of months worked during the income reference period.
[b]This threshold corresponds to 60% of the national median equivalized disposable income after social transfers.
[c]Overeducation and undereducation mean that workers have more or less education than is required to carry out their job (International Labour Organization 2014b).

2. *Prevalently in employment*: Long employment spells (at least 12 consecutive months); few spells of nonemployment (unemployment, inactivity, or education); low number of status changes (three at most); and, overall, more months in employment than in unemployment and inactivity.

3. *Prevalently in unemployment*: Long unemployment spells (at least 12 consecutive months); few spells of employment or inactivity/education; low number of status changes (three at most); and, overall, more months in unemployment/inactivity than in employment. This category also includes individuals who were always out of employment, with more months in unemployment than in inactivity.

4. *Prevalently in inactivity*: Long inactivity spells (at least 12 consecutive months); few short spells (less than 6 months) in employment and education;[14] low number of status changes (three at most); and, overall, more months in inactivity than in unemployment.

5. *In & out employment*: More than three status changes; individuals enter and exit paid employment at least four times during the 36 months considered.

6. *Return to education*: Returned to full-time education for at least 6 consecutive months.

A representation of individual trajectories pertaining to the different EST types can be found in Berloffa et al. (2015).

8.4. YOUTH TRAJECTORIES IN EUROPE: A DESCRIPTIVE ANALYSIS

Differences in youth transitions, both from school to work and within the labor market, may be explained by cross-country differences in education systems, labor market institutions, youth unemployment rates, and other macroeconomic conditions (Müller and Gangl 2003; Scherer 2005; Schomburg and Teichler 2006; Wolbers 2007). But individual trajectories vary greatly also with respect to some individual characteristics, particularly gender and education level.

8.4.1. First Phase: From School to Work

Table 8.2 shows the unconditional distribution of the six EST types (in the first 3 years after leaving full-time education) by gender, highest education level attained, across European countries,[15] and before and during the economic crisis.[16]

Approximately 66% of young individuals in our sample reach a relevant employment spell within 3 years after leaving education, with no major gender differences. Within the unsuccessful group, women have a slightly higher share of continuous unemployment/inactive pathways, whereas men slightly more frequently have in & out unsuccessful trajectories. Level of education plays a relevant role in leading to a successful EST: 73% of university graduates have a speedy pathway, compared to 59% of those with a high school diploma and 44% of those with primary education. Only 10% of individuals with tertiary education have an unsuccessful trajectory, whereas this share is substantially higher among people with secondary and primary education (21% and 41%, respectively). Within this unsuccessful group, the relative distribution between continuous unemployment/inactivity and in & out is similar across education levels.

Successful trajectories are more frequent in the Nordic countries, which exhibit the highest shares of young people in both speedy (74%) and in & out successful pathways (5%). The Nordic countries also have the lowest percentage of young people who are continuously unemployed/inactive (6%). The Southern countries show the worst youth labor market outcomes. Only 43% of young people have a speedy trajectory, whereas more than 31% are continuously unemployed or inactive.

The impact of the economic crisis on ESTs is significant: The share of young people with speedy trajectories decreases by 11 percentage points (pp) between 2005–2007 and 2009–2011 (from 63% to 52%). Also apparent is an increase in individuals who experience continuous unemployment/inactivity trajectories (from 16% to 24%) and in & out unsuccessful pathways (from 4% to 7%). Moreover, return to education pathways record an increase (from 6% to 9%), suggesting higher investment in human capital during economic downturns, as would be expected.

Table 8.2 Descriptive statistics on ESTs in the first 3 years after leaving education (first phase) in 17 European countries

	Successful trajectories			Unsuccessful trajectories			
	Speedy	Long search	In & out successful	In & out unsuccessful	Continuously unemployed/ inactive	Return to education	No. of observations
All sample	0.57	0.06	0.03	0.05	0.21	0.08	6,924
Gender							
Male	0.57	0.06	0.03	0.06	0.20	0.07	3,256
Female	0.56	0.06	0.03	0.04	0.22	0.09	3,668
Education							
Low	0.44	0.04	0.03	0.08	0.33	0.09	3,016
Medium	0.59	0.07	0.03	0.04	0.17	0.10	1,856
High	0.73	0.08	0.04	0.02	0.08	0.04	2,052
Country group							
Nordic	0.74	0.01	0.05	0.05	0.06	0.08	974
Continental	0.60	0.06	0.03	0.06	0.20	0.05	1,727
Southern	0.43	0.06	0.03	0.06	0.31	0.12	2,239
Eastern	0.60	0.09	0.03	0.04	0.19	0.06	1,984
ESTs observed in							
2005–2007	0.63	0.07	0.04	0.04	0.16	0.06	1,230
2009–2011	0.52	0.06	0.03	0.07	0.24	0.09	1,156

Notes: ESTs, individual employment status trajectories. Sample: young individuals (aged 16–34 years) observed for 36 months. Education: low, lower secondary education; medium, upper secondary education; high, tertiary education. Country groups: Nordic = DK, FI, and SE; Continental = AT, BE, and FR; the UK is also added to this group because the sample size is too small to be considered separately and because the distribution of UK individuals across EST types is more similar to Continental countries than to other country groups; Southern = EL, ES, IT, and PT; Eastern = CZ, EE, HU, PL, SI, and SK.

Source: Authors' calculations based on EU-SILC longitudinal data (2006–2012).

8.4.2. Second Phase: Employment Quality and ESTs Approximately 5 Years After Leaving Education

Table 8.3 shows the shares of young people who, approximately 5 years after leaving education, achieve each of the four dimensions used to define their employment quality. Inspection of Table 8.3 reveals that 67% of young individuals in our sample experience employment security, whereas 42% enjoy income security. Overall, 40% of young individuals have a "secure employment condition" (combining employment security with income security). Major differences by gender emerge: Young males are more likely than young females to have a secure employment condition, whatever the dimension of security taken into account. Moreover, education plays a crucial role in ensuring a "secure employment condition": Almost half of all university graduates experience security, compared to only 16% of those with a lower secondary education. The Southern countries stand out as featuring the lowest share of young people enjoying security. Finally, the impact of the economic crisis results in an overall reduction in the share of young people enjoying security: 36% in 2009–2010 compared to 45% in 2006–2007.

The share of young people in our sample enjoying a successful employment condition (i.e., income success and education–occupation success) is only 16%. More than half of young individuals enjoy a good match between their educational attainments and the type of their occupation, but only one out of five is income successful.[17] Because economic success is defined with respect to the education-specific earnings distribution, differences between university and high school graduates disappear when we examine the "success" dimension.

The differences across country groups are relatively small, with the Southern countries recording the lowest shares of young people in terms of both dimensions of success. Although we define income success using year-specific monthly earnings, there is a modest reduction over time in the share of young people experiencing income success. Because our definition of the latter also requires that monthly earnings are nondecreasing during the 2-year observation period, this result suggests that since the onset of the crisis, it has become more likely for youth to experience a reduction in their monthly earnings over time. During the crisis, young people encounter increasing difficulties not only in finding a job but also in finding one that matches their education level.

What is really striking in this scenario is the strong disadvantage suffered by young women—in terms of both income success and education–occupation success. As a result, only 11% of women, versus 21% of men, enjoy a successful employment condition. These results clearly reflect the issues of occupational segregation and wage penalty for females (Dalla Chiara, Matteazzi, and Petrarca 2014).

As noted in Section 8.3.2, the group of people who do not achieve a secure or successful employment condition is quite heterogeneous. Table 8.4 shows

Table 8.3 Descriptive statistics of employment quality of young people approximately 5 years after leaving education (second phase) in 15 European countries

	Secure employment condition			Successful employment condition		
	Employment security	Income security	Employment and income security	Income success	Education–occupation success	Income and education–occupation success
All sample	0.67	0.42	**0.40**	0.21	0.53	**0.16**
Gender						
Male	0.72	0.46	**0.44**	0.28	0.57	**0.21**
Female	0.61	0.38	**0.35**	0.15	0.49	**0.11**
Education						
Low	0.40	0.18	**0.16**	0.14	0.36	**0.10**
Medium	0.65	0.41	**0.39**	0.21	0.55	**0.17**
High	0.78	0.51	**0.48**	0.24	0.58	**0.18**
Country group						
Nordic	0.69	0.41	**0.37**	0.22	0.60	**0.18**
Continental	0.74	0.44	**0.42**	0.23	0.56	**0.17**
Southern	0.58	0.37	**0.33**	0.19	0.44	**0.14**
Eastern	0.69	0.45	**0.43**	0.22	0.57	**0.18**
Employment quality in						
2006–2007	0.68	0.48	**0.45**	0.24	0.55	**0.18**
2009–2010	0.66	0.38	**0.36**	0.19	0.49	**0.14**

Notes: See Table 8.1 and notes to Table 8.2. DK and UK are not included in the analysis.
Source: Authors' calculations based on EU-SILC longitudinal data (2006–2012).

Table 8.4 Descriptive statistics on ESTs approximately 5 years after leaving education (second phase) in 15 European countries

	Almost always in employment	Prevalently in employment	Prevalently in unemployment	Prevalently in inactivity	In & out	Return to education	No. of observations
All sample	0.55	0.19	0.09	0.06	0.06	0.05	8,070
Unsuccessful and/or insecure people	0.49	0.21	0.11	0.07	0.07	0.06	6,824
The relative distribution of young people with unsuccessful and/or insecure ESTs							
Gender							
Male	0.53	0.20	0.11	0.02	0.08	0.06	3,277
Female	0.45	0.22	0.10	0.11	0.07	0.06	3,547
Education							
Low	0.24	0.22	0.23	0.07	0.09	0.15	816
Medium	0.45	0.22	0.11	0.08	0.08	0.06	3,510
High	0.62	0.19	0.05	0.05	0.05	0.03	2,498
Country group							
Nordic	0.51	0.20	0.03	0.06	0.15	0.06	358
Continental	0.57	0.20	0.05	0.03	0.08	0.07	1,289
Southern	0.40	0.22	0.17	0.04	0.08	0.10	2,130
Eastern	0.51	0.21	0.10	0.10	0.06	0.03	3,047
ESTs observed in							
2005–2007	0.50	0.19	0.12	0.06	0.07	0.05	1,284
2009–2011	0.48	0.21	0.11	0.05	0.08	0.07	1,280

Notes: See notes to Table 8.2. DK and UK are not included in the analysis.
Source: Authors' calculations based on EU-SILC longitudinal data (2006–2012).

the unconditional distribution of the six second-phase EST types described in Section 8.3.2 for the whole sample and for the unsuccessful/insecure group. As to be expected, unsuccessful and/or insecure young people are less likely to be almost always in employment. Among the young individuals unable to achieve success and/or security, young women are less likely than men to be almost always in employment and are more likely to be prevalently inactive. No relevant gender differences emerge for the other EST types in this set.

University and high school graduates are much more likely to be almost always in employment compared to individuals with low education, and they are much less likely to be prevalently in unemployment. Only 15% of young people with a low education level choose to return to education.

Again, the Southern countries stand out for the difficulties that young people face in the labor market: Only 62% are almost always or prevalently employed, compared to 72% or more in the other country groups. Southern Europe also exhibits the highest share of young individuals who are prevalently unemployed. No important differences are observed in the distribution of young people by EST types before and during the crisis.

8.5. THE DETERMINANTS OF YOUTH TRAJECTORIES AND EMPLOYMENT QUALITY

We estimate various multinomial logit models for the first and the second phase of young people's labor market experience in order to check the extent to which socioeconomic factors impact on the probability of experiencing various types of outcomes. For the first phase, the outcome considered is the EST type. For the second phase, the explained variable is the interaction between the secure or successful employment condition and the EST types. We also estimate a multinomial logit model for the interaction between the employment security condition and the EST types because we want to compare the results of this model with those for the first phase.

Among the explanatory variables,[18] we include individual characteristics (sex, age, education level, and potential labor market experience), country and quarter of the interview dummies,[19] gross domestic product (GDP) growth rate corresponding to the first and second year of the sequence, and variables accounting for the role of labor market institutions. These include employment protection legislation (EPL) and active labor market policy (ALMP) expenditure. For EPL, we enter separately the two Organization for Economic Co-operation and Development (OECD) indicators of the strictness of regulation on regular contracts (EPL-P) and on temporary contracts (EPL-T),[20] whereas for ALMP we consider annual expenditure on active policies per unemployed, as a share of per capita GDP.[21] For the first phase, the analysis could suffer from right censoring, especially for individuals who left education in the last year of observation (approximately 16% of our sample).[22] Because approximately half of these are continuously unemployed or inactive, our analysis might slightly overestimate the percentage of young people continuously at the margin of the labor market and might underestimate those engaged in lengthy job search.

8.5.1. School-to-Work Trajectories: The Role of Individual Characteristics and Institutions

Table 8.5 shows the predicted probabilities and some selected marginal effects for the first phase of labor market entry. No major gender differences emerge in the likelihood of following various trajectory types, with two exceptions: Males have a higher probability of moving in and out of employment without reaching a relevant employment spell, and they have a lower probability of returning to education. Education is crucial for rapid labor market entry and for avoiding the risk of being continuously unemployed/inactive. Previous working experiences contribute to gaining stable and relevant employment after leaving education, and they reduce the probability of experiencing continuous unemployment/inactivity or of returning to education. However, they also have a small positive and significant effect on the probability of remaining in an unsuccessful in & out pathway.

More stringent regulation of the use of temporary contracts (i.e., a higher level of the EPL-T index) is associated with a lower probability of following both an in & out unsuccessful and a long-search successful pathway. It also increases female probability of being in & out successful. This result suggests that encouraging the use of temporary contracts by reducing the strictness of the rules regulating their use (as has been done mainly by Southern countries)[23] is not an effective policy tool with which to improve employment outcomes; indeed, it may even have undesirable effects.[24]

The effects associated with EPL for regular contracts are more diverse across the subgroups. In general, a more stringent regulation of firings and dismissals (i.e., a higher level of the EPL-P index) appears to have positive effects on the school-to-work transition because it reduces the probability of following an in & out unsuccessful pathway. However, for medium- and highly educated individuals, it also increases the probability of being continuously unemployed/inactive while reducing the likelihood of undergoing a (successful) long search for high school graduates and that of being speedy for university graduates. Thus, a higher EPL-P index is associated with a more difficult school-to-work transition for more educated individuals. It also makes the transition more difficult for females, who have to cope with an even lower probability of rapidly entering paid work.

Finally, ALMP expenditure positively affects the probability of being speedy, and it reduces the probability of being in & out unsuccessful. The latter effect is larger for highly educated young people and females. The magnitude of these effects is, however, quite small.[25]

Table 8.5 Predicted probabilities (Pr) and selected marginal effects for ESTs in the first 3 years after leaving education (first phase) in 17 European countries

| | Successful pathways | | | | | | Unsuccessful pathways | | | | | |
| | Speedy | | Long search | | In & out successful | | In & out unsuccessful | | Continuously unemployed/inactive | | Return to education | |
Predicted probabilities	Pr	St. Err.	Pr	St. Err.	Pr	St. Err.	Pr	St. Err.	Pr	St. Err.	Pr	St. Err.
	0.616***	0.008	0.048***	0.003	0.025***	0.002	0.049***	0.003	0.203***	0.007	0.059***	0.005
Marginal effects	dy/dx	St. Err.	dy/dx	St. Err.	dy/dx	St. Err.	dy/dx	St. Err.	dy/dx	St. Err.	dy/dx	St. Err.
Male	−0.169	0.106	0.068	0.050	−0.010	0.033	0.092**	0.050	0.115	0.108	−0.096**	0.053
Medium education	0.153*	0.090	0.085	0.061	0.014	0.047	0.077	0.059	−0.322***	0.095	−0.006	0.068
High education	1.226***	0.228	−0.051	0.087	−0.018	0.081	−0.184	0.203	−0.882***	0.192	−0.091	0.107
Age	0.138***	0.026	−0.004	0.016	0.007	0.012	0.006	0.013	−0.118***	0.023	−0.028	0.017
Potential labor experience	0.042***	0.008	−0.003	0.005	0.002	0.001	0.008***	0.002	−0.040***	0.006	−0.009***	0.003
EPL-T	0.034	0.025	−0.024**	0.013	0.011	0.010	−0.051**	0.023	−0.004	0.026	0.034	0.025
EPL-T* medium education	−0.020	0.020	0.022	0.014	0.006	0.007	0.006	0.009	−0.018	0.012	0.004	0.014
EPL-T* high education	0.009	0.032	0.013	0.017	−0.003	0.007	0.009	0.015	−0.002	0.026	−0.026	0.020
EPL-T* female	−0.005	0.019	0.006	0.008	0.008**	0.004	0.001	0.006	−0.007	0.014	−0.003	0.010
EPL-P	0.099	0.206	0.163	0.107	0.064	0.066	−0.232**	0.118	−0.083	0.207	−0.011	0.166

EPL-P* medium education	−0.009	0.034	−0.049**	0.024	−0.005	0.019	−0.030	0.023	0.101***	0.037	−0.008	0.028
EPL-P* high education	−0.410***	0.085	0.001	0.036	0.009	0.032	0.072	0.070	0.300***	0.069	0.028	0.039
EPL-P* female	−0.071*	0.041	0.022	0.019	−0.015	0.013	0.033**	0.018	0.060	0.041	−0.030	0.023
ALMPs	0.011**	0.005	−0.003	0.002	−0.001	0.002	−0.007***	0.003	−0.003	0.005	0.003	0.004
ALMPs* medium education	−0.006	0.005	−0.003	0.003	−0.002	0.003	−0.004	0.003	0.011**	0.005	0.004	0.003
ALMPs* high education	0.010	0.017	0.007	0.007	0.005	0.003	−0.020**	0.009	−0.013	0.015	0.011	0.009
ALMPs* female	0.002	0.005	−0.001	0.003	0.002**	0.001	−0.005**	0.003	−0.002	0.004	0.003	0.002

Notes: Sample of young individuals (aged 16–34 years) observed for 36 months. Complete estimation results are available from the authors.
*$p < .10$.
**$p < .05$.
***$p < .01$.
Source: Authors' estimations based on EU-SILC longitudinal data (2006–2012).

The effect of the economic crisis on the transition from school to work is illustrated in Figure 8.2, which shows the predicted probabilities by trajectory type in various European countries for the subperiods 2005–2007 and 2009–2011. The graphs highlight the overall negative impact of the Great Recession on school-to-work trajectories, but they also reveal some heterogeneity across countries. All countries record a reduction in the probability of following speedy trajectories and of undergoing a successful search period (with the sole exception of Austria).

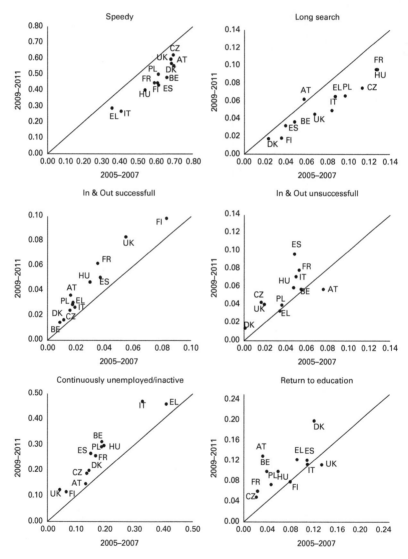

Figure 8.2 Conditional distribution of young individuals by (first-phase) EST types in 12 European countries, 2005–2007 versus 2009–2011.
Source: Authors' estimations based on EU-SILC longitudinal data (2006–2012).

Moreover, young people in all the countries studied face a higher degree of instability, with an increase in the likelihood of experiencing in & out pathways, both successful and unsuccessful (again with the sole exception of Austria). Finally, the economic crisis has increased the likelihood of being at the margin of the labor market by increasing the probability of being continuously unemployed/ inactive but, fortunately, also by increasing the probability of returning to education (with the exception of the United Kingdom).

8.5.2. Employment Quality: The role of Individual Characteristics and Institutions

Table 8.6 shows the predicted probabilities and some selected marginal effects for employment security and different pathways of employment-insecure individuals approximately 5 years after education exit. In contrast with the first phase, in this second phase, females have a significantly lower probability of achieving employment security compared to males and a higher probability of experiencing inactivity and returning to education. Thus, although males and females have similar chances of obtaining good employment outcomes immediately after leaving education, women's labor market conditions deteriorate over the following few years, with females being substantially less likely to be employment secure approximately 5 years after having left education.

The employment condition of women in couples is even worse.[26] In addition to having much lower chances of being employment secure, they are also considerably more likely to have a fragmented career pathway (being prevalently employed and insecure) or to be out of paid employment (prevalently unemployed and inactive). In contrast, males in a couple have a higher probability of being employment secure. Educational attainments are crucial also in this phase of labor market experience. Higher levels of education are associated with a higher probability of being employment secure and with a lower probability of being in all the other trajectory types (except for return to education). Potential work experience also increases the probability of achieving employment security by reducing the risk of experiencing unemployment and the probability of returning to education.

Regarding the mix of EPL and ALMP expenditure, some interesting results emerge. A more stringent regulation of the use of fixed-term contracts (i.e., a higher EPL-T index) increases young people's probability of being employment secure and reduces their probability of experiencing either short employment spells or long unemployment spells from one employment spell to the next (i.e., being prevalently employed but employment insecure). This is in line with what we found in Section 8.5.1 for the first phase, in which a higher level of the EPL-T index was associated with a lower probability of following both in & out unsuccessful and long-search pathways. However, in this second phase, the effects associated with EPL-T are greater for women and low-educated individuals. In

Table 8.6 Predicted probabilities (Pr) and selected marginal effects for employment security approximately 5 years after leaving education (second phase) in 15 European countries

	Employment secure		Employment insecure											Return to education	
			Prevalently employed		In & out		Prevalently unemployed		Prevalently inactive						
Predicted probabilities	Pr	St. Err.	Pr	St. Err.	Pr	St. Err.	Pr	St. Err.	Pr	St. Err.			Pr	St. Err.
	0.752***	0.006	0.089***	0.004	0.051***	0.003	0.057***	0.004	0.029***	0.003			0.022***	0.002
Marginal effects	dy/dx	St. Err.	dy/dx	St. Err.	dy/dx	St. Err.	dy/dx	St. Err.	dy/dx	St. Err.			dy/dx	St. Err.
Female	-0.221 ***	0.060	0.055	0.040	0.025	0.031	0.032	0.029	0.063 ***	0.021			0.046 ***	0.015
Female in couple	-0.143 ***	0.019	0.082 ***	0.013	-0.003	0.009	0.030 ***	0.010	0.055 ***	0.006			-0.021 ***	0.006
Male in couple	0.060 **	0.025	-0.005	0.017	-0.010	0.011	-0.022	0.014	-0.013	0.011			-0.010	0.007
Living in family	-0.039 **	0.017	0.031 ***	0.012	-0.021 ***	0.008	0.028 ***	0.009	0.002	0.005			0.000	0.004
Medium education	0.293 ***	0.104	-0.112 *	0.066	-0.005	0.051	-0.142 ***	0.040	-0.060 **	0.027			0.026	0.024
High education	0.690 ***	0.116	-0.222 ***	0.072	-0.115 **	0.059	-0.252 ***	0.051	-0.086 ***	0.032			-0.014	0.028
Age	0.008	0.005	0.001	0.003	-0.004*	0.003	0.002	0.002	-0.001	0.001			-0.005 ***	0.001
Potential labor experience	0.019 ***	0.002	0.001	0.001	0.001	0.001	-0.014 ***	0.001	0.000	0.001			-0.006 ***	0.001
EPL-T	0.128 ***	0.049	-0.116 ***	0.034	0.014	0.026	-0.044 **	0.021	0.021	0.014			-0.003	0.012
EPL-T* medium education	-0.053 **	0.023	0.041 ***	0.015	0.000	0.011	0.012	0.009	0.003	0.008			-0.003	0.005
EPL-T* high education	-0.052 **	0.024	0.013	0.015	0.014	0.011	0.019 *	0.010	0.001	0.008			0.006	0.005

EPL-T* female	0.052 ***	0.014	−0.015 *	0.009	−0.001	0.007	−0.013 *	0.007	−0.009	0.006	−0.014 ***	0.004
EPL-P	0.077	0.176	−0.042	0.100	−0.195*	0.117	0.108	0.086	−0.029	0.034	0.082	0.085
EPL-P* medium education	0.027	0.028	−0.021	0.019	−0.008	0.015	0.009	0.012	0.005	0.008	−0.011 **	0.005
EPL-P* high education	−0.084 ***	0.030	0.028	0.019	0.015	0.016	0.031 **	0.014	0.008	0.009	0.003	0.006
EPL-P* female	0.020	0.021	−0.008	0.014	−0.007	0.011	−0.001	0.010	−0.006	0.007	0.002	0.004
ALMPs	0.886 ***	0.341	0.087	0.221	−0.304*	0.158	−0.562 ***	0.146	−0.049	0.112	−0.060	0.069
ALMPs* medium education	−1.063 ***	0.267	0.263	0.165	0.104	0.122	0.338 ***	0.116	0.159 **	0.082	0.199 ***	0.054
ALMPs* high education	−1.221 ***	0.291	0.370**	0.178	0.138	0.134	0.342 **	0.146	0.165 *	0.092	0.206 ***	0.062
ALMPs* female	0.082	0.150	0.029	0.099	0.018	0.069	0.048	0.084	−0.106 *	0.064	−0.071 **	0.034

Notes: Sample of young individuals (aged 16–34 years) observed for 36 months. Complete estimation results are available from the authors.

*p < .10.

**p < .05.

***p < .01.

Source: Authors' estimations based on EU-SILC longitudinal data (2006–2012).

other words, a more stringent regulation of the use of temporary contracts is likely to reduce the probability of having fragmented trajectories in both phases, facilitating the achievement by young people of an employment-secure condition approximately 5 years after leaving education,[27] with more marked effects over time for the weakest groups (women and low-educated young people). This finding may be related to the gender and educational segmentation in employment contracts—that is, to the fact that women and low-educated individuals are overrepresented in fixed-term contracts (Petrongolo 2004; Muffels 2008).

The effects associated with EPL-P are similar to those that emerged in Section 8.5.1. A more stringent regulation of individual dismissals (i.e., a higher EPL-P index) is associated with a lower probability of being in & out and with some adverse effects for highly educated individuals (a lower probability of being employment secure and a higher probability of being prevalently unemployed). In other words, where the regulation of individual dismissals is more restrictive, the relative advantage of highly educated workers (compared to individuals with medium or low education) in terms of rapid labor market entry and of employment security is reduced. A possible explanation is that the higher the individual wage, the higher is the expected (discounted) total labor cost that firms face when it is more difficult for them to fire a worker. In any case, the magnitude of these effects decreases over time.

ALMP expenditure has positive effects as in the first phase, but in this second phase it is more differentiated across education levels. Higher ALMP expenditure is associated with a lower probability of being prevalently unemployed for all young people, but with larger effects for low-educated individuals. This lower probability of being prevalently unemployed is compensated by a higher probability of being employment secure for low-educated young people and by a higher probability of returning to education for high school and university graduates. In this case, the magnitude of the effects is much larger than those presented in Section 8.5.1.[28]

In Table 8.7, we consider the combined condition of employment and income security (outcome "secure") and the combined condition of income success and a good education–occupation match (outcome "success"). We report the predicted probabilities and the marginal effects for the secure/success outcomes and for only three trajectory types among the insecure/unsuccessful groups (almost always in employment, prevalently employed, and in & out). For the other trajectory types (prevalently unemployed, prevalently inactive, and return to education), the predicted probabilities and marginal effects are very similar in sign, magnitude, and significance to those obtained for employment security.

The first interesting result is that females and males have the same chances of achieving a secure employment condition. The reason is that although females are more likely to be employment insecure, they are less likely to be income insecure when following a continuous/stable employment pathway (i.e., to be almost always employed and income insecure).[29] By contrast, women living in a couple

Table 8.7 Selected predicted probabilities (Pr) and marginal effects for security and success approximately 5 years after leaving education (second phase) in 15 European countries

	Secure		Insecure						Successful		Unsuccessful					
			Almost always employed		Prevalently employed		In & out				Almost always employed		Prevalently employed		In & out	
Predicted probabilities	Pr	St. Err.	Pr	St. Err.	Pr	St. Err.	Pr	St. Err.	Pr	St. Err.	Pr	St. Err.	Pr	St. Err.	Pr	St. Err.
	0.44***	0.01	0.24***	0.01	0.15***	0.01	0.06***	0.00	0.17***	0.01	0.46***	0.01	0.19***	0.01	0.06***	0.00
Marginal effects	dy/dx	St. Err.	dy/dx	St. Err.	dy/dx	St. Err.	dy/dx	St. Err.	dy/dx	St. Err.	dy/dx	St. Err.	dy/dx	St. Err.	dy/dx	St. Err.
Female	0.10	0.07	-0.29***	0.06	0.01	0.05	0.03	0.03	-0.14***	0.05	-0.11	0.07	0.05	0.05	0.05	0.03
Female in couple	-0.18***	0.02	0.01	0.02	0.12***	0.02	-0.01	0.01	-0.11***	0.02	-0.08***	0.02	0.13***	0.02	-0.01	0.01
Male in couple	0.03	0.03	0.04**	0.02	-0.01	0.02	-0.01	0.01	0.00	0.02	0.04	0.03	0.01	0.02	-0.01	0.01
Living in family	-0.05**	0.02	0.01	0.02	0.03**	0.02	-0.03***	0.01	-0.10***	0.01	0.03*	0.02	0.06***	0.02	-0.02***	0.01
Medium education	0.53***	0.16	-0.21	0.14	-0.13	0.09	-0.01	0.06	0.08	0.11	0.14	0.15	-0.06	0.10	-0.01	0.06
High education	0.67***	0.17	0.01	0.15	-0.19**	0.10	-0.13**	0.06	0.09	0.12	0.48***	0.16	-0.11	0.11	-0.12*	0.07
Age	0.01**	0.01	0.00	0.01	0.00	0.00	-0.01*	0.00	0.02***	0.00	0.00	0.01	0.00	0.00	-0.01*	0.00
Potential labor experience	0.01***	0.00	0.01***	0.00	0.00	0.00	0.00	0.00	0.00	0.00	0.02***	0.00	0.00	0.00	0.00	0.00
EPL-T	0.18***	0.06	-0.02	0.05	-0.14***	0.04	0.02	0.03	0.05	0.04	0.09	0.06	-0.12***	0.05	0.01	0.03
EPL-T* medium education	-0.12***	0.04	0.04	0.03	0.06***	0.02	0.00	0.01	-0.01	0.03	-0.03	0.03	0.03	0.02	0.00	0.01

(continued)

Table 8.7 Continued

	Insecure								Unsuccessful							
	Secure		Almost always employed		Prevalently employed		In & out		Successful		Almost always employed		Prevalently employed		In & out	
Marginal effects	dy/dx	St. Err.	dy/dx	St. Err.	dy/dx	St. Err.	dy/dx	St. Err.	dy/dx	St. Err.	dy/dx	St. Err.	dy/dx	St. Err.	dy/dx	St. Err.
EPL-T* high education	-0.10 ***	0.04	0.03	0.03	0.02	0.02	0.02 *	0.01	-0.01	0.03	-0.02	0.03	0.00	0.02	0.02	0.01
EPL-T* female	0.03 **	0.02	0.03 **	0.01	-0.02 *	0.01	-0.01	0.01	0.03 ***	0.01	0.03 *	0.02	-0.02	0.01	-0.01	0.01
EPL-P	0.19	0.18	-0.15	0.16	0.01	0.14	-0.24 *	0.13	-0.15	0.12	0.16	0.18	0.06	0.15	-0.21 *	0.12
EPL-P* medium education	-0.09 **	0.04	0.11 ***	0.04	-0.01	0.02	0.00	0.02	-0.02	0.03	0.07 *	0.04	-0.04	0.03	-0.01	0.02
EPL-P* high education	-0.14 ***	0.04	0.07	0.04	0.01	0.02	0.02	0.02	-0.04	0.03	0.01	0.04	-0.02	0.03	0.01	0.02
EPL-P* female	-0.08 ***	0.02	0.07 ***	0.02	0.02	0.02	-0.01	0.01	-0.01	0.02	0.02	0.02	0.01	0.02	-0.01	0.01
ALMPs	-1.38 ***	0.49	1.76 ***	0.39	0.42	0.29	-0.28 *	0.17	0.18	0.34	1.15 ***	0.46	-0.31	0.33	-0.32 *	0.18
ALMPs* medium education	0.80 **	0.42	-1.26 ***	0.32	-0.12	0.23	0.04	0.13	-0.51 *	0.28	-0.85 ***	0.37	0.47 *	0.26	0.17	0.14
ALMPs* high education	0.78 *	0.43	-1.43 ***	0.32	-0.02	0.24	0.09	0.15	-0.43	0.28	-1.04 ***	0.38	0.54 **	0.27	0.19	0.15
ALMPs* female	-0.08	0.16	0.16	0.13	0.02	0.13	0.03	0.07	0.11	0.10	0.02	0.15	0.01	0.13	-0.01	0.07

Notes: Complete estimation results are available from the authors. Marginal effects for the other trajectory types are comparable to those obtained for employment security (see Table 8.6).

*p < .10.

**p < .05.

***p < .01.

Source: Authors' estimations based on EU-SILC longitudinal data (2006–2012).

have a significantly lower probability of achieving security because, in addition to the usual effects on unemployment and inactivity, they have a higher probability of being prevalently employed but income insecure.

Major gender differences are observed also when we consider the probability of achieving a successful employment condition. Females have substantially lower chances than men of achieving success. This is true both when we consider the unconditional probability and when we compute the probability of being successful conditional on having a stable employment pathway.[30] Again, women in a couple have worse labor market outcomes. They are even less likely to be successful and, among the unsuccessful group, they are considerably less likely to have a stable/continuous pathway and to be prevalently employed.

Thus, gender differences in labor market outcomes emerge quite soon after leaving education, and they are mainly related to the greater difficulties experienced by women in remaining continuously employed, earning high wages, and achieving a good match between education and occupation. This clearly suggests that well-known gender differences in labor market outcomes (career interruptions due to motherhood, job segregation, and wage penalties) have not yet been resolved, given that the younger generation of women encounters similar problems to the older generation of women.

Higher education levels are associated with a significantly higher probability of achieving a secure employment condition. Moreover, young people with a university degree are substantially less likely than low-educated individuals to be in & out and prevalently employed. Education has no effects on the probability of achieving success because of the way in which we have defined it. However, among the unsuccessful group, young individuals with a university degree have a significantly higher probability of being almost always employed and a lower probability of being in & out. Potential labor market experience increases young people's probability of being secure and having a continuous/stable pathway.

The effects of EPL-T on security are very similar to those described at the beginning of this subsection, confirming that the regulation of temporary contracts affects mainly the type of employment trajectory that individuals follow. By contrast, the EPL of regular contracts appears to have some additional effects on income security. Indeed, a higher EPL-P index is associated with a lower probability of being secure not only for university graduates but also for medium-educated individuals, and even more so for females. This additional effect for the latter two groups is driven mainly by an income effect because both high school graduates and females have a higher probability of being always employed but income insecure where the EPL-P index is higher. In other words, a more stringent regulation of individual dismissals generates some problems in terms of employment security for highly educated individuals, but it also generates problems in terms of low income for those high school graduates and females who are able to enter a stable employment trajectory. Higher expenditure on ALMP has a similar income effect for low-educated individuals (and to a much lower extent for high school graduates). As a result, the positive effect on employment security described at the beginning of this subsection is reversed, and higher ALMP expenditure is associated with lower overall security for low-educated individuals.[31]

The effect of our policy variables is less widespread for the successful dimension of employment quality. Interestingly, a higher EPL-T index increases the female probability of being successful, and higher ALMP expenditure again increases the probability of being almost always employed but unsuccessful for low-educated individuals.

8.6. CONCLUSIONS

This chapter has highlighted the importance of studying various aspects of youth labor market performance from a dynamic perspective. Given that labor markets are increasingly characterized by workers moving quite frequently between jobs, with possible unemployment spells in between, we argue that it is important to go beyond (or to complement) the analysis of jobs' characteristics and to develop new concepts of employment security and employment quality that account for various features of individuals' employment conditions over a certain period of time. Our definition of employment quality encompasses four dimensions: employment security, income security, income success, and a successful match between education and occupation, which are identified using information pertaining to a 2-year period. We have also presented a new methodology with which to analyze ESTs, based on whether they contain a prespecified major outcome and some other minor features that are relevant for the research question being addressed.

We have used this approach for the analysis of young Europeans' labor market experience during the period 2006–2012. We have examined two phases of youth working life: entry into the labor market (i.e., the transition from school to the first relevant employment experience) and the subsequent phase, approximately 5 years after leaving full-time education. For the first phase, we have analyzed the type and the determinants of ESTs followed in the first 3 years after education exit. For the second phase, we have focused on young people's probability of achieving a secure employment condition (employment security and income security) and a successful employment condition (income success and a successful match between education and occupation). For those who were not able to achieve these outcomes, we have examined their employment pathway.

The descriptive analysis shows that successful school-to-work trajectories are more frequent in Nordic countries but that this relative advantage vanishes in the second phase. By contrast, Southern countries record the worst performance in both phases. The impact of the economic crisis on employment trajectories is large in the first phase but negligible in the second phase. In the latter phase, the crisis has reduced young people's probability of achieving income security and a successful employment condition.

Our econometric analysis shows that although males and females have similar chances of obtaining good employment outcomes immediately after leaving education (they have almost the same chances of accessing paid employment rapidly), the labor market condition of women deteriorates during the following few years. More precisely, women are less likely than men to have achieved employment security approximately 5 years after leaving education; that is, they are considerably more likely to experience career interruptions and have more fragmented career pathways. However, if they are able to follow a stable employment trajectory, they have better chances than men of having a stable labor income above the poverty line. On the contrary, they always have less chances of being successful even when they manage to remain continuously employed.

The regulation of temporary contracts mainly affects the type of employment trajectory followed by individuals, whereas the EPL regarding regular contracts appears to have some additional effects on income security. Stricter rules on the use of temporary contracts tend to reduce the probability of fragmented trajectories in both phases, facilitating the achievement by young people of employment security approximately 5 years after leaving education, with more marked effects over time for women and low-educated young people. A more stringent regulation of individual dismissals generates difficulties in the school-to-work transition for highly educated individuals and for females, who have to cope with a lower probability of entering paid work rapidly. These negative effects remain also in the second phase, reducing the chances of being secure not only for university graduates and females but also for high school graduates. For the latter two groups, stricter rules on individual dismissals seem to have adverse effects on income security. Indeed, a higher EPL-P increases the likelihood of having a labor income below the poverty line when following a continuous employment trajectory. This could be the result of a trade-off between earnings levels and job security. ALMP expenditures have overall positive effects in the first phase, increasing the speed of youth labor market entry, whereas in the second phase (approximately 5 years after education exit), they are associated with an increase in youth employment security but also a decrease in overall security (especially for the low educated), presumably because of an increase in income insecurity. Thus, these policies must be considered with caution because ALMPs seem to improve labor market outcomes in terms of stability and permanence in employment but to have side effects on earnings.

From a policy perspective, our findings suggest that there is still a pressing need to enhance women's chances of remaining continuously in employment and moving up the labor income distribution. Indeed, it appears that the well-known gender differences in labor market outcomes (career interruptions due to motherhood, job segregation, wage penalty, etc.) have not yet been removed.

Relaxing the rules on the use of temporary contracts (as has been done mainly by Southern countries), besides generating more difficulties for women (and low-educated individuals), does not appear to be an effective policy tool with which to improve youth employment outcomes in general. In fact, it reduces the chances of reaching a relevant employment spell within 3 years after leaving education, as well as the chances of achieving a sufficiently secure employment condition within the subsequent few years.

NOTES

1 The International Labour Organization has also developed an analytical framework to study individuals' school-to-work transitions. The school-to-work transition is defined as the passage from the end of schooling to a stable or satisfactory employment condition (Matsumoto and Elder 2010). Young people are classified into three categories: (1) "transited" if the job held at the moment of the survey is either stable/secure or satisfactory; (2) "in transition" if the job is unstable/insecure and unsatisfactory or if the person is unemployed or inactive (aims to work later); and (3) "not started transition yet" if the person is in education or inactive (not aiming to work later). Young people who have transited are further categorized by their "speed" of transition into "short," "middling," and "lengthy" based on the type and the lengths of spells experienced.

2 The OM method calculates the minimum distance between any two sequences by considering the number of steps that must be enacted in order to make both sequences equal, associating a cost with each step. The corresponding matrix of minimum distances is then used in a cluster analysis to group sequences into similar "types" or in a discrepancy analysis (Studer et al. 2011) to examine the association between activity sequences and one or more categorical predictors.

3 See Aisenbrey and Fasang (2010) for a discussion of criticisms of traditional OM. See Cornwell (2015) for a review of the OM technique and an update on the latest methodological improvements.

4 The outcome that drives our grouping methodology in the first phase of youth labor market experience is the achievement of a "relevant" employment spell, whereas in the second phase it is the prevailing labor market status.

5 Other dimensions considered in the literature include education and training, working environment, work–life balance, and gender balance.

6 According to recent estimates, nearly 15% of EU employees aged 25–64 years are overqualified (European Commission 2012, 360, 388 (Annex 2)). The studies reviewed by Quintini (2011)—based on educational

qualifications—estimate that one in four workers in OECD countries could be overqualified and that one in three could be underqualified for their jobs.

7 For the second phase, we consider young people who left education 3–5 years before the first interview, evaluating their labor market performance in the following 2 years (first 2 years of the survey). This means that for some individuals, we evaluate labor market performance at 3 or 4 years after exiting full-time education, whereas for others we refer to 4 or 5 or to 5 or 6 years.

8 IE, LU, NL, and NO are excluded from the analysis because the sample size was too small. BG, CY, LT, LV, MT, and RO are excluded because the policy variables that we use in the econometric analysis are not available for these countries.

9 See Berloffa, Mazzolini, and Villa (2015) and Berloffa et al. (2015) for details about the sample selection rules.

10 EU-SILC does not provide daily data. However, by using monthly information instead of daily data, we have a sample with less noise due to the exclusion of individuals who change their status very frequently. The monthly activity status declared by respondents must have been their status for at least 2 out of 4 week in 1 month. If there are more than two activities, the main activity is the one in which the individual spent the most time.

11 The definition of a relevant employment spell follows the EU-SILC convention, according to which a 6-month period identifies the first regular job and whether individuals ever worked. The time frame of 6 months is a reference length also for some labor market policies, such as the UK government's Youth Contract wage incentive, which was in place from 2012 to 2014, paying an incentive to firms that recruited long-term unemployed young people for at least 26 weeks.

12 We consider a 24-month period in order to have all the dimensions of employment quality referring to the same reference period. Indeed, information about income and monthly employment statuses, which is used to identify income security, income success, and employment security, refers to the calendar year preceding the interview. In contrast, information about the type of occupation, which is used to identify education–occupation success, refers to the year of the interview. Thus, the only overlapping years for information about all four dimensions are the two calendar years preceding the third interview.

13 Employment quality is evaluated during the two calendar years corresponding to the first two interviews. In contrast, ESTs cover a 3-year period that starts in the calendar year before the first interview. This means that we have a time span of 2–4 years between education exit and the beginning of the observation period for second-phase ESTs.

14 We exclude from the analysis those individuals who were inactive for the entire length of the sequence.

15 Countries are grouped on the basis of geographic criteria, largely for presentational purposes. This grouping is used only for the descriptive analysis, whereas the econometric analysis uses country dummies.

16 The data on monthly employment status refer to the year preceding the interview. Thus, for those interviewed in 2006–2008, the ESTs refer to the period 2005–2007.

17 This share is computed over the entire sample (including those who were never employed); if we consider only those who have at least 1 month in employment in both years, the share of income successful young people rises to 27%.

18 See Berloffa, Mazzolini, and Villa (2015) and Berloffa et al. (2015) for further details about the control variables included in the analysis.

19 Because we had a small sample size for some countries (e.g., the Nordic countries), we also estimated our models controlling for country-group dummies instead of country dummies. The results remained consistent across specifications.

20 EPL-P measures the strictness of employment protection against individual dismissals, whereas EPL-T measures the strictness of regulation on the use of fixed-term and temporary-work agency contracts.

21 ALMPs include training, job rotation and job sharing, employment incentives, supported employment and rehabilitation, direct job creation, and start-up incentives. We are well aware that this variable only provides information about the input—that is, how much money was spent and how many people participated—but there is no other information available to account for the efficiency of these ALMP expenditures.

22 Right censoring was considerably more limited in the second phase because we examined the prevalent employment condition and the number of status changes in defining trajectories. Hence, the employment condition at the end of the sequence is less relevant for the definition.

23 The EPL-T index of Spain declined in 2006–2007 and in 2010–2011, that of Portugal and Sweden declined in 2007–2008, and that of Greece declined in 2010–2011 and in 2011–2012.

24 This is in line with the data presented in *Employment and Social Developments in Europe 2014* (European Commission 2014, 77–78), suggesting that reductions in EPL either for permanent workers (during economic downturns) or for temporary contracts do not appear to be clearly correlated with improvements in the transition from unemployment to employment.

25 The estimated coefficients imply that, for example, an increase in ALMP expenditure as a share of per capita GDP from 0.10 to 0.20 increases (decreases) the probability of being speedy (in and out unsuccessful) only by 0.11 (0.07) pp.

26 Instead of controlling for partnership, we could have controlled for parenthood. However, we believe that the decision to have children may be more

endogenous than the decision to form a couple. Indeed, many authors have developed and estimated models of joint fertility and labor supply decisions, whereas few studies have explored the interdependencies between females' labor market participation and the choice of living in a couple.

27 Note, however, that this does not necessarily mean that they stay in the same job. Berloffa et al. (2016) show that an increase in the strictness of the regulations on the use of fixed-term contracts raises the likelihood of staying almost continuously in the labor market, although not with the same employer.

28 An increase in ALMP expenditure as a share of per capita GDP from 0.10 to 0.20 increases the probability of being employment secure by 8.9 pp and decreases the probability of being prevalently unemployed by 5.6 pp.

29 Indeed, estimation of a multinomial logit model specifically for income security shows that males are much less likely to be at the margin of the labor market (the probability of being continuously unemployed/inactive or returning to education is 8% for males vs. 22% for females) but much more likely to be always employed and income insecure (25% vs. 11%). If we compute the probability of being income secure conditionally on having continuous/stable employment, men are actually worse off (the conditional probability becomes 68% for males vs. 80% for females).

30 Thus, when women are able to follow a stable employment trajectory, they are more likely than men to be income secure but less likely to be successful.

31 The magnitude of the effect is larger than that estimated for employment security. An increase in ALMP expenditure as a share of per capita GDP from 0.10 to 0.20 decreases the probability of being secure by 13.8 pp.

REFERENCES

Aisenbrey, Silke, and Anette Eva Fasang. 2010. "New Life for Old Ideas: The 'Second Wave' of Sequence Analysis Bringing the 'Course' Back into the Life Course." *Sociological Methods & Research* 38 (3): 420–62.

Berloffa, Gabriella, Eleonora Matteazzi, Alina Şandor, and Paola Villa. 2015a. "The Quality of Employment in the Early Labor Market Experience." In *Youth School-to-Work Transitions: From Entry Jobs to Career Employment*, edited by Gabriella Berloffa et al., 25–40. Brighton, UK: CROME, University of Brighton. http://www.style-research.eu/publications/working-papers

Berloffa, Gabriella, Eleonora Matteazzi, Alina Şandor, and Paola Villa. 2016. "Youth Employment Security and Labor Market Institutions: A Dynamic Perspective." ECINEQ Working Paper 392. Verona: Society for the Study of Economic Inequality.

Berloffa, Gabriella, Gabriele Mazzolini, and Paola Villa. 2015b. "From Education to the First Relevant Employment Spell." In *Youth School-to-Work*

Transitions: From Entry Jobs to Career Employment, edited by Gabriella Berloffa et al., 14–25. Brighton. UK: CROME, University of Brighton. http://www.style-research.eu/publications/working-papers

Berloffa, Gabriella, Francesca Modena, and Paola Villa. 2014. "Changing Labor Market Opportunities for Young People in Italy and the Role of the Family of Origin." *Rivista Italiana degli Economisti* 19 (2): 227–51.

Brzinsky-Fay, Christian. 2007. "Lost in Transition? Labor Market Entry Sequences of School Leavers in Europe." *European Sociological Review* 23 (4): 409–22.

Cappellari, Lorenzo, and Stephen Jenkins. 2008. "Estimating Low Pay Transition Probabilities Accounting for Endogenous Selection Mechanisms." *Journal of the Royal Statistical Society, Series C (Applied Statistics)* 57: 165–86.

Cornwell, Benjamin. 2015. *Social Sequence Analysis: Methods and Applications.* New York: Cambridge University Press.

Dalla Chiara, Elena, Eleonora Matteazzi, and Ilaria Petrarca. 2014. "From the Glass Door to the Glass Ceiling: An Analysis of the Gender Wage Gap by Age Groups." ECINEQ Working Paper 347. Verona: Society for the Study of Economic Inequality.

Dorsett, Richard, and Paolo Lucchino. 2013a. "Visualising the School-to-Work Transition: An Analysis Using Optimal Matching." NIESR Discussion Paper 414. London: National Institute for Economic and Social Research.

Dorsett, Richard, and Paolo Lucchino. 2013b. "Young People's Labor Market Transitions: The Role of Early Experiences." NIESR Discussion Paper 419. London: National Institute for Economic and Social Research.

European Central Bank. 2014. "The Impact of the Economic Crisis on the Euro Area Labor Markets." *ECB Monthly Bulletin* (October): 49–68.

European Commission. 2012. "The Skill Mismatch Challenge in Europe." In *Employment and Social Developments in Europe 2012*, edited by the European Commission, 351–94. Luxembourg: Publications Office of the European Union.

European Commission. 2014. "The Future of Work in Europe: Job Quality and Work Organisation for a Smart, Sustainable and Inclusive Growth." In *Employment and Social Developments in Europe 2014*, edited by the European Commission, 137–204. Luxembourg: Publications Office of the European Union.

European Commission. 2016. "Labour Markets Are Gradually Recovering but Substantial Differences Remain and a Stronger Economic Recovery Is Needed." In *Employment and Social Developments in Europe 2015*, edited by the European Commission, 20–30. Luxembourg: Publications Office of the European Union.

European Commission Employment Committee. 2009. "Monitoring and Analysis of Flexicurity Policies." EMCO Report 2. Brussels: European Commission Employment Committee.

Green, Francis. 2006. *Demanding Work: The Paradox of Job Quality in the Affluent Economy*. Princeton, NJ: Princeton University Press.

International Labour Organization. 2014a. *Skills Mismatch in Europe: Statistics Brief*. Geneva: International Labour Office.

International Labour Organization. 2014b. *Key Indicators of the Labor Market*. 8th ed. Geneva: International Labour Office.

International Labour Organization. 2015. *Global Employment Trends for Youth 2015: Scaling up Investments in Decent Jobs for Youth*. Geneva: International Labour Office.

Levine, Joel H. 2000. "But What Have You Done for Us Lately? Commentary on Abbot and Tsay." *Sociological Methods & Research* 29 (1): 34–40.

Kalwij, Adriaan S. 2004. "Unemployment Experiences of Young Men: On the Road to Stable Employment." *Oxford Bulletin of Economics and Statistics* 66 (2): 205–37.

Korpi, Tomas, Paul de Graaf, John Hendrickx, and Richard Layte. 2003. "Vocational Training and Career Employment Precariousness in Great Britain, the Netherlands and Sweden." *Acta Sociologica* 46 (1): 17–30.

Matsumoto, Makiko, and Sara Elder. 2010. "Characterizing the School-to-Work Transition of Young Men and Women: Evidence from the ILO School-to-Work Transition Surveys." ILO Employment Working Paper 51. Geneva: International Labour Organization.

Mroz, Thomas A., and Timothy H. Savage. 2006. "The Long-Term Effects of Youth Unemployment." *Journal of Human Resources* 41 (2): 259–93.

Muffels, Ruud. 2008. *Flexibility and Employment Security in Europe: Labor Markets in Transition*. Cheltenham, UK: Edward Elgar.

Muller, Walter, and Markus Gangl. 2003. *Transitions from Education to Work in Europe: The Integration of Youth into EU Labor Markets*. Oxford: Oxford University Press.

Petrongolo, Barbara. 2004. "Gender Segregation in Employment Contracts." *Journal of the European Economic Association* 2 (2/3): 331–45.

Quintini, Glenda. 2011. "Over-Qualified or Under-Skilled: A Review of Existing Literature." OECD Social, Employment and Migration Working Paper 121. Paris: Organization for Economic Co-operation and Development.

Quintini, Glenda, and Thomas Manfredi. 2009. "Going Separate Ways? School-to-Work Transitions in the United States and Europe." OECD Social, Employment and Migration Working Paper 90. Paris: Organization for Economic Co-operation and Development.

Russell, Helen, and Philip J. O'Connell. 2001. "Getting a Job in Europe: The Transition from Unemployment to Work Among Young People in Nine European Countries." *Work, Employment and Society* 15 (1): 1–24.

Scherer, Stefani. 2005. "Pattern of Labor Market Entry: Long Wait or Career Instability? An Empirical Comparison of Italy, Great Britain and West Germany." *European Sociological Review* 21 (5): 427–40.

Schomburg, Harald, and Ulrich Teichler. 2006. *Higher Education and Graduate Employment in Europe: Results from Graduates Surveys from Twelve Countries.* Dordrecht: Springer.

Shanahan, Michael J. 2000. "Pathways to Adulthood in Changing Societies: Variability and Mechanisms in Life Course Perspective." *Annual Review of Sociology* 26: 667–92.

Stewart, Mark. 2007. "Inter-Related Dynamics of Unemployment and Low Wage Employment." *Journal of Applied Econometrics* 22 (3): 511–31.

Studer, Matthias, Gilbert Ritschard, Alexis Gabadinho, and Nicolas S. Muller. 2011. "Discrepancy Analysis of State Sequences." *Sociological Methods and Research* 40 (3): 471–510.

Uhlendorff, Arne. 2006. "From No Pay to Low Pay and Back Again? A Multi-State Model of Low Pay Dynamics." IZA Discussion Paper 2482. Bonn: Institute for the Study of Labor.

Wolbers, Maarten H. J. 2007. "Patterns of Labor Market Entry: A Comparative Perspective on School-to-Work Transitions in 11 European Countries." *Acta Sociologica* 50 (3): 189–210.

Wu, Lawrence. 2000. "Some Comments on 'Sequences Analysis and Optimal Matching Methods in Sociology: Review and Prospects.'" *Sociological Research and Methods* 29 (1): 41–64.

9

YOUTH TRANSITIONS AND JOB QUALITY

HOW LONG SHOULD THEY WAIT AND WHAT DIFFERENCE DOES THE FAMILY MAKE?

Marianna Filandri, Tiziana Nazio, and Jacqueline O'Reilly

9.1. INTRODUCTION

Much attention has been devoted to the issues of job quality, the effects of prolonged unemployment, and the influence of families on youth transitions, whereas very little has been given to date to examining the interrelationship between these dimensions. In this chapter, we explore the effects of both persistent unemployment and employment continuity on the likelihood of obtaining a good-quality job 3 years after acquiring a secondary or tertiary educational qualification. We are also interested in understanding how family of origin affects these strategic transitions for young people in Europe. Specifically, we examine the following questions:

1. Does a longer period in unemployment lead to accessing a better job?
2. Does employment continuity influence the chances of accessing a better job?
3. Does a bad entry job lead to more adverse employment outcomes later?
4. How does the social class of the family of origin mediate young people's labor market outcomes?

European countries differ significantly in their labor market institutional settings (particularly in terms of "youth transition regimes"; see Hadjivassiliou et al., this volume) and also with regard to the effects of the Great Recession on employment and unemployment (particularly in terms of differences between young people and prime-age individuals; see Flek, Hála, and Mysíková, this volume). Our main hypothesis is that the mechanisms that enable young people to pursue a successful strategy for securing good employment outcomes in the long term (3–5 years after acquiring an educational qualification) are similar across countries. More precisely, the features of a "successful strategy" are similar across countries, notwithstanding their institutional specificities (youth transition regime, labor market settings, welfare systems, etc.) and their macroeconomic conditions. We also hypothesize that the family of origin has a strong influence on its children's employment outcomes and that the effects of the family social background are similar across countries. Families from the upper social classes should be better able to secure successful employment outcomes for their offspring, not only by making higher investments in their education but also by guiding them toward pursuing more effective employment strategies.

We explore such strategies by testing whether experience of unemployment or of discontinuity in employment, or a certain type of entry job, at the time when young people complete a level of education reflects on the occupational conditions (pay, skill levels, or both) they achieve in employment 3 years later. Using monthly employment-status data from the 2005–2012 longitudinal waves of EU-SILC (European Union Statistics on Income and Living Conditions), we construct individual trajectories covering a period of 36 months following the completion of an education level; in addition, we use the cross-sectional ad hoc 2011 module to explore the effects of the family of origin on these transitions. First, we distinguish between different types of good and bad jobs. Second, we test for associations with successful transitions to good jobs in five selected European countries: Finland, France, Italy, Poland, and the United Kingdom. Third, we examine the impact of family background on the types of transitions young people make.

We hypothesize that families have different capacities—in line with the resources that characterize their social class—to guide, empower, and provide backing for their young adult children as these make their initial steps in the labor market. Depending on their familial resources, young people from less advantaged backgrounds might be required to move into work earlier, or they may not have the necessary resources to enable them to wait for, gain access to, select, or take up promising job opportunities that entail initial losses or higher risks. Our findings show that young people from higher social class families were able to make transitions into better quality jobs than was the case for youth from lower class families. These findings reinforce established knowledge on patterns of stratification and raise significant questions about the best locus for policy interventions that are designed to reduce inequalities.

9.2. THEORETICAL DEBATES ON YOUTH TRANSITIONS: QUALITY AND TIME

9.2.1. Job Quality

A considerable body of empirical studies has found that job quality affects well-being and happiness. Low-quality employment has been associated with lower levels of self-reported life satisfaction and happiness, compared to those of people with higher quality jobs (Gallie 2013a; Sánchez-Sánchez and McGuinness 2013; Green et al. 2014; Keller et al. 2014), and this association holds true across different institutional settings (Gallie 2007; Kattenbach and O'Reilly 2011). Although those in poor-quality jobs have lower levels of life satisfaction, they are often more satisfied than people who remain unemployed (Grün, Hauser, and Rhein 2010). Overall levels of (dis)satisfaction can be traced to a range of different factors, including overeducation, underemployment, and poor employment conditions (contractual forms and salary levels) (Peiró, Agut, and Grau 2010). Several factors associated with job characteristics affect levels of well-being, such as task autonomy in a job, economic and personal rewards, a stimulating and supportive environment, training opportunities, contract security, and work pressure and job control (Gallie 2012; Gallie, Felstead, and Green 2012; Gallie 2013b).

"Good" and "bad" jobs can be distinguished in terms of a number of features related to material (monetary and nonmonetary) and nonmaterial characteristics (Jencks, Perman, and Rainwater 1988; Warhurst et al. 2012; Keller et al. 2014). There have been many definitions of "good" and "bad" jobs involving both objective and subjective aspects (Russell, Leschke, and Smith 2015). Here, we focus on a simple indicator that uses the level of employment and wages to distinguish between good and bad jobs. Higher quality jobs are frequently associated with higher education levels; involve more task complexity, autonomy, and control; pay better salaries; and the workers report greater degrees of satisfaction. This hierarchy is represented in Figure 9.1, which shows the association between different labor market statuses and a hierarchy of skills, wages, and reported satisfaction, as found in the literature (Layard 2004). At the bottom are the unemployed, followed by the inactive (whose lack of economic autonomy is to a certain degree chosen or accepted without bearing the cost of searching for a job as well as the additional psychological loss), those employed in low-quality jobs, and, at the top, those with high-quality, "good" jobs.

Very limited attention has been given in these debates to how occupational positioning specifically affects young people's entrance to work (as an exception, see Russell et al. 2015). It has been well established that early job mismatch and precarious employment trajectories have deleterious effects in later life. McGuinness and Wooden (2009) illustrate how early transitions resulting in skill mismatch have long-term consequences that render it difficult for young people

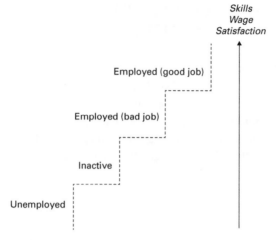

Figure 9.1 Scale of occupational positioning based on skills, wage, and satisfaction.

to make up for the costs of an early mismatch in their later careers. Empirical evidence shows that beginning a professional career with a "bad job" (i.e., low skilled, low paid, or both) can become a career trap (Scherer 2004; Blossfeld et al. 2008; Gash 2008; Barbera, Filandri, and Negri 2010; Barone, Lucchini, and Schizzerotto 2011; Bukodi and Goldthorpe 2011; Hillmert 2011; Wolbers, Luijkx, and Ultee 2011; Reichelt 2015; Mooi-Reci and Dekker 2016).

9.2.2. How Long Should They Wait?

Longer periods in unemployment can result from two different circumstances: not finding employment or waiting for the right opportunity. The decision to be selective and risk waiting for a better opportunity—rather than accepting "any" job—prolongs the duration in unemployment. But it could also be seen as a strategic move, if there is a possibility it could lead to better outcomes over time. This is a particularly salient decision for young people moving into work for the first time. Especially during the early stages of one's career, it is possible that poor-quality jobs can lead to better opportunities later on. For example, internships and short-term training contracts can be used as signaling and screening devices by employers who will later offer better employment opportunities (Scherer 2004). However, in the process of waiting, young people will incur a longer unemployment spell(s), increasing their risk of not finding an entry opportunity at all (Flek et al., this volume).

The apparent individualized choice of a young person also needs to be contextualized in relation to the person's family resources and his or her ability to wait (Bernardi 2007; Medgyesi and Nagy, this volume). Wealthier families have a range of resources that can allow their children to wait longer, be more selective, and be guided more effectively toward successful employment routes (McKnight

2015). Those from less advantaged backgrounds might be required to move into work earlier, depending on the resources available from their families or the welfare state, or they may not have the necessary resources to enable them to avail of opportunities and may thus instead become NEETs—young people not in education, employment, or training (see Mascherini, this volume; Zuccotti and O'Reilly, this volume).

Youth labor markets are frequently characterized by high levels of turbulence and transitions (Flek et al., this volume; Berloffa et al., this volume). "Flexible" forms of employment are often associated with poor job quality, although for some, these options may be the only practical way to remain in employment (O'Reilly et al. 2015; Gebel and Giesecke 2016; Grotti, Russell, and O'Reilly, this volume). Some authors have suggested that "any kind of job, be it short-term, part-time or subsidized, is better than no job at all to forestall unemployment hysteresis and deskilling" (Hemerijck and Eichhorst 2010, 327). The implication is that any form of inclusion in the labor market is better than being excluded. But is it really always the case that any job is better than none? How long should young people wait to find a good match? And what factors affect the opportunity to be able to wait for a better offer?

We are not interested here in highlighting existing differences across the five countries considered in the study. Rather, we intend to identify the characteristics of a "successful strategy" and to test whether such strategies are associated with individual and family characteristics. We test if families have a different ability to empower, guide, and support their offspring in line with their social class positioning and whether family (dis)advantages have similar effects across countries.

9.2.3. Data and Methods

To answer these questions, we use longitudinal (from 2005 to 2012) and cross-sectional (2011) data from EU-SILC surveys. Although the data cover young people's transitions through the labor market before and during the recession—with its different moments of onset and different impacts across countries—the empirical analyses do not focus on how the crisis affected young people's degree of success in employment. We test instead for the role of the families of origin in helping their children secure a successful placing in the labor market. For the longitudinal part, which focuses on later outcomes of early experiences, we selected all young people (aged 19–34 years) who had successfully completed a spell in higher education by their second interview and then followed them for the subsequent 3 years; this provided us with four valid interviews. For the cross-sectional part, which explores the effects of the family of origin, we selected young people (aged 19–34 years) who had obtained a high school diploma or a third-level degree within the 5 years previous to the time of the interview in 2011.[1] We adopted this strategy to maximize the sample size and the statistical power for the first two sets of analyses. The third analysis—of the impact

Table 9.1 Analytical sample size by country (number of cases)

Database	Finland	France	Italy	Poland	United Kingdom
Cross-sectional, 2011	238	720	814	695	223
Longitudinal, 2005–2012	329	1,016	896	965	309

of family background on young people's occupational condition—considers a longer period of 5 years.[2]

We focus our examination on five countries that exemplify the five transition regimes developed by Pohl and Walther (2007) and discussed by Hadjivassiliou et al. (this volume): universalistic (Finland), employment-centered (France), subprotective (Italy), post-socialist (Poland), and liberal (United Kingdom) (Table 9.1). The choice of these countries has the benefit of drawing on their larger sample size in the EU-SILC data, as well as their correspondence to theoretical predictions about different youth transition regimes.

The first set of multivariate analyses uses separate logit models to predict the effect of early unemployment on the likelihood of young people being in skilled and/or well-paid occupations 3 years after completing their education. We explore the overall duration and frequency of unemployment spells. The second set of models explores successful transitions to good jobs in a selection of European countries—by level of education achieved. The final analyses use cross-sectional multinomial logit models to examine the impact of family background on the types of transitions young people have been making. The chapter concludes with a discussion of the inequalities emerging from this examination.

9.3. GOOD AND BAD JOBS: A TYPOLOGY OF SUCCESSFUL OUTCOMES

Using the dimensions of skills and wages, we develop a typology to compare transitions to one of four possible outcomes: "successful," "investment," "need," and "failure" jobs (Figure 9.2). A "successful" state is when young people enter a skilled and well-paid job. An "investment" state is when a skilled position has been achieved with the trade-off of a lower salary (skilled but low-paid job). Jobs requiring higher skills or qualifications may initially be poorly paid (entry positions as a screening device) but over time result in increasing wage returns. Well paid is defined as above the median wage of all employed individuals by all ages in each country each year.[3] A "need" state is when the job is low or unskilled, and the wages can be either high or low. A "failure" state is when the wages are low and the job is unskilled; a failed transition also includes those who end up in unemployment or inactivity. Individuals still in education (students) are excluded from this analysis.

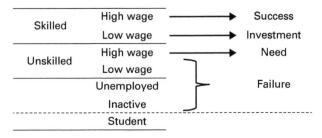

Figure 9.2 Typology of occupational positioning based on skills and wage.

Skilled occupations are defined on the basis of ISCO-88 codes (International Standard Classification of Occupations): high-skilled nonmanual occupations (ISCO 11–34), low-skilled nonmanual occupations (ISCO 41–52), skilled manual occupations (ISCO 61–83), and elementary occupations (ISCO 91–93) (Pintelon et al. 2011, 56–7). We consider both manual and nonmanual skilled occupations.

9.3.1. Unemployment Duration and Employment Outcomes

Having completed their studies, young people ideally achieve speedy insertion into the labor market and then maintain continuous employment.[4] However, they may instead remain out of employment for a longer period of time either voluntarily, because they choose to wait, or involuntarily, because they are unable to find a suitable job. We test the effect of unemployment duration in the early phase of young people's careers on their probability of accessing a high-wage occupation, a skilled occupation, or both conditions jointly (a "success" state).

We codified the overall duration in unemployment over the 48 observation months (Figure 9.3). "None" refers to individuals who had either no time or a maximum of 1 month in unemployment; "short" refers to those with up to 6 months of unemployment; and "medium-long" refers to those who experienced a total duration of an (accumulated) unemployment spell(s) lasting longer than 6 months. The sample is composed of all individuals with four completed interviews who were employed in the final observation.

We ran separate logit models on the EU-SILC longitudinal monthly data, predicting—for those employed—the occupational condition reached 3 years after completing a secondary or tertiary qualification. Three different models explored the probability that these employed would be found in a high-wage occupation, in a skilled occupation, or in a state of occupational "success" (both high-wage and skilled occupation). The results for the effect of the average duration in unemployment in the three models are shown jointly in Figure 9.3. All models use controls for age, gender, country, and number of employment interruption episodes; they also account for the differences based on education level.

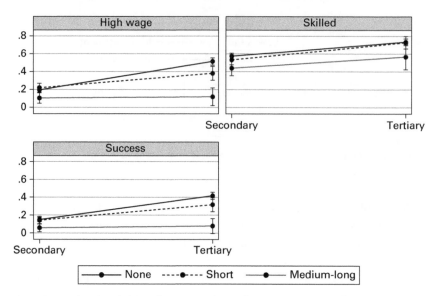

Figure 9.3 Predicted probability of young people (aged 19–34 years; 3 years after acquiring a qualification) being in a high-wage, skilled, or successful job by level of education and unemployment duration.
Source: Authors' calculations based on EU-SILC longitudinal data (2005–2012).

We find no significantly observable difference in any of the outcomes analyzed for those who had been unemployed for up to 6 months (a relatively short period of unemployment) compared to those who had never been unemployed; the exception to this result regarded third-level graduates, who had a lower probability of being in a high-wage job if they had been unemployed. Differences in the effect of unemployment duration were more perceptible in wage attainment than in achieving a skilled occupation after 3 years (Figure 9.3, top graphs), especially for those with a tertiary level of education. The probability of having a high-wage position after 3 years (Figure 9.3, top left graph) was considerably lower for graduates who had been unemployed for more than 6 months (medium-long duration) than for those who had never been unemployed (none) or those who had been unemployed for 6 months or less (short duration).

The relationship between unemployment duration and labor market outcome seems to be similar in the five countries studied. There are, of course, differences in the "baseline" probabilities of being in each state (high skills, high wage, or successful occupation) in the five countries, which reflect the specificities of the different national labor markets. However, the differences in the effects of the *duration of unemployment* are not statistically significant between countries (the interaction effects with country dummy variables were not statistically significant). Although small sample sizes of young people in each country might make country-specific effects difficult to detect, we found empirical evidence of a similar mechanism, across contexts, linking length of unemployment to successful outcomes (especially wages).[5] The results reveal how, in these countries—especially around the initial stage of the employment career—experiencing a small amount of turbulence (up to 6 months of unemployment) does not seem to weigh heavily on short-term employment outcomes.

9.3.2. Continuity in Employment and Employment Outcomes

We further explore any effects of the entry process on the employment outcome 3 years after obtaining a qualification. Specifically, we test for effects due to the timing of unemployment. We distinguish between those with few or no unemployment spells during job search and those with a greater number of unemployment spells in the early search period (i.e., the number of employment interruptions they experienced). We examine the effect of continuity in employment, where "continuity" is defined as having at most one spell of unemployment. In other words, the current employment situation is achieved with no employment interruptions, or with only one, as opposed to those with more frequent interruptions creating a more intermittent employment trajectory.

The outcomes of those employed 3 years after obtaining a secondary- or tertiary-level qualification (Figure 9.4) show that continuity in employment does not seem to affect the skills level of the occupation achieved, and that it only slightly affects the chances of "successful" transitions for those with a secondary-level qualification. This indicates a greater likelihood of higher wages being

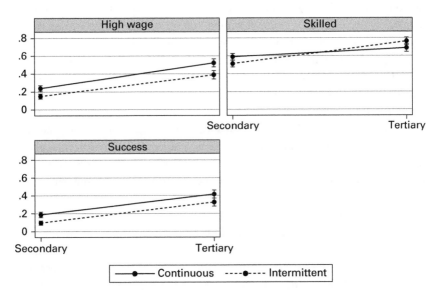

Figure 9.4 Predicted probability of young people (aged 19–34 years; 3 years after acquiring a qualification) being in a high-wage, skilled, or successful job by level of education and employment continuity.
Source: Authors' calculations based on EU-SILC longitudinal data (2005–2012).

reached by those who have been continuously employed (Figure 9.4, top left graph).

Continuity has a marginally significant effect on the probability of being in a "successful occupation" for those with secondary-level education (Figure 9.4, bottom left graph; confidence intervals at the 95% level). This result points to a small positive effect of quick entry (at most one unemployment spell after leaving education): The shorter the search (the quicker the entry after finishing education), the slightly more likely the young person is to be found in a successful occupation. Again, no statistically significant effect was found for the differences in the relationship between continuity and occupational outcome across countries. Although each country has a unique labor market structure (reflected in the different chances of being employed or having experienced continuity), the effect of employment continuity again seems to be working in the same direction in each separate context.

In summary, the previous results suggest that both employment continuity and taking less time to find the first job are associated with some advantages but that these are quite small. We detected some minor effects on the employment outcomes investigated (high wage, skilled employment, or "successful" occupation) from entering employment quickly or not spending too long in unemployment during this relatively brief window of observation (3 years). This result could be specific to the early stage in the employment career, confirming that despite a clear but weak advantage of continuous employment and an early start, a brief period of unemployment does not appear to impair subsequent outcomes as much as we might have expected. In fact, it is the medium- to long-term experience of unemployment (of 6 or more months during the 3 years) that has a more substantial impact. Whether this experience consists of a single short spell or of the accumulation of several shorter spells, longer periods of unemployment clearly have a negative effect on the chances of occupational success, especially in terms of wages and for those with tertiary education (see Figure 9.3). A slightly longer initial delay before first entering employment, or a turbulent beginning (see Figure 9.4), seems to have affected the wage dimension the most for university graduates. For younger workers, these factors have more of an impact on their likelihood of making a transition to a "successful" job. And although the specific institutional arrangements of each country are crucial in defining the chances of being employed and the duration of unemployment (Hipp, Bernhardt, and Allmendinger 2015), our data reveal the relevance of continuity in employment or unemployment in excess of 6 months on later occupational outcomes regardless of the national context. Having examined the likelihood of transitions into successful jobs measured in terms of their wages or skill profiles, we now turn to examining access to occupations after graduating from school or college and the effect on the kind of job achieved 3 years later.

9.4. COMPARING EMPLOYMENT OUTCOMES: WELL BEGUN IS HALF DONE

The analyses presented so far support the idea that a quick transition into any job is always better than joblessness, although the effects are not very substantial and are mostly statistically significant only for longer unemployment durations. But does this give us the full picture? The empirical evidence presented so far is not enough to show how young people are being trapped into poorly paid and low qualified jobs. We have shown an association between speedier entry with fewer interruptions and an overall slightly more favorable employment outcome. To enrich our understanding, it is important to further explore young people's initial position in the labor market and how this changes over time: We compare initial job status on completion of education with that observed 3 years later (for those who were employed).

Here, we do not focus directly on how the occupational conditions of young people change across different countries (reflecting their institutional contexts and already investigated in the literature). Rather, we examine whether the strategies pursued by young people are different across countries *in their effects*. In other words, regardless of the larger or smaller amount of "successful" positions observed in each country, we investigate which are the most effective strategies for young people to achieve these positions. Specifically, we focus on the relevance of a "good employment entry" for a good match in skilled occupations. Occupational characteristics, especially task complexity (as a proxy for occupational skills in this study), are a predictor of likelihood of employment success (Reichelt 2015).

Moving from a cross-sectional to a longitudinal perspective (Figure 9.5), we can observe that all countries' trends move in the same direction over time. In general, we can observe that despite similar trends across countries, the starting levels are rather different, particularly for the United Kingdom, which has a higher share of young people either unemployed or employed in unskilled or low-paid occupations even before the completion of an education. In a context of prevailing stability during the 4-year period considered here, the statistically significant differences are concentrated in the bottom two graphs in Figure 9.5: the conditions of "failure" and "student." On the one hand, "student" decreased—as individuals achieved a secondary or tertiary education—and, on the other hand, "failure" transitions increased.

The trends for the share of students deserve additional consideration regarding the education level achieved. As reflected in the literature, the probabilities of being enrolled in education or being in a condition of "success" vary substantially between graduates from secondary and tertiary education. Achieving a secondary-level qualification is associated with higher chances of continuing in education, whereas obtaining a tertiary degree is associated with higher chances

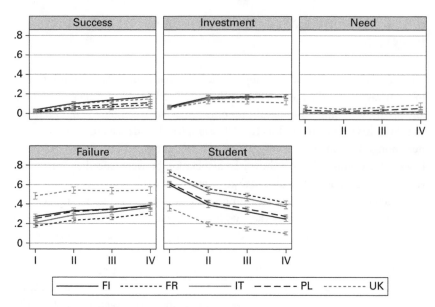

Figure 9.5 Shares of young people (aged 19–34 years; observed in their transition after acquiring a qualification) by occupational typology and country over the 4 years observed.
Source: Authors' calculations based on EU-SILC longitudinal data (2005–2012).

of reaching a skilled position, either well paid or not. In line with the literature, our data confirm a competitive advantage of tertiary graduates compared to upper secondary school-leavers. This is shown at aggregate level in Figure 9.6, but it is true for all countries considered: The secondary educated are more frequently found in the "failure" transitions compared to graduates; they are also less likely than graduates to be in "success" transitions.

Turning to analyzing the early development of occupational conditions after completion of education (separately by education level achieved), we explore the effect of entry occupational conditions on the job held 3 years later (using the typology devised in Figure 9.2). We estimated multinomial logit models with EU-SILC longitudinal data separately for the secondary and tertiary educated, adopting controls for age, sex, and country.

For every initial condition, the results in Figures 9.7 and 9.8 show the difference in probabilities for every final occupational status compared to being students. In other words, positive (above the central horizontal line) or negative (below the line) estimates illustrate how more(/less) likely it is for a young person to be found in the referred occupational condition (titles of graphs) rather than in education after 3 years, given the initial condition (*x* axis of each graph). Figure 9.7 shows a high stability over time for all statuses. For those who accomplished a secondary level of education, being in a "failure" state is associated with a higher probability of remaining so after 3 years (Figure 9.7, "Failure" graph, point above the line). A high degree of stability is also true for all other

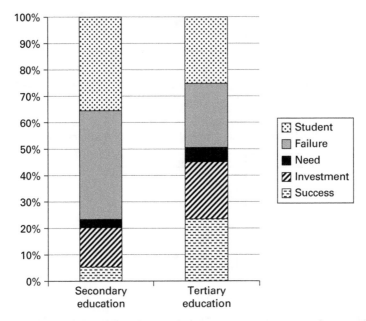

Figure 9.6 Shares of young people (aged 19–34 years; 3 years after acquiring a qualification) by typology and educational qualification.
Source: Authors' calculations based on EU-SILC longitudinal data (2005–2012).

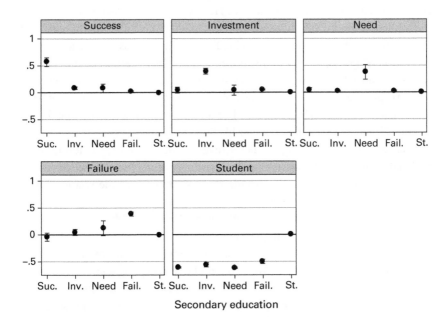

Figure 9.7 Difference in predicted probabilities for every occupational status compared to being students (young people aged 19–34 years; 3 years after concluding secondary education).
Source: Authors' calculations based on EU-SILC longitudinal data (2005–2012).

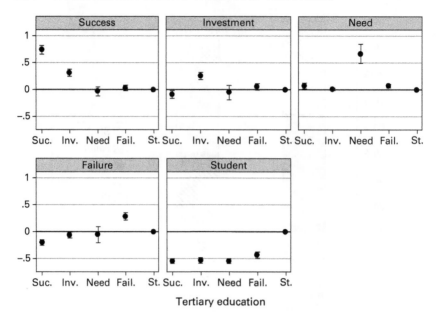

Figure 9.8 Difference in predicted probabilities for every occupational status compared to being students (young people aged 19–34 years; 3 years after concluding tertiary education).
Source: Authors' calculations based on EU-SILC longitudinal data (2005–2012).

statuses: need, investment, and success. However, as can be seen in the graph at the top left of Figure 9.7, those who were initially in an "investment" state also have somewhat higher chances of being found in a "success" state later (Figure 9.7, "Success" graph, second point above the line). This effect is small but statistically significant. The results are very similar for the tertiary educated (Figure 9.8), except for an even stronger effect of "investment" on the likelihood of "success"; that is, those who began in a skilled job that was initially poorly paid ("investment" status) have a much higher likelihood of later success.

The relevance of entering the labor market with a good job is found in all national contexts, with no statistically significant difference across countries. Therefore, even if we cannot conclude that the strength of the relationship is necessarily the same—due to the small sample sizes—our results suggest that the strategy of securing a good entry is valid everywhere.

In summary, we found a high persistence in statuses over the initial years of young people's employment careers, which highlights the relevance of the characteristics of the entry job. We also found that accepting a job that matches the jobseeker's level of education, even if poorly paid at the beginning but with increasing returns over time, qualifies "investment" choices as a possible real strategic move in the labor market that is associated with a higher likelihood of "success." Finding a good job to start with makes a major difference, especially for third-level graduates.

9.5. WHAT DIFFERENCE DO FAMILIES MAKE WITH REGARD TO HOW LONG ONE CAN WAIT?

The probability of being in one of the four outcome states of the proposed typology (success, investment, need, or failure; see Figure 9.2) varies according to the duration experienced in unemployment, the continuity of employment, and the conditions of entry into the labor market. To understand how this varies according to young people's social class of origin, we used the cross-sectional EU-SILC 2011 data, which contain a special ad hoc module on intergenerational transmission of disadvantages. In this module, it is possible to obtain information on the education level achieved by young people's parents and also for those who have already left the family of origin.[6] The subsample for our analysis comprises all young people aged 19–34 years who had obtained a secondary or tertiary educational qualification less than 5 years previously, for a total of 11,824 young people. We estimated the probability of being found in one of the four states illustrated in the typology described in Section 9.3 (see Figure 9.2). We tested for the social class of origin as defined on the basis of the higher education level between young people's mothers and fathers (criteria of dominance; Erikson and Goldthorpe 1992). Social class of origin, as based on education, is classified in three categories: high (tertiary), middle (upper secondary), and low (primary and lower secondary).

Multinomial logit models are controlled for sex, age, living independently or with parents, and country. For ease of interpretation, we again present the main results in the form of average predicted probabilities (marginal effects). Specifically, we illustrate the differences in probability for each category with respect to living with one's own parents and coming from a lower class (Figure 9.9, "IN Low class").

Results from Figure 9.9 clearly show a statistically significant effect of social class of origin on young people's occupational conditions within 5 years of obtaining an educational qualification. Among those who have left the parental household, we see that belonging to a high or middle social class increases the probability of being in a "success" status (Figure 9.9, first two lines of top left graph). All else being equal, success is more likely for the more advantaged strata of young people (a result in line with McKnight (2015) for the United Kingdom). We also show that among those who reside with their parents, youth from the high class have a lower probability of being in an "investment" condition (i.e., skilled job but low paid) compared to their peers from the low and the middle class (Figure 9.9, top right graph). These results point to a better capacity of wealthier families to have their children proceed more frequently and rapidly into skilled and well-paid occupations (be it through counseling, guidance, referrals, soft skills, or social networks), whereas lengthy co-residence with one's parents and resorting to initially low-paid occupations might be the most

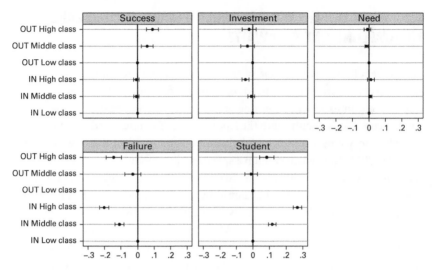

Figure 9.9 Differences in the predicted probability of being in each employment condition by social class of origin for young people (aged 19–34 years and who obtained a high school diploma or a third-level degree within the previous 5 years).
Source: Authors' calculations based on EU-SILC cross-sectional data (2011).

effective strategy for children from other backgrounds for finding employment that is consistent with their qualifications.

Longer co-residence could be an effective way for young people from the middle class to be able to obtain/accept skilled jobs, albeit (at least initially) poorly paid, but with interesting prospects of future opportunities. We also show that the probability of being found in a "failure" condition is lower for young people from the higher class, regardless of their residential independence from their parents, whereas it is lower for children from the middle class only when they still live in the parental home (Figure 9.9, "Failure" graph). Finally, a similar effect of social class of origin and co-residence with one's parents is also found around the decision to continue education (Berloffa et al. 2015; Berloffa, Matteazzi, and Villa, this volume). It is young people from the high class, and those from the middle class living with their parents, who have a higher probability of remaining enrolled in the education system and making further educational investments (Figure 9.9, bottom graph). The role of the family of origin is relevant in all countries. In this last analysis, we tested again for the interaction effect with the country of residence of the young people, and it did not prove to be statistically significant. We believe that all these findings highlight the persistence of a clear class divide for young people, regardless of the country context. The pursuit of "higher profile" career paths, here skilled jobs, is made easier for youth from the higher social class, whereas for children from other social backgrounds, the routes to success are strewn with obstacles. Staying longer in the parental home seems the most viable option for securing better employment prospects for children from the middle class, whereas prospects are not as promising for children from the lower class.

9.6. CONCLUSIONS

In this chapter, we have shown that although both an early start and continuous employment are associated with more favorable outcomes (especially for the highly educated), these effects are relatively small and do not support the idea that any job is necessarily always better than joblessness, at least for a brief initial period. We have also shown, given a high degree of status stability over time, that the starting employment is highly predictive of subsequent outcomes. This explains why a well-matched start in terms of skills level, even if it entails a trade-off in accepting a lower salary or taking longer to find the right job, often seems to be a more successful strategy for securing better outcomes in the long term, especially for third-level graduates; similar results for Germany were found by Voßemer and Schuck (2016). Overall, careful career planning might include the risk of some initial turbulence, or a slightly longer period of unemployment, caused by giving up on unskilled job offers, but it can also enable the chance to find a better job fit.

Exploring the effects of initial occupations on later outcomes of qualified young people, we have also demonstrated that being poorly paid initially but in skilled occupations (an "investment" strategy) can represent an opportunity for young people that can result in a more successful positioning in the labor market. In contrast, unskilled occupations for qualified young people ("need" and "failure" strategies) can become an employment trap that is difficult to reverse in the long term; Reichelt (2015) presented similar findings for Germany. For qualified young people, it appears easier to pursue wage increases with tenure than it is to move from an unskilled to a skilled occupational position.

Finally, higher education still provides a significant stepping stone to a professional job and a successful position in the labor market. However, the capacity of young people to pursue tertiary education is still strongly stratified by family social class background and family/household work intensity (Berloffa, Matteazzi, and Villa, this volume).

Our analyses find support for a strong influence of the family social background on the strategies pursued and the occupational conditions (in terms of pay and skill levels) achieved by young individuals within 5 years of completing their education. These findings suggest a strong familial influence on young peoples' (un)successful employment outcomes. They point to mechanisms related to higher class families' greater success in informing (through advice and guidance), supporting (possibly through social networks, building aspirations, and more effective guidance through the education and employment systems), and possibly providing backup (through economic support and/or longer co-residence) for young peoples' employment strategies. We have shown that the more effective strategies—those more likely to lead to better outcomes—often entail initial losses such as higher risks (longer or more likely unemployment) or investments (lower pay). These findings are in line with analyses on the risk of education and skill mismatch (McGuinness, Bergin, and Whelan, this volume), search methods for first employment, and the impact of unemployment duration on a successful job search (Flek et al., this volume).

Concerning country differences, we found different baseline shares of young people in each occupational status across countries, reflecting differences in the national institutional and economic contexts. However, we found no statistically significant evidence of different mechanisms linking duration in unemployment, continuity of employment, entry jobs, or social class of the family of origin to the degree of success in employment 3–5 years after acquiring an educational qualification in the five selected cases from the youth transition regimes typology. Our understanding is that mechanisms linking class influences to young people's employment outcomes, net of country-specific baseline levels, overtake specificities of youth transition regimes. We found young adults from the high social class to be in a more favorable position than those from the low class. We suppose that this advantage could be further exacerbated by the persistence of the recent economic downturn, which has led young people to increasingly struggle to make their way into stable employment in all countries analyzed (see Grotti et al., this volume). However, we did not focus on the effects of the Great Recession; thus, how the crisis affects the degree of success in employment for young people remains to be to be explored. Younger people and later entrants tend to be more affected than adults by recessions and stagnation and also to be more exposed to the differing capacities of their families to shield and support them. This is not only because the unemployment rate of young people rises more than that of adults during a recession but also because young people caught by the crisis are more vulnerable to its effects. They are likely to suffer the economic downturn for longer (being unemployed or in underemployment) and to have its effects spill over into their subsequent career steps (reduced contributions, weaker career opportunities, and higher unemployment risks). Young people will have to endure the consequences of their current fragility for a lengthier period also because they are at a formative stage in their lives. We limit our analysis to the initial 3–5 years for reasons of data availability, but further analyses should explore longer term consequences (Mooi-Reci and Wooden 2017). The quality of employment is also important (Van Lancker 2012). We considered wages and skills levels, but contractual security and long-term perspectives are also extremely important for young people's transitions to adulthood (Blossfeld et al. 2005). The growing incidence of temporary contracts is an issue of concern, particularly in those countries more strongly affected by the crisis in Europe. Although temporary jobs may facilitate the entry of young people into work, they might lead to a precarious career rather than to permanent employment (Scherer 2005; Brzinsky-Fay 2007; O'Higgins 2010; Gebel and Giesecke 2016).

Our results suggest that as inequalities widen, parents' ability to invest in their children's success not only remains salient but also becomes even more important in determining life chances and sustaining inequalities. Given the strong influence that households' characteristics and families of origin exert in the strategies pursued by young people in accessing and establishing employment careers, further rises in unequal access to employment and income for households would jeopardize lower class young peoples' life chances and opportunities. Alternatively, they would unevenly strain families who have to compensate for retrenched welfare and increasingly fragile markets, with the higher pressure placed on more fragile families. Because the outcomes of employment careers seem so strongly influenced by what happens in the early period of establishment in the labor market, a comprehensive investment strategy in young people's transitions to employment should become a priority.

NOTES

1   Our sample selection might include some university dropouts but cannot include high school dropouts, given that we define success as "matching" between (at least) secondary level of education and a skilled job; thus, we are studying entrance into skilled employment (i.e., requiring at least a secondary-level qualification).

2   Had it been possible, we would also have chosen 5 years for the first two sets of analyses, but EU-SILC data do not allow this. Narrowing the observation window for the analyses of family influences to only approximately 3 years—when a longer time span was available—would have unnecessarily reduced the sample size.

3   Country- and yearly based figures computed on annual wages of full-time employed.

4   Employment continuity in this case does not necessarily imply continuity in the same job; rather, we modeled it as an absence of periods of unemployment.

5   In other words, we cannot exclude that the effect of the duration in unemployment is stronger in one country than in another, but the direction of the relationship is definitely similar and relevant. This also applies when we examine the descriptive statistics.

6   Building an indicator of the social class of origin on the basis of available EU-SILC data is subject to two limitations. The first concerns the framing of the question: The ad hoc module asks about parents' education level when the respondent was aged 14 years, whereas for those who live with their parents the measure is taken at the time of interview. The second, more serious limitation is that information about the parents of those who live independently is only requested of people aged between 25 and 59 years. This means that we

are lacking information on those who had already left the parental home at the time of interview but are not yet 25 years old. In our sample, this group amounts to approximately 17%.

REFERENCES

Barbera, Filippo, Marianna Filandri, and Nicola Negri. 2010. "Conclusioni: Cittadinanza e politiche di ceto medio." In *Restare di ceto medio. Il passaggio alla vita adulta nella società che cambia*, edited by Nicola Negri and Marianna Filandri, 213–38. Bologna: Il Mulino.

Barone, Carlo, Mario Lucchini, and Antonio Schizzerotto. 2011. "Career Mobility in Italy." *European Societies* 13 (3): 377–400.

Berloffa, Gabriella, Marianna Filandri, Eleonora Matteazzi, Tiziana Nazio, Nicola Negri, Jacqueline O'Reilly, Paola Villa, and Carolina Zuccotti. 2015. "Work-Poor and Work-Rich Families: Influence on Youth Labour Market Outcomes." STYLE Working Paper 8.1. Brighton, UK: CROME, University of Brighton. http://www.style-research.eu/publications/working-papers

Bernardi, Fabrizio. 2007. "Movilidad social y dinámicas familiares: Una aplicación al estudio de la emancipación familiar en España." *Revista Internacional de Sociología* 48: 33–54.

Blossfeld, Hans-Peter, Erik Klijzing, Melinda Mills, and Karin Kurz, eds. 2005. *Globalization, Uncertainty and Youth in Society*. London: Routledge.

Blossfeld, Hans-Peter, Karin Kurz, Sandra Buchholz, and Erzsébet Bukodi, eds. 2008. *Young Workers, Globalization and the Labor Market: Comparing Early Working Life in Eleven Countries*. Cheltenham, UK: Elgar.

Brzinsky-Fay, Christian. 2007. "Lost in Transition? Labour Market Entry Sequences of School Leavers in Europe." *European Sociological Review* 23 (4): 409–22.

Bukodi, Erzsébet, and John Goldthorpe. 2011. "Class Origins, Education and Occupation Attainment in Britain." *European Societies* 13 (3): 347–75.

Erikson, Robert, and Goldthorpe, John H. 1992. *The Constant Flux: a Study of Class Mobility in Industrial Societies*. Oxford: Clarendon Press. p. 429.

Gallie, Duncan. 2007. *Employment Regimes and the Quality of Work*. Oxford: Oxford University Press.

Gallie, Duncan. 2012. "Skills, Job Control and the Quality of Work: The Evidence from Britain." *Economic and Social Review* 43 (3): 325–41.

Gallie, Duncan. 2013a. *Economic Crisis, Quality of Work and Social Integration: The European Experience*. Oxford: Oxford University Press.

Gallie, Duncan. 2013b. "Direct Participation and the Quality of Work." *Human Relations* 66 (4): 453–73.

Gallie, Duncan, Alan Felstead, and Francis Green. 2012. "Job Preferences and the Intrinsic Quality of Work: The Changing Attitudes of British Employees 1992–2006." *Work Employment and Society* 26 (5): 806–21.

Gash, Vanessa. 2008. "Bridge or Trap? Temporary Workers' Transitions to Unemployment and to the Standard Employment Contract." *European Sociological Review* 24 (5): 651–68.

Gebel, Michael, and Johannes Giesecke. 2016. "Does Deregulation Help? The Impact of Employment Protection Reforms on Youths' Unemployment and Temporary Employment Risks in Europe." *European Sociological Review* 32 (4): 486–500. doi:10.1093/esr/jcw022.

Green, Francis, Alan Felstead, Duncan Gallie, and Hande Inanc. 2014. "Job-Related Well-Being Through the Great Recession." *Journal of Happiness Studies* 17 (1): 389–411.

Grün, Carola, Wolfgang Hauser, and Thomas Rhein. 2010. "Is Any Job Better Than No Job? Life Satisfaction and Re-employment." *Journal of Labour Research* 31 (3): 285–306.

Hemerijck, Anton, and Werner Eichhorst. 2010. "Whatever Happened to the Bismarckian Welfare State? From Labor Shedding to Employment-Friendly Reforms." In *A Long Goodbye to Bismarck? The Politics of Welfare Reforms in Continental Europe,* edited by Bruno Palier, 301–32. Amsterdam: Amsterdam University Press.

Hillmert, Steffen. 2011. "Occupational Mobility and Developments of Inequality Along the Life Course." *European Societies* 13 (3): 401–23.

Hipp, Lena, Janine Bernhardt, and Jutta Allmendinger. 2015. "Institutions and the Prevalence of Nonstandard Employment." *Socio-Economic Review* 13 (2): 351–77.

Jencks, Christopher, Lauri Perman, and Lee Rainwater. 1988. "What Is a Good job? A New Measure of Labor-Market Success." *American Journal of Sociology* 93: 1322–57.

Kattenbach, Ralph, and Jacqueline O'Reilly. 2011. "Introduction: New Perspectives on the Quality of Working Life." *Management Revue* 22 (2): 107–13.

Keller, Anita C., Robin Samuel, Manfred Max Bergman, and Norbert K. Semmer, eds. 2014. *Psychological, Educational and Sociological Perspectives on Success and Well-Being in Career Development.* New York: Springer.

Layard, Richard. 2004. "Good Jobs and Bad Jobs." Centre for Economic Performance Occasional Paper CEPOP19. London: Centre for Economic Performance.

McGuinness, Seamus, and Mark Wooden. 2009. "Overskilling, Job Insecurity, and Career Mobility." *Industrial Relations* 48 (2): 265–86. doi:210.1111/j.1468-1232X.2009.00557.x.

McKnight, Abigail. 2015. "Downward Mobility, Opportunity Hoarding and the 'Glass Floor.'" CASE Research Report. London: Centre for Analysis of Social Exclusion, London School of Economics.

Mooi-Reci, Irma, and Ronald Dekker. 2016. "Fixed-Term Contracts: Short-Term Blessings or Long-Term Scars? Empirical Findings from the Netherlands 1980–2000." *British Journal of Industrial Relations* 53 (1): 112–35.

Mooi-Reci, Irma, and Mark Wooden. 2017. "Casual Employment and Long-Term Wage Outcomes." *Human Relations* 70 (9): 1064–1090.

O'Higgins, Shane. 2010. *The Impact of the Economic and Financial Crisis on Youth Employment: Measures for Labour Market Recovery in the European Union, Canada and the United States*. Geneva: International Labour Office.

O'Reilly, Jacqueline, Werner Eichhorst, András Gábos, Kari Hadjivassiliou, David Lain, Janine Leschke, Seamus McGuinness, Lucia Mýtna Kureková, Tiziana Nazio, Renate Ortlieb, Helen Russell, and Paola Villa. 2015. "Five Characteristics of Youth Unemployment in Europe: Flexibility, Education, Migration, Family Legacies, and EU Policy." *Sage Open* 5 (1): 1–19.doi:10.1177/2158244015574962.

Peiró, José M., Sonia Agut, and Rosa Grau. 2010. "The Relationship Between Overeducation and Job Satisfaction Among Young Spanish Workers: The Role of Salary, Contract of Employment, and Work Experience." *Journal of Applied Social Psychology* 40: 666–89. doi:10.1111/j.1559-1816.2010.00592.x.

Pintelon, Olivier, Bea Cantillon, Karel Van den Bosch, and Christopher T. Whelan. 2011. "The Social Stratification of Social Risks: Class and Responsibility in the 'New' Welfare State." GINI Discussion Paper 13. Amsterdam: AIAS.

Pohl, Axel, and Andreas A. Walther. 2007. "Activating the Disadvantaged—Variations in Addressing Youth Transitions Across Europe." *International Journal of Lifelong Education* 26 (5): 533–53.

Reichelt, Malte. 2015. "Career Progression from Temporary Employment: How Bridge and Trap Functions Differ by Task Complexity." *European Sociological Review* 31 (5): 558–72.

Russell, Helen, Janine Leschke, and Mark Smith. 2015. "Balancing Flexibility and Security in Europe: The Impact on Young Peoples' Insecurity and Subjective Well-Being." STYLE Working Paper 10.3. Brighton, UK: CROME, University of Brighton. http://www.style-research.eu/publications/working-papers

Sánchez-Sánchez, Nuria, and Seamus McGuinness. 2013. "Decomposing the Impacts of Overeducation and Overskilling on Earnings and Job Satisfaction: An Analysis Using REFLEX data." *Education Economics* 23 (4): 419–32.

Scherer, Stefani. 2004. "Stepping-Stones or Traps? The Consequences of Labour Market Entry Positions on Future Careers in West Germany, Great Britain and Italy." *Work, Employment & Society* 18 (2): 369–94.

Scherer, Stefani. 2005. "Pattern of Labour Market Entry—Long Wait or Career Instability? An Empirical Comparison of Italy, Great Britain and West Germany." *European Sociological Review* 21 (5): 427–40.

Van Lancker, Wim. 2012. "The European World of Temporary Employment: Gendered and Poor?" *European Societies* 14 (1): 83–111.

Voßemer, Jonas, and Bettina Schuck. 2016. "Better Overeducated Than Unemployed? The Short- and Long-Term Effects of an Overeducated Labour Market Re-entry." *European Sociological Review* 32 (2): 251–65.

Warhurst, Chris, Françoise Carré, Patricia Findlay, and Chris Tilly, eds. 2012. *Are Bad Jobs Inevitable? Trends, Determinants and Responses to Job Quality in the Twenty-First Century*. London: Palgrave Macmillan.

Wolbers, Marteen H. J., Ruud Luijkx, and Wout Ultee. 2011. "Educational Attainment, Occupational Achievements, Career Peaks." *European Societies* 13 (3): 425–50.

10

THE WORKLESSNESS LEGACY

DO WORKING MOTHERS MAKE A DIFFERENCE?

Gabriella Berloffa, Eleonora Matteazzi, and Paola Villa

10.1. INTRODUCTION

The analysis of intergenerational inequality and social mobility has attracted increasing attention in the past few decades. Several contributions have analyzed the influence of family background on educational and occupational attainments, highlighting either an intergenerational income inequality (Corak 2006; d'Addio 2007; Bjorklund and Jäntti 2009; Blanden 2013) or an intergenerational correlation of jobs and occupations between fathers and sons (Solon 1992; Black and Devereux 2011). A number of studies have focused on the intergenerational transmission of worklessness (see Section 10.2 for details). However, almost all of these contributions focus on a single country and on the influence of the occupational condition of either the father or the mother on their children's labor market outcomes. This chapter analyzes the intergenerational transmission of worklessness in a cross-country comparative perspective, investigating whether this transmission varies according to the gender of parents and the gender of their children and also across European country groups.

The contribution made by this chapter is threefold. First, this is the first comparative study at the European level on the influence of parents' employment status during their children's adolescence on the risk of worklessness among young people (aged 24–35 years). In fact, national-specific socioeconomic structures and labor market institutions are likely to affect the various channels of the intergenerational transmission of worklessness: economic, genetic, cultural/

familial, and social. As we argue in Section 10.2, the intergenerational correlation of worklessness should be higher in countries characterized by prolonged permanence of youth in the family of origin, low levels of borrowing among young people, social norms based on traditional gender roles within families, less developed and less efficient public employment and youth support services, low participation in active labor market policies (ALMPs), and less liberal labor markets. Thus, this chapter enhances the understanding of how labor market institutions and welfare systems affect labor market outcomes in a comparative perspective (Scruggs and Allan 2006; Gallie 2007; Halleröd, Ekbrand, and Bengtsson 2015).

Second, we consider the employment condition of both parents. When controlling for the employment status of a single parent, the estimated effect might also capture the spouse's effect due to assortative mating in marriage. Controlling for the employment condition of both parents limits this type of problem. Furthermore, it allows us to study the extent to which a young person's probability of being workless varies according to the family employment structure. For instance, we can compare the outcomes for children who grew up in a dual-earner family, in a male-breadwinner family, or with a lone working mother.

Third, we consider the effect of the mother-in-law's employment condition. Indeed, there may be a positive correlation between the participation in employment of women and that of their mother-in-laws via their husbands'/sons' attitudes toward domestic work and female labor market participation (Del Boca, Locatelli, and Pasqua 2000; Fernández, Fogli, and Olivetti 2004; Kawaguchi and Miyazaki 2009; Farré and Vella 2013).

Our empirical findings show that having had a working mother during adolescence considerably reduces the likelihood of being workless for both sons and daughters in all country groups except the Nordic countries. In contrast, the effects of fathers' and mother-in-laws' working condition are less widespread across countries.

The chapter is structured as follows: Section 10.2 reviews the relevant literature, Section 10.3 presents the data and the estimation methodology, Section 10.4 discusses the main empirical findings, and Section 10.5 concludes the chapter.

10.2. LITERATURE REVIEW AND THEORETICAL BACKGROUND

A number of studies have dealt with the intergenerational correlation of worklessness.[1] There is a robust consensus on the existence of a positive correlation between the worklessness of fathers and their sons (O'Neill and Sweetman 1998; Corak, Gustafsson, and Österberg 2004; Oreopoulos, Page, and Huff Stevens 2008; Macmillan 2010, 2013; Mader et al. 2015), between fathers and all their children (Johnson and Reed 1996; Bratberg, Nilsen, and Vaage 2008; Ekhaugen

2009; Gregg, Macmillan, and Nasim 2012; Zwysen 2015), and between mothers and their daughters' labor market participation (Del Boca et al. 2000; Fortin 2005; Fernández 2007; Farré and Vella 2013). However, almost all of these studies focus on the effect of the employment condition of only the father or only the mother on their children's worklessness. Only Ekhaugen (2009) considers the unemployment status of both parents, but she does not distinguish between fathers' and mothers' unemployment experiences.[2]

Several explanations for the existence of an intergenerational transmission of labor outcomes within households have been advanced in the literature. To begin with, parents' economic resources affect their offspring's labor market outcomes through higher investments in educational achievements (Becker and Tomes 1986). However, some authors have recently emphasized the direct impact of the family of origin on offspring employment and earnings, even when controlling for education (Mocetti 2007; Raitano 2011; Franzini, Raitano, and Vona 2013). Thus, other types of effects need to be considered. First, household income and wealth may affect children's employment status and their job search process by leading to different reservation wages or by making it easier to start an independent economic activity. Second, in addition to economic resources, there are other possible channels of influence that interact with each other: (1) genetic, (2) cultural/familial, and (3) social. The genetic channel operates through the inheritance of cognitive traits and soft skills that may influence career advancements (Bowles and Gintis 2002). The cultural/familial channel works through the parental effect on offspring's preferences, values, and attitudes. Specifically, parental work experience can modify young adults' aspirations and attitudes toward education and labor market participation—that is, their evaluation of paid work and their sense of stigma, their attitudes toward relying on welfare benefits and toward gender roles, and so on (Ekhaugen 2009; Macmillan 2010; Schoon et al. 2012; Zwysen 2015). Last, the social channel works through family networks. It is well known that family members' employment status can play a role through the social network on which young individuals are able to rely when they are searching for a job (Montgomery 1991; Granovetter 1995; Rees 1996; Petersen, Saporta, and Seidel 2000; Topa 2001). In particular, several studies find that children of nonworking parents are more disadvantaged in the labor market compared with young people whose parents are working and maintain a network of social contacts (O'Neill and Sweetman 1998; Corak and Piraino 2010).[3]

These three distinct channels might work differently across European countries, depending on national-specific socioeconomic structures and institutional contexts. To the best of our knowledge, there are no studies in the literature dealing with this issue. We now present some hypotheses about the influence of various institutions on the ways in which these channels might operate (they are summarized in Table A10.1 in the Appendix).[4] Recall that we are interested in effects other than those on education.

First, the effect of household economic resources on an individual's reservation wage might be low or even null in countries in which attitudes toward independence are strong and young people leave the family of origin quite early. The economic channel should also be less important in those countries in which it is easier or "more normal" for young people to have debts—for example, housing debts or student loans. As a consequence, the intergenerational correlation of worklessness related to the economic channel should be lower in countries in which youth economic independence occurs earlier (e.g., Nordic, English-speaking, and Continental countries) and in which borrowing is more common among young people (e.g., Nordic and English-speaking countries, but also Eastern countries regarding student loans).[5]

Second, regarding the cultural channel, we expect that children's imitation of their parents' condition will be stronger in contexts in which values are shared by the majority of people. Thus, the intergenerational correlation of worklessness should be lower in countries in which social norms are in favor of female participation in the labor market (e.g., Nordic, Continental, and Eastern countries) and should be higher in countries in which women are expected to be the main family caregivers (e.g., Mediterranean countries). However, it may also be that the transmission of attitudes toward paid work within families prevails over the social norms. Parental views about the importance of paid work may have persistent effects on their children's choices (Mooi-Reci and Bakker 2015).

Third, the extent of the effect related to the social channel (i.e., family networks) is likely to be affected by labor market institutions, such as the development and efficiency of public employment services (PES), the extent of ALMP, and so forth. The intergenerational correlation of worklessness should be lower in countries in which recourse to PES for finding a job is more widespread (e.g., Continental and Eastern countries) and in which participation in ALMP is high (e.g., Nordic and Continental countries). It should also be lower in countries in which hiring is more competitive and labor markets are more liberal (e.g., English-speaking countries), whereas it should be higher in countries in which family and informal networks matter more for finding a job (e.g., Mediterranean countries).

Finally, the genetic channel should become more relevant in countries with more competitive labor markets and education systems and with higher youth unemployment rates.

Based on the preceding discussion, our hypothesis is that the extent of the intergenerational correlation of worklessness is greater in countries characterized by prolonged permanence in the parental home, low levels of borrowing among young people, social norms based on traditional gender roles and a familialistic welfare system (in which women are expected to provide care to frail family members), less efficient and/or developed PES and education and training institutions, less efficient youth support services, low participation in ALMP, and a less liberal labor market. In particular, we expect the extent of the intergenerational correlation of worklessness to be lower in Nordic, English-speaking, and Continental countries and to be greater in Mediterranean and Eastern countries.

This chapter contributes to the existing literature on the intergenerational correlation of worklessness by distinguishing between the effect of mothers' and fathers' worklessness on their sons' and daughters' employment status (considered separately). From previous studies, we expect that having had a working mother reduces female worklessness, whereas having had a working father reduces male worklessness. However, we have no prior hypotheses about the effect of fathers' working conditions on their daughters' employment or about the effect of mothers' working conditions on their sons' employment. Indeed, whereas the effect of the economic channel should be similar for both sons and daughters, the effects related to the cultural and social channels might be more differentiated across genders.

In addition to parental gender role attitudes, husbands' attitudes can also influence female participation in paid employment. There is evidence in the literature of a link between the labor market participation of women and that of their mother-in-laws via their husbands/sons (Fernández et al. 2004; Kawaguchi and Miyazaki 2009; Farré and Vella 2013). In other words, women married to men whose mothers worked are more likely to be employed themselves. Fernández et al. (2004) identify two possible channels: Growing up with a working mother may either shape men's preferences for a working wife or provide men with a set of household skills and attitudes toward housework that make them better partners for working women. In this chapter, we examine whether the working condition of the mother-in-law plays a role in explaining female employment in all European countries or only in some of them.

10.3. DATA AND ESTIMATION METHODOLOGY

This study is based on European Union Statistics on Income and Living Conditions (EU-SILC) data, which encompass extensive and comparable cross-sectional and longitudinal microdata at both the household and the individual level in 26 European countries. We use the 2011 wave because it provides substantial information on parental education and occupation through the ad hoc module on the intergenerational transmission of disadvantages. We select a sample of young people aged 25–34 years.[6] We then model their employment status (employed; not in employment, education, or training (NEET);[7] or in education) as a function of individual characteristics at the time of the interview and of family educational and occupational background in the period when the individual was approximately 14 years old. In order to estimate the intergenerational correlation of worklessness, we consider as workless young adults who are

NEET at the time of the interview and parents who were not in paid work when their children were adolescents.

The descriptive and econometric analyses are carried out separately for five groups of countries that are representative of the great heterogeneity of European labor market institutions and welfare systems:[8] Nordic (DK, FI, NO, and SE), Continental (AT, BE, CH, DE, FR, and NL), English-speaking (IE and UK), Mediterranean (CY, EL, ES, IT, MT, and PT), and Eastern European (BG, CZ, EE, HU, HR, PL, RO, and SK). We grouped countries according to our expectations about the effects of the various intergenerational transmission channels discussed in Section 10.2. These country groups also correspond to the classification adopted by Walther (2006), who defines different regimes of youth transitions. Eastern European countries are treated as a separate group because, according to Fenger (2007), half a century of communist rule has left institutional legacies that set Eastern European countries apart from other welfare systems.

We model the individual choice with respect to employment status as a multinomial logit model. Given that fathers' and mothers' employment conditions during their children's adolescence may impact differently on the labor market outcomes of their sons and daughters, we run separate analyses for young males and females. The set of control variables includes the following:

1. *Individual characteristics*: Age, educational attainment (at most lower secondary, at most upper secondary, and tertiary education), citizenship (individuals from non-EU countries), and motherhood status (young females with at least one child)[9]
2. *Partner's educational attainment* (at most lower secondary, at most upper secondary, and tertiary education)
3. *Cohabitation with parents* at the time of the interview
4. *Presence of parents when the young person was 14 years old* (both parents present, only one parent present, or no parents present)
5. *Parents' characteristics when the young person was 14 years old*: Employment status (employed), occupation (in a high-status occupation such as manager, professional, technician, or associate professional), and education level (tertiary education)
6. *Mother-in-law's employment status* (employed) when the husband/wife was aged approximately 14 years[10]
7. *Country and quarter* of the interview dummies

Table 10.1 shows some descriptive statistics regarding our sample of analysis. Cross-country differences in individual characteristics are in line with what is expected from official statistics. Nordic and Continental countries exhibit the highest shares of employed young people: More than 80% of males and more than 70% of females are in employment. They also show the lowest shares of NEETs. By contrast, Mediterranean and Eastern European countries record the

Table 10.1 Descriptive statistics of young people by country group and gender (individuals aged 25–34 years in 2011)

	Nordic countries		English-speaking countries		Continental countries		Mediterranean counties		Eastern countries	
	Males	Females	Males	Females	Males	Females	Males	Females	Males	Females
Employment status										
Employed	0.84	0.73	0.81	0.66	0.85	0.72	0.75	0.63	0.80	0.65
NEET	0.10	0.18	0.16	0.31	0.09	0.23	0.21	0.32	0.17	0.33
In education	0.07	0.09	0.07	0.03	0.05	0.04	0.05	0.05	0.02	0.02
Education										
Low	0.12	0.07	0.09	0.09	0.10	0.10	0.33	0.25	0.14	0.25
Medium	0.51	0.37	0.39	0.40	0.52	0.47	0.40	0.37	0.62	0.37
High	0.37	0.56	0.52	0.52	0.38	0.43	0.27	0.38	0.24	0.38
Parenthood status										
Parent	0.37	0.56	0.40	0.63	0.33	0.51	0.22	0.42	0.35	0.60
Cohabiting with parents (at the time of the interview)										
Yes	0.05	0.02	0.14	0.08	0.18	0.09	0.56	0.40	0.59	0.42
Presence of parents (when the young person was approximately age 14 years)										
Two parents	0.81	0.79	0.82	0.78	0.82	0.81	0.90	0.89	0.85	0.84
One parent	0.18	0.19	0.16	0.19	0.16	0.17	0.07	0.08	0.13	0.14
No parents	0.02	0.01	0.02	0.03	0.02	0.02	0.02	0.02	0.01	0.02

Household occupational structure (when the young person was approximately age 14 years)

Two-parent households (%)

Both parents working	0.80	0.80	0.58	0.56	0.59	0.62	0.43	0.45	0.82	0.81
Only father working	0.12	0.13	0.35	0.36	0.36	0.33	0.53	0.51	0.14	0.14
Only mother working	0.04	0.05	0.02	0.02	0.02	0.02	0.01	0.01	0.02	0.02
Neither parent working	0.03	0.03	0.05	0.05	0.03	0.03	0.02	0.03	0.03	0.03

One-parent households (%)

Lone working mother	0.71	0.70	0.43	0.42	0.64	0.70	0.58	0.55	0.77	0.77
Lone nonworking mother	0.12	0.14	0.23	0.27	0.20	0.20	0.23	0.25	0.08	0.10

Notes: Nordic countries: DK, FI, NO, and SE; Continental countries: AT, BE, CH, DE, FR, and NL; English-speaking countries: IE and UK; Mediterranean countries: CY, EL, ES, IT, MT, and PT; Eastern European countries: BG, CZ, EE, HU, HR, PL, RO, and SK.

Source: Authors' calculation based on EU-SILC 2011 cross-sectional data.

highest shares of NEETs—approximately 20% of males and more than 30% of females—whereas the English-speaking countries are somewhere in between, with high shares of employed young men and high shares of young women as NEETs.[11] The five groups of countries are quite different in terms of youth educational attainments: Nordic and English-speaking countries record the highest shares of highly educated young people, whereas Mediterranean and Eastern countries have remarkably high shares of young individuals with low education levels. Generally, females are more educated than males. Mediterranean countries stand out for the lowest share of young people with at least one child and for a very high proportion of young adults living with their parents.

Our main interest is in examining the way in which young people's employment outcomes vary according to their parents' working condition when the young people were aged approximately 14 years. First, we consider both one- and two-parent families because this is a policy-relevant distinction and also because the share of young people who grew up with only one parent is not negligible. Indeed, as shown in Table 10.1, in Nordic, English-speaking, and Continental countries, for almost one out of five individuals in our sample, only one parent was present when the individual was aged approximately 14 years. However, for this group we consider only lone mother households, distinguishing between working and nonworking mothers, because the share of lone father families is very low and generally the lone father is employed.

Second, for two-parent households, we distinguish between dual-earner (or work-rich) families (in which both parents were working), male-breadwinner families (in which only the father was working), female-breadwinner families (in which only the mother was working), and workless (or work-poor) families (in which neither parent was working).[12] Table 10.1 confirms the findings of Anxo et al. (2007) and Van Dongen (2009), showing that the dual-earner model predominates in Nordic and Eastern countries, whereas the male-breadwinner model predominates in the Mediterranean countries.

Table 10.2 reports the key descriptive statistics for our subsequent empirical analysis: It shows the shares of young people (aged 25–34 years in 2011) by employment status (employed, NEET, and in education), household employment structure during adolescence, and group of countries. As expected, the share of NEETs increases for both males and females, moving from work-rich to work-poor households (in both one- and two-parent households). Three other, not so well known stylized facts appear in Table 10.2. First, no systematic differences emerge in the shares of students (in this age group) across household employment structures. Second, within workless families, the youth employment condition is more problematic in two-parent than in one-parent families (with the sole exception of males in Nordic countries). Third, in all country groups, daughters of lone working mothers display better employment outcomes than those who grew up in a male-breadwinner family. For sons, this is not always the case: Sons of lone working mothers are better off in English-speaking countries, whereas

Table 10.2 Youth employment status by household employment structure, country group, and gender (individuals aged 25–34 years in 2011)

	Nordic countries		English-speaking countries		Continental countries		Mediterranean countries		Eastern countries	
	Males	Females	Males	Females	Males	Females	Males	Females	Males	Females
Two-parent household with both parents working										
Employed	0.85	0.77	0.88	0.72	0.88	0.77	0.76	0.68	0.83	0.68
NEET	0.08	0.14	0.09	0.25	0.09	0.18	0.19	0.26	0.14	0.29
In education	0.07	0.09	0.03	0.03	0.03	0.04	0.06	0.06	0.02	0.02
Two-parent household with only father working										
Employed	0.87	0.63	0.76	0.64	0.85	0.67	0.76	0.61	0.75	0.55
NEET	0.09	0.27	0.21	0.34	0.10	0.29	0.21	0.36	0.23	0.44
In education	0.04	0.10	0.03	0.02	0.05	0.04	0.03	0.03	0.02	0.01
Two-parent household with only mother working										
Employed	0.75	0.66	0.87	0.55	0.84	0.67	0.59	0.55	0.74	0.61
NEET	0.18	0.20	0.13	0.45	0.11	0.27	0.33	0.35	0.24	0.38
In education	0.07	0.14	0.00	0.00	0.05	0.06	0.09	0.09	0.02	0.01
Two-parent household with neither parent working										
Employed	0.77	0.61	0.57	0.42	0.68	0.59	0.58	0.52	0.66	0.45
NEET	0.18	0.31	0.40	0.50	0.23	0.37	0.38	0.43	0.32	0.51
In education	0.05	0.08	0.03	0.08	0.09	0.04	0.04	0.04	0.02	0.04

(continued)

Table 10.2 Continued

	Nordic countries		English-speaking countries		Continental countries		Mediterranean countries		Eastern countries	
	Males	**Females**	**Males**	**Females**	**Males**	**Females**	**Males**	**Females**	**Males**	**Females**
One-parent household with working mother										
Employed	0.83	0.70	0.84	0.75	0.82	0.72	0.75	0.64	0.76	0.63
NEET	0.11	0.20	0.14	0.25	0.12	0.23	0.19	0.32	0.22	0.34
In education	0.06	0.10	0.02	0.10	0.06	0.05	0.05	0.04	0.03	0.03
One-parent household with nonworking mother										
Employed	0.72	0.57	0.66	0.54	0.80	0.64	0.70	0.57	0.65	0.56
NEET	0.16	0.36	0.31	0.43	0.17	0.33	0.28	0.40	0.33	0.44
In education	0.13	0.07	0.03	0.03	0.03	0.03	0.02	0.03	0.02	0.00

Notes: For country groups, see notes to Table 10.1. Household employment structure refers to when young people were aged approximately 14 years.
Source: Authors' calculation based on EU-SILC 2011 cross-sectional data.

no relevant differences emerge in the other country groups. In Section 10.4, we verify whether these differences remain after controlling for individual and country characteristics.

10.4. RESULTS

This section presents the estimated marginal effects of the multinomial logit models and predicted outcome probabilities.

10.4.1. Marginal effects

The estimated marginal effects of the multinomial logit models for the five country groups are shown in Tables S10.1–S10.5 (see Supplementary Material). Selected results regarding the effect of parents' working status on youth employment outcomes are reported in Table A10.2 in the Appendix. Regarding individual characteristics, age increases females' employment probability in all country groups and reduces their probability of being NEET, whereas it has only weak effects on male employment outcomes. Educational attainments have, as expected, very large and significant effects in all country groups for both men and women: The higher the education level, the higher is the employment probability and the lower is the probability of being NEET. It is worth noting that the marginal effects are greater for females than for males, suggesting that education plays a more important role for women in avoiding poor labor market outcomes and accessing employment.[13] For young women, both living in a couple and having children generally reduce the probability of being employed and increase that of being NEET. However, although the effects of motherhood are significant in all country groups, those associated with living in a couple are significant only in Mediterranean and Eastern countries.[14] For young men, living in a couple either has no effect on their employment outcomes or the effects go in the opposite direction than for women. English-speaking countries are the only exception: Here, young males living with a partner have a higher probability of being NEET. Young individuals who still live with their family of origin are less likely to be employed and more likely to be NEET in all country groups, although the magnitude of the effect is smaller for men than for women.[15]

The cultural and social capital of parents, captured by their education level and type of occupation when their children were aged approximately 14 years, does not appear to have systematic effects on the employment status of young adults.[16] The working conditions of parents during their children's adolescence, instead, seem to play a more decisive role, with noticeable differences between young women and young men across Europe. For young women, having had a working mother increases the probability of being employed and reduces that of being NEET in all country groups but the Nordic countries. In English-speaking,

Mediterranean, and Eastern countries, the father's employment condition reinforces the effect of the mother's working condition by further increasing the employment probability and reducing the probability of being NEET. For young men, having had a working father during adolescence matters only in Nordic, Mediterranean, and Eastern countries, where it increases the probability of being employed and decreases that of being NEET. These effects are reinforced in Mediterranean and Eastern countries if the individual also had a working mother. Interestingly, having had a working mother positively affects male labor market outcomes also in English-speaking and Continental countries, where the working status of the father has no significant effects.

In other words, having had a working mother during adolescence reduces the likelihood of being workless for both sons and daughters in all country groups except the Nordic countries. The effects of fathers' working conditions, by contrast, are less widespread. Fathers' employment is important for both sons and daughters in the Mediterranean and Eastern countries, only for daughters in the English-speaking countries, and only for sons in the Nordic countries.

Interestingly, we find evidence of a significant "mother-in-law effect" for women in Continental, Mediterranean, and Eastern countries. Being married to a partner whose mother was working during his adolescence is associated with a higher probability for women of being employed and a lower probability of being NEET, with larger effects in the Mediterranean countries. As expected, the effect associated with the working condition of the mother-in-law is generally not significant for men, with the exception of Eastern countries, where having a mother-in-law who was working during his spouse's adolescence increases male employment probability and decreases the probability of being NEET.

10.4.2. Predicted outcome probabilities

Considering only marginal effects does not allow us to fully capture the differences between young people with respect to their parents' working condition during adolescence. Thus, in this section, we compare, ceteris paribus, the overall effect of having lived in a specific household type—for example, in a two-parent work-rich household, in a two-parent work-poor household, or with a nonworking lone mother. To do this, we first predict the probability of being NEET for "fictitious" individuals who have all the individual characteristics equal to the sample mean of their country group, except for education level and the presence and work experience of parents.[17] Second, we test whether the probability associated with a particular household type is larger or smaller than the others, and we compute the odds of being NEET for young adults who grew up in two different household types.[18] Table 10.3 shows some selected odds ratios for young adults with a high school diploma and a university degree, who represent the majority of our sample.

Table 10.3 NEET odds ratios of young people by household employment structure, gender, and country groups (individuals aged 25–34 years in 2011)

	2P-0W 2P-2W	P(N|2P-FW) P(N|2P-2W)	P(N|2P-0W) P(N|2P-FW)	P(N|1P-0W) P(N|1P-1W)	P(N|1P-0W) P(N|2P-0W)	P(N|1P-1W) P(N|2P-FW)
Young individuals with a high school diploma (medium-educated individuals)						
Females						
Nordic countries	1.00	1.00	1.00	1.00	1.00	1.00
English-speaking countries	1.52	1.21	1.26	1.00	1.00	1.00
Continental countries	1.60	1.33	1.00	1.00	1.00	1.00
Mediterranean countries	1.41	1.20	1.17	1.00	1.00	1.00
Eastern countries	1.59	1.38	1.16	1.00	0.83	0.82
Males						
Nordic countries	1.92	1.00	1.81	1.00	1.00	1.00
English-speaking countries	1.68	1.55	1.00	1.96	1.00	1.00
Continental countries	1.51	1.33	1.00	1.00	1.00	1.00
Mediterranean countries	2.35	1.17	2.01	1.00	1.00	1.38
Eastern countries	2.06	1.42	1.45	1.39	1.00	1.00
Young individuals with a university degree (highly educated individuals)						
Females						
Nordic countries	1.00	1.00	1.00	1.00	1.00	1.00
English-speaking countries	1.77	1.28	1.39	1.00	1.00	1.00
Continental countries	1.67	1.36	1.00	1.00	1.00	1.00
Mediterranean countries	1.50	1.23	1.22	1.00	1.00	1.00
Eastern countries	1.70	1.44	1.19	1.00	0.80	0.80

(continued)

Table 10.3 Continued

	2P-0W 2P-2W	P(N|2P-FW) P(N|2P-2W)	P(N|2P-0W) P(N|2P-FW)	P(N|1P-0W) P(N|1P-1W)	P(N|1P-0W) P(N|2P-0W)	P(N|1P-1W) P(N|2P-FW)
Males						
Nordic countries	**1.94**	1.00	**1.83**	1.00	1.00	1.00
English-speaking countries	**1.71**	**1.57**	1.00	**2.06**	1.00	1.00
Continental countries	**1.53**	**1.34**	1.00	1.00	1.00	1.00
Mediterranean countries	**2.43**	**1.18**	**2.07**	1.00	1.00	**1.40**
Eastern countries	**2.20**	**1.46**	**1.51**	**1.45**	1.00	1.00

Notes: For country groups, see notes to Table 10.1. Household employment structure refers to when young people were aged approximately 14 years. Numbers in bold are significantly different from 1 at 5% significance level.

2P-2W, two-parent households with both parents working; 2P-FW, two-parent households with only the father working; 2P-MW, two-parent households with only the mother working; 2P-oW, two-parent households with neither parent working; 1P-MW, lone mother households with working mother; 1P-oW, lone mother households with nonworking mother.

Source: Authors' calculation based on EU-SILC 2011 cross-sectional data.

Inspection of Table 10.3 shows that, ceteris paribus, the probability of being NEET is substantially higher for young people who grew up in two-parent work-poor households as opposed to work-rich families. Females with a high school diploma and whose parents were workless during their adolescence have an approximately 40%–60% higher probability of being NEET than those whose parents were working (except in the Nordic countries). For medium-educated males, the difference is much larger: It ranges from 50% to more than 100% (and is very large even in the Nordic countries). These percentages are even larger for highly educated young people.

The odds between work-poor and male-breadwinner families, and between the latter and dual-earner households, reveal the significant and widespread effect of the mother's working condition and the less generalized (but relevant where it occurs) effect of fathers' employment. Young people who grew up in male-breadwinner families have, independently of their gender, a 20%–60% higher probability of being NEET than those who grew up in dual-earner households in all country groups except the Nordic countries. In other words, having had a working mother reduces the NEET probability by 15%–38% for both males and females, whatever their education level.

Fathers' employment has more differentiated effects both by gender and across countries. In English-speaking, Mediterranean, and Eastern countries, females who grew up in work-poor households have a 15%–40% higher probability of being workless compared to those who grew up in male-breadwinner families. In other words, having had a working father reduces females' NEET probability by 13%–29% in these countries, whereas it has no significant effects in Nordic and Continental countries. For males, fathers' worklessness during their adolescence has very large effects in Nordic and Mediterranean countries, moderate effects in Eastern countries, and no effects in English-speaking and Continental countries. In the Nordic and Mediterranean countries, males' probability of being NEET is 80%–100% higher if they grew up in a work-poor household, compared to those who grew up in a male-breadwinner family, whatever the education level. In Eastern countries, medium-educated (highly educated) males coming from work-poor households have a 45% (51%) higher likelihood of being NEET compared to young men who grew up in male-breadwinner families.

Among children of lone mothers, in all country groups, no significant differences emerge in females' risk of being NEET according to the lone mother's working condition. Sons of workless lone mothers, by contrast, have a much higher risk of being workless than sons of working lone mothers in English-speaking and Eastern countries (approximately 100% and 40%, respectively).

Finally, we can compare the situation of children who grew up in one- and two-parent households. Two comparisons deserve attention: (1) between work-poor families with one and two parents and (2) between lone working mothers and male-breadwinner families. Ceteris paribus, children who grew up in work-poor families have the same probability of being NEET, independently of whether both parents or only one parent was present. The only exception regards young women in Eastern countries, for whom the presence of only the mother actually reduces their probability of being workless. Interestingly, children who grew up with a lone working mother are not disadvantaged compared to those who grew up in a male-breadwinner two-parent household, except for young men in Mediterranean countries. In Eastern countries, daughters whose lone mother was working are even less likely to be workless compared to those who grew up in male-breadwinner families. These results suggest that the relative advantage of children of lone working mothers (compared to young people coming from male-breadwinner families) that emerged from the descriptive analysis is generally explained by different individual characteristics. Indeed, when controlling for individual attributes, no significant differences in the NEET risk are found between young people who grew up in these two household types, with very few exceptions.

In summary, some unexpected qualitative results emerge from our analysis. First, male worklessness is affected only by mothers' employment in English-speaking and Continental countries and only by fathers' employment in Nordic countries. Both parents play a role in Eastern and Mediterranean countries. They have similar effects in Eastern countries, whereas fathers' employment is much more relevant in Mediterranean countries. Second, young females' worklessness depends on the working condition of both parents in English-speaking, Mediterranean, and Eastern countries, whereas only mothers' employment seems to matter in Continental countries. Third, the presence of only one parent does not lead to a systematic disadvantage. In particular, no differences emerge in children's worklessness risk between one- and two-parent work-poor households or between lone working mothers and male-breadwinner families (with very few exceptions).

In order to compare the magnitude of these effects, we consider the percentage increase in the NEET risk associated with the worklessness status of parents (ceteris paribus). We use this percentage increase as our measure of the extent of the intergenerational transmission of worklessness in the various countries. In Section 10.2, we expected to find a larger intergenerational correlation of worklessness in Mediterranean and Eastern countries and a smaller correlation in Nordic, English-speaking, and Continental countries. Our empirical results are partly in line with these expectations, and partly they contradict them.

As expected, the intergenerational transmission of worklessness is small, actually null, in Nordic countries, but only for daughters. Surprisingly, the transmission of worklessness from fathers to sons is particularly large in this country group (males' NEET risk increases by 80% if the father was workless during their adolescence compared to the case in which he was working). As expected, the intergenerational transmission of worklessness is larger in Mediterranean countries, but only for sons, and only with respect to fathers' employment. For daughters, the effect of mothers' worklessness (and of both parents) is actually lower in Mediterranean countries than in other country groups.

Considering the two types of relationship that received more attention in the literature (that between mothers and daughters and that between fathers and sons), our results show that, unexpectedly, the transmission of worklessness between mothers and daughters is similar in all country groups (except the Nordic countries), although it is slightly larger in Eastern and Continental countries. The transmission between fathers and sons, by contrast, is more differentiated: It is higher in Mediterranean and Nordic countries and null in English-speaking and Continental countries.

Given that in our analysis we control for variables that possibly capture the influence of intergenerational transmission channels (i.e., parental employment status, education level, and type of occupation), unexpected findings may be the result of the effect of unobserved cultural factors or attitudes (i.e., unobservable family traits for which we cannot control) that are transmitted within the family and that induce individuals to adopt a labor market behavior that deviates from social norms. Or, their behavior may result from the role of informal social networks. In other words, social networks, which are supposed to play a role mainly in Mediterranean countries, matter in helping people find a job also in the other country groups.

Finally, our analysis reveals some important innovative evidence of the effects of these relationships, which has not to date been acknowledged in the literature on intergenerational transmission of inequalities and access to employment. Interestingly, the transmission of worklessness between mothers and sons is present in all country groups (except the Nordic countries); it is highest in English-speaking countries and lowest in Mediterranean countries. The transmission of worklessness between fathers and daughters is less widespread: null in Continental and Nordic countries, highest in English-speaking countries, and somewhat lower in Mediterranean and Eastern countries.

10.5. CONCLUSIONS

This chapter has examined how the intergenerational transmission of worklessness varies across different groups of European countries—characterized by distinct labor market institutions and welfare systems—and according to the gender of parents and the gender of their children. To this end, we have used a sample of young males and females aged 25–34 years from the EU-SILC cross-sectional data (2011), as well as information about the working conditions of their parents when the young people were aged approximately 14 years (from the ad hoc module on the intergenerational transmission of disadvantages).

Our empirical analysis has revealed that, ceteris paribus, having had a workless mother during adolescence increases the likelihood of being workless at approximately 30 years of age for both sons and daughters in all country groups but the Nordic countries. The magnitude of the effect is quite similar across all country groups: The NEET risk for both males and females increases by approximately 20%–35% if the mother was workless, with somewhat larger effects in Eastern countries (by 40%) and between mothers and sons in English-speaking countries (by 55%).

Conversely, the effects of fathers' working conditions are less widespread. Fathers' employment is important for both sons and daughters in Mediterranean and Eastern countries, only for daughters in English-speaking countries, and only for sons in Nordic countries. The magnitude of the effect is also more differentiated: Males' NEET risk increases by 80%–100% if their father was workless in Mediterranean and Nordic countries and only by 48% if he was workless in Eastern countries. The transmission between fathers and daughters is much smaller: Approximately 15%–20% in Mediterranean and Eastern countries and 30% in English-speaking countries.

Unexpectedly, the percentage increase in the NEET risk associated with fathers' worklessness (ceteris paribus) is very large in Nordic countries and quite similar to that in Mediterranean countries. Again unexpectedly, the effect of mothers' worklessness is quite similar in all country groups (except in Nordic countries) and actually lower in Mediterranean countries. These results suggest that the consequences of different labor market institutions, family models, and welfare systems for the intergenerational transmission of worklessness are not very clear-cut. In particular, more research is needed to understand the link between fathers' and sons' employment experiences in Nordic and Mediterranean countries.

Another interesting result of our analysis is that the presence of only one parent does not lead to a systematic disadvantage. In particular, no differences emerge in the probability of being workless for young people growing up in one- and two-parent work-poor households or between those who grew up with lone working mothers or in male-breadwinner families (with very few exceptions). These results suggest that a key challenge for policymakers is that policies should not be limited to enhancing the employment probability of disadvantaged youth; rather, they should consider in parallel the difficulties faced by parents of teenagers. In fact, the adolescents who grew up in the years of the Great Recession with workless parents, particularly workless mothers, might suffer in the future when they start their working life. Perhaps the strongest policy implication that can be drawn from our analysis is that policymakers should pay attention to mothers' employment not only when their children are in their early years of life but also during the children's adolescence. Helping mothers to remain in or re-enter the labor market might have important consequences for their children's future employment prospects. Last, our results also suggest a need for policy initiatives aimed at fostering equality of opportunities by reducing the effects of parental background characteristics on individuals' own life chances.

NOTES

1 For the purpose of this research, people are defined as "workless" if they are unemployed or inactive. We do not distinguish between these latter two states because of the difficulties involved in differentiating between them. In particular, discouraged worker effects or entitlement rules for welfare benefits may bias the responses of individuals. Moreover, discouraged workers (i.e., available to work but not searching for a job), usually classified as inactive, are more similar in terms of behavior to the unemployed than to other inactive individuals (Centeno and Fernandes 2004).

2 Some of these studies are interested in determining whether there is a causal link between fathers' and children's worklessness. Empirical findings for Norway (Ekhaugen 2009), Sweden (Corak, Gustafsson, and Österberg 2004), the United Kingdom (Johnson and Reed 1996; O'Neill and Sweetman 1998; Macmillan 2010), and Germany (Mader et al. 2015) indicate a positive intergenerational correlation of unemployment but not a clear causal effect. Differently, Corak, Gustafsson, and Österberg (2004) and Oreopoulos et al. (2008) find evidence of a causal intergenerational effect in Canada.

3 Reliance on friends and relatives when searching for a job has increased over time. The effectiveness of networks depends on the characteristics of the jobseeker, his or her social ties, and the labor market institutions. For instance, unemployed women are less likely than unemployed men to rely on informal networks, and more educated jobseekers are more likely to count on friends and relatives when searching for a job (Ioannides and Datcher Loury 2004).

4 These hypotheses have been formulated on the basis of the review of the literature on the various channels through which parents' employment status during young people's adolescence might affect their children's employment outcomes when adults. See Berloffa, Matteazzi, and Villa (2017) for a review of the literature highlighting the channels through which the intergenerational transmission of worklessness might operate.

5 According to Eurostat statistics, the mean age of leaving the parental home is 21 years in Nordic countries, 24.5 years in English-speaking and Continental countries, and approximately 29 years in Mediterranean and Eastern countries. According to statistics from the Organization for Economic Co-operation and Development (OECD), the household debt is approximately 203% of net disposable income in Nordic countries, 180% in English-speaking countries, 135% in Continental countries, 118% in Mediterranean countries, and 65% in Eastern countries. Approximately 89% of British students enrolled in tertiary education have a student loan, compared to 70% in Norway; 43% in Sweden; 30% in Denmark, Finland, and the Netherlands; and slightly less than 20% in Hungary and Estonia.

6 We cannot include individuals younger than age 25 years because all the variables concerning family characteristics in the period when the individual was approximately 14 years old can be collected only for individuals aged between 25 and 60 years at the time of the interview.

7 Individual employment status is defined on the basis of the self-reported economic status at the time of the interview.

8 We cannot perform single-country analyses because of limited sample size at the country level. However, in order to account for cross-country heterogeneity within country groups, we control for country-fixed effects in our econometric models.

9 We do not control for fatherhood status because of the very low percentage of young fathers in education or NEET.

10 This information is not available for Nordic countries because only the respondent reports parental background information.

11 The share of NEETs is higher in Finland than in the other Nordic countries, and it is similar to what is observed in English-speaking countries. Within the Continental group, the Netherlands stands out for the lowest share of NEETs, which is close to that of the Nordic countries.

12 In the literature, two main methods are adopted to classify households according to the employment status of household members. The first distinguishes between workless and non-workless households (as in our approach); the second classifies households according to a work-intensity indicator (Cantillon and Vandenbroucke 2014). We cannot use this indicator because retrospective information on hours and months worked is not available in our data set.

13 For young women, we find an additional positive effect on the probability of still being in education in Mediterranean and Eastern countries, probably linked to the longer duration of tertiary education in these countries. This effect is observed also for young men in all country groups, except for the English-speaking countries.

14 In Continental, Mediterranean, and Eastern countries, motherhood also reduces the probability of being in education.

15 Generally, young people still living with their parents are also more likely to be in education.

16 When the results are significant, they generally increase the probability that the young person will still be in education (see also Filandri, Nazio, and O'Reilly, this volume).

17 For these variables, we set the relevant dummies equal to either 1 or 0 according to the type of family that we want to consider. To compute the probabilities, we use the estimated coefficients of the multinomial logit models, independently of their significance level.

18 We perform a series of one-sided tests because the direction of the difference between two probabilities is relevant for the analysis. For those pairs

of household types whose probabilities were not statistically different, we report an odds ratio equal to 1.

REFERENCES

Anxo, Dominique, Colette Fagan, Inmaculada Cebrián, and Gloria Moreno. 2007. "Patterns of Labour Market Integration in Europe—A Life Course Perspective on Time Policies." *Socio-Economic Review* 5 (2): 233–60.

Becker, Gary S., and Nigel Tomes. 1986. "Human Capital and the Rise and Fall of Families." *Journal of Labor Economics* 4 (3): 1–47.

Berloffa, Gabriella, Eleonora Matteazzi, and Paola Villa. 2017. "The Intergenerational Transmission of Worklessness in Europe: The Role of Fathers and Mothers." DEM Working Paper 04. Trento: Trento University, Department of Economics and Management.

Bjorklund, Anders, and Markus Jäntti. 2009. "Intergenerational Income Mobility and the Role of Family Background." In *Oxford Handbook of Economic Inequality*, edited by Wiemer Salverda, Brian Nolan, and Timothy Smeeding, 491–521. Oxford: Oxford University Press.

Black, Sandra E., and Paul J. Devereux. 2011. "Recent Developments in Intergenerational Mobility." In *Handbook of Labor Economics*, vol. 4 (part B), edited by Orley Ashenfelter and David Card, 1487–541. Amsterdam: North-Holland.

Blanden, Jo. 2013. "Cross-Country Rankings in Intergenerational Mobility: A Comparison of Approaches from Economics and Sociology." *Journal of Economic Surveys* 27 (1): 38–73.

Bowles, Samuel, and Herbert Gintis. 2002. "The Inheritance of Inequality." *Journal of Economic Perspectives* 16 (3): 3–30.

Bratberg, Espen, Øivind Anti Nilsen, and Kjell Vaage. 2008. "Job Losses and Child Outcomes." *Labour Economics* 15 (4): 591–603.

Cantillon, Bea, and Frank Vandenbroucke, eds. 2014. *Reconciling Work and Poverty Reduction: How Successful Are Welfare States?* Oxford: Oxford University Press.

Centeno, Mário, and Pedro Afonso Fernandes. 2004. "Labour Market Heterogeneity: Distinguishing Between Unemployment and Inactivity." *Banco de Portugal, Economic Bulletin* (March): 61–68.

Corak, Miles. 2006. "Do Poor Children Become Poor Adults? Lessons from a Cross-Country Comparison of Generational Earnings Mobility." In *Dynamics of Inequality and Poverty*, edited by John Creedy and Guyonne Kalb, 143–88. Bingley: Emerald Group.

Corak, Miles, Björn Gustafsson, and Torun Österberg. 2004. "Intergenerational Influences on the Receipt of Unemployment Insurance in Canada and

Sweden." In *Generational Income Mobility in North America and Europe*, edited by Miles Corak, 245–88. Cambridge: Cambridge University Press.

Corak, Miles, and Patrizio Piraino. 2010. "Intergenerational Earnings Mobility and the Inheritance of Employers." IZA Discussion Paper 4876. Bonn: Institute for the Study of Labor.

d'Addio, Anna Cristina. 2007. "Intergenerational Transmission of Disadvantage: Mobility or Immobility Across Generations? A Review of the Evidence for OECD Countries." OECD Social, Employment and Migration Working Paper 52. Paris: Organization for Economic Co-operation and Development.

Del Boca, Daniela, Marilena Locatelli, and Silvia Pasqua. 2000. "Employment Decisions of Married Women: Evidence and Explanations." *Labour* 14 (1): 35–52.

Ekhaugen, Tyra. 2009. "Extracting the Causal Component from the Intergenerational Correlation in Unemployment." *Journal of Population Economics* 22 (1): 97–113.

Farré, Lídia, and Francis Vella. 2013. "The Intergenerational Transmission of Gender Role Attitudes and Its Implications for Female Labour Force Participation." *Economica* 80 (318): 219–47.

Fenger, H. J. Menno. 2007. "Welfare Regimes in Central and Eastern Europe: Incorporating Post-Communist Countries in a Welfare Regime Typology." *Contemporary Issues and Ideas in Social Sciences* 3 (2): 1–30.

Fernández, Raquel. 2007. "Women, Work and Culture." *Journal of the European Economic Association* 4 (2/3): 305–32.

Fernández, Raquel, Alessandra Fogli, and Claudia Olivetti. 2004. "Mothers and Sons: Preference Formation and Female Labor Force Dynamics." *Quarterly Journal of Economics* 119 (4): 1249–99.

Fortin, Nicole M. 2005. "Gender Role Attitudes and the Labour-Market Outcomes of Women Across the OECD Countries." *Oxford Review of Economic Policy* 21 (3): 416–38.

Franzini, Maurizio, Michele Raitano, and Francesco Vona. 2013. "The Channels of Intergenerational Transmission of Inequality: A Cross-Country Comparison." *Rivista Italiana degli Economisti* 28 (2): 201–26.

Gallie, Duncan. 2007. *Employment Regimes and the Quality of Work.* Oxford: Oxford University Press.

Granovetter, Mark. 1995. *Getting a Job: A Study of Contacts and Careers*, 2nd ed. Chicago: University of Chicago Press.

Gregg, Paul, Lindsey Macmillan, and Bilal Nasim. 2012. "The Impact of Fathers' Job Loss During the Recession of the 1980s on Their Children's Educational Attainment and Labour Market Outcomes." *Fiscal Studies* 33 (2): 237–64.

Halleröd, Björn, Hans Ekbrand, and Mattias Bengtsson. 2015. "In-Work Poverty and Labour Market Trajectories: Poverty Risks Among the Working

Population in 22 European Countries." *Journal of European Social Policy* 25 (5): 473–88.

Ioannides, Yannis M., and Linda Datcher Loury. 2004. "Job Information Networks, Neighborhood Effects and Inequality." *Journal of Economic Literature* 42 (4): 1056–93.

Johnson, Paul, and Howard Reed. 1996. "Intergenerational Mobility Among the Rich and Poor: Results from the National Child Development Survey." *Oxford Review of Economic Policy* 12 (1): 127–42.

Kawaguchi, Daiji, and Junko Miyazaki. 2009. "Working Mothers and Sons' Preferences Regarding Female Labour Supply: Direct Evidence from Stated Preferences." *Journal of Population Economics* 22 (1): 115–30.

Macmillan, Lindsey. 2010. "The Intergenerational Transmission of Worklessness in the UK." CMPO Working Paper 231. Bristol: Centre for Market and Public Organisation.

Macmillan, Lindsey. 2013. "The Role of Non-Cognitive and Cognitive Skills, Behavioural and Educational Outcomes in Accounting for the Intergenerational Transmission of Worklessness. DoQSS Working Paper 01. London: University of London, Department of Quantitative Social Science.

Mader, Miriam, Regina T. Riphahn, Caroline Schwientek, and Steffen Müller. 2015. "Intergenerational Transmission of Unemployment: Evidence from German Sons." *Jahrbücher für Nationalökonomie und Statistik* 235 (4/5): 355–75.

Mocetti, Sauro. 2007. "Intergenerational Earnings Mobility in Italy." *BE Journal of Economic Analysis & Policy* 7 (2): 1–25.

Montgomery, James D. 1991. "Social Networks and Labor-Market Outcomes: Toward an Economic Analysis." *American Economic Review* 81 (5): 1408–18.

Mooi-Reci, Irma, and Bart Bakker. 2015. "Parental Unemployment: How Much and When Does It Matter for Children's Educational Attainment?" LCC Working Paper 03. Queensland: Institute for Social Science Research, Life Course Centre.

O'Neill, Donal, and Olive Sweetman. 1998. "Intergenerational Mobility in Britain: Evidence from Unemployment Patterns." *Oxford Bulletin of Economics and Statistics* 60 (4): 431–47.

Oreopoulos, Philip, Marianne Page, and Ann Huff Stevens. 2008. "The Intergenerational Effect of Worker Displacement." *Journal of Labour Economics* 26 (3): 455–83.

Petersen, Trond, Ishak Saporta, and Marc-David L. Seidel. 2000. "Offering a Job: Meritocracy and Social Networks." *American Journal of Sociology* 106 (3): 763–816.

Raitano, Michele. 2011. "La riproduzione intergenerazionale delle diseguaglianze in Italia: istruzione, occupazione e retribuzioni." *Politica Economica* 27 (3): 345–74.

Rees, Albert. 1966. "Information Networks in the Labour Market." *American Economic Review* 56 (1/2): 559–66.

Schoon, Ingrid, Meichu Chen, Dylan Kneale, and Justin Jager. 2012. "Becoming Adults in Britain: Lifestyles and Wellbeing in Times of Social Change." *Longitudinal and Life Course Studies* 3 (2): 173–89.

Scruggs, Lyle, and James Allan. 2006. "Welfare-State Decommodification in 18 OECD Countries: A Replication and Revision." *Journal of European Social Policy* 16 (1): 55–72.

Solon, Gary. 1992. "Intergenerational Income Mobility in the United States." *American Economic Review* 82 (3): 393–408.

Topa, Giorgio. 2001. "Social Interactions, Local Spillovers, and Unemployment." *Review of Economic Studies* 68 (2): 261–95.

Van Dongen, Walter. 2009. *Towards a Democratic Division of Labour in Europe? The Combination Model as a New Integrated Approach to Professional and Family Life*. Bristol: Policy Press.

Walther, Andreas. 2006. "Regimes of Youth Transitions: Choice, Flexibility and Security in Young People's Experiences Across Different European Contexts." *Young* 14 (2): 119–39.

Zwysen, Wouter. 2015. "The Effects of Father's Worklessness on Young Adults in the UK." *IZA Journal of European Labour Studies* 4 (2): 1–15.

APPENDIX

Table A10.1 Hypotheses about the intergenerational correlation (IC) of worklessness in different country groups by various channels of influence and related institutions

	Economic channel		Cultural channel	Social channel		Genetic channel	Expected IC of worklessness
	Leaving the parental home (average age on leaving the parental home)[a]	Levels of borrowing (housing debts and student loans)[b]	Social norms—female activity rate[c]	PES (% of jobseekers using PES)[d]	Activation support (ALMP participants per 100 persons wanting to work)[e]		
Nordic countries	Low IC (early economic independence)	Low IC (high levels of borrowing)	Low IC (high female activity rate)	High IC (low %) Exception: SE (quite high %)	Low IC (high %)	Low IC	Low IC
English-speaking countries	Medium IC (quite early economic independence)	Low IC (high levels of borrowing)	Medium-low IC (quite high female activity rate) Exception: IE (moderate activity rate)	High IC (low %)	n.a.	High IC	Medium IC
Continental countries	Medium IC (quite early economic independence)	Medium IC (medium levels of borrowing) Exception: low IC in NL (high levels of borrowing)	Medium-low IC (quite high female activity rate) Exceptions: BE and LU (quite low activity rate)	Medium IC (quite high %) Exception: NL (low %)	Low IC (high %)	Medium IC	Medium-Low IC
Mediterranean countries	High IC (late economic independence)	Medium IC (medium levels of borrowing)	High IC (low female activity rate) Exception: PT (quite high activity rate)	High IC (low %) Exceptions: EL and MT (moderate %)	Medium IC (moderate %) Exception: ES (high %)	High IC	High IC

(continued)

Table A10.1 Continued

| | Economic channel | | Cultural channel | Social channel | | Genetic channel | Expected IC of worklessness |
	Leaving the parental home (average age on leaving the parental home)[a]	Levels of borrowing (housing debts and student loans)[b]	Social norms—female activity rate[c]	PES (% of jobseekers using PES)[d]	Activation support (ALMP participants per 100 persons wanting to work)[e]	Genetic channel	Expected IC of worklessness
Eastern European countries	High IC (late economic independence)	High IC (low levels of borrowing) Exceptions: HU and EE (quite high use of student loans)	Medium-high IC (medium female activity rate) Exceptions: HU and RO (low activity rate)	Low IC (high %) Exceptions: RO, EE, and BG (moderate to low %)	High IC (low %)	High IC	Medium-High IC

Notes: Country groups: Nordic (DK, FI, NO, and SE); Continental (AT, BE, CH, DE, FR, and NL); English-speaking (IE and UK); Mediterranean (CY, EL, ES, IT, MT, and PT); and Eastern European (BG, CZ, EE, HU, HR, PL, RO, and SK). See Section 10.3 for more details.
[a] Eurostat's estimated average age of young people leaving the parental household by sex (2011).
[b] OECD's data on household debt as a percentage of net disposable income (2014) and on public loans to students in tertiary type A education (2011).
[c] Eurostat's activity rate for women aged 15–64 years (2011).
[d] Public employment services (European Commission, Directorate-General for Employment, Social Affairs and Inclusion).
[e] Eurostat's database on labor market policies.
ALMPs, active labor market policies; PES, public employment services; n.a. = not available; PES, public employment services.

Table A10.2 Predicted outcome probabilities (Pr) and marginal effects (M) for selected variables from the estimation of multinomial logit models

Country group	Estimate (E)	Females						Males					
		Employed		NEET		In education		Employed		NEET		In education	
		E	St. Err.	E	St. Err.	E	St. Err.	E	St. Err.	E	St. Err.	E	St. Err.
Nordic	Pr	0.798 ***	0.013	0.139 ***	0.011	0.063 ***	0.008	0.907 ***	0.009	0.066***	0.007	0.028***	0.005
	M: Working father	0.023	0.042	0.006	0.035	-0.029	0.025	0.059**	0.023	-0.040**	0.020	-0.019*	0.011
	M: Working mother	0.027	0.033	-0.036	0.026	0.009	0.020	-0.003	0.022	-0.004	0.018	0.006	0.012
	M: Working lone mother	0.022	0.070	-0.031	0.051	0.009	0.046	0.049	0.041	-0.009	0.035	-0.040**	0.020
	M: Working mother-in-law	—		—		—		—		—		—	
English-speaking	Pr	0.710 ***	0.015	0.160 ***	0.015	0.022 ***	0.004	0.886 ***	0.012	0.110 ***	0.012	0.005***	0.002
	M: Working father	0.090*	0.052	-0.086*	0.052	-0.003	0.007	0.010	0.032	-0.009	0.032	0.000	0.004
	M: Working mother	0.061 *	0.035	-0.059*	0.035	-0.002	0.006	0.047 *	0.027	-0.048*	0.027	0.001	0.003
	M: Working lone mother	0.024	0.073	-0.014	0.072	-0.010	0.011	0.041	0.053	-0.036	0.052	-0.005	0.006
	M: Working mother-in-law	0.039	0.036	-0.033	0.036	-0.006	0.007	0.045	0.030	-0.036	0.030	-0.008*	0.005

(continued)

Table A10.2 Continued

Country group	Estimate (E)	Females						Males					
		Employed		NEET		In education		Employed		NEET		In education	
		E	St. Err.	E	St. Err.	E	St. Err.	E	St. Err.	E	St. Err.	E	St. Err.
Continental	Pr	0.759***	0.006	0.187***	0.006	0.018***	0.002	0.921***	0.005	0.063***	0.004	0.016***	0.002
	M: Working father	0.031	0.029	−0.037	0.028	0.006	0.008	0.011	0.016	−0.008	0.015	−0.003	0.006
	M: Working mother	0.059***	0.013	−0.055***	0.013	−0.004	0.003	0.024***	0.008	−0.018**	0.008	−0.005*	0.003
	M: Working lone mother	−0.033	0.033	0.026	0.032	0.007	0.009	−0.028	0.018	0.015	0.017	0.013*	0.007
	M: Working mother-in-law	0.032**	0.013	−0.034***	0.013	0.002	0.004	0.007	0.011	−0.008	0.011	0.001	0.004
Mediterranean	Pr	0.682***	0.006	0.306***	0.006	0.012***	0.002	0.808***	0.006	0.184***	0.006	0.009***	0.002
	M: Working father	0.069**	0.030	−0.060**	0.030	−0.010***	0.004	0.144***	0.025	−0.140***	0.024	−0.004	0.003
	M: Working mother	0.056***	0.014	−0.056***	0.014	0.000	0.002	0.031***	0.012	−0.028**	0.012	−0.003*	0.002
	M: Working lone mother	0.008	0.045	−0.010	0.045	0.002	0.006	0.023	0.041	−0.022	0.041	−0.001	0.004
	M: Working mother-in-law	0.099***	0.018	−0.089***	0.017	−0.011*	0.006	0.000	0.022	0.000	0.021	0.000	0.008

Eastern												
Pr	0.691 ***	0.005	0.307 ***	0.005	0.002 ***	0.000	0.859 ***	0.004	0.139 ***	0.004	0.002***	0.000
M: Working father	0.053 *	0.027	−0.055 **	0.027	0.002	0.002	0.057 ***	0.017	−0.057***	0.017	−0.001	0.001
M: Working mother	0.104 ***	0.015	−0.104 ***	0.015	0.000	0.001	0.050***	0.010	−0.049***	0.010	0.000	0.000
M: Working lone mother	−0.056	0.038	0.053	0.038	0.003 *	0.001	0.002	0.024	−0.003	0.024	0.001	0.001
M: Working mother-in-law	0.033 **	0.015	−0.033 **	0.015	0.000	0.001	0.036 ***	0.012	−0.035***	0.012	−0.001	0.001

Notes: Dummies for country, quarter of interview, and missing information about parents' working status and education level are introduced. −, not controlled for. Marginal effects are computed at the sample mean of the variables.

Source: EU-SILC 2011 data for young people aged 25–34 years; see text for details.

*p < .10.

**p < .05.

***p < .01.

SUPPLEMENTARY MATERIAL

Table S10.1 Predicted outcome probability (Pr) and marginal effects (Mfx) in Nordic countries by gender

	Females						Males					
	Employed		NEET		In education		Employed		NEET		In education	
	Pr	St. Err.	Pr	St. Err.	Pr	St. Err.	Pr	St. Err.	Pr	St. Err.	Pr	St. Err.
Predicted outcome probability	0.798***	0.013	0.139***	0.011	0.063***	0.008	0.907***	0.009	0.066***	0.007	0.028***	0.005
	Mfx	St. Err.	Mfx	St. Err.	Mfx	St. Err.	Mfx	St. Err.	Mfx	St. Err.	Mfx	St. Err.
Individual characteristics at the time of the interview												
Age	0.027***	0.004	-0.011***	0.003	-0.016***	0.002	0.009***	0.003	0.000	0.002	-0.010***	0.001
Own education: medium	0.158***	0.041	-0.147***	0.035	-0.012	0.023	0.060***	0.021	-0.088***	0.015	0.028**	0.014
Own education: high	0.217***	0.043	-0.180***	0.036	-0.037	0.024	0.072***	0.022	-0.106***	0.016	0.034**	0.015
Partner's education: medium	0.059	0.041	-0.055*	0.033	-0.005	0.026	0.021	0.036	-0.050**	0.023	0.029	0.028
Partner's education: high	0.036	0.042	-0.034	0.034	-0.002	0.027	0.021	0.037	-0.048**	0.024	0.028	0.029
Citizenship	-0.298***	0.067	0.189***	0.054	0.109***	0.030	-0.052	0.051	0.081**	0.040	-0.029	0.028
Living with parents	-0.167***	0.057	0.162***	0.047	0.005	0.032	-0.017	0.024	0.039**	0.020	-0.022	0.014
Living in couple	-0.024	0.044	0.056	0.037	-0.033	0.026	0.075**	0.035	-0.026	0.021	-0.049*	0.028
Motherhood	-0.129***	0.024	0.140***	0.021	-0.010	0.013	—	—	—	—	—	—

Presence of parents when the young person was aged 14 years

	(1)		(2)		(3)		(4)		(5)		(6)	
Lone parent family	-0.005	0.069	0.039	0.049	-0.034	0.046	-0.035	0.037	-0.003	0.030	0.039*	0.021
Parentless	0.050	0.066	-0.023	0.050	-0.027	0.043	0.028	0.037	-0.004	0.031	-0.023	0.019
Family background information												
Working father	0.023	0.042	0.006	0.035	-0.029	0.025	0.059**	0.023	-0.040**	0.020	-0.019*	0.011
Working mother	0.027	0.033	-0.036	0.026	0.009	0.020	-0.003	0.022	-0.004	0.018	0.006	0.012
Working lone mother	0.022	0.070	-0.031	0.051	0.009	0.046	0.049	0.041	-0.009	0.035	-0.040**	0.020
Working mother-in-law	—		—		—		—		—		—	
Father's occupation	-0.036	0.032	0.038	0.028	-0.002	0.017	0.006	0.021	-0.022	0.019	0.016*	0.008
Mother's occupation	0.058*	0.031	-0.053*	0.027	-0.005	0.015	-0.019	0.021	0.012	0.019	0.008	0.009
Father's education	-0.016	0.029	0.001	0.026	0.015	0.016	-0.005	0.019	0.006	0.018	-0.001	0.008
Mother's education	-0.071***	0.027	0.038	0.024	0.033**	0.014	-0.003	0.019	-0.010	0.017	0.013	0.008
Observations	1,119		281		140		1,282		146		102	

Notes: Dummies for country, quarter of interview, and missing information about parents' working status and education level are introduced. –, not controlled for. Marginal effects are computed at the sample mean of the variables.

*p < .10.

**p < .05.

***p < .01.

Table S10.2 Predicted outcome probability (Pr) and marginal effects (Mfx) in English-speaking countries by gender

	Females						Males					
	Employed		NEET		In education		Employed		NEET		In education	
Predicted outcome probability	Pr	St. Err.	Pr	St. Err.	Pr	St. Err.	Pr	St. Err.	Pr	St. Err.	Pr	St. Err.
	0.710 ***	0.015	0.160 ***	0.015	0.022 ***	0.004	0.886 ***	0.012	0.110 ***	0.012	0.005 ***	0.002
	Mfx	St. Err.	Mfx	St. Err.	Mfx	St. Err.	Mfx	St. Err.	Mfx	St. Err.	Mfx	St. Err.
Individual characteristics at the time of the interview												
Age	0.016 ***	0.006	-0.013 **	0.006	-0.003 **	0.001	0.001	0.004	0.000	0.004	-0.001 *	0.001
Own education: medium	0.187 ***	0.055	-0.189 ***	0.053	0.002	0.008	0.120 ***	0.035	-0.123 ***	0.034	0.003	0.006
Own education: high	0.386 **	0.058	-0.384 ***	0.056	-0.001	0.009	0.156 ***	0.034	-0.157 ***	0.033	0.001	0.005
Partner's education: medium	0.104 **	0.052	-0.080	0.051	-0.024 ***	0.009	0.110 *	0.065	-0.160 ***	0.058	0.051 *	0.030
Partner's education: high	0.065	0.054	-0.050	0.053	-0.015	0.010	0.188 ***	0.067	-0.241 ***	0.060	0.053 *	0.029
Citizenship	-0.206 ***	0.065	0.186 ***	0.064	0.020 **	0.009	-0.110 **	0.055	0.097 *	0.054	0.014 **	0.007
Living with parents	-0.049	0.064	0.056	0.063	-0.007	0.007	-0.049 *	0.029	0.048 *	0.029	0.001	0.002
Living in couple	-0.035	0.053	0.039	0.052	-0.004	0.008	-0.083	0.065	0.144 **	0.057	-0.061 *	0.032
Motherhood	-0.320 ***	0.037	0.314 ***	0.037	0.006	0.005	—		—		—	

Presence of parents when the young person was aged 14 years

Lone parent family	0.003	0.054	−0.006	0.053	0.003	0.008	−0.086 **	0.040	0.083 **	0.039	0.002	0.005
Parentless	0.565	0.404	−0.411	0.389	−0.155 ***	0.052	−0.240 **	0.101	0.299 ***	0.095	−0.058 *	0.032
Family background information											
Working father	0.090 *	0.052	−0.086 *	0.052	−0.003	0.007	0.010	0.032	−0.009	0.032	0.000	0.004
Working mother	0.061 *	0.035	−0.059 *	0.035	−0.002	0.006	0.047 *	0.027	−0.048 *	0.027	0.001	0.003
Working lone mother	0.024	0.073	−0.014	0.072	−0.010	0.011	0.041	0.053	−0.036	0.052	−0.005	0.006
Working mother-in-law	0.039	0.036	−0.033	0.036	−0.006	0.007	0.045	0.030	−0.036	0.030	−0.008 *	0.005
Father's occupation	−0.017	0.035	0.013	0.034	0.004	0.006	0.075 ***	0.029	−0.076 ***	0.028	0.001	0.002
Mother's occupation	0.008	0.045	−0.015	0.045	0.007	0.007	−0.001	0.033	−0.002	0.032	0.002	0.003
Father's education	−0.025	0.045	0.022	0.045	0.003	0.008	−0.035	0.033	0.037	0.032	−0.003	0.003
Mother's education	−0.017	0.049	0.028	0.049	−0.011	0.009	−0.069 **	0.030	0.064 **	0.029	0.005	0.003
Observations	849		406		37		740		149		30	

Notes: Dummies for country, quarter of interview, and missing information about parents' working status and education level are introduced. –, not controlled for. Marginal effects are computed at the sample mean of the variables.

*p < .10.

**p < .05.

***p < .01.

Table S10.3 Predicted outcome probability (Pr) and marginal effects (Mfx) in Continental countries by gender

| | Females | | | | | | Males | | | | | |
| | Employed | | NEET | | In education | | Employed | | NEET | | In education | |
	Pr	St. Err.	Pr	St. Err.	Pr	St. Err.	Pr	St. Err.	Pr	St. Err.	Pr	St. Err.
Predicted outcome probability	0.759***	0.006	0.187***	0.006	0.018***	0.002	0.921***	0.005	0.063***	0.004	0.016***	0.002
	Mfx	St. Err.	Mfx	St. Err.	Mfx	St. Err.	Mfx	St. Err.	Mfx	St. Err.	Mfx	St. Err.
Individual characteristics at the time of the interview												
Age	0.011***	0.002	-0.006***	0.002	-0.005***	0.001	0.004***	0.001	0.001	0.001	-0.005***	0.001
Own education: medium	0.119***	0.020	-0.136***	0.019	0.017**	0.008	0.035***	0.011	-0.060***	0.009	0.026***	0.007
Own education: high	0.192***	0.022	-0.203***	0.021	0.011	0.008	0.061***	0.013	-0.081***	0.010	0.020***	0.008
Partner's education: medium	0.063***	0.022	-0.057***	0.020	-0.007	0.008	0.037**	0.017	-0.048***	0.013	0.011	0.012
Partner's education: high	0.020	0.023	-0.027	0.022	0.007	0.008	0.043**	0.018	-0.060***	0.015	0.017	0.011
Citizenship	-0.189***	0.026	0.170***	0.025	0.020***	0.006	-0.076***	0.014	0.048***	0.013	0.028***	0.006
Living with parents	-0.063***	0.024	0.054**	0.024	0.010***	0.004	-0.031***	0.009	0.025***	0.008	0.007***	0.003
Living in couple	-0.036	0.025	0.052**	0.024	-0.016*	0.008	0.055***	0.016	-0.023*	0.013	-0.032***	0.011
Motherhood	-0.254***	0.014	0.263***	0.013	-0.009**	0.004	—		—		—	

Presence of parents when the young person was aged 14 years

Lone parent family	0.023	0.029	−0.022	0.028	−0.002	0.008	0.006	0.016	0.005	0.014	−0.011 *	0.007
Parentless	−0.096 *	0.050	0.084 *	0.048	0.012	0.013	−0.024	0.031	0.006	0.028	0.018 *	0.010
Family background information												
Working father	0.031	0.029	−0.037	0.028	0.006	0.008	0.011	0.016	−0.008	0.015	−0.003	0.006
Working mother	0.059 ***	0.013	−0.055 ***	0.013	−0.004	0.003	0.024 ***	0.008	−0.018 **	0.008	−0.005 *	0.003
Working lone mother	−0.033	0.033	0.026	0.032	0.007	0.009	−0.028	0.018	0.015	0.017	0.013 *	0.007
Working mother-in-law	0.032 **	0.013	−0.034 ***	0.013	0.002	0.004	0.007	0.011	−0.008	0.011	0.001	0.004
Father's occupation	0.003	0.014	−0.007	0.014	0.004	0.003	0.001	0.009	−0.007	0.008	0.006 **	0.003
Mother's occupation	−0.002	0.018	−0.001	0.018	0.003	0.003	−0.006	0.010	0.005	0.010	0.002	0.003
Father's education	−0.021	0.017	0.012	0.017	0.009 ***	0.004	−0.010	0.010	0.002	0.010	0.008 **	0.003
Mother's education	0.017	0.020	−0.022	0.020	0.005	0.003	−0.004	0.011	−0.004	0.010	0.008 ***	0.003
Observations	4,111		1,327		248		4,333		480		257	

Notes: Dummies for country, quarter of interview, and missing information about parents' working status and education level are introduced. −, not controlled for. Marginal effects are computed at the sample mean of the variables.

*$p < .10$.

**$p < .05$.

***$p < .01$.

Table S10.4 Predicted outcome probability (Pr) and marginal effects (Mfx) in Mediterranean countries by gender

	Females						Males					
	Employed		NEET		In education		Employed		NEET		In education	
Predicted outcome probability	Pr	St. Err.	Pr	St. Err.	Pr	St. Err.	Pr	St. Err.	Pr	St. Err.	Pr	St. Err.
	0.682 ***	0.006	0.306***	0.006	0.012 ***	0.002	0.808 ***	0.006	0.184 ***	0.006	0.009***	0.002
	Mfx	St. Err.	Mfx	St. Err.	Mfx	St. Err.	Mfx	St. Err.	Mfx	St. Err.	Mfx	St. Err.
Individual characteristics at the time of the interview												
Age	0.014 ***	0.002	-0.011 ***	0.002	-0.003***	0.001	0.010 ***	0.002	-0.007***	0.002	-0.003***	0.001
Own education: medium	0.088 ***	0.016	-0.106 ***	0.016	0.018 ***	0.004	0.076 ***	0.012	-0.089***	0.012	0.014 ***	0.003
Own education: high	0.181 ***	0.018	-0.190 ***	0.017	0.009***	0.003	0.104 ***	0.015	-0.116 ***	0.014	0.012 ***	0.003
Partner's education: medium	0.049 ***	0.019	-0.053 ***	0.018	0.004	0.006	0.074 ***	0.023	-0.074 ***	0.022	-0.001	0.010
Partner's education: high	0.062 ***	0.024	-0.071 ***	0.024	0.009	0.007	0.149 ***	0.030	-0.147 ***	0.029	-0.001	0.010
Citizenship	-0.095 ***	0.022	0.104 ***	0.022	-0.009*	0.005	-0.044 **	0.023	0.061***	0.022	-0.017 *	0.009
Living with parents	-0.141 ***	0.018	0.128 ***	0.018	0.013 ***	0.004	-0.097	0.014	0.088***	0.014	0.009***	0.003
Living in couple	-0.110 ***	0.022	0.119 ***	0.022	-0.009*	0.005	0.034	0.021	-0.018	0.020	-0.016 *	0.009
Motherhood	-0.175 ***	0.016	0.187 ***	0.016	-0.012 ***	0.003						
Presence of parents when the young person was aged 14 years												
Lone parent family	-0.012	0.038	0.021	0.037	-0.009	0.006	0.028	0.032	-0.029	0.032	0.001	0.003
Parentless	0.047	0.048	-0.053	0.047	0.006	0.006	0.098***	0.037	-0.095***	0.037	-0.003	0.005

Family background information

	(1)		(2)		(3)		(4)		(5)		(6)	
Working father	0.069 **	0.030	−0.060**	0.030	−0.010 ***	0.004	0.144 ***	0.025	−0.140 ***	0.024	−0.004	0.003
Working mother	0.056 ***	0.014	−0.056***	0.014	0.000	0.002	0.031 ***	0.012	−0.028**	0.012	−0.003*	0.002
Working lone mother	0.008	0.045	−0.010	0.045	0.002	0.006	0.023	0.041	−0.022	0.041	−0.001	0.004
Working mother-in-law	0.099 ***	0.018	−0.089***	0.017	−0.011 *	0.006	0.000	0.022	0.000	0.021	0.000	0.008
Father's occupation	0.022	0.018	−0.028	0.018	0.006***	0.002	−0.029 **	0.014	0.026**	0.013	0.003*	0.002
Mother's occupation	−0.009	0.026	0.002	0.026	0.008***	0.003	−0.009	0.020	0.003	0.020	0.006**	0.002
Father's education	−0.034	0.028	0.028	0.028	0.006**	0.003	−0.028	0.020	0.020	0.020	0.008***	0.002
Mother's education	−0.039	0.031	0.041	0.031	−0.001	0.003	0.000	0.024	−0.001	0.024	0.001	0.002
Observations	4,396		2,214		321		4,991		1,382		302	

Notes: Dummies for country, quarter of interview, and missing information about parents' working status and education level are introduced. Marginal effects are computed at the sample mean of the variables.

*p < .10.
**p < .05.
***p < .01.

Table S10.5 Predicted outcome probability (Pr) and marginal effects (Mfx) in Eastern countries by gender

	Females						Males					
	Employed		NEET		In education		Employed		NEET		In education	
Predicted outcome probability	Pr	St. Err.	Pr	St. Err.	Pr	St. Err.	Pr	St. Err.	Pr	St. Err.	Pr	St. Err.
	0.691***	0.005	0.307***	0.005	0.002***	0.000	0.859***	0.004	0.139***	0.004	0.002***	0.000
	Mfx	St. Err.	Mfx	St. Err.	Mfx	St. Err.	Mfx	St. Err.	Mfx	St. Err.	Mfx	St. Err.
Individual characteristics at the time of the interview												
Age	0.019***	0.002	-0.018***	0.002	-0.001***	0.000	0.002	0.001	-0.001	0.001	-0.001***	0.000
Own education: medium	0.219***	0.018	-0.222***	0.018	0.003***	0.001	0.125***	0.009	-0.127***	0.009	0.002***	0.001
Own education: high	0.310***	0.020	-0.313***	0.020	0.002*	0.001	0.198***	0.013	-0.200***	0.013	0.002**	0.001
Partner's education: medium	0.008	0.021	-0.037*	0.020	0.029***	0.005	0.053***	0.015	-0.070***	0.015	0.017***	0.004
Partner's education: high	0.002	0.025	-0.033	0.025	0.030***	0.005	0.098***	0.020	-0.118***	0.019	0.020***	0.004
Citizenship	-0.076*	0.045	0.078*	0.045	-0.002	0.002	-0.063***	0.021	0.062***	0.021	0.001	0.001
Living with parents	-0.056***	0.012	0.055***	0.012	0.001**	0.000	-0.039***	0.010	0.038***	0.009	0.001***	0.000
Living in couple	-0.053**	0.025	0.084***	0.025	-0.031***	0.005	0.026*	0.015	-0.005	0.015	-0.020***	0.005
Motherhood	-0.265***	0.014	0.267***	0.014	-0.001**	0.000						

Presence of parents when the young person was aged 14 years

Lone parent family	0.073**	0.034	-0.070**	0.034	-0.004***	0.001	-0.027	0.023	0.027	0.023	0.000	0.001
Parentless	0.002	0.035	-0.007	0.035	0.004***	0.002	0.054**	0.022	-0.054**	0.022	0.000	0.001
Family background information												
Working father	0.053*	0.027	-0.055**	0.027	0.002	0.002	0.057***	0.017	-0.057***	0.017	-0.001	0.001
Working mother	0.104***	0.015	-0.104***	0.015	0.000	0.001	0.050***	0.010	-0.049***	0.010	0.000	0.000
Working lone mother	-0.056	0.038	0.053	0.038	0.003*	0.001	0.002	0.024	-0.003	0.024	0.001	0.001
Working mother-in-law	0.033**	0.015	-0.033**	0.015	0.000	0.001	0.036***	0.012	-0.035***	0.012	-0.001	0.001
Father's occupation	-0.008	0.017	0.007	0.017	0.001	0.001	0.012	0.012	-0.013	0.012	0.001***	0.000
Mother's occupation	0.005	0.015	-0.006	0.015	0.000	0.000	0.009	0.011	-0.009	0.011	0.001*	0.000
Father's education	-0.008	0.021	0.007	0.021	0.001	0.001	0.010	0.015	-0.011	0.015	0.000	0.000
Mother's education	0.005	0.021	-0.006	0.021	0.001*	0.000	-0.026*	0.014	0.025*	0.014	0.001*	0.000
Observations	6,406		3,239		226		7,939		1,710		231	

Notes: Dummies for country, quarter of interview, and missing information about parents' working status and education level are introduced. Marginal effects are computed at the sample mean of the variables.

*p < .10.

**p < .05.

***p < .01.

11

STUCK IN THE PARENTAL NEST?

THE EFFECT OF THE ECONOMIC CRISIS ON YOUNG
EUROPEANS' LIVING ARRANGEMENTS

Fernanda Mazzotta and Lavinia Parisi

11.1. INTRODUCTION

The Great Recession has had a profound impact on the process of young
people's transitions into adulthood. In particular, youth unemployment has
increased disproportionately during the economic crisis, often leading young
people to remain living with their parents. In fact, a number of studies have
found that the share of young people living with their parents increased in
many European countries in the early years of the crisis (Aassve, Cottini, and
Vitali 2013). This chapter aims to expand on previous studies by providing a
comparative analysis of home-leaving and home-returning by young people
in 14 European countries during the period 2005–2013, which covers the
years prior to, during, and after the recession of 2008–2009.[1] Drawing on the
European Union Statistics on Income and Living Conditions (EU-SILC), the
chapter analyzes, first, the probability of youth (aged 18–34 years) leaving
home and, second, the probability of youth (aged 20–36 years) returning home
(i.e., "boomeranging").

Exploiting the nature of EU-SILC's longitudinal data, we consider the two
phenomena—leaving home and returning home—in a dynamic way; in other
words, the same individual is observed in two consecutive years by living arrangement (i.e., living in the parental home or independently in the first year
and living independently or returning to the parental home in the subsequent

year). Living arrangements are strongly linked to employment and partnership.[2] For this reason, we simultaneously model these three outcomes: living independently, finding employment, and being in a partnership (either married or cohabiting with the partner). Our main hypothesis regarding the effects of the Great Recession is that it reduces the probability of leaving home and increases the probability of returning home.

Three main research questions are investigated in this chapter: Is there a negative (positive) effect of the Great Recession on leaving (returning) home? Does the effect persist after considering the two main drivers of leaving and returning home (i.e., employment and partnership)? Are there significant differences across country groups?

The chapter is organized as follows. Section 11.2 provides a literature review, and Section 11.3 discusses the data used and the research design. In Section 11.4, we present descriptive statistics with regard to the effect of the crisis on leaving and returning home. We present our econometric model in Section 11.5 and discuss the empirical results in Section 11.6.

11.2. LITERATURE REVIEW

The literature analyzing the decision of young adults to live with their parents (or, conversely, to leave the parental home) identifies four different sets of determinants: (1) age-related events (in particular, employment and partnership), (2) institutional and cultural factors (labor market regulations, welfare provisions, and social norms), (3) macrostructural factors (i.e., labor market characteristics, economic cycles, and housing market conditions), and (4) rational choice/exchange perspectives and preferences of children and parents.

The first group of determinants deals with young adults' involvement in age-related events such as completing school, getting a job, starting a career, forming a family, or bearing children. Any of these events can lead to a decision to leave the parental home (Berngruber 2015). Among these events, partnership and employment are found to play a crucial role. Indeed, partnership is the most widely reported factor behind young adults' decisions to leave home: Adult children in partnerships are more likely to leave the parental home than are their unpartnered peers (O'Higgins 2006; Hank 2007; Lei and South 2016). Getting a job is widely reported as another crucial event. For instance, Jacob and Kleinert (2008) find that, in Germany, nonemployment delays household formation and that the longer young adults have been unemployed, the less likely they are to leave home. Ayllón (2015) finds that employment and leaving home are two closely linked phenomena in Southern Europe but that the same is not true in Nordic countries. Mazzotta and Parisi (2015a) provide evidence that employed young people in Italy are more likely to leave the family of origin than are jobless youth, after controlling for parental background.

The second group of determinants concerns institutional and cultural factors such as labor market regulations, welfare provisions (unemployment benefits and social assistance), and social norms (Billari 2004; Chiuri and Del Boca 2010; Settersten and Ray 2010). Labor market regulations (e.g., employment protection legislation or active labor market policies) and the generosity of the welfare state (i.e., social assistance and unemployment benefits)—both of which differ across countries—affect both the economic independence of young people and access to affordable accommodation. It has been shown that leaving the parental home is closely linked to the probability of young people receiving social assistance in the Nordic countries (Ayllón 2015). Social norms and culture differ significantly by country (as discussed later in this section) and by gender, albeit with some similarities across countries (related to gender roles in paid and unpaid work), which explains some differences between women and men in the decision to leave home. Women have a lower threshold for economic independence and are more likely to start a family during unemployment than are men (Ermisch 1999).

The third group of determinants concerns macrostructural factors, such as labor market characteristics (youth/prime-age unemployment rate and labor market segmentation), the economic cycle (i.e., economic growth and downturn), and housing conditions. In particular, the prices and the scarcity of rented housing are acknowledged in the literature as reasons that explain young people delaying leaving the parental home (Aassve et al. 2002; Iacovou 2002; Gökşen et al. 2016). Martins and Villanueva (2006) show that differences in mortgage markets across Europe can explain up to 20% of the cross-country variance in establishment of new households. Given that comparable data on housing market conditions are not available for a large number of EU countries or over time (2005–2013), we limit the focus of our empirical analysis to the other two key determinants of leaving and returning home, namely employment and partnership.

Finally, the fourth set of determinants considered in the literature concerns rational choice/exchange perspectives and preferences. Children are assumed to compare the costs and benefits of living with their parents with alternative living arrangements and to then choose the arrangement that offers the most highly valued net benefits. This could depend on the intra-household transfer of time and money, the personal income of young adult children, family income, or the health of parents (Ermisch 1999; Manacorda and Moretti 2006; Mazzotta and Parisi 2015b). Medgyesi and Nagy (this volume) study the extent to which young adults living with their parents contribute to household expenses. They find that the majority of young adults benefit from intra-household sharing of resources within the family. However, a small group of young adults living at home (mainly in Eastern European countries) tend to support their parents: Their contribution to the household budget is higher than that of their parents.

Differences across countries in the share of young people living at home are explained in the literature mainly on the basis of both institutional/cultural factors and macrostructural determinants. Jones (1995) and Reher (1998) identify Southern and Eastern European cultural roots as reasons for late home-leaving and also for the strong synchronization between leaving and first marriage. Others emphasize the poor economic conditions (related to labor market conditions) for young adults in Southern countries (Saraceno 2015). Esping-Andersen (1999) focuses on the peculiarities of the Southern European welfare system, which is characterized by a lack of support for young unemployed people and by the crucial role played by the family in helping them. Reher argues that Northern countries, characterized by early home-leaving, have "weak" family ties and a sense of "social," rather than familial, solidarity with elderly or frail members of society. In Nordic and Continental countries, parents with high incomes help their children leave home, whereas in Southern and some Eastern European countries, parents seem to use their high incomes to delay the departure of children (Iacovou 2010). The decision to co-reside could also depend on parents' economic needs (Medgyesi and Nagy, this volume).

Studies on young people returning home are scarce and mainly focus on returning migrants (see Le Mare, Promphaking, and Rigg 2015; Masso et al., this volume).[3]

The four groups of determinants outlined previously for the analysis of young people's reasons for leaving the parental home can also apply to their reasons for returning home. For instance, young people are more likely to return to the parental home at the end of formal education. Stone, Berrington, and Falkingham (2014) indicate the awarding of a final degree as a key turning point for students deciding to return home.[4] Several other studies highlight the importance of a change in economic activity status (i.e., becoming unemployed) in fostering a potential return to the parental home. Separation and divorce increase the likelihood of returning to live with one's parents (DaVanzo and Goldscheider 1990; Mitchell, Wister, and Gee 2000); however, the association between partnership dissolution and returning home is moderated by gender and parenthood (Stone et al. 2014). Overall, men are more likely than women to return to the parental home following the dissolution of marriage or cohabitation (Ongaro, Mazzuco, and Meggiolaro 2009). Studies have also found that returning home is related to institutional factors, such as welfare provisions (Berrington, Stone, and Falkingham 2013) and cultural norms (Boyd and Pryor 1989). Returns to the parental home at the end of formal education are likely to increase as a result of rising levels of student debt and a weaker graduate jobs market (Andrew 2010; Clapham et al. 2012); economic status and employment conditions can also increase the likelihood of returning home (Goldscheider and Goldscheider 1999). Finally, with regard to the economic crisis, together with later home-leaving, studies have found evidence of a "boomerang" phenomenon in France, Spain, and the United Kingdom, with increasing numbers of young people returning to their parents' home after having lived independently (Plantenga, Remery, and Samek Lodovici 2013).

11.3. RESEARCH DESIGN

In order to examine the phenomena of both leaving and returning home in 14 EU countries (AT, BE, CY, CZ, EE, ES, FR, IT, LT, LU, LV, PL, PT, and SI),[5] we used EU-SILC longitudinal data. We considered eight panels covering the period from 2005 to 2013.[6] For each panel, we considered periods of 2 years each (e.g., for the panel from 2005 to 2008, there are three 2-year periods: 2005–2006, 2006–2007, and 2007–2008), and for each 2-year period we considered the change (or not) in living arrangements between the two points in time (i.e., the beginning, time t, and the end, time $t + 1$). Thus, the first dependent variable is the observed transition of *l*eaving the parental home (L). L describes whether young people who were living in the family of origin at time t are still living with their parents at $t + 1$ or have left.[7] The second dependent variable is the observed transition of *r*eturning to the parental home (R). R describes whether young Europeans who were living on their own at time t are still living without their parents at $t + 1$ or have returned to live with at least one of them.[8]

We constructed two samples—one for those leaving and one for those returning. The leaving-home sample consists of young people aged 18–34 years the first time they are observed. The returning-home sample consists of young people aged 20–36 years the first time they are observed. We excluded students from both samples so as to make the results comparable across countries.[9] In order to improve the interpretation of the results, we grouped countries in four classes: Continental, Southern, Eastern, and Baltic countries. Both the descriptive and the econometric analyses are carried out separately for the four groups of countries. The small sample size at the single-country level (above all for the sample of returning home) makes it necessary to group countries.

Given the great heterogeneity of European labor market institutions and welfare systems, to group countries we follow the classification developed by the European Commission (2006, 2007). Using a principal component analysis, the European Commission groups 18 European countries according to three dimensions of labor market/flexicurity systems: income/employment security, numerical external flexibility/employability, and tax distortions.

The Continental group of countries (AT, BE, FR, and LU) is characterized by (1) intermediate to high security, (2) intermediate to low flexibility, and (3) intermediate to high taxation. In this group, social benefits are targeted at individuals who belong to specific categories, such as a specific type of family or a specific type of worker. In the Southern group of countries (CY, ES, IT, and PT), welfare coverage tends to be "residual" and largely left to the family. It tends to be characterized by (1) relatively low security, (2) low flexibility, and (3) no clear pattern on taxation. The Eastern group (CZ, PL, and SI) is characterized by (1) insecurity, (2) intermediate to high flexibility, and (3) intermediate to high taxation. Finally, we distinguish the Baltic group of countries (EE, LT, and LV) from the Eastern European group because the Baltic countries are more similar to the Continental countries with regard to family formation (Eurofound 2014) and implemented flexibility/protection patterns (Anca 2012).

11.4. DESCRIPTIVE STATISTICS

In this section, we provide descriptive statistics on key variables, focusing on the role of the economic crisis across the four groups of countries. Table 11.1 shows the share of young people (aged 18–34 years) leaving home during the period under consideration (2005–2013). The lowest percentage of youth leaving the parental home is found in the Eastern, Baltic, and Southern European countries (on average, 3.0%, 4.5%, and 5.9%, respectively, over the entire period). The highest percentage is found in the Continental countries (13.6%, on average, over the entire period). Except for the Eastern countries, where the exit rate is very low for all the years considered, descriptive statistics show that the other three groups of countries register a decrease in the share of young people leaving home between 2005 and 2013.[10] However, whereas for the Continental countries we detect two decreases—one just after the onset of the crisis (2009–2010), from

Table 11.1 Observed rate of home-leaving at time $t + 1$ for young people (aged 18–34 years) living with their parents at time t (students are excluded) by group of countries, 2005–2013 (%)

Year	Continental	Southern	Eastern	Baltic	Total
2005–2006	15.5	6.3	3.3	6.9	9.4
2006–2007	15.6	5.8	3.3	5.5	8.8
2007–2008	12.8	7.0	3.1	3.7	8.3
2008–2009	15.3	6.2	3.3	3.4	9.1
2009–2010	10.8	5.0	2.7	4.9	6.7
2010–2011	14.3	7.3	2.7	4.5	9.2
2011–2012	12.5	4.8	3.4	3.4	7.4
2012–2013	9.8	4.1	2.2	3.9	5.5
Total	13.6	5.9	3.0	4.5	8.2
Sample size	2,890	4,492	1,640	1,021	10,043

Notes: Percentages are calculated each year as the number of young people who have left home at time $t + 1$ divided by the total number of young people (excluding students) living in the parental home at time t. Continental countries: Austria, Belgium, France, and Luxembourg; Southern countries: Cyprus, Italy, Portugal, and Spain; Eastern countries: Czech Republic, Poland, and Slovenia; Baltic countries: Estonia, Latvia, and Lithuania.

Table 11.2 Observed rate of home-returning at time *t* + 1 for young people (aged 20–36 years) living away from parents at time *t* (students are excluded) by group of countries, 2005–2013 (%)

Year	Continental	Southern	Eastern	Baltic	Total
2005–2006	0.5	0.9	1.1	0.6	0.6
2006–2007	0.6	0.7	0.4	0.6	0.6
2007–2008	0.6	1.0	0.5	0.6	0.7
2008–2009	0.4	1.1	0.4	1.4	0.6
2009–2010	1.2	1.2	0.5	1.4	1.1
2010–2011	0.5	1.0	0.7	1.0	0.6
2011–2012	0.8	1.4	0.4	0.4	0.9
2012–2013	0.3	1.1	0.3	0.4	0.5
Total	0.6	1.0	0.5	0.8	0.7
Sample size	543	803	378	262	1,986

Notes: Percentages are calculated each year as the number of young people who returned home at time *t* + 1 divided by the total number of young people (excluding students) living independently at time *t*. Continental countries: Austria, Belgium, France, and Luxembourg; Southern countries: Cyprus, Italy, Portugal, and Spain; Eastern countries: Czech Republic, Poland, and Slovenia; Baltic countries: Estonia, Latvia, and Lithuania.

15.3% to 10.8%, and another (in 2011) from 14.3% to 12.5%—the effect in the Southern countries is postponed to 2011 (with a decline from 7.3% to 4.8%).

With regard to returning to the parental home (Table 11.2), all four groups of countries show very low rates (less than 1% on average). However, we do find differences during the economic crisis. Whereas in Continental countries we observe an increase from 0.4% to 1.2% at the beginning of the recession (2008–2009), in Southern countries the increase does not occur until 2011–2012. Overall, the rate of home-returning decreases for all groups of countries in 2012–2013 (see Table 11.2).[11]

When studying the effect of the economic crisis on leaving and returning home, we should consider, separately, the probability of finding a job and the decision to form a family. Figure 11.1a presents the percentage of employed among young people who are still living with their parents at time *t* + 1, compared to those who have left home at time *t* + 1. Figure 11.1b presents the percentage of individuals in partnerships among young people who are still living with their parents at time *t* + 1, compared to those who have left home to live independently.

Young people who have left home are more likely to be employed than those who are still living with their parents (83% vs. 70%, on average),[12] and this difference is higher for Continental countries, suggesting that young people decide to leave the parental home once they have found a job (see Figure 11.1a). The same pattern is found for partnerships:[13] Young people who have left home are more likely to be in a partnership than those who are still living with their parents. On average, 55% of those leaving home are in a partnership at *t* + 1 (for Eastern

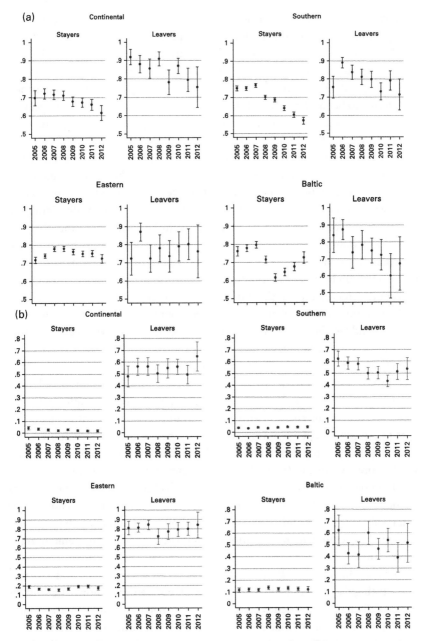

Figure 11.1 (a) Share of young people employed at time $t + 1$ by group of countries, distinguishing between those who stayed at home (stayers) and those who left home (leavers) in the period under consideration (confidence interval at 95% level). (b) Share of young people in a partnership at time $t + 1$ by group of countries, distinguishing between those who stayed at home (stayers) and those who left home (leavers) in the period under consideration (confidence interval at 95% level).

countries, the percentage is particularly high at approximately 70%), compared to approximately 4% for those who stayed at home (17% and 12%, respectively, for the Eastern and Baltic countries; see Figure 11.1b). The Baltic and Eastern European countries have particularly high shares of people in a partnership and living with their parents. In general, for all groups of countries, partnership seems to be more important than employment in explaining home-leaving (there are statistically significant differences in the percentages of partnership among leavers and stayers).

As a result of the depth and duration of the economic crisis, young people are less likely to be in employment in Continental, Southern, and Baltic countries (see Figure 11.1a).[14] Whereas the differences are statistically significant for those who remained in the parental home, there are no statistically significant differences for those who left. Our results are in line with those found by the European Commission (2014, 32, Table 15) and are consistent with the hypothesis that during the economic crisis, young people have a greater need to find a job as a precondition for leaving home. Finally, we do not find statistically significant differences for the share of young people in a partnership across time periods among stayers, whereas the changes found for leavers do not follow a precise trend (see Figure 11.1b). In summary, young people who leave home are likely to be working or in a partnership, especially in the Southern countries.

In Continental countries, being employed is the main factor associated with leaving the parental home, given that in these countries young people also leave when they are single.[15] Thus, we find different cultural patterns (in accordance with the literature), with (single) young people in Continental countries becoming independent (much earlier), whereas in Southern and Eastern countries they mainly leave home in order to start a family (and/or a relationship). Moreover, in Continental countries, employment status is more important than partnership status in explaining the decision to leave home, whereas the opposite is true for the other country groups. This finding does not change as a result of the economic crisis; in fact, in Southern countries, the crisis has worsened the employment conditions of young individuals who remain in the parental home.

Figures 11.2a and 11.2b show the patterns for employment and partnership, distinguishing between those who had not returned home (labeled as alone or living independently) and those who had returned home at time $t + 1$. Figure 11.2a shows that even though individuals who return home are on average more likely not to be employed than those who continue to live independently,[16] we find the most important differences across time periods. There is a very low proportion of not employed at the beginning of the period in the sample of youth living independently, with no differences in the Southern and Baltic countries between not employed as a share of those who returned home and not employed as a share of those who did not return home. For the Southern countries, we observe an increase in the share of people who are not employed

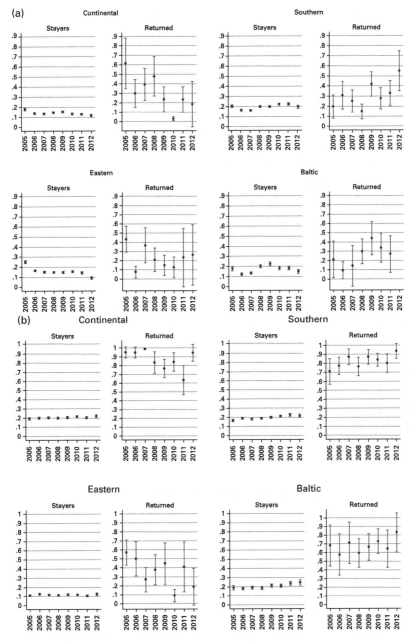

Figure 11.2 (a) Share of young people not employed at time $t + 1$ by group of countries, distinguishing between those who lived independently (stayers) and those who returned home (returned) in the period under consideration (confidence interval at 95% level). (b) Share of young people not in a partnership at time $t + 1$ by group of countries, distinguishing between those who lived independently (stayers) and those who returned home (returned) in the period under consideration (confidence interval at 95% level).

across all the periods, with sharper differences among those who return home (see Figure 11.2a). Moreover, there is a large proportion of people not employed in the very last period for all the countries, above all for those who return home in the Eastern, Baltic, and Southern countries (approximately 26% for Eastern and Baltic countries and approximately 60% for Southern countries). For Continental countries, the percentages of not employed among the young people living independently (defined as stayers in Figure 11.2a) are very low and stable across all periods observed, whereas the shares of not employed among those who return home (defined as returned in Figure 11.2a) show a decrease in 2010 (stable across the years for stayers, decreasing in 2010 for returners).

The effect of partnership dissolution is statistically significant for almost all countries (Eastern Europe being the exception): Young people without a partner return home more often than do young people with a partner, and the proportion is quite high (approximately 90% in some countries). This pattern is less strong for Eastern countries, where (in line with Iacovou 2010) young people are often found living with a partner in the same house as their parents. In short, partnership status does not appear to influence the decision to return home.

The difference in the percentage of not employed young people among those who return home and those who do not return home is lower than the difference in the percentage of returners and non-returners who are not in a partnership. With regard to leaving home, it seems that partnership is more important than not having a job in predicting the probability of returning home. Across subperiods, there are neither clear nor significant patterns in the Continental or Baltic countries, whereas in the Southern countries the percentage of partnership breakups increases among those who return home, and the opposite is true in Eastern countries (these effects are statistically significant).

11.5. ECONOMETRIC ANALYSIS: METHODOLOGY

The aim of the econometric analysis is to disentangle the effect of the economic crisis on the probability of leaving (returning) home after controlling for employment and the partnership status of young people.[17] The method used to estimate the two probabilities is a trivariate probit model. This is a simulation method for maximum likelihood estimation of a multivariate probit regression model. The model controls for unobservable factors that influence the probability of leaving (returning) home, of being employed (not employed), and of being in a couple (not in a couple). It is necessary to consider the mutual correlation between the three outcomes in order to avoid biased results.[18] Moreover, this is a type of first-order Markov approach. It takes into account pairs of observations in two consecutive years, namely t and $t + 1$ for each individual. In year t, the young person lives with his or her parents (or independently), and in year $t + 1$ he or she has left (returned) home. This strategy improves the existing models in the literature by controlling for feedback effects; unobserved heterogeneity; nonrandom selection of the sample; and unobserved cross-process correlations between living arrangement, employment, and partnership.

The model for leaving home considers three dependent variables: the probability of leaving home (L_{t+1}), the probability of being employed (E_{t+1}), and the probability of having a partner (P_{t+1}). The model can be identified by functional form, but we also include the following variables (in only one equation at a time): the household crowding index at time t in equation L_{t+1}, the employment status at time t in equation E_{t+1}, and whether or not the person is living not just with one but with both parents at time t in equation P_{t+1}. To examine the effect of employment and partnership on the probability of leaving home, we also include, in equation L_{t+1}, the probability of being employed and of being in a relationship at time $t+1$. Other control variables (i.e., gender—male or not; age and age squared; education—two dummies for secondary education and tertiary education, with compulsory education as the reference category; and general health status—good health or not) have been chosen in accordance with the literature. We further include in equation L_{t+1} parents' income at time t (expressed as the logarithm of the sum of the income of both parents) and personal income of the young person at time t (expressed as the logarithm of his or her personal income).

The model for returning home simultaneously estimates the probability of returning home (R_{t+1}), the probability of not being in partnership (UP_{t+1}), and the probability of not being employed (NE_{t+1}). We include the following variables to identify the model: the crowding index and whether the person has children at time $t+1$ in equation R_{t+1}, whether the person has children and whether the person is not employed at $t+1$ in equation UP_{t+1}, and whether the person is not employed at time t in equation NE_{t+1}. We also include, in R_{t+1}, the probability of not being employed at $t+1$ and the probability of not being in a relationship at $t+1$. Other control variables (i.e., gender, age and age squared, education, general health status, and personal income at time $t+1$) are included as described for the home-leaving model.

The three outcomes (for the models for both leaving and returning home) can be correlated independently. The correlations relate to unobservable traits such as ability, intelligence, personality traits, ambition, quality of the relationship with parents, family background, and so forth. We estimate the correlation among the three error terms as follows: whether positive, unobservable individual factors determining the outcome of primary interest (i.e., leaving or returning) are also positively associated with the other two outcomes (being employed and having a partner for leaving, and not being employed and not being in a partnership for returning).

We claim that only by acknowledging correlation effects between the three processes can we properly deal with endogeneity problems that may arise when studying life transitions that possibly take place in a sequential manner and/or simultaneously (Siegers, de Jong-Gierveld, and van Imhoff 1991; Mulder and Wagner 1993; Billari, Philipov, and Baizán 2001).

Together with the estimated coefficients (provided in Tables 11.3 and 11.4), we also calculate predicted probabilities (Figures 11.3 and 11.4) and their confidence intervals so as to analyze whether there is evidence of a time trend or not across groups of countries.

Table 11.3 Trivariate probit model for probability of leaving home by group of countries

Probability of leaving home	Continental	Southern	Eastern	Baltic
Log parents' income at t	−0.027**	−0.017***	0.008	−0.028***
Log personal income at t	0.065***	0.027***	0.046***	0.040***
2005–2006	0.170**	0.109**	0.061	0.111
2006–2007	0.150**	0.055	0.09	0.030
2007–2008	0.019	0.116***	0.057	−0.151**
2008–2009	0.220***	0.122***	0.119*	−0.249***
2010–2011	0.152**	0.245***	−0.059	−0.063
2011–2012	0.142*	0.000	0.081	−0.186**
2012–2013	−0.100	−0.085	−0.111	−0.131
Male	−0.080*	−0.036	−0.094**	−0.174***
Age	0.093	0.117***	−0.027	0.208***
Age squared	−0.003**	−0.002***	0.000	−0.004***
Tertiary education	0.789***	0.175***	−0.05	−0.077
Secondary education	0.394***	0.059**	−0.119**	−0.002
Good health at t	0.120*	0.089**	−0.041	−0.179***
House crowded at t	0.217***	0.231***	0.031	0.095*
In a partnership at $t + 1$	2.169***	1.644***	1.458***	0.975***
Employed at $t + 1$	0.215***	0.199***	−0.062	0.000
Country dummies	Yes	Yes	Yes	Yes
Constant	−4.015***	−4.413***	−1.525**	−4.178***
No. of observations	27,386	75,774	44,544	21,445
Log likelihood	−2.74E + 08	−2.51E + 08	−1.30E + 08	−1.40E + 07

Notes: Continental countries: Austria, Belgium, France, and Luxembourg; Southern countries: Cyprus, Italy, Portugal, and Spain; Eastern countries: Czech Republic, Poland, and Slovenia; Baltic countries: Estonia, Latvia, and Lithuania. The likelihood ratio test for the hypothesis $\rho_{21} = \rho_{31} = \rho_{32} = 0$ is statistically different from zero at the 1% level. Estimates do not consider students. Estimates are clustered at the individual level.
*$p < .10$.
**$p < .05$.
***$p < .01$.

Table 11.4 Trivariate probit model for probability of returning home by group of countries

Probability of returning home	Continental	Southern	Eastern	Baltic
Log personal income at $t + 1$	0.013	0.000	0.008	−0.008
2005–2006	−0.408***	−0.012	0.256***	−0.241**
2006–2007	−0.335***	−0.145*	−0.059	−0.235**
2007–2008	−0.372***	0.006	0.001	−0.244*
2008–2009	−0.485***	0.005	−0.05	0.082
2010–2011	−0.437***	−0.081	0.166	−0.097
2011–2012	−0.138	0.058	−0.068	−0.371***
2012–2013	−0.594***	−0.027	−0.151	−0.396***
Male	0.078	0.055	−0.041	0.218***
Age	−0.177**	−0.247***	−0.151**	−0.162*
Age squared	0.002	0.003***	0.003**	0.003
Tertiary education	−0.482***	−0.119**	−0.530***	−0.300***
Secondary education	−0.165**	−0.05	−0.272***	−0.002
Is a parent	−0.196**	−0.351***	−0.167**	−0.173**
Good health at t	−0.049	−0.072	−0.047	0.111
House crowded at t	−0.092***	−0.237***	−0.155***	−0.119**
Not in a partnership at $t + 1$	1.021***	1.138***	0.506***	0.796***
Not employed at $t + 1$	0.238***	0.222***	0.105	0.189**
Country dummies	Yes	Yes	Yes	Yes
Constant	0.835	2.869***	0.585	0.738
No. of observations	97,157	74,607	63,122	28,931
Log likelihood	−7.91E + 08	−2.92E + 08	−1.14E + 08	−2.17E + 07

Notes: See notes to Table 11.3.

11.6. RESULTS AND DISCUSSION

This section presents and discusses estimates for both models regarding the probability of leaving and returning home. The models are estimated separately for the four groups of countries. We present estimates that include country dummies (within each country group—not reported) and year dummies. Table 11.3 shows estimates for the probability of leaving home.[19] To disentangle the effect of the economic crisis, we include year dummies, excluding the period 2009–2010, and we calculate predicted probabilities for each year plotted in Figure 11.3.

The correlation between the error terms (ρ) is significantly different from zero.[20] Thus, the three equations are strongly related: The same unobservable factors positively affect the probability of leaving, of being employed, and of

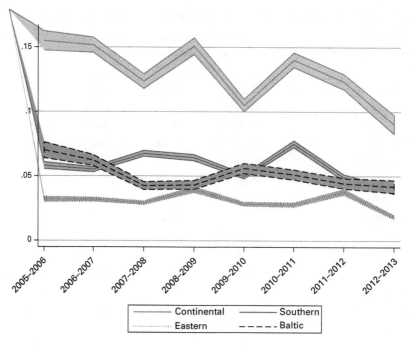

Figure 11.3 Marginal predicted probabilities of leaving home by group of countries and across time periods with 95% confidence interval bands.

being in a relationship. This indicates that a trivariate probit technique is appropriate in this context.

Looking at the coefficients of the time dummies, we can see that young people are more likely to leave home before and after 2009–2010; in other words, there is a crisis effect, given that the probability of leaving is lower just after the onset of the Great Recession compared to the other periods (i.e., the coefficients of all time dummies are positive compared to 2009–2010; see Table 11.3). And the effect also holds after including employment and partnership. Figure 11.3 plots the marginal predicted probabilities of leaving home. The results confirm the descriptive statistics, showing that in Southern, Baltic, and Eastern European countries, the probability of leaving home is lower compared to that in Continental countries (approximately 3%–6% and 12%–15%, respectively). There are no striking differences over time with the exception of the Continental countries, where we observe a decrease in the probability of leaving (in particular, there are two declines: one in 2009–2010 and another in 2012–2013).

Thus, the probability of leaving home in Southern and Eastern European countries (the lowest in comparative terms) turns out to be rather stable in the period considered (2005–2013), whereas a decrease is recorded in Continental countries. The crisis has therefore reduced the probability of leaving home in those countries that were both less affected by the economic downturn and where young people were used to living independently at a relatively young age. In the Southern and Eastern countries, by contrast, where young people were hit hardest by the economic crisis, we do not observe the sharp decrease in the probability of home-leaving one might have expected (Aassve et al. 2013). This may be due to the fact that these countries already recorded the highest percentage of young adults living in the parental home at the beginning of the observed period (i.e., before the Great Recession). This implies that the economic crisis hit a large share of those young individuals (aged 18–34 years) who were already somehow "protected" by their family of origin (i.e., living with their parents). Therefore, the change observed in the probability of youth leaving home during the Great Recession is smaller in these two groups of countries (Southern and Eastern) than in the others. Moreover, in these countries, cultural factors (which tend to be relatively stable over time) may play a stronger role than economic conditions (which fluctuate with the economic cycle) in explaining living arrangements.

As already seen in the descriptive statistics (see Section 11.4), leaving home is strongly connected to partnership, and indeed it seems to be more closely linked to partnership than to employment: In all groups of countries considered, the coefficient of partnership is positive and strongly significant compared to that of employment, which is smaller and not significant in the Eastern and Baltic countries. Partnership thus has a strong effect on leaving home: The more young people enter a partnership (including marriage), the more likely they are to leave home. Employment is a good predictor of leaving home in Continental and Southern countries: Being employed positively affects the probability of leaving. However, employment has an indirect effect through partnership in those countries (Baltic and Eastern) where we do not find a direct effect.

With regard to demographic variables, the results are in line with the literature. Women have a lower income threshold for independence: They leave the parental home more often than men in all countries except the Southern countries. The difference observed between men and women may be due to the fact that the impact of unemployment differs by gender: Women may be more inclined to start a family, whereas men try to find a more stable job first (Plantenga et al. 2013); also, women enter partnerships at a lower age (Eurostat 2009).

High parental income (in Southern, Continental, and Baltic countries) is associated with a lower probability of leaving home. Higher personal education and good health unambiguously increase the probability of leaving home in Continental and Southern countries. A downward correlation exists between age and leaving, such that the most likely to leave are individuals aged approximately 29 and 26 years, respectively, for the Baltic and Southern countries.

Table 11.4 presents estimates for a trivariate probit model for the probability of returning home, and Figure 11.4 plots the marginal predicted probabilities across time periods. Looking at the dummies that explain the difference between time periods, we find that there is a time effect only in the Continental and Baltic countries, where the probability of returning home is always lower compared

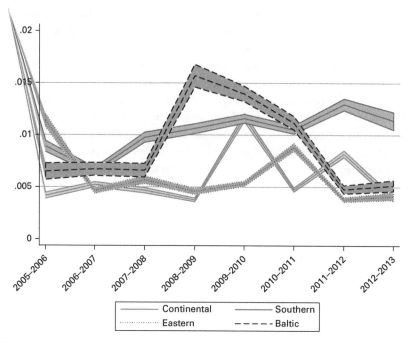

Figure 11.4 Predicted probabilities of returning home by group of countries and across time periods with 95% confidence interval bands.

to 2009. In contrast with Stone, Berrington, and Falkingham's results (2012), the period is still statistically significant when we include what they call turning points (e.g., separation or unemployment). This result implies that the economic crisis has a direct effect on returning home, given that it produces uncertainty about the future. However, when we plot the predicted marginal probability of returning home (see Figure 11.4), we observe that, also in Southern countries, the probability of returning home constantly increases for all the periods considered. This increase—observed already in 2007 (before the crisis) in the Southern countries—may be due to structural or cultural factors, but it has been exacerbated by the Great Recession.

Continental and Eastern countries have the lowest percentage of individuals returning home, with a jump just after the onset of the crisis (2009–2010), whereas in Eastern countries the effect does not appear until 2011 (but the difference is not significant). In Baltic countries, we record an increase that lasts longer—from 2008–2009 until 2010–2011. The predicted probability of returning to the parental home for countries in these three groups becomes stable at approximately 0.5%. This low rate (especially in the Continental countries) has been related to relatively generous welfare-state benefits and to cultural factors, given that both young people and their parents greatly value independence compared to their Southern counterparts (Iacovou 2010). For the Eastern and Baltic countries, this result may depend on emigration—that is, on the necessity for young people to leave their country of origin.

Thus, the result that merits highlighting is that Southern European countries show an increase in boomeranging throughout the entire period considered (beginning in 2005), which may indicate a long-term as opposed to a cyclical trend. This finding differs from that for the Continental countries, where the increase starts just after the onset of the crisis (2009–2010), whereas in the Baltic countries we record an increase that lasts longer—from 2008–2009 until 2010–2011.

Again, we confirm the hypothesis already observed for leaving: Just as partnership had a strong effect on leaving home, being single has a very strong effect on returning home. In fact, union dissolution is a key determinant of returning home. Similarly, not being employed increases the probability of returning home in the Continental, Southern, and Baltic countries (the result also holds if we exclude inactives).

With regard to the other control variables, the most important result is that being alone increases the likelihood of returning to the parental home. In fact, young parents (both mothers and fathers) are less likely to return to the parental home than are individuals without children, just as individuals living in crowded families (usually with more than one child or other relatives) are less likely to return to living with their parents. Higher education decreases the probability of returning home, whereas health does not have any effect. Men are more likely to return home only in the Baltic countries.

11.7. CONCLUSIONS

This chapter has examined the influence of the Great Recession on the probability of leaving or returning to the parental home in Europe. The transition into adulthood in the form of leaving the parental home to establish an autonomous household is highly variable across European countries. Our findings reveal that Southern, Baltic, and Eastern European countries have lower leaving rates compared to Continental countries and that the crisis has not exacerbated this difference. In the former groups of countries, leaving the family of origin is not as highly valued as in Continental countries. Also, before the Great Recession, a high share of young adults were living in the family of origin in Southern, Baltic, and Eastern European countries. Thus, in these countries, cultural factors (which tend to be relatively stable over time) may play a stronger role than economic conditions in decisions to leave home. So when youth unemployment started to increase dramatically, many young adults in these countries were still living at home. In short, these youth were caught by the crisis and by its effects, but they were already under the protection of the family of origin.

What is striking are the changes observed in Continental countries. We observe a decrease in the probability of leaving home during the crisis (in particular, the percentage of home-leavers rises and falls between 2009 and 2011). Continental countries are still characterized by higher levels of home-leaving compared to the other groups of countries, but the deterioration in labor market conditions for young people (i.e., difficult school-to-work transitions, youth unemployment, and economic hardship) increased the uncertainty of youth integration into secure employment, thus lowering the probability of leaving home in 2009.

All country groups experience an increase in the percentage of people returning home, with the exception of the Eastern countries. There are also noticeable differences across countries regarding timing: Southern European countries register an increase throughout the entire period; Continental countries show an increase in the very first period, after the onset of the crisis; and in the Baltic countries, the effect occurs earlier (in 2008–2009) and lasts longer. However, for the latter group of countries, the returning rate stabilizes at its lowest percentage toward the end of the period considered. Previous studies analyzing home-leaving have shown that in Southern European countries, late home-leaving contributes to a lower probability of returning (Iacovou and Parisi 2009). We find instead that returning home has increased in Southern countries and that this trend has been exacerbated by the Great Recession. In these countries, young people are less likely to be entitled to welfare benefits/assistance compared to their Continental counterparts; moreover, living with parents is more socially acceptable in Southern countries so that they are more likely to return home during a long-term economic downturn.

The results regarding the effect of the Great Recession also hold after controlling for partnership and employment. Partnership has a strong effect on the probability of both leaving and returning home. Young people in a partnership are more likely to leave, just as young people not (or no longer) in a partnership are more likely to return home. Employment is a good predictor of leaving home in Continental and Southern countries, but it has an indirect effect through partnership on leaving home in the Baltic and Eastern European countries. Similarly, losing one's job increases the probability of returning home in Continental, Southern, and Baltic countries (the result also holds if we exclude inactives).

Our findings support the hypothesis that parental monetary resources play a crucial role in adulthood transitions. More than in previous recessions, the family plays a protective role, allowing their adult children to stay longer at home—that is, allowing young adults to overcome the economic difficulties faced during the Great Recession. This is noticeable especially in those countries (i.e., Continental countries, in our study) where economic independence is highly valued (both by parents and by children) and school-to-work transitions tend to be smoother. In these countries, it is relatively uncommon for older youth to live with their parents; therefore, staying at home longer might imply a higher psychological cost for both parents and adult children. Conversely, in those countries where cultural norms render it socially acceptable for older youth to live with their parents, the psychological costs of postponing home-leaving because of the difficulties faced by young people in the labor market might be lower.

NOTES

1 Four Continental countries (AT, BE, FR, and LU), four Southern countries (CY, ES, IT, and PT), three Eastern countries (CZ, PL, and SI), and three Baltic countries (EE, LT, and LV).

2 Individuals in a partnership are defined here as people who are either married or cohabiting.

3 See, for instance, for Europe: Iacovou and Parisi (2009); and for the United States: DaVanzo and Goldscheider (1990), Goldscheider and Goldscheider (1999), Kaplan (2009), Dettling and Hsu (2014), and Lei and South (2016). For specific European countries, see Konietzka and Huinink (2003); Konietzka (2010); Stone, Berrington, and Falkingham (2012, 2014); and Berngruber (2015).

4 The "turning point" is a key concept in life course theory, referring to an event, an experience, or a change in circumstances that significantly alters the individual's subsequent life course trajectory (Stone et al. 2012).

5 We selected 14 countries because of data restrictions. We excluded countries that are not included in all the waves from 2005 to 2013 (BG, CH, HR, IE, MT, RO, and TR). Greece had to be excluded because of missing information for some key variables. The Nordic countries (DK, FI, IS, NO, and SE) were excluded because of their sampling design strategy, which is not suitable for our dynamic approach. Another four countries (HU, NL, SK, and UK) were excluded because they do not collect net personal income for all the waves, and this is one of the key variables in the empirical analysis.

6 For each panel, the same individuals were tracked for a maximum of 4 years.

7 The nature of the data does not permit a distinction between those who have left home for the first time and those who had previously left, subsequently returned, and then left a second time.

8 Because of the relatively short observation period, we do not know when exactly the young people in this sample left the parental home; we only know that they left home some time previously and have now returned.

9 Students may bias the results because their attitude toward living arrangements is different across countries. In some countries, it is common for students to leave home and then return after getting a degree. In other countries, young people stay at home to complete their tertiary education, which increases the share of individuals living in the parental home only for education purposes. We are not interested here in leaving and/or returning for educational reasons.

10 The differences between the two percentages at the beginning and at the end of the period (2005–2006 and 2012–2013) are statistically significant at the

1% level—except for the Eastern countries, for which the statistical significance is at the 5% level.

11 Between 2011 and 2012, the decrease is significant at the 1% level for both
Continental and Southern countries, and for the entire sample.

12 The mean differences are statistically significant in almost all the periods for
the Continental and the Southern countries. There are significant differences
only in some years in the Eastern and in the Baltic countries.

13 The differences are all statistically significant at the 1% level.

14 In the Eastern countries, the differences are not statistically significant for
either leavers or stayers across the period observed.

15 See Mazzotta and Parisi (2016) for descriptive statistics on different
destinations after leaving.

16 The differences are statistically significant at the 1% level.

17 As argued in Section 11.2, it is not possible to control for housing conditions
given that data on housing markets are not easily available for a large number
of EU countries or over time.

18 The maximum likelihood estimates of the implied trinomial probit model
differ sharply from those obtained when either being employed or household
membership is taken as exogenous (McElroy 1985).

19 Estimates for the probability of being employed and being in a partnership
are available from the authors on request.

20 Accordingly, the overall likelihood ratio test of $\rho_{21} = \rho_{31} = \rho_{32} = 0$ is always not
accepted with Prob $> \chi^2 = 0.0000$.

REFERENCES

Aassve, Arnstein, Francesco C. Billari, Stefano Mazzuco, and Fausta Ongaro.
2002. "Leaving Home: A Comparative Analysis of ECHP Data." *Journal of
European Social Policy* 12 (4): 259–75.

Aassve, Arnstein, Elena Cottini, and Agnese Vitali. 2013. "Youth Vulnerability
in Europe During the Great Recession." Dondena Working Paper 57.
Milan: Università Bocconi.

Anca, Ionete. 2012. "The Worlds of Flexicurity—Labour Market Policies in
Europe." *Annals of Faculty of Economics, University of Oradea* 1 (1): 133–38.

Andrew, Mark. 2010. "The Changing Route to Owner Occupation: The Impact of
Student Debt." *Housing Studies* 25 (1): 39–62.

Ayllón, Sara. 2015. "Youth Poverty, Employment, and Leaving the Parental Home
in Europe." *Review of Income and Wealth* 61 (4): 651–76.

Berngruber, Anne. 2015. "'Generation Boomerang' in Germany? Returning
to the Parental Home in Young Adulthood." *Journal of Youth Studies* 18
(10): 1274–90.

Berrington, Ann, Juliet Stone, and Jane Falkingham. 2013. "The Impact of Parental Characteristics and Contextual Effects on Returns to the Parental Home in Britain." ESRC-CPC Working Paper 29. Southampton: ESRC Centre for Population Change.

Billari, Francesco. 2004. "Becoming an Adult in Europe: A Macro(/Micro)-Demographic Perspective." *Demographic Research* 3 (2): 15–44.

Billari, Francesco, Dimiter Philipov, and Pau Baizán. 2001. "Leaving Home in Europe: The Experience of Cohorts Born Around 1960." *International Journal of Population Geography* 7 (5): 339–56.

Boyd, Monica, and Edward Pryor. 1989. "The Cluttered Nest: The Living Arrangements of Young Canadian Adults." *Canadian Journal of Sociology* 14 (4): 461–77.

Chiuri, Maria Concetta, and Daniela Del Boca. 2010. "Home-Leaving Decisions of Daughters and Sons." *Review of Economics of the Household* 8 (3): 393–408.

Clapham, David, Peter Mackie, Scott Orford, Kelly Buckley, and Ian Thomas. 2012. "Housing Options and Solutions for Young People in 2020." Joseph Rowntree Foundation Report. York: Joseph Rowntree Foundation.

DaVanzo, Julie, and Frances Kobrin Goldscheider. 1990. "Coming Home Again: Returns to the Parental Home of Young Adults." *Population Studies* 44 (2): 241–55.

Dettling, Lisa J., and Joanne W. Hsu. 2014. "Returning to the Nest: Debt and Parental Co-Residence Among Young Adults." FEDS Working Paper 80. Washington, DC: Federal Reserve Board.

Ermisch, John. 1999. "Prices, Parents, and Young People's Household Formation." *Journal of Urban Economics* 45 (1): 47–71.

Esping-Andersen, Gøsta. 1999. *Social Foundations of Postindustrial Economies.* Oxford: Oxford University Press.

Eurofound. 2014. *Mapping Youth Transitions in Europe.* Luxembourg: Publications Office of the European Union.

European Commission. 2006. *Employment in Europe 2006.* Luxembourg: Office for Official Publications of the European Communities.

European Commission. 2007. Employment in Europe 2007. Luxembourg: Office for Official Publications of the European Communities.

European Commission. 2014. "The Effect of the Crisis on Young People's Ability to Live Independently." Research Note 5. Brussels: European Commission.

Eurostat. 2009. "Eurostat Archive: Youth in Europe." http://ec.europa. eu/eurostat/statistics-explained/index.php?title=Archive:Youth_in_ Europe&oldid=214773#Further_Eurostat_information

Gökşen, Fatoş, Deniz Yükseker, Alpay Filiztekin, İbrahim Öker, Sinem Kuz, Fernanda Mazzotta, and Lavinia Parisi. 2016. "Leaving and Returning to the Parental Home During the Economic Crisis." STYLE Working Paper 8.3. Brighton, UK: CROME, University of Brighton. http://www.style-research. eu/publications/working-papers

Goldscheider, Frances Kobrin, and Calvin Goldscheider. 1999. *The Changing Transition to Adulthood: Leaving and Returning Home*. Thousand Oaks: Sage.

Hank, Karsten. 2007. "Proximity and Contacts Between Older Parents and Their Children: A European Comparison." *Journal of Marriage and Family* 69 (1): 157–73.

Iacovou, Maria. 2002. "Regional Differences in the Transition to Adulthood." *Annals of the American Academy of Political and Social Science* 580: 40–69.

Iacovou, Maria. 2010. "Leaving Home: Independence, Togetherness and Income in Europe." *Advances in Life Course Research* 15 (4): 147–60.

Iacovou, Maria, and Lavinia Parisi. 2009. "Leaving Home." In *Changing Relationships*, edited by John Ermisch and Malcolm Brynin, 59–72. New York: Routledge.

Jacob, Marita, and Corinna Kleinert. 2008. "Does Unemployment Help or Hinder Becoming Independent? The Role of Employment Status for Leaving the Parental Home." *European Sociological Review* 24 (2): 141–53.

Jones, Gill. 1995. *Leaving Home*. Buckingham, UK: Open University Press.

Kaplan, Greg. 2009. "Boomerang Kids: Labor Market Dynamics and Moving Back Home." Working Paper 675. Minneapolis: Federal Reserve Bank.

Konietzka, Dirk. 2010. *Zeiten des Übergangs. Sozialer Wandel des Übergangs in das Erwachsenenalter*. Wiesbaden: VS Verlag für Sozialwissenschaften.

Konietzka, Dirk, and Johannes Huinink. 2003. "Die De-Standardisierung einer Statuspassage? Zum Wandel des Auszugs aus dem Elternhaus und des Übergangs in das Erwachsenenalter in Westdeutschland." *Soziale Welt* 54 (3): 285–312.

Le Mare, Ann, Buapun Promphaking, and Jonathan Rigg. 2015. "Returning Home: The Middle-Income Trap and Gendered Norms in Thailand." *Journal of International Development* 27 (2): 285–306.

Lei, Lei, and Scott South. 2016. "Racial and Ethnic Differences in Leaving and Returning to the Parental Home." *Demographic Research* 34 (January): 109–42.

Manacorda, Marco, and Enrico Moretti. 2006. "Why Do Most Italian Youths Live with Their Parents? Intergenerational Transfers and Household Structure." *Journal of the European Economic Association* 4 (4): 800–29.

Martins, Nuno, and Ernesto Villanueva. 2006. "Does Limited Access to Mortgage Debt Explain Why Young Adults Live with Their Parents?" Documentos de Trabajo 0628. Madrid: Banco de España.

Mazzotta, Fernanda, and Lavinia Parisi. 2015a. "The Effect of Employment on Leaving Home in Italy." CRISEI Discussion Paper 08. Naples: University of Naples Parthenope.

Mazzotta, Fernanda, and Lavinia Parisi. 2015b. "Leaving Home and Poverty Before and After the Economic Crisis in Southern European Countries." In *Youth and the Crisis*, edited by Gianluigi Coppola and Niall O'Higgins, 170–94. Oxford: Routledge.

Mazzotta, Fernanda, and Lavinia Parisi. 2016. "What Are the Role of Economic Factors in Determining Leaving and Returning to the Parental Home in Europe During the Crisis?" STYLE Working Paper 8.3.2. Brighton, UK: CROME, University of Brighton. http://www.style-research.eu/publications/working-papers

McElroy, Marjorie B. 1985. "The Joint Determination of Household Membership and Market Work: The Case of Young Men." *Journal of Labor Economics* 3 (3): 293–316.

Mitchell, Barbara, Andrew V. Wister, and Ellen M. Gee. 2000. "Culture and Co-Residence: An Exploration of Variation in Home-Returning Among Canadian Young Adults." *Canadian Review of Sociology* 37 (2): 197–222.

Mulder, Clara H., and Michael Wagner. 1993. "Migration and Marriage in the Life Course: A Method for Studying Synchronized Events." *European Journal of Population* 9 (1): 55–76.

O'Higgins, Niall. 2006. "Still with Us After All These Years: Trends in Youth Labour Market Entry, Home-Leaving and Human Capital Accumulation in Italy 1993–2003." CELPE Discussion Paper 99. Salerno: University of Salerno.

Ongaro, Fausta, Stefano Mazzuco, and Silvia Meggiolaro. 2009. "Economic Consequences of Union Dissolution in Italy: Findings from the European Community Household Panel." *European Journal of Population* 25 (1): 45–65.

Plantenga, Janneke, Chantal Remery, and Manuela Samek Lodovici. 2013. "Starting Fragile: Gender Differences in the Youth Labour Market." Luxembourg: Publications Office of the European Union.

Reher, David Sven. 1998. "Family Ties in Western Europe: Persistent Contrasts." *Population and Development Review* 24 (2): 203–34.

Saraceno, Chiara. 2015. *Il lavoro non basta: La povertà in Europa negli anni della crisi*. Milano: Feltrinelli.

Settersten, Richard A., and Barbara Ray. 2010. "What's Going on with Young People Today? The Long and Twisting Path to Adulthood." *The Future of Children* 20 (1): 19–41.

Siegers, Jacques, Jenny de Jong-Gierveld, and Evert van Imhoff. 1991. *Female Labour Market Behaviour and Fertility: A Rational-Choice Approach.* Berlin: Springer.

Stone, Juliet, Ann Berrington, and Jane Falkingham. 2012. "Is the Boomerang Generation of Young Adults a Real Phenomenon? Returning Home in Young Adulthood in the UK." Paper presented at the European Population Conference, Stockholm, June 2012.

Stone, Juliet, Ann Berrington, and Jane Falkingham. 2014. "Gender, Turning Points, and Boomerangs: Returning Home in Young Adulthood in Great Britain." *Demography* 51 (1): 257–76.

12
INCOME SHARING AND SPENDING DECISIONS OF YOUNG PEOPLE LIVING WITH THEIR PARENTS

Márton Medgyesi and Ildikó Nagy

12.1. INTRODUCTION

Co-residence rates have increased in many countries during the economic downturn (Aassve, Cottini, and Vitali 2013) as the crisis has induced young adults to postpone leaving the parental home or, in some cases, even to return there (see Mazzotta and Parisi, this volume). In order to evaluate the consequences of rising co-residence with parents for the income situation and material well-being of young adults, one needs to understand how incomes are shared in such households. This chapter provides quantitative evidence on how young adults in co-residence with their parents participate in household finances—an issue that is rarely studied in the literature.[1]

Studies analyzing poverty—including those on youth poverty—are based on the usual assumption that income is shared equally among members of the same household. This literature thus typically neglects the issue of income sharing within households and assumes the nonexistence of intra-household inequality. The literature on household money management most often studies couples, whereas evidence—especially of a quantitative nature—is scarce regarding other household types, including households in which parents live together with adult children. Research in demography and related disciplines (family sociology and population economics) studies the timing and determinants of the transition to independent living, whereas literature on household money management in co-residential living is scarce.

This chapter examines the extent to which young adults living with their parents contribute to household expenses and also the extent to which they are able to decide autonomously about their expenses on personal consumption and leisure activities. The analysis is based on data covering 17 European countries from the European Union Statistics on Income and Living Conditions (EU-SILC 2010 special module) on intra-household sharing of resources. The chapter also explores the implications of taking into account intra-household sharing of resources for the assessment of the income situation of the young. In particular, we investigate the roles of absolute household income, household members' economic needs, and relative income in shaping the observed patterns, also describing cross-country differences.

The study finds that income sharing in the household tends to attenuate income differences between household members and tends to help household members with low resources. The study also finds that there are inequalities in young adults' experience of co-residence with parents: young adults in low-income households tend to contribute more to the household finances and to enjoy less independence in their consumption and leisure decisions. Our results also show that although the majority of young adults benefit from intra-household sharing of resources, there is a smaller group of young adults who tend to support their parents in the sense that their contribution to the household budget is higher. The most significant cross-country differences can be seen between the Eastern European and the other European countries, with young adults in Eastern Europe making higher contributions to the household budget and having less independence in consumption decisions.

The following section presents the related literature and formulates hypotheses about the determinants behind the contributions of young adults to household budgets and about the financial independence of young adults living in the parental home. In Section 12.3, we present the data and the methods used in the analysis. Section 12.4 presents our results concerning the determinants of young adults' contributions to household budgets and their ability to decide about personal spending. In Section 12.5, we attempt to evaluate the effect of taking into account survey results regarding intra-household sharing of income in the estimation of the income situation of young adults. Section 12.6 concludes the chapter.

12.2. LITERATURE REVIEW AND HYPOTHESES

In many advanced societies, the transition from adolescence to independent adulthood has become a slower and more variable process. This prolonged life phase between adolescence and adulthood often goes together with longer periods of co-residence between young adults and their parents.

Co-residential living arrangements can be the result of different life course trajectories, however. These include both adult children who have never left the parental home and those who have returned home after finishing education, after divorcing, or during spells of unemployment ("boomerang kids"). Finally, there are also cases in which a parent moves in with an adult child (Dykstra et al. 2013). Co-residence can be particularly important in times of crisis, when staying with or moving back to one's parents' home can be an element of the "safety net" provided by the family (Mazzotta and Parisi, this volume). Studies such as those by Aassve, Iacovou, and Mencarini (2006) and Aassve et al. (2007) show that co-residence can protect the young from falling into poverty.[2]

The benefits of co-residence for the young adult are the support, security, and company that living at home provides, as well as the financial advantages of such an arrangement. Co-residence with parents may imply some financial benefits for the young as they save on paying for rent and utilities, can enjoy better housing standards than they could otherwise afford, and the household can also benefit from economies of scale. On the other hand, co-residence with parents inevitably entails lower levels of autonomy compared to independent living (White 2002; Sassler, Ciambrone, and Benway 2008). The young adult has to accept the rules of the parental house and has to accept some parental oversight over work/education, free time, social activities, and also money spending. In many cases, the parents ask their young adult children to pay for room and board and/or to do housework.

The monetary contributions that young adults make when living in the parental home are rarely studied in the literature. For instance, the literature on income distribution and poverty generally assumes that income (or economic well-being) is shared equally among members of the same household and that an individual cannot be poor when living in a household that has adequate income. Although several studies suggest that significant inequalities might exist within the same family (e.g., Haddad and Kanbur 1990), the assumption of equal sharing is adopted by most of the studies, including those on poverty among young adults (e.g., Aassve et al. 2006, 2013; Ward et al. 2012).

Most of the research on the living arrangements of young adults concerns the timing and determinants of the transition to independent living, whereas literature on financial arrangements in co-residential living and how such households manage finances is scarce. Several studies assume that an intensive monetary exchange is taking place between parents and their adult children when they live in the same household—without explicitly analyzing such an exchange (White 1994).[3] Financial arrangements in multigenerational households are not at the focus of the literature on intra-household inequality, nor is money management, because this literature tends to analyze couple households (Yodanis and Lauer 2007; Nagy, Medgyesi, and Lelkes 2012).

A central concept of the literature on intra-household inequality is "pooling of incomes." Full pooling of incomes means that all incomes of all household members are pooled and all members have full access to the pooled income. Partial pooling means that household members contribute only a share of their own income to the household budget and keep the rest (Ponthieux 2013). Here, we are interested in financial arrangements between young adults and their parents living in the same household. Specifically, we study the extent to which young adults pool their incomes with other household members or keep their incomes separate. We describe the determinants of young adults' contributions to the household budget and assess their effects on the measurement of intra-household inequality. In the following, we formulate hypotheses regarding the determinants of young adults' contributions to household budgets when they are co-residing with their parents.

12.2.1. Household Income and Young Adults' Contributions

The overall level of monetary resources in the household is said to shape households' money management strategies (Yodanis and Lauer 2007). For poor households, making ends meet (paying utility bills and having money at the end of the month) requires the careful management of the totality of household incomes. Under a certain level of household income, there is no "discretionary" income that household members can keep for themselves. Thus, we expect that in low-income households, the young adult members will keep a lower share of their income separate and will contribute more to the common budget. In parallel, we expect that young adults in poorer households will have less control over spending decisions (*hypothesis H1*).

12.2.2. Household Members' Lack of Resources and Young Adults' Contributions

Both economic theories of altruistic transfers (Cox 1987) and sociological theories about contingent transfers (Swartz et al. 2011) imply that household members will be inclined, when they can, to help other members in need of monetary support. Thus, we expect that young adults will increase their contributions to the household budget when their parents have insufficient economic resources—for instance, when the parent is single, when parents have no work, or when parents live with health limitations. On the other hand, young adults' contributions to the household budget should be lower when they find themselves in difficult life circumstances and with insufficient resources. Such difficulties might arise from an unfavorable labor market situation (e.g., in the case of students or unemployed young people) or might also be associated with certain stages of the life course—for instance, young adults with dependent children may be more in need of support (Schenk, Dykstra, and Maas 2010) (*hypothesis H2*).

12.2.3. Relative Income and Young Adults' Contributions

The relative income of household members is assumed to influence intra-household income allocation. According to altruistic theories of intra-household transfers, a skewed distribution of income in the household would increase the incentive of the higher earning household member to pool re-sources and help household members with lower incomes (Cox 1987; Bennett 2013). When a young adult's income is significantly lower than that of his or her parents, this implies a lower contribution to the household budget by the young adult and higher contributions from the parents. When the income dis-tribution of the household is more equilibrated, contributions to the house-hold budget should be more equilibrated as well; thus, higher relative income of young adults should go together with higher contributions to the house-hold budget (*hypothesis H3*).

12.2.4. Cross-Country Differences in Young Adults' Contributions

Cross-country differences in household financial arrangements between young adults and their parents might be expected for several reasons. First, differing patterns of nest leaving and co-residence lead to differences in the composition of the young adult population living with their parents. As the literature documents (Mulder 2009), young adults tend to leave the parental nest later in the Southern than in the Northern European countries, where young adults tend to leave the parental home early (in their early twenties).[4] Western Europe occupies an intermediate position between these two country groups, whereas co-residence rates are relatively high in Eastern European countries (Dykstra et al. 2013). The composition of the young population still living at home is thus likely to be very different across countries, which could be partly responsible for cross-country differences in contributions to the household budget.

Cross-country differences in income sharing in households might also be linked to differences in family norms. For instance, Reher (1998) describes the Southern European countries as "strong family countries," where kin relations and family solidarity are of prime importance. By contrast, in Western and Northern European countries, more individualistic conceptions of the family prevail, and the norm prescribes that young adults should attain economic in-dependence and leave the parental home at an early age. In more individual-istic countries, young adults are expected to be independent in their decisions regarding leisure and consumption and could also be more likely to contribute to the household budget (*hypothesis H4*).

12.3. DATA AND METHODOLOGICAL ISSUES

This study uses data for 17 European countries from the EU-SILC 2010 ad hoc module on intra-household sharing of resources in the EU. This module contains household-level and individual-level questions about management of household finances, covering aspects of income pooling and decision-making about expenses and savings. Two questions are particularly relevant for our research topic because they provide substantial information on two dependent variables.

The first dependent variable in our analysis measures the degree to which respondents contribute to the household budget. The survey question PA010 asks respondents, "What is the share of income kept separate from the household budget?" According to the survey description, income that is kept separate from the "common household pot" is viewed by the respondent to be his or hers and can be used as he or she wishes (Eurostat 2010). By "common household budget," the survey means expenses and savings not primarily concerning one person only in the household. The following responses were coded on a 5-point scale: (1) all my personal income, (2) more than half, (3) about half, (4) less than half, (5) none, and (6) no personal income.

The second dependent variable measures the extent to which other household members (in this case, parents) have control over the spending decisions of young adults. The relevant question (PA090) asks about the "ability to decide about expenses for personal consumption, leisure activities, hobbies." The response categories are the following: (1) yes, always, almost always; (2) yes, sometimes; and (3) never or almost never. Here, we reverse the coding of this item and use the recoded version as a second dependent variable in our analysis. One way parents can gain control over the spending decisions of young adults is to ask for monetary contributions to the household budget. Thus, young adults who contribute a high share of their income to the household budget will have less opportunity to decide about spending on personal consumption.

We restricted our analysis to 17 EU countries representing different geographical areas in Europe.[5] The analysis includes 3 countries from Western Europe (Belgium and Luxembourg together with Germany in the case of the first dependent variable and together with Ireland in the case of the second dependent variable), 6 countries from Southern Europe (Cyprus, Greece, Italy, Malta, Portugal, and Spain), 3 countries from Central–Eastern Europe (Czech Republic, Hungary, and Slovakia), 3 Baltic states (Estonia, Latvia, and Lithuania), and 2 countries from Southeastern Europe (Bulgaria and Romania). Our analysis studies young adults in the 18- to 34-year-old age group and their households in all these countries.

In the following, we present the measurement of the key explanatory variables that are used in the multivariate analysis to investigate the hypotheses described previously.

Absolute income of the household is measured using total equivalent household income. In order to focus on within-country differences in income, we divided equivalent household income by the median of the given country and used the logarithm of income divided by the country median as an explanatory variable.

Lack of personal resources concerns household members who find themselves in difficult life circumstances with insufficient personal resources for various reasons. Here, we consider three types of such situations: labor market difficulties (e.g., unemployment), difficulties related to family structure (e.g., having dependent children or being single), and difficulties arising from poor health conditions. In the case of young adults, these are captured by measures of labor market status (five categories: working full-time, working part-time, unemployed, student, and other nonworking) and of whether they have children in the household (dummy variable).[6] In the case of parents, difficulties are captured by measures of parental labor market status (three categories of parental work intensity:[7] 0–0.5, 0.5–0.99, and 1), health status (dummy variable showing whether either of the parents is seriously limited in daily activities because of health problems), and parental family status (three categories: single mother, single father, or both parents—or one parent with a partner—live in the household).

Relative income is measured by the personal income of the young adults relative to the average income of their parents. When calculating relative income, all income types that are recorded at an individual level in the EU-SILC data set (income from employment, self-employment, unemployment benefits, old-age and survivors' benefits, sickness and disability benefits, and education-related allowances) were included. Relative income was then transformed into a five-category variable: The first category is composed of young adults with incomes below 30% of average parental income; in the second group, young adults have 31%–50% of average parental income; in the third, young adults have 50%–80% of parental income; the fourth category consists of cases in which young adults have income roughly equal to that of average parental income (between 80% and 120%); and the fifth category is made up of cases in which young adults have higher incomes than those of their parents (above 120%).

12.4. DETERMINANTS OF FINANCIAL ARRANGEMENTS

In this section, we first provide some descriptive statistics about young adults who are living in the parental household in 17 EU countries. We then show differences in our two dependent variables before proceeding with the description of the results of the multivariate analysis. Finally, we analyze cross-country differences in household financial arrangements.

12.4.1. Young Adults Living in the Parental Home in Europe

The share of young adults living at their parents' home varies significantly across the countries covered by the study. Among those in the 18- to 24-year-old age group, the great majority of young adults (more than 75%) are still living in the parental home in all countries. The highest percentage of co-resident young adults in this age group can be found in Slovakia (96%), whereas the lowest is found in Germany (78%). One can find more important differences between the country groups regarding co-residence with parents in the 25- to 34-year-old age group. In this group, the percentage of those living with their parents is lowest in Germany and Belgium (13%–17%), whereas the highest percentages are found in Slovakia, Bulgaria, Malta, and Greece, where more than half of those in this age group are living in the parental home.

Differences in the share of co-resident youth lead to differences in the composition of the population of young adults living with parents. Because this population is typically older in the case of the Southern and Southeastern European countries, it is not surprising that a relatively high percentage of them have a job, whereas the percentage of students is lower compared to Western European countries. The percentage of working youth is highest among those residing in the parental home in Malta (61%), Portugal (53%), and Greece (48%).

Differences in the age and labor market status of co-resident young adults lead to differences between countries in terms of their relative income situation. The relative income situation of the young adult is described by comparing his or her personal income with the average income of parents, as described in the methodological section (see Figure 12.1). Whereas the majority of youth aged 18–24 years have a lower income compared to their parents in every country, in the case of the 25- to 34-year-old age group, this is only true for 5 out of 17 countries. The share of young adults who have similar or higher income compared to their parents is lowest in Germany, whereas it is highest in Malta. There is considerable variation among Western European and Southern European countries. Belgium and Luxembourg, unlike Germany, have a relatively high percentage of young adults with similar or higher income compared to their parents, whereas—except for Malta—the other Southern European countries do not exhibit high percentages in this regard.

12.4.2. Descriptive Analysis

Our first dependent variable describes the proportion of youth personal income that is contributed to the household budget and not kept separately. Figure 12.2 shows the percentage of those contributing at least half of their income to the

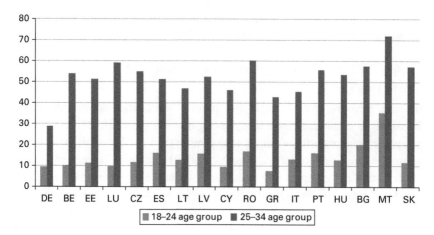

Figure 12.1 Percentage of young adults with income higher than 80% of average parental income in 17 EU countries, 2010.
Source: Authors' calculations based on the EU-SILC 2010 ad hoc module on intra-household sharing of resources.

household budget in the countries included in the analysis (the whole distribution is shown in Table A12.1 in the Appendix). In all countries, only a minority of young adults contribute at least half of their incomes. The percentage of young adults contributing at least half of their income is highest in Romania (44%), Bulgaria (37%), Hungary (34%), and Latvia (30%). The lowest figures are found in the Western European countries (5%–10%), whereas the Southern European

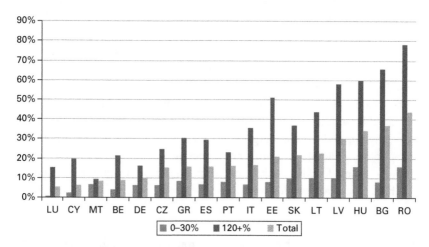

Figure 12.2 Percentage of young adults (aged 18–34 years) contributing at least half of income to household budget by relative income in 17 EU countries, 2010.
Source: Authors' calculations based on the EU-SILC 2010 ad hoc module on intra-household sharing of resources.

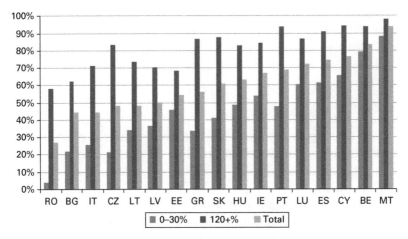

Figure 12.3 Percentage of young adults (aged 18–34 years) always able to decide about personal spending by relative income in 17 EU countries, 2010.
Source: Authors' calculations based on the EU-SILC 2010 ad hoc module on intra-household sharing of resources.

countries are in between (approximately 16% or 17%), with the exception of Cyprus and Malta, where the percentage is lower.

The second dependent variable shows whether young adults are able to decide about spending on their personal consumption, hobbies, and so forth. Figure 12.3 shows the percentage of those who are always able to decide about this issue (the whole distribution is shown in Table A12.2 in the Appendix). The highest percentage is found in Malta, where 94% of young adults are always able to decide about spending on personal consumption, and the second highest percentage is detected in Belgium (84%). In Cyprus, Spain, and Luxembourg, this is true for 72%–76% of young adults, whereas in Portugal, Hungary, Slovakia, and Ireland, the percentage of those who are always able to decide is somewhat lower (61%–69%). The lowest figure is found in Romania, where only 27% of young adults responded that they are always able to decide about their personal expenses. The second lowest figure is found in both Bulgaria and Italy, where 44% of young adults who live with their parents are always able to decide about spending on personal consumption. In this case, there is thus more heterogeneity within country groups, especially in the case of the Southern and Central–Eastern European countries.

Figures 12.2 and 12.3 also show the association between our dependent variables and the income of young adults relative to their parents. In every case, there is a clear correlation between relative income and contribution to household expenses. Young adults who have higher income relative to their parents are more likely to contribute more than half of their income to the household budget compared to young adults who have low income relative to their parents. At the same time, it is also true that young adults with high income relative to their parents are more likely to be able to decide about spending on personal consumption. The descriptive evidence thus supports our hypothesis regarding the role of relative income. In the following multivariate analysis, we investigate our hypotheses while taking into account cross-country differences in the composition of our sample.

12.4.3. Multivariate Analysis

To study our hypotheses about the determinants of young adults' financial contributions to the household, and their ability to decide about personal expenses, ordinal probit regressions were run on pooled models with country dummies included.

In addition to the main explanatory variables described previously (measuring need for support, absolute income, and relative income position), the models control for variables that have been identified by the literature as affecting income sharing in households. The first group of controls are basic sociodemographic variables: gender (Ward and Spitze 1996), age, and education. According to Bonke and Uldall-Poulsen (2007), income pooling will be more frequent when there is a need for partners to coordinate their economic behavior. A case of coordination that is relevant to our research topic is that of common goods in the household (e.g., shared rental of an apartment and shared car). In our analysis, we control for tenure status of the dwelling where the household is living (three categories: owner occupied/rented for free, rented at reduced rate, and rented at market price). To quantify crowding in the household, we also include a measure of the number of rooms per household member. Other controls included in the analysis are parental migrant status and parental contributions to the household budget. Migrant origin was defined as those born in a country different from the country of residence, and we also measure the share of parental income contributed to the household budget by parents. It can be expected that, ceteris paribus, the contribution of the young adult will be higher in households in which there is a norm of income pooling, where parents pool a large share of their incomes.

Regarding our first dependent variable—which measures the monetary contributions of young adults to the household budget as a percentage of their income—the estimated coefficients for all explanatory variables are shown in Table A12.3 in the Appendix. To assess the magnitude of the effects, Table 12.1 provides average marginal effects of the most important explanatory variables on the probability that a young adult will contribute all personal income to the household budget (this is the highest category of the dependent variable). In Model 1, the sample has been restricted to young adults with positive income because respondents with zero income cannot contribute to the household budget. As a robustness analysis, we also run the same model on the sample of those aged 25–34 years (Model 2) because this is the age group for which the issue of

Table 12.1 Dependent variable: Proportion of co-resident young adults' (aged 18–34 years) personal income contributed to common household budget, average marginal effects on the probability of "contributing all personal income" for selected explanatory variables, 2010

	Model 1: Those with positive income	Model 2: Those aged 25–34 years	Model 3: All those aged 18–34 years
Log household income	−0.0212***	−0.0170***	−0.0090***
Young adult's relative income			
0%–30%	0	0	0
30%–50%	0.0306***	0.0554***	0.0424***
50%–80%	0.0392***	0.0622***	0.0482***
80%–120%	0.0432***	0.0687***	0.0506***
120+%	0.0411***	0.0684***	0.0485***
Young adult's labor market status			
Works full-time	0	0	0
Works part-time	−0.0060	0.0041	0.0011
Unemployed	−0.0604***	−0.0690***	−0.0590***
Student	−0.0782***	−0.0762***	−0.0731***
No work, other	−0.0041	−0.0170	−0.0264***
Partner in household	0.0774***	0.0793***	0.0519***
Child in household	0.0413***	0.0449***	0.0389***
Number of parents in household			
Only mother	0	0	0
Only father	−0.0073	−0.0158	−0.0089
Two parents	−0.0528***	−0.0475***	−0.0388***
Parental work intensity			
0–0.5	0	0	0
0.5–0.99	−0.0042	−0.0002	−0.0032
1	−0.0082*	−0.0035	−0.0053*
Parental health limitations	0.0000	−0.0044	0.0030

Note: Pooled models include all controls and country dummies (see Table A12.3 in the Appendix).
*$p < .10$.
**$p < .05$.
***$p < .01$.
Source: Authors' calculations based on the EU-SILC 2010 ad-hoc module on intra-household sharing of resources in 17 EU countries.

monetary contributions is more relevant. We also present results on the entire sample of those aged 18–34 years living in the parental home (Model 3).

The results confirm the role of absolute household income, which has a statistically negative effect: The higher the household income, the lower is the probability of young adults contributing significantly to the household budget. Hypothesis H1 about the role of absolute income is thus confirmed. The variables related to the lack of economic resources of young adults and their parents show mixed results. The results regarding the employment status of young adults are in line with our hypothesis H2. As Table 12.1 shows, students are 8 points less likely and unemployed youth are 6 points less likely to contribute all income compared to working young adults. Those neither in employment nor in education also have a lower probability of contributing to household expenses, but this is visible only in Model 3, which includes all members of the 18- to 34-year-old age group living in the parental home. Contrary to our expectations, having a child in the household actually increases the probability that the young adult will contribute all income to the household budget (by 4 points). This might be a result of more intensive reciprocity between parents and young adults with dependent children, where parents help with grandchild care and young adults increase monetary contributions to the household budget.

Also in line with hypothesis H2, young adults contribute a higher fraction of their income when the parent is single. The probability that the young adult contributes all personal income to the household budget is 5 points lower when both parents live in the household (or one parent with a spouse/partner). Contributions to household income are also less likely if parents work full-time during the whole year (work intensity equals 1). Contrary to our hypothesis, parental health problems are not associated with a higher probability of household budget contributions by young adults.

The relative income position of parents and the young is important in determining the contribution of young adults to the household budget. The higher the income of young adults compared to that of their parents, the higher the contributions they are likely to make to the household budget. Young adults whose incomes are between 31% and 50% of the average income of their parents are 3 points more likely to contribute all income to the household budget compared to young adults whose incomes amount to 30% or less of their parents' average income. Young adults whose incomes exceed 50% of average parental income are 4 points more likely to contribute all their income.

Most control variables exhibit the expected sign (see Table A12.3 in the Appendix, Model 1). Higher contributions to the household budget become more likely with age. Somewhat surprisingly, education level (ceteris paribus) has a negative effect: Those with tertiary education are less likely to make a higher contribution to the household budget. This might be a result of shorter labor market experience on the part of those with tertiary education. Young adults in migrant households make higher contributions to the household budget. The contribution to the household budget is larger if parents contribute more from their own incomes to the budget. The contribution is also higher if the apartment/house is rented compared to owner-occupied housing. Parental age, overcrowding (number of rooms per household member), and the number of young adults in the household have no significant effect.

We checked the robustness of our results concerning the determinants of young adults' financial contributions to households by estimating the pooled model for the sample of all young adults aged 25–34 years (Model 2 in Table 12.1). The reason for selecting this age group is that the issue of contribution to household expenses might be more meaningfully studied among those aged between 25 and 34 years because many of those aged between 18 and 24 years are still obtaining their education. Finally, we also estimated the model for all those aged between 18 and 34 years (Model 3 in Table 12.1). As can be seen from Table 12.1, the results obtained with different subsamples show similar signs and significance to the original estimates. In some cases, the magnitude of the effects seems to be different: for instance, total household income or the effect of having no partner in the household has a stronger effect on contribution to the household budget in the case of the subsamples.

Regarding our second dependent variable—which measures the freedom of young adults to decide about their personal expenses—detailed results are shown in Table A12.4 in the Appendix, and the average marginal effects for the most important explanatory variables can be found in Table 12.2. The first model includes only total household income, relative income, and country dummies on the right-hand side. In the second model, we add other explanatory variables that relate to young adults, whereas the third model also adds parental character-istics. Ability to decide about expenses on personal consumption is also related to the absolute income of the household: Young adults living in more affluent households are more likely to be able to decide about spending on personal con-sumption. This result thus confirms hypothesis H1, similarly to the case of our first dependent variable. The pattern among variables related to the lack of per-sonal resources is also similar. Part-time workers, the unemployed, students, and other inactive young adults are less likely to be able to decide about expenses on personal consumption compared to those who are working full-time. The effect of not working reduces the probability that the young adult is always able to de-cide about personal expenses by approximately 22–28 points. Having children decreases the probability that young adults can always decide about expenses on personal consumption, but the effect is not statistically significant. The variables measuring parental needs are expected to have a negative effect. This is con-firmed in the case of parental family status: When a young adult is living together with a single mother, the probability of being able to decide about expenses is lower. On the other hand, parents having health limitations does not have a sta-tistically significant effect. Relative income is also related to the ability to decide about personal consumption. In households in which the income of the young adult is roughly equal to or higher than the average income of parents, the young adult is 7 or 8 points more likely to be able to decide about expenses on personal

Table 12.2 Dependent variable: Ability of co-resident young adults (aged 18–34 years) to decide about expenses for personal consumption, average marginal effects on the probability of "always able to decide" for selected explanatory variables, 2010

	Model 1	Model 2	Model 3
Log household income	0.1417***	0.0762***	0.0630***
Relative income			
0%–30%	0	0	0
30%–50%	0.0896***	0.0207	0.0279*
50%–80%	0.1388***	0.0368**	0.0520***
80%–120%	0.1780***	0.0556***	0.0669***
120+%	0.2020***	0.0641***	0.0795***
Labor market status			
Works full-time		0	0
Works part-time		−0.0523**	−0.0539**
Unemployed		−0.2280***	−0.2205***
Student		−0.2348***	−0.2293***
No work, other		−0.2934***	−0.2823***
Partner in household		−0.0732***	−0.0841***
Child in household		−0.0126	−0.0051
Number of parents in household			
Only mother			0
Only father			0.0382
Two parents			0.0267**
Parental work intensity			
0–0.5			0
0.5–0.99			0.0276*
1			0.0063
Parental health limitations			0.0098

Note: Pooled models include country dummies and control variables (see Table A12.4 in the Appendix).
*$p < .10$.
**$p < .05$.
***$p < .01$.
Source: Authors' calculations based on the EU-SILC 2010 ad hoc module on intra-household sharing of resources in 17 EU countries.

consumption compared to young adults who have less than 30% of parental income. These results confirm hypothesis H3.

The results regarding the control variables are shown in Table A12.4 in the Appendix. There is no statistically significant effect of gender or age. Influence over decisions regarding personal consumption increases with educational attainment. Young adults living in more spacious housing are more likely to have influence over such decisions. Finally, the number of young adults in the household increases the likelihood that young adults can decide about expenses on personal consumption.

12.4.4. Differences Between Countries

We study differences between countries by examining estimates for country dummies in the pooled models. The country intercepts show the difference in the dependent variable that exists between the given country and the country of reference (Belgium) after controlling for a wide set of explanatory variables. Figure 12.4 shows the estimates of these country effects for the two dependent variables. According to the estimates, the probability that young adults contribute to the household budget is highest in Romania, Bulgaria, and Hungary. Other Eastern European countries and the Baltic states follow in the country ranking. The likelihood of contributions is, ceteris paribus, lowest in Luxembourg, Malta, and Cyprus. Germany and Belgium follow in the lower part of the country ranking, but Portugal, Spain, and Greece are also relatively close to these countries. It is clear from the figure that in the case of our two dependent variables, the country effects are negatively correlated: countries where young adults are less likely to contribute to the household budget are those where they are more likely to be able to decide about personal expenses. The main difference between the two

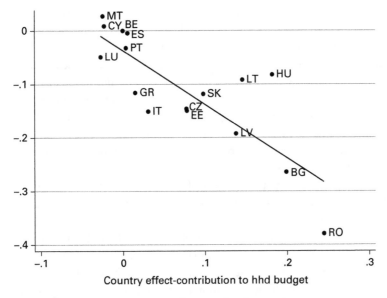

Figure 12.4 Differences between countries after controlling for covariates.
Source: Authors' calculations based on the EU-SILC 2010 ad hoc module on intra-household sharing of resources.

cases is that Greece and Italy are closer to the Eastern European countries in the case of the dependent variable on independence in consumption.

Overall, our results do not seem to show the expected pattern regarding cross-country differences, although information about more countries would be needed to properly test our fourth hypothesis. Our expectation was that more individualistic values in Western European countries would result in higher contributions to the household budget. In contrast to this, Belgium, Luxembourg, and Germany do not actually seem to be very different from the Southern European countries with regard to contributions to the household budget. The more important division seems to be between the Eastern European countries and the rest, with young adults being less independent and contributing more to household finances in Eastern Europe. This latter group seems to be heterogeneous, however, because Bulgaria and Romania show higher levels of contributions and lower levels of independence in consumption compared to other countries.

12.5. IMPACT OF TAKING ACCOUNT OF INTRA-HOUSEHOLD RESOURCE SHARING ON THE RELATIVE INCOMES OF THE YOUNG

As the last step in our analysis, we evaluate the consequences of taking into account intra-household sharing of resources on the income situation of young adults living together with their parents. Our method follows that of Ponthieux (2014), who constructs a measure of modified equivalized income, taking into account the intra-household sharing of income in households. In the usual calculation of household equivalized income, all incomes of all household members are added up and divided by the number of consumption units in the household. However, the modified equivalent income studied here takes into account the fact that household members pool only a part of their incomes. Pooled income (or "public" income) in a household is composed of the personal incomes of household members that are contributed to the household budget plus other household-level income types (e.g., income from capital or income from certain social transfers). The total income of a household member is the sum of an individual's personal income kept separate from the household budget plus his or her part of the public income of the household.[8] To divide the personal incomes of household members into income contributed to the household budget and income kept separate for personal purposes, one can make use of responses to the survey question discussed in Section 12.3 about the share of income kept separate from the household budget. To make a numeric illustration possible, one needs to make assumptions about the precise share of income corresponding to each of the response categories. Here, we assume that keeping less than half of income separate from the budget means keeping 25% of income for one's own use, whereas keeping more than half means keeping 75% of personal income separate from the household budget.

As discussed previously, the standard measure of equivalized income used in inequality and poverty measurement assumes full pooling of incomes of household members and thus assumes equality among household members. The modified measure of equivalized income allows household members to keep a certain part of their income separate from the household budget (partial pooling). Moving from the standard measure to the modified measure is "beneficial" to young adults if their modified equivalized income is higher than standard equivalized income. Whether moving to the modified measure is beneficial, neutral, or detrimental to young adults depends on the relative incomes of young adults and parents and on their relative contribution levels. The proportion of such cases in the sample studies is shown in Table 12.3.

Table 12.3 shows the distribution of young adults in these groups. In all countries, the majority of young adults would benefit from moving from the standard

Table 12.3 The effect of taking into account intra-household sharing on the incomes of young adults (aged 18–34 years) in 17 EU countries (%)

Country	Modified income lower than original equivalized income	Modified and original equivalized income equal	Modified income higher than equivalized income	Total
BE	15.9	7.5	76.7	100
BG	19.7	12.4	67.9	100
CZ	24.3	6.3	69.4	100
DE	18.3	12.9	68.7	100
EE	22.8	6.4	70.8	100
EL	24.8	6.3	68.9	100
ES	11.3	9.8	79.0	100
HU	15.1	17.0	67.9	100
IT	16.9	5.5	77.6	100
LT	15.5	10.3	74.2	100
LU	12.8	4.5	82.7	100
LV	27.7	6.7	65.5	100
MT	33.2	4.1	62.7	100
PT	18.1	9.5	72.5	100
RO	28.6	9.2	62.3	100
SK	30.2	5.9	63.9	100

Note: By equal is meant between ±2% of the original equivalized income.
Source: Authors' calculations based on the EU-SILC 2010 ad hoc module on intra-household sharing of resources.

equivalized income to the modified version. This is mainly due to the fact that parents typically contribute a higher share of their income to the household budget compared to young adults. The highest percentage of young adults who would end up with lower incomes under the modified version can be found in Malta (33%), Slovakia (30%), and Romania (29%), whereas the lowest figures were found for Spain (11%) and Luxembourg (13%).

The standard assumption of inequality and poverty studies about intra-household equality thus means that we underestimate the incomes of the majority of young adults living with their parents. In reality, their income situation is likely to be more favorable than shown by the conventional statistics. There is, however, a smaller group of this young adult population for which the conventional estimates overestimate true incomes. This group is in a minority, but it is far from negligible; indeed, in some countries, it is close to one-third of the young adult population still living in the parental home.

12.6. CONCLUSIONS

This study uses the 2010 EU-SILC special module on intra-household sharing of resources to shed light on practices of income sharing in households in which young adults live together with their parents. The chapter is novel in two respects. First, it provides new quantitative comparative evidence on how young adults in co-residence with their parents participate in household finances and also on their financial independence. Monetary exchanges in such households are rarely studied either in research on family processes or in the literature on intra-household allocation. In particular, we studied the main determinants—the role of absolute household income, the status of individual economic need by household members (parents and adult children), and the relative income of young adults—of the contributions of young adults to the household budget and their freedom to decide about personal spending. The study also tries to quantify the effect of taking into account intra-household income sharing on the measurement of the income situation of young adults.

Our findings on the determinants of contributions to household budgets and on the ability to decide about personal expenses broadly confirm our hypotheses about the effects of household income, relative income of household members, and household members' material needs. We found that income sharing in households tends to benefit household members in need and with low relative income. The young pay lower contributions when they are in need (e.g., unemployed or students), but they pay higher contributions if the parents are in need of support. Contributions to the household budget increase with the relative income of young adults, albeit sometimes non-monotonically. Overall, this pattern is consistent with the view that income sharing in the household tends to attenuate income differences between household members.

Although income sharing moderates differences within households, we found inequality between low- and high-income households in the extent to which young adults can benefit from intra-household transfers. In households with high absolute incomes, young adults contribute less to the household budget and are more free to decide about their personal expenses, whereas in low-income households, young adults contribute more to the household budget and have less independence in consumption decisions. Our hypothesis on cross-country differences was only partially confirmed. Young adults living in the parental home in Western European countries are the most independent in deciding about personal expenses, and they contribute less to the household budget. Moreover, Western European countries are not very different from some of the Southern European countries. The most important difference is between the Eastern European countries and the rest, with young adults being less independent and contributing more to household finances in Eastern Europe.

Our results show that the majority of young adults benefit from intra-household sharing of monetary resources compared to the conventional assumption of intra-household equality. This happens because parents typically have higher incomes than their young adult children and share a larger fraction of their incomes with other household members. There is, however, a smaller group of young adults (between 11% and 33%) who support their parents economically in the sense that their contribution to the household budget is higher. Overall, our results suggest that young adults have differing motivations for and experiences with co-residence with parents. Some young adults stay at home longer in order to enjoy better economic well-being, some stay at home longer as a strategy to overcome the difficulties faced in the labor market or on the housing market or both, whereas others stay at home longer in order to support their family of origin.

The 2010 special module of the EU-SILC on intra-household sharing of resources is a valuable data set for studying intra-household allocation, which is seldom covered by large comparative surveys. There are, however, certain drawbacks of the survey that impose constraints on the current study. One constraint is that we are unable to differentiate between different cases of co-residence, such as young adults returning to the parental home and young adults who have never left home. Another limitation is that the question about income sharing does not explicitly ask what percentage of their income respondents keep separate or put into the household budget, so assumptions are required when this information is used in calculations.

NOTES

1   Earlier versions of the chapter were presented at the International Sociological Association RC28 spring meeting in Budapest (May 8–10, 2014); at the STYLE

Project Consortium Meeting, Grenoble School of Management (March 23–24, 2015); and at various seminars. The authors benefitted from comments from the editors; from Fatoş Gökşen, Chiara Saraceno, András Gábos, and Gábor Hajdu; and also from conference and seminar participants. Research assistance was provided by Orsolya Mikecz. Financial support from Bolyai János Kutatási Ösztöndíj to Márton Medgyesi is gratefully acknowledged.

2 In the case of the United States, Kahn, Goldscheider, and García-Manglano (2013) affirm that young adults have become the more financially dependent generation in multigenerational households. This evidence also suggests that co-residence with parents might protect the young from falling into poverty.

3 Although financial arrangements between parents and co-resident young adults are not at the forefront of research on co-residence or intra-household arrangements, there are some studies that cover this area, such as Aquilino and Supple (1991), Ward and Spitze (1996), White (2002), and Sassler et al. (2008).

4 Several reasons have been put forward for this difference. Some explanations highlight the difficulties that young adults face on the labor market and the housing market in Southern European countries (Buchmann and Kriesi 2011). Others focus on preferences and norms. According to Manacorda and Moretti (2006), parental preference for co-residence with young adult children can be strong, and parents can bribe children to stay in the parental home. Giuliano (2007) also shows the effect of cultural norms on the home-leaving behavior of young adults. She demonstrates that value changes (e.g., the sexual revolution in the 1970s) have different effects on the living arrangements of second-generation immigrants in the United States, depending on the cultural norms prevailing in their countries of origin.

5 The so-called register countries (Denmark, Finland, the Netherlands, Slovenia, and Sweden) had to be omitted because only one respondent was selected per household to answer the personal questionnaire. Other countries were not included because of substantive modifications to the expected question wording (Austria, France, and Ireland in the case of the first explanatory variable) or differences in response categories (France and Ireland) that make comparison with other countries difficult. Three other countries were not included because of a high percentage of missing values in the case of the population aged 18–34 years (Austria, Poland, and the United Kingdom). In the case of the second explanatory variable, Germany had to be excluded, but we were able to use the data for Ireland.

6 Health status for young adults is not included in the analysis because this is relevant for only a small subsample and these people tend to be outside the labor market. This makes it difficult to arrive at a reliable estimate of poor health in the case of the young.

7 The work intensity of a household is the ratio of the number of months that all working-age household members (aged 16–64 years) have worked during

the income reference year to the total number of months the same household members theoretically could have worked during the same period.

8 The part of public income assigned to one household member equals P/N_{eq}, where P is the amount of public income of the household, and N_{eq} measures the number of consumption units in the household.

REFERENCES

Aassve, Arnstein, Elena Cottini, and Agnese Vitali. 2013. "Youth Prospects in a Time of Economic Recession." *Demographic Research* 29: 949–62.

Aassve, Arnstein, María Davia, Maria Iacovou, and Stefano Mazzuco. 2007. "Does Leaving Home Make You Poor? Evidence from 13 European Countries." *European Journal of Population* 23 (3/4): 315–38.

Aassve, Arnstein, Maria Iacovou, and Letizia Mencarini. 2006. "Youth Poverty and Transition to Adulthood in Europe." *Demographic Research* 15 (1): 21–50.

Aquilino, William S., and Khalil R. Supple. 1991. "Parent–Child Relations and Parent's Satisfaction with Living Arrangements When Adult Children Live at Home." *Journal of Marriage and Family* 53 (1): 13–27.

Bennett, Fran. 2013. "Researching Within-Household Distribution: Overview, Developments, Debates, and Methodological Challenges." *Journal of Marriage and Family* 75 (3): 582–97.

Bonke, Jens, and Hans Uldall-Poulsen. 2007. "Why Do Families Actually Pool Their Income? Evidence from Denmark." *Review of Economics of the Household* 5 (2): 113–28.

Buchmann, Marlis C., and Irene Kriesi. 2011. "Transition to Adulthood in Europe." *Annual Review of Sociology* 37: 481–503.

Cox, Donald. 1987. "Motives for Private Income Transfers." *Journal of Political Economy* 95 (3): 508–46.

Dykstra, Pearl A., Thijs van den Broek, Cornelia Muresan, Mihaela Haragus, Paul T. Haragus, Anita Abramowska-Kmon, and Irena E. Kotowska. 2013. "State-of-the-Art Report: Intergenerational Linkages in Families." Family and Societies Working Paper 1. Rotterdam: Erasmus University.

Eurostat. 2010. *EU-SILC Module on Intra-Household Sharing of Resources: Assessment of the Implementation.* Brussels: European Commission.

Giuliano, Paola. 2007. "Living Arrangements in Western Europe: Does Cultural Origin Matter?" *Journal of the European Economic Association* 5 (5): 927–52.

Haddad, Lawrence, and Ravi Kanbur. 1990. "How Serious Is the Neglect of Intra-Household Inequality?" *Economic Journal* 100 (402): 866–81.

Kahn, Joan R., Frances Goldscheider, and Javier García-Manglano. 2013. "Growing Parental Economic Power in Parent–Adult Child Households: Coresidence and Financial Dependency in the United States, 1960–2000." *Demography* 50 (4): 1449–75.

Manacorda, Marco, and Enrico Moretti. 2006. "Why Do Most Italian Youths Live with Their Parents? Intergenerational Transfers and Household Structure." *Journal of the European Economic Association* 4 (4): 800–29.

Mulder, Clara. H. 2009. "Leaving the Parental Home in Young Adulthood." In *Handbook of Youth and Young Adulthood: New Perspectives and Agendas,* edited by Andy Furlong, 203–10. London: Routledge.

Nagy, Ildikó, Márton Medgyesi, and Orsolya Lelkes. 2012. "The 2010 Ad Hoc EU SILC Module on the Intra-Household Sharing of Resources." Social Situation Observatory Research Note 3. Brussels: European Commission.

Ponthieux, Sophie. 2013. "Income Pooling and Equal Sharing Within the Household—What Can We Learn from the 2010 EU-SILC Module? Eurostat Methodologies and Working Papers. Luxembourg: Publications Office of the European Union.

Ponthieux, Sophie. 2014. "Intra-Household Sharing of Resources: A Tentative 'Modified' Equivalised Income." Paper presented at Net-SILC2 Conference, October 16–17, Lisbon.

Reher, David S. 1998. "Family Ties in Western Europe: Persistent Contrasts." *Population and Development Review* 24 (2): 203–34.

Sassler, Sharon, Desiree Ciambrone, and Gaelan Benway. 2008. "Are They Really Mama's Boys/Daddy's Girls? The Negotiation of Adulthood upon Returning to the Parental Home." *Sociological Forum* 23 (4): 670–98.

Schenk, Niels, Pearl Dykstra, and Ineke Maas. 2010. "The Role of European Welfare States in Intergenerational Money Transfers: A Micro-Level Perspective." *Ageing and Society* 30 (8) 1315–42.

Swartz, Teresa T., Minzee Kim, Mayumi Uno, Jeylan Mortimer, and Kirsten B. O'Brien. 2011. "Safety Nets and Scaffolds: Parental Support in the Transition to Adulthood." *Journal of Marriage and Family* 73 (2): 414–29.

Ward, Russell, and Glenna Spitze. 1996. "Gender Differences in Parent–Child Coresidence Experiences." *Journal of Marriage and the Family* 58 (3): 718–25.

Ward, Terry, Erhan Özdemir, Annamária Gáti, and Márton Medgyesi. 2012. "Young People in the Crisis." Social Situation Observatory Research Note 5. Brussels: European Commission.

White, Lynn. 1994. "Coresidence and Leaving Home: Young Adults and Their Parents." *Annual Review of Sociology* 20: 81–102.

White, Naomi R. 2002. "'Not Under My Roof!' Young People's Experience of Home." *Youth & Society* 34 (2): 214–31.

Yodanis, Carrie, and Sean Lauer. 2007. "Managing Money in Marriage: Multilevel and Cross-National Effects of the Breadwinner Role." *Journal of Marriage and Family* 69 (5): 1307–25.

APPENDIX

Table A12.1 Proportion of personal income contributed by co-resident young adults (aged 18-34 years) to common household budget in 17 EU countries, 2010

Country	All income separate	Less than half in common pot	About half in common pot	More than half in common pot	All income in common pot	No income	Total	n
BE	31.3	6.8	0.9	3.2	4.7	53.1	100.0	1,311
BG	7.8	12.2	8.6	13.7	14.6	43.1	100.0	2,538
CY	39.4	4.9	1.7	2.4	2.0	49.5	100.0	1,784
CZ	17.8	22.6	6.4	4.1	4.7	44.2	100.0	2,875
DE	47.3	12.8	2.2	3.2	4.3	30.3	100.0	2,146
EE	19.7	9.1	8.2	6.9	5.7	50.5	100.0	1,477
EL	30.9	11.8	5.6	6.5	3.5	41.8	100.0	2,295
ES	35.4	7.2	3.7	3.8	8.4	41.6	100.0	4,572
HU	11.8	10.8	6.9	11.6	15.6	43.3	100.0	3,595
IT	23.2	6.9	3.9	7.6	5.1	53.3	100.0	5,727
LT	9.7	14.3	5.4	6.7	10.7	53.1	100.0	1,792
LU	36.2	7.3	2.1	0.7	2.7	51.1	100.0	1,498
LV	11.0	10.3	7.7	16.7	5.7	48.6	100.0	2,221
MT	65.4	4.3	1.5	4.5	2.4	22.0	100.0	1,838
PT	37.4	9.4	3.4	4.8	8.1	37.0	100.0	1,814
RO	4.9	7.7	7.8	25.2	10.9	43.4	100.0	2,783
SK	17.5	22.1	4.5	12.6	4.5	38.8	100.0	3,344

Source: Authors' calculations based on the EU-SILC 2010 ad hoc module on intra-household sharing of resources.

Table A12.2 Ability of co-resident young adults (aged 18–34 years) to decide about spending on personal consumption in 17 EU countries, 2010

Country	No	Yes, sometimes	Yes, always	Total	n
BE	6.2	10.3	83.5	100.0	1,313
BG	22.8	33.0	44.3	100.0	2,538
CY	6.2	17.6	76.2	100.0	1,784
CZ	21.7	30.3	48.0	100.0	2,855
EE	15.8	30.1	54.1	100.0	1,551
EL	18.0	25.7	56.2	100.0	2,295
ES	8.4	17.2	74.4	100.0	4,573
HU	10.9	25.9	63.3	100.0	3,595
IE	20.7	12.2	67.1	100.0	1,277
IT	29.7	25.8	44.5	100.0	5,727
LT	12.4	39.4	48.2	100.0	1,772
LU	12.5	15.1	72.4	100.0	1,488
LV	25.2	24.8	50.1	100.0	2,221
MT	1.6	4.7	93.7	100.0	1,832
PT	14.6	16.3	69.1	100.0	1,819
RO	36.5	36.6	26.9	100.0	2,783
SK	17.6	21.4	61.0	100.0	3,345

Source: Authors' calculations based on the EU-SILC 2010 ad hoc module on intra-household sharing of resources.

Table A12.3 Dependent variable: Proportion of personal income contributed by co-resident young adults (aged 18–34 years) to common household budget, coefficients of ordinal probit model, pooled models

	Model 1: Those with positive income	Model 2: Those aged 25–34 years	Model 3: Those aged 18–34 years
Log household income	−0.0961***	−0.1737***	−0.1306***
Relative income			
0%–30%	0	0	0
30%–50%	0.5270***	0.3000***	0.5582***
50%–80%	0.5783***	0.3681***	0.6072***
80%–120%	0.5984***	0.3985***	0.6522***
120+%	0.5805***	0.3826***	0.6507***
Female	0.0112	0.0319	0.0167
Age	0.0230***	0.0247***	0.0226***
Education, three categories			
Below upper secondary	0	0	0
Upper secondary	0.0147	−0.0637*	−0.0721
Tertiary	−0.0946**	−0.1941***	−0.1890***

Table A12.3 Continued

	Model 1: Those with positive income	Model 2: Those aged 25–34 years	Model 3: Those aged 18–34 years
Labor market status			
Works full-time	0	0	0
Works part-time	0.0084	−0.0421	0.0277
Unemployed	−0.6501***	−0.5652***	−0.6643***
Student	−0.9736***	−0.8640***	−0.7811***
No work, other	−0.2270***	−0.0286	−0.1227
Partner in household	0.5563***	0.6351***	0.6098***
Child in household	0.4167***	0.3385***	0.3455***
Number of parents in household			
Only mother	0	0	0
Only father	−0.0738	−0.0458	−0.1004
Two parents	−0.3735***	−0.3915***	−0.3362***
Parents' average age	−0.0023	−0.0029	−0.0024
Parental education level			
All below upper secondary	0	0	0
With and without upper secondary	0.0085	−0.0640	−0.0842
All at least upper secondary	−0.1298***	−0.1248**	−0.1430**
Parental work intensity			
0–0.5	0	0	0
0.5–0.99	−0.0343	−0.0342	−0.0015
1	−0.0574*	−0.0675*	−0.0272
Parent has health limitations	0.0323	0.0004	−0.0337
Parent migrant origin	0.2196***	0.2551***	0.2660***
Contribution of parent to household budget			
No contribution	0	0	0
Half or less	0.3852***	0.4020***	0.4648***
More than half	0.4480***	0.5348***	0.5663***
No income	0.5121***	0.5743***	0.5886***
Home ownership			
Owner/no rent	0	0	0
Reduced rent	0.0740	0.0917	0.0426
Market rent	0.1921***	0.2650***	0.2644***

(continued)

Table A12.3 Continued

	Model 1: Those with positive income	Model 2: Those aged 25–34 years	Model 3: Those aged 18–34 years
Rooms per household member	−0.0531	−0.0268	−0.1142*
No. of household members aged <18 years	0.0035	0.0042	0.0133
No. of household members aged 18–34 years	−0.0148	−0.0246	−0.0620*
N			
Pseudo R^2			

Note: Pooled models include control dummies (coefficients not shown).
*p < .10.
**p < .05.
***p < .01.
Source: Authors' calculations based on the EU-SILC 2010 ad hoc module on intra-household sharing of resources.

Table A12.4 Ability to decide about spending on personal consumption, coefficients of ordinal probit model, pooled models

	Model 1	Model 2	Model 3
Log household income	0.5276***	0.3055***	0.2561***
Relative income			
0%–30%	0	0	0
30%–50%	0.2832***	0.0774	0.1047*
50%–80%	0.4570***	0.1400**	0.1999***
80%–120%	0.6107***	0.2159***	0.2616***
120+%	0.7146***	0.2514***	0.3156***
Female		0.0075	0.0103
Age		0.0022	0.0033
Education, three categories			
Below upper secondary		0	0
Upper secondary		0.1998***	0.1482***
Tertiary		0.3086***	0.2402***
Labor market status			
Works full-time		0	0
Works part-time		−0.2311***	−0.2409***
Unemployed		−0.8278***	−0.8147***
Student		−0.8481***	−0.8415***
No work, other		−1.0199***	−0.9994***
Partner in household		−0.2935***	−0.3422***

Table A12.4 Continued

	Model 1	Model 2	Model 3
Child in household		−0.0503	−0.0206
Number of parents in household			
Only mother			0
Only father			0.1544
Two parents			0.1063**
Parents' average age			0.0036
Parental education level			
All below upper secondary			0
With and without upper secondary			0.0573
All at least upper secondary			0.1662***
Parental work intensity			
0–0.5			0
0.5–0.99			0.1143*
1			0.0255
Parent has health limitations			0.0397
Parent migrant origin			−0.0984
Contribution of parent to household budget			
No contribution			0
Half or less			0.1148
More than half			0.0573
No income			−0.1565
Home ownership			
Owner/no rent			0
Reduced rent			−0.0088
Market rent			−0.0858
Rooms per household member			0.1374**
No. of household members aged <18 years			0.0381
No. of household members aged 18–34 years			0.0450*
N	19,861	19,708	18,596
Pseudo R^2	0.094	0.125	0.129

Note: Pooled models include control dummies (coefficients not shown).

*$p < .10$.

**$p < .05$.

***$p < .01$.

Source: Authors' calculations based on the EU-SILC 2010 ad hoc module on intra-household sharing of resources.

PART III

TRANSITIONS ACROSS EUROPE

13

WHAT HAPPENS TO YOUNG PEOPLE WHO MOVE TO ANOTHER COUNTRY TO FIND WORK?

Mehtap Akgüç and Miroslav Beblavý

13.1. INTRODUCTION

The freedom of movement of citizens across all of Europe has been one of the most important achievements of the European Union (EU).[1] The size, composition, and direction of migration flows in Europe have evolved in a continuously changing pattern, reflecting various social, economic, and political conjunctures and circumstances resulting from both diverse and dynamic pull and push factors (Castles 1986, 2006; Constant and Massey 2003). Recent evidence suggests, however, that the mobility patterns of the past decade in Europe are mostly dominated by youth flows (Eurostat 2011). In particular, educated youth from Eastern and Southern Europe have been migrating to regions to the west and north that offer relatively more favorable labor market opportunities (Kahanec and Zimmermann 2010). However, the recent economic downturn, which has contributed to rising youth unemployment, and the challenges faced by young people transitioning from education to labor markets have put a strain on the labor market transitions of youth. Added to these difficulties are the challenges migrants normally face in integrating into destination-country labor markets.

Against the background of human capital and neoclassical models explaining migration patterns and motivations (Sjaastad 1962; Bowles 1970; Greenwood, Hunt, and McDowell 1986; Borjas, Bronars, and Trejo 1992), and given the evidence that migrants are ever more frequently young, female, and relatively well educated, these population movements raise questions concerning the ability of destination-country labor markets to integrate migrants in accordance with

389

their human capital endowments. Economic theory predicts a strong correlation between the circumstances of the labor market at origin and in the destination countries (Martin 2009). Based on this theory, if young individuals move mainly to escape stressful economic circumstances in their countries of origin, then one wonders what happens to them once they arrive in the destination country's labor markets. Previous results from the migration literature generally find relatively worse labor market outcomes for foreign-born individuals vis-à-vis native peers. In this vein, if international transferability of skills or qualification recognition is an issue, then it is possible to observe education–occupation mismatches among migrant individuals (Chiswick 2009). In addition to sociodemographic differences such as education and age, the role of ethnic background in the labor market has also been highlighted in explaining some of the observed differences compared to native peers (Akgüç and Ferrer 2015). Furthermore, young migrants sometimes face a double disadvantage: the first for their youthfulness, which usually means that they lack work experience and therefore have difficulty in making the transition from education to the labor market (Brzinsky-Fay 2007), and a second one in the form of the differential and discriminatory treatment that is commonly meted out to migrants. All in all, analyzing the labor market integration of young migrants has important policy relevance because it evidences the (in)effectiveness of labor market institutions (e.g., in terms of recognition of foreign qualifications) in tackling possible labor market mismatches faced by foreign-born residents in destination countries.

To this end, this chapter addresses the following research questions: Do recently arrived young migrants in Europe differ from native peers with respect to socioeconomic and labor market indicators? How do recently arrived young migrants from different regions of origin differ among themselves? To what extent do the observable differences in sociodemographic characteristics explain the gaps in the labor market outcomes of young migrants from various regions relative to native peers? Do we observe gender gaps in labor market outcomes among young migrants?

To address these questions, this chapter conducts a comparative econometric analysis of the labor market integration of young migrants of different origins. In a departure from the main literature on labor market integration (one exception is Spreckelsen, Leschke, and Seeleib-Kaiser, this volume), the chapter focuses on youth aged 35 years or younger because this age group accounts for a large share of the migrants in Europe in the past two decades. In particular, the analysis considers recent migrants who arrived within the past 10 years. Regarding labor market integration, the chapter examines a wide range of outcomes, such as (un)employment, type of job contract (temporary or permanent), self-employment, hours worked, and various indicators of occupational mismatch.[2] Unlike the general approach in much of the previous research, migrants are not treated as a homogeneous group, and attention is paid to differences in ethnic origins. In line with the recent mobility patterns in Europe, the focus is on young migrants from

Eastern and Southern Europe, but other migrant groups are also considered so as to give a broader picture. Moreover, the novelty of the chapter is that it analyzes the labor market integration of young migrants in a cross-country framework. Last, because the gender gap is highlighted as an important factor in migrants' experience, the chapter also contributes to the literature by embedding gender aspects in the analysis of the labor market integration of young migrants.

The descriptive findings point to differences in socioeconomic characteristics (e.g., age and education) as well as in labor market indicators (e.g., employment and occupational mismatch) across different migrant groups and between migrants and native peers. Econometric analysis suggests that observable characteristics explain part, although not all, of the differential labor market outcomes of migrants. Young Eastern European migrants are found to be overqualified for their occupations compared to native peers of destination countries. Young Southern Europeans are more likely to be self-employed and to be on a temporary employment contract. Regarding broader age groups, the younger cohorts seem to be performing worse than the older cohorts in terms of unemployment, self-employment, contract type, and overqualification, but these differences are not always statistically significant and they vary by the origin of individuals. Furthermore, important gender gaps are observed among youth in favor of men with regard to employment and hours worked per week, and this pattern holds for all migrant groups considered.

The remainder of the chapter is organized as follows. We first provide a brief literature review with a short background on recent migration trends in Europe. We next provide a description of the data, variables of interest, and the econometric methodology used for the micro-level cross-country analysis, followed by a presentation of the descriptive analysis and the estimation results. Finally, we discuss the results along the youth and gender dimensions and provide concluding remarks, suggesting areas for future research and discussing issues related to policymaking aimed at alleviating migrant and youth vulnerabilities in destination labor markets.

13.2. LITERATURE REVIEW

The majority of the literature has focused on migrant integration into English-speaking countries, examining single-country cases (Chiswick 1978, 1979; Borjas 1987; Ferrer and Riddell 2008; Constant, Nottmeyer, and Zimmermann 2012). Most of these papers examine a limited number of labor market outcomes, such as wages (Chiswick 1978; Borjas 1987; Ferrer and Riddell 2008). There are a few studies comparing several countries, but even these do not always use comparable data sources (Constant and Zimmermann 2005; Antecol, Kuhn, and Trejo 2006; Algan et al. 2010). One novelty of this chapter is that it takes a comparative approach and conducts an analysis using harmonized cross-country data on labor market integration covering various outcomes. Notwithstanding a number of caveats—discussed in Section 13.3—pooled cross-country data add to our understanding of differences in the integration of migrant populations across countries (Adsera and Chiswick 2007).

Most contributions find relatively worse outcomes for migrants compared to native peers in the labor markets for various reasons (Chiswick 1978; Adsera and Chiswick 2007; Jean et al. 2007). Although part of the nativity gap is related to socioeconomic background, such as education—where the latter has been obtained (Akgüç and Ferrer 2015)—and previous labor market experience, another part could be caused by skills recognition or transferability issues in destination countries (Chiswick 2009). Earlier studies also emphasize the assimilation process, whereby migrants catch up—if ever—with native outcomes only after a certain amount of time has been spent in the country and after obtaining country-specific skills (Chiswick 1978). Country of origin and cultural background are another set of related factors that determine labor market outcomes (Fernández and Fogli 2009; Blau, Kahn, and Papps 2011). Migration motivations, such as economic goals, education, political beliefs, or family reunification, might also be associated with integration patterns (Akgüç 2014), whereby the experience of economic and student migrants seems to more closely approximate that of native peers. Last, differential treatment in the form of discrimination might also lie behind native–immigrant gaps. Considering these dimensions, this chapter contributes to the literature by providing further insights into the labor market integration of recent young migrants in Europe by controlling for socioeconomic and ethnic backgrounds.

In the migration literature, the main focus is usually on working-age individuals rather than on migrating youth, except in some contributions, such as Seeleib-Kaiser and Spreckelsen (2016) and Spreckelsen et al. (this volume). Examining recent young European migrants in the United Kingdom, Seeleib-Kaiser and Spreckelsen find that although these migrants are highly integrated in terms of employment, they end up in poor-quality jobs. Similarly, Clark and Drinkwater (2008) find that recent Eastern European migrants to the United Kingdom experience relatively low returns on their education and work in unskilled occupations. This chapter likewise focuses on young migrants, but in a cross-country framework; the findings are nevertheless similar to those of previous papers. Although most of the aforementioned reasons for poor integration outcomes can be valid for young migrants as well, this group might also face the additional challenge of being young and the related risks to labor market transitions posed by lack of previous market experience and particularly of skills that are specific to the destination country. Finally, to our knowledge, none of the earlier studies addresses gender gaps while examining the labor market integration of youth migrant groups, as is done in this chapter.

As mentioned in Section 13.1, the chapter mainly focuses on Southern and Eastern European young migrants, even though other origins are included in order to have a complete picture. The main reason for the focus on these groups are the recent mobility patterns in Europe. Regarding Southern Europe, Spain has turned from a migration destination during the boom years of 1995–2000 into an emigration country during the recent recession, whereby many young native peers and foreign residents have left to find employment elsewhere as jobs have become scarce (González Gago and Kirzner 2013; Izquierdo, Jimeno, and Lacuesta 2016). In the Italian case, despite the stable emigration in the pre- and postcrisis periods, the recent composition of migrants has changed to include more highly educated youth older than age 25 years, which suggests that the usual out-migration for study abroad has been replaced by work motives with lower return rates (Constant and D'Agosto 2008; Ciccarone 2013), thus raising the issue of brain drain (Beine, Docquier, and Özden 2011; Docquier and Rapoport 2012). Regarding migrants from Eastern Europe, the major policy change influencing their mobility has been the Eastern enlargement of the EU. However, EU accession did not immediately give the right of free movement and work to the citizens of the new member states,[3] with transitional measures of up to 7 years restricting free movement for work purposes (Galgóczi, Leschke, and Watt 2011; Galgóczi and Leschke 2012).[4] Regardless of the transition measures, a striking feature of recent migrant flows from Eastern Europe is that they are mainly dominated by young and well-educated individuals, as will be shown in the empirical analysis.

13.3. DATA AND METHODOLOGY

To conduct the econometric analysis of labor market integration of migrants within a cross-country framework, we have at least two options regarding data sources: the European Union Labour Force Survey (EU-LFS) and the European Social Survey (ESS). Given the focus on Southern and Eastern European origins, we opted for the ESS, mainly because it provides detailed country-of-origin information. For example, we are not able to distinguish Southern European migrants in the EU-LFS, which gives only a broader country-of-origin categorization, such as EU15.

The ESS is a biennial—partly repetitive—cross-section survey including conventional demographic and socioeconomic variables as well as labor market indicators relating to diverse populations in more than 30 countries. The survey covers all persons aged 15 years or older who are residents within private households—regardless of their nationality, citizenship, language, or legal status—in the 36 participating countries (mainly in Europe). The survey is accessible via the Norwegian Social Science Data Services.

Using the ESS, we focus on 15 destinations, namely Austria, Belgium, Denmark, Finland, France, Germany, Ireland, Italy, Luxembourg, the Netherlands, Norway, Spain, Sweden, Switzerland, and the United Kingdom. These are countries that have received important migrant flows during the past few decades not only from within but also from outside Europe (Brücker, Capuano, and Marfouk 2013). The migration flows to these destinations have been influenced by and have evolved through various economic, social, and political developments during this period—for example, the Eastern enlargement of the EU, occasional amnesties offered to illegal migrants (e.g., in Spain), rising youth unemployment, and widening socioeconomic inequalities. Not all of the 15 countries participated in all rounds of the survey, but quite a few of them participated in almost all rounds (see Table A13.1 in the Appendix). The total sample has 145,564 observations, composed of native- and foreign-born individuals from diverse origins; in fact, the sample includes 198 different countries of origin.

In order to have a large enough sample for the econometric analysis, we use all available ESS rounds (1–7) during the period 2002–2015. We pool the countries together and over time and include individuals aged 15–65 years at the time of the survey. Given that young people from various origins have been more mobile in Europe in recent years, we pay particular attention to the youth dimension, searching for possible heterogeneities and patterns across various countries of origin. To this end, we create two age bands using 35 years as the cut-off age, whereby individuals are defined as being young if they are aged 35 years or younger. In addition to providing standard summary statistics including everyone, we report additional descriptive information on the youth dimension so as to inspect the differences in outcomes by age group.

Regarding the definition of migrants, an individual is defined as a migrant if his or her country of birth is different from his or her country of residence at the time of the survey. However, this definition of migration, although standard in the literature, can be rather broad because it can also include migrants who arrived as small children and hence would be considered second-generation migrants, which is not the focus of this chapter. Because the focus is mainly on first-generation migrants who move for work, we address this potential issue by limiting the sample to "recent" migrants who migrated within the previous 10 years. In this way, we capture—to a large extent—individuals who recently migrated as adults or youth. Moreover, because there is no particular information on seasonal, circular, or cross-border migration in the data, we are not able to capture such temporary migration here.

Given the focus on Southern and Eastern European migrants, because they have been among the most mobile groups in Europe recently, we create aggregate categories of origins for migrants, in addition to the *native peers*:[5] (1) *Southern Europe*, which includes individuals from Greece, Italy, Portugal, and Spain; (2) *Eastern Europe*, which includes individuals from EU10 countries—that is, Bulgaria, Czech Republic, Estonia, Hungary, Latvia, Lithuania, Poland, Romania, Slovakia, and Slovenia; (3) *intra-EU*, which consists of individuals from other EU countries, excluding Southern and Eastern Europeans; and (4) *non-EU*, which consists of individuals from countries other than the 28 member states of the European Union.[6] The main focus is on Southern and Eastern European individuals, but to give a complete picture, residents from non-EU origins as well as the other intra-EU countries are also included. In total, approximately 10.3% of the population in the sample is foreign born of diverse origins.

While carrying out the descriptive analysis, we also run several t-tests (not reported here but available upon request) of mean differences in characteristics across various groups in order to check whether the observed unconditional differences are statistically significant, in which case analysis across groups is justified. Results from these tests point to statistically significant heterogeneities in almost all observed characteristics across diverse origins. Therefore, we distinguish these various subgroups, taking native peers as the reference in the remainder of the econometric analysis.

For a comparative analysis of the socioeconomic characteristics and the labor market integration of various populations, we initially examine the unconditional differences in individual characteristics such as age, gender, household size, marital status, number of children, residential area, and educational attainment, in addition to several labor market indicators, such as employment, unemployment, self-employment, weekly total hours worked in main job (overtime included), contract type (temporary/permanent), and education–occupation mismatch. With regard to mismatch, we mainly have in mind overqualification, referring to individuals who are capable of handling more complex tasks and whose skills are underused, as defined by the Organization for Economic Cooperation and Development (OECD 2012; see also McGuinness, Bergin, and Whelan, this volume).[7] Technically, we construct the overqualification indicator based on the definition used by Chiswick and Miller (2010) and Aleksynska and Tritah (2013): Using information on the average years of educational attainment per occupation in each country, an individual is defined to be overqualified if his or her education is one standard deviation above the average within the occupation.[8]

The different access years for citizens from Eastern Europe to the labor markets of the old member states because of various transitional measures can potentially raise issues when one analyzes migration for work, but it is outside the scope of this chapter to analyze labor market integration incorporating all possible restrictive transitional periods. However, evidence from aggregate data by Akgüç and Beblavý (2015) suggests that there has already been a substantial and continuous migrant flow from Eastern European countries to Western and Northern European countries since the early 1990s. Moreover, taking into account country and time effects in the econometrics analysis partially captures the differential transition periods as well.[9]

We address the differences in labor market integration by controlling for socioeconomic characteristics and their interactions across different groups analyzed within a multivariate regression framework. For the baseline model, each binary dependent variable (employment, unemployment, self-employment, contract type, and overqualification) Y_{ict} of individual i in country c at time t is estimated by probit using the following model:[10]

$$P\left(Y_{ict} = 1 \middle| X\right) = \Phi\left(X\beta\right) \tag{13.1}$$

where X includes dummy variables (ORI_{ic}) for five broad origin groups for each individual i in country c (native peers, Southern Europeans, Eastern Europeans, intra-EU, and non-EU migrants); demographic/socioeconomic controls (X_{ict}) such as age and age squared, gender, household size, marital status, children, educational attainment in years, and residential area; and country-fixed effects (η_c), year effects (μ_t), and a random error term (ε_{ict}). To facilitate the interpretation of the coefficients, all the estimation results with binary variables report the estimated marginal effects of the respective control variable.

For the continuous dependent variable (weekly total hours worked) of individual i in country c at time t, we estimate an ordinary least squares version of Eq. (13.1):

$$Y_{ict} = \beta_0 + \beta_1 ORI_{ic} + \beta_2 X_{ict} + \eta_c + \mu_t + \varepsilon_{ict} \tag{13.2}$$

where the same notation as before follows. For self-employment, contract type, hours worked, and overqualification, we add the condition of "being employed." In this way, we compare, for example, the number of hours worked among employed individuals only and not also among unemployed. In the models, the coefficients of interest are those in front of the origin dummies as well as the youth dummy—where relevant—and they are interpreted as the deviation in the outcomes from the reference population, consisting of native-born and older individuals.

Next, with the aim of exploring heterogeneities in these initial results for different age cohorts by origin, we estimate the previous models by interacting the origin dummies with the youth dummy. This implies adding the term $\beta_1 ORI_{ic} * YOUTH_{ict}$ into the previous equations, where $YOUTH_{ict}$ is an indicator of youth (1 if aged 35 years or younger). Furthermore, we explore the gender dimension in the analysis by running similar interaction models as with the youth dimension but replacing the youth dummy by the gender dummy $FEMALE_{ict}$. Finally, we estimate gender gaps across native-born and migrant groups for selected labor market outcomes among young individuals only. This last exercise allows us to explore the potential heterogeneities and vulnerabilities experienced by young migrant women.

With respect to the pooling of data across different countries and over time, as we have elected to do in this chapter, there are both advantages and disadvantages to this exercise. We acknowledge that pooling different destination countries with different economic and welfare-state configurations combined with changes over time makes it difficult to interpret the results—especially in a causal way for a particular country. For this reason, we note that outcomes would be likely to differ from one destination to another if countries were analyzed separately (see Spreckelsen et al., this volume). At the same time, pooling helps smooth out heterogeneities between countries and years and provides a comprehensive overview of the general situation that is complementary to the single-country analysis at a point in time or over time. Pooling also boosts the sample size, particularly for migrants. Furthermore, inclusion of country and time effects in models with pooled data—as done in this chapter—takes into account part of the cross-country and period-related heterogeneities. Finally, in order to have representative results both nationally and across countries, we include country and design weights provided by ESS when pooling all countries throughout the empirical analysis.

13.4. DESCRIPTIVE STATISTICS

13.4.1. Summary Statistics of Main Variables

Table 13.1 displays the main summary statistics for native peers and recent migrant groups of all age groups in the sample. The female ratio is mainly approximately 50% across various population groups, reaching between 55% and 60% for Eastern European and intra-EU migrants. This finding is consistent with the feminization of migration during recent decades. Migrants tend to live in more urban areas than do native peers. The latter finding might be related to the prediction by Harris and Todaro (1970) that individuals from less developed rural regions are more likely to move to developed urban areas.[11] Regarding educational attainment, the numbers suggest that recent migrants from Eastern Europe, followed by those from intra-EU countries, have acquired more years of education compared to native-born individuals. The educational profiles of migrants overall seem to be in line with the human capital theory of migration, which postulates that migrants tend to be relatively well educated notwithstanding differences across different origins.

Regarding the labor market variables, the employment rate is approximately two-thirds for all groups, whereas unemployment is approximately 5% or 6%, on average, for native-born individuals, Southern migrants, and intra-EU migrants, and it is higher for Eastern European and non-EU migrants (8%–10%). Self-employment is more common among intra-EU migrants and Southern European migrants. The average number of weekly hours worked is approximately 39 hours for everyone. Regarding contract type, migrants from Eastern European and non-EU countries are more likely to be on temporary contracts compared to the rest of the sample. This could be due to the fact that these groups are younger than the others. At the same time, there has been a general increase in the share of temporary

Table 13.1 Summary statistics of main variables (all age groups)

	Native peers	Southern European migrants	Eastern European migrants	Intra-EU migrants	Non-EU migrants
Female	0.515	0.496	0.549	0.597	0.512
	(0.500)	(0.500)	(0.497)	(0.492)	(0.500)
Household size	3.050	3.115	3.062	2.800	3.430
	(1.377)	(1.394)	(1.423)	(1.330)	(1.619)
Married	0.533	0.688	0.587	0.559	0.623
	(0.499)	(0.463)	(0.492)	(0.497)	(0.485)
No. of children	0.803	0.993	0.781	0.815	1.124
	(1.067)	(1.094)	(1.028)	(1.096)	(1.284)
Residence in urban area	0.274	0.352	0.362	0.314	0.459
	(0.446)	(0.478)	(0.481)	(0.464)	(0.498)
Education (years)	13.21	11.52	13.41	14.36	12.96
	(3.837)	(4.984)	(3.538)	(4.213)	(4.500)
Employed	0.643	0.682	0.653	0.639	0.596
	(0.479)	(0.466)	(0.476)	(0.480)	(0.491)
Unemployed	0.053	0.062	0.083	0.062	0.099
	(0.224)	(0.240)	(0.275)	(0.241)	(0.294)
Self-employment	0.135	0.143	0.114	0.148	0.120
	(0.341)	(0.351)	(0.318)	(0.355)	(0.325)
Total hours of work (week)	38.98	38.80	39.46	38.48	39.25
	(13.46)	(12.80)	(16.02)	(13.54)	(13.80)
Contract type (temporary)	0.107	0.109	0.170	0.093	0.165
	(0.309)	(0.311)	(0.376)	(0.290)	(0.371)
Education–occupation mismatch	0.147	0.152	0.201	0.199	0.223
Overqualified	(0.354)	(0.359)	(0.401)	(0.399)	(0.416)
No. of observations	129,395	1,389	2,011	3,832	8,711

Notes: Means are reported, standard deviations are in parentheses. Only migrants who arrived within the previous 10 years are included. Intra-EU refers to EU countries other than Southern and Eastern Europe. *Source:* ESS (2002–2015).

contracts since the early 2000s. Therefore, an econometric estimation that controls for sociodemographic characteristics together with time trends can shed light on this finding. Finally, the constructed overqualification indicator suggests that native peers are the least likely to be overqualified in their jobs, whereas non-EU migrants are the most likely to be overqualified. Southern Europeans are relatively similar to native peers in this regard, whereas Eastern Europeans and intra-EU migrants are more likely to be overqualified compared to native peers.

13.4.2. Further Inspection of Age Structures, Migrant Backgrounds, and Gender Gaps

Regarding the age structure, a comparative report by Eurostat (2011) on the migrant population in Europe suggests that compared to native peers, the foreign-born population is younger and more concentrated in the lower working-age group. The figures from the ESS sample, as displayed in Table 13.2, suggest parallel results. Although the share of native peers aged 35 years or younger is approximately one-third, the numbers jump almost twofold among migrants who arrived within the past 10 years; for example, approximately two out of three migrants from Eastern Europe and non-EU countries are young, whereas slightly more than half of Southern Europeans are young. In line with the youth shares, recent migrants are, on average, much younger than the native-born population (aged 41 vs. aged in their early 30s, respectively).

The youth dimension among migrants is given further inspection in Figure 13.1, which shows the evolution of youth shares among migrants from the main sending regions per survey year. Each column gives the composition of migrants aged 35 years or younger by region of origin. For example, in 2002, the majority of young migrants (almost 70%) were from non-EU countries, whereas less than 10% were from Southern and Eastern Europe combined. In 2009, the total share of young European migrants increased to more than 40%. Moreover, the relative share of young Eastern Europeans has increased significantly since 2008, which is likely due both to the changing economic circumstances brought on by the global recession and to the Eastern enlargement of the EU. Overall, an increasing number of young people of diverse origins seem to be on the move in Europe during the past decade.

Table 13.3 examines the gender gaps in different age cohorts in general, without distinguishing between migratory origins. To do this, we first estimate the mean gaps in outcome between men—the reference group—and women for a selected set of variables that are closely associated with labor market performance (e.g., educational attainment, employment status, hours worked, contract type, and mismatch indicators). In order to investigate whether gender gaps differ by age structure, we repeat the first step for young individuals younger than age 35 years and for individuals aged 35 years or older, respectively. In this

Table 13.2 Youth shares and average age by country of origin

	Native peers	Southern Europe	Eastern Europe	Intra-EU	Non-EU
Youth population share (%; recent migrants only)	33.6	53.5	65.5	45.4	65.1
Average age (years)	41.1	33.6	32.1	36.4	32.3

Source: Authors' calculations based on ESS (2002–2015).

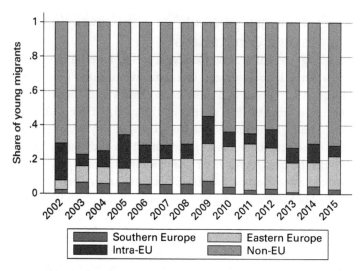

Figure 13.1 Distribution of youth share among migrant groups by survey year.
Source: Authors' calculations based on ESS (2002–2015).

way, we get a hint as to how gender gaps in selected outcomes evolve across the life cycle.[12] From the results shown in Table 13.3, we observe that young women have significantly more years of education (0.25) compared to young men, whereas the difference goes in the opposite direction among older individuals. Young women are also 8% less likely to be employed compared to young men, and this gap widens to 12% among the older cohorts. In terms of unemployment, women in general (regardless of their age cohort) are 1% less likely than men to be unemployed, which could be explained by the higher inactivity shares among women. The gender gap in self-employment is also in favor of men and widens with age, whereas the gender gap in weekly working hours widens by almost half in favor of men aged 35 years or older. For the remaining outcomes (e.g., contract type and overqualification), the gender gaps remain significant but do not differ across age groups. Without claiming causal relations, the econometric analysis in Section 13.4.3 acknowledges these differences by taking into account sociodemographic and ethnic background as well as variation across countries and time.

13.4.3. Baseline Estimation Results for Recent Migrants

Table 13.4 reports the baseline results of estimating Eqs. (13.1) and (13.2). By default, we always include the broad origin variables (first column of each outcome variable) and then add the common set of explanatory variables, comprising age, age squared, female dummy, household size, children, education, marital status, and urban dummy (second column of each outcome variable) in order to

Table 13.3 Mean gender gaps in labor market outcomes by age groups

	(1)	(2)
	35 years or younger	**35+ years**
Education (years)	0.249***	−0.088***
	(8.02)	(−3.39)
Employed	−0.080***	−0.121***
	(−18.02)	(−41.59)
Unemployed	−0.010***	−0.009***
	(−4.67)	(−6.73)
Self-employment	−0.038***	−0.096***
	(−12.83)	(−35.51)
Hours worked (week)	−7.076***	−9.702***
	(−46.17)	(−100.47)
Temporary contract	0.03***	0.024***
	(6.15)	(12.64)
Overqualified	−0.013***	−0.016***
	(−2.87)	(−5.79)
No. of observations	49,068	96,459

Notes: t statistics in parentheses. Reference group is men.
*$p < .10$.
**$p < .05$.
***$p < .01$.
Source: ESS (2002–2015).

determine whether holding observed characteristics constant modifies the initial effects of origins on the labor market outcomes of interest among native-born individuals and recent migrants. The improvement of the (pseudo/adjusted) R^2 when additional explanatory variables are added implies a better fit of the models when the positive influence on this coefficient due to the increase in the number of covariates is taken into account.

The results of the baseline employment regressions before introducing additional controls suggest that there is no significant difference in employment across groups, except for migrants from non-European countries. Once we take into account differences in personal characteristics, however, significant gaps emerge: For example, migrants from Eastern Europe and intra-EU have lower employment levels compared to the native-born population. The explained employment gap between native-born individuals and non-EU migrants rises to 12 percentage points once individual controls are held constant. The change from column 1 to column 2 in Table 13.4 suggests that migrants have characteristics that lead to lower employment compared to native peers. The remaining coefficients in column 2 have expected signs: Age increases employment at a

Table 13.4 Baseline estimations of labor market performance with full set of control variables

	Employment		Unemployment		Self-employment	
	(1)	(2)	(3)	(4)	(5)	(6)
South	0.030	−0.021	0.014	0.012	0.023	0.022
	(0.028)	(0.029)	(0.011)	(0.010)	(0.023)	(0.022)
East	−0.026	−0.072***	0.027***	0.021***	−0.030*	−0.000
	(0.020)	(0.021)	(0.007)	(0.007)	(0.018)	(0.018)
Intra-EU	−0.015	−0.078***	0.016	0.017*	0.017	0.022
	(0.017)	(0.019)	(0.010)	(0.009)	(0.014)	(0.014)
Non-EU	−0.073***	−0.120***	0.039***	0.033***	−0.023***	−0.015*
	(0.009)	(0.010)	(0.004)	(0.003)	(0.009)	(0.009)
Age		0.098***		0.007***		0.010***
		(0.001)		(0.000)		(0.001)
Age squared		−0.001***		−0.000***		−0.000***
		(0.000)		(0.000)		(0.000)
Female		−0.153***		−0.004***		−0.072***
		(0.004)		(0.002)		(0.003)
Household size		−0.006**		0.001		0.006**
		(0.003)		(0.001)		(0.003)
Education (years)		0.017***		−0.004***		0.002***
		(0.001)		(0.000)		(0.000)
Married		0.055***		−0.034***		−0.006
		(0.005)		(0.002)		(0.004)
No. of children		−0.024***		−0.005***		0.001
		(0.004)		(0.001)		(0.003)
Living in urban area		−0.019***		0.003		−0.004
		(0.005)		(0.002)		(0.004)
Pseudo R^2	0.008	0.198	0.023	0.062	0.024	0.063
No. of observations	140,813	139,641	140,813	139,641	92,543	91,960

Table 13.4 Continued

	Temporary contract		Hours of work (weekly)		Overqualified	
	(7)	(8)	(9)	(10)	(11)	(12)
South	0.033*	0.046**	−0.436	−0.529	0.020	0.022*
	(0.019)	(0.018)	(0.781)	(0.726)	(0.023)	(0.013)
East	0.060***	0.042***	1.615	0.679	0.048**	0.030***
	(0.014)	(0.013)	(1.385)	(0.762)	(0.019)	(0.009)
Intra-EU	−0.001	0.004	−0.229	−0.347	0.071***	−0.000
	(0.012)	(0.012)	(0.612)	(0.553)	(0.014)	(0.007)
Non-EU	0.073***	0.064***	0.605*	0.580*	0.075***	0.037***
	(0.007)	(0.006)	(0.356)	(0.338)	(0.008)	(0.004)
Age		−0.017***		0.965***		−0.001*
		(0.001)		(0.055)		(0.001)
Age squared		0.000***		−0.011***		0.000
		(0.000)		(0.001)		(0.000)
Female		0.017***		−9.524***		−0.019***
		(0.003)		(0.127)		(0.002)
Household size		0.007***		−0.214		0.003**
		(0.002)		(0.139)		(0.001)
Education (years)		−0.000		0.242***		0.031***
		(0.000)		(0.018)		(0.001)
Married		−0.032***		−0.462***		−0.008***
		(0.003)		(0.158)		(0.002)
No. of children		−0.007***		−0.737***		−0.003*
		(0.002)		(0.162)		(0.002)
Living in urban area		0.001		−0.643***		−0.009***
		(0.003)		(0.138)		(0.002)
Pseudo R^2	0.026	0.113	0.017	0.159	0.008	0.409
No. of observations	92,543	91,960	89,902	89,445	92,226	91,670

Notes: Reference group is native-born individuals. Robust standard errors are in parentheses. Individual controls include age, age squared, gender, household size, education, marital status, children, and urban residence. Only recent migrants who arrived in the destination countries within the previous 10 years are included. Intra-EU refers to EU countries other than Southern and Eastern Europe.
*$p < .10$.
**$p < .05$.
***$p < .01$.
Source: ESS (2002–2015).

decreasing rate, being female is negatively related to employment, and an additional year of education increases employment. Regarding unemployment, migrants from Eastern Europe and of non-EU origins have higher chances of being unemployed, and adding individual controls does not modify the results to any great extent. In terms of self-employment, Eastern Europeans and non-EU migrants are less likely (although the significance of the coefficient is barely 10% for the former group) to be self-employed compared to native peers; however, this difference almost disappears once individual controls are introduced. Regarding contract duration, most migrants—except for intra-EU migrants—are more likely (to a varying extent by origin) than native peers to hold a temporary job. The estimated gaps in temporary contracts between native-born workers and migrants remain significant even after introducing individual controls.

As seen in the unconditional means from the descriptive statistics, weekly hours of work do not differ across groups in general for the main groups of interest, except for the non-EU migrants, who work slightly more hours than the others. Concerning occupational mismatch, all migrants except Southern Europeans have a higher chance of being overqualified compared to native-born individuals, but this picture changes somewhat once sociodemographic controls are introduced. For example, whereas migrants from intra-EU no longer differ from native peers, Southern Europeans now appear to be overqualified in terms of their educational attainments (although only at 10% significance), together with individuals from Eastern Europe and non-EU countries, even though the extent of mismatch is reduced for the latter origins once control variables are added.

13.4.4. Results with Youth Interactions and Gender Gaps Among Youth

Following the baseline estimations, we investigate the labor market outcomes of various migrant groups by distinguishing between different age cohorts in order to obtain insights into the possible vulnerabilities that young people might experience in destination labor markets. To this end, we conduct several additional exercises.[13] First, we rerun similar models by adding an interaction term for the youth indicator and the origin dummies (Table 13.5). Next, based on these estimation results with youth interactions, we choose the migrant origins in which we are interested—Eastern and Southern Europe—and conduct a post-estimation mean-differences test (i.e., a t-test) to compare the labor market outcomes of young migrants to those of native-born young people (Table 13.6). We illustrate the results with youth interactions graphically for selected labor market outcomes by origin and by age group, broken down by the 35-year cutoff (see Figure 13.2). Finally, we augment the econometric analysis thus far with the gender dimension by estimating labor market performance models across different migrant origins by gender and by age groups only among individuals

Table 13.5 Estimations of labor market performance with youth interactions (with full set of controls)

	Employment	Unemployment	Self-employment	Temporary contract	Hours (weekly)	Overqualified
	(1)	(2)	(3)	(4)	(5)	(6)
South	0.049	0.018	0.003	0.044*	-0.607	0.012
	(0.034)	(0.014)	(0.025)	(0.024)	(0.838)	(0.018)
East	-0.076***	0.044***	-0.015	0.052***	-0.115	0.030**
	(0.028)	(0.010)	(0.023)	(0.019)	(0.917)	(0.014)
Intra-EU	-0.108***	0.019*	0.015	0.031**	-0.666	-0.006
	(0.022)	(0.012)	(0.016)	(0.014)	(0.662)	(0.008)
Non-EU	-0.064***	0.047***	-0.018*	0.069***	0.960**	0.048***
	(0.013)	(0.005)	(0.010)	(0.008)	(0.418)	(0.005)
Young (age < 35)	-0.071***	0.016***	-0.082***	0.083***	-1.091***	0.017***
	(0.005)	(0.002)	(0.005)	(0.003)	(0.184)	(0.002)
South*Young	-0.038	-0.002	0.081	0.001	1.243	0.030
	(0.062)	(0.021)	(0.052)	(0.036)	(1.684)	(0.025)
East*Young	0.119***	-0.036***	0.025	-0.024	2.038	0.002
	(0.041)	(0.014)	(0.035)	(0.026)	(1.505)	(0.018)
Intra-EU*Young	0.145***	0.001	0.020	-0.069***	1.389	0.016
	(0.039)	(0.019)	(0.032)	(0.023)	(1.187)	(0.014)
Non-EU*Young	-0.006	-0.018***	-0.004	-0.013	-0.683	-0.026***
	(0.020)	(0.007)	(0.019)	(0.012)	(0.715)	(0.009)
Female	-0.138***	-0.006***	-0.073***	0.018***	-9.501***	-0.019***
	(0.004)	(0.002)	(0.003)	(0.003)	(0.128)	(0.002)
Household size	-0.055***	-0.003***	-0.001	0.018***	-0.778***	0.004***
	(0.003)	(0.001)	(0.003)	(0.002)	(0.137)	(0.001)

(continued)

Table 13.5 Continued

	Employment	Unemployment	Self-employment	Temporary contract	Hours (weekly)	Overqualified
	(1)	(2)	(3)	(4)	(5)	(6)
Education (years)	0.028***	−0.003***	0.002***	−0.001**	0.284***	0.031***
	(0.001)	(0.000)	(0.000)	(0.000)	(0.018)	(0.001)
Married	0.056***	−0.035***	0.009**	−0.049***	−0.008	−0.011***
	(0.005)	(0.002)	(0.004)	(0.003)	(0.151)	(0.002)
No. of children	0.103***	0.005***	0.004	−0.020***	0.229	−0.003**
	(0.003)	(0.001)	(0.003)	(0.002)	(0.152)	(0.002)
Living in urban area	−0.020***	0.003	−0.004	0.000	−0.650***	−0.010***
	(0.004)	(0.002)	(0.004)	(0.003)	(0.139)	(0.002)
Individual controls	Yes	Yes	Yes	Yes	Yes	Yes
Year effects	Yes	Yes	Yes	Yes	Yes	Yes
Country-fixed effects	Yes	Yes	Yes	Yes	Yes	Yes
Pseudo R^2	0.099	0.048	0.057	0.099	0.149	0.408
No. of observations	139,641	139,641	91,960	91,960	89,445	91,670

Notes: See notes to Table 13.4.
Source: ESS (2002–2015).

Table 13.6 Labor market performance differences between native-born youth and young Southern/Eastern migrants

	Young Southern European migrants vs. young native-born	Young Eastern European migrants vs. young native-born
Employment	+	+
Unemployment	+	+
Self-employment	+**	+
Temporary contract	+*	+
Hours of work (weekly)	+	+**
Overqualified	+	+***

Notes: The table displays post-estimation *t*-test results of linear combinations of origin interacted with youth dummies. A plus sign indicates that the respective migrant group has a higher value of the outcome variable compared to native-born. Asterisks indicate the significance level of the *t*-tests based on conventional notation. No asterisk means nonsignificance of the tested coefficients. Only recent migrants who arrived in the destination countries within the previous 10 years are included in the analysis.
*$p < .10$.
**$p < .05$.
***$p < .01$.
Source: ESS (2002–2015).

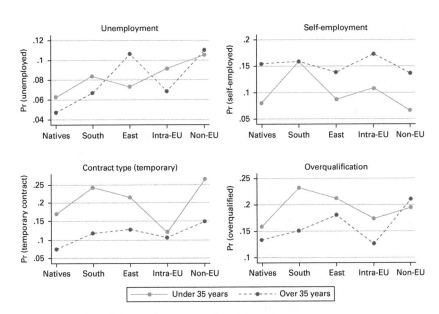

Figure 13.2 Predicted labor market outcomes by origins and age groups.
Source: ESS (2002–2015).

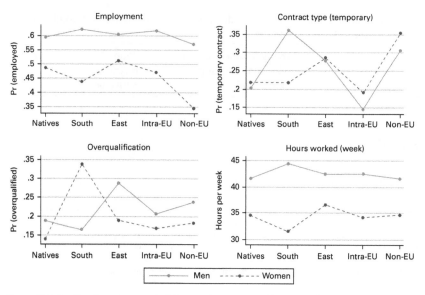

Figure 13.3 Predicted gender gaps in labor market outcomes by origin of youth.
Source: ESS (2002–2015).

younger than age 35 years. We display the predicted gender gaps among young people and by origin in selected labor market outcomes (see Figure 13.3)

In Table 13.5, the single coefficients of the origin dummies for Southern and Eastern Europe give the average effect for these groups without distinguishing the age group, whereas the interacted terms with the youth dummy give the effects for young individuals from these regions. Therefore, to obtain the overall effect of being young and being of a particular origin on the outcome variable, we need to add these coefficients together. Before assessing the overall effects, a quick glance at the estimated coefficients suggests that compared to older individuals, young individuals are less likely to be employed or self-employed, are more likely to be unemployed or have temporary job contracts, and are more likely to be overqualified for their occupations.

In order to determine whether the joint effect of being young and from a particular migratory origin on labor market outcome is statistically significant, we run post-estimation significance tests of linear combinations of the coefficients of the youth and respective origin dummies from Table 13.5. Table 13.6 summarizes these post-estimation test results for young Southern and Eastern European migrants by taking native-born young people as the reference group.[14]

The results show that young Southern and Eastern Europeans are not significantly more likely than young native peers to be employed or unemployed. However, young Southern Europeans are more likely than young native peers to be self-employed (which is not a general result for Southern migrants of all ages, as seen in Table 13.4). Finally, the results suggest that young migrants from both Eastern and Southern Europe are more likely than young native peers to be overqualified for their occupations, where the gap compared to native peers is statistically significant for Eastern Europeans, in particular.

To further illustrate these results visually, Figure 13.2 shows the predicted probabilities of selected labor market indicators—such as unemployment, self-employment, contract type, and overqualification—across origins for two age bands (cut-off age is 35 years). The graphs in Figure 13.2 are based on the estimated probit models with the full set of controls, and each point in the figure gives the marginal effect of a particular age group on the predicted outcome for a given origin. The top left panel shows that unemployment is generally higher for all young groups of different origins except for Eastern Europe and that the overall predicted unemployment is highest among non-EU migrants. Regarding self-employment, young individuals of all origins have lower predicted self-employment compared to older individuals. Among young people, Southern Europeans have the highest level of self-employment. Similar to self-employment, young individuals of all origins are more likely than older individuals to have a temporary contract, but among the youth of different origins, there is quite a bit of heterogeneity in predicted outcomes. For example, young migrants from non-EU countries and Southern Europe have higher predicted values for having a temporary contract compared to young intra-EU migrants and native-born workers. Finally, younger individuals are generally more likely to be overqualified across all groups, except for non-EU migrants. However, as the post-estimation test from Table 13.4 suggested, the difference is significant mainly for Eastern Europeans.

Finally, we examine the gender gaps among individuals of different origins and aged 35 years or younger for selected labor market outcomes, such as employment, contract type, overqualification, and hours worked per week. We choose the labor market outcomes for which we observed significant (unconditional) gender differences, as reported previously (see Table 13.3). Figure 13.3 is based on the estimation of predicted probabilities for these selected outcomes after including all control variables as before. We see that there is an important gender gap in favor of men in employment and hours worked per week and that this pattern holds for all migrant groups considered. As observed previously for other outcomes, there are also variations in the outcomes among the migrant origins. For example, young women of non-EU origins have the lowest employment and hours worked per week compared to young women of other origins and compared to young men in general. Concerning contract type, we observe that the previous gender-gap patterns are somewhat broken but that they still seem to exist. For example, young migrant men from Southern Europe have a higher probability of having a temporary job compared to their female counterparts of the same origin, whereas the predicted probability of being on a temporary job contract is almost the same for young native-born individuals and for Eastern European male and female migrants. Regarding the gender gap in the overqualification outcome, it seems that there is again a slight gender pattern, although this time it is more in favor of women, whereby young men of most origins, including native-born men (except for Southern Europe), are more likely than young women to be overqualified for the jobs they hold.

13.5. DISCUSSION

Overall, regarding the main groups of interest in the destination countries analyzed, the results from baseline estimations show clearly that migrants from Eastern Europe and non-EU countries (as well as from Southern Europe, to a lesser extent) display important differences in certain labor outcomes, such as employment, unemployment, and overqualification for the occupation held, even after taking into account differences in their socioeconomic characteristics. This comes as a surprise given the strong educational and socioeconomic background of some migrants. At the same time, examining the fit of the models in different columns, we observe that the performance of the model estimation varies across outcomes of interest, whereby the fit of the models for employment, hours worked, and overqualification is better than for the rest.

The finding of a relatively worse labor market performance of migrants compared to native peers is not very new in the literature (Chiswick 1978; Adsera and Chiswick 2007; Jean et al. 2007; Akgüç and Ferrer 2015). Chiswick asserts that the earnings gap between native-born individuals and immigrants in the labor markets narrows the longer the migrant stays in the destination country and that this assimilation period can last for a relatively long time (10–15 years). The fact that we focus our analysis only on recent migrants could partially explain these nativity gaps because it might take a longer time for recent migrants to accumulate country-specific skills. Other reasons behind the persisting gaps between various populations in European destination labor markets could be related to factors not accounted for here, such as individual unobserved heterogeneity, language proficiency gaps, and so on. A further explanation for labor market outcome gaps between native-born individuals and migrants could be related to differential labor market treatment in the form of discrimination.

Regarding the main results with youth interactions, we find that youth generally have worse outcomes in employment, unemployment, contract type, and education–occupation match compared to older cohorts but that these differences are not always significant. This is in line with the findings from the literature pointing to various transitional challenges faced by youth in general (Brzinsky-Fay 2007). Moreover, this differential performance varies by the origin of the young individuals. Our results also suggest that Eastern and Southern migrants are more likely than native-born people to be overqualified and that the overqualification of Eastern Europeans seems to be mainly found among young migrants. These findings, again, could be associated with the theses that there is imperfect international skills transferability across countries (Chiswick 2009) or that these young migrants need more time to fully assimilate and accumulate skills that are specific to the destination country so that they can catch up with the native-born individuals (Chiswick 1978). Moreover, we note that because the estimated models are based on pooled data from a number of relatively hetero-geneous destination countries with different labor market institutions, welfare systems, and compositions of migrant populations, it is impossible to pin down the exact mechanism explaining why the migrant–native gaps persist in the labor markets.

Regarding the gender dimension in labor market integration among youth migrants, our findings highlight the fact that the gender gaps seem to generally exist among young individuals regarding certain labor outcomes such as employ-ment and hours worked, although some differential patterns are also observed in contract type and occupational mismatch. Moreover, the predicted outcomes also vary by different migratory origins. In summary, various factors—such as different labor market institutions in terms of their flexibility for work–life bal-ance, differences in childcare access, as well as different cultural attitudes toward labor market participation among various migrant groups—could be behind these gender gaps. A comprehensive understanding of the causal mechanisms behind these differences is beyond the scope of this chapter; however, we high-light these gender differences among youth migrants by controlling for various sociodemographic and ethnic backgrounds and by exploiting the variation across countries and time.

13.6. CONCLUSIONS

Using a microeconometric framework, this chapter examined the labor market integration of recent migrant populations vis-à-vis native-born individuals, with a focus on youth in major European countries that have received impor-tant inflows in recent decades. Although the quantitative analysis is carried out including all migratory origins, particular attention is paid to migrants from Southern and Eastern Europe, given that these two regions have been the largest source of young migrants within Europe especially during the past decade. In this vein, examining the recent migration flows from within Europe, Akgüç and Beblavý (2015) point to a shift from Southern Europe to Eastern Europe as an important region of origin. The stock figures suggest, however, that Southern European migrant stocks are still larger than those of Eastern Europeans across many destinations in Europe, such as France, Germany, and the United Kingdom.

This chapter focused on youth migrant integration and investigated outcomes following migration because—based on several theories outlined previously—(1) migration is an essential part of a strategic transition in an individual's life and (2) youth is a particular group with possibly different migration behavior and human capital endowment compared to the rest of the population. With this aim in mind, the microeconometric analysis using individual-level data from the ESS across 15 European countries specifically examined how young migrants differ from older migrants and from native peers, and especially whether young migrants from Southern and Eastern Europe have different labor market outcomes compared to young migrants from the rest of Europe and from outside the EU. The chapter treated migrants as a heterogeneous group and distinguished ethnic origins via broader country clusters. The descriptive analysis highlighted that recent migrants (who arrived within the past 10 years) are, on average, much younger than the native-born population. The findings from the micro-level analysis suggest that migrants from Eastern and Southern Europe show important differences compared to native-born people regarding certain outcomes, such as employment, unemployment, contract type, and overqualification, even after taking into account differences in socioeconomic characteristics such as education, gender, age, and country-fixed and year effects. Furthermore, young migrants from both Eastern and Southern Europe are more likely to be overqualified compared to young native-born workers. These findings imply that individual characteristics explain only part of the differential performance of migrants in the destination-country labor markets. Moreover, we also find important gender gaps in favor of men in employment and hours worked per week and that this pattern holds for all migrant groups considered (and very significantly so for non-EU migrants).

There could be various reasons for the unexplained gaps between different young migrant groups and native peers, such as differential treatment of these groups in destination countries. Regarding the vulnerabilities faced by—especially female—migrants in the labor markets, there is also the issue of their selection into the labor force (and employment), which could lie behind the discrepancies compared to the performance of native-born workers. However, dealing with selection issues, in general, is outside the scope of this chapter and has been left for future research. Last, we note that given the pooled nature of the cross-country data, we can expect different outcomes and findings if the analysis is carried out on a single country; nevertheless, these findings on differential outcomes for migrants in destination-country labor markets call for further research on the underlying channels leading to native–migrant gaps. In this vein, panel data would prove very useful in controlling for unobserved individual heterogeneity.

To tackle issues of persisting native–migrant gaps in labor market performance, policies could be geared toward further integration and nondiscriminatory treatment of foreign-born residents in the destination labor markets. Employers could adopt anonymous job applications to avoid discriminatory hiring based on ethnicity. On the education–occupation mismatch issue, better screening and more transparent evaluation schemes could be developed to compare and recognize the degrees, qualifications, and skills possessed by the migrants so that their skills and competences could be put to better use in destination countries. Similarly, mechanisms that facilitate international skill transferability and on-the-job training possibilities could be offered to (young) migrants so as to avoid skill mismatches in occupations. Regarding the persisting gender gap found among migrants, especially in outcomes such as employment and hours worked, policymakers could take a targeted approach, whereby they inform migrant women about existing facilities, such as family-friendly work schedules and access to childcare, depending on the destination-country context and labor market flexibilities.

NOTES

1   We thank Silvana Weiss, Paweł Kaczmarczyk, and the editors of this volume—Jacqueline O'Reilly, Janine Leschke, Renate Ortlieb, Martin Seeleib-Kaiser, and Paola Villa—for valuable comments and feedback.
2   We are not able to analyze wages because the data we used contain no information on this point.
3   Except for countries such as Ireland, Sweden, and the United Kingdom, which opened their labor markets immediately to migrants from the new member states.
4   See http://ec.europa.eu/social for more information regarding the year when free access to the receiving-country labor markets in the old member states was given to citizens of new member states.
5   We acknowledge the existence of further heterogeneities among migrants within country-of-origin clusters; however, this compromise is offset by the possibility of getting an overall effect for these broader groups of origin, which still have certain sociodemographic characteristics in common. We leave the more detailed analysis of the peculiarities of migration experiences by specific origins to future research.
6   In this construction, non-EU also includes Switzerland and Norway; however, given the relatively low emigration rates from these countries compared to the rest of the non-EU, the data are not significantly affected by this inclusion. Moreover, the results are also not sensitive to including these two countries in the intra-EU cluster.
7   We also estimated models with indicators for underqualification and correct matches; the results are not reported here but are available from the authors upon request.

8 There may be other ways to define overqualification that take into account migrant niches in certain occupations, where migrants might be overrepresented (see Kacmarczyk and Tyrowicz 2015).

9 We also ran the analysis dropping the first round of the survey (hence, years 2002 and 2003) so as to account for the first year of the enlargement period, but the results remained substantially the same. Therefore, we decided to use all the survey rounds.

10 As a robustness check, we estimated the mismatch variables using a multinomial logit specification; the results (available upon request) remain qualitatively unchanged compared to binary probit estimations.

11 Of course, there could also be network effects, in which the existing migrant networks in urban areas attract further migrants.

12 Note that we do not observe the same individuals over their exact life cycle in the ESS data set; rather, we observe different cohorts of representative individuals at various cycles in their lives.

13 We also ran models without native-born individuals and included controls for years since migration, but the results did not change substantially; thus, we present the findings with the full set of population groups.

14 We note that the comparison of young migrants to older native-born individuals would be a different exercise, which we also performed but have not reported here (available upon request). We also note that these results are based on pooled country estimations and hence might show different patterns if applied to and tested in separate country studies.

REFERENCES

Adsera, Alicia, and Barry R. Chiswick. 2007. "Are There Gender and Country of Origin Differences in Immigrant Labor Market Outcomes Across European Destinations?" *Journal of Population Economics* 20: 495–526.

Akgüç, Mehtap. 2014. "Do Visas Matter? Labor Market Outcomes of Immigrants in France by Visa Classes at Entry." TSE Working Paper. Toulouse: Toulouse School of Economics.

Akgüç, Mehtap, and Miroslav Beblavý. 2015. "From South or East? Re-emerging European Migration Patterns and Labor Market Outcomes." STYLE Working Paper 6.3. Brighton, UK: CROME, University of Brighton. http://www.style-research.eu/publications/working-papers

Akgüç, Mehtap, and Ana Ferrer. 2015. "Educational Attainment and Labor Market Performance: An Analysis of Immigrants in France." IZA Discussion Paper 8925. Bonn: Institute for the Study of Labor.

Aleksynska, Mariya, and Ahmed Tritah. 2013. "Occupation–Education Mismatch of Immigrant Workers in Europe: Context and Policies." *Economics of Education Review* 36: 229–44.

Algan, Yann, Christian Dustmann, Albrecht Glitz, and Alan Manning. 2010. "The Economic Situation of First- and Second-Generation Immigrants in France, Germany and the United Kingdom." *Economic Journal* 120: 4–30.

Antecol, Heather, Peter Kuhn, and Stephen J. Trejo. 2006. "Assimilation via Prices or Quantities? Sources of Immigrant Earnings Growth in Australia, Canada, and the United States." *Journal of Human Resources* 41 (4): 821–40.

Beine, Michel, Frédéric Docquier, and Çağlar Özden. 2011. "Diasporas." *Journal of Development Economics* 95 (1): 30–41.

Blau, Francine D., Lawrence M. Kahn, and Kerry L. Papps. 2011. "Gender, Source Country Characteristics, and Labor Market Assimilation Among Immigrants: 1980–2000." *Review of Economics and Statistics* 93 (1): 43–58.

Borjas, George J. 1987. "Self-Selection and the Earnings of Immigrants." *American Economic Review* 77 (4): 531–53.

Borjas, George J., Stephen G. Bronars, and Stephen J. Trejo. 1992. "Self-Selection and Internal Migration in the United States." *Journal of Urban Economics* 32 (2): 159–85.

Bowles, Samuel. 1970. "Migration as Investment: Empirical Tests of the Human Investment Approach to Geographical Mobility." *Review of Economic Statistics* 52 (4): 356–62.

Brücker, Herbert, Stella Capuano, and Abdeslam Marfouk. 2013. "Education, Gender and International Migration: Insights from a Panel-Dataset 1980–2010." Mimeo. Nuremberg: IAB Institute for Employment Research.

Brzinsky-Fay, Christian. 2007. "Lost in Transition? Labour Market Entry Sequences of School Leavers in Europe." *European Sociological Review* 23 (4): 409–22.

Castles, Stephen. 1986. "The Guest-Worker in Western Europe: An Obituary." *International Migration Review* 20 (4): 761–78.

Castles, Stephen. 2006. "Guestworkers in Europe: A Resurrection?" *International Migration Review* 40 (4): 741–66.

Chiswick, Barry R. 1978. "The Effect of Americanization on the Earnings of Foreign-Born Men." *Journal of Political Economy* 86 (5): 897–922.

Chiswick, Barry R. 1979. "The Economic Progress of Immigrants: Some Apparently Universal Patterns." In *Contemporary Economic Problems*, edited by William J. Fellner, 357–99. Washington, DC: American Enterprise Institute.

Chiswick, Barry R. 2009. "The International Transferability of Immigrants' Human Capital." *Economics of Education Review* 28 (2): 162–69.

Chiswick, Barry R., and Paul W. Miller. 2010. "Does the Choice of Reference Levels of Education Matter in the ORU Earnings Equation?" *Economics of Education Review* 29 (6): 1076–85.

Ciccarone, Giuseppe. 2013. "Geographical Labour Mobility in the Context of the Crisis: Italy." Ad-hoc Request. Brussels: European Employment Observatory.

Clark, Ken, and Stephen Drinkwater. 2008. "The Labour-Market Performance of Recent Migrants." *Oxford Review of Economic Policy* 24 (3): 496–517.

Constant, Amelie F., and Elena D'Agosto. 2008. "Where Do the Brainy Italians Go?" IZA Discussion Paper 3325. Bonn: Institute for the Study of Labor.

Constant, Amelie F., and Douglas S. Massey. 2003. "Self-Selection, Earnings and Out-Migration: A Longitudinal Study of Immigrants." *Journal of Population Economics* 16: 630–53.

Constant, Amelie F., Olga Nottmeyer, and Klaus F. Zimmermann. 2012. "Cultural Integration in Germany." In *Cultural Integration of Immigrants in Europe*, edited by Yann Algan, Alberto Bisin, Alan Manning, and Thierry Verdier, 69–124. Oxford: Oxford University Press.

Constant, Amelie F., and Klaus F. Zimmermann. 2005. "Legal Status at Entry, Economic Performance, and Self-Employment Proclivity: A Bi-National Study of Immigrants. IZA Discussion Paper 1910. Bonn: Institute for the Study of Labor.

Docquier, Frédéric, and Hillel Rapoport. 2012. "Globalization, Brain Drain, and Development." *Journal of Economic Literature* 50 (3): 681–730.

Eurostat. 2011. *Migrants in Europe: A Statistical Portrait of the First and Second Generation.* Luxembourg: Publications Office of the European Union.

Fernández, Raquel, and Alessandra Fogli. 2009. "Culture: An Empirical Investigation of Beliefs, Work, and Fertility." *American Economic Journal: Microeconomics* 1 (1): 146–77.

Ferrer, Ana, and W. Craig Riddell. 2008. "Education, Credentials, and Immigrant Earnings." *Canadian Journal of Economics* 41 (1): 186–216.

Galgóczi, Béla, and Janine Leschke. 2012. "Intra-EU Labor Migration After Eastern Enlargement and During the Crisis." ETUI Working Paper 13. Brussels: European Trade Union Institute.

Galgóczi, Béla, Janine Leschke, and Andrew Watt. 2011. "Intra-EU Labor Migration: Flows, Effects and Policy Responses." ETUI Working Paper 03. Brussels: European Trade Union Institute.

González Gago, Elvira, and Marcelo Segales Kirzner. 2013. "Geographical Labour Mobility in the Context of the Crisis: Spain." Ad-hoc Request. Brussels: European Employment Observatory Publication.

Greenwood, Michel J., Gary L. Hunt, and John M. McDowell. 1986. "Migration and Employment Change: Empirical Evidence on the Spatial and Temporal Dimensions of the Linkage." *Journal of Regional Science* 26 (2): 223–34.

Harris, John R., and Michael P. Todaro. 1970. "Migration, Unemployment and Development: A Two-Sector Analysis." *American Economic Review* 60 (1): 125–42.

Izquierdo, Mario, Juan F. Jimeno, and Aitor Lacuesta. 2016. "Spain: From (Massive) Immigration to (Vast) Emigration?" *IZA Journal of Development and Migration* 5 (10).

Jean, Sebastian, Orsetta Causa, Miguel Jimenez, and Isabelle Wanner. 2007. "Migration in OECD Countries: Labour Market Impact and Integration Issues." OECD Economics Department Working Paper 562. Paris: Organization for Economic Co-operation and Development.

Kacmarczyk, Paweł, and Joanna Tyrowicz. 2015. "Winners and Losers Among Skilled Migrants: The Case of Post-Accession Polish Migrants to the UK." IZA Discussion Paper 9057. Bonn: Institute for the Study of Labor.

Kahanec, Martin, and Klaus F. Zimmermann. 2010. "Migration in an Enlarged EU: A Challenging Solution?" In *Five Years of an Enlarged EU: A Positive Sum Game*, edited by Filip Keereman and Istvan Szekely, 63–94. Berlin: Springer.

Martin, Philip. 2009. "The Recession and Migration: Alternative Scenarios." International Migration Institute Working Paper 13. Oxford: University of Oxford.

Organization for Economic Co-operation and Development (OECD). 2012. *Better Skills, Better Lives: A Strategic Approach to Skills Policies.* Paris: OECD.

Seeleib-Kaiser, Martin, and Thees Spreckelsen. 2016. "Dimensions of Labour Market Integration Among Young EU Migrant Citizens in the UK." Barnett Working Paper 01. Oxford: Department of Social Policy and Intervention, University of Oxford.

Sjaastad, Larry A. 1962. "The Costs and Returns of Human Migration." *Journal of Political Economy* 70 (5): 80–93.

APPENDIX

Table A13.1 European Social Survey (2002–2015)

Country	ESS Round							Total sample
	1	2	3	4	5	6	7	
Austria	✓	✓	✓	o	o	o	✓	7,322
Belgium	✓	✓	✓	✓	✓	✓	✓	10,266
Denmark	✓	✓	✓	✓	✓	✓	✓	8,729
Finland	✓	✓	✓	✓	✓	✓	✓	11,314
France	✓	✓	✓	✓	✓	✓	✓	10,209
Germany	✓	✓	✓	✓	✓	✓	✓	16,294
Ireland	✓	✓	✓	✓	✓	✓	✓	12,435
Italy	✓	✓	o	o	o	✓	✓	2,993
Luxembourg	✓	✓	o	o	o	o	o	2,712
Netherlands	✓	✓	✓	✓	✓	✓	✓	10,678
Norway	✓	✓	✓	✓	✓	✓	✓	9,868
Spain	✓	✓	✓	✓	✓	✓	✓	10,823
Sweden	✓	✓	✓	✓	✓	✓	✓	10,200
Switzerland	✓	✓	✓	✓	✓	✓	✓	9,890
United Kingdom	✓	✓	✓	✓	✓	✓	✓	11,831
Total sample	23,827	23,742	20,901	19,228	18,498	19,774	19,594	145,564

Note: A checkmark indicates that the country was included in the survey round.
Source: ESS (2002–2015; rounds 1–7).

14

EUROPE'S PROMISE FOR JOBS?

LABOR MARKET INTEGRATION OF YOUNG EUROPEAN UNION MIGRANT CITIZENS IN GERMANY AND THE UNITED KINGDOM

Thees F. Spreckelsen, Janine Leschke, and Martin Seeleib-Kaiser

14.1. INTRODUCTION

Migrant youth are faced with the double disadvantage of labor market entry and problems associated with assimilation and discrimination in the broad context of migrant life courses (Kogan et al. 2011, 75). In the words of Hooijer and Picot (2015, p. 5), "Migrants are by definition labour market entrants" (see also Kogan 2006). Although there is some literature on barriers to labor market integration for recent immigrants in general (Kogan 2006; Andrews, Clark, and Whittaker 2007; Clark and Lindley 2009; Demireva 2011; Altorjai 2013), little country-comparative evidence is available on the working conditions of recent *young* EU migrant workers. Also, to date, only a few studies have explicitly compared migrant citizens from different European Union (EU) countries of origin with regard to their labor market outcomes (Akgüç and Beblavý 2015; Höhne and Schulze Buschoff 2015; Recchi 2015) while simultaneously taking into account the different institutional contexts in the countries of destination.

Against this backdrop, this chapter focuses on the quantitative and qualitative labor market integration of recent young *EU migrant citizens*[1] from Central and Eastern Europe (CEE, EU8),[2] Romania and Bulgaria (EU2), and Southern European countries (South-EU),[3] who are living in Germany and the United Kingdom.[4] To contextualize our analysis, results are also presented for the old EU member states (EU-Rest)[5] and for third-country nationals (TCNs). Quantitative labor market integration is captured by examining the levels of employment of each group compared to nationals. Qualitative labor market integration is captured by comparing income, forms of nonstandard employment, and particularly marginal, fixed-term, and (solo) self-employment, as well as skills/qualification mismatch of each group against nationals. Germany and the United Kingdom were selected as destinations because these two countries not only have very different labor markets and welfare regimes but also are major destination countries for intra-EU migration (Galgóczi and Leschke 2015). A comparison between the two countries is of special interest given that intra-EU migration—in contrast to the openness of the British labor market in the past—was one of the key issues in the debate leading up to the 2016 Brexit referendum in the United Kingdom, whereas major European politicians, such as the German chancellor Angela Merkel, are outspoken advocates of freedom of movement.

On the basis of the quantitative and qualitative labor market indicators outlined previously, this chapter addresses the following research questions: How well are recent young migrants integrated in the labor market relative to their peers in the respective destination countries? Does the degree of labor market integration reflect structural differences between the regions of origin (in particular, CEE and Southern European countries) and macroeconomic changes caused by the economic crisis after 2008? Is there evidence that quantitative and qualitative labor market integration of recent young EU migrants varies across welfare regimes?

The novelty of our research is its comparative perspective at the level of both country group of origin and destination countries. The analyses describe the situation in both Germany and the United Kingdom using—for the most part—proportions and means across the different migration groups. Furthermore, in line with the public debates reflecting on "migrants" as a holistic group, characteristics such as skill levels are not controlled for, nor are young EU citizens' undoubtedly various motives for migrating (Verwiebe, Wiesböck, and Teitzer 2014) taken into account. Thus, this chapter investigates the aggregate differences between young nationals and the recent EU migrant population in Germany and the United Kingdom, with a focus on the precrisis and postcrisis periods, in order to provide an assessment of their situation.[6]

The following section briefly presents the economic and welfare-state context of the two receiving countries in order to formulate expectations with regard to the labor market integration of EU citizens. Section 14.3 presents the data, definitions, and measures. Section 14.4 contains the empirical results, focusing on forms of nonstandard employment, skills/qualification mismatches, and income. Finally, the discussion draws out commonalities and differences in relation to the region of origin and receiving countries.

14.2. ECONOMIC AND WELFARE-STATE CONTEXTS

Young migrants face the same risks and challenges with regard to labor market integration as all young people, as well as those difficulties that are specific to migrants. Labor market "outsiderness"—inactivity, unemployment, low income, and low employment protection—is increasingly problematic for young people across Europe (Seeleib-Kaiser and Spreckelsen 2018), leading to a "new generation with higher exposure to systematic labor market risks" (Chung, Bekker, and Houwing 2012, 301). Youth vulnerability to labor market outsiderness is due in part to limited work experience, which impacts on the transition from education to employment (Brzinsky-Fay 2007; Schmelzer 2008). Early career insecurity is exacerbated by a prevalence of fixed-term contracts and "last-in, first-out" principles. In addition, the dualization literature (Emmenegger et al. 2012) has highlighted the risk of migrants becoming labor market outsiders who are exposed to (insecure) precarious employment and low wages (Standing 2009).

Access to the labor market by EU migrant citizens from EU8 countries has differed significantly between Germany and the United Kingdom. Whereas EU8 migrant citizens had more or less immediate access to the UK labor market after the accession of the CEE countries in 2004, Germany applied strict transition rules until 2011 (Fihel et al. 2015). Prior to the 2008–2009 economic crisis, and after 2012, the United Kingdom had strong economic pull factors for EU migrants—low unemployment, overall good economic performance, and a liberal regulatory regime coupled with language advantages. By contrast, weak economic growth and comparatively high unemployment rates made Germany less attractive up until the economic crisis. Nevertheless, long-term traditions of migration from CEE countries, including particular inflows for seasonal labor, the existence of migration networks, and geographic proximity, played important roles in attracting EU migrant workers to Germany (for details, see Kogan 2011). EU2 migrants were restricted from entering the German and the UK labor markets as employees for the maximum possible transition period of 7 years following the 2007 EU enlargement.

As a result of the asymmetric economic development within the EU after 2008, the growing German economy became much more attractive for intra-EU labor migrants, whereas the crisis had a dampening effect on the UK labor market. Given rising unemployment and a shift in migration policies (transitional measures for workers from Romania and Bulgaria and changes in benefit entitlements), the United Kingdom became comparatively less attractive during the crisis period (Tilly 2011). Hence, the labor market integration of migrants in Germany is likely to have improved over time, whereas an inverse trend might be visible in the United Kingdom. The impact of transition measures is expected to be visible in particular with regard to the share of (solo) self-employed migrant citizens in the economy because the freedom of establishment can be used to "circumvent" employment restrictions (for more details on self-employment, see Ortlieb, Sheehan, and Masso, this volume).

Quantitative labor market integration of (young) EU migrant citizens might be easier in the United Kingdom than in Germany given the two countries' different school-to-work transition regimes (Walther and Pohl 2005; Hadjivassiliou et al., this volume) and, in particular, the prevalence of general skills in the United Kingdom. Strongly institutionalized vocational education systems and a relatively strong reliance on specific skills, as found in Germany (Hall and Soskice 2001), can represent an entry barrier to migrant employment and might thus potentially also lead to more segmentation between nationals and migrants in qualitative labor market outcomes. Irrespective of institutional labor market and welfare-state differences (Esping-Andersen 1990; Hall and Soskice 2001; Hall 2007), both Germany and the United Kingdom have highly segmented labor markets, as evidenced in the low-wage sectors. Similarly, both countries have institutionalized job categories at the outer fringes of the labor market: "minijobs" in Germany and "zero-hours contracts" in the United Kingdom. In addition, trade union density has been declining substantially during recent decades in both countries. The German labor market is also segmented with regard to job security, partly as a result of strict employment protection for insiders, which differs significantly from the relatively low overall level of employment protection in the United Kingdom (Organization for Economic Co-operation and Development (OECD) 2013).

Empirical research by Fleischmann and Dronkers (2010) suggests that country-of-origin effects can be more significant for labor market integration than the nature and characteristics of the destination labor market. There are several reasons for potential differences in labor market integration by country or region of origin. Wage differentials between country of origin and destination country and differences in reservation wages might be a result of much lower (exportable) unemployment benefits. As Bruzelius, Reinprecht, and Seeleib-Kaiser (2016) have shown, the exportable weekly unemployment benefit of an ideal-typical unemployed Romanian worker moving to another EU member state is approximately €27/$32, compared to the benefit of €228/$267 for an unemployed German worker. Low exportable benefits are likely to expose migrants from CEE countries and Southern Europe to precarious work. Compared to migrants from EU-Rest countries, they might thus also be more likely to take up jobs below their skill levels or that do not reflect their formal qualifications, leading to qualification and skill mismatches (McGuinness, Bergin, and Whelan, this volume). This problem will be even more pronounced for youth migrants, given that young people typically are less often eligible for unemployment benefits compared to adults because of insufficient contribution records (Leschke and Finn, this volume).

Overall, our expectation is to find a clear stratification of labor market integration by EU migrant citizens' region of origin as a result of differences in reservation wages and variations in the application of transition measures. We expect to find less labor market integration overall and more segmentation compared to nationals in Germany than in the United Kingdom. This would reflect the stronger reliance of the German labor market on specific compared to general skills and the recent precarization and dualization trends (Lehndorff 2015), which indeed are also found in the United Kingdom (Leschke and Keune 2008). We expect

> a segmentation of labor market integration by region of origin in terms of employment (quantitative integration), income, and quality of jobs (qualitative integration), with potentially more segmentation in Germany;
> higher rates of solo self-employment of EU8 and EU2 migrants in Germany and of EU2 migrants in the United Kingdom as a result of institutional and transition arrangements; and
> improving quantitative and qualitative labor market integration of EU youth migrants over time in Germany, with an inverse trend in the United Kingdom because of economic developments.

14.3. DATA, DEFINITIONS, AND MEASURES

In our analysis, we define youth as *young people* aged 20–34 years. As a consequence of data restrictions, migrants are identified slightly differently between the United Kingdom and Germany.[7] This chapter studies recent migrants, specifically those who arrived in the respective receiving country within the previous 5 years (Rienzo 2013). The region-of-origin effects regarding EU migrant citizens are best studied among those who have arrived recently because after 5 years of residence, EU migrant citizens have the same social rights as nationals, irrespective of their economic activity or economic status. Moreover, more established migrants might have already caught up with or assimilated with their national peers.

The analyses utilized the German Microcensus[8] and the UK Quarterly Labour Force Survey (UK-LFS),[9] both of which are the national inputs to the European Labour Force Survey (EU-LFS), rendering them relatively comparable in terms of sampling and indicators. However, the UK-LFS has been known to underestimate migrant populations (Martí and Ródenas 2007; Longhi and Rokicka 2012). The same is likely to be true for the German Microcensus because the questionnaire is only available in German (with translation assistance into English for the interviewers).[10] Because of the sampling design, both data sets largely exclude short-term migrants (e.g., seasonal workers) and cross-border or posted workers. Furthermore, the numbers for youth migrant workers are comparatively small, particularly when broken down by region of origin. Consequently, the data were pooled across waves to increase estimation samples and reliability. The results are provided with confidence intervals reflecting often small case numbers.[11]

The chapter combines data for 2004–2009 and 2010–2014 for the United Kingdom and for 2005–2008 and 2009–2012 for Germany so as to assess differences between the precrisis and crisis periods. Proportions and means were estimated for national youth and EU migrant citizen youth using the standard weights from the Microcensus and the UK-LFS. These account for nonresponse and adjust for demographic factors, namely age, nationality, and gender.

Table 14.1 summarizes the dimensions of labor market integration and their corresponding indicators in the German and UK data. Comparable measures and international standard classifications were used. Thus, employment is operationalized according to the International Labour Organization convention.[12]

Table 14.1 Measuring dimensions of labor market integration

	Germany	United Kingdom
Quantitative integration		
Employment, unemployment, inactivity	ILO	ILO
Qualitative integration		
Marginal employment	Minijobs (earnings < €400/approx. $470)	Gross hourly wages at or below the national minimum wage according to age group[a]
Fixed-term employment	Employees only	Employees only
(Solo) self-employment	Self-employed without employees	Self-employed without employees
Skill/qualification mismatch	Mean ISEI[b] score for skill level (low, medium, and high: ISCED[c])	Mean ISEI score by origin of education (school, work-related, and university)
Income	Net hourly income (broad: including social benefits) adjusted for inflation (CPI)—only persons whose main source of income is employment	Net hourly income (pay)[d] adjusted for inflation (CPI)

[a]UK minimum wage limits differed over time: prior to 2010, the minimum wage increased at age 18 years and at age 22 years; subsequent to 2010, the age thresholds were 18 and 21 years, with a lower minimum for apprentices (GOV.UK 2016b).
[b]International Socio-Economic Index of Occupational Status (ISEI; Ganzeboom and Treiman 2003), calculated using syntax from the GESIS Institute (http://193.175.238.45/missy-qa/de/materials/MZ/tools/isei); for a critical account of the ISEI measure, see Schimpl-Neimanns (2004).
[c]The International Standard Classification of Education (ISCED) was created using routines available at GESIS (Lechert, Schroedter, and Lüttinger 2006).
[d]Proportions estimated using a zero-inflated Poisson regression, adjusted for illness/absence in reference week (United Kingdom only).
CPI, consumer price index; ILO, International Labour Organization.

Marginal employment is the key dimension that was conceptualized differently in the two countries. Marginal employment in Germany is characterized by the prevalence and recent increase of so-called "minijobs." Minijobs pay a maximum monthly wage of €450/$525 (€400/$470 until 2013) and are, in principle, exempt from social insurance contributions (Voss and Weinkopf 2012). These low-paying jobs are often topped up with in-work benefits (Bruckmeier et al. 2015)—similar to tax credits in the United Kingdom and United States. They are of particular relevance given the absence of a statutory minimum wage in Germany until 2015. In the United Kingdom, marginal employment was measured as employment at or below the national minimum wage. Temporary employment was operationalized as employees being on fixed-term contracts.

Self-employment can be very heterogeneous, taking place at both the high end and the low end of the labor market (Ortlieb and Weiss 2015), whereby self-employed workers without employees (solo self-employed) have worse labor market outcomes than do self-employed with employees. Self-employed workers in Germany, unlike the United Kingdom, are not obliged to contribute to social insurance. Hence, self-employed workers with comparatively low earnings are likely to have insufficient social insurance coverage (Schulze Buschoff and Protsch 2008).

Qualification mismatch and skill mismatch were assessed by comparing the average occupational status for a qualification (skill level) among natives against the corresponding status for the same qualification (skill level) among migrants (see Section 14.4.3.2 for an explanation of the distinction between the two types of mismatch). Although this is a fairly standard way of comparing skills–occupation mismatch, such a relative measure has the disadvantage that immigrants may be clustered in specific immigrant occupation niches (Joassart-Marcelli 2014), which could potentially distort the results. In this regard, subjective measures on qualification mismatch would be more appropriate, but they are not available in the context of the research presented here. Income was measured somewhat differently in Germany and the United Kingdom. In both countries, net hourly income is analyzed; however, in Germany this refers to income including social benefits and is only recorded for persons whose main source of income is employment. By contrast, income in the United Kingdom refers to pay from employment only, which in principle will exclude all benefits because even (Working or Child) Tax Credits are paid directly to claimants (GOV.UK 2016a). However, the respective survey question does not explicitly exclude other income. Income is adjusted for inflation using the respective country's consumer price index (Destatis 2016; Office of National Statistics 2015b).

14.4. RESULTS

14.4.1. Demographic Characteristics of Young European Union Migrant Citizens

In Germany and the United Kingdom, EU migrant citizens, especially those from EU8 and EU2 countries, increased as a share of all recent migrants from pre- to postcrisis (for details, see Leschke et al. 2016). Notably, and despite the economic crisis, we observe no *relative* increase for Southern European migrant citizens in the United Kingdom compared to the precrisis period. A relative increase can be observed for this group for the entire period in Germany, as well as a steep *absolute* increase since the crisis (Destatis 2012).

Recent EU migrant citizens in Germany and the United Kingdom are predominantly young, aged 20–34 years (Table 14.2). In Germany, gender proportions differ considerably across migrant groups, with relatively more female CEE youth and fewer female EU-South and EU-Rest youth. Gender proportions seem similar among youth migrant groups in the United Kingdom, except for fewer females among EU-South youth. Postcrisis, more young migrant citizens are students in Germany (13%–30%) than in the United Kingdom (9%–23%).

14.4.2. Quantitative Labor Market Integration: Economic Activity

Figure 14.1 records the employment, unemployment, and inactivity levels of young EU migrant citizens. Overall, they are well integrated compared to TCNs, and several groups have improved their status over time. In the United Kingdom, CEE migrants have higher employment rates compared to their native peers, whereas in Germany they have lower employment rates, which, however, have increased from pre- to postcrisis. This result is consistent with a labor demand argument, given the comparatively robust economic growth in Germany, the gradual opening up of the labor market in particular for qualified CEE migrants, and the end of transition measures for CEE nationals in 2011. The different proportions of youth in the respective employment statuses reflect the different shares of students among the migrant groups (e.g., larger proportions of students correspond to higher proportions of inactive youth because the inactive status is defined as including students; see Table 14.2).

14.4.3. Qualitative Labor Market Integration: Prevalence of Nonstandard Employment

Despite finding (relatively) positive quantitative employment integration levels, particularly in the postcrisis period, the results presented here demonstrate significant shortcomings in the quality of employment. Quality of employment is gauged by the prevalence of nonstandard employment, skills–occupation and qualification–occupation mismatch, and wages. Forms of nonstandard employment are reported separately; however, they tend to overlap and often correlate with low wages (Leschke 2015; on youth labor market outsiderness, see Seeleib-Kaiser and Spreckelsen 2018).

Table 14.2 Demographics of recent migrants to Germany and the United Kingdom, precrisis and postcrisis periods

Destination	Region of origin	Youth, % (aged 20–34 years)		Females, % (of youth migrants)		Students, % (of youth migrants)	
		Precrisis	Postcrisis	Precrisis	Postcrisis	Precrisis	Postcrisis
Germany	CEE (EU8)	72.5	65.0	67.4	58.4	18.1	12.8
	Bulgaria/Romania (EU2)	52.4	52.9	66.0	50.2	36.1	19.0
	EU-South	66.9	63.5	46.3	43.0	24.2	29.8
	EU-Rest	67.0	58.2	48.5	45.4	24.2	26.5
	Third country (TCN)	68.7	71.4	53.7	54.7	25.2	28.7
United Kingdom	CEE (EU8)	70.0	60.7	46.2	51.3	12.4	8.6
	Bulgaria/Romania (EU2)	68.7	67.1	50.1	51.1	17.7	14.9
	EU-South	63.3	61.6	53.4	44.0	17.7	14.3
	EU-Rest	53.3	53.2	50.4	55.8	15.9	14.3
	Third country (TCN)	55.9	57.4	49.4	50.3	24.0	23.1

CEE, Central and Eastern Europe; TCN, third-country nationals.
Sources: Pooled German Microcensus (2005–2012) and pooled UK-LFS Survey (2004–2014).

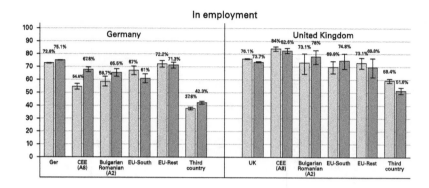

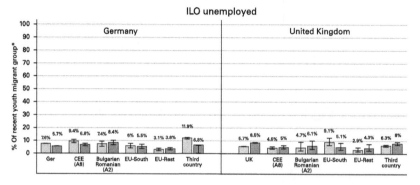

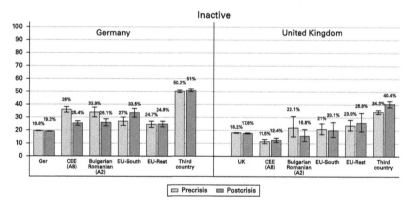

Figure 14.1 Employment status of recent youth migrants compared to nationals (Germany/United Kingdom, precrisis/postcrisis periods). Weighted estimates adjusted for sampling design.
Source: Pooled German Microcensus (2005–2012) and pooled UK-LFS (2004–2014).

14.4.3.1. Nonstandard Employment

In both countries, the results (Figure 14.2) show higher fixed-term employment levels among all migrant groups compared to their native peers, with larger differences in Germany, partially reflecting the weaker overall employment protection in the United Kingdom (OECD 2013). The higher level of fixed-term

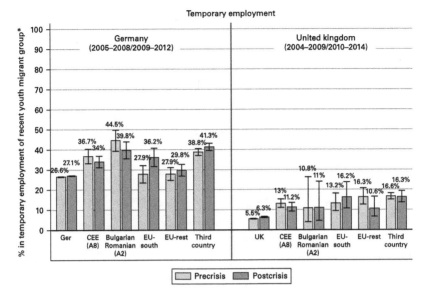

Figure 14.2 Temporary employment of recent youth migrants compared to nationals (Germany/United Kingdom, precrisis/postcrisis periods). Weighted estimates adjusted for sampling design.
Source: Pooled German Microcensus (2005–2012) and pooled UK-LFS (2004–2014).

contracts very likely reflects the labor market entrant status of recent migrants, irrespective of the host country. German nationals (postcrisis) have the longest fixed-term contracts and cite "being in education or training" as the main reason, whereas CEE nationals frequently mention probation periods (Leschke et al. 2016, Table 4a). CEE and EU-South nationals state "not finding a permanent job" as the main reason for *involuntary fixed-term employment*—more than other migrant groups and especially more than Germans (Leschke et al. 2016, Table 4a). Notably, one cannot discern consistent substantial changes in temporary employment from pre- to postcrisis.

The proportions of *solo self-employment* (self-employed without an employee; Figure 14.3) attest strongly to the labor market impact of the post-enlargement transition regimes (Fihel et al. 2015). Restrictions on the freedom of movement of labor applied to EU8 and EU2 migrants in Germany and to EU2 migrants in the United Kingdom. Consequently, EU migrant citizens from these countries were able to use the freedom of establishment to gain access to the labor market on the basis of self-employment (with some sectoral restrictions in place for Germany, including construction and commercial cleaning), which led to higher shares of solo self-employed EU8 and EU2 youth in Germany and to significantly higher solo self-employment among EU2 youth migrant citizens in the United Kingdom. These proportions declined slightly in Germany for EU8 nationals in the postcrisis period when transition measures were phased out.

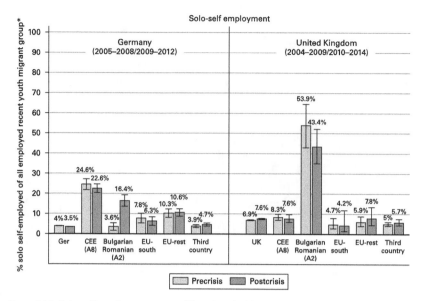

Figure 14.3 Solo self-employment (i.e., self-employed without employees) of recent youth migrants compared to nationals (Germany/United Kingdom, precrisis/postcrisis periods). Weighted estimates adjusted for sampling design.
Source: Pooled German Microcensus (2005–2012) and pooled UK-LFS (2004–2014).

In addition to solo self-employment, it seems pertinent to analyze *marginal employment*. In Germany, youth from EU8, EU2, and Southern European countries have higher shares in minijobs compared to natives. Nationals from the EU-Rest countries have the lowest and TCNs the highest shares in this form of employment (Figure 14.4).[13]

Although the United Kingdom has a lower earnings limit for national insurance contributions, somewhat similar to German minijobs, employment at the national minimum wage constitutes the main form of marginal employment (more than 5% of all jobs).[14] Youth from CEE are more likely to earn a minimum or below-minimum hourly wage compared to their United Kingdom peers. This also holds for EU2 but not for EU-South or EU-Rest youth. If anything, the latter have a lower share working at the minimum wage. Mirroring the German findings, a larger proportion of TCNs compared to nationals earn a minimum hourly wage in the United Kingdom (Figure 14.5).

14.4.3.2. Skill Mismatch and Qualification Mismatch

Several studies highlight a skills–occupation mismatch, particularly among CEE migrant workers in EU15 countries (European Integration Consortium 2009; Bettin 2012; Engels et al. 2012). This mismatch refers to situations in which the occupation a person works in requires a different skill level from what the person has at the present time. The "requirement" should be viewed in relative terms, referring, for example, to the average skill level in an occupation.

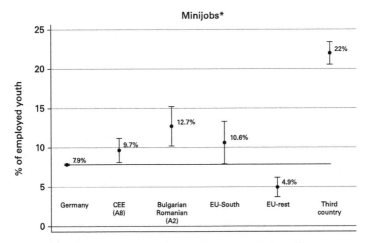

Figure 14.4 Share of minijobs among employed recent youth migrants compared to nationals (Germany, postcrisis period). * Maximuum pay <€450/$525, no social insurance contributions.
Source: Pooled German Microcensus (2009–2012).

Similarly, a qualification–occupation mismatch refers to the difference between the formal qualification a person holds and the qualification level of the person's occupation.

The measures of both skill and qualification mismatches are relative here, using the mean occupational status of the native youths in a skills/qualification category as a reference point (their status level is indicated by the horizontal line in each panel of Figures 14.6 and 14.7). Pooled data are presented here combining

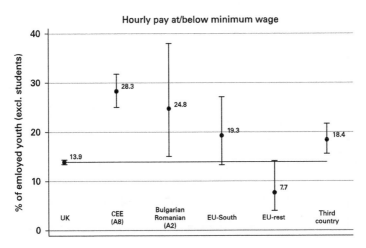

Figure 14.5 Hourly pay at/below the minimum wage for recent youth migrants compared to nationals (United Kingdom, postcrisis period). Estimates based on hourly pay ≤ minimum wage threshold.
Source: Pooled UK-LFS (2010–2014).

the pre- and postcrisis periods because of the low case numbers resulting from the division of the migrants into three groups according to their skill levels. The following results should be viewed with caution, given the differences between the indicators used (see Table 14.1), namely skills (Germany) and qualifications (United Kingdom). Therefore, the following sections refer correspondingly to skill mismatch and qualification mismatch in order to highlight the limited comparability of the measures.

Recent youth migrants from EU8 and EU2 work consistently in lower status jobs compared to their German peers (Figure 14.6). In the United Kingdom (Figure 14.7), the same holds for EU8 youth migrants (on the low rate of return to education for Polish migrants in the United Kingdom, see Kacmarczyk and Tyrowicz 2015) but not for their Bulgarian and Romanian peers. Consistently, young recent migrants from the Rest-EU find higher status jobs in the same skills bracket as their native peers in both Germany and the United Kingdom.

EU-South migrants with tertiary education seem to achieve on average higher status jobs compared to their native peers in Germany. Those with medium- or low-skilled backgrounds fare consistently worse than their native peers. For the United Kingdom, in contrast, EU-South nationals with tertiary education have comparatively poor occupational outcomes. The same holds true, although with smaller gaps, for those with work-related qualifications.

In Germany, migrant workers with medium skill levels (secondary and postsecondary nontertiary education) might have particular problems applying their skills (Engels et al. 2012), which again might follow from the importance of specific rather than general skills in the German economy.

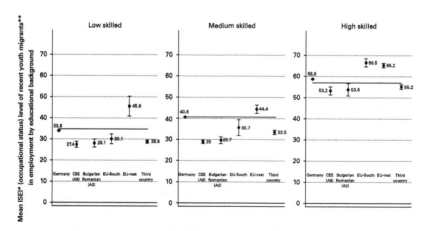

Figure 14.6 Levels of skill mismatch in Germany for recent youth migrants compared to nationals. *Mean ISEI-08 by educational background (**ISCED).
Source: Pooled German Microcensus (2005–2012).

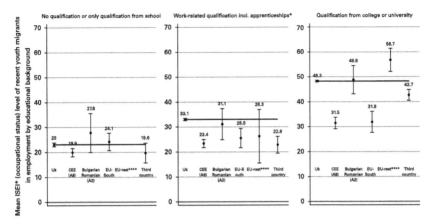

Figure 14.7 Levels of qualification mismatch in the United Kingdom for recent youth migrants compared to nationals. *Mean ISEI-08. Weighted estimates adjusted for sampling design. *Source*: Pooled UK-LFS (2004–2014).

14.4.3.3. Income Differentials

Migrant–native income differentials have long been studied (Andrews et al. 2007) in their own right. The focus here is instead on the comparison between youth migrant groups: Figure 14.8 presents the average hourly income levels of the different groups as a percentage of those of their German/UK peers.

Using the broad Microcensus income measure including social benefits (see Table 14.1), but restricting it to those people who state that their main income derives from work, Germany appears to be comparatively equal in terms of income, with slightly lower net income among EU2 migrants and considerably higher income among EU-South and EU-Rest youth (+11% and +31%, respectively). By contrast, EU8 migrants and, to a lesser extent, EU-South migrants and TCNs report lower income compared to their national peers in the United Kingdom. The experience of lower wages does not apply to migrants from the EU-Rest; both in the United Kingdom and in Germany, these EU migrant citizens do better than their native peers.

14.5. DISCUSSION

14.5.1. Quantitative and Qualitative Labor Market Integration

European Union migrant citizens have generally high employment rates, especially in the United Kingdom. However, EU migrant citizens from CEE countries are more often in precarious employment compared to Southern European and particularly EU-Rest migrants. The latter's qualitative labor market integration is close to or better than that of nationals. Both countries show by far the worst

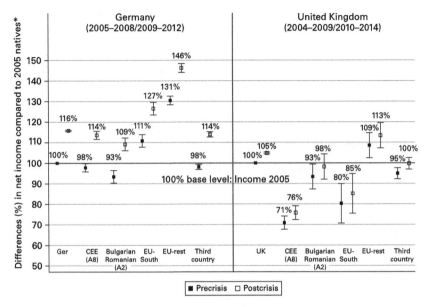

Figure 14.8 Wage–income differentials for recent youth migrants compared to nationals in Germany and the United Kingdom. Estimates: Logarithm of net income adjusted for inflation (GER: Destatis, 2016; UK: CPI base 2005, Source: Office for National Statistics 2015).
Source: Net hourly income from German Microcensus (2005–2012); net hourly income from pooled UK-LFS (2004–2014).

outcomes for TCNs on quantitative labor market integration (low employment rates and high inactivity).

These better results for EU migrant citizens might be due to their privileged status compared to that of TCNs, based on the principle of nondiscrimination in relation to nationals. Given free labor mobility, their migration channels differ substantially from those of TCNs, who often come as asylum seekers or under family reunification regulations.

The United Kingdom seems to achieve better quantitative labor market integration of EU migrant citizens (particularly from CEE countries) compared to Germany. This might be explained by the UK economy's orientation toward general rather than specific skills, which facilitates the integration of youth migrants. Furthermore, the improvements in EU migrants' quantitative labor market integration that are visible in Germany during our second observation period are consistent with a labor demand argument, for unemployment significantly declined during this period.

In terms of qualitative labor market integration, the over-representation of migrant workers in nonstandard employment in Germany is not surprising. Given the high degree of dualization of the German labor market, flexibility needs are achieved at the margins—for example, through higher levels of fixed-term employment, solo self-employment (particularly for CEE migrant citizens during the transition period), and minijobs.

The findings on wage income and skill and qualification mismatches—in addition to reflecting issues such as linguistic barriers, transferability of skills, and potential migrant niche effects generated by migrant networks—point to an interesting segmentation of EU migrants according to region of origin. For the United Kingdom, which arguably provides a more clear-cut wage measure than the German data, our analysis points to lower wages for young recent CEE migrants compared to their national peers, higher wages for EU-Rest migrants, and no significant wage differences between nationals and EU-South migrants. EU8 migrants show pronounced skill (Germany) and qualification (United Kingdom) mismatches in their occupations; the results for EU-South migrants are more mixed; and EU-Rest migrants, particularly in Germany, seem to perform better than nationals on this indicator.

These intra-EU differences in qualitative labor market outcomes might partly be explained by destination-country wage differentials and by differences in reservation wages because of much lower (exportable) unemployment benefits (Bruzelius et al. 2016). These potentially render migrant citizens from CEE countries and, to some degree, EU-South migrants more willing than EU-Rest migrants to work under precarious conditions, for low wages, and below their skill/qualification levels. The results for EU2 and EU-South migrants differ between Germany and the United Kingdom, potentially pointing to migrant network effects and the role of general versus specific skills. Crucially, the segmentation of labor market integration outcome seems to reflect structural differences by regions of origin.

The analysis shows that contextual factors, such as transition arrangements, had a clear impact on migration movements, for the share of EU migrant citizens, especially those from CEE countries, increased in both destination countries. In addition, their levels of solo self-employment indicate a response to the previous transition arrangements even though this calls for further analysis taking selectivity into account. The analysis did not identify large relative increases of EU-South migrants, which were quite salient in UK media reporting in the run-up to the Brexit referendum. By contrast, we were able to identify an increasing trend for this group in Germany.

14.5.2. Limitations

The analysis has a number of limitations. First, the pooling of data makes it difficult to identify the effects of the transition periods. The limited panel possibilities of the UK-LFS data mean the labor market outcomes of recent youth migrant workers are only examined in two time periods. Thus, improved labor market integration due to better language skills, acquaintance with working culture norms, and better networks is not accounted for (see Prokic-Breuer and McManus's (2016) notion of "apparent qualification mismatch").

Sampling biases mean that the data capture "better integrated" recent migrants, who might not fully represent migrants as such. In both countries, the data mainly capture residents, thus under-representing seasonal workers, posted workers, or more recent migrants (see Section 13.3 on methods).

Comparability issues arise from the use of partially harmonized data (e.g., migrant definition, marginal employment, and skill and qualification mismatch with one's occupation). Most of these reflect data constraints, but also country-specific labor market arrangements (e.g., minijobs). Despite these limitations, the findings are rather consistent across measures and with our theoretical expectations.

14.6. CONCLUSIONS

Despite institutional differences between labor markets and welfare regimes, as well as the different transition regimes, we identified significant similarities in the labor market integration of young EU migrant citizens across Germany and the United Kingdom.

Young EU citizens who recently migrated are well integrated in the respective labor markets (particularly in the United Kingdom), as measured by overall employment rates. However, EU youth migrants' qualitative labor market integration as measured here by income, marginal, fixed-term, and (solo) self-employment, as well as skills/qualification mismatch, is segmented by their region of origin: EU8 and EU2 citizens often work in precarious and nonstandard employment, youth from Southern Europe take a middle position, and youth from the remaining EU countries do as well or better than their native peers on several indicators. Notably, this segmentation can be observed for these migrant groups without a detailed analysis of demographic characteristics.

A number of broad questions for future research derive from the previously discussed findings. Crucially for labor market and social policy research, does the availability and *exportability of unemployment benefits* influence the segmentation of labor market integration outcomes by region of origin? For example, do these result in observable differences in EU migrant citizens' reservation wages and support options, which in turn affect their labor market positions in the countries of destination?

Finally, and more generally, the question arises as to whether, at the micro level, EU cross-border labor mobility simply replicates the existing stratification of young people across Europe or whether migration gives young EU citizens an opportunity to improve their relative labor market position compared to their position in the country of origin and their initial position in the country of destination. The corresponding question on the macro EU-wide level is whether, and in what way, young EU citizens' migration can contribute to an economically and socially ever closer European Union.

NOTES

1 Throughout the chapter, we use the term *EU migrant citizen* because our analysis focuses on those EU citizens who have migrated from one member state to another. Working EU migrant citizens have the same rights as nationals and can be differentiated from the category of EU mobile workers (e.g., posted or cross-border workers), for whom different regulations apply; see Bruzelius and Seeleib-Kaiser (2017).

2 The EU8 countries acceded the union in May 2004 and are composed of the Czech Republic, Estonia, Hungary, Latvia, Lithuania, Poland, Slovakia, and Slovenia.

3 Greece, Italy, Portugal, and Spain; Malta and Cyprus.

4 Throughout the text, reference is made to the United Kingdom, in line with the main data source, the UK-LFS.

5 Austria, Belgium, Denmark, France, Ireland, Luxembourg, Netherlands, Sweden (and, for Germany only, the European Free Trade Association countries), Germany (UK analysis only), and the United Kingdom (German analysis only).

6 We particularly thank Silvana Weiss, Franziska Meinck, and Jonas Felbo-Kolding for helpful comments on earlier drafts of this chapter. The chapter also received two reviews from María González Menéndez and Paweł Kaczmarczyk, which were motivating and insightful. Previous versions of the chapter received comments in January 2016 and January 2017 at the STYLE meetings. We further thank Noor Abdul Malik and Magnus Paulsen Hansen for their help with preparing the manuscript and Niamh Warde for her excellent language editing. Finally, we thank Renate Ortlieb for her guidance, support, and patience as section editor and Jackie O'Reilly for getting us all there in the end.

7 For the United Kingdom, migrants are defined as having a different country of birth than the United Kingdom, no UK citizenship, and UK residency for between 1 and 5 years. For Germany, migrants are defined as having non-German citizenship and having migrated to Germany within the previous 5 years.

8 The Microcensus is a representative sample containing demographic and labor market information from 1% of all households in Germany. All persons who have right of residence in Germany, whether living in private or collective households, or at their main or secondary residence, are sampled and are obliged to participate (Research Data Center of the Federal Statistical Office and Statistical Offices of the Länder).

9 The LFS is the largest social survey in the United Kingdom. All adult members from a rotating sample of 41,000 private households are interviewed in five consecutive quarters. The sample size makes it the best data set available for

analyzing the labor market situation of recent migrants (Office for National Statistics 2015a).

10 In the German case, there is an obligation to participate, and nonparticipation is penalized. The UK-LFS makes efforts to conduct face-to-face interviews with the help of interpreters if no household member speaks English.

11 Analysis of the German data was carried out by Janine Leschke (FDZ Forschungsprojekt: 2014-2631), and that of the UK data and figures was performed by Thees F. Spreckelsen.

12 According to the EU-LFS definition, persons working at least 1 hour in the reference week are counted as employed and are asked questions relating to their employment status. The analyses, unless otherwise stated, thus include students and those in vocational training.

13 Only information for 2009-2012 has been used. Because the earlier measure is incomparable, these data also capture short-term employment (often seasonal) and "one-Euro-jobs"—an employment integration measure under the subsidiary welfare scheme.

14 See Office for National Statistics workforce statistics at http://webarchive. nationalarchives.gov.uk/20160105160709/http://www.ons.gov.uk/ons/ about-ons/business-transparency/freedom-of-information/what-can-i-request/previous-foi-requests/labour-market/workforce-statistics/index. html.

REFERENCES

Akgüç, Mehtap, and Miroslav Beblavý. 2015. "Re-Emerging Migration Patterns: Structures and Policy Lessons." STYLE Working Paper 6.3. Brighton, UK: CROME, University of Brighton. http://www.style-research. eu/publications/working-papers

Altorjai, Szilvia. 2013. "Over-Qualification of Immigrants in the UK." ISER Working Paper 11. Essex, UK: Institute for Social and Economic Research.

Andrews, Martyn, Ken Clark, and William Whittaker. 2007. "The Employment and Earnings of Migrants in Great Britain." IZA Discussion Paper 3068. Bonn: Institute for the Study of Labor.

Bettin, Giulia. 2012. "Migration from the Accession Countries to the United Kingdom and Italy: Socio-Economic Characteristics, Skills Composition and Labour Market Outcomes." In *EU Migration and Labour Markets in Troubled Times: Skills Mismatch, Return and Policy Responses*, edited by Béla Galgóczi, Janine Leschke, and Andrew Watt, 47–80. Aldershot, UK: Ashgate.

Bruckmeier, Kerstin, Johannes Eggs, Carina Sperber, Mark Trappmann, and Ulrich Walwei. 2015. "Arbeitsmarktsituation von Aufstockern: Vor allem Minijobber suchen nach einer anderen Arbeit." IAB-Kurzbericht 19. Nuremberg: Institut für Arbeitsmarkt- und Berufsforschung.

Bruzelius, Cecilia, Constantin Reinprecht, and Martin Seeleib-Kaiser. 2016. "EU Migrant Citizens, Welfare States and Social Rights." Paper prepared for presentation at the 23rd International Conference of Europeanists, Philadelphia, April 14–16.

Bruzelius, Cecilia, and Martin Seeleib-Kaiser. 2017. "European Citizenship and Social Rights." In *A Handbook of European Social Policy*, edited by Patricia Kennett and Noemi Lendvai-Bainton, 155–168. Cheltenham, UK: Elgar.

Brzinsky-Fay, Christian. 2007. "Lost in Transition? Labour Market Entry Sequences of School Leavers in Europe." *European Sociological Review* 23 (4): 409–22.

Chung, Heejung, Sonja Bekker, and Hester Houwing. 2012. "Young People and the Post-Recession Labour Market in the Context of Europe 2020." *Transfer: European Review of Labour and Research* 18 (3): 301–17.

Clark, Ken, and Joanne Lindley. 2009. "Immigrant Assimilation Pre and Post Labour Market Entry: Evidence from the UK Labour Force Survey." *Journal of Population Economics* 22 (1): 175–98.

Demireva, Neli. 2011. "New Migrants in the UK: Employment Patterns and Occupational Attainment." *Journal of Ethnic and Migration Studies* 37 (4): 637–55.

Destatis. 2012. "Bevölkerung und Erwerbstätigkeit: Vorläufige Wanderungsergebnisse." Wiesbaden: Statistisches Bundesamt. https://www.destatis.de/DE/Publikationen/Thematisch/Bevoelkerung/Wanderungen/vorlaeufigeWanderungen5127101127004.pdf?__blob=publicationFile

Destatis. 2016. "Verbraucherpreisindizes für Deutschland Lange Reihen ab 1948." Wiesbaden: Statistisches Bundesamt. www.destatis.de/DE/Publikationen/Thematisch/Preise/Verbraucherpreise/VerbraucherpreisindexLangeReihenPDF_5611103.pdf;jsessionid=88883693162273CDCE9B9930135E252E.cae1?__blob=publicationFile

Emmenegger, Patrick, Silja Häusermann, Bruno Palier, and Martin Seeleib-Kaiser, eds. 2012. *The Age of Dualization: The Changing Face of Inequality in Deindustrializing Societies*. New York: Oxford University Press.

Engels, Dietrich, Regine Köhler, Ruud Koopmans, and Jutta Höhne. 2012. *Zweiter Integrations indikatorenbericht*. Berlin: Die Beauftragte der Bundesregierung für Migration, Flüchtlinge und Integration.

Esping-Andersen, Gøsta. 1990. *The Three Worlds of Welfare Capitalism*. Princeton, NJ: Princeton University Press.

European Integration Consortium. 2009. "Labour Mobility Within the EU in the Context of Enlargement and the Functioning of the Transitional Arrangements." http://doku.iab.de/grauepap/2009/LM_finalreport.pdf

Fihel, Agnieszka, Anna Janicka, Paweł Kaczmarczyk, and Joanna Nestorowicz. 2015. *Free Movement of Workers and Transitional Arrangements: Lessons from the 2004 and 2007 Enlargements*. Warsaw: Centre of Migration Research.

Fleischmann, Fenella, and Jaap Dronkers. 2010. "Unemployment Among Immigrants in European Labour Markets: An Analysis of Origin and Destination Effects." *Work, Employment and Society* 24 (2): 337–54.

Galgóczi, Béla, and Leschke Janine. 2015. "Intra-EU Labour Mobility: A Key Pillar of the EU Architecture Under Challenge." *International Journal of Public Administration* 38 (12): 860–73.

Ganzeboom, Harry B. G., and Donald J. Treiman. 2003. "International Stratification and Mobility File: Conversion Tools." Amsterdam: Department of Social Research Methodology. http://www.harryganzeboom.nl/ismf/index.htm

GOV.UK. 2016a. "Working Tax Credit—What You'll Get." https://www.gov.uk/working-tax-credit/what-youll-get

GOV.UK. 2016b. "National Minimum Wage and National Living Wage Rates." https://www.gov.uk/national-minimum-wage-rates

Hall, Peter A. 2007. "The Evolution of Varieties of Capitalism in Europe." In *Beyond Varieties of Capitalism*, edited by Bob Hancké, Martin Rhodes, and Mark Thatcher, 39–88. Oxford: Oxford University Press.

Hall, Peter A., and David Soskice, eds. 2001. *Varieties of Capitalism: The Institutional Foundations of Comparative Advantage*. Oxford: Oxford University Press.

Höhne, Jutta, and Karin Schulze Buschoff. 2015. "Die Arbeitsmarktintegration von Migranten und Migrantinnen in Deutschland. Ein Überblick nach Herkunftsländern und Generationen." *WSI Mitteilungen* 68 (5): 345–54.

Hooijer, Gerda, and Georg Picot. 2015. "European Welfare States and Migrant Poverty: The Institutional Determinants of Disadvantage." *Comparative Political Studies* 48 (14): 1879–1904.

Joassart-Marcelli, Pascale. 2014. "Gender, Social Network Geographies, and Low-Wage Employment Among Recent Mexican Immigrants in Los Angeles." *Urban Geography* 35 (6): 822–51.

Kacmarczyk, Paweł, and Joanna Tyrowicz. 2015. "Winners and Losers Among Skilled Migrants: The Case of Post-Accession Polish Migrants to the UK." IZA Discussion Paper 9057. Bonn: Institute for the Study of Labor.

Kogan, Irena. 2006. "Labour Markets and Economic Incorporation Among Recent Immigrants in Europe." *Social Forces* 85 (2): 697–721.

Kogan, Irena. 2011. "New Immigrants–Old Disadvantage Patterns? Labour Market Integration of Recent Immigrants into Germany." *International Migration* 49 (1): 91–117.

Kogan Irena, Frank Kalter, Elisabeth Liebau, and Yinon Cohen. 2011. "Individual Resources and Structural Constraints in Immigrants: Labour Market Integration." In *A Life-Course Perspective on Migration and Integration*, edited by Matthias Wingens, Michael Windzio, Helga de Valk, and Can Aybek, 75–100. Dordrecht: Springer.

Lechert, Yvonne, Julia Schroedter, and Paul Lüttinger. 2006. "Die Umsetzung der Bildungsskala ISCED-1997 für die Volkszählung 1970, die Mikrozensus-Zusatzerhebung 1971 und die Mikrozensen 1976–2004." ZUMA-Methodenbericht 2006–08. Mannheim: Zentrum für Umfragen, Methoden und Analysen.

Lehndorff, Steffen. 2015. "Model or Liability? The New Career of the 'German Model,' Divisive Integration." In *The Triumph of Failed Ideas in Europe—Revisited*, edited by Steffen Lehndorff, 149–78. Brussels: European Trade Union Institute.

Leschke, Janine. 2015. "Non-Standard Employment of Women in Service Sector Occupations: A Comparison of European Countries." In *Non-Standard Employment in Post-Industrial Labour Markets: An Occupational Perspective*, edited by Werner Eichhorst and Paul Marx, 324–52. Cheltenham, UK: Elgar.

Leschke Janine, and Maarten Keune. 2008. "Precarious Employment in the Public and Private Sectors: Comparing the UK and Germany." In *Privatisation and Liberalisation of Public Services in Europe: An Analysis of Economic and Labour Market Impacts*, edited by Maarten Keune, Janine Leschke, and Andrew Watt, 197–231. Brussels: European Trade Union Institute.

Leschke, Janine, Martin Seeleib-Kaiser, Thees F. Spreckelsen, Christer Hyggen, and Hans Christian Sandlie. 2016. "Labour Market Outcomes and Integration of Recent Youth Migrants from Central-Eastern and Southern Europe in Germany, Norway and Great Britain." STYLE Working Paper 6.4. Brighton, UK: CROME, University of Brighton. http://www.style-research.eu/publications/working-papers

Longhi, Simonetta, and Magdalena Rokicka. 2012. "Eastern European Immigrants in the UK Before and After the 2004 European Enlargement." ISER Working Paper 22. Essex, UK: Institute for Social and Economic Research.

Martí, Mónica, and Carmen Ródenas. 2007. "Migration Estimation Based on the Labour Force Survey : An EU-15 Perspective." *International Migration Review* 41 (1): 101–26.

Office for National Statistics. 2015a. *Quarterly Labour Force Survey: Special Licence Access*. Essex, UK: UK Data Archive.

Office for National Statistics. 2015b. "Consumer Price Index 1988–2015 (2005 Prices)." http://www.ons.gov.uk/ons/datasets-and-tables/data-selector.html?cdid=D7BT&dataset=mm23&table-id=1.1

Organization for Economic Co-operation and Development (OECD). 2013. *Protecting Jobs, Enhancing Flexibility: A New Look at Employment Protection Legislation*. OECD Employment Outlook 2013. Paris: OECD.

Ortlieb, Renate, and Silvana Weiss. 2015. "Business Start-Ups and Youth Self-Employment in Germany: A Policy Literature Review." STYLE Working Paper 7.1. Brighton, UK: CROME, University of Brighton. http://www.style-research.eu/publications/working-papers

Prokic-Breuer, Tijana, and Patricia A. McManus. 2016. "Immigrant Educational Mismatch in Western Europe, Apparent or Real?" *European Sociological Review* 32 (3): 411–38.

Recchi, Ettore. 2015. *Mobile Europe—The theory and practice of free movement in the EU*. New York: Palgrave Macmillan.

Rienzo, Cinzia. 2013. *Migrants in the UK Labour Market: An Overview—Migration Observatory Briefing*. Oxford: COMPAS, University of Oxford.

Schimpl-Neimanns, Bernhard. 2004. "Zur Umsetzung des Internationalen Sozioökonomischen Index des beruflichen Status (ISEI)." *ZUMA-Nachrichten* 54 (28): 154–70.

Schmelzer, Paul. 2008. "Increasing Employment Instability Among Young People? Labor Market Entries and Early Careers in Great Britain Since the 1980s." In *Young Workers, Globalization and the Labour Market: Comparing Early Working Life in Eleven Countries*, edited by Hans-Peter Blossfeld, Sandra Buchholz, Erzsébet Bukodi, and Karin Kurz, Ch. 8, 181–206. Cheltenham, UK: Elgar.

Schulze Buschoff, Karin, and Paula Protsch. 2008. "(A-)Typical and (In-)Secure? Social Protection and 'Non-Standard' Forms of Employment in Europe." *International Social Security Review* 61 (4): 51–73.

Seeleib-Kaiser, Martin, and Thees F. Spreckelsen. 2018. "Youth Labour Market Outsiderness: The 'Nordic Model' Compared with Britain and Germany." In *Youth Diversity and Employment: Comparative Perspective on Labour Market Policies*, edited by Rune Halvorsen and Bjørn Hvinden. Cheltenham, UK: Elgar.

Standing, Guy. 2009. *Work After Globalization: Building Occupational Citizenship*. Cheltenham, UK: Elgar.

Tilly, Chris. 2011. "The Impact of the Economic Crisis on International Migration: A Review." *Work, Employment & Society* 25 (4): 675–92.

Verwiebe, Roland, Laura Wiesböck, and Roland Teitzer. 2014. "New Forms of Intra-European Migration, Labour Market Dynamics and Social Inequality in Europe." *Migration Letters* 11 (2): 125–36.

Voss, Dorothea, and Claudia Weinkopf. 2012. "Niedriglohnfalle Minijobs." *WSI-Mitteilungen, Schwerpunktheft Minijobs* 1: 5–12.

Walther, Andreas, and Axel Pohl. 2005. "Thematic Study on Policy Measures Concerning Disadvantaged Youth: Study Commissioned by the European Commission—Final Report." Tübingen: Institute for Innovation and Social Research.

15

HOW DO LABOR MARKET INTERMEDIARIES HELP YOUNG EASTERN EUROPEANS FIND WORK?

Renate Ortlieb and Silvana Weiss

15.1. INTRODUCTION

Mainstream economists view the geographic mobility of workers as a prerequisite for well-functioning labor markets.[1] Relatedly, policy measures aimed at increasing the mobility of young people, such as the Youth on the Move flagship initiative launched by the European Commission in 2010, are said to be effective means to combat youth unemployment (European Commission 2010; O'Reilly et al. 2015). Against the background of the high relevance of youth mobility, as endorsed by both academics and policymakers, and given the high numbers of young migrants from Eastern Europe working in Western Europe (Kahanec and Fabo 2013; Akgüç and Beblavý, this volume), the following question arises: How did these young migrants find work in a foreign country? This question is important because the existing literature suggests that migrants from Eastern Europe struggle to find jobs with good working conditions in Western Europe (Favell 2008; Galgóczi and Leschke 2012; Spreckelsen, Leschke, and Seeleib-Kaiser, this volume). Thus, in order to be able to develop theoretical models explaining these difficulties and to design policy measures aimed at improving the labor market opportunities of young migrants from Eastern Europe, detailed knowledge about their routes into employment is crucial.

In the migration literature, entering a foreign labor market is typically conceived as a process in which several actors are involved. Apart from the migrants themselves, employers are key actors in that they may fill vacant job positions with migrants (Moriarty et al. 2012; Ortlieb and Sieben 2013; Scott

2013; Cangiano and Walsh 2014; Ortlieb, Sieben, and Sichtmann 2014). In addition, migrants often draw on informal networks of friends and relatives to find a job and to (temporarily) settle abroad (Agunias 2009; Lindquist, Xiang, and Yeoh 2012). Finally, an important role may be played by labor market intermediaries (LMIs) such as public employment services, online job portals, and temporary work agencies. Previous research shows that LMIs act as significant facilitators of globalized labor markets (Freeman 2002; Coe, Johns, and Ward 2007; Elrick and Lewandowska 2008). Nonetheless, despite the increasing numbers of LMIs worldwide within the past few years (Bonet, Cappelli, and Hamori 2013; CIETT 2016) and the growing body of LMI research in Europe (Andersson and Wadensjö 2004; Findlay and McCollum 2013; Friberg and Eldring 2013; Sporton 2013), the role of these actors in trans-European job search and recruiting is not yet fully understood.

This chapter addresses this knowledge gap. We concentrate on young EU8 citizens—that is, people younger than age 35 years from Estonia, Latvia, Lithuania, Poland, the Czech Republic, Slovakia, and Hungary. We examine the role of LMIs for young EU8 migrants entering the Austrian labor market, thereby taking the perspectives of young EU8 migrants, Austrian employers, and LMIs into account. Austria is particularly suitable for studying East–West youth migration in Europe because it is a receiving country with geographical proximity and historically strong ties to Eastern Europe, it has a comparatively good overall labor market situation, and it hosts a large number of EU8 migrants (Benton and Petrovic 2013). At the same time, we posit that our findings offer insights into underlying labor market processes that prevail in other countries as well.

In order to capture specific features of the role of LMIs, we focus on three industrial sectors: high-tech/information technology (IT), hospitality, and 24-hour domestic care. Our choice was determined both by the high number of EU8 migrants and by the strong labor demand that characterize these three sectors, enabling good observation of entry processes. Furthermore, this selection allows us to account for different skill levels, gender compositions, and types of employment relations. To theorize on differences between the three sectors, we apply a framework proposed by Benner (2003). According to this framework, LMIs fulfill three specific functions for both employers and workers: They reduce transaction costs, build social networks, and help manage risks. We suppose that these functions are of different importance in the three sectors. Thus, the role of LMIs for young EU8 migrants entering the Austrian labor market will vary across the three chosen sectors.

Our research relies on 60 semistructured interviews with young EU8 migrants, employers, LMIs, and labor market experts. We find that young EU8 migrants across the three sectors use a broad range of entry ports, including different types of LMIs. They mainly use informal networks and online platforms providing information on job vacancies, working conditions, and general country characteristics. In addition, in the 24-hour domestic care sector, young

EU8 migrants contact agencies that match caregivers with private households and assist with various kinds of paperwork. We also find that, especially in the high-tech/IT and 24-hour domestic care sectors, LMIs reduce transaction costs and risks for both employers and workers. LMIs play a more important role in job search and recruiting processes in these sectors than in the hospitality sector, in which the transaction costs and risks attached to employment relations are comparatively low.

Overall, our research shows that LMIs are important facilitators of youth transitions from Eastern Europe to the West. LMIs can help reduce youth unemployment in Eastern Europe by providing informational, matchmaking, and administrative services to both employers and jobseekers. Our research findings provide a more nuanced understanding of the labor market entry paths of young migrants and the many-faceted role of LMIs in these processes. Taking account of the perspectives of both employers and young migrants, and focusing on sectoral specificities, we go beyond the existing literature on youth migration in Europe.

The chapter is structured as follows. In Section 15.2, we summarize the literature on LMIs, focusing on different types of LMIs and their services. In Sections 15.3 and 15.4, we elucidate our theoretical framework and describe our methods, including the research context of Austria. In Sections 15.4–15.6, we present findings regarding the salience of different LMI types and services in the three sectors and then turn, in Section 15.7, to specific functions of LMIs in the three sectors. In the concluding Section 15.8, we suggest avenues for future research.

15.2. TYPES AND SERVICES OF LABOR MARKET INTERMEDIARIES

Labor market intermediaries serve to mediate the relationship between employers and workers. The controversy associated with LMIs has centered on whether or not they exploit vulnerable workers and whether or not they facilitate job matching. On the one hand, the types of LMIs that receive heightened media attention related to exploitative practices are, in general, a marginal part of this market. On the other hand, the range of legal LMIs is considerably varied. They include traditional public employment services, online job portals, temporary work agencies, and highly specialized executive search firms, as well as non-governmental organizations (NGOs) and social enterprises concerned with the labor market integration of vulnerable people.

To enable a systematic view of these different kinds of institutions, scholars have proposed several frameworks that categorize LMIs in terms of diverse criteria. Table 15.1 presents prototypes of LMIs, drawing on the categorizations by Benner (2003), Agunias (2009), Autor (2009), and Bonet et al. (2013). We categorize different types of LMIs based on their

Table 15.1 Types of labor market intermediaries

Type of LMI	Organizational structure and funding		Services offered to employers and jobseekers		
	Private sector	Public sector	Information provider	Matchmaker	Administrator
Public employment service (e.g., Austrian/AMS, European/EURES)		X	X	X	
Temporary work agencies (e.g., Adecco, ISS, Manpower)	X			X	X
Recruitment agencies, executive search firms (e.g., Kienbaum, Hill, Boyden)	X			X	
Online job portals (e.g., monster.com, karriere.at, ams.at, ec.europa.eu/eures)	X	X	X	X	
Social media (e.g., LinkedIn, Facebook)	X		X		
Educational institutions (e.g., universities, vocational schools)	X	X	X		

AMS, Austrian Public Employment Service; EURES, European Employment Services; LMI, labor market intermediary.
Sources: Authors' compilation based on Benner (2003), Agunias (2009), Autor (2009), and Bonet et al. (2013).

organizational structure and funding as either private-sector or public-sector intermediaries. Thereby, private-sector LMIs typically are paid by employers, whereas their services are cost-free to jobseekers.[2] Depending on the services LMIs offer to employers and jobseekers, we further distinguish between information providers, matchmakers, and administrators. Information providers either sell or offer cost-free information about vacancies, job profiles, and candidate profiles. Matchmaking services include job and candidate diagnosis, assignment of qualified candidates to jobs, and monitoring of a probation period. Administrative services refer to the full spectrum of human resource management, such as payroll, training, and career planning. Administrator LMIs such as temporary work agencies often act as an employer who hires out personnel to client firms.

Previous research on the role of LMIs for labor market outcomes of (young) migrants has produced mixed results. There is evidence that migrants recruited by LMIs obtain better employment contracts compared to migrants using informal social networks; for example, they are more likely to obtain higher wages (Bonet et al. 2013; Findlay and McCollum 2013). However, LMIs have also been found to increase the risk of devaluation of foreign professional skills (Samaluk 2016). Moreover, their recruiting and selection procedures are not always free of discriminating biases against migrants (Bonet et al. 2013). Also, in some cases, LMIs have been associated with fraud and exploitation of migrant workers (Agunias 2009; van den Broek, Harvey, and Groutsis 2016).

A considerable body of research revolves around temporary work agencies. This type of LMI can have a negative impact on the labor market outcomes of its employees, especially the highly vulnerable group of (young) migrants (McDowell, Batnitzky, and Dyer 2008; Autor and Houseman 2010; Sporton 2013). At the same time, for persons with otherwise limited employment prospects, temporary work agencies can act as stepping stones into employment (Andersson and Wadensjö 2004; Arrowsmith 2006; Heinrich, Mueser, and Troske 2007; Voss et al. 2013).

However, it is unclear whether these findings can be applied to the context of East–West youth migration in Europe. In addition, although previous research suggests that the role of LMIs differs between sectors (see Section 15.3), there is currently no systematic comparative evidence with regard to youth labor migration. In the following, we explore the role of LMIs in shaping East–West youth migration in Europe in greater detail.

15.3. THEORETICAL FRAMEWORK: FUNCTIONS OF LABOR MARKET INTERMEDIARIES ACROSS INDUSTRIAL SECTORS

Prior research based on either single-sector (Benner 2003; Fitzgerald 2007; Findley and McCollum 2013; Thörnquist 2013) or multisector studies (Friberg and Eldring 2013; Sporton 2013; Cangiano and Walsh 2014; van den Broek et al. 2016) indicates that the role of LMIs varies across sectors. However, there is as yet no coherent theoretical framework explaining these differences. A promising approach has been suggested by Benner, who theorizes on the relationship between LMI activities and regional development. Based on a case study on Silicon Valley, the author argues that distinctive functions of LMIs can help firms adapt to changing labor markets, which in turn is crucial for doing business in an environment driven by knowledge work and rapid innovation. This reasoning can be applied to explaining the role of LMIs in shaping East–West youth migration in Europe.

According to Benner (2003), LMIs fulfill three functions in the labor market. First, LMIs *reduce transaction costs* for both employers and workers. Because LMIs specialize in certain fields, they possess information and access to other resources that help both employers and workers minimize search costs as well as costs related to contracting and monitoring. Second, LMIs function as *network builders* for both employers and workers. By connecting various individuals and institutions with one another, LMIs can replace informal networks, facilitating person–job matching processes as well as key business activities such as innovation. Third, LMIs help employers and workers *manage risks*, such as firms' risks related to volatile demand in product markets and workers' risks related to job loss. Although these three functions of LMIs may be observed throughout the entire labor market, we maintain that their importance varies across sectors, depending on the transaction costs and the need to build networks and manage risks.

15.4. METHODS

15.4.1. Research Context: EU8 Migrants Working in Austria

Austria belongs to the group of EU15 countries that restricted labor movement for EU8 citizens following the enlargement of the European Union in May 2004. Austria and Germany were the only countries that maintained their restrictions until the end of the period of transitional arrangements in April 2011. After the restrictions had been fully removed in May 2011, a growing number of EU8 citizens entered the Austrian labor market. However, it is important to note that EU8 citizens had the opportunity also before May 2011 to (legally) work in Austria, with or without the assistance of LMIs. Work permits were issued for sectors suffering from labor shortages, and self-employed migrants were allowed to offer their services if they fulfilled certain occupational requirements.

Figure 15.1 presents the number of EU8 migrants working in Austria between 2007 and 2015, differentiated by age. In accordance with the available data, EU8 migrants are defined for this figure based on their citizenship. The graph includes

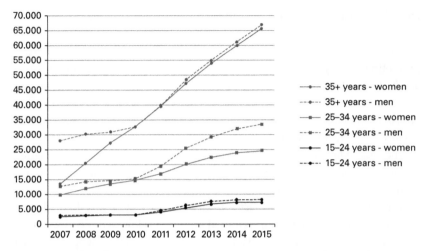

Figure 15.1 Number of EU8 migrants working in Austria, 2007–2015 (employees and self-employed).
Source: Austrian Labor Market Service Monitoring of Occupational Careers (Erwerbskarrieremonitoring, AMS 2016, personal communication); authors' calculations.

both EU8 citizens who migrated themselves and second-generation migrants. However, the vast majority of these people, and especially those who trigger variation within the curves, are first-generation migrants—that is, EU8 citizens who migrated themselves.

According to Figure 15.1, a total of 206,294 EU8 migrants worked in Austria in 2015 as either salaried employees or self-employed, which is more than 5% of the Austrian labor force and almost three times as many EU8 migrant workers as in 2007 (68,965 persons). People younger than age 35 years account for 36% of the EU8 migrants (73,650 persons). Men outnumber women, with the major differences emerging for the group of adults aged older than 35 years at the beginning of the period of data availability in 2007 and for the group of adults aged between 25 and 34 years after May 2011—when the restrictions for labor movement had been lifted. Although the available data do not allow for conclusive interpretation of these gaps, we suggest that they reflect gender segregation of the labor market in association with both increasing business trends in women-dominated sectors and political efforts to legalize the work of migrants in such sectors.

15.4.2. Key Characteristics of the Selected Sectors

We selected three sectors to gain deeper insight into the role of LMIs by juxtaposing the specific types and functions of LMIs in these different sectors, namely high-tech/IT, hospitality, and 24-hour domestic care. The selection is based on the following three criteria: (1) Both the number of young EU8 migrants working in these sectors and the labor demand should be considerably high; (2) the skill level should vary across these sectors; and (3) the gender composition should vary across these sectors.[3] The three sectors are briefly described next.

The *high-tech/IT sector* is characterized by a long-lasting labor shortage, prompting employers to recruit employees from abroad. The skill level is generally high, and the majority of employees are men. In comparison with the hospitality and the 24-hour domestic care sectors, firms in the high-tech/IT sector are larger, they more often operate in international markets and with business alliances, and their personnel management is more professional.

The *hospitality sector* is characterized by a high share of young migrants among employees, a fairly high labor demand, high labor fluctuation, low or medium skill level, and a balanced gender composition.

The *24-hour domestic care sector* is characterized by a very high share of migrants among caregivers. The required skill level is low, and the vast majority of caregivers are women.[4] A particularity of this sector is that caregivers usually work as self-employed on the basis of service contracts with private households. For the sake of simplicity, in the following we refer to private households as "employers," given that the relationships between private households and caregivers resemble those between employers and employees. Caregivers usually live in the same household as their clients for a period of 2 weeks, followed by a break of 2 weeks. During the absence of one caregiver, a colleague takes over. These caregiver tandems usually remain the same over a longer period of time, often up until the client moves into a care home or dies. Legislation related to this sector is complex as a result of the self-employment status of caregivers.

15.4.3. Data

The data we use in this chapter originate from a larger research project comparing East–West and North–North youth migration in Europe (Hyggen et al. 2016). Our empirical material comprises data from 60 semistructured interviews conducted with young EU8 migrants, representatives of employers and LMIs, and labor market experts. We conducted the interviews between September 2014 and August 2015. Each interview lasted between 30 and 90 minutes. Table 15.2 presents the number of interviews we conducted with the different types of interviewees in the three selected employment sectors.

Of the interviewed EU8 migrants, the majority were from Hungary or Slovakia. Fifteen were women and seven were men. Their average age was 28.8 years (ranging from 18 to 36 years), with an average age at the time of migration of 25.4 years. The period of time they had been working in Austria ranged from a few months to 14 years (median, 2 years). The employers were of varying sizes, ranging from one-person "companies" in the case of private households and small companies typical of the hospitality sector to large companies with a few thousand employees, especially in the high-tech/IT sector. LMIs were private-sector agencies, public-sector institutions, and NGOs of varying sizes.

Table 15.2 Sample characteristics: Type of interviewees and industrial sectors

Interviewees	Sector				
	High-tech/IT	Hospitality	Care	General	Total
Young migrants	5	9	8		22
Employers	5	5	5		15
LMIs	5	2	6	2	15
Labor market experts	1	1	1	5	8
Total	16	17	20	7	60

IT, information technology; LMIs, labor market intermediaries.

15.5. WHAT TYPES OF LABOR MARKET INTERMEDIARIES DO EU8 MIGRANTS AND AUSTRIAN EMPLOYERS USE?

In our sample, private-sector LMIs appear to be more relevant for connecting employers with jobseekers compared to public-sector LMIs. In the high-tech/IT sector, the EU8 migrants mainly used cost-free online job portals. In addition, they found jobs via direct search on the websites of potential employers in Austria. None of the young interviewees working in this sector had been in contact with an agency. Many employers in the high-tech/IT sector have long-standing business relationships with different kinds of for-profit agencies. For instance, they use executive search firms to fill top management positions, recruitment agencies to find employees with specific skills, and temporary work agencies for large-scale projects.[5]

Although employers from all the sectors stated that they use the informal networks of their (migrant) employees to recruit personnel from abroad, some employers in the high-tech/IT sector strategically use the informal recruitment channel by providing financial bonuses to employees who recommend job candidates. The employers' representatives stated that this strategy is highly effective because employees who recommend a job candidate not only are familiar with the candidate but also informally instruct and supervise their new co-worker. In addition, some of the employers in our sample recruit personnel from their subsidiaries in EU8 countries. Others collaborate with public-sector or private-sector universities in EU8 countries.

In the hospitality sector, EU8 migrants stated that in addition to public-sector or commercial online job portals, unsolicited applications via phone calls or personal visits to restaurants and hotels are effective ways to find a job in Austria. Some employers use public-sector online job portals also for validating the professional skills and the foreign certificates of job candidates. Some of them found employees via the public employment service or social media. One employer in our sample collaborated with a vocational school in Hungary, from which this employer directly recruited graduates. In general, employers in the hospitality sector only very seldom use recruitment agencies. Exceptions include the filling of high-level positions such as chef de rang. The majority do not use LMIs at all; rather, they recruit personnel via informal networks, or they select candidates from the pool of unsolicited job applications.

In the 24-hour domestic care sector, for-profit agencies are by far the most prevalent LMIs. A particularity of this sector is that agencies receive fees from both private households and caregivers. According to one of the intermediaries interviewed, an estimated one-third of caregivers from EU8 countries use agencies. However, our interviewees indicated that EU8 migrants prefer finding a family through their own networks in order to save money. The caregivers interviewed also stated that they switched between different agencies and sometimes searched for a family without an agency. Likewise, private households use either informal networks or for-profit agencies because they lack the competence and the time to find an appropriate caregiver. Often, they need a caregiver on short notice—for instance, after a family member has suffered a stroke.

Overall, the interviewed young EU8 migrants from all three sectors use LMIs whenever they are searching for information and cannot draw on their informal networks of friends and family. According to them, some jobseekers neither intentionally contacted an LMI to find a job in Austria nor did they notice that they were interacting with a recruitment agency and not with an employer. Because LMIs often place job offers in their own name and do the first screening of job candidates, it is not always clear to applicants that they would factually be working for another employer. Neither is it always clear to them that the job is located in a foreign country. For instance, one woman from Hungary working in the hospitality sector reported that she had searched for a job in her home country. It was only during the job interview that she learned that her future workplace would be in Austria. The agency doing the job interview also managed her travel to Austria and all registration formalities. Although this procedure enabled the woman to find employment, she expressed personal fears associated with this journey into the unknown.

15.6. WHAT KINDS OF SERVICES OFFERED BY LABOR MARKET INTERMEDIARIES DO EU8 MIGRANTS AND AUSTRIAN EMPLOYERS USE?

According to our interview data, of the variety of services made available, jobseekers and employers from all three sectors most often use the *information services* of LMIs. In contrast, matchmaking and administrative services are less salient. EU8 migrants search for information not only regarding job vacancies but also regarding working conditions and general host-country characteristics. Employers are especially interested in information on the skills and work experience of job candidates. They use online job portals to obtain information on their counterparts and simultaneously to provide information about themselves. A special informational service offered by an agency in the 24-hour domestic care sector was the provision of data related to the criminal records of caregivers from Slovakia.

Compared with information services, *matchmaking services* are far less often used. Matchmaking services are especially relevant in the high-tech/IT and the 24-hour domestic care sectors. In the hospitality sector, employers only sporadically use matchmaking services by LMIs to fill high-skill positions. Recruitment agencies and matching algorithms implemented in online job portals usually preselect job applications and provide a short list of the best qualified job candidates to employers. In some cases, recruitment agencies additionally monitor a probation period of job candidates. If it turns out that a proposed candidate is less qualified for the position than expected, the agency suggests another candidate.

In our sample, *administrative services* offered by LMIs were less prevalent than informational or matchmaking services. However, in the 24-hour domestic care sector, they are highly relevant. Although the agencies in the 24-hour care sector do not act as the employers of the caregivers, they offer further services before and after matchmaking. For example, they assist caregivers with paperwork, for instance, regarding the obligatory registration as self-employed at the Austrian Economic Chamber and in the social insurance system. Often, they organize the caregivers' travel between their home towns and their places of work in Austria. Some of them additionally offer training, for instance, in caring or in the German language. A particularly important service, as stated by caregivers, is the assignment to a new household at short notice if a client moves into a care home or dies. Private households also avail of the paperwork assistance provided by LMIs, for example, in relation to applications for state subsidies. In addition, they use a replacement service in the event that a caregiver becomes unavailable. These "full-service" arrangements are unique for the 24-hour domestic care sector. In the high-tech/IT sector, if employers use the administrative services of agencies, these typically include payroll, performance monitoring, and replacement of hired workers in the event of longer absences or other kinds of failure. In the hospitality sector, employers almost never use the administrative services offered by LMIs.

Beyond existing categorizations of LMI services into informational, matchmaking, and administrative services, in our interviews we identified a further kind of service, namely the provision of access to job candidates from abroad (without preselection of candidates, matchmaking, or provision of further information). Specifically, employers in the high-tech/IT and the hospitality sectors use special activities of universities and other educational institutions in EU8 countries to find qualified personnel. Examples include universities in EU8 countries hosting student job fairs at which Austrian employers can present themselves and universities or other educational institutions in EU8 countries organizing student competitions for internships in Austrian firms. Although such access services are typically related to high-skill positions, our interview data indicate that employers from all three sectors use access services when they face an extreme scarcity of qualified job candidates in Austria. In addition, LMIs enable access to job candidates from EU8 countries through close collaboration with LMIs in these countries. For instance, some agencies operating in the 24-hour domestic care sector draw on a "chain of LMIs" consisting of several agents in Slovakia, some of whom had previously worked as caregivers in Austria. These LMI chains help bridge language barriers and geographic distance.

15.7. WHAT FUNCTIONS DO LABOR MARKET INTERMEDIARIES FULFILL?

15.7.1. Transaction Cost Reduction

In our sample, the eminent importance of LMIs as reducers of transaction costs becomes clearly visible across all three sectors. The fact that employers and jobseekers act in a transnational context complicates the search for and the validation of information. Thus, the costs associated with establishing contracts are higher than those in local or national contexts. Different languages or state regulations related to required professional certificates, for instance, further increase transaction costs.

In all three sectors, LMIs in the form of online job portals effectively lower information costs for both employers and jobseekers. Depending on the sector, further types of LMIs are used to lower different kinds of transaction costs. In the high-tech/IT sector, even firms with a professional personnel management department face high transaction costs in certain situations, leading them to use various kinds of agencies. In the hospitality sector, personnel management is usually less professionalized because of the smaller firm sizes. However, given that these firms receive many unsolicited job applications and screening of job candidates is comparatively easy, transaction costs are lower. Thus, with the exception of a few high-level positions, there is little need for employers in the hospitality sector to use other LMIs than online job portals. In the 24-hour domestic care sector, private households usually lack the competence and time to search for an appropriate caregiver. Moreover, as lay employers, they can be challenged by comparatively complex legislation. Thus, transaction costs are relatively high. Specialized agencies reduce these transaction costs for the employers, and they also reduce the search costs of the caregivers. Given that Austrian agencies often collaborate with other institutions located in an EU8 country, EU8 citizens can easily obtain information closer to where they live and in their first language. Finally, for both private households and caregivers, agencies reduce contracting costs by assisting with the required paperwork.

15.7.2. Risk Management

Partly interrelated with their function as reducers of transaction costs, LMIs also reduce the risks attached to recruitment and job search, particularly if they act as matchmakers or administrators. This function is especially relevant in the 24-hour domestic care sector, in which LMIs reliably replace caregivers or private households when a relationship terminates. For caregivers, agencies reduce the general risks associated with job search because the assignment of a new client usually takes less than 2 weeks. In addition, for both private households and caregivers, agencies reduce the risk of unintended illegal activities due to nonfamiliarity with social protection or trade legislation. Furthermore, some agencies in this sector reduce risks by securing acceptable working conditions (including fair pay) by acting as a contact point for caregivers who otherwise would be at the private households' mercy.

Unlike in the 24-hour domestic care sector, the risk management function plays a minor role only in the high-tech/IT and the hospitality sectors. Specifically, interviewees in the hospitality sector stressed that the risk of inappropriate matching of job candidates with positions is very low. Because newly hired employees only need little training and because fluctuation in this sector is generally high, employees and employers can be comparatively easily replaced. In the high-tech/IT sector, in cases in which recruitment agencies monitor a probation period of job candidates and replace failing candidates, they manage the risks associated with candidate misfit.

15.7.3. Network Building

The network-building function of LMIs is less pronounced in our sample than the functions as reducers of transaction costs and risks. Although LMIs replace informal networks of both jobseekers and employers with regard to their function as information providers, they contribute less to the development of new networks. Rare examples of the network-building function include online job portals and social media, creating communities that especially help the interviewed young EU8 migrants to obtain further information. Although such communities exist in all industries, agencies in the 24-hour domestic care sector additionally connect their clients with other businesspeople, such as drivers who manage caregivers' travel between their home towns and their places of work in Austria.

15.8. CONCLUSIONS

Our research provides in-depth insight regarding the entry ports of young EU8 migrants into the Austrian labor market and regarding the role of LMIs in different sectors. The findings indicate that young EU8 migrants across sectors preferably use informal networks or cost-free informational services provided by online job portals. In addition, in the high-tech/IT sector, young EU8 migrants search for information on company websites; in the hospitality sector, they spontaneously call or visit potential employers of their own accord; and in the 24-hour domestic care sector, they pay agencies to establish relationships with private households. These search strategies are often complemented with recruitment activities by employers using LMIs to gain access to job candidates in EU8 countries.

LMIs facilitate entry into the Austrian labor market especially in the high-tech/IT and the 24-hour domestic care sectors, in which they are important substitutes for informal networks. In these two sectors, LMIs—also in the form of agencies—play an important role in that they reduce transaction costs and risks for both young EU8 migrants and Austrian employers. In contrast, in the hospitality sector, agencies are far less important, which can be explained by the lower transaction costs and risks attached to employment relations in this sector.

Although this chapter offers a more nuanced understanding of EU8 migrants' routes into employment in Austria, the quality of this employment remains an open question. Relatedly, the impact of the different entry ports on job quality cannot be fully assessed. In other words, although our findings indicate that LMIs are important facilitators of youth transitions from Eastern Europe to the West, the question of the consequences of these transitions for the labor market outcomes of young people from Eastern Europe remains open. LMIs may either secure good working conditions or hamper them by exploiting the weak power position of young EU8 migrants in the Austrian labor market.

Another limitation of our research is sample and response bias. Specifically, it was difficult to approach agencies operating in the 24-hour care sector, which reflects the complex circumstances in which these LMIs work. Those agencies that granted an interview were apparently not among the "black sheep" exploiting migrant caregivers that were mentioned by some interview partners. Moreover, the overall positive description of recruiting processes and working conditions, as perceived by interviewees across all sectors and interview types, should be carefully interpreted because social desirability may have contributed to these depictions.

In view of these limitations, further research on the role of LMIs in shaping East–West youth migration in Europe is needed, in particular regarding the impact of different entry ports on labor market outcomes. In addition, although we have argued that Austria is a particularly apt case for studying East–West migration, future research focusing on other receiving countries is required. Given that our research findings indicate that the importance of entry ports and the importance of LMIs vary across sectors, future research should take account of these differences.

NOTES

1 We thank Christer Hyggen and Hans-Christian Sandlie for productive and stimulating collaboration in our research on this topic. Jan Brzozowski provided helpful comments on a previous version of the chapter. We are also grateful to Sabrina Franczik and Isabella Bauer for their assistance in data collection, as well as to Janine Leschke, Jacqueline O'Reilly, and Martin Seeleib-Kaiser for their guidance in preparing the text.

2 We exclude membership-based LMIs—which are the third type identified by Autor (2009)—from our analysis because neither the activities of guilds nor the collective action of unions are relevant to our research question.

3 A theoretical rationale for selecting the three sectors is provided by labor market segmentation theory (Reich, Gordon, and Edwards 1973; Piore 1986). According to this theory, labor markets consist of a primary segment characterized by stable employment relations, higher wages, and better opportunities for training and career development; and a secondary segment characterized by higher turnover rates, low wages, and poor opportunities for training and career development. We maintain that these differences between labor market segments are associated with differences in the role of LMIs. Whereas the high-tech/IT sector is a prototypical example for the primary segment, the hospitality and the 24-hour domestic care sectors are examples for the secondary segment. Thereby, the 24-hour domestic care sector differs from the hospitality sector in that legislation is much more complex in the former sector. Given that previous research highlights the impact of legislation on migration (Garapich 2008; Lindquist et al. 2012; Cangiano and Walsh 2014), we posit that the role of LMIs also varies between the hospitality sector and the 24-hour domestic care sector.

4 Depending on the needs of the client, specific training of caregivers is required—for instance, in palliative care. However, the typical caregivers in our study are people who only look after the client and do some housework, without providing any medical treatment or special care.

5 Although temporary work agencies often are associated with low-skill work in the secondary labor market segment, they also operate in high-skill areas such as engineering and IT design.

REFERENCES

Agunias, Dovelyn R. 2009. "Guiding the Invisible Hand: Making Migration Intermediaries Work for Development." United Nations Human Development Research Paper 22. New York: United Nations.

Andersson, Pernilla, and Eskil Wadensjö. 2004. "Temporary Employment Agencies: A Route for Immigrants to Enter the Labor Market?" IZA Discussion Paper 1090. Bonn: Institute for the Study of Labor.

Arrowsmith, James. 2006. *Temporary Agency Work in an Enlarged European Union*. Luxembourg: Office for Official Publications of the European Communities.

Autor, David H. 2009. "Studies of Labor Market Intermediation: Introduction." In *Studies of Labor Market Intermediation*, edited by David H. Autor, 1–23. Chicago: University of Chicago Press.

Autor, David H., and Susan N. Houseman. 2010. "Do Temporary-Help Jobs Improve Labor Market Outcomes for Low-Skilled Workers? Evidence from 'Work First.'" *American Economic Journal: Applied Economics* 2 (3): 96–128.

Benner, Chris. 2003. "Labor Flexibility and Regional Development: The Role of Labor Market Intermediaries." *Regional Studies* 37 (6–7): 621–33.

Benton, Meghan, and Milica Petrovic. 2013. *How Free Is Free Movement? Dynamics and Drivers of Mobility Within the European Union*. Brussels: Migration Policy Institute Europe.

Bonet, Rocio, Peter Cappelli, and Monika Hamori. 2013. "Labor Market Intermediaries and the New Paradigm for Human Resources." *Academy of Management Annals* 7 (1): 341–92.

Cangiano, Alessio, and Kieran Walsh. 2014. "Recruitment Processes and Immigration Regulations: The Disjointed Pathways to Employing Migrant Carers in Ageing Societies." *Work, Employment and Society* 23 (3): 372–89.

CIETT. 2016. "Economic Report 2016 Edition." International Confederation of Private Employment Services. http://www.wecglobal.org/economicreport2016

Coe, Neil M., Jennifer Johns, and Kevin Ward. 2007. "Mapping the Globalization of the Temporary Staffing Industry." *Professional Geographer* 59 (4): 503–20.

Elrick, Tim, and Emilia Lewandowska. 2008. "Matching and Making Labor Demand and Supply: Agents in Polish Migrant Networks of Domestic Elderly Care in Germany and Italy." *Journal of Ethnic and Migration Studies* 34 (5): 717–34.

European Commission. 2010. *Youth on the Move: An Initiative to Unleash the Potential of Young People to Achieve Smart, Sustainable and Inclusive Growth in the European Union*. Luxembourg: Publications Office of the European Union.

Favell, Adrian. 2008. "The New Face of East–West Migration in Europe." *Journal of Ethnic and Migration Studies* 34 (5): 701–16.

Findlay, Allan, and David McCollum. 2013. "Recruitment and Employment Regimes: Migrant Labour Channels in the UK's Rural Agribusiness Sector, from Accession to Recession." *Journal of Rural Studies* 30: 10–19.

Fitzgerald, Ian. 2007. *Working in the UK: Polish Migrant Worker Routes into Employment in the North East and North West Construction and Food Processing Sectors*. London: Trade Union Congress.

Freeman, Richard B. 2002. "The Labor Market in the New Information Economy." *Oxford Review of Economic Policy* 18 (3): 288–305.

Friberg, Jon Horgen, and Line Eldring, eds. 2013. *Labour Migrants from Central and Eastern Europe in the Nordic Countries: Patterns of Migration—Working Conditions and Recruitment Practices.* Copenhagen: TemaNord.

Galgóczi, Béla, and Janine Leschke. 2012. "Intra-EU Labour Migration After Eastern Enlargement and During the Crisis." ETUI Working Paper 13. Brussels: European Trade Union Institute.

Garapich, Michał P. 2008. "The Migration Industry and Civil Society: Polish Immigrants in the United Kingdom Before and After EU Enlargement." *Journal of Ethnic and Migration Studies* 34 (5): 735–52.

Heinrich, Carolyn J., Peter R. Mueser, and Kenneth R. Troske. 2007. "The Role of Temporary Help Employment in Low-Wage Worker Advancement." NBER Working Paper 13520. Cambridge, MA: National Bureau of Economic Research.

Hyggen, Christer, Renate Ortlieb, Hans-Christian Sandlie, and Silvana Weiss. 2016. "East–West and North–North Migrating Youth and the Role of Labour Market Intermediaries: The Case of Austria and Norway. STYLE Working Paper 6.2. Brighton, UK: CROME, University of Brighton. http://www.style-research.eu/publications/working-papers

Kahanec, Martin, and Brian Fabo. 2013. "Migration Strategies of the Crisis-Stricken Youth in an Enlarged European Union." IZA Discussion Paper 7285. Bonn: Institute for the Study of Labor.

Lindquist, Johan, Biao Xiang, and Brenda S. A. Yeoh. 2012. "Opening the Black Box of Migration: Brokers, the Organization of Transnational Mobility and the Changing Political Economy in Asia." *Pacific Affairs* 85 (1): 7–19.

McDowell, Linda, Adina Batnitzky, and Sarah Dyer. 2008. "Internationalization and the Spaces of Temporary Labor: The Global Assembly of a Local Workforce." *British Journal of Industrial Relations* 46 (4): 750–70.

Moriarty, Elaine, James Wickham, Torben Krings, Justyna Salamonska, and Alicja Bobek. 2012. "'Taking on Almost Everyone?' Migrant and Employer Recruitment Strategies in a Booming Labour Market." *International Journal of Human Resource Management* 23 (9): 1871–87.

O'Reilly, Jacqueline, Werner Eichhorst, András Gábos, Kari Hadjivassiliou, David Lain, Janine Leschke, et al. 2015. "Five Characteristics of Youth Unemployment in Europe: Flexibility, Education, Migration, Family Legacies, and EU Policy." *Sage Open* 5 (1): 1–19. doi:10.1177/2158244015574962.

Ortlieb, Renate, and Barbara Sieben. 2013. "Diversity Strategies and Business Logic: Why Do Companies Employ Ethnic Minorities?" *Group & Organization Management* 38 (4): 480–511.

Ortlieb, Renate, Barbara Sieben, and Christina Sichtmann. 2014. "Assigning Migrants to Customer Contact Jobs: A Context-Specific Exploration of the Business Case for Diversity." *Review of Managerial Science* 8 (2): 249–73.

Piore, Michael J. 1986. "The Shifting Grounds for Immigration." *Annals of the American Academy for Political and Social Science* 485 (May): 23–33.

Reich, Michael, David M. Gordon, and Richard C. Edwards. 1973. "Dual Labor Markets: A Theory of Labor Market Segmentation." *American Economic Review* 63 (2): 359–65.

Samaluk, Barbara. 2016. "Migrant Workers' Engagement with Labour Market Intermediaries in Europe: Symbolic Power Guiding Transnational Exchange." *Work, Employment and Society* 30 (3): 455–71.

Scott, Sam. 2013. "Migration and the Employer Perspective: Pitfalls and Potentials for a Future Research Agenda." *Population, Space and Place* 19 (6): 702–13.

Sporton, Deborah. 2013. "'They Control My Life': The Role of Local Recruitment Agencies in East European Migration to the UK." *Population, Space and Place* 19 (5): 443–58.

Thörnquist, Annette. 2013. "False (Bogus) Self-Employment in East–West Labour Migration: Recent Trends in the Swedish Construction and Road Haulage Industries." TheMES Report 41. Linköping: Institute for Research on Migration, Ethnicity and Society.

Van den Broek, Diane, William Harvey, and Dimitria Groutsis. 2016. "Commercial Migration Intermediaries and the Segmentation of Skilled Migrant Employment." *Work, Employment and Society* 30 (3): 523–34.

Voss, Eckhard, Katrin Vitols, Nico Farvaque, Andrea Broughton, Felix Behling, Francesca Dota, Salvo Leonardi, and Frédéric Naedenoen. 2013. *The Role of Temporary Agency Work and Labor Market Transitions in Europe: Institutional Frameworks, Empirical Evidence, Good Practice and the Impact of Social Dialogue*. Brussels: European Confederation of Private Employment Agencies.

16

WHAT ARE THE EMPLOYMENT PROSPECTS FOR YOUNG ESTONIAN AND SLOVAK RETURN MIGRANTS?

Jaan Masso, Lucia Mýtna Kureková, Maryna Tverdostup, and Zuzana Žilinčíková

16.1. INTRODUCTION

Free mobility is an important aspect of European integration that was widely realized for those Central and Eastern European (CEE) countries that joined the European Union (EU) in 2004 and 2007. Many young and highly educated people from these countries have since sought employment in Western Europe (Kahanec and Zimmermann 2010). The key findings about East–West migration refer to the selection of emigrants on the basis of age and level of education, to emigrants' employment in low-skilled and low-paid jobs, and to their relatively weak upward occupational mobility (Drinkwater, Eade, and Garapich 2009; Kahanec and Zimmermann 2010; Voitchovsky 2014). The quality of the employment of CEE migrants in the West is significantly worse than that of young migrants originating from Western countries (Akgüç and Beblavý, this volume; Spreckelsen, Leschke, and Seeleib-Kaiser, this volume). At the same time, CEE migrants in the West have very high employment levels (Kahanec and Zimmermann 2010; Kahanec and Kureková 2013), which even during the economic crisis exceeded the employment levels of nationals in some host countries (Kahanec and Kureková 2016). To date, researchers have mainly focused on understanding the impact of East–West mobility on the receiving countries (Barrett and Duffy 2008; Clark and Drinkwater 2008; House of Lords 2008; Pollard,

Latorre, and Sriskandarajah 2008) and on evaluating the effects of the outflows for the sending countries (Rutkowski 2007; Galgóczi, Leschke, and Watt 2009; Pryymachenko and Fregert 2011; Organization for Economic Co-operation and Development (OECD) 2012; Zaiceva 2014).

With the onset of the 2008–2009 economic crisis, many observers anticipated that the CEE migrants would return home. The economic literature mostly refers to return migration as a positive phenomenon for the home country, with returnees being viewed as agents of modernization and development, given that they bring home economic and social capital acquired abroad (King 1978). The existing evidence suggests that return patterns in the EU since the crisis have been diverse across both host and home countries (Galgóczi, Leschke, and Watt 2012). This chapter seeks to enhance our knowledge about return migration patterns in two small CEE economies—Estonia and Slovakia.[1] Although some comparative studies have recently analyzed return migration to CEE countries (Barcevičius et al. 2012; Lang et al. 2012; Coniglio and Brzozowski 2016), Estonia and Slovakia, in particular, are rarely selected as case studies, and knowledge about return migration in these countries is patchy. We chose these two countries because of their similar post-accession emigration rates, the variation in the severity of the 2008–2009 economic crisis and in respective labor market conditions, and the differences in their institutional models in terms of welfare-state spending changes (Bohle and Greskovits 2012).

We focus our analysis on young emigrants (15–34 years old) who have returned home to Estonia or Slovakia, calling them "returnees" here. Thus, we define a returnee as a person who emigrated from the home country, worked abroad for a period, and subsequently returned home. A "current emigrant," by contrast, is a person who emigrated from the home country and has remained abroad. A "stayer" is a person who never left the home country (within our observation period) to work abroad. More exact definitions are provided in Section 16.3. We rely on the Estonian and Slovak Labor Force Surveys (LFS) as our source of data. Although the two data sets involve to some extent different types of variables, they enable us to compare the two countries in a structured way. The LFS is a natural choice of data for the comparative analysis of return migration in Europe (concerning earlier studies, see Zaiceva and Zimmermann 2016) because within both the Estonian and the Slovak data, the variable of workplace location—home country or abroad—can be used to identify returnees.

The chapter conducts the analysis in two areas. First, we investigate what might lie behind the decision of some emigrants to return home (selection of returnees), and we seek to identify specific characteristics of returnees relative to those who remained at home (stayers) and those who remained abroad (current emigrants). Second, the chapter provides an analysis of the labor market status of young returnees after they have re-entered the domestic labor market. In summary, our research is centered on two questions: (1) Who are returnees compared to both stayers and current emigrants—among both young people and older adults? and (2) How successful are returnees in the home-country labor markets in terms of observed labor market status—that is, how often are they employed, unemployed, or inactive?

The value of our contribution lies in the comparative design of the study, which enables us to test the relative importance of some institutional and macroeconomic factors vis-à-vis micro-level characteristics such as education, gender, and labor market status. On the micro level, we pay particular attention to understanding the impact of being occupationally mismatched while abroad on the selection of returnees and on their short-term labor market outcomes. We also measure the effect of macroeconomic factors—gross domestic product (GDP) per capita and unemployment rate—on the returnees' labor market performance.

Our findings suggest that among young returnees, level of education has no effect on the decision to return in either of the country-specific samples. At the same time, level of occupation has a significant effect on the selection of young returnees, but only in the Estonian sample. In fact, an education–occupation mismatch significantly affects the decision to return among young and highly educated Estonian emigrants. By contrast, no mismatch effect is found for young Slovak returnees. The analysis of post-return labor market status reveals that both Estonian and Slovak returnees are more likely to face short-term unemployment (after re-entering the domestic labor market) compared to either current emigrants or stayers. This result could be attributed to a higher reservation wage and longer job search periods, both of which returnees can probably afford due to savings accumulated while abroad and possibly also the opportunity to transfer unemployment benefits from the host country to the home country (Hazans 2008; Zaiceva and Zimmermann 2016). These advantages appear to create conditions that enable returnees to find jobs that match their qualification levels and preferences (e.g., wage and type of work). We also find that Estonian returnees have a lower risk of unemployment compared to Slovak returnees. We attribute this difference to better labor market conditions and a broader response of the Estonian social security system to the crisis, both of which facilitate smoother reintegration of returnees in Estonia.

16.2. LITERATURE REVIEW: MACRO- AND MICRO-LEVEL DETERMINANTS OF RETURN MIGRATION

On a theoretical level, it has been established that economic actors self-select into migration (Borjas 1987) and that emigrants differ from stayers in terms of both observable (e.g., age, family status, and labor market status) and unobservable (e.g., attitudes and risk aversion) characteristics. The type of selection and how it compares to stayers or to citizens of the host country depends on the home- and host-country characteristics. Similar factors affect the selection of returnees. This is most widely analyzed with respect to selection according to skill and ability, as anchored in the theoretical framework of the Roy model (Roy 1951). This model predicts that where migration flows are negatively selected on the basis of skills (i.e., those who emigrate have lower than average skills), return migrants are the best of this negative selection. On the other hand, where the original migrants were positively selected (i.e., those who emigrate have higher than average skills), the return migrants are "the worst of the best" (Borjas and Bratsberg 1996). The aspect of selectivity is important because it signals the characteristics of returnees relative to stayers and is likely to affect returnee behavior in the home labor market, not least via their competitiveness with stayers.

However, the Roy model of selection into return migration overlooks the issue of occupational mismatch, whereas CEE migrants are often mismatched in the host countries, working in jobs below their qualifications (Akgüç and Beblavý, this volume; Spreckelsen et al., this volume). For example, Voitchovsky (2014) argues that the severity of the occupational downgrading of CEE migrants and the related wage penalty stand out relative to those of other migrant groups in Ireland (and the United Kingdom), including third-country nationals. The mismatch is strongest for workers with higher secondary and tertiary education (Drinkwater et al. 2009; Turner 2010). There is some evidence supporting a link between mismatch and return decisions. For instance, overeducation of migrants has been identified as a key variable associated with the intention to return for Estonian migrants working in Finland (Pungas et al. 2012). Similarly, Currie (2007) found that Polish returnees commonly framed their decision to return to Poland within a context of frustration with limited labor market progress in the United Kingdom.

Scholars theorize different reasons for return migration. It may follow, for example, from an initial plan regarding the country of residence over the life cycle, where the return home is already envisaged at the moment of emigration. In an analysis of determinants of return among Moroccan emigrants, for instance, De Haas, Fokkema, and Fassi Fihri (2015) showed that the decision to return can be driven by economic success in the host country. However, the return may also result from mistakes in the initial migration decision; that is, it follows from an unsuccessful migration experience (failed migration) (Rooth and Saarela 2007). The individual and collective success of the return process may vary depending on the individual characteristics of the migrant and his or her household, networks, and community, as well as country-level features in the home and host states (Kveder 2013). Furthermore, precautionary savings may be related to the return decision (Dustmann 1997; McCormick and Wahba 2001). Along these lines, Dumont and Spielvogel (2008, 178) define the key reasons for return migration as a failure to integrate in the host country, changes in the economic situation in the home country (macroeconomic environment), personal preference for the home country, the achievement of a savings objective, or improved employment opportunities at home following experience gained abroad.

The variety of factors that can contribute to the success of a return (individual-level characteristics, networks, country-level factors, motive for return, migration experience, and timing of return) is reflected in the mixed empirical findings on the characteristics of returnees and especially on their post-return labor market trajectories and performance across different CEE countries and over time (Iara 2006; Hazans 2008; Martin and Radu 2012; Pungas et al. 2012; Zaiceva and Zimmermann 2016). Coniglio and Brzozowski (2016) document that skill mismatch in the host country is significantly associated with post-return nonconformance of skills and employment, which ultimately reduces the likelihood of successful reintegration.

The majority of studies found that returnees to CEE countries are positively selected in terms of education (Hazans and Philips 2010; Martin and Radu 2012; Smoliner, Förschner, and Nova 2012; Masso, Eamets, and Mõtsmees 2014; Zaiceva and Zimmermann 2016). This positive selection into return migration is reflected in the significant wage premiums of CEE returnees (Iara 2006; Ambrosini et al. 2011; Martin and Radu 2012). However, evidence found by De Coulon and Piracha (2005) indicates that Albanian emigrants are negatively selected on skills, relative to stayers, which to a large extent explains the relatively worse performance of Albanian returnees on the home labor market. Another strand of literature has documented that returnees have a higher probability of falling into unemployment or inactivity (Smoliner et al. 2012; Coniglio and Brzozowski 2016). However, Piracha and Vadean (2010) found that the association between return migration to Albania and unemployment vanishes after a 1-year period of reintegration.

In addition to individual-level factors, institutional and macroeconomic aspects also play a role. Friberg et al. (2014) found that the performance of immigrants to a great extent depends on their structural position in the host labor market, which is largely determined by the institutional configuration of the host-country labor market. Other evidence by Findlay and McCollum (2013) highlights the significance of recruitment and employment regimes in the context of rural agricultural migrant labor. Napierała and Fiałkowska (2013) emphasize the importance of host-country employment agencies in preventing skill–occupation mismatch and, hence, in reducing return migration driven by overqualification. The macroeconomic environment is framed by changing external conditions, such as the Great Recession of 2008–2009, which significantly affected several host and home countries. White (2014), analyzing the return migration of young Polish migrants from the United Kingdom and Ireland following the crisis, questions the strength of a causal effect of the crisis on their decision to return. She argues that migrants prefer to stay in the host country because of the persistence of significant wage differentials compared to Poland. The existing evidence suggests that patterns of return in response to the economic crisis have been diverse across both host and home countries (Galgóczi et al. 2012).

To date, systematic work exploring the impact of welfare policies on patterns of return is absent. As stated previously, some studies view returning emigrants as being selected on the basis of a lack of economic success in the host country; return migration would thus correct for the failure of the initial migration. Being unemployed in the host country, therefore, significantly increases the probability of returning to the homeland (Pungas et al. 2012; Bijwaard, Schluter, and Wahba 2014). This might not be quite the case in the context of intra-EU mobility because migrants with a sufficient employment record become eligible for social insurance and other types of welfare benefits in the host country (Kureková 2013). Moreover, under EU legislation, unemployment benefits can be transferred to the country of origin.[2] However, if access to welfare is employment based, it continues to exclude the least successful migrants. The few existing studies have noted that choosing to stay or to return home can be influenced by where (at home or in the host country) the emigrant has access to social security benefits (for a discussion regarding Poland during the economic crisis, see Anacka and Fihel 2012) and that the decision of returnees to register as unemployed can depend on the country of previous employment (Kahanec and Kureková 2016). Other findings indicate that unemployment benefits enable emigrants to survive a period of unemployment abroad (White 2014) and that public programs might be important for the successful integration of poorly prepared return migrants (Cassarino 2004).

The contextual factors of the home and host countries go beyond economic and institutional variables. Some studies argue that return decisions are influenced mainly by the home countries rather than the host countries (Martin and Radu 2012) or that private and social motives play a key role (Barcevičius et al. 2012; Lang et al. 2012). Furthermore, cultural factors might be behind a return due to failed migration, such as an inability to integrate in the host country because of prejudices and stereotypes encountered abroad (Cerase 1974), whereas changed cultural and social patterns in the country of origin may also pose challenges to successful reintegration on return (Dumon 1986). Cross-border social network theory emphasizes that cross-border networks of social and economic relationships secure and sustain return migration (Cassarino 2004). For instance, having lost networks of social relationships may be the factor that causes returnees to fail to pursue their interests in the home country. Networks provide access to resources influencing performance on return, whereas return migration may help establish and maintain networks spanning several societies (Cassarino 2004). As an example of the importance of social factors for successful reintegration, Barrett and Mosca (2013) highlight the high degrees of loneliness and social isolation among elderly Irish returnees who had spent long periods abroad compared to those who had stayed at home. However, Kureková and Žilinčíková (2018), using web-survey data for Slovak returnees, find that returning for family reasons adds to the success of reintegration. Given this existing body of evidence, understanding the consequences for returning youth emigrants to Estonia and Slovakia can provide a novel and pertinent lens for examining some of the effects of youth migration during the recent crisis period.

16.3. DATA

The EU Labor Force Survey (EU-LFS) is a random representative household survey collected on a quarterly basis. The data set is restricted to individuals who are at least 15 years old, and we added an upper limit of 64 years for our study. The EU-LFS employs a rotational panel design, whereby every individual is interviewed for five consecutive quarters of the survey and subsequently leaves the sample. We use this panel structure of the data set to identify those who have work experience abroad. Within both the Estonian and the Slovak data, the variable of workplace location—home country or abroad—is used to identify returnees. The variable of country of residence a year previously, used by other return migration studies (Zaiceva and Zimmerman 2016), does not provide a sufficient sample size in the case of Estonian and Slovak data. A disadvantage of our approach is that we cannot use the data set to observe longer integration patterns and can only comparatively assess labor market outcomes for one quarter (the last quarter of the survey). However, we are able to go beyond the descriptive approach prevalent in most other studies that use EU-LFS data (Martin and Radu 2012; Smoliner et al. 2012).

For the analysis of the Slovak data, we keep only individuals who were interviewed in at least two out of the five available quarters in the sample. We define returnee as a person who worked at least one quarter abroad but returned to Slovakia in the last observed quarter. A current emigrant is an individual who is working abroad in the last observed quarter. In the Estonian LFS data, the labor market history of individuals is available for the past 2 years. Therefore, we define Estonian returnees as those who have worked abroad for at least one quarter during the past 2 years and are back in Estonia in the last quarter. This longer time span for observing emigrants and returnees yields a much larger sample of returnees in Estonia than in Slovakia.

A general disadvantage of the EU-LFS is the fact that it only captures emigration and return migration of short-term emigrants and returnees. A condition of participation in the survey is that an individual is considered a member of a surveyed household; therefore, the survey does not cover emigration of economically independent units (e.g., young people who emigrated and live abroad and are considered economically independent by the household members). However, individuals engaging in temporary or seasonal work abroad (or commuters) are considered household members, even if they work abroad for more than a year, and are therefore included in the survey (Bahna 2013). An important implication of this survey design is that the EU-LFS more precisely captures emigrants who live with a broader family and engage in circular or temporary mobility and at the same time is likely to underestimate the mobility of young people who have not established a family and are more footloose. We interpret our results in the light of these limitations.

16.4. KEY FACTS ABOUT ESTONIA AND SLOVAKIA

Estonia and Slovakia are understudied countries in the return migration literature. We selected these cases because they experienced similar post-accession emigration rates (Kureková 2011) but showed differences in the severity of the 2008–2009 economic crisis, as well as varying today in their labor market conditions and in their institutional models in terms of changes in welfare spending. The key comparative data for the two countries are presented in Table 16.1.

Slovakia and Estonia have had very different experiences of the economic crisis. They entered the crisis with different levels of youth unemployment, converging by 2010 on very high rates—from which Estonia recovered more quickly than Slovakia, however. Estonian youth unemployment rates skyrocketed from approximately 10% in 2007 to 34% in 2010 and then declined to approximately 19% in 2013. In contrast, the youth unemployment rate in Slovakia was nearly double that of Estonia at the onset of the crisis: It was 19% in 2008 and increased to 34% by 2012, remaining at this level in 2013.

Estonia experienced significant declines in GDP in 2008 and 2009 of 5.4% and 14.7%, respectively. Subsequently, economic growth returned, contributing to a decline in the general unemployment rate from 16.7% in 2010 to 8.6% in 2013. Although Slovakia experienced only a mild GDP decline in 2009 (−4.9%), its success in fighting unemployment has been limited. From this perspective, we might expect that the integration of return migrants to the Estonian labor market would be smoother than that of Slovak returnees.

Moreover, social protection spending has increased considerably in Estonia. Whereas in the mid-2000s, Estonia had a lower level of social protection spending than that of Slovakia (12.4% vs. 15.9%, respectively, in 2005), the levels converged at the peak of the crisis in 2009, with social protection spending amounting to 18.8% versus 18.2% of GDP in Estonia and Slovakia, respectively. This change indicates that Estonia invested significantly in assisting its citizens with weathering the misfortunes of the economic crisis. This increased investment in welfare may have assisted return migrants, but it also discouraged further outmigration from Estonia (Kureková 2013). Which country was more successful in integrating returnees is an important question. Based on these aggregate indicators, we might expect that returnees to Estonia on average perform better at reintegrating into the labor market because of higher levels of labor market flexibility (Eamets et al. 2015), contributing to higher outflows from

Table 16.1 Key economic indicators: Estonia and Slovakia

	2000	2001	2002	2003	2004	2005	2006	2007	2008	2009	2010	2011	2012	2013
Unemployment rate														
EU25	8.8	8.5	8.8	9.1	9.2	9.1	8.2	7.2	7.1	9.1	9.7	9.7	10.5	10.9
EE	14.6	13.0	11.2	10.3	10.1	8.0	5.9	4.6	5.5	13.5	16.7	12.3	10.0	8.6
SK	18.9	19.5	18.8	17.7	18.4	16.4	13.5	11.2	9.6	12.1	14.5	13.7	14.0	14.2
Youth unemployment rate (age 15–24 years)														
EU25	17.3	16.9	17.4	18.4	18.8	18.7	17.3	15.5	15.7	20.1	21.0	21.2	22.8	23.2
EE	23.9	22.2	17.9	20.9	23.9	15.1	12.1	10.1	12.0	27.4	32.9	22.4	20.9	18.7
SK	37.3	39.6	38.1	33.8	33.4	30.4	27.0	20.6	19.3	27.6	33.9	33.7	34.0	33.7
GDP growth														
EU27	3.9	2.0	1.3	1.5	2.6	2.2	3.4	3.2	0.4	-4.5	2.0	1.7	-0.4	0.1
EE	9.7	6.3	6.6	7.8	6.3	8.9	10.1	7.5	-4.2	-14.1	2.6	9.6	3.9	0.8
SK	1.4	3.5	4.6	4.8	5.1	6.7	8.3	10.5	5.8	-4.9	4.4	3.0	1.8	0.9
Social protection expenditures (% GDP)														
EU25	25.6	25.7	26.0	26.5	26.3	26.4	26.0	25.5	26.2	28.9	28.7	28.4	28.8	—
EE	13.8	13.0	12.7	12.6	13.0	12.5	12.0	12.0	14.7	18.8	17.6	15.6	15.0	14.8
SK	19.1	18.7	18.8	18.0	16.9	16.2	16.0	15.7	15.7	18.5	18.3	17.9	18.1	18.4
Strictness of employment protection—individual and collective dismissals: regular contracts														
EE	—	—	—	—	—	—	—	—	2.33	2.33	2.07	2.07	2.07	2.07
SK	—	—	—	—	—	—	—	—	2.63	2.63	2.63	2.63	2.16	2.26
Strictness of employment protection—temporary contracts														
EE	—	—	—	—	—	—	—	—	2.29	2.29	2.29	2.29	2.29	3.04
SK	—	—	—	—	—	—	—	—	2.17	2.17	2.17	2.42	2.29	2.42

EE, Estonia; SK, Slovakia.
Sources: OECD (employment protection) and Eurostat (all other data series).

Table 16.2 Estonia: Numbers of emigrants, returnees, and stayers (full sample)

	2008	2009	2010	2011	2012	2013	Total
Stayers	17,763	15,526	15,634	16,660	18,556	18,346	152,456
Returnees	275	413	491	608	778	785	3,570
Emigrants	332	307	365	390	507	492	3,002
Total	18,370	16,246	16,490	17,658	19,841	19,623	159,028
Share of returnees	1.50	2.54	2.98	3.44	3.92	4.00	2.24
Share of emigrants	1.81	1.89	2.21	2.21	2.56	2.51	1.89
Returnees per emigrants	82.8	134.5	134.5	155.9	153.5	159.6	118.9

Source: EE-LFS; authors' calculations.

unemployment and better labor market conditions. In fact, Estonian returnees show lower unemployment rates than has been the case for returnees to Slovakia.

For the analysis of return migration, we work with a pooled sample of EU-LFS data from 2008 to 2013. The overall Slovak sample consists of 96,821 individuals, of whom 3,211 are current emigrants and 329 are returnees. The total Estonian sample includes 159,028 respondents, of whom 3,002 are current emigrants and 3,570 are returnees. Of the returnees, 62% of the Slovaks and 65% of the Estonians are young (aged 15–34 years).

The rate of return migration increased over time in both countries, but the growth has been especially significant in Estonia (Tables 16.2 and 16.3). By 2013, the rate of return had exceeded the rate of outmigration, resulting in positive net intra-EU mobility in Estonia. The rate of return to Slovakia has been more modest. Between 2008 and 2013, on average every tenth person who worked abroad returned, but the rate of return varies significantly over the years analyzed, reaching close to 20% in 2009 and 2012 but only approximately 7% in all other years.[3] The share of current emigrants out of Slovakia relative to

Table 16.3 Slovakia: Numbers of migrants, returnees, and stayers (full sample)

	2008	2009	2010	2011	2012	2013	Total
Stayers	14,618	14,402	13,563	14,172	13,550	22,976	93,281
Returnees	69	83	30	30	68	49	329
Emigrants	695	484	437	440	357	798	3,211
Total	15,382	14,969	14,030	14,642	13,975	23,823	96,821
Share of returnees	0.5	0.6	0.2	0.2	0.5	0.2	0.3
Share of emigrants	4.5	3.2	3.1	3.0	2.6	3.4	3.3
Returnees per emigrants	9.9	17.1	6.9	6.8	19.0	6.1	10.2

Source: SK-LFS; authors' calculations.

returnees to Slovakia exceeds the share of current emigrants out of Estonia relative to returnees to Estonia, especially in the crisis years 2008 and 2009.

The EU-LFS does not include information about the main migrant destination countries for Estonia. Other studies document that Finland was, and remains, the most important destination country for temporary labor mobility among young Estonians (aged 15–35 years); the United Kingdom, Austria, Norway, Sweden, and Russia are also popular destinations. The key migration destinations for Slovaks are the United Kingdom, Czech Republic, Hungary, Italy, Austria, and Germany (Masso et al. 2016).

Tables 16.4 and 16.5 present descriptive statistical evidence for key demographic features of returnees, current emigrants, and stayers and for different age brackets. Estonian return migrants are substantially different from both current emigrants and stayers (see Table 16.4). Return migrants are on average younger than those who stay in Estonia; returnees are also more often male, compared to the relevant age group of stayers. Among young returnees, the share of married individuals is 39%, which is higher relative to that of stayers (31%) but lower relative to that of their peers who are still working abroad (49%). In terms of education, young returnees are more educated (e.g., the share of those with a lower level education is 32%, compared to 41% among stayers of the corresponding age group) and predominantly hold a secondary-level education (54%). The examination of labor market status revealed that approximately 72% of young returnees were employed while abroad; however, after returning, the share of those employed dropped to 52%, along with an increase in the share of unemployed from 12% a year previously to 26% in the current year.[4] However, despite the better educational attainments of returnees, they are still more likely to be unemployed than are stayers. Among returnees who found work, their occupational profile was lower compared to that recorded in their last quarter abroad. Consequently, young returnees with high education levels more frequently reported themselves to be overeducated in the last quarter working abroad compared to those who had stayed in Estonia (16% relative to 10% among stayers).

For Slovakia (see Table 16.5), we find that returnees significantly differ both from stayers (nonmigrants) and from Slovak emigrants currently working abroad with regard to the main demographic and labor market characteristics. Similar to current emigrants, returnees are more likely to be males. Returnees are younger, more frequently overeducated for the jobs they performed abroad, and more skilled than both current emigrants and stayers. Most young returnees have a secondary education (90%); however, approximately two-thirds of returnees were unemployed in the last quarter of the survey, which exceeds the share of unemployed among stayers and especially among Slovak emigrants abroad.

However, returnees are also much less likely to be inactive compared to stayers in the relevant age categories. Returnees are less likely than stayers to be self-employed, which might be related to their better performance in the labor market (e.g., no need to enter bogus self-entrepreneurship; see Ortlieb, Sheehan, and

Table 16.4 Estonia: Descriptive statistics based on EE-LFS

	Returnees				Stayers				Current emigrants			
	15–35 years	Youth 15–24 years	Youth 25–35 years	>35 years	15–35 years	Youth 15–24 years	Youth 25–35 years	>35 years	15–35 years	Youth 15–24 years	Youth 25–35 years	>35 years
Sociodemographic characteristics												
Average age, years	41				45				39			
Gender (male = 1)	71.8	68.8	78.2	61.2	50.5	52.5	53.5	44.5	87.2	79.9	89.9	85.7
Nationality (Estonian = 1)	80	82.3	78.4	66.4	78.2	81.4	73.7	73	79.1	85.8	76.1	77.8
Citizenship (Estonian = 1)	92.3	95.4	90.3	79.7	91.5	94	87.9	84.3	94	97.2	92.6	88.2
Marital status (married = 1)	39	16.7	56.7	77.5	30.8	10.3	63.7	75.4	48.9	20.1	59.8	81.1
Education												
Higher	13.9	5.2	21.5	18.9	14.2	5.2	28.5	21.9	11.1	4.7	13.5	8.2
Secondary	53.9	60.5	50.4	59.1	44.7	44.6	49.5	50.5	57.8	66.8	54.4	68.3
Lower	32.2	34.3	28.2	22	41.1	50.3	22	27.6	31.1	28.4	32.2	23.5
Employment												
Employed	51.9	38.2	60.4	59.5	49.1	23.1	76.2	58.1	100	100	100	100
Unemployed	25.8	26.9	25.2	15.6	8.8	8.6	9	5	—	—	—	—
Inactive	22.3	35	14.4	24.9	42.1	68.3	14.9	36.9	—	—	—	—

Employment 1 year previously

Employed	72	58.2	79.3	77	61.8	35.7	78.5	60.1	79.9	62.2	85.3	78.5
Unemployed	12	11.6	11.2	6.8	3.3	3.4	3.3	3.3	6.9	13.5	4.9	7.2
Inactive	16	30.2	8.5	16.2	34.9	60.9	18.3	36.6	13.2	24.3	9.8	14.3
ISCO (last quarter abroad for returnees)												
High	7.7	6.2	8.8	11.3	37.9	22.5	42.8	39.2	8.7	5	10.1	13.1
Medium	7.2	9.9	5.1	8.1	23.1	32.4	20.1	20.2	9.8	16	7.5	7.3
Low	85.1	83.9	86.1	80.5	38	44.8	35.8	40.2	81.2	79	82.4	79.5
Overeducation (last quarter abroad for returnees)												
Among medium educated	11.1	12.9	9.6	7.8	8.2	11.2	7	11	11.2	13.5	10.1	8.9
Among highly educated	16.1	36.4	13.2	3.7	10.2	13.8	9.8	10.6	32.6	60	29	18.9
Self-employed (last quarter abroad for returnees)	2.8	4.5	1.5	2.9	6.2	2.6	7.4	9	1.5	0.9	1.7	3.7
No. of observations	1,042	280	701	1,563	29,770	15,189	14,581	106,009	794	219	575	1,424

Notes: The level of occupation corresponds to the International Standard Classification of Occupations (ISCO) code: low (9), medium (4–8), and high (0–3). Overeducation was measured as a combination of education and occupational level. Overeducation among the medium educated was defined as the combination of medium education (ISCED 3 or 4) and low occupational level (ISCO 9); overeducation among the highly educated was defined by high education (ISCED 5 or 6) and a low or middle level of occupation (ISCO > 3).

Table 16.5 Slovakia: Descriptive statistics based on SK-LFS

	Returnees				Stayers				Current emigrants			
	15–34 years	Youth 15–24 years	Youth 25–34 years	>35 years	15–34 years	Youth 15–24 years	Youth 25–34 years	>35 years	15–34 years	Youth 15–24 years	Youth 25–34 years	>35 years
Sociodemographic characteristics												
Average age, years	n.a.				n.a.				n.a.			
Gender (male = 1)	63.7	50.6	72.4	73.6	51.1	50.9	51.2	46.9	67.6	62.7	69.7	70.5
Nationality (Slovak = 1)	85.3	85.2	85.4	83.2	90.2	90.4	89.9	89.1	88.2	90.7	87.1	87.9
Citizenship (Slovak = 1)	99.5	100	99.2	99.2	99.9	100	99.7	99.8	99.7	100	99.6	99.7
Marital status (married = 1)	13.7	0	22.8	70.4	22.1	2.9	42	75.7	21	3.6	28.4	74.3
Education												
Higher	7.4	3.7	9.8	2.4	15	5.8	24.6	13.7	10.9	4.3	13.8	5
Secondary	89.7	91.4	88.6	91.2	57.9	46.9	69.4	75.3	86.1	90	84.4	91.1
Lower	2.9	4.9	1.6	6.4	27	47.4	6	11.1	3	5.7	1.8	3.9
Employment												
Employed	33.3	28.4	36.6	32.8	42.8	17.5	68.9	62.3	98	99.1	97.5	98.7
Unemployed	59.3	60.5	58.5	53.6	12	10.6	13.4	9.8	0.1	0	0.2	0
Inactive	7.4	11.1	4.9	13.6	45.3	71.9	17.7	27.9	1.9	0.9	2.3	1.3

Employment 1 year previously

Employed	70.6	61.7	76.4	85.6	39.2	13.6	65.8	63.3	84.9	73.2	89.8	94.2
Student	10.8	23.5	2.4	0.0	40.1	74.2	4.8	0.0	4.8	12.7	1.5	0.0
Unemployed	17.2	14.8	18.7	10.4	11.4	9.1	13.8	10.5	8.8	13.9	6.6	4.7
Inactive	1.5	0	2.4	4.0	9.2	3.1	15.6	26.2	1.6	0.2	2.1	1.2
No. of observations	204	81	123	125	34,582	17,595	16,987	58,698	1,473	440	1,033	1,738

Labor market characteristics

Occupation/ISCO (last quarter abroad for returnees), N = 56,789

High	11	6.2	14.2	8.8	36.6	22.6	40.4	36.2	15	9.1	17.6	7.9
Medium	62.2	66.7	59.2	72	56.1	66.2	53.4	54.3	66	67.1	65.6	79.5
Low	26.9	27.2	26.7	19.2	7.3	11.1	6.2	9.5	19	23.7	16.9	12.7

Overeducation (last quarter abroad for returnees)

Among medium educated	25.9	24.7	26.7	14.4	5.7	8.1	5	7	16.8	20.3	15.2	11.1
Among highly educated	3	1.2	4.2	0.8	3.3	1.8	3.8	1.8	4.2	2.1	5.1	1.7
Self-employed	6.0	2.5	8.3	13.6	12.7	8.6	13.8	15.3	19.2	14.8	21.0	35.7
No. of observations	201	81	120	125	15,248	3,261	11,987	38,031	1,451	438	1,013	1,733

Notes: Overeducation was measured as a combination of education and occupational level. Overeducation among the medium educated was defined as the combination of medium education (ISCED 3 or 4) and low occupational level (ISCO 9); overeducation among the highly educated was defined by high education (ISCED 5 or 6) and a low or middle level of occupation (ISCO > 3).

Masso, this volume). But this may also be associated with the lower frequency of opportunity entrepreneurship (Bosma et al. 2012) among return migrants. These findings contrast with some other previous findings (McCormick and Wahba 2001; Piracha and Vadean 2010); however, the EU-LFS might not be the appropriate data source for studying the degree of self-employment among returnees because they may require more time after their return home to become engaged in entrepreneurship.[5] In the empirical analysis that follows, we examine whether these differences are statistically salient and to what degree these compositional effects impact on the labor market performance of returnees relative to stayers and current emigrants.

16.5. ECONOMETRIC ANALYSIS OF SELECTIVITY AND LABOR MARKET STATUS

16.5.1. Models

The econometric analysis has two foci. First, a set of logistic regressions is used to investigate how the characteristics of returnees differ from those of both stayers and current emigrants. Second, the labor market status of returnees is investigated in comparison to the rest of the respondents—stayers and current emigrants. A multinomial logistic regression is fitted for the variable indicating labor market status in the last observed quarter: employed, unemployed, or inactive. All models are estimated for the full sample (M1–M3), as well as for the youth sample only (M4–M6). Results are shown in Tables 16.6 and 16.7 for Estonia and in Tables 16.8 and 16.9 for Slovakia.

The models include two broad types of variables: individual-level variables and macroeconomic variables. In particular, the models include sociodemographic variables: gender; marital status (single or married); age; nationality (Estonian/Slovak or non-Estonian/non-Slovak); and education—low (International Standard Classification of Education (ISCED) 1–2), medium (ISCED 3–4), and high (ISCED 5–6). The models addressing the selectivity of returnees further employ variables related to the economic activity of respondents: self-employment (a dummy variable), labor market status a year previously (employed [ref.], student, unemployed, or inactive), skill level of job after return, and overqualification while abroad. We distinguish between two types of overqualification: overqualified among medium-educated and overqualified among highly educated workers.

Macro-level characteristics include measures of GDP per capita and unemployment rate in the home country. Based on the findings of secondary literature, host-country conditions appear more important than home-country conditions for the return and reintegration of emigrants. We are not able to use these macro-level variables in the host countries (or their differences in the host and home countries) because of the lack of information on the migrants' destination

Table 16.6 Estonia: Selectivity analysis

| | Returnee–stayer | | | | | | Returnee–emigrant | | | | | |
| | All sample | | | Youth sample (15–34 years) | | | All sample | | | Youth sample (15–34 years) | | |
	M1	M2	M3	M4	M5	M6	M7	M8	M9	M10	M11	M12
Male	0.003*	0.003**	0.004**	0.008**	0.008**	0.01***	−0.294***	−0.293***	−0.299***	−0.314***	−0.314***	−0.308***
	(0.001)	(0.001)	(0.002)	(0.003)	(0.003)	(0.004)	(0.020)	(0.020)	(0.020)	(0.041)	(0.041)	(0.042)
Married	−0.001	−0.001	−0.001	−0.003	−0.003	−0.003	−0.025	−0.028	−0.026	−0.009	−0.011	−0.011
	(0.001)	(0.001)	(0.002)	(0.003)	(0.003)	(0.003)	(0.023)	(0.023)	(0.023)	(0.029)	(0.029)	(0.029)
Age 15–24 years	0.017***	0.02***	0.022***				−0.022	−0.027	−0.029			
	(0.003)	(0.003)	(0.003)				(0.042)	(0.042)	(0.042)			
Age 25–34 years	0.012***	0.013***	0.015***				−0.115***	−0.119***	−0.12***			
	(0.002)	(0.002)	(0.002)				(0.036)	(0.035)	(0.036)			
Age 35–44 years	0.011***	0.012***	0.014***				−0.075**	−0.079**	−0.081**			
	(0.002)	(0.002)	(0.002)				(0.034)	(0.034)	(0.034)			
Age 45–54 years	0.006***	0.007***	0.008***				−0.104***	−0.108***	−0.109***			
	(0.002)	(0.002)	(0.002)				(0.035)	(0.035)	(0.036)			
Other non-Estonian nationality	−0.001	−0.001	−0.001	−0.008***	−0.008**	−0.009**	0.013	0.011	0.015	−0.038	−0.036	−0.029
	(0.001)	(0.001)	(0.002)	(0.003)	(0.003)	(0.004)	(0.022)	(0.022)	(0.022)	(0.037)	(0.037)	(0.037)
Secondary education	0.011***	0.008***	0.009***	0.008**	0.005	0.007*	0.03	0.028	0.035	0.036	0.046	0.059*
	(0.002)	(0.002)	(0.002)	(0.003)	(0.003)	(0.004)	(0.023)	(0.023)	(0.023)	(0.031)	(0.031)	(0.031)
Higher education	0.017***	0.014***	0.016***	0.008	0.004	0.005	0.145***	0.145***	0.156***	0.012	0.022	0.04
	(0.003)	(0.003)	(0.004)	(0.007)	(0.007)	(0.008)	(0.035)	(0.035)	(0.036)	(0.06)	(0.06)	(0.061)

(continued)

Table 16.6 Continued

| | Returnee–stayer | | | | | | Returnee–emigrant | | | | | |
| | All sample | | | Youth sample (15–34 years) | | | All sample | | | Youth sample (15–34 years) | | |
	M1	M2	M3	M4	M5	M6	M7	M8	M9	M10	M11	M12
Overeducated among medium educated	−0.018***	−0.019***	−0.022***	−0.059***	−0.06***	−0.07***	−0.196***	−0.199***	−0.193***	−0.564***	−0.556***	−0.554***
	(0.004)	(0.004)	(0.004)	(0.022)	(0.022)	(0.025)	(0.053)	(0.054)	(0.054)	(0.192)	(0.193)	(0.190)
Overeducated among highly educated	−0.004	−0.004	−0.005	0.021***	0.019***	0.022***	−0.051	−0.052	−0.057	0.15**	0.155**	0.145*
	(0.004)	(0.004)	(0.005)	(0.007)	(0.007)	(0.008)	(0.055)	(0.055)	(0.056)	(0.076)	(0.075)	(0.077)
Medium-level occupation	−0.01***	−0.01***	−0.013***	−0.019***	−0.02***	−0.024***	−0.347***	−0.343***	−0.339***	−0.511***	−0.503***	−0.5***
	(0.003)	(0.003)	(0.004)	(0.006)	(0.006)	(0.007)	(0.046)	(0.046)	(0.047)	(0.067)	(0.067)	(0.068)
High-level occupation	0.02***	0.02***	0.023***	0.015***	0.014***	0.016***	−0.181***	−0.177***	−0.182***	−0.321***	−0.316***	−0.317***
	(0.003)	(0.003)	(0.003)	(0.005)	(0.005)	(0.006)	(0.024)	(0.024)	(0.024)	(0.033)	(0.034)	(0.034)
Self-employed	−0.015***	−0.015***	−0.017***	−0.013*	−0.012*	−0.014	−0.02	−0.016	−0.012	0.046	0.056	0.049
	(0.003)	(0.003)	(0.004)	(0.007)	(0.007)	(0.009)	(0.056)	(0.056)	(0.057)	(0.098)	(0.095)	(0.096)
Labor market status 1 year ago—student	−0.002	−0.002	−0.002	−0.006	−0.006	−0.007	0.022	0.024	0.026	0.023	0.024	0.037
	(0.003)	(0.003)	(0.003)	(0.004)	(0.004)	(0.005)	(0.042)	(0.043)	(0.043)	(0.052)	(0.05)	(0.049)
Unemployed	0.009***	0.007***	0.008***	0.008	0.005	0.006	−0.05*	−0.045	−0.051*	−0.074*	−0.066	−0.063
	(0.002)	(0.002)	(0.003)	(0.005)	(0.005)	(0.005)	(0.029)	(0.03)	(0.030)	(0.042)	(0.042)	(0.043)
Inactive	−0.008***	−0.008***	−0.01***	−0.007*	−0.007*	−0.01**	−0.131***	−0.129***	−0.146***	−0.051	−0.048	−0.077
	(0.002)	(0.002)	(0.003)	(0.004)	(0.004)	(0.005)	(0.037)	(0.037)	(0.037)	(0.051)	(0.05)	(0.05)

	(1)	(2)	(3)	(4)	(5)	(6)	(7)	(8)	(9)	(10)	(11)	(12)
GDP last quarter			0.018***			0.031***			0.011			0.053
			(0.003)			(0.007)			(0.04)			(0.061)
Unemployment rate last quarter			0.001***			0.001***			−0.004			−0.008*
			(0.000)			(0.000)			(0.003)			(0.004)
Year dummies	No	Yes	No	No	Yes	No	No	Yes	No	No	Yes	No
No. of observations	48,664	48,664	41,373	13,305	13,305	11,223	2,389	2,389	2,336	938	938	915
Pseudo R^2	0.064	0.085	0.071	0.0526	0.0703	0.0638	0.1335	0.1368	0.1393	0.155	0.162	0.1694

Notes: The level of occupation corresponds to the standard categorization of the ISCO code: low (9), medium (4–8), and high (0–3). Overeducation was measured as a combination of education and occupational level. Overeducation among the medium educated was defined as the combination of medium education (ISCED 3 or 4) and low occupational level (ISCO 9); overeducation among the highly educated was defined by high education (ISCED 5 or 6) and a low or middle level of occupation (ISCO > 3). The figures reported in the table are the marginal effects with standard errors in parentheses. The reference categories in the regressions are male, single, age 55–65 years, Estonian nationality, primary education, overeducated among primary education, low-level education, and salaried employee.

*p < .10.

**p < .05.

***p < .01.

Table 16.7 Estonia: Labor market status analysis

| | All sample | | | | | | Young sample (15–34 years) | | | | | |
| | M1 | | M2 | | M3 | | M4 | | M5 | | M6 | |
	Unemployed	Inactive	Unemployed	Inactive	Unemployed	Inactive	Unemployed	Inactive	Unemployed	Inactive	Unemployed	Inactive
Returnee	0.062***	−0.06***	0.051***	−0.066***	0.057***	−0.064***	0.093***	−0.21***	0.082***	−0.219***	0.091***	−0.215***
	(−0.004)	(−0.011)	(−0.004)	(0.011)	(0.004)	(0.011)	(0.007)	(0.021)	(0.007)	(0.021)	(0.007)	(0.021)
Male	0.019***	−0.086***	0.018***	−0.086***	0.021***	−0.084***	0.021***	−0.182***	0.02***	−0.183***	0.024***	−0.174***
	(0.001)	(0.002)	(0.001)	(0.002)	(0.002)	(0.002)	(0.002)	(0.004)	(0.002)	(0.004)	(0.003)	(0.004)
Married	−0.019***	−0.065***	−0.019***	−0.065***	−0.018***	−0.061***	−0.011***	−0.286***	−0.011***	−0.286***	−0.011***	−0.274***
	(0.002)	(0.003)	(0.002)	(0.003)	(0.002)	(0.003)	(0.003)	(0.004)	(0.003)	(0.004)	(0.003)	(0.004)
Age 15–24 years	0.041***	0.005***	0.043***	0.006*	0.048***	0.007*						
	(0.002)	(0.003)	(0.002)	(0.003)	(0.003)	(0.004)						
Age 25–34 years	0.063***	−0.283***	0.065***	−0.282***	0.072***	−0.274***						
	(0.002)	(0.003)	(0.002)	(0.003)	(0.003)	(0.004)						
Age 35–44 years	0.058***	−0.371***	0.059***	−0.369***	0.061***	−0.366***						
	(0.002)	(0.003)	(0.002)	(0.003)	(0.003)	(0.004)						
Age 45–54 years	0.057***	−0.357***	0.059***	−0.355***	0.064***	−0.354***						
	(0.002)	(0.003)	(0.002)	(0.003)	(0.003)	(0.004)						
Other non-Estonian nationality	0.041***	−0.013***	0.042***	−0.012***	0.045***	−0.019***	0.051***	−0.081***	0.052***	−0.079***	0.056***	−0.09***
	(0.001)	(0.002)	(0.001)	(0.002)	(0.002)	(0.003)	(0.002)	(0.005)	(0.002)	(0.005)	(0.003)	(0.005)
Secondary education	0.005***	−0.141***	−0.002	−0.145***	−0.001	−0.156***	0.013***	−0.207***	0.008***	−0.21***	0.011***	−0.224***
	(0.002)	(0.002)	(0.002)	(0.002)	(0.002)	(0.003)	(0.003)	(0.004)	(0.003)	(0.004)	(0.003)	(0.004)

	(1)	(2)	(3)	(4)	(5)	(6)	(7)	(8)	(9)	(10)	(11)	(12)
Higher education	-0.027***	-0.226***	-0.033***	-0.23***	-0.035***	-0.237***	-0.019***	-0.361***	-0.025***	-0.367***	-0.029***	-0.359***
	(0.002)	(0.003)	(0.002)	(0.003)	(0.003)	(0.004)	(0.004)	(0.006)	(0.004)	(0.006)	(0.005)	(0.007)
GDP per capita					-0.019*	0.016					-0.029	0.003
					(0.011)	(0.016)					(0.021)	(0.029)
Unemployment rate					0.002***	0.002*					0.002	0.001
					(0.001)	(0.001)					(0.002)	(0.002)
Year dummies	No	Yes	Yes	No	Yes	Yes	No	Yes	Yes	No	Yes	Yes
No. of observations	143,017	143,017	143,017	143,017	111,069	111,069	51,559	51,559	51,559	51,559	39,609	39,609
Pseudo R^2	0.0494	0.2562	0.0726	0.2568	0.0732	0.2543	0.0291	0.1766	0.0541	0.178	0.0529	0.1767

Note: See notes to Table 16.6.

Table 16.8 Slovakia: Selectivity analysis

| | Returnee–stayer | | | | | | Returnee–emigrant | | | | | |
| | All sample | | | Youth sample (15–34 years) | | | All sample | | | Youth sample (15–34 years) | | |
	M1	M2	M3	M4	M5	M6	M7	M8	M9	M10	M11	M12
Male	0.002**	0.002**	0.002**	-0.001	-0.001	0	-0.001	-0.002	-0.002	-0.012	-0.014	-0.012
	(0.001)	(0.001)	(0.001)	(0.002)	(0.002)	(0.002)	(0.011)	(0.011)	(0.011)	(0.018)	(0.017)	(0.017)
Married	-0.003***	-0.004***	-0.004***	-0.009***	-0.010***	-0.010***	-0.018	-0.018	-0.02	-0.03	-0.027	-0.029
	(0.001)	(0.001)	(0.001)	(0.002)	(0.002)	(0.002)	(0.012)	(0.012)	(0.012)	(0.021)	(0.021)	(0.021)
Age 15–24 years		0.008***	0.008***				0.008	0.008	-0.008			
		(0.002)	(0.002)				(0.025)	(0.025)	(0.026)			
Age 25–34 years	0.006***	0.005***	0.005***				-0.001	-0.004	-0.011			
	(0.001)	(0.001)	(0.001)				(0.022)	(0.022)	(0.023)			
Age 35–44 years	0.001	0.001	0.001				-0.024	-0.025	-0.029			
	(0.001)	(0.001)	(0.001)				(0.022)	(0.021)	(0.023)			
Age 45–54 years	0	0	0				-0.03	-0.032	-0.035			
	(0.001)	(0.001)	(0.001)				(0.022)	(0.022)	(0.023)			
Other non-Slovak nationality	-0.003**	-0.003**	-0.003**	-0.005	-0.005	-0.005	-0.022	-0.021	-0.022	-0.03	-0.034	-0.032
	(0.001)	(0.001)	(0.001)	(0.003)	(0.003)	(0.003)	(0.014)	(0.014)	(0.014)	(0.023)	(0.023)	(0.023)
Secondary education	0.002	0.002	0.002	-0.001	0	0	0.011	0.005	0.014	-0.008	-0.015	-0.006
	(0.002)	(0.002)	(0.002)	(0.008)	(0.008)	(0.008)	(0.03)	(0.031)	(0.028)	(0.061)	(0.062)	(0.059)

Higher education	-0.002 (0.002)	-0.001 (0.002)	-0.001 (0.002)	-0.007 (0.009)	-0.006 (0.008)	-0.005 (0.009)	-0.033 (0.036)	-0.039 (0.036)	-0.022 (0.036)	-0.049 (0.071)	-0.06 (0.071)	-0.033 (0.071)
Overeducated among medium educated	0.009 (0.007)	0.007 (0.007)	0.007 (0.007)	0.08 (0.069)	0.065 (0.057)	0.069 (0.06)	0.007 (0.044)	0.017 (0.046)	0.004 (0.043)	0.176 (0.147)	0.18 (0.141)	0.174 (0.145)
Overeducated among highly educated	0.002 (0.004)	0.002 (0.004)	0.002 (0.004)	0.003 (0.008)	0.004 (0.008)	0.003 (0.008)	0.007 (0.048)	0.013 (0.05)	0 (0.046)	0.003 (0.057)	0.016 (0.062)	-0.007 (0.053)
Medium-level occupation	0.001 (0.004)	0.000 (0.004)	0.001 (0.004)	0.014 (0.011)	0.012 (0.010)	0.013 (0.010)	-0.022 (0.046)	-0.011 (0.043)	-0.023 (0.046)	0.075 (0.066)	0.079 (0.063)	0.075 (0.066)
High-level occupation	-0.004 (0.003)	-0.005 (0.003)	-0.005 (0.003)	0.001 (0.007)	-0.001 (0.007)	-0.001 (0.007)	-0.025 (0.05)	-0.012 (0.046)	-0.03 (0.049)	0.048 (0.07)	0.054 (0.067)	0.04 (0.068)
Self-employed	-0.002 (0.001)	-0.002 (0.001)	-0.002 (0.001)	-0.008* (0.004)	-0.008* (0.004)	-0.008* (0.004)	-0.100*** (0.017)	-0.099*** (0.017)	-0.091*** (0.017)	-0.125*** (0.032)	-0.128*** (0.032)	-0.118*** (0.032)
LM status one year ago—student	0.006* (0.003)	0.006* (0.003)	0.006* (0.003)	0.013* (0.005)	0.013* (0.005)	0.012* (-0.005)	0.097* (0.039)	0.101** (0.039)	0.103** (0.04)	0.124** (0.044)	0.130** (0.044)	0.125** (0.044)
Unemployed	0.004** (0.002)	0.005** (0.002)	0.005** (0.002)	0.008* (0.004)	0.010* (0.004)	0.010*** (0.004)	0.063** (0.021)	0.068** (0.021)	0.072*** (0.022)	0.073* (0.03)	0.078*** (0.03)	0.084*** (0.031)
Inactive	0 (0.002)	0 (0.002)	0 (0.002)	-0.008* (0.003)	-0.008** (0.003)	-0.008** (0.003)	0.165 (0.085)	0.180* (0.086)	0.183* (0.089)	0.101 (0.18)	0.139 (0.191)	0.144 (0.2)
GDP last quarter			-0.002 (0.002)			-0.007 (0.005)			-0.056* (0.025)			-0.091* (0.041)

(continued)

Table 16.8 Continued

| | Returnee–stayer | | | | | | Returnee–emigrant | | | | | |
| | All sample | | | Youth sample (15–34 years) | | | All sample | | | Youth sample (15–34 years) | | |
	M1	M2	M3	M4	M5	M6	M7	M8	M9	M10	M11	M12
Unemployment rate last quarter			-0.001***			-0.002***			-0.008***			-0.006
			(0.000)			(0.000)			(0.002)			(0.004)
Year dummies	No	Yes	No	No	Yes	No	No	Yes	No	No	Yes	No
No. of observations	53,604	53,604	53,602	15,449	15,449	15,447	3,510	3,510	3,508	1,652	1,652	1,650
Pseudo R^2	0.102	0.116	0.116	0.089	0.111	0.106	0.064	0.092	0.073	0.053	0.089	0.06

Note: See notes to Table 16.6.

Table 16.9 Slovakia: Labor market status analysis

| | All sample | | | | | | Young sample (15–34 years) | | | | | |
| | M1 | | M2 | | M3 | | M4 | | M5 | | M6 | |
	Unemployed	Inactive	Unemployed	Inactive	Unemployed	Inactive	Unemployed	Inactive	Unemployed	Inactive	Unemployed	Inactive
Returnee	0.415***	−0.188***	0.427***	−0.191***	0.432***	−0.191***	0.462***	−0.293***	0.476***	−0.296***	0.479***	−0.296***
	(0.027)	(0.02)	(0.027)	(0.02)	(0.027)	(0.02)	(0.036)	(0.029)	(0.035)	(0.028)	(0.035)	(0.028)
Male	0.008***	−0.138***	0.008***	−0.138***	0.008***	−0.138***	0.022***	−0.198***	0.021***	−0.198***	0.021***	−0.198***
	(0.002)	(0.002)	(0.002)	(0.002)	(0.002)	(0.002)	(0.003)	(0.004)	(0.003)	(0.004)	(0.003)	(0.004)
Married	−0.040***	0.005	−0.038***	0.006	−0.038***	0.006	−0.015***	−0.095***	−0.012**	−0.094***	−0.012**	−0.093***
	(0.002)	(0.003)	(0.002)	(0.003)	(0.002)	(0.003)	(0.004)	(0.005)	(0.004)	(0.005)	(0.004)	(0.005)
Age 15–24	0.020***	0.054***	0.022***	0.055***	0.022***	0.055***						
	(0.003)	(0.006)	(0.003)	(0.006)	(0.003)	(0.006)						
Age 25–34	0.081***	−0.363***	0.083***	−0.362***	0.083***	−0.362***						
	(0.003)	(0.005)	(0.003)	(0.005)	(0.003)	(0.005)						
Age 35–44	0.085***	−0.462***	0.085***	−0.461***	0.085***	−0.461***						
	(0.003)	(0.004)	(0.003)	(0.004)	(0.003)	(0.004)						
Age 45–54	0.083***	−0.449***	0.083***	−0.449***	0.083***	−0.449***						
	(0.003)	(0.004)	(0.003)	(0.004)	(0.003)	(0.004)						
Other non-Slovak nationality	−0.080***	0.039***	−0.079***	0.039***	−0.079***	0.039***	−0.121***	0.126***	−0.120***	0.126***	−0.120***	0.126***
	(0.004)	(0.004)	(0.004)	(0.004)	(0.004)	(0.004)	(0.007)	(0.007)	(0.007)	(0.007)	(0.007)	(0.007)

(continued)

Table 16.9 Continued

| | All sample | | | | | | Young sample (15–34 years) | | | | | |
| | M1 | | M2 | | M3 | | M4 | | M5 | | M6 | |
	Unemployed	Inactive	Unemployed	Inactive	Unemployed	Inactive	Unemployed	Inactive	Unemployed	Inactive	Unemployed	Inactive
Secondary education	-0.108***	-0.278***	-0.110***	-0.277***	-0.110***	-0.277***	0.034***	-0.565***	0.034***	-0.565***	0.034***	-0.565***
	(0.004)	(0.004)	(0.004)	(0.004)	(0.004)	(0.004)	(0.004)	(0.005)	(0.004)	(0.005)	(0.004)	(0.005)
Higher education	-0.162***	-0.312***	-0.165***	-0.312***	-0.165***	-0.312***	-0.017***	-0.619***	-0.021***	-0.622***	-0.022***	-0.622***
	(0.004)	(0.005)	(0.004)	(0.005)	(0.004)	(0.005)	(0.005)	(0.007)	(0.005)	(0.007)	(0.005)	(0.007)
GDP per capita					0.028***	-0.012					0.003	-0.002
					(0.007)	(0.009)					(0.003)	(0.004)
Unemployment rate					0.004**	-0.003					0.040**	-0.040*
					(0.002)	(0.002)					(0.012)	(0.016)
Year dummies	No	Yes	No	No	Yes	No	No	Yes	No	No	Yes	No
No. of observations	96,820		96,820		96,818		36,259		36,259		36,257	
Pseudo R^2	0.254		0.2558		0.2559		0.2212		0.2252		0.2254	

Note: See notes to Table 16.6.

countries in the Estonian data. The variables GDP per capita and unemployment rate are measured at the national level in the home countries, and we use quarterly data for these. We also include year dummies to capture other aggregate-level dynamics. The models are organized in three modifications: baseline models (individual-level variables only), models with year dummies, and models with macroeconomic variables. The models are identical for the two countries.

16.5.2. Results: Estonia
16.5.2.1. Selectivity Analysis

The results of the selectivity analysis for the Estonian sample are presented in Table 16.6. Returnee–stayer and returnee–migrant selections are studied in both the young group (aged 15–34 years) and the total sample. We first focus on the returnee–stayer selection framework. The estimates based on the total sample showed that the likelihood of being a returnee decreases with age; for example, the odds of being a returnee are highest for those aged 15–24 years.[6] Because young returnees are of prime interest, we explicitly analyze their selection patterns. We found that young returnees are more likely to be male, relative to stayers (the same holds in the total sample). Returnees aged 15–34 years are more likely to hold a secondary education qualification (models M4 and M6). However, higher education does not significantly affect the decision to return in the sample of young people, whereas in the total sample both secondary and higher education play a role in the selection of returnees. In terms of job-related characteristics, young returnees are less likely to occupy medium-level positions relative to low-level occupations, and they are more likely to have high-level occupations.[7] This suggests a bimodal selection of returnees with respect to the skill level of occupation in returnee–stayer selection (i.e., we can observe positive selection from both low- and high-level occupations). Compared to stayers aged 15–34 years, returnees have less likelihood of being self-employed, more likelihood of being unemployed, and are less likely to be inactive 1 year before the interview. It is interesting to note that being overeducated shortly before return significantly disincentivized return among medium-educated youth. At the same time, among highly educated youth (but not in the total sample), a mismatch significantly increased the likelihood of return relative to current emigrants. In terms of macro-level variables, as expected, a higher home-country unemployment rate and GDP level are positively linked to the probability of being a returnee in both the young and the total samples.

Second, we analyzed selection of returnees compared to current Estonian emigrants (see Table 16.6). Age affects selection for returning differently for emigrants than for stayers: The likelihood of returning increases with age. Therefore, younger aged people are more likely to experience temporary labor migration, but once abroad they are more likely to return as they grow older. Analysis of the young sample revealed that returnees are likely to be female (the same holds in the total sample). This result, coupled with the evidence on selection by gender in the returnee–stayer framework, implies that men are generally more likely to choose temporary employment abroad, but once in the foreign country, women are more likely to return. Regarding job-related characteristics, young returnees are less likely to occupy medium- and high-level positions in the last quarter abroad. Overeducation in the last quarter abroad significantly affects the decision to return in the young subsample of both medium- and highly educated returnees. At the same time, overeducation only appeared to significantly affect the decision to return among the medium educated in the total sample. Among other employment-related variables, unemployed status a year previously decreases the likelihood of being a returnee in the young sample solely in model M10. Self-employed, student, and inactive labor market status a year previously plays no significant role in the selection of returning youth. Naturally, a higher unemployment rate in the home country is negatively associated with the likelihood of returning; however, a statistically significant effect was found only in the young subsample.

16.5.2.2. The Effect of Migration Status on Labor Market Status (Multinomial Logistic Regression)

Table 16.7 reports the results of the multinomial logistic regression of labor market status (employed, unemployed, or inactive) in the last quarter of the interview across the total sample and the youth subsample. In the baseline model of the young age group (M4), returnees were found to be 9.3 percentage points (pp) more likely to be unemployed and 21 pp less likely to be inactive. A similar pattern holds in the total sample, albeit of a smaller magnitude (6.2 pp and 6 pp, respectively). Regarding the effect of other controls within the youth sample, women are less likely than men to be unemployed, whereas they are more likely to be inactive. Married respondents are less likely to be either unemployed or inactive. Non-Estonians have a 5.1 pp greater likelihood of facing unemployment and are 8.1 pp less likely to be inactive. A higher education degree decreases the likelihood of unemployment by 1.9 pp, whereas the probability of being inactive is negatively and substantially affected by both secondary and higher education. Macroeconomic indicators appeared to have no statistically significant association with the odds of being unemployed or inactive in the young group (M6). However, model M3, based on the total sample, revealed a significant positive effect of the unemployment rate on the probability of unemployment and inactivity, whereas the GDP level negatively affects the likelihood of unemployment in the total sample.

16.5.3. Results: Slovakia
16.5.3.1. Selectivity Analysis

The results for the Slovak sample are presented in Table 16.8 for the general sample and for the youth subsample. Comparing returnee–stayer selection in the general sample, we find that being male, young (aged 15–34 years), single (as opposed to married), and of Slovak nationality all increase the likelihood of being a returnee. Among young returnees, only being single increases the likelihood of return. Young returnees are also more likely to have been either a student or unemployed a year before the interview in the host country, relative to being employed, but are less likely to be economically inactive. Young returnees are also more likely to work in medium-skilled positions and are less likely to be self-employed compared to stayers. We observe similar results for the general sample. Concerning the macroeconomic variables, essentially the same results were observed for both the general sample and the youth sample (M5 and M6). A higher unemployment rate in the home country is associated with a lower probability of returning. Overall, although we find significant differences between returnees and stayers in both samples, they are substantively rather small. Importantly, we do not find any effect from overeducation, skill level of occupation, or the level of education on the selection of returnees relative to stayers.

Comparing returnees to current emigrants, we find no significant differences between these groups in terms of demographic characteristics. We focus on interpreting the results for the youth subsample. The only significant results relate to the nature of employment and previous labor market status. Being self-employed is associated with approximately 13 pp lower probability of being a returnee. Being a student or unemployed a year previously are all associated with a higher probability of returning (approximately 13 pp and 8 pp, respectively). Furthermore, higher GDP is negatively associated with the probability of being a returnee rather than a current emigrant, but we do not find a significant effect of unemployment rate in the youth subsample. Higher unemployment in the home country does, however, deter returns for the general sample.

16.5.3.2. The Effect of Migration Status on Labor Market Status (Multinomial Logistic Regression)

Table 16.9 shows the results of the multinomial logistic regression of labor market status (employed, unemployed, or inactive) in the last quarter of the interview across the total sample (M1–M3) and the youth subsample (M4–M6). We again focus on the interpretation of the youth subsample. Results from the baseline model of the multinomial logistic regression of labor market status in the last quarter of the interview (M4 in Table 16.7) show the probability of being employed, unemployed, or inactive for the whole sample. Compared to stayers and migrants, young returnees are 46 pp more likely to be unemployed—a strikingly stronger relationship compared to Estonia—and 30 pp less likely to be inactive, controlling for gender, age, marital status, education, and nationality. Women have a lower probability of being unemployed but a greater probability of being inactive compared to men. Being married decreases the chances of being unemployed or inactive. Having a higher education decreases the likelihood of unemployment or inactivity, whereas having a secondary education increases the probability of unemployment. Non-Slovaks have a 12 pp lower probability of unemployment, but a 13 pp stronger likelihood of being inactive. These results also hold in the extended specifications of the model. The results for the total subsample are substantively the same on most accounts. Adding macroeconomic variables to the model (M3), we do not observe any effect from the level of GDP on unemployment or inactivity, but we still find a positive effect of rising unemployment rates on unemployment. For the total sample, a higher GDP level and unemployment rate are associated with a higher probability of being unemployed, but there is no such linkage with the probability of being inactive.

16.6. COMPARATIVE SYNTHESIS

The conclusions from the Estonian and Slovakian case studies contribute to previous empirical findings regarding the post-return labor market performance of return migrants, and they also reveal the main characteristics of the labor market integration of young returnees in two small economies in Central and Eastern Europe.

We find a multitude of differences in the return migration patterns, determinants of selection, and labor market integration of returnees. First, return migration is a more widespread phenomenon in Estonia than in Slovakia. In Estonia, net intra-EU migration is positive because more people have started to return than to leave. The Slovak balance continues to be negative. Poor labor market conditions could be the reason for continued outflows of migrants from Slovakia. Second, young returnees do not differ from young stayers or young emigrants in terms of their level of education in either of the two countries. However, Estonian returnees in the total sample are positively selected on the basis of education relative to stayers and migrants. The no-effect findings for youth seem to contradict other studies finding selectivity on the basis of education (Hazans and Philips 2010; Martin and Radu 2012; see also the literature review in Section 16.2), but these studies did not specifically focus on youth.

Third, overeducation plays no role in the selectivity of returnees relative to migrants or stayers in Slovakia. This is in line with other research using web-survey data about returnees (Kureková and Žilinčíková 2018). Kureková and Žilinčíková show that returnees find positions equivalent to their qualifications after returning and that mismatch does not cause a failed return; in other words, there is no negative effect of a mismatch on Slovak returnees. The results are significant in Estonia, where overeducation among highly educated young return migrants has contributed to their return. This finding is in line with several other studies, which argue that a mismatch abroad is a significant factor of return (Currie 2007; Pungas et al. 2012; Coniglio and Brzozowski 2016). This suggests that young highly educated Estonians face difficulties when trying to find a job that corresponds to their qualifications abroad and that the decision to return is partly driven by a mismatch in their occupation and qualifications in the foreign labor market. It may also indicate that highly educated Estonian youth are relatively optimistic about their opportunities in their home country. In the total sample of highly educated Estonians, no statistically significant effect of overqualification on return probability was found.

The patterns observed regarding overeducation in Estonia could be explained in terms of young people gaining more from their good education in the home country compared to older people. Although generally the returns on higher education are high in the Estonian labor market, some labor market groups, such as ethnic minorities, benefit much less from higher education (Hazans 2003). The main destination countries have to be acknowledged in this context, too. Masso et al. (2016) showed that Finland was and remains the key destination country among Estonian emigrants.[8] A highly suppressed income distribution in Finland coupled with the previous evidence on occupational downgrading of Estonian migrants (Masso et al. 2014) may result in lower earnings for highly educated Estonian migrants who fail to find a job that corresponds to their qualifications. At the same time, a lower occupation–qualification match for medium-educated young Estonians in Finland results in higher earnings compared to a better match if they were to remain in Estonia. In other words, they obtain higher earnings in Finland compared to Estonia despite their lower occupation–qualification match. The latter finding is supported by the negative effect of overeducation among the medium educated on selection of returnees.

Fourth, for the young Estonian returnees, labor market status a year previously does not affect their selectivity relative to migrants or stayers, whereas it is an important factor for the Slovak returnees. The crucial role of labor market conditions in Slovakia is also confirmed in the analysis of post-return short-term labor market outcomes. Although we find a higher risk of short-term unemployment for young returnees in both countries, there are some important cross-country differences. The magnitude of the negative effect of returnee status on labor market performance is much stronger in Slovakia than in Estonia. Furthermore, the impact of macroeconomic variables in Estonia is less important in predicting labor market outcomes for young and older returnees. The latter finding might be related to the rather different destination countries of the Estonian and Slovak migrants and possibly to the fact that the business cycles in the home and host countries for migrants are more closely correlated in the case of Estonia. The finding that being a returnee has a negative impact on short-term labor market outcomes is generally in line with the findings of other studies (Smoliner et al. 2012; Coniglio and Brzozowski 2016). We can, however, also anticipate that most returnees integrate relatively smoothly within 6 months of return, as has been shown in other research, not least due to their high levels of education and foreign experience. For example, Tverdostup and Masso (2016) identified a positive, statistically significant effect of temporary mobility on earnings in the young cohort 3 years after returning (based on Estonian Population and Housing Census data linked to Tax Registry data on individual payroll taxes). This result is in line with our finding of a negative short-term impact on labor market performance and suggests that positive returns on foreign labor market experience for youth develop over time after returning home. Masso et al. (2016) found that employers and young returnees generally value foreign work experience positively, although, on the negative side, employers mention higher wage expectations among returnees and the risk of them going abroad again in the future. These authors also document that unemployment benefits appear to facilitate job matching after return, but likewise temporarily increase short-term unemployment as returnees use the time to find adequate jobs. Finally, Masso et al. found that foreign work experience significantly increases the attractiveness of job candidates.

The initial differences in the likelihood of unemployment between the Slovak and Estonian returnees are probably a function of the general performance of the labor market, which has been relatively poor in Slovakia. The labor market situation in the host countries has important implications for the ease of reintegration of returnees. It might also explain the differences in the magnitude of returns, which have been more prominent in Estonia and comparatively weaker in Slovakia. Overall, the labor market situation in the home country affects return decisions and labor market performance. It appears that better labor market conditions and increased welfare support in response to the crisis have contributed to better immediate labor market outcomes for Estonian returnees. Other studies suggest that medium-term integration prospects for returnees are likely to be better relative to the situation immediately after return; that is, over time the prospects of reintegration into the home country labor market are likely to improve (Piracha and Vadean 2010; Masso et al. 2016).

16.7. CONCLUSIONS

This chapter furthers our understanding of the selectivity and labor market integration of return migrants in Estonia and Slovakia. The comparative approach is useful because it helps highlight that selectivity and integration prospects might vary significantly across EU countries. Our findings highlight the complex ways in which various factors intervene and interrelate in affecting different subgroups of returnees (e.g., young returnees) in different ways, including a mediating role of personal, gender, and family-related factors that we are unable to uncover in our analysis. The complexity is further revealed in the two-country comparison showing that across countries, different factors might play a role, depending on, for example, home country labor market conditions. In summary, our research seems to point to different underlying reasons for mobility and return in Estonia and Slovakia, mediated by the role of labor market performance and welfare spending changes. This implies that no uniform conclusions or policy advice that is applicable across the EU are possible in the area of return migration and that specific country contexts should be carefully investigated and evaluated.

We have focused, in particular, on isolating the role of macroeconomic factors in affecting who returns and how they integrate. Although we have been unable to investigate the full range of possible factors, our findings suggest that the quality of the macroeconomic environment affects both the selectivity and the performance of returnees. Better labor market conditions in Estonia and significantly enhanced social support in response to the crisis appear to have encouraged the return of older migrants and facilitated the reintegration of young migrants.

Although our study shows that in both countries, returnees initially enter unemployment registers, evidence suggests that this is a temporary phenomenon facilitated by the possibility of transferring unemployment benefits from the country where they were earning to another EU country (typically the home country) for a period of 3 months. Other research rather consistently shows that the integration prospects of returnees improve soon thereafter and that they find work within 6 months. Employers value foreign work experience because it demonstrates a set of skills valued in the CEE labor markets. A further important finding relates to the role of overeducation and mismatch in shaping return patterns. Especially in the case of Estonia, a mismatch abroad led to a greater propensity to return among highly educated young returnees, but it disincentivized the return of medium-educated migrants. This suggests that receiving countries are losing the most able CEE migrants because of a failure to offer quality employment and career prospects. Although this appears to be an advantage for the sending countries, it is unlikely that these highly educated returnees had enough opportunities to develop their human capital and that, therefore, their contribution to the home country is more limited.

The limitations of our chapter are threefold. First, we only examine how different labor market groups—returnees, stayers, and current emigrants—perform in terms of labor market status. Such an approach naturally has its limitations because return migration might also have an effect on wages (Hazans 2008), the tendency to be self-employed, or occupational mobility (Masso et al. 2014). Second, given the data structure, we are only able to analyze short-term labor market outcomes in the 3 months following the return. Although the results indicate a worse labor market situation for returnees than for emigrants and stayers, other research consistently finds that in the longer term, returnees integrate well and their foreign work experience is valued in the domestic labor market after returning (Masso et al. 2016). Third, because of data limitations, we concentrate on economic factors only and are unable to consider several other factors, such as social networks and some of the specific characteristics of migration that arguably play a role in successful reintegration (Barrett and Mosca 2013; Coniglio and Brzozowski 2016). Although most of the returnees had experienced short-term migration, we were unable to reconstruct the exact length of the migration spell that was previously found to increase difficulties with integration upon return (Coniglio and Brzozowski 2016). We could also not employ a measure of the number of children in our analysis, which had been found to have a positive impact on integration into the home labor market (Coniglio and Brzozowski 2016). Last, we were unable to control for the destination country of emigrants, which might have impacted on the selectivity of return and on integration into the home labor market, given the different employment opportunities in each host country.

One possible solution to some of these issues would be to have panel data following the whole migration process and return—capturing information for before migration (in the home country), while abroad (in the host country), and after return (once back in the home country). Such data, whether collected on a continuous basis or through a series of retrospective interview surveys, would capture the complete migration path and examine the selections more profoundly. It would allow us to analyze "true" returns on migration and re-turning home in a consistent manner, controlling for migrants' labor market performance in the home country before leaving. This kind of data could also be obtained by linking the national registers of home and host countries (e.g., Estonia and Finland). However, the downside of such an approach is that we are likely to learn only about a limited number of countries, which may induce some selectivity issues. Online data, such as reconstructing life histories from online curriculum vitae (CVs), provide another possible source for studying migration and returning home from the perspective of labor market integration (Kureková and Žilinčíková 2018).

Several policy lessons can be drawn from our analysis. First, given that young return migrants constitute a specific subgroup of the returnee population, they should be attracted to the host-country economy because they have significant potential based on high educational attainment accompanied by foreign market experience. Facilitating the acceleration of the labor market integration of young returnees will enable them to fully realize their potential and thus provide benefits for the home-country economy. There is scope for public institutions to provide better assistance upon return and to facilitate integration, especially in underperforming labor markets such as that of Slovakia. Precisely such practices of labor market intermediaries were also identified for EU8 migrants in Austria (Ortlieb and Weiss, this volume). For example, return migrants can become a target category for post-return assistance in labor offices, especially if they return to worse performing regions, as seems to be the case (Barcevičius et al. 2012).

Second, inequalities exist among returnees, and not all returnees are on an equal footing in terms of their abilities. In particular, returnees disadvantaged in terms of gender, age, ethnicity, or geographic location might be in more need of assistance from public authorities in their reintegration process. On the other hand, programs targeted at highly educated youth underperforming in the host countries may help overcome the effects of a brain drain or brain waste. Yet, as demonstrated in the Slovak case, given that overeducation need not be associated with the return decision among the highly skilled, the challenge could also be how many opportunities the home-country labor market offers these individuals. The need for policy intervention seems to be somewhat less pressing in the Estonian case, in which overeducation was shown to be associated positively with returning home among the highly educated.

NOTES

1 Jaan Masso acknowledges financial support from the Estonian Research Agency, project No. IUT20-49, "Structural Change as the Factor of Productivity Growth in the Case of Catching Up Economies." The authors are grateful for comments made on earlier versions by Maura Sheehan, Jan Brzozowski, and the editors of this volume, while assuming full responsibility for the final content.

2 The mechanism of transfer of unemployment benefits allows an individual to carry over unemployment benefits from the EU country in which he or she was last working to another EU country, usually for a period of 3 months. There are two basic conditions under which a worker is entitled to transfer the benefits. First, the worker must be entitled to unemployment benefits in the country of last employment and, second, he or she must register as unemployed with the labor office in another EU member state. The eligibility, duration, and maximum amount of benefits vary widely across EU countries. For example, the level of jobseeker's allowance in the United Kingdom is relatively low—approximately £313 per month for a person aged older than 25 years, which is extremely difficult to live on. The relative value of such benefits may be higher in the home country, where living costs may be lower; hence, an unemployed person might choose to return home to receive this value of benefits in his or her country of origin.

3 Kureková and Žilinčíková (2018), analyzing online CV data, find that return migration to Slovakia is much more sizable. In their sample of young jobseekers, every fifth person had experience of migration. Their sample also significantly differs from the EU-LFS sample of returnees regarding key demographic characteristics, especially the education variable.

4 One may think of the higher unemployment rate among returnees as being related to the scarring effect if the best people do not emigrate. However, the qualitative evidence shows that returnees are rather attractive for employers but that they may have higher wage expectations, resulting in a longer job search period (Masso et al. 2014, 2016). The higher unemployment rate may also be due to savings accumulated abroad that enable returnees to afford a longer period for job search.

5   We are grateful to Jan Brzozowski for drawing our attention to this possibility.
6   The higher share of return migrants among youth may be thought to be associated with student mobility; however, in the current analysis, the definition of returnee is based exclusively on being abroad for work.
7   The results are probably due to the selection rather than, for example, to individuals previously employed in medium-level positions moving to high-level positions because of return migration, given that previous studies did not find any effect of return migration on occupational upgrading (Masso et al. 2014).
8   The evidence from the Estonian job search portal data set (CV Keskus) revealed that among Estonian migrants aged 15–35 years, the share of those moving to Finland increased from 17% in 2004 to 38% in 2012 (Masso et al. 2016).

REFERENCES

Ambrosini, William J., Karin Mayr, Giovanni Peri, and Dragos Radu. 2011. "The Selection of Migrants and Returnees: Evidence from Romania and Implications." NBER Working Paper 16912. Cambridge, MA: National Bureau of Economic Research.

Anacka, Marta, and Agnieszka Fihel. 2012. Return Migration to Poland in the Post-Accession Period. In *EU Labour Migration in Troubled Times: Skills Mismatch, Return and Policy Responses*, edited by Béla Galgóczi, Janine Leschke, and Andrew Watt, 169–210. Aldershot, UK: Ashgate.

Bahna, Miloslav. 2013. "Intra-EU Migration from Slovakia." *European Societies* 15 (3): 388–407. doi:10.1080/14616696.2012.707669.

Barcevičius, Egidijus, Krystyna Iglicka, Daiva Repečkaitė, and Dovilė Žvalionytė. 2012. *Labour Mobility Within the EU: The Impact of Return Migration*. Dublin: Eurofound. http://www.eurofound.europa.eu/publications/htmlfiles/ef1243.htm

Barrett, Alan, and David Duffy. 2008. "Are Ireland's Immigrants Integrating into Its Labor Market?" *International Migration Review* 42 (3): 597–619.

Barrett, Alan, and Irene Mosca. 2013. "Social Isolation, Loneliness and Return Migration: Evidence from Older Irish Adults." *Journal of Ethnic and Migration Studies* 39 (10): 1659–77. doi:10.1080/1369183X.2013.833694.

Bijwaard, Govert E., Christian Schluter, and Jackline Wahba. 2014. "The Impact of Labor Market Dynamics on the Return Migration of Immigrants." *Review of Economics and Statistics* 96 (3): 483–94.

Bohle, Dorothee, and Béla Greskovits. 2012. *Capitalist Diversity on Europe's Periphery*. Ithaca, NY: Cornell University Press.

Borjas, George J. 1987. "Self-Selection and the Earnings of Immigrants." *American Economic Review* 77 (4): 531–53.

Borjas, George J., and Bernt Bratsberg. 1996. "Who Leaves? The Outmigration of the Foreign-Born." *Review of Economics and Statistics* 78: 165–76.

Bosma, Niels, Alicia Coduras, Yana Litovsky, and Jeff Seaman. 2012. "GEM Manual: A Report on the Design, Data and Quality Control of the Global Entrepreneurship Monitor." *Global Entrepreneurship Monitor* 2012–9.

Cassarino, Jean-Pierre. 2004. "Theorising Return Migration: The Conceptual Approach to Return Migrants Revisited." *International Journal on Multicultural Societies* 6 (2): 253–79.

Cerase, Francesco P. 1974. "Expectations and Reality: A Case Study of Return Migration from the United States to Southern Italy." *International Migration Review* 8 (2): 245–62. doi:10.2307/3002783.

Clark, Ken, and Stephen Drinkwater. 2008. "The Labour-Market Performance of Recent Migrants." *Oxford Review of Economic Policy* 24 (3): 496–517.

Coniglio, Nicola Daniele, and Jan Brzozowski. 2016. "Migration and Development at Home: Bitter or Sweet Return? Evidence from Poland." *European Urban and Regional Studies* 25 (1): 85–105. doi:10.1177/0969776416681625.

Currie, Samantha. 2007. "De-Skilled and Devalued: The Labour Market Experience of Polish Migrants in the UK Following EU Enlargement." *International Journal of Comparative Labour Law and Industrial Relations* 23 (1): 83–116.

De Coulon, Augustin, and Matloob Piracha. 2005. "Self-Selection and the Performance of Return Migrants: The Source Country Perspective." *Journal of Population Economics* 18 (4): 779–807.

De Haas, Hein, Tineke Fokkema, and Mohamed Fassi Fihri. 2015. "Return Migration as Failure or Success?" *Journal of International Migration and Integration* 16 (2): 415–29.

Drinkwater, Stephen, John Eade, and Michał Garapich. 2009. "Poles Apart? EU Enlargement and the Labour Market Outcomes of Immigrants in the United Kingdom." *International Migration* 47 (1): 161–90.

Dumon, Wilfried. 1986. "Problems Faced by Migrants and Their Family Members, Particularly Second Generation Migrants, in Returning to and Reintegrating into Their Countries of Origin." *International Migration* 24 (1): 113–28. doi:10.1111/j.1468-2435.1986.tb00105.x.

Dumont, Jean-Christophe, and Gilles Spielvogel. 2008. "Return Migration: A New Perspective." International Migration Outlook SOPEMI, Annual Report, 162–222. Paris: Organization for Economic Co-operation and Development.

Dustmann, Christian. 1997. "Return Migration, Uncertainty and Precautionary Savings." *Journal of Development Economics* 52 (2): 295–316.

Eamets, Raul, Miroslav Beblavý, Kariappa Bheemaiah, Mairéad Finn, Katrin Humal, Janine Leschke, Ilaria Maselli, and Mark Smith. 2015. "Mapping Flexibility and Security Performance in the Face of the Crisis." STYLE Working Paper 10.1. Brighton, UK: CROME, University of Brighton. http://www.style-research.eu/publications/working-papers

Findlay, Allan, and David McCollum. 2013. "Recruitment and Employment Regimes: Migrant Labour Channels in the UK's Rural Agribusiness Sector, from Accession to Recession." *Journal of Rural Studies* 30: 10–19.

Friberg, Jon H., Jens Arnholtz, Line Eldring, Nana W. Hansen, and Frida Thorarins. 2014. "Nordic Labour Market Institutions and New Migrant Workers: Polish Migrants in Oslo, Copenhagen and Reykjavik." *European Journal of Industrial Relations* 20 (1): 37–53.

Galgóczi, Béla, Janine Leschke, and Andrew Watt. 2009. *EU Labour Migration Since Enlargement: Trends, Impacts and Policies*. Aldershot, UK: Ashgate.

Galgóczi, Béla, Janine Leschke, and Andrew Watt. 2012. *EU Labour Migration in Troubled Times: Skills Mismatch, Return and Policy Responses*. Aldershot, UK: Ashgate.

Hazans, Mihails. 2003. "Returns to Education in the Baltic Countries." GDNet Knowledge Base Working Paper 16801. SSRN. https://ssrn.com/abstract=699623

Hazans, Mihails. 2008. "Post-Enlargement Return Migrants' Earnings Premium: Evidence from Latvia." Paper presented at EALE Conference, Amsterdam, September 2008. SSRN. http://ssrn.com/abstract=1269728

Hazans, Mihails, and Kaia Philips. 2010. "The Post-Enlargement Migration Experience in the Baltic Labor Markets." In *EU Labor Markets After Post-Enlargement Migration*, edited by Martin Kahanec and Klaus F. Zimmermann, 255–304. Berlin: Springer.

House of Lords. 2008. "The Economic Impact of Immigration. Volume I: Report." HL Paper 82–I. London: The Stationery Office.

Iara, Anna. 2006. "Skill Diffusion in Temporary Migration? Returns to Western European Working Experience in the EU Accession Countries." Centro Studi Luca d'Agliano Development Studies Working Paper 210. SSRN. https://ssrn.com/abstract=918037

Kahanec, Martin, and Lucia Mýtna Kureková. 2013. "European Union Expansion and Migration." In *The Encyclopedia of Global Human Migration*, edited by Immanuel Ness. Hoboken, NJ: Wiley-Blackwell.

Kahanec, Martin, and Lucia Mýtna Kureková. 2016. "Did Post-Enlargement Labor Mobility Help the EU to Adjust During the Great Recession? The Case of Slovakia." In *Labor Migration, EU Enlargement, and the Great Recession*, edited by Martin Kahanec and Klaus F. Zimmermann, 189–218. Berlin: Springer.

Kahanec, Martin, and Klaus F. Zimmermann. 2010. "Migration in an Enlarged EU: A Challenging Solution?" In *Five Years of an Enlarged EU. A Positive Sum Game,* edited by Filip Keereman and Istvan Szekely, 63–94. Berlin: Springer.

King, Russell. 1978. "Return Migration: A Neglected Aspect of Population Geography." *Area* 10 (3): 175–82.

Kureková, Lucia Mýtna. 2011. "From Job Search to Skill Search: Political Economy of Labor Migration in Central and Eastern Europe." PhD dissertation, Central European University, Budapest.

Kureková, Lucia Mýtna. 2013. "Welfare Systems as Emigration Factor: Evidence from the New Accession States." *JCMS: Journal of Common Market Studies* 55 (4): 721–39. doi:10.1111/jcms.12020.

Kureková, Lucia Mýtna, and Zuzana Žilinčíková. 2018. "What Is the Value of Foreign Work Experience for Young Return Migrants." *International Journal of Manpower* 39 (1): 71–92.

Kveder, Cora Leonie Mezger. 2013. *Temporary Migration: A Review of the Literature*. INED Documents De Travail 188. Paris: French Institute for Demographic Studies.

Lang, Thilo, Aline Hämmerling, Jan Keil, Robert Nadler, Anika Schmidt, Stefan Haunstein, and Stefanie Smoliner. 2012. "Re-Turn Migrant Survey Report: The Migrants' Potential and Expectations." Re-Turn Consortium, Leibniz Institute for Regional Geography. http://www.iom.cz/files/323_Migrant-Survey-Report.PDF

Martin, Reiner, and Dragos Radu. 2012. "Return Migration: The Experience of Eastern Europe." *International Migration* 50 (6): 109–28. doi:10.1111/j.1468-2435.2012.00762.x.

Masso, Jaan, Raul Eamets, and Pille Mõtsmees. 2014. "Temporary Migrants and Occupational Mobility: Evidence from the Case of Estonia." *International Journal of Manpower* 35 (6): 753–75.

Masso, Jaan, Lucia Mýtna Kureková, Maryna Tverdostup, and Zuzana Žilinčíková. 2016. "Return Migration Patterns of Young Return Migrants After the Crises in the CEE Countries: Estonia and Slovakia. STYLE Working Paper 6.1. Brighton, UK: CROME, University of Brighton. http://www.style-research.eu/publications/working-papers

McCormick, Barry, and Jackline Wahba. 2001. "Overseas Work Experience, Savings and Entrepreneurship Amongst Return Migrants to LDCs." *Scottish Journal of Political Economy* 48 (2): 164–78.

Napierała, Joanna, and Kamila Fiałkowska. 2013. "Mapping the Market for Employment Agencies in Poland." In *Labour Migrants from Central and Eastern Europe in the Nordic Countries: Patterns of Migration, Working Conditions and Recruitment Practices*, edited by Jon Horgen Friberg and Line Eldring, 169–200. Copenhagen: Nordic Council of Ministers.

Organization for Economic Co-operation and Development (OECD). 2012. *Free Movement of Workers and Labour Market Adjustment. Recent Experiences from OECD Countries and the European Union*. Paris: OECD. http://www.oecd-ilibrary.org/social-issues-migration-health/free-movement-of-workers-and-labour-market-adjustment_9789264177185-en

Piracha, Matloob, and Florin Vadean. 2010. "Return Migration and Occupational Choice: Evidence from Albania." *World Development* 38 (8): 1141–55.

Pollard, Naomi, Maria Latorre, and Dhananjayan Sriskandarajah. 2008. *Floodgates or Turnstiles? Post-EU Enlargement Migration Flows to (and from) the UK*. London: Institute for Public Policy Research.

Pryymachenko, Yana, and Klas Fregert. 2011. "The Effect of Emigration on Unemployment in Source Countries: Evidence from the Central and Eastern European EU Member States." Master's thesis, Lund University, Lund, Sweden.

Pungas, Enel, Ott Toomet, Tiit Tammaru, and Kristi Anniste. 2012. "Are Better Educated Migrants Returning? Evidence from Multi-Dimensional Education Data." Norface Migration Discussion Paper 18. London: Department of Economics, University College London. http://www.norface-migration.org/publ_uploads/NDP_18_12.pdf

Rooth, Dan-Olof, and Jan Saarela. 2007. "Selection in Migration and Return Migration: Evidence from Micro Data." *Economics Letters* 94 (1): 90–95.

Roy, Andrew Donald. 1951. "Some Thoughts on the Distribution of Earnings." *Oxford Economic Papers* 3 (2): 135–46.

Rutkowski, Jan. 2007. "Labor Markets in EU8+2: From the Shortage of Jobs to the Shortage of Skilled Workers." IZA Discussion Paper 3202. Bonn: Institute for the Study of Labor.

Smoliner, Stefanie, Michael Förschner, and Jana Nova. 2012. "Comparative Report on Re-Migration Trends in Central Europe." Re-Turn Consortium, Leipzig Institute for Regional Geography.

Turner, Thomas. 2010. "The Jobs Immigrants Do: Issues of Displacement and Marginalisation in the Irish Labour Market." *Work, Employment & Society* 24 (2): 318–36. doi:10.1177/0950017010362148.

Tverdostup, Maryna, and Jaan Masso. 2016. "The Labour Market Performance of Young Return Migrants After the Crisis in CEE Countries: The Case of Estonia." *Baltic Journal of Economics* 16 (2): 192–220.

Voitchovsky, Sarah. 2014. "Occupational Downgrading and Wages of New Member States Immigrants to Ireland." *International Migration Review* 48: 500–537. doi:10.1111/imre.12089.

White, Anne. 2014. "Polish Return and Double Return Migration." *Europe-Asia Studies* 66 (1): 25–49. doi:10.1080/09668136.2013.855021.

Zaiceva, Anželika. 2014. "Post-Enlargement Emigration and New EU Members' Labor Markets." *IZA World of Labor* 40. doi:10.15185/izawol.40.

Zaiceva, Anželika, and Klaus F. Zimmermann. 2016. "Returning Home at Times of Trouble? Return Migration of EU Enlargement Migrants During the Crisis." In *Labor Migration, EU Enlargement, and the Great Recession*, edited by Martin Kahanec and Klaus F. Zimmermann, 397–418. Berlin: Springer.

PART IV

CHALLENGING FUTURES FOR YOUTH

17

ORIGINS AND FUTURE OF THE CONCEPT OF NEETS IN THE EUROPEAN POLICY AGENDA

Massimiliano Mascherini

17.1. INTRODUCTION

Deeply concerned about the risk of a "lost generation" and seeking to better understand the complex nature of youth disadvantage, researchers and government officials began to adopt new ways of estimating the prevalence of labor market vulnerability among young people by using the concept of NEETs: young people not in employment, education, or training. Originating in studies carried out in the United Kingdom in the 1980s, the concept was adopted by the European Commission Employment Committee (EMCO), which agreed in 2010 on a definition and the methodology for an indicator to measure and monitor trends in the NEET population of the European Union (EU) as part of the Horizon 2020 strategy.

Once it had entered the European policy debate, the term NEET quickly became a powerful tool for attracting public attention to the multifaceted vulnerabilities of young people and for mobilizing researchers' and policymakers' efforts in addressing the problem of labor market participation by young people. The concept of NEETs has since been widely used in the European policy debate: Reducing the number of NEETs is one of the objectives of the European Youth Guarantee and, more recently, prevalence of NEETs has been included as one of the indicators for strengthening the social dimension of the Economic and Monetary Union.

Despite the rapid success of the NEET concept, it is often criticized for its grouping of a highly heterogeneous set of young people under one single term.

Although the term NEET captures all young people who are in a status of not accumulating human capital through formal channels—namely the labor market or education—this is actually a very diverse population with very different characteristics and needs. The heterogeneity of the NEET population has important consequences for policy responses. Although governments and social partners are rightly setting targets to reduce the overall NEET rate, it is argued here that greater attention should be given to disaggregating the heterogeneous NEET category. Policy interventions sensitive to the needs and barriers faced by particular groups of young people will be more effective than a blanket policy imposed on a heterogeneous group.

This chapter discusses the origin and the future of the NEETs indicator in the European policy framework and proposes a distinction between seven different types within the NEET categorization with a view to better informed targeted policies. First, we examine the origins of the concept of NEETs and how it entered into the European policy debate. This is followed by a critical evaluation of the value added by the concept and of its limitations for policymaking. We then examine the main characteristics of the NEET population in Europe and the risk factors associated with becoming NEET. Finally, a disaggregation of the NEET indicator is proposed and applied to data from the European Union Labour Force Survey (EU-LFS), followed by a discussion of policy implications.

17.2. ORIGINS AND EVOLUTION OF THE NEET INDICATOR

The need for an additional indicator able to capture young people who are not in employment, education, or training first emerged in the United Kingdom in the late 1980s as an alternative way of categorizing young people aged 16–17 years. This came about as a result of changes in the UK benefit regime: Specifically, the 1986 Social Security Act and its 1988 implementation withdrew entitlement to Income Support/Supplementary Benefit from young people aged 16–17 years in return for a "youth training guarantee" (Williamson 2010).

As a result of this change and the consequent emergence of this new group, researchers and government officials started to adopt new ways of estimating the prevalence of labor market vulnerability among young people. Williamson (1985) was the first to highlight the emerging crisis of young adulthood. Subsequently, a study of young people in South Glamorgan in Wales (funded by the South Glamorgan Training and Enterprise Council) was the first to produce quantitative estimates of the number of young people aged 16–17 years who were not in education, training, or employment (Istance, Rees, and Williamson 1994). Using more qualitative material, this study also illustrated how some of these young people had arrived at this status, how they were getting by, and what they expected for their futures. Here, Istance and colleagues (1994) used the term Status 0/Status Zer0 (later changed to "Status A") to refer to a group of people aged 16–17 years who were not covered by any of the main categories of labor market status (employment, education, or training). The term Status 0/Status Zer0 was merely a technical term derived from careers service records, where Status 1 referred to young people in post-16 education, Status 2 to those in training, and Status 3 to those in employment. The study concluded with the shocking finding that 16%–23% of the age group in question was in Status Zer0 in the United Kingdom during the 1980s. Without making any claim as to representativeness, Istance and colleagues acknowledged the heterogeneity of the group, depicting different routes into Status Zer0 and different experiences within it. The term Status Zer0 was by no means intended as a negative label; it was more about reflecting societal abandonment of this group. However, the term soon came to represent "a powerful metaphor" for the fact that Status Zer0 young people appeared to "count for nothing and were going nowhere" (Williamson 1997:82). The study captured the media's imagination (Bunting 1994; McRae 1994), and the term entered into the policy debate in the summer of 1994 as Status A (where A stood for abandoned, as in "the abandoned generation"). In this context, Liberal–Democrat MPs raised questions about the Status A phenomenon in Parliament and convened a debate in the House of Lords (Williamson 2010).

Against this background, the term NEET was coined in March 1996 by a senior Home Office civil servant who had detected resistance on the part of policymakers working with the original and often controversial terms of Status Zer0 and Status A. Embracing the concept previously introduced by Istance et al. (1994), the term NEET replaced the other labels and was then formally introduced at the political level in the United Kingdom in 1999 with the publication of the government's *Bridging the Gap* report from the Social Exclusion Unit of the New Labour government (SEU 1999).

The term NEET rapidly gained importance outside the United Kingdom, too. By the beginning of the new millennium, similar definitions had been adopted in almost all EU member states; similar concepts referring to disengaged youth were also emerging in popular discourse in Japan, New Zealand, Taiwan, Hong Kong, and—most recently—China (Mizanur Rahman 2006; Liang 2009; Eurofound 2012; Pacheco and Dye 2013). Some of these new concepts went beyond the original meaning of NEET, also attaching a negative stigma to these newly identifiable categories of youth. For example, *hikikomori* in Japan means "withdrawal" and is used to refer to young Japanese NEETs, usually young men, who live with their parents, spend their time alone in their rooms, are without friends, and engage only in activities on the Internet or in watching movies (Jones 2006; Wang 2015). In Spain, the term *generación ni-ni* became popular before the crisis as a means to identify young people who did not want to grow up by studying or going to work (Navarrete Moreno 2011); similar terms with negative connotations were also used in Italy (*bamboccioni*) and Germany (*Nesthocker*)—usually for young men who appeared unwilling to leave home and "grow up." Thus, although it had originated in the United Kingdom, the concept of NEETs was gradually being recognized in a number of other economically advanced countries.

17.2.1. NEETs at the European level

As the term became more popular across Europe, "NEETs" came to refer to young people aged 15–24 or 15–29 years who were not in employment, education, or training, and it was measured and mapped using national labor force surveys. Nevertheless, this seemingly simple definition masks considerable diversity between countries with regard to the characteristics of the young people classified as NEET. In the UK context, NEETs were frequently associated with problematic labor market transitions. In other countries—with well-functioning transmission paths into education and employment—NEETs were not present and youth transitions were not problematized in the same manner (Wallace and Bendit 2009; Filandri, Nazio, and O'Reilly, this volume).

The totality of those classified as NEETs can also include a diversity of experiences ranging from unemployed graduates taking their time to find work to unqualified early school-leavers and those taking on family caring responsibilities. Some of this diversity has been captured in a number of studies from the Organization for Economic Co-operation and Development and the European Commission (Walther and Pohl 2005; Carcillo et al. 2015). A study by Eurofound (2012) provided the first comparative analysis of the extent of the NEET phenomenon in Europe, examining the economic and societal costs of not integrating youth into the labor market.

At the European policymaking level, EMCO and its Indicators Group (European Commission, DG EMPL) agreed on a definition and a methodology for a standardized indicator to measure and compare the NEET population in Europe as part of its monitoring of the Europe 2020 strategy in April 2010 (European Commission 2011a, 2011b). The definition of NEETs implemented by Eurostat refers to young people aged 15–24 years who are unemployed or inactive according to the International Labour Organization (ILO) definition[1] and who are not in any form of education or training.

The Eurostat definition of NEET is constructed as follows: The numerator of the indicator refers to persons who are not employed (i.e., unemployed or inactive) and/or have not received any education or training during the 4 weeks preceding the survey; the denominator consists of the total population of the same age and gender. The NEET indicator is calculated using cross-sectional data from the EU-LFS, observing established rules for statistical quality and reliability (European Commission 2010b, 2011a).

The main NEET indicator produced by Eurostat covers various age groups. For analytical purposes, and given a conceptualization of youth as an age group that varies substantially across different countries (Wallace and Bendit 2009), the indicator is then disaggregated by gender and is available for different age groups (15–17/15–19/15–24/15–29/15–34/18–24/20–24/20–34/25–29 years).

Breakdowns by labor market status (unemployed and inactive) and education level (at most lower secondary attainment/at least upper secondary attainment) are also available on the Eurostat website (European Commission 2011a).

The NEET indicator is constructed each year using the EU-LFS according to the following equation:

$$NEET_{Rate} = \frac{Number\,of\,young\,people\,not\,in\,employment,education,or\,training}{Total\,population\,of\,young\,people}$$

The NEET indicator thus measures the share of young people who are not in employment, education, or training among the *total* youth population. This is not the same as the youth unemployment rate, which measures the share of young people who are unemployed among the population of young people who are *economically active* (i.e., employed or searching for work, and excluding students). For this reason, although the youth unemployment rate is generally higher than the NEET rate, in absolute terms, the overall number of NEETs is generally higher than the overall number of young unemployed people (Figure 17.1). For example, although in 2015 the youth unemployment and NEET rates in Europe were 20.3% and 12%, respectively, the population of unemployed youth accounted for 4,640,000 individuals, whereas the population of NEETs was 6,604,000 individuals.

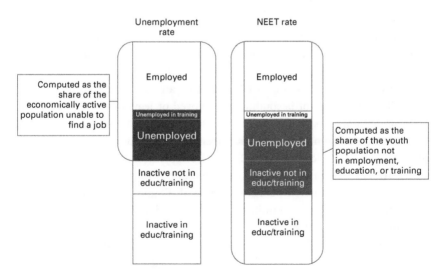

Figure 17.1 Unemployment compared to NEET.
Source: Eurofound (2012).

17.2.2. NEETs in the European policy agenda

Once a standardized definition had been agreed and operationalized at the EU level, the term NEET became increasingly central to the European policy agenda: NEETs were explicitly targeted for the first time in the Europe 2020 flagship initiative Youth on the Move (European Commission 2010a). The initiative states its mission as "unleashing all young people's potential," and emphasizes the importance of reducing the "astonishingly" high number of NEETs in Europe by providing pathways back into education or training and by enabling contact with the labor market. Most important, and going beyond youth unemployment, the initiative places special emphasis on ensuring the labor market integration of young people with disabilities or health problems.

Building on Youth on the Move, NEETs consequently became central to the new set of integrated guidelines for economic and employment policies. In 2011, the Youth Opportunities Initiative drew attention to the increasing share of young people not in employment, education, or training (European Commission 2011a), proposing a combination of concrete actions by member states and the EU to tackle the issue (Hadjivassiliou et al., this volume; Petmesidou and González Menéndez, this volume).

By 2012, several documents drawn up as part of the employment package Towards a Job-rich Recovery (European Commission 2012) emphasized the importance of tackling the NEET crisis and suggested making greater use of the European Social Fund for the next program period (2014–2020). One proposal was to make the sustainable integration of NEETs into the labor market (through youth guarantees and other measures) one of the investment priorities for the new program period. NEETs were identified as the most problematic group in terms of labor market trends and challenges (European Commission 2012).

Against this background, NEETs are at the heart of the Youth Guarantee, which aims to reduce NEET rates by ensuring that all young people aged 15–24 years not in employment, education, or training receive a good-quality offer of employment, continued education, or an apprenticeship or traineeship within 4 months of becoming unemployed or leaving formal education. Following a long debate starting in 2005, the Youth Guarantee was proposed by the European Commission in December 2012 and endorsed by the Council of the European Union on April 23, 2013 (Council of the European Union 2013). To make the practical implementation of the Youth Guarantee a reality, the European Commission published the Youth Employment Initiative (YEI), supported by €6 billion of funding, which targeted young NEETs (European Commission 2013a, 2013b).

Furthermore, NEETs are now regularly referred to in the documents of the European Employment, Social Policy, Health and Consumer Affairs Council, and the topic of NEETs has been a priority for recent European Council presidencies.

In the first half of 2013, the Irish Council presidency focused extensively on youth unemployment; in fact, it was during this period that the establishment of the Youth Guarantee was recommended. Subsequent presidencies frequently referred to the situation of NEETs (Council of the European Union 2013, 2014, 2015). Similarly, the European Parliament also took on board the NEET concept, as in a recent briefing on the youth employment situation in Greece (European Parliament 2015), but also in more generic publications examining the social situation in the EU (European Parliament 2014). When the pre-financing of the YEI was discussed in 2015, the NEET indicator played an important role in policy formulations.

17.3. VALUE ADDED AND LIMITATIONS OF NEET AS A CONCEPT FOR POLICYMAKING

As with every new concept entering the policy debate, the NEET concept has often struggled to be understood in terms of what exactly it is and what it was designed to do. NEET and youth unemployment are related concepts, but there are important differences between the two. NEET goes beyond unemployment in that it captures all young people who, for various reasons, are unemployed or inactive and are not accumulating human capital through formal channels (Eurofound 2012, 2016).

Although the NEET indicator is easily defined and captures a very general and heterogeneous population of all young people who—regardless of their education level and sociodemographic characteristics—are not in employment, education, or training, the term is sometimes used as a shortcut to identify solely the most vulnerable and the population most at risk of being socially excluded. The misuse of the NEET acronym can probably be traced back to the origins of the concept in the United Kingdom: Being NEET was more closely associated with early school-leaving and other severe patterns of vulnerability that lead to a higher risk of social exclusion and a lack of employment.

However, today this correspondence between risk of social exclusion and NEET status is far from being univocal. By enlarging the age category to the 15- to 24-year-old age group (or even to 15- to 29-year-olds), NEET captures all young people who are not currently participating in the labor market or in education. This includes vulnerable groups and those with accumulated disadvantages (including lower education levels, immigration background, health issues, young mothers, or young people with a difficult family background). But it also includes more privileged youth who voluntarily become NEET—while waiting for a particular opportunity or while attempting to pursue alternative careers (see Filandri et al., this volume; Zuccotti and O'Reilly, this volume). The heterogeneity of this group means that the concept of NEET, when applied to the older youth cohort, no longer provides the same shortcut to identify the most vulnerable youth. In addition, there is a negative association in the media and public discourse in which NEET implies that young people do not *want* to work or study (Serracant 2013); this has been particularly true in some of the public discourse preceding the financial crisis.

The concept of NEET has been adopted in very different ways by governments and international organizations (Elder 2015). NEET is often associated with is-sues of joblessness, discouragement, or marginalization of youth, but it cannot be equated only with one of these areas; rather, it lies at the intersection of the three issues. The Eurofound (2012) study strongly related NEET to a lack of human capital accumulation through formal channels, whereas Elder (2015) concludes that the best interpretation of the term goes beyond a "productivist" approach and that the best fit is offered by marginalization/exclusion/disaffection. Williamson, who coined the concept under the name Status Zer0 (subsequently changed to NEET), rejects the use of the term "disaffection" to characterize NEETs, arguing for language that is less judgmental; hence his advocacy of "dis-engagement" or "exclusion," which in turn allow for re-engagement and inclu-sion (Williamson 2010).

Despite the relative novelty of the NEET concept, it has had a strong catalyzing effect in attracting and mobilizing policymakers and public opinion. As well as having entered the youth policies lexicon, the concept of NEET is now highly popular among European media. Given the country's high share of NEETs, Italian media, for example, have defined Italy as the nation of NEETs (Corriere della Sera 2015; L'Espresso 2015). Similarly, in the United Kingdom, the BBC has repeatedly called for greater attention to be paid to the situa-tion of NEETs (BBC 2012, 2014), while the Spanish newspaper El País has described the apathy and passiveness of NEETs and their general situation (El País 2014, 2015). The NEET concept has the capability to increase the under-standing of the various vulnerabilities of young people by placing particular groups such as the low educated, early school dropouts, young mothers, or young people with disabilities at the center of policy debates. These groups would otherwise simply be classified as inactive, usually with very limited attention being dedicated to them from a policy perspective (see Berloffa, Matteazzi, and Villa, this volume). Making the reduction of the NEET rate a policy target, as the Youth Guarantee does, means preparing policies to re-integrate young people into education and the labor market that go beyond the issue of unemployment and the needs of the conventionally unemployed. Although there is no doubt that policy focused on reducing NEET rates is im-portant, recognition of the heterogeneity of this group requires tailored policy interventions (Furlong 2007; Eurofound 2012).

17.4. THE CHARACTERISTICS OF NEETS IN EUROPE

Despite its limitations, the standardized indicator proposed by EMCO and operationalized by Eurostat in 2010 makes it possible to estimate the number of young people who are disengaged from the labor market and from education in Europe and to perform cross-country comparisons on the basis of the usual socioeconomic variables (Eurofound 2012, 2016).

According to the latest Eurostat data, the share of young people aged 15–29 years in Europe who were not in employment, education, or training was 14.8% in 2015. In absolute numbers, this corresponds to approximately 13 million young people belonging to the NEET group. As shown in Figure 17.2, the prevalence of NEETs varies substantially across member states. The Netherlands, Sweden, Luxembourg, and Denmark record the lowest NEET rates (approximately 7%). Croatia, Romania, Bulgaria, Greece, and Italy record the highest rates (greater than 20%), which implies that at least one out of five young people in these countries is not in employment, education, or training. In absolute terms, the NEET population is highest in Italy, with more than 2 million young people belonging to this group.

Before the economic crisis of 2008–2009, NEET rates were decreasing across Europe: The lowest level of NEETs was recorded for all age categories in 2008. However, with the beginning of the economic crisis, this improvement ended abruptly, and NEET rates increased markedly. European NEET rates were at

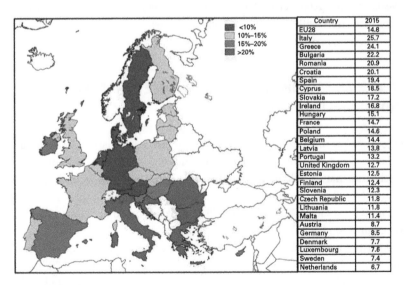

Country	2015
EU28	14.8
Italy	25.7
Greece	24.1
Bulgaria	22.2
Romania	20.9
Croatia	20.1
Spain	19.4
Cyprus	18.5
Slovakia	17.2
Ireland	16.8
Hungary	15.1
France	14.7
Poland	14.6
Belgium	14.4
Latvia	13.8
Portugal	13.2
United Kingdom	12.7
Estonia	12.5
Finland	12.4
Slovenia	12.3
Czech Republic	11.8
Lithuania	11.8
Malta	11.4
Austria	8.7
Germany	8.5
Denmark	7.7
Luxembourg	7.6
Sweden	7.4
Netherlands	6.7

Legend: <10%; 10%–15%; 15%–20%; >20%

Figure 17.2 NEET rates across Europe (young people aged 15–29 years).
Source: Eurostat (EU-LFS).

their highest in 2013, when 15.9% of young people aged 15–29 years were NEET, compared to 13% in 2008. NEET rates have now started to decrease slowly, falling to below 15% in 2015 for those aged 15–29 years.

In terms of socioeconomic characteristics, analysis of the EU-LFS reveals considerable heterogeneity across member states. At the European level, there are more female than male NEETs. In the age category 15–29 years, the female NEET rate was 16.7% at the European level in 2015, compared to 13% for males. This gap of 3.7% constitutes a considerable reduction compared to the 6% recorded in the precrisis period. Although considerable gender variability is found at the member-state level, only in Luxembourg, Cyprus, Croatia, and Finland is the share of young males higher than that of young women among NEETs. Conversely, the gender NEET gap is larger in the United Kingdom, Germany, Malta, Hungary, and the Czech Republic, where the great majority of NEETs in this age category are young women.

In terms of education, at the European level, 39% of young NEETs (aged 15–29 years) have a lower education level, 47% have an upper secondary level of education, and 14% have tertiary education. Substantial heterogeneity is observed across member states with regard to educational attainment. In countries such as Spain, Malta, and Germany, more than 50% of NEETs have a low education level. Conversely, in Poland, Greece, and Croatia, more than 60% of NEETs hold an upper secondary diploma. Finally, in Cyprus, more than 30% of NEETs have completed tertiary education. Furthermore, the disaggregation of upper education levels between general courses and vocational education and training (VET) reveals that the group of NEETs with a VET-oriented upper education level is larger than those with more general qualifications.

17.5. RISK FACTORS FOR BECOMING NEET: DISADVANTAGE AND DISAFFECTION

As reviewed in the Eurofound (2012) study, there is reasonable agreement in the literature about the range of social, economic, and personal factors that increase the chances that an individual might become NEET, and it is generally perceived that the NEET status arises from a complex interplay of institutional, structural, and individual factors (Hodkinson 1996; Hodkinson and Sparkes 1997; Bynner 2005; Eurofound 2012).

Focusing on the vulnerable groups (i.e., involuntary NEETs), the literature suggests that there are two principal risk factors relating to NEET: disadvantage and disaffection. Whereas educational disadvantage is associated with social factors such as the family, school, and personal characteristics, disaffection concerns the attitudes young people have toward education and schooling specifically, as expressed by truancy or behavior that leads to expulsion from school.

There also seems to be a clear correlation between both educational disadvantage and disaffection prior to age 16 years and later disengagement (SEU 1999). Both educational disadvantage and disaffection are linked to a number of background factors, such as family disadvantage and poverty; having an unemployed parent(s); living in an area with high unemployment; membership in an ethnic minority group; or having a chronic illness, disability, and/or special education needs (Coles et al. 2002; see also Berloffa, Matteazzi, and Villa, this volume; Zuccotti and O'Reilly, this volume).

Although it should be emphasized that it is often not easy to differentiate between those factors that cause or lead to NEET status and those factors that are simply correlated with being NEET (Farrington and Welsh 2003, 2007), existing research places great emphasis on family background and individual characteristics as determinants of the NEET status (Stoneman and Thiel 2010). At the individual level, characteristics that are over-represented among the NEET population are low academic attainment (Dolton et al. 1999; Meadows 2001; Coles et al. 2002); teenage pregnancy and lone parenthood (Morash and Rucker 1989; Cusworth et al. 2009); special education needs and learning difficulties (Cassen and Kingdon 2007; Social Exclusion Task Force 2008); health problems and mental illness (Meadows 2001); involvement in criminal activities; and low motivation and aspiration, including lack of confidence, sense of fatalism, and low self-esteem (Strelitz and Darton 2003). Moreover, motivation is often identified as one of the key factors among the nonvulnerable who may be in a "voluntary NEET status"—that is, those who are more likely to come from a privileged background and remain briefly outside the labor market and education in order to sample jobs and educational courses (Furlong et al. 2003; Pemberton 2008).

In order to perform a pan-European investigation of the NEET phenomenon in this chapter, the Eurostat definition of NEET is implemented in the European Values Study survey (EVS), focusing on young people aged 15–29 years. The EVS is a large-scale, cross-national, and longitudinal survey research program on basic human values, which provides insights into the ideas, beliefs, preferences, attitudes, values, and opinions of citizens for 47 European countries and regions. It is an important source of data for investigating how Europeans think about life, family, work, religion, politics, and society, and specific attention is dedicated to individual socioeconomic and family-related variables. On this basis, we explore the characteristics of NEETs in Europe by making use of the set of key characteristics identified in the literature, which includes, especially, the investigation of individual and family background characteristics. In particular, in our analysis, we use the 2008 wave (the most recent) of the EVS by considering data from all 27 EU member states, with an overall sample of more than 40,000 observations that are representative for the EU population. NEETs are identified in the EVS as those young people aged 15–29 years who declared not being in paid employment because of being unemployed, disabled, young carers, housewives, or not otherwise employed for undeclared reasons. This operationalization of the definition of NEET is equivalent to that implemented by Eurostat using the EU-LFS, and the computed rates are comparable. Data refer to 2008, so they capture the scenario only at the beginning of the crisis.

The characteristics of the NEETs in Europe have been investigated using a logit model that accounts for a broad set of individuals' sociodemographic and family-related variables while also controlling for countries' heterogeneity. We investigated a large set of individual characteristics: gender, age, immigration background, perceived health status, education level, religiosity, and living with parents. Furthermore, at the family level, we considered household income, education level of parents, unemployment history of parents, and the area where the household is located. The analysis is performed at the European and also at the cluster level, which are identified on the basis of the extent of the NEET phenomenon observed at country level and the mediating role of different welfare-state models (Marshall 1950; Hadjivassiliou et al., this volume). In this respect, the established categorization of member states in five clusters is adopted here: employment-centered (AT, BE, DE, FR, LU, and NL), universalistic (DK, FI, and SE), liberal (IE and UK), subprotective (CY, ES, GR, IT, MT, and PT), and post-socialist (BG, CZ, EE, HU, LT, LV, PL, RO, SI, and SK). The results of our analysis show a high level of consistency with the general literature and reveal some heterogeneity among the risk factors observed in the different geographical clusters. In particular, the findings indicate that the probability of ending up NEET is influenced by the following factors and characteristics (Table 17.1):

- Regarding gender, young women are more likely than men to be NEET. The interpretation of the odds ratio shows that because of family responsibilities, young European women are 62% more likely than men to be NEET. Interestingly, this effect is stronger in the subprotective and post-socialist clusters than in the universalistic, liberal, or employment-centered clusters.

- As indicated in the literature, those perceiving their health status as bad or very bad and who are suffering from some kind of disability are 38% more likely to be NEET compared to those with a good health status. This effect is stronger in the liberal and universalistic clusters than in the rest of Europe.

- Young people with an immigration background are 68% more likely to become NEET compared to nationals. This effect is strongest in the liberal cluster, whereas it is not significant in the universalistic or in the subprotective cluster.

- Young people living in a partnership are 67% more likely to be NEET compared to those living alone or with parents. This effect is mainly driven by young women with family responsibilities. It is strongest in the liberal, subprotective, and post-socialist clusters, whereas it is not significant elsewhere.

Table 17.1 Logistic regression results

Variable	European Union		Cluster 1: AT, BE, DE, FR, LU, NL		Cluster 2: DK, FI, SE		Cluster 3: IE, UK		Cluster 4: CY, ES, EL, IT, MT, PT		Cluster 5: BG, CZ, EE, HU, LT, LV, PL, RO, SI, SK	
	Odds ratio	SE	Odds ratio	SE	Odds ratio	SE	Odds ratio	SE	Odds ratio	SE	Odds ratio	SE
Gender (male)	0.381***	0.034	0.615***	0.116	0.399***	0.137	0.111***	0.069	0.393***	0.080	0.289***	0.040
Age (years)	1.066***	0.015	1.118***	0.037	0.993	0.062	0.997	0.099	1.053*	0.033	1.073***	0.024
Health (not good)	1.388***	0.159	1.938***	0.475	2.580**	0.995	3.175*	2.105	2.149***	0.624	0.930	0.160
Immigration background	1.689***	0.261	1.969**	0.529	1.621	0.993	8.965***	6.431	1.287	0.390	2.803***	0.970
Living with parents (ref.)	(dropped)		(dropped)		(dropped)		(dropped)		(dropped)		(dropped)	
Living alone	0.804	0.114	0.703	0.204	0.754	0.436	2.185	1.882	0.755	0.220	0.723	0.187
Living with partner	1.673***	0.183	1.057	0.268	1.402	0.711	4.248*	3.634	1.621*	0.405	2.051***	0.317
Experienced divorce	1.265**	0.142	1.338	0.283	1.677	0.572	1.353	0.877	1.499	0.479	1.044	0.188
Education level: primary (ref.)	(dropped)		(dropped)		(dropped)		(dropped)		(dropped)		(dropped)	
Education level: secondary	0.448***	0.048	0.452***	0.105	0.514	0.247	0.151***	0.098	0.754	0.186	0.375***	0.061
Education level: tertiary	0.320***	0.048	0.148***	0.055	0.490	0.307	0.183***	0.135	0.568*	0.191	0.321***	0.072
Income	0.443***	0.042	0.356***	0.084	3.395	2.751	0.112***	0.079	0.683	0.165	0.391***	0.063
Income squared	1.051***	0.013	1.094**	0.043	0.603**	0.153	1.332***	0.123	0.997	0.042	1.056***	0.018

(continued)

Table 17.1 Continued

Variable	European Union		Cluster 1: AT, BE, DE, FR, LU, NL		Cluster 2: DK, FI, SE		Cluster 3: IE, UK		Cluster 4: CY, ES, EL, IT, MT, PT		Cluster 5: BG, CZ, EE, HU, LT, LV, PL, RO, SI, SK	
	Odds ratio	SE	Odds ratio	SE	Odds ratio	SE	Odds ratio	SE	Odds ratio	SE	Odds ratio	SE
Highest education parents: primary (ref.)	(dropped)		(dropped)		(dropped)		(dropped)		(dropped)		(dropped)	
Highest education parents: secondary	0.656***	0.071	0.626**	0.146	1.007	0.445	0.104**	0.099	0.618**	0.151	0.646***	0.107
Highest education parents: tertiary	0.524***	0.079	0.531**	0.158	1.338	0.640	0.323	0.257	0.353**	0.156	0.527**	0.131
Unemployment history (father)	1.199	0.223	0.832	0.357	0.428	0.462	1.912	1.582	2.504*	1.238	1.113	0.301
Country dummies	Omitted		Omitted		Omitted		Omitted		Omitted		Omitted	
No. of observations	4,470		1,259		344		156		779		1,933	
Pseudo R^2	0.168		0.194		0.169		0.42		0.135		0.198	

- Education is the main driver affecting the probability of being NEET: Young people with lower level education are two times more likely to be NEET compared to those with secondary education, and they are more than three times more likely to be NEET compared to those with tertiary education. The effect of education is strongest in the liberal cluster, whereas it is very limited in the subprotective cluster.
- Capturing both the heterogeneity of the NEET population and its composition (both vulnerable and nonvulnerable youth), the marginal effect of income emerges as a U-shaped curve. The probability of being NEET is higher for those with a lower income, then decreases for the middle-level income, and increases again for higher incomes. Again, the effect of income is strongest in the liberal cluster, whereas it is more limited in the subprotective and universalistic clusters.

In addition to these individual characteristics, the following intergenerational influences and family backgrounds play a significant role in increasing the probability of being NEET:

- Having parents who experienced unemployment is not significant at the EU level, whereas it is only marginally significant in the subprotective cluster.
- Those with parents with a low level of education are up to 50% more likely to be NEET compared to young people with parents with a secondary level of education, and they are up to twice as likely to be NEET compared to those with parents with a tertiary level of education. This effect is strongest in the liberal cluster, whereas it is not significant in the universalistic cluster.
- Young people who experienced the divorce of their parents are almost 30% more likely to be NEET compared to those who did not.

Despite some heterogeneity at the cluster level, the results of the investigation indicate that NEET status can be described as both an outcome and a defining characteristic of disadvantaged youth, who are at much greater risk of social exclusion. Education is the most important variable, and it has the strongest effect in influencing the probability of being NEET: This is true at both the individual level and the family level and in all clusters considered. Moreover, suffering some kind of disadvantage, such as a disability or having an immigration background, strongly increases the probability of being NEET, and this effect is strongest in the liberal cluster (Zuccotti and O'Reilly in this volume suggest that these effects also vary by ethnic group and appear to diminish somewhat for second-generation migrants). The importance of family background is confirmed as increasing the risk of becoming NEET. In particular, young people with a difficult family background, such as those with divorced parents or with parents who have experienced unemployment, are more likely to be NEET (as in the subprotective cluster) (see Berloffa, Matteazzi, and Villa, this volume). The heterogeneity of the NEET population, as a mix of vulnerable and nonvulnerable situations, is, however, confirmed by the effect of income, which is common to all clusters but the universalistic.

17.6. POLICIES TO TACKLE THE HETEROGENEITY OF NEETS

Understanding the composition of the NEET population is essential for policy design and for implementing reintegration measures. Armed with information about the size and the characteristics of each subgroup of the NEET population, member states can also better understand how to prioritize their actions and know which tools are most needed in order to reintegrate young people into the labor market or education.

Several alternative theoretical categorizations of NEETs have already been proposed in the literature. Williamson (1997) suggested disaggregating NEETs into three groups: "essentially confused," "temporarily side-tracked," and "deeply alienated." According to Williamson, whereas members of the first group are willing and ready to re-engage as long as the right support and encouragement are provided, those in the second group need some understanding and patience while they deal with what they consider to be more important matters in their lives right now. Williamson considers the third group to be at the highest risk of disengagement and disaffection. This group may include those who have discovered "alternative ways of living" within the informal and illegal economies and those whose lives revolve around the consumption of alcohol and illegal drugs. Although it would be possible to re-engage the "temporarily side-tracked" and the "essentially confused" into the labor market or education, it could be very difficult to persuade the "deeply alienated" to return.

An alternative categorization has been developed by Eurofound (2012, 2016) and Mascherini (2017), who identified five categories within the NEET population with varying degrees of vulnerability and needs: the conventionally unemployed, the unavailable, the disengaged, opportunity seekers, and voluntary NEETs. The "conventionally unemployed" were expected to be the largest group within the NEET population, which could be further divided into short- and long-term unemployed. The "unavailable" include young people who are unavailable because of family responsibilities or because of illness or disability. The "disengaged" include all young people who are not seeking a job or following any education or training and who do not have other obligations that stop them from doing so. This category includes discouraged workers and young people who are pursuing dangerous and asocial lifestyles. The "opportunity seekers" include young people who are seeking work or training but are holding out for the right opportunity. The "voluntary NEETs" are constructively engaged in other activities, such as art, music, or self-directed learning.

Although the previous categorizations are quite rich, their implementation is rather difficult because of data constraints that do not allow their operationalization through the EU-LFS, the survey officially used to compute the NEET rate. The EU-LFS has the undoubted advantage of having the largest sample base of any European survey, but it offers a restricted number of variables. This makes it difficult to capture the sociodemographic qualities and behaviors that are essential to a better understanding of the characteristics of NEETs, the reasons for their status, and their vulnerabilities. The limited range of variables also makes it impossible to use the previously described categorizations of vulnerable and nonvulnerable NEETs because the variables that would capture these characteristics are missing.

Building on findings from previous research and using the EU-LFS, a new categorization is proposed here. This categorization revolves around seven descriptions created using the available five variables that make it possible to understand why those in each particular group responded during the survey that they were not searching for employment and were not able to start work within the next 2 weeks.[2] Similarly, duration of unemployment has been used to disaggregate the short- and long-term unemployed.

The seven subcategories that emerged from this exercise are as follows:

Re-entrants: This category captures those young people who will soon re-enter employment, education, or training and will soon begin or resume accumulation of human capital through formal channels. They are people who have already been hired or have enrolled in education or training and will soon start this activity.[3]

Short-term unemployed: This category is composed of all young people who are unemployed, seeking work, and available to start within 2 weeks and who have been unemployed for less than 1 year.[4]

Long-term unemployed: This category is composed of all young people who are unemployed, seeking work, and available to start within 2 weeks and who have been unemployed for more than 1 year. People in this category are at high risk of disengagement and social exclusion.[5]

Unavailable because of illness or disability: This category includes all young people who are not seeking employment or are not available to start a job within 2 weeks because of illness or disability. This group includes those who need more social support because the nature of their illness or disability means they cannot carry out paid work.[6]

Unavailable because of family responsibilities: This group includes those who are not seeking work or who are not available to start a new job because they are caring for children or incapacitated adults or have other less specific family responsibilities. Young people in this group are a mix of the vulnerable and nonvulnerable; some are not able to participate in the labor market because they cannot afford to pay for care for their child or adult family member, whereas others voluntarily withdraw from the labor market or education to take up family responsibilities.[7]

Discouraged workers: This group encompasses all young people who have stopped searching for work because they believe that there are no job opportunities for them. They are mostly vulnerable young people at high risk of social exclusion who are very likely to experience poor employment outcomes over the course of their working lives and are at high risk of lifelong disengagement.[8]

Other inactive: This group contains all NEETs whose reasons for being NEET do not fall into any of the previous six categories. This group is a statistical residual category made up of those who did not specify any reason for their NEET status. It is likely to be an extremely heterogeneous mix that includes people at all extremes of the spectrum of vulnerability: the most vulnerable, the difficult to reach, those at risk of being deeply alienated, the most privileged, and those who are holding out for a specific opportunity or who are following alternative paths.[9]

The proposed categorization allows investigation of the composition of the NEET population by identifying seven major groups, four of which are labor-market driven (re-entrants, short-term unemployed, long-term unemployed, and discouraged workers), whereas three are inactivity driven (unavailable because of illness or disability, unavailable because of family responsibilities, and other inactive). Although the categorization is not exhaustive, it can be implemented every year through the EU-LFS, providing a useful tool for measuring the extent of NEET populations and the broad types of policy initiative among the various EU member states, showing not only the heterogeneity of the NEET population but also the heterogeneity of the member states, where NEET status differs in terms of not only rate but also composition.

17.6.1. Differentiating the composition of the NEET population and appropriate policy responses

Focusing on young people aged 15–29 years, we implemented the categorization outlined previously on data from the 2013 EU-LFS.[10] Figure 17.3 thus shows that in 2013, the largest category of NEETs was the short-term unemployed (25.5%), followed by the long-term unemployed (23.1%). The group of those unavailable because of family responsibilities is also large (20.3%). Discouraged workers account for 5.8% of the total, whereas 7% are young people with an illness or

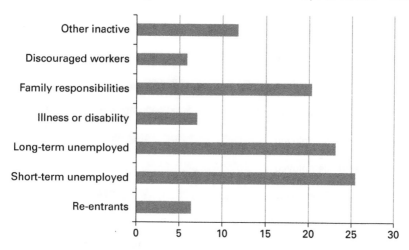

Figure 17.3 Composition of the NEET population aged 15–29 years at the EU level, percentage shares, 2013.
Source: Eurostat (EU-LFS 2013).

disability. Finally, 11.7% are young people who are inactive without having indicated the reason, and 6.4% are re-entrants. Looking at the total population of young people in Europe in 2013, 4% of those aged 15–29 years were short-term unemployed, whereas 3.6% were long-term unemployed and approximately 3.1% were outside the labor market and education because of family responsibilities.

According to the proposed decomposition, we can say in broad terms that at the European level, the share of young people who are NEET for labor-market driven reasons amounts to 60.8% of the total, which corresponds to the sum of re-entrants, short- and long-term unemployed, and discouraged workers. Of these, half are at risk of long-term disengagement (being both long-term unemployed and discouraged workers) and will require more ad hoc reactivation measures in order to be reintegrated into the labor market.

The need for targeted measures becomes even more evident when the distribution of the composition of the NEET population is examined by gender. The gender composition of the various categories reveals that whereas young men dominated the categories of labor market-driven NEETs, more than 92% of NEETs attributing this status to family responsibilities are women (Figure 17.4). Although it is unfortunately not possible to determine how many in this category are voluntarily in this situation, the clear gender imbalance in the category suggests room for maneuver for policy interventions, including the promotion of support to young women through childcare and other social care for family members so as to foster their reintegration into the labor market or education.

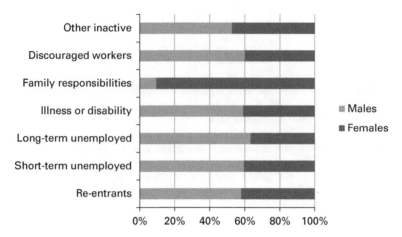

Figure 17.4 Gender composition of the NEET population aged 15–29 years, 2013.
Source: Eurostat (EU-LFS 2013)

17.6.2. Heterogeneity of NEETs in a heterogeneous Europe

The unemployed are the largest group of NEETs in most countries, although there are some significant differences with regard to the proportions in long- or short-term unemployment (Figure 17.5).

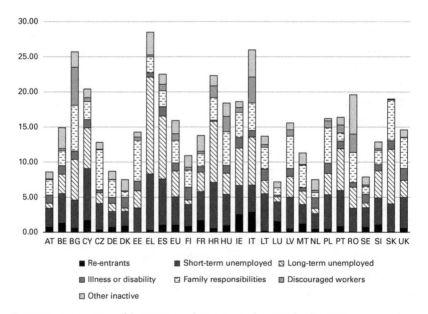

Figure 17.5 Composition of the NEET population at member-state level in 2013.
Source: Eurostat (EU-LFS 2013).

The short-term unemployed are the largest category among NEETs in Austria, Belgium, Denmark, Finland, France, Germany, Luxembourg, the Netherlands, Sweden, and the United Kingdom. This group ranges from 39% in Luxembourg to 28% in Belgium and Finland. All of these countries are also characterized by a NEET rate below the EU average, indicating that young people manage to enter the labor market more rapidly (see Berloffa et al., this volume; Flek, Hála, and Mysíková, this volume). It is interesting to highlight that in almost all these countries, the share of those who are NEET because of illness or disability is higher than the EU average and that the proportion of discouraged workers is also (marginally) higher than average.

Conversely, in Ireland and in some Mediterranean and Central European countries, such as Croatia, Greece, Italy, Portugal, Slovenia, and Spain, the largest group of NEETs is composed of the long-term unemployed. Some of this is a result of the economic crisis, but it also indicates deeper structural problems in youth transitions from school to work. The size of this cohort ranges from 48% in Greece to 26% in Italy, and in all these member states it is well above the EU average. In both Italy and Croatia, the percentage of young people who are discouraged workers is also well above the EU average.

The gender composition of the NEET group is strongly polarized, and in the United Kingdom, Ireland, and Italy, the percentage of NEETs with family responsibilities is well above the EU average. This suggests that in most of these countries, being NEET not only appears to be driven by structural barriers in accessing the labor market but also may be largely attributable to additional disadvantages and family responsibilities (Gökşen et al. 2016).

The NEET rate in Eastern European countries varies across countries—from 12% in the Czech Republic to 25% in Bulgaria. The largest proportion of the NEET population in Eastern member states is attributable to those with family responsibilities—a category composed almost entirely of women. Although the gender dimension and family responsibilities are common drivers, member states differ as to how labor market factors affect the composition of the NEET population. In the Czech Republic, Latvia, Lithuania, and Poland, the share of those closer to the labor market—re-entrants and the short-term unemployed— is higher than the EU average. Conversely, the share of long-term unemployed and discouraged workers is well above the EU average in Bulgaria, Hungary, Romania, and Slovakia.

Considerable efforts have been made by EU member states to reintegrate some groups of NEETs through the use of the Youth Guarantee, especially the short-term unemployed and re-entrants. In many cases, member states have included provisions that address young people who are NEET because of illness or disability. Despite these efforts, few measures currently focus on long-term youth unemployment and especially on young mothers and those young people who cannot participate in the labor market because of family responsibilities

(Eurofound 2015). A more general observation is that some member states have tended to target job-ready young people with Youth Guarantee interventions rather than those who are furthest from the labor market (Eurofound 2016).

17.7. CONCLUSIONS

The concept of NEET and the NEET indicator have attempted to go beyond traditional indicators for youth labor market participation so as to provide a better understanding of youth vulnerability on the labor market. Although from a statistical standpoint it is very easy to capture the NEET population, NEETs are by definition a heterogeneous category combining groups with very different experiences, characteristics, and needs, which include both vulnerable and nonvulnerable young people. Addressing the heterogeneity of the NEET population is of key importance in order to make successful and optimal use of the NEET indicator for policymaking.

Although the overall NEET indicator does not allow us to understand the characteristics of this diverse population, this chapter disentangles the heterogeneity of the NEET population by proposing a disaggregation of the main indicator in seven types, each of which identifies a particular subgroup of young people with its own needs. If applied to the EU-LFS, the categorization could be used every year to monitor trends in the composition of the NEET population and the effectiveness of specific targeted policy interventions.

On the one hand, policy is rightly aimed at reducing overall NEET rates because these are clear indicators of the difficulties young people find in making the transition to work. On the other hand, addressing the heterogeneity of the NEET population has important consequences for appropriate policy responses for different groups of young people.

In particular, when used carefully and disaggregated in the manner outlined in this chapter, the NEET indicator can illustrate the particular needs of specific young people, such as young mothers and those with disabilities. This is preferred to a more traditional categorization implied by the label "inactive." In order to effectively reintegrate NEETs, the different needs and characteristics of the various subgroups have to be taken into account because there will be no one-size-fits-all policy solution. Only a tailored approach for different subgroups has the potential to effectively and successfully reintegrate NEETs into the labor market and education.

The key groups who are still overlooked are those in the gray areas of education, training, and employment. Those who are in temporary or insecure forms of work and those who are underemployed, for example, are frequently in vulnerable and marginalized positions. Similarly, there are young people in education and training who can be regarded as reluctant conscripts: They have been "forced" to engage under threat of benefit withdrawal or have been discouraged from entering the labor market by a perceived lack of opportunities. In this context, although new concepts will be difficult to operationalize, future analysis to map the landscape of youth opportunities needs to pick up both objective and subjective dimensions of vulnerability that characterize modern youth transitions so as to understand how effective policy implementation can address these different dimensions of disadvantage.

NOTES

1 The ILO definition of unemployment covers all people who are without work or were not in paid employment during the previous 4 weeks, who have actively sought work during the previous 4 weeks, and who are available to start work within the next fortnight (International Labour Organization 1982).

2 (1) Seeking employment during the previous 4 weeks (SEEKWORK); (2) reasons for not looking for a job (SEEKREAS); (3) availability to start job within 2 weeks (AVAIBLE); (4) reasons for not being available to start a job (AVAIREAS); and (5) duration of unemployment (SEEKDUR).

3 (SEEKWORK = 1–2) or (SEEKWORK = 3 and SEEKREAS = 1,5); or (SEEKWORK = 4 and AVAIBLE = 2 and AVAIREAS = 1).

4 (SEEKWORK = 4 and AVAIBLE = 1 and SEEKDUR = 0–4).

5 (SEEKWORK = 4 and AVAIBLE = 1 and SEEKDUR = 6–8).

6 (SEEKWORK = 3 and SEEKREAS = 2) and (SEEKWORK = 4 and AVAIBLE = 2 and AVAIREAS = 5).

7 (SEEKWORK = 3 and SEEKREAS = 3,4) and (SEEKWORK = 4 and AVAIBLE = 2 and AVAIREAS = 4).

8 (SEEKWORK = 4 and SEEKREAS = 7).

9 (SEEKWORK = 3 and SEEKREAS = 6,8,–1) and (SEEKWORK = 4 and AVAIBLE = 2 and AVAIREAS = –1,6,2).

10 The most recent available data at the time of writing.

REFERENCES

BBC. 2012. "Young Jobless Neets Still Top One Million." *BBC News*. November 22. https://www.bbc.com/news/education-20444524

BBC. 2014. "Large Drop in Young Jobless Total, Official Data Shows." *BBC News*. May 22. https://www.bbc.com/news/education-27522404

Bunting, Michael. 1994. "The Abandoned Generation." *The Guardian*, June 1, 18.

Bynner, John. 2005. "Rethinking the Youth Phase of the Life-Course: The Case for Emerging Adulthood?" *Journal of Youth Studies* 8: 367–84.

Carcillo, Stéphane, Rodrigo Fernández, Sebastian Königs, and Andreea Minea. 2015. "NEET Youth in the Aftermath of the Crisis." OECD Social, Employment and Migration Working Paper 164. Paris: Organization for Economic Co-operation and Development.

Cassen, Robert, and Geeta Kingdon. 2007. "Tackling Low Educational Achievement." Joseph Rowntree Foundation Report. York, UK: Joseph Rowntree Foundation.

Coles, Bob, Sandra Hutton, Jonathan Bradshaw, Gary Craig, Christine Godfrey, and Julie Johnson. 2002. "Literature Review of the Costs of Being 'Not in Education, Employment or Training' at Age 16–18." DfES Research Report 347. Norwich, UK: Her Majesty's Stationery Office. https://www.york.ac.uk/inst/spru/pubs/pdf/RR347.pdf

Corriere della Sera. 2015. "Giovani senza studio né lavoro, la carica dei Neet: In Italia sono 2,5 milioni, i peggiori d'Europa." October 6.

Council of the European Union. 2013. "Council Recommendation of 22 April 2013 on Establishing a Youth Guarantee." *Official Journal of the European Union* C120: 1.

Council of the European Union. 2014. "Decision No 573/2014/EU of the European Parliament and of the Council of 15 May 2014 on Enhanced Cooperation Between Public Employment Services (PES)." *Official Journal of the European Union* L159: 32.

Council of the European Union. 2015. "Outcome of the Council Meeting: 3398th Council Meeting, Luxembourg, June 18–19," 10088/15. Brussels: EU Press Office.

Cusworth, Linda, Jonathan Bradshaw, Bob Coles, Antonia Keung, and Yekaterina Chzhen. 2009. "Understanding the Risks of Social Exclusion Across the Life Course: Youth and Young Adulthood." Social Exclusion Task Force Research Report. London: Cabinet Office.

Dolton, Peter, Gerald Makepeace, Steve Hutton, and Robert Audas.1999. "Making the Grade." Joseph Rowntree Foundation Research Report. York, UK: Joseph Rowntree Foundation.

El País. 2014. "La apatía de un 'nini.'" October 22.

El País. 2015. "El número de 'ninis' baja por primera vez en España desde 2008." May 15.

Elder, Sarah. 2015. "What Does NEETs Mean and Why Is the Concept So Easily Misinterpreted?" Work 4 Youth Technical Brief. Geneva: ILO.

Eurofound. 2012. *NEETs–Young People Not in Employment, Education or Training: Characteristics, Costs and Policy Responses in Europe.* Luxembourg: Publications Office of the European Union.

Eurofound. 2015. *Social Inclusion of Young People.* Luxembourg: Publications Office of the European Union.

Eurofound. 2016. *Exploring the Diversity of NEETs.* Luxembourg: Publications Office of the European Union.

European Commission. 2010a. *Youth on the Move*. Luxembourg: Publications Office of the European Union.

European Commission. 2010b. "Proposal for a Council Decision on Guidelines for the Employment Policies of the Member States–Part II of the Europe 2020 Integrated Guidelines." SEC (2010) 488 final. http://eur-lex.europa.eu/legal-content/EN/ALL/?uri=celex:52010PC0193

European Commission. 2011a. "Youth Opportunities Initiative." COM (2011) 933 final. Brussels: European Commission.

European Commission. 2011b. "Youth Neither in Employment Nor Education and Training (NEET): Presentation of Data for the 27 Member States." EMCO Contribution. Brussels: European Commission (DG-EMPL).

European Commission. 2012. "Towards a Job-Rich Recovery." Communication from the Commission COM (2012) 173 final. http://ec.europa.eu/social/main.jsp?catId=89&langId=en&newsId=1270&moreDocuments=yes&tableName=news

European Commission. 2013a. "Working Together for Europe's Young People: A Call to Action on Youth Unemployment." Communication from the Commission COM (2013) 447 final. Brussels: European Commission.

European Commission. 2013b. *Barcelona Objectives: The Development of Childcare Facilities for Young Children in Europe with a View to Sustainable and Inclusive Growth*. Luxembourg: Publications Office of the European Union.

European Parliament. 2014. "Austerity and Poverty in the EU." Study for the Employment Committee. Brussels: European Parliament Policy Department A.

European Parliament. 2015. "Youth Unemployment in Greece—Situation Before the Government Change." Briefing. Brussels: European Parliament Policy Department A.

Farrington, David P., and Brandon C. Welsh. 2003. "Family-Based Prevention of Offending: A Meta-Analysis." *Australian and New Zeeland Journal of Criminology* 36 (2): 127–51.

Farrington, David P., and Brandon C. Welsh. 2007. *Saving Children from a Life of Crime: Early Risk Factors and Effective Intervention*. New York: Oxford University Press.

Furlong, Andy. 2007. *Young People and Social Change: New Perspectives*. Maidenhead, UK: Open University Press.

Furlong, Andy, Fred Cartmel, Andy Biggart, Helen Sweeting, and Patrick West. 2003. *Youth Transitions: Patterns of Vulnerability and Processes of Social Inclusion*. Edinburgh, UK: Scottish Executive.

Gökşen, Fatoş, Deniz Yükseker, Alpay Filiztekin, İbrahim Öker, Sinem Kuz, Fernanda Mazzotta, and Lavinia Parisi. 2016. "Leaving and Returning to the Parental Home During the Economic Crisis." STYLE Working Paper 8.3. Brighton, UK: CROME, University of Brighton. http://www.style-research.eu/publications/working-papers

Hodkinson, Phil. 1996. "Careership: The Individual, Choices and Markets in the Transition to Work." In *Knowledge and Nationhood: Education, Politics and Work*, edited by James Avis, Martin Bloomer, Geoff Esland, Denis Gleeson, and Phil Hodkinson, 121–39. London: Cassell.

Hodkinson, Phil, and Andy Sparkes. 1997. "Careership: A Sociological Theory of Career Decision Making." *British Journal of Sociology and Education* 18 (1): 29–44.

International Labour Organization. 1982. "Resolutions Concerning Economically Active Population, Employment, Unemployment and Underemployment, Adopted by the 13th International Conference of Labour Statisticians (October 1982). http://www.ilo.org/public/english/bureau/stat/download/res/ecacpop.pdf

Istance, David, Gareth Rees, and Howard Williamson. 1994. *Young People Not in Education, Training or Employment in South Glamorgan*. Cardiff, UK: South Glamorgan Training and Enterprise Council.

Jones, Maggie. 2006. "Shutting Themselves In." *New York Times*. January 15. https://www.nytimes.com/2006/01/29/opinion/magazine/shutting-themselves-in-656348.html

L'Espresso. 2015. "Italia, siamo il paese dei giovani "Neets": Nessuno in Europa fa peggio di noi." April 16. http://espresso.repubblica.it/attualita/2015/04/16/news/all-italia-un-record-europeo-quello-dei-neets-1.208415

Liang, Ellie K. 2009. "Have NEET's Become an Important Societal Issue in Asian Countries?" *Journal of Asian Studies* 1 (1): 17–21.

Marshall, Thomas H. 1950. *Citizenship and Social Class*. Cambridge, MA: Cambridge University Press.

Mascherini, Massimiliano. 2017. "NEETs in European Agenda: Characteristics and Policy Debate." In *Routledge Handbook of Youth and Young Adulthood*, edited by Andy Furlong, 2nd ed., 164–71. London: Routledge.

McRae, Hamish. 1994. "Too Young and too Precious to Waste." *The Independent*. May 11. https://www.independent.co.uk/voices/too-young-and-too-precious-to-waste-1435390.html

Meadows, Pamela. 2001. *Young Men on the Margins of Work: An Overview Report*. York, UK: Joseph Rowntree Foundation.

Mizanur Rahman, Khondaker. 2006. "Neets' Challenge to Japan: Causes and Remedies." In *Arbeitswelten in Japan 18*, edited by René Haak, 221–44. Munich: Iudicium.

Morash, Merry, and Lila Rucker. 1989. "An Exploratory Study of the Connection of Mother's Age at Childbearing to Her Children's Delinquency in Four Data Sets." *Crime and Delinquency* 35 (1): 45–93.

Navarrete Moreno, Lorenzo. 2011. "Desmontando a ni-ni: Un estereotipo juvenil en tiempos de crisis." Technical Report. Madrid: InJuve.

Pacheco, Gail, and Jessica Dye. 2013. "Estimating the Cost of Youth Disengagement in New Zealand." Department of Economics Working Paper 04. Auckland: University of Auckland.

Pemberton, Simon. 2008. "Tackling the NEET Generation and the Ability of Policy to Generate a 'NEET' Solution—Evidence from the UK." *Environment and Planning C: Politics and Space* 26 (1): 243–59.

Serracant, Pau. 2013. "A Brute Indicator for a NEET Case: Genesis and Evolution of a Problematic Concept and Results from an Alternative Indicator." *Social Indicator Research* 177 (2): 401–19.

SEU. 1999. *Bridging the Gap: New Opportunities for 16–18 Year Olds Not in Education, Employment or Training*. London: The Stationery Office.

Social Exclusion Task Force. 2008. *Think Family: Improving the Life Chances of Families at Risk*. London: Cabinet Office.

Stoneman, Paul, and Darren Thiel. 2010. *NEET in Essex: A Review of the Evidence*. Colchester, UK: University of Essex.

Strelitz, Joseph, and David Darton. 2003. "Tackling Disadvantage: Place." In *Tackling UK Poverty and Disadvantage in the Twenty-First Century: An Exploration of the Issues,* edited by David Darton and Joseph Strelitz, 91–103. Joseph Rowntree Foundation Report. York, UK: Joseph Rowntree Foundation.

Wallace, Claire, and René Bendit. 2009. "Youth Policies in Europe: Towards a Classification of Different Tendencies in Youth Policies in the European Union." *Perspectives on European Politics and Society* 10: (3) 441–58.

Walther, Andreas, and Axel Pohl. 2005. "Thematic Study on Policy Measures Concerning Disadvantaged Youth." Study Commissioned by the European Commission. Tübingen: Institute for Regional Innovation and Social Research.

Wang, Shirley. 2015. "The Fight to Save Japan's Young Shut-Ins." *Wall Street Journal*. January 26. https://www.wsj.com/articles/the-fight-to-save-japans-young-shut-ins-1422292138

Williamson, Howard. 1985. "Struggling Beyond Youth." *Youth in Society* 98 (January).

Williamson, Howard. 1997. "Status Zer0 Youth and the 'Underclass': Some Considerations." In *Youth, the "Underclass" and Social Exclusion,* edited by Robert MacDonald, 70–82. London: Routledge.

Williamson, Howard. 2010. "Delivering a 'NEET' Solution: An Essay on an Apparently Intractable Problem." In *Engaging Wales' Disengaged Youth,* edited by Stevie Upton, 7–20. Cardiff, UK: Institute of Welsh Affairs.

18

YOUTH OVEREDUCATION IN EUROPE

IS THERE SCOPE FOR A COMMON POLICY APPROACH?

Seamus McGuinness, Adele Bergin, and Adele Whelan

18.1. INTRODUCTION

Overeducation describes the situation in which individuals are employed in jobs for which the level of education required to either get or do the jobs in question is below the level of schooling held by the workers. Overeducation has become an increasingly important issue for discussion both within national governments and at the European and Organization for Economic Cooperation and Development (OECD) levels, and policymakers have become ever more concerned about the apparent inability of large shares of new labor market entrants to acquire jobs that are commensurate with their levels of education. Overeducation is costly at an individual level, with mismatched workers typically earning 15% less than their well-matched counterparts with similar levels of education. Furthermore, overeducation tends to reduce levels of job satisfaction and increase rates of job mobility (for a review of the evidence, see Quintini 2011). At the firm level, although there is some evidence that overeducated workers raise productivity levels somewhat,[1] higher rates of job mobility imply that overeducation can impose additional hiring costs on firms. At the macroeconomic level, total output will be lower as a consequence of a significant proportion of the workforce operating below their full potential productivity, while public finances are adversely affected as a consequence of lower income tax receipts and suboptimal investments in educational provision. Given the various impacts of overeducation, it is extremely important to assess the evolution of its rates over time (both within and between countries) so as to develop our understanding of the phenomenon and ascertain the extent to which policies combating overeducation can be coordinated at a European level or whether country-specific responses are likely to be more appropriate.

Currently, almost all of the research on labor market mismatch, measured in terms of either overeducation or overskilling, has relied on country-specific, cross-sectional, or panel data sets. To date, the research has focused on identifying the individual- or firm-level determinants of mismatch and/or the impact of mismatch on individual outcomes such as income or job satisfaction. Although such insights are crucial to understanding mismatch, it is only by studying the phenomenon at a more aggregate level that we can come to an understanding of the macroeconomic, demographic, and institutional forces that drive it. In this study, we use the European Union Labour Force Survey (EU-LFS) to construct quarterly time series of both youth and adult overeducation rates between 1997 and 2012 for 29 European countries. This chapter has a number of objectives, including (1) providing a descriptive assessment of trends in overeducation in European countries over time, (2) assessing the extent to which the rate of overeducation among youth and adult cohorts moves together within countries, (3) measuring the degree of interdependence and convergence in the evolution of overeducation between countries over time, and (4) identifying some of the underlying drivers of youth overeducation.

From a policy perspective, the extent to which overeducation could be suitable for a common policy approach, at either a European or a national level, will largely depend on the similarities in the evolution of overeducation over time both between and within countries. In this chapter, we adopt advanced econometric techniques that can confirm if two time series are driven by a common underlying economic relationship, as opposed to merely trending together in a spurious, noncausal manner. If overeducation has evolved in different directions at different rates across countries, this will provide a strong indication that it is driven by a range of factors that will vary in terms of both their magnitude and their significance across countries. Conversely, if movements in overeducation are confirmed through econometric testing to be driven by the same underlying causal factors over time, this would be supportive of a centralized policy approach aimed at targeting the common underlying causal influences driving both series. We consider a range of potential drivers relating to labor market demand, labor market supply, the structure of education systems, and macroeconomic factors. The potential for a future common policy approach to overeducation, at either a national or a pan-European level, is consequently assessed on the basis of this analysis.

18.1.1. Existing evidence on international variations in overeducation

Although the general literature on overeducation has expanded rapidly, particularly during the past two decades (for reviews, see McGuinness 2006; Quintini 2011; McGuinness et al., 2018), there has been little assessment of overeducation from an aggregate country-level perspective; nevertheless, some exceptions do exist. Pouliakas (2013), also using data from the EU-LFS and analyzing the average rate of overeducation between 2001 and 2011, demonstrates the existence of considerable variation in overeducation rates across European countries. Pouliakas further concludes that although the average level of overeducation among EU25 member states exhibited a relatively stable time series between 2001 and 2009, there was substantial credentialism present in the labor market, with the growth in overeducation being largely subdued by higher occupational entry requirements.[2] Despite the relatively constant trend, the Pouliakas study does indicate that during the financial crisis, the average rate of overeducation in Europe increased during the years 2008 and 2009, implying that levels of overeducation may vary with the business cycle. In support of this view, Mavromaras and McGuinness (2012) argue that there are grounds to expect the rate of mismatch to vary with macroeconomic conditions, on the basis that fluctuations in the economy will change the composition in the demand for labor and, consequently, how workers are utilized within firms. Ex ante, we might reasonably expect rates of overeducation to rise during times of recession and to fall during periods of economic growth. However, it is also reasonable to suppose that business-cycle impacts will be more heavily felt among newly qualified younger workers and that variations in the overall rate of overeducation are likely to be less affected by variations in aggregate output. These hypotheses will be further explored in Sections 18.3 and 18.5.

With respect to the potential drivers of overeducation at the macroeconomic level, there is limited research primarily because of the paucity of cross-country data sets. A number of possible effects could potentially explain the existence and persistence of overeducation at a national level. Overeducation could arise when the supply of educated labor outstrips demand, primarily as a result of the tendency of governments in developed economies to continually seek to raise the proportion of individuals with third-level qualifications. Alternatively, it may be that the quantity of educated labor does not exceed supply but that there are imbalances in composition; in other words, individuals are being educated in areas in which there is little demand, leading to people from certain fields of study being particularly prone to overeducation.[3] Furthermore, labor demand and supply might be perfectly synchronized yet overeducation might still arise because of frictions deriving from asymmetric information, institutional factors that prevent labor market clearance, or variations in individual preferences related to either job mobility or work–life balance.

Applying a multilevel model to a cross-country graduate cohort database, Verhaest and van der Velden (2012) derive a number of variables from the individual-level data to explain cross-country differences in the incidence of overeducation. Explanatory variables in the Verhaest and van der Velden study include measures for the composition of higher education supply in terms of vocational versus academic orientation and field of study, proxies for educational quality,[4] measures of the output and unemployment gaps,[5] indicators of employment protection legislation within each country, and the level of education oversupply. In their study, Verhaest and van der Velden calculate the share of graduates in the population older than age 25 years and gross expenditure on research and development (R&D). Graduate oversupply is then taken as the difference in the standardized values of these two variables. Verhaest and van der Velden find that cross-country differences in overeducation are related to their measures, which, they argue, capture variations in quality and orientation (general vs. specific) of the education system, business-cycle effects, and the relative oversupply of highly skilled labor.

Davia, McGuinness, and O'Connell (2017) attempt a similar exercise using EU-SILC data. Similar to Verhaest and van der Velden (2012), Davia et al. find evidence to support the notion that overeducation is more prevalent in regions where the level of educated labor supply exceeds demand and where university enrolment levels are highest.[6] These authors also report that the overeducation rate is positively related to the share of migrants in the labor market and is lower for females in regions with strong employment protection. Thus, although some concerns may be raised regarding the quality of some of the indicator variables derived in studies relying on cross-sectional international data, the studies by Verhaest and van der Velden and Davia et al. demonstrate the potential importance of aggregate-level variables in explaining overeducation, with both studies pointing toward education oversupply as an important driving force. Recently, McGuinness and Pouliakas (2017), using cross-country European data, have attempted to assess the relative importance of the various explanations for overeducation in terms of the proportion of the overeducation pay penalty that can be attributed to them. McGuinness and Pouliakas argue that there is merit to the view that overeducation is related to differences in the human capital of overeducated and matched workers; however, differences in job conditions and skill requirements were also important. Furthermore, McGuinness and Pouliakas suggest that the quality of information that workers acquire before accepting a job is also an important component in explaining the impact of overeducation among European graduates.

18.2. DATA AND METHODS

To our knowledge, there are no reliable time-series data on overeducation that would allow a systematic cross-country comparison across time, and the data-development aspect is a key contribution of the current study. The data used in this study are the quarterly anonymized country-level files of the EU-LFS for the period up to the fourth quarter of 2012. Because there is no subjective question within the EU-LFS related to the level of schooling necessary to get, or undertake, a person's current job, overeducation is measured objectively. There are essentially three standard methods of measuring overeducation. The subjective measure is based on individual responses comparing attained education levels with perceived job-entry requirements; the occupational-dictionary approach compares individual-level education with the required level of schooling detailed for specific occupations in the documentation accompanying occupational classification systems; finally, the objective approach compares individual levels of schooling with either the mean or the mode level of schooling of the respective occupation. The goal of this chapter is to examine overeducation over time across a large number of EU countries. In this regard, the EU-LFS is one of the only data sets that enables this type of analysis; however, using this data set means that the only measure of overeducation we can exploit is the objective approach. Existing studies indicate that although the correlation between the various definitional approaches tends not to be particularly high, they generate very similar results with respect to both the incidence and the impacts of overeducation (for review, see McGuinness 2006).

For each country, in each quarter, overeducation is defined as the proportion of employees in employment whose International Standard Classification of Education (ISCED) level of schooling lies one level or more above the occupational mode. The occupational modal level of education is the most common qualification possessed by workers in each two-digit International Standard Classification of Occupations (ISCO) occupation group. Overeducation is calculated within two-digit occupational codes and using five ISCED categories of <2, 3, 4, 5B, and 5A + 6. Thus, if the modal level of schooling in a particular two-digit occupation were measured at ISCED-3, then all individuals educated to ISCED levels 4 and above would be deemed to be overeducated in our approach. We calculate the overall rate of overeducation in each country for each quarter, and we also calculate the rates for individuals aged 15–24 and 25–64 years. Given that we are dealing with a large number of countries, for the purposes of our analysis we group these into three categories on the basis of an initial inspection of patterns in the data. Moreover, the selected groupings are likely to have common linkages in terms of geographical proximity, levels of economic development, and access to the single market. The first category is composed of the countries that acceded to the EU from 2004—which include Bulgaria, the Czech Republic, Estonia, Hungary, Latvia, Lithuania, Poland, Romania, the Slovak Republic, and Slovenia—and are referred to as the "Eastern" states. The second category refers to Portugal, Ireland, Italy, Greece, and Spain—the traditional "Periphery" of the EU. The third group ("Central") is made up of the remaining countries located in Central and Northern Europe and includes Austria, Belgium, Denmark,

Finland, France, Iceland, Luxembourg, the Netherlands, Norway, Sweden, and the United Kingdom.[7] Generally, we found that the average rate of overeducation is lowest in the Eastern European countries, highest in the Periphery, and somewhere in between in the Central European countries (see descriptive evidence in Section 18.3).

In terms of the empirical approach, we are interested in determining the extent to which youth and adult overeducation move together within countries and also the degree to which long-term relationships in the rates of overeducation exist between countries. We classify these long-term equilibrium relationships as "completed convergence" on the grounds that, if detected, they indicate that certain series are sufficiently correlated that overeducation is likely to be driven by a common set of macroeconomic and/or institutional factors. We might expect a link between youth and general overeducation within countries on the grounds that they are likely to be driven by a common set of macroeconomic variables related to, for instance, the nature of labor market demand, labor supply, or wage-setting institutions. The overall overeducation rate is closely related to a stock measure that will react more slowly to major changes in determining factors. However, the youth overeducation rate is more of a flow measure that may react with more volatility to changes in labor market conditions. This raises uncertainties related to the extent to which the two series will be highly synced even if they do share common determinants. Regarding intercountry completed convergence, there are grounds to believe that convergence could prevail within an EU context. This could happen, for example, when cross-country differences in key labor market variables such as unemployment and, possibly, overeducation are reduced by the free movement of workers. Conversely, completed convergence (a tendency for the overeducation rates across countries to equalize over time) may be limited for Eastern European countries or between countries where language or other noneconomic barriers prevent equalizing labor flows.

In this chapter, we are dealing with time-series data, which should not be approached using a traditional regression methodology. Historically, econometricians have tended to assume that most time-series data are "nonstationary" and, crucially, this had no impact on their empirical analysis. Time-series data tend to increase or decrease over time and, therefore, do not have a constant "stationary" mean and variance. Running regressions on data of this nature (nonstationary) can give rise to misleading results and essentially lead to erroneous conclusions about the existence of a relationship between variables where one may not in fact exist; this is commonly known as the spurious regression problem. Spurious regressions occur when two variables are statistically related to each other but no causal relationship exists, meaning they are related purely by coincidence or they are both influenced by another external variable. For example, in examining ice cream sales, we may find that sales are highest when the rate of drowning is highest. To imply that ice cream sales cause drowning or vice versa is an example of a spurious relationship. In fact, a contemporaneous increase in these two variables could be caused by a heat wave. Consequently, when we test for common underlying trends between the overeducation series, we take account of the spurious regression problem. In order to overcome such issues, we adopt a cointegration estimation approach. Two nonstationary variables are said to be cointegrated when they move together in a similar manner over time—for example, variables such as household income and expenditure—and, in this case, the regression results are meaningful.

We begin by establishing whether each respective series is stationary or nonstationary by applying standard Phillips–Perron unit root tests (Phillips 1987; Phillips and Perron 1988).[8] The Phillips–Perron test is written formally for a time series y_t in Eq. (18.1), where t is a time trend. The null hypothesis of the Phillips–Perron test is that there is a unit root or that the series is nonstationary; that is, $\beta_1 = 0$:

$$y_t = \beta_0 + \gamma t + \beta_1 y_{t-1} + \varepsilon_t \qquad (18.1)$$

If we establish that two overeducation time series are nonstationary, then we adopt the Phillips–Ouliaris test for a cointegrating relationship. If both series are stationary, we perform ordinary least squares (OLS) on the basis that spurious regressions are no longer an issue. Finally, if one series is stationary and the other nonstationary, we do not undertake any further tests for an underlying relationship.

The Phillips–Ouliaris test is a residual-based test for cointegration involving a two-step estimation approach. In the first stage, Eq. (18.2) is estimated:

$$X_{it} = \alpha + \beta_1 y_{it} + u_t \qquad (18.2)$$

$\hat{\beta}$ is a cointegrating vector if $u_t = X_{it} - \alpha - \beta_i Y_{it}$, and the second stage of the procedure tests whether the regression residuals from Eq. (18.2) are stationary using the Phillips–Perron test.

In addition to testing for long-term relationships in overeducation rates both within and between countries, we also examine the extent to which overeducation rates in Europe have been converging or diverging over time by estimating a Barro regression (Eq. 18.3; Barro 1997). This investigates the relationship between a country's initial level of overeducation and how the rate has evolved over time. In instances in which completed convergence has not been achieved (where overeducation rates across countries have not equalized over time), overeducation rates may converge as workers from saturated graduate labor markets relocate to areas with greater levels of job opportunity and lower levels of overeducation (see Akgüç and Beblavý, this volume). For example, the lack of convergence could arise from some countries remaining outside of the monetary union. Under these circumstances, the consequence of labor market inflows would be to raise overeducation levels in areas of oversupply. At the same time, labor market outflows, in the form of outmigration, would tend to reduce overeducation rates in highly saturated labor markets.

The application of the Barro model involves examining the relationship between the growth rate of overeducation and the initial level of overeducation using a regression model. If a country with a lower initial level of overeducation tended to have a higher growth in overeducation over time, then the estimate of the coefficient of interest—β_1 in Eq. (18.3)—would be negative and significant. This implies that this country's overeducation rate would converge to the average prevailing in other countries. Therefore, disparities in rates across countries over time would tend to dissipate. In contrast, a positive coefficient would point toward divergence in overeducation rates across countries. In addition to the Barro regression, we also check for convergence by plotting the cross-country variance in overeducation rates for specific groups of countries:

$$\frac{\ln Ov(t) - \ln Ov(0)}{t} = \beta_0 + \beta_1 Ov(0) + \varepsilon \tag{18.3}$$

Finally, we examine the determinants of youth overeducation for countries with a stationary series. Twenty-one of the 28 youth overeducation series were found to be stationary in nature, suggesting that the application of standard OLS is appropriate.[9] For the stationary series, we estimate the following model for all countries initially and then for our three country groupings:

$$y_{it} = \beta_0 + \beta_1 y_{it-1} + \beta_j X_{ijt} + \alpha_i + \varepsilon_{it} \tag{18.4}$$

where y_{it} is the dependent variable observed for country i in time t, y_{it-1} is the lagged dependent variable, X_{ijt} represents a number of j independent variables with β_j the associated coefficients, α_i is the unobserved time-invariant country effect that allows us to control for institutional factors (fixed effect), and ε_{it} is the error term. Using this fixed-effect approach allows us to model the determinants of youth overeducation, but we cannot exclude the possibility that some variables may be endogenous and, in further analysis, we plan to build on this approach using panel data in a dynamic framework.[10]

18.3. DESCRIPTIVE EVIDENCE

The average levels of overeducation, based on quarterly data for the period 2001–2011, are reported in the first column of Table 18.1. Our sample is restricted to employees in full-time employment and so will largely exclude the student population but include paid apprenticeships and traineeships. The estimated rate of overeducation varies from 8% in the Czech and Slovak Republics to 30% or greater in Ireland, Cyprus, and Spain. In general, we observe the estimated

Table 18.1 Overeducation rates: Comparison of estimates from EU-LFS data averaged over 2001–2011 and estimates based on PIAAC data for 2014

	(1)	(2)
Country	Estimates based on EU-LFS (2001–2011 average)	Estimates based on PIAAC (2014)
Austria	0.19	0.23
Belgium	0.26	0.24
Bulgaria	0.11	
Cyprus	0.31	0.31
Czech Republic	0.08	0.12
Germany	0.18	0.22
Denmark	0.18	0.31
Estonia	0.24	0.26
Spain	0.30	0.34
Finland	0.14	0.17
France	0.17	0.17
Greece	0.28	
Hungary	0.13	
Ireland	0.33	0.33
Italy	0.24	0.24
Lithuania	0.25	
Luxembourg	0.17	
Latvia	0.19	
Netherlands	0.22	0.22
Poland	0.11	0.11
Portugal	0.18	
Romania	0.10	
Sweden	0.14	0.19
Slovenia	0.09	
Slovak Republic	0.08	0.10
United Kingdom	0.21	0.20

Sources: Column (1), authors' calculations based on EU-LFS data; column (2), Flisi et al. (2014).

incidence of overeducation to be lowest in the Eastern countries (e.g., the Czech Republic, Slovenia, and the Slovak Republic) and highest in the Peripheral countries (e.g., Spain and Ireland), with the Central countries lying somewhere in the middle. There are, however, some exceptions to this general pattern; for instance, overeducation rates were relatively high in Lithuania and Estonia, whereas overeducation in Portugal was well below the level observed in other

Peripheral countries. The second column of Table 18.1 provides a comparison with a number of estimates for 2014 generated by Flisi et al. (2014), who applied a comparable approach to the OECD Programme for the International Assessment of Adult Competencies (PIAAC) data. In general, our overeducation estimates match closely with those from the PIAAC-based study, with the exception of the estimate for Denmark, where a relatively large discrepancy exists.

We plot the country rates for total overeducation and for the 15- to 24-year-old and 25- to 64-year-old age groups for each country in Figure 18.1.[11] The length of the time series varies depending on data availability. There is a high

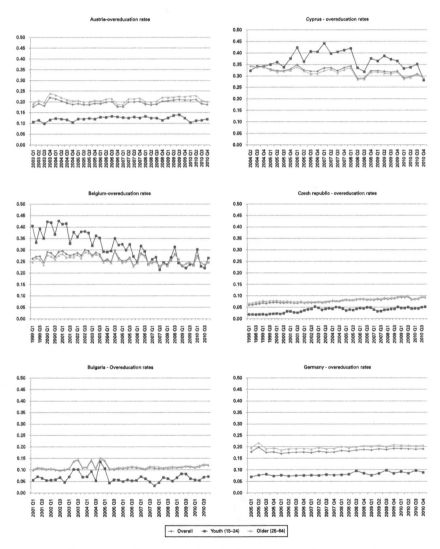

Figure 18.1 Quarterly overeducation rates (restricted to full-time employees) for each country plotted for the time periods available from Q1/1998 to Q4/2010.

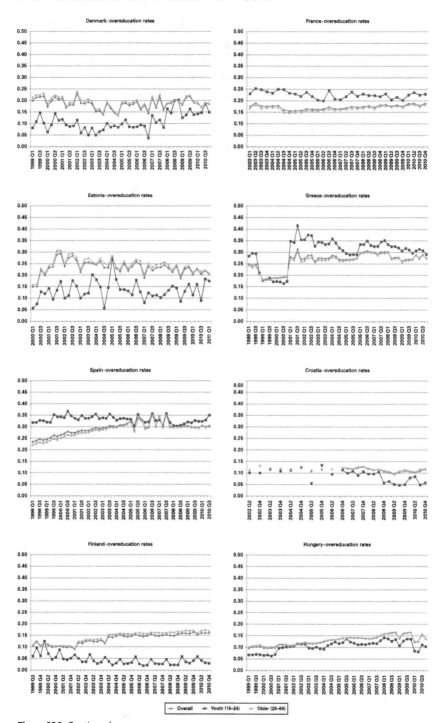

Figure 18.1 Continued

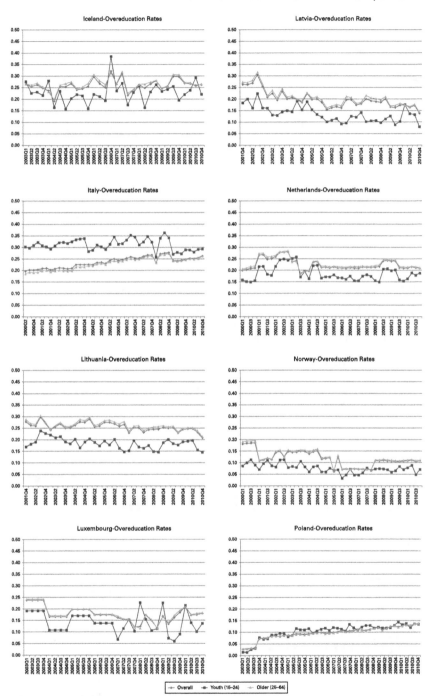

Figure 18.1 Continued

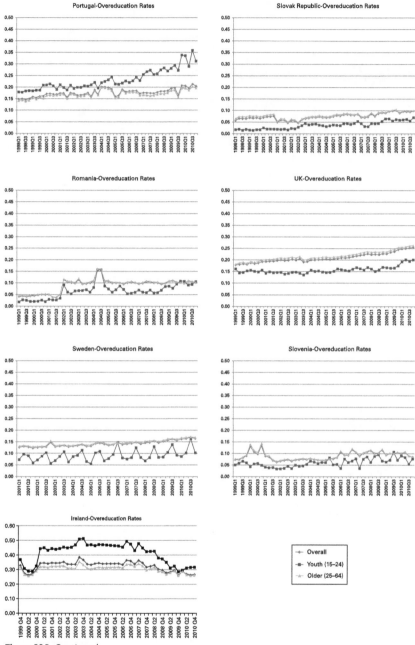

Figure 18.1 Continued

degree of cross-country variation in terms of the level of overeducation, the general direction of the trend over time, and the relationship between youth and adult overeducation within countries.

For slightly less than half of the countries, overeducation appears to be trending upward over time. However, although the rate of increase seems quite slight, a much steeper slope is observed for most countries in the Peripheral group (Spain, Greece, Portugal, and Italy) and also in Poland. Furthermore, overeducation appears *not* to have risen in any observable way in 12 countries, including Austria, Belgium, Denmark, Germany, Iceland, Ireland, and Luxembourg, whereas it has fallen over time in Cyprus, Croatia, Lithuania, and Latvia.

With respect to youth overeducation, the pattern appears much more volatile relative to adult overeducation. Youth overeducation lies below the average in the vast majority of countries; however, it has been consistently above the average in the Peripheral group and in Belgium, Cyprus, France, and Poland. It may be the case that the consistently high levels of youth overeducation in countries in the Peripheral group are also contributing to the observed trend increase in total overeducation over time. For example, this may happen as a consequence of higher proportions of consecutive generations of young people failing to achieve an appropriate labor market match. The main characteristics of the country-level overeducation series are summarized in Table 18.2.

18.4. HAVE OVEREDUCATION RATES CONVERGED OR ARE THEY CONTINUING TO CONVERGE?

To investigate the existence of a long-term relationship between overeducation rates across countries, we adopt the Phillips–Ouliaris approach (described in Section 18.2) and perform pairwise analysis of overeducation rates. Cointegration tests should reveal whether overeducation rates move together over a longer time period. A finding of a common trend in the rates across countries may signify that an international policy approach to overeducation is appropriate. Even if there is no finding of cointegration across countries, overeducation may still respond to the same underlying processes, which we explore in Section 18.5.

For each country, the tests for stationarity are performed either with or without a time trend. The decision to include a time trend or not depends on the evolution of the overall overeducation rate over time in each country. The null hypothesis (that the series is nonstationary) is the presence of a unit root. We conclude that we cannot reject the null hypothesis of a unit root for any series where the test statistic is below the critical value at the 10% level of significance. These countries are then included in the cointegration analysis to ascertain if the overeducation rates move together over time in an equilibrium manner. We perform pairwise OLS on the other countries where we conclude that the overeducation rate is stationary and include a time trend depending on the nature of the stationarity. For example, a series is trend stationary if the underlying series is stationary after removing the time trend.

The finding of nonstationarity means that the overeducation rate has a nonconstant mean and/or variance, suggesting that the phenomenon is somewhat unstable over time. Conversely, a finding of stationarity implies relative

Table 18.2 Key characteristics of country-level overeducation series based on estimates from EU-LFS data, 2001–2011

Country	Youth > adult	Youth < adult	Positive trend	Negative trend	No trend
Austria		X			X
Belgium	X				X
Bulgaria		X			X
Cyprus	X			X	
Czech Republic		X	X		
Germany		X			X
Denmark		X			X
Estonia		X			X
Spain	X		X		
Finland		X	X		
France	X				X
Greece	X				X
Croatia		X		X	
Hungary		X	X		
Ireland	X				X
Iceland		X			X
Italy	X		X		
Lithuania		X		X	
Luxembourg		X			X
Latvia		X		X	
Netherlands		X			X
Norway		X	X		
Poland	X		X		
Portugal	X		X		
Romania		X	X		
Sweden		X	X		
Slovenia		X	X		
Slovak Republic		X	X		
United Kingdom		X			X

Table 18.3 Country-level Phillips–Perron stationarity tests

Country	Phillips–Perron test statistic	Trend
Austria	−4.066***	No
Belgium	−4.302***	No
Bulgaria	−5.161***	No
Cyprus	−3.098	Yes
Czech Republic	−3.468*	Yes
Germany	−2.824*	No
Denmark	−4.842***	No
Estonia	−4.937***	No
Spain	−3.032	Yes
Finland	−4.189***	Yes
France	−2.836*	No
Greece	−1.962	No
Hungary	−2.063	Yes
Ireland	−2.594	No
Iceland	−3.899***	No
Italy	−2.177	Yes
Lithuania	−5.368***	Yes
Luxembourg	−2.985**	No
Latvia	−3.485*	Yes
Netherlands	−2.704*	No
Norway	−2.573	Yes
Poland	−2.006	Yes
Portugal	−5.670***	Yes
Romania	−2.367	Yes
Sweden	−5.548***	Yes
Slovenia	−3.749**	Yes
Slovak Republic	−3.078	Yes
United Kingdom	−2.272	Yes

$*p < .10.$
$**p < .05.$
$***p < .01.$
Source: EU-LFS.

stability, suggesting that overeducation rates are generally stable in the sense that they are constant over time or increase/decrease at a constant rate with no volatility. Table 18.3 shows that for the majority of countries, overeducation is stationary, meaning the average rates are stable over time. The null hypothesis of nonstationarity could not be rejected for Cyprus, Hungary, Poland, Romania, the Slovak Republic, Norway, the United Kingdom, Greece, Italy, Ireland, and Spain, indicating that these series are nonstationary and therefore should be included in the pairwise cointegration analysis. In the sense that the tests suggest that the development of overeducation is somewhat unpredictable, it appears more likely to be erratic in most countries in the Peripheral group, which could reflect their greater exposure to macroeconomic shocks.

Table 18.4 shows the test results from the cointegration analysis. Although the patterns are not clear-cut, the table provides some evidence of cointegrating relationships within the Peripheral group, indicating completed convergence. For example, Greece, Italy, Ireland, and Spain are all bilaterally cointegrated at varying levels of statistical significance. This implies that overeducation in these countries responds in a similar manner to external shocks; in other words, there is some evidence of a long-term relationship in overeducation rates between these countries. This arguably suggests that they should be subject to a particular policy response. Outside of this, the table indicates no clear pattern, with some evidence of cointegration between countries in the Central, Eastern, and Peripheral groups.[12] The pairwise OLS results, presented in Table 18.5, reveal similar patterns. These findings of long-term relationships between several of the Central group countries and also between the Central and Eastern groups indicate that there are similarities in the general evolution of overeducation across certain countries, and they may justify a common policy approach for these countries. However, in a minority of countries, overeducation series were found not to be heavily correlated with those of other European countries; examples are Austria, Portugal, and Sweden, which exhibit little or no commonality in their overeducation series. This finding suggests that a common policy approach may not be appropriate for these countries.

In summary, the completed convergence evidence suggests that overeducation in Europe is likely to respond to a coordinated policy approach. However, overeducation in the Peripheral group appears to behave somewhat differently from the rest of Europe, suggesting that a separate policy response is likely to be required for this block of countries.

Although there is some evidence of completed convergence within and between the Central group countries and some Eastern group countries, it is still possible that the countries in our study are converging to a common overeducation rate. Ongoing convergence is feasible given that many countries were found to be stationary with a common trend, suggesting that they continue to rise or fall over time, whereas others were found to follow no discernible pattern or trend.

Next, we test for the presence of ongoing convergence over the period first quarter Q1/2003 to Q1/2010. This time period was chosen so as to maximize the number of countries that could be included in the model; nevertheless, the results remained unchanged when the model was tested on a longer time series including fewer countries.

Table 18.4 Phillips–Ouliaris cointegration statistics testing the existence of a long-term relationship (null hypothesis of no cointegration between paired countries against alternative hypothesis of stable cointegration relationship), 2001–2011

Country	Hungary	Poland	Romania	Slovak Republic	Norway	United Kingdom	Greece	Italy	Ireland	Spain
Cyprus	-3.242	-3.208	-3.292	-3.026	-3.921*	-3.585	-3.189	-3.346	-3.171	-3.613
Hungary		-3.122	-2.635	-2.401	-4.326**	-3.674*	-2.779	-4.951***	-2.221	-5.050***
Poland			-2.642	-2.846	-2.313	-3.111	-3.142	-3.451	-2.167	-3.674*
Romania				-3.161	-2.861	-2.594	-3.190	-2.978	-3.037	-3.660*
Slovak Republic					-4.108*	-3.793*	-5.204***	-4.674***	-4.683***	-4.463**
Norway						-3.280	-2.160	-4.651***	-2.810	-5.659***
United Kingdom							-2.824	-3.108	-2.558	-3.387
Greece								-4.348**	-3.814*	-3.912*
Italy									-1.976	-6.471***
Ireland										-3.903*

*$p < .10$.
**$p < .05$.
***$p < .01$.
Source: EU-LFS.

Table 18.5 Pairwise OLS estimates to examine the existence of long-term relationships between pairs of countries

Country	AT	BE	DE	DK	FI	FR	NL	SE	IS	LU	PT	BG	CZ	EE	LT	LV	SI
AT		−0.065	0.458***	0.056	0.002	0.385**	0.025	0.026	0.008	−0.017	0.101	−0.130	0.294	0.076	0.051	0.046	−0.045
BE			−0.468	−0.070	−0.447***	0.063	0.336***	−0.348*	−0.162*	0.113	−0.242	−0.303	−1.352***	0.066	0.245*	0.202**	−0.170
DE				0.175**	0.107	0.129	0.335**	0.014	0.111**	0.105	0.024	−0.148	0.725*	0.003	0.067	0.145*	−0.212*
DK					−0.319**	0.255	0.270***	−0.103	0.156	−0.090	−0.531***	−0.704***	−0.466	−0.090	0.039	0.121	−0.084
FI						−0.496***	−0.087	−0.516*	0.038	−0.054	−0.039	0.153	1.250***	−0.044	0.254**	−0.144**	−0.029
FR							0.050	0.306***	−0.056	−0.017	0.213**	0.011	0.346	−0.053	−0.259***	−0.092	0.142
NL								−0.709***	0.064	−0.032	−0.578***	−0.684***	−1.185***	0.311***	0.433***	0.442***	−0.579***
SE									−0.031	0.063**	0.074	−0.020	−0.418**	−0.041	−0.086	0.050	−0.088
IS										0.265	−0.854**	−0.436	−0.010	0.294	0.571**	0.315	−0.270
LU											−0.678*	0.462	−3.373***	0.514**	0.647***	0.699***	−1.286***
PT												0.144	−0.294	−0.078	0.062	−0.090	−0.050
BG													0.139	−0.023	−0.037	−0.079	−0.030
CZ														−0.015	0.062	−0.034	0.028
EE															0.792***	0.478***	−1.009***
LT																0.033	−0.080
LV																	−0.316
SI																	

Country	AT	BE	DE	DK	FI	FR	NL	SE	IS	LU	PT	BG	CZ	EE	LT	LV	SI
AT																	
BE	-0.222																
DE	0.439***	-0.112															
DK	0.234	-0.084	0.811**														
FI	-0.064	-0.186***	0.143	-0.047													
FR	0.302**	0.014	0.128	0.048	0.057												
NL	0.044	0.402***	0.493**	0.307**	-0.461***	0.112											
SE	-0.032	0.081**	0.094	0.031	-0.138*	0.106	0.105***										
IS	0.073	-0.452*	1.601**	0.361	-0.451	-0.689	0.351	-0.851**									
LU	-0.159	0.301	0.752	-0.198	-1.363***	-0.198	-0.165	-1.135***	0.252								
PT	0.142	0.095	0.119	-0.097	-0.042	0.160	-0.061	0.331	-0.095	0.035							
BG	-0.184	-0.105	-0.128	-0.232***	0.116	0.021	-0.188**	0.085	-0.064	0.071	0.167						
CZ	0.073	-0.088***	0.165**	0.053**	0.154***	-0.090	-0.012	-0.213**	0.054***	-0.053**	-0.034	-0.016					
EE	0.388	0.142	0.020	-0.184	-0.389**	-0.348	0.561***	-1.142***	0.157	0.288**	-0.687***	-0.112	-1.108**				
LT	0.280	0.041	0.261	-0.031	0.566***	-0.724***	0.056	-0.680	0.092	-0.020	0.104	-0.030	0.898	0.212**			
LV	0.348	0.229	0.670**	0.218	-0.690***	0.317	0.725***	0.844	-0.018	0.050	-0.322	-0.531***	-1.066	0.294*	0.070		
SI	-0.195	0.043	-0.470**	0.092	-0.075	-0.155	-0.277***	-0.390	0.062	-0.189***	-0.121	-0.214	0.594	-0.326***	-0.042	-0.077	

*p < .10.
**p < .05.
***p < .01.

Source: EU-LFS.

Table 18.6 Barro regression results: Time period Q1/2003–Q1/2012 for 26 countries

Overeducation shares	Coefficients
Total overeducation	−0.033***(0.009)
Female overeducation	−0.036**(0.011)
Male overeducation	−0.032***(0.008)

*p < .10.
**p < .05.
***p < .01.

Ongoing convergence would imply that overeducation increased at a faster rate between 2003 and 2010 in countries that had a lower initial overeducation rate in 2003. This is equivalent to a negative and significant β_1 coefficient in the Barro regression from Eq. (18.3). Conversely, a positive and significant coefficient would be indicative of divergence. The coefficients from the Barro models are presented in Table 18.6 and indicate that ongoing convergence was a feature of the time period. The results suggest that there is a tendency for countries to converge toward a common overeducation rate over time for all measures of overeducation.

It may be the case that the degree of ongoing convergence varies among groups of countries with common structural, geographical, and historical features. It is not possible to estimate Barro regressions separately for our three groups because the sample size is too small. In order to overcome this difficulty, we assess the rate of ongoing convergence by plotting the variance of overeducation rates across countries, on the grounds that ongoing convergence would be consistent with a falling variance over time. Plotting the variance across all countries confirms the results from Table 18.6 that ongoing convergence did occur over the time period (Figures 18.2–18.4). However, the aggregate picture appears to conceal substantial variation because it is apparent that ongoing convergence was more modest in the Central group relative to the Eastern and Peripheral groups (Figures 18.5–18.7).

18.5. DETERMINANTS OF YOUTH OVEREDUCATION

We now bring the analysis full circle by using the EU-LFS data to calculate a number of additional variables that can potentially explain movements in youth overeducation within countries. Specifically, for each country for each quarter, we compute variables measuring the labor force shares of migrants, the employment shares of workers who are part-time and workers who are temporary, the shares of workers employed in various sectors (administration, sales, and

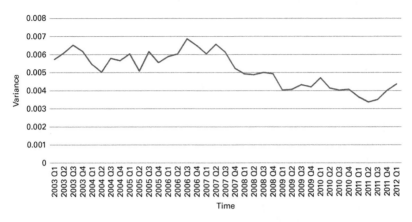

Figure 18.2 Variance in total overeducation across countries from Q1/2003 to Q1/2012 (26 countries).

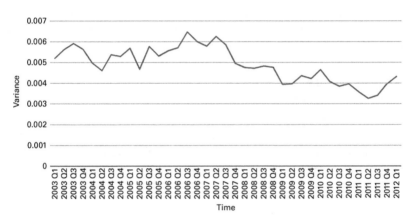

Figure 18.3 Variance in adult overeducation across countries from Q1/2003 to Q1/2012 (26 countries).

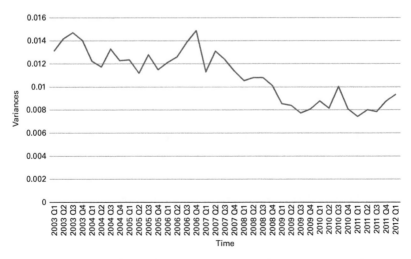

Figure 18.4 Variance in youth overeducation across countries from Q1/2003 to Q1/2012 (26 countries).

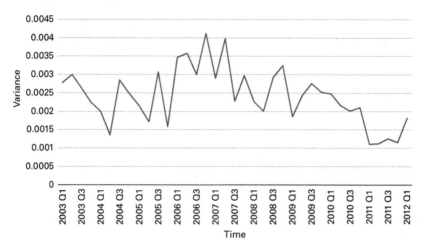

Figure 18.5 Variance in total overeducation across Central group countries from Q1/2003 to Q1/2012 (Austria, Belgium, Denmark, Finland, France, Iceland, Luxembourg, Netherlands, Norway, Sweden, and United Kingdom).

manufacturing), the unemployment rate, and the participation rate. We also compute a number of variables related to relative educational supply, specifically (1) the ratio of workers employed in professional occupations to graduates in employment and (2) the ratio of workers employed in professional occupations to workers in low-skilled occupations. Whereas the first variable is designed as a straightforward measure of graduate oversupply, the second is intended to pick up

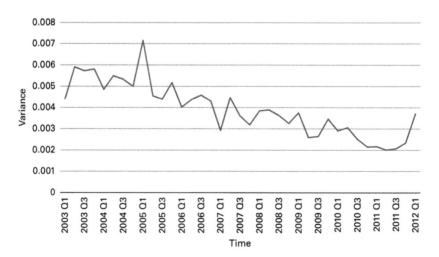

Figure 18.6 Variance in total overeducation across Eastern group countries from Q1/2003 to Q1/2012 (Bulgaria, Czech Republic, Estonia, Hungary, Romania, Slovak Republic, and Slovenia).

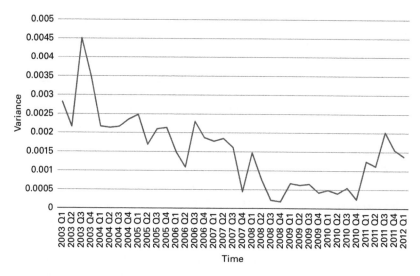

Figure 18.7 Variance in total overeducation across Peripheral group countries from Q1/2003 to Q1/2012 (Greece, Ireland, Italy, Portugal, and Spain).

the effects of skill-biased technological change, which is generally associated with a shift in relative demand away from high-skilled and toward low-skilled labor and in many countries with a general hollowing out of mid-skilled occupations. In addition to the variables calculated from the individual labor force surveys, we also derive some indicators from external data sources, and where necessary, annual data are interpolated to quarterly data series. Information on gross domestic product (GDP) per capita and R&D spending was sourced from Eurostat and the OECD.[13] Information on the number of students enrolled in tertiary and vocational programs was sourced from the OECD and standardized by age cohort using the EU-LFS data.[14]

   A number of patterns are present in the results shown in Table 18.7. In the model that combines the data across all countries, the results suggest that overeducation declines with an increase in part-time employment, labor force participation, and manufacturing employment. Conversely, overeducation was found to rise with increases in the share of temporary workers and in employment in the sales and hotel sectors. The results are difficult to interpret because, on the one hand, the finding with respect to part-time workers suggests that overeducation tends to be lower in more flexible labor markets, whereas on the other hand, the finding related to temporary workers suggests the opposite. The estimates suggest that the higher the overall participation rate and GDP per capita, the lower the youth overeducation rate. To the extent that a rise in the participation rate is generally accompanied by increases in wage rates and general labor demand, the results suggest that youth overeducation will tend to

Table 18.7 Determinants of youth overeducation for countries with stationary series (fixed-effects model)

Dependent variable: Youth overeducation	(1)	(2)	(3)	(4)
Variable	All countries	Central group	Eastern group	Peripheral group
Lagged youth overeducation	0.45***	0.35***	0.17***	0.35***
	(0.030)	(0.041)	(0.063)	(0.101)
% Migrants in labor force	−0.03	0.09	−0.11**	−0.26
	(0.042)	(0.077)	(0.056)	(0.455)
% Temporary workers	0.13**	−0.02	0.20	0.46*
	(0.060)	(0.091)	(0.152)	(0.269)
Overall unemployment rate	0.01	0.18	−0.07	0.06
	(0.052)	(0.144)	(0.078)	(0.249)
% Part-time workers	−0.33***	−0.38***	0.04	−0.78**
	(0.070)	(0.091)	(0.176)	(0.352)
% Employed in public administration	−0.14	0.52	−0.40	0.62
	(0.244)	(0.365)	(0.376)	(1.023)
% Employed in sales and hotels	0.44***	0.69***	−0.03	−0.66
	(0.149)	(0.237)	(0.227)	(0.648)
Overall participation rate	−0.21***	−0.22	−0.02	0.79
	(0.078)	(0.134)	(0.118)	(0.511)
Ratio of employed in occupations 2, 3 to grads in employment	−0.02	−0.01	−0.07***	−0.00
	(0.011)	(0.021)	(0.019)	(0.055)
Ratio of workers in high (2, 3) to low (7, 8, 9) ISCO	0.03**	0.02	0.03	0.06
	(0.010)	(0.012)	(0.032)	(0.086)
Share of manufacturing	−0.20*	−0.31**	−0.26	0.16
	(0.107)	(0.150)	(0.167)	(0.694)
Ratio of tertiary students to population (aged 20–24 years)	0.06***	0.05**	−0.15**	3.41**
	(0.022)	(0.028)	(0.072)	(1.327)
Ratio of vocational students to population (aged 15–19 years)	−0.04**	−0.04*	0.03	−2.35**
	(0.016)	(0.021)	(0.048)	(1.121)
Ln GDP per capita	−0.04***	−0.09**	−0.06***	0.03
	(0.016)	(0.036)	(0.021)	(0.086)
R&D expenditure	0.02***	0.02***	−0.01	−0.02
	(0.005)	(0.008)	(0.010)	(0.030)
Constant	0.57***	0.99***	0.80***	−0.55
	(0.140)	(0.354)	(0.173)	(0.664)

Table 18.7 Continued

Dependent variable: Youth overeducation	(1)	(2)	(3)	(4)
Variable	All countries	Central group	Eastern group	Peripheral group
No. of observations	903	491	284	128
R^2	0.32	0.31	0.24	0.76
No. of countries	21	11	7	3
Prob > F	0.00	0.00	0.00	0.00

Note: Standard errors in parentheses. Ln = Natural Log.
*$p < .10$.
**$p < .05$.
***$p < .01$.

decline as general labor market conditions tighten. In the context of the model, the participation rate and GDP per capita tend to capture changing labor market demand more effectively compared to the unemployment rate. The measure relating to skill-biased technological change is positive, suggesting that youth overeducation is increasing as a consequence of declining relative demand for unskilled labor. This suggests that as the labor market restructures, jobs that were traditionally occupied by poorly educated workers are now being occupied by workers with higher levels of schooling. The results suggest that higher R&D spending has a positive effect on the youth overeducation rate. At first glance, this result seems counterintuitive because one would expect countries with higher R&D spending to have more high-skilled jobs so that, all else being equal, this would have a negative impact on overeducation. However, it could be the case that this does not apply to the youth cohort given that a certain level of experience may be required for such jobs. Finally, the aggregate model provides consistent support for the view that overeducation will be higher in countries with comprehensive-based education systems and lower in countries providing viable vocational alternatives.

When the model is estimated separately for country groupings, we find that many of the results hold, although some variations exist. For example, within the Eastern group, the relative balance between vocational and comprehensive-based education appears less important, whereas overeducation was found to decrease along with an increase in the availability of graduate-level jobs and in migrants in the labor force. Within the Central and Peripheral groups, the share of part-time employment was found to have a strong negative effect, but no significant effect was found for the Eastern group. The positive temporary worker effect observed within the aggregate model was only evident for the Peripheral group.

18.6. CONCLUSIONS

Overeducation is known to be costly to workers, and it also has negative implications for firms and the wider macroeconomy. To date, the vast body of research in the area has focused on examining the incidence and impacts of overeducation within countries. This chapter represents one of the few existing attempts to examine patterns of overeducation within countries, while the adoption of a time-series approach enables the identification of common trends across Europe. The evidence suggests that although overeducation rates in Europe are converging upward over time, the general pattern of overeducation is linked across many countries, suggesting that the phenomenon responds in a similar way to external shocks and, consequently, is likely to react in similar ways to appropriate policy interventions. However, the research indicates that overeducation within the Peripheral group is evolving somewhat differently compared to the rest of Europe, suggesting that a separate policy response is likely to be appropriate.

Although the overall model results are complex for the determinants of youth overeducation, a number of impacts are consistently present for all or most country groupings. Specifically, youth overeducation is highly driven by the composition of education provision and will tend to be lower in countries with more developed vocational pathways. Furthermore, youth overeducation tends to be heavily related to the level of aggregate labor demand, proxied in the model by variations in the participation rate and GDP per capita. Finally, youth overeducation tends to be lower the higher the employment share of part-time workers, suggesting that the phenomenon may be partly driven by labor market flexibility.

So what form are appropriate policy interventions likely to take? Although much remains unknown with respect to the drivers of overeducation, a number of recent studies have identified some key factors that influence overeducation across countries. The research by Verhaest and van der Velden (2012) and by Davia et al. (2017) suggests that overeducation is, at least to some degree, related to an excess supply of university graduates, implying that education policy should take closer account of the demand for graduate labor before agreeing to further increases in the number of university places. However, responsible education expansion is likely to be only part of the policy response, given that the study by McGuinness and Pouliakas (2017) identified a number of policy areas likely to be effective in tackling the problem of overeducation. Overeducation is partly related to inferior human capital, suggesting that policies aimed at improving the job readiness of students will help alleviate the problem (McGuinness and Pouliakas 2017; McGuinness, Whelan, and Bergin 2016). For example, increasing the practical aspects of degree programs, irrespective of the field of study, was found to reduce the incidence of initial mismatch for graduates (McGuinness et al. 2016). Job conditions are also part of the problem, with the research suggesting that policies targeted at improving job quality and flexibility will also make a positive contribution (McGuinness and Pouliakas 2017). Finally, the quality of information that individuals acquire about a potential job before deciding to accept the post is also important, as is the method of job search that is undertaken (McGuinness and Pouliakas 2017; McGuinness et al. 2016), leading to the conclusion that policy initiatives that facilitate a smoother and more informed route into the labor market should also be pursued. For example, higher education work placements with the potential to develop into permanent posts and the provision of higher education job-placement assistance were found to have substantial impacts in reducing the incidence of graduate mismatch (McGuinness et al. 2016). Therefore, there are many initiatives that have the potential to lessen the impact of overeducation, and the research presented here suggests that many of these can be facilitated and coordinated at a central European level.

NOTES

1   Although their earnings are penalized relative to matched workers with similar levels of schooling, overeducated workers enjoy a wage premium relative to workers with lower levels of education doing the same job (McGuinness 2006).

2   Pouliakas (2013) measured overeducation subjectively by comparing individual levels of education with the modal level of education in the chosen occupation. The study demonstrates that overeducation in the EU25 would have increased much more rapidly between 2001 and 2009 had occupational entry requirements remained at their 2001 levels.

3   There is ample evidence in the literature of a higher prevalence of overeducation among graduates from fields such as Arts and Social Sciences.

4   Derived from factor analyses carried out on subjective variables.

5   Deviations of the observed rate from the natural rate.

6   Measured by the ratio between the share of workers with ISCED-5 educational attainment and the share of workers in professional-directive occupations— that is, ISCO groups I and II, which consist of legislators; senior officials and managers; corporate managers; managers of small enterprises; physical, mathematical, and engineering science professionals; life science and health professionals; teaching professionals; and other professionals.

7   The descriptive analysis and the tests for long-term relationships also include Cyprus, Croatia, and Germany. These countries are excluded from later analysis because of missing or incomplete data.

8   The augmented Dickey–Fuller (ADF) test is the most commonly used test for this purpose, but it can behave poorly, especially in the presence of serial correlation. Dickey and Fuller correct for serial correlation by including

lagged difference terms in the regression; however, the size and power of the ADF test are sensitive to the number of these terms. The nonparametric test developed by Phillips (1987) and Phillips and Perron (1988) allows for both heteroskedasticity and serial correlation in the error term.

9 For the remaining seven countries, where overeducation was found to be more volatile, OLS can only be applied after each series is differenced a sufficient number of times to induce stationarity.

10 Our dependent variable runs from 0 to 1, and a standard panel regression may generate predicted values that lie outside the 0 to 1 interval. However, the incidence of overeducation typically lies in the range of 10%–30%. This implies that there is no clustering around the extreme values of 0 or 1 and suggests that the use of a fractional outcome variable is not highly problematic in this instance.

11 The 15- to 24-year-old age group was chosen on the basis that it allowed us to observe overeducation among young people across all levels of educational attainment.

12 The results for the Slovak Republic are somewhat implausible and should be treated with caution because a visual inspection of the data suggests that the series is stationary, contrary to the test statistic result.

13 Gross domestic expenditure on R&D from the OECD was used.

14 Some existing research has indicated that overeducation tends to be lower in countries with more developed vocational pathways (Mavromaras and McGuinness 2012).

REFERENCES

Barro, Robert J. 1997. *Determinants of Economic Growth: A Cross-Country Empirical Study*. Cambridge, MA: MIT Press.

Davia, M. A., McGuinness, S., and O'Connell, P. J. 2017. "Determinants of regional differences in rates of overeducation in Europe." *Social Science Research* 63: 67–80.

Flisi, Sara, Valentina Goglio, Elena Meroni, Margarida Rodrigues, and Esperanza Vera-Toscano. 2014. "Occupational Mismatch in Europe: Understanding Overeducation and Overskilling for Policy Making." JRC Science and Policy Report. Luxembourg: European Commission.

Mavromaras, Kostas, and Seamus McGuinness. 2012. "Overskilling Dynamics and Education Pathways." *Economics of Education Review* 31 (5): 619–28.

McGuinness, Seamus. 2006. "Overeducation in the Labour Market." *Journal of Economic Surveys* 20 (3): 387–418.

McGuinness, Seamus, Adele Whelan, and Adele Bergin. 2016. "Is There a Role for Higher Education Institutions in Improving the Quality of First Employment?" *BE Journal of Economic Analysis and Policy* 16 (4): 12–23.

McGuinness, Seamus, and Pouliakas, K. 2017. "Deconstructing theories of overeducation in Europe: a wage decomposition approach." In S. Polachek, K. Pouliakas, G. Russo, and K. Tatsiramos (eds) *Skill Mismatch in Labor Markets* (Research in Labor Economics, Volume 45), Emerald. Publishing Limited, Bingley, UK, 81–127.

McGuinness, S., Pouliakas, K., and Redmond, P. 2018. "Skills mismatch: concepts, measurement and policy approaches." *Journal of Economic Surveys.* doi:10.1111/joes.12254

Phillips, Peter C. B. 1987. "Time Series Regression with a Unit Root." *Econometrica* 55: 227–301.

Phillips, Peter C. B., and Pierre Perron. 1988. "Testing for Unit Roots in Time Series Regression." *Biometrika* 75: 335–46.

Pouliakas, Konstantinos. 2012. "The skill mismatch challenge in Europe." In *European Commission* (ed.). Employment and social developments in Europe. Luxembourg: Publications Office, 351–394.

Quintini, Glenda. 2011. "Over-Qualified or Under-Skilled: A Review of the Existing Literature." OECD Social, Employment and Migration Working Paper 121. Paris: Organization for Economic Co-operation and Development.

Verhaest, Dieter, and Rolf van der Velden. 2012. "Cross-Country Differences in Graduate Overeducation." *European Sociological Review* 29 (3): 642–53.

19

DO SCARRING EFFECTS VARY BY ETHNICITY AND GENDER?

Carolina V. Zuccotti and Jacqueline O'Reilly

19.1. INTRODUCTION

There is a substantive literature showing that the poor labor market integration of young people can have long-term negative impacts on their adult lives—for example, by increasing the probability of subsequent periods of unemployment or by affecting their income (for the United Kingdom, see Gregg 2001; for the Netherlands, see Luijkx and Wolbers 2009; for Germany, see Schmillen and Möller 2012; Schmillen and Umkehrer 2013; for the United States, see Mroz and Savage 2006). We also know that migrants and their children perform differently in the labor market compared to majoritarian populations. In particular, those coming from developing countries are often disadvantaged in terms of access to jobs, as shown both in cross-national (Heath and Cheung 2007) and in country-specific studies (Carmichael and Woods 2000; Silberman and Fournier 2008; Heath and Li 2010; Kogan 2011; Zuccotti 2015a). However, research that focuses on dynamics into and out of employment, or on the impact of early labor market outcomes on later employment or occupational outcomes for different ethnic groups, is less common (some exceptions are Kalter and Kogan 2006; Demireva and Kesler 2011; Mooi-Reci and Ganzeboom 2015). In particular, surprisingly little is known about how early job insecurity affects different ethnic groups in the labor market over time.

In this chapter, we address this gap in the literature by examining the impact of the early labor market status of young individuals in the United

Kingdom (in 2001) on their employment probabilities and occupational status 10 years later (in 2011), focusing on how this varies across ethnic groups and by gender. In particular, we are interested in whether an early experience of being NEET (not in employment, education, or training) affects later labor market outcomes. Our analysis is based on the Office for National Statistics Longitudinal Study (ONS-LS), a data set linking census records for a 1% sample of the population of England and Wales across five successive censuses (1971, 1981, 1991, 2001, and 2011). We study individuals who are aged between 16 and 29 years in 2001 and follow them up in 2011, when they are between 26 and 39 years old. The focus is on second-generation minority groups born in the United Kingdom; we also include individuals who arrived in the United Kingdom at a young age.

Understanding how early labor market experiences affect later outcomes for different ethnic groups (and genders within them) is of crucial importance (see Berloffa et al., this volume), especially in countries where the number of ethnic minorities is considerable and increasing. On the one hand, this knowledge enables a better understanding of integration processes over time; on the other hand, it can contribute to the development of more targeted policies, given the dramatic rise in youth unemployment since the 2008 crisis (Bell and Blanchflower 2010; Eurofound 2014; O'Reilly et al. 2015). The United Kingdom represents a valuable opportunity for a case study for this purpose, given its long-standing ethnic minority population, which includes a large and diverse number of second-generation minorities. The groups studied here—Indian, Pakistani, Bangladeshi, and Caribbean (compared with White British)—are also very varied in terms of levels of educational and economic resources, cultural values and religion, and degrees of spatial segregation (Modood et al. 1997; Phillips 1998; Platt 2007; Longhi, Nicoletti, and Platt 2013; Catney and Sabater 2015; Crawford and Greaves 2015; Catney 2016). These differences allow us to explore a range of expectations as to why "scars" related to poor early labor market integration might differ across groups.

We find that the transmission of disadvantage occurs differently across ethnic groups and genders: Some groups/genders perform better (and others worse) in terms of overcoming an initial disadvantaged situation. In particular, Asian men appear to be in a better relative position compared to White British men— a finding that challenges preconceptions about ethnic minorities always performing poorly in the British labor market.

In the next section, we present previous studies on scarring effects and ethnic inequalities, identifying the main mechanisms and discussing why these might vary across ethnic groups and genders. After outlining the data and methods used, we perform the analyses separately for employment and occupational outcomes. Finally, we conclude and discuss our findings.

19.2. LITERATURE REVIEW AND THEORY

19.2.1. The long-term effects of youth nonemployment

Experiencing periods of unemployment or inactivity while young has been shown to have both short- and long-term negative effects for labor market outcomes. In the United Kingdom, several studies have addressed this issue (Kirchner Sala et al. 2015). Using the National Child Development Study (NCDS; a UK data set following a cohort born in 1958), Gregg (2001) examines the extent to which nonemployment[1] (i.e., unemployment or another inactive situation, excluding students) experienced between the ages of 16 and 23 years (measured when individuals were 23 years old in 1981) has an effect on later work experiences (when individuals are aged between 28 and 33 years). He shows that conditional on background characteristics such as education, family socioeconomic status, and neighborhood unemployment, men who experience an extra 3 months of being nonemployed before age 23 years face an extra 1.3 months out of employment between the ages of 28 and 33 years, whereas for women the effect is approximately half as strong. Kalwij (2004), who follows individuals who turned 18 years between 1982 and 1998 and were registered as unemployed at least once during this period, presents evidence pointing in the same direction. He demonstrates that the longer the previous spell of unemployment, the lower the probability of finding a job later. Specifically, 2 years in unemployment decreases the probability of becoming employed by 31%. Similarly, analyzing the British Household Panel Survey (BHPS), Crawford et al. (2010) show that individuals who were NEET at 18 or 19 years old have an almost 20% greater chance of being unemployed 10 years later, compared to individuals who were either studying or working at the same age. More recently, Dorsett and Lucchino (2014), using the BHPS to study transitions up to age 24 years, show that the longer one remains in employment, the lower the chance of becoming unemployed, whereas the longer an individual remains unemployed or inactive, the less likely he or she is to find employment.

Some authors have examined scarring effects in terms of wage outcomes. For example, using the NCDS, Gregg and Tominey (2005) find that given equal characteristics (including education), 13 months of unemployment between ages 16 and 23 years (vs. being always employed) reduces income by 20% at ages 23 and 33 years and by 13% at age 43 years. They also find that even when individuals do not experience unemployment after the age of 23 years, a wage scar of between 9% and 11% remains. Crawford et al. (2010) demonstrate that individuals who were NEET at ages 18 or 19 years had significantly lower wages when aged 28 or 29 years compared to individuals who were either working or studying at the same age; this held even when they shared similar characteristics, such as comparable education and parental background.

Scarring effects may vary in their intensity depending on the highest level of education achieved or the qualifications of individuals. Kalwij (2004), for example, shows that highly skilled men have greater chances of exiting and weaker chances of re-entering unemployment compared to low-skilled men. Burgess et al. (2003), analyzing data from the UK Labour Force Survey (UK-LFS), show that although the effect of early career unemployment is to reduce later employment chances for those with lower or no educational qualifications, the opposite occurs among those with higher educational qualifications. Schmelzer (2011), examining occupational outcomes, arrives at a similar finding. He shows that individuals with higher levels of education do not suffer as a result of early career unemployment; in fact, their stronger resources allow them to stay longer in this situation while waiting for better job offers (see Filandri, Nazio, and O'Reilly, this volume). Individuals with lower education levels, by contrast, are penalized in terms of their future occupations—an outcome that is generally attributed to gaps in their human capital accumulation. It is also possible that these periods outside of employment or education send negative signals to employers.

In summary, a wealth of research on early labor market experiences reveals how crucial these are for later life outcomes. These experiences vary by educational attainment, with the lowest qualified being the most negatively affected later in life. Clearly, such findings are very significant, given the heightened rates of youth unemployment being seen across Europe—both preceding and exacerbated by the 2008 financial crisis (O'Reilly et al. 2015).

19.2.2. Ethnicity and labor market outcomes in the United Kingdom

Western European countries have a long history of immigration, often connected to processes of economic reconstruction. In the United Kingdom, there has been a long-term pattern of Irish migration; however, immigration intensified in the postwar period with the arrival of the first waves of Caribbean migrants in the late 1940s, who were subsequently followed by Indians and Pakistanis and—later—by Chinese, Bangladeshis, and Africans. Today, more than 10% of the population in the United Kingdom self-defines as non-White, and this includes both first-generation migrants and their second-generation children.

In general, studies are in agreement that although problems such as unemployment (Heath and Cheung 2007) and low income (Longhi et al. 2013) are still faced by several ethnic groups in Western European countries, especially the visible non-White groups, the children of immigrants are in a better situation compared to their parents in terms both of education (Brinbaum and Cebolla-Boado 2007; van de Werfhorst and van Tubergen 2007) and of labor market outcomes (Heath and Cheung 2007; Alba and Foner 2015). In the United Kingdom, efforts have been made to develop policies and laws to help these groups integrate (Cheung and Heath 2007), and these initiatives have probably encouraged the processes of social mobility we observe today (Platt 2007). For example, whereas first generations are more often concentrated in low-qualified jobs (Zuccotti 2015b), their children have similar (Pakistanis, Bangladeshis, and Caribbeans) or even higher (Indian) rates of participation in professional and managerial occupations compared to White British. Regarding access to jobs, unemployment has historically been one of the main problems concerning ethnic minorities' labor market integration. However, trends show an improvement in employment levels for all groups in the adult population. For example, the unemployment level for Pakistanis and Bangladeshis declined from 25% in 1991 to approximately 10% in 2011; Indians had practically the same unemployment level as the White British (approximately 6%) in 2011; and the unemployment level of Caribbean men, although still relatively high (16%), has improved since 1991 (Nazroo and Kapadia 2013). Of course, there are also gender differences in this respect, with Pakistani and Bangladeshi women still being characterized by high unemployment and inactivity levels (House of Commons Women and Equalities Committee 2016). Moreover, although studies have shown that some of the differences in employment levels across groups are connected to education (Cheung and Heath 2007), social origins, and neighborhood deprivation (Zuccotti 2015b), discrimination continues to be a key problem faced by ethnic minorities (Heath and Cheung 2006).

19.2.3. A longitudinal view on ethnicity and labor market outcomes

The studies on ethnic inequalities presented so far are either restricted to certain time points or, if applied to several years, do not really discuss changes within individuals or individual-level changes in labor market performance over time. A recent work by Demireva and Kesler (2011) sheds some light on this matter. Using data from the UK Quarterly Labour Force Survey (1992–2008), Demireva and Kesler study transitions into and out of employment for different migrant and native groups. In accordance with previous studies, they corroborate the idea that higher education plays a positive role in these transitions. In terms of ethnicity, they show that men born in the New Commonwealth (which includes the Caribbean, India, Pakistan, and Bangladesh) are more likely than the White British to remain in or to move into unemployment/inactivity between two consecutive quarters of a year. Among second-generation immigrants, the authors note that men are more likely to remain in unemployment compared to equivalent White British; women are also more likely to move from unemployment to inactivity compared to their White British counterparts. However, group differences within second generations are not further developed—a limitation of this work that we address in the current study.

Related studies have been carried out in other European countries (see Reyneri and Fullin 2011 and other articles in the same journal issue) and in comparison with North America (Alba and Foner 2015), with results varying according to institutional factors and labor market characteristics. An analysis of 10 (pooled)

Western European countries found that non-EU15 immigrants generally have higher probabilities of remaining in unemployment between two years (Reyneri and Fullin 2011). More recently, a study in the Netherlands (Mooi-Reci and Ganzeboom 2015)—a country that, like the United Kingdom, has a relatively long history of immigration—has examined the concept of scars and how these might vary according to the migrant status of individuals. Using the Dutch Labor Supply Panel (covering data between 1980 and 2000), the authors examine income as an outcome and explore how previous unemployment experiences affect re-employment income for native Dutch and foreign-born individuals. They find that individuals born outside of the Netherlands receive lower re-employment income compared to Dutch counterparts with similar unemployment experiences.

Often, ethnic minorities and foreign-born individuals are more exposed to unemployment/inactivity compared to their majoritarian host-country counterparts. Most important, these events seem to have particularly pronounced scarring effects in later life for these groups, including weaker employment chances and lower re-employment income. This chapter focuses on how the early labor market experiences of young people in different second-generation minority groups affect their later outcomes. Although, according to the literature discussed previously, more severe scarring might be expected among second-generation ethnic minorities, the recent improvements in terms of employment and occupation might actually point in the opposite direction.

19.2.4. Highlighting mechanisms: Human capital decay versus stigma

When searching for explanations as to why an early experience of inactivity or unemployment might affect later labor market outcomes, the literature has highlighted two in particular: human capital decay and stigma (Omori 1997; Schmelzer 2011). These explanations focus mainly on employers' recruitment practices. Human capital decay suggests that in periods of nonemployment, individuals lose vital work experience, which in turn might reduce their future employability and earnings. Stigma-related explanations, on the other hand, suggest that employers judge future employees' capabilities based on their unobserved trajectory of employment and nonemployment. In other words, they infer workers' qualities based on their past employment status. In this context, previous unemployment spells have a negative stigma (e.g., when one assumes that individuals are unemployed because they are lazy), which might then affect later employment probabilities and income prospects. However, as suggested by Mooi-Reci and Ganzeboom (2015), stigma might also be related to how employers infer characteristics of individuals based on their ethnic origins. For example, if employers believe that an ethnic minority group has certain negative characteristics in terms of employability—such as an educational degree obtained abroad, language deficiencies, or their concentration in deprived neighborhoods—a period of unemployment or inactivity might exacerbate these negative preconceptions and stereotypes, affecting future employment probabilities, type of occupation, or income. These authors' empirical analysis regarding the Netherlands presents evidence in this direction.

To what extent can we see stigma mechanisms connected to ethnicity occurring in the United Kingdom? First, there is evidence of discrimination in the labor market (Heath and Cheung 2006; Wood et al. 2009). In particular, experimental studies have demonstrated that employers usually prefer White British compared to other ethnic groups, especially Asians and Blacks. Although the reasons behind this preference are still to be explored, we could argue that a period of unemployment or inactivity might affect some ethnic minority groups in particular negative ways and independently of whether they were born in the United Kingdom or abroad. For example, Pakistani and Bangladeshi populations have historically worked in relatively lower qualified jobs and have been spatially concentrated in the most deprived areas (Phillips 1998; Robinson and Valeny 2005). This negative signal in terms of where employers view these populations in the social structure (which could affect their views on these groups' productivity, for instance) might contribute to how they perceive their nonemployment experiences and thus help create a particularly profound scar for them.

However, for other groups, we might observe other processes taking place. We argued that scars are lighter (or not present) among highly educated individuals, partly because employers do not view a period of unemployment for highly educated individuals particularly negatively (Schmelzer 2011), assuming them to be searching for an appropriately qualified job. In terms of ethnic differences and how employers perceive groups, this might benefit Indians, in particular. This group has very high rates of university achievement, which could be observed as a positive signal for employers in terms of group characteristics. A period of unemployment or inactivity might therefore be more "legitimate" for Indians than for other groups, which would be observed in a lower scarring effect of unemployment/inactivity on this group.

Mooi-Reci and Ganzeboom (2015) also suggest that employers' perceptions might vary by gender. They argue that immigrant women from poorer countries are more likely to be perceived as more nurturing and obedient, which might weaken the stigma of joblessness. In the United Kingdom, this might apply to Pakistani and Bangladeshi women, who are also embedded in cultural contexts in which women are expected to stay at home (Peach 2005).

The group context or group characteristics, and how employers observe these, are therefore an argument for expecting variation in scars across ethnic groups. In line with this reasoning, Omori (1997) found that individuals who experienced unemployment in periods when unemployment was high were less penalized in terms of future employability compared to individuals who had been unemployed when unemployment levels were low. The context perceived by employers or, in our case, the perceived group context may therefore matter.

Until now, we have discussed employers; however, groups' perspectives, culture, and networks might also affect outcomes. For example, although it is true that Bangladeshi men are usually concentrated in poor areas and have low social backgrounds, there is evidence that second-generation Bangladeshis are doing quite well in the labor market: Not only do they not seem to experience ethnic penalties in employment (Zuccotti 2015b) but also they overperform compared to the White British in terms of the occupations they obtain. This finding might be connected to specific characteristics of Bangladeshis that make them more resilient to adverse situations. Hence, we might argue that they manage to better overcome a situation of early unemployment or inactivity. Similarly, with regard to the arguments concerning gender, given the strong role models in some Asian ethnic groups and the family and community pressures on women to remain out of the labor market (Dale et al. 2002a, 2002b; Kabeer 2002), we could argue that it might actually be particularly difficult for women to become employed if they have had early experiences of unemployment or inactivity. In summary, these arguments suggest that the role of (increased or decreased) stigma might not be the only explanation behind differences in the effect of early labor market statuses across groups.

19.3. DATA AND METHODS

19.3.1. The Office for National Statistics Longitudinal Study

Our analysis is based on the ONS-LS,[2] a unique data set collected by the Office for National Statistics in the United Kingdom that links census information for a 1% sample of the population of England and Wales, following individuals in 1971, 1981, 1991, 2001, and 2011. The original sample was selected from the 1971 Census, incorporating data on individuals born on one of four selected dates. The sample was updated at each successive census by taking individuals with the same four dates of birth in each year and linking them to the existing data (Hattersley and Creeser 1995). Life-event information has been added to the ONS-LS since the 1971 Census. New members enter the study through birth and immigration, and existing members leave through death and emigration. Some individuals might also exit the study (e.g., someone who goes to live abroad for a period) and then re-enter at a later census point; however, individuals are never "removed" from the data set, nor do they actively "leave" it.

Slightly more than 500,000 individuals can be found at each census point; however, information for people in the 1% sample who participated in more than one census point is more limited. For example, there is information on approximately 400,000 people at two census points, on average, whereas information is available on approximately 200,000 people for all five census points. In total, approximately 1,000,000 records are available for the entire period (1971–2011).

One of the most interesting aspects of this data set—in addition to its large sample size—is that both household and aggregated census data for small geographical areas can be attached to each individual and for each census point. This provides a reasonable idea of the "family contexts" and "neighborhoods" in which individuals live at different moments of their lives.

19.3.2. Sample

Our focus is on young individuals aged between 16 and 29 years in 2001, whom we follow through 2011, when they are between 26 and 39 years old. Different definitions have been given as to what it means to be young or to belong to the "youth population." The Office for National Statistics in the United Kingdom, for example, usually considers an age range of 16–24 years. We decided to use a slightly wider age range for two main reasons. First, we wanted to capture the increasingly lengthy and blurred trajectories into adulthood (Aassve, Iacovou, and Mencarini 2006); second, we could thus cover a larger sample of ethnic minorities. We performed robustness checks excluding individuals aged 25–29 years and found that the results remained robust to the findings shown here.

We constructed our sample in a way that permits more than one measurement per individual. Where individuals had more than one measurement for "family context" and "origin neighborhood" (obtained when they were between 0 and 15 years old, in 1981–1991), we counted these as two units of analysis. For example, we counted an individual twice if he or she was 21 years old in 2001 and had household and neighborhood information in both 1991 (when he or she was 11 years old) and 1981 (when he or she was 1 year old). This structure follows a model used previously by Platt (2007) and is common in works using panel-like data. In order to account for double measurement, we control for "origin year" (1981/1991) and we use clustered standard errors in the regression models. We have also estimated a model in which one origin year per individual is randomly chosen and the results remain the same. The total sample consists of 77,180 cases, out of which 73% are "unique" individuals.

19.3.3. Variables and methods

We study two outcome variables in 2011: employment status and occupational status. These are examined in relation to labor market status in 2001. We observe individuals with different statuses in 2001—NEET (i.e., "unemployed and inactive," including individuals doing housework, with long-term illness or disability, and other inactive), employed, and students—and ascertain their employment and occupational trajectories in 2011. The focus is on the potential negative effect that being out of employment and out of education might have on later labor market outcomes and how this varies by ethnicity and gender (for a discussion on the concept of NEET, see Mascherini, this volume). Employment in 2011 is a dummy variable that determines whether the person was employed or not in 2011 (the reference category is unemployed/inactive, excluding students). Occupational status, on the other hand, is measured using the National Statistics Socio-economic Classification (NS-SEC) (Erikson and Goldthorpe 1992). The NS-SEC includes seven categories ranging from higher managerial/professional occupations to routine occupations. We study the probability of having a Class 1 or Class 2 occupation (vs. any other): Class 1 consists of higher managerial, administrative, and professional occupations, whereas Class 2 consists of lower managerial, administrative, and professional occupations. The occupations within these two classes are often regulated by so-called service relations, where "the employee renders service to the employer in return for compensation, which can be both immediate rewards (for example, salary) and long-term or prospective benefits (for example, assurances of security and career opportunities)" (Office for National Statistics 2010, 3). Note that occupational status refers to the current or most recent job.

We examine these trajectories across five ethnic groups: White British, Indian, Pakistani, Bangladeshi, and Caribbean. In this study, White British are those who identify themselves as White English/Welsh/Scottish/Northern Irish/British[3] and have both parents (or one parent, in the case of individuals raised in single-parent households) born in the United Kingdom. Ethnic minorities, on the other hand, are those who identify themselves as belonging to one of the main ethnic groups and have one (single-parent households) or two parents born abroad.[4] The parental country of birth is measured when individuals were between 0 and 15 years old in 1981–1991.

In studies of scarring effects, efforts are usually made to measure the actual scar in the best possible way. Often, we do not know all the variables that might affect an outcome. If such variables are present but we do not control for them, then we might be over(under)estimating the size of the scar. For example, if individuals of a certain group have characteristics that make them more likely to be unemployed, this will affect both the 2001 and the 2011 outcomes and will make the relationship between the two unemployment variables at the respective time points stronger than it is in reality. In order to reduce unobserved heterogeneity, we control for a wide range of key predictors of labor market status, including family arrangements and education in 2011 and the socioeconomic characteristics of the households in which individuals lived when they were between 0 and 15 years old. Household-level variables (found in the 1981 and 1991 census files) include number of cars, housing tenure, level of overcrowding in the home, and parental occupation (taking the highest status between the father and the mother). In addition, we also control for current-neighborhood deprivation and origin-neighborhood deprivation (when individuals were between 0 and 15 years old), both measured with the Carstairs Index (Norman, Boyle, and Rees 2005; Norman and Boyle 2014).[5] This measure is a summary of four dimensions: percentage male unemployment, percentage overcrowded households, percentage no car/van ownership, and percentage low social class.

The inclusion of variables that denote neighborhood characteristics—current and, most important, past—has been a commonly used tool by some authors (e.g., Gregg 2001) to control for the self-selection of individuals into their initial condition (in our case, labor market status in 2001) and hence reduce the impact of unobserved heterogeneity. In terms of our study, neighborhood deprivation when individuals are young is likely to affect labor market status in 2001 but less so labor market status in 2011, except through neighborhood deprivation in 2011 (which we control for). Most important, this variable has the advantage that young individuals probably did not choose the neighborhood where they lived when they were young (rather, their parents did).

Our model has, nevertheless, some limitations. First, we are not able to use (as Gregg (2001) does) more detailed neighborhood unemployment levels or types of jobs available in the area, which would be a better indicator of labor market conditions and availability of jobs. The ONS has restrictions regarding the use of neighborhood variables, and neighborhood deprivation is easy to access and is a commonly used variable among ONS-LS users. Note, however, that because we include students in our initial labor market statuses, neighborhood deprivation is probably a better variable than, for example, neighborhood unemployment alone, given that it includes indicators such as social class and socioeconomic resources of households, which might impact on decisions regarding school attendance. Second, we do not use an instrumental variable approach, as Gregg does: In other words, origin-neighborhood characteristics is not an instrument in our model (as it is in Gregg's study) but, rather, a control variable. The program we use to analyze our data (Stata 14) has limitations in terms of the commands for instrumental variables, and some tests led us to prefer a classic regression model.[6] Finally, a third limitation (that would also be present even with an instrumental variable approach) is that there might be unmeasured parental or group characteristics (e.g., parental aspirations or group preferences for certain areas) that affect individuals' outcomes as well as their selection of neighborhoods. If present, these unmeasured characteristics will weaken the origin-neighborhood deprivation's potential ability to randomize the allocation of individuals into areas and, hence, into initial statuses. In summary, we are aware that we cannot fully randomize the selection of individuals into their initial statuses in 2001, which means that we cannot be certain that the relationship between initial status and employment in 2011 is casual. The observed scar might therefore include some unmeasured characteristics of individuals, their parents, or the ethnic groups to which they belong.

Our multivariate analyses are based on average marginal effects derived from logistic regressions. In addition to the previously mentioned variables, other controls include age in 2001, country of birth, and number of census points in which the individual participated.

19.4. ANALYSIS

19.4.1. Descriptive statistics

Table 19.1 shows the percentage of individuals employed in 2011 and the percentage of individuals who declare a high occupational status (either presently or in the most recent job), distinguished by their labor market status in 2001, ethnic group, and gender.

For most groups, and as expected, having been employed or in education in 2001 leads to a greater likelihood of being employed in 2011 and to a greater likelihood of having a higher occupational status—compared to individuals who were unemployed or inactive (i.e., NEET) in 2001. In particular, those who were students in 2001 have high proportions in both employment and professional/managerial occupations in 2011, probably attributable to having a university degree. However, the extent to which education and employment in 2001 act as "protectors" in the labor market or, conversely, the extent to which unemployment and inactivity make people more "vulnerable" or generate "scars" varies greatly across ethnic groups and genders.

Having been NEET in 2001 (compared to having been employed) is not particularly detrimental for the labor market prospects of ethnic minorities compared to the White British. Only Caribbean women seem to follow this pattern as regards their employment probabilities (note that among those who were employed in 2001, White British and Caribbean women have similar employment probabilities in 2011, whereas this is 9% lower for Caribbeans among those who were NEET). In contrast, it is White British men who seem to experience deeper scars regarding employment, especially compared to Asian groups (Indian, Pakistani, and Bangladeshi). We observe that among those who were employed in 2001, employment probabilities in 2011 are similar across all groups, but having been NEET has a more detrimental effect on the likelihood of White British men being in employment in 2011. Approximately 59% of White British men who were NEET in 2001 are employed in 2011; for Indians, in particular, but also for Pakistani and Bangladeshi men, the percentage of employed is higher.

Table 19.1 also shows that although, in general, ethnic minority groups do not suffer very strongly from previous periods of unemployment or inactivity, sometimes having been employed in 2001 is not as protective for them as it is for the White British. For example, Caribbean men are similar to White British in terms of their employment probabilities among those who were NEET in 2001; however, they do not benefit from having been employed in 2001 to the same degree as White British men (they have approximately 10 percentage points less probability of being employed in 2011). A similar finding is observed among Pakistani and Bangladeshi men and women when studying occupational status. We observe that although differences with respect to White British are relatively small among those who were NEET in 2001, of those who were employed in

Table 19.1 Employed individuals and individuals with (current or most recent) professional/managerial status in 2011, by labor market status in 2001, ethnic group, and gender (%)

	Employed				Professional/managerial status			
	NEET	S	E	Total	NEET	S	E	Total
Men								
White British	58.9	92.0	93.6	89.8	22.8	59.1	42.8	44.4
Indian	77.6	91.8	91.0	90.1	37.7	69.8	55.2	60.2
Pakistani	64.8	86.0	91.2	84.1	21.6	45.8	32.9	37.0
Bangladeshi	64.5	100.0	87.5	87.7	25.0	61.0	35.9	41.8
Caribbean	58.3	76.2	84.9	78.3	40.0	47.2	47.6	46.2
Women								
White British	50.2	89.2	85.6	80.0	19.3	62.7	44.5	44.5
Indian	50.9	87.1	82.4	80.3	28.7	74.6	55.5	60.7
Pakistani	29.9	61.6	67.5	52.2	18.4	56.4	38.2	38.4
Bangladeshi	33.7	64.2	68.1	53.5	18.0	53.6	34.8	34.9
Caribbean	41.0	74.6	84.8	74.4	30.3	60.0	51.2	50.2
Totals: Men								
White British	3,471	6,878	24,791	35,140	2,768	6,674	24,354	33,796
Indian	85	413	434	932	77	397	422	896
Pakistani	88	222	181	491	74	212	173	459
Bangladeshi	31	60	80	171	40	59	78	177
Caribbean	24	42	86	152	25	36	82	143
Totals: Women								
White British	6,875	8,158	23,315	38,348	5,704	7,970	22,988	36,662
Indian	110	357	403	870	87	343	389	819
Pakistani	224	198	203	625	152	172	191	515
Bangladeshi	89	67	72	228	61	56	69	186
Caribbean	39	59	125	223	33	55	121	209

Notes: Labor market status in 2001: NEET, unemployed or inactive; S, student; E, employed.
Population: Individuals between 16 and 29 years old in 2001.
Source: Authors' calculations based on ONS-LS.

2001, White British have higher probabilities of attaining a professional/managerial position by 2011.

Finally, other well-known patterns that emerge from Table 19.1 are the overperformance of Indians in terms of access to high-status occupations and the low employment probabilities of Pakistani and Bangladeshi women (see House of Commons Women and Equalities Committee 2016). In this respect, note that although there is no clear evidence of a stronger employment scarring effect for these women (the difference in employment probabilities with respect to White British is approximately 18–20 percentage points among both those who were employed and those who were NEET in 2001), we do observe a particularly strong scar connected to having been a student in 2001: The ethnic gap in terms of employment chances grows to 30 percentage points for this category.

These results, however, need to be studied after we have controlled for a series of factors that might also affect the outcomes. In fact, there is great variation across ethnic groups in terms of educational achievements, socioeconomic backgrounds, and family arrangements, as shown in Table 19.2.

Table 19.2 Social origins and individual-level characteristics, by ethnic group

	British	Indian	Pakistani	Bangladeshi	Caribbean	Total
Social origins						
Parental social class						
No earners/no code	5.6	4.9	18.8	29.3	14.5	5.9
Manual (V + VI + VII)	33.4	47.0	56.7	51.7	33.7	34.1
Routine nonmanual (III)	15.1	11.3	3.6	3.2	26.8	14.8
Petite bourgeoisie (IV)	11.8	15.8	12.5	11.3	3.3	11.9
Professional/managerial (I + II)	34.1	20.9	8.5	4.4	21.7	33.2
Cars						
No cars	18.7	22.5	39.5	69.0	46.7	19.5
1 car	53.4	57.0	51.8	28.3	45.9	53.3
2 cars	27.9	20.5	8.7	2.7	7.4	27.2
Tenure						
Owner	70.4	86.9	86.8	41.9	46.9	70.8
Social rent	22.8	7.7	7.4	42.9	46.4	22.5
Private rent	6.7	5.4	5.8	15.3	6.6	6.7
Persons per room						
>1.5 persons	0.7	8.8	22.5	36.2	6.1	1.4
1.5 persons	0.5	3.7	6.5	8.9	5.4	0.8
>1 and <1.5 persons	6.1	20.3	31.2	28.8	13.8	6.9
1 person	16.3	23.8	18.7	12.3	25.5	16.6
≥0.75 and <1 person	29.9	22.0	12.9	9.4	21.7	29.3
<0.75 person	46.5	21.4	8.2	4.4	27.6	45.0
Carstairs quintiles						
Q1 (less deprivation)	22.0	7.2	2.1	2.5	2.8	21.2
Q2	21.7	7.7	3.7	3.4	5.1	20.9

(continued)

Table 19.2 Continued

	British	Indian	Pakistani	Bangladeshi	Caribbean	Total
Q3	20.8	11.8	5.8	5.9	7.1	20.2
Q4	19.7	21.5	16.8	8.9	22.4	19.6
Q5 (more deprivation)	15.8	51.7	71.6	79.3	62.5	18.0
Individual characteristics						
Age (2001)						
Mean age	22.6	22.1	21.9	21.8	23.0	22.6
Education (2011)						
None and other	10.7	4.9	12.6	12.3	4.8	10.6
Level 1	14.2	9.2	18.5	22.2	14.0	14.1
Level 2	18.8	11.7	16.3	17.0	17.6	18.5
Level 3	18.2	11.5	12.6	12.3	17.1	17.9
Level 4+	38.2	62.7	40.0	36.2	46.4	38.8
Family type (2011)						
Single, no children	25.8	37.0	22.1	20.0	45.9	26.1
Couple, no children	22.3	18.3	8.2	8.4	12.0	21.9
Single with children	8.6	8.2	14.6	18.7	22.2	8.8
Couple with children	43.2	36.4	55.1	53.0	19.9	43.2
Country of birth						
UK-born	99.0	93.4	81.1	45.6	97.7	98.3
N	74,796	1,830	1,147	406	392	78,571

Note: Population: Individuals between 16 and 29 years old in 2001.
Source: Authors' calculations based on ONS-LS.

There are two clear and interesting findings from Table 19.2. On the one hand, ethnic minorities tend, in general, to have lower or more deprived social origins. For example, they are more likely to have been raised in areas with high neighborhood deprivation and to have parents with lower occupational status. This is particularly evident for the Pakistani and Bangladeshi populations. These factors might impact negatively not only on their labor market outcomes but also on the transitions they make in the labor market. On the other hand, ethnic minorities also tend to be more educated, revealing their upward educational mobility (given their low parental social backgrounds). For instance, the high percentage of Indians who reach university level (level 4+) is striking. Bearing in mind the positive role that education plays in the labor market, including making good-quality transitions, a higher education level among ethnic minorities might actually help counterbalance their poorer social origins. Recent research (Zuccotti 2015a; Zuccotti, Ganzeboom, and Guveli 2017) shows the importance of considering both education and social origins (see also Berloffa, Matteazzi, and Villa, this volume) in the estimation of ethnic inequalities in the labor market. Variation is also observed in terms of family type, with Pakistani and Bangladeshi populations having particularly large shares of households composed of a couple with children. This might be an explanation as to why we see such low employment levels among women from these groups.

The next section examines all these factors together using multivariate logistic regression models. In addition to the socioeconomic, educational, and family variables observed in Table 19.2, we also control for the year in which the origin variables were measured (1981 or 1991) and for the number of census points in which the individuals participated. Finally, note that although the majority of ethnic minorities were born in the United Kingdom, we also consider the country of birth in our analyses (with a dummy as to whether they were born in the United Kingdom or not). Bangladeshis, in particular, have the highest proportion of foreign-born young individuals (see Table 19.2)—a factor that might have a negative impact on labor market transitions.

19.4.2. Multivariate models

This section examines whether the trends found in Table 19.1 still hold after we control for individual and social-origin characteristics, including current and past residential neighborhood deprivation levels. First, we show the average effect of labor market status in 2001 and of ethnic group on labor market outcomes in 2011 (employment and occupational status) before (Model a) and after (Model b) controlling for key individual, social-origin, and neighborhood variables (see Tables 19.3 and 19.4). The results are presented separately for men and women; the coefficients represent average marginal effects derived from logistic regressions (models with all controls are shown in Table A19.1 in the Appendix).

Next, we introduce interactions between labor market status in 2001 and ethnicity in order to study whether scarring varies in relation to an individual's ethnic group. Models with interactions are used to answer the main question in this chapter: What is the effect of having been unemployed or inactive (NEET), compared to having been employed or in education, in 2001 on the probability of being employed/having a high occupational status in 2011—for different ethnic minority groups and for White British? In particular, to what extent is being out of education and out of the labor market particularly detrimental (or not) for some ethnic groups? Because we work with logistic regression models, we calculated predicted values for the groups from the interaction models (keeping all control variables at their mean; see Table A19.2 in the Appendix) and created graphs.[7] Predicted values and graphs serve not only to observe the magnitude of the effects but also to explore at which levels of the dependent variable they occur for an individual with "average" characteristics. Assuming that the variable

Table 19.3 Probability of being employed in 2011, by labor market status in 2001 and ethnic group; AME (clustered standard errors)

	Men		Women	
	Model a	Model b	Model a	Model b
Labor market status in 2001 (ref. Employed)				
NEET (unemployed or inactive)	−0.338***	−0.175***	−0.357***	−0.173***
	(0.0103)	(0.0078)	(0.0079)	(0.0073)
Student	−0.005	−0.041***	0.056***	−0.012*
	(0.0045)	(0.0063)	(0.0052)	(0.0071)
Ethnic group (ref. White British)				
Indian	0.003	0.004	−0.028	−0.061***
	(0.0120)	(0.0109)	(0.0176)	(0.0185)
Pakistani	−0.020	0.007	−0.211***	−0.160***
	(0.0164)	(0.0130)	(0.0250)	(0.0223)
Bangladeshi	0.002	0.042***	−0.180***	−0.100***
	(0.0243)	(0.0159)	(0.0393)	(0.0325)
Caribbean	−0.067*	−0.023	−0.064*	−0.073**
	(0.0347)	(0.0246)	(0.0343)	(0.0324)
N	36,886	36,886	40,294	40,294
Basic controls	X	X	X	X
Individual, social origin, and neighborhood controls		X		X

Notes: Basic controls: Age, country of birth, origin year, and number of census points. Individual, social origin, and neighborhood controls: Education, family type, parental social class, number of cars, tenure, level of overcrowding, and neighborhood deprivation (past and current). Population: Individuals between 16 and 29 years old in 2001.
*$p < .10$.
**$p < .05$.
***$p < .01$.
Source: Authors' calculations based on ONS-LS.

"labor market status in 2001" has a certain "order" in the categories, we explore "slopes" for different ethnic groups: how steep they are and whether they touch or not.

19.4.2.1. Employment scarring

Overall, our findings indicate that having been NEET in 2001, compared to having been employed, reduces by more than 30 percentage points the probability of being employed in 2011—for both men and women (Model a). After we control for social-origin and individual characteristics, as well as for current and past levels of deprivation of the neighborhood of residence (Model b), the effect

Table 19.4 Probability of having a (current or most recent) professional/managerial occupation in 2011, by labor market status in 2001 and ethnic group; AME (clustered standard errors)

	Men		Women	
	Model a	Model b	Model a	Model b
Labor market status in 2001 (ref. Employed)				
NEET (unemployed or inactive)	–0.172***	–0.098***	–0.240***	–0.105***
	(0.0105)	(0.0117)	(0.0072)	(0.0088)
Student	0.276***	0.037***	0.278***	0.036***
	(0.0085)	(0.0092)	(0.0081)	(0.0087)
Ethnic group (ref. White British)				
Indian	0.105***	0.082***	0.105***	0.063***
	(0.0208)	(0.0183)	(0.0209)	(0.0187)
Pakistani	–0.113***	–0.021	–0.041	0.010
	(0.0270)	(0.0273)	(0.0265)	(0.0238)
Bangladeshi	–0.025	0.075*	–0.040	0.057
	(0.0446)	(0.0433)	(0.0429)	(0.0387)
Caribbean	0.017	0.038	0.037	0.041
	(0.0510)	(0.0451)	(0.0409)	(0.0358)
N	35,453	35,453	38,391	38,391
Basic controls	X	X	X	X
Individual, social origin, and neighborhood controls		X		X

Notes: Basic controls: Age, country of birth, origin year, and number of census points. Individual, social origin, and neighborhood controls: Education, family type, parental social class, number of cars, tenure, level of overcrowding, and neighborhood deprivation (past and current). Population: Individuals between 16 and 29 years old in 2001.
*p < .10.
**p < .05.
***p < .01.
Source: Authors' calculations based on ONS-LS.

declines, but it is still quite substantive (approximately 17%). Poor labor market integration at a young age creates scarring for both men and women.

Table 19.3 shows that although the effect of having been in education in 2001 on the probability of being employed in 2011 is similarly positive to the effect of having been employed in 2001 (for women it is actually more positive), the education effect becomes negative after we control for key variables. In other words, after we control for the fact that individuals with more socioeconomic resources are usually more likely to continue in higher/university education, and for the fact that higher education levels lead to better employment chances, a situation of employment (vs. any other) in 2001 seems to have more positive long-term effects than studying. Although this does not mean that individuals should invest less in education, it does suggest that early experiences of employment—perhaps simultaneously with an educational activity—can have positive long-term effects in terms of accessing work in the UK labor market. As previously argued, this might be connected to the extra skills acquired due to longer lasting work experience but also to sending a positive "signal" to employers.

In terms of average group differences, we observe that men from ethnic minority backgrounds (especially Bangladeshis) have similar or even higher probabilities of being in work in 2011 compared to White British. This finding is similar to previous results obtained for a slightly older age group (aged 20–45 years; Zuccotti 2015b). For women, on the contrary, all ethnic minority groups have lower employment probabilities compared to White British women. Differences that emerge from our analysis range from 6 percentage points lower for Indian women to 16 percentage points lower for Pakistani women.

We identified several statistically significant interactions. For men, having been NEET in 2001 (vs. having been employed) is not as detrimental for Indian and Bangladeshi men as it is for White British men. This denotes lower scarring effects for the ethnic minorities. A similar relative advantage is observed for Indian and Pakistani men when comparing NEET with students in 2001. Among women, the results suggest that Pakistani and Caribbean women have deeper scars connected to having been NEET than is the case for White British women. These findings are better understood by looking at Figures 19.1 and 19.2, which show the predicted values of employment in 2011 for Indian, Pakistani, and Bangladeshi men (vs. White British men) and for Pakistani and Caribbean women (vs. White British women) for each labor market status in 2001 (keeping all control variables at their mean).

In visual terms, the weaker detrimental effect of having been NEET, versus having been employed or a student, for Indian, Pakistani, and Bangladeshi men is expressed in the flatter slopes for these three ethnic groups. In particular, for Indians and Bangladeshis, there is a much higher probability of employment among those who were NEET in 2001: This difference is approximately 9 percentage points for Indians and approximately 12 percentage points for Bangladeshis. Note that Bangladeshis are also greatly advantaged among those who were students in 2001. Conversely, these groups have more similar employment probabilities among those who were employed in 2001 (only Indians seem to present a negative and relatively small gap with respect to White British).

The graph for women (see Figure 19.2), in contrast, shows a steeper slope for Pakistanis and Caribbeans than for White British, denoting a deeper scar for the ethnic minority. Looking at the predicted values, we observe, for example, that

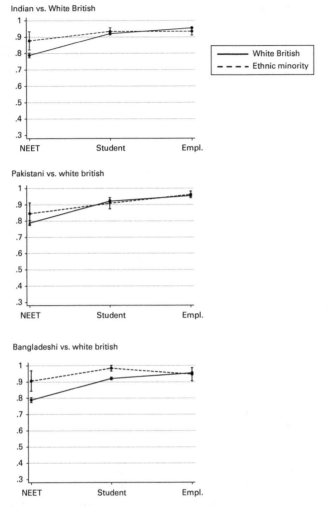

Figure 19.1 Predicted values of male employment in 2011 (90% confidence interval).
Source: Authors' calculations based on ONS-LS.

the employment probabilities among those who were employed in 2001 are approximately 74% for Pakistanis and 88% for White British (a 14% gap), whereas among those who were NEET in 2001, the values are 47% and 70%, respectively (a gap that grows to 23%).

Overall, the results on employment scarring show that ethnic minority men are not particularly penalized; On the contrary, being NEET in 2001 has a similar or reduced scarring effect on later employment probabilities compared to White British. Among women, the results suggest higher scarring effects on employment for Pakistani and Caribbean women.

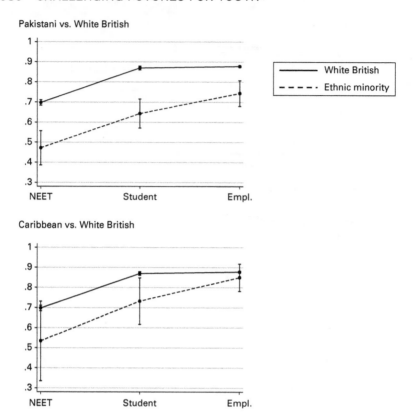

Figure 19.2 Predicted values of female employment in 2011 (90% confidence interval). *Source*: Authors' calculations based on ONS-LS.

19.4.2.2. Scarring of occupational status

As with the results for employment, the results for occupational status show that having been NEET leads to lower probabilities (approximately 10 percentage points less; Model b) of attaining a high occupational status, even after controlling for key variables. However, having been a student in 2001 is actually better than having been employed as regards future occupational status. Although much of this effect is explained by the education of individuals (introduced in Model b), probably driven by individuals acquiring a university degree, there is still a small residual effect. This might suggest that having been to university provides additional skills on top of the degree itself and/or access to a wider and better qualified network. Following previous findings (Cheung and Heath 2007; Zuccotti 2015b), Table 19.4 also shows that given equality in their labor market situations in 2001 and their individual and socioeconomic background characteristics (Model b), ethnic minorities do as well as or even better, on average, than White British in terms of occupational attainment. In particular, this is the case for Indian and Bangladeshi men.

Regarding interactions, the results show that for Bangladeshi men, having been a student in 2001 (vs. having been employed) exerts a more positive effect on occupational status than is the case for White British. This can be clearly observed in Figure 19.3, which shows that Bangladeshi men have higher probabilities of achieving a professional/managerial position compared to White British and that this is particularly strong among those who were students in 2001: These have a 70% probability of attaining a higher occupational status (compared to approximately 50% for equivalent White British).

Among women, the results are neither substantive nor statistically significant. In fact, the findings show that the general tendency is for the labor market status in 2001 to have a similar effect across ethnic groups. This can also be interpreted in terms of ethnic gaps remaining similar across statuses in 2001.

In summary, the results of the occupational analysis show that for all groups, having been NEET in 2001 leads, in general, to lower probabilities of attaining a professional/managerial position. However, unemployment/inactivity scars do not vary by ethnicity, nor are ethnic minorities particularly disadvantaged if they were NEET in 2001 compared to White British. On the contrary, some groups (Bangladeshi men) are particularly well positioned with respect to White British: In particular, they have higher probabilities of achieving a professional/managerial position if they were a student in 2001.

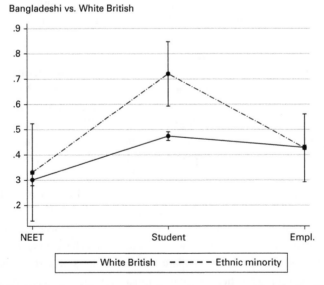

Figure 19.3 Predicted values of male access to (current or most recent) professional/managerial occupation in 2011.
Source: Authors' calculations based on ONS-LS.

19.5. CONCLUSIONS

This chapter has sought to bridge a gap between two research agendas that have only marginally interacted: ethnic inequalities and labor market scarring effects for young people. A further dimension we have included here—and that is even less evident in previous research—is the systematic comparison of gender differences between different ethnic groups. The use of the ONS-LS enabled us to follow young individuals over time and to have a sufficiently large number of ethnic minority groups, accompanied with rich and detailed information on their socioeconomic backgrounds, including neighborhood deprivation information attached to individuals.

Our results support previous research indicating the effects of early experiences on subsequent labor market outcomes. On average, we found that those who were not in employment, education, or training in 2001 had an approximately 17 percentage points less chance of being employed in 2011 and an approximately 10 percentage points less chance of being in a professional/managerial position compared to those who were employed in 2001; these results were found after controlling for comparable levels of education, social background, and neighborhood deprivation. We also found that whereas having been employed in 2001 leads to the highest employment probabilities in 2011, having been a student in 2011 leads to the greatest likelihood of attaining a professional/managerial position. This is an interesting finding that might indicate different mechanisms playing a role: Although a previous employment experience seems to be crucial for improving future employability, it is participation in the education system (and the additional benefits it may have in addition to the university degree) that makes the greatest difference in terms of acquiring a good-quality job (see Filandri et al., this volume).

Moving to the core question of the chapter, we found that scarring connected to a previous experience of unemployment or inactivity indeed varies across ethnic groups, and it also depends on the gender of individuals. In particular, examining employment probabilities in 2011, the NEET scar is weaker among Indian and Bangladeshi men by more than half compared to White British men. For women, by contrast, scarring appears to be stronger among Pakistani and Caribbean women than among White British women. The nonemployment of Asian women is an issue of current political concern in the United Kingdom (House of Commons Women and Equalities Committee 2016).

Occupational attainment is not affected by ethnic differences for those with a period of being NEET in 2001. However, Bangladeshis have a particularly high probability of attaining a high occupational status if they were students in 2001, even after controlling for their own educational attainment. Interestingly, we also observe these results for Indian and Bangladeshi students when studying access to employment.

Overall, our results for men contradict previous findings for the United Kingdom (Demireva and Kesler 2011) and for other European countries (Reyneri and Fullin 2011; Mooi-Reci and Ganzeboom 2015). The penalties associated with coming from an ethnic minority background do not accrue with being unemployed or inactive, as the stigma argument predicted. On the contrary, some male groups actually showed the opposite trajectory. In the case of Indians, it could be argued that their high educational attainment at the group level might compensate for any experience of unemployment or inactivity in the eyes of employers recruiting them. This might be one of the reasons why we observe relatively higher employment probabilities among Indians who were NEET in 2001. Previous findings (Zuccotti and Platt 2017) also show that Indian men benefit in terms of labor market outcomes from being raised in areas with a higher share of coethnics, which might point to networking mechanisms as potential additional causes. The findings are more puzzling for Pakistani and, especially, for Bangladeshi men because these groups have historically been located in the lower sector of the social structure, and we would expect this to send a negative signal to employers. Further research to untangle this puzzle, as well as to explain the advantage found for Indians, might focus on unmeasured characteristics of these groups, including parental aspirations, motivational factors, the role of networks at the neighborhood and the university level (especially for Indians and Bangladeshis), the exploitation of resources such as internships, and the type of university degrees chosen. Note that these factors might be potential explanations for the scar, but they may also belong to the mechanisms of self-selection into initial conditions, given the limits of our model.

Regarding women, youth unemployment or inactivity leads to lower employment probabilities later in life for Pakistanis and Caribbeans compared to equivalent White British. Group stigmatization might be an explanation for the Caribbeans' disadvantage; this might also be connected with their overrepresentation as single mothers. The result for Pakistanis might be connected to the role in this group of women, who are often occupied with caring activities, and the low value attached to paid work for them (Peach 2005). Evidence suggesting that these cultural values might actually influence labor market transitions is the fact that having been raised in a neighborhood with a higher share of coethnics negatively impacts on Asian women's employment probabilities as adults (Zuccotti and Platt 2017). White British women, on the other hand, often combine caring with part-time work (O'Reilly and Fagan 1998; Dale et al. 2002a, 2002b). Interestingly, we do not find particularly strong scarring effects for Bangladeshi women (despite the fact that, independently of their origin status in 2001, they have lower employment probabilities compared to White British women). Pakistani and Bangladeshi women therefore seem to be following different transition trajectories—a finding that deserves further examination.

Finally, in addition to showing that scars vary by ethnicity, this chapter challenges the idea that ethnic minorities are always disadvantaged in terms of access to jobs. The fact that some ethnic minority groups—especially second-generation men—are less penalized by a previous unemployment/inactivity experience compared to some of their White British counterparts is in part good news in terms of integration processes. Although much of recent UK policy has focused on limiting new immigration, this has gone hand in hand with efforts to promote integration (Cheung and Heath 2007), as well as new legislation to prevent discrimination and to promote "social cohesion" at the local level (Heath and Yu 2005; Rattansi 2011; Cantle 2012; Meer and Modood 2013). Our results are likely to be in part connected to these measures, although the extent to which they imply a decrease in ethnic discrimination in the labor market requires further exploration.

Significant concerns remain regarding employment probabilities for ethnic minority women and young White British men, who are increasingly "left behind" (Organization for Economic Co-operation and Development 2012). The findings raise questions regarding the groups that policymakers should target. Often, being an ethnic minority is equated with being disadvantaged, but our results show that this is not universally the case in the United Kingdom. Among men, scarring connected to having experienced a period of unemployment or inactivity is particularly high for White British. Our evidence is also supported by previous findings showing that--given equality of education and social background--employment probabilities increased for all ethnic minorities between 2001 and 2011 but declined for White British individuals (Zuccotti 2015b). Among women, however, we do observe a clear "ethnic minority disadvantage" in the labor market. Here, the mechanisms behind these disadvantages deserve greater attention: Although discrimination might be part of the story, and here policymaking should definitely have a role, cultural values (especially among Asians) and possibly fewer employment opportunities in their communities might also contribute to the explanation. Policy to address these multiple and complex outcomes clearly needs to be sensitive to the differential effects and outcomes of gender and ethnicity on young people's employment transitions.[8]

NOTES

1 In this section, we use nonemployment to identify individuals who are either unemployed or engaged in any other activity that does not involve working or studying. Some studies include students in their comparisons (hence identify NEET populations), whereas others do not.

2 Some cell counts, percentages, and totals shown in the tables created with ONS-LS data have been modified in order to comply with publication rules

established by the Office for National Statistics. These modifications, however, do not affect the main findings derived from the regression models. The permission of the Office for National Statistics to use the Longitudinal Study is gratefully acknowledged, as is the help provided by staff at the Centre for Longitudinal Study Information and User Support (CeLSIUS). CeLSIUS is supported by the ESRC Census of Population Programme (Award ref. ES/K000365/1). The authors alone are responsible for the interpretation of the data. This work contains statistical data from ONS, which is Crown Copyright. The use of the ONS statistical data in this work does not imply the endorsement of the ONS in relation to the interpretation or analysis of the statistical data. This work uses research data sets, which may not exactly reproduce National Statistics aggregates.

3   Ethnicity is measured by a question on self-identification (measured in 2011; when missing, self-identification in 2001 is used). In 2011, the question is formulated as follows: "What is your ethnic group?" The options are White (English/Welsh/Scottish/Northern Irish/British; Irish; Gypsy or Irish traveler; other White), Mixed/multiple ethnic groups (White and Black Caribbean; White and Black African; White and Asian; any other Mixed/multiple ethnic background; open question), Asian/Asian British (Indian, Pakistani, Bangladeshi, Chinese; any other Asian background; open question), Black/African/Caribbean/Black British (African; Caribbean; any other Black/African/Caribbean background; open question), and Other ethnic group (Arab; any other ethnic group). Note that the "Gypsy or Irish traveler" and "Arab" categories were not specified separately in the 2001 census form.

4   Individuals of whom one parent is born abroad and the other in the United Kingdom are therefore excluded from the analysis. White British with foreign-born parents (or a foreign-born parent in the case of single-parent households) and ethnic minorities with UK-born parents (or a foreign-born parent in the case of single-parent households) are also excluded. African and Chinese were excluded due to the small number of cases.

5   Neighborhood deprivation is expressed in population-weighted quintiles and is obtained at the ward level. The ward is the key building block of UK administrative geography and is used to elect local government councilors. Wards vary in terms of size and population, with the average population amounting to 4,000. In general, the smallest and most populous wards are in metropolitan areas, where the majority of ethnic minorities are found. The permission of Dr. Paul Norman, School of Geography, University of Leeds, to use the 2011 Carstairs Index of Deprivation he created is gratefully acknowledged. Please see Norman and Boyle (2014) for use of the Carstairs Index in conjunction with the ONS-LS.

6   "Ivprobit," which is the command we should use given that our outcomes are dichotomous, does not allow factorial endogenous variables (i.e., status in 2001), but only continuous variables. We have, nevertheless, run a model (without

interactions) in which a recoded version of status in 2001—being NEET (vs. being in employment or in education)—is used as an endogenous dummy variable, and neighborhood deprivation when individuals were 0–15 years old is used as an instrument. The results are similar to those presented here. Another option would be to use the command "ivregress" and ignore the fact that our dependent variable is dichotomous. We have tried this model as well, but the outcomes are difficult to interpret (predictions are out of range, i.e., they exceed 1, and have very large standard errors). All results are available on request.

7   To identify relevant interactions (shown in Figures 19.1–19.3), we plotted all interactions in graphs and also created "contrasts," which show the size of the interaction effect and whether or not it is statistically significant. In the study of employment in 2011, we have identified contrasts that are statistically significant at $p < .10$ for Indian and Bangladeshi men, for whom the effect of being employed in 2001 versus being NEET is different compared to White British men. We have also found, in the analysis of occupations in 2011, that the effect of being a student versus being NEET is different for Bangladeshi men ($p < .10$) compared to White British men. Finally, we have identified relevant interactions when the observed effects were quite substantive (but the contrasts were statistically significant at larger p values). In the analysis of employment, the effect of being employed in 2001 versus being NEET is different for Pakistani men and women ($p < .14$) and for Caribbean women ($p < .30$) compared to White British men and women.

8   An earlier version of this chapter was published in the journal Human Relations.

REFERENCES

Aassve, Arnstein, Maria Iacovou, and Letizia Mencarini. 2006. "Youth Poverty and Transition to Adulthood in Europe." *Demographic Research* 15 (2): 21–50.

Alba, Richard, and Nancy Foner. 2015. *Strangers No More: Immigration and the Challenges of Integration in North America and Western Europe*. Princeton, NJ: Princeton University Press.

Bell, David N. F., and David G. Blanchflower. 2010. "UK Unemployment in the Great Recession." *National Institute Economic Review* 214 (1): 3–25.

Brinbaum, Yael, and Hector Cebolla-Boado. 2007. "The School Careers of Ethnic Minority Youth in France: Success or Disillusion?" *Ethnicities* 7 (3): 445–74.

Burgess, Simon, Carol Propper, Hedley Rees, and Arran Shearer. 2003. "The Class of 1981: The Effects of Early Career Unemployment on Subsequent Unemployment Experiences." *Labour Economics* 10 (3): 291–309.

Cantle, Ted. 2012. *Interculturalism: The New Era of Cohesion and Diversity*. Hampshire, UK: Palgrave Macmillan.

Carmichael, Fiona, and Robert Woods. 2000. "Ethnic Penalties in Unemployment and Occupational Attainment: Evidence for Britain." *International Review of Applied Economics* 14 (1): 71–98.

Catney, Gemma. 2016. "Exploring a Decade of Small Area Ethnic (De-) Segregation in England and Wales." *Urban Studies* 53 (8): 1691–1709.

Catney, Gemma, and Albert Sabater. 2015. *Ethnic Minority Disadvantage in the Labour Market: Participation, Skills and Geographical Inequalities.* York, UK: Joseph Rowntree Foundation.

Cheung, Sin Yi, and Anthony Heath. 2007. "Nice Work If You Can Get It: Ethnic Penalties in Great Britain." In *Unequal Chances: Ethnic Minorities in Western Labour Markets,* edited by Anthony Heath and Sin Yi Cheung, 507–50. New York: Oxford University Press.

Crawford, Claire, Kathryn Duckworth, Anna Vignoles, and Gill Wyness. 2010. "Young People's Education and Labour Market Choices Aged 16/17 to 18/19." Research Report DFE-RR182. London: Department for Education.

Crawford, Claire, and Ellen Greaves. 2015. "Socio-Economic, Ethnic and Gender Differences in HE Participation." BIS Research Paper 186. London: Department for Business, Innovation and Skills.

Dale, Angela, Nusrat Shaheen, Virinder Kalra, and Edward Fieldhouse. 2002a. "The Labour Market Prospects for Pakistani and Bangladeshi Women." *Work, Employment and Society* 16 (1): 5–25.

Dale, Angela, Nusrat Shaheen, Virinder Kalra, and Edward Fieldhouse. 2002b. "Routes into Education and Employment for Young Pakistani and Bangladeshi Women in the UK." *Ethnic and Racial Studies* 25 (6): 942–68.

Demireva, Neli, and Christel Kesler. 2011. "The Curse of Inopportune Transitions: The Labour Market Behaviour of Immigrants and Natives in the UK." *International Journal of Comparative Sociology* 52 (4): 306–26.

Dorsett, Richard, and Paolo Lucchino. 2014. "Young People's Labour Market Transitions: The Role of Early Experiences." NIESR Discussion Paper 419. London: National Institute of Economic and Social Research.

Erikson, Robert, and John Goldthorpe. 1992. *The Constant Flux: A Study of Class Mobility in Industrial Societies.* Oxford: Clarendon.

Eurofound. 2014. *Mapping Youth Transitions in Europe.* Luxembourg: Publications Office of the European Union.

Gregg, Paul. 2001. "The Impact of Youth Unemployment on Adult Unemployment in the NCDS." *Economic Journal* 111 (475): 626–53.

Gregg, Paul, and Emma Tominey. 2005. "The Wage Scar from Male Youth Unemployment." *Labour Economics* 12 (4): 487–509.

Hattersley, Lin, and Rosemary Creeser. 1995. "Longitudinal Study 1971–1991: History, Organisation and Quality of Data." Series LS 7. London: Her Majesty's Stationery Office.

Heath, Anthony, and Sin Yi Cheung. 2006. "Ethnic Penalties in the Labour Market: Employers and Discrimination." Research Report 341. Leeds, UK: Corporate Document Services for the Department for Work and Pensions.

Heath, Anthony, and Sin Yi Cheung, eds. 2007. *Unequal Chances: Ethnic Minorities in Western Labour Markets.* Oxford: Oxford University Press.

Heath, Anthony, and Yaojun Li. 2010. "Struggling onto the Ladder, Climbing the Rungs: Employment and Class Position of Minority Ethnic Groups in Britain." In *Spatial and Social Disparities: Understanding Population Trends and Processes*, edited by John Stillwell, Paul Norman, Claudia Thomas, and Claudia Surridge, 83–97. London: Springer.

Heath, Anthony, and Soojin Yu. 2005. "Explaining Ethnic Minority Disadvantage." In *Understanding Social Change*, edited by Anthony Heath, John Ermisch, and Duncan Gallie, 187–225. Oxford: Oxford University Press.

House of Commons Women and Equalities Committee. 2016. "Employment Opportunities for Muslims in the UK." Second Report of Session 2016–17. London: House of Commons.

Kabeer, Naila. 2002. *The Power to Choose: Bangladeshi Women and Labour Market Decisions in London and Dhaka*. London: Verso.

Kalter, Frank, and Irena Kogan. 2006. "Ethnic Inequalities at the Transition from School to Work in Belgium and Spain: Discrimination or Self-Exclusion?" *Research in Social Stratification and Mobility* 24 (3): 259–74.

Kalwij, Adriaan S. 2004. "Unemployment Experiences of Young Men: On the Road to Stable Employment?" *Oxford Bulletin of Economics and Statistics* 66 (2): 205–37.

Kirchner Sala, Laura, Vahé Nafilyan, Stefan Speckesser, and Arianna Tassinari. 2015. "Youth Transitions to and Within the Labour Market: A Literature Review." BIS Research paper 255a. London: Department for Business, Innovation and Skills.

Kogan, Irena. 2011. "New Immigrants—Old Disadvantage Patterns? Labour Market Integration of Recent Immigrants into Germany." *International Migration* 49 (1): 91–117.

Longhi, Simonetta, Cheti Nicoletti, and Lucinda Platt. 2013. "Explained and Unexplained Wage Gaps Across the Main Ethno-Religious Groups in Great Britain." *Oxford Economic Papers* 65 (2): 471–93.

Luijkx, Ruud, and Maarten H. J. Wolbers. 2009. "The Effects of Non-Employment in Early Work–Life on Subsequent Employment Chances of Individuals in the Netherlands." *European Sociological Review* 25 (6): 647–60.

Meer, Nasar, and Tariq Modood. 2013. "The 'Civic Re-balancing' of British Multiculturalism, and Beyond . . ." In *Challenging Multiculturalism: European Models of Diversity*, edited by Raymond Taras, 75–96. Edinburgh, UK: Edinburgh University Press.

Modood, Tariq, Richard Berthoud, Jane Lakey, James Nazroo, Patten Smith, Satnam Virdee, and Sharon Beishon. 1997. *Ethnic Minorities in Britain: Diversity and Disadvantage—Fourth National Survey of Ethnic Minorities*. London: Policy Studies Institute.

Mooi-Reci, Irma, and Harry B. G. Ganzeboom. 2015. "Unemployment Scarring by Gender: Human Capital Depreciation or Stigmatization? Longitudinal Evidence from the Netherlands, 1980–2000." *Social Science Research* 52: 642–58.

Mroz, Thomas A., and Timothy H. Savage. 2006. "The Long-Term Effects of Youth Unemployment." *Journal of Human Resources* 41 (2): 259–93.

Nazroo, James, and Dharmi Kapadia. 2013. "Have Ethnic Inequalities in Employment Persisted Between 1991 and 2011?" ESRC Series Dynamics of Diversity: Evidence from the 2011 Census. Manchester, UK: Centre on Dynamics of Ethnicity.

Norman, Paul, and Paul Boyle. 2014. "Are Health Inequalities Between Differently Deprived Areas Evident at Different Ages? A Longitudinal Study of Census Records in England and Wales, 1991–2001." *Health & Place* 26: 88–93.

Norman, Paul, Paul Boyle, and Philip Rees. 2005. "Selective Migration, Health and Deprivation: A Longitudinal Analysis." *Social Science & Medicine* 60 (12): 2755–71.

Office for National Statistics. 2010. *Standard Occupational Classification 2010: The National Statistics Socio-economic Classification: (Rebased on the SOC2010) User Manual.* Basingstoke, UK: Palgrave Macmillan.

Omori, Yoshiaki. 1997. "Stigma Effects of Nonemployment." *Economic Inquiry* 35 (2): 394–416.

O'Reilly, Jacqueline, Werner Eichhorst, András Gábos, Kari Hadjivassiliou, David Lain, Janine Leschke, et al. 2015. "Five Characteristics of Youth Unemployment in Europe: Flexibility, Education, Migration, Family Legacies, and EU Policy." *Sage Open* 5 (1): 1–19. doi:10.1177/2158244015574962.

O'Reilly, Jacqueline, and Colette Fagan, eds. 1998. *Part-Time Prospects: An International Comparison of Part-Time Work in Europe, North America and the Pacific Rim.* London: Routledge.

Organization for Economic Co-operation and Development (OECD). 2012. *OECD Employment Outlook 2012.* Paris: OECD.

Peach, Ceri. 2005. "Social Integration and Social Mobility: Spatial Segregation and Intermarriage of the Caribbean Population in Britain." In *Ethnicity, Social Mobility and Public Policy*, edited by Glenn C. Loury, Tariq Modood, and Steven M. Teles, 178–203. Cambridge: Cambridge University Press.

Phillips, Deborah. 1998. "Black Minority Ethnic Concentration, Segregation and Dispersal in Britain." *Urban Studies* 35 (10): 1681–1702.

Platt, Lucinda. 2007. "Making Education Count: The Effects of Ethnicity and . Qualifications on Intergenerational Social Class Mobility." *Sociological Review* 55 (3): 485–508.

Rattansi, Ali. 2011. *Multiculturalism: A Very Short Introduction.* Oxford: Oxford University Press.

Reyneri, Emilio, and Giovanna Fullin. 2011. "Ethnic Penalties in the Transition to and from Unemployment: A West European Perspective." *International Journal of Comparative Sociology* 52 (4): 247–63.

Robinson, Vaughan, and Rina Valeny. 2005. "Ethnic Minorities, Employment, Self-Employment, and Social Mobility in Postwar Britain." In *Ethnicity, Social*

Mobility and Public Policy, edited by Glenn C. Loury, Tariq Modood, and Steven M. Teles, 414–47. Cambridge: Cambridge University Press.

Schmelzer, Paul. 2011. "Unemployment in Early Career in the UK: A Trap or a Stepping Stone?" *Acta Sociologica* 54 (3): 251–65.

Schmillen, Achim, and Joachim Möller. 2012. "Distribution and Determinants of Lifetime Unemployment." *Labour Economics* 19 (1): 33–47.

Schmillen, Achim, and Matthias Umkehrer. 2013. "The Scars of Youth—Effects of Early-Career Unemployment on Future Unemployment Experience." IAB Discussion Paper 6/2013. Leibniz: Institute for Employment Research, German Federal Employment Agency.

Silberman, Roxane, and Irène Fournier. 2008. "Second Generations on the Job Market in France: A Persistent Ethnic Penalty." *Revue Française de Sociologie* 49 (5): 45–94.

Van de Werfhorst, Herman G., and Frank van Tubergen. 2007. "Ethnicity, Schooling, and Merit in the Netherlands." *Ethnicities* 7 (3): 416–44.

Wood, Martin, Jon Hales, Susan Purdon, Tanja Sejersen, and Oliver Hayllar. 2009. "A Test for Racial Discrimination in Recruitment Practice in British Cities." Research report No. 607. London: Department for Work and Pensions.

Zuccotti, Carolina V. 2015a. "Do Parents Matter? Revisiting Ethnic Penalties in Occupation Among Second Generation Ethnic Minorities in England and Wales." *Sociology* 49 (2): 229–51.

Zuccotti, Carolina V. 2015b. "Shaping Ethnic Inequalities: The Production and Reproduction of Social and Spatial Inequalities Among Ethnic Minorities in England and Wales." PhD dissertation, European University Institute.

Zuccotti, Carolina V., Harry B. G. Ganzeboom, and Ayse Guveli. 2017. "Has Migration Been Beneficial for Migrants and Their Children?" *International Migration Review* 51 (1): 97–126. doi:10.1111/imre.12219.

Zuccotti, Carolina V., and Lucinda Platt. 2017. "Does Neighbourhood Ethnic Concentration in Early Life Affect Subsequent Labour Market Outcomes? A Study Across Ethnic Groups in England and Wales." *Population, Space and Place* 23 (6): e2041. doi:10.1002/psp.2041.

APPENDIX

Table A19.1 Probability of being employed and probability of having a (current or most recent) professional/managerial occupation in 2011; AME (clustered standard errors)—full models

| | Employment | | | | Professional/managerial | | | |
| | Men | | Women | | Men | | Women | |
	Model a	Model b	Model a	Model b	Model a	Model b	Model a	Model b
Status in 2001 (ref. Employed)								
NEET (unemployed or inactive)	-0.338***	-0.175***	-0.357***	-0.173***	-0.172***	-0.098***	-0.240***	-0.105***
	(0.0103)	(0.0078)	(0.0079)	(0.0073)	(0.0105)	(0.0117)	(0.0072)	(0.0088)
Student	-0.005	-0.041***	0.056***	-0.012*	0.276***	0.037***	0.278***	0.036***
	(0.0045)	(0.0063)	(0.0052)	(0.0071)	(0.0085)	(0.0092)	(0.0081)	(0.0087)
Ethnic group (ref. White British)								
Indian	0.003	0.004	-0.028	-0.061***	0.105***	0.082***	0.105***	0.063***
	(0.0120)	(0.0109)	(0.0176)	(0.0185)	(0.0208)	(0.0183)	(0.0209)	(0.0187)
Pakistani	-0.020	0.007	-0.211***	-0.160***	-0.113***	-0.021	-0.041	0.010
	(0.0164)	(0.0130)	(0.0250)	(0.0223)	(0.0270)	(0.0273)	(0.0265)	(0.0238)
Bangladeshi	0.002	0.042***	-0.180***	-0.100***	-0.025	0.075*	-0.040	0.057
	(0.0243)	(0.0159)	(0.0393)	(0.0325)	(0.0446)	(0.0433)	(0.0429)	(0.0387)
Caribbean	-0.067*	-0.023	-0.064*	-0.073**	0.017	0.038	0.037	0.041
	(0.0347)	(0.0246)	(0.0343)	(0.0324)	(0.0510)	(0.0451)	(0.0409)	(0.0358)

(continued)

Table A19.1 Continued

| | Employment | | | | Professional/managerial | | | |
| | Men | | Women | | Men | | Women | |
	Model a	Model b	Model a	Model b	Model a	Model b	Model a	Model b
Family type (ref. Single, no children)								
Couple, no children		0.092***		0.077***		0.074***		0.035***
		(0.0048)		(0.0062)		(0.0077)		(0.0087)
Single with children		−0.010		−0.084***		0.022		−0.094***
		(0.0123)		(0.0079)		(0.0199)		(0.0107)
Couple with children		0.076***		−0.079***		0.047***		−0.056***
		(0.0044)		(0.0061)		(0.0070)		(0.0078)
Education (ref. Level 1)								
No education		−0.149***		−0.289***		−0.046***		−0.041*
		(0.0117)		(0.0228)		(0.0152)		(0.0250)
Other		−0.043***		−0.086***		0.076***		0.044*
		(0.0095)		(0.0207)		(0.0137)		(0.0234)
Level 2		−0.014		−0.015		0.142***		0.088***
		(0.0091)		(0.0203)		(0.0135)		(0.0231)
Level 3		0.022**		0.049**		0.191***		0.154***
		(0.0089)		(0.0204)		(0.0137)		(0.0233)
Level 4+		0.044***		0.085***		0.525***		0.497***
		(0.0085)		(0.0202)		(0.0130)		(0.0230)

Tenure (ref. Owner)

Social rent	-0.019***	-0.024***	-0.040***	-0.039***
	(0.0044)	(0.0055)	(0.0076)	(0.0071)
Private rent	-0.005	-0.014*	-0.008	-0.012
	(0.0060)	(0.0080)	(0.0104)	(0.0100)
Number of cars (ref. None)				
1 car	0.012***	0.009	0.008	0.016**
	(0.0043)	(0.0053)	(0.0077)	(0.0071)
2+ cars	0.017***	0.020***	0.020**	0.038***
	(0.0055)	(0.0069)	(0.0094)	(0.0088)
Persons per room (ref. 1 person per room)				
>1.5 persons	0.001	-0.026*	-0.030	-0.008
	(0.0111)	(0.0153)	(0.0235)	(0.0212)
1.5 persons	0.006	-0.016	0.029	-0.055*
	(0.0157)	(0.0181)	(0.0300)	(0.0283)
>1 and <1.5 persons	-0.006	-0.004	-0.015	-0.007
	(0.0064)	(0.0074)	(0.0117)	(0.0106)
≥0.75 and <1 person	0.010**	0.003	0.004	-0.001
	(0.0043)	(0.0054)	(0.0073)	(0.0069)
<0.75 person	0.009**	0.001	0.025***	0.012*
	(0.0044)	(0.0055)	(0.0073)	(0.0069)

(continued)

Table A19.1 Continued

	Employment				Professional/managerial			
	Men		Women		Men		Women	
	Model a	Model b	Model a	Model b	Model a	Model b	Model a	Model b
Parental social class (ref. Manual [V + VI + VIII])								
No earners/no code		−0.015**		−0.026***		0.043***		0.013
		(0.0064)		(0.0076)		(0.0126)		(0.0114)
Routine nonmanual (III)		0.003		−0.004		0.048***		0.026***
		(0.0046)		(0.0058)		(0.0076)		(0.0072)
Petite bourgeoisie (IV)		0.003		−0.001		−0.007		−0.006
		(0.0053)		(0.0067)		(0.0088)		(0.0083)
Professional/managerial (I + II)		0.005		−0.009		0.085***		0.053***
		(0.0045)		(0.0057)		(0.0073)		(0.0069)
Carstairs quintile in origin (ref. Q1: Least deprived)								
Q2		−0.004		0.005		−0.009		0.002
		(0.0051)		(0.0064)		(0.0073)		(0.0070)
Q3		−0.002		0.003		−0.003		−0.001
		(0.0052)		(0.0067)		(0.0079)		(0.0074)
Q4		−0.008		0.012*		−0.023***		0.003
		(0.0054)		(0.0069)		(0.0084)		(0.0079)
Q5		−0.010*		0.010		−0.017*		−0.002
		(0.0059)		(0.0075)		(0.0096)		(0.0091)
Carstairs quintile in 2011 (ref. Q1: Least deprived)								
Q2		−0.003		0.013*		−0.016*		−0.007

		(0.0058)		(0.0074)		(0.0088)		(0.0083)
Q3		−0.015***		0.022***		−0.034***		−0.027***
		(0.0058)		(0.0072)		(0.0089)		(0.0084)
Q4		−0.021***		0.018**		−0.047***		−0.020**
		(0.0059)		(0.0075)		(0.0093)		(0.0087)
Q5		−0.031***		0.005		−0.042***		−0.022**
		(0.0065)		(0.0082)		(0.0105)		(0.0100)
Age								
Age in 2001	0.001*	−0.001	0.004***	0.004***	0.016***	0.006***	0.013***	0.005***
	(0.0007)	(0.0007)	(0.0009)	(0.0008)	(0.0012)	(0.0011)	(0.0011)	(0.0010)
Origin year (ref. 1981)								
1991	0.000	−0.007***	0.005**	−0.004*	0.010***	−0.022***	0.013***	−0.019***
	(0.0018)	(0.0020)	(0.0023)	(0.0026)	(0.0030)	(0.0032)	(0.0028)	(0.0030)
Number of census points (ref. 3)								
4 census points	0.017***	−0.003	0.031***	0.005	0.098***	0.023***	0.090***	0.022***
	(0.0055)	(0.0050)	(0.0069)	(0.0064)	(0.0091)	(0.0084)	(0.0087)	(0.0080)
Country of birth								
UK-born	0.008	0.026**	−0.020	−0.017	−0.010	0.035	−0.011	0.015
	(0.0135)	(0.0118)	(0.0179)	(0.0170)	(0.0251)	(0.0228)	(0.0237)	(0.0207)
N	36,886	36,886	40,294	40,294	35,453	35,453	38,391	38,391

Notes: Robust (clustered) standard errors in parentheses. Population: Individuals between 16 and 29 years old in 2001.
Source: Authors' calculations based on ONS-LS.

Table A19.2 Predicted values of employment and professional/managerial occupation in 2011, by labor market status in 2001, ethnic group, and gender

	Employment				Professional/managerial occupation			
	Men		Women		Men		Women	
	Value	SE	Value	SE	Value	SE	Value	SE
NEET								
White British	0.79	0.01	0.70	0.01	0.30	0.01	0.30	0.01
Indian	0.88	0.03	0.59	0.07	0.39	0.08	0.33	0.07
Pakistani	0.85	0.04	0.47	0.05	0.33	0.09	0.28	0.06
Bangladeshi	0.91	0.04	0.59	0.07	0.33	0.12	0.44	0.11
Caribbean	0.85	0.07	0.53	0.12	0.45	0.17	0.33	0.10
Student								
White British	0.92	0.00	0.87	0.01	0.47	0.01	0.48	0.01
Indian	0.93	0.01	0.82	0.03	0.63	0.03	0.59	0.04
Pakistani	0.91	0.02	0.64	0.04	0.43	0.05	0.55	0.05
Bangladeshi	0.98	0.01	0.71	0.06	0.72	0.08	0.56	0.08
Caribbean	0.90	0.04	0.73	0.07	0.46	0.11	0.55	0.10
Employed								
White British	0.95	0.00	0.88	0.00	0.43	0.00	0.44	0.01
Indian	0.93	0.01	0.81	0.03	0.50	0.03	0.51	0.04
Pakistani	0.96	0.01	0.74	0.04	0.40	0.06	0.42	0.05
Bangladeshi	0.95	0.02	0.79	0.06	0.43	0.08	0.47	0.08
Caribbean	0.92	0.03	0.85	0.04	0.49	0.08	0.49	0.06

Notes: Variables set to their mean: Age, country of birth, origin year, number of census points, parental social class, number of cars, tenure, level of overcrowding, neighborhood deprivation (past and current), education, and family type. Population: Individuals between 16 and 29 years old in 2001.
Source: Authors' calculations based on ONS-LS.

20

DO BUSINESS START-UPS CREATE HIGH-QUALITY JOBS FOR YOUNG PEOPLE?

Renate Ortlieb, Maura Sheehan, and Jaan Masso

20.1. INTRODUCTION

Since the onset of the recent economic crisis, there has been a renewed interest among policymakers across Europe in measures to stimulate self-employment and entrepreneurship as an alternative to unemployment (e.g., within the Europe 2020 strategy; European Commission 2010, 2013). However, fundamental questions about policies promoting self-employment, especially among young people, remain unanswered. For instance, do such policies create new jobs or just promote new forms of precarious, poor-quality employment? (For an overview of policies targeted at youth transitions in general across Europe, see Petmesidou and González Menéndez, this volume.) Despite considerable interest among policymakers, there is little evidence regarding the quality of jobs that young people create for either themselves or for further employees. Indeed, Shane's (2008) detailed analysis of entrepreneurship in the United States critically concluded, "Start-ups don't generate as many jobs as most people think, and the jobs that they create aren't as good as the jobs in existing companies" (p. 161). Focusing on EU27 countries, this chapter addresses the question as to whether business start-ups create high-quality jobs for young people.[1]

New economic business models have recently seen a flourishing of self-employment for young people, as exemplified by the growth of companies such as Deliveroo and Uber operating in the "sharing" economy (Cushing 2013; Eichhorst et al. 2016). Young people working for these companies frequently have a self-employment status as own-account workers rather than a traditional employment relationship with the organization. So-called "gig" workers are typically contracted through virtual "human cloud" platforms such as Amazon's Mechanical Turk, TaskRabbit, and Upwork. The European Commission (2016a) is generally quite positive in its outlook for these new business models and the associated employment opportunities. However, the rise of "gig" workers is also receiving increased media and policy attention, with workers demanding better pay deals and questions being raised about the extent to which these young people really are self-employed or not (BBC 2016; Valenduc and Vendramin 2016). As an emerging form of employment, it is not always clear to what extent these new self-employed workers are protected by domestic labor law (De Stefano 2016), given that they do not have employment contracts but, rather, service contracts on the basis of so-called clickwrap agreements—that is, the workers agree to the terms of a service contract by clicking an "OK" button on the company website.

Encouraging self-employment for young people requires an understanding of what the long-term implications of this work are in terms of job quality. The aim of this chapter is to examine the job quality of self-employed women and men younger than age 35 years and the related job-creation potential. The analysis uses an explorative approach based on current conceptualizations of job quality and secondary data sources such as the European Union Labour Force Survey, the European Working Conditions Survey, and the European Union Statistics on Income and Living Conditions, as well as semistructured interviews with self-employed young people in selected countries and industries. After mapping youth self-employment in EU27 countries, the chapter presents findings concerning the job quality of young self-employed and the job-creation potential of youth self-employment. The analysis takes gender-related differences into account, given that the existing literature indicates that job quality differs substantially between women and men (Smith et al. 2008; Mühlau 2011; Beblo and Ortlieb 2012).

20.2. DEFINING SELF-EMPLOYMENT

In this chapter, we define self-employment in accordance with the definition used by the European Union Labour Force Survey. That is, with the term "self-employment," we refer to a form of employment engaged in by people who work in their own business, farm, or professional practice and who receive some form of economic return for their labor. Thereby, in our analysis we consider both self-employed with employees working for them and self-employed without employees. Alternative terms commonly used in the literature include "employers" and "owner–managers" for self-employed with employees and "sole traders," "solo self-employed," "own-account workers," and "freelancers" for self-employed without employees. With the term "salaried employees," we refer to people employed by organizations.

Defining self-employment is a challenging endeavor because the empirical boundary between self-employment and salaried employment is blurred (Jorens 2008; Muehlberger and Pasqua 2009; Eichhorst et al. 2013; Oostveen et al. 2013). According to definitions typically used by social security institutions and state authorities, people are categorized as self-employed if they fulfill the following criteria: Self-employed individuals autonomously choose the content, time, and place of their work without being bound by the instructions of other persons—such as formal supervisors within a hierarchically structured company—and they take responsibility for business risks on their own (for an overview of legal definitions in selected European countries, see Sheehan and McNamara 2015).

However, within the past few decades, "false" or "bogus" forms of self-employment have been emerging as a consequence of an increase in outsourcing activities by firms (Jorens 2008; Flecker and Hermann 2011). Bogus self-employed people formally deliver their services as an independent firm based on a service contract or a general commercial contract, but factually, they depend on another organization to the same degree as salaried employees depend on their employers. Typically, these people work as sole traders without employees working for them, they have only one client, they are not able to hire staff if necessary, and/or they are not able to make the most important decisions about how to organize their work and run the business (Ostveen et al. 2013). This form of self-employment is related to employers circumventing social insurance contributions and other issues subject to labor law, such as employment protection, working-time limits, maternity/paternity and sick pay, or paid holidays (Román, Congregado, and Millán 2011). In addition, bogus self-employment has been related in the past to circumventing access restrictions to the labor market for migrants from European Union (EU) accession countries (Thörnquist 2013). Thus, although bogus self-employment sometimes may remain the only viable option for youth to find paid work, it is often associated with a quite significant lack of employment protection and social welfare entitlements (Eichhorst et al. 2013). As a consequence, in those countries and occupations in which such institutions exist, bogus self-employed people are at a disadvantage in this regard compared to salaried employees. Moreover, the (bogus) self-employed cannot avail of benefits negotiated from the collective bargaining agreements commonly found in Denmark, Germany, and Sweden, for example.

Both the difficulties related to the empirical distinction between self-employed, bogus self-employed, and salaried employees and the differences between these three forms of employment with respect to dependencies and risks should be kept in mind when interpreting the empirical findings presented in this chapter. We shed more light on bogus self-employment in Section 20.8 on job-creation potential.

20.3. JOB QUALITY: CONCEPTS AND EMPIRICAL EVIDENCE

For policymakers, unions, and many employers alike, the quality of jobs is a highly important issue. For example, one of the declared aims of the Lisbon Strategy launched by the European Council in 2000 reads, "More and better jobs for Europe" (European Council 2000). For unions and other workers' associations, job quality can be viewed as the overarching aim of different kinds of activities. This aim is also reflected in the International Labour Organization's (2015) Decent Work Agenda, which emphasizes fair labor income, security in the workplace, and workers' voice, among other issues. Only recently, management scholars, too, have called for a reinvigoration of research on quality of working life, which also should have a policy impact (Grote and Guest 2017).

A number of studies seek to map job quality in Europe using survey data (Gallie 2003; Smith et al. 2008; Olsen, Kalleberg, and Nesheim 2010; Green and Mostafa 2012; Oinas et al. 2012; Green et al. 2013; Holman 2013). According to these studies, job quality tends to be better in Nordic and Continental European countries than in Southern Europe and especially in Eastern Europe. However, although some studies establish nuanced pictures of job quality in Europe, very few consider the job quality of young people (Russell, Leschke, and Smith 2015), and none explicitly examine the consequences for young self-employed.

Within the job-quality literature, various conceptualizations of job quality have been proposed. Although scholars do not have a common understanding of what "good jobs" or "bad jobs" mean, we can identify workers' well-being as a comprehensive aim. As Muñoz de Bustillo et al. (2011) state in their extensive review, "At a very high level of generality, we can more or less agree that job quality refers to the characteristics of work and employment that affect the well-being of the worker" (p. 460).

The question as to what concrete job characteristics constitute job quality has not yet been conclusively answered. However, review articles indicate that there is agreement on the shortcomings of subjective concepts focusing on factors such as job satisfaction and feelings of well-being (Leschke, Watt, and Finn 2008; Muñoz de Bustillo et al. 2011; Hauff and Kirchner 2014). Although subjective concepts might suit research purposes related to work motivation or general life satisfaction, they fall short with regard to identifying the sources of these attitudes and their long-term consequences for the well-being of both workers and their families. In contrast, objective concepts of job quality directly focus on "the features of jobs that meet workers' needs from work" (Green and Mostafa 2012, 10), which can be summarized under the umbrella concept of workers' well-being. Examples of objective measures include pay, working time, autonomy, health and safety, skills and career development, and participation in decision-making. Objective concepts have a subjective component, too, because they center on the perspective of the working individuals. Correspondingly, research typically relies on self-reported data. Overall, however, objective concepts rely on measures related to the universal needs of (all) workers rather than on subjective feelings.

In our analysis of the job quality of self-employed youth in Europe, we focus on both objective and subjective job characteristics. These indicators include the following: pay, working hours, work intensity, feeling of social belonging, health and safety, learning and development, perceived job security, and subjective satisfaction with pay and working hours.

20.4. RESEARCH DESIGN AND DATA

With the aim of understanding and comparing the job quality of self-employed youth in Europe, we draw on a range of complementary methodological approaches. The analysis of secondary data relies on three cross-EU individual-level representative surveys. First, the European Union Labour Force Survey (EU-LFS)—run by the national statistical authorities—is the standard household-based survey of labor market information, such as rates of unemployment and inactivity, in the EU. In the analysis, we used data for EU27 countries from 2002 until 2014. In recent years, the number of annual observations has ranged from approximately 20,000 to 600,000. Second, the European Working Conditions Survey (EWCS) run by Eurofound is the source of information for working conditions and the quality of work in the EU. We used the most recent available data (year 2010) for 27 countries, with the number of observations per country being in the range of 1,000 to 4,000. Third, the European Union Statistics on Income and Living Conditions (EU-SILC) is the source for comparative statistics on income distribution and social inclusion in the EU, with a focus on income. In the analysis, we used three waves from 2004, 2008, and 2012 for 31 countries (for details, see Masso et al. 2015, 61).

The quantitative data are supplemented by case study data originating from semistructured interviews with 72 young self-employed under 35 years of age and by additional company information gathered from websites and personal visits. Applying purposeful sampling, we conducted the case studies in six selected countries: Estonia, Germany, Ireland, Poland, Spain, and the United Kingdom. We selected these countries because they represent very different business environments in terms of institutional, economic, and cultural contexts. Specifically, these countries cover different types of Hall and Soskice's (2001) *Varieties of Capitalism* typology and of Pohl and Walther's (2007) categorization of school-to-work transition regimes.

Germany reflects many elements of coordinated market capitalism and has an employment-centered transition regime, Ireland and the United Kingdom both have liberal market economies and liberal transition regimes, Spain has some degree of market coordination and a subprotective transition regime, and Estonia and Poland both have liberal market economies and post-socialist transition regimes. We sought to take account of different regimes in our sample because we expected that these frameworks would help provide a theoretical explanation for patterns of youth self-employment in the six study countries and possibly across the EU. In addition, hypothesizing that national unemployment rates and youth self-employment rates reflect more general labor market and institutional conditions, we selected the countries in such a way that the sample covers different labor market contexts.

The six countries differ in terms of youth unemployment rates (ranging from 7.2% in Germany to 48.3% in Spain in 2014; Eurostat 2016) and youth self-employment rates (ranging from 4.3% in Germany to 11.1% in Poland in 2014; authors' calculations based on EU-LFS data; see also Section 20.5). Regarding social protection systems, in all six countries the self-employed have access to health care and pension insurance. Differences between the countries relate to the degree of compulsion, the cost of social insurance, and the related benefits (for details on selected European countries, see Schulze Buschoff and Protsch 2008). For instance, in Germany, health care and pension insurance are compulsory, with contributions depending on the amount of tax paid. In contrast, all self-employed in the United Kingdom receive health care benefits without paying contributions. In Spain, the self-employed can voluntarily contribute to a special system that also provides cash benefits in the event of sickness (for further details, see European Commission 2014). The fact that the sample does not include a country with a very high rate of self-employment—for example, Greece or Italy—is recognized as a limitation of this study.

In the six countries, we focus on two selected industrial sectors so as to reduce complexity. We selected the cultural and creative industry (CCI) and the information/communication technologies sector (ICT) because they provide comparatively good opportunities for youth, especially, to start a business. Moreover, the ICT industry represents 4.8% of the European economy, where investments in ICT account for half of the productivity growth in Europe (European Commission 2016b), whereas the CCI industry is perceived as one of Europe's most dynamic sectors, providing approximately 5 million jobs across the EU27 (European Commission 2010). In addition, the importance of these two sectors within the European economy is expected to increase in the future so that they could become a significant source of future self-employment opportunities for young people (for details, see McNamara et al. 2016).

The value of this case study research is to provide insights into perceptions of job quality and into the job-creation potential associated with youth self-employment that go beyond those available from an interpretation of more quantitative aggregate data. In this sense, our research design incorporates both a macro, comparative dimension and a more specific, micro perspective to evaluate the issue of job quality for the young self-employed in Europe.

20.5. YOUTH SELF-EMPLOYMENT RATES ACROSS EUROPE

The extent and significance of youth self-employment in Europe are indicated by the figure of more than 5.6 million EU27 citizens younger than age 35 years who were self-employed in 2014 (according to EU-LFS data). Within the group of working people aged 25–34 years, more than every tenth person was self-employed. The self-employment rate—that is, the share of self-employed among all employed—within this group of older youth is more than twice as high as the rate for younger youth aged 15–24 years, but it is decidedly lower than that for adults aged 35–65 years (older youth, 10.1%; younger youth, 4.2%; older adults, 17.0%). During the past decade, the self-employment rate has been fairly stable. The overall rate across EU27 countries has oscillated within the range of 14.2% to 14.7%, with a peak in 2004 and a decreasing trend during the past 5 years.

Self-employment rates in EU27 countries are presented in Figure 20.1, which compares youth younger than age 35 years and older adults in the years 2002 and 2014. The graph shows that youth self-employment rates vary significantly across the EU. For example, in 2014, the rates for youth younger than age 35 years were highest in Greece and Italy (18.3% and 17.8%, respectively), whereas they were lowest in Denmark and Germany (3.6% and 4.3%, respectively). Regarding age groups, Figure 20.1 indicates that the largest gaps in self-employment rates between youth younger than age 35 years and older adults exist in Ireland and Austria. By contrast, the self-employment rates of youth younger than age 35 years and older adults are similar in Italy and Slovakia.

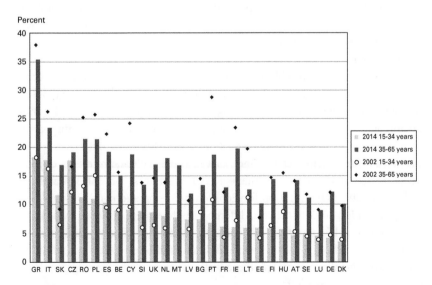

Figure 20.1 Self-employment rates of youth (aged 15–34 years) and older adults (aged 35–65 years) across EU27 countries: 2002 and 2014.
Source: EU-LFS.

A comparison of the years 2002 and 2014—spanning a period that may entail effects of the recent economic and financial crisis but is still long enough to shed light on longer term trends—indicates that self-employment rates decreased especially in those countries that were characterized by comparatively high self-employment rates in 2002 and poor general economic environments. Examples include Portugal, Poland, and Romania. Interestingly, countries such as Estonia, Latvia, and Slovakia, where self-employment rates increased, faced similarly difficult economic conditions. But because self-employment rates in these countries were comparatively low in 2002, they apparently subsequently caught up with the other EU countries. Western European countries with increased self-employment rates include France, the Netherlands, and the United Kingdom. In these countries, self-employment rates possibly increased because of both improved governmental support for entrepreneurship and increased outsourcing activities—resulting in bogus self-employment.

A further interesting finding is that in some countries, youth self-employment rates changed differently over time from those for older adults, whereas in most countries the rates for youth and older adults changed in a similar way—that is, between 2002 and 2014, the rates for both age groups increased, decreased, or they remained at the same level. Specifically, in Spain and Italy, youth self-employment rates increased, whereas rates for older adults decreased. Similarly, in Cyprus and Greece, rates for older adults considerably decreased, whereas those for the young remained nearly stable. Because these four countries are among those EU countries with the highest youth unemployment rates, the patterns suggest that a high number of young people may have tried to escape from unemployment by working as self-employed, although they might have preferred salaried employment had it been available.[2]

Although we are not able to identify a clear pattern of differences across countries according to Hall and Soskice's (2001) *Varieties of Capitalism* typology, we interpret these findings as reflecting country specificities, such as the youth unemployment rate, the size of the informal sector, the relative importance of sectors typical of self-employment (e.g., agriculture), institutions related to starting a business and social welfare, as well as the skills and mindsets of young people (Packard, Koettl, and Montenegro 2012; Eichhorst et al. 2013; Mascherini and Bisello 2015; Organization for Economic Co-operation and Development/ European Union 2015). Likewise, differences between age groups may be traced back to different labor market opportunities, economic structures, and mindsets. Furthermore, although young people and adults of one country act within the same institutional environment, these institutions may affect young people differently compared to adults.

20.6. WHO ARE THE SELF-EMPLOYED AND WHAT KIND OF BUSINESSES DO THEY RUN?

Confirming previous research findings on the sociodemographic character-istics of the self-employed (Dawson, Henley, and Latreille 2009; Barnir and McLaughlin 2011; Poschke 2013; Caliendo, Fossen, and Kritikos 2014; Simoes, Crespo, and Moreira 2015), our analyses based on EU-LFS data show that the probability of being self-employed increases with age. In addition, this proba-bility is higher for men than for women, for nationals than for non-nationals, for less educated people (below secondary education) than for the better ed-ucated, and for those whose parents are self-employed (for details, see Masso et al. 2015, 20–21). Self-employment does not appear to be very attractive to the rising number of "overeducated" young people across the EU (for a comprehen-sive analysis of youth overeducation across the EU, see McGuinness, Bergin, and Whelan, this volume).

Regarding industrial sectors, according to EWCS data for 2010, young self-employed under 35 years of age tend to cluster in the wholesale, retail, food, and accommodation sectors (22.6%); other services (21.8%); and agriculture (20.5%). Figure 20.2 displays their distribution across sectors compared to all self-employed and all young working people under 35 years of age. In addition, it presents the distribution of young self-employed women under 35 years of age.

Figure 20.2 shows a very similar pattern for young self-employed aged under 35 years and for all self-employed, with approximately 3% of the young working less in the agricultural sector and 3% more providing other services. These trends might result from a cohort effect, shaped by the general decline of

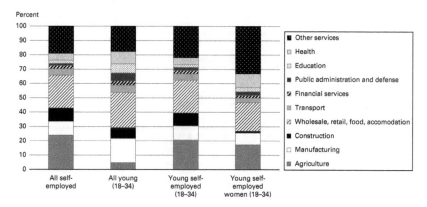

Figure 20.2 Sectors of all self-employed (aged 18–65 years), all young working people (aged 18–34 years), young self-employed (aged 18–34 years), and young self-employed women (aged 18–34 years) in EU27 countries: 2010.
Source: EWCS.

the agricultural sector and the emergence of the service sector during the past few decades. Nevertheless, agriculture is still an important sector for young self-employed, particularly in comparison to young salaried employees. Furthermore, Figure 20.2 indicates typical gender segregation within the group of young self-employed under 35 years, with young women strongly over-represented in the health sector and in other services.

Altogether, these findings support previous evidence, according to which young people tend to focus on sectors with low entry barriers and low capital requirements (Parker 2009). At the same time, because these sectors are characterized by high shares of low-skill jobs and poorly paid work, they are often associated with lower job quality (see Grotti, Russell, and O'Reilly, this volume).

20.7. JOB QUALITY OF YOUNG SELF-EMPLOYED

Using EWCS data for the EU27 countries (the wording of the items is provided in the Appendix to this chapter), this section concentrates on selected job characteristics, as outlined in Section 20.3 on concepts of job quality (for an overview of youth transitions and job quality in general, see Filandri, Nazio, and O'Reilly, this volume). Figure 20.3 depicts the median net earnings and average working hours, as well as ratings concerning further working conditions, of all self-employed, all young working people under 35 years, young self-employed people under 35 years, and young self-employed women.

Figure 20.3 shows that the young self-employed under 35 years receive a median income of €1,158, which is higher than the income of young salaried

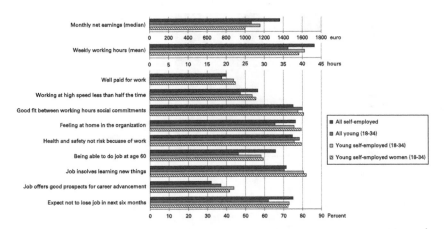

Figure 20.3 Working conditions of all self-employed (aged 18–65 years), all young working people (aged 18–34 years), young self-employed (aged 18–34 years), and young self-employed women (aged 18–34 years) in EU27 countries: 2010.
Source: EWCS.

employees but lower than the income of older adult self-employed. Within the group of the young self-employed under 35 years, women—with a median income of €1,000—receive less than men.[3] Interestingly, among the young self-employed under 35 years, and thereof among women in particular, the share of those who believe they are well paid for their work is larger than in the groups of older adult self-employed and young salaried employees under 35 years.

Regarding working hours, young self-employed under 35 years work 40.8 hours per week, on average, which is more than 4 hours above the mean for all young working people (36.5 hours) and 2.6 hours less than the mean for all self-employed (43.4 hours). Young self-employed women, on average, work 38.6 hours per week. However, the median working hours of young self-employed women and men equal those of all young working people and all employees, amounting to 40 hours per week. According to Figure 20.3, young self-employed under 35 years—and, in particular, young self-employed women—perceive a good fit between their job duties and their social commitments. Although the share of those perceiving a good fit is smaller than that of the young salaried employees, this finding indicates satisfactory working-time arrangements, also in comparison with older adult self-employed.

Likewise, young self-employed aged under 35—and, especially, young self-employed women—report comparatively low work intensity. According to figure 20.3, the ratings of this job feature correspond with those of the following three items, where young self-employed perceive themselves as having better working conditions than their salaried employed peers, but (slightly) worse conditions than older adult self-employed: "Feeling at home in the organization worked for," "Being able to do job at age 60," and "Expect not to lose job in next 6 months." The finding that young self-employed at least partly perceive these job features more negatively than older adult self-employed can be traced back to effects related to age and experience. For example, it is less likely that a 30-year-old person would envision doing her/his job at the age of 60, as compared to a 50-year-old person, simply because the time horizon for the 30-year-old is much longer.

Besides satisfaction with pay, the young self-employed evaluated two further job characteristics more positively than the other groups, namely "Job involves learning new things" and "Job offers good prospects for career advancement." Figure 20.3 additionally shows that young self-employed women rate learning opportunities more positively than their male peers, but career prospects more negatively. These gender differences might be associated with the different industrial sectors women and men work in, as described in section 6 above. Notwithstanding these differences, this finding is particularly notable because good learning and development opportunities are especially crucial for young people, both in their current situation and for their future.

However, although young self-employed perceive comparatively good learning opportunities, they also view themselves as lacking skills. According to EWCS data, compared to all self-employed and all young working people, young self-employed under 35 years more often report that their present skills do not correspond well with their job duties (for details, see Masso et al. 2015, 30–31). In particular, the share of those who perceive themselves as lacking skills is largest among young self-employed women. The share of young self-employed under 35 years reporting that they need further training is particularly large in Austria (58.2%), Estonia (41.1%), and Denmark (37.5%). Although this finding points, on the one hand, to the potentially problematic situation of high demands faced by young self-employed, it can be viewed, on the other hand, as a positive indicator of the fact that these people work not just in low-skill jobs.

In summary, compared to other groups of working people, young self-employed generally report good job quality. However, the overall good ratings should not hide the fact that a large share of young self-employed indicated that they do not believe they are well paid for their work and that their job does not offer good career prospects. Moreover, even if they express less job insecurity than peers working as salaried employees, the consequences of losing their jobs are more severe because in many countries they are not entitled to unemployment benefits (for details, see Schulze Buschoff and Protsch 2008).

20.8. JOB-CREATION POTENTIAL

This section takes a closer look at the job-creation potential for both the young self-employed and additional people working for them. Indicators of the job-creation potential of self-employment relate to the following three questions: Do young people leave unemployment by becoming self-employed? Are young self-employed to be classified as bogus self-employed? and Do young self-employed have further employees working for them?

20.8.1. Do young people leave unemployment by becoming self-employed?

Regarding this question, analyses of labor market status transition rates based on EU-LFS data reveal a mixed picture (for details, see Masso et al. 2015, 14–17). Table 20.1 presents results for transitions between different labor market statuses in 2011 and 2012.

Table 20.1 shows that 1.4% of young unemployed under 25 years in 2011 and 2.8% of older youth aged 25–34 years in 2011 became self-employed in the following year—that is, in 2012. Of both youth age groups, approximately two-thirds remained unemployed in the following year; one-fourth became salaried employees; and 6.1% or 7.0%, respectively, moved into labor market inactivity (e.g., by entering further training). The small shares of those young unemployed who moved from unemployment into self-employment indicate that opportunities for young people to escape unemployment by founding their own

Table 20.1 Labor market status transitions of young youth (aged 15–24 years), older youth (aged 25–34 years), and older adults (aged 35–64 years) in EU27 countries, 2011–2012

| | | Labor market status in 2012 (row %) | | | |
Age group	Labor market status in 2011	Unemployed	Self-employed	Salaried employed	Labor market inactive
15–24 years	Unemployed	67.9	1.4	23.8	7.0
	Self-employed	6.1	78.1	8.1	7.7
	Salaried employed	9.2	0.6	82.5	7.7
	Labor market inactive	5.5	0.2	6.2	88.1
25–34 years	Unemployed	66.4	2.8	24.8	6.1
	Self-employed	3.1	89.0	4.7	3.2
	Salaried employed	6.1	0.8	90.4	2.7
	Labor market inactive	10.2	1.3	13.4	75.1
35–64 years	Unemployed	72.4	2.0	16.9	8.7
	Self-employed	2.0	92.5	2.2	3.3
	Salaried employed	3.9	0.5	92.8	2.9
	Labor market inactive	2.2	0.5	2.2	95.1

Notes: Authors' calculations; no data for Germany, Ireland, or the United Kingdom.
Source: EU-LFS.

business are limited. Even so, these numbers are slightly higher for older youth aged 25–34 years compared to older adults aged 35 years or older.

Relatedly, the transition rates of young self-employed under 25 years suggest that for many younger youth, self-employment is a temporary option only (for details, see Masso et al. 2015, 14–17, 65–67, 70–73). Of the self-employed aged 15–24 years in 2011, in the following year 6.1% were unemployed, 8.1% were working as salaried employees, and 7.7% were inactive in the labor market. Overall, transition rates out of self-employment decrease with increasing age. Of the older self-employed youth aged 25–34 years in 2011, in the following year 3.1% were unemployed, 4.7% were working as salaried employees, and 3.2% were labor market inactive. The shares for self-employed adults aged 35–64 years amounted to 2% being unemployed in the following year, 2.2% becoming salaried employees, and 3.3% being labor market inactive.

The finding that transition rates out of self-employment decrease by increasing age can be interpreted as partly resulting from a higher share of involuntary self-employment among youth. For some of those young self-employed who moved into salaried employment, running their own business may have functioned as a steppingstone to a less insecure job. On the other hand, young people may, on average, change jobs more often than older adults because they still have to determine what kind of work suits them. However, the high transition rates of young self-employed—especially of those younger than age 25 years—into unemployment or labor market inactivity point to larger problems.

20.8.2. Are young self-employed to be classified as bogus self-employed?

To analyze bogus self-employment, our second indicator of job-creation potential, we apply the criteria suggested by Oostveen et al. (2013) and outlined previously. Data from the 2010 wave of the EWCS show that young self-employed under 35 years of age are likely to a similar degree as older adults to belong to the category of bogus self-employed (for details, see Masso et al. 2015, 22–23). Among the young self-employed under 35 years without employees working for them, 13.4% indicate that they have only one client (all self-employed: 14.0%), 40.9% are not able to hire staff (all self-employed: 43.6%),[4] and 9.7% do not make the most important decisions on how to run their business (all self-employed: 7.9%). Furthermore, 28.1% receive regular payments from their client(s) (all self-employed: 25.4%). We interpret regular payments as an indicator of bogus self-employment, too, because they are associated with dependencies typical of employer–employee relationships. These findings indicate that a large share of young self-employed people factually work in jobs resembling salaried employment rather than self-employment. In terms of job-creation potential, the question is whether these jobs would exist if the same work had to be done on the basis of an employment contract.

20.8.3. Do young self-employed have further employees working for them?

Our third indicator refers to the employment of further people. According to EU-SILC data for 2012, the majority of young self-employed run their business without employees working for them (for details, see Masso et al. 2015, 17–20). Within the group of the younger self-employed under 25 years of age, only 11.2% have one or more employees working for them. For older youth aged 25–34 years, this share increases to 21.8%, whereas 27.7% of the self-employed adults aged 35–64 years have at least one employee. Within all age groups, compared to men, fewer women have employees. The correlation of age with number of employees could be due to various reasons, such as longer life of the business associated with growth or different sectors. These findings appear to curb the hope that young self-employed serve as a source of further job creation.

Altogether, these findings provide a comprehensive insight into youth self-employment in Europe. However, although the statistical analyses showed that youth self-employment has many shapes (e.g., in terms of the size and the sector of the business), they cannot identify what exactly is behind a statistical case. To obtain a better understanding of the concrete circumstances under which young self-employed people work, further investigation at the micro level of analysis is needed. In Section 20.9, we take such a micro perspective, focusing on selected cases of young self-employed people.

20.9. FINDINGS FROM INTERVIEWS WITH YOUNG SELF-EMPLOYED PEOPLE

Building on the findings from a macro perspective on youth self-employment in Europe, we turn in this section to a micro perspective. Our case studies in the CCI and ICT sectors based on semistructured interviews and further company information offer deeper insight into job quality and job-creation potential. In the analysis of this qualitative material, certain patterns emerged in these regards—related to the business success of the start-up and subjective concerns of the founders regarding social protection. We identified four such patterns that we present next by describing one prototypical case standing for each pattern. We chose the four cases that are best suited to illustrating details related to the job quality and the job-creation potential of young self-employed people.

Originating from Germany, Estonia, and Ireland, the four selected cases are embedded in different institutional, economic, and cultural contexts (see the description in Section 20.4). However, because of the small sample size of 12 cases in each country, our findings are not intended to make generalizations about country differences. Rather, by presenting these 4 cases from three countries, we aim at a condensed illustration of the larger trends we have identified in the empirical material.

Here, we first describe the four cases. Then we juxtapose the cases in order to carve out the specific details related to job quality and job-creation potential. The cases are real, but the names are pseudonyms and several details have been omitted to ensure the anonymity of the interviewees. We indicate the number of cases in our empirical material that belong to the same category as the prototypical example.

The case of Hanna from Germany, exemplifying young self-employed people who work hard and receive considerable income but face challenges related to staff (14 cases in the empirical material)

Hanna provides post-production services related to photography and video clips. Holding a master's degree in arts, she taught herself how to use graphics software. Her company is located in a large city, where Hanna can draw on a large pool of national and international clients. She migrated from another

European country and started working as a freelancer 5 years before the interview. After a few months, she had earned the initial capital for a limited company. Hanna did not apply for financial assistance from the state because she had been generating revenue from the outset and because she lacked the German language skills she would have needed to complete application forms.

Hanna works between 50 and 80 hours per week, often including working in the evenings and on bank holidays, and sometimes working during the night, on weekends, and during holidays. She would prefer to work less hours and spend more time with her two children, but she is afraid of losing her clients if she works less. Although Hanna perceives the financial performance of her business to be below the industry average, her income amounts to €6,000 per month before tax.[5] Her skills match the job requirements very well.

Asked about risks associated with her work as self-employed, Hanna indicates that at the time of founding her business she was unsure whether clients would like her work. Sickness is a risk, as her clients rely on her. Because the business depended on her, a challenging period was when she gave birth to her two children. Although she usually works even if she is sick, she perceives the risk that if something serious happened to her, the whole business would be affected. She tries to invest in real estate so as to have a pension when she is old.

Hanna has one full-time and one part-time employee, both aged younger than 35 years. Because she has many orders, Hanna can afford to employ more staff. However, she has difficulties in finding and retaining qualified employees. The major challenge is that job candidates expect to receive both training and a salary, but Hanna is too busy to devote much of her time to instructing new staff because she has to carry out the regular work herself. In addition, she has had bad experiences regarding employees who quit their job once they have received training from her. She wishes to find employees with appropriate skills or the willingness to earn only a little during the training stage and to stay with her company for a longer period of time.

The case of Bettina from Germany, exemplifying young self-employed people who are creative and perfectionists but in a precarious economic situation (21 cases in the empirical material)

Bettina is a sole trader in fashion design. After obtaining a master's degree and working for several years abroad at a large, high-quality fashion company, she realized a long-cherished desire and founded her own label. Bettina has no employees but does have a few temporary interns. Although she learned a lot during her previous job, she thinks that it would have been better if she had entered self-employment immediately after her studies when she had more energy and better social networks. Setting up her own label initially went well, but then Bettina became pregnant and had to take a break for several months. She is currently a single parent without financial support from the child's father.

Bettina works approximately 40 hours per week. She never works on Sundays, but sometimes she works in the evening or at night, on Saturdays, on bank holidays, and during holidays. She perceives herself as having a good work–life balance, particularly when she compares the current working hours with those of her previous job as a salaried employee in a leadership position. The financial performance of the business is comparatively low. Bettina has difficulty assessing her monthly takings from the business and her total income. Roughly, monthly takings are less than €2,000, and Bettina earns less than €500 per month after tax. She receives financial assistance from the public employment service, supplemented by social benefits. An investor had been interested in her company, but Bettina decided to stay independent because she highly appreciates her autonomy regarding design, materials, and working style. Although her move from salaried employment to self-employment was associated with a considerable loss of income and social security, Bettina prefers her current situation over the previous one. She regularly contributes to a sickness insurance scheme and a pension scheme, which is covered by the social benefits she receives.

Bettina would like to hire staff in the future because she still has many ideas she would like to follow through on. However, it is unclear at what time the financial performance of her label will be good enough to pay salaries.

The case of Sofia from Estonia, exemplifying young self-employed people with a good business partner, a solid business, and a down-to-earth mindset (20 cases in the empirical material)

Sofia runs a company specializing in embroidery, sewing, and female fashion design. She jointly founded the company with another woman. The two women decided to start their own firm when one of them moved to another city and could not find a job matching her skills and the other had been made redundant and was thus also searching for a job in which she could utilize her professional skills in fashion design. The two women started with their own funds and took loans from their relatives. After a few months in business, they successfully applied for state funding to invest in machinery. The company operates on the local market; there is good demand, and the financial performance is above industry average.

Sofia earns less than €500 per month.[6] She works 40 hours per week, sometimes in the evenings and at night or on Saturdays, but never on Sundays, during holidays, or on bank holidays. Living with her husband and small children, she perceives her work–life balance as being good. Her skills set perfectly matches the job requirements. She does not see any risks related to social security. Rather, when she founded the company, she was concerned about her products and the size of her customer base. Later, she perceived difficulties associated with lack of managerial skills and lack of skilled staff.

Sofia's company employs three full-time employees, all of whom are aged older than 50 years. Because the order situation is good, she could hire further employees. However, Sofia and her partner lack the time and money to strategically invest in the company's growth. Sofia also sees a shortage of skilled job candidates, and in the past she had to deal with employees who had a poor work ethic, especially young employees.

The case of David from Ireland, exemplifying young self-employed people who are innovative, run a growing business, and postpone thinking about social insurance to the future (17 cases in the empirical material)

David runs a company that provides an Internet platform to connect customers with cleaning professionals. He holds a bachelor's degree related to information technology (IT) and founded the company immediately after finishing his studies. He rejected a job offer by an IT company and preferred entering self-employment, aiming at doing something he loved to do, working for himself, and developing his own idea. Although less than 1 year in operation, the business has already created revenue. However, the monthly takings are less than €1,000 before tax.[7] The company has no employees, and David does not receive a salary from his company. Because he has a convincing business plan, David receives financial assistance from several state programs.

David works between 60 and 70 hours per week; he works sometimes in the evenings but never at night, usually on Saturdays and during holidays, and sometimes on Sundays and bank holidays. He is single and lives alone. He perceives himself as having a good work–life balance and especially enjoys flexibility because he can work from anywhere. He can utilize his skills, and he appreciates the fact that through running his own business he can learn a lot.

David expressed no concerns about social protection regarding his job status as self-employed. He does not contribute to any insurance schemes. Given his young age, he plans to go 2 or 3 years without any social security and to look more, as he gets older, into pensions, health care, and other insurance. The major risk factors he saw when he started his own business included lack of finances and the risk of personal failure. David is less concerned about financial losses, but he fears that if his business fails, people would question his ability. At the time of the interview, David sees the major risks as originating from upcoming competitors on the market and from having employees that have to be paid.

David plans to employ staff in the future. He wants to hire 15 full-time employees within the next 3 years. He perceives no challenges related to hiring employees because he believes that many people want to work for a start-up, which—according to his experience—is seen as a "cool thing" to do.

20.9.1. Discussion of the interview findings

The micro perspective highlights several topics related to youth self-employment that were hidden in the macro perspective. Regarding job quality, the presented cases illustrate different patterns of working hours and income as well as underlying reasons. Whereas all four interviewees indicated that their job requires them to work long hours, Hanna does so because she is interested in retaining clients and has difficulty delegating work. David works long hours, too, but it seems that he does so more voluntarily than Hanna. Bettina and Sofia work less hours. The working times of the latter two women are restricted by their family responsibilities, whereby Sofia has the advantage that she can share working tasks with her business partner. All interviewees emphasized that one of the major advantages of self-employment is flexibility of working time—despite the long working hours overall—and working place. Because the three women have children, they especially benefit from flexibility, but David also highly appreciates the flexibility.

Whereas Hanna and Sofia earn their living from work, Bettina and David depend on subsistence provided by the state. David appears to be in a less difficult situation compared to Bettina. David receives a large amount of financial assistance related to planned investments and business growth. Living without a family, for a certain period of time he can make ends meet even without a regular salary from his company. In contrast, Bettina belongs to the group of precarious workers. Working without pay may be more prevalent among young self-employed compared to older adults because young people may believe that they are still at a stage of learning and training within their vocational career. Even Hanna, who was able to make a living from the beginning and at the time of the interview was receiving a high salary, trained herself without getting paid. Later on, she accepted poorly paid orders because she needed them to build up her service portfolio, a customer base, and her reputation.

At the time of the interviews, Hanna's income was more than 10 times as high as Sofia's, reflecting different service/product markets and national income levels. However, Sofia appears to be more satisfied with both her business and her co-workers compared to Hanna. The underlying reasons may include the different points of reference in terms of national contexts and the different experiences related to colleagues and employees: Sofia has worse alternative job opportunities in the Estonian fashion industry compared to Hanna in her market segment in Germany. At the same time, whereas Sofia perceived the financial performance of her company as above average, Hanna viewed her company's performance as below average. Furthermore, although both women reported that they were disappointed by former employees and job candidates, Sofia eventually found three employees with whom she was satisfied. In addition, Sofia benefits from the professional and social support of her business partner.

A further important topic related to job quality is professional skills and the degree to which skills sets match job requirements. Echoing our findings based on EWCS data, all the interviewees emphasized that they can utilize their skills and that they continue to learn while running their business. In particular, for Sofia, a major incentive for founding her own business was that she wanted to utilize her skills. Although for all working people the utilization of skills and further learning opportunities are viewed as important, this particularly holds true for young people because they need to create a solid body of knowledge, skills, and abilities for their future career. Thereby, all interviewees expressed their strong desire to do at work those things at which they are best. They repeatedly described their work as something they really love to do. Especially for youth, this typical feature of self-employment will contribute to personal development.

On the other hand, the interviewees also perceived several risks related to self-employment. However, although in the interviews we explicitly asked about risks related to social protection, the interviewees actually mainly referred to business failure. In contrast, their long-term future and social insurance coverage only played a minor role. Apparently, business comes first, and the interviewees were much more concerned about potential competitors, lack of clients, or lack of money. Although the interviewees were well aware of the consequences of business failure, such as poverty or unemployment, they put far more emphasis on their business than on their private situation. This finding holds true for the whole sample of 72 interviews. Even if interviewees expressed their concerns about becoming sick without sickness pay or if they said it was unfair that social protection legislation differentiates between self-employed and salaried employed, their major concerns basically revolved around their businesses.

Of the four cases presented previously, David is illustrative of those young self-employed who believe they are too young to think about social insurance. Hanna and Bettina are aware that they must take care of social security, and they act accordingly. Sofia perceives that the question about social security risks was not relevant in the Estonian context. However, although in some European countries social security legislation provides self-employed with buffers against socioeconomic downfall, these people may be at disadvantage. For instance, young self-employed persons may have lower entitlements to social security over their entire life cycle if their earnings have been low and/or if their contributions were discontinuous. Indeed, after a detailed analysis of social protection for dependent self-employed across the EU, Eichhorst et al. (2013) concluded, "It is doubtful that most dependent self-employed workers sufficiently improve their income over time and save enough to compensate for insufficient public pension entitlements" (p. 9). These authors express serious concerns for potentially high levels of risk of old-age poverty among self-employed EU citizens in the future.

Regarding the job-creation potential of youth self-employment, apparently all four interviewees created jobs that would not exist otherwise, as they invented new services or products. Thereby, the jobs of Bettina and David are not self-sustaining so far but, rather, financed by the public employment service and state programs, respectively. In contrast, both Hanna's and Sofia's work generate sufficient income. In addition, Hanna and Sofia created jobs for further employees. However, they faced challenges related to personnel recruitment. In particular, they reported on negative experiences related to employees' lack of skills and poor work ethic. Although these issues present challenges for all kinds of firms, they will affect young self-employed more than older adults because the young may more often lack professional skills in human resource management. Moreover, apparently there is a danger that young self-employed seek out people with skills and work ethics very similar to their own, leading to disappointment if they see that there are no "clones" of themselves on the labor market.

In summary, although our analyses based on the EWCS suggest that the job-creation potential of youth self-employment is moderate only, the case studies shed light on experiences of young self-employed and rationales behind these findings. Furthermore, the four cases illustrate that the job quality of young self-employed is intertwined with job-creation potential because the interviewees were searching for employees who were willing to work under the same conditions as the interviewees themselves. However, because many job candidates refuse to accept these working conditions, the job-creation potential is only small, in both qualitative and quantitative terms.

It is important to note several limitations related to our case-study analysis. To reduce complexity, we concentrated on very few countries and relatively small labor market segments. In particular, because we selected the creative and ICT sectors, the finding that the young self-employed appreciate autonomy and the opportunity to realize their wishes may be more pronounced than in the transport/logistics, retail, or food service industry. Thus, future case study research should also take account of sectors such as these. Thereby, job quality related to bogus self-employment could be considered—a topic that did not arise in our study because none of the interviewees are categorized as bogus self-employed. In addition, our analyses are based on cross-sectional data. Although our sample comprised self-employed people at different stages, ranging from less than 1 year after founding their business to more than 4 years later, we were not able to trace them over time. Accordingly, future research applying a longitudinal design should cover longer time periods. Specifically, consideration of (formerly) self-employed at older ages and after business failure would be important.

20.10. CONCLUSIONS

This chapter examined the job quality and the job-creation potential of self-employed people younger than age 35 years. The analysis on the basis of EWCS data revealed a somewhat mixed picture in terms of pay and hours worked. The young self-employed report comparatively low work intensity, indicating scope for a good work–life balance. On the other hand, this finding may also reflect under-employment. Importantly, young self-employed see good opportunities for learning and career development. Among the young self-employed, women tend to report better working conditions compared to men. Nevertheless, large shares of the total group of young self-employed do not believe they are well paid for their job and believe that their job offers limited career advancement. The case studies of young self-employed in the creative and ICT sectors additionally showed that despite the long working hours and sometimes very low income, self-employment has the advantage of providing young people with autonomy and an opportunity to utilize their skills. However, the interviews also highlighted that young self-employed see more risks related to their business than related to their private situation in terms of social protection. Because young self-employed have only limited social protection in many European countries (Eichhorst et al. 2013; European Commission 2014), a lack of awareness of the associated risks or insufficient financial means for contributing to optional insurance schemes is worrying. Thus, policies that expand the social security of salaried employees to the self-employed are needed and should address various issues, such as health insurance, sickness and disability pay, maternity/paternity pay, unemployment benefits, and pension coverage.

There already exist national welfare systems that take account of the particularities of self-employed workers. Examples include the health care system of the United Kingdom, which provides high-quality health care for all citizens without monthly contributions to be paid by the beneficiaries. Spain has a comprehensive legal framework related to its special system for the self-employed, including the establishment of benefits for the cessation of self-employment activity and temporary sick leave, along with maternity/paternity pay. In Austria and Germany, the self-employed can opt in to public unemployment insurance. However, as long as young self-employed are not concerned about their futures or if their business profits are too small to cover insurance contributions, they may not take this option.

This chapter has also highlighted that the job-creation potential associated with youth self-employment is only limited. The analysis based on EU-LFS data showed that only a few young people exit unemployment by means of becoming self-employed. At the same time, a non-negligible share of young self-employed become unemployed. A considerable share of young self-employed are categorized as bogus self-employed, and only a small share have employees.

Our case study findings in the creative and ICT sectors indicate that the main obstacles to hiring employees are financial costs and difficulties in finding candidates with appropriate skills and work ethic. Accordingly, policies that promote job creation should comprise measures to address these issues, such as wage subsidies, assistance in finding qualified personnel, or targeted training of job candidates.

Our findings related to bogus self-employment and the hiring of employees also point to the need for policymakers to specify the target groups of policies aiming at the promotion of self-employment (for details, see Sheehan et al. 2016). Likewise, evaluation of policy measures should consider different forms of self-employment. Furthermore, there is a need to carefully assess the employment status of the self-employed working in "human clouds" and organizations that rely on the self-employed for their competitive advantage. For example, Uber regards contracted drivers as "partners," who are thus not protected by labor law. Despite the heavy critique coming from trade unions, Uber's competitors, researchers, and the courts (for a summary, see Adam et al. 2016), presumably other firms will adopt this business model in the future. In general, the so-called "collaborative" and "sharing" economy is in need of specification and regulation. Although the European Commission (2016a) has indicated general support for these rapidly growing forms of economy, new questions of social security arise. For instance, it is difficult to distinguish between those people who provide services on an occasional basis and those who do so in a professional way. However, those people who view their activities within the collaborative economy as a main source of earning a living face the problem that they lack both social protection and protection by labor law.

In summary, for some young people, self-employment presents an option that offers high-quality jobs, as perceived by the young self-employed themselves. In particular, young self-employed people report that they can use and further develop their skills, and they appreciate the high degrees of autonomy and flexibility. However, job quality is impaired by poor social protection, with severe negative consequences especially in the long term. The actual volume of jobs created through self-employment lags behind what politicians had expected, and further policy measures are needed in order to realize existing job-creation potential in the future. Such policy measures would include mentoring and job-shadowing initiatives between established self-employed and young people exploring this career trajectory, as well as easier access to seed funding and other kinds of support for aspiring self-employed. Policies will also need to address the high risks associated with self-employment, especially in relation to unemployment, health care, and pension benefits. Overall, given the large amount of resources targeted at promoting self-employment within the EU, there is an important need for policies that address the current and future well-being of the young self-employed.

NOTES

1 We thank the following colleagues for dedicated and fruitful collaboration: Beata Buchelt, Begoña Cueto, Anna Fohrbeck, María C. González
   Menéndez, Robin Hinks, Eneli Kindsiko, Andrea McNamara, Nigel
   Meager, Kadri Paes, Urban Pauli, Aleksy Pocztowski, Sam Swift, and
   Silvana Weiss. We are also grateful to Brendan Burchell and Traute Meyer,
   who provided helpful comments on previous versions of the chapter, as
   well as to Janine Leschke, Jacqueline O'Reilly, and Martin Seeleib-Kaiser
   for their guidance in preparing the text. Jaan Masso acknowledges financial support from the Estonian Research Agency project No. IUT20–49,
   "Structural Change as the Factor of Productivity Growth in the Case of
   Catching Up Economies."
2 Increases in youth self-employment rates can also reflect a decline in salaried
   employment. The absolute numbers of salaried employed and self-employed
   in Spain, Italy, Cyprus, and Greece for 2002 and 2014 based on EU-LFS data
   do not support this reasoning, however.
3 The means and confidence intervals are as follows: All self-employed: €1,588
   (1,533; 1,643); all young (aged 18–24 years): €1,103 (1,087; 1,120); young self-
   employed (aged 25–34 years): €1,272 (1,182; 1,361); and young self-employed
   women (aged 18–34 years): €1,160 (1,041; 1,279).
4 The high share of young self-employed who indicated that they are not able to
   hire staff may have resulted from a misunderstanding because the respondents
   may have evaluated their (lacking) resources for hiring staff instead of the
   mere freedom to make a decision.
5 In 2015, the median gross labor income in Germany amounted to €1,928 per
   month (Eurostat 2017).
6 In 2015, the median gross labor income in Estonia amounted to €834 per
   month (Eurostat 2017).
7 In 2015, the median gross labor income in Ireland amounted to €2,246 per
   month (Eurostat 2017).

REFERENCES

Adam, Duncan, Mitchell Bremermann, Jessica Duran, Francesca Fontanarosa,
   Birgit Kraemer, Hedvig Westphal, Annamaria Kunert, and Lisa Tönnes
   Lönnroos. 2016. "Digitalisation and Working Life: Lessons from the Uber
   Cases Around Europe." *EurWORK, European Observatory of Working
   Life*, January 25. Dublin: Eurofound. https://www.eurofound.europa.eu/
   observatories/eurwork/articles/working-conditions-law-and-regulation-
   business/digitalisation-and-working-life-lessons-from-the-uber-cases-
   around-europe

Barnir, Anat, and Erin McLaughlin. 2011. "Parental Self-Employment, Start-Up Activities and Funding: Exploring Intergenerational Effects." *Journal of Developmental Entrepreneurship* 16 (3): 371–92.

BBC. 2016. "Deliveroo Offers Concessions in Pay Row." *BBC News*, August 14. https://www.bbc.com/news/business-37076706

Beblo, Miriam, and Renate Ortlieb. 2012. "Absent from Work? The Impact of Household and Work Conditions in Germany." *Feminist Economics* 18 (1): 73–97.

Caliendo, Marco, Frank Fossen, and Alexander S. Kritikos. 2014. "Personality Characteristics and the Decision to Become and Stay Self-Employed." *Small Business Economics* 42 (4): 787–814.

Cushing, Ellen. 2013. "Amazon Mechanical Turk: The Digital Sweatshop." *UTNE Reader*, January/February. https://www.utne.com/science-and-technology/amazon-mechanical-turk-zm0z13jfzlin.aspx

Dawson, Christopher J., Andrew Henley, and Paul L. Latreille. 2009. "Why Do Individuals Choose Self-Employment?" IZA Discussion Paper 3974. Bonn: Institute for the Study of Labor.

De Stefano, Valerio. 2016. "The Rise of the 'Just-in-Time Workforce': On-Demand Work, Crowdwork and Labour Protection in the 'Gig-Economy.'" *Comparative Labor Law & Policy Journal* 37 (3): 471–504.

Eichhorst, Werner, Michela Braga, Ulrike Famira-Mühlberger, Maarten Gerard, Thomas Horvath, Martin Kahanec, et al. 2013. "Social Protection Rights of Economically Dependent Self-Employed Workers." Study commissioned by the European Parliament's Committee on Employment and Social Affairs. Brussels: European Union.

Eichhorst, Werner, Holger Hinte, Ulf Rinne, and Verena Tobsch. 2016. "How Big Is the Gig? Assessing the Preliminary Evidence on the Effects of Digitalization on the Labor Market." IZA Policy Paper 117. Bonn: Institute for the Study of Labor.

European Commission. 2010. "Europe 2020: A Strategy for Smart, Sustainable and Inclusive Growth." Communication from the Commission COM (2010) 2020 final. https://eur-lex.europa.eu/LexUriServ/LexUriServ.do?uri=COM:2010:2020:FIN:EN:PDF

European Commission. 2013. "Entrepreneurship 2020 Action Plan." Communication from the Commission COM (2012) 795 final. https://eur-lex.europa.eu/LexUriServ/LexUriServ.do?uri=COM:2012:0795:FIN:en:PDF

European Commission. 2014. "Social Protection of the Self-Employed: Situation on 1 January 2014." In *Social Protection in the Member States of the European Union, of the European Economic Area and in Switzerland.* Luxembourg: Publications Office of the European Union.

European Commission. 2016a. "A European Agenda for the Collaborative Economy." Communication from the Commission COM (2016) 356 final. https://ec.europa.eu/transparency/regdoc/rep/1/2016/EN/1-2016-356-EN-F1-1.PDF

European Commission. 2016b. "ICT Research & Innovation." Horizon 2020. https://ec.europa.eu/programmes/horizon2020/en/area/ict-research-innovation

European Council. 2000. "Presidency Conclusions: Lisbon European Council 23 and 24 March 2000." European Parliament. http://www.europarl.europa.eu/summits/lis1_en.htm

Eurostat. 2016. "Unemployment Statistics." Statistics Explained. http://ec.europa.eu/eurostat/statistics-explained/pdfscache/1163.pdf

Eurostat. 2017. "Mean and Median Income by Most Frequent Activity Status—EU-SILC Survey (ilc_di05)." *Eurostat.* http://appsso.eurostat.ec.europa.eu/nui/show.do?dataset=ilc_di05&lang=en

Flecker, Jörg, and Christoph Hermann. 2011. "The Liberalization of Public Services: Company Reactions and Consequences for Employment and Working Conditions." *Economic and Industrial Democracy* 32 (3): 523–44.

Gallie, Duncan. 2003. "The Quality of Working Life: Is Scandinavia Different?" *European Sociological Review* 19 (1): 61–79.

Green, Francis, and Tarek Mostafa. 2012. *Trends in Job Quality in Europe.* Luxembourg: Publications Office of the European Union.

Green, Francis, Tarek Mostafa, Agnès Parent-Thirion, Greet Vermeylen, Gijs Van Houten, Isabella Biletta, and Maija Lyly-Yrjanainen. 2013. "Is Job Quality Becoming More Unequal?" *ILR Review* 66 (4): 753–84.

Grote, Gudela, and David Guest. 2017. "The Case for Reinvigorating Quality of Working Life Research." *Human Relations* 70 (2): 149–67.

Hall, Peter A., and David Soskice. 2001. *Varieties of Capitalism: The Institutional Foundations of Comparative Advantage.* Oxford: Oxford University Press.

Hauff, Sven, and Stefan Kirchner. 2014. "Cross-National Differences and Trends in Job Quality: A Literature Review and Research Agenda." Discussion Paper 13. Hamburg: Schwerpunkt Unternehmensführung am Fachbereich BWL der Universität Hamburg.

Holman, David. 2013. "Job Types and Job Quality in Europe." *Human Relations* 66 (4): 475–502.

International Labour Organization. 2015. "The 2030 Agenda for Sustainable Development." Governing Body Document GB.325/INS/6. Geneva: International Labour Office.

Jorens, Yves. 2008. *Self-Employment and Bogus Self-Employment in the European Construction Industry. A Comparative Study of 11Member States.* Brussels: European Federation of Builders and Woodworkers.

Leschke, Janine, Andrew Watt, and Mairéad Finn. 2008. "Putting a Number on Job Quality? Constructing a European Job Quality Index." ETUI Working Paper 03. Brussels: European Trade Union Institute.

Mascherini, Massimiliano, and Martina Bisello. 2015. *Youth Entrepreneurship in Europe: Values, Attitudes, Policies.* Luxembourg: Publications Office of the European Union.

Masso, Jaan, Maryna Tverdostup, Maura Sheehan, Andrea McNamara, Renate Ortlieb, Silvana Weiss, et al. 2015. "Mapping Patterns of Self-Employment: Secondary Analysis Synthesis Report." STYLE Working Paper 7.2. Brighton, UK: CROME, University of Brighton. http://www.style-research.eu/publications/working-papers

McNamara, Andrea, Maura Sheehan, Renate Ortlieb, Silvana Weiss, Aleksy Pocztowski, Beata Buchelt, et al. 2016. "Business Start-Ups & Youth Self-Employment: Case Study Findings Synthesis Report. STYLE Working Paper 7.3. Brighton, UK: CROME, University of Brighton. http://www.style-research.eu/publications/working-papers

Muehlberger, Ulrike, and Silvia Pasqua. 2009. "Workers on the Border Between Employment and Self-Employment." *Review of Social Economy* 67 (2): 201–28.

Mühlau, Peter. 2011. "Gender Inequality and Job Quality in Europe." *Management Revue* 22 (2): 114–31.

Muñoz de Bustillo, Rafael, Enrique Fernández-Macías, Fernando Esteve, and José-Ignacio Antón. 2011. "E Pluribus Unum? A Critical Survey of Job Quality Indicators." *Socio-Economic Review* 9 (3): 447–75.

Oinas, Tomi, Timo Anttila, Armi Mustosmäki, and Jouko Nätti. 2012. "The Nordic Difference: Job Quality in Europe 1995–2010." *Nordic Journal of Working Life Studies* 2 (4): 135–51.

Olsen, Karen M., Arne L. Kalleberg, and Torstein Nesheim. 2010. "Perceived Job Quality in the United States, Great Britain, Norway and West Germany." *European Journal of Industrial Relations* 16 (3): 221–40.

Oostveen, Adriaan, Isabella Biletta, Agnès Parent-Thirion, and Greet Vermeylen. 2013. "Self-Employed or Not Self-Employed? Working Conditions of 'Economically Dependent Workers.'" Background Paper. Dublin: Eurofound.

Organization for Economic Co-operation and Development (OECD)/European Union. 2015. *The Missing Entrepreneurs 2015: Policies for Self-Employment and Entrepreneurship.* Paris: OECD.

Packard, Truman G., Johannes Koettl, and Claudio Montenegro. 2012. *In from the Shadow: Integrating Europe's Informal Labor.* Washington, DC: World Bank.

Parker, Simon C. 2009. *The Economics of Self-Employment and Entrepreneurship.* Cambridge: Cambridge University Press.

Pohl, Axel, and Andreas Walther. 2007. "Activating the Disadvantaged: Variation in Addressing Youth Transitions Across Europe." *International Journal of Lifelong Education* 26 (5): 533–53.

Poschke, Markus. 2013. "Who Becomes an Entrepreneur? Labor Market Prospects and Occupational Choice." *Journal of Economic Dynamics and Control* 37 (3): 693–710.

Román, Concepción, Emilio Congregado, and José María Millán. 2011. "Dependent Self-Employment as a Way to Evade Employment Protection Legislation." *Small Business Economics* 37 (3): 363–92.

Russell, Helen, Janine Leschke, and Mark Smith. 2015. "Balancing Flexibility and Security in Europe: The Impact on Young People's Insecurity and Subjective Well-Being." STYLE Working Paper 10.3. Brighton, UK: CROME, University of Brighton. http://www.style-research.eu/publications/working-papers

Schulze Buschoff, Karin, and Paula Protsch. 2008. "(A-)Typical and (In-)Secure? Social Protection and Non-Standard Forms of Employment in Europe." *International Social Security Review* 61 (4): 51–73.

Shane, Scott A. 2008. *The Illusions of Entrepreneurship: The Costly Myths That Entrepreneurs, Investors, and Policy Makers Live By.* New Haven, CT: Yale University Press.

Sheehan, Maura, and Andrea McNamara. 2015. "Business Start-Ups and Youth Self-Employment: A Policy Literature Review Synthesis Report. STYLE Working Paper 7.1. Brighton, UK: CROME, University of Brighton. http://www.style-research.eu/publications/working-papers

Sheehan, Maura, Andrea McNamara, Renate Ortlieb, Silvana Weiss, Jaan Masso, Kadri Paes, et al. 2016. "Policy Synthesis and Integrative Report on Youth Self-Employment in Europe." STYLE Working Paper 7.4. Brighton, UK: CROME, University of Brighton. http://www.style-research.eu/publications/working-papers

Simoes, Nadia, Nuno Crespo, and Sandrina B. Moreira. 2015. "Individual Determinants of Self-Employment Entry: What Do We Really Know?" *Journal of Economic Surveys* 30 (4): 783–806. doi:10.1111/joes.12111.

Smith, Mark, Brendan Burchell, Colette Fagan, and Catherine O'Brien. 2008. "Job Quality in Europe." *Industrial Relations Journal* 39 (6): 586–603.

Thörnquist, Annette. 2013. "False (Bogus) Self-Employment in East–West Labour Migration: Recent Trends in the Swedish Construction and Road Haulage Industries." TheMES Report 41. Linköping: Institute for Research on Migration, Ethnicity and Society.

Valenduc, Gérard, and Patricia Vendramin. 2016. "Work in the Digital Economy: Sorting the Old from the New." ETUI Working Paper 03. Brussels: European Trade Union Institute.

APPENDIX

Wording of the items capturing working conditions and response categories considered in Figure 20.3, as taken from the EWCS:

Well paid for work: "I am well paid for the work I do"—strongly agree; agree (not: neither agree nor disagree; disagree; strongly disagree).

Working at high speed less than half the time: "Does your job involve working at very high speed?"—never; almost never; around ¼ of the time (not: around half of the time; around ¾ of the time; almost all of the time; all of the time).

Good fit between working hours and social commitments: "Do your working hours fit in with your family or social commitments outside work?"—very well; well; (not: not very well; not at all well).

Feeling at home in the organization: "I feel at home in this organization"—strongly agree; agree (not: neither agree nor disagree; disagree; strongly disagree).

Health and safety not at risk because of work: "Do you think your health or safety is at risk because of your work?"—no (not: yes).

Being able to do job at age 60: "Do you think you will be able to do the same job you are doing now when you are 60 years old?"—yes, I think so (not: no, I don't think so; I wouldn't want to).

Job involves learning new things: "Generally, does your main paid job involve learning new things?"—yes (not: no).

Job offers good prospects for career advancement: "My job offers good prospects for career advancement"—strongly agree; agree (not: neither agree nor disagree; disagree; strongly disagree).

Expect not to lose job in next 6 months: "I might lose my job in the next 6 months"—strongly agree; agree (not: neither agree nor disagree; disagree; strongly disagree).

21

ARE THE WORK VALUES OF THE YOUNGER GENERATIONS CHANGING?

Gábor Hajdu and Endre Sik

21.1. INTRODUCTION

A common stereotype emerging in political speeches and everyday intellectual conversations about the younger generations paints them as increasingly less work oriented. Specifically, they are seen to be increasingly less motivated with regard to finding a job and working hard in the interests of developing a career. In comparison to older generations, the value of work as a significant part of personal identity is believed to be declining. It is often assumed that one of the consequences of increased labor market flexibility and precarious employment has been to create weaker incentives to build a career or invest in long-term human capital. The seeming impossibility of achieving what previous generations obtained in terms of career jobs (with attractive benefits and pensions) may generate attempts to reduce cognitive dissonance by rejecting the value of these achievements. It is thought that these attitudinal trends are likely to be exacerbated by the growing obstacles to labor market entry, lengthening spells of unemployment, and/or the spread of precarious work. If these arguments are true, youth-oriented European Union (EU) or national labor market policies will fail because the new entrants to the labor market (and even more so those who cannot enter at all) will in any case not respond positively to them.

In this chapter, instead of testing the existing theories of generational differences, our research aim is exploratory: We test empirically whether work values indeed differ between birth cohorts (with an emphasis on the youngest cohorts), age groups, and time periods. Specifically, we analyze whether the centrality of work varies by birth date, age, and time period,[1] using large cross-national surveys from more than 30 countries (most of the European countries and some Organization for Economic Co-operation and Development (OECD) countries from the Euro-Atlantic area).

Sections 21.2 and 21.3 describe the conceptual basis of the analysis, the main characteristics of the data, and the methodology applied. In Section 21.4, we first illustrate the trends for attitudes regarding the centrality of work and then test the role of age, time period, and birth cohorts with respect to these trends. Section 21.5 concludes that given the lack of evidence of significant gaps between birth cohorts with regard to relative centrality of work, there is not a generational divide in contemporary Europe with respect to work values.

21.2. BACKGROUND

21.2.1. Birth cohort versus generation

We decided to use the concept of birth cohort as opposed to generation for our analysis because the latter concept is rife with ambiguities. The term *generation* refers to individuals born at approximately the same time. From this, it follows that they experience more or less similar historical and life events during their early years. The underlying assumption is that because in their childhood and adolescent periods they are influenced by actors with similar value systems and are exposed to identical events and developments (news, economic or social booms and crises, technological innovation, policy and political influences, etc.), the values they hold will be rather similar, and they will be different from those of all other generations. It is also assumed that this impact is the strongest during an individual's childhood and adolescence and remains relatively stable from then on (Harpaz and Fu 2002). The stability of such generation-specific values offers a chance for a generation to develop into a social group with a shared loose form of self-consciousness and identity (Diepstraten, Ester, and Vinken 1999).

The consciousness of a generation is a stochastic and dynamic social phenomenon. In other words, if it emerges at all, there should be a significant event such as a war or a revolution, a brand-new technology, or some other major phenomenon to lay the foundation of the new generation. If such an impetus is strong enough to mobilize a group of young people who are in a position to influence their fellows from the same cohort in identifying themselves as an "imagined generational community," then the nucleus of a generation may appear. If such a feeling of generational community takes hold, then the shared set of values and goals becomes the common denominator of a generation.

The essence of this generation concept is well captured by the concept of generation subculture theory, which is defined by Egri and Ralston (2004) as follows:

Significant macro-level social, political, and economic events that occurred during a birth cohort's impressionable pre-adult years result in a generational identity comprised of a distinctive set of values, beliefs, expectations, and behaviors that remain relatively stable throughout a generation's lifetime. . . . A generation's values orientation becomes more pervasive in a national culture as it becomes the majority in societal positions of power and influence. (p. 210)

Although seemingly concise and elegant, there are several problems with the generation concept. For example,

- It is much too loosely defined timewise, in that it sometimes covers more than a decade, which might be too long to assume that the members of a generation indeed have similar experiences.
- The characteristics used to capture the main features of generations are often based on anecdotal evidence or on invalid and unreliable survey data.
- The assumption that there are global generations (i.e., a generation can be defined by the same characteristics all over the planet) is very likely a myth.[2] Even if generations are rather similar across different countries, they can be very different in terms of historical moment: Their periodization depends on a country's specific timeline of technological, political, and policy development.

Unlike the generational approach, the *birth cohort* is usually narrowly defined—in demography, for example, usually as a 5-year-wide "mini-generation." Moreover, the birth cohort does not fluctuate according to vague, quasi-theoretical assumptions usually based on technological–political changes in the United States.

21.2.2. Work values

Work values form a core subset of the general value system (Wuthnow 2008; Jin and Rounds 2012). They have been the target of several large-scale comparative projects since the 1970s and 1980s that use quantitative databases to describe the differences between citizens from various countries with respect to the centrality of work in their lives (Roe and Ester 1999). Most of these studies have treated work-related values (Roe and Ester 1999)

as expressions of more general life values. . . . All definitions treat values as latent constructs that refer to the way in which people evaluate activities or outcomes. . . . Holders of values are not necessarily individuals but may also be collectivities, i.e. the people belonging to a certain occupational group, a firm, a subculture, a community, a national category, or a country. (pp. 2–4)

To understand the association between values and other socioeconomic characteristics of society, as well as the relationship between value systems in general and work values in particular, large quantitative data sets have been used since the 1980s for comparative analysis of work values (Wuthnow 2008). Since the late 1990s, a promising new direction in comparative quantitative research on values (cultural economics) has emerged, rephrasing old questions in a new format using large-scale surveys carried out in several countries (e.g., the World Value Survey, the European Values Study, and the International Social Survey Programme) to analyze the high inertia of culture.[3]

In the course of our analysis, we used "centrality of work" as the dependent variable. This term covers both paid and unpaid work and measures the attitude of the respondent toward work in general—in other words, how important work is for a respondent as a part of his or her life and identity.[4] Centrality of work (under various names) is a core concept in organization, business, and management sciences, in which it is considered a crucial aspect of activity in a workplace. From the employees' viewpoint, it is necessary to achieve higher income and subjective well-being, satisfaction, a career, and so forth; from the employers' viewpoint, it is the primary source of commitment to hard work, efficiency, informal and on-the-job training, and so on (Hansen and Leuty 2012).

21.2.3. Previous literature

The most widely accepted hypothesis regarding the trend followed by centrality of work is that generations have different attitudes toward work to the extent that (Tolbize 2008)

> the perceived decline in work ethic is perhaps one of the major contributors of generational conflicts in the workplace. Generation X for instance, has been labelled the "slacker" generation, and employers complain that younger workers are uncommitted to their jobs and work only the required hours and little more. Conversely, Boomers may be workaholics . . . while "Traditionals" have been characterized as the most hardworking generation. (p. 5)

This hypothesis dominates the discourse despite the fact that a meta-analysis of generation-specific work values (Costanza et al. 2012) found moderate or zero differences between generational membership and work-related attitudes.

Other research combining longitudinal panel data between 1981 and 1993 and a representative survey of the Israeli Jewish labor force in 1993 analyzed how time period, cohort, and life course (in our vocabulary, age group) affect work values (primarily the importance of work). The study concluded that in contrast to other developed countries, the centrality of work has strengthened in Israel since the early 1980s (Sharabi and Harpaz 2007, 103–4).

Kowske, Rasch, and Wiley (2010) analyzed the role of time period, age, and cohort on work values (satisfaction with company/job, recognition, career, security, pay, and turnover intentions) among generations of Americans with a special focus on the so-called millennial generation. According to their research,

> Work attitudes differed across generations, although effect sizes were relatively small and depended on the work attitude. Compared to Boomers and GenXers, Millennials reported higher levels of overall company and job satisfaction, satisfaction with job security, recognition, and career development and advancement, but reported similar levels of satisfaction with pay and benefits and the work itself, and turnover intentions. (p. 265)

According to these authors, the role of generations is significantly weaker than a set of labor-market sensitive individual factors such as gender, industry, and occupation (p. 273).

Regarding the impact of different generations, Kowske et al. (2010) found curvilinear trends (i.e., U-shaped curves) in the case of all work values. This means that the least satisfied with the various aspects of work were the late baby boomers, whereas the "GI" (born around the time of World War II) and millennial generations were the most satisfied (the latter especially with recognition and career). However, the most important conclusion of their analysis was that contrary to the popular view of the role of generation with respect to the labor market, "generational differences might be re-named 'generational similarities'" (p. 275).

To conclude, we quote a more recent overview in which the authors convincingly summarize the theoretical and methodological state of the art of research on generations (Becton, Walker, and Jones-Farmer 2014):

> Considering the extent to which generational stereotypes are commonly accepted, it is surprising that empirical evidence of generational differences is relatively sparse, and the research that exists is somewhat contradictory. . . . There exists a great deal of controversy about whether or not generational differences exist at all with some suggesting that perceived generational differences are a product of popular culture versus social science. Scholars have also noted that observed generational differences may be explained, at least in part, by age, life stage, or career stage effects instead of generation. (pp. 175–76)

21.3. DATA AND METHODS

The basic problem in analyzing generations stems from the fact that the effects of age, time period, and birth cohort are closely intertwined. Any change over time can be determined by any of the three effects, as can be illustrated with the following fictional dialogue (based on Suzuki 2012, 452):

> ENDRE: I'm very tired, I must be getting old. (*Age effect*)
>
> GÁBOR: You're no spring chicken indeed, but maybe you're crawling into bed early every night because life is so stressful nowadays. (*Period effect*)
>
> ENDRE: Could be, but you seem to be tired too. The truth is, you young people are not as fit as we used to be at your age. (*Cohort effect*)

21.3.1. The problem of decomposing the effects of age, period, and birth cohort

Because age, time period (year of the survey), and birth cohort (year of birth) are linearly interdependent, their effects cannot be simultaneously estimated using standard regression models (Firebaugh 1997; Yang and Land 2006, 2008). A possible solution to this identification problem is to use a hierarchical age–period–cohort (HAPC) regression model (Yang and Land 2006, 2008).[5]

To minimize the effect of multicollinearity between age, birth cohort, and period, we defined fixed and equal-period (year of the survey) clusters.[6] In this grouped data, age, period (with 5-year intervals), and birth cohort (year of birth) are not perfectly dependent. In other words, we are no longer able to directly calculate the year of birth from age and period (with 5-year intervals); nonetheless, remarkable multicollinearity still remains.

Moreover, whereas age is an individual-level variable, period and cohort are macro-level variables.[7] This means that we have a multilevel data structure assuming that the attitudes of the individuals in the same birth cohort, or interviewed in the same year, will be more similar than those from other periods or birth cohorts.

Yang and Land (2006, 2008) propose cross-classified hierarchical models to represent clustering effects in individual survey responses by period and birth cohorts when using repeated cross-sectional data. In this analysis, we use these models where it is assumed that individuals are nested simultaneously within the two second-level variables (period and cohort); thus, we use cross-classified hierarchical regression models.[8]

Bell and Jones (2014), however, argue that there is no statistically and mathematically correct solution to the age–period–cohort identification problem in the absence of preliminary theoretical assumptions: "There is no technical solution to the identification problem without the imposition of strong (and correct) a priori assumptions" (p. 335). They show with simulations that in several scenarios, the results of the HAPC model are biased: For example, if there is quadratic age effect and linear cohort trend, these effects are estimated as a period trend. In other words, the effects of the three time-related variables might be assigned to each other or be combined by the effects of the other two variables. However, Bell and Jones also show that the model works if there are no trends for periods or cohorts. Given that our results show that the cohort and period effects are quite small, our findings should be "probably justifiable," according to Bell and Jones (i.e., because the results are not biased by strong cohort and/or period effects, the use of the HAPC model is feasible).

Twenge (2010) recommends another solution to avoid the identification problem mentioned previously by taking one step backward. She suggests using the time-lag method, in which individuals of the same age at different points in time are compared: "With age held constant, any differences are due to either generation (enduring differences based on birth cohort) or time period (change over time that affects all generations)" (p. 202). Twenge argues that because the impact of period is often the weakest, a time-lag design should be able to isolate generational differences.

Here, we first provide a descriptive analysis in which we separately model age, period, and birth cohort effects on work values to illustrate the main trends. Some of these descriptive analyses are equivalent to Twenge's (2010) time-lag method; however, the results might be biased by omitted variables because they are based on bivariate relationships in which the sociodemographic characteristics of the respondents are uncontrolled. In the second step, we develop HAPC regression models to avoid problems stemming from the linear dependency of these three dimensions of time (Yang and Land 2006, 2008). As part of this exercise, we also separately run models for the youngest respondents (aged 18–40 years) so as to meet the requirements of the time-lag method recommended by Twenge; in other words, individuals with more homogeneous ages are compared.

21.3.2. Data

Given that our strategy of analyzing the changing (or unchanging) attitudes of generations toward work was based on secondary analysis of existing large, repeated cross-sectional, cross-national databases, we first had to select those precious few questions that were asked either similarly in these surveys or could be made identical by recoding and therefore be used as proxies of work values.[9]

Questions about the importance of work and other aspects of life were asked in the questionnaires of the World Values Survey/European Values Study (WVS/EVS). Respondents were asked to answer the question, "How important is *[life aspect]* in your life?" on a 4-point scale.[10] We used four variables: importance of work, importance of family, importance of friends, and importance of leisure time. We calculated the relative importance of work as the difference between the importance of work and the average importance of the other three life aspects (i.e., family, friends, and leisure time). Thus, positive values of the variable indicate that work is more important in the respondent's life than other life aspects, whereas negative values indicate that it is less important than other life aspects—in other words, that work plays a relatively minor role in the respondent's life.

Our analysis covers most of the European countries and some OECD countries from the Euro-Atlantic area. Table A21.1 in Appendix 2 contains the list of countries (arranged into three groups: post-socialist, EU15, and other OECD countries) included in the various waves.

Because the question was not asked in the first wave of WVS/EVS and the number of observations between 2000 and 2004 was relatively low, we only have data from three periods.[11] Because our analysis is extremely time sensitive to the year of the information the analysis is based on, we decided to use the year of the fieldwork country by country.[12]

The number of observations and the means of the variable of relative centrality of work by period are shown in Table 21.1. The aggregate value of relative centrality of work is highest in 1990–1994, somewhat lower in 1995–1999, and lowest in the mid-2000s. This means that compared to the importance of other aspects of life, work was more important in the 1990s and became less so in the second half of the 2000s.

In the descriptive analysis, the period, the age of the respondent, and the birth cohorts were coded into 5-year intervals, which are conventional in age–period–cohort analyses (Yang, Fu, and Land 2008) and significantly shorter than those used in the sociological or management literature on generations. The result of this operation was 12 age groups (from 18–22 to 73+ years), 3 period groups (1990–1994, 1995–1999, and 2005–2009), and 16 cohort groups (from –1916 to 1987–1991).

In the multivariate models, age was allowed to have a nonlinear (curvilinear) effect (squared age is also included in the models), cohorts were included as birth year, and periods (year of the survey) were grouped into 5-year intervals as in the descriptive analysis.

Table 21.1 Number of observations and average relative centrality of work by period

Period	N	Mean	SD	Min	Max
1990–1994	36,370	0.050	0.805	–3	3
1995–1999	64,407	0.023	0.810	–3	3
2005–2009	65,563	–0.105	0.832	–3	3
Total	166,340	–0.022	0.821	–3	3

To control for the changing composition along the basic socioeconomic characteristics of subsequent generations in our multivariate models, we used the following control variables:

- Gender (binary variable, 1 = female)
- Education (binary variable, 1 = more than secondary education)
- Marital status (married/living with partner, divorced/separated, widowed or never married)
- Labor force status (binary variable, 1 = respondent has a job; i.e., his or her employment status is "working")
- Type of settlement (binary variable, 1 = respondent lives in a city (with population >100,000))

In addition, every model contained country-fixed effects in order to control for time-invariant country characteristics.

21.4. RESULTS

21.4.1. The cumulated impact of age and period on the relative centrality of work

Table 21.2 displays the mean relative centrality of work by age group and period. The last column (age effect) shows that the centrality of work increases until age 43–52 years and then decreases continuously. In other words, people slowly "learn" the importance of work, but this (centrality of work) holds only as long as they are in their active years. If we focus on the bottom row, we find an aggregate decrease in the mean relative centrality of work (period effect) between 1995–1999 and 2005–2009. This can be interpreted as indicating that work in general is losing its importance.

The differences by age groups and birth cohorts (the final column in Table 21.3) show that work seems to be relatively most important in the birth cohorts 1947–1961 and less important for the earlier and later cohorts.

To visualize the main differences and similarities of the trends between age and period, we designed two closely related figures (Figure 21.1a and Figure 21.1b). Figure 21.1a shows the trend of the relative centrality of work by age, controlling for period. The general pattern (the inverted U-curve) is rather similar in the three periods, but the highest level of the centrality of work lasts longer (from age 43–47 to age 53–57 years) in the first period than in the second or the third period. For every age group, the importance of work is lowest in the final period (2005–2009). Among those aged older than 53 years, work is relatively more important in the first period (1990–1994), whereas among the younger age groups, there is no real difference between the first two periods.

Table 21.2 Means of relative centrality of work by age group and period (cohort uncontrolled)

Age group (years)	Period			
	1990–1994	1995–1999	2005–2009	Total
18–22	−0.095	−0.115	−0.236	−0.155
23–27	−0.028	−0.006	−0.090	−0.042
28–32	−0.008	0.028	−0.035	−0.004
33–37	0.054	0.062	−0.027	0.028
38–42	0.120	0.128	0.037	0.091
43–47	0.189	0.165	0.043	0.122
48–52	0.181	0.170	0.049	0.123
53–57	0.176	0.100	−0.018	0.066
58–62	0.111	0.009	−0.113	−0.018
63–67	0.036	−0.077	−0.312	−0.144
68–72	−0.038	−0.116	−0.334	−0.186
73+	−0.152	−0.245	−0.409	−0.308
Total	0.050	0.023	−0.105	−0.022

Figure 21.1b focuses on the trend for the relative centrality of work by period in six age groups.[13] Although the general trend is a slight decrease between the first two periods and a steeper decrease after 1995–1999, centrality of work declines sharply after 1990–1994 in the two oldest age groups. In the middle age groups, the trend is similar to the average, and they have the highest level of relative centrality of work throughout all periods. As for the youngest age groups, there is a slight increase between 1990–1994 and 1995–1999 in the group aged 23–27 years, whereas subsequently the decrease for both age groups is less sharp than in general.

21.4.2. The HAPC models of the relative centrality of work

The HAPC regression models (Table 21.4) contain the three time-related and all control variables. Whereas age and squared age are included as individual-level variables, period (year of the survey) and cohort (year of birth) are second-level predictors. Random period and cohort intercepts allow level 1 intercepts to vary randomly by cohorts and periods; that is, they allow variation from the mean for each cohort and period. The models in columns 0–5 show results from the entire sample, whereas the model in column 6 covers the young (age 18–40 years) individuals only.[14]

Comparing the six models, the sign and the size of the coefficients are fairly stable. Age differences become smaller with the inclusion of the other variables,

Table 21.3 Means of relative centrality of work by birth cohort and age group (period uncontrolled)

Cohort	18–22	23–27	28–32	33–37	38–42	43–47	48–52	53–57	58–62	63–67	68–72	73+	Total
–1916												-0.225	-0.225
1917–1921											-0.107	-0.250	-0.190
1922–1926										-0.004	-0.082	-0.312	-0.173
1927–1931									0.056	-0.073	-0.081	-0.429	-0.138
1932–1936								0.151	0.064	-0.034	-0.408	-0.339	-0.081
1937–1941							0.154	0.118	0.032	-0.403	-0.300		-0.056
1942–1946						0.168	0.169	0.121	-0.201	-0.266			0.006
1947–1951					0.107	0.168	0.185	-0.106	-0.073				0.074
1952–1956				0.046	0.113	0.178	0.009	0.023					0.087
1957–1961			-0.028	0.059	0.141	0.036	0.068						0.069
1962–1966		-0.035	0.009	0.066	0.014	0.046							0.028
1967–1971	-0.097	-0.042	0.042	-0.057	0.048								-0.004
1972–1976	-0.114	0.012	-0.032	-0.012									-0.021
1977–1981	-0.112	-0.095	-0.036										-0.079
1982–1986	-0.168	-0.088											-0.114
1987–1991	-0.268												-0.268
Total	-0.155	-0.042	-0.004	0.028	0.091	0.122	0.123	0.066	-0.018	-0.144	-0.186	-0.308	-0.022

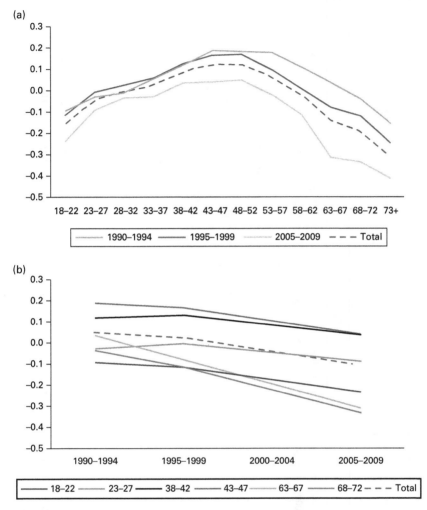

Figure 21.1 Means of centrality of work by (a) age in the three periods and (b) period in seven age groups.

given that there is collinearity between age and other variables (e.g., labor force status or marital status). Focusing on the role of the three time variables, we find that although they have a significant impact on the centrality of work, this is small compared to the impact of the non-age individual variables and the country-fixed effects.

The visualized results (Figure 21.2) show that—controlling for period, birth cohort, and relevant sociodemographic characteristics—the centrality of work increases from age 18 years, reaches a peak at approximately age 50 years, and decreases thereafter. This result is similar to that of the uncontrolled inverted

Table 21.4 HAPC models of centrality of work

Individual effect	(0) All		(1) All		(2) All		(3) All		(4) All		(5) All		(6) Youth (18–40 years)	
	B	SE	B	SE	B	SE	B	SE	B	SE	B	SE	B	SE
Age			−0.0011***	(0.000)	−0.0008***	(0.000)	0.0024***	(0.000)	0.0021***	(0.000)	0.0026***	(0.000)	−0.0013	(0.003)
Age squared			−0.0004***	(0.000)	−0.0004***	(0.000)	−0.0004***	(0.000)	−0.0003***	(0.000)	−0.0003***	(0.000)	−0.0003***	(0.000)
Female									−0.0659***	(0.004)	−0.0646***	(0.004)	−0.0687***	(0.006)
Education: More than secondary									−0.0710***	(0.005)	−0.0339***	(0.005)	−0.0676***	(0.006)
Employment status: Working									0.1831***	(0.005)	0.2064***	(0.005)	0.1160***	(0.006)
Type of settlement: City									−0.0607***	(0.004)	−0.0491***	(0.004)	−0.0518***	(0.006)
Marital status														
Single									Ref.		Ref.		Ref.	
Married/living with partner									0.0122**	(0.006)	−0.0007	(0.006)	0.0150**	(0.007)
Divorced/separated									0.0603***	(0.009)	0.0769***	(0.009)	0.1002***	(0.013)
Widowed									0.0051	(0.010)	−0.0381***	(0.010)	0.0623*	(0.036)
Intercept	−0.0233***	(0.002)	0.0899***	(0.003)	0.0987***	(0.040)	0.1294**	(0.051)	0.0540	(0.046)	0.0236	(0.060)	0.0180	(0.044)

Variance component	Variance	SE	Variance	SE	Variance	SE	Variance	SE	Variance	SE	Variance	SE	Variance	SE
Individual	0.6822***	(0.001)	0.6661***	(0.001)	0.6613***	(0.001)	0.6600***	(0.001)	0.6510***	(0.001)	0.6175***	(0.001)	0.0028***	(0.001)
Period					0.0047***	(0.002)	0.0076***	(0.003)	0.0061***	(0.003)	0.0074***	(0.003)	0.0224***	(0.003)
Cohort							0.0055***	(0.002)	0.0030***	(0.001)	0.0024***	(0.000)	0.0004***	(0.000)
Country											0.0381***	(0.004)	0.5059***	(0.001)
N	166,340		166,340		166,340		166,340		166,340		166,340		70,664	
AIC	408,443.9		404,466.7		403,287.3		403,187.4		400,861.9		392,271.8		152,622.9	
Deviance (df)	408,439.9(2)		404,458.7(4)		403,277.3(5)		403,175.4(6)		400,835.9(13)		392,243.8(14)		152,594.9(14)	

*$p < 0.10$.
**$p < 0.05$.
***$p < 0.01$.

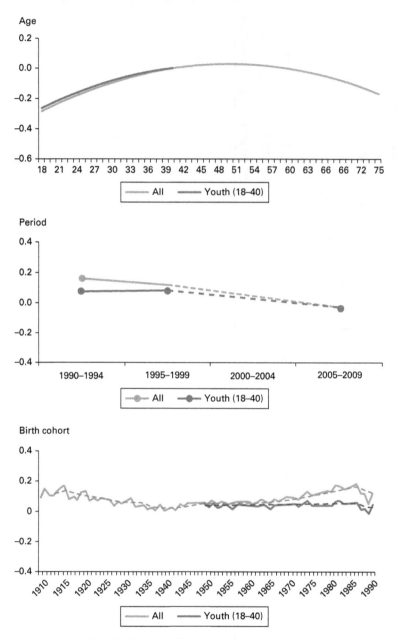

Figure 21.2 Age, period, and birth cohort effects on relative centrality of work in total sample and in young (aged 18–40 years) cohorts (HAPC regression model).

U-curve (Figure 21.1a) and is in accordance with a life course concept of economic activity: Because younger people are not yet involved and older people are no longer involved in income-generating activities, it makes sense that their attitude toward the importance of work should be lower compared to that of people for whom work plays the central role in their identity (i.e., career-oriented, human capital investing, etc., individuals in (early) middle age), who are in their active household and labor market cycles (i.e., entering the labor market, becoming adults, establishing a family, having children, etc.).

The results shown in the second panel in Figure 21.2 confirm that—controlling for age, cohort, and relevant sociodemographic characteristics—the centrality of work is significantly lower in 2005–2009 than in the 1990s. However, period accounts for only 1.17% of the variance of the centrality of work; that is, the effect size is rather small.

Finally, after controlling for age and period and relevant sociodemographic characteristics, work is somewhat less important for birth cohorts born in the mid-20th century compared to the earlier and later-born cohorts. This result may be interpreted as a generational effect: For those who entered the labor market in approximately 1968, the centrality of work has temporarily decreased. However, because the effect size is quite small (cohort accounts for only 0.38% of the variance in the centrality of work), we are better to conclude that there is no generational effect.

The cohort and period differences among the youngest group (aged 18–40 years) are even smaller compared to those of the full sample. Period differences are slightly smaller than in the whole sample, suggesting that relative importance of work seems to have decreased less among the younger generation. However, in general, it seems that our findings regarding the full sample are valid in the case of the young subsample as well.

21.4.3. Gender differences

To test whether the determinants of the relative centrality of work differ by gender, we ran the HAPC models for men and women separately. The results (the detailed results in Table 21.5 and the visualized effects of the three time-related variables in Figure 21.3) show that the differences by gender are very small.[15] The effect of the three time-related variables does not differ between men and women, whereas cohort differences are somewhat larger among women, although the effect size is very small.

There are, however, other significant gender differences, such as the following:

- Being married or living with a partner has a positive but insignificant effect on the centrality of work among men, but it has a negative and significant effect among women.
- The effect of employment status is larger among men than among women.
- Work is more important for an average man than for an average woman.[16]

These findings might be explained by gender norms, such as the traditional prescription that a man has to work more and has to be the main earner in the family.

Table 21.5 HAPC models of centrality of work among men and women

Individual effect	Men		Women	
	B	SE	B	SE
Age	0.0018***	(0.000)	0.0013***	(0.000)
Age squared	−0.0003***	(0.000)	−0.0003***	(0.000)
Education: More than secondary	−0.0305***	(0.007)	−0.0388***	(0.007)
Employment status: Working	0.2313***	(0.007)	0.1926***	(0.006)
Type of settlement: City	−0.0392***	(0.007)	−0.0577***	(0.006)
Marital status				
Single	Ref.		Ref.	
Married/living with partner	0.0144	(0.009)	−0.0277***	(0.008)
Divorced/separated	0.0857***	(0.014)	0.0625***	(0.012)
Widowed	−0.0440***	(0.017)	−0.0518***	(0.012)
Intercept	−0.0350	(0.051)	−0.0349	(0.062)
Variance component	Variance	SE	Variance	SE
Period	0.0055***	(0.002)	0.0071***	(0.003)
Cohort	0.0270***	(0.003)	0.0509***	(0.006)
Country	0.0001***	(0.000)	0.0009***	(0.000)
Individual	0.6063***	(0.002)	0.6248***	(0.001)
N	76,477		89,863	
AIC	178,982.0		213,068.7	
Deviance (df)	178,956.0(13)		213,042.7(13)	

$*p < 0.10.$
$**p < 0.05.$
$***p < 0.01.$

21.4.4. Regional differences

We compared the impact of age, period, and birth cohort in two subgroups of European countries:[17] post-socialist and EU15 countries.[18] We hypothesized that because state socialism as a "natural experiment" influenced post-socialist countries for five decades in terms of their state-induced work-oriented ideology, we might detect path-dependent, cohort-specific characteristics for the value of work. For instance, the work values at least at the beginning of the post-socialist period might be stronger than those of people living in EU15 countries—that is, in societies without this socialist heritage.

The results of two HAPC models for the two groups of countries (the detailed results in Table 21.6 and the visualized effects of the three time-related variables in Figure 21.4) show that the coefficients of the control variables are mostly similar: The centrality of work is significantly higher for men, for divorced people

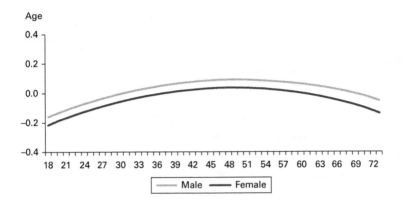

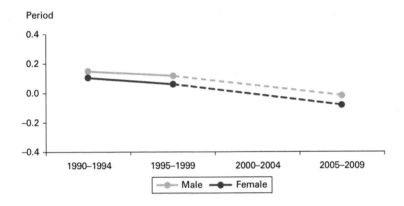

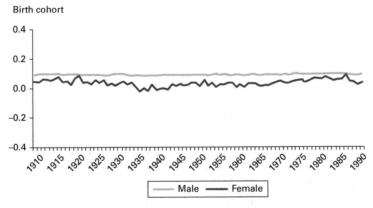

Figure 21.3 Age, period, and birth-cohort effect on centrality of work among men and women (HAPC regression model).

Table 21.6 HAPC models of centrality of work in EU15 and post-socialist countries

	EU15		Post-socialist	
Individual effect	**B**	**SE**	**B**	**SE**
Age	0.0010***	(0.000)	0.0081***	(0.001)
Age squared	−0.0002***	(0.000)	−0.0005***	(0.000)
Female	−0.0761***	(0.006)	−0.0438***	(0.006)
Education: More than secondary	−0.0534***	(0.008)	−0.0196***	(0.007)
Employment status: Working	0.1918***	(0.007)	0.1966***	(0.007)
Type of settlement: City	−0.0316***	(0.007)	−0.0736***	(0.006)
Marital status				
Single	Ref.		Ref.	
Married/living with partner	−0.0194**	(0.009)	0.0263***	(0.009)
Divorced/separated	0.0343**	(0.014)	0.1154***	(0.013)
Widowed	−0.0863***	(0.016)	0.0101	(0.014)
Intercept	−0.0699	(0.067)	0.2159***	(0.075)
Variance component	Variance	SE	Variance	SE
Period	0.0045***	(0.002)	0.0141***	(0.006)
Cohort	0.0004***	(0.000)	0.0221***	(0.003)
Country	0.0436***	(0.008)	0.0085***	(0.002)
Individual	0.0436***	(0.008)	0.0085***	(0.002)
N	66,400		77,405	
AIC	157,627.8		179,739.0	
Deviance (*df*)	157,599.8 (14)		179,711.0 (14)	

*$p < 0.10$.
**$p < 0.05$.
***$p < 0.01$.

(compared to single individuals), and for working people, whereas it is lower for city dwellers and for more highly educated people in both country groups. However, there are system-specific differences as well, including the following:

- In the EU15 countries, the overall level of centrality of work is lower.
- In the EU15 countries, high education has a more negative effect on the centrality of work.
- Being widowed has a negative effect in the EU15 countries but no effect in the post-socialist countries.
- The signs of gender and higher education effects are the same in the two groups, but the sizes of the coefficients are twice as large in the EU15 countries compared to the post-socialist countries.
- The effect of being married or living with a partner is negative in the EU15 countries, whereas it is positive in the post-socialist countries.

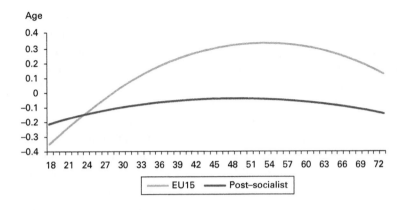

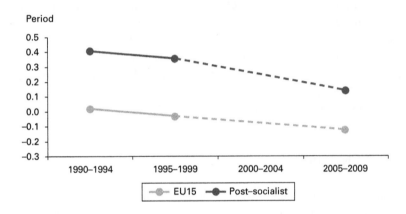

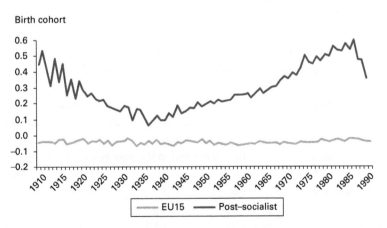

Figure 21.4 Age, period, and birth cohort effect on centrality of work in EU15 and post-socialist countries (HAPC regression model).

If we compare the effects of the three time-related variables, we can see that age differences are smaller in EU15 countries, whereas the curve is more similar to an inverted U-shape for post-socialist countries. However, the effect size is notable in EU15 countries as well: Work is 0.15 points less important for an 18-year-old individual than for an individual in his or her fifties. This effect size is close to that of working people and higher than the effect of education. The period trends are similar in the two country groups, but the centrality of work declines somewhat more in the post-socialist countries than in the EU15 countries. Period accounts for 0.7% and 2.2% of the variance in the centrality of work in the EU15 and the post-socialist countries, respectively. Finally, centrality of work falls and remains very low among those born in the 1940s in post-socialist countries and starts increasing thereafter. In the EU15 countries, however, there are no real differences between cohorts. Cohort accounts for only 0.1% of the variance in the centrality of work in the EU15 countries and for 3.5% in the post-socialist countries. It is worth noting that cohort differences in post-socialist countries might not be detectable if we analyze single countries, but a more detailed analysis goes beyond the scope of this chapter. However, some analyses in the working paper version of this chapter suggest that cohort differences within single countries do not exist (Hajdu and Sik 2015).

21.5. CONCLUSIONS

We did not find significant gaps between birth cohorts with respect to relative centrality of work and thus claim that in contemporary Europe, the generations are not divided significantly with regard to their work values. In this respect, our findings reinforce the results of Clark (2010), Kowske et al. (2010), Costanza et al. (2012), Jin and Rounds (2012), and Becton et al. (2014): Rather than pointing to generational differences, we should instead emphasize the lack of them.

There are, however, different trends in the centrality of work by age and birth cohort. The effect of the former is close to an inverted U-shaped curve—the centrality of work is higher in the middle age groups than among the younger or older groups—whereas the effect of the latter is closer to a curvilinear curve—the centrality of work is higher in the earlier and in the later-born cohorts. However, it is worth noting that although this effect can be regarded as statistically significant, the effect size is rather small. Regarding the impact of period, it is characterized by a linear and slightly decreasing trend.

The interpretation of the inverted U-shape of the relative centrality of work by age is rather straightforward: Because younger people are not yet involved and older people are no longer involved in income-generating activities, it is logical to find that work is less central for both of these groups compared to individuals in their active household and labor market cycles. The decreasing linear trend of the centrality of work by period fits well into what the literature proposes: It indicates a shift from modernity toward postmodernity (Egri and Ralston 2004; Twenge et al. 2010).

The U-curve for the centrality of work by birth cohort might mean that work is less central for the cohort born between 1940 and 1959 compared to the earlier and later-born cohorts. This result may be interpreted as a rather weak generational effect in the sense that for those who entered the education system and the labor market in the 1960s and 1970s, intrinsic values became more important than work (or other extrinsic aspects of life). However, this change was quite quickly reversed, and the values of those who entered the labor market after the mid-1970s became more extrinsically oriented again.

The first conclusion from a policy standpoint is that we could not identify any relevant gap between the birth cohorts. From this follows that the generational differences often referred to in public debates and used in political discourses are a myth. Kowske et al. (2010) quite rightly summarized their findings as indicating that instead of generational differences, we should speak about "generational similarities." Our results imply that in contemporary Europe, generations follow a similar age trend: As the younger generations become older, their work values change similarly. Of course, this does not mean that within a country (and especially in smaller social units such as a region, a settlement, or a workplace) generational effects could not emerge, but these do not add up in our aggregated analysis as a generational trend.

If there are no significant differences between the generations, for policymakers this means that those social and economic efforts made in the interest of decreasing youth unemployment will not be hindered by changing generational attitudes toward work.

In summary, our assumption that younger generations are increasingly less work oriented, have less faith that they will achieve a career, and are less optimistic about getting a job and making ends meet on the basis of a salary turned out to be wrong. Therefore, if there sound EU policies are implemented to cope with youth unemployment, they will not fail because of generation-specific attitudes. Moreover, if the proposition of the management literature is correct that work values have a significant impact on values in general as well as on behavior in the workplace and on the labor market, then the unchanging nature of work values provides policymakers with firm ground to act.

The second conclusion is based on the fact that although birth cohort does not have a strong impact on work values, we did detect differences in work values by both age and time period. Thus, we should be aware that generational stability does not mean full-scale similarity. For example, the slow but steady decrease in the centrality of work by period might call for the development of policies that relax the association between life and work for future generations. It seems likely that instead of having work as the central social phenomenon that gives meaning to life, multiple centrality (having work as one important life aspect) is becoming increasingly more common among Europeans.

NOTES

1   In the course of our analysis, we use "centrality of work" as the dependent variable because it refers to work in the widest sense (i.e., work as a basic human activity). As we note in Section 21.2.2, the working paper version of this chapter covers other variables of work values as well, such as employment commitment and extrinsic/intrinsic values (Hajdu and Sik 2015).

2   Usually, political/economic/technological periodizations relating to the United States are the basis of these global generational definitions, as defined, for example, by Twenge et al. (2010):

- Baby boomers by the civil rights and women's movements, the Vietnam War, and the assassinations of John F. Kennedy and Martin Luther King
- GenX by the AIDS epidemic, economic uncertainty, and the fall of the Soviet Union
- GenY by being "wired" and "tech savvy," liking "informality," learning quickly, and embracing "diversity"

On the other hand, Diepstraten et al. (1999), for example, identified "prewar," "silent," "protest," "lost," and "pragmatic" generations for the Netherlands on the basis of an entirely different national "story."

3   For example, on redistribution, see Luttmer and Singhal (2011); on trust, see Dinesen (2013); on subjective well-being, see Senik (2014) and Hajdu and Hajdu (2016); and on female labor force participation, see Fernández and Fogli (2009) and Alesina and Giuliano (2010). The most notable example of illustrating the impact of ethnicity on work values is the analysis of the role of an ethnic border (the so-called *Röstigraben*) in Switzerland (Brügger, Lalive, and Zweimüller 2009).

4   In the working paper version of this chapter, employment commitment and extrinsic/intrinsic work values were used as dependent variables as well. *Employment commitment*—that is, paid work only—was considered as a more restricted form of the centrality of work. From this viewpoint, work is conceptualized as the source of income, and the question is whether the respondents consider paid work as a standard economic resource (and therefore work only until its aggregate return does not start to decrease) or not (i.e., they do paid work for its own sake). *Extrinsic/intrinsic work values* are widely used in the organization, business, and management literature. An extrinsic work value is "dependent on a source external to the immediate task-person situation . . . such as status, respect, power, influence, high salary." An intrinsic value, on the contrary, is "derived from the task per se; that is, from outcomes which are not mediated by a source external to the task–person situation. Such a state of motivation can be characterized as a

self-fulfilling experience" (Brief and Aldag 1977, 497–98). In the working paper, we used three extrinsic work values (good income, security, and flexibility) and two intrinsic values (interesting job and having a job that is useful to society) that are considered important by the respondents in evaluating a job (Hajdu and Sik 2015).

5 Hierarchical age–period–cohort (HAPC) regression models have been used to analyze repeated cross-sectional data by Yang and Land (2006, 2008) in examining verbal test scores; by Schwadel (2014) in examining the changing association between higher education and reporting no religious affiliation in the United States; by Down and Wilson (2013) in examining life cycle and cohort effects on support for the EU; and by Kowske et al. (2010) in examining the effect of generation on job satisfaction and on satisfaction with other job aspects.

6 This can only be done artificially, so it is ultimately a subjective decision by the researcher. However, we grouped our data by taking account of waves of surveys so that data from each wave were grouped together into 5-year intervals, which can be considered the most "natural" (i.e., "theory-blind") grouping principle.

7 Yang and Land (2008) argue that whereas the age variable is related to the biological process of individual aging, period and cohort effects reflect the influences of external (political, technological, economic, etc.) forces; thus, the latter two variables can be treated as level 2 (or macro-level) variables. Suzuki (2012, 453) shows a data structure in which individuals are nested simultaneously within periods and birth cohorts, whereas age is an attribute of individuals rather than a random sample of age categories from a population of age groupings.

8 Detailed descriptions of the models are provided in Appendix 1.

9 Other researchers using these variables created complex scales (Wollack et al. 1971; Ros, Schwartz, and Surkiss 1999; Den Dulk et al. 2013), but we wanted to keep our variables simple so as to ensure that they are understood identically by respondents in subsequent surveys and different cultures.

10 The coding was as follows: 1 (very important), 2 (quite important), 3 (not important), and 4 (not important at all).

11 Although the second wave of WVS/EVS was conducted between 1989 and 1993, the date of the fieldwork was between 1990 and 1993 in all but two of the participating countries. We excluded from this wave two countries (Poland and Switzerland)—where the year of the fieldwork was 1989—in order to avoid a small sample size for this year (or in the period 1985–1989) and also to avoid results driven by only two countries. Moreover, because the number of observations between 2000 and 2004 is relatively low, given that the fourth (1999–2004) wave of WVS/EVS was conducted in most countries in 1999, we excluded this period from the analysis as well.

12 The same applies to defining the age of the respondent: It was calculated as the difference between the year of the fieldwork and the respondent's birth year.

13 We show only six age groups (two of the youngest groups, two from the middle-aged groups, and two of the oldest groups) in order to have a less cluttered table.

14 Because we analyze respondents of similar age, this model can be conceptualized as a special form of the time-lag method recommended by Twenge (2010).

15 This lack of differences between men and women has also been found by other authors examining various work values (e.g., Clark 2010).

16 An "average man" is a man who has average characteristics (average values of the control variables among the men), and an "average woman" is a woman who has average characteristics (average values of the control variables among the women).

17 As Table A21.2 in Appendix 2 shows, the relative centrality of work differs significantly across countries. However, because a comparative analysis of the trend for relative centrality of work at the country level would require a separate paper, we restrict ourselves to a regional (i.e., semi-aggregated version of country-specific) comparative analysis.

18 Germany is split into two parts: federal states from the former West Germany as an EU15 country and federal states from the former East Germany as a post-socialist country.

REFERENCES

Alesina, Alberto, and Paola Giuliano. 2010. "The Power of the Family." *Journal of Economic Growth* 15 (2): 93–125.

Becton, John Bret, Harvell Jack Walker, and Allison Jones-Farmer. 2014. "Generational Differences in Workplace Behavior." *Journal of Applied Social Psychology* 44 (3): 175–89. doi10.1111/jasp.12208.

Bell, Andrew, and Kelvyn Jones. 2014. "Another 'Futile Quest'? A Simulation Study of Yang and Land's Hierarchical Age–Period–Cohort Model." *Demographic Research* 30 (February): 333–60. doi:10.4054/DemRes.2014.30.11.

Brief, Arthur P., and Ramon J. Aldag. 1977. "The Intrinsic–Extrinsic Dichotomy: Toward Conceptual Clarity." *Academy of Management Review* 2 (3): 496–500. doi:10.5465/AMR.1977.4281861.

Brügger, Beatrix, Rafael Lalive, and Josef Zweimüller. 2009. "Does Culture Affect Unemployment? Evidence from the Röstigraben." CEPR Discussion Paper 7405. London: Centre for Economic Policy Research. https://ideas.repec.org/p/cpr/ceprdp/7405.html

Clark, Andrew E. 2010. "Work, Jobs, and Well-Being Across the Millennium." In *International Differences in Well-Being*, edited by Ed Diener, John F. Helliwell, and Daniel Kahneman, 436–68. Oxford: Oxford University Press.

Costanza, David P., Jessica M. Badger, Rebecca L. Fraser, Jamie B. Severt, and Paul A. Gade. 2012. "Generational Differences in Work-Related Attitudes: A Meta-Analysis." *Journal of Business and Psychology* 27 (4): 375–94. doi:10.1007/s10869-012-9259-4.

Den Dulk, Laura, Sandra Groeneveld, Ariane Ollier-Malaterre, and Monique Valcour. 2013. "National Context in Work–Life Research: A Multi-Level Cross-National Analysis of the Adoption of Workplace Work–Life Arrangements in Europe." *European Management Journal* 31 (5): 478–94. doi:10.1016/j.emj.2013.04.010.

Diepstraten, Isabelle, Peter Ester, and Henk Vinken. 1999. "Talkin' 'Bout My Generation: Ego and Alter Images of Generations in the Netherlands." *The Netherlands Journal of Social Sciences* 35 (2): 91–109.

Dinesen, Peter Thisted. 2013. "Where You Come from or Where You Live? Examining the Cultural and Institutional Explanation of Generalized Trust Using Migration as a Natural Experiment." *European Sociological Review* 29 (1): 114–28. doi:10.1093/esr/jcr044.

Down, Ian, and Carole J. Wilson. 2013. "A Rising Generation of Europeans? Life-Cycle and Cohort Effects on Support for 'Europe.'" *European Journal of Political Research* 52 (4): 431–56. doi:10.1111/1475-6765.12001.

Egri, Carolyn P., and David A. Ralston. 2004. "Generation Cohorts and Personal Values: A Comparison of China and the United States." *Organization Science* 15 (2): 210–20. doi:10.1287/orsc.1030.0048.

Fernández, Raquel, and Alessandra Fogli. 2009. "Culture: An Empirical Investigation of Beliefs, Work, and Fertility." *American Economic Journal: Macroeconomics* 1 (1): 146–77. doi:10.1257/mac.1.1.146.

Firebaugh, Glenn. 1997. *Analyzing Repeated Surveys*. Sage University Paper 115. Thousand Oaks, CA: Sage.

Hajdu, Gábor, and Tamás Hajdu. 2016. "The Impact of Culture on Well-Being: Evidence from a Natural Experiment." *Journal of Happiness Studies* 17 (3): 1089–110. doi:10.1007/s10902-015-9633-9.

Hajdu, Gábor, and Endre Sik. 2015. "Searching for Gaps: Are Work Values of the Younger Generations Changing?" STYLE Working Paper 9.1. Brighton, UK: CROME, University of Brighton. http://www.style-research.eu/publications/working-papers

Hansen, Jo-Ida C., and Melanie E. Leuty. 2012. "Work Values Across Generations." *Journal of Career Assessment* 20 (1): 34–52. doi:10.1177/1069072711417163.

Harpaz, Itzhak, and Xuanning Fu. 2002. "The Structure of the Meaning of Work: A Relative Stability Amidst Change." *Human Relations* 55 (6): 639–67. doi:10.1177/0018726702556002.

Jin, Jing, and James Rounds. 2012. "Stability and Change in Work Values: A Meta-Analysis of Longitudinal Studies." *Journal of Vocational Behavior* 80 (2): 326–39. doi:10.1016/j.jvb.2011.10.007.

Kowske, Brenda J., Rena Rasch, and Jack Wiley. 2010. "Millennials' (Lack of) Attitude Problem: An Empirical Examination of Generational Effects on Work Attitudes." *Journal of Business and Psychology* 25 (2): 265–79. doi:10.1007/s10869-010-9171-8.

Luttmer, Erzo F. P., and Monica Singhal. 2011. "Culture, Context, and the Taste for Redistribution." *American Economic Journal: Economic Policy* 3 (1): 157–79. doi:10.1257/pol.3.1.157.

Roe, Robert A., and Peter Ester. 1999. "Values and Work: Empirical Findings and Theoretical Perspective." *Applied Psychology* 48 (1): 1–21. doi:10.1111/j.1464-0597.1999.tb00046.x.

Ros, Maria, Shalom H. Schwartz, and Shoshana Surkiss. 1999. "Basic Individual Values, Work Values, and the Meaning of Work." *Applied Psychology* 48 (1): 49–71. doi:10.1111/j.1464-0597.1999.tb00048.x.

Schwadel, Philip. 2014. "Birth Cohort Changes in the Association Between College Education and Religious Non-Affiliation." *Social Forces* (August): 1–28. doi:10.1093/sf/sou080.

Senik, Claudia. 2014. "The French Unhappiness Puzzle: The Cultural Dimension of Happiness." *Journal of Economic Behavior & Organization* 106 (October): 379–401. doi:10.1016/j.jebo.2014.05.010.

Sharabi, Moshe, and Itzhak Harpaz. 2007. "Changes in Work Centrality and Other Life Areas in Israel: A Longitudinal Study." *Journal of Human Values* 13 (2): 95–106. doi:10.1177/097168580701300203.

Suzuki, Etsuji. 2012. "Time Changes, So Do People." *Social Science & Medicine* 75 (3): 452–56. doi:10.1016/j.socscimed.2012.03.036.

Tolbize, Anick. 2008. *Generational Differences in the Workplace.* Minneapolis: Research and Training Center on Community Living, University of Minnesota.

Twenge, Jean M. 2010. "A Review of the Empirical Evidence on Generational Differences in Work Attitudes." *Journal of Business and Psychology* 25 (2): 201–10. doi:10.1007/s10869-010-9165-6.

Twenge, Jean M., Stacy M. Campbell, Brian J. Hoffman, and Charles E. Lance. 2010. "Generational Differences in Work Values: Leisure and Extrinsic Values Increasing, Social and Intrinsic Values Decreasing." *Journal of Management* 36 (5): 1117–42. doi:10.1177/0149206309352246.

Wollack, Stephen, James G. Goodale, Jan P. Wijting, and Patricia C. Smith. 1971. "Development of the Survey of Work Values." *Journal of Applied Psychology* 55 (4): 331–38. doi:10.1037/h0031531.

Wuthnow, Robert. 2008. "The Sociological Study of Values." *Sociological Forum* 23 (2): 333–43. doi:10.1111/j.1573-7861.2008.00063.x.

Yang, Yang, Wenjiang Fu, and Kenneth C. Land. 2008. "The Intrinsic Estimator for Age–Period–Cohort Analysis: What It Is and How to Use It." *American Journal of Sociology* 113 (6): 1697–736.

Yang, Yang, and Kenneth C. Land. 2006. "A Mixed Models Approach to the Age–Period–Cohort Analysis of Repeated Cross-Section Surveys, with an Application to Data on Trends in Verbal Test Scores." *Sociological Methodology* 36 (1): 75–97. doi:10.1111/j.1467-9531.2006.00175.x.

Yang, Yang, and Kenneth C. Land. 2008. "Age–Period–Cohort Analysis of Repeated Cross-Section Surveys: Fixed or Random Effects?" *Sociological Methods & Research* 36 (3): 297–326. doi:10.1177/0049124106292360.

APPENDIX 1

We use cross-classified hierarchical regression models. The level 1 model is as follows:

$$Y_{ijk} = \beta_{0jk} + \beta_1 AGE_{ijk} + \beta_2 AGE_{ijk}^2 + \beta_3 \mathbf{X}_{ijk} +$$

The level 2 model is

$$\beta_{0jk} = \gamma_0 + u_{0j} + v_{0k}$$

The combined model is

$$Y_{ijk} = \gamma_0 + \beta_1 AGE_{ijk} + \beta_2 AGE_{ijk}^2 + \beta_3 \mathbf{X}_{ijk} + u_{0j} + v_{0k} + e_{ijk}$$

where, within each cohort j and period k, respondents' work attitude is a function of their age, squared age, and other individual characteristics (vector of $\mathbf{X}$). This model allows level 1 intercepts to vary randomly by cohorts and periods. β_{0jk} is the mean of the work-attitude variable of individuals in cohort j and period k (cell mean); β_1, β_2, and β_3 are the level 1 fixed effects; e_{ijk} is the random individual variation, which is assumed to be normally distributed with mean 0 and within-cell variance σ^2; γ_0 is the grand mean (across all cohorts and periods) or the model intercept; u_{0j} is the residual random effect of cohort j; and v_{0j} is the residual random effect of period k. Both u_{0j} and v_{0j} are assumed to be normally distributed with mean 0 and variance τ_u and τ_v, respectively.

APPENDIX 2

Table A21.1 Number of observations of relative centrality of work by country and year of fieldwork

Country	1990	1991	1992	1993	1995	1996	1997	1998	1999	2005	2006	2007	2008	2009	Total
EU15															
AT	1,395	0	0	0	0	0	0	0	1,495	0	0	0	1,505	0	4,395
BE	2,578	0	0	0	0	0	0	0	1,785	0	0	0	0	1,490	5,853
DE-W	3,276	0	0	0	0	0	1,954	0	1,990	0	1,908	0	1,999	0	11,127
DK	994	0	0	0	0	0	0	0	998	0	0	0	1,386	0	3,378
ES	3,404	0	0	0	1,202	0	0	0	1,193	0	0	1,175	1,483	0	8,457
FI	48	0	0	0	0	901	0	0	0	973	0	0	0	1,061	2,983
FR	786	0	0	0	0	0	0	0	1,541	0	963	0	1,484	0	4,774
GB	1,405	0	0	0	0	0	0	0	847	0	918	0	0	895	4,065
EL	0	0	0	0	0	0	0	0	1,039	0	0	0	1,489	0	2,528
IE	991	0	0	0	0	0	0	0	902	0	0	0	541	0	2,434
IT	1,960	0	0	0	0	0	0	0	1,970	978	0	0	0	1,409	6,318
LU	0	0	0	0	0	0	0	0	1,107	0	0	0	1,592	0	2,699
NL	976	0	0	0	0	0	0	0	959	0	950	0	1,533	0	4,418
PT	1,088	0	0	0	0	0	0	0	995	0	0	0	1,527	0	3,610
SE	909	0	0	0	0	990	0	0	740	0	984	0	0	987	4,610

(continued)

Table A21.1 Continued

Country	1990	1991	1992	1993	1995	1996	1997	1998	1999	2005	2006	2007	2008	2009	Total
Post-socialist															
BA	0	0	0	0	0	0	0	1,178	0	0	0	0	1,356	0	2,534
BG	942	0	0	0	0	0	986	0	974	0	963	0	1,397	0	5,262
CS	0	0	0	0	0	1,455	0	0	0	0	0	0	0	0	1,455
CZ	770	2,082	0	0	0	0	0	1,084	1,879	0	0	0	1,696	0	7,512
EE	960	0	0	0	0	1,000	0	0	989	0	0	0	1,502	0	4,452
HR	0	0	0	0	0	0	0	0	933	0	0	0	1,410	0	2,343
HU	0	981	0	0	0	0	0	630	975	0	0	0	1,506	0	4,093
LT	0	0	0	0	0	0	969	0	993	0	0	0	1,462	0	3,425
LV	813	0	0	0	0	1,160	0	0	984	0	0	0	1,488	0	4,445
PL	960	0	0	0	0	0	0	0	1,082	979	0	0	1,448	0	4,469
RO	0	0	0	1,077	0	0	0	1,226	1,131	1,709	0	0	1,430	0	6,573
RU	1,000	0	0	0	2,007	0	0	0	2,454	0	1,865	0	1,442	0	8,769
SI	0	0	948	0	970	0	0	0	987	1,024	0	0	1,337	0	5,266
SK	381	1,104	0	0	0	0	0	1,037	1,323	0	0	0	1,493	0	5,337
UA	0	0	0	0	0	2,662	0	0	1,142	0	967	0	1,478	0	6,249

Other

														Total
AU	0	0	0	1,857	0	0	0	1,216	0	0	0			3,073
CA	1,675	0	0	0	0	0	0	0	2,015	0	0			3,690
CH	0	0	0	0	1,149	0	0	0	0	0	1,228			2,377
IS	0	0	0	0	0	0	930	0	0	0	0			930
MT	0	0	0	0	0	988	0	0	0	685				1,673
NO	1,139	0	0	0	1,114	0	0	0	0	0	2,096			4,349
NZ	0	0	0	0	0	1,025	0	0	0	0	0			1,025
US	1,662	0	0	1,379	0	0	1,184	0	1,163	0	0			5,388
Total	30,115	4,168	948	1,077	7,416	10,432	3,910	6,181	36,513	6,879	12,694	1,175	38,991	5,842	16,6340

Source: World Values Survey/European Values Study.

Table A21.2 Mean of relative centrality of work by country and year of fieldwork

Country	1990	1991	1992	1993	1995	1996	1997	1998	1999	2005	2006	2007	2008	2009	Total
EU15															
AT	0.126								0.082				-0.117		0.028
BE	0.001								0.027					-0.114	-0.020
DE-W	-0.195						-0.148		-0.223		-0.140		-0.234		-0.189
DK	-0.173								-0.358				-0.309		-0.283
ES	0.116				0.051				0.161				0.016		0.052
FI	0.069					-0.196				-0.345				-0.435	-0.325
FR	0.170								0.109		0.072		0.102		0.110
GB	-0.339								-0.542		-0.580			-0.625	-0.499
EL									0.044				0.045		0.045
IE	0.033								-0.255				-0.349		-0.159
IT	0.136								0.151	0.074				0.168	0.138
LU									-0.075				0.125		0.043
NL	-0.158								-0.284		-0.506		-0.331		-0.320
PT	0.105								0.166				0.131		0.133
SE	-0.042					-0.090			-0.258		-0.280			-0.334	-0.200
Post-socialist															
BA								0.104					-0.005		0.046
BG	0.151						0.065		0.186		-0.107		0.070		0.073
CS						0.126									0.126

CZ	0.135	0.293			-0.095				0.141					-0.187	0.075
EE	-0.019		0.248						0.159					-0.016	0.082
HR									0.041					-0.017	0.006
HU	0.199							0.008	0.067					-0.048	0.047
LT						0.157			0.216					0.049	0.128
LV	0.041		0.296						0.508					0.192	0.261
PL	0.285								0.362	-0.001				-0.027	0.140
RO				0.401	0.293				0.418	0.183				0.124	0.267
RU	-0.019						-0.003		0.168		-0.115			-0.090	0.005
SI			0.409			0.100			0.176	-0.147				0.031	0.104
SK	0.203	0.260			-0.052				0.147					0.042	0.106
UA					-0.032				0.086		-0.264			-0.069	-0.055
Other															
AU	-0.130					-0.263				-0.463					-0.342
CA											-0.295				-0.220
CH					-0.203									-0.038	-0.118
IS									-0.021						-0.021
MT									0.233					0.118	0.186
NO	0.068				-0.068									-0.183	-0.088
NZ					-0.271										-0.271
US	-0.115				-0.265						-0.534	-0.222	-0.037		-0.268
Total	-0.003	0.262	0.409	0.401	-0.095	0.011	-0.019	0.008	0.058	-0.097	-0.258	-0.198	-0.037	-0.220	-0.022

Source: World Values Survey/European Values Study.

22

HOW CAN TRADE UNIONS IN EUROPE CONNECT WITH YOUNG WORKERS?

Kurt Vandaele

22.1. INTRODUCTION

Trade union density has almost universally declined across Europe in recent decades (Visser 2016), although substantial cross-country variation still exists. Among the different categories of under-represented groups in unions, young workers are considered the "most problematic group" in this regard (Pedersini 2010, 13). There is ample evidence that they are generally less inclined to unionize (see Section 22.2). Three major (and not mutually exclusive) explanations for this group's low unionization rate have been identified in the literature (Payne 1989; Serrano Pascual and Waddington 2000).

The first involves the assumption that the propensity of young workers to unionize has decreased because of intergenerational shifts in values and attitudes. The second explanation is that the opportunity to unionize has been structurally hampered by the individualization of working conditions (driven by human resource management policies), new developments in work organization (e.g., telework), and changing labor markets for young workers (Blossfeld et al. 2008). These workers are more likely to be employed in nonstandard employment arrangements and in those workplaces, occupations, and economic sectors marked by weak union representation.[1] Finally, the sociology of unionism matters: In light of the developments outlined previously, the current policies and organizational structures of many unions are likely to be ineffective for engaging and organizing young workers, and their predominant (decision-making) culture could be considered unattractive and unfavorable for youth participation in union democracy and action (Vandaele 2012, 2015). We need to understand that the ways in which unions perceive and prioritize (or not) young workers play a pivotal role in shaping their efforts to address this problem (Esders, Bailey, and McDonald 2011). Moreover, given that there is a significant overlap between young workers and the phenomenon of precariousness, unions' strategies toward precarious work have, by definition, important consequences for these workers (Murphy and Simms 2017).

Based for the most part on a literature review, the aim of this chapter is to explore what kind of strategies unions in Europe could develop to reconnect with the new generation on the labor market.[2] In developing our main argument, we refer first to the main motives for union membership because their *relative* presence in a sector or country will influence unions' strategies and policies for organizing young workers (Heery and Adler 2004). The chapter broadly focuses on three areas of motivation (Ebbinghaus, Göbel, and Koos 2011): the significance of union membership as a traditional custom embedded in social networks; instrumental/rational motives that are influenced by a favorable institutional framework for unions to lower the costs of organizing and servicing (young) workers; and, finally, the principle of solidarity, the identity-forming function of union membership, and the ideological convictions promoted by unions. In the literature on youth unionization, each motive largely corresponds to a different research focus (as shown in Table 22.1), and the different sections of this chapter are accordingly built around this framework. Bearing in mind the diminishing impact of traditional motives and the pressure that employer organizations or governments exert upon "union-friendly" institutional frameworks in the labor market, the argument will be made that union agency takes on a particular importance in the effort to counteract the deunionization trend. Decisive union action in the form, for instance, of comprehensive campaigning can be instrumental in reviving or strengthening these traditional and instrumental/rational motives (Ibsen and Tapia 2017).

If the difficulties in organizing young workers continue unabated, this situation will represent an increasingly serious challenge for existing unions. It could impede their generational and imaginative renewal, exacerbate their already biased representation of today's more diversified workforce, and even seriously call

Table 22.1 The linkage between motives of union membership and the research focus

Motives of union membership	Research focus
Traditional social customs	Young people themselves: Their believes and attitudes
Instrumental/rational motives	Young people in the labor market: School-to-work transitions
Union agency	Young people and unions: Sociology of unionism

Source: Author's own typology.

into question their legitimacy vis-à-vis employers and political authorities, as well as their own organizational survival. Eventually, other or new organizations or social movements might emerge or gain further prominence for representing young (vulnerable) workers (and particularly in specific segments of the labor market such as the "gig economy"). At the same time, many young workers could potentially benefit from union representation. Since the Great Recession, inequalities in the labor market between adults and young people have accelerated, with labor market flexibility tending to disproportionally affect young workers (France 2016). Therefore, the idea will also be developed that young people's early labor market experiences should be placed center stage in any union recruitment or organizing drive toward the young. However, young people entering the labor market are not a homogeneous bloc, a fact that becomes especially clear in their transition from school to work. This crucial phase in young people's lives is marked by differences in the timing, duration, and sequence of labor market events. Distinctive trajectories in the school-to-work transition imply different challenges and opportunities for unions in terms of recruiting and retaining young workers, as well as engaging their participation in union activities, because their exposure to unionism is not uniform.

The chapter is organized as follows. Section 22.2 explores the extent to which an individual's age influences his or her decision to join a union, and it examines the patterns in youth unionization across Europe. Section 22.3 focuses on young people themselves in a discussion of their beliefs and attitudes toward unionization. It then explores the demise of unionization as a traditional social custom as an alternative explanation to simple cohort effects. Section 22.4 examines the significance of school-to-work transition regimes for organizing young people: The opportunities and costs of organizing are dependent on the degree of union integration in those regimes. The internal adaptation and diverse initiatives of unions across Europe toward engaging and organizing young workers are discussed in Section 22.5. Section 22.6 concludes the chapter.

22.2. YOUNG WORKERS AS A DEMOGRAPHIC CHALLENGE FOR UNIONS

In this section, we explore the relationship between age and unionization to assess to what extent there exists an "age deficit" within unions. Based on a literature review on the determinants of unionization (of studies from the 1980s until the early 1990s), Riley (1997, 272) found "conflicting evidence," with age only sometimes having a significant effect on union membership. Some years later, however, in the UK context, Machin (2004, 430) claimed that age is "a more important determinant of who joins trade unions now than it used to be." A seminal study by Blanchflower (2007) concluded that union density in 34 of the

38 advanced economies investigated follows a similar pattern: An inverted U-curve in regard to age shows that workers in their mid- to late forties have the highest likelihood of being unionized, compared to lower membership rates for both younger and older workers. Controlling for existing cohort effects in the United Kingdom and the United States, Blanchflower found that the concave age effect on unionization remains. More recent research on individual countries or across countries has either confirmed the concave age/unionization pattern (Kirmanoğlu and Başlevent 2012, 695; Turner and D'Art 2012, 47) or questioned it (Scheuer 2011; Schnabel and Wagner 2012). Thus, in the latter cases, it is found that the probability of unionization increases monotonically with age.

At first glance, the typical pattern of relatively low youth unionization should not, in itself, worry unions excessively because there might be an age effect at play. As young workers grow older and settle into (if it can be assumed) stable working careers, they might naturally "mature" into unionism. However, Figure 22.1 illustrates that in most European countries considered in this study, the median age of union members increased between 2004 and 2014; the same cohort effect applies to union activists and representatives in many sectors.[3] In fact, in some countries, the median age indicates that a great number of union members are in their mid-forties to early fifties. Because middle-aged workers currently dominate the overall union membership composition, the median voter theorem would suggest that their policy preferences are dominating union strategies (Ebbinghaus 2006). If indeed unions are primarily representing the interests and needs of "insiders" (i.e., older workers), they might appear relatively unattractive

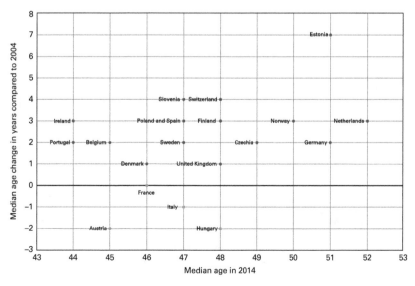

Figure 22.1 Median age of union members in 2014 and its change compared to 2004 in Europe. *Source*: European Social Survey.

to "outsiders" (i.e., young workers). However, such a rationale, based on assumed member preferences, ignores the structural context of labor market dualization and betrays a biased reasoning regarding statistical labor market outcomes. Apart from its rather manicheistic tendencies, this framework disregards "the constraints under which unions operate and the drivers of union strategies beyond their members' interests" (Benassi and Vlandas 2016, 6).

Nevertheless, today's smaller birth cohorts and young people's later labor market entrance (due to higher tertiary education rates) might further contribute to this "graying" of unions.[4] Figure 22.2 provides evidence that, by and large, most unions in many countries are struggling to organize young people or, at least, cannot keep membership developments in line with growing employment rates. The figure compares the unionization rates among "youth" and "adults" at the aggregated level (thus masking sectoral differences) in 2004 and 2014. Here, "youth" is defined as unionization until the age of 24 years and "adult" as unionization between 25 and 54 years. In practice, unions generally use a broader definition by setting the maximum age for "youth" at 35 years (Vandaele 2012, 208). Yet the definition of "youth" used in Figure 22.2 makes it easier to discern the possible difficulties unions have with attracting young people; it is also more in line with youth studies. Three observations can be made from the figure.

First, country differences in adult and youth unionization are *generally* persistent over time. Looking at, for instance, the level of youth unionization, there is a strong positive relationship between the country rankings in 2004 and 2014

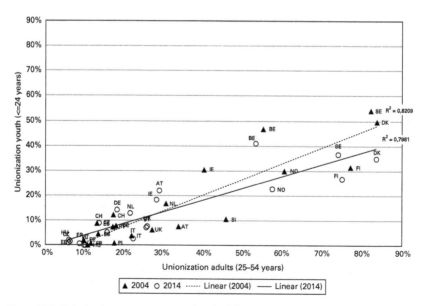

Figure 22.2 Unionization rates among youth and adults in Europe, 2004 and 2014.
Source: European Social Survey.

$(r_s(20) = .86, p < .00)$. Second, there is an equally strong positive association between youth and adult unionization in 2004, which still holds 10 years later. Although the youth/adult gap in unionization in the Nordic countries is relatively substantial because of the very high levels of adult membership, youth unionization is still higher in those countries compared to the others. Finally, there is a drop in both youth and adult unionization rates in most, but not all, countries, with a relatively stronger decline in youth unionization. In other words, during the past 10 years in most European countries considered here, less young people have joined a union, more often than not resulting in a widening of the youth/adult gap in unionization. The fall in youth unionization is especially conspicuous in Denmark, Ireland, and Sweden. Youth unionization has increased in only a small number of countries, notably Austria and Germany.

Figure 22.2 illustrates the strong self-perpetuating tendencies of early union membership and demonstrates that early unionization is key. Indeed, although a typical union member is middle-aged, the first experience with unionism is very likely to happen when a worker is still young (Booth, Budd, and Munday 2010a, 48). Evidence from, for instance, Denmark (Toubøl and Jensen 2014, 150) and the Netherlands (Visser 2002, 416) suggests that the likelihood of first-time union membership is higher when workers are young and entering the labor market than it is later on: They seem "sensitive to reputational effects even at low levels of workplace union density" (Ibsen, Toubøl, and Jensen 2017, 10). In other words, there are many "first-timers" but far fewer "late bloomers" in unions (Booth, Budd, and Munday 2010b). This essentially implies that the window of opportunity for unions to organize workers becomes decidedly smaller the older they get (Budd 2010). Moreover, the early stages of unionization are crucial because the first years of union membership are the period when the probability of member outflow seems to be at its highest (Leschke and Vandaele 2015, 3–5). However, the crucial question for many (but not all) unions is not so much why young workers are resigning from membership but, rather, why so many of them "do not join a union (or at least join a union once they get a stable job)" at all (Peetz, Price, and Bailey 2015, 64).

Further contributing to this bleak picture of the continued existence of unions is the increasing percentage of workers who have never become a union member, a trend that has been evident in Germany (Schnabel and Wagner 2006), the United Kingdom, and the United States (Booth et al. 2010a), as well as across other European countries (Kirmanoğlu and Başlevent 2012, 695). The rise of never-membership can be considered a "demographic time bomb" for unions if organizing young workers is not prioritized. Crucially, although the employment shift—from the traditionally highly unionized manufacturing industries to the less unionized private service sector—has significantly contributed to the rise of never-membership, this is not the whole story. Deunionization would have occurred even in the absence of such a structural employment shift in the labor market (Ebbinghaus and Visser 1999).

22.3. THE YOUNG PEOPLE THEMSELVES: THEIR BELIEFS AND ATTITUDES TOWARD UNIONS

Among many other causes (see Vachon, Wallace, and Hyde 2016), intergenerational change in beliefs and attitudes toward unions is considered an additional explanation for deunionization. Cohort effects in attitudes and beliefs toward collectivism are consequently a central concern in this section, which investigates whether such effects can explain the low youth unionization rate. Many young people do actually seem to demonstrate trade union sympathies (although they have less knowledge about unions), but the traditional sources for the transmission of favorable attitudes and beliefs toward unionization are disappearing. Therefore, instead of "problematizing youth," it is important to understand how young people develop their behavioral attitudes toward unions rather than simply comparing them to those of previous generations.

22.3.1. Framing young people's attitudes and beliefs via cohort effects

Studies on youth unionization that focus on young people *themselves* predominantly emphasize cohort effects. Such a social generation approach claims that young people's attitudes and beliefs toward collective behavior diverge sharply from those of previous generations. There is no consensus here as to how a young worker should be defined, in the sense that different age boundaries are used; when these are too large, this entails the danger of masking significant in-group variance (Tailby and Pollert 2011), which in turn might be influenced by differences in school-to-work regimes (Booth et al. 2010b). Thus, it remains an empirical question whether the attitudes of *very* young workers, with little labor market experience, are always similar to those of *older* young workers with more experience.

Above all other factors contributing to the low level of youth unionization, it has been speculated that young workers, being associated with increasingly individualistic beliefs and values, are less motivated by the collective ethos of unionism compared to previous generations (Allvin and Sverke 2000; Kirmanoğlu and Başlevent 2012). However, there are good reasons to be cautious about this claim. First, *conceptually*, individualism does not necessarily exclude the belief that collective behavior is required to achieve common goals (Goerres 2010). Nevertheless, collective behavior needs backing by collective mechanisms, which are increasingly breaking down or are no longer supported by the state or employer organizations (Peetz 2010). Second, *methodologically*, findings on differential intergenerational attitudes toward unions are often based on small-scale sociological studies, sometimes even of an anecdotal nature, so generalizing them is problematic (Haynes, Vowles, and

Boxall 2005, 96). Finally, *empirically*, pointing to period effects, there is little evidence that young union members are more individualistic than their older counterparts, although there may be differences between the unionized and the nonunionized (Paquet 2005). Instead, employers' hostility to union membership and a fear of victimization among young people may play an important and dissuasive role (Mrozowicki, Krasowska, and Karolak 2015; Hodder 2016; Alonso and Fernández Rodríguez 2017).

Although a narrow interpretation of young people's individualism often negatively associates it with "Thatcher's children" (in the UK context; see Waddington and Kerr 2002; Bryson and Gomez 2005), recent studies referring to "millennials" cast young people in a good light in terms of political engagement (despite their individualism). Again assuming cohort effects, millennials are considered a generational group that is loosely defined as those people who reached adulthood after the onset of the new millennium. Thus, specific attitudes and beliefs have been attributed to this "tech-savvy generation," especially concerning work, such as the minor importance of paid work in their value system. However, many of the intergenerational differences in the workplace could be explained by age and period as opposed to cohort effects (Hajdu and Sik, this volume). It has also been claimed that millennials constitute a new political generation whose differences from their predecessors have become especially apparent in the anti-austerity/pro-democracy movements that have been active since the Great Recession (Milkman 2017).

Although the participants in the anti-austerity/pro-democracy movements differ in their sociodemographic composition—being younger and more educated—and they are more likely to identify with the middle class, these youthful activists do share the same discontent and left-leaning political orientations as unionists (Peterson, Wahlstrom, and Wennerhag 2015). Still, tensions between them, if employed (and more often in vulnerable employment positions), and established union confederations rose notably in those European countries that were heavily affected by the Great Recession, such as Greece (Kretsos 2011) and Spain (Fernández Rodríguez et al. 2015; Köhler and Calleja Jiménez 2015). In these countries, the union confederations' original strategy of political inclusion through co-managing the crisis has contributed to a general decline in trust in them or to a perception of them being "bureaucratic dinosaurs" (Hyman 2015). But the union strategies adopted in the early stages of the recession also show that the disconnection between millennials and unions in those countries should be considered in a specific context. In fact, compared to previous generations, there is little reason to believe that most young people today are born with an "antipathetic union gene." Studies examining their attitudes toward unions paint a less negative picture than the assumed cohort effects suggest; in fact, strong antagonistic attitudes toward unionism *in principle* are not at all common among young people.

22.3.2. Virulent anti-unionism is not the problem

Studies actually point to an underlying and unmet demand for unionization among young workers. Basing their research on European Social Survey data, D'Art and Turner (2008) report largely positive attitudes toward unions, irrespective of age, and the persistence and even strengthening of this view among workers since the early 1980s. In fact, young workers seem even more inclined to join unions compared to their older counterparts. Such findings come from studies in Australia (Pyman et al. 2009), Canada (Gomez, Gunderson, and Meltz 2002), New Zealand (Haynes et al. 2005), the United States (Booth et al. 2010a), and the United Kingdom (Payne 1989; Serrano Pascual and Waddington 2000; Waddington and Kerr 2002; Freeman and Diamond 2003; Tailby and Pollert 2011). Also, as a corollary, a comparison between Canada, the United Kingdom, and the United States concludes that "workers have broadly similar preferences for unionization across age groups and borders" (Bryson et al. 2005, 166).

Significantly, this pattern of unmet demand for unionization can be confirmed for a large range of very different countries beyond the Anglophone world, including Belgium (Vendramin 2007), Denmark (Caraker et al. 2015, 97–111), France (Contrepois 2015, 94–95), Germany (Oliver 2011, 246; TNS Infratest 2015, 36–37; Nies and Tullius 2017), the Netherlands (Huiskamp and Smulders 2010), Sweden (Furåker and Berglund 2003; Bengtsson and Berglund 2011), and elsewhere across Europe (Turner and D'Art 2012); Hungary seems to be an exception (Keune 2015, 15). Furthermore, although results based on focus groups or individual interviews cannot readily be extended to young workers in general, such research methods do allow for a more enhanced differentiation between various youth segments in the labor market.[5] Again, interview-based research in, for instance, Poland (Mrozowicki et al. 2015), Portugal (Kovács, Dias, and da Conceição Cerdeira 2017), and the United Kingdom (Hodder 2016; TUC 2017, 25–28; the latter confirming previous results) highlights the (critical) support toward unions among certain labor market youth segments.

Although young people's attitude toward unionization is generally positive, it has been found that young workers possess very limited knowledge about unions (Fernández Rodríguez et al. 2015, 147; Hodder 2016, 13). Because young people are largely unaware as to what unions actually do, the overall majority of young people seem to be largely "blank slates" (Freeman and Diamond 2003, 40) when they enter the labor market. Even if they have some understanding about unions, it tends to be a stereotyped view, especially because the press and mass media are "biased toward selecting events about actual or impeding strike actions" (Gallagher 1999, 249).[6] Unions' negative public image might feed into the view that they are "representing a different type and culture of work and dynamics in employment to that experienced by young people" (Fernández Rodríguez et al. 2015, 157). In Australia, for example, it was found that young people think that only "victims" on the labor market need unions, being powerless to bargain effectively for themselves (Bulbeck 2008).

Young workers' lack of knowledge about unionism is particularly evident when they experience concrete problems at work (Paquet 2005). When this is the case, at least in the Australian (McDonald et al. 2014, 321–23) and UK contexts (Tailby and Pollert 2011, 511; Hodder 2016, 66), unions are rarely considered a source of advice. For basic information and assistance on employment-related matters, popular internet search engines are common resources.[7] Young workers also informally approach management for advice. Finally, young workers rely on parental and family support and their circle of friends as a source of information to address job-related dissatisfaction. The literature on union attitude formation has specifically identified parents, family, and friends as socialization agents who could shape young people's union attitudes prior to their labor market entrance; it is to these pre-employment sources that we turn now.

22.3.3. Union attitude formation before labor market entrance

Two theoretical approaches are helpful for identifying sources that could influence young people's attitudes toward unions before their first entry into the labor market. First, applying insights from marketing theory, the "experience-good" model of unionism emphasizes that workers can only truly appreciate unions if they sample membership or become a member (Gomez, Gunderson, and Meltz 2002, 2004; Gomez and Gunderson 2004; Bryson et al. 2005). Joining a union requires some degree of prior knowledge, given that most union-provided benefits are rather unclear for nonunion members; in particular, nonmembers may have difficulty discerning the nonpecuniary benefits of union membership. This problem is especially relevant for young people because most of them do not have first-hand experience with unions. Still, the importance of unionism as an "experience good" should not be overemphasized, for indirect experience through contacts and networks is also important for learning about union benefits. Second, social learning theory likewise highlights the importance of embeddedness in union-friendly social networks in which positive union attitudes are socialized (Kelloway and Newton 1996; Griffin and Brown 2011). Social interaction with parents, relatives, and friends who support unionization increases the probability of young people having favorable union attitudes, and this might also act as a counterbalance to the predominantly negative public image of unions.

Thus, if favorable attitudes toward unionism (as a social custom) are transmitted from one generation to another, family and parental socialization can be identified as a potential source for the development of positive union attitudes among young people (Blanden and Machin 2003; Oliver 2010, 515;

2011, 253; Ebbinghaus et al. 2011, 109). However, it can be expected that such intergenerational social learning has *relatively* lost its importance in most countries because, given the rise of never-membership in a union, parental union membership has itself diminished (Freeman and Diamond 2003, 33–35; Schnabel and Wagner 2006; Kirmanoğlu and Başlevent 2012, 699). Even in a high-union-density country such as Belgium, the traditional social custom of union membership has become a less important motive for unionization among the younger age categories (Swyngedouw, Abts, and Meuleman 2016, 35). Favorable attitudes to unions can also come from young people's union-friendly social networks (Griffin and Brown 2011, 95–96); in fact, with regard to joining a union, peers seem to be a more important source of influence on young workers compared to older people (Freeman and Diamond 2003, 45). Yet, particularly in low-union-density countries, it is again questionable whether such pro-union networks are still strong enough for sustaining the norm of union membership. Finally, social networks in the context of education could also be a source of union attitude formation. Thus, students in certain fields of study, such as the arts and social sciences, seem to be particularly receptive to unionism (Oliver 2010, 515; 2011, 253; Griffin and Brown 2011, 96). Whether this is a consequence of the self-selecting tendencies of these disciplines, which perhaps mainly attract students who already have pro-union attitudes, or whether other factors (e.g., the curriculum of certain courses) are more significant has yet to be ascertained.

One question that arises is whether the initial socializing agents continue to have an influence on young people's union attitudes as they gain experience on the labor market. Based on the experience-good model of unionism, it is expected that the agents will lose their influence somewhat when young people have left full-time education and fully entered the labor market, for the youngsters will then gradually rely more on their own, individually accumulated "sampling history" (Gomez and Gunderson 2004, 108). This point is confirmed by a study on labor market experiences via student employment in Australia (Oliver 2010, 2011): Once young people begin to gain experience on the labor market, norms and influences at the workplace seem to gain greater importance as determinants of union membership compared to parental socialization (Cregan 1991). As Figure 22.2 indicates, the key period for unions to organize young workers is when they first enter the labor market because this gives unions a crucial opportunity to shape young workers' attitudes (Booth et al. 2010b, 66–68). This timing does not necessarily correspond with the completion of education or labor market entrance on a full-time basis; it could also concern student employment. Analyzing the influence of these early labor market experiences and transitions from school to work on union attitude formation is therefore vital.

22.4. EARLY LABOR MARKET EXPERIENCES AND SCHOOL-TO-WORK TRANSITIONS

Concerning the *timing* of labor market entry, one event in the school-to-work transition that deserves special attention is student employment. It provides unions with an opportunity to specifically target students, and it enables students to gauge the benefits of union membership for themselves first-hand (Oliver 2010, 2011). A crucial question is whether these first-time experiences with unionism in student employment serve as lasting impressions for when young people begin their careers after graduating. This exposure to unionism might be particularly different to what young people go on to experience in their future sectors of employment (Booth et al. 2010b, 61–62). Although there are few studies on young people's attitudes toward unionism during student employment, their development does seem to be influenced by these formative experiences of work. Two conclusions can be made.

First, young people in lower quality (student) jobs or who have encountered concrete labor market difficulties (e.g., temporary or involuntary part-time employment or unemployment) seem to have a greater desire to become union members compared to their counterparts with higher quality jobs (Lowe and Rastin 2000; Vendramin 2007, 59–61; Oliver 2010, 2011). This indicates that those in lower quality (student) jobs believe that unions could improve their job quality, which is especially the case among young workers with a longer involvement in the labor market, suggesting that they realize that "exit and different jobs are not necessarily solutions to problems at work which repeat themselves" (Tailby and Pollert 2011, 514). Second, workers with previous union experience generally hold more positive views about the ability of unions to improve working conditions and job security compared to never-members (Kolins Givan and Hipp 2012). Likewise, those who were union members during their period of student employment are more likely to join a union after finishing their studies compared to those young people who have never been a union member (Oliver 2010). However, confirming the experience-good model, it is not union membership per se that seems to matter but, rather, the *positive experience* of that membership during student employment. Communicating with new young members in a personal way and educating them about their social rights could contribute to such a positive experience (Paquet 2005).

Of great importance, naturally, is whether unions are embedded in the workplace, because the extent of union representation influences (young) workers' perception of the effectiveness of unions (Waddington 2014). It is no coincidence that unions' diminishing access to the workplace (linked to the firm size via legal eligibility requirements about union representation) is clearly associated with lower youth unionization (Spilsbury et al. 1987; Payne 1989). It is therefore crucial to map what proportion of those in student employment are exposed to unionism and to analyze their experiences at work; the same principle, of course, applies for young workers in general (TUC 2016, 2017). It is certain that being in paid employment alongside studying has become widespread throughout Europe (especially for those in tertiary education) out of the need to finance costs or to improve the standard of living (Hauschildt et al. 2015, 95–102). Notable variation in student employment rates exists between countries and between study disciplines, for instance, which alludes to different patterns in school-to-work transitions. At the same time, student employment is especially concentrated in the wholesale, retail, accommodation, and food sectors in most European countries (calculations based on Grotti, Russell, and O'Reilly, this volume)—the very sectors in which union density is far below the national average. Thus, in most countries, the odds are not very high that young people have direct experience with unions at the workplace for the first time during student employment, especially in low-union-density countries. But even in unionized workplaces, one particular finding is that nonunionized students or young workers are not always *actively* recruited: In other words, nobody asks them to join (Cregan and Johnston 1990, 94; Pyman et al. 2009, 12–13; Oliver 2010, 511).

School-to-work transitions are marked not only by variation in young people's labor market entry speed (via student employment or otherwise) but also by differences in the sequence and duration of employment statuses. The distinctive patterns of school-to-work transitions are associated with different degrees of job stability and security, and they have long-lasting effects on labor market outcomes (Berloffa et al., this volume). Patterns depend on differences in educational and training systems, sectoral and national labor market institutions regarding employment regulation, and changing macroeconomic conditions such as the outbreak of the Great Recession (Grotti et al., this volume). Individual characteristics such as gender and educational attainment also clearly influence young people's early employment and career history. All of this explains why the dominance of certain patterns in school-to-work transitions varies across sectors and countries (Brzinsky-Fay 2007). Based on several institutional characteristics, five country clusters or regimes of school-to-work transitions have been identified (Pohl and Walther 2007; Pastore 2016; Hadjivassiliou et al., this volume). It is beyond the scope of this chapter to explore each regime in detail; rather, it is sufficient here to give an account of the degree of integration of unions into the institutional framework of these regimes and how they are (perceived as) helpful in smoothing young people's entrance into the labor market. Thus, in the Northern European universalistic regime, unions play a role (together with public employment services) in the management of income-support schemes and active labor market policies, which increases the probability of young workers' union exposure. Above all, union-managed voluntary unemployment insurance schemes (the "Ghent system") act as a selective incentive for unionization in Denmark, Finland, and Sweden (Ebbinghaus et al. 2011). However, the *state-led* "erosion" of this Ghent system or the promotion of

new institutional alternatives or both have weakened the close relationship between unions and insurance schemes, especially for new labor market entrants
(Høgedahl and Kongshøj 2017). Nonetheless, these countries, together with
Norway and Belgium (the latter a quasi-Ghent system country; Vandaele 2006),
record high youth unionization in both selected years (see Figure 22.2).

While belonging to the employment-centered regime, Belgium has a fairly
stable youth unionization rate, explained by the relatively unchanging de facto
Ghent system and the quadrennial social elections in large firms in the private
sector, which offer unions an opportunity to reach out to young workers (Faniel
and Vandaele 2012). In other countries belonging to the employment-centered
regime, especially Austria and Germany, the dual educational system plays a
central role, helping young people gain specific occupational skills while still
at school by providing vocational training opportunities via apprenticeships.
Historically supported by a legal framework of firm-level representation (the
Jugend- und Auszubildendenvertretung), apprenticeships have been unions' dominant and most successful channel for organizing young workers in Germany
(Holst, Holzschuh, and Niehoff 2014). Since the late 1980s, however, vocational
training has slowly lost its significance as an entry point into the labor market.
German school-to-work transitions have become characterized by precarious
employment or by tertiary education students entering the labor market directly or via dual studies, with those taking the latter route combining study with
practical training or work experience in a company. These different school-to-
work trajectories have prompted German unions to strategically rethink their
organizing approaches; for instance, the different strategies toward organizing
young workers of the IG Metall union have been identified as key to its success
(Schmalz and Thiel 2017). Nevertheless, apprenticeships remain a significant
recruitment channel for unions in large firms, especially in the manufacturing
industry (which continues to be an important provider of employment in
Germany). It has therefore been suggested that German unions would do better
to focus on young people's apprenticeships and traineeships within their field
of study rather than on their possible experiences in non-study-related student
employment because this is weakly clustered in particular sectors (Oliver 2011).

Finally, in the three other school-to-work transition regimes—with obvious
differences between the liberal, subprotective, and post-socialist regimes—the
education, training, and welfare systems *generally* allow less room for union involvement. In the case of the subprotective regimes, it should be noted that unions'
associational power is less oriented toward organizing union members. Their
power is predominantly based on their mobilization capacity for demonstrations
and strikes (as in France, although it belongs to the employment-centered regime;
Sullivan 2010) or on the social election results at the company level (as in Spain;
Martínez Lucio, Martino, and Connolly 2017). Although these different union
identities reveal the various ways in which unions prioritize the organization of
young workers (and to what extent), it is important for all unions to renew their

base of union activists, candidates for social elections, or union representatives. In any case, across the five regimes, today's school-to-work transitions are more often than not complex, unstable, and nonlinear. From a historical perspective, this level of complexity and nonlinearity is not typical for contemporary school-to-work transitions (Goodwin and O'Connor 2015). Even so, today's employment has been increasingly plagued by precariousness and the quality of youth jobs has deteriorated, with an increase in part-time and temporary jobs since the Great Recession (Lewis and Heyes 2017; Grotti et al., this volume; Hadjivassiliou et al., this volume). In this respect, given young people's turnover rates, it has been claimed that unions should opt for a life cycle approach to organizing instead of a job-centered approach (Budd 2010).

22.5. UNION AGENCY: UNIONS REACHING OUT TO YOUNG PEOPLE?

Historically, and highlighting their weaknesses in terms of field-enlarging organizing strategies, unions have long found their relationship with young workers to be a challenge (Williams and Quinn 2014): The "generation gap" in unionization between young workers and their older counterparts is not new. But today's positive attitude formation regarding unionization through socializing agents and union exposure at the workplace is becoming a less effective means of reaching out to *all* young workers. However, the shaping of union attitudes also depends on the agency of the union—in the efforts it makes toward developing the collective consciousness, identity, and actions of the young workers (Blackwood et al. 2003). Unions across Europe have gradually (although too slowly) begun undertaking different (small-scale) actions to better engage with young people. Unions' growing awareness of low youth unionization and the economic context of the Great Recession, with its increase in youth unemployment, have both enhanced this engagement (Vandaele 2013).

As illustrated by brochures on "good examples" from the United Kingdom's largest union Unite (2014) and the European Federation of Building and Woodworkers (Lorenzini 2016), among others (Pedersini 2010; Keune 2015), several unions are using a vast array of (not necessarily new) tactics to engage young workers. Reach-out activities include visits to vocational schools, higher education institutions, and job-information conventions; self-promotion; and providing information about young people's social rights and challenges in their school-to-work transitions where unions can provide specific services.[8] Fostering alliance-building between unions and relevant youth organizations, such as student organizations, is another way to achieve a better understanding of school-to-work transitions and young people's problems, also outside the workplace. Some unions are also present at youth events such as music festivals or advertise in cinemas. Furthermore, although face-to-face communication and traditional forms of mass communication continue to be of importance, young people's media consumption is heavily oriented toward the internet and social media via apps on mobile computer devices. Although unions have increased their presence and activity in this regard, there is often a lack of strategic coherence, meaning that their potential communication power is underutilized (Hodder and Houghton 2015), especially because young people's preferences toward social media communications are based on the opportunities it offers for participation (Wells 2014).

There are also abundant examples of unions offering a reduced-price or free union membership so that students and young workers, often in low-paid or even unpaid work (e.g., in the creative industries), can sample the benefits of union membership. Meanwhile, some unions—for instance, in Italy, the Netherlands, and Slovenia—have set up separate organizations or networks for representing atypical or freelance workers, whose jobs are often characterized by precariousness (Gumbrell-McCormick 2011; Lorenzini 2016). Furthermore, regarding recent labor market developments, so-called "self-employed" workers in the "gig economy" (more likely to be younger) have been building solidarity outside of the traditional unions to deal with employment issues. They have set up their own grassroots campaigns, collective actions, (virtual) community-based self-organizations, and "labor mutuals" (Bauwens and Niaros 2017; Tassinari and Maccarrone 2017). Alliance-building between these self-organizations and existing unions, as well as imaginative and diversified union strategies that make innovative use of technology to connect spatiotemporally distributed workers, is needed now more than ever to "#YouthUp"—that is, to attract the millennials and future generations. However, apart from legal arrangements, current union statutes and representation structures might often act as obstacles to union membership for those workers who frequently change employment status (including "gig workers").

Furthermore, some unions have set up targeted campaigns demonstrating the benefits of collective representation and action in order to alter their media profile and public image among potential (young) members and the wider public (Bailey et al. 2010). Although the findings presented here are solely from the perspective of an observer, the relative success of the Dutch "Young & United" campaign illustrates the possibilities of union agency. In 2015, the *Federatie Nederlandse Vakbeweging* (Dutch Federation of Trade Unions), together with a diverse range of youth organizations, launched this campaign to reach a dispersed young workforce that is difficult to organize, given that many young people are employed in companies and sectors with a high turnover rate. Shining a spotlight on age discrimination, the well-prepared Young & United campaign was launched with the aim of abolishing the low "youth minimum wage" for young workers aged between 18 and 23 years.[9] Intriguingly, this issue-based campaign was successful in terms of political agenda setting and the partial abolishment of the youth minimum wage, despite the fact that this low wage had not been a public issue in the Netherlands for several decades.

Because the sharing of media content is a social driver, and union-friendly networks are socializing agents for union attitude formation, one of the key challenges of any union youth campaign is "to tap into these networks of young people and provide information in a way that can be easily shared" (Geelan 2015, 77; see also Johnson and Jarley 2005). The Young & United campaign seemed largely effective in gaining a foothold in youth networks by using a language, visuals, and messages that appealed to young people. Inspired by methods from the "community organizing model" (Lorenzini 2016, 24–25), the campaign made heavy use of social media and escalating direct action, often with a festive dimension and led by a large and diverse group of young people who were engaged via like-by-like recruitment. However, research is needed on the extent to which the campaign succeeded in raising awareness among young people about unionism and triggered an ongoing increase in youth union activism. Furthermore, new young members might develop false expectations if they think of unions as primarily social movements, for this ignores the realities of daily, routine union work and the fact that most unions are hardly permanent mobilization machines, especially in the Dutch context. Nevertheless, the Young & United campaign turned its attention in 2017 to problematizing temporary and zero-hour contracts for young workers and putting better employment contracts on the political agenda.

The Young & United campaign demonstrates that, if it is successful, comprehensive campaigning can forge a collective identity and sense of solidarity based on salient (workplace) issues that are politicized and could be addressed by better regulation (Murphy and Turner 2016). The potential for better regulation is crucial, given that young people's interest in unionism is based on the condition that "they feel that their contribution can make a difference" (Byford 2009, 237). From the perspective of union membership as an experience good, campaigns that make *sole or predominant* use of formal advertising channels are likely to be relatively unsuccessful in influencing young people's union attitudes (Gomez and Gunderson 2004, 107). The Danish "Are you OK?" campaign, launched in 2012, illustrates this point. Although this campaign highlighted the importance of collective organization and the concrete benefits of collective agreements, its network embeddedness among young people was weak because of its top-down character; thus, young people's union attitudes were only marginally altered (Geelan 2015). In contrast to a simple marketing campaign, comprehensive campaigning combines a top-down approach with youth-led activism at the workplace or beyond.

Furthermore, it is doubtful whether campaigns that address young workers uniformly as an age-defined or homogeneous group will be successful. A demographic characteristic such as age might be a meager basis for identifying issues of concern because young workers do not necessarily think of themselves as a group with shared interests (Kahmann 2002). Given the variety of school-to-work transition regimes, young workers' different labor market experiences give rise to different interests and needs, although not necessarily different from those of older generations; still, the precariousness of young people's working conditions might be an issue that is salient and common across the different regimes.[10] Although union campaigns might capitalize on issue-based forms of civic and political participation and the "resurgence in youth activism," youth engagement seems largely to mirror existing national patterns of political participation, which can be clustered into country groups that are similar to the school-to-work transition regimes (Sloam 2016; Bassoli and Monticelli 2018). This indicates that campaign strategies should be contextualized within these regimes.

Finally, if unions want to help young workers develop agency in their working lives, effective internal structures for youth representation are also a necessity, insofar as they make unions more responsive to and knowledgeable about the aspirations, interests, and needs of young people (Vandaele 2012, 2015; Bielski Boris et al. 2013). Increasing unions' responsiveness toward young workers might help disprove the pessimistic stereotype that they are hostile to unions because of individualistic tendencies. In addition, although it could be speculated that "generational differences have perhaps been more apparent to activists than to academics" (Williams and Quinn 2014, 140), the possible misconception about young workers' excessive individualism is certainly not without risk for unions; it could turn into a self-fulfilling prophecy if the resulting behavior of union officials and activists ends up impeding a satisfactory engagement with the new generation on the labor market (Esders et al. 2011). Similarly, certain groups of young workers, at least in the United Kingdom, have internalized the principles of today's labor market flexibility (Bradley and Devadason 2008, 131), which indicates that "how they see the world differs from the union officials who seek to organise them" (TUC 2016, 33). A simple replication of formal union decision-making structures via parallel structures for youth entails the danger of a ghettoization based on age, weakening the articulation of young workers' own agendas and ideas (Dufour-Poirier and Laroche 2015). Furthermore, such age-based structures, unlike gender structures or those for under-represented groups such as migrants, would face regular changes in the membership composition (because of maximum age criteria). Integrating young workers into union activities solely through forms of representative democracy seems insufficient for instigating a more *transformative* change in union strategies and practices. New forms of participatory democracy and self-expression, informal engagement around issues (e.g., precariousness), and training and education (also via mentoring and union leadership development programs) may contribute to a greater—and more politicized—involvement of young unionists in union life and activities and also empower them (Laroche and Dufour-Poirier 2017).

22.6. CONCLUSIONS

Demographic change is a fundamental issue for membership-based organizations, and this is equally applicable to unions. Many of them are in trouble today because union membership is not only heavily skewed toward workers in industry and the public sector but also noticeably "graying." Although youth unionization is persistently higher in the Northern European countries and Belgium than in all other European countries considered here, a decline in youth unionization, at the aggregated level, almost represents a common trend. This representation gap in unionization between younger and older workers is not new. However, it is often explained by attributing specific attitudes and beliefs to the new generation of workers. This is a recurrent popular narrative: Public perceptions, media representations, and political discourses tend to stress intergenerational shifts, although empirical evidence of cohort effects is often lacking. Rather than a deficiency of collectivist beliefs and values, there are other, more significant reasons for unions' difficulties in engaging and organizing young workers.

Thus, socialization via parents and social networks is a less effective means of positive attitude formation for unionism than in the past. Furthermore, young workers are predominantly employed in workplaces, occupations, and sectors in which the social norm of union membership is simply weak. If union leadership continues to hold generational stereotypes about young people, the risk is that it will not be self-reflective or self-critical enough to tackle low youth unionization. Apart from a broad strategic vision on the future of unions, a vast shift in resource allocation is needed for overcoming the widening representation gap and for turning small-scale, local initiatives into large-scale organizing efforts, especially in those growing occupations and sectors in which young workers are employed and need unions the most. In this area, early unionization and demonstration of the effectiveness of unions is crucial. The research on unions and student employment highlights that only student workers with a positive experience have a higher probability of future membership, compared to workers reporting that unions made either a negative impression or little impression at all. Rather than providing historical accounts of the achievements of the labor movement, union activities for engaging young people would do better to emphasize how unions are addressing salient issues that matter to them today.

Furthermore, the continued cross-country variation in youth unionization points to the relevance of unions' institutional embeddedness in school-to-work transitions, inter-related with different union approaches to organizing young workers. In other words, it appears that age itself is a less important factor for explaining low youth unionization; the decision to become a union member is rather "embedded in the context of an individual's work history" (Lowe and Rastin 2000, 217). It is young people's early experiences on the labor market and their (workplace) issues—either via student employment or when they begin their career after graduating—that matter, along with their direct exposure to unions at the workplace. Analyzing in detail the institutional arrangements within education, training, and welfare systems could contribute to a better understanding of how unions can strengthen their relevance for school-leavers in their transition from school to work by designing tailor-made union strategies for young people in precarious work and other nonstandard forms of employment. Youth unionization is not doomed to failure because of an intergenerational shift, and unions should therefore not resign themselves to such a fate but, rather, should recognize—it must be stressed, the sooner the better—that there is still room for maneuver.

NOTES

1 This latter issue has been the result of either a lack of legal provision for such representation or a lack of deliberate managerial or state strategies of avoiding or resisting union representation in the (fissured) workplace (due to contracting out and subcontracting).

2 I am very grateful for the constructive remarks and suggestions from Carl Roper, Mark Stuart, and the editors of this book.

3 Retired members and other categories of passive members are included in Figure 22.1 because they can also influence union decision-making. Notably in Italy, pensioners have an incentive to become or remain union members because specialized union offices help them access welfare benefits (Frangi and Barisione 2015). Obviously, the overall median age in each country drops slightly if only active union members are included in the count; the country trends over time remain, however.

4 Youth emigration could be another explanatory factor.

5 Disaggregating survey data within the young age group is seldom done because the size of the survey sample usually does not allow for this.

6 In particular, a public transport strike might disproportionally distress young people because they often make use of this means of transport (Schnake, Dumler, and Moates 2016).

7 It remains an open question whether unions are found at the top of the search engine results page.

8 In several countries, unions are legally prohibited from going to schools or campuses, but creative tactics can be employed to get around this restriction.

9 See https://www.youngandunited.nl.

10 Those problems could include issues beyond the workplace, such as affordable housing.

REFERENCES

Alonso, Luis Enrique and Carlos Jesús Fernánd Rodríguez. 2017. "Young Workers in Europe: Perceptions and Discourses on the Labour Market." In: *The Palgrave Handbook of Age Diversity and Work*, edited by Emma Parry and Jean McCarthy. 371–395. Basingstoke, UK: Palgrave Macmillan.

Allvin, Michael, and Magnus Sverke. 2000. "Do New Generations Imply the End of Solidarity? Swedish Unionism in the Era of Individualization." *Economic and Industrial Democracy* 21 (1): 79–95.

Bailey, Janis, Robin Price, Lin Esders, and Paula McDonald. 2010. "Daggy Shirts, Daggy Slogans? Marketing Unions to Young People." *Journal of Industrial Relations* 52 (1): 43–60.

Bassoli, Matteo, and Lara Monticelli. 2018. "What About the Welfare State? Exploring Precarious Youth Political Participation in the Age of Grievances." *Acta Politica* 53 (2): 204–230. doi:10.1057/s41269-017-0047-z.

Bauwens, Michel, and Vasilis Niaros. 2017. "The Emergence of Peer Production: Challenges and Opportunities for Labour and Unions." ETUI Policy Brief 3. Brussels: European Trade Union Institute.

Benassi, Chiara, and Tim Vlandas. 2016. "Union Inclusiveness and Temporary Agency Workers: The Role of Power Resources and Union Ideology." *European Journal of Industrial Relations* 22 (1): 5–22.

Bengtsson, Mattias, and Tomas Berglund. 2011. "Negotiating Alone or Through the Union? Swedish Employees' Attitudes in 1997 and 2006." *Economic and Industrial Democracy* 32 (2): 223–41.

Bielski Boris, Monica, Jeff Grabelsky, Ken Margolies, and David Reynolds. 2013. "Next Up: The Promise of AFL–CIO-Affiliated Young Worker Groups." *Working USA: The Journal of Labor and Society* 16 (2): 227–52.

Blackwood, Leda, George Lafferty, Julie Duck, and Deborah Terry. 2003. "Putting the Group Back into Unions: A Social Psychological Contribution to Understanding Union Support." *Journal of Industrial Relations* 45 (4): 485–504.

Blanchflower, David G. 2007. "International Patterns of Union Membership." *British Journal of Industrial Relations* 45 (1): 1–28.

Blanden, Jo, and Stephen Machin. 2003 "Cross-Generation Correlations of Union Status for Young People in Britain." *British Journal of Industrial Relations* 41 (3): 391–415.

Blossfeld, Hans-Peter, Sandra Buchholz, Erzsébet Bukodi, and Karin Kurz, eds. 2008. *Young Workers, Globalization and the Labor Market: Comparing Early Working Life in Eleven Countries.* Cheltenham, UK: Elgar.

Booth, Jonathan E., John W. Budd, and Kristen M. Munday. 2010a. "Never Say Never? Uncovering the Never-Unionized in the United States." *British Journal of Industrial Relations* 48 (1): 26–52.

Booth, Jonathan E., John W. Budd, and Kristen M. Munday. 2010b. "First-Timers and Late-Bloomers. Youth-Adult Unionization Differences in a Cohort of the U.S. Labor Force." *Industrial and Labor Relations Review* 64 (1): 53–73.

Bradley, Harriet, and Ranji Devadason. 2008. "Fractured Transitions: Young Adults' Pathways into Contemporary Labour Markets." *Sociology* 42 (1): 119–36.

Bryson, Alex, and Rafael Gomez. 2005. "Why Have Workers Stopped Joining Unions? The Rise in Never-Membership in Britain." *British Journal of Industrial Relations* 43 (1): 67–92.

Bryson, Alex, Rafael Gomez, Morley Gunderson, and Noah Meltz. 2005. "Youth-Adult Differences in the Demand for Unionization: Are American, British, and Canadian Workers All That Different?" *Journal of Labor Research* 26 (1): 155–67.

Brzinsky-Fay, Christian. 2007. "Lost in Transition? Labour Market Entry Sequences of School Leavers in Europe." *European Sociological Review* 23 (4): 409–22.

Budd, John W. 2010. "When do U.S. Workers First Experience Unionization? Implications for Revitalizing the Labor Movement." *Industrial Relations* 49 (2): 209–25.

Bulbeck, Chilla. 2008. "Only 'Victim' Workers Need Unions? Perceptions of Trade Unions Amongst Young Australians." *Labour & Industry* 19 (1–2): 49–71.

Byford, Iona. 2009. "Union Renewal and Young People: Some Positive Indications from British Supermarkets." In *The Future of Union Organising: Building for Tomorrow*, edited by Gregor Gall, 223–38. Basingstoke, UK: Palgrave Macmillan.

Caraker, Emmett, Laust Kristian Høgedahl, Henning Jørgensen, and Rasmus Juul Møberg. 2015. *Fællesskabet før forskellene. Hovedrapport fra APL III-projektet om nye lønmodtagerværdier og interesser.* Copenhagen: FTF og LO.

Contrepois, Sylvie. 2015. "Mobilised But Not Unionized? An Analysis of the Relationship Between Youth and Trade Unions in France." In *Young Workers and Trade Unions: A Global View*, edited by Andy Hodder and Lefteris Kretsos, 90–106. Basingstoke, UK: Palgrave Macmillan.

Cregan, Christina. 1991. "Young People and Trade Union Membership: A Longitudinal Analysis." *Applied Economics* 23 (9):1511–18.

Cregan, Christina, and Stewart Johnston. 1990. "An Industrial Relations Approach to the Free Rider Problem: Young People and Trade Union Membership in the UK." *British Journal of Industrial Relations* 28 (1): 84–104.

D'Art, Daryl, and Thomas Turner. 2008. "Workers and the Demand for Trade Unions in Europe: Still a Relevant Social Force?" *Economic and Industrial Democracy* 29 (2): 165–91.

Dufour-Poirier, Mélanie, and Mélanie Laroche. 2015. "Revitalising Young Workers' Union Participation: A Comparative Analysis of Two Organisations in Quebec (Canada)." *Industrial Relations Journal* 46 (5–6): 418–33.

Ebbinghaus, Bernhard. 2006. "Trade Union Movements in Post-Industrial Welfare States: Opening Up to New Social Interests?" In *The Politics of Post-Industrial Welfare States: Adapting Post-War Social Policies to New Social Risks*, edited by Klaus Armingeon and Giuliano Bonoli, 123–43. London: Routledge.

Ebbinghaus, Bernhard, Claudia Göbel, and Sebastian Koos. 2011. "Social Capital, 'Ghent' and Workplace Context Matter: Comparing Union Membership in Europe." *European Journal of Industrial Relations* 17 (2): 107–24.

Ebbinghaus, Bernhard, and Jelle Visser. 1999. "When Institutions Matter: Union Growth and Decline in Western Europe." *European Sociological Review* 15 (2): 135–58.

Esders, Linda, Janis Bailey, and Paula McDonald. 2011. "Declining Youth Membership: The Views of Union Officials." In *Young People and Work*, edited by Robin Price, Paula McDonald, Janis Bailey, and Barbara Pini, 263–81. Farnham, UK: Ashgate.

Faniel, Jean, and Kurt Vandaele. 2012. "Implantation syndicale et taux de syndicalisation 2000–2010." *Courrier hebdomadaire* 2146/2147. Brussels: Crisp.

Fernández Rodríguez, Carlos J., Rafael Ibáñez Rojo, Pablo López Calle, and Miguel Martínez Lucio. 2015. "Young Workers and Unions in Spain: A failed Meeting?" In *Young Workers and Trade Unions: A Global View*, edited by Andy Hodder and Lefteris Kretsos. 142–61. Basingstoke, UK: Palgrave Macmillan.

France, Alan. 2016. *Understanding Youth in the Global Economic Crisis*. Bristol, UK: Policy Press.

Frangi, Lorenzo, and Mauro Barisione. 2015. "'Are You a Union Member?' Determinants and Trends of Subjective Union Membership in Italian Society (1972–2013)." *Transfer* 21 (4): 451–69.

Freeman, Richard, and Wayne Diamond. 2003. "Young Workers and Trade Unions." In *Representing Workers: Union Recognition and Membership in Britain*, edited by Howard Gospel and Stephen Wood, 29–50. London: Routledge.

Furåker, Bengt, and Tomas Berglund. 2003. "Are the Unions Still Needed? Employees' Views of Their Relations to Unions and Employees." *Economic and Industrial Democracy* 24 (4): 573–94.

Gallagher, Daniel G. 1999. "Youth and Labor Representation." In *Young Workers: Varieties of Experience*, edited by Julian Barling and E. Kevin Kelloway, 235–58. Washington, DC: American Psychological Association.

Geelan, Torsten. 2015. "Danish Trade Unions and Young People." In *Young Workers and Trade Unions: A Global View*, edited by Andy Hodder and Lefteris Kretsos. 71–89. Basingstoke, UK: Palgrave Macmillan.

Goerres, Achim. 2010. "Being Less Active and Outnumbered? The Political Participation and Relative Pressure Potential of Young People in Europe." In *A Young Generation Under Pressure? The Financial Situation and the "Rush Hour" of the Cohorts 1970–1985 in a Generational Comparison*, edited by Joerg Tremmel, 207–24. Berlin: Springer.

Gomez, Rafael, and Morley Gunderson. 2004. "The Experience Good Model of Trade Union Membership." In *The Changing Role of Unions: New Forms of Representation*, edited by Phanindra V. Wunnava, 92–112. New York: Sharp.

Gomez, Rafael, Morley Gunderson, and Noah M. Meltz. 2002. "Comparing Youth and Adult Desire for Unionization in Canada." *British Journal of Industrial Relations* 40 (3): 519–42.

Gomez, Rafael, Morley Gunderson, and Noah M. Meltz. 2004. "From Playstations to Workstations: Young Workers and the Experience-Good Model of Union Membership." In *Unions in the 21st Century: An International Perspective*, edited by Anil Verma and Thomas A. Kochan, 239–49. Basingstoke, UK: Palgrave Macmillan.

Goodwin, John, and Henrietta O'Connor. 2015. *Norbert Elias's Lost Research: Revisiting the Young Worker Project*. Farnham, UK: Ashgate.

Griffin, Leanne, and Michele Brown. 2011. "Second Hand Views? Young People, Social Networks and Positive Union Attitudes." *Labour & Industry* 22 (1–2): 83–101.

Gumbrell-McCormick, Rebecca. 2011. "European Trade Unions and Atypical Workers." *Industrial Relations Journal* 42 (3): 293–310.

Hauschildt, Kristina, Christoph Gwosć, Nicolai Netz, and Shweta Mishra. 2015. *Social and Economic Conditions of Student Life in Europe: Synopsis of Indicators— Eurostudent Volumes 2012-2015*. Bielefeld, Germany: Bertelsmann Verlag.

Haynes, Peter, Jack Vowles, and Peter Boxall. 2005. "Explaining the Younger– Older Worker Union Density Gap: Evidence from New Zealand." *British Journal of Industrial Relations* 43 (1): 93–116.

Heery, Edmund, and Lee Adler. 2004. "Organizing the Unorganized." In *Varieties of Unionism: Strategies for Union Revitalization in a Globalizing Economy*, edited by Carola Frege and John Kelly, 45–69. Oxford: Oxford University Press.

Hodder, Andy. 2016. *Young People: Attitudes to Work, Unions and Activism*. Birmingham, UK: University of Birmingham.

Hodder, Andy, and David Houghton. 2015. "Union Use of Social Media: A Study of the University and College Union on Twitter." *New Technology, Work and Employment* 30 (3): 173–89.

Høgedahl, Laust, and Kristian Kongshøj. 2017. "New Trajectories of Unionization in the Nordic Ghent Countries: Changing Labour Market and Welfare Institutions." *European Journal of Industrial Relations* 23 (4): 365–80. doi:10.1177/0959680116687666.

Holst, Hajo, Madeleine Holzschuh, and Steffen Niehoff. 2014. *YOUnion: Country Report Germany*. Jena, Germany: Friedrich-Schiller-Universität Jena.

Huiskamp, Rien, and Peter Smulders. 2010. "Vakbondslidmaatschap in Nederland: Nooit serieus over nagedacht!" *Tijdschrift voor Arbeidsmarktvraagstukken* 26 (2): 197–210.

Hyman, Richard. 2015. "Austeritarianism in Europe: What Options for Resistance?" In *Social Policy in the European Union: State of Play 2015*, edited by David Natali and Bart Vanhercke, 97–126. Brussels: European Trade Union Institute/European Social Observatory.

Ibsen, Christian Lyhne, and Maite Tapia. 2017. "Trade Union Revitalization: Where Are We Now? Where to Next?" *Journal of Industrial Relations* 59 (2): 170–91. doi:10.1177/0022185616677558.

Ibsen, Lyhne Christian, Jonas Toubøl, and Daniel Sparwath Jensen. 2017. "Social Customs and Trade Union Membership: A Multi-Level Analysis of Workplace Union Density Using Micro-Data." *European Sociological Review* 33 (4): 504–17.

Johnson, Nancy Brown, and Paul Jarley. 2005. "Unions as Social Capital: The Impact of Trade Union Youth Programmes on Young Workers' Political and Community Engagement." *Transfer* 11 (4): 605–16.

Kahmann, Marcus. 2002. *Trade Unions and Young People: Challenges of the Changing Age Composition of Unions.* Brussels: European Trade Union Institute.

Kelloway, E. Kevin, and Tricia Newton. 1996. "Preemployment Predictors of Union Attitudes: The Effects of Parental Union and Work Experiences." *Canadian Journal of Behavioural Science* 28 (2): 113–20.

Keune, Maarten. 2015. "Trade Unions and Young Workers in Seven EU Countries." Final report for YOUnion (Union for Youth). http://adapt.it/englishbulletin/wp/?p=1578

Kirmanoğlu, Hasan, and Cem Başlevent. 2012. "Using Basic Personal Values to Test Theories of Union Membership." *Socio-Economic Review* 10 (4): 683–703.

Köhler, Holm-Detlev, and José Pablo Calleja Jiménez. 2015. "They Don't Represent Us!" Opportunities for a Social Movement Unionism Strategy in Spain." *Relations Industrielles* 70 (2): 240–61.

Kolins Givan, Rebecca, and Lena Hipp. 2012. "Public Perceptions of Union Efficacy: A Twenty-Four Country Study." *Labor Studies Journal* 37 (1): 7–32.

Kovács, Ilona, João Dias, and Maria da Conceição Cerdeira. 2017. "Young Workers' Perceptions of Trade Unions in Portugal" *Relations Industrielles/ Industrial Relations* 72 (3): 574–95.

Kretsos, Lefteris. 2011. "Union Responses to the Rise of Precarious Youth Employment in Greece." *Industrial Relations Journal* 45 (5): 453–72.

Laroche, Mélanie, and Mélanie Dufour-Poirier. 2017. "Revitalizing Union Representation Through Labor Education Initiatives: A Close Examination of Two Trade Unions in Quebec." *Labor Studies Journal* 42 (2): 99–123. doi:10.1177/0160449X17697442.

Lewis, Paul, and Jason Heyes. 2017. "The Changing Face of Youth Employment in Europe." *Economic and Industrial Democracy.* Advance online publication. doi:10.1177/0143831X17720017

Leschke, Janine, and Kurt Vandaele. 2015. "Explaining Leaving Union Membership by the Degree of Labour Market Attachment: Exploring the Case of Germany." *Economic and Industrial Democracy* 39 (1): 64–86. doi:10.1177/0143831X15603456.

Lorenzini, Chiara, ed. 2016. *Just Go for It! A Compendium of Best Practices from All Over Europe on Involving Young People in Trade Unions*. Brussels: European Federation of Building and Woodworkers.

Lowe, Graham S., and Harvey Krahn. 2000. "Work Aspirations and Attitudes in an Era of Labour Market Restructuring: A Comparison of Two Canadian Youth Cohorts." *Work, Employment and Society* 14 (1): 1–22.

Lowe Graham S., and Sandra Rastin. 2000. "Organizing the Next Generation: Influences on Young Workers' Willingness to Join Unions in Canada." *British Journal of Industrial Relations* 38 (2): 203–22.

Machin, Stephen. 2004. "Factors of Convergence and Divergence in Union Membership." *British Journal of Industrial Relations* 42 (2): 423–38.

Martínez Lucio, Miguel, Stefania Marino, and Heather Connolly. 2017. "Organising as a Strategy to Reach Precarious and Marginalised Workers: A Review of Debates on the Role of the Political Dimension and the Dilemmas of Representation and Solidarity." *Transfer* 23 (1): 31–46.

McDonald, Paula, Janis Bailey, Robin Price, and Barbara Pini. 2014. "School-Aged Workers: Industrial Citizens in Waiting?" *Journal of Sociology* 50 (3): 315–30.

Milkman, Ruth. 2017. "A New Political Generation: Millennials and the Post-2008 Wave of Protest." *American Sociological Review* 82 (1): 1–31.

Mrozowicki, Adam, Agata Krasowska, and Mateusz Karolak. 2015. "'Stop the Junk Contracts!' Young Workers and Trade Union Mobilisation Against Precarious Employment in Poland." In *Young Workers and Trade Unions: A Global View*, edited by Andy Hodder and Lefteris Kretsos, 123–41. Basingstoke, UK: Palgrave Macmillan.

Murphy, Caroline, and Melanie Simms. 2017. "Tripartite Responses to Young Workers and Precarious Employment in the European Union." In *The Palgrave Handbook of Age Diversity and Work*, edited by Emma Parry and Jean McCarthy, 345–95. Basingstoke, UK: Palgrave Macmillan.

Murphy, Caroline, and Thomas Turner. 2016. "Organising Precarious Workers: Can a Public Campaign Overcome Weak Grassroots Mobilization at Workplace Level?" *Journal of Industrial Relations* 58 (5): 589–607.

Nies, Sarah, and Knut Tullius. 2017. "Zwischen Übergang und Etablierung. Beteiligungsansprüche und Interessenorientierungen jüngerer Erwerbstätiger." Study der Hans-Böckler-Stiftung Nr. 357. https://www.boeckler.de/pdf/p_study_hbs_357.pdf

Oliver, Damian. 2010. "Union Membership Among Young Graduate Workers in Australia: Using the Experience Good Model to Explain the Role of Student Employment." *Industrial Relations Journal* 41 (5): 505–19.

Oliver, Damian. 2011. "University Student Employment in Germany and Australia and Its Impact on Attitudes Toward Union Membership." In *Young*

People and Work, edited by Robin Price, Paula McDonald, Janis Bailey, and Barbara Pini, 243–62. Farnham, UK: Ashgate.

Paquet, Renaud. 2005. "Vers une explication de la faible implication syndicale des jeunes." *Revue international sur le travail et la sociéte* 3 (1): 29–60.

Pastore, Francesco. 2016. "A Classification of School-to-Work Transition Regimes." In *Varieties of Economic Equality,* edited by Sebastiano Fadda and Pasquale Tridico, 170–96. Abingdon, UK: Routledge.

Payne, Joan. 1989. "Trade Union Membership and Activism Among Young People in Great Britain." *British Journal of Industrial Relations* 27 (1): 111–32.

Pedersini, Roberto. 2010. *Trade Union Strategies to Recruit New Groups of Workers.* Dublin: Eurofound.

Peetz, David. 2010. "Are Individualistic Attitudes Killing Collectivism?" *Transfer* 16 (3): 383–98.

Peetz, David, Robin Price, and Janis Bailey. 2015. "Ageing Australian Unions and the 'Youth Problem.'" In *Young Workers and Trade Unions: A Global View,* edited by Andy Hodder and Lefteris Kretsos, 54–70. Basingstoke, UK: Palgrave Macmillan.

Peterson, Abby, Mattias Wahlstrom, and Magnus Wennerhag. 2015. "European Anti-Austerity Protests—Beyond 'Old' and 'New' Social Movements?" *Acta Sociologica* 58 (4): 293–310.

Pohl, Axel, and Andreas Walther. 2007. "Activating the Disadvantaged: Variations in Addressing Youth Transitions Across Europe." *International Journal of Lifelong Education* 26 (5): 533–53.

Pyman, Amanda, Julian Teicher, Brian Cooper, and Peter Holland. 2009. "Unmet Demand for Union Membership in Australia." *Journal of Industrial Relations* 51 (1): 5–24.

Riley, Nicola-Maria. 1997. "Determinants of Union Membership: A Review." *Labour* 11 (2): 265–301.

Scheuer, Steen. 2011. "Union Membership Variation in Europe: A Ten-Country Comparative Analysis." *European Journal of Industrial Relations* 17 (1): 57–73.

Schmalz, Stefan, and Marcel Thiel. 2017. "IG Metall's Comeback: Trade Union Renewal in Times of Crisis." *Journal of Industrial Relations* 59 (4): 465–86.

Schnabel, Claus, and Joachim Wagner. 2006. "Who Are the Workers Who Never Joined a Union? Empirical Evidence from Western and Eastern Germany." *Industrielle Beziehungen* 13 (2): 118–31.

Schnabel, Claus, and Joachim Wagner. 2012. "With or Without U? Testing the Hypothesis of an Inverted U-Shaped Union Membership–Age Relationship." *Contemporary Economics* 6 (4): 28–34.

Schnake, Mel E., Michael P. Dumler, and K. Nathan Moates. 2016. "The Effect of Union Protest Behavior on Attitudes Towards Unions: An Experimental Analysis." *American Journal of Management* 16 (2): 90–7.

Serrano Pascual, Amparo, and Jeremy Waddington. 2000. *Young People: The Labour Market and Trade Unions. Research Prepared for the Youth Committee of the European Trade Union Confederation.* Brussels: ETUC.

Sloam, James. 2016. "Diversity and Voice: The Political Participation of Young People in the European Union." *British Journal of Politics and International Relations* (18) 3: 521–37.

Spilsbury, Mark, M. Hoskins, David Ashton, and Malcolm Maguire. 1987. "A Note on the Trade Union Membership Patterns of Young Adults." *British Journal of Industrial Relations* 15 (2): 267–74.

Sullivan, Richard. 2010. "Labour Market or Labour Movement? The Union Density Bias as Barrier to Labour Renewal." *Work, Employment and Society* 24 (1): 145–56.

Swyngedouw, Marc, Koen Abts, and Bart Meuleman. 2016. "Syndicats et Syndicalisme: Perceptions et Opinions." *Courrier hebdomadaire* 2298. Brussels: Crisp.

Tailby, Stephanie, and Anna Pollert. 2011. "Non-Unionized Young Workers and Organizing the Unorganized." *Economic and Industrial Democracy* 32 (3): 499–522.

Tassinari, Arianna, and Vincenzo Maccarrone. 2017. "Striking the Startups." *Jacobin.* https://www.jacobinmag.com/2017/01/foodora-strike-turin-gig-economy-startups-uber

TNS Infratest. 2015. *Persönliche Lage und Zukunftserwartungen der "Jungen Generation" 2015. Eine Erhebung der TNS Infratest Politikforschung im Auftrag des Vorstands der IG Metall.* Berlin: TNS Infratest.

Toubøl, Jonas, and Carsten Strøby Jensen. 2014. "Why Do People Join Trade Unions? The Impact of Workplace Union Density on Union Recruitment." *Transfer* 20 (1): 135–54.

TUC. 2016. *Living for the Weekend? Understanding Britain's Young Core Workers.* London: Trades Union Congress.

TUC. 2017. *"I Feel Like I Can't Change Anything": Britain's Young Core Workers Speak out About Work.* London: Trades Union Congress.

Turner, Thomas, and Daryl D'Art. 2012. "Public Perceptions of Trade Unions in Countries of the European Union: A Causal Analysis." *Labor Studies Journal* 37 (1): 33–55.

Unite. 2014. *Our Time Is Now—Young People and Unions: Lessons from Overseas.* London: Unite.

Vachon, Todd E., Michael Wallace, and Allen Hyde. 2016. "Union Decline in a Neoliberal Age: Globalization, Financialization, European Integration, and Union Density in 18 Affluent Democracies." *Socius: Sociological Research for a Dynamic World.* doi:10.1177/2378023116656847.

Vandaele, Kurt. 2006. "A Report from the Homeland of the Ghent System: Unemployment and Union Membership in Belgium." *Transfer* 13 (4): 647–57.

Vandaele, Kurt. 2012. "Youth Representatives' Opinions on Recruiting and Representing Young Workers: A Twofold Unsatisfied Demand?" *European Journal of Industrial Relations* 18 (3): 203–18.

Vandaele, Kurt. 2013. "Union Responses to Young Workers Since the Great Recession in Ireland, the Netherlands and Sweden: Are Youth Structures Reorienting the Union Agenda?" *Transfer* 19 (3): 381–97.

Vandaele, Kurt. 2015. "Trade Unions' 'Deliberative Vitality' Towards Young Workers: Survey Evidence Across Europe." In *Young Workers and Trade Unions: A Global View,* edited by Andy Hodder and Lefteris Kretsos, 16–36. Basingstoke, UK: Palgrave Macmillan.

Vendramin, Patricia. 2007. *Les jeunes, le travail et l'emploi. Enquête auprès des jeunes salariés en Belgique francophone.* Namur, Belgium: Fondation Travail–Université (FTU).

Visser, Jelle. 2002. "Why Fewer Workers Join Unions in Europe: A Social Custom Explanation of Membership Trends." *British Journal of Industrial Relations* 40 (3): 403–30.

Visser, Jelle. 2016. *ICTWSS Database. Version 5.1.* Amsterdam: Amsterdam Institute for Advanced Labour Studies, University of Amsterdam.

Waddington, Jeremy. 2014. "Workplace Representation, Its Impact on Trade Union Members and Its Capacity to Compete with Management in the European Workplace." *Transfer* 20 (4): 537–58.

Waddington, Jeremy, and Allan Kerr. 2002. "Unions Fit for Young Workers?" *Industrial Relations Journal* 33 (4): 298–315.

Wells, Chris. 2014. "Two Eras of Civic Information and the Evolving Relationship Between Civil Society Organizations and Young Citizens." *New Media & Society* 16 (4): 615–36.

Williams, Glynne, and Martin Quinn. 2014. "Macmillan's Children? Young Workers and Trade Unions in the Early 1960s." *Industrial Relations Journal* 45 (2): 137–52.

23

INTEGRATING PERSPECTIVES ON YOUTH LABOR IN TRANSITION

ECONOMIC PRODUCTION, SOCIAL REPRODUCTION, AND POLICY LEARNING

Jacqueline O'Reilly, Janine Leschke, Renate Ortlieb, Martin Seeleib-Kaiser, and Paola Villa

23.1. INTRODUCTION

Youth unemployment has received considerable political and media attention since its staggering rise in certain areas of Europe in the wake of the Great Recession. In particular, the European Union (EU) flagship program, Youth Guarantee (YG), has been critically examined to assess its effectiveness in addressing youth unemployment and inactivity throughout the EU (Dhéret and Morosi 2015; O'Reilly et al. 2015; European Court of Auditors 2017). Using this program as a focus to understand how innovative policy practices have been developed, Petmesidou and González Menéndez (this volume) illustrate why this policy initiative has only been partially successful, with a significant distinction between active countries and regions and those exhibiting considerable inertia with regard to policy learning and innovation. The contributions to this volume also show that youth labor market challenges are by no means confined to youth unemployment and that a broader perspective on youth transitions is needed to inform policymakers.

In this concluding chapter, we provide an integrated analysis of the findings presented in the volume. First, we discuss the main challenges by comparing youth transitions across countries, and we also discuss the importance of using a wider range of indicators and a more comprehensive policy focus. Second, we argue that the concept of economic production encapsulates some of the key dimensions and foci for policy initiatives related to labor market flexibility, mobility, and reforms of vocational education and training (VET) systems; where appropriate, we also include some policy pointers.[1] Third, we contend that an exclusive focus on this domain of economic production risks undervaluing the continued importance of the sphere of social reproduction and the role of family legacies and how these affect established and emerging forms of inequality. Fourth, we propose that given the complexity and variety of youth transitions, policy initiatives need to focus simultaneously on both dimensions so as to develop multifocused strategies that will ensure successful youth transitions. We conclude by identifying key issues for future research and policy intervention resulting from this comprehensive analysis that take into consideration the consequences of increasingly precarious patterns of mobility and labor market transitions, the need to engage employers, and the effect of inequalities rooted in the family.

23.2. COMPARING YOUTH TRANSITIONS ACROSS COUNTRIES

A central tenet of European employment research is the value of cross-country comparisons (O'Reilly 2006). These are often motivated by a desire to understand what drives similarities and differences between social and institutional arrangements, or what policies work better in different countries. Why do some countries perform better than others? What can we learn from these cases? How can this influence change where performance is weaker? And, is it possible to transfer best practice? These are some of the questions that catalyze an interest in conducting comparative research in the first place. However, how we go about conducting these comparisons raises a few methodological and empirical issues.

When faced with an array of potential sources of data, one of the greatest challenges to researchers is finding an analytical framework that will allow them to order this material in a coherent manner. For this reason, it has become increasingly common for researchers to rely on comparative regime typologies, such as those proposed by Esping-Andersen (1990), Pohl and Walther (2007), Hall and Soskice (2001), and Wallace and Bendit (2009). These frameworks provide heuristic devices that enable comparisons across countries and between regime types. Typologies simplify and help us understand the complexities of institutional arrangements. They allow us to compare characteristics and trends between groups of countries seen as sharing key institutional characteristics and then to compare differences between these groupings. Typologies can also help with the formulation of hypotheses concerning expected similarities and differences (Ferragina and Seeleib-Kaiser 2011).

23.2.1. The value and limits of youth transition typologies

One of the most popular typologies for examining youth transition regimes has been that of Pohl and Walther (2007). This is discussed extensively by Hadjivassiliou et al. (this volume) and is also used in several other chapters in this book. However, one of the doubts raised about typologies that were developed before the Great Recession is how well they can accommodate change. Hadjivassiliou et al. suggest that the recent economic crisis has led to a hybridization of youth transition regimes as a result of policy learning, innovation, and reform; one catalyst for this development has been the implementation of the YG. Hybridization challenges the static picture suggested by established typologies. This does not imply second- or third-order regime change (Hall 1993), nor has it led to a process of "conversion" (Thelen 2004; Streeck and Thelen 2005). But it does illustrate attempts at policy learning, adoption, and transfer that can result in "layering," in which new policy elements are grafted onto existing institutions (Petmesidou and González Menéndez, this volume). The introduction of new policies targeting joblessness (i.e., unemployment and inactivity) among youth, such as the YG, creates a complex picture. On the one hand, policy initiatives recommended to all member states can propagate practices encouraging common elements toward convergence between regime types—for example, toward the strengthening of apprenticeships—as well as encouraging the development of a mode of governance that supports regional/local partnerships between key stakeholders (Hadjivassiliou et al., this volume). On the other hand, the implementation of these common goals illustrates the persistence of divergence in the institutional capability to make these policies effective. This has resulted in an increasing hybridization within regime types.

Examples of the values and limits of these typologies can be seen, for instance, in two chapters in this volume. First, Petmesidou and González Menéndez start out with the youth transitions typology to examine the role of policy innovation in building resilient bridges for youth transitions. However, they find that this established typology is less helpful for distinguishing between countries that frequently experiment with new proactive measures and those exhibiting considerable inertia. The distinction between innovative and inert countries cuts across established youth transition typologies. Second, the chapter by Spreckelsen, Leschke, and Seeleib-Kaiser builds on the *Varieties of Capitalism* approach (Hall and Soskice 2001), which positions the United Kingdom and Germany as diametrically contrasting labor markets. As a result, one might expect to find significant differences in the integration of youth EU migrant citizens in each country. In fact, the authors find that youth EU migrant citizens are well integrated in both countries in terms of finding employment but that the quality of these jobs is hierarchically segmented and closely related to their region of origin. Intra-EU youth migration can provide new opportunities as well as reproduce existing inequalities in a new form. The authors suggest that the region of origin appears to have a stronger determining effect than the characteristics of the youth transition regime into which these young people enter. These findings raise novel questions that sometimes challenge established knowledge and assumptions when categorizing countries into particular "regime" types.

A further limitation with the use of typologies arises because some countries, such as France, sit awkwardly in "ideal types." Others, such as the Netherlands, are sometimes relegated to different categories depending on the focus of the typology—that is, welfare systems versus labor market institutions—or because of the methods used to develop the typology (Arts and Gelissen 2002; O'Reilly 2006; Ferragina and Seeleib-Kaiser 2011). There is also considerable diversity within types. For example, there is more variability among the Baltic states and other Eastern European countries than the "post-socialist" label would suggest (Deacon 2000). Established youth transition typologies can provide useful abstract "regime" types, but once we move down the ladder of abstraction, we find a greater degree of diversity within regimes than the initial macro picture would suggest.

As a consequence, a number of chapters in this book employ alternative approaches to comparing countries that go beyond the established youth transitions regimes. Mazzotta and Parisi prefer to use the classification of EU member states into groups based on models of flexicurity as developed by the European Commission on the basis of principal component analysis in 2006. Hajdu and Sik are interested in comparing countries along an East–West divide; they want to understand whether there is any difference in young peoples' values regarding work and, to this end, examine differences by birth cohorts, age groups, and time periods. Other authors use geographical regions that largely correspond to the categories found in youth transition regimes without assuming that there will be institutional effects (Berloffa et al.). Others again prefer not to be constrained by any typology; for instance, the questions examined by Medgyesi and Nagy on how households pool resources between family members go beyond the dimensions usually considered in comparative approaches to youth transitions.

In other cases, the research focus encourages the authors to make comparisons of different measures that are universally experienced across the EU, albeit at different levels. So, for example, Leschke and Finn base their comparative analysis on benefit eligibility, levels of benefits, and forms of labor market regulation; Berloffa, Matteazzi, and Villa compare the legacy of workless households on youth employment probabilities across the EU; and Mascherini examines the variation in NEET (not in employment, education, or training) rates and how this has been adopted as a policy target throughout the EU. Comparing which economic sectors are more "youth friendly," Grotti, Russell, and O'Reilly provide the added value of allowing more straightforward policy recommendations vis-á-vis how youth can be integrated more effectively in the labor market and what role employers can play. The units of comparison are not always common components of established typologies, but they are identified as having a determining effect on youth transitions, and they draw our attention to shared experiences as well as identify country differences in outcomes and policy reach.

Two chapters focus their comparison on a single country. Ortlieb and Weiss examine the integration of Eastern European migrants across a range of economic sectors in Austria. By keeping constant the destination country, they are able to explore similarities and differences related to the types of young people recruited to different sectors. The second single-country study (Zuccotti and O'Reilly) compares the scarring effects of being a NEET by gender for five different ethnic groups in the United Kingdom. This choice is in part driven by the fact that the ethnic composition of the youth population varies significantly across countries in Europe so that it is difficult to find good-quality, comparable cross-national data on this issue that do not conflate ethnicity as a synonym for migrant or exclude nationals of color. In this case, a national comparison of ethnic and gender differences provides a more refined understanding of differences between ethnic groups, including White nationals, than a simple White versus non-White or migrant versus nonmigrant comparison would provide.

Overall, the collection of chapters in this book illustrates both the strengths and the limits of using established cross-national typologies. The chapters also show how alternative approaches can be used, depending on specific research questions concerned with understanding the variety of existing youth labor transitions. These approaches are able to identify both country specificities and shared universal trends as they seek to distinguish between institutional effects and other influential factors.

23.2.2. Using a wide range of indicators

To capture the diversity of youth labor transitions, we need to draw on a broad range of indicators. First, we need to go beyond conventional analysis focused solely on systems of vocational education and training. Hadjivassiliou et al. (this volume) show convincingly how this broader perspective involves examining recent changes in the underlying logic and design of school-to-work (STW) transitions. This requires analysis of the reach and effectiveness of both active labor market policies and specific policies targeted at NEETs, as well as employment protection legislation (EPL) to complement our understanding of how different labor market institutions within the economic sphere of production shape transition trajectories for young people.

Second, we need to take account also of inactivity rather than a narrower focus only on those who are unemployed. This is particularly relevant from a youth and gender perspective, as illustrated by Mascherini's (this volume) examination and differentiation between various categories of NEETs. Likewise, Flek, Hála, and Mysíková (this volume) advocate that youth labor market transitions are different from those of prime-age workers, examining simultaneously movements between employment, unemployment, and inactivity.

Third, we need to develop a better understanding of youth early career insecurity. Several chapters in this volume use standard indicators to this end (Grotti, Russell, and O'Reilly; Akgüç and Beblavý; Spreckelsen, Leschke, and Seeleib-Kaiser). Examples on the outcome side are temporary employment, (solo) self-employment, and part-time or marginal employment shares. Examples on the policy side inspired by the flexicurity agenda are EPL, capturing job security, and active and passive labor market policy indicators, capturing, respectively, employability security and income security (Hadjivassiliou et al.; Smith et al.; Leschke and Finn). Further distinctions are made between measures of job quality in terms of skill–occupation match and wages, as well as examining the effect of family background on successful transitions (Filandri, Nazio, and O'Reilly). Berloffa et al. use a particularly innovative and comprehensive approach to capture early career insecurities. Rather than examining a specific employment status or a single transition at a fixed point in time, they develop a dynamic approach. This involves examining youth labor market integration by focusing on individual trajectories—that is, monthly sequences of employment statuses over at least 2 years—and considering the timing, order, and length of employment, unemployment, and inactivity spells. Smith et al. emphasize the importance of not focusing only on objective measures of early career insecurity, such as temporary employment, but also including subjective measures, such as perceived vulnerability to job loss, underemployment, and concerns about future prospects. By taking inspiration in the transitional labor markets approach (Schmid and Gazier 2002; Schmid 2008), the contributions to this volume go beyond standard indicators and conventional analysis of youth unemployment to illustrate how youth joblessness and early career insecurity are experienced and addressed from a policy perspective.

23.3. YOUTH TRANSITIONS BETWEEN ECONOMIC PRODUCTION, SOCIAL REPRODUCTION, AND POLICY LEARNING

In the years preceding the Great Recession of 2008–2009, there was evidence that the labor market for young people in Europe had been improving (Grotti, Russell, and O'Reilly, this volume, Figure 2.1). The Great Recession and the austerity years that followed knocked this trend off course: Where things were already difficult for young people, it made them even worse. Along with the worsening of labor market conditions, we can identify a structural shift in job opportunities for young people between various economic sectors (Grotti, Russell, and O'Reilly, this volume). The economic crisis, in most countries, resulted in the nonrenewal of temporary contracts, followed by the destruction of full-time and permanent jobs; in the recovery, job creation for youth has shifted toward temporary and part-time work in many countries. Moreover, the economic crisis amplified the differences in labor market outcomes between young adults and prime-age workers (Flek, Hála, and Mysíková, this volume), and thereby increased the pressure on policymakers to act.

However, what we have learned about youth labor market transitions goes beyond the effects of the Great Recession, and it also reflects back on some more deep-rooted causes of inequalities among youth. Although there has been some improvement in countries that were least affected by the crisis, in others the situation has not improved significantly (O'Reilly et al., this volume; Grotti, Russell, and O'Reilly, this volume, Figure 2.2). Causes of youth joblessness and labor market insecurity are related not only to differences in VET systems, STW transition regimes, and EPL but also to socioeconomic inequalities rooted in families. The role of these factors, and the findings from this book, can be understood in terms of the inter-relationship between three key domains: economic production, social reproduction, and policy interventions. These domains affect patterns of inequality, mobility, and the form of policy intervention.

23.3.1. Economic production: Labor market flexibility, mobility, education, and skills

The sphere of "economic production" (i.e., the locus of where labor is employed) in our approach is shaped, among other things, by labor market institutions as well as the quantity and quality of the new generations entering the labor market. More precisely, we define the sphere of economic production as including the impact of labor market flexibility, new labor resources made available through mobility and migration, as well as reforms of education and training.

23.3.1.1. Labor market flexibility

The idea that labor market flexibility had to be encouraged in order to improve the efficiency of the labor market and favor the smooth transition of young people into employment has failed to recognize the impact on increasing inequality among young adults (Smith et al., this volume). Flexicurity, despite its ambition to achieve both increased flexibility and transition security (i.e., employment security instead of job security), has delivered only partly and continues to have different interpretations and unequal outcomes both across countries and for different labor market groups, including youth. Overall, only a fraction of school-leavers and university graduates manage to find a stable and satisfactory job within a relatively short period of time, with noticeable differences by age group, gender, education level, ethnicity, and across countries (Berloffa et al., this volume; Zuccotti and O'Reilly, this volume). Instead, many young adults experience unemployment or frequent job changes combined with repeated unemployment spells, also later in their working life, when the turbulent STW period should already be overcome (Berloffa et al., this volume). Often, unemployment spells of young people are not sufficiently buffered with income security to allow them to search for an adequate job (Leschke and Finn, this volume). Youth are thus pushed into temporary and marginal employment as well as increasingly into (solo) self-employment (Ortlieb, Sheehan, and Masso, this volume). To address this issue, forms of non-standard employment should be covered by unemployment and other social security schemes (Leschke and Finn, this volume; Ortlieb, Sheehan, and Masso, this volume). The increasing diffusion and promotion of flexible employment is likely to have long-term negative consequences for young people's quality of employment and labor market attachment.

Labor market flexibility, often implemented via deregulation at the margins, means, first, that labor markets are increasingly characterized by young workers moving quite frequently between jobs, with possible unemployment/inactivity spells in between; and, second, that one needs to consider not only the early years of working life (i.e., STW transition) but also the subsequent years (early career of young adults). This calls for a life course perspective that allows us to understand how earlier experiences affect longer term trajectories both with regard to labor market outcomes and in establishing independent households. A shift from a focus on STW transitions to a life course perspective also widens the possible policy responses: In addition to career guidance and job search support, they should include comprehensive investment strategies geared at young people and their families, as well as new measures having a focus on aspirations and motivation and the development of soft skills.

23.3.1.2. Labor market mobility

Migration from Eastern and Southern Europe to the North and the West has significantly increased during the past decade, since the EU enlargements (in 2004 and 2007) and the economic downturn (in the years of the Great Recession and of austerity). Increasing geographic mobility within the EU is often viewed as one key instrument to address the consequences of asymmetric shocks, uneven economic development, and high youth unemployment, especially in Central–Eastern and Southern European countries. Intra-EU mobility, migration, and return migration have been supported by various EU policy initiatives and services (O'Reilly et al. 2015). These policy tools include the coordination of entitlement to social benefits, specific directives regulating the working conditions of groups of cross-border workers such as posted workers, and comprehensive information for EU citizens and businesses on rights in the country of destination and support when these rights are breached by public authorities (SOLVIT centers).[2] The European job placement service, European Employment Services (EURES),[3] provides support for jobseekers, employers, and students, including information on rules and regulations as well as living and working conditions in the country of destination (Masso et al., this volume).

The analyses in this book show that young EU migrant citizens are largely rather well integrated and that labor market intermediaries play an important role in terms of reducing transaction costs, managing risks associated with the employment relationship, and building networks (Ortlieb and Weiss, this volume). However, labor market intermediaries are not necessarily neutral and often serve interests of employers first, which is particularly the case for private labor market intermediaries such as temporary work agencies. This calls for careful monitoring and regulation of private intermediaries, as well as a strengthening and promotion of public labor market intermediaries such as EURES. There is also evidence that young EU migrant citizens are often overqualified and tend to have a higher risk of being employed in nonstandard employment relationships (Akgüç and Beblavý, this volume). The country of origin appears to contribute to the stratification of young people at least as much as the institutional arrangements in the countries to which they migrate (Spreckelsen, Leschke, and Seeleib-Kaiser, this volume).

The reintegration of young returnees into their country-of-origin labor markets also poses a policy challenge that is nearly uniform across countries (Masso et al., this volume). Of those who return "home," some are able to reap the benefits of their time abroad, having developed their soft and hard skills. However, returnees might need additional support from public institutions, such as employment offices in the country of origin, given the fact that not all of them will be able to benefit from their experiences abroad. Also, access to services especially with respect to family-related issues (i.e., maternity benefits and health care) is part of the process leading to the return migration decision. The balance of rewards from migration, both for the individuals who left or returned and for the countries of origin and destination, is not a simple calculus (Fihel et al. 2007). Without question, intra-EU mobility has reduced youth unemployment across Europe, and many young people value the opportunity to work and live in a different country. At the same time, however, some patterns of intra-EU migration have also contributed to labor shortages in specific occupations or sectors in Central and Eastern Europe (Polakowski and Szelewa 2016).

23.3.1.3. The role of education and training

It is the interaction between systems of education and training and labor demand to absorb young people that lie at the heart of many of the problems in youth labor markets (McGuinness, Bergin, and Whelan, this volume). Many chapters in this book show that higher education is associated with a lower risk of being unemployed (Flek, Hála, and Mysíková, this volume), with having a higher job quality (Berloffa et al., this volume; Filandri, Nazio, and O'Reilly, this volume), and with having a lower probability of returning to the family of origin's household (Mazzotta and Parisi, this volume). However, young people from lower class backgrounds often have less educational opportunities than their peers from higher class backgrounds, which perpetuates socioeconomic inequalities (Berloffa, Matteazzi, and Villa, this volume; Filandri, Nazio, and O'Reilly, this volume). The chapters in this book also show that VET as well as apprenticeships are considered to have been effective in smoothing the process of STW transitions. In liberal (e.g., United Kingdom) and subprotective (e.g., Greece and Spain) countries, policymakers have recently begun to experiment with various policy initiatives—for example, through the European Alliance for Apprenticeships (Hadjivassiliou et al., this volume; Petmesidou and González Menéndez, this volume) and, in the United Kingdom, through the Apprenticeship Levy. [4] However, effective VET and apprenticeship schemes require a mode of policy governance that supports regional/local partnerships, networks, and active involvement of all relevant stakeholders, which are occasionally lacking and very difficult to emulate. In particular, measures need to focus on overcoming governance barriers that may result from excessive fragmentation of competencies between distinct partners as well as overcome rigidities created by overcentralization.

At the same time, there is evidence of overeducation for some young workers (McGuinness, Bergin, and Whelan, this volume), particularly among migrants (Akgüç and Beblavý, this volume; Ortlieb and Weiss, this volume; Masso et al., this volume). Core to the assessment of policy interventions in the VET system, it is necessary to understand how the supply of qualified labor will be absorbed by domestic or international labor demand. At the individual level, this translates into improving the quality and accessibility of information about potential education pathways and jobs. Also, increasing the practical aspects of degree programs can reduce the incidence of initial mismatch for graduates (McGuinness, Whelan, and Bergin 2016). Although there is greater understanding and recognition of EU qualifications across borders today than there was 20 years ago,[5] there are still many obstacles for young EU migrant citizens and third-country nationals that are only beginning to be addressed.

Together, the three dimensions of flexibility, mobility, and education are key to understanding how youth unemployment in Europe can be examined under the rubric of the sphere of economic production. VET systems and STW regimes interact and engage employers and trade unions in concert with domestic and international policymakers. This approach provides a more comprehensive analysis to understand how youth opportunities are shaped by the demand for, and availability of, youth labor both at home and abroad.

23.3.2. Social reproduction: Family legacies and new and emerging forms of inequality

Emerging patterns of segmentation in youth labor markets along the lines of education, gender, and ethnicity require a holistic analytical approach, including an analysis of the legacy of family differences from the sphere of "social reproduction" (i.e., the locus where the labor force is produced) to understand how these interact with the sphere of "economic production" (i.e., the locus where labor is employed) (O'Reilly, Smith, and Villa 2017). The family provides an interface for youth transitions into the public realm: It acts as both a source of stratification and potentially as a source of protection.

23.3.2.1. Family legacies

Parental employment status plays a significant role in explaining youth labor market outcomes. A number of chapters in this volume show how employment probabilities, decisions to leave/return to the parental home, and the pooling of household finances are differentially affected by the type of household in which young people grew up. Although some effects are universal (e.g., having grown up in a household in which no one was working increases the likelihood of that young person also being without work), the extent varies by country (Berloffa et al., this volume) as well as by different ethnic group (Zuccotti and O'Reilly, this volume). Without the role of families providing support and welfare for young people, it is very likely that the social consequences of the sharp increase in youth unemployment in Europe would have been much more severe. Families can provide support in difficult times, but this can also constrain young people's steps toward economic independence and independent living. Also since the outbreak of the economic crisis, an increasing proportion of youth are staying longer in the family of origin or are returning to the family home after finishing education and/or not finding employment. Simultaneously, in some families, it is not only youth who benefit from cohabitation: Among some of the poorest families in Europe, youth employment is providing resources to be shared with other family members in need (Medgyesi and Nagy, this volume). Accrued worklessness across generations exacerbates household and youth inequalities between work-rich and work-poor households.

In summary, family legacies play a significant role providing support to their jobless children but with the side effect of increasing inequalities of opportunities among youth. Young people from higher social classes are better equipped to achieve good educational and labor market outcomes. Universal access to employment services—providing services also to less advantaged young people in low work-intensity households—might help address these inequalities. In addition, as some chapters suggest (Berloffa, Matteazzi, and Villa, this volume; Filandri, Nazio, and O'Reilly, this volume), the family of origin plays a crucial role in the transmission of gender roles during adolescence, shaping the attitudes of young women and men toward female participation. In order to enhance the participation of young women in particular, and youth employment in general, it is also crucial to strengthen policies focused on increasing parental employment, especially that of mothers.

23.3.2.2. New contours of labor market segmentation: Gender, ethnicity, class, and migrant status

Although young women have been increasingly successful in education systems and in participating in higher education, the evidence in this book highlights the emergence of gender gaps opening up early in young people's labor market experiences. Men and women (aged 16–34 years) have similar chances of accessing paid employment rapidly, but as Berloffa et al. (this volume) show, young women's labor market conditions deteriorate relatively quickly during their early working life in terms of both security and success, even before motherhood.

Young women also have a higher likelihood of becoming NEET (Mascherini, this volume), and young self-employed women often find themselves in more precarious situations compared to their male counterparts (Ortlieb, Sheehan, and Masso, this volume). These gaps reflect segregation of education and training choices and different sectoral choices (Grotti, Russell, and O'Reilly, this volume; Ortlieb, Sheehan, and Masso, this volume).

Specific gendered processes in the parental home and in the labor market (e.g., discrimination in recruitment, job allocation, and training) reinforce gender roles that subsequently produce lower quality labor market outcomes. Gender gaps emerging in early adulthood have long-term consequences over the life course. This suggests that well-known gender differences in labor market outcomes (not fully explained by early parenthood) have not yet been equalized for younger women, who are still encountering similar problems as those of older generations. A wide range of policies are needed to tackle the weaker position of young women in the labor market—from policies aiming to ensure equal access to employment and career opportunities to reconciliation policies (e.g., paid leave for fathers and affordable care services and flexible working hours for parents with small children).

Gender impacts are also intertwined in different ways with the effects of other social dimensions, such as ethnicity and class/family background. Zuccotti and O'Reilly's (this volume) analysis of gender and ethnic differences in the United Kingdom found that young White British men and those of Caribbean origin are more likely to be affected than any other group by the negative consequences of being NEET; however, young Asian women, especially those from Pakistani communities, have lower employment probabilities. Patterns of gender inequalities are changing at the margins, but often as a result of the situation for young men deteriorating rather than that of young women improving.

Policies need to take account of such intersectionalities in order to be effective and thereby also consider that age is a significant dimension of intersectionality (Hanappi-Egger and Ortlieb 2015). However, analysis of the policy environment for young people reveals, for example, that such policies are often gender blind (Petmesidou and González Menéndez, this volume), and there is limited evidence of consistent gender mainstreaming. The substantial variation in gender differences between countries is only partially captured by STW regime frames of analysis. Greater attention to the differential outcomes for specific categories of youth (e.g., in the United Kingdom, young White British men or some young women of specific ethnic minorities) could make policies more effective if they were used to inform targeted policymaking. Although there is some evidence of good practices that acknowledge these differences, these policies are exceptions rather than the rule.

23.3.3. Policy transfer and policy learning

The third key component required to understand the form of youth transitions is related to the role of policymakers and to the possibilities for policy transfer and learning between countries. Across Europe, the policy architectures for addressing youth problems are very different: These range from countries with specific ministries, or transversal organizations, to those with no dedicated institutions (Wallace and Bendit 2009). Similarly, the design and capacity of public employment services vary significantly across Europe. It is frequently the case that policies affecting young people are spread across a range of very different institutions; but these often do not have consistent strategies, and they are frequently decentralized to local and regional levels (Petmesidou and González Menéndez, this volume).

We have argued that one of the distinctive characteristics of the current phase of youth unemployment has been an increased Europeanization of youth policies (O'Reilly et al. 2015), a process referred to as "transversalism" by Wallace and Bendit (2009). This reflects a broader project from the European Commission to encourage an exchange of information, good practice, and benchmarks. This includes, for example, the European Network of Public Employment Services,[6] which allows public employment services to collaborate, share good practice, and participate in learning events geared toward improving services for jobseekers. It also contributes to facilitating intra-EU labor mobility.

There have also been attempts to bring together a range of measures from different levels of government and ministries to develop a coherent and coordinated employment strategy to foster youth employment, including technical support from the EU. However, EU intervention is often focused on softer policy instruments, such as guidelines, recommendations, periodic reporting through the open method of coordination (Smith et al., this volume), the EU Agenda for new skills and jobs, and, since 2013, through the initiative of the European YG. Since 2010, through the EU Agenda for new skills and jobs,[7] there have been EU-level attempts to give new impetus to labor market reforms that help people gain suitable qualifications. The EU Agenda primarily aims at skills upgrading to cope with a shrinking working-age population and to stimulate young people to gain appropriate skills by prevention of early school leaving and increasing the number of young people in higher education or equivalent vocational education.

The YG, launched in 2013, was held up as the flagship program to address youth unemployment, and in many countries it was linked to attempts to strengthen the dual vocational training system, in particular by mobilizing employers to play a more active role. In Greece, Slovakia, and Spain, EU influence regarding the dual VET system created "windows of opportunity" for domestic policy entrepreneurs (or for negotiated agreements at the regional level in the case of Spain) to experiment with novel practices that promote work-based learning. However, recent assessments of the YG by the European Court of Auditors (2017) have been quite critical. They suggest that although there has been some progress, the initiative falls short of the initial expectations raised when it was launched. In particular, none of the countries evaluated (Croatia, France, Ireland, Italy, Portugal, Slovakia, and Spain) had succeeded in ensuring that NEETs had taken up an opportunity within 4 months. Part of this problem was attributed to the lack of resources available from the EU budget. But part of the lack of success was due to the difficulties faced by member states in carefully planning the implementation of the YG on the basis of their national specificities and limited institutional capacities to carry out implementation by the established public employment services. The European Court of Auditors' evaluation suggests that the YG was insufficient to provide paradigmatic shifts in the key STW transitions mechanisms, partly as a result of path dependency combined with cultural and institutional stickiness. Any policy transfer or policy learning will need to take into account these different dimensions and levels of policymaking in order to be more effective in the future (Petmesidou and González Menéndez, this volume).

Being sensitive to such differences makes any discussion of policy implications of our complex analyses a difficult task. Nevertheless, some generalizable observations with regard to the policy implications of our research can be made. First, we need to highlight that we are aware of the potential interaction effects of any policy recommendations aiming at the reduction of youth unemployment and the improvement of STW transitions with macroeconomic conditions as well as with other policies. For instance, in cases of a lack of demand for young workers (Grotti, Russell, and O'Reilly, this volume), it would seem very unlikely that policies improving the supply side will be sufficient to address the issue of youth unemployment in the short term (Smith et al., this volume). Second, austerity policies implemented immediately after the Great Recession have very likely limited the effectiveness of new labor market policy initiatives that required additional financial resources—in particular, investment in education and training, in addition to active and passive labor market policies—as observed in a number of countries.

23.4. DIRECTIONS FOR FUTURE RESEARCH

In conclusion, the extensive evidence provided in this volume can be summarized in relation to three key features for future research encapsulated by our analysis of the relationship between economic production, social reproduction, and policy interventions. These three areas capture increasingly precarious patterns of youth mobility and transition trajectories, the absence of employer engagement, and emerging inequalities linked to family origins.

First, we have seen that new job opportunities are becoming increasingly precarious. Where there has been job growth, it is more likely to be in temporary or part-time jobs, whereas more permanent full-time positions have been lost during the Great Recession. Our analysis of youth transitions has consistently indicated that many of these transitions are associated with a growing margin of precariousness. One dimension of this is also related to the encouragement of self-employment for young people, which can unleash a welcomed form of youthful entrepreneurship and creativity or can increase social insecurity and lead to indebtedness. The question as to whether some of these jobs are genuine self-employment or a disguised form of dependent employment has been gaining increased media and legal attention in discussions of the expansion of the "gig economy." The form and characteristics of future jobs for youth and their long-term consequences will clearly become an increasingly important area for research and policy.

Second, one key dimension that is insufficiently addressed in the vast body of research has been the role of employers. Much research approaches this issue tangentially, by illustrating how more stable pathways for young people to find better quality jobs are found where employers are more integrated into VET systems. These systems clearly reflect that employers see advantages to participating in the collective organization and the shared costs of recruiting young people through these channels. Where these systems are more fragile, employers do not perceive an advantage in being actively involved in collectivist collaborations. Their ability to absorb young people coming onto the labor market is curtailed either because they do not perceive young people to have the skills they require or because they do not have the financial capability to integrate young people into their firms in a way that they would find profitable. This might be due to a lack of incentives in the policy instruments designed to integrate young people that sufficiently alleviate their anticipated long-term costs or because they have alternative sources of labor. Some country differences in this absorption capacity are related not only to firm size but also to the institutions encompassed in the sphere of economic production, including VET systems and EPL. Future research agendas clearly need to give this aspect more attention, alongside the uneven sectoral distribution of jobs for youth.

Third, we have also evidenced how the family plays a significant role both in contributing to the stratification of opportunities for young people and in protecting vulnerable youth in times of crisis. It is the interaction between inequalities in the sphere of social reproduction with an effect on which groups of youth labor are trained and employed in the sphere of economic production that provides a key nexus in the analysis presented in this volume.

The evidence of growing inequalities can be seen in the polarization between NEETs and those experiencing the negative consequences of overeducation. The NEET population illustrates the fact that a significant proportion of young people "fall out of the system." A large proportion of these young people are more likely to come from already disadvantaged families. On the other hand, the consequences of overeducation for an increasingly better educated generation of young people run the risks of occupational mismatch and wage penalties in the long term. Evidence suggests that some of the negative effects of overeducation are also associated with coming from less advantaged parental backgrounds, as well as how young people are segregated into different educational pathways.

In addition to these polarizing trends, there is an emerging fragmentation of inequality between different subgroups of young people. This presents itself in new forms of inequalities that will shape young peoples' attitudes and values around work, trade unions, and other collective organizations. Future analyses of youth labor market transitions need to take account not only of how reforms to VET institutions in the sphere of economic production will adapt to the challenges resulting from the growing digitalized and increasingly "personalized" service economy but also of how disadvantages in the sphere of social reproduction affect where different groups of young people are able to access pathways into the field of economic production and where there are spaces for policymakers to intervene effectively.

NOTES

1   For more detailed information on the policy level, we refer our readers to the STYLE Policy Briefs that have been produced as part of the project: http://www.style-research.eu/publications/policy-briefs.

2   http://ec.europa.eu/solvit/index_en.htm.

3   https://ec.europa.eu/eures/public/en/homepage.

4   The Apprenticeship Levy was introduced on April 6, 2017, in the United Kingdom. This amounts to a compulsory tax on employers' payroll that is to be used to fund apprenticeships, unless employers show evidence of creating these kinds of jobs for young people within their organization. For an explanation of how this policy will work, see https://www.gov.uk/government/publications/apprenticeship-levy-how-it-will-work/apprenticeship-levy-how-it-will-work.

5   For example, through Erasmus+ (https://www.erasmusplus.org.uk) or initiatives to recognize skills.

6   For more information, see http://ec.europa.eu/social/main.jsp?catId=1100&langId=en.

7   The most recent update in 2016 particularly emphasized digital skills; see http://ec.europa.eu/social/main.jsp?catId=1223.

REFERENCES

Arts, Wil, and John Gelissen. 2002. "Three Worlds of Welfare Capitalism or More? A State-of-the-Art Report." *Journal of European Social Policy* 12 (2): 137–58.

Deacon, Bob. 2000. "Eastern European Welfare States: The Impact of the Politics of Globalization." *Journal of European Social Policy* 10 (2): 146–61.

Dhéret, Claire, and Martina Morosi. 2015. "One Year After the Youth Guarantee: Policy Fatigue or Signs of Action?" EPC Policy Brief, May 27. Brussels: European Policy Centre.

Esping-Andersen, Gøsta. 1990. *The Three Worlds of Welfare Capitalism.* Princeton, NJ: Princeton University Press.

European Court of Auditors. 2017. "Youth Unemployment—Have EU Policies Made a Difference? An Assessment of the Youth Guarantee and the Youth Employment Initiative." Luxembourg: Publications Office of the European Union. http://www.eca.europa.eu/Lists/ECADocuments/SR17_5/SR_YOUTH_GUARANTEE_EN.pdf

Ferragina, Emanuele, and Martin Seeleib-Kaiser. 2011. "Thematic Review: Welfare Regime Debate—Past, Present, Futures?" *Policy & Politics* 39 (4): 583–611.

Fihel, Agnieszka, Paweł Kaczmarczyk, Nina Wolfeil, and Anna Żylicz. 2007. "Brain Drain, Brain Gain and Brain Waste." In *Labour Mobility Within the EU in the Context of Enlargement and the Functioning of the Transitional Arrangements,* edited by Centre of Migration Research. Warsaw: University of Warsaw.

Hall, Peter A. 1993. "Policy Paradigms, Social Learning, and the State: The Case of Economic Policymaking in Britain." *Comparative Politics* 25 (3): 275–96.

Hall, Peter A., and David Soskice, eds. 2001. *Varieties of Capitalism: The Institutional Foundations of Comparative Advantage.* Oxford: Oxford University Press.

Hanappi-Egger, Edeltraud, and Renate Ortlieb. 2015. "The Intersectionalities of Age, Ethnicity, and Class in Organizations." In *The Oxford Handbook of Diversity in Organizations,* edited by Regine Bendl, Inge Bleijenbergh, Elina Henttonen, and Albert J. Mills, 454–68. Oxford: Oxford University Press.

McGuinness, Seamus, Adele Whelan, and Adele Bergin. 2016. "Is There a Role for Higher Education Institutions in Improving the Quality of First Employment?" *BE Journal of Economic Analysis and Policy* 16 (4): 12–23.

O'Reilly, Jacqueline. 2006. "Framing Comparisons: Gendering Perspectives on Cross-National Comparisons of Welfare and Work." *Work, Employment and Society* 20 (4): 731–50. http://journals.sagepub.com/doi/abs/10.1177/0950017006069812

O'Reilly, Jacqueline, Werner Eichhorst, András Gábos, Kari Hadjivassiliou, David Lain, Janine Leschke, et al. 2015. "Five Characteristics of Youth Unemployment in Europe: Flexibility, Education, Migration, Family Legacies, and EU Policy." *Sage Open* 5 (1): 1–19. doi:10.1177/2158244015574962.

O'Reilly, Jacqueline, Mark Smith, and Paola Villa. 2017. "The Social Reproduction of Youth Labour Market Inequalities: The Effects of Gender, Households and Ethnicity." In *Making Work More Equal: A New Labour Market Segmentation Approach*, edited by Damian Grimshaw, Colette Fagan, Gail Hebson, and Isabel Tavora, 249–67. Manchester, UK: Manchester University Press.

Pohl, Axel, and Andreas Walther. 2007. "Activating the Disadvantaged— Variations in Addressing Youth Transitions Across Europe." *International Journal of Lifelong Education* 26 (5): 533–53.

Polakowski, Michał and Dorota Szelewa. 2016. "Poland in the Migration Chain: Causes and Consequences." *Transfer: European Review of Labour and Research* 22 (2): 207–18.

Schmid, Günther. 2008. *Full Employment in Europe: Managing Labour Market Transitions and Risks*. Cheltenham, UK: Elgar.

Schmid, Günther, and Bernard Gazier, eds. 2002. *The Dynamics of Full Employment: Social Integration Through Transitional Labour Markets*. Cheltenham, UK: Elgar.

Streeck, Wolfgang, and Kathleen Thelen, eds. 2005. *Beyond Continuity: Institutional Change in Advanced Political Economies*. Oxford: Oxford University Press.

Thelen, Kathleen. 2004. *How Institutions Evolve*. Cambridge: Cambridge University Press.

Wallace, Claire, and René Bendit. 2009. "Youth Policies in Europe: Towards a Classification of Different Tendencies in Youth Policies in the European Union." *Perspectives on European Politics and Society* 10 (3): 441–58. doi:10.1080/15705850903105868.

INDEX